Berkley Books by Dean R. Koontz

DARKFALL
THE FACE OF FEAR
LIGHTNING
THE MASK
MIDNIGHT
NIGHT CHILLS
PHANTOMS
THE SERVANTS OF TWILIGHT
SHATTERED
STRANGERS
TWILIGHT EYES
THE VISION
WATCHERS
WHISPERS
THE BAD PLACE
COLD FIRE
THE HOUSE OF THUNDER
THE VOICE OF THE NIGHT

DEAN R. KOONTZ

A NEW COLLECTION

DEAN R. KOONTZ

A NEW COLLECTION

SHATTERED

WHISPERS

WATCHERS

WINGS BOOKS
New York · Avenel, New Jersey

This edition contains the complete and unabridged texts of the original
editions. They have been completely reset for this volume.
This omnibus was originally published in separate volumes under the titles:
Shattered, copyright © 1973 by Nkui, Inc.
(Previously published under the pseudonym of K. R. Dwyer.)
Whispers, copyright © 1980 by Nkui, Inc.
Watchers, copyright © 1987 by Nkui, Inc.
This 1992 edition is published by Wings Books
distributed by Outlet Book Company, Inc., a Random House Company,
40 Engelhard Avenue, Avenel, New Jersey 07001
by arrangement with The Berkley Publishing Group.

Printed and bound in the United States of America

Library of Congress Cataloging-in-Publication Data
Koontz, Dean R. (Dean Ray), 1945–
Dean Koontz : a new collection : watchers, whispers, shattered /
Dean Koontz.
p.   cm.
Originally published: New York : Random House, 1973.
ISBN 0-517-07369-2
1. Horror tales, American.   I. Title.
PS3561.O55A6   1992
813′.54—dc20
92-7597
CIP

8 7 6 5 4 3 2

CONTENTS

SHATTERED

To Lee Wright—
in return for much kindness,
advice, and patience

MONDAY

CHAPTER 1

ONLY FOUR BLOCKS from the furnished apartment in Philadelphia, with more than three thousand miles to drive before they joined Courtney in San Francisco, Colin began one of his games. Colin thrived on his games, not those which required a board and movable pieces but those which were played inside the head—word games, idea games, elaborate fantasies. He was a very garrulous and precocious eleven-year-old with more energy than he was able to use. Slender, shy in the company of strangers, bothered by a moderately severe astigmatism in both eyes that required him to wear heavy eyeglasses at all times, he was not much for sports. He could not exhaust himself in a fast game of football, because none of the athletic boys his own age wanted to play with someone who tripped over his own feet, dropped the ball, and was devastated by even the most delicate tackle. Besides, sports bored him. He was an intelligent kid, an avid reader, and he found his own games more fun than football. Kneeling on the front seat of the big car and looking out the rear window at the home he was leaving forever, he said, "We're being followed, Alex."

"Are we now?"

"Yeah. He was parked down the block when we put the suitcases in the trunk. I saw him. Now he's following us."

Alex Doyle smiled as he wheeled the Thunderbird onto Lansdowne Avenue. "Big black limousine, is it?"

5

Colin shook his head, his thick shoulder-length mop of brown hair flopping vigorously. "No. It's some kind of van. Like a panel truck."

Alex looked in the rear-view mirror. "I don't see him."

"You lost him when you turned the corner," Colin said. He pressed his stomach against the backrest, head thrust over the back seat. "There he is! See him now?"

Nearly a block behind them, a new Chevrolet van turned the corner onto Lansdowne Avenue. At five minutes past six o-clock on a Monday morning, it was the only other moving vehicle in sight.

"I thought it was always a black limousine," Alex said. "In the movies, the heroes are always followed by a big black limousine."

"That's only in the movies," Colin said, still watching the van, which remained a full block behind them. "Nobody's that obvious in real life."

The trees on their right cast long black shadows across half the street and made dizzying, flickering patterns on the windshield. The first sun of May had risen somewhere to the east, still too far down the sky for Alex to see it. Crisp spring sunlight bathed the old two-story frame houses and made them new and fresh again.

Invigorated by the early-morning air and by the spray of green buds on the trees, almost as excited as Colin was about the journey ahead of them, Alex Doyle thought he had never been happier. He handled the heavy car with ease, enjoying the quiet power at his disposal. They were going to be on the road a long time in terms of both hours and miles; but as imaginative as he was, Colin would provide better company than most adults.

"He's still back there," Colin said.

"I wonder *why* he's following us."

Colin shrugged his thin shoulders but did not turn around. "Could be lots of reasons."

"Name one."

"Well . . . He could have heard that we were moving to California. He knows we'll take our valuables with us, see? Family treasures, things like that. So he follows us and runs us into a ditch on some lonely stretch of road and robs us at gunpoint."

Alex laughed. "Family treasures? All you have is clothes enough for the trip. Everything else went out on the moving van a week ago, or it went with your sister on the plane. And I assure you that I've brought nothing more valuable than my wristwatch."

Colin was unperturbed by Doyle's amusement. "Maybe he's an enemy of yours. Someone with an old grudge to settle. He wants to get hold of you before you leave town."

"I don't have any real friends in Philly," Alex said. "But I don't have any real enemies, either. And if he wanted to beat me up, why didn't he just catch me when I was putting our bags in the trunk?"

Fluttering laces of sunshine and shadow flipped rapidly over the windshield. Ahead, a stoplight turned green just in time to spare Alex the inconvenience of braking.

After a while Colin said, "Maybe he's a spy."

"A spy?" Alex asked.

"A Russian or something."

"I thought we were friends with the Russians these days," Alex said, looking at the van in the rear-view mirror and smiling again. "And even if we aren't friends with the Russians these days—why would a spy be interested in you or me?"

"That's easy," Colin said. "He has us mixed up with someone else. He was assigned to tail someone living on our block, and he got confused."

"I'm not scared of any spy who's that inept," Alex said. He reached out and fiddled with the air-conditioning controls, brought a gentle, cool breeze into the stuffy car.

"He might not be a spy," Colin said, his attention captured by the unimposing little van. "He might be something else."

"Like what?"

"Let me think about it awhile," the boy said.

While Colin thought about what the man in the van might be, Alex Doyle watched the street ahead and thought about San Francisco. That hilly city was not just a geographical identity so far as Alex was concerned. To him, it was a synonym for the future and a symbol for everything that a man wanted in life. The new job was there, the innovative advertising agency that recognized and cultivated talented young commercial artists. The new house was there, the three-bedroom Spanish stucco on the edge of Lincoln Park, with its spectacular view of the Golden Gate area and the shaggy palm outside the master-bedroom window. And Courtney was there, of course. If she had not been, the new job and the house would not have meant anything. He and Courtney had met in Philadelphia, had fallen in love there, had been married in the city hall on Market Street, with her brother, Colin, as honorary best man and a woman from the Justice Department steno pool as their required adult witness. Then Colin had been packed off to stay two weeks with Alex's Aunt Pauline in Boston, while the newlyweds flew to San Francisco to honeymoon, to meet Alex's new employers to whom he had spoken only over the telephone, and to find and buy the house in which they would start their life together. It was in San Francisco, more than Philly, that the future took shape and meaning. San Francisco *became* the future. And Courtney became inextricably entwined with that city. In Doyle's mind, she *was* San Francisco, just as San Francisco *was* the future. She was golden and even-tempered, exotic, sensuous, intellectually intriguing, comfortable yet exciting—everything that San Francisco was. And now, as he thought about Courtney, the hilly streets and the crisp blue bay rose clearly on the screen behind his eyes.

"He's still back there," Colin said, peering through the narrow rear window at the van.

"At least he hasn't tried to run us into a ditch yet," Alex said.

"He won't do that," Colin said.

"Oh?"

"He'll just tail us. He's a government man."

"FBI, is he?"

"I think so," Colin said, grimly compressing his lips.

"Why would he be after us?"

"He's probably got us mixed up with someone else," Colin said. "He was assigned to tail some—radicals. He saw our long hair and got confused. He thinks *we're* the radicals."

"Well," Alex said, "our own spies are just as inefficient as the Russians', aren't they?"

Doyle's smile was too large for his face, a generous curve that was punctuated at each end with a dimple. He held the smile both because he felt so damned fine and because he knew it was the best thing about his face. In all his thirty years, no one had ever told him that he was handsome. Despite the fact that he was one-quarter Irish, there was too much strong-jawed Italian in him, too much of a Roman nose. Three months after they met, when they began to sleep together, Courtney had said, "Doyle, you are just not a handsome man. You're *attractive,* certainly, but not handsome. When you say that I look smashing, I want to reciprocate—but I just can't lie to you. But your smile . . . Now, *that's* perfect. When you smile, you even look a little bit like Dustin Hoffman." Already they were too honest with each other for Doyle to be hurt by what she'd said. Indeed, he had been delighted by the comparison: "Dustin Hoffman? You really think so?" She had studied him a moment, putting her hand under his chin and turning his face this way and that in the weak orange light of the bedside lamp. "When you smile, you look *exactly* like Hoffman—when he's trying to look ugly, that is." He had gaped at her. "When he's trying to look *ugly,* for Christ's sake?" She grimaced. "I meant . . . Well, Hoffman can't really look ugly, even when he tries. When you smile, then, you look like Hoffman but not as handsome . . ." He watched her trying to extricate herself from the embarrassing hole she'd dug, and he had begun to laugh. His laughter had infected her. Soon they were giggling like idiots, expanding on the joke and making it funnier, laughing until they were sick and then settling down and then making love with a paradoxically fierce affection. Ever since that night Doyle tried to remember to smile a lot.

On the right-hand side of the street a sign announced the entrance to the Schuylkill Expressway. "Give your FBI man a break," Alex told the boy. "Let him tail us in peace for a while. The expressway's coming up, so you better turn around and buckle your seatbelt."

"Just a minute," Colin said.

"No," Alex said. "Get your seatbelt on, or I'll also make you use the shoulder strap." Colin despised being bound up by both belts.

"*Half* a minute," the boy said, straining even harder against the back of the seat as Alex drove the car onto the approach ramp leading up to the superhighway.

"Colin—"

The boy turned around and bounced down onto the seat. "I just wanted to see if he followed us onto the expressway. He did."

"Well, of course he did," Alex said. "An FBI man wouldn't be restricted to the city limits. He could follow us anywhere."

"Clear across the country?" the boy asked.

"Sure. Why not?"

Colin laid his head back against the seat and laughed. "That'd be funny. What would he do if he followed us clear across country and found out we weren't the radicals he was after?"

At the top of the ramp, Alex looked southeast at the two empty lanes of blacktop. He eased his foot down on the accelerator, and they started west. "You going to put your seatbelt on?"

"Oh, sure," Colin said, fumbling for the half of the buckle that was rolled up in the trough beside the passenger's door. "I forgot." He had not forgotten, of course. Colin never forgot anything. He just didn't like to wear the belt.

Briefly taking his eyes from the empty highway ahead of them, Alex glanced sideways at the boy and saw him struggling with the two halves of the seatbelt. Colin grimaced, cursed the apparatus, making problems with it so Doyle would know just what he thought of being tied down like a prisoner.

"You might as well grin and bear it," Alex said, grinning himself as he looked ahead at the highway again. "You're going to wear that belt the whole way to California, whether you like it or not."

"I won't like it," Colin assured him. The seatbelt in place, he smoothed the wrinkles out of his King Kong T-shirt until the silk-screened photograph of the gigantic, raging gorilla was neatly centered on his frail chest. He pushed his thick hair out of his eyes and straightened the heavy wire-framed glasses which his button nose was hard-pressed to hold in place. "Thirty-one hundred miles," he said, watching the gray roadway roll under and behind them. The Thunderbird's power seat elevated high enough to give him a good view. "How long will it take to drive that far?"

"We won't be lolling around," Alex said. "We ought to get into San Francisco Saturday morning."

"Five days," Colin said. "Hardly more than six hundred miles a day." He sounded disappointed by the pace.

"If you could spell me at the wheel," Alex said, "we'd do better. But I wouldn't want to handle much more than six hundred a day all by myself."

"So why didn't Courtney drive out with us?" Colin asked.

"She's getting the house ready. She met the movers there, and she's arranging for drapes and carpeting—all that stuff."

"Did you know that when I flew up to Boston to stay with Pauline while you two were on your honeymoon—that was my first plane ride?"

"I know," Alex said. Colin had talked about it for two solid days after he came back.

"I really liked that plane ride."

"I know."

Colin frowned. "Why couldn't we sell this car and fly out to California with Courtney?"

"You know the answer to that," Alex said. "The car's only a year old. A new car depreciates the most in its first year. If you want to get your money out of it, you keep it for three or four years."

"You could afford the loss," Colin said, beginning to beat a quiet but insistent rhythm on his dungareed knees. "I heard you and Courtney talking. You'll be making a *fortune* in San Francisco."

Alex held one palm out to dry it in the hushed breath of the air-conditioning vent on the dashboard. "Thirty-five thousand dollars a year is not a fortune."

"I only get a three-dollar allowance," the boy said.

"True enough," Alex said. "But I've got nineteen years of experience and training on you."

The tires hummed pleasantly on the pavement.

A huge truck hurtled by on the other side of the road, going in toward the city. It was the first traffic, besides the van, that they had seen.

"Thirty-one hundred miles," Colin said. "That's just about one-eighth of the way around the world."

Alex had to think a minute. "That's right."

"If we kept driving and didn't stop in California, we'd need about forty days to circumnavigate the earth," Colin said, holding his hands around an imaginary globe at which he was staring intently.

Alex remembered when the boy had first learned the word "circumnavigate" and had been fascinated with the sound and concept of it. For weeks he did not walk around the room or the block—he "circumnavigated" everything. "Well, we'd probably need more than forty days," Alex said. "I don't know what kind of driving time I can make on the Pacific Ocean."

Colin thought that was funny. "I meant we could do it if there was a bridge," he said.

Alex looked at the speedometer and saw that they were only making a moderate fifty miles an hour, twenty less than he had intended to maintain on this first leg of the journey. Colin was good company. Indeed, he was too good. If he kept distracting Alex, they'd need a month to get across the damn country.

"Forty days," Colin mused. "That's half as long as they needed when Jules Verne wrote about it."

Though he knew that Colin had been skipped ahead one grade in school and that his reading ability was still a couple of years in advance of that of his classmates, Alex was always surprised at the extent of the kid's knowledge. "You've read *Around the World in Eighty Days,* have you?"

"Sure," Colin said. "A long time ago." He held his hands out in front of another vent and dried them as he had seen Doyle do.

Though it was a small thing, that gesture made an impression on Doyle. He, too, had been a skinny, nervous kid whose palms were always damp. Like Colin, he had been shy with strangers, not much good at sports, an outcast among his contemporaries. In college he had begun a rigorous weight-lifting program, determined to develop himself into another Charles Atlas. By the time his chest filled out and his biceps hardened, he grew bored with weight-lifting and quit bothering with it. At five-ten and a hundred-sixty pounds, he was no Charles Atlas. But he was slim and hard, and he was no longer the skinny kid, either. Still, he was awkward with people whom he had just met—and his palms were often damp with nervous perspiration. Deep inside, he had not forgotten what it was like to be constantly self-conscious and never self-confident enough. Watching Colin dry his slender hands, Alex understood why he had taken an immediate liking to the boy and why they had seemed comfortable with each other from the day they met eighteen months before. Nineteen years separated them. But little else.

"He still back there?" Colin asked, breaking into Alex's thoughts.

"Who?"

"The van."

Alex checked the mirror. "He's there. FBI doesn't give up easily."

"Can I look?"

"You keep your belt on."

"This is going to be a bad trip," Colin said morosely.

"It will be if you don't accept the rules at the start," Alex agreed.

Traffic picked up on the other side of the expressway as the early-bird commuters began their day and as an occasional truck whistled by on the last lap of a long cargo haul. On the westbound lanes, their own car and the van were the only things in sight.

The sun was behind the Thunderbird, where it could not bother them. Ahead, the sky was marred by only two white clouds. The hills, on both sides, were green.

When they got on the Pennsylvania turnpike at Valley Forge and went west toward Harrisburg, Colin said, "What about our tail?"

"Still there. Some poor FBI agent tracking the wrong prey."

"He'll probably lose his job," Colin said. "That'll make an opening for me."

"You want to be an FBI agent?"

"I've thought about it," Colin admitted.

Alex pulled the Thunderbird into the left lane, passed a car pulling a horse trailer. Two little girls about Colin's age were in the back seat of the car. They pressed against the side window and waved at Colin, who blushed and looked sternly ahead.

"It wouldn't be dull in the FBI," Colin said.

"Oh, I don't know about that. It might be pretty boring when you have to follow a crook for weeks before he does something exciting."

"Well, it can't be any more boring than sitting under a seatbelt all the way to California," Colin said.

God, Alex thought, I walked into that one. He took the car into the right lane again, set the automatic accelerator for an even seventy miles per hour so that if Colin got too interesting they would still make decent time. "When that guy following us gets us on a lonely stretch of road and runs us into a ditch, you'll thank me for making you wear your belt. It'll save your life."

Colin turned and looked at him, his big brown eyes made even larger by the eyeglasses. "I guess you aren't going to give in."

"You guessed right."

Colin sighed. "You're more or less my father now. Aren't you?"

"I'm your sister's husband. But . . . Since your sister has custody of you, I guess you could say I have a father's right to make rules you'll live by."

Colin shook his head, brushed his long hair out of his eyes. "I don't know. Maybe it was better being an orphan."

"Oh, you think so, do you?" Doyle asked, full of mock anger.

"If you hadn't come along, I wouldn't have gotten a plane ride to Boston," Colin admitted. "I wouldn't get to go to California, either. But . . . I don't know."

"You're too much," Doyle said, ruffling the boy's hair with one hand.

Sighing loudly, as if he needed the patience of Job in order to get along with Doyle, the boy smoothed his mussed hair with a comb he kept in his hip pocket. He put the comb away, straightened his King Kong T-shirt. "Well, I'll have to think about it. I'm just not sure yet."

The engine was silent. The tires made almost no noise on the well-surfaced roadbed.

Five minutes slipped by without awkwardness; they were comfortable enough with each other to endure silence. However, Colin grew restless and began to tap wildly elaborate rhythms on his bony knees.

"You want to find something on the radio?" Alex asked.

"I'll have to unbuckle my seatbelt."

"Okay. But just for a minute or two."

The boy relished the slithering retreat of the cloth belt. In an instant he was on his knees on the seat, turned and looking out the rear window. "He's still behind us!"

"Hey!" Alex said. "You're supposed to be finding a radio station."

Colin turned and sat down. "Well, you'd have thought I was slipping if I didn't *try*." His grin was irresistible.

"Get some music on that thing," Alex said.

Colin fiddled with the AM-FM radio until he located a rock-and-roll show. He set the volume, then suddenly popped up on his knees and looked out the rear window. "Staying right on our tail," he said. Then he dropped into his seat and grabbed for his belt.

"You're a real troublemaker, aren't you?" Alex asked.

"Don't worry about me," the boy said. "We have to worry about that guy following us."

At eight-fifteen they stopped at a Howard Johnson's restaurant outside of Harrisburg. The moment Alex slotted the car into a parking space in front of the orange-roofed building, Colin was looking for the van. "He's here. Like I expected."

Alex looked out his side window and saw the van pass in front of the restaurant, heading for the service station at the other end. On the side of the white Chevrolet, brilliant blue and green letters read: AUTOMOVER. ONE-WAY MOVE-IT-YOURSELF CONVENIENCE! Then the van was out of sight.

"Come on," Alex said. "Let's get some breakfast."

"Yeah," Colin said. "I wonder if he'll have the nerve to walk in after us?"

"He's just here to get gas. By the time we come out, he'll be fifty miles down the turnpike."

When they came outside again nearly an hour later, the parking spaces in front of the restaurant were all occupied. A new Cadillac, two ageless Volkswagens, a gleaming red Triumph sports car, a battered and muddy old Buick, their own black Thunderbird, and a dozen other vehicles nosed into the curb like several species of animals sharing a trough. The rented van was nowhere in sight.

"He must have phoned his superiors while we were eating—and discovered he was following the wrong people," Alex said.

Colin frowned. He jammed his hands into his dungaree pockets, looked up and down the row of cars as if he thought the Chevrolet were really there in some clever new disguise. Now he would have to make up a whole new game.

Which was just as well, so far as Doyle was concerned. It was not likely that even Colin would devise *two* games with built-in excuses for his popping out of his seatbelt every fifteen minutes.

They walked slowly back to the car, Doyle savoring the crisp morning air, Colin squinting at the parking lot and hoping for a glimpse of the van.

Just as they were to the car, the boy said, "I'll bet he's parked around the side of the restaurant." Before Doyle could forbid him, Colin jumped back onto the sidewalk and ran around the corner of the building, his tennis shoes slapping loudly on the concrete.

Alex got in the car, started it, and set the air conditioning a notch higher to blow out the stale air that had accumulated while they were having breakfast.

By the time he had belted himself in, Colin was back. The boy opened the passenger's door and climbed inside. He was downcast. "Not back there either." He shut and locked the door, slumped down, thin arms folded over his chest.

"Seatbelt." Alex put the car in gear and reversed out of the parking lot.

Grumbling, Colin put on the belt.

They pulled across the macadam to the service station and stopped by the pumps to have the tank topped off.

The man who hurried out to wait on them was in his forties, a beefy farmer-type with a flushed face and gnarled hands. He was chewing tobacco, not a common sight in Philly or San Francisco, and he was cheerful. "Help you folks?"

"Fill it with regular, please," Alex said, passing his credit card through the window. "It probably only needs half a tank."

"Sure thing." Four letters—CHET—were stitched across the man's shirt pocket. Chet bent down and looked past Alex at the boy. "How are you, Chief?"

Colin looked at him, incredulous. "F-f-ine," he stammered.

Chet showed a mouthful of stained teeth. "Glad to hear it." Then he went to the back of the car to put in the gasoline.

"Why did he call me Chief?" Colin asked. He was over his incredulity now, and he was embarrassed instead.

"Maybe he thinks you're an Indian," Alex said.

"Oh, sure."

"Or in charge of a fire company."

Colin scrunched down in the seat and looked at him sourly. "I should have gone on the plane with Courtney. I can't take your bad jokes for five days."

Alex laughed. "You're too much." He knew that Colin's perceptions and vocabulary were far in advance of his real age, and he had long ago grown accustomed to the boy's sometimes startling sarcasm and occasional good turn of phrase. But there was a forced quality to this precocious banter. Colin was trying hard to be grown up. He was straining out of childhood, trying to grit his teeth and *will* his way through adolescence and into adulthood. Doyle was familiar with that temperament, for it had been his own when he was Colin's age.

Chet came back and gave Doyle his credit card and sales form on a hard plastic holder. While Alex took the pen and scrawled his name, the attendant peered at Colin again. "Have a long trip ahead of you, Chief?"

Colin was as shaken this time as he had been when Chet had first addressed him. "California," he said, looking at his knees.

"Well," Chet said, "ain't that something? You're the second in an hour on his way to California. I always ask where people's going. Gives me a sense of helping them along, you know? An hour ago this guy's going to California, and now you. Everyone's going to California except me." He sighed.

Alex gave back the clipboard and tucked his credit card into his wallet. He glanced at Colin and saw that the boy was intently cleaning one fingernail with the other in order to have something to occupy his eyes if Chet should want to resume their one-sided conversation.

"Here you go." Chet handed Alex the receipt. "Way out to the coast?" He shifted his wad of tobacco from the left to the right side of his mouth.

"That's right."

"Brothers?" Chet asked.

"Excuse me?"

"You two brothers?"

"Oh, no," Alex said. He knew there was no time or reason for a full explanation of his and Colin's relationship. "He's my son."

"Son?" Chet seemed not to have heard the word before.

"Yes." Even if he was not Colin's father, he was old enough to be.

Chet looked at Doyle's coarse hair, at the way it spilled over his collar. He looked critically at Doyle's brightly patterned shirt with its large wooden buttons. Alex almost thanked the man for implying that he was not old enough to have a son Colin's age—and then he realized that the attendant's mood had changed. The man was not saying Doyle was too young to be father to an eleven-year-old, but that a father ought to set a better example. Doyle could look and dress strangely if he were Colin's brother, but if he were Colin's father, it was inappropriate—at least, it was to Chet's way of thinking.

"Thought you was twenty, twenty-one," Chet said, tonguing his tobacco.

"Thirty," Alex said, wondering why he bothered to answer.

The attendant looked at the sleek black car. A subtle hardness came into his eyes. Clearly, he thought that while it was fine for Doyle to be driving a Thunderbird that belonged to his father, it was a different thing if Doyle owned the car himself. If a man who looked like Doyle could have a fancy car and trips to California, while a workingman half again his age could not—there was no justice. "Well," Alex said, "have a good day."

Chet stepped back onto the pump island without wishing them a good trip. He frowned at the car. When the power window hummed up in one smooth motion, he frowned more deeply, the lines in his red brow bunched together like rolls in corrugated sheet metal.

"Such a nice man." Alex put the car in gear and got out of there.

When they were on the turnpike going west again, Colin suddenly laughed aloud.

"What's so funny?" Alex asked. He was shivering inside, angry with Chet out of proportion to what the man had done. Indeed, the man had done nothing except reveal a rather quiet prejudice.

"When he said you looked twenty-one, I thought he was going to call you Chief like he did me," Colin said. "That would have been good."

"Oh, sure! That would have been just hysterical."

Colin shrugged. "You thought it was funny when he called *me* Chief."

As Doyle's anger and fear settled, he realized that his own reaction to the attendant's unvoiced hatred was only a milder version of that overreaction which Colin had shown to the man's friendly small talk. Had the boy seen through Chet's original folksy persona to the not-so-folksy core? Or had he just been his usual shy self? It really did not matter. Whatever the case, the fact remained that an injustice had been done both of them. "I apologize, Colin. I should never have approved of the condescending tone he used with you."

"He treated me like I was a child."

"It's a natural trap for adults to fall into," Alex said. "But it isn't right. Are you going to accept my apology?"

Colin was especially serious, sitting straight and stiff, for this was the first time an adult had asked his forgiveness. "I accept," he said soberly. Then his gamin face broke into a wide smile. "But I still wish that he had called *you* Chief just like he did me."

Thick pines and black-trunked elms crowded against the sides of the road now, swaying gently in the spring wind.

The highway rose nearly a mile. At the crest it did not slope down again but continued across a flat table of land toward another gradual slope a mile away. The forest still loomed up, the tall sentinel pines in grand array, the sprawling elms like generals inspecting the troops.

Halfway along this flat stretch, on the right, was a picnic and rest area. The brush had been cleared from beneath the trees. A few wooden tables—anchored to concrete stanchions to guard against theft—and several trash baskets were fixed at intervals under the scattered pines. A sign announced public rest rooms.

At this hour of the morning there was no one at the picnic tables. However, at the far western end of the miniature park, stopped in the exit lane and waiting to pull back onto the pike, was the delivery van.

Automover
One-Way Move-It-Yourself
Convenience!

It was unquestionably the same van.

"There he is again!" Colin said, pressing his nose against the window as they swept past the van at seventy miles an hour. "It really is him!"

Doyle looked in the rear-view mirror and watched the delivery van pull onto the main road. It accelerated rapidly. In three or four minutes it caught up with them, settling in a quarter of a mile behind, pacing them as it had before.

Doyle knew that it was just coincidence. There was no reality in Colin's game. It was as much make-believe as all the games he had played with the boy in the past. No one in the world had a grudge against them. No one in the world had a reason to follow them with sinister intent. Coincidence . . .

Nevertheless, a chill lay the length of his back, a crust of imaginary ice.

CHAPTER 2

GEORGE LELAND HANDLED the rented twenty-foot Chevrolet van as if he were pushing a baby carriage, not even rattling the furniture and household goods which were packed into the cargo space behind the front seat. The land whizzed past, and the road rumbled underneath, and Leland was in command of it all.

He had grown up with trucks and other big machines, and he had a special talent for making them perform as they had been built to perform. On the farm near Lancaster, he had driven a hay truck by the time he was thirteen, touring his father's fields and loading from the separate baler beds. Before he was out of high school, he had operated the mower, bailer, plow, and all the other powerful equipment that brought a farm full circle from planting to harvesting to planting once more. When he went away to college, he helped pay his tuition by driving a delivery van much like the one he was now pushing across Pennsylvania. Later, when he was of age, he drove a full-size rig for a fuel-oil company, and in two summers of that he had not put a single nick on his truck or any passing automobile. He had been offered a job with the oil company after that second summer, but he had turned it down, of course. A year later, when he received his second degree in civil engineering and took his first *real* job, he often hopped up on one of the gigantic earth-moving machines and ran it through its paces—not because he was worried that the job was going badly, but because he enjoyed using the machine, enjoyed knowing that his touch with it was sure.

Now, all Monday morning and then past noon, he nursed the rented van westward. He stayed the same distance behind the black Thunderbird at all times. When the car slowed down, he slowed down too. When it accelerated, he quickly caught up with it. For the most part, however, the Thunderbird maintained a precise seventy miles an hour. Leland knew that the top-of-the-line model T-Bird had a speed-set control on the steering wheel which took some of the effort out of long-distance driving. Doyle was probably using that device. But it did not matter. Effortlessly, skillfully, George Leland matched the car's automatically controlled pace for hour after hour, almost as if he were a machine himself.

Leland was a big man, six-three and over two hundred pounds. He had once been twenty pounds heavier, but lately he had suffered a weight loss because he forgot to eat regular meals. His broad shoulders were more hunched than they had once been, his narrow waist even narrower. He had a square face framed with blond, almost white, hair. His eyes were blue, complexion clear except for a spray of freckles across his blunt nose. His neck was all muscle, gristle, and corded veins. When he gripped the steering wheel with his big hands and made his biceps swell with the unconscious fierceness of his grip, he looked absolutely immovable, as if he were welded to the vehicle.

He did not switch on his radio.

He did not look at the scenery.

He did not smoke, chew gum, or talk to himself.

Mile after mile, his attention was on the road, the car ahead, the machine that hummed satisfactorily all around him. Not once in those first hours of the journey did he think specifically about the man and the boy in the Thunderbird. His discordant thoughts, but for his driving, were vague and undetailed. Mostly he was riveted by a broad mesmeric hatred that had no single focus.

Somehow the car ahead would eventually become that focus. He knew this. But for the moment he only followed like a machine.

From Harrisburg, the Thunderbird went west on the turnpike, switched from that to Interstate 70, and passed across the northernmost sliver of West Virginia. Past Wheeling, barely inside of Ohio, the car signaled its intention to take an exit lane into a service area full of gasoline stations, motels, and restaurants.

The moment he saw the flashing signal, Leland braked and allowed the van to fall a mile behind Doyle. When he took the ramp a minute after the Thunderbird, the big black car was nowhere in sight. At the bottom of the ramp, Leland hesitated only a second, then turned west toward the heaviest concentration of tourist facilities. He drove slowly, looking for the car. He found it parked in front of a rectangular aluminum diner that looked like an old-fashioned railroad passenger car. The T-Bird was cooling in the shade of a huge sign that proclaimed HARRY'S FINE FOOD.

Leland drove until he came to Breen's, the last diner in the chrome, plastic, fake-stone, neon jungle of the interchange. He parked the Chevrolet on the far side of the small structure so that no one down at Harry's Fine Food, five hundred yards away, would see it. He got out, locked the van, and went to have his own lunch.

Breen's was, at least on the outside, much like the restaurant where Doyle and the kid had stopped. It was eighty feet long, an aluminum tube designed to look like a railroad passenger car, with one long narrow window row around three sides and an entrance cubicle tacked on the front almost as an afterthought.

Inside, a single width of cracked plastic coated booths was built onto the wall beside the contiguous windows. Each booth was equipped with a scarred ashtray, cylindrical glass sugar dispenser, glass salt and pepper shakers, a stainless-steel napkin dispenser, and a selector for the jukebox that stood next to the rest rooms at the extreme east end of the restaurant. A wide aisle separated the booths from the counter that ran from one end of the place to the other.

Leland turned right when he went in, walked to the end of the counter, and sat on the curve where he could occasionally look out the windows beyond the booths and see the Thunderbird down at Harry's.

Because it was the last restaurant in the complex, and because the lunch-hour rush had passed by two-thirty in the afternoon, Breen's was almost deserted. In a booth just inside the door, a middle-aged couple worked at hot roast beef sandwiches in mutual stony silence. An Ohio State Police lieutenant occupied the booth behind them, facing Leland. He was busy with a cheeseburger and French fries. In the booth at the far end of the room from Leland, a frowsy waitress with bleached hair smoked a cigarette and stared at the yellowed tile ceiling.

The only other person in the place was the counter waitress, who came to see what Leland wanted. She was perhaps nineteen, a fresh and pretty blonde with eyes as blue as Leland's. Her uniform was off the rack of a discount house, but she had personalized it. The skirt was hemmed eight inches above her shapely knees. A small embroidered chipmunk capered on one skirt pocket, a rabbit on the other. She had replaced the uniform's original white buttons with red ones. On her left breast stood an embroidered bird, and on her right breast was her name in fancy script: *Janet.* And a cheerful greeting just below the name: *Hi there!* She had a sweet smile, a curiously charming way of cocking her head, an almost Mickey Mouse cuteness—and she was obviously an easy lay.

"Seen the menu?" she asked. Her voice was at once throaty and childlike.

"Coffee and a cheeseburger," Leland said.

"French fries, too? They're already made."

"Well, okay," he said.

She wrote it down, then winked at him. "Back in a jiff."

He watched her walk up the service aisle behind the counter. Her trim legs scissored prettily. Her tight uniform clung to the well-delineated halves of her round ass. Suddenly, though the transformation was impossible, she was nude. To his eye, her clothes vanished in an instant. He saw all of her long legs, the divided globe of her behind, the exquisite line of her slim back . . .

He looked guiltily down at the counter top as he felt his loins tighten, and he was abruptly confused, disoriented. In that instant he could not even say where he was.

Janet came back with the coffee and put it in front of him. "Cream?"

"Yes, please."

She reached under the counter and came up with a two-inch-high cardboard container shaped like a milk bottle. She laid out his silverware, inspected her work, and approved. Instead of leaving him to his coffee, however, she leaned her elbows on the counter, propped her chin in her hands, gave him a saucy grin. "Where are you moving to?" she asked.

Leland frowned. "How did you know I'm moving?"

"Saw you pull in. Saw the Automover. You moving around here someplace?"

"No," he said, pouring cream into his coffee. "California."

"Oh, wow!" she said. "Great! Palm trees, sunshine, surfing . . ."

"Yeah," he said, wishing she would go away.

"I'd love to learn to surf," she said. "I like the sea. Summers, I take two weeks in Atlantic City, lay around on the beach and get real brown. I tan well. I have this *very* skimpy bikini that browns me all over." She laughed with false modesty. "Well . . . *Almost* all over. They don't approve of bikinis *that* small in Atlantic City."

Leland looked at her over the rim of his coffee cup.

She met his eyes and held them until he looked down again.

"Burg and fries?" the cook called from the serving window which connected the restaurant to the kitchen.

"Yours," she said quietly. She went and got the food, put it down before him. "Anything else!"

"No," he said.

She leaned against the counter again, talking while he ate. She worked hard at her ingenuousness. She giggled, did a lot of blinking and practiced blushing. He decided she was five years older than he had first thought.

"Could I have another cup of coffee?" he asked at last, just to be rid of her for a few moments.

"Sure," she said, picking up his empty cup and walking back toward the tall chrome brewer.

Watching her, Leland felt an odd vibration pass through him—and then he was seeing her without her clothes, just as he had before. He was not just imagining what she would look like when she was nude. He actually *saw* her as clearly as he saw the normal features of the diner around her. Her long legs and round buttocks were taut as she stood on her toes to check the filter in the top of the huge pot. When she turned, her breasts swayed, nipples swelling even as he watched.

Closing his eyes, Leland tried desperately to erase the vision. Opening them, he saw that it remained. And second by second, the longer it remained, the stranger he felt.

He closed his hand around the knife she had given him. He lifted the knife and held it before his face and looked at the bright serrated edge. Then the blade softened, diffused, as he looked beyond it to the nude girl walking slowly toward him, walking toward him as if through syrup, her bare breasts moving sensuously with each step . . . He thought of putting the knife between her ribs, deep between them, then twisting it back and forth until she stopped screaming and gave him a rictus of welcome . . .

Then, when she was almost up to him, the overfilled coffee cup balanced carefully in both her slim hands, Leland realized that someone was watching him. He turned slightly on his stool and looked at the middle-aged couple in the booth by the door. The man had a mouthful of food, but he was not chewing it. Cheeks bulging, he was watching Leland, watching the tight expression on Leland's face and the knife held up like a torch in the engineer's big right hand. In the second booth, the policeman had also stopped eating to watch Leland. He was frowning, as if he didn't quite know what to make of the knife.

Leland put the knife down and slid off the stool just as the waitress arrived with the coffee. He fumbled for his wallet and threw two dollars on the counter.

"You aren't leaving, are you?" she asked. Her voice was faraway and so icy that it made Leland shiver.

He did not answer her. He walked quickly to the door and went outside. The day seemed fiercely bright as he hurried to the van.

Sitting behind the wheel of the Chevrolet, he heard his heart pounding relentlessly against the walls of his chest. He drew breath in great wracking sobs and shuddered like a cold, wet dog.

Though she was not in sight now, and though he held his eyes tightly shut, Leland could see the young waitress: her supple body, long bare legs, widely spaced breasts . . . He could see himself leaning into her with the blade, her fair skin parting, could see himself clambering over the counter and taking her right there on the floor. No one would have stopped him, because he would have kept the knife. Everyone would have been afraid. Even the cop. He could have pressed the waitress down on the dirty tiles behind the counter, could have ravaged her as often as he wanted . . .

He thought about the knife and the blood that would have been and about the girl's breasts and the feel of her body moving against him, and he saw the stunned looks the others in the diner would have given him if he had actually done it. And, gradually, the mood left him. His heart grew quiet. His breath came less raggedly than it had.

He raised his head and unexpectedly caught sight of himself in the wide rear-view mirror fixed beside the driver's window. He looked into his own eyes, and for a moment he knew where he was and what he was doing. Suddenly, lucid, he realized why he was following the Thunderbird, what he intended to do to the people inside of it. And he knew it was all wrong. He was sick, confused, disoriented.

Looking away from his own eyes, sickened by what he saw in them, he discovered that the cop had come out of the diner and was walking toward the van. Irrationally, he was certain the trooper knew everything. The trooper somehow knew all that Leland would have liked to do to the girl and all that he would do to the pair in the Thunderbird. The trooper knew.

Leland started the van.

The trooper called to him.

Unable to hear what the man said, certain that he did not *want* to hear it, Leland put the van in gear and tramped the accelerator.

The cop shouted again.

The truck jerked, slewed sideways, kicking up loose gravel. Leland eased up on the gas and settled the machine. He drove out of the lot and picked up speed going through the clutter of motels and service stations.

He was breathing hard again. He was whimpering.

At the east end of the complex, he took the entrance ramp to Interstate 70 much faster than he should have. He did not check the traffic, but drove unheedingly onto the throughway. Fortunately, both westbound lanes were deserted.

Though in the back of his mind Leland knew that these roads were well patrolled and even monitored by radar, he let the needle on the speedometer climb and climb. When it hit close to a hundred, the van trembled slightly and fell into its maximum pace like a thoroughbred into the proper trot.

In the cargo space, the furniture rattled and banged against the walls. A table lamp fell with a crash of broken glass.

Leland looked in the mirror. The cop either had not started after him or had not started quickly enough. The road back there was empty.

Nevertheless, he held the van at a hundred miles an hour. The road roared beneath him. The flat land spun past like rapidly changed stage settings. And little by little the panic died in him. He gradually lost the feeling that everyone was watching him, that everyone's hand was against him, that he was transparent, and that he was being relentlessly pursued by forces connected with but not really identified by that state policeman. As he barreled westward, he quickly became a part of his machine once more. He guided it with a safe and measured touch. When he had gone seven or eight miles, he let the speed fall back to the legal limit; and even though only minutes had passed since he left the diner, he could not recall what had made him panic in the first place.

However, he suddenly *did* remember Doyle and Colin. The Thunderbird was somewhere behind him, to the east. Perhaps it was still parked in the shadow of that enormous sign at Harry's Fine Food. Even if it were on the road again, Doyle and the kid were miles to the rear, out of sight. Leland did not like that at all.

He let his speed drop even further. As he began to realize that now *they* were following *him,* his ever-present fear took on a familiar edge. The gray road seemed like a tunnel now, a trap with one exit and no way to turn back.

Then, ahead, another rest area loomed on the right, shielded from the highway by a double row of pines. Leland braked and drove in there, went up a slight incline. He parked on the square graveled plateau, facing the highway so that he could watch the traffic between the thick brown trunks of the trees.

All he had to do now was wait and watch the road. When the Thunderbird passed, he could fall in behind it, catch up to it in two or three minutes. He was enormously relieved.

The trooper was getting out of the patrol car even before George Leland realized that he had driven into the rest area. Leland had been watching the highway beyond the pines for a full five minutes, and he must have been somewhat mesmerized by the bright sunshine and the spurts of westbound traffic. One moment he thought he was alone—and the next moment he was aware of the Ohio State Police patrol car angled in beside the van. Half in the shadows cast by the pines and half in the slanting sunlight, it looked unreal. The dome light was flashing, though the siren had not been used. The trooper who got out was in his early thirties, sober and hard-jawed. He was the same man who had been taking his lunch in Breen's, the one who had called to Leland outside the little diner.

Leland remembered some of the reasons for his previous panic. Again the world appeared to close in on him. Darkness swept up at the corners of his vision, inward-spreading ink stains. He felt bottled up and vulnerable, an easy target for those who meant him harm. These days everyone seemed to be after him. He was always running.

He rolled down his window as the cop approached.

"You alone?" the lieutenant asked, stopping far enough from the van to be out of the way of the door if Leland should suddenly swing it open. He had one hand on the butt of his holstered revolver.

"Alone?" Leland asked. "Yes, sir."

"Why didn't you stop when I called to you?"

"Called to me?"

"At the restaurant," the lieutenant said, his voice crisp and older than his smooth face.

Leland looked perplexed. "I didn't see you. You called me?"

"Twice."

"I'm sorry," Leland said. "I didn't hear." He frowned. "Did I do something wrong? I'm usually a careful driver."

The trooper watched him carefully for a moment, searched his blue eyes, took in his sun-darkened face and neatly trimmed hair, then relaxed. He let his hand drop from the gun. He took the last few steps to the van. "It wasn't your driving," he said. "Just the same, I'd like to have a look at your license and the rental papers for the truck."

"Sure," Leland said. "Always glad to cooperate." Moving as if he were reaching for his wallet, he took the .32-caliber pistol out of the tissue box on the seat beside him. In one fluid movement he raised it to the window and centered the barrel on the trooper's face and pulled the trigger. The single shot echoed in the copse of pines behind the van and slapped sharply across the highway out front.

Leland sat and watched the traffic on the throughway for several minutes before he realized that he ought to conceal the corpse. Any minute someone could pull into the rest area, see the cop sprawled between the patrol car and the van, and run for help. These days everyone was on his trail. He had stayed alive this long only by keeping one step ahead of them. Now was no time to let his thinking get fuzzy.

He pushed open the van door and got out.

The trooper was lying face down in the gravel, dark blood pooled around his head. He looked much smaller now, almost like a child.

During the past year, when he sensed the conspiracy working against him, Leland had wondered whether he would be able to kill to protect himself. He knew it would come to that. Kill or be killed. And until this moment he had not been sure which it would be. Now he could not understand why he had ever been in doubt. When it was kill or be killed, even a non-violent man could act to save himself.

Expressionlessly Leland bent down and grabbed hold of the dead man's ankles, dragged him around to the open door of the squad car. The short-wave radio in there was sputtering noisily. Leland heaved the corpse inside, let it slump over the steering wheel. But that was no good. Even from a distance the man looked dead. Aware that he would have to completely conceal it, Leland pushed the body across the vinyl seat and climbed into the car after it.

He touched the steering wheel, unaware he was leaving fingerprints.

He touched the back of the vinyl seat.

Oblivious to the thickening blood, he bent the dead man's ruined face down to his knees, then shoved the compacted hulk onto the floor in front of the passenger's seat.

Inadvertently he touched the window on that side of the car, pressing all five fingers firmly to the glass.

He had to force the corpse to slip halfway back into the cavity beneath the dashboard, but when he was done he was confident that no one would find the body unless they opened the door looking for it.

Climbing out, he touched the bench of the vinyl seat.

He touched the steering wheel again.

He closed the door, fingers clasped around the chrome handle.

It never occurred to him that he ought to take a rag and wipe down everything that he had touched. Already he had half forgotten the dead man crammed in the corner of the official car.

He went back to the van and got in and closed the door. On the highway, traffic flashed by, casting off a golden shower of late-afternoon sunlight. For ten minutes or more Leland watched the road, waiting for the Thunderbird to pass.

With his physical attention focused on so small an area, his thoughts drifted until they eventually settled on the young waitress who had served him at the diner, the girl with the rabbits and chipmunks on her uniform. Now he saw why she had confused and upset him. With her long natural-platinum hair and elfin features, she looked a little bit like Courtney. Not much, but some. Therefore she had precipitated his spell. He knew, now, that he did not want to put his knife into her, had never wanted to put his knife into her. He did not want to make love to her, either. Indeed, he had no interest in that girl at all. He was strictly a one-woman man. He cared only for his lovely Courtney.

As quickly as his thoughts passed from the waitress to Courtney, they flicked from Courtney to Doyle and the boy. Leland was shocked at the suddenly perceived possibility that the Thunderbird had passed while he was putting the dead trooper into the squad car. Perhaps they had gone by twenty minutes ago. They could be miles and miles out in front of him . . .

What if Doyle changed his intended route? What if he did not follow the road that was marked on his map?

Leland felt a hard lump of fear rise in his throat.

If he lost Doyle and the kid, wouldn't he be losing Courtney? If he lost Courtney, lost his way to Courtney, hadn't he then lost everything?

Droplets of sweat standing out on his broad forehead despite the air conditioning, he slipped the van in gear and backed out of there. The front wheels arced through the bloodied gravel. He shifted into drive and took the Chevrolet out of the rest area. The dome light on the squad car still went around and around, but Leland was not aware of that. There was no reality for him except the road ahead and the Thunderbird which must be even now escaping from him.

CHAPTER 3

WHEN THEY HAD been back on the road for fifteen minutes after their lunch break and still the rented Chevrolet van had not appeared in the rear-view mirror, Doyle stopped watching for it. He had been shaken when the van pulled behind them again after their breakfast stop near Harrisburg, but of course that had been merely coincidence. It had trailed them across all of Pennsylvania and through a sliver of West Virginia, then into Ohio—but that was because it happened to be going west on the same Interstate they were using. The driver of the van, whoever he was, had chosen his route from a map, just as Doyle had; there was nothing sinister in the other man's mind when he outlined his trip. Belatedly Alex realized that he could have relieved his own mind at any time during the morning just by pulling to the side of the road and letting the van go past. He could have waited for it to build up a fifteen-minute lead and could have dispensed immediately with the whole crazy idea that they were being pursued. Well, it did not matter much now. The van was gone, way out ahead of them somewhere.

"He back there?" Colin asked.

"No."

"Shucks."

"Shucks?"

"I'd really like to know what he was up to," Colin said. "Now I guess we'll never find out."

Alex smiled. "I guess we never will."

Compared to Pennsylvania, Ohio was almost a plains state. Vistas of open green land stretched out on both sides of the highway, marred only by an occasional shabby town, neat farm, or oddly isolated and routinely filthy factory. The sameness of it, stretching away into the distance under an equally bland blue sky, bored and depressed them. The car seemed to crawl at a quarter of its real speed.

When they had been on the road only twenty minutes, Colin began to twist and squirm uncomfortably. "This seatbelt isn't made right," he told Doyle.

"Oh?"

"I think they made it too tight."

"It can't be too tight. It's adjustable."

"I don't know . . ." Colin tested it with both hands.

"You aren't getting out of it with excuses as contrived as that one."

Colin looked at the open fields, at a herd of fat cows grazing on a hill above a white-and-red barn. "I didn't know there were so many cows in the world. Ever since we left home I've seen cows everywhere I look. If I see one more cow, I think I might puke."

"No you won't," Alex said. "I'd make you clean it up."

"Is the rest of the country going to be like this?" Colin asked, indicating the mundane landscape with one slim, upturned hand.

"You know it isn't," Doyle said patiently. "You'll see the Mississippi River, the deserts, the Rocky Mountains . . . You've taken enough imaginary trips around the world to know it far better than I do."

Colin quit tugging at his seatbelt when he saw he was not getting anywhere with Doyle. "By the time we find these *interesting* places, my brain will be all rotten inside. If I watch too much of this *nothing*, I'll turn into a zombie. You know what a zombie's like?" He made a face like a zombie for Doyle's benefit: mouth agape, flesh slack, eyes open wide but taking in nothing.

While he liked Colin and was amused by him, Doyle was also disturbed. He knew that the boy's persistent campaign to be let out of his belt was as much a test of Doyle's talent for discipline as it was an expression of real discomfort. Before Alex had married Courtney, the boy obeyed his sister's suitor as he might his own father. And even when the honeymooners came home to tie up their affairs in Philadelphia, Colin had behaved. But now that he was alone with Doyle and out of his sister's sight, he was testing their new relationship. If he could get away with anything, he would. In that respect, he was the same as all other boys his age.

"Look," Alex said, "when you talk to Courtney on the phone tonight, I don't want you complaining about your seatbelt and the scenery. She and I both thought this trip would be good for you. I might as well tell you that we also thought it would let you and me get used to each other, throw us together and smooth out any wrinkles. Now, I won't have you complaining and groaning when we call her from Indianapolis. She's out in San Francisco getting people to put down the carpet, install the drapes, deliver the furniture . . . She has enough on her mind without worrying about you."

Colin thought about that as they rushed directly westward toward Columbus. "Okay," he said at last. "I surrender. You have nineteen years on me."

Alex glanced at the boy, who gave him a shy under-the-eyebrows look, and laughed quietly. "We'll get along. I always thought we would."

"Tell me one thing," the boy said.

"What's that?"

"You have nineteen years on me. And—six on Courtney?"

"That's right."

"Do you make the rules and regulations for Courtney, too?"

"*Nobody* makes rules and regulations for Courtney," Doyle said.

Colin folded his skinny arms over his chest and nodded smugly. "That's sure the truth. I'm glad you understand her. I wouldn't give this marriage six months if you thought you could tell Courtney to wear *her* seatbelt."

On both sides, flat fields spread out. Cows grazed. Scattered puffs of clouds drifted lazily across the open sky.

After a while Colin said, "I'll bet you half a buck I can estimate how many cars will pass us going east in the next five minutes—and come within ten of the real number."

"Half a buck?" Alex asked. "You're on."

The dashboard clock ticked off the five minutes as they counted the eastbound cars, announcing each one aloud. Colin was only three off his estimate.

"Double or nothing?" the boy asked.

"What have I got to lose?" Alex asked, grinning, his confidence in the trip and himself and the boy now all restored.

They played the game again. Colin's estimate was only four cars off, and he won another fifty cents. "Double or nothing?" he asked again, rubbing his long-fingered hands together.

"I don't think so," Alex said suspiciously. "How'd you manage that?"

"Easy. I counted them to myself for half an hour until I saw what an average five minutes brought. Then I asked you if you wanted to bet."

"Maybe we ought to take a detour down to Las Vegas," Alex said. "I'll just tag along with you in the casinos and do what you tell me."

Colin was so pleased by the compliment that he could not think of anything to say. He hugged himself and dropped his head, then looked out the side window and smiled toothily at his own vague reflection in the glass.

Although the boy was not aware of it, Doyle could see that reflection when he took a quick look at Colin to see why he had become silent so suddenly. Understanding, he grinned himself and relaxed against the seat, the last bit of tension draining out of him. He saw that he had not fallen in love with one person, but with two. He loved this skinny, overly intellectual boy almost as much as he loved Courtney. It was the sort of realization that could make a man forget the uncertainty and shallow, disquieting fear of the morning.

When he originally mapped the trip and called ahead from Philly to make reservations, and again when he mailed the room-deposit check four days ago, Doyle had told the people at the Lazy Time Motel that he and Colin would arrive between seven and eight o'clock Monday evening. At seven-thirty, precisely in the middle of his estimate, he drove into the motel's lot, just east of Indianapolis, and parked by the office.

Their rooms were reserved ahead for the entire trip. Doyle did not want to drive six hundred miles only to spend half the night looking for a vacancy.

He shut off the headlights, then the car. The silence was eerie. Gradually the traffic sounds from the Interstate came to him, forlorn cries on the early-night air. "How's this for a schedule?" he asked Colin. "A hot shower, a good supper. Then we call Courtney—and hit the sack for eight hours."

"Sure," Colin said. "But could we eat first?"

The request was an unusual one for him. He was as light an eater as Doyle had been at his age. When they had stopped for lunch today, Colin nibbled at one piece of chicken, ate some cole slaw, a dish of sherbet, drank a Coke—then proclaimed himself "stuffed."

"Well," Doyle said, "we're not so grubby they'll refuse to let us in the restaurant. But I want to get our rooms first." He opened his door and let the chill but muggy night air into the car. "You wait here for me."

"Sure," Colin said. "If I can get out of this seatbelt now."

Alex smiled, unfastened his own belt. "I really scared you, did I?"

Colin gave him a lopsided smile. "If you want to look at it that way."

"Okay, okay," Doyle said. "Take off your seatbelt, Colin, me boy."

When he got out of the car and stretched his legs, he saw that the Lazy Time Motel was just what the tour-guide book said it was: clean, pleasant, but inexpensive. It was built as a large L, with the neon-framed office at the junction of the two wings. Forty or fifty doors, all alike and spaced as evenly as the slats in a fence, were set into undistinguished red-brick walls. A concrete promenade fronted both wings and was covered by a corrugated aluminum awning supported by black wrought-iron posts every ten feet. A soda machine stood just outside the office door, humming and clinking to itself.

The office was small, but the walls were bright yellow, the tile floor clean and polished. Doyle crossed to the counter and struck the bell for service.

"Just a *minute!*" a woman called from behind a bamboo-curtained doorway at the end of the work area on the business side of the counter.

Beside the counter was a rack of magazines and paperback books. A sign above the rack read: TONIGHT, WHY NOT READ YOURSELF TO SLEEP? While Doyle waited for the clerk, he looked at the books, though he would not need anything to make him sleepy after all day on the road.

"Sorry to make you wait," she said, shouldering through the bamboo curtain. "I was—" Halfway from the curtain to the counter, she got a look at Doyle, and she stopped talking. She stared at him the same way Chet, at the service station, had stared. "Yes?" Her voice was decidedly cool.

"You've got reservations for Doyle," Alex said. Now he was doubly glad he had made reservations. He was fairly sure she would have turned him away, even if he could see there was not a car in front of every room and even if the neon vacancy sign *was* lighted.

"Doyle?" she asked.

"Doyle."

She came the rest of the way to the counter, brightened as she reached for the file cards by the registry book. "Oh, the father and son from Philadelphia!"

"That's right," Doyle said, trying to smile.

She was in her middle fifties, an attractive woman despite the extra twenty pounds she carried. She wore her hair in a 1950's bouffant, her broad forehead revealed, spit curls at her ears. Her knit dress clung to a full if matronly bosom. The lines of a girdle showed at hips and waist.

"That was one of our seventeen-dollar rooms," she said.

"Yes."

She took the file card from the green metal box, looked closely at it, then flipped open the registration book. She carefully completed a third-of-a-page form, then turned the book around and held out the pen. "If you'll sign here . . . Oh," she said as he reached for the pen, "maybe your father should sign. The room *is* reserved in his name."

Doyle looked at her uncomprehendingly until he realized she had more in common with Chet than he had first thought. "I *am* the father. I'm Alex Doyle."

She frowned. When she tilted her head, the bouffant seemed about to slide right down over her face in one well-sprayed piece. "But it says here—"

"My boy's eleven." He took the pen and scribbled his signature on the form.

She looked at the freshly inked name as if it were an ugly spot on her new slipcovers. Any minute now she would run for the solvent and scrub the nasty thing away.

"Which room have we got?" Alex asked, prodding her along against her will.

She took in his hair and clothes again. He was not accustomed to such frank disapproval in cities like Philly and San Francisco, and he resented her manner.

"Well," she said, "you must be aware that you pay—"

"In advance," he finished for her. "Yes, silly of me not to think of it." He counted out twelve dollars onto the registration book. "I sent in a five-dollar deposit, you may recall."

"But there's tax," she said.

"How much?"

When she told him, he paid from the loose change in the pocket of his wrinkled dark-gray jeans.

She counted the money into the cash drawer even though she had seen him count it himself a minute ago. Reluctantly she took a key from the pegboard and gave it to him. "Room 37," she said, staring at the key as if it were diamond jewelry she was committing to his care. "That's way down the long wing."

"Thank you," he said, hoping to avoid a scene. He walked back across the clean, well-lighted room toward the door.

"The Lazy Time has very nice rooms," she said as he reached the door.

He looked back. "I'm sure it does."

"We like to keep them that way," she said.

He nodded grimly and got the hell out of there.

Despite the fact that he had lost sight of the Thunderbird, George Leland began to calm down. For fifteen minutes he pushed the van along at top speed, desperately surveying the traffic ahead for a glimpse of the big car. But his natural empathy with machines acted as a sedative. The fear left him. He let the van slow down. With a growing confidence in his ability to catch up with the Thunderbird, he drove only a few miles an hour over the speed limit. Like a man in a light trance, he was aware only of the road and of the Chevy's engine revving at just the right pitch, and he was considerably quieted by these things.

For the first time all day Leland smiled. And he wished, for the first time in a long time, that he had someone to whom he could talk . . .

"You look happy, George," she said, startling him.

He glanced away from the road.

She was sitting in the passenger's seat, only a couple of feet away from him. But how was that possible?

"Courtney," he said, voice a dry whisper. "I . . ."

"It's nice to see you so happy," she said. "You're usually so sober."

He looked back at the road, confused.

But his eyes were drawn to her magnetically an instant later. The sunlight pierced the windshield and passed through her as if she were a spirit. It touched her golden hair and skin, then kept right on going. He could see the door panel on the other side of her. He could see through her lovely face to the window behind her head and the countryside beyond the window—as if she were transparent. He could not understand. How could she be here? How could she know that he was following Doyle and the boy?

A horn blared nearby.

Leland looked up, surprised to find he had drifted out of the right lane and almost collided with a Pontiac trying to pass him. He wheeled hard right and brought the van back into line.

"How have you been, George?" she asked.

He looked at her, then quickly back at the highway. She was wearing the same outfit she had worn when he saw her last: clunky shoes, a short white skirt, fancy red blouse with long pointed collar. When he followed her to the airport a week ago and watched her board the 707, he had been so excited by the way she looked in that trim little suit that he had wanted her more than he had ever wanted a woman before. He almost rushed up to her—but he had realized that she would think it was strange of him to be following her.

"How have you been, George?" she asked again.

She had been worried about his problems even before he recognized that he had any, even before he had seen that everything was going wrong. When she dissolved their two-year-old affair and would only talk to him on the telephone, she had still called him twice a month to see how he was getting along. Of course, she has stopped calling eventually. She had forgotten him completely.

"Oh," he said, keeping his eyes on the road, "I'm fine."

"You don't look fine." Her voice was faraway, hollow, only slightly like her real voice. Yet there she was, sitting beside him in broad daylight.

"I'm doing very well," he assured her.

"You've lost weight."

"I needed to lose some."

"Not *that* much, George."

"It can't hurt."

"And you have bags under your eyes."

He took one hand from the wheel and touched the discolored, puffy flesh. "Haven't you been getting enough sleep?" she asked.

He did not respond. He did not like this conversation. He hated her when she badgered him about his health and said his emotional problems with other people must come from a basic *physical* illness. Sure, the problems had come on suddenly. But he wasn't at fault. It was other people. Lately, everyone had it in for him.

"George, have people been treating you better since we last talked?"

He admired her long legs. They were not transparent now. The flesh was golden, firm, beautiful. "No, Courtney. I lost another job."

Now that she had stopped nagging him about his health, he felt better. He wanted to tell her everything, no matter how embarrassing. She would under-stand. He would put his head in her lap and cry until he had no tears left. Then he would feel better . . . He would cry while she smoothed his hair, and when he sat up he would have as few problems as he had had more than two years ago, before this trouble had come along and everyone had gotten nasty with him.

"Another job?" she asked. "How many jobs have you held these last two years?"

"Six," he said.

"What did you get fired for this time?"

"I don't know," Leland said, genuine misery in his voice. "We were putting up an office building—two years of work. I was getting along with everyone. Then my boss, the chief engineer, started in on me."

"Started in on you?" she asked, flat and faraway, barely audible above the buzz of the wide tires. "How?"

He shifted uneasily behind the wheel. "You know, Courtney. Just like all the other times. He talked about me behind my back, set the other men against me. He countermanded my job assignments and encouraged Preston, the steel foreman, to—"

"He did all this behind your back?" she asked.

"Yes. He—"

"If he said all this behind your back, how do you really know he said anything at all?" He could not tolerate the sympathy in her voice, for it was too much like pity. "Did you hear him? You didn't hear him yourself, did you, George?"

"Don't talk to me like that. Don't try to say it was my imagination."

She was quiet, as ordered.

He looked to see if she was still there. She smiled at him, more solid than she had been a few minutes before.

He looked at the setting sun, but did not see it. He was now only minimally conscious of the highway ahead. Unsettled by her magical presence, he no longer handled the Chevrolet van as well as he could. It drifted back and forth within the right-hand lane, now and then running onto the gravel shoulder.

After a while he said, "Did you know that after I called you that day just to ask for a date, after I found you were already three weeks married—I almost went out of my mind? I followed you for a week, day in and day out, just watching you. Did you know? You had said you were flying to Frisco, that this man Doyle and your brother would follow in a week, and you said you didn't think you'd ever come back to Philly again. That nearly killed me, Courtney. Everything was going so badly for me. I remembered how good we had it once . . . So I called to see if maybe we could get together again. I was going to ask for a date. Did you know that? You didn't, I'll bet. I was all ready to ask for a date . . . And then I find out you're married and running clear across country." His voice got hard, cold, almost mean. He paused to collect his thoughts. "You were my good luck— two, three, four years ago. When we were together, everything was fine. Now you're going to be out of touch, out of sight . . . I knew I had to be near you, Courtney. When I followed you to the airport and saw you leave on that 707, I knew I'd have to follow Doyle and Colin and find out where you were living."

She said nothing.

He drove and talked on, hoping to get a positive reaction from her, no longer perplexed by her sudden appearance. "I had lost my job again. There was nothing to keep me in Philly. Of course, I didn't have money to pay movers like this Doyle did. I had to pack and haul my own things. So I'm driving this clumsy van with its poor air conditioning instead of a fancy Thunderbird. I'm not having a run of luck like this Doyle of yours. People aren't treating me as well as they're treating him. But I knew I had to come out to California anyway, to be near you. To be near you, Courtney . . ."

Pretty, quiet, unmoving, she sat there, her slim hands folded in her lap, a nimbus of the day's last light encircling her head.

"It wasn't easy staying on their trail," he told her. "I had to be smart. When they were eating breakfast, I realized they must have a marked map in the car, something that would show me which way they were going. I checked." He gave her a quick glance, grinning, looked at the road again. "I put a wire coat hanger through the rubber seal between the windows and popped the lock button. The maps were on the seat. An address book, too. Your man Doyle is extremely efficient. He'd written down the names and addresses of the motels where he had reservations. I copied them. And I studied the maps. I know every road they're taking and every place they'll stay overnight between here and San Francisco. Now I can't lose them. I'll just trail along behind. I don't have them in sight this minute, but I'll connect with them later." He talked very fast, running his words together. He was eager for her to understand the trouble he had gone to so that he might be near her.

She surprised him. "George, did you ever see a doctor about your headaches, about your other problems?"

"I'm not sick, damn you!" he shouted. "I've got a healthy mind, healthy brain, healthy body. I'm in good shape. I don't want to hear anything more about that. Just forget about that."

"*Why* are you following them?" she asked, changing the subject as ordered.

Perspiration ran off his brow in several steady streams, fat crystal droplets that tickled his cheeks and neck. "Didn't I just tell you? I want to find out where you'll be living. I want to be near you."

"But if you copied the addresses in Alex's book, you have our new home address in San Francisco. You don't have to follow them to find me. You already know where I am, George."

"Well . . ."

"George, *why* are you following Alex and Colin?"

"I told you."

"You did not."

"Shut up!" he said. "I don't like what you're implying. I won't listen to any more of this. I'm healthy. I'm not sick. There's nothing at all wrong with me. So just go away. Leave me alone. I don't want to have to look at you."

The next time he looked, she was gone. She had vanished.

Although he had been momentarily confused by her unexpected and unexplained appearance, he was not at all surprised by her disappearance. He had *told* her to go away. Toward the end of their affair, just before she broke off with him two years ago, Courtney had said that he frightened her, that these recent black moods of his made her uneasy. She was still scared of him. When he said "Go," she went. She knew better than to argue. The thoughtless bitch had betrayed him by marrying this Doyle, and now she would do anything to stay in his good graces.

He smiled at the darkening highway.

In the last light of day, with the land drenched in almost eerie orange radiance, Ohio State Police officer Eric James Coffey drove off Interstate 70 into a picnic and rest area on the right-hand side of the road. He went up the slight incline to the pine-shielded clearing, and he saw the empty squad car at once. The dome light still swiveled, transmitting a red pulse to the trees on all sides.

Since four o'clock, when Lieutenant Richard Pulham had been one hour late returning his cruiser to the division garage at the end of his shift, more than twenty of his fellow troopers had been scouring the Interstate and all the secondary access roads leading to and from it. And now Coffey had found the car—identified it by the numerals on the front door—at the extreme west end of Lieutenant Pulham's patrol circuit.

Coffey wished he had not been the one to find it, for he suspected what he would discover. A dead cop. So far as Coffey could see, there was no other possibility.

He picked up the microphone, thumbed the button. "This is 166, Coffey.

I've found our cruiser." He repeated the message and gave his position to the dispatcher. His voice was thick and quavery.

Reluctantly he shut off the engine and got out of his own car.

The evening air was chilly. A wind had sprung up from the northwest.

"Lieutenant Pulham! Rich Pulham!" he shouted. The name came back to him in whispered imitations of his own voice. He received no other answer.

Resignedly Coffey went to Pulham's cruiser, bent and stared into the passenger's window. With the sun down, the car was full of shadows.

He opened the door. The interior light came on, weak and insufficient because the dome flasher had nearly drained the battery. Still, dim as it was, it illuminated the blackening blood and the body jammed rudely into the space before the front seat.

"Bastards," Coffey said quietly. "Bastards, bastards, bastards." His voice rose with each repetition. "Cop killers," he told the onrushing darkness. "We'll get the sons of bitches."

Their room at the Lazy Time Motel was large and comfortable. The walls were an off-white color, the ceiling a couple of feet higher than it would be in any motel built since the end of the fifties. The furniture was heavy and utilitarian, though not spartan by any means. The two easy chairs were well padded and upholstered, and the desk, if surfaced with plastic, gave plenty of knee room and working space. The two double beds were firm, the sheets crisp and redolent of soap and softener. The scarred mahogany nightstand between the beds held a Gideon Bible and a telephone.

Doyle and Colin sat on separate beds, facing each other across the narrow walk space between them. By mutual agreement, Colin was the first to talk to his sister. He held the receiver in both hands. His thick eyeglasses had slipped down his nose and now rested precariously on the very tip of it, though the boy did not seem to notice. "We were followed all the way from Philadelphia!" he told Courtney as soon as she came on the line.

Alex grimaced.

"A man in a Chevrolet van," Colin said. "No. We couldn't get a look at him. He was much too smart for that." He told her all about their imaginary FBI man. When he tired of that, he told her how he had won a dollar from Doyle. He listened to her for a moment, laughed. "I tried, but he wouldn't make any more bets."

Listening to the boy's half of the conversation, Doyle was momentarily jealous of the warm, intimate relationship between Courtney and Colin. They were entirely at ease with each other, and neither one needed to pretend—or disguise—his love. Then the envy passed as Doyle realized his own relationship with Courtney was much the same—and that he and the boy would soon be as close as they both were to the woman.

"She says I'm costing you too much," Colin said, passing the receiver to Doyle.

He took it. "Courtney?"

"Hi, darling." Her voice was rich and full. She might have been beside him instead of at the other end of twenty-five hundred miles of telephone wire.

"Are you okay?"

"Lonely," she said.

"Not for long. How's the house coming?"

"The carpets are all down."

"No hassles?"

"Not until the bill arrives," she said.

"Painters?"

"Been and gone."

"Then you just have the furniture deliveries to worry about," he said.

"I can't *wait* for our bedroom suite to get here."

"Every bride's greatest concern," he said.

"That's not what I mean, sexist. It's just that this damn sleeping bag gives me a backache."

He laughed.

"And," she said, "have you ever tried camping out in the middle of an empty, lushly carpeted twenty-by-twenty master bedroom? It's eerie."

"Maybe we should have all flown out," Alex said. "Maybe a furnitureless house would be easier to endure if you had company."

"No," she said. "I'm okay. I just like to gripe. How are you and Colin getting along?"

"Famously," he said, watching Colin as the boy pushed his glasses up on his pug nose.

"What about this guy following you in the Automover?" she asked.

"It's nothing."

"One of Colin's games?"

"That's all," he assured her.

"Hey, did he really take you for a dollar?"

"He really did. He's a sneaky kid. He's a lot like you."

Colin laughed.

"How's the car handling?" Courtney asked. "Is six hundred miles a day too much for you, by yourself?"

"Not at all," he said. "My back's probably not aching as much as yours. We'll be able to stay right on schedule."

"I'm glad to hear you say that. I'm a little bit of a sexist myself—and I can't wait to get you in that new bed."

"Likewise," he said, smiling.

"I've had several nights to appreciate the view from this damn bedroom window," she said. "It's even more spectacular tonight than it was last night. You can see the city lights on the bay, all distorted and glimmering."

"I'm homesick for a home I've never slept in," Doyle said. He was also lovesick, and he was made more feverish by the sound of her voice.

"I love you," she said.

"Likewise."

"Say it."

"I've got an audience," Doyle said, looking at Colin. The boy was listening, rapt, as if he could hear both sides of the conversation.

"Colin won't be embarrassed by that," she said. "Love doesn't embarrass him at all."

"Okay," he said. "I love you."

Colin grinned and hugged himself.

"Call tomorrow night."

"As scheduled," he promised.

"Say goodnight to Colin for me."

"I will."

"Goodbye, darling."

"Goodbye, Courtney."

He missed her so profoundly that breaking the connection was a little bit like drawing a sharp knife across his own flesh.

When George Leland pulled the rented Chevrolet van into the macadamed lot in front of the Lazy Time Motel, the No VACANCY sign was on, large green neon letters. He was not disturbed by that, for he had never intended to stay there. He was not as flush as Alex Doyle, not as lucky; he was unable to afford even the Lazy Time's prices. He just drove slowly along the short arm of the L, then down the long branch until he saw the Thunderbird.

He smiled, satisfied with himself. "Just like in the address book," he said. "Doyle, you're nothing if not efficient."

He drove away from the Lazy Time, then, before he might be seen. He went on down the road, past two dozen other motels, some of them like the Lazy Time and some much fancier. At last he came to a shabby wooden motel with a small vacancy sign out front and a spare, undecorated neon sign at the entrance: DREAMLAND. It looked like an eight-dollar-a-night dive. He drove in and parked near the office.

He rolled down the window and turned the rear-view mirror so that he could get a look at himself. As he took his comb from his pocket, he noticed several dark streaks on his face. He rubbed at the stains, sniffed the residue, then put it on his tongue. Blood. Surprised, he opened the door and examined himself in the glow of the ceiling light. Dried blood was spattered over his trousers and smeared all over his short-sleeved shirt. The soft white hairs on his left arm were now stiff and purple with dried blood.

Where had it come from?

And when?

He knew he had not hurt himself, yet he could not understand whose blood this was if not his own. Thinking about it, he sensed the approach of one of his fierce migraine headaches. Then, in the back of his mind, something ugly stirred and turned over heavily; and although he still could not recall whose blood had been spilled on him, he knew that he dared not attempt to rent a room for the night while he was wearing the stuff.

Praying that his headache would hold off for a while, he readjusted the mirror, closed the door, started the truck, and drove away from the motel. He went half a mile down the road and parked in front of an abandoned service station. He opened his suitcase and took out a change of clothes. He undressed, washed his face and hands with paper tissues and his own spittle, then put on the clean clothes.

He still felt travel-weary and headachy, but he was now presentable enough to face the night clerk at the motel.

Fifteen minutes later he was in his room in Dreamland. It was not much of a room. Ten-foot square, with a tiny attached bath, it seemed more like a place where a man was *put* than like one to which he went voluntarily. The walls were a dirty yellow, scarred, finger-stained, even marked with dust webs in the high corners. The easy chair was new and functional yet ancient. The desk was green tubular steel with a Masonite work surface darkened with the wormlike marks of cigarette burns. The bed was narrow, soft, the sheets patched.

George Leland did not really notice the condition of the room. It was merely a place to him, like any other place.

At the moment he was chiefly concerned with staving off the headache which he could feel building behind his right eye. He dropped his suitcase at the foot of the sagging bed and stripped out of his clothes. In the tiny bathroom's bare shower stall, he let the spray of hot water sluice the weariness from him. For long minutes he stood with the water drumming pleasantly against the back of his skull and neck, for he had found that this would, on rare occasion, lessen the severity of and even cure altogether an oncoming migraine.

This time, however, the water did no good. When he toweled off, all the warning signs of the migraine were still there: dizziness, a pinpoint of bright light whirling round and round and growing larger behind his right eye, clumsiness, a faint but persistent nausea . . .

He remembered that he had skipped breakfast and supper and had taken only half a lunch in-between. Perhaps the headache was caused by hunger. He was not hungry—or at least he did not suffer the pangs of unconscious self-denial. Nevertheless, he dressed and went outside, where he bought food from vending machines by the pay telephones in the motel's badly lighted breezeway. He dined on two bottles of Coke, a package of peanut-butter crackers, and a Hershey Bar with almonds.

He suffered the headache anyway. It pulsed out from the core of him, rhythmic waves of pain that forced him to be perfectly still lest he make the agony unbearable. Even when he lifted a hand to his forehead, the responding thunder of pain brought him close to the edge of delirium. He stretched out on his bed, flat on his back, twisting the gray sheets in both big hands, and after a while he was not merely approaching the edge of delirium but had leapt deep into it. For more than two hours he lay as rigid as a wooden construction, perspiration rolling off him like moisture from an icy cold water glass. Exhausted, wrung dry, moaning softly, he eventually passed from a half-aware trance into a troubled but comparatively painless sleep.

As always, there were nightmares. Grotesque images flickered through his shattered mind like visions formed at the bottom of a satanic kaleidoscope, each independent of the other, each a horrifying minim to recall later: long slender knives dripping blood into a woman's cupped palm, maggots crawling in a corpse, enormous breasts enfolding him and smothering him in a damp warm sexless caress, acres of scuttling cockroaches, herds of watchful red-eyed rats waiting to leap upon him, bloody lovers writhing ecstatically on a marble floor, Courtney nude and writhing on a bloody floor, a revolver snapping bullets into a woman's slim stomach . . .

The nightmares passed. Soon after, sleep passed as well. Leland groaned and sat up in bed, held his head in both hands. The headache was gone, but the memory of it was a new agony. Afterward he always felt crushingly helpless, vulnerable. And lonely. Lonelier than a man could endure to be.

"Don't feel lonely," Courtney said. "I'm here with you."

Leland looked up and saw her sitting on the foot of the bed. This time he was not the least bit surprised by her magical materialization. "It was so bad, Courtney," he said.

"Headache?"

"And nightmares."

"Did you ever go back to Dr. Penebaker?" she asked.

"No."

Her gentle voice came to him as if she were speaking from the far end of a tunnel. The hollow, distant tone was curiously in harmony with the shabby room. "You should have let Dr. Penebaker—"

"I don't want to *hear* about Penebaker!"

She said nothing more.

Several minutes later he said, "I stood by you when your parents were killed in the accident. Why didn't you stand by *me* when things first started to go sour?"

"Don't you remember what I told you then, George? I would have stood by you, if you had been willing to get help. But when you refused to admit that your headaches and your emotional problems might be caused by some—"

"Oh, for Christ's sake, shut up! Shut up! You're a rotten, nagging, holier-than-thou bitch, and I don't want to listen to you."

She did not vanish, but neither did she speak again.

Quite some time later he said, "We could have it as good as it once was, Courtney. Don't you agree?" He wanted her to agree more than he had ever wanted anything else.

"I agree, George," she said.

He smiled. "It could be just like it was. The only thing that's really keeping us apart is this Doyle. And Colin, too. You were always closer to Colin than to me. If Doyle and Colin were dead, I'd be all you had. You would have to come back to me, wouldn't you?"

"Yes," she said, just as he wanted her to say.

"We'd be happy again, wouldn't we?"

"Yes."

"You'd let me touch you again."

"Yes, George."

"Let me sleep with you again."

"Yes."

"Live with me?"

"Yes."

"And people would stop being nasty to me."

"Yes."

"You're my lucky piece, always were. With you back, it would almost be as if the last two years never even happened."

"Yes," she said.

But it was no good. She was not as responsive and warm and open as he would have liked. Indeed, talking with her was almost like talking with himself, a curiously masturbatory enterprise.

Angry with her, he turned away and refused to talk any more. A few minutes later, when he looked back to see if she was showing any signs of contrition, he found that she had vanished. She had left him again. She was always leaving him. She always going away to Doyle or Colin or somebody else and leaving him alone. He did not think that he could tolerate much more of that sort of treatment.

A police cruiser blocked the entrance to the rest area off Interstate 70, dome light and emergency blinkers flashing. Behind it, up on the clearing in the shelter of the pines, half a dozen other official cars were parked in a semicircle with their headlights on and engines running. Several portable kliegs had been hooked up to auxiliary batteries and arranged in another semicircle at the south edge of the clearing, facing the automobiles. In that vicinity, at least, night did not exist.

The focus of all this was, of course, Lieutenant Pulham's cruiser. The bumpers and chrome trim glinted with cold, white light. In the glare, the windshield had been transformed into a mirror.

Detective Ernie Hoval, who was in charge of the Pulham investigation, watched a lab technician photograph the five bloody fingerprints which were impressed so clearly on the inside of the right front car window, hundreds of fine red whirls. "They Pulham's prints?" he asked the lab man when the last of the shots had been aligned and taken.

"I'll check in a minute." The technician was thin, sallow, balding, with hands as delicate and soft as a woman's. Yet he apparently was not intimidated by Hoval. Everyone else was. Hoval used both his rank and his two hundred and forty pounds to dominate everyone who worked under him, and he was annoyed with the technician when the man failed to be impressed. The soft white hands packed the camera away with deliberately maddening care. Only when that was all secured as it should be, did they pick through the other contents of the leather satchel beside the squad car and come up with file copies of Lieutenant Pulham's fingerprints. The technician raised the yellow sheet and held it beside the bloody prints on the window.

"Well?" Hoval asked.

The lab man took a full minute, studying the two sets of prints. "They aren't Pulham's," he said at last.

"Son of a bitch," Hoval said, slamming one meaty fist into the other open palm. "It's going to be easier than I thought."

"Not necessarily."

Hoval looked down at the pale, narrow man. "Oh?"

The technician got to his feet and dusted his hands together. He noticed that in the cross-glare of all the lights, neither he nor Hoval nor any of the others cast a shadow. "Not everyone in the United States has his prints on file," the technician said. "Far less than half of us, in fact."

Hoval gestured impatiently with one strong hand. "Whoever did this is on file, believe me. Probably arrested in a dozen different protest marches—maybe even on a previous assault charge. FBI probably has a full file on him."

The lab man wiped one hand across his face, as if he were trying to pull away his perpetually sorrowful expression. "You think it was a radical, a new leftist, somebody like that?"

"Who else?" Hoval asked.

"Maybe just a nut."

Hoval shook his square, long-jawed head. "No. Don't you read the papers any more? Policemen getting killed all over the country these days."

"It's the nature of their job," the technician said. "Policemen have always gotten killed in the line of duty. Percentage of deaths is still the same as it always was."

Hoval was adamant as he watched the other lab men and the uniformed troopers comb the murder site. "These days there's an organized effort to slaughter policemen. Nationwide conspiracy. And it's finally touched us. You wait and see. This asshole's prints will be on file. And he'll be just the kind of bastard I'm telling you he is. We'll have him nailed to a post in twenty-four hours."

"Sure," the technician said. "That'll be nice."

TUESDAY

CHAPTER 4

ON THE SECOND day of May they rose early and ate a light breakfast, checked out of the Lazy Time Motel, and were on the road again shortly after eight o'clock.

The day was as bright and fresh as the previous one had been. The sky was high and cloudless. The sun, behind them once more, seemed to propel them on toward the coast.

"Does the scenery get better today?" Colin asked.

"Some," Alex said. "For one thing, you'll get to see the famous Gateway Arch in St. Louis."

"How many miles to St. Louis?"

"Oh . . . maybe two-fifty."

"And this Gateway Arch is the very first thing that we have to look forward to?"

"Well—"

"Christ," the boy said, shaking his head sorrowfully, "this is going to be a long, *long* morning."

Interstate 70 took them west-southwest toward the border of Illinois, a straight multi-lane avenue carved out of the flatlands of America. It was a convenient, fairly safe, controlled access throughway made for fast travel, designed for a nation always in a hurry. Though Doyle was, himself, in a hurry, anxious to be with Courtney again, he shared some of Colin's dissatisfaction with their route. Though simple and quick, it was characterless.

Fields of spring wheat, short and tender and green, began to fill the open spaces on both sides of the highway. Initially, these crisp green vistas and the complex of irrigation pipelines that sprayed them proved moderately interesting. Before too long, however, the fields grew boringly repetitious.

Despite his professed pessimism about the long morning which lay ahead of them, Colin was in a particularly garrulous mood, and he made their first two hours on the road pass more pleasantly and swiftly. They talked about what it would be like to live in California, talked about space travel, astronauts, science fiction, rock-and-roll, pirates, sailing ships, and Count Dracula—this last, chiefly because Colin was wearing a green-and-black Count Dracula T-shirt today, his narrow chest gruesomely decorated with a menacing fierce-eyed, fanged Christopher Lee.

As they passed the Indiana-Illinois border, there was a lull in the conversation, at last. With Doyle's permission, Colin unbuckled his seatbelt long enough to slide forward and locate a new radio station.

To make certain that nothing was coming up on them too fast while the boy was in such a vulnerable position on the edge of the seat, Alex looked in the rear-view mirror at the light flow of traffic on the broad throughway behind them.

That was when he saw the Chevrolet van.

He looked quickly away from it, looked at the road ahead.

At first he did not want to believe what he had seen, he was sure it must be his imagination. Then he argued with himself that since there were thousands of Automovers on the roads of America, this was most likely *another* of them, not at all the same vehicle that had hung behind them on their first leg of the journey.

Colin slid back onto his seat and buckled his seatbelt without argument. As he carefully smoothed down his T-shirt, he said, "Is that one okay?"

"What one?"

Colin tilted his head and stared curiously at Doyle. "The radio station, naturally. What else?"

"Sure. It's fine."

But Alex was so distracted that he was not actually aware of what sort of music the boy had selected for them. Reluctantly he glanced at the rear-view mirror a second time.

The Automover was still cruising in their wake, no mere figment of his overworked imagination to be lightly dismissed, hanging back there a little less than a quarter of a mile, well silhouetted in the morning sun, nevertheless darkly sinister.

Unaccountably, Doyle thought of the service station attendant whom they had encountered near Harrisburg, and of the stout anachronism behind the desk of the Lazy Time Motel. That familiar and uncontrollable shudder, the embarrassment of his childhood which he had never fully outgrown, started in his stomach and bowels and seemed to generate, of itself, a quiet and possibly irrational fear. However, deep down inside, Doyle admitted to himself what he had been first forced to face up to more than twenty years ago: he was an unmitigated coward. His pacifism was not based on any real moral precepts, but on an abiding terror of violence. When you really thought about it, what danger did that van pose? What injury or threat of injury had it done? If it seemed sinister, the blame was in his own mind. His fear was not only irrational, it was premature and simple-minded. He had no more cause to be frightened by the Chevrolet than he had to be frightened by Chet or the woman at the Lazy Time.

"He's back there again, isn't he?" Colin said.

"Who?"

"Don't play dumb with me," the boy said.

"Well, there *is* an Automover behind us."

"It's him, then."

"Could be another one."

"That's too coincidental," Colin said, quite sure of himself.

For a long moment Doyle was silent. Then: "Yes, I'm afraid you're right. That's too coincidental. He's behind us again, all right."

CHAPTER 5

"I'M GOING TO pull over and stop on the shoulder of the road," Alex said, lightly pumping the power brakes.

"Why?"

"To see what he does."

"You think he'll stop behind us?" Colin asked.

"Maybe." Doyle sincerely hoped not.

"He won't. If he really is an FBI man, he'll be too smart to fall for that kind of trick. He'll just zoom on by as if he doesn't notice us, then pick us up later."

Alex was too tense to play the boy's game. His lips set in a tight, grim line, he slowed the car even more, looked back and saw that the rental van was also slowing down. His heart beating too rapidly, he drove onto the berm, gravel crunching under the wide tires, and came to a full stop.

"Well?" Colin asked, excited by this turn of events.

Alex tilted the rear-view mirror and watched the Automover pull off the highway and stop just a quarter of a mile behind them. "Well, he's not an FBI man, then."

"Hey, great!" the boy said, apparently delighted by the unexpected turn the day had taken. "What could he be?"

"I don't like to think about that," Doyle said.

"I do."

"Think quietly, then."

He let off the brake and drove back onto the interstate, accelerated smoothly into the traffic pattern. Two cars came between them and the van, providing an illusory sense of isolation and safety. However, within a very few minutes the Chevrolet passed the other vehicles and insinuated itself behind the Thunderbird once more.

What does he want? Doyle wondered.

It was almost as if the stranger behind the wheel of the van somehow knew of Alex Doyle's secret cowardice and was playing on it.

The land was now even flatter than it had been, like a gigantic gameboard, and the road was straighter and more mesmeric.

They had passed the exit ramp for Effingham; and now all the signs were warning far in advance of the connecting route for Decatur, and marking the tens of miles to St. Louis.

Alex kept the Thunderbird moving five miles faster than the speed limit, sweeping around the slower traffic but staying mostly within the right-hand lane.

The van would not be shaken.

Ten miles after their first stop, he slowed down and pulled over to the berm again, watched as the Chevrolet followed suit. "What the hell does he *want?*" Doyle asked.

"I've been thinking about that," Colin said, frowning. "But I just can't figure him."

When Doyle took the car back on the road again, he said, "We can make more speed than a van like that. Lots more. Let's leave him in our dust."

"Just like in the movies," Colin said, clapping his hands. "Tromp it down all the way!"

Although he was not as pleased as Colin was about the prospect of a high-speed escape and pursuit, Doyle gradually pressed the accelerator pedal to the floor. He felt the big car tremble, shimmy, then steady down as it raced toward the performance peak which was being demanded of it. In spite of the Thunderbird's nearly airtight insulation, the road noises came to them now: a dull but building background roar underlying the rhythmic pounding of the engine and the shrill, protesting cry of the gusting wind which strained through the bar grille.

When the speedometer registered a hundred miles an hour, Alex looked in the mirror again. Incredibly, the Chevrolet was pacing them. It was the only other vehicle in sight which was using the left-hand lane.

The Thunderbird picked up speed: one-oh-five (with the road noise like a waterfall crashing down all around them), one-fifteen (the shimmy back, the frame sighing and groaning), then the top of the gauge, beyond the last white numerals and still moving, still increasing speed . . .

The median posts flashed past in a single faultless blur, a wall of gray steel. Beyond that wall, in the eastbound lanes, cars and trucks went past in the opposite direction as if they had been shot out of a cannon.

The van lost ground.

"We're really moving!" Colin cried, his voice a mixture of glee and outright horror.

"And he isn't keeping up!" Alex said.

The van dwindled, disappeared behind them.

The highway was deserted up ahead. Doyle did not take his foot from the accelerator.

Startling the drivers of the other cars which they passed, eliciting a symphony of angrily blaring horns, they rocketed across Illinois at top speed for another five minutes, putting miles between themselves and the stranger in the van. They were half exhilarated and half panicked, caught up in the excitement of the chase.

However, with the Chevrolet out of sight now, and the sense of being hotly pursued thus dimmed, Doyle was made aware of the risk that he was taking by maintaining such a terribly high speed even in this light traffic. If a tire blew . . .

Above the shrieking wind and the manic music of the pavement rushing under them, Colin said, "What about radar?"

If they were stopped for speeding, would any right-thinking highway patrolman believe that they were fleeing from a mysterious man in a rented Automover? Fleeing from a man they did not even know, had never met—had never really even seen? Fleeing from a man who had neither harmed nor threatened to harm them? Fleeing from a complete stranger whom Alex feared only because—well, only because he had always been afraid of that which he could not fully understand? No, that kind of story would look like a lie, a clumsy excuse. It was too fantastic and, at the same time, far too shallow. It would only antagonize a cop.

Reluctantly Doyle eased back on the accelerator. The speedometer needle fell rapidly to the one-hundred mark, quivered there like a hesitant finger, then dropped even lower.

Doyle looked in the mirror.

The van was nowhere in sight. For a few minutes, anyway, they would be unobserved by the driver of the Chevrolet.

"He's probably coming up fast," Colin said.

"Exactly."

"What are we going to do?"

Immediately ahead was the exit for Route 51 and signs announcing the distance to Decatur.

"We'll use secondary roads for the rest of the day," Alex said. "Let him hunt for us along Route 70 if he wants."

He used the Thunderbird's brakes for the first time in a long while, drove down the exit ramp into that flat country.

CHAPTER 6

FROM DECATUR, THEY took the secondary Route 36 west to the end of the state, then followed it into Missouri. The land was even flatter than it had been during the morning; the fabled prairies were a monotonous spectacle. Just past noon, Alex and the boy ate a quick lunch at a trim white-clapboard café and then pressed on.

Not far beyond the turnoff from Jacksonville, Colin said, "What do you think, then?"

"About what?"

"The man in the Chevrolet."

The westering sun glared on the windshield.

"What about him?" Doyle asked.

"Who could he be?"

"Isn't he FBI?"

"That was just a game."

For the first time Alex realized how much the ubiquitous van had affected the boy, how much it had unsettled him. If Colin was no longer interested in his games, he must be quite disturbed, and he deserved a straightforward reply.

"Whoever he is," Doyle said, shifting his aching buttocks on the vinyl seat, "he's dangerous."

"Somebody we know?"

"No. I think he's a complete stranger."

"Then why is he after us?"

"Because he needs to be after *someone*."

"That's no answer."

Doyle thought about that special breed of madmen which had grown out of the previous decade, out of those pressure-cooker years when the very fabric of society had been heated to the boiling point and very nearly melted away. He thought about men like Charles Manson, Richard Speck, Charles Whitman, Arthur Bremer . . . Though Charles Whitman, the Texas tower sniper who had shot more than a dozen innocent people, might have been suffering from an undiagnosed brain tumor, the others had not required any physical illness or rational explanations for the bloodletting they had caused. The slaughter— which had been legitimized by a government which gloated over the "body counts" from Vietnam—had been, in itself, the reason and explanation for the event. There were at least a dozen other names that Doyle could no longer recall, men who had murdered wantonly but not sufficiently to gain immortality. Since 1963 a madman had to be either clever in his methods, selective enough to choose the famous as his targets, or ruthless enough to cut down a dozen or more people before he was at all memorable. The videotape replay of an assassination and the nightly broadcasting of a bloody war had dulled American sensitivities. The single murderous impulse had become far too common to be at all noteworthy . . . Doyle attempted to convey these thoughts to Colin, couching them in grisly terms only when no other terms would do.

"You think he's crazy, then?" the boy asked when Doyle was finished.

"Perhaps. Actually, he hadn't done much of anything yet. But if we had stayed on the throughway and let him follow us, given him time and plenty of opportunity . . . Who knows what he might have done, eventually?"

"This all sounds para—"

"Paranoid?"

"That's the word," Colin said, shaking his head approvingly. "It sounds very paranoid."

"These days you have to be somewhat paranoid," Doyle said. "It's almost a vital requirement for survival."

"Do you think he'll find us again?"

"No." Doyle blinked as the sun glimmered especially brightly against the windshield. "He'll stay on the Interstate, trying like hell to catch up with us again."

"Sooner or later he's going to realize we got off."

"But he won't know where or when," Doyle said. "And he can't know where, exactly, we'll be going."

"What if he finds someone else to pick on?" Colin asked. "If he just started to tail us because we happened to be going west on the same road he was using—won't he choose some other victim when he realizes that we've gotten away from him?"

"What if he does?" Doyle asked.

"Shouldn't we let the police know about him?" the boy asked.

"You've got to have proof before you can accuse anyone," Doyle said. "Even if we had proof, incontrovertible proof, that the man in the Chevrolet intended to hurt us, we couldn't do anything with it. We don't know *whom* to accuse, not by name. We don't know where he's headed, except westward. We don't have a number for the van, anything the cops could use to trace it." He looked at Colin, then back at the blacktop road. "All we can do is thank our stars we got rid of him."

"I guess so."

"You better believe it."

Much later Colin said, "When he was following us, pulling off the road behind us, speeding to catch up with us—were you scared?"

Doyle hesitated only a second, wondering if he should admit to some less unmanly reaction: uneasiness, disquiet, alarm, anxiety. But he knew that, with Colin, honesty was always the best. "Of course I was scared. Just a little bit, but scared nonetheless. There was reason to be."

"I was scared too," the boy said without embarrassment. "But I always thought that when you got to be an adult, you didn't have to be scared of anything any more."

"You'll outgrow some fears," Doyle said. "For instance . . . are you afraid of the dark at all?"

"Some."

"Well, you will outgrow that. But you don't outgrow everything. And you find new things to be afraid of."

They crossed the Mississippi River at Hannibal instead of St. Louis, missing the Gateway Arch altogether. Just before the turnoff to Hiawatha, Kansas, they left Route 36 for a series of connecting highways that took them south once more to Interstate 70 and, by eight-fifteen, to the Plains Motel near Lawrence, Kansas, where they had reservations for the night.

The Plains Motel was pretty much like the Lazy Time, except that it had only one long wing and was built of gray stone and clapboard instead of bricks. The signs were the same orange and green neon. The Coke machine by the office door might have been moved, during the day, from the Lazy Time near Indianapolis; the air around it was cool and filled with robotic noises.

Alex wondered if the desk clerk would be a stout woman with a beehive hair style.

Instead, it was a man Doyle's age. He was clean-shaven, his hair neatly trimmed. He had a square, honest, *American* face, perfect for recruitment posters. He could have made a fortune doing television commercials for Pepsi, Gillette, Schick, the full-page ads for Camel cigarettes in all the magazines.

"I noticed a no-vacancy sign outside," Doyle said. "I wondered if you'd held our room. We're an hour later than the reservations called for, but—"

"Is it Doyle?" the man asked, revealing perfect white teeth.

"Yes."

"Sure, I held it." He produced a flimsy form from the desk.

"Hey, good news! I know you must have been worried about getting stuck—"

"Wasn't worried at all, Mr. Doyle. If you hadn't reserved it, I'd have had to rent it to coons."

Doyle was weary from a long day on the road, and he could not decide what the clerk meant. "Coons?"

"Niggers," the clerk said. "Three times they came in. If I didn't have your reservation, I'd have had to let one of them take 22 for the night. And I hate that. I'd rather let a room stand empty all night then rent to one of them."

Doyle felt as if he were giving his approval to the man's bigotry when he signed the registration paper. He wondered, briefly, why he, dressed and groomed as he was, made any better impression than the blacks who had stopped before him.

When the handsome young man gave Doyle the room key, he said, "What kind of gas mileage you get on that T-Bird?"

Alex had known his share of bigots, and he was expecting this one, like the others, to continue with his practiced invective. He was surprised, then, by the change of subject. "Mileage? I don't know. I never checked."

"I'm saving for a car like that. Gas hogs, but I love them. Car like that tells you about a man. You see a man in a T-Bird, you know he's making it."

Alex looked at the room key in his hand. "Twenty-two? Where's that?"

"To the right clear at the end. Nice room, Mr. Doyle."

Alex went out to the car. He knew why the clerk accepted him. The Thunderbird was, for that man, a symbol which eclipsed reality. A car like that transformed a counterculture freak into a mere eccentric, so far as the clerk was concerned. That attitude depressed Alex. He had not expected that here in the heartlands a man was defined by his possessions.

* * *

George Leland spent Tuesday night in a cheaper place three miles west of the Plains Motel. Though it was a tiny single room, he was not always alone. Courtney was often there. Sometimes he saw her standing in a corner, her back to the wall. Other times she sat on the foot of the bed or in the poorly padded plank chair by the bathroom door. He got angry with her more than once and told her to go away. She would vanish as quietly as she appeared. But then he would miss her and long for her—and she would return, making the cheaper place seem far more luxurious and grand than the Plains Motel.

He slept fitfully.

Two hours before dawn, unable to sleep at all any more, he got up and showered and dressed. He sat on the bed, several maps opened on the covers, and studied the route that would be followed Wednesday. He traced and re-traced it with his blunt fingers.

Leland knew that somewhere in those six hundred miles he would have to take care of Doyle and the boy. He no longer needed to conceal this truth from himself. Courtney had helped him face up to it. He must kill them, just as he had killed that highway patrolman who tried to stand between him and Court-ney. It was much too dangerous to put this thing off any longer. By tomorrow night they would be well over halfway to San Francisco. If Doyle decided to change their route for the last long leg of the journey, Leland might lose them for good.

Tomorrow, then. Somewhere between Lawrence, Kansas, and Denver. Le-land would finally be striking back at Them, at everyone who had put him down and worked against him these last two years. This was the new beginning. From now on, he was not going to be pushed around. He would teach everyone to respect him. His luck would pick up, too. With Doyle and the kid out of the way, he and Courtney could go on together with their wonderful life. He would be all that she had, and she would cling to him.

A few minutes past six o'clock Tuesday evening, a call came through from the police lab. Detective Ernie Hoval took it in his sparsely furnished office on the second floor of the divisional headquarters building. "This about the Pul-ham case?" he asked before the man on the other end of the line could say anything. "If it's not, take it to someone else. I'm on the Pulham until it's solved, and nothing else."

"You'll want this," the lab man said. He sounded like the same balding, sallow, narrow man who had not been humbled by Detective Hoval the night before. "We got the fingerprint report from Washington. Just came in on the teletype."

"And?"

"No record."

Hoval hunched over his big desk, dwarfing it, the receiver clenched tightly in one hand, his other hand fisted on the blotter. His knuckles were white and sharp. "No record?"

"I told you it might be that way," the technician said, almost as if he enjoyed Hoval's disappointment. "I think this looks more like a nut case with every passing minute."

"It's political," Hoval insisted, his fist opening and closing again and again. "Organized cop killing."

"I don't agree."

"You got proof otherwise?" Hoval asked angrily.

"No," the technician admitted. "We're still going over the car, but it looks hopeless. We've taken paint samples from every nick and scrape. But who knows if one of them was made by the killer's vehicle? And if one of them was—which one?"

"You sweep out the cruiser?" Hoval asked.

"Of course," the technician said. "We found a few hairs, pubic and otherwise. Nail clippings. Various kinds of mud. Blades of grass. Bits of food. Most of it had no connection with the killer. And even if some of it does—the hair, a couple of torn threads we picked off the door catch—we can't do much with it until we have a suspect to apply it to."

"The case won't be solved with lab work," Hoval agreed.

"What other leads you have?"

"We're reconstructing Pulham's shift," Hoval said. "Starting with the moment he took the squad car out of the garage."

"Anything?"

"There are lots of minutes to account for, lots of people to talk with," Hoval said. "But we'll come up with something."

"A nut," the technician said.

"You're all wrong about that." Hoval hung up.

Twenty years ago Ernie Hoval had become a cop because it was a profession and not just a job; it was work that brought a man a measure of honor and respect. It was hard work, the hours long, the pay only adequate, but it gave you the opportunity to contribute something to your community. The fringe benefits of police work—the gratitude of your neighbors and the respect of your own children—were more important than the salary. At least, that had been true in the past . . .

These days, Hoval thought, a cop was nothing more than a target. Everyone was after the police. Blacks, liberals, spics, peaceniks, women's liberationists—all the lunatic fringe reveled in making fools of the police. These days a cop was looked upon, at best, as a buffoon. At worst, he was called a fascist, and he was marked for death by these revolutionary groups that no one but other cops seemed to give a damn about . . .

It had all started in 1963, with Kennedy and Dallas. And it had gotten much, much worse through the war. Hoval knew that, although he could not understand why the assassinations and the war had so fundamentally changed so many people. There were other political murders in America's history, all without profound effect on the nation. And there had been other wars which had, if anything, strengthened our moral fiber. This war had had the opposite effect. He could not say why—except to point out that the communists and other revolutionary forces had long been looking for excuses to act—but he knew it to be true.

He thought about Pulham, latest victim of these changes, and he fisted both big hands. It *was* political. Sooner or later they *would* get the bastards.

WEDNESDAY, 7:00 A.M.—
THURSDAY, 7:00 A.M.

CHAPTER 7

THE MORNING HELD the threat of rain. Gently undulating fields of tender new wheat shoots touched the far horizons, a green carpet under the low gray ceiling of fast-moving clouds. Here and there on the maddeningly level land, enormous concrete grain elevators thrust up like gigantic lightning rods to test the mettle of the pending storm.

Colin liked it. He kept pointing to the grain elevators and to the occasional skeletal oil derricks which stood like prison watchtowers in the distance. "It's great, isn't it?"

"This land's every bit as flat as that back in Indiana and Missouri," Doyle said.

"But there's *history* here." Today the boy was wearing a red-and-black Frankenstein T-shirt. It had pulled up out of his corduroy trousers, but he paid it no attention now.

"History?" Doyle asked.

"Haven't you ever heard of the Old Chisholm Trail? Or the Santa Fe Trail? All the famous Old West towns are here," the boy said, excited about it. "You have Abilene and Fort Riley, Fort Scott, Pawnee Rock, Wichita, Dodge City, and the old Boot Hill."

"I didn't know you were a cowboy-movie fan," Doyle said.

"I'm not, that much. But it's still exciting."

Alex looked at the great plains and tried to picture them as they had once

44

been: shifting sands, dust, cactus, a stark and foreboding landscape that had barely been touched by man. Yes, once it must have been a romantic place.

"There were Indian wars here," Colin said. "And John Brown caused a small civil war in Kansas back in 1856, when he and his boys killed five slave owners at Pottawatomie Creek."

"But you can't say that five times, fast."

"A dollar?" Colin asked.

"You're on."

"Pottawatomie, Pottawatomie, Pottawatomie, Pottawatomie, Pottawatomie!" he said, breathless at the end of it. "You owe me a buck."

"Put it on my tab," Doyle said. He felt loose and easy and good again, now that the trip was turning out to be what they had planned.

"You know who else came from Kansas?"

"Who?"

"Carrie Nation," Colin said, giggling. "The woman who went around breaking up saloons with an ax."

They passed another grain elevator sitting at the end of a long, straight blacktop road.

"Where did you learn all this?" Doyle asked.

"Just picked it up," Colin said. "Bits and pieces from here and there."

Now and then they passed fields which were standing idle, rich brown patches of land like neatly opened tablecloths. In one of these, a fifty-foot-high whirlwind gathered dust in a compact column of whining spring air.

"This is also where Dorothy lived," Colin said, watching the whirlwind.

"Dorothy who?"

"The girl in *The Wizard of Oz*. Remember how she got carried to Oz by a tremendous tornado?"

Alex was about to answer when he was startled by the brash roar of an automobile horn immediately behind him. He looked in the mirror—and sucked air between his teeth when he saw the Chevrolet van. It was no more than six feet from their rear bumper. The unseen driver was pounding the palm of his hand into the horn ring: *beep, beep, beep, beep, beep, beeeeeep!*

Doyle looked at the speedometer, saw that they were doing better than seventy. If he had been so surprised by the horn that he had stomped the brake pedal, the Chevrolet would have run right over them. And they would all be dead.

"Stupid sonofabitch," he said.

Beep, beeeeeeep, beeeeeep . . .

"Is it him?" Colin asked.

"Yes."

The van moved up, so close now that Doyle could not even see its bumper or the bottom third of its grille.

"Why's he blowing his horn?" Colin asked.

"I don't know . . . I guess—to make sure we know he's back."

CHAPTER 8

THE VAN'S HORN played a monotonous dirge.

"Do you think he wants you to stop?" Colin asked, gripping his knees in his delicate hands and leaning forward as if bent by the tension.

"I don't know."

"Are you going to stop?"

"No."

Colin nodded. "Good. I don't think we should stop. I think we should keep going no matter what."

Doyle expected that any second now the stranger would stop blowing his horn and let the van fall back to its customary quarter of a mile. Instead, it just hung in there, only three feet away from their back end now, cruising at seventy miles an hour, horn blaring.

Whether or not the man in the Chevy was as dangerous as Charles Manson or Richard Speck, he was most certainly unbalanced. He was getting some sort of kick out of terrorizing complete strangers, and that was far from normal. More than ever before, Doyle knew he did not want to confront this man face-to-face and test the limits of his madness.

Beep, beep, beeeeeep . . .

"What can we do?" the boy asked.

Doyle glanced at him. "Seatbelt on?"

"Of course."

"We'll outrun him again."

"And go to Denver on the back roads?"

"Yeah."

"He'll pick us up again tomorrow morning when we leave Denver on the way to Salt Lake City."

"No, he won't," Doyle said.

"How can you be sure?"

"He's not clairvoyant," Doyle said. "He's just been lucky, that's all. By chance, he's stayed in the approximate area where we've stayed each night—and equally by chance, he's started out around the same hour each morning that we started out. It's purely coincidental, the way he keeps catching up to us." He knew that this was the only rational explanation, as weak as it was, the only thing that made any sense. Yet he did not believe a word of it. "You read about dozens of wilder coincidences in the newspapers. All the time." He was talking, now, only to calm the boy. That old, familiar, dreaded fear of his had returned, and he knew that he would not be calm again, himself, until they were safely in San Francisco.

He pressed down on the accelerator.

The Thunderbird surged forward, opening a gap between them and the Chevrolet. The gap rapidly widened, even though the Automover put on its own burst of speed.

"You'll have a lot more driving to do if we go the back way," the boy said, a vague apprehension in his voice.

"Not necessarily. We can go north and pick up Route 36 again," Doyle said, watching the van dwindle in the rearview mirror. "That's a pretty good road up there."

"It'll still mean an extra couple of hours. Yesterday you were really tired when we got to the motel."

"I'll be all right," Doyle said. "Don't you worry about me."

They took Connecting Route 77 north to Route 36 and went west across the top of the state.

Colin no longer found the fields, grain elevators, oil derricks, and dust storms especially interesting. He hardly looked at the scenery. He tucked in his Frankenstein T-shirt and smoothed it down, played tunes on his bony knees, cleaned his thick glasses, and smoothed his shirt some more. The minutes passed like snails.

Leland let the van slow down to seventy, quieting the furniture and household goods which rattled noisily in the cargo hold when he drove any faster. He looked at the golden, transparent girl beside him. "They must have turned off somewhere along the way. We won't catch up with them until we get into Denver this evening."

She said nothing.

"I should have stayed back a ways until I saw a chance to run them off the road. I shouldn't have pressured him like that right away."

She only smiled.

"Well," he said, "I guess you're right. The highway's too public a place to take care of them. Tonight, at the motel, will be better. I might be able to do it with the knife, if I can sneak up on them. No noise that way. And they won't be expecting anything there."

The fields flashed past. The leaden sky grew lower, and rain spattered across the windshield. The wipers thumped hypnotically, like a club slammed again and again into something soft and warm.

CHAPTER 9

〰

THE ROCKIES MOTOR HOTEL, on the eastern edge of Denver, was an enormous complex in the shape of a two-story tick-tack-toe grid, with one hundred rooms in each of its four long wings. Despite its size—nearly two miles of concrete-floored, open-air, metal-roofed corridors—the place seemed small, for it stood in the architectural shadow of the city's high-rise buildings and, more impressively, in view of the magnificent snow-capped Rocky Mountains which loomed up to the west and south. During the day the high country sun gleamed on the ranks of precisely duplicated windows and on the steel rain spouting, transformed the tops of the long walkway awnings into corrugated mirrors, shimmered on the Olympic swimming pool in the enclosed center of the courtyard grid. At night warm orange lamps glowed behind the curtains in most of the rooms, and there were also lights in the pool and around the pool; and the front of the motel was a blaze of yellow, white, and red lights which were there chiefly to draw attention to the office, lobby, restaurant, and Big Rockies Cocktail Lounge.

At ten o'clock Wednesday night, however, the motel was dim and drab. Although all the usual lights were burning, they could not cast back the driving gray rain and the thin night mist which carried a reminder of the winter chill that had not been long gone from the city. The cold rain bounced on the macadam parking lot, thundered on the rows of cars, and pattered against the sheet-glass walls of the lobby and restaurant. It drummed insistently on the roofs and on the rippled awnings that covered the promenades on every wing, a pleasant sound which lulled most of the overnight guests into a quick, deep sleep. The rain chattered noisily into the swimming pool and puddled at the base of the spruce trees and other evergreens which dotted the well-landscaped grounds. It sloshed out of the rain spouting and swirled along curb gutters, and made momentary lakes around drainage grilles. The mist reached what the rain could not, beading on sheltered windows and on the slick red enamel of the numbered room doors.

In room 318, Alex Doyle sat on the edge of one of the twin beds and listened both to the rain on the roof and to Colin talking on the telephone to Courtney.

The boy did not mention the stranger in the rented van. The man had not caught up to them again during the long afternoon. And he had no way of knowing where they were spending the night . . . Even if this game had begun to intrigue him enough to send him out of his way in order to keep it going, he would be discouraged by the bad weather; he would not be searching all the motels along the Interstate in hopes of locating the Thunderbird—not tonight, not in the rain. There was no need to worry Courtney with the details of a danger which had passed and which, Doyle felt now, had never been much of a danger to begin with.

Colin finished and handed the receiver to Doyle.

"How did *you* like Kansas?" she asked when he said hello.

"It was an education," Doyle said.

"With Colin as your teacher."

"That sums it up."

"Alex, is anything wrong with him?"

"Colin?"

"Yes."

"Nothing's wrong. Why do you ask?"

She hesitated. The open line hissed softly between them like a subdued echo of the cold rain thundering across the motel roof. "Well . . . He's not as exuberant as usual."

"Even Colin gets tired," Doyle said, winking at the boy.

Colin nodded grimly. He knew what his sister was asking and what Alex was trying to avoid telling her. When he had spoken to her, Colin had tried to be natural. But his practiced chatterboxiness had not been able to fully cover over the simmering fear he'd kept on the back burner since the van had appeared early this morning.

"That's all?" Courtney asked Doyle. "He's just tired?"

"What else?"

"Well—"

"We're both road-weary," Doyle interrupted. He knew that she sensed more to it than just that. Sometimes she was positively psychic. "It's true that there's a lot to see on a cross-country drive—but most of it is exactly what you saw ten minutes ago, and ten minutes before *that*." He changed the subject before she could press for more details. "Any furniture arrive yet?"

"Oh yes!" she said. "The bedroom suite."

"And?"

"Just like it looked in the showroom. And the mattress is firm but full of bounce."

He assumed a mock suspicious tone. "How would you know about that— what with your husband halfway across the country?"

"I jumped up and down on it for about five minutes," she said, chuckling quietly. "Testing it, you know?"

He laughed, picturing the slim, long-haired, elfin-faced girl romping happily on their bed as if it were a trampoline.

"And you know what, Alex?"

"What?"

"I was nude when I tested it. How's that strike you?"

He stopped laughing. "Strikes me fine." His voice caught in the back of his throat. He felt himself smile idiotically, even though Colin was watching and listening. "Why torture me like this?"

"Well, I keep thinking you might meet some saucy woman on the highway and run off with her. I don't want you to forget me."

"I couldn't," he said, speaking beyond sex now. "I couldn't forget."

"Well, I like to be sure. And—hey, I think I found a job."

"Already?"

"There's a new city magazine starting up, and they need a photographer to work full time. No tedious layout jobs. Just straight photography. I made an appointment to show them my portfolio tomorrow."

"Sounds great."

"It'll be good for Colin, too," she said. "It's not an office job. I'll be running all over the city, setting up shots. That ought to make a pretty full summer for him."

They talked only a few minutes more, then said their goodbyes. When he hung up the phone, the drumming rain seemed to get suddenly louder.

Later, in the intensely dark room as they lay in their beds waiting for sleep to come, Colin sighed and said, "Well, she knew that something was wrong, didn't she?"

"Yes."

"You can't fool Courtney."

"Not for very long, anyway," Doyle said, staring at the lightless ceiling and thinking about his wife.

The darkness seemed to swell and shrink and swell again, to pulse as if it were alive, to press warmly down around them like a blanket.

"You really think we've lost him?" the boy asked.

"Sure."

"We thought we'd lost him before."

"This time we can be certain."

"I hope you're right," Colin said. "He's a real crazy, whoever he is."

The shushing snare-drum music of the spring storm soon put the boy, and then Doyle, to sleep . . .

Rain was falling as steadily as ever when Colin woke him. He stood beside Doyle's bed, shaking the man by the shoulder and whispering urgently. *"Alex! Alex, wake up. Alex!"*

Doyle sat up in bed, groggy and somewhat confused. His mouth felt furry and stale. He kept blinking his eyes, trying to see something, until he realized it was the middle of the night and the room was still pitch-black.

"Alex, are you awake?"

"Yeah. What's the matter?"

"There's someone at the door," the boy said.

Alex stared straight at the voice but could see nothing of the boy. "At the door?" he asked stupidly, still not clear-headed enough to understand what was happening.

"He woke me up," Colin whispered. "I've been listening to him maybe three or four minutes. I think he's trying to pick the lock."

NOW, ABOVE THE background noise of the rain, Alex could hear the strange fumbling noises on the other side of the door. In the warm, close, anonymous darkness, the sounds of the wire probing back and forth in the lock seemed much louder than they really were. His fear acted as an amplifier.

"You hear him?" Colin asked. His voice cracked between the last two words, leaping up the scale.

Doyle reached out and found the boy and put one hand on his skinny shoulder. "I can hear him, Colin," he whispered, hoping his own voice would remain steady. "It's okay. Nobody's going to come in here. Nobody's going to hurt you."

"But it must be *him*."

Doyle looked at his wristwatch, which was the only source of light in the small room. The irradiated numerals jumped up at him, sharp and clear: seven minutes after three in the morning. At this hour no one had a legitimate reason for picking a lock on a room that . . . What was he thinking? There was no legitimate reason for such a thing at *any* hour, day or night.

"Alex, what if he gets in here?"

"Ssshh," Doyle said, kicking back the covers and sliding out of bed.

"What if he *does*?"

"He won't."

Doyle went to the door, aware that Colin was right behind him, and he bent down to listen at the lock. Metal rasped on metal, clinked, snickered, rasped again.

He stepped sideways to the room's only window, just to the left of the door. Careful not to make a sound, he lifted the heavily lined drapes and then the cold venetian blinds. He tried to look to the right along the covered promenade where the man would be bent over the lock, but he found that the outside of the glass was sheathed in a fine white mist which made the window completely opaque. He could not see anything through it except the vague, diffused glow of several scattered motel lights that made the darkness beyond somewhat less intense and more manageable than that within the room.

With as much care as he had employed in raising them away from the window, he dropped the blinds and the drapes back into place. He could not see any good reason for continued silence, but he took the precaution anyway, in order to waste a few more precious seconds . . . Any moment, he knew, the time would come for him to make a decision, to chart some response to this— yet he did not know for sure if he was capable of acting against whoever was out there.

He went back to the door.

The carpet was nubbed and prickly against his bare feet.

Colin had remained by the door, silent, invisible in the onyx shadows, perhaps too frightened to move or speak.

The icy sound of the wire scraping inside the lock was insistent and as loud as ever. It made Alex think of the surgeon's scalpel worrying at the hard surface of a bone.

"Who's there?" Doyle finally asked. He was surprised at the strength and self-possession so evident in his voice. Indeed, he was surprised that he could even speak at all.

The wire stopped moving.

"Who's there?" Doyle demanded once more, louder this time but with less genuine courage and more false bravado than before.

Rapid footsteps—certainly those of a large man—sounded on the concrete promenade floor and were quickly swallowed up in the steady roar of the storm.

They waited, listening intently. But the man was gone.

Alex fumbled for the light switch by the door, found it.

For a moment they were both blinded by the sudden glare. Then the familiar lines of the tritely designed motel room filtered back to them.

"He'll return," Colin said.

The boy was standing by the desk, wearing only his skivvies and his Coke-bottle glasses. His thin brown legs were trembling uncontrollably, the bony knees nearly knocking together. Doyle, also standing there in his underwear, wondered if his own body was betraying his state of mind.

"Maybe not," he said. "Now that he knows we're up and around, he might not risk coming back."

Colin was adamant. "He will."

Doyle knew what the situation demanded, but he did not want to face up to it. He did not want to go out there in the rain, looking for the man who had tried to pick the room lock.

"We could call the police," Colin said.

"Oh? We still haven't anything to tell them, any proof. We'd sound like a couple of raving lunatics."

Colin went back to his bed and sat down, pulled the blanket around himself, so that he looked like a miniature American Indian.

In the bathroom, Doyle drew a glass of tap water and drank it slowly, swallowing with some difficulty.

As he rinsed the glass and put it on the fake-marble shelf beside the porcelain sink, he caught sight of his face in the mirror. He was pale and haggard. The fear was etched in painfully obvious lines at the corners of his bloodless mouth and all around his eyes. He did not like what he saw, and he could barely meet his own gaze.

Christ, he thought, doesn't the frightened little boy ever fade away and let the man come through? Won't you ever outgrow it, Alex? Are you going to be so easily terrified all the rest of your life? Now that you have a wife to protect? Do you think that maybe Colin will grow up fast enough so that he will be able to look after both you and Courtney?

Angry with himself, half ashamed, but still undeniably frightened, he turned away from the mirror and his own accusing countenance, and went back into the main room.

Colin had not moved from the bed or dropped the blanket from his shoulders. He looked at Doyle, his large eyes magnified by the eyeglasses, the speck of fear magnified as well. "What would he have done if he'd been able to pick the lock without waking us?"

Doyle stood there in the middle of the room, unable to answer.

"When he got in here with us," the boy said, "what would he have done? Like you said when all this started—we don't have anything worth stealing."

Doyle nodded stupidly.

"I think he's just what you said," Colin want on. "I think he's like one of those people you read about in the papers. I think he's a maniac." His voice had become almost inaudible.

Though he knew that it was no real answer and was probably even untrue, Alex said, "Well . . . he's gone now."

Colin just looked at him.

The boy's expression might have meant anything, or nothing at all. But Alex saw in it the beginnings of doubt and a subtle shift of judgment. The boy, he felt certain, was reevaluating him just as surely as the rain pattered on the roof overhead. And although Colin was far too intelligent to sum up anyone in an absolute term or category, too clever to think in blacks and whites, his opinion of Doyle was this minute changing for the worse, no matter how minimally.

But, Doyle asked himself, did one child's opinion mean all that much to him? And he knew immediately that when it was this child, the answer was yes. All of his life Doyle had been afraid of people, too timid to let himself be close to anyone. He had been too unsure of himself to risk loving. Until he had met Courtney. And Colin. And now their opinions of him were more important than anything else in the world.

He heard his own voice as if it had come from someone else. "I guess I better go outside and have a look around. If I can get a glimpse of him, see what he looks like, get the license number for that van of his . . . Then we'll at least know something about our enemy. He won't be such a cipher—and he'll seem less frightening."

"And if he does try anything serious," Colin said, "we'll have a description to give the cops."

Doyle nodded numbly, then went to the closet and took out the rumpled, soiled clothes he had worn the day before. He got dressed.

At the door a few minutes later, he looked back at Colin. "Will you be all right here by yourself?"

The boy nodded and drew the blanket tightly around himself.

"I'll lock the door when I go out—and I won't take a key. Don't open up for anyone but me. And don't even open for me until you're certain that you recognize my voice."

"Okay."

"I won't be long."

Colin nodded again. Then, as frightened as he was for himself and Alex, he managed a bit of gallows humor. "You better be careful. It would be utterly tasteless for an artist to let himself be killed in a cheap, dismal place like this."

Doyle smiled grimly. "No chance." Then he went outside, making sure the door had locked behind him.

Earlier in the evening and fifteen hundred miles to the east, Detective Ernie Hoval opened the front door of a thirty-thousand-dollar three-bedroom ranch house in a pleasant middle-class development between Cambridge and Cadiz, Ohio, just off Route 22, and stepped into an entrance foyer which was liberally splashed with blood. Long red stains smeared the walls on both sides where desperate hands had slid down the plaster. Thick droplets of blood spotted the beige carpet and the yellow-brocade loveseat by the coat closet.

Hoval closed the door and walked into the living room, where a dead woman lay half on the sofa and half on the floor. She had been in her late forties, rather handsome if not pretty, tall and dark. She had taken a shotgun blast in the stomach.

Newspaper reporters and lab photographers circled her like wolves. Four lab technicians, as silent as a quartet of deaf-mutes, crawled all over the big room on their hands and knees, measuring and charting the spray patterns of the blood, which seemed to have reached into every nook and cranny. They were most likely fighting to keep from being sick.

"Christ," Hoval said.

He went through the living room and down the narrow hall to the first bathroom, where there was an extremely pretty teenage girl sprawled at the foot of a bloodstained commode. She was wearing skimpy blue panties, nothing else, and had been shot once in the back of the head. The bathroom was even bloodier than the foyer and the living room combined.

In the smallest bedroom, a good-looking, long-haired, bearded boy in his early twenties was lying on his back in bed, covers drawn up to his chin, his hands folded peacefully on his chest. The pastel blanket was soaked with blood and shredded in the center by shotgun pellets. The poster of the Rolling Stones stapled to the wall above the bed was streaked with red and curled damply at the edges.

"I thought you were only working on the Pulham case."

Hoval turned to see who had spoken and confronted the ineffectual-looking lab man who had lifted the killer's fingerprints from Rich Pulham's squad car. "I heard the report of the initial find and thought maybe this was tied in. It is kind of similar."

"It was a family thing," the lab man said.

"They already have a suspect?"

"They already have a *confession*," the technician said, glancing uninterestedly at the dead boy on the bed.

"Who?"

"Husband and father."

"He killed his own family?" This was not the first time Hoval had encountered a thing like that, but it never failed to shock him. His own wife and kids meant too much to him, were too intricate a part of his life for him to ever understand how another man could bring himself to slaughter his own flesh and blood.

"He was waiting for the arresting officers," the technician said. "He was the one who telephoned for them."

Hoval felt ill.

"Anything on the Pulham situation?"

Hoval leaned against the wall, remembered the blood, pulled away and checked for stains. But the wall here was clean. He leaned back again, uneasy, a chill coursing along his spine. "We think we have something," he told the technician. "It might have started at Breen's Café back at the interchange." He summarized what they had learned from Janet Kinder, the waitress who had served an unnamed oddball his lunch Monday afternoon. "If Pulham went after the man—and it looks more and more like he did—then our killer is driving a rented van on his way to California."

"Hardly enough data for you to put out an APB, is there?"

Hoval nodded glumly. "Must be a thousand Automovers going west on I-70. It'll take weeks to go through them all, trace the drivers, winnow it down to the bastard that did it."

"This waitress give a description?" the lab man asked.

"Yeah. She's man-crazy, so she remembers these things well." He repeated the description they had gotten from the waitress.

"He doesn't sound like a left-wing revolutionary to me," the lab man said. "More like an ex-marine."

"There's no way to tell these days," Ernie Hoval said. "The SDS and some of these other crazies are cutting their hair, shaving, bathing, blending right in with your decent average citizens." He was impatient with the sallow man and did not want to pursue the subject; quite obviously, they were not on the same wavelength. He leaned away from the wall and looked once more into the bloody bedroom. "Why?"

"Why this? Why'd he kill his own family?"

"Yes."

"He's very religious," the technician said, smiling again.

Hoval didn't get it. He said so.

"He's a lay preacher. Very dedicated to Christ, you know. Spreads the Good Word as much as he can, reads the Bible for an hour every night . . . Then he sees his boy going off the deep end with drugs—or at least pot. He thinks his daughter's got loose morals or maybe no morals at all, because she won't tell him who she's dating or why she stays out so late. And the mother took up for both the kids a little too much. She was encouraging them to sin, as it were."

"And what finally set him off?" Hoval asked.

"Nothing much. He says that all the little day-to-day things mounted up until he couldn't stand it any longer."

"And the solution was murder."

"For him, anyway."

Hoval shook his head sadly, thinking of the pretty girl lying on the bathroom floor. "What's the world coming to these days?"

"Not the world," the slim man said. "Not the *whole* world."

CHAPTER 11

IT WAS A hard rain, a downpour, a seemingly perpetual cloudburst. The wind from the east pushed it across high Denver in vicious, eroding sheets. It streamed off the peaked black-slate roofs of the four motel wings, chuckled rather pleasantly along the horizontal sections of spouting, roared down the wide vertical spouts, and gushed noisily into the drainage gratings in the ground. Everywhere, trees dripped, shrubs dripped, and flat surfaces glistened darkly. Dirty water collected in depressions in the courtyard lawn. The hard-driven droplets shattered the crystalline tranquillity of the swimming pool, danced on the flagstones laid around the pool, flattened the tough grass that encircled the flagstones.

The gusting wind brought the rain under the awning and into the second-level promenade outside of Doyle's room. The moment he closed the door, locking Colin inside, a whirlwind of cold water raced along the walkway and spun over him, soaking his right side. His blue work shirt and one leg of his well-worn jeans clung uncomfortably to his skin.

Shivering, he looked southward, down the longest stretch of the walkway, to the courtyard steps at the far end. The shadows were deep. None of the rooms had light in them; and the weak night lights on the promenade were spaced fifty or sixty feet apart. The night mist complicated the picture, curling around the iron awning supports and eddying in the recessed entrances to the rooms. Nevertheless, Doyle was fairly sure that there was no one prowling about in that direction.

Thirty feet to the north, two rooms beyond their own, another wing of the motel grid intersected this one, forming the northeast corner of the courtyard overlook. Whoever had been at their door might have run up there in a second, might have ducked quickly out of sight . . . Alex tucked his head down to keep the rain out of his face, hurried up that way and peered cautiously around the corner.

There was nothing down the short arm of that corridor except more red doors, the night mist, darkness, and wet concrete. A blue safety bulb burning behind a protective wire cage marked another set of open steps that led down to the first level, this time to the parking lot which completely ringed the complex.

The last segment of his own walkway, running off to the north, was equally deserted, as was the remainder of the second-level east-west wing.

He walked back to the wrought-iron railing and looked down into the courtyard at the pool and the landscaped grounds around it. The only things that moved down there were those stirred by the wind and the rain.

Suddenly Alex had the eerie notion that he was not merely alone out here— but that he was the only living soul in the entire motel. He felt as if all the rooms were empty, the lobby empty, the manager's quarters empty, all of it abandoned in the wake—or perhaps the approach—of some great cataclysm. The overbearing silence, except for the rain, and the black concrete hallways generated and fed this odd fantasy until it became disturbingly real and a bit upsetting.

Don't let the frightened little kid come to the surface again, Doyle warned himself. You've done well so far. Don't lose your cool now.

After a few minutes of observation, during which he leaned with both hands on the fancy iron safety railing, Doyle was convinced that the miniature pine trees and the neatly trimmed shrubbery in the courtyard below did not conceal anyone; their shadows were entirely their own.

The crisscrossing promenades remained quiet, deserted.

The windows were all dark.

Underneath the steadily drumming rain and the occasional banshee cries of the storm wind, the sepulcher silence continued undisturbed.

Standing by the rail, Alex had been without protection, and now he was thoroughly drenched. His shirt and trousers were sodden. Water had even gotten into his boots and had made his socks all cold and squishy. His arms were decorated with rank on rank of goose pimples, and he was shivering uncontrollably. His nose was running, and his eyes were teary from squinting out at the rain and fog.

Nevertheless, Doyle felt better than he had for some time. Although he had not found the stranger who was harassing them, he had at least *tried* to confront the man. Finally, he had done something more than run away from the situation. He could have remained in the room despite Colin's accusing look, could have made it through the night without taking this risk. But he *had* taken the risk, after all, and now he felt somewhat better, pleased with himself.

Of course, there was nothing more to be done. Whoever the stranger was, and whatever the hell he had intended to do once he had picked their lock, the man had obviously lost interest in his game when he realized that they were awake and onto him. He would not be back tonight. Perhaps they would never see him again at all, here or anywhere.

When he turned and started back toward their room, all of his good humor was abruptly forgotten . . .

Two hundred feet along the same walkway which he had first examined on coming out of the room, along a corridor that had appeared to be absolutely empty and safe, a man stepped out of a recess in front of a door and hurried to the courtyard steps in the southeast corner of the overlook, thumped down them two at a time. He was very nearly invisible, thanks to the mist and the rain and the darkness. Doyle saw him only as a shapeless figure, a shadowy phantom . . . However, the hollow sound of his footsteps on the open stairs was proof that he was no imagined spirit.

Doyle went to the railing and looked down.

A big man dressed in dark clothes, made otherwise featureless by the night and the storm, loped across the lawn and the flagstones by the pool. He ducked under the floor of the second-level walkway which served as the roof over the first-level promenade.

Before he quite realized what he was doing, Alex started after the man. He ran to the head of the courtyard steps and went down fast, came out on the lawn where the rain and wind roiled openly.

The stranger was no longer over there on the ground-floor walkway where he had been when Doyle had last seen him. Indeed, he seemed to have vanished into thin air.

Doyle looked at the pines and shrubs from this new prospective, and he realized that the stranger might have doubled back to wait for him. The feathery shadows were menacing, far too deep and too dangerous . . .

Taking advantage of the yellow and green lights that surrounded the swimming pool and avoiding the shadows, Doyle crossed the courtyard without incident. However, he had no sooner gotten out of the worst of the wind and rain than he heard footsteps again. This time they were at the back of the complex, to the north, going up to the second level on this wing. He followed the hauntingly hollow *thump-thump-thump* which was barely audible above the rain sounds.

The stairwell was deserted when he got to it, a straight flight of wet and mottled gray-brown risers.

He stood at the bottom for a minute, looking up, thinking. He was quite aware of the easy target that he would make when he came out at the top, all too vulnerable to a gun or knife or even to a quick shove that would carry him back down the way he had come.

Nevertheless, he started up, more than a little bit exhilarated and surprised at his own daring in having come even this far. Tonight he had begun to discover a new Alex Doyle inside the old one. There was a Doyle who could overcome the cowardliness when faced with a responsibility for the well-being of those he loved, when more than his own pride was affected.

He was not set upon when he came off the last step and into the northwest corner of the courtyard overlook. There was no one waiting for him. He was greeted by lightless windows, concrete, and red doors.

Again he experienced the strange feeling that he was the last man alive in the motel—indeed, that he was the last man in the world. He did not know if the fantasy was based on megalomania or paranoia, but the sense of isolation was complete.

Then Alex saw the stranger again. Shapeless, shadow-swathed, mist-draped, the man stood at the extreme north end of the promenade, at the head of the stairs which went down to the parking lot behind the motel complex. Another blue safety bulb behind another wire cage did nothing to illuminate the phantom. He took the first step, seemed to turn and look back at Doyle, took the second step, then the third, disappeared once more.

It's almost as if he *wants* me to follow him, Alex thought.

He went north along the promenade and down the rain-washed steps.

CHAPTER 12

FOUR MERCURY-VAPOR arc lamps towered over the parking area behind the Rockies Motor Hotel, making the night above them twice as dark as it was elsewhere, but somewhat illuminating the rows of cars beneath. The irritating, fuzzy purple light glinted dully in the falling raindrops and in the water that flushed across the black macadam. It made stark shadows. It leeched the color out of everything it touched, transforming the once-bright cars into depressing, green-brown look-alikes.

Doyle, tinted a light purple himself, stood on the walk at the bottom of the stairwell and looked left and right along the lot.

The stranger was nowhere in sight.

Of course, the man might be hidden between two of the cars, crouched expectantly . . . But if the chase were to degenerate into a game of hide-and-seek in a playground of two or three hundred automobiles, they could waste all night darting around the silent machines and in and out of the shadows between them.

He supposed he had come to the end of it now; there was nothing to be gained by this expedition, after all. He was not going to get a look at the man or at the rented Automover. He would have no description or license number to work with or to give to the police—if it came to that. Therefore, he might as well go back to the room, get out of these wet clothes, towel off, and . . .

But he could not walk away from the challenge quite as easily as that. If he were not exactly drunk with courage, he was at least somewhat inebriated with his own appreciation for his new-found bravery. This brand-new Alex Doyle, this suddenly responsible Doyle, this Doyle who was capable of coping with and perhaps even overcoming his long-held fear, fascinated and pleased him immensely. He wanted to see just how far this previously unknown, even unsuspected, but certainly welcome strength would carry him, how deep this vein which he had tapped.

He went looking for the stranger.

The vending-machine room at the back of the motel complex did not have any doors on its two entrances. Cold white light fanned out in twin semicircles from both narrow archways, dispelling the sickly purple glow of the mercury-vapor lamps overhead.

Doyle went to the doorway and peered inside.

The room was well lighted and appeared untenanted. However, there were a number of blind spots formed by the bulky machines, a dozen places where a man could hide.

He stepped across the raised threshold.

The room was about twenty feet by ten feet. It contained twelve machines, which stood against the two longest walls and faced one another like teams of futuristic heavy-weight prize fighters waiting for the bell to ring and the match to begin: three humming soda machines that could dispense six different flavors of bottled and canned refreshment; two squat cigarette machines; one cracker and cookie vender full of stale and half-stale goods; two candy machines with an especially twenty-first-century look about them; a coffee and hot chocolate dispenser with stylized cups of steaming brown liquid painted on the mirrored front along with the bold legend **Sugar Cream Marshmallow**; a vender of peanuts, potato chips, pretzels, and cheese popcorn; and an ice machine which rattled noisily, continually, spitting newly made cubes into a shiny steel storage bin.

He walked slowly down the room, flanked by the murmuring dispensers, looking into the niche between each pair of them, expecting someone to jump out at him any second now. His tension and fear were qualitatively different from what he had known in the past; they were almost beneficial, clean, purgative. He felt a great deal like a small boy prowling through a most forbidding, decaying graveyard on Halloween night, a rag bag of conflicting emotions.

But the stranger was not in the room.

Doyle went outside again into the wind and rain, no longer much concerned with the bad weather, a man caught up in his own changes.

He walked along the parked cars, hoping to find the stranger kneeling between two of them. But he crossed from the end of one north-south wing to the end of the other north-south wing without noticing any movement or unlikely shadows.

He was just about to call it quits when he saw the weak light spilling out of the half-opened maintenance-room door. He had passed this way less than five minutes ago when he had been on his way to the vending machines, and this door had not been open then. And it was hardly an hour when the motel janitor would be coming to work . . .

Alex put his back to the wet concrete wall, his head resting in the center of the neatly stenciled black-and-white sign which was painted there (Maintenance and Supplies—Motel Employees Only), and listened for movement inside the room.

A minute passed in silence.

Cautiously he reached out and pushed the oversized metal door all the way open. It swung inward without a sound, and an equally soundless gray light came out.

Doyle looked inside. Directly across the large room, a second door, also metal and also oversized, stood wide open to the rain. Beyond it was a section of the amoeboid parking lot. Good enough. The stranger had been here and had already gone.

He went into the room and looked around. It was slightly larger than the place that contained the vending machines. Toward the back, along the wall, were barrels of industrial cleaning compounds: soaps, abrasives, waxes, furniture polish. There were also electric floor waxers and buffers, a forest of long-handled mops and brooms and window-washing sponges. Two riding lawn mowers stood in the middle of the room with a host of gardening tools and huge coils of transparent green plastic hose. At the front, closer to the doors, were the workbenches, carpentry tools, a standing jigsaw, and even a small wood lathe. To Doyle's right, the entire wall was covered with pegboard; the silhouettes of dozens of tools had been painted on the pegboard and the tools themselves hung over their own black outlines. The gardening ax was missing, but everything else was clean and hung neatly in place.

The barrels of cleaning compounds were too widely spaced and too small to effectively conceal a man, especially a man as tall and broad-shouldered as the one whom he had seen crossing the courtyard earlier in the night.

Doyle walked farther into the room and was halfway to the second door, only fifteen feet from it, when he suddenly understood the full implications of the missing ax on the pegboard. He almost froze in place. Then, warned by some sixth sense, he crouched and turned with more speed and agility than he had ever shown in his life.

Looming immediately behind him, nightmarishly large, the wild-eyed blond man raised both hands and swung the gardening ax.

CHAPTER 13

NOT ONCE IN his entire thirty years had Alex Doyle been in a fight—not a fist fight, wrestling match, or even a juvenile push-and-shove. He had never dealt out physical punishment to anyone, and neither had he taken any himself. Whether coward or genuinely committed pacifist or both, he had always managed to avoid controversial subjects in casual discussions, had avoided arguments and taking sides and forming relationships which might conceivably have led to violence. He was a civilized man. His few friends and acquaintances had always been as gentle as he was himself, and often even gentler. He was singularly unprepared to handle a raging maniac who was wielding a well-sharpened gardener's ax.

However, instinct served where experience failed. Almost as if he had been combat-trained, Alex fell backward, away from the glittering blade, and rolled across the grease-stained cement floor until he came up hard against the two riding lawn mowers.

His intellectual acceptance of the situation lagged far behind his automatic physical-emotional realization of the danger. He had heard the ax whistle past, inches from his head, and he knew what it would have done to him if it had found its mark . . . Yet, it was inconceivable that anyone could want to take his life, especially in such a sudden bloody fashion. He was Alex Doyle. The man without enemies. The man who had walked softly and carried no stick at all—the man who had often sacrificed his pride to save himself from just this sort of madness.

The stranger moved fast.

Dazed as he was, numb with surprise at the suddenness and extreme ferocity of the attack, Alex still saw the man coming.

The stranger lifted the ax.

"Don't!" Doyle said. He barely recognized his own voice. He had not lost all of his new-found courage. However, it was now tempered by a healthy fear which put it in the proper perspective.

The five-inch razored blade swept up, reached the top of its arc in one smooth movement, almost a precision instrument in those strong hands. Sharp slivers of light danced brightly on the cutting edge. The blade hesitated up there, high and cold and fantastic—and then it fell.

Alex rolled.

The ax dropped in his wake. It made the moist air whistle once again, and it thudded into a solid rubber tire on one of the lawn mowers, splitting the deep tread.

Doyle came to his feet, and once more powered by a mindless drive for self-preservation, vaulted over one of the work-benches, clearing the four-foot width with more ease then he would ever have thought possible. He stumbled, though, and nearly fell flat on his face when he came down on the other side.

Behind him, the madman cursed: a curiously wordless, low grunt of anger and frustration.

Doyle turned, fully expecting the ax to cleave either his head or the surface of the wooden bench behind him. He had, at last, come to terms with his predicament. He knew that he might die here.

Across the room, the stranger hunched his broad shoulders and put all his strength into them, wrenched the blade free of the solid, uninflated tire in which it had become wedged. He turned, his wet shoes scraping unpleasantly on the concrete floor, and he clutched the ax in both hands as if it were some sacred and all-powerful talisman which would ward off evil magic and protect the bearer from the work of malevolent sorcerers. There *was* something of the superstitious savage in this man, especially in and around those enormous dark-ringed eyes . . .

Those same eyes now located Doyle. Incredibly, the stranger bobbed his head and smiled.

Alex did not return the smile.

He *could not* return it. He was almost physically ill with premonitions of death, and he wished that he had never left the room.

He was still too far away from the doors to make a run for either of them. Before he could have crossed the open floor and gained the threshold, he would almost certainly have felt the ax blade bite down between his shoulder blades . . .

Rain dripping from his clothes, the stranger moved in on Doyle, quiet and swift for such a large man. The noises which he had made outside, on the steps and promenades, could not have been accidental. He had been luring Doyle along those shadowy corridors, drawing him to a place where he might be trapped.

A place like this.

Now only the wooden bench separated them.

"Who are you?" Doyle asked.

The stranger was no longer smiling when he stopped on the other side of the waist-high bench. In fact, he was frowning intensely, even wincing, as if he were being cruelly pinched or jabbed with pins. What was it, what was on his mind? More than murder, now? He was annoyed considerably by *something*; that much was obvious. His mouth was set in a tight, straight, grim line, and he appeared to be struggling desperately to choke back a reaction to an inner pain.

"What do you want from us?" Doyle asked.

The man only glared at him.

"We've never hurt you."

No answer.

"You don't even know us, do you?"

Even though his voice was weak, an involuntary whisper, and even though the terror that it betrayed might have goaded the madman into even bolder action, Doyle had to ask the questions. All of his life he had been able to settle other people's anger with sympathetic words, and now it became essential that he elicit some response—at least contrition—from this man. "What have you to gain by hurting me?"

The madman swung the ax horizontally this time, from right to left, trying to chop Doyle's torso from his legs.

It was close. His long arms had sufficient reach and strength to make the trick work, even with the bench between them. But Doyle saw it coming just in time to avoid it. He scrambled backward, out of the murderous arc.

Then he tripped over a large metal toolbox which he had not noticed. He windmilled his arms in a hopeless attempt to recover, lost his balance altogether. The room tilted around him. In that instant Doyle knew that he probably did not have a chance of getting out of this place alive. He was not going to return to Room 318, where Colin waited for him, was never going to finish the drive to San Francisco or see the new furniture in the new house or begin his wonderful new job with the agency or make love to Courtney again. Never. Falling, he saw the tall blond man start around the end of the workbench.

He did not stay down on the floor any measurable length of time, or even a second. The moment he hit, he pushed to his feet and staggered backward, trying to keep out of the madman's reach for at least one more precious minute.

In three short steps, however, he backed straight into the pegboard wall where the tools were hung.

Even as Doyle realized that he had nowhere left to run, the stranger stepped in front of him and swung the ax from right to left.

Doyle crouched.

The blade skimmed the pegboard above his head.

Rising even as he heard the ax whine by him, Doyle grabbed a heavy claw hammer which dangled from a hook on the wall. He had it in his hand when he was knocked sideways and down by a blow from the ax.

The hammer clattered across the floor.

But losing the hammer, Doyle thought, was the least of his troubles. The oppressive, pulsing pain in his side and chest made him all but helpless. Had he been cut up? Torn open? The pain . . . pain was terrible, the worst he had ever endured. But please, God, no . . . Please, please, not this. Not death. Not all the blood and having to lie in all the blood while the ax rose and fell and methodically dismembered him. Not death, dammit. Anything else. All he could see on the other side of death was nothingness, perpetual blackness; and the vision was so complete and vivid and horrifying that he never even recognized the incongruity and futility of praying to a God in whose existence he did not believe. Just: God, God, please . . . Not this. Anything but this. Please . . .

All of this flashed through his mind in a fraction of a second, before he realized that he had not been caught by the ax blade. Instead, he had been hit on the backswing of the first blow. He had taken the *head* of the ax, the three-inch-wide top of it, just below the ribs on his right side. There had been enough force in the blow to knock the wind out of him and to leave him with a welt and eventually a bruise. But that was all. There was no torn flesh. No blood.

But where was the madman—and the ax?

Doyle looked up, blinked tears out of his eyes.

The stranger had dropped the weapon. He was pressing the palms of his hands against his temples, grimacing furiously. Perspiration had popped out on his forehead and was trickling down his reddened face.

Gasping for breath, Alex clambered to his feet and leaned back against the wall, too weak and pain-wracked to move any farther.

The stranger saw him. He bent down to pick up the ax, but stopped short of it. He gave a strangled cry, turned, and stumbled out of the room, out into the night and the rain.

For a long while, as he struggled to regain his breath and to overcome the pain which stitched his side, Alex was certain that he had been granted only a temporary reprieve. It made no sense for this stranger to walk away from a job so nearly finished. The man had desperately *needed* to kill Doyle. There had been nothing playful or joking about him. Each time that he had swung that ax, he had intended to sever flesh and spill blood. Certainly, he was insane. And the insane were unpredictable. But it was likewise true that a madman's violent compulsions were not easily or rapidly dissipated.

Yet the man did not return.

The pain in Doyle's side gradually eased until he could stand erect, could walk. His breath came much less raggedly than it had, although he could not inhale too deeply without amplifying the pain. His heartbeat softened and slowed.

And he was left alone.

He walked slowly to the door, his right hand pressed to his side, and he leaned against the frame for a moment, then stepped outside. The rain and wind struck him with more force than ever, chilling him.

The parking lot was deserted. The green-brown cars sparkled with water, all still and unremarkable.

He listened to the night.

The only sounds were the steady drumming of the rain and the fluting of the wind along the building.

It seemed almost as if the events in the maintenance room had been nothing but a bad dream. If he had not had the pain in his side to convince him of its reality, he might have gone back to look for the ax and the other signs of what had happened.

He walked back toward the courtyard in the center of the motel complex, splashing through puddles rather than walk around them, wary of every velvety shadow, stopping half a dozen times to listen for imagined footsteps following close behind him.

But there were no footsteps other than his own.

At the top of the stairs which led to the second level, in the northeast corner of the courtyard overlook, he leaned against the iron safety rail to catch his breath and to clamp down on the renewed thump of dull pain in his side and chest.

He was cold. Deep-down cold and shivering. The raindrops struck him like chips of ice and melted down his face.

As he sucked the crisp air, he looked at the dozens of identical doors and windows, all of them closed and lightless . . . And he wondered, suddenly, why he had not screamed for help when the stranger had first attacked him with the ax. Even though they had been clear at the back of the motel, and even though the thunder of rain and wind was a blanket over other sounds, his voice would have carried into these rooms, would have awakened these people. If he screamed as loudly as he could, surely someone would have to come to see what was wrong. Someone would have called the police. But he had been so frightened that the thought of crying out for help had never occurred to him. The battle had been strangely noiseless, a nightmare of nearly silent thrust and counter-thrust which had not reached the motel guests.

And then, remembering various newspaper stories he had read, accounts of the average man's indifference to the commission of a rape or murder in front of his eyes, Doyle wondered if anyone *would* have answered his call for help? Or would they all have turned and put pillows over their heads? Would these people in these identical rooms have reacted unemotionally and identically: with reluctance and perhaps apathy?

It was not a nice thought.

Shaking violently now, he tried to stop thinking about it as he pushed away from the rail and walked down the rainwashed promenade toward their room.

CHAPTER 14

WHEN DOYLE FINISHED drying his hair, Colin folded the white motel towel and carried it into the bathroom, where he draped it over the shower rail with the rain-soaked clothes. Trying to handle himself in a calm and dignified manner— even though he was wearing only undershorts and eyeglasses, and even though he was obviously quite frightened—the boy came back into the main room and sat down in the middle of his own bed. He stared openly at Doyle's bruised right side.

Alex cautiously explored the tender flesh with the tips of his fingers, until he was satisfied that nothing was broken or so seriously damaged that it demanded a doctor's attention.

"Hurt?" Colin asked.

"Like a bitch."

"Maybe we should get some ice to put on it."

"It's just a bruise. Not much to be done."

"You *think* it's just a bruise," Colin said.

"The worst of the pain is gone already. I'll be stiff and sore for a few days, but there isn't any way to avoid that."

"What do we do now?"

Doyle had, of course, told the boy everything about the ax battle and the tall, gaunt man with the wild eyes. He had known that Colin would recognize a lie and would probe for the truth until he got it. This was not a child whom you could treat like a child.

Doyle stopped massaging his discolored flesh and considered the boy's question. "Well . . . We definitely have to change the route we'd planned on taking from here to Salt Lake City. Instead of using Route 40, we'll take either Interstate 80 or Route 24 and—"

"We changed plans before," Colin said, blinking owlishly behind his thick, round glasses. "And it didn't work. He picked us up again."

"He picked us up again only when we returned to I-70, the road that *he* was using," Doyle said. "This time we won't go back to the main roads at all. We'll take the longer way around. We'll figure a new way into Reno from Salt Lake City—then a secondary road from Reno to San Francisco."

Colin thought about that for a minute. "Maybe we should stay at new motels, too. Pick them at random."

"We have reservations and deposits waiting for us," Doyle said.

"That's what I mean." The boy was somber.

"That sounds like paranoia," Doyle said, surprised.

"I guess."

Doyle sat up straighter against the headboard. "You think that this character knows where we intend to stop each night?"

"He keeps picking us up in the mornings," the boy said defensively.

"But how would he know our plans?"

Colin shrugged.

"He would have to be somebody we know," Doyle said, not warming to the idea at all, afraid to warm to it. "I don't know him. Do you?"

Colin just shrugged again.

"I've already described him," Doyle said. "A big man. Light, almost white hair, cut short. Blue eyes. Handsome. A little gaunt . . . Does he sound like somebody you know?"

"I can't tell from a description like that," Colin said.

"Exactly. He's like ten million guys. So we'll operate under the assumption that he *is* a total stranger, that he's just your average American madman, the kind you read about in the newspapers every day."

"He was waiting for us in Philly."

"Not *waiting*. He happened to—"

"He started out with us," Colin said. "He was right there behind us from the first."

Doyle did not want to consider that the man might know them, might have some real or imagined grudge against them. If that were the case, this whole crazy thing would not end with the trip. If this maniac knew them, he could pick them up again in San Francisco. He could come after them any time he wanted. "He's a stranger," Alex insisted. "He's nuts. I saw him in action. I saw his eyes. He is not the sort of man who could plan and execute a cross-country pursuit."

Colin said nothing.

"And why would he pursue us? If he wants us dead—why not kill us back in Philly? Or out on the coast? Why chase us this way?"

"I don't know," the boy admitted.

"Look, you have to accept some coincidence in this thing," Doyle said. "By sheer coincidence, he began his trip the same time we did, from the same block of the same street that we did. And he's crazy. A madman might very well become obsessed with a coincidence like that. He would make more of it than it was, use it as the foundation for some paranoid delusion. And everything that has happened since would explain itself."

Colin hugged himself and rocked slowly back and forth on the bed. "I guess you're right."

"But you still aren't convinced."

"No."

Doyle sighed. "Okay. We'll forfeit the room deposits we've made. We'll pick motels at random the next two nights—if we can find any vacancies." He smiled, somewhat relieved even though he could not believe Colin's vague hypothesis. "You feel better now?"

"I won't really feel better until we're in San Francisco, until we're home," Colin said.

"That makes two of us." Doyle slid down in bed until he was flat on his back. The movement made his bruise throb again. "You want to turn out the light so we can catch a few winks?"

"Can you sleep after all this?" Colin asked.

"Probably not. But I'm going to try. I'm certainly not going to leave the motel now—not in the dark. And if we're going to take back roads and add hours of driving time to our schedule, I'll need all the rest I can get."

Colin turned out the lights, but he did not slip under the covers. "I'll just sit here awhile," he said. "I can't sleep now."

"You better try."

"I will. In a little while."

As exhausted as he was, Doyle slept, though fitfully. He dreamed of flashing ax blades and gouting blood and maniacal laughter, and he woke repeatedly, sheathed in cold sweat. Awake, he thought about the stranger and wondered who he might be. And he thought, as well, about his own new courage. He realized that it was his love for Courtney and for Colin that had provided him with the key to this strength. When he had no one to look out for except himself, he could always run from trouble. But now . . . Well, three could not run as easily or as quickly as one. Therefore, he had been compelled to call upon resources which he had not known he possessed. Knowing, he felt more at peace with himself than he had ever been before in his life. Content, he slept. Sleeping, he dreamed again and woke with the shakes and countered the shakes with the knowledge that he could now handle the cause of them.

For two long hours Colin sat up in bed, wrapped in darkness, listening to Doyle breathe. Occasionally, the man woke from a bad dream and turned over and wrestled with the bedclothes until he could sleep again. At least he *was* dozing. Doyle's equanimity in these dangerous circumstances impressed Colin quite a bit.

Of course, he had always been impressed with Alex Doyle—more than he had ever been able to let the man know. Sometimes he wanted to grab hold of Doyle and hug him and hold onto him forever. He was afraid, all through the courtship, that Courtney would lose Doyle. He knew how much they cared for each other and suspected the intensity of their physical relationship, yet he had been sure Doyle would leave them. Now that Doyle was theirs, he wanted to hug him and be around him and learn from him. But he was not capable of that hug, for it seemed too juvenile a means of expressing what he felt. He had worked too hard and too long at being an adult to let himself slip now, no matter how much he loved, liked, and admired Alex Doyle. Therefore, he had to let his feelings be known in small ways, in hundreds of separate, simple gestures that would say it all as well as that one hug would say it, if less forcefully.

He got off his bed when the first morning light found its way around the edges of the heavy drapes, and he went into the bathroom to shower. With Alex in the room beyond, with the warm water cascading down on him and the yellow soap foaming pleasantly against his thin limbs, Colin worried less and less about the stranger in the Chevrolet van. With just a little bit of luck, everything would be fine. It *had* to come out all right in the end, because Alex Doyle was here to make certain that nothing really bad happened to him or to Courtney.

By the time George Leland reached the Automover which was parked near the front of the Rockies Motor Hotel, he had forgotten all about Doyle and the boy. He fumbled with his keys, dropped them. He pawed clumsily in an inch-deep puddle until he found them again. Unlocking the cab door, he climbed into the truck, unable to recall the silent chase through the motel corridors or the ax-swinging madness in the maintenance room when he had come within seconds and inches of killing a man. He was too beaten down with pain to care about this sudden amnesia.

It was the worst headache yet. The pain was most fierce in and around the right eye, but now it also fanned out across his entire forehead and back to the top of his skull. It brought tears to his eyes. He could even hear his teeth grinding together like sandstone wheels, but he could not stop the hard, involuntary chewing motion; it was as if he were possessed, and as if his possessor thought that the pain could be masticated, shredded into fine pieces, swallowed, and digested away.

There had been no warning signs. Usually, at least one hour in advance of the first wave of pain, he grew dizzy and nauseated, and he saw that spiral of hot multicolored light turning around and around behind his eye. But not tonight. One moment he had felt just fine, even exhilarated, and the next, pain had hit him like a hammer blow. It had been an ugly but comparatively small pain to begin with—hadn't it? A small pain at the start? He could not remember exactly where he had been when it first struck him, but he was sure the pain had been only mild, initially. Certainly bearable. However, it had rapidly gotten worse until, now, he despaired of reaching his own motel before he was completely incapacitated.

He drove out of the motel lot, slammed off a four-inch curb and onto the highway, the van's springs squealing beneath him. He did not feel like a part of the vehicle tonight. He was no extension of it. He had lost his usual empathy with machines. He was a stranger in this contraption, and the steering wheel felt like an alien artifact, an inhuman device, under his large hands.

He squinted at the wet pavement as he drove, tried to push back the rain and the ghostly tendrils of fog.

A low, sleek car approached from the opposite direction, flashed past in a violent spray of water. Its four headlights were much too bright; they sliced into Leland's eyes like a quartet of knives and drew a painful wound across his forehead.

Unconsciously he pulled the wheel hard to the right, away from the light which so offended him. The van crunched onto the shoulder of the road, nosed down, bounced in a rut, came up again with a prolonged shudder. In the cargo hold, furniture shifted noisily. Suddenly, immediately ahead, a waist-high brown-brick wall loomed out of the night, stark and deadly, Leland cried out and wheeled hard to the left. The right front fender nicked the bricks. Then the Chevrolet jumped back onto the pavement, sliding in the rainwater for a long, dangerous moment before it finally, reluctantly came back under his control.

He reached the motel only because he encountered no other traffic. If even one other car had passed him, he would have demolished the Chevrolet and killed himself.

At the door of his room, rain beating against his back, he had trouble inserting the key in the lock, and he cursed nearly loudly enough to wake the other guests.

Inside, as he closed the door, the pain abruptly worsened, driving him to his knees on the stained carpet. He was sure that he was dying.

But the new pain passed, and the agony became merely unbearable pain.

He went to the bed and almost lay down before he realized that he had to get out of his clothes first. They were wet clear through. If he passed the rest of the night in them, he would be ill in the morning . . . Slowly, with exaggerated movements, he undressed and dried himself on the tufted bedspread. Even then, he was chilled to the bone. Trembling, he got into bed and pulled the cover up to his chin. He gave himself over to the unrelenting pain and tried to ride with it.

It lasted more than twice as long as usual. And when, well after dawn, it was finally gone, the nightmares which always followed it were also worse than they had ever been. The only lovely thing in that parade of grisly images was Courtney. She kept popping up. Nude and beautiful. Her full, round breasts and delightfully long legs were welcome relief from the other visions . . . Yet, each time she did appear in the dreams, an imaginary dream-Leland killed her with an imaginary knife. And the murder was, without exception, curiously satisfying.

THURSDAY

CHAPTER 15

Interstate 25 ran north from Denver and connected with Interstate 80 just inside the Wyoming border. That was all well-paved, four-lane, controlled-access highway that would carry them straight into San Francisco without a single intersection to get in the way.

But they did not take it, because it seemed like *too* obvious an alternative to the route which they had originally planned to use. If the madman in the Chevrolet van *had* become obsessed with them—and with killing them—then he might make the effort to think one step ahead of them. And if he realized that they would now leave their pre-planned route, he would see, with one quick glance at a map, that I-25 and I-80 was their next best bet.

"So we'll take Route 24," Doyle said.

"What kind of road is it?" Colin asked, leaning across the seat to look at the map which Doyle had propped against the steering wheel.

"Pieces of it are four-lane. Most of it isn't."

Colin reached out and traced it with one finger. Then he pointed to the gray-shaded areas. "Mountains?"

"Some. High plateaus. But there are a good many deserts, alkali and salt flats . . ."

"I'm glad we've got air conditioning."

Doyle folded the map and handed it to the boy. "Belt yourself in."

Colin put the map in the glove compartment, then did as he had been told.

As Doyle drove out of the Rockies Motor Hotel parking lot, the boy tucked in his orange-and-black Phantom of the Opera T-shirt, smoothed the wrinkles out of the phantom's hideously deformed face, and took a couple of minutes to comb his thick brown hair until it fell straight to his shoulders just the way he liked it. Then he sat up straight and watched the sunscorched landscape whisk past as the mountains drew nearer.

The electric-blue sky was streaked with narrow bands of gray-white clouds, but it was no longer a storm sky. Last night's downpour had ended as abruptly as it had begun, leaving few traces. The sandy soil alongside the road looked almost parched, dusty.

The traffic was not heavy this morning, and what there was of it moved so well and orderly that Doyle did not have to pass a single car all the way out of the Denver area.

And there was no van behind them.

"You're awfully quiet this morning," Alex said after fifteen minutes had passed in silence. He glanced away from the twisting snakes of hot air that danced above the highway, looked at the boy. "You feeling okay?"

"I was thinking."

"You're *always* thinking."

"I was thinking about this—maniac."

"And?"

"We aren't being followed, are we?"

"No."

Colin nodded. "I bet we never see him again."

Doyle frowned, accelerated slightly to keep up with the flow of cars around them. "How can you be so sure?"

"Just a hunch."

"I see. I thought you might have a theory . . ."

"No. Only a hunch."

"Well," Doyle said, "I'd feel a whole lot better if you *did* have some reasons for thinking we've seen the last of him."

"So would I," the boy said.

Even as he drove into the parking lot that encircled the Rockies Motor Hotel, George Leland knew that he had missed them. The headache had been so damned long and intense . . . And the period of unconsciousness, afterward, had lasted at least two hours. They might not be too far out in front of him, but they had surely gotten a head start.

The Thunderbird was not where it had been the night before. That space was empty.

He refused to panic. Nothing was lost. They had not escaped. *He knew exactly where they were going.*

He parked where the Thunderbird had been, shut off the engine. There was a map on top of the same tissue box which held the .32-caliber pistol. Leland unfolded it on the seat and turned sideways to study it, traced the meager system of highways that crossed Colorado and Utah.

"They don't have many choices," he told the golden girl in the seat next to him. "Either they stay on the planned route—or they take one of these other two."

She said nothing.

"After last night, they'll change their plans."

When his headache was gone, Leland had also lost his selective amnesia. He could now recall everything: arriving at the motel an hour before they did, watching the lobby until they arrived, cautiously following them to their room, coming back in the middle of the night and trying to pick the lock on their door, the silent chase, and the ax . . . If that damned headache had only held off for a few minutes, if it had not come on him when it did, he would have finished off Alex Doyle.

Leland was not disturbed by the realization that he had tried to kill a man. After suffering so much at the hands of others, he had finally come to understand that there was only one thing that would destroy this far-reaching conspiracy that was working against him: force, violence, counterattack. He must smash this entire evil association which had been formed solely to drive him to complete despair. And since Alex Doyle—and the boy, as well—formed the keystone of this conspiracy, murder was quite justified. He had acted in self-defense.

On Monday, when he had caught sight of his own eyes in the mirror, he had been confused, shocked by what he saw. Now, when he looked in the mirror, he saw nothing but a reflection, a flat image. After all, he was only doing what Courtney wanted, so that they could be together again, so that everything could be as wonderful as it had been two years ago.

"They can either go up to Wyoming and catch Interstate 80, or go southwest on Route 24. What do you think?"

"Whatever you say, George," the golden girl replied, her voice faint but pleasant, like a happy memory.

Leland studied the map for several minutes. "Damn . . . They probably went up and caught I-80 outside of Cheyenne. But even if they did, and even if we went that way and managed to catch up with them, we wouldn't be able to do anything to them. That's a major highway. Too much traffic, too many police patrols. All we could do would be follow them—and that's not enough." He was quiet for a while, thinking. "But if they went the other way, it's a whole different ballgame. That's desolate country. Not as much traffic. Fewer cops. We could really make up for lost time. Might get a chance at them somewhere along the way."

She waited, silently.

"We'll take Route 24," he said at last. "And if they *did* go the other way . . . Well, we can always pick them up again tonight, at their motel."

She said nothing.

He smiled at her, folded the map and placed it on top of the tissue box, where it covered the blue-gray pistol.

He started the van.

He drove away from the Rockies Motor Hotel and then from Denver, going southwest toward Utah.

During the morning they came out of the mountains and down the piney valleys of Colorado, from winter's leftover snow to sun and sand again. They went through Rifle and Debeque, crossing the Colorado River twice, then passed Grand Junction and, soon after, the border. In Utah, the mountains fell back into the distance and the land became sandier, and there was less traffic than there had been. For long minutes theirs was the only car in sight on the level stretches of open road.

"What if we had a flat tire now?" Colin asked, indicating the vistas of unpopulated land.

"We won't."

"We might."

"We have all new tires," Doyle said.

"But what if?"

"Then we'd change it."

"And if the spare went flat too?"

"We'd fix it."

"How?"

Alex realized that they were playing one of the boy's games, and he smiled. Maybe the kid's hunch was a good one. Maybe it was all over now. Perhaps they could yet restore to the trip that fun which they had known at the beginning of it. "In the emergency kit in the trunk of this car," Doyle said in an exaggerated professorial voice, "there is a large spraycan which you can attach to the valve of the flat tire. It inflates the tire and simultaneously seals the puncture. You will then be able to drive until you locate a service station which will attend to your needs."

"Pretty clever."

"Isn't it?"

Colin held an imaginary aerosol dispenser in one hand, pushed on the unseen button, and made a sputtering noise. "But what if the spraycan doesn't work?"

"Oh, it will."

"Okay . . . But what if we have *three* flats?"

Doyle laughed.

"It could happen," Colin said.

"Sure. And we could have *four* flats."

"And what would we do?"

As Doyle started to tell him that they would get out of the car and walk, a horn blared behind them. It was loud and close and uncomfortably familiar. It was the van.

CHAPTER 16

BEFORE ALEX COULD react properly, before the fear could well up and he could tramp down on the accelerator and rocket away from the Automover, the van swung into the left-hand lane and started to go around him, its strident horn still wailing. Far out ahead on the gray, heat-twisted road—clear to the high, rocky, multi-layered Capitol Reefs which stood miles away—there was not any east-bound traffic to get in the van's path.

"You can't let him go around us!" Colin said.

"I know."

If the bastard got out in front of them, he would be able to blockade the entire roadway. The cracked stone shoulders on both sides were too narrow and the sand beyond them too dry and soft and loose for the Thunderbird to leave the pavement and regain the lead once that was lost.

Doyle put his foot down.

The big car surged ahead.

But the stranger in the van, though mad, was not stupid. He had been expecting that maneuver. He put speed on, too, and at least for the moment, he was able to stay even with Doyle.

Wind roared between the two parallel vehicles as they hurtled westward.

"We'll outpace him," Alex said.

Colin did not respond.

The slim speedometer needle climbed smoothly to eighty and then on up to eighty-five. Doyle glanced at it once. Tense and frightened, Colin watched it with real dread.

The flat land whipped past them in a shimmering white blur of sand and heat and free-lying salt.

And the Automover hung in beside them.

"He can't keep up," Alex said.

Ninety. Ninety-five . . .

Then, as they were rushing toward a hundred-miles-an-hour, with the wind whooping between them, the madman pulled his wheel to the right. Not much. Just a little bit. And only for an instant. The whole side of the Automover made light, brief contact with the full length of the Thunderbird.

Sparks showered up and skittered like a fall of bright stars across the windshield in front of Doyle. Tortured sheet metal screamed and coughed and crumpled up on itself.

The steering wheel was nearly torn out of Doyle's hand. He grappled with it, held on as the car lurched onto the stone shoulder, kicking up gravel that rattled noisily in the undercarriage. Their speed fell, and they began a slow sideways turn. Alex was certain that they were going to plow into the van, which was still alongside of them. But then the car began to right itself . . . He took them back onto the highway, touching the gas pedal when he would have preferred to go with the brakes.

"You all right?" he asked Colin.

The boy swallowed hard. "Yes."

"Better hold on, then. We're going to get the hell out of here," he said as the Thunderbird gradually picked up the speed which it had lost, casting its pale shadow on the side of the Chevrolet.

Doyle risked one quick glance away from the road, looked up at the van's side window, which was no more than three or four feet away. Despite the short distance between them, he could not see the other driver, not even his silhouette. The man was sitting up higher than Doyle, on the far side of the cab, and he was very well hidden by the yellow-white desert sunlight that played upon the window glass.

Eighty miles an hour again, making up for lost time and for lost ground. And now on up to eighty-five, with the speedometer needle quivering slightly. It hesitated on the eighty-five, in fact; for a moment it looked as if it would stick there, and then it jerked and rose slowly.

Alex watched the Chevrolet out of the corner of his eyes. When he first sensed it moving in to brush against them a second time, he would take the car into the stony berm and try to avoid another collision. They could not tolerate much more of that banging around. Though it was half again as expensive as the Automover van, the big luxury car would come apart much sooner and more completely than the Chevrolet. It would dissolve around them like a flimsy paper construction, roll over and over like a weightless model, and burn faster than a cardboard carton.

At ninety miles an hour, the car began to shake badly, making a noise like stones rolling in the bottom of a washtub. The steering wheel vibrated furiously in Doyle's hands. And then, worse, it started to spin uselessly back and forth.

Doyle eased up on the accelerator, although that was the last thing he wanted to do.

The needle fell. At eighty-five, the ride was smooth and the car was under control.

"Something's broken!" Colin shouted over the roar of the wind and the two competing engines.

"No. It must have been a section of bad road."

Though he knew that their luck was not running that way, Alex hoped to God that what he had told the boy was true. Let it be true. Let it be nothing more serious than a piece of bad road, a section of rain-runneled pavement. Don't let anything happen to the Thunderbird. It must not break down. They must not be stranded out here in the sand and the salt flats, not alone, not so far from help, and not with the madman as their only company.

He tried the accelerator.

The car picked up, hit ninety . . .

And the violent shudder returned, as if the frame and body were no longer firmly joined and were slamming into each other, parting, slamming together again. This time, as he lost control of the wheel, he felt the horrible quaking in the gas pedal as well. Their top speed was going to be eighty-five. Otherwise, the car would fall apart. Therefore, they were not going to outpace the Chevrolet.

The driver of the van seemed to realize this the same moment that Doyle did. He tooted his horn, then pulled away from them, out in front where he had command of the highway.

"What are we going to do?" Colin asked.

"Wait and see what *he* does."

When the Automover was approximately a thousand yards out ahead of them, wrapped up in the deceptively undulating streams of hot air that were rising off the superheated pavement, it slowed down to a steady eighty-five and maintained a consistent half-mile lead.

A mile passed.

On both sides of the road, the land became even whiter, as if it had been bleached by the raw sun. It was punctuated only by rare, ugly clumps of struggling scrub and by occasional dark rock teeth that were all stained and rotted by the desert wind and heat.

Two miles.

The van was still out there, taunting them.

The dashboard vents spewed crisp, cold air, and still the interior of the Thunderbird was too warm and close. Alex felt perspiration bead on his forehead. His shirt was sticking to him.

Three miles.

"Maybe we should stop," Colin said.

"And turn back?"

"Maybe."

"He would see us," Doyle said. "He would turn right around and follow— and before long, he'd be out in front of us again."

"Well . . ."

"Let's wait and see what he does," Doyle said again, trying to keep the fear out of his voice. He was aware that the boy needed an example of strength. "You want to get the map and see how far it is to the next town?"

Colin understood the significance of the question. He grabbed the map and opened it on his knees. It covered him like a quilt. Squinting through his Coke-bottle glasses, he found their last known position, estimated the distance they had come since then, and marked the spot with one finger. He located the nearest town, checked the key at the bottom of the map, then did some figuring in his head.

"Well?" Doyle asked.

"Sixty miles."

"You sure?"

"Positive."

"I see."

It was too damned far.

Colin folded the map and put it away. He sat like a stone sculpture, staring at the back of the Chevrolet van.

The highway crested a gentle slope, dropped away into a broad alkali basin. It looked like an ink line drawn across a clean sheet of typewriter paper. For miles and miles to the west, the road was empty. Nothing moved out there.

This complete isolation was precisely what the driver of the van wanted. He braked hard, pulled the Chevrolet toward the right berm, then swung it around to the left in a broad loop. The van stopped, sideways in the road, blocking most of both lanes.

Doyle tapped the brakes, then realized that there was no percentage in slowing down or stopping altogether. He put his foot on the accelerator again. "Here we go!"

Holding at a steady eighty-five, the Thunderbird bore down on the van, aimed straight at the center of the green-and-blue advertisement painted on its flank. Seven hundred yards lay between them. Now only six hundred—five, four, three hundred . . .

"He isn't going to move!" Colin said.

"Doesn't matter."

"We'll hit!"

"No."

"Alex—"

Fifty yards from the truck, Doyle wheeled to the right. Tires squealed. The car rushed across the graveled berm, bounced as wildly as if the springs had turned to rubber, and kept on going.

Doyle realized that he was attempting to pull off a stunt which only a short while ago he had thought impossible. Now, whether it was impossible or not, it was their only hope. He was terrified.

The car plowed into the grainy white soil that edged the highway, and alkali dust plumed up behind them like a vapor trail. Their speed was cut by a third in the first few seconds, and the Thunderbird lurched sickeningly in the sandy earth.

It'll stop us, Doyle thought. We'll be stranded here.

He stomped the accelerator to the floor.

Although they were still doing better than fifty, the wide tires protested the loss of traction, spun furiously. The car slewed sideways, fishtailed back before picking up the speed demanded of it.

They passed the Automover.

Doyle angled back toward the highway. He kept the accelerator pressed all the way down. Through the partially unresponsive steering wheel, he felt the treacherous land shifting beneath them. However, before the sand could capture one or more of the wheels, they reached the shoulder of the road and kicked up hundreds of small stones as they plunged back onto the pavement.

In seconds, they were doing eighty-five again, heading west, the van behind them.

"You did it!" Colin said.

"Not yet."

"But you did!" He was still frightened, but he also sounded pleasantly excited.

Doyle looked in the mirror.

Far back there, the van was starting after them, a white speck against the whiter land.

"He's coming?" Colin asked.

"Yes."

"See if it'll go past ninety now."

Doyle tried, but the car began to shake and rattle. "No good. Something was damaged when he slammed into us."

"Well, at least we know you can drive us around any roadblock he throws up," the boy said.

Doyle looked at him. "You've got more faith in my driving than I do. That was pretty hairy back there."

"You can do it," Colin said. Desert sunlight, coming through the window, made his wire-framed glasses look like tiny tubes of light.

Three minutes later the van was on their tail.

But when it tried to come around them, Doyle swung the Thunderbird into the left-hand lane, blocking the van and forcing it to fall back. When the Chevy attempted to move in on their right, Doyle weaved in front of it and blew his own horn to counter the other's savage blaring.

For several minutes and miles they played that game with an unsportsman-like disregard for rules, cruising from one side of the road to the other. Then, inevitably, the van found an opening and took advantage of it, drawing even with them.

"Here we go again," Doyle said.

As if he had cued it, the Automover closed the space between them and brushed the car. Sparks showered up and sputtered out in an instant, and metal whined, though not as loudly or as gratingly as it had the first time that they had collided.

Alex fought the wheel. They plummeted along the gravel shoulder for a thousand yards before he could get them back onto the highway.

The van hit them again, harder than before.

This time Alex lost control. He could not hold onto the sweat-slicked steering wheel which spun through his hands. It was slippery as a stick of butter. Only when they were off the road, grinding crazily through the ridged sand, was he able to get a good grip on the wet plastic and regain command of their fates.

They were doing forty-five when they came back onto the road, and they were a few yards ahead of the van. But it caught up with them a moment later and hung beside them until they were doing eighty-five again. The whole right side of the Automover was scraped and dented. Doyle knew, as he looked anxiously at the other vehicle, that the left side of the Thunderbird was in much worse condition.

The van swept in at them again. There was a sudden *bang!* so loud that Alex thought they had been hit a fourth time. However, there was no impact with the sound. And, abruptly, the Chevrolet lost speed, fell behind them.

"What's he doing?" Colin asked.

It was too good to be true, Doyle thought. "One of his tires blew."

"You're kidding."

"I'm not kidding."

The boy slumped back against the seat, pale and shaking, limp, wrung out. In a thin, almost whispered voice, he said, *"Jesus!"*

CHAPTER 17

THE TOWN SURVIVED despite the inhospitable land in which it stood. The low buildings—whether they were of wood, brick, or stone—had all turned a dull yellow-brown in order to coexist with the merciless sun and the wind-blown sand. Here and there, alkaline encrustations limed the edges of walls, but that was only variation in the drabness. The main highway—which became the borough's most important street—had been a harsh gray-black line through the desert ever since they had crossed over from Colorado; but now it succumbed to the influence of the town, became dun and dusty. Out on the open land, the wind had scoured the road clean; but here, the buildings blocked the wind and let the dust collect. A soft powder filmed the automobiles, taking the shine out of them. The dust seemed like the hands of the living desert, gradually stealing back this meager plot which men had taken from it.

The police station, three blocks west along the main street, was as dreary as everything else, a one-story building that was losing the mortar between its mustard-colored stones.

The officer in charge of the station, a man who called himself Captain Ackridge, wore a brown uniform that fit in with his town and a hard, experienced face which did not. He was six-foot, two hundred pounds, perhaps ten years older than Doyle but with a body ten years younger. His close-cropped hair was black, his eyes darker than that. He held himself like a soldier on parade, stiff and proud.

He came out and looked at the Thunderbird. He walked the whole way around it and seemed to be as interested in the undamaged angles as he was in the long scars down the driver's side. He leaned close to the tinted windshield and peered in at Colin as if the boy were a fish in an aquarium. Then he looked at the damage on the car's left side again and was satisfied with his inspection.

"Come on back inside," he told Doyle. His voice was crisp and precise in spite of the underlying Southwest accent. "We'll talk about it."

They returned to the station, crossed the public room where two secretaries were pounding on typewriters and one uniformed, overweight cop was taking a coffee break and munching on an eclair. They went through the door to Ackridge's office, and the big man closed it behind them.

"What do you think can be done?" Alex asked as Ackridge went around behind his neatly ordered desk.

"Have a seat."

Doyle went to the chair that faced the scarred metal desk, but he did not sit down. "Look, that flat tire won't slow the bastard up for long. And if he—"

"Please sit down, Mr. Doyle," the policeman said, sitting down himself. His well-worn spring-backed chair squeaked as if there were a live mouse in the cushion.

Somewhat irritated, Doyle sat down. "I think—"

"Let's just do this my way," Ackridge said, smiling briefly. It was an imitation smile, utterly false. The policeman seemed to understand that it was a bad copy, for he gave it up right away. "You have some identification?"

"Me?"

"It was you I asked."

The officer's voice contained no real malice, yet it chilled Doyle. He got his wallet from his hip pocket, withdrew his driver's license from one of the plastic windows, and pushed it across the desk.

The policeman studied it. "Doyle."

"That's right."

"Philadelphia?"

"Yes, but we're moving to San Francisco. Of course, I don't have my California license yet." He knew he was on the verge of babbling, his tongue loosened not so much by the residual fear of their encounter with the madman in the van as by Ackridge's penetrating black eyes.

"You have an owner's card for that T-Bird?"

Doyle found it, held the wallet open to the proper plastic envelope, and passed the whole thing over to the policeman.

Ackridge looked at it for a long time. The billfold was small in his large, hard hands. "First Thunderbird you've owned?"

Alex could not see what that had to do with anything, but he answered the question anyway. "Second."

"Occupation?"

"Mine? Commercial artist."

Ackridge looked up at him, seemed to stare through him. "Exactly what is that?"

"I do advertising artwork," Doyle said.

"And you get paid well for that?"

"Pretty well," Doyle said.

Ackridge started to leaf through the other cards in the wallet, taking a couple of seconds with each. His sober, intense interest in these private things was almost obscene.

What in the hell is going on here? Doyle wondered. I came here to report a crime. I'm a good, upstanding citizen—not the suspect!

He cleared his throat. "Excuse me, Captain."

Ackridge stopped flipping through the cards. "What is it?"

Last night, Doyle told himself, I faced a man who was trying to kill me with an ax. Today I can surely face this two-bit police chief.

"Captain," he said, "I don't see why you're so interested in who I am. Isn't the most important thing—well, going after this man in the Automover?"

"I always believe it pays to know the victim as well as the victimizer," Ackridge said. With that, he went back to the cards in Doyle's wallet.

It was all wrong. How on earth could it have gone sour like this—and why had it?

So that he would not be humiliated by watching the cop pry through his wallet, Alex looked around the room. The walls were institutional-gray and brightened by only three things: a poster-sized framed photograph of the President of the United States; an equally large photograph of the late J. Edgar Hoover; and a four-foot-square map of the immediate area. Filing cabinets stood side by side along one wall, breaking only for a window and an air-conditioning unit. There were three straight-backed chairs, the desk, the chair in which Ackridge sat, and a flagstand bearing a full-sized cotton-and-silk Old Glory.

"Conscientious objector?" Ackridge asked.

Alex looked at him, surprised. "What did you say?"

Ackridge showed him the selective service card in his wallet. "You have a CO rating here."

Why had he ever kept that card? He was under no legal obligation to carry it with him, especially not now that he was thirty years old. They had long ago stopped drafting men over twenty-six. Indeed, the draft was pretty much of a forgotten thing for *everyone*. Yet he had transferred the card from one billfold to the next—through maybe three or four of them. Why? Subconsciously had he believed that possession of the card was proof that his non-violent philosophy was based on principle and not cowardice? Or had he simply given in to that common American neurosis—the reluctance and sometimes the inability to throw away anything with a vaguely official look to it, no matter how dated it might be?

"I did alternate service in a veterans' hospital," Doyle said, though he did not feel he needed to justify himself to Ackridge.

"I was too young for Korea and too old for Nam," the cop said. "But I served in the regular army, in-between wars." He handed back the driver's license and the wallet.

Alex put the license in the wallet, the wallet in his pocket, and he said, "About the man in the Chevrolet—"

"You ever try marijuana?" Ackridge asked.

Easy, Doyle thought. Be damn careful. Be damn nice.

"Long time ago," he told the cop. He no longer tried to find a way to get back to the man in the Automover, because he saw that for whatever reasons, Ackridge didn't care about that.

"Still use it?"

"No."

Ackridge smiled. It was the same bad imitation. "Even if you did use it every day of the week, you wouldn't tell a crusty old cop like me."

"I'm telling the truth," Doyle said, feeling new perspiration on his forehead.

"Other things?"

"What do you mean?"

Leaning across the desk, his voice lowered to a melodramatic whisper, Ackridge said, "Barbiturates, amphetamines, LSD, cocaine . . ."

"Drugs are for people who don't really care for life," Doyle said. He believed what he was saying, but he knew it must sound hollow to the cop. "I happen to love life. I don't need drugs. I can make myself happy without them."

Ackridge watched him closely for a moment, then leaned back in his chair, crossed his heavy arms on his chest. "You want to know why I'm asking all these questions?"

Alex did not respond, for he was not sure whether or not he wanted to know.

"I'll tell you," Ackridge said. "I've got two theories about this story of yours—about the man in the Automover. First one is—none of it happened. You hallucinated it all. Could be. Could be like that. If you were really high on something, maybe LSD, you could have given yourself a real bad spook."

The thing to do, now, was just to listen. Don't argue. Just let him go on and, hopefully, get out of here as soon as possible. Still, Alex could not help saying, "What about the side of my car? The paint's gone. The body is all torn up. My door won't open . . ."

"I'm not saying *that* is imaginary," Ackridge told him. "But it could be that you side-swiped a retaining wall or an outcropping of rock—anything."

"Ask Colin," Doyle said.

"The boy in the car? Your—brother-in-law?"

"Yes."

"How old is he?"

"Eleven."

Ackridge shook his burly head. "He's too young for me to touch. And he'd probably just say anything he supposed you wanted him to say."

Alex cleared his throat, which was tight and dry. "Search the car. You won't find any drugs."

"Well," Ackridge said, purposely emphasizing his drawl, "let me tell you my other theory before you go getting your dander up. I think it's a better one, anyway. Know what it is?"

"No."

"I think maybe you were tooling along in that big black car of yours, playing king of the road, and you passed some local boy who was driving the only broken-down old pickup he could afford." Ackridge smiled again, and this time it was a genuine smile. "He probably looked at you with your loud clothes and long hair and effeminate ways, and he wondered why you could have the big car while he had to settle for the truck. And, naturally, the more he thought on it, the madder he got. So he caught up with you and held a little duel on the highway. Couldn't of hurt his old wreck. You were the only one with something fancy to lose."

"Why would I tell you it was an Automover? Why would I make up an elaborate story about a cross-country pursuit?" Doyle asked, barely able to control his anger but painfully aware that any expression of it would land him in jail, or worse.

"That's easy."

"I'd like to hear it."

Ackridge stood up and pushed his chair back, walked over and stood by the flag, his hands clasped behind his back. "You figured that I might not go after a local boy, that I'd favor one of ours over someone like you. So you made up this other thing to get me onto the case. Once I'd gone on record, started a full investigation, I couldn't have backed out of it so easily when I learned the real story."

"That is far-fetched," Doyle said. "And you know it."

"Sounds reasonable to me."

Alex got to his feet, his damp hands fisted at his sides. Once it had been easy for him to take this kind of abuse and crawl away without another thought. But now, with the changes that had taken place in him during the last couple of days, excessive humility was not his best suit. "Then you aren't going to help us?"

Ackridge looked at him with real hatred now. For the first time there was genuine malice in his voice. "I'm not a man you can call a pig one day—then run to for help the next."

"I've never called any policeman a pig," Alex said.

But the cop was not listening. He appeared to be looking straight through Doyle when he said, "For fifteen years or better, this country's been like a sick man. It's been absolutely delirious, staggering around and bumping into things, not sure where it was or where it was going or even if it would survive. But it isn't so sick any more. It's casting off the parasites that made it ill. Soon there won't be any parasites at all."

"I get you," Alex said, shaking uncontrollably with both fear and rage.

"It will up and kill *all* the germs and be as healthy as it once was," Ackridge said, grinning broadly, hands still clasped behind his back, rocking on his heels.

"I understand you perfectly," Alex said. "May I leave?"

Ackridge laughed in short, sharp barks. "Leave? Gee, I really would appreciate it if you did."

Colin climbed out of the car and let Alex slide inside, then followed him and pulled the door shut, locked it. "Well?"

Alex gripped the steering wheel as hard as he could and stared at his whitened knuckles. "Captain Ackridge thinks I might have been taking drugs and imagined the whole thing."

"Oh, great."

"Or that maybe some local boys were harassing us in a pickup. He sure doesn't want to favor us over some good old boys having their fun."

Colin buckled his seatbelt. "Was it really that bad?"

"I think he'd have jailed me if you hadn't been along," Doyle said. "He didn't know what to do with an eleven-year-old boy."

"What now?" He pulled at his Phantom of the Opera T-shirt.

"We'll fill the gas tank," Alex said. "Buy some take-out food and drive straight through to Reno."

"What about Salt Lake City?"

"We'll skip it," Doyle said. "I want to get into San Francisco as soon as I can—and get as far off our schedule as possible, in case that bastard *does* know our route."

"Reno isn't just around the corner," the boy said, remembering how far it had seemed on the map. "How long will it take us to get there?"

Doyle surveyed the dusty street, the yellow-brown buildings, and the alkali-skinned automobiles. These were all inanimate objects without intentions of their own, malevolent or otherwise. Yet he feared and hated them. "I could get us into Reno a little after dawn tomorrow."

"Without sleeping?"

"I won't sleep tonight anyway."

"Driving will wear you out, though. No matter how you feel now, you'll fall asleep at the wheel."

"No," Alex said. "If I feel myself nodding off, I'll pull over to the side of the road and take a fifteen- or twenty-minute nap."

"What about the maniac?" the boy asked, jerking a thumb toward the road behind them.

"That flat will slow him up some. It won't be easy handling the van by himself, jacking it up . . . And once he's on the road again, he won't drive all night. He'll figure that we stopped at a motel somewhere. If he knows we planned to be in Salt Lake City tonight—and I still don't see *how* he could know—then he'll be up there looking for us. We can get away from him for good, this time." He started the car. "If the T-Bird holds together, that is."

"Want me to plan a route?" Colin asked.

Alex nodded. "Back roads. But roads we can make decent time on."

"This might even be fun," Colin said, opening the map once more. "A real adventure."

Doyle looked at him, incredulous. Then he saw, in the boy's eyes, a haunted look that must have matched his own, and he realized that the statement had been sheer bravado. Colin was trying as best he could to stand up under the incredible stress—and he was doing remarkably well for an eleven-year-old.

"You're really something else," Doyle said.

Colin blushed. "You too."

"We make quite a pair."

"Don't we?"

"Zooming off into the unknown," Alex said, "without even blinking an eye. Wilbur and Orville."

"Lewis and Clark," the boy said, grinning.

"Columbus and—Hudson."

"Abbott and Costello," Colin said.

It might have been just the circumstances, but Doyle thought that was the funniest line he had heard in years. It brought tears to his eyes. "Laurel and Hardy," he said when he was finished laughing. He put the car in gear and drove away from the police station.

* * *

The van was as difficult to handle as a stubborn cow. After half an hour of constant struggle, Leland got the wheels blocked and the jack pumped up enough to remove the punctured tire. The wind coming across the sand flats made the Chevy sway lightly on its metal crutch. And if the furniture in the cargo hold shifted without warning . . .

An hour after he had begun, Leland tightened the last nut on the spare and let the van down again. When he heaved the ruined tire into the truck, he realized he should stop at the first service station to get it repaired. But . . .

Doyle and the kid had gotten too much of a head start already. Though it was true that he could pick them up again tonight in Salt Lake City, he did not want to lose the chance of finishing them out here on the open road. The closer they got to San Francisco, the less sure he was of himself and his ability to dispose of them.

And if he didn't get them out of the picture, what would Courtney think? Courtney was depending on him. If he didn't take care of those two, then he and Courtney could never be together like they wanted.

Therefore, the tire could wait.

He closed the rear doors of the van, locked them, and went around to the cab. Five minutes later he was doing ninety-five on the flat, deserted highway.

Detective Ernie Hoval of the Ohio State Police ate supper in an interchange diner which most of the cops in the area favored. The atmosphere was pretty bad, but the food was good. And policemen were given a twenty percent discount.

He was halfway through his club sandwich and French fries when the sallow, smart-ass lab technician sat down in the other half of the booth, facing him. "Do you mind some company?" the man said.

Hoval winced. He did mind, but he shrugged.

"I didn't know a man like you took advantage of thinly disguised bribes like restaurant discounts," the technician said, opening the menu which the waitress brought him.

"I didn't when I first started," Hoval said, surprised to find that he actually *wanted* to talk to this man. "But everyone else does . . . And there's not much else you can take advantage of—if you want to keep being a good cop."

"Ah, you're just like all the rest of us," the technician said, dismissing Hoval with a brisk wave of the hand.

"Poor."

The other man's pale face crinkled in a grin, and he even allowed himself a soft laugh. "How's the club sandwich?"

"Fine," Hoval said, around a mouthful of it.

The technician ordered one, without French fries, and a coffee. When the girl had gone, he said, "What about the Pulham investigation?"

"I'm not on it full time now," Hoval said.

"Oh?"

"Not much I can do," Hoval explained. "If the killer was going to California in an Automover, he's way out of my territory. The FBI is checking on the names they got from Automover's central records. They've narrowed it down to a few dozen. Looks like maybe a couple of weeks until they find our guy."

The technician frowned, picked up the salt shaker and turned it around and around in his bony hands. "A couple of weeks could be too late. When a fruitcake starts to go, he goes fast."

"You still on that kick?" Hoval asked, putting down his sandwich.

"I think we're dealing with a psychotic. And if we are, he'll add a few more murders to his record in the next week or two. Maybe even kill himself."

"This isn't any nut," Hoval insisted. "It's one of your political cases. He won't kill anyone else—not until he gets a chance to set up another cop."

"You're wrong about him," the technician said.

Hoval shook his head, took a long drink of his lemon blend. "You bleeding-heart liberals astound me. Can't stop looking for simple answers."

The waitress brought the pale man's coffee. When she went away, he said, "I haven't noticed any blood on my shirt in the vicinity of my heart. And I am not a political liberal. And I think *your* answer is more simplistic than mine."

"The country's going to hell in a handbasket, and you're blaming it all on psychotics and fruitcakes."

"Well," the technician said, finally putting down the salt shaker, "I almost hope you're right. Because if this guy *is* a nut, and if he *is* loose another week or two . . ."

FRIDAY

CHAPTER 18

By two o'clock Friday morning, sixteen hours after they had left Denver, Alex felt as if he belonged in a hospital ward for terminally ill patients. His legs were cramped and heavy. His buttocks pinched and burned as if they were jammed full of needles, and his back ached all the way from the base of his spine to the back of his skull. And these were only the first in a long list of complaints: he was sweat-damp, rumpled, and unclean from having missed last night's shower; his eyes were bloodshot, grainy, and sore; the crisp black stubble of his one-day beard itched badly; his mouth was fuzzy and dry and tasted like sour milk; his arms ached dully from holding the damned steering wheel for hour after hour, mile after mile . . .

"You awake?" he asked Colin. In the darkness, with the gentle country music coming out of the radio, the boy should have been asleep.

"I'm here," Colin said.

"Should try to catch a few winks."

"I'm afraid the car is going to break down," Colin said. "I can't sleep for worrying about it."

"The car's okay," Doyle said. "The body got dented in a little, but that's all. The only reason it begins to shake when we go past eighty-five is that the wheel starts brushing against the indented metal."

"I'll still worry," Colin said.

"We'll stop at the next likely place and freshen up," Doyle said. "We both need it. And the car's low on gas."

Late Thursday afternoon they had headed southwest across Utah on a series of back roads, then picked up the secondary two-lane Route 21, which carried them northwest again. The swift desert sunset came, faded rapidly from a fiery orange-red to solemn purple and then a deep and velvety black. And still they drove, crossing into Nevada and switching over to Route 50, which they intended to follow from one end of the Silver State clear to the other.

Shortly after ten o'clock they stopped to get gasoline and to call Courtney from a pay phone. They pretended that they were at their motel, because Alex could not see any good reason to worry her now. Though they *had* been through a harrowing ordeal, it was probably all finished now. They had lost their stalker. There was no need to alarm her unnecessarily. They could give her the full story when they finally got into San Francisco.

From ten-thirty Thursday night until two o'clock Friday morning, they passed through what had once been the heart of the romantic Old West. The forbidding sand plains lay dark and empty to the left and right. Hard, barren mountains thrust up without warning and fell sharply away, out of place even if they had spent millennia here. Cactus loomed at both sides of the road, and rabbits occasionally fled across the pavement in the yellow glare of their headlights. If the trip had gone differently, if there had been no madman on their tail for the last two thousand miles, perhaps Nevada would have been a pleasure, a chance to indulge in nostalgia and a few of Colin's games. But now it was a bore, just something to be passed through before they could get to San Francisco.

At two-thirty they stopped at a combination service station and all-night diner. While the Thunderbird was topped off with gas and oil, Colin used the bathroom, freshened up for the next long leg of the marathon drive. In the diner, they ordered hamburgers and French fries. And while those were sizzling, Alex went into the men's room to shave and wash his face.

And to take two caffeine tablets.

He had bought a package of them earlier in the night, at the service station where they had stopped just before leaving Utah. Colin had been in the car at the time and had not witnessed the purchase. Alex did not want the boy to know about the tablets. Colin was already too tense for his own good. It would not be good for him to find out that Doyle, despite all his assurances, was getting sleepy at the wheel.

He looked at his reflection in the cracked mirror above the dirty washbasin, grimaced. "You look terrible."

The reflection remained mute.

They by-passed the exit to Reno and stayed on Route 50 until they found a motel just east of Carson City. It was a shabby place, decaying at the edges. But neither of them had the energy to look any farther. The dashboard clock read eight-thirty—more than twenty-two hours since they had left Denver.

In their room, Colin went straight for his bed and flopped down. "Wake me in six months," he said.

Alex went into the bath and closed the door. He used his electric razor to touch up the shave he had taken six hours before, brushed his teeth, took a hot shower. When he came back into the main room, Colin was asleep; the boy had not even bothered to undress. Doyle put on clean clothes, then woke him.

"What's the matter?" the boy asked, nearly leaping off the bed when Doyle touched his shoulder.

"You can't sleep yet."

"Why not?" Colin rubbed at his face.

"I'm going out. I won't leave you alone, so I guess you'll have to come with me."

"Out? Where?"

Alex hesitated a moment. "To . . . to buy a gun."

Now Colin was wide awake. He stood up and straightened his Phantom of the Opera shirt. "Do you really think we need a gun? Do you think that man in the Automover—"

"He probably won't show up again."

"Then—"

"I only said he *probably* won't. But I just don't know any more . . . I've thought about it all night, all the way across Nevada, and I can't be sure of anything." He wiped at his own face, pulling off his weariness. "And then, when I'm pretty sure that we've lost him—well, I think about some of the people we've run into. That service station attendant near Harrisburg. The woman at the Lazy Time Motel. I think about Captain Ackridge . . . I don't know. It's not that I think those people are dangerous. It's just that they represent something that's happening . . . Well, it seems to me we ought to have a gun, more to keep it in the house in San Francisco than to protect us for the last few hours of this trip."

"Then why not buy it in San Francisco?"

"I think I'll sleep better if we get it now," Alex said.

"But I thought you were a pacifist."

"I am."

Colin shook his head. "A pacifist who carries a gun?"

"Stranger things happen every day," Doyle said.

A few minutes past eleven o'clock, an hour and a half after they had gone out, Doyle and the boy returned to the motel room. Alex closed the door, shutting out the insufferable desert heat. He twisted the dead lock and put the guard chain in place. He tried the knob, but it would not turn.

Colin took the small, heavy pasteboard box to the bed and sat down with it. He lifted the lid and looked inside at the .32-caliber pistol and the box of ammunition. He had stayed in the car when Doyle went to buy it, and he had not been allowed to open the box on the short ride back. This was his first look at the weapon. He made a sour face. "You said the man in the sporting goods store called it a *lady's* gun."

"That's right," Doyle said, sitting down on the edge of his bed and taking off his boots. He knew he was not going to be able to stay awake more than another minute or two.

"Why did he say that?"

"Compared to a .45, it has less punch, less kick, and makes a great deal less noise. It's the kind of pistol a woman usually buys."

"Did you have any trouble buying it, since you're from out of state and all?"

Doyle stretched out on the bed. "No. In fact, it was too damned easy."

CHAPTER 19

FRIDAY AFTERNOON, GEORGE LELAND drove across the Nevada badlands toward Reno, his eyes brimming with pain even though the sunglasses he wore cut out half the glare from the white-white sand. He did not make good time. He was unable to keep his mind on his driving.

Since that especially severe headache he had suffered early Thursday morning when he had gone after Alex Doyle with a garden ax, Leland had found his thoughts wandering freely, almost beyond his control. He was not able to concentrate on anything for more than five minutes at a stretch. His mind jumped from subject to subject like a motion picture full of quick-cuts.

Time and again he snapped back from a daydream, surprised to find himself behind the wheel of the van. He had driven miles and miles while his mind was elsewhere . . . Apparently some fraction of his attention *was* on the road ahead and the traffic around him; but it was a very *small* fraction. If he had been on a heavily used freeway instead of out here in the flat, open wastelands, he would have killed himself, would have demolished the van during one of those daydreams.

Courtney was always there with him, in and out of the dreams. Now, as he came back again to the sand-flanked highway and the reality of the Chevrolet grumbling crankily beneath him, she was perched only a couple of feet away, her long legs drawn up on the seat beneath her.

"I almost had them yesterday," Leland said contritely. "But these damn worn tires . . ."

"That's okay, George," she said, close yet faraway.

"No, Courtney. I should have nailed them. And . . . Last night, when I checked the motel in Salt Lake, *they were not there.*" He was puzzled by that. "In that book of his, it said they'd stay at the Highlands Motel in Salt Lake City. What happened to them?"

She must not have known, for she did not answer.

Leland wiped his left hand on his trousers while he held the wheel in his right, repeated the gesture and drove with the left. "I looked in all the motels near the Highlands. They weren't staying in any of them. I've lost them. Somehow, they got away from me."

"You'll pick them up again," she said. He had hoped that she would be sympathetic and would encourage him. Lovely Courtney. You could always depend on Courtney.

"Maybe I will," he said, squinting out at the rolling hills of sand and the distant blue-and-rose mountains. "But how? And where?" He hoped she had the answer to that.

She did. "In San Francisco, of course."

"San Francisco?"

"You have my address there," Courtney said. "And that's where they're going. Isn't it?"

"Yes," he said. "It sure is."

"There you are."

"But . . . Maybe I can catch them in Reno tonight."

The lovely, soft-voiced, ethereal girl said, "They'll change motels again. You won't find them."

He nodded. It was true.

For a while, then, he went away from her. He was not in Nevada now, but in Philadelphia. Three months ago. He had gone downtown to see a film which had been entertaining and which . . . Well, the girl in it had looked so much like Courtney that he had been unable to sleep that night. He saw the film the next night too, and he learned from the lobby posters that the actress who fascinated him was Carol Lynley. But he soon forgot that. He went back to the film night after night, and she became the *real* Courtney. She was perfect. Long yellow-white hair, elfin features, those eyes that seemed to pierce him . . . Gradually, the sixth and seventh and eighth and ninth times he saw the movie, he began to experience a regeneration of sexual desire—which was odd, because the film was family fare. Finally, though, he had gone bar-hopping and had picked up a girl. He had made it with her . . . But she looked nothing like Courtney. Afterward, when he was spent, lying atop her, he looked into her face and saw that she was not Courtney, and he was angry. He felt that he had been tricked. She had cheated him. And so he started hitting her, slamming his hard fists into her face, over and over until—

He blinked at the blue sky, white sand, gray-black road. "Well," he said to the girl on the seat beside him, "I guess I will skip Reno. They won't stay in the right motel, anyway. I'll just go right on in to Frisco."

The golden girl smiled.

"Right on in to Frisco," Leland said. "They won't expect me there. They won't be ready for anything. I can take care of them real easy. And then we can be together. Can't we?"

"Yes," she said, just as he wanted her to say.

"We'd be happy again, wouldn't we?"

"Yes."

"You'd let me touch you again."

"Yes, George."

"Let me sleep with you again."

"Yes."

"Live with me?"

"Yes."

"And people would stop being nasty to me."

"Yes."

"You don't have to worry about me hurting you, Courtney," he said. "When you first left me, I wanted to hurt you. I wanted to kill you. But not any more. We're going to be together again, and I wouldn't hurt you for the world."

CHAPTER 20

━━━━━

COURTNEY ANSWERED THE telephone on the first ring, and she was even more exuberant than usual. "I've been waiting for your call," she said. "I've got some good news."

Alex was ready for a piece of good news, especially if it was delivered in that warm, throaty voice of hers. "What is it?"

"I got the job, Alex!"

"At the magazine?"

"Yes!" She laughed into the phone, and he could almost see her standing there with her golden head thrown back and her taut throat exposed. "Isn't it wonderful?"

Her happiness almost made up for everything that had gone wrong in the last few days. "You're absolutely sure it's what you wanted?"

"It's better than what I wanted."

"So . . . You and Colin will be old San Franciscans in short order—and I'll have to take a month off just to catch up with you."

"You know what the pay is?"

"Ten dollars a week?" he asked.

"Be serious."

"Fifteen?"

"Eighty-five hundred a year. To start."

He whistled. "Not bad for your first really professional job. But look, you aren't the only one with good news."

"Oh?"

Doyle looked at Colin, who was squeezed into the telephone booth with him, and he tried not to sound like a liar when he told the lie: "We got into Reno a few minutes ago." In fact, they had never gone to Reno at all, but to Carson City. And they had arrived early this morning, not minutes ago. They had slept all afternoon, right through the supper hour, and had awakened at half past eight, little more than an hour ago. "Neither one of us is sleepy." This was true enough, though he did not want to have to explain *why* neither one of them was sleepy, since they were not supposed to have been dozing in a motel all day. "It's about two hundred and fifty miles to San Francisco, so . . ."

"You're coming home tonight?" she asked.

"We thought we might as well."

"Look, if you're sleepy—sleep."

"We aren't sleepy."

"One day doesn't matter," she said. "Don't get in a big rush to finish the trip. If you fall asleep at the wheel—"

"You'll lose a new Thunderbird but gain valuable insurance money," he finished for her.

"That isn't funny."

"No, I guess it isn't. I'm sorry." He was irritable, he knew, only because he did not like to lie to her. He felt cheap and somehow dirty, even though he was only lying to save her unnecessary worry.

"You're *sure* you feel up to it?"

"Yes, Courtney."

"Then I'll keep the bed warm."

"*That* I might not feel up to."

"You will," she said. She laughed again, more softly this time. "You always are *up* to it."

"Bad joke," he said. "Bad joke."

"But one of those that just had to be made. So . . . What time can I expect you and the Marvelous Mite?"

Doyle looked at his wristwatch. "It's a quarter of ten now. Give us forty-five minutes for supper . . . We should get to the house around three in the morning, if we don't get *too* lost."

She gave him a noisy kiss via telephone. "Until three, darling."

At eleven o'clock George Leland passed a sign which gave the mileage to San Francisco. He looked down at the speedometer and did some figuring. He was not as quick about it as he once would have been. The numbers were slippery. He could not seem to add with even a third-grader's skill. And he was not as sure of himself as he had once been, either, for he had to refigure the thing three times before he was satisfied with the answer.

He looked at the shimmering golden girl beside him. "We'll reach your place by one o'clock. Maybe one-thirty," he said.

SATURDAY

CHAPTER 21

Courtney gathered up the stacks of trash that had accumulated from moving and taking delivery on new furniture—empty wooden packing crates, cardboard boxes, mounds of shredded newspapers, plastic and paper wrappings, wire, cord, rope—and put it all in the guest bedroom, which had not yet been furnished. It made quite a large, unsightly hill of rubble in the center of the carpet. She stepped into the hall and closed the door on the junk. There. Now they wouldn't have to look at it or think about it until Monday, when it would become necessary to haul the whole lot away somewhere to make room for the guest-room furniture. It was a bit like sweeping dirt under a carpet, she supposed. But as long as no one lifted up the carpet to look, what was wrong with that?

She went back to their bedroom and stood in the doorway, surveying it. The dresser, highboy, nightstands, and bed were all of matching heavy, dark wood which looked as if it had been hand-carved and hand-polished. The carpet was a deep-blue shag. The bedspread and drapes were a rich dark-gold velvet that looked almost as soft and honied as her own skin when she had a good tan. All in all, she thought, it was a damned sexy room.

Of course, the spread didn't hang perfectly even all around. And there was a cluster of perfume and make-up bottles on the dresser. And maybe the full-length mirror needed polishing . . . But all these things were what made it a Courtney Doyle Room. She left her mark of casual, minimal, harmless disarray wherever she lived.

"Remember," she had warned Alex on the night before their wedding, "you aren't getting a good housekeeper."

"I don't *want* to marry a housekeeper," he said. "Hell, I can *hire* housekeepers by the dozen!"

"And I'm not a really terrific cook."

"Why did God make restaurants?" he asked.

"And," she had said, scowling at the thought of her own sloppiness and slothfulness, "I usually let the laundry pile up until I either have to do the wash or buy all new clothes."

"Courtney, why do you think God invented Chinese laundries? Huh?"

Remembering that exchange, how they had broken into fits of laughter and giggled helplessly, holding each other and rocking on the floor like silly children, she smiled and went over to their new bed and sat down on it, testing the springs.

She actually had tested them before. She had stripped off all her clothes and jumped up and down in the center of the mattress, just as she had told Alex on the telephone. It had seemed a splendid idea at the time. But the exercise and the cool air on her bare skin had given her ideas and an appetite for loving. She could hardly get to sleep that night for wanting him. She kept thinking of Alex, of what it was like with him, kept thinking how perfect they were together and how bedtime with him was unlike anything she had ever known with anyone else.

They were good together in many ways, not just in bed. They liked the same books, the same movies, and usually the same people. If it was true that opposites attract, then duplicates attract even more.

"Do you think we'll ever get bored with each other?" she had asked him toward the end of the first week of their honeymoon.

"Bored?" he had asked, faking an enormous yawn.

"Seriously."

"We won't be bored for a minute," he said.

"But we're so similar, so—"

"Only three kinds of people bore me," he had said. "First: someone who can only talk about himself. And you're not an egomaniac."

"Second?"

"Someone who can't talk about *anything*. That kind bores me to tears. But you are an intelligent, active, exciting woman who always has something going. You'll never be without something to say."

"Third?"

"The most boring person of all is the one who doesn't listen when I talk about myself," Alex said, half serious but trying to get a laugh out of her as well.

"I always listen," she said. "I like to hear you talk about yourself. You are a fascinating subject."

Now, sitting on the bed which they would share tonight, she realized that *listening* to each other was the main thing that made their relationship work so well. She wanted to *know* him, and he wanted to fully understand her. He wanted to know what she was thinking and doing, and she wanted to be a part of all that concerned him. When you got right down to it, maybe they were not duplicates at all. Maybe, because they listened so well, they came to understand and appreciate each other's tastes and, soon, to share them. They did not duplicate each other so much as they helped each other expand and grow.

The future seemed so promising, and she was so happy that she hugged herself, an unconscious expression of satisfaction and delight which she had unknowingly passed on to Colin.

Downstairs, the doorbell rang.

She looked at the bedside clock: ten minutes past two.

Could they be here an hour early? Could he have overestimated the length of the drive by that much?

She got off the bed and hurried into the hall, took the stairs two at a time. She was excited at the prospect of seeing them and asking lots of questions about the trip, but . . . At the same time she was a bit angry. Had he just mistaken the length of time they would need to drive in from Reno? Or had he broken all the speed limits getting here? If he did . . . How dare he risk their future only to shave an hour off a five-day trip? By the time she reached the front door, she was almost as angry as she was pleased to know they were finally home.

She pulled off the chain and opened the door.

"Hello, Courtney," he said, reaching out to gently touch her face.

"George? What are you doing here?"

CHAPTER 22

BEFORE SHE COULD turn and run, before she could even grasp that there was something sinister about his unexpected appearance, he took her arm in a viselike grip and walked her over to the Spanish sofa, sat down with her. He looked around the room and nodded, smiled. "It's nice. I'll like it here."

"George? What—"

Still gripping her arm in one hand, he touched her face, traced the delicate line of her jaw. "You're so lovely," he said.

"George, why are you here?" She was somewhat afraid, though not quite terrified. His appearance did not make any sense, but it was no reason for her to go to pieces.

He let his hand slide along her throat, felt her pulse with his fingertips, then dropped the hand and cupped one of her heavy, unrestrained breasts. "Just as lovely as ever," he said.

"Please. Don't touch me like that," she said. She tried to pull away from him.

He held her tightly, and his free hand fondled her. He caressed the other breast now. "You said that you'd let me touch you again."

"What do you mean?" His fingers were digging into her arm so deeply that shooting pains exploded in her shoulder.

"You said I could make love to you again." His voice was low and dreamy. "Like before."

"No. I never said that."

"Yes, Courtney. You did."

She looked into his dark-ringed, bloodshot eyes, into the vaguely unfocused blue circles, and for the first time in her life she experienced the fear which belonged solely to women. She knew he might try to rape her. And she knew that even as gaunt as he was, he would be strong enough to do it . . . But wasn't it ridiculous to fear him this way? Hadn't she been to bed with him dozens of times in the past, before he had started to change? What was there to fear, then? But she knew it. It was not the sex that she feared. It was the force involved, the violent potential, the humiliation and the sense of being *used*. She did not know how he had gotten here or how he had learned their address. She did not know his circumstances or full intentions. But none of that mattered worth a damn. All that mattered right now was whether or not he would rape her. She felt weak, helpless, and oppressed. She was cold and hollow inside, trembling at the prospect of having to accept his forced attentions.

"You better not stay here any longer," she said, despising herself for the tremor in her voice. "Alex will be here in a few minutes."

Leland smiled. "Well, of course he will. I *know* that."

She could not figure out what he wanted, what he thought he could achieve beyond the brief, vicious taking of her. "Then why are you here?"

"We talked about that before."

"No. No, we did not."

"Sure, Courtney. You remember. In the van, we talked. On the way here. You and me. We've talked about it for several days now—how we could take care of them and then be together again."

She was no longer merely frightened. She was terrified. Finally he had gone over the edge. Whatever was wrong with him—some physical illness or a psychological disease—it had at last pushed him beyond sanity. "George, you've got to listen. Are you listening to me?"

"Sure, Courtney. I like your voice."

She shuddered involuntarily. "George, you're not well. Whatever has been wrong with you for the past two years—"

The smile faded from his face as he interrupted her. "I'm perfectly healthy. Why do you always insist I'm not?"

"Did you ever have those X-rays that the doctor—"

"Shut up!" he said. "I don't want to talk about it."

"George, if you're sick, maybe there's still something—"

She saw the blow coming, but she could not pull away from it in time. His big calloused hand struck her hard alongside the head. Her teeth rattled. She thought that was an almost funny sound . . .

But then the darkness rushed up at her, and she knew that she was going to faint. Unconscious, she would be even more helpless. And she realized, suddenly, that rape might be the least of her worries. He might not rape her at all. He might kill her.

She cried out, or thought that she did, and then she fell away into an inky pool.

Leland went out to the van and got the .32-caliber pistol which he had forgotten to bring with him the first time. He came back into the living room and stood by the sofa, looking down at her, admiring her golden hair and her freckles, the exquisite line of her face.

Why couldn't she have been nice to him? All the way across the country, she had been nice. When he told her to stop nagging him about something, she had stopped at once. But now she was the bitch again, picking at him, trying to say his mind was going on him. Didn't she know that was impossible? It was his mind that had gotten him all the scholarships, years ago. It was his superb mind which had gotten him off that damn farm, away from the poverty and the Bible-thumping and his father's paddle. So he *couldn't* be losing his mind. She only said that to frighten him.

He put the pistol barrel in her ear.

But he could not pull the trigger.

"I love you," he told her, although she could not hear him. He sat down on the floor beside the couch, and he started to cry. He snapped back from a daydream and realized that he was undressing her. While his thoughts had been elsewhere, he had pulled off her thin blue sweater, and now he was fumbling at the catch on her jeans. He stopped what he was doing and looked at her. Naked to the waist, she looked like a little girl despite the firm lines of her breasts. She seemed defenseless and weak and in need of protection.

This was not the way.

Leland knew, suddenly, that if he just tied her up and put her on ice until he had dealt with Doyle and the boy, she would be all right. When they were dead, she would realize that Leland was all she had. And then they could be together.

Lifting her as easily as he would have an infant, he carried her upstairs and put her on the bed in the master bedroom. He retrieved her sweater from the living-room floor and somehow slipped it onto her again.

Fifteen minutes later he had tied her hands and feet with rope that he found on the junk heap in the guest bedroom, and he had used a length of adhesive tape to seal her mouth.

He was sitting on the bed beside her, staring into her eyes, when they fluttered open and found him.

"Don't be afraid," he said.

She cried out behind the gag.

"I won't hurt you," he said. "I love you." He touched her long, fine hair. "In a little while everything will be okay. We'll be happy together, because we won't have anyone else in the world but each other."

CHAPTER 23

"THIS IS OUR STREET?" Colin asked as the Thunderbird labored up the steep lane toward a cluster of lights near the top.

"That's right."

Beyond an aisle of well-shaped cherry trees, the darkness of Lincoln Park lay on their left. To the right, the land shelved down through more darkness to the city's lights and the glimmering necklace of the harbor and the bay bridge. It was a stunning sight, even at three o'clock in the morning.

"This is *some* place," the boy said.

"You like it, huh?"

"It beats Philadelphia."

Doyle laughed. "It sure does."

"That our house up there?" Colin asked, pointing toward the only lights ahead of them.

"Yes. And a real nice lot with plenty of big trees." Coming home to the place for the first time now, he knew that it was worth every penny they had paid for it, though the price had initially seemed exorbitant. He thought of Courtney there, waiting. He remembered the tree outside the bedroom window, and he wondered if they would keep each other awake until dawn, when they could see the morning sun slanting down on the blue bay . . .

"I hope Courtney isn't too mad about the lies we told her," Colin said, still looking out across the edge of the city toward the dark ocean. "If she was, it would spoil this."

"She won't be angry," Doyle said, knowing that she would be, just a little and for just a few minutes. "She'll be glad we're safe and sound."

The house lights were close now, though the outline of the structure was hidden by a wall of deeply shadowed trees that rose behind it.

Doyle slowed down, looking for the entrance to the driveway. He found it and turned in. Thousands of small oval stones crunched under the tires.

He had to drive clear around to the side of the house before he saw the Chevrolet van parked by the garage.

CHAPTER 24

━━━━━

DOYLE GOT OUT of the damaged car on the passenger's side, put one hand on Colin's thin shoulder. "You get back in there," he said. "Stay here. If you see anyone but me come out of the house, leave the car and run to the neighbors. The nearest ones are downhill."

"Shouldn't we call the cops and—"

"There isn't time for that. He's inside with Courtney." Alex felt his stomach twist, and he thought he was going to vomit. A bitter fluid touched the back of his throat, but he choked it down.

"Another couple of minutes—"

"Might make all the difference."

Doyle turned away from the Thunderbird and hurried across the dark lawn toward the front door, which was ajar.

How was it possible? Who was this man who could follow them wherever they went, who could catch up with them no matter how much they changed their plans? Who in the hell was he that he could drive ahead and wait for them here? He seemed more than maniacal. He was almost superhuman, satanic.

And what had he done to Courtney? If he had hurt her in any way . . . Alex was caught up between rage and terror. It was frightening to realize that even when you had the courage to face up to violence, you could not protect those you loved. More than that, you couldn't know where the danger would come from or in what form.

He reached the front door, pushed it open, and stepped into the house before he thought that he might have walked into a trap. Suddenly he remembered all too clearly the cunning and ferocity which the madman had shown when he had been swinging that ax . . .

Doyle crouched against the wall, sheltering behind a telephone stand, making as small a target of himself as he could. He looked quickly around the front room.

It was deserted.

All the lights were blazing, but no madman here. And no Courtney.

The house was very quiet.

Too quiet?

Keeping his back to the wall, he went from the living room to the dining room, the shag carpet absorbing the noise of each footstep. But the dining room was also empty.

In the kitchen, three plates, knives, forks and spoons had been laid out on the butcher-block table along with various other utensils. She had planned a late-night snack for them.

Doyle's heart was pounding painfully. His breathing was so harsh and deep that he felt certain it would be heard from one end of the house to the other.

He kept thinking: Courtney, Courtney, Courtney . . .

The sunken den and the screened-in back porch were also deserted. Everything was neat and orderly—or, rather, as neat and orderly as things could be in Courtney's house. And that must be a good sign. Right? No traces of a struggle, no overturned furniture, no blood . . .

"Courtney!"

He had intended to remain silent. But now it seemed terribly important to call her name—as if the spoken word were a magic charm that would heal whatever the madman had done to her.

"Courtney!"

No reply.

"Courtney, where are you?"

In the back of his mind, Doyle knew that he should calm down. He should shut up for a minute and rethink the situation, consider his options once more before making another move. He was not going to help either Courtney or Colin if he acted stupidly, precipitously, and got himself killed.

However, with the silent house pressing in on him, he was temporarily incapable of rational behavior.

"Courtney!"

Bent forward like a soldier landing on an enemy-held beach, he ran up the main stairs two at a time. At the top, he grabbed the head of the banister to keep his balance, and he gasped for breath.

Along the second-floor hallway, all the doors were closed, each like the lid of a surprise package.

The guest bedroom was the nearest. He took three steps across the hall and threw that door open.

For a moment he could not understand what he was seeing. Boards, boxes, papers, and other junk were stacked in the middle of the room, a pile of rubble in the center of the nice new carpet. He took several steps forward, past the threshold, curiously disquieted by the incongruity of what lay there.

The thick, slow voice came from the doorway immediately behind him: "You took her away from me."

Alex made himself fall to the left as he turned. But it was hopeless. In spite of that maneuver, the bullet slammed into him and knocked him all the way down.

The tall, broad-shouldered man stood in the doorway, smiling. He held a pistol quite like the one which Doyle had bought in Carson City—and had thoughtlessly left in the car when he needed it most.

He thought: It just proves that you can't turn a pacifist into a violent man overnight. You can pump him up with courage, but you can't make him think in terms of guns . . .

It was a ridiculous thing to be running through his mind just then. Therefore, he stopped thinking about it and gave himself up to the ruby-colored darkness.

When George Leland came back from a daydream about the farm and his father, he was sitting on the edge of Courtney's bed. He was caressing her face with one hand.

Her body was as stiff as a plaster statue as she strained against her bonds. She was trying to say something behind the adhesive tape, and she had begun to weep.

"It's okay," Leland said. "I took care of him."

She tossed back and forth, trying to shake off his hand.

Leland looked at the pistol in his other hand, and he realized that he had only shot Doyle once. Maybe the sonofabitch was not dead. He ought to go back and make sure.

But he did not want to leave Courtney. He wanted to touch her some more, maybe even make love to her. Feel her soft, warm skin gliding over the calloused pads of his fingers. Enjoy her. Enjoy being with her. The two of them together again . . . He spread his hands on her chest and pressed down with enough force to make her be still. He petted her face and sifted her golden hair through his fingers.

For the moment he had all but forgotten Alex Doyle.

He did not think of Colin at all.

The boy heard the shot. It was muffled by the walls of the house, but it was instantly identifiable.

He opened the door and jumped out of the car. He ran halfway down the drive, then stopped when he suddenly realized that he had nowhere to go.

Downhill, the houses remained dark, as did those uphill. Apparently no one had been awakened by the shot.

Okay. But he could still go wake them up and tell them what happened, couldn't he? Even as he considered that, he knew it was useless. He thought of the way Captain Ackridge had treated Alex. And while he knew that the neighbors would be friendly, he also knew that they would not believe him—at least not in time to help Alex and Courtney. An eleven-year-old boy? He would be humored, perhaps scolded. But never believed.

He turned and ran back to the car, stopped at the open door and looked at the house. No one had come outside.

Get on with it, he thought. Alex wouldn't hesitate. He went right in after Courtney, didn't he? You want to be an adult or a frightened child?

He sat on the edge of the car seat and opened the glove compartment, took out the small pasteboard box. He lifted out the pistol and put it on the seat, fumbled for ammunition. In his eleven years he had never handled a gun before, but he thought the loading procedure looked pretty elementary. The safety was marked by tiny letters which he could just make out in the dim overhead light: SAFETY ON—OFF. He pushed it to OFF.

CHAPTER 25

ALEX STARED AT the broken crates, shredded newspapers, and other garbage for a minute or two before he realized where he was and remembered what had happened. The madman, with a gun this time . . .

"Courtney?" he asked softly.

When he moved, he triggered the pain. It came in waves and made him feel old and weak. He had been hit high in the left shoulder blade, and he felt as if someone had liberally salted the wound.

Missed the heart, at least, he thought. Must have missed everything vital. But that was only slightly comforting.

He got one hand under himself and pushed up to his knees, dripping blood on the carpet under him. The pain increased; the waves crashed through him with greater force and more speed.

He kept expecting to hear another shot and to be knocked forward into the boxes and newspapers. But he climbed laboriously to his feet and turned around to find the doorway empty, the madman gone.

Clutching his shoulder with his good hand, blood bubbling between his fingers, he started across the room. He was halfway to the hall door when he thought it would be a good idea to have some sort of weapon before he went looking for the man. But what? He turned around again and looked at the stack of junk, saw just what he needed. He went back and picked up a four-foot-long, three-inch-wide board from a broken wooden packing crate. Three long bent nails protruded from one side of it. It would do. Again he turned toward the doorway and crossed the room.

Those eight steps seemed more like eight hundred. By the time he had taken them, he needed to stop and rest. His chest was tight, and his breath did not come easily. He leaned against the wall just inside the door, out of sight of anyone in the second-floor hallway.

You've got to do better than this, he told himself, closing his eyes to block out the dizzying movements of the room. Even if you do find him, you won't be able to stop him from doing whatever he pleases to Courtney and Colin. You *can't* be this weak. It's shock. You were shot. You're bleeding. And you're suffering from shock. Anyone would be. But you have to overcome it soon, or you might as well sit down and bleed to death.

Leland pulled the tape off her mouth and touched her bloodless lips. "It's all right now, Courtney. Doyle is dead. We don't have to worry about him. It's just you and me against everyone."

She was unable to speak. She was no longer the golden girl, but was as pale as milk.

"I'm going to let you up now," he said, smiling. "If you're good, that is. If you behave yourself, I'll untie your feet and hands—so that we can make love. Would you like that?" She shook her head no.

"Sure you would."

On the first level, toward the back of the house, a window broke and crashed across a bare floor.

"It's the police," she said, not knowing for sure who it was, wanting to frighten him.

He stood up without untying her. "No," he said. "It's the boy. How could I have forgotten the boy?" Perplexed, he turned away from the bed and started for the door.

"Don't hurt him!" she cried. "For God's sake, leave him alone!"

Leland did not hear her. He was able to fully perceive and think about only one thing at a time. Right now, that was the boy. He had to find the boy and kill him, eliminate this last obstacle between himself and Courtney.

He left the master bedroom, went down the hall to the stairs.

When Alex heard the glass shattering downstairs, he thought that Colin must have brought help. But then he remembered that the front door was standing open. Why would anyone not use it?

He knew, at once, that Colin had not gone for help. Instead, the boy had taken the pistol from the glove compartment, the pistol Doyle had not remembered at the right time. Colin had distrusted the open front door and had gone around to the back of the house to find a way in. He was coming to the rescue all by himself. It was a very brave thing to do. It would also get him killed.

Doyle pushed away from the wall just as Courtney screamed, and he nearly tripped over his own feet in surprise. She was alive! Of course, he had been telling himself that she would be okay—but he had not believed it. He had expected to find a corpse.

He turned toward the door to the hall just in time to see the madman reach the top of the stairs and start down.

In the master bedroom down the hall, Courtney screamed again. "Don't you hurt him! Don't you kill my brother too!"

Too? Then she believes that I'm already dead, Doyle thought.

"Courtney!" He did not care if the man downstairs heard him. "I'm okay. Colin will be okay."

"Alex? Is that *you?*"

"It's me," he said. Holding the crude weapon tightly in his good hand, he went across the landing and down the steps, hurrying after the madman.

CHAPTER 26

COLIN TRIED THE kitchen door. It was locked. He did not want to waste time trying all the windows, and he was not about to walk through the front entrance which had so completely swallowed Alex. He hesitated only a second, then reversed the pistol, held it by the barrel, and used the butt to smash in one of the large panes of glass in the door.

He thought he ought to be able to get inside quickly enough to find a good hiding place before the madman reached the kitchen. Then he would come out of concealment and shoot the man in the back.

But he could not find the latch. He thrust one arm through the empty windowpane, scratching it on the remaining shards of glass, and he felt around on the inside of the door. But the lock mechanism escaped his fingers. There did not seem to *be* a lock switch.

He looked at the other end of the well-lighted kitchen, at the door the man would come through.

Precious seconds passed while he fumbled noisily, desperately for the unseen latch.

And, suddenly, he found it. He cried out, twisted it, and pushed the door open, stumbling into the kitchen with the .32 held out in front of him.

Before he could look for a place to hide, George Leland came through the other door. Colin recognized the man at once, though he had not seen him in two years. But the recognition did not freeze him. He pointed the gun at Leland's chest and pulled the trigger.

The recoil numbed his arms clear up to the elbows.

Leland moved in like an express train, roaring wordlessly. He swung one open hand and sent the boy sprawling on the shiny tile floor.

Colin's pistol clattered among the table and chair legs, out of reach. And the boy knew, as he watched the gun spin away, that his first and only shot had missed the mark.

Alex was halfway through the dining room, closing in on the stranger's unprotected back while the man was still unaware of him, when the shot exploded in the kitchen. He heard the madman shout, saw him leap forward. He heard Colin squeal and something overturn an instant later.

But he did not know who had shot whom.

Running the last few feet into the kitchen, he raised the spiked board over his head.

On the floor by the refrigerator, Colin was trying to get to his feet. Two yards away, the stranger raised his pistol . . .

Crying out in terror and a sort of savage glee, Alex brought his club down, swung it with all his strength. The three spikes raked the back of the other man's skull.

The stranger howled, dropped his gun, grabbed at his head with both hands. He staggered two steps and was brought up by the heavy butcher-block table.

Alex struck again. The spikes pierced the man's hands this time, briefly nailing them to his skull before Doyle jerked the board away.

The madman came around to face his attacker, his bleeding hands thrown up to ward off the next blow.

Alex met the wide blue eyes, and he thought that there was definitely more than a trace of sanity in them now, something clean and rational. The madness had temporarily fallen away.

Alex did not care about that. He swung the club again. The spikes grazed the stranger's face, furrowed the flesh, drew three red streaks across one cheek.

"Please," the man said, leaning back over the table, crossing his arms in front of his face. "Please! Please stop!"

But Doyle knew that if he stopped now, the insanity might well return to those eyes quickly and with a vengeance. The big man might lunge forward and regain the advantage. And then *he* would show no mercy.

Doyle thought of what the sonofabitch might have done to Courtney, what he would have done to Colin. He struck again. And again. He struck harder and faster each time, ripping the nails into the man's arms, neck, the sides of his skull . . . Doyle whimpered, painfully aware that he was now the maniac and that the man on the table had become the right man. But he went on anyway, slashing and tearing with all of his strength.

The stranger fell to the floor and cracked his head on the tiles. He looked sadly up at Doyle and tried to say something. Blood ran from a hundred cuts and, suddenly, it poured out of his nose like water from a set of faucets. He died.

For a full minute Alex stood over the corpse, staring down at his handiwork. He was numb. He felt nothing: not anger, shame, pity, sorrow, not anything at all. It did not seem right to have killed a man and feel no remorse.

Waves of pain spread out again from his wounded shoulder. He realized that he had been using both hands to hold the club, that he had put both of his shoulders into each brutal swing of it. He dropped the board on top of the corpse and turned away from both of them.

Colin was standing in the corner by the refrigerator. He was sheet-white and trembling. He looked smaller and skinnier than ever.

"Are you okay?" Doyle asked.

The boy looked at him, unable to speak.

"Colin."

The boy only shook.

Doyle took a step toward him.

Suddenly crying out, Colin ran forward, flung himself against Doyle, hugged the man around the waist. He was sobbing hysterically. He looked up, eyes glistening behind the thick glasses, and said, "You won't ever leave us, will you?"

"Leave you? Of course not," Doyle said. He grabbed the boy under the arms, lifted him and held him tightly.

"Say you won't leave us!" Colin demanded. Tears streamed down his face. He was shaking so hard that he could not be settled no matter how firmly Doyle held him. "Say it! Say it!"

"I'll never leave you," Doyle said, squeezing him even tighter. "Oh, God, Colin, the two of you are all I have now. I've lost everything else now."

The boy cried against his neck.

Carrying Colin, he went out of the kitchen and through the dining room, out to the main steps. "We'll go see how Courtney is," he told the boy, hoping his voice would calm him.

It did not.

They were halfway up the steps toward the second floor when the boy began to shake worse than ever in Doyle's arms. "Are you telling the truth? You really won't leave us?"

"Truth." Doyle kissed the boy's tearstained nose.

"Not ever?"

"Never. I told you . . . The two of you are all that's left. I've just lost everything else."

Holding the boy against his chest as he went to see about Courtney, Alex thought that one of the things he had lost was the ability to cry as freely as a child. And right now, more than anything, he wanted to cry.

WHISPERS

*This book is dedicated to
Rio and Battista Locatelli,
two very nice people who
deserve the very best*

PART ONE

THE LIVING AND THE DEAD

The forces that affect our lives, the
influences that mold and shape us, are
often like whispers in a distant room,
teasingly indistinct, apprehended only
with difficulty.

—Charles Dickens

CHAPTER 1

TUESDAY AT DAWN, Los Angeles trembled. Windows rattled in their frames. Patio wind chimes tinkled merrily even though there was no wind. In some houses, dishes fell off shelves.

At the start of the morning rush hour, KFWB, all-news radio, used the earthquake, as its lead story. The tremor had registered 4.8 on the Richter Scale. By the end of the rush hour, KFWB demoted the story to third place behind a report of terrorist bombings in Rome and an account of a five-car accident on the Santa Monica Freeway. After all, no buildings had fallen. By noon, only a handful of Angelenos (mostly those who had moved west within the past year) found the event worthy of even a minute's conversation over lunch.

The man in the smoke-gray Dodge van didn't even feel the earth move. He was at the northwest edge of the city, driving south on the San Diego Freeway, when the quake struck. Because it is difficult to feel any but the strongest tremors while in a moving vehicle, he wasn't aware of the shaking until he stopped for breakfast at a diner and heard one of the other customers talking about it.

He knew at once that the earthquake was a sign meant just for him. It had been sent either to assure him that his mission in Los Angeles would be a success—or to warn him that he would fail. But which message was he supposed to perceive in this sign?

He brooded over that question while he ate. He was a big strong man—

six-foot-four, two hundred and thirty pounds, all muscle—and he took more than an hour and a half to finish his meal. He started with two eggs, bacon, cottage fries, toast and a glass of milk. He chewed slowly, methodically, his eyes focused on his food as if he were entranced by it. When he finished his first plateful, he asked for a tall stack of pancakes and more milk. After the pancakes, he ate a cheese omelet with three pieces of Canadian bacon on the side, another serving of toast, and orange juice.

By the time he ordered the third breakfast, he was the chief topic of conversation in the kitchen. His waitress was a giggly redhead named Helen, but each of the other waitresses found an excuse to pass by his table and get a better look at him. He was aware of their interest, but he didn't care.

When he finally asked Helen for the check, she said, "You must be a lumberjack or something."

He looked up at her and smiled woodenly. Although this was the first time he had been in the diner, although he had met Helen only ninety minutes ago, he knew exactly what she was going to say. He had heard it all a hundred times before.

She giggled self-consciously, but her blue eyes fixed unwaveringly on his. "I mean, you eat enough for three men."

"I guess I do."

She stood beside the booth, one hip against the edge of the table, leaning slightly forward, not-so-subtly letting him know that she might be available. "But with all that food . . . you don't have an ounce of fat on you."

Still smiling, he wondered what she'd be like in bed. He pictured himself taking hold of her, thrusting into her—and then he pictured his hands around her throat, squeezing, squeezing, until her face slowly turned purple and her eyes bulged out of their sockets.

She stared at him speculatively, as if wondering whether he satisfied *all* of his appetites with such single-minded devotion as he had shown toward the food. "Must get a lot of exercise."

"I lift weights," he said.

"Like Arnold Schwarzenegger."

"Yeah."

She had a graceful, delicate neck. He knew he could break it as if it were a dry twig, and the thought of doing that made him feel warm and happy.

"You sure do have a set of big arms," she said, softly, appreciatively. He was wearing a short-sleeved shirt, and she touched his bare forearm with one finger. "I guess, with all that pumping iron, no matter how much you eat, it just turns into more muscle."

"Well, that's the idea," he said. "But I also have one of those metabolisms."

"Huh?"

"I burn up a lot of calories in nervous energy."

"You? Nervous?"

"Jumpy as a Siamese cat."

"I don't believe it. I bet there's nothing in the world could make you nervous," she said.

She was a good-looking woman, about thirty years old, ten years younger than he was, and he figured he could have her if he wanted her. She would need a little wooing, but not much, just enough so she could convince herself that he had swept her off her feet, playing Rhett to her Scarlett, and had tumbled her into bed against her will. Of course, if he made love to her, he would have to kill her afterward. He'd have to put a knife through her pretty breasts or cut her throat, and he really didn't want to do that. She wasn't worth the bother or the risk. She simply wasn't his type, he didn't kill redheads.

He left her a good tip, paid his check at the cash register by the door, and got out of there. After the air conditioned restaurant, the September heat was like a pillow jammed against his face. As he walked toward the Dodge van, he knew that Helen was watching him, but he didn't look back.

From the diner he drove to a shopping center and parked in a corner of the large lot, in the shade of a date palm, as far from the stores as he could get. He climbed between the bucket seats, into the back of the van, pulled down a bamboo shade that separated the driver's compartment from the cargo area, and stretched out on a thick but tattered mattress that was too short for him. He had been driving all night without rest, all the way from St. Helena in the wine country. Now, with a big breakfast in his belly, he was drowsy.

Four hours later, he woke from a bad dream. He was sweating, shuddering, burning up and freezing at the same time, clutching the mattress with one hand and punching the empty air with the other. He was trying to scream, but his voice was stuck far down in his throat; he made a dry, gasping sound.

At first, he didn't know where he was. The rear of the van was saved from utter darkness only by three thin strips of pale light that came through narrow slits in the bamboo blind. The air was warm and stale. He sat up, felt the metal wall with one hand, squinted at what little there was to see, and gradually oriented himself. When at last he realized he was in the van, he relaxed and sank back onto the mattress again.

He tried to remember what the nightmare had been about, but he could not. That wasn't unusual. Nearly every night of his life, he suffered through horrible dreams from which he woke in terror, mouth dry, heart pounding; but he never could recall what had frightened him.

Although he knew where he was now, the darkness made him uneasy. He kept hearing stealthy movement in the shadows, soft scurrying sounds that put the hair up on the back of his neck even though he knew he was imagining them. He raised the bamboo shade and sat blinking for a minute until his eyes adjusted to the light.

He picked up a bundle of chamois-textured cloths that lay on the floor beside the mattress. The bundle was tied up with dark brown cord. He loosened the knot and unrolled the soft cloths, four of them, each rolled around the other. Wrapped in the center were two big knives. They were very sharp. He had spent a lot of time carefully honing the gracefully tapered blades. When he took one of them in his hand, it felt strange and wonderful, as if it were a sorcerer's knife, infused with magic energy that it was now transmitting to him.

The afternoon sun had slipped past the shadow of the palm tree in which he had parked the Dodge. Now the light streamed through the windshield, over his shoulder, and struck the ice-like steel; the razor-edge glinted coldly.

As he stared at the blade, his thin lips slowly formed a smile. In spite of the nightmare, the sleep had done him a lot of good. He felt refreshed and confident. He was absolutely certain that the morning's earthquake had been a sign that everything would go well for him in Los Angeles. He would find the woman. He would get his hands on her. Today. Or Wednesday at the latest. As he thought about her smooth, warm body and the flawless texture of her skin, his smile swelled into a grin.

Tuesday afternoon, Hilary Thomas went shopping in Beverly Hills. When she came home early that evening, she parked her coffee-brown Mercedes in the circular driveway, near the front door. Now that fashion designers had decided women finally would be allowed to look feminine again, Hilary had bought all the clothes she hadn't been able to find during the dress-like-an-army-sergeant fever that had seized everyone in the fashion industry for at least the past five years. She needed to make three trips to unload the trunk of the car.

As she was picking up the last of the parcels, she suddenly had the feeling that she was being watched. She turned from the car and looked toward the street. The low westering sun slanted between the big houses and through the feathery palm fronds, streaking everything with gold. Two children were playing on a lawn, half a block away, and a floppy-eared cocker spaniel was padding happily along the sidewalk. Other than that, the neighborhood was silent and almost preternaturally still. Two cars and a gray Dodge van were parked on the other side of the street, but as far as she could see, there wasn't anyone in them.

Sometimes you act like a silly fool, she told herself. Who would be watching?

But after she carried the last of the packages inside, she came out to park the car in the garage, and again she had the unshakeable feeling that she was being observed.

Later, near midnight, as Hilary was sitting in bed reading, she thought she heard noises downstairs. She put the book aside and listened.

Rattling sounds. In the kitchen. Near the back door. Directly under her bedroom.

She got out of bed and put on a robe. It was a deep blue silk wrapper she had bought just that afternoon.

A loaded .32 automatic lay in the top drawer of the nightstand. She hesitated, listened to the rattling sounds for a moment, then decided to take the gun with her.

She felt slightly foolish. What she heard was probably just settling noises, the natural sounds a house makes from time to time. On the other hand, she had lived here for six months and had not heard anything like it until now.

She stopped at the head of the stairs and peered down into the darkness and said, "Who's there?"

No answer.

Holding the gun in her right hand and in front of her, she went downstairs and across the living room, breathing fast and shallow, unable to stop her gun hand from shaking just a bit. She switched on every lamp that she passed. As she approached the back of the house, she still could hear the strange noises, but when she stepped into the kitchen and hit the lights, there was only silence.

The kitchen looked as it should. Dark pegged pine floor. Dark pine cabinets with glossy white ceramic fixtures. White tile counters, clean and uncluttered. Shining copper pots and utensils hanging from the high white ceiling. There was no intruder and no sign that there had been one before she arrived.

She stood just inside the doorway and waited for the noise to begin again.

Nothing. Just the soft hum of the refrigerator.

Finally she walked around the gleaming central utility island and tried the back door. It was locked.

She turned on the yard lights and rolled up the shade that covered the window above the sink. Outside, off to the right, the forty-foot-long swimming pool shimmered prettily. The huge shadowy rose garden lay to the left, a dozen bright blossoms glowing like bursts of phosphorescent gas in the dark green foliage. Everything out there was silent and motionless.

What I heard was the house settling, she thought. Jeez. I'm getting to be a regular spooky old maid.

She made a sandwich and took it upstairs with a cold bottle of beer. She left all the lights burning on the first floor, which she felt would discourage any prowler—if there actually was someone lurking about the property.

Later, she felt foolish for leaving the house so brightly lit.

She knew exactly what was wrong with her. Her jumpiness was a symptom of the I-don't-deserve-all-this-happiness disease, a mental disorder with which she was intimately acquainted. She had come from nowhere, from nothing, and now she had everything. Subconsciously, she was afraid that God would take notice of her and decide that she didn't deserve what she'd been given. Then the hammer would fall. Everything she had accumulated would be smashed and swept away: the house, the car, the bank accounts. . . . Her new life seemed like a fantasy, a marvelous fairytale, too good to be true, certainly too good to last.

No. Dammit, no! She had to stop belittling herself and pretending that her accomplishments were only the result of good fortune. Luck had nothing to do with it. Born into a house of despair, nurtured not with milk and kindness but with uncertainty and fear, unloved by her father and merely tolerated by her mother, raised in a home where self-pity and bitterness had driven out all hope, she had of course grown up without a sense of real worth. For years she had struggled with an inferiority complex. But that was behind her now. She had been through therapy. She understood herself. She didn't dare let those old doubts rise again within her. The house and car and money would *not* be taken away; she *did* deserve them. She worked hard, and she had talent. Nobody had given her a job simply because she was a relative or friend; when she'd come to Los Angeles, she hadn't known anyone. No one had heaped money in her lap just because she was pretty. Drawn by the wealth of the entertainment industry and by the promise of fame, herds of beautiful women arrived every day in L.A. and were usually treated worse than cattle. She had made it to the top for one reason: she was a good writer, a superb craftsman, an imaginative and energetic artist who knew how to create the motion pictures that a lot of people would pay money to see. She earned every dime she was paid, and the gods had no reason to be vindictive.

"So relax," she said aloud.

No one had tried to get in the kitchen door. That was just her imagination. She finished the sandwich and beer, then went downstairs and turned out the lights.

She slept soundly.

The next day was one of the best days of her life. It was also one of the worst.

Wednesday began well. The sky was cloudless. The air was sweet and clear. The morning light had that peculiar quality found only in Southern California and only on certain days. It was crystalline light, hard yet warm, like the sunbeams in a cubist painting, and it gave you the feeling that at any moment the air would part like a stage curtain to reveal a world beyond the one in which we live.

Hilary Thomas spent the morning in her garden. The walled half-acre behind the two-story neo-Spanish house was adorned with two dozen species of roses—beds and trellises and hedges of roses. There were the Frau Karl Druschki Rose, the Madame Pierre Oger Rose, the rosa muscosa, the Souvenir de la Malmaison Rose, and a wide variety of modern hybrids. The garden blazed with white roses and red roses, orange and yellow and pink and purple and even green roses. Some blooms were the size of saucers, and others were small enough to pass through a wedding ring. The velvety green lawn was speckled with windblown petals of every hue.

Most mornings, Hilary worked with the plants for two or three hours. No matter how agitated she was upon entering the garden, she was always completely relaxed and at peace when she left.

She easily could have afforded a gardener. She still received quarterly payments from her first hit film, *Arizona Shifty Pete*, which had been released more than two years ago and which had been an enormous success. The new movie, *Cold Heart*, in the theaters less than two months, was doing even better than *Pete*. Her twelve-room house in Westwood, on the fringes of Bel Air and Beverly Hills, had cost a great deal, yet six months ago she had paid cash for the place. In show business circles, she was called a "hot property." That was exactly how she felt, too. Hot. Burning. Ablaze with plans and possibilities. It was a glorious feeling. She was a damned successful screenwriter, a hot property indeed, and she could hire a platoon of gardeners if she wanted them.

She tended to the flowers and the trees herself because the garden was a special place for her, almost sacred. It was the symbol of her escape.

She had been raised in a decaying apartment building in one of Chicago's worst neighborhoods. Even now, even here, even in the middle of her fragrant rose garden, she could close her eyes and see every detail of that long-ago place. In the foyer, the mailboxes had been smashed open by thieves looking for welfare checks. The hallways were narrow and poorly lit. The rooms were tiny, dreary, the furniture tattered and worn. In the small kitchen, the ancient gas range had seemed about to spring a leak and explode; Hilary had lived for years in fear of the stove's irregular, spurting blue flames. The refrigerator was yellow with age; it wheezed and rattled, and its warm motor attracted what her father called "the local wildlife." As she stood now in her lovely garden, Hilary clearly remembered the wildlife with which she'd spent her childhood, and she shuddered. Although she and her mother had kept the four rooms spotlessly clean, and although they had used great quantities of insecticide, they had never been able to get rid of the cockroaches because the damned things came through the thin walls from the other apartments where people were *not* so clean.

Her most vivid childhood memory was of the view from the single window in her cramped bedroom. She had spent many lonely hours there, hiding while her father and mother argued. The bedroom had been a haven from those terrible bouts of cursing and screaming, and from the sullen silences when her parents weren't speaking to each other. The view from the window wasn't inspiring: nothing more than the soot-streaked brick wall on the far side of the four-foot-wide serviceway that led between the tenements. The window would not open; it was painted shut. She'd been able to see a thin sliver of sky, but only when she'd pressed her face against the glass and peered straight up the narrow shaft.

Desperate to escape from the shabby world in which she lived, young Hilary learned to use her imagination to see *through* the brick wall. She would set her mind adrift, and suddenly she would be looking out upon rolling hills, or sometimes the vast Pacific Ocean, or great mountain ranges. Most of the time, it was a garden that she conjured up, an enchanted place, serene, with neatly trimmed shrubs and high trellises twined about with thorny rose vines. In this fantasy there was a great deal of pretty wrought-iron lawn furniture that had been painted white. Gaily striped umbrellas cast pools of cool shadow in the coppery sunlight. Women in lovely long dresses and men in summer suits sipped iced drinks and chatted amiably.

And now I'm living in that dream, she thought. That make-believe place is real, and I own it.

Maintaining the roses and the other plants—palms and ferns and jade shrubs and a dozen other things—was not a chore. It was a joy. Every minute she worked among the flowers, she was aware of how far she had come.

At noon, she put away her gardening tools and showered. She stood for a long while in the steaming water, as if it were sluicing away more than dirt and sweat, as if it were washing off ugly memories as well. In that depressing Chicago apartment, in the minuscule bathroom, where all the faucets had dripped and where all the drains had backed up at least once a month, there never had been enough hot water.

She ate a light lunch on the glassed-in patio that overlooked the roses. While she nibbled at cheese and slices of an apple, she read the trade papers of the entertainment industry—*Hollywood Reporter* and *Daily Variety*—which had come in the morning mail. Her name appeared in Hank Grant's column in the *Reporter*, in a list of movie and television people whose birthday it was. For a woman just turned twenty-nine, she had come a long, long way indeed.

Today, the chief executives at Warner Brothers were discussing *The Hour of the Wolf*, her latest screenplay. They would decide either to buy or reject by the close of the business day. She was tense, anxious for the telephone to ring, yet dreading it because it might bring disappointing news. This project was more important to her than anything else she'd ever done.

She had written the script without the security of a signed contract, strictly on speculation, and she had made up her mind to sell it only if she was signed to direct and was guaranteed final cut. Already, Warners had hinted at a record offer for the screenplay if she would reconsider her conditions of sale. She knew she was demanding a lot; however, because of her success as a screenwriter, her demands were not entirely unreasonable. Warners reluctantly would agree to let her direct the picture; she would bet anything on that. But the sticking point would be the final cut. That honor, the power to decide exactly what would appear on the screen, the ultimate authority over every shot and every frame and every nuance of the film, usually was bestowed upon directors who had proven themselves on a number of money-making movies; it was seldom granted to a fledgling director, especially not to a fledgling *female* director. Her insistence on total creative control might queer the deal.

Hoping to take her mind off the pending decision from Warner Brothers, Hilary spent Wednesday afternoon working in her studio, which overlooked the pool. Her desk was large, heavy, custom-made oak, with a dozen drawers and two dozen cubbyholes. Several pieces of Lallique crystal stood on the desk, refracting the soft glow from the two brass piano lamps. She struggled through the second draft of an article she was writing for *Film Comment*, but her thoughts constantly wandered to *The Hour of the Wolf.*

The telephone rang at four o'clock, and she jerked in surprise even though she'd been waiting all afternoon for that sound. It was Wally Topelis.

"It's your agent, kid. We have to talk."

"Isn't that what we're doing now?"

"I mean face to face."

"Oh," she said glumly. "Then it's bad news."

"Did I say it was?"

"If it was good," Hilary said, "you'd just give it to me on the phone. Face to face means you want to let me down easy."

"You're a classic pessimist, kid."

"Face to face means you want to hold my hand and talk me out of suicide."

"It's a damned good thing this melodramatic streak of yours never shows up in your writing."

"If Warners said no, just tell me."

"They haven't decided yet, my lamb."

"I can take it."

"Will you listen to me? The deal hasn't fallen through. I'm still scheming, and I want to discuss my next move with you. That's all. Nothing more sinister than that. Can you meet me in half an hour?"

"Where?"

"I'm at the Beverly Hills Hotel."

"The Polo Lounge?"

"Naturally."

As Hilary turned off Sunset Boulevard, she thought the Beverly Hills Hotel looked unreal, like a mirage shimmering in the heat. The rambling building that thrust out of stately palms and lush greenery, a fairytale vision. As always, the pink stucco did not look as garish as she remembered it. The walls seemed translucent, appeared almost to shine with a soft inner light. In its own way, the hotel was rather elegant—more than a bit decadent, but unquestionably elegant nonetheless. At the main entrance, uniformed valets were parking and delivering cars: two Rolls-Royces, three Mercedes, one Stuts, and a red Maserati.

A long way from the poor side of Chicago, she thought happily.

When she stepped into the Polo Lounge, she saw half a dozen movie actors and actresses, famous faces, as well as two powerful studio executives, but none of them was sitting at table number three. That was generally considered to be the most desirable spot in the room, for it faced the entrance and was the best place to see and be seen. Wally Topelis was at table three because he was one of the most powerful agents in Hollywood and because he charmed the maître d' just as he charmed everyone who met him. He was a small lean man in his fifties, very well dressed. His white hair was thick and lustrous. He also had a neat white mustache. He looked quite distinguished, exactly the kind of man you expected to see at table number three. He was talking on a telephone that had been plugged in just for him. When he saw Hilary approaching, he hastily concluded his conversation, put the receiver down, and stood.

"Hilary, you're lovely—as usual."

"And you're the center of attention—as usual."

He grinned. His voice was soft, conspiratorial. "I imagine everyone's staring at us."

"I imagine."

"Surreptitiously."

"Oh, of course," she said.

"Because they wouldn't want us to know they're looking," he said happily. As they sat down, she said, "And we dare not look to see if they're looking."

"Oh, heavens no!" His blue eyes were bright with merriment.

"We wouldn't want them to think we care."

"God forbid."

"That would be gauche."

"Trés gauche." He laughed.

Hilary sighed. "I've never understood why one table should be so much more important than another."

"Well, I can sit and make fun of it, but I understand," Wally said. "In spite of everything Marx and Lenin believed, the human animal thrives on the class system—so long as that system is based primarily on money and achievement, not on pedigree. We establish and nurture class systems everywhere, even in restaurants."

"I think I've just stumbled into one of those famous Topelis tirades."

A waiter arrived with a shiny silver ice bucket on a tripod. He put it down beside their table, smiled and left. Apparently, Wally had taken the liberty of ordering for both of them before she arrived. But he didn't take this opportunity to tell her what they were having.

"Not a tirade," he said. "Just an observation. People *need* class systems."

"I'll bite. Why?"

"For one thing, people must have aspirations, desires beyond the basic needs of food and shelter, obsessive wants that will drive them to accomplish things. If there's a best neighborhood, a man will hold down two jobs to raise money for a house there. If one car is better than another, a man—or a woman, for that matter; this certainly isn't a sexist issue—will work harder to be able to afford it. And if there's a best table in the Polo Lounge, everyone who comes here will want to be rich enough or famous enough—or even infamous enough—to be seated there. This almost manic desire for status generates wealth, contributes to the gross national product, and creates jobs. After all, if Henry Ford hadn't wanted to move up in life, he'd never have built the company that now employs tens of thousands. The class system is one of the engines that drive the wheels of commerce; it keeps our standard of living high. The class system gives people goals—and it provides the maître d' with a satisfying sense of power and importance that makes an otherwise intolerable job seem desirable."

Hilary shook her head. "Nevertheless, being seated at the best table doesn't mean I'm automatically a better person than the guy who gets second-best. It's no accomplishment in itself."

"It's a *symbol* of accomplishment, of position," Wally said.

"I still can't see the sense of it."

"It's just an elaborate game."

"Which you certainly know how to play."

He was delighted. "Don't I though?"

"I'll never learn the rules."

"You should, my lamb. It's more than a bit silly, but it helps business. No one likes to work with a loser. But everyone playing the game wants to deal with the kind of person who can get the best table at the Polo Lounge."

Wally Topelis was the only man she knew who could call a woman "my lamb" and sound neither patronizing nor smarmy. Although he was a small man, about the right size to be a professional jockey, he somehow made her think of Cary Grant in movies like *To Catch a Thief*. He had Grant's style: excellent manners observed without flourish; balletic grace in every movement, even in casual gestures; quiet charm; a subtle look of amusement, as if he found life to be a gentle joke.

Their captain arrived, and Wally called him Eugene and inquired about his children. Eugene seemed to regard Wally with affection, and Hilary realized that getting the best table in the Polo Lounge might also have something to do with treating the staff as friends rather than servants.

Eugene was carrying champagne, and after a couple of minutes of small talk, he held the bottle for Wally's inspection.

Hilary glimpsed the label. "Dom Perignon?"

"You deserve the best, my lamb."

Eugene removed the foil from the neck of the bottle and began to untwist the wire that caged the cork.

Hilary frowned at Wally. "You must *really* have bad news for me."

"What makes you say that?"

"A hundred-dollar bottle of champagne. . . ." Hilary looked at him thoughtfully. "It's supposed to soothe my hurt feelings, cauterize my wounds."

The cork popped. Eugene did his job well; very little of the precious liquid foamed out of the bottle.

"You're such a pessimist," Wally said.

"A realist," she said.

"Most people would have said, 'Ah, champagne. What are we celebrating?' But not Hilary Thomas."

Eugene poured a sample of Dom Perignon. Wally tasted it and nodded approval.

"*Are* we celebrating?" Hilary asked. The possibility really had not occurred to her, and she suddenly felt weak as she considered it.

"In fact, we are," Wally said.

Eugene slowly filled both glasses and slowly screwed the bottle into the shaved ice in the silver bucket. Clearly, he wanted to stick around long enough to hear what they were celebrating.

It was also obvious that Wally wanted the captain to hear the news and spread it. Grinning like Cary Grant, he leaned toward Hilary and said, "We've got the deal with Warner Brothers."

She stared, blinked, opened her mouth to speak, didn't know what to say. Finally: "We don't."

"We do."

"We can't."

"We can"

"Nothing's that easy."

"I tell you, we've got it."

"They won't let me direct."

"Oh, yes."

"They won't give me final cut."

"Yes, they will."

"My God."

She was stunned. Felt numb.

Eugene offered his congratulations and slipped away.

Wally laughed, shook his head. "You know, you could have played that a lot better for Eugene's benefit. Pretty soon, people are going to see us celebrating, and they'll ask Eugene what it's about, and he'll tell them. Let the world think you always knew you'd get exactly what you wanted. Never show doubt or fear when you're swimming with sharks."

"You're not kidding about this? We've actually got what we wanted?"

Raising his glass, Wally said, "A toast. To my sweetest client, with the hope she'll eventually learn there *are* some clouds with silver linings and that a lot of apples *don't* have worms in them."

They clinked glasses.

She said, "The studio must have added a lot of tough conditions to the deal. A bottom of the barrel budget. Salary at scale. No participation in the gross rentals. Stuff like that."

"Stop looking for rusty nails in your soup," he said exasperatedly.

"I'm not eating soup."

"Don't get cute."

"I'm drinking champagne."

"You know what I mean."

She stared at the bubbles bursting in her glass of Dom Perignon.

She felt as if hundreds of bubbles were rising within her, too, chains of tiny, bright bubbles of joy; but a part of her acted like a cork to contain the effervescent emotion, to keep it securely under pressure, bottled up, safely contained. She was afraid of being too happy. She didn't want to tempt fate.

"I just don't get it," Wally said. "You look as if the deal fell through. You did hear me all right, didn't you?"

She smiled. "I'm sorry. It's just that . . . when I was a little girl, I learned to expect the worst every day. That way, I was never disappointed. It's the best outlook you can have when you live with a couple of bitter, violent alcoholics."

His eyes were kind.

"Your parents are gone," he said, quietly, tenderly. "Dead. Both of them. They can't touch you, Hilary. They can't hurt you ever again."

"I've spent most of the past twelve years trying to convince myself of that."

"Ever consider analysis?"

"I went through two years of it."

"Didn't help?"

"Not much."

"Maybe a different doctor—"

"Wouldn't matter," Hilary said. "There's a flaw in Freudian theory. Psychiatrists believe that as soon as you fully remember and understand the childhood traumas that made you into a neurotic adult, you can change. They think finding the key is the hard part, and that once you have it you can open the door in a minute. But it's not that easy."

"You have to want to change," he said.

"It's not that easy, either."

He turned his champagne glass around and around in his small well-manicured hands. "Well, if you need someone to talk to now and then, I'm always available."

"I've already burdened you with too much of it over the years."

"Nonsense. You've told me very little. Just the bare bones."

"Boring stuff," she said.

"Far from it, I assure you. The story of a family coming apart at the seams, alcoholism, madness, murder, and suicide, an innocent child caught in the middle. . . . As a screenwriter, you should know that's the kind of material that never bores."

She smiled thinly. "I just feel I've got to work it out on my own."

"Usually it helps to talk about—"

"Except that I've already talked about it to an analyst, and I've talked about it to you, and that's only done me a little bit of good."

"But talking has helped."

"I've got as much out of it as I can. What I've got to do now is talk to *myself* about it. I've got to confront the past alone, without relying on your support or a doctor's, which is something I've never been able to do." Her long dark hair had fallen over one eye; she pushed it out of her face and tucked it behind her ears. "Sooner or later, I'll get my head on straight. It's only a matter of time."

Do I really believe that? she wondered.

Wally stared at her for a moment, then said, "Well, I suppose you know best. At least, in the meantime, drink up." He raised his champagne glass. "Be cheerful and full of laughter so all these important people watching us will envy you and want to work with you."

She wanted to lean back and drink lots of icy Dom Perignon and let happiness consume her, but she could not totally relax. She was always sharply aware of that spectral darkness at the edges of things, that crouching nightmare waiting to spring and devour her. Earl and Emma, her parents, had jammed her into a tiny box of fear, had slammed the heavy lid and locked it; and since then she had looked out at the world from the dark confines of that box. Earl and Emma had instilled in her a quiet but ever-present and unshakable paranoia that stained everything good, everything that should be right and bright and joyful.

In that instant, her hatred of her mother and father was as hard, cold, and immense as it had ever been. The busy years and the many miles that separated her from those hellish days in Chicago suddenly ceased to act as insulation from the pain.

"What's wrong?" Wally asked.

"Nothing. I'm okay."

"You're so pale."

With an effort, she pushed down the memories, forced the past back where it belonged. She put one hand on Wally's cheek, kissed him. "I'm sorry. Sometimes I can be a real pain in the ass. I haven't even thanked you. I'm happy with the deal, Wally, I really am. It's wonderful! You're the best damned agent in the business."

"You're right," he said. "I am. But this time I didn't have to do a lot of selling. They liked the script so much they were willing to give us almost anything just to be sure they'd get the project. It wasn't luck. And it wasn't just having a smart agent. I want you to understand that. Face it, kid, you deserve success. Your work is about the best thing being written for the screen these days. You can go on living in the shadow of your parents, go on expecting the worst, as you always do, but from here on out it's going to be nothing but the best for you. My advice is, get used to it."

She desperately wanted to believe him and surrender to optimism, but black weeds of doubt still sprouted from the seeds of Chicago. She saw those familiar lurking monsters at the fuzzy edges of the paradise he described. She was a true believer in Murphy's Law: *If anything can go wrong, it will.*

Nevertheless, she found Wally's earnestness so appealing, his tone so nearly convincing, that she reached down into her bubbling cauldron of confused emotions and found a genuine radiant smile for him.

"That's it," he said, pleased. "That's better. You have a beautiful smile."

"I'll try to use it more often."

"I'll keep making the kind of deals that'll force you to use it more often."

They drank champagne and discussed *The Hour of the Wolf* and made plans and laughed more than she could remember having laughed in years. Gradually her mood lightened. A macho movie star—icy eyes, tight thin lips, muscles, a swagger in his walk when he was on screen; warm, quick to laugh, somewhat shy in real life—whose last picture had made fifty million dollars, was the first to stop by to say hello and inquire about the celebration. The sartorially impeccable studio executive with the lizard eyes tried subtly, then blatantly, to learn the plot of *Wolf*, hoping it would lend itself to a quick cheap television movie-of-the-week rip-off. Pretty soon, half the room was table-hopping, stopping by to congratulate Hilary and Wally, flitting away to confer with one another about her success, each of them wondering if there was any percentage in it for him. After all, *Wolf* would need a producer, stars, someone to write the musical score. . . . Therefore, at the best table in the room, there was a great deal of back-patting and cheek-kissing and hand-holding.

Hilary knew that most of the glittery denizens of the Polo Lounge weren't actually as mercenary as they sometimes appeared to be. Many of them had begun at the bottom, hungry, poor, as she had been herself. Although their fortunes were now made and safely invested, they couldn't stop hustling; they'd been at it so long that they didn't know how to live any other way.

The public image of Hollywood life had very little to do with the facts. Secretaries, shopkeepers, clerks, taxi drivers, mechanics, housewives, waitresses, people all over the country, in everyday jobs of all kinds came home weary from work and sat in front of the television and dreamed about life among the stars. In the vast collective mind that brooded and murmured from Hawaii to Maine and from Florida to Alaska, Hollywood was a sparkling blend of wild parties, fast women, easy money, too much whiskey, too much cocaine, lazy sunny days, drinks by the pool, vacation in Acapulco and Palm Springs, sex in the back seat of a fur-lined Rolls-Royce. A fantasy. An illusion. She supposed that a society long abused by corrupt and incompetent leaders, a society standing upon pilings that had been rotted by inflation and excess taxation, a society existing in the cold shadow of sudden nuclear annilation, needed its illusions if it were to survive. In truth, people in the movie and television industries worked harder than almost anyone else, even though the product of their labor was not always, perhaps not even often, worth the effort. The star of a successful television series worked from dawn till nightfall, often fourteen or sixteen hours a day. Of course, the rewards were enormous. But in reality, the parties were not so wild, the women no faster than women in Philadelphia or Hackensack or Tampa, the days sunny but seldom lazy, and the sex exactly the same as it was for secretaries in Boston and shopkeepers in Pittsburgh.

Wally had to leave at a quarter past six in order to keep a seven o'clock engagement, and a couple of the table-hoppers in the Polo Lounge asked Hilary to have dinner with them. She declined, pleading a prior commitment.

Outside the hotel, the autumn evening was still bright. A few high clouds tracked across the technicolor sky. The sunlight was the color of platinum-blonde hair, and the air was surprisingly fresh for mid-week Los Angeles. Two young couples laughed and chattered noisily as they climbed out of a blue Cadillac, and farther away, on Sunset Boulevard, tires hummed and engines roared and horns blared as the last of the rush hour crowd tried to get home alive.

As Hilary and Wally waited for their cars to be brought around by the smiling valets, he said, "Are you really having dinner with someone?"

"Yeah. Me, myself, and I."

"Look, you can come along with me."

"The uninvited guest."

"I just invited you."

"I don't want to spoil your plans."

"Nonsense. You'd be a delightful addition."

"Anyway, I'm not dressed for dinner."

"You look fine."

"I vant to be alone," she said.

"You do a terrible Garbo. Come to dinner with me. Please. It's just an informal evening at The Palm with a client and his wife. An up and coming young television writer. Nice people."

"I'll be okay, Wally. Really."

"A beautiful woman like you, on a night like this, with so much to celebrate—there ought to be candlelight, soft music, good wine, a special someone to share it with."

She grinned. "Wally, you're a closet romantic."

"I'm serious," he said.

She put one hand on his arm. "It's sweet of you to be concerned about me, Wally. But I'm perfectly all right. I'm happy when I'm alone. I'm very good company for myself. There'll be plenty of time for a meaningful relationship with a man and skiing weekends in Aspen and chatty evenings at The Palm after *The Hour of the Wolf* is finished and in the theaters."

Wally Topelis frowned. "If you don't learn how to relax, you won't survive for very long in a high-pressure business like this. In a couple of years, you'll be as limp as a rag doll, tattered, frayed, worn out. Believe me, kid, when the physical energy is all burnt up, you'll suddenly discover that the mental energy, the creative juice, has also evaporated with it."

"This project is a watershed for me," she said. "After it, my life won't be the same."

"Agreed. But—"

"I've worked hard, damned hard, single-mindedly, toward this chance. I'll admit it: I've been obsessed with my work. But once I've made a reputation as a good writer *and* a good director, I'll feel secure. I'll finally be able to cast out the demons—my parents, Chicago, all those bad memories. I'll be able to relax and lead a more normal life. But I can't rest yet. If I slack off now, I'll fail. Or at least I think I will, and that's the same thing."

He sighed. "Okay. But we would have had a lot of fun at The Palm."

A valet arrived with her car.

She hugged Wally. "I'll probably call you tomorrow, just to be sure that this Warner Brothers thing wasn't all a dream."

"Contracts will take a few weeks," he told her. "But I don't anticipate any serious problems. We'll have the deal memo sometime next week, and then you can set up a meeting at the studio."

She blew him a kiss, hurried to the car, tipped the valet, and drove away.

She headed into the hills, past the million-dollar houses, past lawns greener than money, turning left, then right, at random, going nowhere in particular, just driving for relaxation, one of the few escapes she allowed herself. Most of the streets were shrouded in purple shadows cast by canopies of green branches; night was stealing across the pavement even though daylight still existed above the interlaced palms, oaks, maples, cedars, cypresses, jacarandas, and pines. She switched on the headlights and explored some of the winding canyon roads until, gradually, her frustration began to seep away.

Later, when night had fallen above the trees as well as below them, she stopped at a Mexican restaurant on La Cienega Boulevard. Rough beige plaster walls. Photographs of Mexican bandits. The rich odors of hot sauce, taco seasoning, and corn meal tortillas. Waitresses in scoop-necked peasant blouses and many-pleated red skirts. South-of-the-border Muzak. Hilary ate cheese enchiladas, rice, refried beans. The food tasted every bit as good as it would have tasted if it had been served by candlelight, with string music in the background, and with someone special seated beside her.

I'll have to remember to tell Wally that, she thought as she washed down the last of the enchiladas with a swallow of Dos Equis, a dark Mexican beer.

But when she considered it for a moment, she could almost hear his reply: "My lamb, that is nothing but blatant psychological rationalization. It's true that loneliness doesn't change the taste of food, the quality of candlelight, the sound of music—but that doesn't mean that loneliness is desirable or good or healthy." He simply wouldn't be able to resist launching into one of his fatherly lectures about life; and listening to that would not be made any easier by the fact that whatever he had to say would make sense.

You better not mention it, she told herself. You are never going to get one up on Wally Topelis.

In her car again, she buckled her seatbelt, brought the big engine to life, snapped on the radio, and sat for a while, staring at the flow of traffic on La Cienega. Today was her birthday. Twenty-ninth birthday. And in spite of the fact that it had been noted in Hank Grant's *Hollywood Reporter* column, she seemed to be the only one in the world who cared. Well, that was okay. She was a loner. Always had been a loner. Hadn't she told Wally that she was perfectly happy with only her own company?

The cars flashed past in an endless stream, filled with people who were going places, doing things—usually in pairs.

She didn't want to start for home yet, but there was nowhere else to go.

* * *

The house was dark.

The lawn looked more blue than green in the glow of the mercury-vapor streetlamp.

Hilary parked the car in the garage and walked to the front door. Her heels made an unnaturally loud *tock-tock-tock* sound on the stone footpath.

The night was mild. The heat of the vanished sun still rose from the earth, and the cooling sea wind that washed the basin city in all seasons had not yet brought the usual autumn chill to the air; later, toward midnight, it would be coat weather.

Crickets chirped in the hedges.

She let herself into the house, found the entranceway light, closed and locked the door. She switched on the living room lights as well and was a few steps from the foyer when she heard movement behind her and turned.

A man came out of the foyer closet, knocking a coat off a hanger as he shouldered out of that confining space, throwing the door back against the wall with a loud *bang!* He was about forty years old, a tall man wearing dark slacks and a tight yellow pullover sweater—and leather gloves. He had the kind of big, hard muscles that could be gotten only from years of weightlifting; even his wrists, between the cuffs of the sweater and the gloves, were thick and sinewy. He stopped ten feet from her and grinned broadly, nodded, licked his thin lips.

She wasn't quite sure how to respond to his sudden appearance. He wasn't an ordinary intruder, not a total stranger, not some punk kid or some shabby degenerate with a drug-blur in his eyes. Although he didn't belong here, she knew him, and he was just about the last man she would expect to encounter in a situation of this sort. Seeing gentle little Wally Topelis come out of that closet was the only thing that could have shocked her more than this. She was less frightened than confused. She had met him three weeks ago, while doing research for a screenplay set in the wine country of Northern California, a project meant to take her mind off Wally's marketing of *The Hour of the Wolf*, which she had finished about that time. He was an important and successful man up there in the Napa Valley. But that didn't explain what the hell he was doing in her house, hiding in her closet.

"Mr. Frye," she said uneasily.

"Hello, Hilary." He had a deep, somewhat gravely voice which seemed reassuring and fatherly when she had taken an extensive private tour of his winery near St. Helena, but which now sounded coarse, mean, threatening.

She cleared her throat nervously. "What are you doing here?"

"Come to see you."

"Why?"

"Just had to see you again."

"About what?"

He was still grinning. He had a tense, predatory look. His was the smile of the wolf just before it closed hungry jaws on the cornered rabbit.

"How did you get in?" she demanded.

"Pretty."

"What?"

"So pretty."

"Stop it."

"Been looking for one like you."

"You're scaring me."

"You're a real pretty one."

He took a step toward her.

She knew then, beyond doubt, what he wanted. But it was crazy, unthinkable. Why would a wealthy man of his high social position travel hundreds of miles to risk his fortune, reputation, and freedom for one brief violent moment of forced sex?

He took another step.

She backed away from him.

Rape. It made no sense. Unless. . . . If he intended to kill her afterwards, he would not be taking much of a risk at all. He was wearing gloves. He would leave no prints, no clues. And no one would believe that a prominent and highly-respected vintner from St. Helena would drive all the way to Los Angeles to rape and murder. Even if some would believe it, they'd have no reason to think of him in the first place. The homicide investigation would never move in his direction.

He kept coming. Slowly. Relentlessly. Heavy steps. Enjoying the suspense. Grinning more than ever as he saw comprehension enter her eyes.

She backed past the huge stone fireplace, briefly considered grabbing one of the heavy brass implements on the hearth, but realized that she would not be quick enough to defend herself with it. He was a powerful, athletic man in excellent physical condition; he would be all over her before she could seize the poker and swing it at his damned thick skull.

He flexed his big hands. The knuckles strained at the snug-fitting leather.

She backed past a grouping of furniture—two chairs, a coffee table, a long sofa. She started moving toward her right, trying to put the sofa between her and Frye.

"Such pretty hair," he said.

A part of her wondered if she were losing her mind. This could not be the Bruno Frye she had met in St. Helena. There had been not even the slightest hint of the madness that now contorted his broad, sweat-greased face. His eyes were blue-gray chips of ice, and the frigid passion that shone in them was surely too monstrous to have been concealed when she last saw him.

Then she saw the knife, and the sight of it was like a blast of furnace heat that turned her doubts to steam and blew them away. He meant to kill her. The knife was fixed to his belt, over his right hip. It was in an open sheath, and he could free it simply by popping the metal snap on a single narrow leather strap. In one second, the blade could be slipped from the holder and wrapped tightly in his fist; in two seconds, it could be jammed deep into her soft belly, slicing through warm meat and jelly organs, letting loose the precious store of blood.

"I've wanted you since I first saw you," Frye said. "Just wanted to get at you."

Time seemed to stop for her.

"You're going to be a good little piece," he said. "Real good."

Abruptly, the world was a slow-motion movie. Each second seemed like a minute. She watched him approach as if he were a creature in a nightmare, as if the atmosphere had suddenly become as thick as syrup.

The instant that she spotted the knife, Hilary froze. She stopped backing away from him, even though he continued to approach. A knife will do that. It chokes you up, freezes your heart, brings an uncontrollable tremor to your guts. Surprisingly few people have the stomach to use a knife against another living thing. More than any other weapon, it makes you aware of the delicacy of flesh, the terrible fragility of human life; in the damage that he wreaks, the attacker can see all too clearly the nature of his own mortality. A gun, a draught of poison, a firebomb, a blunt instrument, a strangler's piece of rope—all can be used relatively cleanly, most of them at a distance. But the man with a knife must be prepared to get dirty, and he must get in close, so close that he can feel the heat escaping from the wounds as he makes them. It takes a special courage, or insanity, to slash at another person and not be repelled by the warm blood spurting over your hand.

Frye was upon her. He placed one large hand on her breasts, rubbed and squeezed them roughly through the silky fabric of her dress.

The rude contact snapped her out of the trance into which she'd fallen. She knocked his hand away, twisted out of his grasp, and ran behind the couch.

His laugh was hearty, disconcertingly pleasant, but his hard eyes glinted with a macabre amusement. It was a demon joke, the mad humor of hell. He wanted her to fight back, for he enjoyed the chase.

"Get out!" she said. "Get out!"

"Don't want to get out," Frye said, smiling, shaking his head. "I want to get *in*. Oh yeah. That's it. I want to get in you, little lady. I want to rip that dress off your back, get you naked, and get right up in there. All the way up, all the way inside where it's warm and wet and dark and soft."

For a moment, the fear that made her legs rubbery and turned her insides to water was supplanted by more powerful emotions: hate, anger, fury. Hers was not the reasoned anger of a woman toward an arrogant man's usurpation of her dignity and rights; not an intellectual anger based on the social and biological injustices of the situation; it was more fundamental than that. He had entered her private space uninvited, had pushed his way into her modern cave, and she was possessed by a primitive rage that blurred her vision and made her heart race. She bared her teeth at him, growled in the back of her throat; she was reduced to an almost unconscious animal response as she faced him and looked for a way out of the trap.

A low, narrow, glass-topped display table stood flush against the back of the sofa. Two eighteen-inch-high pieces of fine porcelain statuary rested upon it. She grabbed one of the statues and hurled it at Frye.

He ducked with a primitive, instinctual quickness of his own. The porcelain struck the stone fireplace and exploded like a bomb. Dozens of chunks and hundreds of chips of it rained down on the hearth and on the surrounding carpet.

"Try again," he said, mocking her.

She picked up the other porcelain, hesitated. She watched him through narrowed eyes, weighed the statue in her hand, then faked a pitch.

He was deceived by the feint. He dipped down and to one side to avoid the missile.

With a small cry of triumph, she threw the statue for real.

He was too surprised to duck again, and the porcelain caught him on the side of the head. It was a glancing blow, less devastating then she'd hoped, but he staggered back a step or two. He didn't go down. He wasn't seriously injured. He wasn't even bleeding. But he was hurt, and the pain transformed him. He was no longer in a perversely playful mood. The crooked smile disappeared. His mouth was set in a straight, grim line, lips tightly compressed. His face was red. Fury wound him up as if he were a watch spring; under the strain, the muscles in his massive neck popped up, taut, impressive. He crouched slightly, ready to charge.

Hilary expected him to come around the couch, and she intended to circle it, staying away from him, keeping the couch between them until she could reach something else worth throwing. But when he moved at last, he didn't stalk her as she'd anticipated. Instead, he rushed straight at her without finesse, as if he were a bull in a blind rage. He bent in front of the couch, gripped it with both hands, tilted it up, and in one smooth movement pushed it over backwards as if it weighed only a few pounds. She jumped out of the way as the big piece of furniture crashed down where she'd been standing. Even as the sofa fell, Frye vaulted over it. He reached for her, and he would have had her if he hadn't stumbled and gone down on one knee.

Her anger gave way to fear again, and she ran. She headed toward the foyer and the front door, but she knew she would not have time to throw off both bolt locks and get out of the house before he got hold of her. He was too damned close, no more than two or three steps away. She darted to the right and dashed up the winding stairs, two at a time.

She was breathing hard, but over her own gasping she heard him coming. His footfalls were thunderous. He was cursing her.

The gun. In the nightstand. If she could get to her bedroom far enough ahead of him to slam and lock the door, that ought to hold him for a few seconds, at least, certainly long enough for her to get the pistol.

At the top of the stairs, as she came into the second-floor hallway, when she was certain she had put another few feet between them, he caught her right shoulder and yanked her back against him. She screamed, but she didn't try to pull away, as he evidently expected her to do. Instead, the instant he grabbed her, she turned on him. She pushed into him before he could get a restraining arm around her, pressed so tight against him that she could feel his erection, and she drove one knee hard into his crotch. He reacted as if he'd been hit by lightning. The red flush of anger went out of his face, and his skin flashed bone-white, all in a fraction of a second. He lost his grip on her and staggered back and slipped on the edge of the first step and windmilled his arms and toppled over, cried out, threw himself to one side, clutched the bannister and was lucky enough to arrest his fall.

Apparently, he hadn't had much experience with women who fought back effectively. She had tricked him twice. He thought he was on the trail of a nice, fluffy, harmless bunny, timid prey that could be subdued easily and used and then broken with a flick of the wrist. But she turned and showed long fangs and claws to him, and she was exhilarated by his shocked expression

She had hoped he would tumble all the way to the bottom of the staircase, breaking his neck as he went. Even now, she thought the blow to his privates would take him out of action at least a minute or two, long enough for her to get the upper hand. She was shocked when, after only the briefest pause, before she could even turn and run, he shoved away from the bannister and, wincing with pain, struggled up toward her.

"Bitch," he said between clenched teeth, barely able to get his breath.

"No," she said. "No. Stay back."

She felt like a character in one of those old horror movies that Hammer Films used to do so well. She was in a battle with a vampire or a zombie, repeatedly astonished and disheartened by the beast's supernatural reserves of strength and endurance.

"Bitch."

She ran down the shadow-draped hallway, into the master bedroom. She slammed the door, fumbled for the lock button in the dark, finally hit the light switch, engaged the lock.

There was a strange and frightening noise in the room. It was a loud hoarse sound filled with terror. She looked around wildly for the source of it before she realized that she was listening to her own ragged and uncontrollable sobbing.

She was dangerously close to panic, but she knew she must control herself if she wanted to live.

Suddenly, Frye tried the locked door behind her, then threw his weight against it. The barrier held. But it would not hold much longer, certainly not long enough for her to call the police and wait for help.

Her heart was beating furiously, and she was shaking as if she were standing naked on a vast field of ice; but she was determined not to be incapacitated by fear. She hurried across the big room, around the bed, toward the far night-stand. On the way, she passed a full-length wall mirror that seemed to throw back to her the image of a total stranger, an owl-eyed and harried woman with a face as pale as the painted visage of a mime.

Frye kicked the door. It shook violently in the frame but didn't let go.

The .32 automatic was on top of three pairs of folded pajamas in the night-stand drawer. The loaded magazine lay beside it. She picked up the gun and, with jittery hands that nearly failed her, rammed the magazine into the butt. She faced the doorway.

Frye kicked the lock again. The hardware was flimsy. It was the kind of interior lock primarily meant to keep children and nosy house guests out of a room. It was useless against an intruder like Bruno Frye. On the third kick, the workings burst from the mounting, and the door clattered open.

Panting, sweating, he looked more than ever like a mad bull as he lumbered out of the dark hall and crossed the threshold. His broad shoulders were hunched, and his hands were fisted at his sides. He wanted to lower his head and charge, smash and destroy everything that stood in his way. Blood lust shone in his eyes as clearly as his reflection glowered back at him from the wall mirror beside Hilary. He wanted to smash his way through the china shop and stomp on the proprietor.

Hilary pointed the pistol at him, holding it firmly with both hands.

He kept coming.

"I'll shoot! I will! I swear to God I will!" she said frantically.

Frye stopped, blinked at her, saw the gun for the first time.

"Out," she said.

He didn't move.

"Get the hell out of here!"

Incredibly, he took one more step toward her. It was no longer the smug, calculating, game-playing rapist she had faced downstairs. Something had happened to him; deep inside, relay switches had clicked into place, setting up new patterns in his mind, new wants and needs and hungers that were more disgusting and perverted than any he had revealed thus far. He was no longer even half rational. His demeanor was that of a lunatic. His eyes flashed, not icy as they had been, but watery and hot, fevered. Sweat streamed down his face. His lips worked ceaselessly, even though he was not speaking; they writhed and twisted, pulled back over his teeth, then pushed out in a childish pout, formed a sneer, then a weird little smile, then a fierce scowl, then an expression for which there was no name. He was no longer driven by lust or the desire to utterly dominate her. The secret motor that drove him now was darker in design than the one that had powered him just a few minutes ago, and she had the terrible crazy feeling that it would somehow provide him with enough energy to shield him from harm, to let him advance untouched through a hail of bullets.

He took the large knife from the sheath on his right hip and thrust it in front of him.

"Back off," she said desperately.

"Bitch."

"I mean it."

He started toward her again.

"For God's sake," she said, "be serious. That knife's no good against a gun."

He was twelve or fifteen feet from the other side of the bed.

"I'll blow your goddamned head off."

Frye waved the knife at her, drew small rapid circles in the air with the point of the blade, as if it were a talisman and he were chasing off evil spirits that stood between him and Hilary.

And he took another step.

She lined up the forward sight with the center of his abdomen, so that no matter how high the recoil kicked her hands and no matter whether the gun pulled to the left or the right, she would hit something vital. She squeezed the trigger.

Nothing happened.

Please, God!

He took two steps.

She stared at the pistol, stunned. She had forgotten to throw off the safety catches.

He was maybe eight feet from the other side of the bed. Maybe only six.

Swearing at herself, she thumbed the two tiny levers on the side of the pistol, and a pair of red dots appeared on the black metal. She aimed and pulled the trigger a second time.

Nothing.

Jesus! What? It can't be jammed!

Frye was so completely disassociated from reality, so thoroughly possessed by his madness, that he did not realize immediately that she was having problems with the weapon. When he finally saw what was happening, he moved in fast, while the advantage was his. He reached the bed, scrambled onto it, stood up, started straight across the mattress like a man walking a bridge of barrels, swaying on the springy surface.

She had forgotten to jack a bullet into the chamber. She did that and retreated two steps until she backed into the wall. She squeezed off a shot without taking aim, fired up at him as he loomed directly over her like a demon leaping out of a crack in hell.

The sound of the shot filled the room. It slapped off the walls and reverberated in the windows.

She saw the knife shatter, saw the fragments arc out of Frye's right hand. The sharp steel flew up and back, sparkling for a moment in the shaft of light that escaped through the open top of the bedside lamp.

Frye howled as the knife spun away from him. He fell backwards and rolled off the far side of the bed. But he was up as soon as he went down, cradling his right hand in his left.

Hilary didn't think she had hit him. There wasn't any blood. The bullet must have struck the knife, breaking it and tearing it out of his grasp. The shock would have stung his fingers worse than the crack of a whip.

Frye wailed in pain, screamed in rage. It was a wild sound, a jackal's bark, but it was definitely not the cry of an animal with its tail between its legs. He still intended to come after her.

She fired again, and he went down again. This time he stayed down.

With a little whimper of relief, Hilary sagged wearily against the wall, but she did not take her eyes off the place where he had gone down and where he now lay out of sight beyond the bed.

No sound.

No movement.

She was uneasy about not being able to see him. Head cocked, listening intently, she moved cautiously to the foot of the bed, out into the room, then around to the left until she spotted him.

He was belly-down on the chocolate-brown Edward Fields carpet. His right arm was tucked under him. His left arm was flung straight out in front, the hand curled slightly, the still fingers pointing back toward the top of his head.

His face was turned away from her. Because the carpet was so dark and plush and eye-dazzlingly textured, she had some difficulty telling from a distance if there was any blood soaked into it. Quite clearly, there was not an enormous sticky pool like the one she had expected to find. If the shot had hit him in the chest, the blood might be trapped under him. The bullet might even have taken him squarely in the forehead, bringing instant death and abrupt cessation of heartbeat; in which case, there would be only a few drops of blood.

She watched him for a minute, two minutes. She could not detect any movement, not even the subtle rise and fall of his breathing.

Dead?

Slowly, timidly, she approached him.

"Mr. Frye?"

She didn't intend to get too close. She wasn't going to endanger herself, but she wanted a better look at him. She kept the gun trained on him, ready to put another round into him if he moved.

"Mr. Frye?"

No response.

Funny that she should keep calling him "Mr. Frye." After what had happened tonight, after what he had tried to do to her, she was still being formal and polite. Maybe because he was dead. In death, the very worst man in town is accorded hushed respect even by those who know that he was a liar and a scoundrel all his life. Because every one of us must die, belittling a dead man is in a way like belittling ourselves. Besides, if you speak badly about the dead, you somehow feel that you are mocking that great and final mystery—and perhaps inviting the gods to punish you for your effrontery.

Hilary waited and watched as another minute dragged past.

"You know what, Mr. Frye? I think I won't take any chances with you. I think I'll just put another bullet in you right now. Yeah. Fire a round right in the back of your head."

Of course, she wasn't able to do that. She wasn't violent by nature. She had fired the gun on a shooting range once, shortly after she bought it, but she had never killed a living thing larger than the cockroaches in that Chicago apartment. She had found the will to shoot at Bruno Frye only because he had been an immediate threat and she had been pumped full of adrenalin. Hysteria and a primitive survival instinct had made her briefly capable of violence. But now that Frye was on the floor, quiet and motionless, no more menacing than a pile of dirty rags, she could not easily bring herself to pull the trigger. She couldn't just stand there and watch as she blew the brains out of a corpse. Even the thought of it turned her stomach. But the threat of doing it was a good test of his condition. If he was faking, the possibility of her shooting pointblank at his skull ought to make him give up his act.

"Right in the head, you bastard," she said, and she fired a round into the ceiling.

He didn't flinch.

She sighed and lowered the pistol.

Dead. He was dead.

She had killed a man.

Dreading the coming ordeal with police and reporters, she edged around the outstretched arm and headed for the hall door.

Suddenly, he was not dead any more.

Suddenly, he was very much alive and moving.

He anticipated her. He'd known exactly how she was trying to trick him. He'd seen through the ruse, and he'd had nerves of steel. He hadn't even flinched!

Now he used the arm under him to push up and forward, striking at Hilary as if he were a snake, and with his left hand he seized her ankle and brought her down, screaming and flailing, and they rolled over, a tangle of arms and legs, then over again, and his teeth were at her throat, and he was snarling like a dog, and she had the crazy fear that he was going to bite her and tear open her jugular vein and suck out all of her blood, but then she got a hand between them, got her palm under his chin and levered his head away from her neck as they rolled one last time, and then they came up against the wall with jarring impact and stopped, dizzy, gasping, and he was like a great beast on her, so rough, so heavy, crushing her, leering down at her, his hideous cold eyes so frighteningly close and deep and empty, his breath foul with onions and stale beer, and he had one hand under her dress, shredding her pantyhose, trying to get his big blunt fingers under her panties and gain a grip on her sex, not a lover's grip but a fighter's grip, and the thought of the damage he might do to her softest tissues made her gag with horror, and she knew it was even possible to kill a woman that way, to reach up inside and claw and rip and pull, so she tried frantically to scratch his cobalt eyes and blind him, but he swiftly drew his head back, out of range, and then they both abruptly froze, for they realized simultaneously that she had not dropped the pistol when he had pulled her down onto the floor. It was wedged between them, the muzzle pressed firmly into his crotch—and although her finger was on the trigger guard instead of the trigger itself, she was able to slip it back a notch and put it in the proper place even as she became aware of the situation.

His heavy hand was still on her pubis. An obscene thing. A leathery, demonic, disgusting hand. She could feel the heat of it even through the glove he was wearing. He was no longer clawing at her panties. Trembling. His big hand was trembling.

The bastard's scared.

His eyes seemed to be fastened to hers by an invisible thread, a strong thread that would not break easily. Neither of them could look away.

"If you make one wrong move," she said weakly, "I'll blow your balls off."

He blinked.

"Understand?" she asked, unable to put any force in her voice. She was wheezing and breathless with exertion and, mostly, with fear.

He licked his lips.

Blinked slowly.

Like a goddamned lizard.

"*Do you understand?*" she demanded, putting bite into it this time.

"Yeah."

"You can't fool me again."

"Whatever you say."

His voice was deep and gruff, as before, and it did not waver. There wasn't anything in his voice or eyes or face to betray his hard-muscled tough guy image. But his gloved hand continued to spasm nervously on the sensitive juncture of her thighs.

"Okay," she said. "What I want you to do is move very slowly. Very, very slowly. When I give the word, we're going to roll over very slowly, until you're on the bottom and I'm on the top."

Without being the least amused, she was aware that what she had said bore a grotesque resemblance to an eager lover's suggestion in the middle of the sex act.

"When I tell you to, and not a second before I tell you to, you'll roll to your right," she said.

"Okay."

"And I'll move with you."

"Sure."

"Nice and easy."

"Sure."

"And I'll keep the gun where it is."

His eyes were still hard and cold, but the insanity and the rage had gone out of them. The thought of having his sex organs shot off had snapped him back into the real world—at least temporarily.

She poked the barrel of the gun hard against his privates, and he grimaced with pain.

"Now roll over *easy*," she said.

He did exactly what she had instructed him to do, moved onto his side with exaggerated care, then onto his back, never taking his eyes from hers. He slipped his hand out from under her dress as they reversed positions, but he didn't attempt to take the pistol from her.

She clung to him with her left hand, the gun clenched in her right, and she went over with him, keeping the muzzle firmly in his crotch. Finally she was atop him, one arm trapped between them, the .32 automatic still strategically placed.

Her right hand was beginning to go numb because of the awkward position, but also because she was squeezing the pistol with all of her might and was afraid to hold it any less surely. Her grip was so fierce that her fingers and the muscles up the length of her arm ached with the effort. She was worried that somehow he would sense the growing weakness in her hand—or that she would actually let go of the gun against her will as her fingers lost all feeling.

"Okay," she said. "I'm going to slide off you. I'm going to keep the gun where it is, and I'm going to slip off beside you. Don't move. Don't even blink."

He stared at her.

"You got that?" she asked.

"Yeah."

Keeping the .32 on his scrotum, she disengaged herself from him as if she were rising from a bed of nitroglycerin. Her abdominal muscles were painfully tight with tension. Her mouth was dry and sour. Their noisy breathing seemed to fill the bedroom like rushing wind, yet her hearing was so acute that she could detect the soft ticking of her Cartier watch. She slid to one side, got up on her knees, hesitated, finally pushed all the way to her feet and shuffled quickly out of his reach before he could trip her again.

He sat up.

"No!" she said.

"What?"

"Lie down."

"I'm not coming after you."

"Lie down."

"Just relax."

"Dammit, lie down!"

He would not obey her. He just sat there. "So what happens next?"

Waving the pistol at him, she said, "I told you to lie down. Flat on your back. Do it. Now."

He twisted his lips into one of those ugly smiles that he did so well. "And I asked *you* what happens next."

He was trying to regain control of the situation, and she did not like that. On the other hand, did it really matter whether he was sitting or lying down? Even sitting up, he could not get to his feet and cross the space between them faster than she could put a couple of bullets into him.

"Okay," she said reluctantly. "Sit up if you insist. But you make one move toward me, and I'll empty the gun on you. I'll spread your guts all over the room. I swear to Christ I will."

He grinned and nodded.

Shivering, she said, "Now, I'm going to the bed. I'll sit down there and phone the police."

She moved sideways and backwards, crablike, one small step at a time, until she got to the bed. The telephone was on the nightstand. The moment she sat down and lifted the receiver, Frye disobeyed her. He stood up.

"Hey."

She dropped the receiver and clutched the pistol with both hands, trying to keep it steady.

He held his hands out placatingly, palms toward her. "Wait. Just wait a second. I'm not going to touch you."

"Sit down."

"I'm not coming anywhere near you."

"Sit down right now."

"I'm going to walk out of here," Frye said.

"Like hell you are."

"Out of this room and out of this house."

"No."

"You won't try to shoot me if I just leave."

"Try me and you'll be sorry."

"You won't," he said confidently. "You aren't the type to pull the trigger unless you don't have any other choice. You couldn't kill me in cold blood. You couldn't shoot me in the back. Not in a million years. Not you. You don't have that kind of strength. You're weak. Just too damned weak." He gave her that ghastly grin again, that wide death's head smile, and he took one step toward the door. "You can call the cops when I'm gone." Another step. "It would be different if I was a stranger. Then I might have a chance to get away scot-free. But after all, you can tell them who I am." Another step. "See, you've already won, and I've lost. All I'm doing is buying a little time. A very little bit of time."

She knew he was right about her. She could kill him if he attacked, but she was not capable of shooting him while he retreated.

Sensing her unspoken acknowledgment of the truth in what he had said, Frye turned his back on her. His smug self-confidence infuriated her, but she could not pull the trigger. He had been sidling carefully toward the exit. Now, he strode boldly out of the room, not bothering to glance back. He disappeared through the broken door, and his footsteps echoed along the hallway.

When Hilary heard him thumping down the stairs, she realized that he might not leave the house. Unobserved, he could slip into one of the downstairs rooms and hide in a closet, wait patiently until the police had come and gone, then slither out of his hole and strike her by surprise. She hurried to the head of the stairs and got there just in time to see him turn right, into the foyer. A moment later, she heard him rattling the locks; then he went out and threw the door shut behind him with a loud *wham!*

She was three-quarters of the way down the stairs when she realized he might have faked his departure. He might have slammed the door without leaving. He might be waiting for her in the foyer.

Hilary was carrying the pistol at her side, the muzzle directed safely at the floor, but she raised it in dread anticipation. She descended the stairs, and on the bottom step she paused for a long while, listening. At last, she eased forward until she could see into the foyer. It was empty. The closet door stood open. Frye wasn't in there either. He was really gone.

She closed the closet door.

She went to the front door and double-locked it.

Weaving slightly, she walked across the living room, in the study. The room smelled of lemon-scented furniture polish; the two women from the cleaning agency had been in yesterday. Hilary switched on the light and drifted to the big desk. She put the gun in the center of the blotter.

Red and white roses filled the vase on the window table. They added a sweet contrasting fragrance to the lemon air.

She sat down at the desk and pulled the telephone in front of her. She looked up the number for the police.

Suddenly, unexpectedly, her vision blurred with hot tears. She tried to hold them back. She was Hilary Thomas, and Hilary Thomas did not cry. Not ever. Hilary Thomas was tough. Hilary Thomas could take all the crap the world wanted to throw at her and keep on taking it and never break down. Hilary Thomas could handle herself perfectly well, thank you. Even though she squeezed her eyes shut, the flood would not be contained. Fat tears tracked down her cheeks and settled saltily in the corners of her mouth, then dribbled over her chin. At first she wept in eerie silence, emitting not even the shallowest whimper. But after a minute or so, she began to twitch and shiver, and her voice was shaken loose. In the back of her throat, she made a wet choking sound which swiftly grew into a sharp little cry of despair. She broke. She let out a terrible quaverous wail and hugged herself. She sobbed and sputtered and gasped for breath. She pulled Kleenex from a decorator dispenser on one corner of the desk, blew her nose, got hold of herself—then shuddered and began to sob again.

She was not crying because he had hurt her. He hadn't caused her any lasting or unbearable pain—at least not physically. She was weeping because, in some way she found difficult to define, he had violated her. She boiled with outrage and shame. Although he had not raped her, although he had not even managed to tear off her clothes, he had demolished her crystal bubble of privacy, a barrier that she had constructed with great care and upon which she had placed a great value. He had smashed into her snug world and had pawed everything in it with his dirty hands.

Tonight, at the best table in the Polo Lounge, Wally Topelis had begun to convince her that she could let down her guard at least a fraction of an inch. For the first time in her twenty-nine years, she seriously had considered the possibility of living much less defensively than she had been accustomed to living. With all the good news and Wally's urging, she had been willing to look at the idea of a life with less fear, and she had been attracted to it. A life with more friends. More relaxation. More fun. It was a shining dream, this new life, not easily attained but worth the struggle to achieve it. But Bruno Frye had taken that fragile dream by the throat and had throttled it. He had reminded her that the world was a dangerous place, a shadowy cellar with nightmare creatures crouching in the dark corners. Just as she was struggling out of her pit, before she had a chance to enjoy the world above ground, he kicked her in the face and sent her tumbling back where she came from, down into doubt and fear and suspicion, down into the awful safety of loneliness.

She wept because she felt violated. And because she was humiliated. And because he had taken her hope and stomped on it the way a schoolyard bully crushes the favorite toy of a weaker child.

CHAPTER 2

PATTERNS.

They fascinated Anthony Clemenza.

At sundown, before Hilary Thomas had even gone home, while she was still driving through the hills and canyons for relaxation, Anthony Clemenza and his partner, Lieutenant Frank Howard, were questioning a bartender in Santa Monica. Beyond the enormous windows in the room's west wall, the sinking sun created constantly changing purple and orange and silver-fleck patterns on the darkening sea.

The place was a singles' bar called Paradise, meeting ground for the chronically lonely and terminally horny of both sexes in an age when all the traditional meeting grounds—church suppers, neighborhood dances, community picnics, social clubs—had been leveled with real (and sociological) bulldozers, the ground where they once stood now covered with highrise offices, towering cement and glass condominiums, pizza parlors, and five-story parking garages. The singles' bar was where space-age boy met space-age girl, where the macho stud connected with the nymphomaniac, where the shy little secretary from Chatsworth met the socially inept computer programmer from Burbank, and, where, sometimes, the rapist met the rapee.

To Anthony Clemenza's eye, the people in Paradise made patterns that identified the place. The most beautiful women and the handsomest men sat very erect on barstools and at minuscule cocktail tables, legs crossed in geometric perfection, elbows bent just so, posing to display the clean lines of their faces and their strong limbs; they made elegantly angular patterns as they watched and courted one another. Those who were less physically attractive than the *crème de la crème*, but who were nonetheless undeniably appealing and desirable, tended to sit and stand with less than ideal posture, choosing to make up in attitude and image what they lacked in form. Their posture made a statement: I am at ease here, relaxed, unimpressed with those gorgeous straight-backed girls and guys, confident, my own person. This group slouched and slumped gracefully, using the eye-pleasing rounded lines of a body at rest to conceal slight imperfections of bone and muscle. The third and largest group of people in the bar was composed of the plain ones, neither pretty nor ugly, who made jagged anxious patterns as they huddled in corners and darted from table to table to exchange gaping smiles and nervous gossip, worried that no one would love them.

The overall pattern of Paradise is sadness, Tony Clemenza thought. Dark strips of unfulfilled need. A checkered field of loneliness. Quiet desperation in a colorful herringbone.

But he and Frank Howard were not there to study the patterns in the sunset and the customers. What they were there to do was get a lead on Bobby "Angel" Valdez.

Last April, Bobby Valdez had been released from prison after serving seven years and a few months of a fifteen-year sentence for rape and manslaughter. It looked like letting him go had been a big mistake.

Eight years ago, Bobby had raped as few as three and as many as sixteen Los Angeles women. The police could prove three; they suspected the others. One night, Bobby accosted a woman in a parking lot, forced her into his car at gunpoint, drove her to a little-traveled dirt connecting road high in the Hollywood Hills, tore off her clothes, raped her repeatedly, then pushed her out of the car and drove off. He had been parked on the verge of the lane, and the narrow shoulder had opened on a long nasty drop. The woman, thrust naked from the car, lost her balance and went over the edge. She landed on a broken-down fence. Splintery wooden fence posts. With rusted wire. Barbed wire. The wire lacerated her badly, and a jagged four-inch-wide section of weathered pine railing slammed through her belly and out her back, impaling her. Incredibly, while submitting to Bobby in the car, she had put her hand upon a flimsy copy of a Union 76 credit card purchase slip, had realized what it was, and had held on to it all the way down to the fence, all the way down into death. Furthermore, police learned that the deceased wore only one kind of panties, a gift from her boyfriend. Every pair she owned bore this embroidered legend on the silky crotch: HARRY'S PROPERTY. A pair of those panties, torn and soiled, were found in a collection of underthings in Bobby's apartment. Those and the scrap of paper in the victim's hand led to the suspect's arrest.

Unfortunately for the people of California, circumstances conspired to get Bobby off lightly. The arresting officers made a minor procedural error when they took him into custody, just the sort of thing to stir some judges to passionate rhetoric about constitutional guarantees. The district attorney at that time, a man named Kooperhausen, had been busy responding to charges of political corruption in his own office. Aware that the improper handling of the accused at the time of arrest might have jeopardized the state's case, preoccupied with saving his own ass from the muckrakers, the D.A. had been receptive to the defense attorney's offer to plead Bobby guilty to three counts of rape and one of manslaughter in return for the dropping of all other and more serious charges. Most homicide detectives, like Tony Clemenza, felt that Kooperhausen should have tried to get convictions for second-degree murder, kidnapping, assault, rape, and sodomy. The evidence was overwhelmingly in favor of the state's position. The deck was stacked against Bobby—and then fate dealt him an unexpected ace.

Today, Bobby was a free man.

But maybe not for long, Tony thought.

In May, one month after his release from prison, Bobby "Angel" Valdez failed to keep an appointment with his parole officer. He moved out of his apartment without filing the required change of address form with the proper authorities. He vanished.

In June, he started raping again. Just as easy as that. As casually as some men start smoking again after shaking the habit for a few years. Like renewed interest in an old hobby. He molested two women in June. Two in July. Three in August. Two more in the first ten days of September. After eighty-eight months behind bars, Bobby had a craving for womanflesh, an insatiable need.

The police were convinced that those nine crimes—and perhaps a few others that had gone unreported—were the work of one man, and they were equally certain the man was Bobby Valdez. For one thing each of the victims had been approached in the same way. A man walked up to her as she got out of her car alone, at night, in a parking lot. He put a gun in her ribs or back or belly, and said, "I'm a fun guy. Come to the party with me, and you won't get hurt. Turn me down, and I'll blow you away right now. Play along, and you've got no worries. I'm really a fun guy." He said pretty much the same thing every time, and the victims remembered it because the "fun guy" part sounded so weird, especially when spoken in Bobby's soft, high-pitched, almost girlish voice. It was identical to the approach Bobby had used more than eight years ago, during his first career as a rapist.

In addition to that, the nine victims gave strikingly similar descriptions of the man who had abused them. Slender. Five-foot-ten. A hundred and forty pounds. Dusky complexion. Dimpled chin. Brown hair and eyes. The girlish voice. Some of Bobby's friends called him "Angel" because of his sweet voice and because he had a cute baby face. Bobby was thirty years old, but he looked sixteen. Each of the nine victims had seen her assailant's face, and each had said he looked like a kid, but handled himself like a tough, cruel, clever, and sick man.

The chief bartender in Paradise left the business to his two subordinates and examined the three glossy mug shots of Bobby Valdez that Frank Howard had put on the bar. His name was Otto. He was a good-looking man, darkly tanned and bearded. He wore white slacks and a blue body shirt with the top three buttons undone. His brown chest was matted with crisp golden hairs. He wore a shark's tooth on a gold chain around his neck. He looked up at Frank, frowned. "I didn't know L.A. police had jurisdiction in Santa Monica."

"We're here by sufferance of the Santa Monica P.D.," Tony said.

"Huh?"

"Santa Monica police are cooperating with us in this investigation," Frank said impatiently. "Now, did you ever see the guy?"

"Yeah, sure. He's been in a couple of times," Otto said.

"When?" Frank asked.

"Oh . . . a month ago. Maybe longer."

"Not recently?"

The band, just returned from a twenty-minute break, struck up a Billy Joel song.

Otto raised his voice above the music. "Haven't seen him for at least a month. The reason I remember is because he didn't look old enough to be served. I asked to see some ID, and he got mad as hell about that. Caused a scene."

"What kind of scene?" Frank asked.

"Demanded to see the manager."

"That's all?" Tony asked.

"Called me names." Otto looked grim. "Nobody calls me names like that."

Tony cupped one hand around his ear to funnel in the bartender's voice and block some of the music. He liked most Billy Joel tunes, but not when they were played by a band that thought enthusiasm and amplification could compensate for poor musicianship.

"So he called you names," Frank said. "Then what?"

"Then he apologized."

"Just like that? He demands to see the manager, calls you names, then right away apologizes?"

"Yeah."

"Why?"

"I asked him to," Otto said.

Frank leaned farther over the bar as the music swelled into a deafening chorus. "He apologized just because you asked him to?"

"Well . . . first, he wanted to fight."

"Did you fight him?" Tony shouted.

"Nah. If even the biggest and meanest son of a bitch in the place gets rowdy, I don't ever have to touch him to quiet him down."

"You must have a hell of a lot of charm," Frank yelled.

The band finished the chorus, and the roar descended from a decibel level high enough to make your eyeballs bleed. The vocalist did a bad imitation of Billy Joel on a verse played no louder than a thunderstorm.

A stunning green-eyed blonde was sitting at the bar next to Tony. She had been listening to the conversation. She said, "Go on, Otto. Show them your trick."

"You're a magician?" Tony asked Otto. "What do you do—make unruly customers disappear?"

"He scares them," the blonde said. "It's neat. Go on, Otto. Show them your stuff."

Otto shrugged and reached under the bar and took a tall beer glass from a rack. He held it up so they could look at it, as if they had never seen a beer glass before. Then he bit off a piece of it. He clamped his teeth on the rim and snapped a chunk out of it, turned, spat the sharp fragment into a garbage can behind them.

The band exploded through the last chorus of the song and gifted the audience with merciful silence.

In the sudden quiet between the last note and the burst of scattered applause, Tony heard the beer glass crack as Otto took another bite out of it.

"Jesus," Frank said.

The blonde giggled.

Otto chomped on the glass and spat out a mouthful and chomped some more until he had reduced it to an inch-thick base too heavy to succumb to human teeth and jaws. He threw the remaining hunk in the can and smiled. "I chew up the glass right in front of the guy who's making trouble. Then I look mean as a snake, and I tell him to settle down. I tell him that if he doesn't settle down I'll bite his goddamned nose off."

Frank Howard gaped at him, amazed. "Have you ever done it?"

"What? Bitten off someone's nose? Nah. Just the threat's enough to make them behave."

"You get many hard cases here?" Frank asked.

"Nah. This is a class place. We have trouble maybe once a week. No more than that."

"How do you do that trick?" Tony asked.

"Biting the glass? There's a little secret to it. But it's not really hard to learn."

The band broke into Bob Seeger's *Still the Same* as if they were a bunch of juvenile delinquents breaking into a nice house with the intention of trashing it.

"Ever cut yourself?" Tony shouted to Otto.

"Every once in a while. Not often. And I've never cut my tongue. The sign of someone who can do the stunt well is the condition of his tongue," Otto said. "My tongue has never been cut."

"But you have injured yourself."

"Sure. My lips a few times. Not often."

"But that only makes the trick more effective," the blonde said. "You should see him when he cuts himself. Otto stands there in front of the jerk who's been causing all the trouble, and he just pretends like he doesn't know he's hurt himself. He lets the blood run." Her green eyes shone with delight and with a hard little spark of animal passion that made Tony squirm uneasily on his barstool. "He stands there with bloody teeth and with the blood oozing down into his beard, and he warns the guy to stop making a ruckus. You wouldn't believe how fast they settle down."

"I believe," Tony said. He felt queasy.

Frank Howard shook his head and said, "Well. . . ."

"Yeah," Tony said, unable to find words of his own.

Frank said, "Okay . . . let's get back to Bobby Valdez." He tapped the mug shots that were lying on the bar.

"Oh. Well, like I told you, he hasn't been in for at least a month."

"That night, after he got angry with you, after you settled him down with the glass trick, did he stick around for a drink?"

"I served him a couple."

"So you saw his ID."

"Yeah."

"What was it—driver's license?"

"Yeah. He was thirty, for God's sake. He looked like he was in maybe eleventh grade, a high school junior, maybe at most a senior, but he was thirty."

Frank said. "Do you remember what the name was on the driver's license?"

Otto fingered his shark's tooth necklace. "Name? You already know his name."

"What I'm wondering," Frank said, "is whether or not he showed you a phony driver's license."

"His picture was on it," Otto said.

"That doesn't mean it was genuine."

"But you can't change pictures on a California license. Doesn't the card self-destruct or something if you mess around with it?"

"I'm saying the whole card might be a fake."

"Forged credentials," Otto said, intrigued. "Forged credentials. . . ." Clearly, he had watched a couple of hundred old espionage movies on television. "What is this, some sort of spy thing?"

"I think we've gotten turned around here," Frank said impatiently.

"Huh?"

"*We're* supposed to be the ones asking questions," Frank said. "You just answer them. Understand?"

The bartender was one of those people who reacted quickly, strongly, and negatively to a pushy cop. His dark face closed up. His eyes went blank.

Aware that they were about to lose Otto while he still might have something important to tell them, Tony put a hand on Frank's shoulder, squeezed gently. "You don't want him to start munching on a glass, do you?"

"I'd like to see it again," the blonde said, grinning.

"You'd rather do it your way?" Frank asked Tony.

"Sure."

"Go ahead."

Tony smiled at Otto. "Look, you're curious, and so are we. Doesn't hurt a thing if we satisfy your curiosity, so long as you satisfy ours."

Otto opened up again. "That's the way I see it, too."

"Okay," Tony said.

"Okay. So what's this Bobby Valdez done that makes you want him so bad?"

"Parole violations," Tony said.

"And assault," Frank said grudgingly.

"And rape," Tony said.

"Hey," Otto said, "didn't you guys say you were with the homicide squad?"

The band finished *Still the Same* with a clatter-bang-boom of sound not unlike the derailment of a speeding freight train. Then there were a few minutes of peace while the lead singer made unamusing small talk with the ringside customers who sat in clouds of smoke that, Tony felt sure, had come partly from cigarettes and partly from burning eardrums. The musicians pretended to tune their instruments.

"When Bobby Valdez comes across an uncooperative woman," Tony explained to Otto, "he pistol-whips her a little to make her more eager to please. Five days ago, he went after victim number ten, and she resisted, and he hit her on the head so hard and so often that she died in the hospital twelve hours later. Which brought the homicide squad into it."

"What I don't understand," the blonde said, "is why any guy would take it by force when there's girls willing to give it away." She winked at Tony, but he didn't wink back.

"Before the woman died," Frank said, "she gave us a description that fit Bobby like a custom-made glove. So if you know anything about the slimy little bastard, we've got to hear it."

Otto hadn't spent all his time watching spy movies. He had seen his share of police shows, too. He said, "So now you want him for murder-one."

"Murder-one," Tony said. "Precisely."

"How'd you know to ask me about him?"

"He accosted seven of those ten women in singles' bar parking lots—"

"None of them in our lot," Otto interrupted defensively. "Our lot is very well lighted."

"That's true," Tony said. "But we've been going to singles bars all over the city, talking to bartenders and regular customers, showing them those mug shots, trying to get a line on Bobby Valdez. A couple of people at a place in Century City told us they thought they'd seen him here, but they couldn't be sure."

"He was here all right," Otto said.

Now that Otto's feathers had been smoothed, Frank took over the questioning again. "So he caused a commotion, and you did your beer glass trick, and he showed you his ID."

"Yeah."

"So what was the name on the ID?"

Otto frowned. "I'm not sure."

"Was it Robert Valdez?"

"I don't think so."

"Try to remember."

"It was a Chicano name."

"Valdez is a Chicano name."

"This was more Chicano than that."

"What do you mean?"

"Well . . . longer . . . with a couple Zs in it."

"Zs?"

"And Qs. You know the kind of name I mean. Something like Velazquez."

"Was it Velazquez?"

"Nah. But like that."

"Began with a V?"

"I couldn't say for sure. I'm just talking about the sound of it."

"What about the first name?"

"I think I remember that."

"And."

"Juan."

"J-U-A-N?"

"Yeah. Very Chicano."

"You notice an address on his ID?"

"I wasn't looking for that."

"He mention where he lived?"

"We weren't exactly chummy."

"He say anything at all about himself?"

"He just drank quietly and left."

"And never came back?"

"That's right."

"You're positive?"

"He's never been back on my shift, anyway."

"You got a good memory."

"Only for the troublemakers and the pretty ones."

"We'd like to show those mug shots to some of your customers," Frank said.

"Sure. Go ahead."

The blonde sitting next to Tony Clemenza said, "Can I get a closer look at him? Maybe I was in here when he was. Maybe I even talked to him."

Tony picked up the photographs and swiveled on his barstool.

She swung toward him as he swung toward her, and she pressed her pretty knees against his. When she took the pictures from him, her fingers lingered for a moment on his. She was a great believer in eye contact. She seemed to be trying to stare right through his brain and out the back of his skull.

"I'm Judy. What's your name?"

"Tony Clemenza."

"I *knew* you were Italian. I could tell by your dark soulful eyes."

"They give me away every time."

"And that thick black hair. So curly."

"And the spaghetti sauce stains on my shirt?"

She looked at his shirt.

"There aren't really any stains," he said.

She frowned.

"Just kidding. A little joke," he said.

"Oh."

"Do you recognize Bobby Valdez?"

She finally looked at the mug shot. "Nope. I must not have been here the night he came in. But he's not all that bad, is he? Kind of cute."

"Baby face."

"It would be like going to bed with my kid brother," she said. "Kinky." She grinned.

He took the pictures from her.

"That's a very nice suit you're wearing," she said.

"Thank you."

"It's cut really nice."

"Thank you."

This was not just a liberated woman exercising her right to be the sexual aggressor. He liked liberated women. This one was something else. Something weird. The whips and chains type. Or worse. She made him feel like a tasty little morsel, a very edible canapé, the last tiny piece of toast and caviar on a silver tray.

"You sure don't see many suits in a place like this," she said.

"I guess not."

"Body shirts, jeans, leather jackets, the Hollywood look—that's what you see in a place like this."

He cleared his throat. "Well," he said uneasily, "I want to thank you for helping us as much as you could."

She said, "I like men who dress well."

Their eyes locked again, and he saw that flicker of ravenous hunger and animal greed. He had the feeling that if he let her lead him into her apartment, the door would close behind him like a set of jaws. She'd be all over him in an instant, pushing and pulling and whirling him around as if she were a wave of digestive juices, breaking him down and sucking the nutrients out of him, using him until he fragmented and dissolved and simply ceased to exist except as a part of her.

"Got to go to work," he said, sliding off the barstool. "See you around."

"I hope so."

For fifteen minutes, Tony and Frank showed the mug shots of Bobby Valdez to the customers in Paradise. As they moved from table to table, the band played Rolling Stones and Elton John and Bee Gees material at a volume that set up sympathetic vibrations in Tony's teeth. It was a waste of time. No one in Paradise remembered the killer with the baby face.

On the way out, Tony stopped at the long oak bar where Otto was mixing strawberry Margaritas. "Tell me something," he shouted above the music.

"Anything," Otto yelled.

"Don't people come to these places to meet each other?"

"Making connections. That's what it's all about."

"Then why the hell do so many singles' bars have bands like that one?"

"What's wrong with the band?"

"A lot of things. But mostly it's too damned loud."

"So?"

"So how can anyone possibly strike up an interesting conversation?"

"Interesting conversation?" Otto said. "Hey man, they don't come here for interesting conversation. They come to meet each other, check each other out, see who they want to go to bed with."

"But no conversation?"

"Look at them. Just look around at them. What would they talk about? If we didn't play music loud and fairly steady, they'd get nervous."

"All those maddeningly quiet spaces to fill."

"How right you are. They'd go somewhere else."

"Where the music was louder and they only needed body language."

Otto shrugged. "It's a sign of the times."

"Maybe I should have lived in another time," Tony said.

Outside, the night was mild, but he knew it would get colder. A thin mist was coming off the sea, not genuine fog yet, but a sort of damp greasy breath that hung in the air and made halos around all the lights.

Frank was waiting behind the wheel of the unmarked police sedan. Tony climbed in on the passenger's side and buckled his seatbelt.

They had one more lead to check out before they quit for the day. Earlier, a couple of people at that Century City singles' bar had said they'd also seen Bobby Valdez at a joint called The Big Quake on Sunset Boulevard, over in Hollywood.

Traffic was moderate to heavy heading toward the heart of the city. Sometimes Frank got impatient and darted from lane to lane, weaving in and out with toots of the horn and little squeals of the brakes, trying to get ahead a few car lengths, but not tonight. Tonight, he was going with the flow.

Tony wondered if Frank Howard had been discussing philosophy with Otto. After a while, Frank said, "You could have had her."

"Who?"

"That blonde. That Judy."

"I was on duty, Frank."

"You could have set something up for later. She was panting for you."

"Not my type."

"She was gorgeous."

"She was a killer."

"She was what?"

"She'd have eaten me up alive."

Frank considered that for about two seconds, then said, "Bullshit, I'd take a crack at her if I had the chance."

"You know where she's at."

"Maybe I'll mosey back there later, when we're done."

"You do that," Tony said. "Then I'll come visit you in the rest home when she's finished with you."

"Hell, what's the matter with you? She wasn't *that* special. That kind of stuff can be handled easy."

"Maybe that's why I didn't want it."

"Send that one by me again."

Tony Clemenza was tired. He wiped his face with his hands as if weariness was a mask that he could pull off and discard. "She was too well-handled, too well-used."

"Since when did you become a Puritan?"

"I'm not," Tony said, "Or . . . yeah . . . okay, maybe I am. Just a little. Just a thin streak of Puritanism in there somewhere. God knows, I've had more than a few of what they now call 'meaningful relationships.' I'm far from pure. But I just can't see myself on the make in a place like Paradise, cruising, calling all the women 'foxes,' looking for fresh meat. For one thing, I couldn't keep a straight face making the kind of chatter that fills in between the band's numbers. Can you hear me making that scene? 'Hi, I'm Tony. What's your name? What's your sign? Are you into numerology? Have you taken est training? Do you believe in the incredible totality of cosmic energy? Do you believe in destiny as an arm of some all-encompassing cosmic consciousness? Do you think we were destined to meet? Do you think we could get rid of all the bad karma we've generated individually by creating a good energy gestalt together? Want to fuck?'"

"Except for the part about fucking," Frank said, "I didn't understand a thing you said."

"Neither did I. That's what I mean. In a place like Paradise, it's all plastic chatter, glossy surface jive talk formulated to slide everyone into bed with as little friction as possible. In Paradise, you don't ask a woman anything really important. You don't ask about her feelings, her emotions, her talents, her fears, hopes, wants, needs, dreams. So what happens is you end up going to bed with a stranger. Worse than that, you find yourself making love to a fox, to a paper cut-out from a men's magazine, an image instead of a woman, a piece of meat instead of a person, which means you aren't making love at all. The act becomes just the satisfying of a bodily urge, no different than scratching an itch or having a good bowel movement. If a man reduces sex to that, then he might as well stay home alone and use his hand."

Frank braked for a red light and said, "Your hand can't give you a blow job."

"Jesus, Frank, sometimes you can be crude as hell."

"Just being practical."

"What I'm trying to say is that, for me at least, the dance isn't worth the effort if you don't know your partner. I'm not one of those people who'd go to a disco just to revel in my own fancy choreography. I've got to know what the lady's steps are, how she wants to move and why, what she feels and thinks. Sex is just so damned much better if she means something to you, if she's an individual, a quirky person all her own, not just a smooth sleek body that's rounded in all the right places, but a unique personality, a character with chips and dents and marks of experience."

"I can't believe what I'm hearing," Frank said as he drove away from the traffic signal. "It's that old bromide about sex being cheap and unfulfilling if love isn't mixed up with it somehow."

"I'm not talking about undying love," Tony said. "I'm not talking about unbreakable vows of fidelity until the end of time. You can love someone for a little while, in little ways. You can go on loving her even after the physical part of the relationship is over. I'm friends with old lovers because we didn't look at each other as new notches on the gun; we had something in common even after we stopped sharing a bed. Look, before I'm going to go for a tumble in the sack, before I'm going to get bare-assed and vulnerable with a woman, I want to know I can trust her; I want to feel she's special in some way, dear to me, a person worth knowing, worth revealing myself to, worth being a part of for a while."

"Garbage," Frank said scornfully.

"It's the way I feel."

"Let me give you a warning."

"Go ahead."

"The best advice you'll ever get."

"I'm listening."

"If you think there's really something called love, if you honest-to-God believe there's actually a thing called love that's as strong and real as hate or fear, then all you're doing is setting yourself up for a lot of pain. It's a lie. A big lie. Love is something writers invented to sell books."

"You don't really mean that."

"The hell I don't." Frank glanced away from the road for a moment, looked at Tony with pity. "You're how old—thirty-three?"

"Almost thirty-five," Tony said as Frank looked back at the street and pulled around a slow-moving truck that was loaded down with scrap metal.

"Well, I'm ten years older than you," Frank said. "So listen to the wisdom of age. Sooner or later, you're going to think you're in true love with some fluff, and while you're bending over to kiss her pretty feet she's gong to kick the shit out of you. Sure as hell, she'll break your heart if you let her know you have one. Affection? Sure. That's okay. And lust. Lust is the word, my friend. Lust is what it's really all about. But not love. What you've got to do is forget all this love crap. Enjoy yourself. Get all the ass you can while you're young. Fuck 'em and run. You can't get hurt that way. If you keep daydreaming about love, you'll only go on making a complete goddamned fool out of yourself, over and over and over again, until they finally stick you in the ground."

"That's too cynical for me."

Frank shrugged.

Six months ago, he had gone through a bitter divorce. He was still sour from the experience.

"And you're not really that cynical, either," Tony said. "I don't think you really believe what you said."

Frank didn't say anything.

"You're a sensitive man," Tony said.

Frank shrugged again.

For a minute or two, Tony tried to revive the dead conversation, but Frank had said everything he intended to say about the subject. He settled into his usual sphinxlike silence. It was surprising that he had said all he said, for Frank was not much of a talker. In fact, when Tony thought about it, the brief discussion just concluded seemed to have been the longest they'd ever had.

Tony had been partners with Frank Howard for more than three months. He still was not sure if the pairing was going to work out.

They were so different from each other in so many ways. Tony *was* a talker. Frank usually did little more than grunt in response. Tony had a wide variety of interests other than his job: films, books, food, the theater, music, art, skiing, running. So far as he could tell, Frank didn't care a great deal about anything except his work. Tony believed that a detective had many tools with which to extract information from a witness, including kindness, gentleness, wit, sympathy, empathy, attentiveness, charm, persistence, cleverness—and of course, intimidation and the rare use of mild force. Frank felt he could get along fine with just persistence, cleverness, intimidation, and a bit more force than the department thought acceptable; he had no use whatsoever for the other approaches on Tony's list. As a result, at least twice a week, Tony had to restrain him subtly but firmly. Frank was subject to eye-bulging, blood-boiling rages when too many things went wrong in one day. Tony, on the other hand, was nearly always calm. Frank was five-nine, stocky, solid as a block-house. Tony was six-one, lean, rangy, rugged looking. Frank was blond and blue-eyed. Tony was dark. Frank was a brooding pessimist. Tony was an optimist. Sometimes it seemed they were such totally opposite types that the partnership never could be successful.

Yet they were alike in some respects. For one thing, neither of them was an eight-hour-a-day cop. More often than not, they worked an extra two hours, sometimes three, without pay, and neither of them complained about it. To-ward the end of a case, when evidence and leads developed faster and faster, they would work on their days off if they thought it necessary. No one asked them to do overtime. No one ordered it. The choice was entirely theirs.

Tony was willing to give more than a fair share of himself to the department because he was ambitious. He did not intend to remain a detective-lieutenant for the rest of his life. He wanted to work his way up at least to captain, perhaps higher than that, perhaps all the way to the top, right into the chief's office, where the pay and retirement benefits were a hell of a lot better than what he would get if he stayed where he was. He had been raised in a large Italian family in which parsimony had been a religion as important as Roman Cathol-icism. His father, Carlo, was an immigrant who worked as a tailor. The old man had labored hard and long to keep his children housed, clothed, and fed, but quite often he had come perilously close to destitution and bankruptcy. There had been much sickness in the Clemenza family, and the unexpected hospital and pharmacy bills had eaten up a frighteningly high percentage of what the old man earned. While Tony was still a child, even before he was old enough to understand about money and household budgets, before he knew anything about the debilitating fear of poverty with which his father lived, he sat through hundreds, maybe thousands, of short but strongly worded lectures on fiscal responsibility. Carlo instructed him almost daily in the importance of hard work, financial shrewdness, ambition, and job security. His father should have worked for the CIA in the brainwashing department. Tony had been so totally indoctrinated, so completely infused with his father's fears and princi-ples, that even at the age of thirty-five, with an excellent bank account and a steady job, he felt uneasy if he was away from work more than two or three days. As often as not, when he took a long vacation, it turned into an ordeal instead of a pleasure. He put in a lot of overtime every week because he was Carlo Clemenza's son, and Carlo Clemenza's son could not possibly have done otherwise.

Frank Howard had other reasons for giving a big piece of himself to the department. He did not appear to be any more ambitious than the next guy, and he did not seem unduly worried about money. As far as Tony could tell, Frank put in the extra hours because he really lived only when he was on the job. Being a homicide detective was the only role he knew how to play, the one thing that gave him a sense of purpose and worth.

Tony looked away from the red taillights of the cars in front of them and studied his partner's face. Frank wasn't aware of Tony's scrutiny. His attention was focused on his driving; he peered intently at the quicksilver flow of traffic on Wilshire Boulevard. The green glow from the dashboard dials and gauges highlighted his bold features. He was not handsome in the classic sense, but he was good-looking in his own way. Broad brow. Deeply-set blue eyes. The nose a bit large and sharp. The mouth well-formed but most often set in a grim scowl that flexed the strong jawline. The face unquestionably contained power and appeal—and more than a hint of unyielding single-mindedness. It was not difficult to picture Frank going home and sitting down and, every night without fail, dropping into a trance that lasted from quitting time until eight the next morning.

In addition to their willingness to work extended hours, Tony and Frank had a few other things in common. Although many plainclothes detectives had tossed out the old dress code and now reported for duty in everything from jeans to leisure suits, Tony and Frank still believed in wearing traditional suits and ties. They thought of themselves as professionals, doing a job that required special skills and education, a job as vital and demanding as that of any trial attorney or teacher or social worker—more demanding, in fact—and jeans simply did not contribute to a professional image. Neither of them smoked. Neither of them drank on the job. And neither of them attempted to foist his paperwork on the other.

So maybe it'll work out between us, Tony thought. Maybe in time I can quietly convince him to use more charm and less force with witnesses. Maybe I can get him interested in films and food, if not in books and art and theater. The reason I'm having so much trouble adjusting to him is that my expectations are far too high. But Jesus, if only he'd talk a little more instead of sitting there like a lump!

For the rest of his career as a homicide detective, Tony would expect a great deal of anyone who rode with him because, for five years, until last May 7, he had worked with a nearly perfect partner, Michael Savatino. He and Michael were both from Italian families; they shared certain ethnic memories, pains, and pleasures. More important than that, they employed similar methods in their police work, and they enjoyed many of the same extracurricular activities. Michael was an avid reader, a film buff, and an excellent cook. Their days had been punctuated by fascinating conversations.

Last February, Michael and his wife, Paula, had gone to Las Vegas for a weekend. They saw two shows. They ate dinner twice at Battista's Hole in the Wall, the best restaurant in town. They filled out a dozen Keno cards and won nothing. They played two-dollar blackjack and lost sixty bucks. And one hour before their scheduled departure, Paula put a silver dollar in a slot machine that promised a progressive jackpot, pulled the handle, and won slightly more than two hundred and twenty thousand dollars.

Police work never had been Michael's first choice for a career. But like Tony, he was a seeker of security. He attended the police academy and climbed relatively quickly from uniformed patrolman to detective because public service offered at least moderate financial security. In March, however, Michael gave the department a sixty-day notice, and in May he quit. All of his adult life, he had wanted to own a restaurant. Five weeks ago, he opened Savatino's, a small but authentic Italian *ristorante* on Santa Monica Boulevard, not far from the Century City complex.

A dream come true.

How likely is it that I could make *my* dream come true the same way? Tony wondered as he studied the night city through which they moved. How likely is it that I could go to Vegas, win two hundred thousand bucks, quit the police force, and take a shot at making it as an artist?

He did not have to ask the question aloud. He didn't need Frank Howard's opinion. He knew the answer. How likely was it? Not very damned likely.

About as likely as suddenly learning he was the long-lost son of a rich Arabian prince.

As Michael Savatino had always dreamed of being a restaurateur, so Tony Clemenza dreamed of earning his living as an artist. He had talent. He produced fine pieces in a variety of media: pen and ink, watercolor, oil. He was not merely technically skilled; he had a sharp and unique creative imagination as well. Perhaps if he had been born into a middle-class family with at least modest financial resources, he would have gone to a good school, would have received the proper training from the best professors, would have honed his God-given abilities, and would have become tremendously successful. Instead, he had educated himself with hundreds of art books and through thousands of hours of painstaking drawing practice and experimentation with materials. And he suffered from that pernicious lack of self-confidence so common to those who are self-taught in any field. Although he had entered four art shows and had twice won top prize in his division, he never seriously considered quitting his job and plunging into the creative life. That was nothing more than a pleasant fantasy, a bright daydream. No son of Carlo Clemenza would ever forsake a weekly paycheck for the dread uncertainties of self-employment, unless he had first banked a windfall from Las Vegas.

He was jealous of Michael Savatino's good fortune. Of course, they were still close friends, and he was genuinely happy for Michael. Delighted. Really. But also jealous. He was human, after all, and in the back of his mind, the same petty question kept blinking off and on, off and on, like a neon sign: *Why couldn't it have been me?*

Slamming on the brakes, jolting Tony out of his reverie, Frank blew the horn at a Corvette that cut him off in traffic. "Asshole!"

"Easy, Frank."

"Sometimes I wish I was back in uniform again, handing out citations."

"That's the last thing you wish."

"I'd nail his ass."

"Except maybe he'd turn out to be out of his skull on drugs or maybe just plain crazy. When you work the traffic detail too long, you tend to forget the world's full of nuts. You fall into a habit, a routine, and you get careless. So maybe you'd stop him and walk up to his door with your ticket book in hand, and he'd greet you with a gun. Maybe he'd blow your head off. No. I'm thankful traffic detail's behind me forever. At least when you're on a homicide assignment, you know the kind of people you're gong to have to deal with. You never forget there's going to be someone with a gun or a knife or a piece of lead pipe up ahead somewhere. You're a lot less likely to walk into a nasty little surprise when you're working homicide."

Frank refused to be drawn into another discussion. He kept his eyes on the road, grumbled sullenly, wordlessly, and settled back into silence.

Tony sighed. He stared at the passing scenery with an artist's eye for unexpected detail and previously unnoticed beauty.

Patterns.

Every scene—every seascape, every landscape, every street, every building, every room in every building, every person, every thing—had its own special patterns. If you could perceive the patterns in a scene, you could then look beyond the patterns to the underlying structure that supported them. If you could see and grasp the method by which a surface harmony had been achieved, you eventually could understand the deepest meaning and mechanisms of any subject and then make a good painting of it. If you picked up your brushes and approached the canvas without first performing that analysis, you might wind up with a pretty picture, but you would not produce a work of art.

Patterns.

As Frank Howard drove east on Wilshire, on the way to the Hollywood singles' bar called The Big Quake, Tony searched for patterns in the city and the night. At first, coming in from Santa Monica, there were the sharp low lines of the sea-facing houses and the shadowy outlines of tall feathery palms—patterns of serenity and civility and more than a little money. As they entered Westwood, the dominant pattern was rectilinear: clusters of office highrises, oblong patches of light radiating from scattered windows in the mostly dark faces of the buildings. These neatly ordered rectangular shapes formed the patterns of modern thought and corporate power, patterns of even greater wealth than had been evident in Santa Monica's seaside homes. From Westwood they went to Beverly Hills, an insulated pocket within the greater fabric of the metropolis, a place through which the Los Angeles police could pass but in which they had no authority. In Beverly Hills, the patterns were soft and lush and flowing in a graceful continuum of big houses, parks, greenery, exclusive shops, and more ultra-expensive automobiles than you could find anywhere else on earth. From Wilshire Boulevard to Santa Monica Boulevard to Doheny, the pattern was one of ever-increasing wealth.

They turned north on Doheny, crawled up the steep hills, and swung right onto Sunset Boulevard, heading for the heart of Hollywood. For a couple of blocks, the famous street delivered a little bit on the promise of its name and legend. On the right stood Scandia, one of the best and most elegant restaurants in town, and one of the half dozen best in the entire country. Glittering discos. A nightclub specializing in magic. Another spot owned and operated by a stage hypnotist. Comedy clubs. Rock and roll clubs. Huge flashy billboards advertising current films and currently popular recording stars. Lights, lights and more lights. Initially, the boulevard supported the university studies and government reports that claimed Los Angeles and its suburbs formed the richest metropolitan area in the nation, perhaps the richest in the world. But after a while, as Frank continued to drive eastward, the blush of glamor faded. Even L.A. suffered from senescence. The pattern became marginally but unmistakably cancerous. In the healthy flesh of the city, a few malignant growths swelled here and there: cheap bars, a striptease club, a shuttered service station, brassy massage parlors, an adult book store, a few buildings desperately in need of renovation, more of them block by block. The disease was not terminal in this neighborhood, as it was in others nearby, but every day it gobbled up a few more bits of healthy tissue. Frank and Tony did not have to descend into the scabrous heart of the tumor, for The Big Quake was still on the edge of the blight. The bar appeared suddenly in a blaze of red and blue lights on the righthand side of the street.

Inside, the place resembled Paradise, except that the decor relied more heavily on colored lights and chrome and mirrors than it did in the Santa Monica bar. The customers were somewhat more consciously stylish, more aggressively *au courant*, and generally a shade better looking than the crowd in Paradise. But to Tony the patterns appeared to be the same as they were in Santa Monica. Patterns of need, longing, and loneliness. Desperate, carnivorous patterns.

The bartender wasn't able to help them, and the only customer who had anything for them was a tall brunette with violet eyes. She was sure they would find Bobby at Janus, a discotheque in Westwood. She had seen him there the previous two nights.

Outside, in the parking lot, bathed in alternating flashes of red and blue light, Frank said, "One thing just leads to another."

"As usual."

"It's getting late."

"Yeah."

"You want to try Janus now or leave it for tomorrow?"

"Now," Tony said.

"Good."

They turned around and traveled west on Sunset, out of the area that showed signs of urban cancer, into the glitter of the Strip, then into greenery and wealth again, past the Beverly Hills Hotel, past mansions and endless marching rows of gigantic palm trees.

As he often did when he suspected Tony might attempt to strike up another conversation, Frank switched on the police band radio and listened to Communications calling black-and-whites in the division that provided protection for Westwood, toward which they were heading. Nothing much was happening on that frequency. A family dispute. A fender-bender at the corner of Westwood Boulevard and Wilshire. A suspicious man in a parked car on a quiet residential street off Hilgarde had attracted attention and needed checking out.

In most of the city's other sixteen police divisions, the night was far less safe and peaceful than it was in privileged Westwood. In the Seventy-seventh, Newton, and Southwest divisions, which served the black community south of the Santa Monica Freeway, none of the mid-watch patrol officers would be bored; in their baliwicks the night was jumping. On the east side of town, in the Mexican-American neighborhoods, the gangs would continue to give a bad name to the vast majority of law-abiding Chicano citizens. By the time the mid-watch went off duty at three o'clock—three hours after the morning watch came on line—there would be several ugly incidents of gang violence on the east side, a few punks stabbing other punks, maybe a shooting and a death or two as the macho maniacs tried to prove their manhood in the wearisome, stupid, but timeless blood ceremonies they had been performing with Latin passion for generations. To the northwest, on the far side of the hills, the affluent valley kids were drinking too damned much whiskey, smoking too much pot, snorting too much cocaine—and subsequently ramming their cars and vans and motorcycles into one another at ghastly speeds and with tiresome regularity.

As Frank drove past the entrance to Bel Air Estates and started up a hill toward the UCLA campus, the Westwood scene suddenly got lively. Communications put out a woman-in-trouble call. Information was sketchy. Apparently, it was an attempted rape and assault with a deadly weapon. It was not clear if the assailant was still on the premises. Shots had been fired, but Communications had been unable to ascertain from the complainant whether the gun belonged to her or the assailant. Likewise, they didn't know if anyone was hurt.

"Have to go in blind," Tony said.

"That address is just a couple of blocks from here," Frank said.

"We could be there in a minute."

"Probably a lot faster than the patrol car."

"Want to assist?"

"Sure."

"I'll call in and tell them."

Tony picked up the microphone as Frank hung a hard left at the first intersection. A block later they turned left again, and Frank accelerated as much as he dared along the narrow, tree-flanked street.

Tony's heart accelerated with the car. He felt an old excitement, a cold hard knot of fear in his guts.

He remembered Parker Hitchison, a particularly quirky, morose, and humorless partner he had endured for a short while during his second year as a patrol officer, long before he won his detective's badge. Every time they answered a call, every damned time, whether it was a Code Three emergency or just a frightened cat stuck in a tree, Parker Hitchison sighed mournfully and said, "Now, we die." It was weird and decidedly unsettling. Over and over again on every shift, night after night, with sincere and unflagging pessimism, he said it—"Now we die"—until Tony was almost crazy.

Hitchison's funereal voice and those three somber words still haunted him in moments like this.

Now we die?

Frank wheeled around another corner, nearly clipping a black BMW that was parked too close to the intersection. The tires squealed, and the sedan shimmied, and Frank said, "That address ought to be right around here somewhere."

Tony squinted at the shadowy houses that were only partly illuminated by the streetlamps. "There it is, I think," he said, pointing.

It was a large neo-Spanish house set well back from the street on a spacious lot. Red tile roof. Cream-colored stucco. Leaded windows. Two big wrought-iron carriage lamps, one on each side of the front door.

Frank parked in the circular driveway.

They got out of the unmarked sedan.

Tony reached under his jacket and slipped the service revolver out of his shoulder holster.

After Hilary had finished crying at her desk in the study, she had decided, in a daze, to go upstairs and make herself presentable before she reported the assault to the police. Her hair had been in complete disarray, her dress torn, her pantyhose shredded and hanging from her legs in ludicrous loops and tangles. She didn't know how quickly the reporters would arrive once the word had gotten on the police radio, but she had no doubt that they would show up sooner or later. She was something of a public figure, having written two hit films and having received an Academy Award nomination two years ago for her *Arizona Shifty Pete* screenplay. She treasured her privacy and preferred to avoid the press if at all possible, but she knew that she would have little choice but to make a statement and answer a few questions about what had happened to her this night. It was the wrong kind of publicity. It was embarrassing. Being the victim in a case like this was always humiliating. Although it should make her an object of sympathy and concern, it actually would make her look like a fool, a patsy just waiting to be pushed around. She had successfully defended herself against Frye, but that would not matter to the sensation seekers. In the unfriendly glare of the television lights and in the flat gray newspaper photos, she would look weak. The merciless American public would wonder why she had let Frye into her house. They would speculate that she had been raped and that her story of fending him off was just a coverup. Some of them would be certain that she had invited him in and had asked to be raped. Most of the sympathy she received would be shot through with morbid curiosity. The only thing she could control was her appearance when the newsmen arrived. She simply could not allow herself to be photographed in the pitiable, disheveled state in which Bruno Frye had left her.

As she washed her face and combed her hair and changed into a silk robe that belted at the waist, she was not aware that these actions would damage her credibility with the police, later. She didn't realize that, in making herself presentable, she was actually setting herself up as a target for at least one policeman's suspicion and scorn, as well as for charges of being a liar.

Although she thought she was in command of herself, Hilary got the shakes again as she finished changing clothes. Her legs turned to jelly, and she was forced to lean against the closet door for a minute.

Nightmarish images crowded her mind, vivid flashes of unsummoned memories. At first, she saw Frye coming at her with a knife, grinning like a death's head, but then he changed, melted into another shape, another identity, and he became her father, Earl Thomas, and then it was Earl who was coming at her, drunk and angry, cursing, taking swipes at her with his big hard hands. She shook her head and drew deep breaths and, with an effort, banished the vision.

But she could not stop shaking.

She imagined that she heard strange noises in another room of the house. A part of her knew that she was merely imagining it, but another part was sure that she could hear Frye returning for her.

By the time she ran to the phone and dialed the police, she was in no condition to give the calm and reasoned report she had planned. The events of the past hour had affected her far more profoundly than she had thought at first, and recovering from the shock might take days, even weeks.

After she hung up the receiver, she felt better, just knowing help was on the way. As she went downstairs, she said aloud, "Stay calm. Just stay calm. You're Hilary Thomas. You're tough. Tough as nails. You aren't scared. Not ever. Everything will be okay." It was the same litany that she had repeated as a child so many nights in that Chicago apartment. By the time she reached the first door, she had begun to get a grip on herself.

She was standing in the foyer, staring out the narrow leaded window beside the door, when a car stopped in the driveway. Two men got out of it. Although they had not come with sirens blaring and red lights flashing, she knew they were the police, and she unlocked the door, opened it.

The first man onto the front stoop was powerfully built, blond, blue-eyed, and had the hard no-nonsense voice of a cop. He had a gun in his right hand. "Police. Who're you?"

"Thomas," she said. "Hilary Thomas. I'm the one who called."

"This your house?"

"Yes. There was a man—"

A second detective, taller and darker than the first, appeared out of the night and interrupted her before she could finish the sentence. "Is he on the premises?"

"What?"

"Is the man who assaulted you still here?"

"Oh, no. Gone. He's gone."

"Which way did he go?" the blond man asked.

"Out this door."

"Did he have a car?"

"I don't know."

"Was he armed?"

"No. I mean, yes."

"Which is it?"

"He had a knife. But not now."

"Which way did he run when he left the house?"

"I don't know. I was upstairs. I—"

"How long ago did he leave?" the tall dark one asked.

"Maybe fifteen, maybe twenty minutes ago."

They exchanged a look that she did not understand but which she knew, immediately, was not good for her.

"What took you so long to call it in?" the blond asked.

He was slightly hostile.

She felt she was losing some important advantage that she could not identify.

"At first I was . . . confused," she said. "Hysterical. I needed a few minutes to get myself together."

"Twenty minutes?"

"Maybe it was only fifteen."

Both detectives put away their revolvers.

"We'll need a description," the dark one said.

"I can give you better than that," she said as she stepped aside to let them enter. "I can give you a name."

"A name?"

"His name. I know him," she said. "The man who attacked me, I know who he is."

The two detectives gave each other that look again.

She thought: *What have I done wrong?*

Hilary Thomas was one of the most beautiful women Tony had ever seen. She appeared to have a few drops of Indian blood. Her hair was long and thick, darker than his own, a glossy raven-black. Her eyes were dark, too, the whites as clear as pasteurized cream. Her flawless complexion was a light milky bronze shade, probably largely the result of carefully measured time in the California sun. If her face was a bit long, that was balanced by the size of her eyes (enormous) and by the perfect shape of her patrician nose, and by the almost obscene fullness of her lips. Hers was an erotic face, but an intelligent and kind face as well, the face of a woman capable of great tenderness and compassion. There was also pain in that countenance, especially in those fascinating eyes, the kind of pain that came from experience, knowledge; and Tony expected that it was not merely the pain she'd suffered that night; some of it went back a long, long time.

She sat on one end of the brushed corduroy sofa in the book-lined study, and Tony sat on the other end. They were alone.

Frank was in the kitchen, talking on the phone to a desk man at headquarters.

Upstairs, two uniformed patrolmen, Whitlock and Farmer, were digging bullets out of the walls.

There was not a fingerprint man in the house because, according to the complainant, the intruder had worn gloves.

"What's he doing now?" Hilary Thomas asked.

"Who?"

"Lieutenant Howard."

"He's calling headquarters and asking someone to get in touch with the sheriff's office up there in Napa County, where Frye lives."

"Why?"

"Well, for one thing, maybe the sheriff can find out how Frye got to L.A."

"What's it matter how he got here?" she asked. "The important thing is that he's here and he's got to be found and stopped."

"If he flew down," Tony said, "it doesn't matter much at all. But if Frye drove to L.A., the sheriff up in Napa County might be able to find out what car he used. With a description of the vehicle and a license number, we've got a better chance of nailing him before he gets too far."

She considered that for a moment, then said, "Why did Lieutenant Howard go to the kitchen? Why didn't he just use the phone in here?"

"I guess he wanted you to have a few minutes of peace and quiet," Tony said uneasily.

"I think he just didn't want me to hear what he was saying."

"Oh, no. He was only—"

"You know, I have the strangest feeling," she said, interrupting him. "I feel like I'm the suspect instead of the victim."

"You're just tense," he said. "Understandably tense."

"It isn't that. It's something about the way you're acting toward me. Well . . . not so much you as him."

"Frank can seem cool at times," Tony said. "But he's a good detective."

"He thinks I'm lying."

Tony was surprised by her perspicacity. He shifted uncomfortably on the sofa. "I'm sure he doesn't think any such thing."

"He does," she insisted. "And I don't understand why." Her eyes fixed on his. "Level with me. Come on. What is it? What did I say wrong?"

He sighed. "You're a perceptive lady."

"I'm a writer. It's part of my job to observe things a little more closely than most people do. And I'm also persistent. So you might as well answer my question and get me off your back."

"One of the things that bothers Lieutenant Howard is the fact that you know the man who attacked you."

"So?"

"This is awkward," he said unhappily.

"Let me hear it anyway."

"Well . . ." He cleared his throat. "Conventional police wisdom says that if the complainant in a rape or an attempted rape knows the accused, there's a pretty good chance that she contributed to the crime by enticing the accused to one degree or another."

"Bullshit!"

She got up, went to the desk, and stood with her back to him for a minute. He could see that she was struggling to maintain her composure. What he had said had made her extremely angry.

When she turned to him at last, her face was flushed. She said, "This is horrible. It's outrageous. Every time a woman is raped by someone she knows, you actually believe she asked for it."

"No. Not every time."

"But *most* of the time, that's what you think," she said angrily.

"No."

She glared at him. "Let's stop playing semantical games. You believe it about *me*. You believe I enticed him."

"No," Tony said. "I merely explained what conventional police wisdom is in a case like this. I didn't say that I put much faith in conventional police wisdom. I don't. But Lieutenant Howard does. You asked me about him. You wanted to know what he was thinking, and I told you."

She frowned. "Then . . . you believe me?"

"Is there any reason I shouldn't?"

"It happened exactly the way I said."

"All right."

She stared at him. "Why?"

"Why what?"

"Why do you believe me when he doesn't?"

"I can think of only two reasons for a woman to bring false rape charges against a man. And neither of them makes any sense in your case."

She leaned against the desk, folded her arms in front of her, cocked her head, and regarded him with interest. "What reasons?"

"Number one, he has money, and she doesn't. She wants to put him on the spot, hoping she can pry some sort of big settlement out of him in return for dropping the charges."

"But I've got money."

"Apparently, you've got quite a lot of it," he said, looking around admiringly at the beautifully furnished room.

"What's the other reason?"

"A man and a woman are having an affair, but he leaves her for another lady. She feels hurt, rejected, scorned. She wants to get even with him. She wants to punish him, so she accuses him of rape."

"How can you be sure that doesn't fit me?" she asked.

"I've seen both your movies, so I figure I know a little bit about the way your mind works. You're a very intelligent woman, Miss Thomas. I don't think you could be foolish or petty or spiteful enough to send a man to prison just because he hurt your feelings."

She studied him intently.

He felt himself being weighed and judged.

Obviously convinced that he was not the enemy, she returned to the couch and sat down in a swish of dark-blue silk. The robe molded to her, and he tried not to show how aware he was of her strikingly female lines.

She said, "I'm sorry I was snappish."

"You weren't," he assured her. "Conventional police wisdom makes me angry, too."

"I suppose if this gets into court, Frye's attorney will try to make the jury believe that I enticed the son of a bitch."

"You can count on it."

"Will they believe him?"

"They often do."

"But he wasn't just going to rape me. He was going to *kill* me."

"You'll need proof of that."

"The broken knife upstairs—"

"Can't be connected to him," Tony said. "It won't be covered with his prints. And it's just a common kitchen knife. There's no way we can trace it to the point of purchase and tie it to Bruno Frye."

"But he looked so crazy. He's . . . unbalanced. The jury would see that. Hell, you'll see it when you arrest him. There probably won't even be a trial. He'll probably just be put away."

"If he's a lunatic, he knows how to pass for normal," Tony said. "After all, until tonight, he's been regarded as an especially responsible and upstanding citizen. When you visited his winery near St. Helena, you didn't realize you were in the company of a madman, did you?"

"No."

"Neither will the jury."

She closed her eyes, pinched the bridge of her nose. "So he's probably going to get away clean."

"I'm sorry to say there's a good chance that he will."

"And then he'll come back for me."

"Maybe."

"Jesus."

"You wanted the unvarnished truth."

She opened her lovely eyes. "I did, yes. And thank you for giving it to me." She even managed a smile.

He smiled back at her. He wanted to take her in his arms, hold her close, comfort her, kiss her, make love to her. But all he could do was sit on his end of the couch like a good officer of the law and smile his witless smile and say, "Sometimes it's a lousy system."

"What are the other reasons?"

"Excuse me?"

"You said *one* reason Lieutenant Howard didn't believe me was because I knew the assailant. What are the other reasons? What else makes him think I'm lying?"

Tony was about to answer her when Frank Howard walked into the room.

"Okay," Frank said brusquely. "We've got the sheriff looking into it up there in Napa County, trying to get a line on when and how this Frye character left town. We also have an APB out, based on your description, Miss Thomas. Now, I went to the car and got my clipboard and this crime report form." He held up the rectangular piece of masonite and the single sheet of paper affixed to it, took a pen from his inside coat pocket. "I want you to walk Lieutenant Clemenza and me through your entire experience just once more, so I can write it all down precisely in your own words. Then we can get out of your way."

She led them to the foyer and began her story with a detailed recounting of Bruno Frye's surprise appearance from the coat closet. Tony and Frank followed her to the overturned sofa, then upstairs to the bedroom, asking questions as they went. During the thirty minutes they needed to complete the form, as she reenacted the events of the evening, her voice now and then became tremulous, and again Tony had the urge to hold and soothe her.

Just as the crime report was completed, a few newsmen arrived. She went downstairs to meet them.

At the same time, Frank got a call from headquarters and took it on the bedroom phone.

Tony went downstairs to wait for Frank and to see how Hilary Thomas would deal with the reporters.

She handled them expertly. Pleading weariness and a need for privacy, she did not allow them into her house. She stepped outside, onto the stone walk, and they gathered in front of her. A television news crew had arrived, complete with a minicam and the standard actor-reporter, one of those men who had gotten his job largely because of his chiseled features and penetrating eyes and deep fatherly voice. Intelligence and journalistic ability had little to do with being a performer in television news; indeed, too much of either quality could be seriously disadvantageous; for optimum success, the career-minded television reporter had to think much the same way that his program was structured—in three- and four- and five-minute segments, never dwelling longer than that on any one subject, and never exploring anything at great depth. A newspaperman and his photographer, not so pretty as the television man and a bit rumpled, were also present. Hilary Thomas fielded their questions with ease, answering only those that she wanted to answer, smoothly turning away all of those that were too personal or impertinent.

The thing that Tony found most interesting about her performance was the way she kept the news people out of the house and out of her most private thoughts without offending them. That was no easy trick. There were many excellent reporters who could dig for the truth and write fine stories without violating the subject's rights and dignity; but there were just as many of the other kind, the boars and the con men. With the rise of what *The Washington Post* glowingly referred to as "advocacy journalism"—the despicable slanting of a story to support the reporter's and the editor's personal political and social beliefs—some members of the press, the con men and the boars, had gone on a power trip of unprecedented irresponsibility. If you bristled at a reporter's manner and methods or at his obvious bias, if you dared to offend him, he might decide to use his pen to make you look like a fool, a liar, or a criminal; and he would see himself as the champion of enlightenment in a battle against evil. Clearly, Hilary was aware of the danger, for she dealt masterfully with them. She answered more questions than not, stroked the news people, accorded them respect, charmed them, and even smiled for the cameras. She didn't say that she knew her assailant. She didn't mention the name Bruno Frye. She didn't want the media speculating about her previous relationship with the man who had attacked her.

Her awareness forced Tony to reevaluate her. He already knew that she was talented and intelligent; now he saw she was also shrewd. She was the most intriguing woman he had encountered in a long time.

She was nearly finished with the reporters, carefully extricating herself from them, when Frank Howard came down the stairs and stepped to the doorway, where Tony stood in the cool night breeze. Frank watched Hilary Thomas as she answered a reporter's question, and he scowled fiercely. "I've got to talk to her."

"What did headquarters want?" Tony asked.

"That's what I've got to talk to her about," Frank said grimly. He had decided to be tight-lipped. He wasn't going to reveal his information until he was damned good and ready. That was another of his irritating habits.

"She's almost through with them," Tony said.

"Strutting and preening herself."

"Not at all."

"Sure. She's loving every minute of it."

"She handles them well," Tony said, "but she really doesn't seem to enjoy it."

"Movie people," Frank said scornfully. "They need that attention and publicity like you and I need food."

The reporters were only eight feet away, and although they were noisily questioning Hilary Thomas, Tony was afraid they might hear Frank. "Not so loud," he said.

"I don't care if they know what I think," Frank said. "I'll even give them a statement about publicity hounds who make up stories to get newspaper coverage."

"Are you saying she made this all up? That's ridiculous."

"You'll see," Frank said.

Tony was suddenly uneasy. Hilary Thomas brought out the chivalrous knight in him; he wanted to protect her. He didn't want to see her hurt, but Frank apparently had something decidedly unpleasant to discuss with her.

"I've got to talk to her now," Frank said. "I'll be damned if I'll stand around cooling my heels while she sucks up to the press."

Tony put a hand on his partner's shoulder. "Wait here. I'll get her."

Frank was angry about whatever headquarters had told him, and Tony knew the reporters would recognize that anger and be irritated by it. If they thought there was progress in the investigation—especially if it looked to be a juicy bit, a scandalous twist—they would hang around all night, pestering everybody. And if Frank actually had uncovered unflattering information about Hilary Thomas, the press would make headlines out of it, trumpet it with that unholy glee they reserved for choice dirt. Later, if Frank's information proved inaccurate, the television people most likely wouldn't make any correction at all, and the newspaper retraction, if there ever was one, would be four lines on page twenty of the second section. Tony wanted her to have an opportunity to refute whatever Frank might say, a chance to clear herself before the whole thing became a tawdry media carnival.

He went to the reporters and said, "Excuse me, ladies and gentlemen, but I believe Miss Thomas has already told you more than she's told us. You've squeezed her dry. Now, my partner and I were scheduled to go off duty a few hours ago, and we're awfully tired. We've put in a hard day, beating up innocent suspects and collecting bribes, so if you would let us finish with Miss Thomas, we would be most grateful."

They laughed appreciatively and began to ask questions of him. He answered a few of them, giving out nothing more than Hilary Thomas had done. Then he hustled the woman into her house and closed the door.

Frank was in the foyer. His anger had not subsided. He looked as if steam should be coming from his ears. "Miss Thomas, I have some more questions to ask you."

"Okay."

"Quite a few questions. It'll take a while."

"Well . . . shall we go into the study?"'

Frank Howard led the way.

To Tony, Hilary said, "What's happening?"

He shrugged. "I don't know. I wish I did."

Frank had reached the center of the living room. He stopped and looked back at her. "Miss Thomas?"

She and Tony followed him into the study.

Hilary sat on the brushed corduroy couch, crossed her legs, straightened her silk robe. She was nervous, wondering why Lieutenant Howard disliked her so intensely. His manner was cold. He was filled with an icy anger that made his eyes look like cross sections of two steel rods. She thought of Bruno Frye's strange eyes, and she could not suppress a shiver. Lieutenant Howard glowered at her. She felt like the accused at a trial during the Spanish Inquisition. She would not have been terribly surprised if Howard had pointed a finger and charged her with witchcraft.

The nice one, Lieutenant Clemenza, sat in the brown armchair. The warm amber light from the yellow-shaded floor lamp fell over him and cast soft shadows around his mouth and nose and deeply set eyes, giving him an even gentler and kinder aspect than he ordinarily possessed. She wished he was the one asking questions, but at least for the moment, his role was evidently that of an observer.

Lieutenant Howard stood over her, looked down at her with unconcealed contempt. She realized that he was trying to make her look away in shame or defeat, playing some police version of a childish staring contest. She looked back at him unwaveringly until he turned from her and began to pace.

"Miss Thomas," Howard said, "there are several things about your story that trouble me."

"I know," she said. "It bothers you that I know the assailant. You figure I might have enticed him. Isn't that conventional police wisdom?"

He blinked in surprise but quickly recovered. "Yes. That's one thing. And there's also the fact that we can't find out how he got into this house. Officer Whitlock and Officer Farmer have been from one end of the place to the other, twice, three times, and they can't find any sign of forced entry. No broken windows. No smashed or jimmied locks."

"So you think I let him in," she said.

"I certainly must consider it."

"Well, consider this. When I was up there in Napa County a few weeks ago, doing research for a screenplay, I lost my keys at his winery. House keys, car keys—"

"You drove all the way up there?"

"No. I flew. But all my keys were on the same ring. Even the keys for the rental car I picked up in Santa Rosa; they were on a flimsy chain, and I was afraid I'd lose them, so I slipped them on my own key ring. I never found them. The rental car people had to send out another set. And when I got back to L.A., I had to have a locksmith let me into my house and make new keys for me."

"You didn't have the locks changed?"

"It seemed like a needless expense," she said. "The keys I lost didn't have any identification on them. Whoever found them wouldn't know where to use them."

"And it didn't occur to you they might have been stolen?" Lieutenant Howard asked.

"No."

"But now you think Bruno Frye took the keys with the intention of coming here to rape and kill you."

"Yes."

"What does he have against you?"

"I don't know."

"Is there any reason he should be angry with you?"

"No."

"Any reason he should hate you?"

"I hardly know him."

"It's an awfully long way for him to come."

"I know."

"Hundreds of miles."

"Look, he's crazy. And crazy people do crazy things."

Lieutenant Howard stopped pacing, stood in front of her, glared down like one of the faces on a totem pole of angry gods. "Doesn't it seem odd to you that a crazy man would be able to conceal his madness so well at home, that he would have the iron control needed to keep it all bottled up until he was off in a strange city?"

"Of course it seems odd to me," she said. "It's weird. But it's true."

"Did Bruno Frye have an opportunity to steal those keys?"

"Yes. One of the winery foremen took me on a special tour. We had to clamber up scaffolding, between fermentation vats, between storage barrels, through a lot of tight places. I couldn't have easily taken my purse with me. It would have been in my way. So I left it in the main house."

"Frye's house."

"Yes."

He was crackling with energy, supercharged. He began to pace again, from the couch to the windows, from the windows to the bookshelves, then back to the couch again, his broad shoulders drawn up, head thrust forward.

Lieutenant Clemenza smiled at her, but she was not reassured.

"Will anyone at the winery remember you losing your keys?" Lieutenant Howard asked.

"I guess so. Sure. I spent at least half an hour looking for them. I asked around, hoping someone might have seen them."

"But no one had."

"That's right."

"Where did you think you might have left them?"

"I thought they were in my purse."

"That was the last place you remembered putting them?"

"Yes. I drove the rental car to the winery, and I was sure I'd put the keys in my purse when I'd parked."

"Yet when you couldn't find them, you never thought they might have been stolen?"

"No. Why would someone steal my keys and not my money? I had a couple hundred dollars in my wallet."

"Another thing that bothers me. After you drove Frye out of the house at gunpoint, why did you take to long to call us?"

"I didn't take long."

"Twenty minutes."

"At most."

"When you've just been attacked and nearly killed by a maniac with a knife, twenty minutes is a hell of a long time to wait. Most people want to get hold of the police right away. They want us on the scene in ten seconds, and they get furious if it takes us a few minutes to get there."

She glanced at Clemenza, then at Howard, then at her fingers, which were tightly laced, white-knuckled. She sat up straight, squared her shoulders. "I . . . I guess I . . . broke down." It was a difficult and shameful admission for her. She had always prided herself on her strength. "I went to that desk and sat down and began to dial the police number and . . . then . . . I just . . . I cried. I started to cry . . . and I couldn't stop for a while."

"You cried for twenty minutes?"

"No. Of course not. I'm really not the crying type. I mean, I don't fall apart easily."

"How long did it take you to get control of yourself?"

"I don't know for sure."

"Fifteen minutes?"

"Not that long."

"Ten minutes?"

"Maybe five."

"When you regained control of yourself, why didn't you call us then? You were sitting right there by the phone."

"I went upstairs to wash my face and change my clothes," she said. "I've already told you about that."

"I know," he said. "I remember. Primping yourself for the press."

"No," she said, beginning to get angry with him. "I wasn't 'primping' my-self. I just thought I should—"

"That's the fourth thing that makes me wonder about your story," Howard said, interrupting her. "It absolutely amazes me. I mean, after you were almost raped and murdered, after you broke down and wept, while you were still afraid that Frye might come back here and try to finish the job he started, you nevertheless took time out to make yourself look presentable. Amazing."

"Excuse me," Lieutenant Clemenza said, leaning forward in the brown armchair. "Frank, I know you've got something, and I know you're leading up to it. I don't want to spoil your rhythm or anything. But I don't think we can make assumptions about Miss Thomas's honesty and integrity based on how long she took to call in the complaint. We both know that people sometimes go into a kind of shock after an experience like this. They don't always do the rational thing. Miss Thomas's behavior isn't all that peculiar."

She almost thanked Lieutenant Clemenza for what he had said, but she sensed a low-grade antagonism between the two detectives, and she did not want to fan that smoldering fire.

"Are you telling me to get on with it?" Howard asked Clemenza.

"All I'm saying is, it's getting late, and we're all very tired," Clemenza told him.

"You admit her story's riddled with holes?"

"I don't know that I'd put it quite like that," said Clemenza.

"How would you put it?" Howard asked.

"Let's just say there are some parts of it that don't make sense yet."

Howard scowled at him for a moment, then nodded. "Okay. Good enough. I was only trying to establish that there are at least four big problems with her story. If you agree, then I'll get on with the rest of it." He turned to Hilary. "Miss Thomas, I'd like to hear your description of the assailant just once more."

"Why? You've got his name."

"Indulge me."

She couldn't understand where he was going with his questioning. She knew he was trying to set a trap for her, but she hadn't the faintest idea what sort of trap or what it would do to her if she got caught in it. "All right. Just once more. Bruno Frye is tall, about six-four—"

"No names, please."

"What?"

"Describe the assailant without using any names."

"But I know his name," she said slowly, patiently.

"Humor me," he said humorlessly.

She sighed and settled back against the sofa, feigning boredom. She didn't want him to know that he was rattling her. What the hell was he after? "The man who attacked me," she said, "was about six-feet-four, and he weighed maybe two hundred and forty pounds. Very muscular."

"Race?" Howard asked.

"He was white."

"Complexion?"

"Fair."

"Any scars or moles?"

"No."

"Tattoos?"

"Are you kidding?"

"Tattoos?"

"No."

"Any other identifying marks?"

"No."

"Was he crippled or deformed in any way?"

"He's a big healthy son of a bitch," she said crossly.

"Color of hair?"

"Dirty blond."

"Long or short?"

"Medium length."

"Eyes?"

"Yes."

"What?"

"Yes, he had eyes."

"Miss Thomas—"

"Okay, okay."

"This is serious."

"He had blue eyes. An unusual shade of blue-gray."

"Age?"

"Around forty."

"Any distinguishing characteristics?"

"Like what?"

"You mentioned something about his voice."

"That's right. He had a deep voice. It rumbled. A gravelly voice. Deep and gruff and scratchy."

"All right," Lieutenant Howard said, rocking slightly on his heels, evidently pleased with himself. "We have a good description of the assailant. Now, describe Bruno Frye for me."

"I just did."

"No, no. We're pretending that you didn't know the man who attacked you. We're playing this little game to humor me. Remember? You just described your assailant, a man without a name. Now, I want you to describe Bruno Frye for me."

She turned to Lieutenant Clemenza. "Is this really necessary?" she asked exasperatedly.

Clemenza said, "Frank, can you hurry this along?"

"Look, I've got a point I'm trying to make," Lieutenant Howard said. "I'm building up to it the best way I know how. Besides, *she's* the one slowing it down."

He turned to her, and again she had the creepy feeling she was on trial in another century and that Howard was some religious inquisitionist. If Clemenza would permit it, Howard would simply take hold of her and shake until she gave the answers he wanted, whether or not they were the truth.

"Miss Thomas," he said, "if you'll just answer all of my questions, I'll be finished in a few minutes. Now, will you describe Bruno Frye?"

Disgustedly, she said, "Six-four, two hundred and forty pounds, muscular, blond, blue-gray eyes, about forty years old, no scars, no deformities, no tattoos, a deep gravelly voice."

Frank Howard was smiling. It was not a friendly smile. "Your description of the assailant and Bruno Frye are exactly the same. Not a single discrepancy. Not one. And of course, you've told us that they were, in fact, one and the same man."

His line of questioning seemed ridiculous, but there was surely a purpose to it. He wasn't stupid. She sensed that already she had stepped into the trap, even though she could not see it.

"Do you want to change your mind?" Howard asked. "Do you want to say that perhaps there's a small chance it was someone else, someone who only resembled Frye?"

"I'm not an idiot," Hilary said. "It was him."

"There wasn't even maybe some slight difference between your assailant and Frye? Some little thing?" he persisted.

"No."

"Not even the shape of his nose or the line of his jaw?" Howard asked.

"Not even that."

"You're certain that Frye and your assailant shared precisely the same hairline, exactly the same cheekbones, the same chin?"

"Yes."

"Are you positive beyond a shadow of a doubt that it was Bruno Frye who was here tonight?"

"Yes."

"Would you swear to that in court?"

"*Yes, yes, yes!*" she said, tired of his badgering.

"Well, then. Well, well. I'm afraid if you testified to that effect, you'd wind up in jail yourself. Perjury's a crime."

"What? What do you mean?"

He grinned at her. His grin was even more unfriendly than his smile. "Miss Thomas, what I mean is—you're a liar."

Hilary was so stunned by the bluntness of the accusation, by the boldness of it, so disconcerted by the ugly snarl in his voice, that she could not immediately think of a response. She didn't even know what he meant.

Lieutenant Clemenza got out of the brown armchair and said, "Frank, are we handling this right?"

"Oh, yeah," Howard said. "We're handling it exactly right. While she was out there talking to the reporters and posing so prettily for the photographers, I got a call from headquarters. They heard back from the Napa County Sheriff."

"Already?"

"Oh, yeah. His name's Peter Laurenski. Sheriff Laurenski looked into things for us up there at Frye's vineyard, just like we asked him to, and you know what he found? He found that Mr. Bruno Frye didn't come to Los Angeles. Bruno Frye never left home. Bruno Frye is up there in Napa County right now, right this minute, in his own house, harmless as a fly."

"Impossible!" Hilary said, pushing up from the sofa.

Howard shook his head. "Give up, Miss Thomas. Frye told Sheriff Laurenski that he *intended* to come to L.A. today for a week-long stay. Just a short vacation. But he didn't manage to clear off his desk in time, so he cancelled out and stayed home to get caught up on his work."

"The sheriff's wrong!" she said. "He couldn't have talked to Bruno Frye."

"Are you calling the sheriff a liar?" Lieutenant Howard asked.

"He . . . he must have talked to someone who was covering for Frye," Hilary said, knowing how hopelessly implausible that sounded.

"No," Howard said. "Sheriff Laurenski talked to Frye himself."

"Did he see him? Did he actually *see* Frye?" she demanded. "Or did he only talk to someone on the phone, someone claiming to be Frye?"

"I don't know if it was a face to face chat or a phone conversation," Howard said. "But remember, Miss Thomas, you told us about Frye's unique voice. Extremely deep. Scratchy. A guttural, gravelly voice. Are you saying someone could have easily imitated it on the phone?"

"If Sheriff Laurenski doesn't know Frye well enough, he might be fooled by a bad imitation. He—"

"It's a small county up there. A man like Bruno Frye, an important man like that, is known to just about everyone. And the sheriff has known him *very* well for more than twenty years," Howard said triumphantly.

Lieutenant Clemenza looked pained. Although she did not care much what Howard thought of her, it was important to Hilary that Clemenza believed the story she had told. The flicker of doubt in his eyes upset her as much as Howard's bullying.

She turned her back on them, went to the mullioned window that looked out on the rose garden, tried to control her anger, couldn't suppress it, and faced them again. She spoke to Howard, furious, emphasizing every word by pounding her fist against the window table: "Bruno—Frye—was—here!" The vase full of roses rocked, toppled off the table, bounced on the thick carpet, scattering flowers and water. She ignored it. "What about the sofa he overturned? What about the broken porcelain I threw at him and the bullets I fired at him? What about the broken knife he left behind? What about the torn dress, the pantyhose?"

"It could be just clever stage dressing," Howard said. "You could have done it all yourself, faked it up to support your story."

"That's absurd!"

Clemenza said, "Miss Thomas, maybe it really was someone else. Someone who looked a lot like Frye."

Even if she had wanted to retreat in that fashion, she could not have done it. By forcing her to repeatedly describe the man who attacked her, by drawing several assurances from her that the assailant had been none other than Bruno Frye, Lieutenant Howard had made it difficult if not impossible for her to take the way out that Clemenza was offering. Anyway, she didn't want to back up and reconsider. She knew she was right. "It was Frye," she said adamantly. "Frye and nobody else but Frye. I didn't make the whole thing up. I didn't fire bullets into the walls. I didn't overturn the sofa and tear up my own clothes. For God's sake, why would I do a crazy thing like that? What reason could I possibly have for a charade of that sort?"

"I've got some ideas," Howard said. "I figure you've known Bruno Frye for a long time, and you—"

"I told you. I only met him three weeks ago."

"You've told us other things that turned out not to be true," Howard said. "So I think you knew Frye for years, or at least for quite a while, and the two of you were having an affair—"

"No!"

"—and for some reason, he threw you over. Maybe he just got tired of you. Maybe it was another woman. Something. So I figure you didn't go up to his winery to research one of your screenplays, like you said. I think you went up there just to get together with him again. You wanted to smooth things over, kiss and make up—"

"No."

"—but he wasn't having any of it. He turned you away again. But while you were there, you found out that he was coming to L.A. for a little vacation. So you made up your mind to get even with him. You figured he probably wouldn't have anything planned his first night in town, probably just a quiet dinner alone and early to bed. You were pretty sure he wouldn't have anyone to vouch for him later on, if the cops wanted to know his every move that night. So you decided to set him up for a rape charge."

"Damn you, this is disgusting!"

"It backfired on you," Howard said. "Frye changed his plans. He didn't even come to L.A. So now you're caught in the lie."

"He was here!" She wanted to take the detective by the throat and choke him until he understood. "Look, I have one or two friends who know me well enough to know if I'd been having an affair. I'll give you their names. Go see them. They'll tell you I didn't have anything going with Bruno Frye. Hell, they might even tell you I haven't had anything going with anyone for a while. I've been too busy to have much of a private life. I work long hours. I haven't had a lot of time for romance. And I sure as hell haven't had time to carry on with a lover who lives at the other end of the state. Talk to my friends. They'll tell you."

"Friends are notoriously unreliable witnesses," Howard said. "Besides, it might have been that one affair you kept all to yourself, the secret little fling. Face it, Miss Thomas, you painted yourself into a corner. The facts are these. You say Frye was in this house tonight. But the sheriff says he was up there, in his own house, as of thirty minutes ago. Now, St. Helena is over four hundred miles by air, over five hundred by car. He simply could not have gotten home that fast. And he could not have been in two places at once because, in case you haven't heard, that's a serious violation of the laws of physics."

Lieutenant Clemenza said, "Frank, maybe you should let me finish up with Miss Thomas."

"What's to finish? It's over, done, kaput." Howard pointed an accusing finger at her. "You're damned lucky, Miss Thomas. If Frye had come to L.A.

and this had gotten into court, you'd have committed perjury. You might have wound up in jail. You're also lucky that there's no sure way for us to punish someone like you for wasting our time like this."

"I don't know that we've wasted our time," Clemenza said softly.

"Like hell we haven't." Howard glared at her. "I'll tell you one thing: If Bruno Frye wants to pursue a libel suit, I sure to God will testify for him." Then he turned and walked away from her, toward the study door.

Lieutenant Clemenza didn't make any move to leave and obviously had something more to say to her, but she didn't like having the other one walk out before some important questions were answered. "Wait a minute," she said.

Howard stopped and looked back at her. "Yeah?"

"What now? What are you going to do about my complaint?" she said.

"Are you serious?"

"Yes."

"I'm going to the car, cancel that APB on Bruno Frye, then call it a day. I'm going home and drink a couple cold bottles of Coors."

"You aren't going to leave me here alone? What if he comes back?"

"Oh, Christ," Howard said. "Will you please drop the act?"

She took a few steps toward him. "No matter what you think, no matter what the Napa County Sheriff says, I'm not putting on an act. Will you at least leave one of those uniformed men for an hour or so, until I can get a locksmith to replace the locks on my doors?"

Howard shook his head. "No. I'll be damned if I'll waste more police time and taxpayers' money to provide you with protection you don't need. Give up. It's all over. You lost. Face it, Miss Thomas." He walked out of the room.

Hilary went to the brown armchair and sat down. She was exhausted, confused, and scared.

Clemenza said, "I'll make sure Officers Whitlock and Farmer stay with you until the locks have been changed."

She looked up at him. "Thank you."

He shrugged. He was noticeably uncomfortable. "I'm sorry there's not much more I can do."

"I didn't make up the whole thing," she said.

"I believe you."

"Frye really was here tonight," she said.

"I don't doubt that someone was here, but—"

"Not just someone. Frye."

"If you'd reconsider your identification, we could keep working on the case and—"

"It was Frye," she said, not angrily now, just wearily. "It was him and no one else but him."

For a long moment, Clemenza regarded her with interest, and his clear brown eyes were sympathetic. He was a handsome man, but it was not his good looks that most pleased the eye; there was an indescribably warm and gentle quality in his Italian features, a special concern and understanding so visible in his face that she felt he truly cared what happened to her.

He said, "You've had a very rough experience. It's shaken you. That's perfectly understandable. And sometimes, when you go through a shock like this, it distorts your perceptions. Maybe when you've had a chance to calm down, you'll remember things a little . . . differently. I'll stop by sometime tomorrow. Maybe by then you'll have something new to tell me."

"I won't," Hilary said without hesitation. "But thanks for . . . being kind."

She thought he seemed reluctant to leave. But then he was gone, and she was alone in the study.

For a minute or two, she could not find the energy to get out of the armchair. She felt as if she had stepped into a vast pool of quicksand and had expended every bit of her strength in a frantic and futile attempt to escape.

At last she got up, went to the desk, picked up the telephone. She thought of ringing the winery in Napa County, but she realized that would accomplish nothing. She knew only the business office number. She didn't have Frye's home phone listing. Even if his private number was available through information—and that was highly unlikely—she would not gain any satisfaction by dialing it. If she tried calling him at home, only one of two things could happen. One, he wouldn't answer, which would neither prove her story nor disprove what Sheriff Laurenski had said. Two, Frye would answer, surprising her. And then what? She would have to reevaluate the events of the night, face the fact that the man with whom she had fought was someone who resembled Bruno Frye. Or perhaps he didn't look like Frye at all. Maybe her perceptions were so askew that she had perceived a resemblance where there was none. How could you tell when you were losing your grip on reality? How did madness begin? Did it creep up on you, or did it seize you in an instant, without warning? She had to consider the possibility that she was losing her mind because, after all, there was a history of insanity in her family. For more than a decade, one of her fears had been that she would die as her father had died; wild-eyed, raving, incoherent, waving a gun and trying to hold off monsters that were not really there. Like father, like daughter?

"I saw him," she said aloud. "Bruno Frye. In my house. Here. Tonight. I didn't imagine or hallucinate it. I saw him, dammit."

She opened the telephone book to the yellow pages and called a twenty-four-hour-a-day locksmith service.

After he fled Hilary Thomas's house, Bruno Frye drove his smoke-gray Dodge van out of Westwood. He went west and south to Marina Del Rey, a small-craft harbor on the edge of the city, a place of expensive garden apartments, even more expensive condominiums, shops, and unexceptional but lushly decorated restaurants, most with unobstructed views of the sea and the thousands of pleasure boats docked along the man-made channels.

Fog was rolling in along the coast, as if a great cold fire burned upon the ocean. It was thick in some places and thin in others, getting denser all the time.

He tucked the van into an empty corner of a parking lot near one of the docks, and for a minute he just sat there, contemplating his failure. The police would be looking for him, but only for a short while, only until they found out that he had been at his place in Napa County all evening. And even while they were looking for him in the L.A. area, he would not be in much danger, for they wouldn't know what sort of vehicle he was driving. He was sure Hilary Thomas had not seen the van when he left because it was parked three blocks from her house.

Hilary Thomas.

Not her real name, of course.

Katherine. That's who she really was. Katherine.

"Stinking bitch," he said aloud.

She scared him. In the past five years, he had killed her more than twenty times, but she had refused to stay dead. She kept coming back to life, in a new body, with a new name, a new identity, a cleverly constructed new background, but he never failed to recognize Katherine hiding in each new persona. He had encountered her and killed her again and again, but she would not stay dead. She knew how to come back from the grave, and her knowledge terrified him more than he dared let her know. He was frightened of her, but he couldn't let her see that fear, for if she became aware of it, she'd overwhelm and destroy him.

But she can be killed, Frye told himself. I've done it. I've killed her many times and buried many of her bodies in secret graves. I'll kill her again, too. And maybe this time she won't be able to come back.

As soon as it was safe for him to return to her house in Westwood, he would try to kill her again. And this time he planned to perform a number of rituals that he hoped would cancel out her supernatural power of regeneration. He had been reading books about the living dead—vampires and other creatures. Although she was not really any of those things, although she was horrifyingly unique, he believed that some of the methods of extermination that were effective against vampires might work on her as well. Cut out her heart while it was still beating. Drive a wooden stake through it. Cut off her head. Stuff her mouth full of garlic. It would work. Oh, God, it *had* to work.

He left the van and went to a public phone close by. The damp air smelled vaguely of salt, seaweed, and machine oil. Water slapped against the pilings and the hulls of the small yachts, a curiously forlorn sound. Beyond the plexiglas walls of the booth, rank upon rank of masts rose from the tethered boats, like a defoliated forest looming out of the night mist. About the same time that Hilary was calling the police, Frye phoned his own house in Napa County and gave an account of his failed attack on the woman.

The man on the other end of the line listened without interruption, then said, "I'll handle the police."

They spoke for a few minutes, then Frye hung up. Stepping out of the booth, he looked around suspiciously at the darkness and swirling fog. Katherine could not possibly have followed him, but nevertheless, he was afraid she was out there in the gloom, watching, waiting. He was a big man. He should not have been afraid of a woman. But he was. He was afraid of the one who would not die, the one who now called herself Hilary Thomas.

He returned to the van and sat behind the wheel for a few minutes, until he realized that he was hungry. Starving. His stomach rumbled. He hadn't eaten since lunch. He was familiar enough with Marina Del Rey to know there was not a suitable restaurant in the neighborhood. He drove south on the Pacific Coast Highway to Culver Boulevard, then west, then south again on Vista Del Mar. He had to proceed slowly, for the fog was heavy along that route; it threw the van's headlight beams back at him and reduced visibility to thirty feet, so that he felt as if he was driving underwater in a murky phosphorescent sea. Almost twenty minutes after he completed the telephone call to Napa County (and about the same time that Sheriff Laurenski was looking into the case up there in behalf of the L. A. police), Frye found an interesting restaurant on the northern edge of El Segundo. The red and yellow neon sign cut through the fog: GARRIDO'S. It was a Mexican place, but not one of those *norte-americano* chrome and glass outlets serving imitation *comida;* it appeared to be authentically Mexican. He pulled off the road and parked between two hotrods that were equipped with the hydraulic lifts so popular with young Chicano drivers. As he walked around to the entrance, he passed a car bearing a bumper sticker that proclaimed CHICANO POWER. Another one advised everyone to SUPPORT THE FARM WORKERS' UNION. Frye could already taste the enchiladas.

Inside, Garrido's looked more like a bar than a restaurant, but the close warm air was redolent with the odors of a good Mexican kitchen. On the left, a stained and scarred wooden bar ran the length of the big rectangular room. Approximately a dozen dark men and two lovely young señoritas sat on stools or leaned against the bar, most of them chattering in rapid Spanish. The center of the room was taken up by a single row of twelve tables running parallel to the bar, each covered with a red tablecloth. All of the tables were occupied by men and women who laughed and drank a lot as they ate. On the right, against the wall, there were booths with red leatherette upholstery and high backs; Frye sat down in one of them.

The waitress who hustled up to his table was a short woman, almost as wide as she was tall, with a very round and surprisingly pretty face. Raising her voice above Freddie Fender's sweet and plaintive singing, which came from the jukebox, she asked Frye what he wanted and took his order: a double platter of chili verde and two cold bottles of Dos Equis.

He was still wearing leather gloves. He took them off and flexed his hands.

Except for a blonde in a low-cut sweater, who was with a mustachioed Chicano stud, Frye was the only one in Garrido's who didn't have Mexican blood in his veins. He knew some of them were staring at him, but he didn't care.

The waitress brought the beer right away. Frye didn't bother with the glass. He put the bottle to his lips, closed his eyes, tilted his head back, and chugged it down. In less than a minute, he had drained it. He drank the second beer with less haste than he had consumed the first, but it was also gone by the time she brought his dinner. He ordered two more bottles of Dos Equis.

Bruno Frye ate with voracity and total concentration, unwilling or unable to look away from his plate, oblivious of everyone around him, head lowered to receive the food in the fevered manner of a graceless glutton. Making soft animal murmurs of delight, he forked the chili verde into his mouth, gobbled up huge dripping bites of the stuff, one after the other, chewed hard and fast, his cheeks bulging. A plate of warm tortillas was served on the side, and he used those to mop up the delicious sauce. He washed everything down with big gulps of icy beer.

He was already two-thirds finished when the waitress stopped by to ask if the meal was all right, and she quickly realized the question was unnecessary. He looked up at her with eyes that were slightly out of focus. In a thick voice that seemed to come from a distance, he asked for two beef tacos, a couple of cheese enchiladas, rice, refried beans, and two more bottles of beer. Her eyes went wide, but she was too polite to comment on his appetite.

He ate the last of the chili verde before she brought his second order, but he did not rise out of his trance when the plate was clean. Every table had a bowl of taco chips, and he pulled his in front of him. He dipped the chips into the cup of hot sauce that came with them, popped them into his mouth whole, crunched them up with enormous pleasure and a lot of noise. When the waitress arrived with more food and beer, he mumbled a thank you and immediately began shoveling cheese enchiladas into his mouth. He worked his way through the tacos and the side dishes. A pulse thumped visibly in his bull neck. Veins stood out boldly across his forehead. A film of sweat sheathed his face, and beads of sweat began to trickle down from his hairline. At last he swallowed the final mouthful of refried beans and chased it with beer and pushed the empty plates away. He sat for a while with one hand on his thigh, one hand wrapped around a bottle, staring across the booth at nothing in particular. Gradually, the sweat dried on his face, and he became aware of the jukebox music again; another Freddie Fender tune was playing.

He sipped his beer and looked around at the other customers, taking an interest in them for the first time. His attention was drawn to a group at the table nearest the door. Two couples. Good-looking girls. Darkly handsome men. All in their early twenties. The guys were putting on an act for the women, talking just a fraction too loud and laughing too much, doing the rooster act, trying too hard, determined to impress the little hens.

Frye decided to have some fun with them. He thought about it, figured out how he would set it up, and grinned happily at the prospect of the excitement he would cause.

He asked the waitress for his check, gave her more than enough money to cover it, and said, "Keep the change."

"You're very generous," she said, smiling and nodding as she went off to the cash register.

He pulled on the leather gloves.

His sixth bottle of beer was still half-full, and he took it with him when he slid out of the booth. He headed toward the exit and contrived to hook a foot on a chair leg as he passed the two couples who had interested him. He stumbled slightly, easily regained his balance, and leaned toward the four surprised people at the table, letting them see the beer bottle, trying to look like a drunk.

He kept his voice low, for he didn't want others in the restaurant to be aware of the confrontation he was fomenting. He knew he could handle two of them, but he wasn't prepared to fight an army. He peered blearily at the toughest looking of the two men, gave him a big grin, and spoke in a low mean snarl that belied his smile. "Keep your goddamned chair out of the aisle, you stupid spic."

The stranger had been smiling at him, expecting some sort of drunken apology. When he heard the insult, his wide brown face went blank, and his eyes narrowed.

Before that man could get up, Frye swung to the other one and said, "Why don't you get a foxy lady like that blonde back there? What do you want with these two greasy wetback cunts?"

Then he made swiftly for the door, so the fight wouldn't start inside the restaurant. Chuckling to himself, he pushed through the door, staggered into the foggy night, and hurried around the building to the parking lot on the north side to wait.

He was only a few steps from his van when one of the men he had left behind called to him in Spanish-accented English. "Hey! Wait a second, man!"

Frye turned, still pretending drunkenness, weaving and swaying as if he found it difficult to keep the ground under his feet. "What's up?" he asked stupidly.

They stopped, side by side, apparitions in the mist. The stocky one said, "Hey, what the hell you think you're doin', man?"

"You spics looking for trouble?" Frye asked, slurring his words.

"*Cerdo!*" the stocky one said.

"*Mugriento cerdo!*" said the slim man.

Frye said, "For Christ's sake, stop jabbering that damn monkey talk at me. If you have something to say, speak English."

"Miguel called you a pig," said the slim one. "And I called you a filthy pig."

Frye grinned and made an obscene gesture.

Miguel, the stocky man, charged, and Frye waited motionless, as if he didn't see him coming. Miguel rushed in with his head down, his fists up, his arms tucked close to his sides. He threw two quick and powerful punches at Frye's iron-muscled midsection. The brown man's granite hands made sharp hard slapping sounds as they landed, but Frye took both blows without flinching. By design, he was still holding the beer bottle, and he smashed it against the side of Miguel's head. Glass exploded and rained down on the parking lot in dissonant musical notes. Beer and beer foam splashed over both men. Miguel dropped to his knees with a horrible groan, as if he had been poleaxed. "Pablo," he called pleadingly to his friend. Grabbing the injured man's head with both hands, Frye held him steady long enough to ram a knee into the underside of his chin. Miguel's teeth clacked together with an ugly noise. As Frye let go of him, the man fell sideways, unconscious, his breath bubbling noisily through bloody nostrils.

Even as Miguel crumpled onto the fog-damp pavement, Pablo came after Frye. He had a knife. It was a long thin weapon, probably a switchblade, probably sharpened into cutting edges on both sides, certain to be as wickedly dangerous as a razor. The slim man was not a charger as Miguel had been. He moved swiftly but gracefully, almost like a dancer, gliding around to Frye's right side, searching for an opening, making an opening by virtue of his speed and agility, striking with the lightning moves of a snake. The knife flashed in, from left to right, and if Frye had not jumped back, it would have torn open his stomach, spilling his guts. Crooning eerily to himself, Pablo pressed steadily forward, slashing at Frye again and again, from left to right, from right to left. As Frye retreated, he studied the way Pablo used the knife, and by the time he backed up against the rear end of the Dodge van, he saw how to handle him. Pablo made long sweeping passes with the knife instead of the short vicious arcs employed by skilled knife fighters; therefore, on the outward half of each swing, after the blade had passed Frye but before it started coming back again, there was a second or two when the weapon was moving away from him, posing no threat whatsoever, a moment when Pablo was vulnerable. As the slim man edged in for the kill, confident that his prey had nowhere to run, Frye timed one of the arcs and sprang forward at precisely the right instant. As the blade swung away from him, Frye seized Pablo's wrist, squeezing and twisting it, bending it back against the joint. The slim man cried out in agony. The knife flew out of the slender fingers. Frye stepped behind him, got a hammerlock on him and ran him face-first into the rear end of the van. He twisted Pablo's arm even farther, got the hand all the way up between the shoulder blades, until it seemed something would have to snap. With his free hand, Frye gripped the seat of the man's trousers, literally lifted him off his feet, all hundred and forty pounds of him, and slammed him into the van a second time, a third, a fourth, a fifth, a sixth, until the screaming stopped. When he let go of Pablo, the slim man went down like a sack of rags.

Miguel was on his hands and knees. He spit blood and shiny white bits of teeth onto the black macadam.

Frye went to him.

"Trying to get up, friend?"

Laughing softly, Frye stepped on his fingers. He ground his heel on the man's hand, then stepped back.

Miguel squealed, fell on his side.

Frye kicked him in the thigh.

Miguel did not lose consciousness, but he closed his eyes, hoping Frye would just go away.

Frye felt as if electricity was coursing through him, a million-billion volts, bursting from synapse to synapse, hot and crackling and sparking within him, not a painful feeling, but a wild and exciting experience, as if he had just been touched by the Lord God Almighty and filled up with the most beautiful and bright and holy light.

Miguel opened his swollen dark eyes.

"All the fight gone out of you?" Frye asked.

"Please," Miguel said around broken teeth and split lips.

Exhilarated, Frye put a foot against Miguel's throat and forced him to roll onto his back.

"Please."

Frye took his foot off the man's throat.

"Please."

High with a sense of his own power, floating, flying, soaring, Frye kicked Miguel in the ribs.

Miguel choked on his own scream.

Laughing exuberantly, Frye kicked him repeatedly, until a couple of ribs gave way with an audible crunch.

Miguel began to do something he had struggled manfully not to do for the past few minutes. He began to cry.

Frye returned to the van.

Pablo was on the ground by the rear wheels, flat on his back, unconscious.

Saying, "Yeah, yeah, yeah, yeah, yeah, yeah," over and over again, Frye circled Pablo, kicking him in the calves and knees and thighs and hips and ribs.

A car started to pull into the lot from the street, but the driver saw what was happening and wanted no part of it. He put the car in reverse, backed out of there, and sped off with a screech of tires.

Frye dragged Pablo over to Miguel, lined them up side by side, out of the way of the van. He didn't want to run over anyone. He didn't want to kill either of them, for too many people in the bar had gotten a good look at him. The authorities wouldn't have much desire to pursue the winner of an ordinary street fight, especially when the losers had intended to gang up on a lone man. But the police would look for a killer, so Frye made sure that both Miguel and Pablo were safe.

Whistling happily, he drove back toward Marina Del Rey and stopped at the first open service station on the right-hand side of the street. While the attendant filled the tank, checked the oil, and washed the windshield, Frye went to the men's room. He took a shaving kit with him and spent ten minutes freshening up.

When he traveled, he slept in the van, and it was not as convenient as a camper; it did not have running water. On the other hand, it was more maneuverable, less visible, and far more anonymous than a camper. To take full advantage of the many luxuries of a completely equipped motor home, he would have to stop over at a campground every night, hooking up to sewer and water and electric lines, leaving his name and address wherever he went. That was too risky. In a motor home, he would leave a trail that even a noseless bloodhound could follow, and the same would be true if he stayed at motels where, if the police asked about him later, desk clerks would surely remember the tall and extravagantly muscled man with the penetrating blue eyes.

In the men's room at the service station, he stripped out of his gloves and yellow sweater, washed his torso and underarms with wet paper towels and liquid soap, sprayed himself with deodorant, and dressed again. He was always concerned about cleanliness; he liked to be clean and neat at all times.

When he felt dirty, he was not only uncomfortable but deeply depressed as well—and somewhat fearful. It was as if being dirty stirred up vague recollections of some intolerable experience long forgotten, brought back hideous memories to the edge of his awareness, where he could sense but not see them, perceive but not understand them. Those few nights when he had fallen into bed without bothering to wash up, his repeating nightmare had been far worse than usual, expelling him from sleep in a screaming flailing terror. And although he had awakened on those occasions, as always, with no clear memory of what the dreams had been about, he had felt as if he'd just clawed his way out of a sickeningly filthy place, a dark and close and foul hole in the ground.

Rather than risk intensifying the nightmare that was sure to come, he washed himself there in the men's room, shaved quickly with an electric razor, patted his face with aftershave lotion, brushed his teeth, and used the toilet. In the morning, he would go to another service station and repeat the routine, and he would also change into fresh clothes at that time.

He paid the attendant for the gasoline and drove back to Marina Del Rey through ever-thickening fog. He parked the van in the same dockside lot from which he had made the call to his house in Napa County. He got out of the Dodge and walked to the public phone booth and called the same number again.

"Hello?"

"It's me," Frye said.

"The heat's off."

"The police called?"

"Yeah."

They talked for a minute or two, and then Frye returned to the Dodge.

He stretched out on the mattress in the back of the van and switched on a flashlight he kept there. He could not tolerate totally dark places. He could not sleep unless there was at least a thread of illumination under a door or a night light burning dimly in a corner. In perfect darkness, he began to imagine that strange things were crawling on him, skittering over his face, squirming under his clothes. Without light, he was assaulted by the threatening but wordless whispers that he sometimes heard for a minute or two after he awakened from his nightmare, the blood-freezing whispers that loosened his bowels and made his heart skip.

If he could ever identify the source of those whispers or finally hear what they were trying to tell him, he would know what the nightmare was about. He would know what caused the recurring dream, the icy fear, and he might finally be able to free himself from it.

The problem was that whenever he woke and heard the whispers, that tailend of the dream, he was in no state of mind to listen closely and to analyze them; he was always in a panic, wanting nothing more than to have the whispers fade away and leave him in peace.

He tried to sleep in the indirect glow of the flashlight, but he could not. He tossed and turned. His mind raced. He was wide awake.

He realized that it was the unfinished business with the woman that was keeping him from sleep. He had been primed for the kill, and it had been denied him. He was edgy. He felt hollow, incomplete.

He had tried to satisfy his hunger for the woman by feeding his stomach. When that had not worked, he had tried to take his mind off her by provoking a fight with those two Chicanos. Food and enormous physical exertion were the two things he had always used to stifle his sexual urges, and to divert his thoughts from the secret blood lust that sometimes burned fiercely within him. He wanted sex, a brutal and bruising kind of sex that no woman would willingly provide, so he gorged himself instead. He wanted to kill, so he spent four or five hard hours lifting progressive weights until his muscles cooked into pudding and the violence steamed out of him. The psychiatrists called it *sublimation*. Lately, it had been less and less effective in dissipating his unholy cravings.

The woman was still on his mind.

The sleekness of her.

The swell of hips and breasts.

Hilary Thomas.

No. That was just a disguise.

Katherine.

That was who she really was.

Katherine. Katherine the bitch. In a new body.

He could close his eyes and picture her naked upon a bed, pinned under him, thighs spread, squirming, writhing, quivering like a rabbit that sees the muzzle of a gun. He could envision his hand moving over her heavy breasts and taut belly, over her thighs and the mound of her sex . . . and then his other hand raising the knife, plunging it down, jamming the silvered blade into her, all the way into her softness, her flesh yielding to him, the blood springing up in bright wet promise. He could see the stark terror and excruciating pain in her eyes as he smashed through her chest and dug for her living heart, trying to rip it out while it was still beating. He could almost feel her slick warm blood and smell the slightly bitter coppery odor of it. As the vision filled his mind and took command of all his senses, he felt his testicles draw tight, felt his penis twitch and grow stiff—another knife—and he wanted to plunge it into her, all the way into her marvelous body, first his thick pulsing penis and then the blade, spurting his fear and weakness into her with one weapon, drawing out her strength and vitality with the other.

He opened his eyes.

He was sweating.

Katherine. The bitch.

For thirty-five years, he had lived in her shadow, had existed miserably in constant fear of her. Five years ago, she had died of heart disease, and he had tasted freedom for the first time in his life. But she kept coming back from the dead, pretending to be other women, looking for a way to take control of him again.

He wanted to use her and kill her to show her that she did not scare him. She had no power over him any more. He was now stronger than she was.

He reached for the bundle of chamois cloths that lay beside the mattress, untied them, unwrapped his spare knife.

He wouldn't be able to sleep until he killed her.

Tonight.

She wouldn't be expecting him back so soon.

He looked at his watch. Midnight.

People would still be returning home from the theater, late dinner, parties. Later, the streets would be deserted, the houses lightless and quiet, and there would be less chance of being spotted and reported to the police.

He decided that he would leave for Westwood at two o'clock.

CHAPTER 3

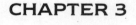

THE LOCKSMITH came and changed the locks on the front and back doors, then went on to another job in Hancock Park.

Officers Farmer and Whitlock left.

Hilary was alone.

She didn't think she could sleep, but she knew for sure she couldn't spend the night in her own bed. When she stood in that room, her mind's eye filled with vivid images of terror: Frye smashing through the door, stalking her, grinning demonically, moving inexorably toward the bed and suddenly leaping onto it, rushing across the mattress with the knife raised high. . . . As before, in a curious dreamlike flux, the memory of Frye became a memory of her father, so that for an instant she had the crazy notion that it had been Earl Thomas, raised from the dead, who had tried to kill her tonight. But it was not merely the residual vibrations of evil in the room that put it off limits. She was also unwilling to sleep there until the ruined door had been removed and a new one hung, a job that couldn't be taken care of until she could get hold of a carpenter tomorrow. The flimsy door that had been there had not held long against Frye's assault, and she had decided to have it replaced with a solid-core hardwood door and a brass deadbolt. But if Frye came back and somehow got into the house tonight, he would be able to walk right into her room while she slept—if she slept.

And sooner or later he would come back. She was as certain of that as she ever had been about anything.

She could go to a hotel, but that didn't appeal to her. It would be like hiding from him. Running away. She was quietly proud of her courage. She never ran away from anyone or anything; she fought back with all of her ingenuity and strength. She hadn't run away from her violent and unloving parents. She had not even sought psychological escape from the searing memory of the final monstrous and bloody events in that small Chicago apartment, had not accepted the kind of peace that could be found in madness or convenient amnesia, which were two ways out that most people would have taken if they'd been through the same ordeal. She had never backed away from the endless series of challenges she had encountered while struggling to build a career in Hollywood, first as an actress, then as a screenwriter. She had gotten knocked down plenty of times, but she had picked herself up again. And again. She persevered, fought back, and won. She would also win this bizarre battle with Bruno Frye, though she would have to fight it alone.

Damn the police!

She decided to sleep in one of the guest rooms, where there was a door she could lock and barricade. She put sheets and a blanket on the queen-size bed, hung towels in the adjoining guest bathroom.

Downstairs, she rummaged through the kitchen drawers, taking out a variety of knives and testing each for balance and sharpness. The large butcher's knife looked deadlier than any of the others, but in her small hand it was unwieldy. It would be of little use in close quarters fighting, for she needed room to swing it. It might be an excellent weapon for attack, but it was not so good for self-defense. Instead, she chose an ordinary utility knife with a four-inch blade, small enough to fit in a pocket of her robe, large enough to do considerable damage if she had to use it.

The thought of plunging a knife into another human being filled her with revulsion, but she knew that she could do it if her life was threatened. At various times during her childhood, she had hidden a knife in her bedroom, under the mattress. It had been insurance against her father's unpredictable fits of mindless violence. She had used it only once, that last day, when Earl had begun to hallucinate from a combination of delirium tremens and just plain lunacy. He had seen giant worms coming out of the walls and huge crabs trying to get in through the windows. In a paranoid schizophrenic fury, he had transformed that small apartment into a reeking charnel house, and she had saved herself only because she'd had a knife.

Of course, a knife was inferior to a gun. She wouldn't be able to use it against Frye until he was on top of her, and then it might be too late. But the knife was all she had. The uniformed patrolmen had taken her .32 pistol with them when they left right behind the locksmith.

Damn them to hell!

After Detective Clemenza and Howard had gone, Hilary and Officer Farmer had had a maddening conversation about the gun laws. She became furious every time she thought of it.

"Miss Thomas, about this pistol. . . ."

"What about it?"

"You need a permit to keep a handgun in your house."

"I know that. I've got one."

"Could I see the registration?"

"It's in the nightstand drawer. I keep it with the gun."

"May Officer Whitlock go upstairs and get it?"

"Go ahead."

And a minute or two later:

"Miss Thomas, I gather you once lived in San Francisco."

"For about eight months. I did some theater work up there when I was trying to break in as an actress."

"This registration bears a San Francisco address."

"I was renting a North Beach apartment because it was cheap, and I didn't have much money in those days. A woman alone in that neighborhood sure needs a gun."

"Miss Thomas, aren't you aware that you're required to fill out a new registration form when you move from one county to another?"

"No."

"You really aren't aware of that?"

"Look, I just write movies. Guns aren't my business."

"If you keep a handgun in your house, you're obliged to know the laws governing its registration and use."

"Okay, okay. I'll register it as soon as I can."

"Well, you see, you'll have to come in and register it if you want it back."

"Get it back?"

"I'll have to take it with me."

"Are you kidding?"

"It's the law, Miss Thomas."

"You're going to leave me alone, unarmed?"

"I don't think you need to worry about—"

"Who put you up to this?"

"I'm only doing my job."

"Howard put you up to it, didn't he?"

"Detective Howard did suggest I check the registration. But he didn't—"

"Jesus!"

"All you have to do is come in, pay the proper fee, fill out a new registration—and we'll return your pistol."

"What if Frye comes back here tonight?"

"It isn't very likely, Miss Thomas."

"But what if he does?"

"Call us. We've got some patrol cars in the area. We'll get here—"

"—just in time to phone for a priest and a morgue wagon."

"You've got nothing to fear but—"

"—fear itself? Tell me, Officer Farmer, do you have to take a college course in the use of the cliché before you can become a cop?"

"I'm only doing my duty, Miss Thomas."

"Ahhh . . . what's the use."

Farmer had taken the pistol, and Hilary had learned a valuable lesson. The police department was an arm of the government, and you could not rely on the government for anything. If the government couldn't balance its own budget and refrain from inflating its own currency, if it couldn't find a way to deal with the rampant corruption within its own offices, if it was even beginning to lose the will and the means to maintain an army and to provide national security, then why should she expect it to stop a single maniac from cutting her down?

She had learned long ago that it was not easy to find someone in whom she could place her faith and trust. Not her parents. Not relatives, every one of whom preferred not to get involved. Not the paper-shuffling social workers to whom she had turned for help when she was a child. Not the police. In fact, she saw now that the only person anyone could trust and rely on was himself.

All right, she thought angrily. Okay. I'll deal with Bruno Frye myself.

How?

Somehow.

She left the kitchen with the knife in her hand, went to the mirrored wet bar that was tucked into a niche between the living room and the study, and poured a generous measure of Remy Martin into a large crystal snifter. She carried the knife and the brandy upstairs to the guest room, defiantly switching off the lights as she went.

She closed the bedroom door, locked it, and looked for some way to fortify it. A highboy stood against the wall to the left of the door, a heavy dark pine piece taller than she was. It weighed too much to be moved as it was, but she made it manageable by taking out all the drawers and setting them aside. She dragged the big wooden chest across the carpet, pushed it squarely against the door, and replaced the drawers. Unlike many highboys, this one had no legs at all; it rested flat on the floor and had a relatively low center of gravity that made it a formidable obstacle for anyone trying to bull his way into the room.

In the bathroom, she put the knife and the brandy on the floor. She filled the tube with water as hot as she could stand it, stripped, and settled slowly into it, wincing and gasping as she gradually submerged. Ever since she had been pinned beneath Frye on the bedroom floor, ever since she'd felt his hand pawing at her crotch and shredding her pantyhose, she had felt dirty, contaminated. Now, she soaked herself with great pleasure, worked up a thick lilac-scented lather, scrubbed vigorously with a washcloth, pausing occasionally to sip Remy Martin. At last, when she felt thoroughly clean again, she put the bar of soap aside and settled down even farther in the fragrant water. Steam rose over her, and the brandy made steam within her, and the pleasant combination of inner and outer heat forced fine drops of perspiration out of her brow. She closed her eyes and concentrated on the contents of the crystal snifter.

The human body will not run for long without the proper maintenance. The body, after all, is a machine, a marvelous machine made of many kinds of tissues and fluids, chemicals and minerals, a sophisticated assemblage with one heart-engine and a lot of little motors, a lubricating system and an air-cooling system, ruled by the computer brain, with drive trains made out of muscles, all constructed upon a clever calcium frame. To function, it needs many things, not the least of which are food, relaxation, and sleep. Hilary had thought she would be unable to sleep after what had happened, that she would spend the night like a cat with its ears up, listening for danger. But she had exerted herself tonight in more ways than one, and although her conscious mind was reluctant to shut down for repairs, her subconscious knew it was necessary and inevitable. By the time she finished the brandy, she was so drowsy that she could hardly keep her eyes open.

She climbed out of the tub, opened the drain, and dried herself on a big fluffy towel as the water gurgled away. She picked up the knife and walked out of the bathroom, leaving the light on, pulling the door halfway shut. She switched off the lights in the main room. Moving languorously in the soft glow and velvet shadows, she put the knife on the nightstand and slid naked into bed.

She felt loose, as if the heat had unscrewed her joints.

She was a bit dizzy, too. The brandy.

She lay with her face toward the door. The barricade was reassuring. It looked very solid. Impenetrable. Bruno Frye wouldn't get through it, she told herself. Not even with a battering ram. A small army would find it difficult to get through that door. Not even a tank would make it. What about a big old dinosaur? she wondered sleepily. One of those tyrannosaurus rex fellas like in the funny monster pictures. Godzilla. Could Godzilla bash through that door . . . ?

By two o'clock Thursday morning. Hilary was asleep.

At 2:25 Thursday morning, Bruno Frye drove slowly past the Thomas place. The fog was into Westwood now, but it was not as turbid as it was nearer the ocean. He could see the house well enough to observe that there was not even the faintest light beyond any of the front windows.

He drove two blocks, swung the van around, and went by the house again, even slower this time, carefully studying the cars parked along the street. He didn't think the cops would post a guard for her, but he wasn't taking any chances. The cars were empty; there was no stakeout.

He put the Dodge between the pair of Volvos two blocks away and walked back to the house through pools of foggy darkness, through pale circles of hazy light from the mist-cloaked streetlamps. As he crossed the lawn, his shoes squished in the dew-damp grass, a sound that made him aware of how ethereally quiet the night was otherwise.

At the side of the house, he crouched next to a bushy oleander plant and looked back the way he had come. No alarm had been set off. No one was coming after him.

He continued to the rear of the house and climbed over a locked gate. In the back yard, he looked up at the wall of the house and saw a small square of light on the second floor. From the size of it, he supposed it was a bathroom window; the larger panes of glass to the right of it showed vague traces of light at the edges of the drapes.

She was up there.

He was sure of it.

He could sense her. Smell her.

The bitch.

Waiting to be taken and used.

Waiting to be killed.

Waiting to kill me? he wondered.

He shuddered. He wanted her, had a fierce hard-on for her, but he was also afraid of her.

Always before, she had died easily. She had always come back from the dead in a new body, masquerading as a new woman, but she had always died without much of a struggle. Tonight, however, Katherine had been a regular tigress, shockingly strong and clever and fearless. This was a new development, and he did not like it.

Nevertheless, he had to go after her. If he didn't pursue her from one reincarnation to the next, if he didn't keep killing her until she finally stayed dead, he would never have any peace.

He did not bother to try opening the kitchen door with the keys he had stolen out of her purse the day she'd been to the winery. She had probably had new locks installed. Even if she hadn't taken that precaution, he would be unable to get in through the door. Tuesday night, the first time he had attempted to get into the house, she had been at home, and he had discovered that one of the locks would not open with a key if it had been engaged from inside. The upper lock opened without resistance, but the lower one would only release if it had been locked from outside, with a key. He had not gotten into the house on that occasion, had had to come back the next night, Wednesday night, eight hours ago, when she was out to dinner and both of his keys were useable. But now she was in there, and although she might not have had the locks replaced, she had turned those special deadbolts from the inside, effectively barring entrance regardless of the number of keys he possessed.

He moved along to the corner of the house, where a big mullioned window looked into the rose garden. It was divided into a lot of six-inch-square panes of glass by thin strips of dark, well lacquered wood. The book-lined study lay on the other side. He took a penlight from one pocket, flicked it on, and directed the narrow beam through the window. Squinting, he searched the length of the sill and the less visible horizontal center bar until he located the latch, then turned off the penlight. He had a roll of masking tape, and he began to tear strips from it, covering the small pane that was nearest the window lock. When the six-inch square was completely masked over, he used his gloved fist to smash through it: one hard blow. The glass shattered almost soundlessly and did not clatter to the floor, for it stuck onto the tape. He reached inside and unlatched the window, raised it, heaved himself up and across the sill. He barely avoided making a hell of a racket when he encountered a small table and nearly fell over it.

Standing in the center of the study, heart pounding, Frye listened for movement in the house, for a sign that she had heard him.

There was only silence.

She was able to rise up from the dead and come back to life in a new identity, but that was evidently the limit of her supernatural power. Obviously, she was not all-seeing and all-knowing. He was in her house, but she did not know it yet.

He grinned.

He took the knife from the sheath that was fixed to his belt, held it in his right hand.

With the penlight in his left hand, he quietly prowled through every room on the ground floor. They were all dark and deserted.

Going up the stairs to the second floor, he stayed close to the wall, in case any of the steps creaked. He reached the top without making a sound.

He explored the bedrooms, but he encountered nothing of interest until he approached the last room on the left. He thought he saw light coming under the door, and he switched off his flash. In the pitch-black corridor only a nebulous silvery line marked the threshold of the last room, but it was more marked than any of the others. He went to the door and cautiously tried the knob. Locked.

He had found her.

Katherine.

Pretending to be someone named Hilary Thomas.

The bitch. The rotten bitch.

Katherine, Katherine, Katherine. . . .

As the name echoed through his mind, he clenched his fist around the knife and made short jabbing motions at the darkness, as if he were stabbing her.

Stretching out face-down on the floor of the hallway, Frye looked through the inch-high gap at the bottom of the door. A large piece of furniture, perhaps a dresser, was pushed up against the other side of the entrance. A vague indirect light spread across the bedroom from an unseen source on the right, some of it finding its way around the edges of the dresser and under the door.

He was delighted by what little he could see, and a flood of optimism filled him. She had barricaded herself in the room, which meant the hateful bitch was afraid of him. *She* was afraid of *him*. Even though she knew how to come back from the grave, she was frightened of dying. Or maybe she knew or sensed that this time she would not be able to return to the living. He was going to be

damned thorough when he disposed of the corpse, far more thorough than he
had been when he'd disposed of the many other women whose bodies she had
inhabited. Cut out her heart. Pound a wooden stake through it. Cut off her
head. Fill her mouth with garlic. He also intended to take the head and the
heart with him when he left the house; he would bury the pair of grisly trophies
in separate and secret graves, in the hallowed ground of two different church-
yards, and far away from wherever the body itself might be interred. Apparently, she was aware that he planned to take extraordinary precautions this
time, for she was resisting him with a fury and a purpose the likes of which she
had never shown before.

She was very quiet in there.

Asleep?

No, he decided. She was too scared to sleep. She was probably sitting up in
bed with the pistol in her hands.

He pictured her hiding in there like a mouse seeking refuge from a prowling
cat, and he felt strong, powerful, like an elemental force. Hatred boiled blackly
within him. He wanted her to squirm and shake with fear as she had made him
do for so many years. An almost overpowering urge to scream at her took hold
of him; he wanted to shout her name—Katherine, Katherine—and fling curses
at her. He kept control of himself only with an effort that brought sweat to his
face and tears to his eyes.

He got to his feet and stood silently in the darkness, considering his options.
He could throw himself against the door, break through it, and push the
obstacle out of the way, but that would surely be suicidal. He wouldn't get
through the fortifications fast enough to surprise her. She would have plenty of
time to line up the sights of the gun and put half a dozen bullets into him. The
only other thing he could do was wait for her to come out. If he stayed in the
hallway and didn't make a sound all night, the uneventful hours might wear the
edges off her watchfulness. By morning, she might get the idea that she was
safe and that he wasn't ever coming back. When she walked out of there, he
could seize her and force her back to the bed before she knew what was
happening.

Frye crossed the corridor in two steps and sat on the floor with his back
against the wall.

In a few minutes, he began to hear rustling sounds in the dark, soft scurrying noises.

Imagination, he told himself. That familiar fear.

But then he felt something creeping up his leg, under his trousers.

It's not really there, he told himself.

Something slithered under one sleeve and started up his arm, something
awful but unidentifiable. And something ran across his shoulder and up his
neck, onto his face, something small and deadly. It went for his mouth. He
pressed his lips together. It went for his eyes. He squeezed his eyes shut. It
went for his nostrils, and he brushed frantically at his face, but he couldn't find
it, couldn't knock it off. *No!*

He switched on the penlight. He was the only living creature in the hallway.
There was nothing moving under his trousers. Nothing under his sleeves.
Nothing on his face.

He shuddered.

He left the penlight on.

At nine o'clock Thursday morning, Hilary was awakened by the telephone.
There was an extension in the guest room. The bell switch accidentally had
been turned all the way up to maximum volume, probably by someone from the

housecleaning service that she employed. The strident ringing broke into Hilary's sleep and made her sit up with a start.

The caller was Wally Topelis. While having breakfast, he had seen the morning paper's account of the assault and attempted rape. He was shocked and concerned.

Before she would tell him any more than the newspaper had done, she made him read the article to her. She was relieved to hear that it was short, just a small picture and a few column inches on the sixth page. It was based entirely on the meager information that she and Lieutenant Clemenza had given the reporters last night. There was no mention of Bruno Frye—or of Detective Frank Howard's conviction that she was a liar. The press had come and gone with perfect timing, just missing the kind of juicy angle that would have put the story at least a few pages closer to page one.

She told Wally all of it, and he was outraged. "That stupid goddamned cop! If he'd made any effort at all to find out about you, what kind of person you are, he'd have known you couldn't possibly make up a story like that. Look, kid, I'll take care of this. Don't worry. I'll get some action for you."

"How?"

"I'll call some people."

"Who?"

"How about the chief of police for starters?"

"Oh, sure."

"Hey, he owes me," Wally said. "For the past five years in a row, who was it that organized the annual police benefit show? Who was it that got some of the biggest Hollywood stars to appear for nothing? Who was it got singers and comedians and actors and magicians all free for the police fund?"

"You?"

"Damn right it was me."

"But what can he do?"

"He can reopen the case."

"When one of his detectives swears it was a hoax?"

"His detective is brain-damaged."

"I have a hunch this Frank Howard might have a very good record," she said.

"Then the way they rate their people is a disgrace. Their standards are either very low or all screwed up."

"You might have a pretty hard time convincing the chief of that."

"I can be very persuasive, my lamb."

"But even if he owes you a favor, how can he reopen the case without new evidence? He may be the chief, but he has to follow the rules, too."

"Look, he can at least talk to the sheriff up there in Napa County."

"And Sheriff Laurenski will give the chief the same story he was putting out last night. He'll say Frye was at home baking cookies or something."

"Then the sheriff's an incompetent fool who took the word of someone on Frye's household staff. Or he's a liar. Or maybe he's even in on this with Frye somehow."

"You go to the chief with that theory," she said, "and he'll have both of us tested for paranoid schizophrenia."

"If I can't squeeze some action out of the cops," Wally said, "then I'll hire a good PI team."

"Private investigators?"

"I know just the agency. They're good. Considerably better than most cops. They'll pry open Frye's life and find all the little secrets in it. They'll come up with the kind of evidence that'll get the case reopened."

"Isn't that expensive?"

"I'll split the cost with you," he said.

"Oh, no."

"Oh, yes."

"That's generous of you, but—"

"It's not generous of me at all. You're an extremely valuable property, my lamb. I own a percentage of you, so anything I pay to a PI team is just insurance. I only want to protect my interests."

"That's baloney, and you know it," she said. "You *are* generous, Wally. But don't hire anyone just yet. The other detective that I told you about, Lieutenant Clemenza, said he'd stop around later this afternoon to see if I remembered anything more. He still sort of believes me, but he's confused because Laurenski shot a big hole in my story. I think Clemenza would use just about any excuse he could find to get the case reopened. Let's wait until I've seen him. Then if the situation still looks bleak, we'll hire your PI."

"Well . . . all right," Wally said reluctantly. "But in the meantime, I'm going to tell them to send a man over to your place for protection."

"Wally, I don't need a bodyguard."

"Like hell you don't."

"I was perfectly safe all night, and I—"

"Listen, kid, I'm sending someone over. That's final. There won't be any arguing with Uncle Wally. If you won't let them inside, he'll just stand by your front door like a palace guard."

"Really, I—"

"Sooner or later," Wally said gently, "you're going to have to face the fact that you can't get through life alone, entirely on your own steam. No one does. No one, kid. Now and then everyone has to accept a little help. You should have called me last night."

"I didn't want to disturb you."

"For God's sake, you wouldn't have disturbed me! I'm your friend. In fact, you disturbed me a whole lot more by not disturbing me last night. Kid, it's all right to be strong and independent and self-reliant. But when you carry it too far, when you isolate yourself like this, it's a slap in the face to everybody who cares about you. Now, will you let the guard in when he arrives?"

She sighed. "Okay."

"Good. He'll be there within an hour. And you'll call me as soon as you've talked to Clemenza?"

"I will."

"Promise."

"I promise."

"Did you sleep last night?"

"Surprisingly, yes."

"If you didn't get enough sleep," he said, "take a nap this afternoon."

Hilary laughed. "You'd make a wonderful Jewish mother."

"Maybe I'll bring over a big pot of chicken soup this evening. Good-bye, dear."

"Good-bye, Wally. Thanks for calling."

When she hung up the receiver, she glanced at the highboy that stood in front of the door. After the uneventful night, the barricade looked foolish. Wally was right: the best way to handle this was to hire around-the-clock bodyguards and then put a first-rate team of private investigators on Frye's trail. Her original plan for dealing with the problem was ludicrous. She simply could not board up the windows and play Battle of the Alamo with Frye.

She got out of bed, put on her silk robe, and went to the highboy. She took the drawers out and put them aside. When the tall chest was light enough to be moved, she dragged it away from the door, back to the indentation in the carpet that marked where it had rested until last night. She replaced the drawers.

She went to the nightstand, picked up the knife, and smiled ruefully as she realized how naive she had been. Hand-to-hand combat with Bruno Frye? Knife-fighting with a maniac? How could she have thought that she would have any chance whatever in such an uneven contest? Frye was many times stronger than she was. She had been fortunate last night when she had managed to get away from him. Luckily, she'd had the pistol. But if she tried fencing with him, he would cut her to ribbons.

Intending to return the knife to the kitchen, wanting to be dressed for the day by the time the bodyguard arrived, she went to the bedroom door, unlocked it, opened it, stepped into the hallway, and screamed as Bruno Frye grabbed her and slammed her up against the wall. The back of her head hit the plaster with a sharp crack, and she struggled to remain above a wave of darkness that washed in behind her eyes. He clutched her throat with his right hand, pinned her in place. With his left hand, he tore open the front of her robe and squeezed her bare breasts, leering at her, calling her a bitch and a slut.

He must have been listening when she talked to Wally, must have heard that the police had taken away her pistol, for he had absolutely no fear of her. She hadn't mentioned the knife to Wally, and Frye was not prepared for it. She rammed the four-inch blade into his flat hard-muscled belly. For a few seconds, he seemed unaware of it; he slid his hand down from her breasts, tried to thrust a couple of fingers into her vagina. As she jerked the knife out of him, he was stricken by pain. His eyes went wide, and he let out a high-pitched yelp. Hilary stuck the blade into him again piercing him high and toward the side this time, just under the ribs. His face was suddenly as white and greasy looking as lard. He howled, let go of her, stumbled backwards until he collided with the other wall and knocked an oil painting to the floor.

A violent spasmodic shiver of revulsion snapped through Hilary as she realized what she had done. But she did not drop the knife, and she was fully prepared to stab him again if he attacked her.

Bruno Frye looked down at himself in astonishment. The blade had sunk deep. A thin stream of blood oozed from him, rapidly staining his sweater and pants.

Hilary did not wait for his expression of amazement to metamorphose into agony and anger. She turned and hurried into the guest room, threw the door shut and locked it. For half a minute she listened to Frye's soft groans and curses and clumsy movements, wondering if he had sufficient strength left to smash through the door. She thought she heard him lumbering down the hall toward the stairs, but she couldn't be sure. She ran to the telephone. With bloodless and palsied hands, she picked up the receiver and dialed the operator. She asked for the police.

The bitch! The rotten bitch!

Frye slipped one hand under the yellow sweater and gripped the lower of the two wounds, the gut puncture, for that was the one doing the most bleeding. He squeezed the lips of the cut together as best he could, trying to stop the life from flowing out of him. He felt the warm blood soaking through the stitching of the gloves, onto his fingers.

He was suffering very little pain. A dull burning in his stomach. An electric tingle along his left side. A mild rhythmic twinge timed to his heartbeat. That was the extent of it.

Nevertheless, he knew that he had been badly hurt and was getting worse by the second. He was pathetically weak. His great strength had gushed out of him suddenly and completely.

Holding his belly with one hand, clutching the bannister with the other, he descended to the first floor on steps as treacherous as those in a carnival funhouse; they seemed to tip and pitch and roll. By the time he reached the bottom, he was streaming sweat.

Outside, the sun stung his eyes. It was brighter than he had ever seen it, a monstrous sun that filled the sky and beat mercilessly upon him. He felt as if it were shining through his eyes and starting tiny fires on the surface of his brain.

Bending over his wounds, cursing, he shuffled south along the sidewalk until he came to the smoke-gray van. He pulled himself up into the driver's seat, drew the door shut as if it weighed ten thousand pounds.

He drove with one hand to Wilshire Boulevard, turned right, went to Sepulveda, made a left, looking for a public telephone that offered a lot of privacy. Every bump in the road was like a blow to his solar plexus. At times, the automobiles around him appeared to stretch and flex and balloon, as if they were constructed of a magical elastic metal, and he had to concentrate to force them back into more familiar shapes.

Blood continued to trickle out of him no matter how tightly he pressed on the wound. The burning in his stomach grew worse. The rhythmic twinge became a sharp pinch. But the catastrophic pain that he knew was coming had not yet arrived.

He drove an interminable distance on Sepulveda before he finally located a pay phone that suited his needs. It was in a back corner of a supermarket parking lot, eighty or a hundred yards from the store.

He parked the van at an angle, screening the phone from everyone at the market and from motorists passing on Sepulveda. It was not a booth, just one of those plastic windscreens that were supposed to provide excellent sound-proofing but which had no effect at all on background noise; but at least it appeared to be in service, and it was private enough. A high cement block fence rose behind it, separating the supermarket property from the fringes of a housing tract. On the right, a cluster of shrubs and two small palms shielded the phone from the side street leading off Sepulveda. No one was likely to see him well enough to realize he was hurt; he didn't want anyone nosing around.

He slid across the seat to the passenger's side and got out that door. When he looked down at the thick red muck oozing between the fingers that were clamped over the worse wound, he felt dizzy, and he looked quickly away. He only had to take three steps to reach the phone, but each of them seemed like a mile.

He could not remember his telephone credit card number, which had been as familiar to him as his birthdate, so he called collect to Napa Valley.

The operator rang it six times.

"Hello?"

"I have a collect call for anyone from Bruno Frye. Will you accept the charges?"

"Go ahead, operator."

There was a soft click as she went off the line.

"I'm hurt real bad. I think . . . I'm dying." Frye told the man in Napa County.

"Oh, Jesus, no. No!"

"I'll have to . . . call an ambulance," Frye said. "And they . . . everyone will know the truth."

They spoke for a minute, both of them frightened and confused.

Suddenly, Frye felt something loosen inside him. Like a spring popping. And a bag of water bursting. He screamed in pain.

The man in Napa County cried out in sympathy, as if he felt the same pain.

"Got to . . . get an ambulance," Frye said.

He hung up.

Blood had run all the way down his pants to his shoes, and now it was dribbling onto the pavement.

He lifted the receiver off the hook and put it down on the metal shelf beside the phone box. He picked up a dime from the same shelf, on which he had put his pocket change, but his fingers weren't working properly; he dropped it and looked down stupidly as it rolled across the macadam. Found another dime. Held this one as tightly as he could. He lifted the dime as if it were a lead disc as big as an automobile tire, finally put it in the proper slot. He tried to dial 0. He didn't even have enough energy to perform that small chore. His muscle-packed arms, his big shoulders, his gigantic chest, his powerful back, his hard rippled belly, and his massive thighs all failed him.

He couldn't make the call, and he couldn't even stand up any longer. He fell, rolled over once, and lay face-down on the macadam.

He couldn't move.

He couldn't see. He was blind.

It was a very black darkness.

He was scared.

He tried to tell himself that he would come back from the dead as Katherine had done. *I'll come back and get her,* he thought. *I'll come back.* But he really didn't believe it.

As he lay there getting increasingly light-headed, he had a surprisingly lucid moment when he wondered if he had been all wrong about Katherine coming back from the dead. Had it been his imagination? Had he just been killing women who resembled her? Innocent women? Was he mad?

A new explosion of pain blew those thoughts away and forced him to consider the smothering darkness in which he lay.

He felt things moving on him.

Things crawling on him.

Things crawling on his arms and legs.

Things crawling on his face.

He tried to scream. Couldn't.

He heard the whispers.

No!

His bowels loosened.

The whispers swelled into a raging sibilant chorus and, like a great dark river, swept him away.

Thursday morning, Tony Clemenza and Frank Howard located Jilly Jenkins, an old friend of Bobby "Angel" Valdez. Jilly had seen the baby-faced rapist and killer in July, but not since. At that time, Bobby had just quit a job at Vee Vee Gee Laundry on Olympic Boulevard. That was all Jilly knew.

Vee Vee Gee was a large one-story stucco building dating from the early fifties, when an entire Los Angeles school of benighted architects first thought of crossing ersatz Spanish texture and form with utilitarian factory design. Tony had never been able to understand how even the most insensitive architect could see beauty in such a grotesque crossbreed. The orange-red tile roof was studded with dozens of firebrick chimneys and corrugated metal vents; steam rose from about half of those outlets. The windows were framed with heavy timbers, dark and rustic, as if this were the *casa* of some great and rich *terrateniente;* but the ugly factory-window glass was webbed with wire. There were loading docks where the verandas should have been. The walls were straight, the corners sharp, the overall shape boxlike—quite the opposite of the graceful arches and rounded edges of genuine Spanish construction. The place was like an aging whore wearing more refined clothes than was her custom, trying desperately to pass for a lady.

"Why did they do it?" Tony asked as he got out of the unmarked police sedan and closed the door.

"Do what?" Frank asked.

"Why did they put up so many of these offensive places? What was the point of it?"

Frank blinked. "What's so offensive?"

"It doesn't bother you?"

"It's a laundry. Don't we need laundries?"

"Is anybody in your family an architect?"

"Architect? No," Frank said. "Why'd you ask?"

"I just wondered."

"You know, sometimes you don't make a whole hell of a lot of sense."

"So I've been told," Tony said.

In the business office at the front of the building, when they asked to see the owner, Vincent Garamalkis, they were given worse than a cool reception. The secretary was downright hostile. The Vee Vee Gee Laundry had paid four fines in four years for employing undocumented aliens. The secretary was certain that Tony and Frank were agents with the Immigration and Naturalization Service. She thawed a bit when she saw their LAPD identification, but she was still not cooperative until Tony convinced her that they hadn't even a smidgen of interest in the nationalities of the people working at Vee Vee Gee. At last, reluctantly, she admitted that Mr. Garamalkis was on the premises. She was about to take them to him when the phone rang, so she gave them hasty directions and asked them to find him on their own.

The enormous main room of the laundry smelled of soap and bleach and steam. It was a damp place, hot and noisy. Industrial washing machines thumped, buzzed, sloshed. Huge driers whirred and rumbled monotonously. The clacking and hissing of automatic folders put Tony's teeth on edge. Most of the workers unloading the laundry carts, and the husky men feeding the machines, and the women tagging linens at a double row of long tables were speaking to one another in loud and rapid Spanish. As Tony and Frank walked from one end of the room to the other, some of the noise abated, for the workers stopped talking and eyed them suspiciously.

Vincent Garamalkis was at a battered desk at the end of the big room. The desk was on a three-foot-high platform that made it possible for the boss to watch over his employees. Garamalkis got up and walked to the edge of the platform when he saw them coming. He was a short stocky man, balding, with hard features and a pair of gentle hazel eyes that didn't match the rest of his face. He stood with his hands on his hips, as if he were defying them to step onto his level.

"Police," Frank said, flashing ID.

"Yeah," Garamalkis said.

"Not Immigration," Tony assured him.

"Why should I be worried about Immigration?" Garamalkis asked defensively.

"Your secretary was," Frank said.

Garamalkis scowled down at them. "I'm clean. I hire nobody but U.S. citizens or documented aliens."

"Oh, sure," Frank said sarcastically. "And bears don't shit in the woods any more."

"Look," Tony said, "we really don't care about where your workers come from."

"So what do you want?"

"We'd like to ask a few questions."

"About what?"

"This man," Frank said, passing up the three mug shots of Bobby Valdez. Garamalkis glanced at them. "What about him?"

"You know him?" Frank said.

"Why?"

"We'd like to find him."

"What for?"

"He's a fugitive."

"What'd he do?"

"Listen," Frank said, fed up with the stocky man's sullen responses. "I can make this hard or easy for you. We can do it here or downtown. And if you want to play Mr. Hardass, we can bring the Immigration and Naturalization Service into it. We don't really give a good goddamned whether nor not you hire a bunch of Mexes, but if we can't get cooperation from you, we'll see that you get busted every which way but loose. You got me? You hear it?"

Tony said, "Mr. Garamalkis, my father was an emigrant from Italy. He came to this country with his papers in order, and eventually he became a citizen. But one time he had some trouble with agents from the Immigration Service. It was just a mistake in their records, a paperwork foul-up. But they hounded him for more than five weeks. They called him at work and paid surprise visits to our apartment at odd hours. They demanded records and documentation, but when Papa provided those things, they called them forgeries. There were threats. Lots of threats. They even served deportation papers on him before it was all straightened out. He had to hire a lawyer he couldn't afford, and my mother was hysterical most of the time until it was settled. So you see, I don't have any love for the Immigration Service. I wouldn't go one step out of my way to help them pin a rap on you. Not one damn step, Mr. Garamalkis."

The stocky man looked down at Tony for a moment, then shook his head and sighed. "Don't they burn you up? I mean, a year or two ago, when all those Iranian students were making trouble right here in L.A., overturning cars and trying to set houses on fire, did the damn Immigration Service even consider booting their asses out of the country? Hell, no! The agents were too busy harrassing my workers. These people I employ don't burn down other people's houses. They don't overturn cars and throw rocks at policemen. They're good hard-working people. They only want to make a living. The kind of living they can't make south of the border. You know why Immigration spends all its time chasing them? I'll tell you. I've got it figured out. It's because these Mexicans don't fight back. They're not political or religious fanatics like a lot of these Iranians. They aren't crazy or dangerous. It's a whole hell of a lot safer and easier for Immigration to come after these people 'cause they generally just go along quietly. Ahh, the whole damned system's a disgrace."

"I can understand your point of view," Tony said. "So if you'd just take a look at these mug shots—"

But Garamalkis was not ready to answer their questions. He still had a few things to get off his chest. Interrupting Tony, he said, "Four years ago, I got fined the first time. The usual things. Some of my Mexican employees didn't have green cards. Some others were working on expired cards. After I settled up in court. I decided to play it straight from then on. I made up my mind to hire only Mexicans with valid work cards. And if I couldn't find enough of those, I was going to hire U.S. citizens. You know what? I was stupid. I was really stupid to think I could stay in business that way. See, I can only afford to pay minimum wage to most of these workers. Even then, I'm stretching myself thin. The problem is Americans won't work for minimum wage. If you're a citizen, you can get more from welfare for not working than you can make at a job that pays minimum wage. And the welfare's tax-free. So I just about went crazy for about two months, trying to find workers, trying to keep the laundry going out on schedule. I nearly had a heart attack. See, my customers are places like hotels, motels, restaurants, barber shops . . . and they all need to get their stuff back fast and on a dependable schedule. If I hadn't started hiring Mexicans again, I'd have gone out of business."

Frank didn't want to hear any more. He was about to say something sharp, but Tony put a hand on his shoulder and squeezed gently, urging him to be patient.

"Look," Garamalkis said, "I can understand not giving illegal aliens welfare and free medical care and like that. But I can't see the sense in deporting them when they're only doing jobs that no one else wants to do. It's ridiculous. It's a disgrace." He sighed again, looked at the mug shots of Bobby Valdez that he was holding, and said, "Yeah, I know this guy."

"We heard he used to work here."

"That's right."

"When?"

"Beginning of the summer, I think. May. Part of June."

"After he skipped out on his parole officer," Frank said to Tony.

"I don't know anything about that," Garamalkis said.

"What name did he give you?" Tony asked.

"Juan."

"Last name?"

"I don't remember. He was only here six weeks or so. But it'll still be in the files."

Garamalkis stepped down from the platform and led them back across the big room, through the steam and the smell of detergent and the suspicious glances of the employees. In the front office he asked the secretary to check the files, and she found the right pay record in a minute. Bobby had used the name Juan Mazquezza. He had given an address on La Brea Avenue.

"Did he really live at this apartment?" Frank asked.

Garamalkis shrugged. "It wasn't the sort of important job that required a background credit check."

"Did he say why he was quitting?"

"No."

"Did he tell you where he was going?"

"I'm not his mother."

"I mean, did he mention another job?"

"No. He just cut out."

"If we don't find Mazquezza at this address," Tony said, "we'd like to come back and talk to your employees. Maybe one of them got to know him. Maybe somebody here's still friends with him."

"You can come back if you want," Garamalkis said. "But you'll have some trouble talking to my people."

"Why's that?"

Grinning, he said. "A lot of them don't speak English."

Tony grinned back at him and said. "*Yo leo, escribo y hablo español.*"

"Ah," Garamalkis said, impressed.

The secretary made a copy of the pay record for them, and Tony thanked Garamalkis for his cooperation.

In the car, as Frank pulled into traffic and headed toward La Brea Avenue, he said, "I've got to hand it to you."

Tony said, "What's that?"

"You got more out of him quicker than I could have."

Tony was surprised by the compliment. For the first time in their three-month association, Frank had admitted that his partner's techniques were effective.

"I wish I had a little bit of your style," Frank said. "Not all of it, you understand. I still think my way's best most of the time. But now and then we run across someone who'd never open up to me in a million years, but he'd pour out his guts to you in about a minute flat. Yeah, I wish I had a little of your smoothness."

"You can do it."

"Not me. No way."

"Of course, you can."

"You've got a way with people," Frank said. "I don't."

"You can learn it."

"Nah. It works out well enough the way it is. We've got the classic mean-cop-nice-cop routine, except we aren't playing at it. With us, it just sort of naturally works out that way."

"You're not a mean cop."

Frank didn't respond to that. As they stopped at a red light, he said, "There's something else I've got to say, and you probably won't like it."

"Try me," Tony said.

"It's about that woman last night."

"Hilary Thomas?"

"Yeah. You liked her, didn't you?"

"Well . . . sure. She seemed nice enough."

"That's not what I mean. I mean, you *liked* her. You had the hots for her."

"Oh, no. She was good looking, but I didn't—"

"Don't play innocent with me. I saw the way you looked at her."

The traffic light changed.

They rode in silence for a block.

Finally, Tony said, "You're right. I don't get all hot and bothered by every pretty girl I see. You know that."

"Sometimes I think you're a eunuch."

"Hilary Thomas is . . . different. And it's not just the way she looks. She's gorgeous, of course, but that's not all of it. I like the way she moves, the way she handles herself. I like to listen to her talk. Not just the sound of her voice. More than that. I like the way she expresses herself. I like the way she thinks."

"I like the way she looks," Frank said, "but the way she thinks leaves me cold."

"She wasn't lying," Tony said.

"You heard what the sheriff—"

"She might have been mixed up about exactly what happened to her, but she didn't create the whole story out of thin air. She probably saw someone who looked like Frye, and she—"

Frank interrupted. "Here's where I've got to say what you won't want to hear."

"I'm listening."

"No matter how hot she made you, that's no excuse for what you did to me last night."

Tony looked at him, confused. "What'd I do?"

"You're supposed to support your partner in a situation like that."

"I don't understand."

Frank's face was red. He didn't look at Tony. He kept his eyes on the street and said, "Several times last night, when I was questioning her, you took her side against mine."

"Frank, I didn't intend—"

"You tried to keep me from pursuing a line of questioning that I *knew* was important."

"I felt you were too harsh with her."

"Then you should have indicated your opinion a whole hell of a lot more subtly than you did. With your eyes. With a gesture, a touch. You handle it that way all the time. But with her, you came charging in like a white knight."

"She had been through a very trying ordeal and—"

"Bullshit," Frank said. "She hadn't been through any ordeal. She made it all up!"

"I still won't accept that."

"Because you're thinking with your balls instead of your head."

"Frank, that's not true. And it's not fair."

"If you thought I was being so damned rough, why didn't you take me aside and ask what I was after?"

"I *did* ask, for Christ sake!" Tony said, getting angry in spite of himself. "I asked you about it just after you took the call from HQ, while she was still out on the lawn talking to the reporters. I wanted to know what you had, but you wouldn't tell me."

"I didn't think you'd listen," Frank said. "By that time, you were mooning over her like a lovesick boy."

"That's crap, and you know it. I'm as good a cop as you are. I don't let personal feelings screw up my work. But you know what? I think you *do*."

"Do what?"

"I think you do let personal feelings screw up your work sometimes," Tony said.

"What the hell are you talking about?"

"You have this habit of hiding information from me when you come up with something really good," Tony said. "And now that I think about it . . . you only do it when there's a woman in the case, when it's some bit of information you can use to hurt her, something that'll break her down and make her cry. You hide it from me, and then you spring it on her by surprise, in the nastiest way possible."

"I always get what I'm after."

"But there's usually a nicer and easier way it could be gotten."

"Your way, I suppose."

"Just two minutes ago you admitted my way works."

Frank didn't say anything. He glowered at the cars ahead of them.

"You know, Frank, whatever your wife did to you through the divorce, no matter how much she hurt you, that's no reason to hate every woman you meet."

"I don't."

"Maybe not consciously. But subconsciously—"

"Don't give me any of that Freud shit."

"Okay. All right," Tony said. "But I'll swap accusation for accusation. You say I was unprofessional last night. And I say you were unprofessional. Stale-mate."

Frank turned right on La Brea Avenue.

They stopped at another traffic signal.

The light changed, and they inched forward through the thickening traffic. Neither of them spoke for a couple of minutes.

Then Tony said, "Whatever weakness and faults you might have, you're a pretty damned good cop."

Frank glanced at him, startled.

"I mean it," Tony said. "There's been friction between us. A lot of the time, we rub each other the wrong way. Maybe we won't be able to work together. Maybe we'll have to put in requests for new partners. But that'll just be a personality difference. In spite of the fact that you're about three times as rough with people as you ever need to be, you're good at what you do."

Frank cleared his throat. "Well . . . you, too."

"Thank you."

"Except sometimes you're just too . . . sweet."

"And you can be a sour son of a bitch sometimes."

"Want to ask for a new partner?"

"I don't know yet."

"Me either."

"But if we don't start getting along better, it's too dangerous to go on together much longer. Partners who make each other tense can get each other killed."

"I know," Frank said. "I know that. The world's full of assholes and junkies and fanatics with guns. You have to work with your partner as if he was just another part of you, like a third arm. If you don't, you're a lot more likely to get blown away."

"So I guess we should think seriously about whether we're right for each other."

"Yeah," Frank said.

Tony started looking for street numbers on the buildings they passed. "We should be just about there."

"That looks like the place," Frank said, pointing.

The address on Juan Mazquezza's Vee Vee Gee pay record was a sixteen-unit garden apartment complex in a block largely taken over by commercial interests: service stations, a small motel, a tire store, an all-night grocery. From a distance the apartments looked new and somewhat expensive, but on closer inspection Tony saw signs of decay and neglect. The exterior walls needed a new coat of stucco; they were badly chipped and cracked. The wooden stairs and railings and doors all needed new paint. A signpost near the entrance said the place was *Las Palmeras Apartments*. The sign had been hit by a car and badly damaged, but it hadn't been replaced. Las Palmeras looked good from a distance because it was cloaked in greenery that masked some of its defects and softened the splintery edges. But even the landscaping, when scrutinized closely, be-trayed the seediness of Las Palmeras; the shrubs had not been trimmed in a long time, and the trees were raggedy, and the jade shrubs were in need of care.

The pattern at Las Palmeras could be summed up in one word: transition. The few cars in the parking area reinforced that evaluation. There were two middle-priced new cars that were lovingly cared for, gleaming with fresh wax. No doubt they belonged to young men and women of optimism and were signs of accomplishment to them. A battered and corroded old Ford leaned on one flat tire, unused and unusable. An eight-year-old Mercedes stood beyond the Ford, washed and waxed, but a bit worse for wear; there was a rusty dent in one rear fender. In better days, the owner was able to purchase a twenty-five-thousand-dollar automobile, but now he apparently couldn't come up with the two-hundred-dollar deductible part of the repair bill. Las Palmeras was a place for people in transition. For some of them, it was a way station on the upward climb to bright and beckoning careers. For others, it was a precarious spot on the cliff, the last respectable toehold on a sad and inevitable fall into total ruin.

As Frank parked by the manager's apartment, Tony realized that Las Palmeras was a metaphor for Los Angeles. This City of Angels was perhaps the greatest land of opportunity the world had ever known. Incredible quantities of money moved through here, and there were a thousand ways to earn a sizable bankroll. L.A. produced enough success stories to fill a daily newspaper. But the truly astounding affluence also created a variety of tools for self-destruction and made them widely available. Any drug you wanted could be found and bought easier and quicker in Los Angeles than in Boston or New York or Chicago or Detroit. Grass, hashish, heroin, cocaine, uppers, downers, LSD, PCP. . . . The city was a junkie's supermarket. Sex was freer, too. Victorian principles and sensibilities had collapsed in Los Angeles faster than they had in the rest of the country, partly because the rock music business was centered there, and sex was an integral part of that world. But there were other vastly more important factors that had contributed to the unchaining of the average Californian's libido. The climate had something to do with it; the warm dry days and the subtropical light and the competing winds—desert and sea winds—had a powerful erotic influence. The Latin temperament of the Mexican immigrants made its mark on the population at large. But perhaps most of all, in California you felt that you were on the edge of the Western world, on the brink of the unknown, facing an abyss of mystery. It was seldom a conscious awareness of being on the cultural edge, but the subconscious mind was bathed in that knowledge at all times, an exhilarating and sometimes scary feeling. Somehow, all of those things combined to break down inhibitions and stir the gonads. A guilt-free view of sex was healthy, of course. But in the special atmosphere of L.A., where even the most bizarre carnal tastes could be indulged with little difficulty, some men (and women) could become as addicted to sex as to heroin. Tony had seen it happen. There were some people, certain personality types, who chose to throw everything away—money, self-respect, reputation—in an endless party of fleshy embraces and brief wet thrills. If you couldn't find your personal humiliation and ruin in sex and drugs, L.A. provided a smorgasbord of crackpot religions and violence-prone radical political movements for your consideration. And of course, Las Vegas was only one hour away by cheap regularly scheduled airlines, free if you could qualify as a high-rolling junketeer. All of those tools for self-destruction were made possible by the truly incomprehensible affluence. With its wealth and its joyous celebration of freedom, Los Angeles offered both the golden apple and the poisoned pear: positive transition and negative transition. Some people stopped at places like Las Palmeras Apartments on their way up, grabbed the apple, moved to Bel Air or Beverly Hills or Malibu or somewhere else on the Westside, and lived happily ever after. Some people tasted the contaminated fruit, and on the way down they made a stop at Las Palmeras, not always certain how or why they'd wound up there.

In fact, the manager of the apartment complex did not appear to understand how the patterns of transition had brought her to her current circumstances. Her name was Lana Haverby. She was in her forties, a well-tanned blonde in shorts and halter. She had a good opinion of her sexual attractiveness. She walked and stood and sat as if she were posing. Her legs were okay, but the rest of her was far from prime. She was thicker in the middle than she seemed to realize, too big in hips and butt for her skimpy costume. Her breasts were so huge that they were not attractive but freakish. The thin halter top exposed canyonesque cleavage and accentuated the large turgid nipples, but it could not give her breasts the shape and uplift they so desperately needed. When she wasn't changing her pose or adjusting it, when she wasn't trying to gauge what effect her body had on Frank and Tony, she seemed confused, distracted. Her eyes didn't always appear to be focused. She tended to leave sentences unfinished. And several times she looked around in wonder at her small dark living room and at the threadbare furniture, as if she had absolutely no idea how she had come to this place or how long she'd been here. She cocked her head as if she heard whispering voices, just out of range, that were trying to explain it all to her.

Lana Haverby sat in a chair, and they sat on the sofa, and she looked at the mug shots of Bobby Valdez.

"Yeah," she said. "He was a sweetie."

"Does he live here?" Frank asked.

"He lived . . . yeah. Apartment nine . . . was it? But not any more."

"He moved out?"

"Yeah."

"When was that?"

"This summer sometime. I think it was. . . ."

"Was what?" Tony asked.

"First of August," she said.

She recrossed her bare legs, put her shoulders back a bit farther to elevate her breasts as much as possible.

"How long did he live here?" Frank asked.

"I guess it was three months," she said.

"He live alone?"

"You mean was there a chick?"

"A girl, a guy, anybody," Frank said.

"Just him," Lana said. "He was a sweetie, you know."

"Did he leave a forwarding address?"

"No. But I wish he would have."

"Why? Did he skip out on the rent?"

"No. Nothing like that. I'd just like to know where I could. . . ."

She cocked her head, listening to the whispers again.

"Where you could what?" Tony asked.

She blinked. "Oh . . . I'd sure like to know where I could visit him. I was kind of working on him. He turned me on, you know. Got my juices running. I was trying to get him into bed, but he was, you know, sort of shy."

She had not asked why they wanted Bobby Valdez, alias Juan Mazquezza. Tony wondered what she would say if she knew her shy little sweetie was an aggressive, violent rapist.

"Did he have any regular visitors?"

"Juan? Not that I noticed."

She uncrossed her legs, sat with her thighs spread, and watched Tony for his reaction.

"Did he say where he worked?" Frank asked.

"When he first moved in, he worked at some laundry. Later, he got something else."

"Did he say what it was?"

"No. But he was, you know, making good money."

"He have a car?" Frank asked.

"Not at first," she said. "But later. A Jaguar two-plus-two. That was beautiful, man."

"And expensive," Frank said.

"Yeah," she said. "He paid a bundle for it and all in cold hard cash."

"Where would he get that kind of money?"

"I told you. He was making good bread at his new job."

"Are you sure you don't know where he was working?"

"Positive. He wouldn't talk about it. But, you know, as soon as I saw that Jaguar, I knew . . . he wasn't long for this place," she said wistfully. "He was moving up fast."

They spent another five minutes asking questions, but Lana Haverby had nothing more of consequence to tell them. She was not a very observant person, and her recollection of Juan Mazquezza seemed to have tiny holes in it, as if moths had been nibbling at her store of memories.

When Tony and Frank got up to leave, she hurried to the door ahead of them. Her gelatinous breasts jiggled and swayed alarmingly, in what she evidently thought was a wildly provocative display. She affected that ass-swinging, tippy-toe-walk that didn't look good on any coquette over twenty-one; she was forty, a grown woman, unable to discover and explore the dignity and special beauty of her own age, trying to pass for a teenager, and she was pathetic. She stood in the doorway, leaning back slightly against the open door, one long leg bent at the knee, copying a pose she'd seen in a men's magazine or on a cheesecake calendar, virtually begging for a compliment.

Frank turned sideways as he went through the door, barely able to avoid brushing against her breasts. He strode quickly down the walk toward the car, not looking back.

Tony smiled and said, "Thanks for your cooperation, Miss Haverby."

She looked up at him, and her eyes focused on his eyes more clearly than they had focused on anything during the past fifteen minutes. She held his gaze, and a spark of something vital glimmered in her eyes—intelligence, genuine pride, maybe a shred of self-respect—something better and cleaner than had been there before. "I'm going to move up and out of here, too, you know, like Juan did. I wasn't always just a manager at Las Palmeras. I moved in some, you know, pretty rich circles."

Tony didn't want to hear what she had to tell him, but he felt trapped and then mesmerized, like the man who was stopped in the street by the Ancient Mariner.

"Like when I was twenty-three," she said. "I was working as a waitress, but I got up and out of that. That was when the Beatles, you know, were just getting started, like seventeen years ago, and the whole rock thing was really exploding then. You know? A good-looking girl back then, she could connect with the stars, make those important connections, you know, and go just about everywhere with the big groups, travel all over the country with them. Oh, wow, man, those were some fantastic times! Like there wasn't anything you couldn't have or do. They had it all, those groups, and they spread it around, you know. And I was with them. I sure was. I slept with some very famous people, you know. Household names. I was very popular, too. They liked me."

She began to list bestselling rock groups from the sixties. Tony didn't know how many of them she'd actually been with and how many she only imagined she'd been with, but he noticed that she never mentioned individuals; she had been to bed with *groups*, not people.

He had never wondered what became of groupies, those bouncy child-women who wasted some of their best years as hangers-on in the rock music world. But now he knew at least one way they could end up. They trailed after the current idols, offering inarticulate praise, sharing drugs, providing convenient receptacles for the sperm of the rich and famous, giving no thought to time and the changes it would bring. Then one day, after a girl like that had been burnt out by too much booze and too much pot and too much cocaine and maybe a little heroin, when the first hard wrinkles came at the corners of the eyes, when the laugh lines grew a shade too deep, when the pneumatic breasts began to show the first signs of sagging, she was eased out of one group's bed—and discovered that, this time, there was no other group willing to take her in. If she wasn't averse to turning tricks, she could still make a living that way, for a few years. But to some of them that was a turnoff; they didn't think of themselves as hookers but as "girlfriends." For a lot of them, marriage was out, for they'd seen too much and done too much to willingly settle for a tame domestic life. One of them, Lana Haverby, had taken a job at Las Palmeras, a position she thought of as temporary, just a way to swing free rent until she could reconnect with the beautiful people.

"So I won't be here much longer," she said. "I'll be moving on soon. Any time now, you know. I feel lots of good things coming. Like really good vibrations, you know?"

Her situation was ineffably sad, and Tony could think of nothing to say that would make a difference to her. "Uh . . . well . . . I sure wish you all the luck in the world," he said stupidly. He edged past her, through the door.

The gleam of vitality vanished from her eyes, and she was suddenly desperately posing again, shoulders back, chest out. But her face was still weary and drawn. Her belly was still straining at the waistband of her shorts. And her hips were still too big for girlish games. "Hey," she said, "if you're ever in the mood for some wine and, you know, a little conversation. . . ."

"Thank you," he said.

"I mean, feel free to stop by when you're not, you know, on duty."

"I might do that," he lied. Then, because he felt he had sounded insincere and didn't want to leave her without anything, he said, "You've got pretty legs."

That was true, but she didn't know how to accept a compliment, gracefully. She grinned and put her hands on her breasts and said, "It's usually my boobs that get all the attention."

"Well . . . I'll be seeing you," he said, turning away from her and heading toward the car.

After a few steps, he glanced back and saw that she was standing in the open door, head cocked to one side, far away from him and Las Palmeras Apartments, listening to those faint whispering voices that were trying to explain the meaning of her life.

As Tony got into the car, Frank said, "I thought she got her claws into you. I was about ready to call up a SWAT team to rescue you."

Tony didn't laugh. "It's sad."

"What?"

"Lana Haverby."

"You kidding me?"

"The whole situation."

"She's just a dumb broad," Frank said. "But what did you think about Bobby buying the Jag?"

"If he hasn't been robbing banks, there's only one way he could get hold of that kind of cash."

"Dope," Frank said.

"Cocaine, grass, maybe PCP."

"It gives us a whole new place to start looking for the little bastard," Frank said. "We can go out on the street and start putting some muscle on the known dealers, guys who've taken falls for selling junk. Make it hot for them, and if they've got a lot to lose and they know where Bobby is, they'll give him to us on a silver platter."

"Meanwhile," Tony said, "I'd better call in."

He wanted a DMV check on a black Jaguar registered to Juan Masquezza. If they could get a license number for the hot sheet, then looking for Bobby's wheels would be part of every uniformed officer's daily duties.

That didn't mean they would find him right away. In any other city, if a man was wanted as badly as Bobby was wanted, he would not be able to live in the open for a long time. He would be spotted or tracked down in a few weeks at most. But Los Angeles was not like other cities; at least in terms of land area, it was bigger than any other urban center in the nation. L.A. was spread over nearly five hundred square miles. It covered half again as much land as all the boroughs of New York City, ten times more than all of Boston, and almost half as much as the state of Rhode Island. Counting the illegal aliens, which the Census Bureau did not do, the population of the entire metropolitan area was approaching nine million. In this vast maze of streets, alleyways, freeways, hills, and canyons, a clever fugitive could live in the open for many months, going about his business as boldly and unconcernedly as any ordinary citizen.

Tony switched on the radio, which they had left off all morning, called Communications, and asked for the DMV check on Juan Mazquezza and his Jaguar.

The woman handling their frequency had a soft appealing voice. After she took Tony's requests, she informed him that a call had been out for him and Frank the past two hours. It was now 11:45. The Hilary Thomas case was open again, and they were needed at her Westwood house, where other officers had answered a call at 9:30.

Racking the microphone, Tony looked at Frank and said, "I knew it! Dammit, I knew she wasn't lying about the whole thing."

"Don't preen your feathers yet," Frank said disagreeably. "Whatever this new development is, she's probably making it up like she made up all the rest of it."

"You never give up, do you?"

"Not when I know I'm right."

A few minutes later, they pulled up in front of the Thomas house. The circular driveway was filled with two press cars, a station wagon for the police laboratory, and a black-and-white.

As they got out of their car and started across the lawn, a uniformed officer came out of the house and walked toward them. Tony knew him; his name was Warren Prewitt. They met him halfway to the front door.

"You guys answered this call last night?" Prewitt asked.

"That's right," Frank said.

"What is it, do you work twenty-four hours a day?"

"Twenty-six," Frank said.

Tony said, "How's the woman?"

"Shaken up," Prewitt said.

"Not hurt?"

"Some bruises on her throat."

"Serious?"

"No."

"What happened?" Frank said.

Prewitt capsulized the story that Hilary Thomas had told him earlier.

"Any proof that she's telling the truth?" Frank asked.

"I heard how you feel about this case," Prewitt said. "But there is proof."

"Like what?" Frank asked.

"He got into the house last night through a study window. A very smart job it was, too. He taped up the glass so she wouldn't hear it breaking."

"She could have done that herself," Frank said.

"Broken her own window?" Prewitt asked.

"Yeah. Why not?" Frank said.

"Well," Prewitt said, "she wasn't the one who bled all the hell over the place."

"How much blood?" Tony asked.

"Not a whole lot, but not a whole little," Prewitt said. "There's some on the hall floor, a big bloody handprint on the wall up there, drops of blood on the stairs, another smeared print on the downstairs foyer wall, and traces of blood on the doorknob."

"Human blood?" Frank asked.

Prewitt blinked at him. "Huh?"

"I'm wondering if it's a fake, a hoax."

"Oh, for Christ's sake!" Tony said.

"The boys from the lab didn't get here till about forty-five minutes ago," Prewitt said. "They haven't said anything yet. But I'm sure it's human blood. Besides, three of the neighbors saw the man running away."

"Ahhh," Tony said softly.

Frank scowled at the lawn at his feet, as if he were trying to wither the grass.

"He left the house all doubled up," Prewitt said. "He was holding his stomach and shuffling kind of hunched over, which fits in with Miss Thomas's statement that she stabbed him twice in the midsection."

"Where'd he go?" Tony asked.

"We have a witness who saw him climb into a gray Dodge van two blocks south of here. He drove away."

"Got a license number?"

"No," Prewitt said. "But the word's out. There's a want on the van."

Frank Howard looked up. "You know, maybe this attack isn't related to the story she fed us last night. Maybe she cried wolf last night—and then this morning she really was attacked."

"Doesn't that strike you as just a bit too coincidental?" Tony asked exasperatedly.

"Besides, it must be related," Prewitt said. "She swears it was the same man."

Frank met Tony's stare and said, "But it can't be Bruno Frye. You know what Sheriff Laurenski said."

"I never insisted it was Frye," Tony said. "Last night, I figured she was attacked by someone who resembled Frye."

"She insisted—"

"Yeah, but she was scared and hysterical," Tony said. "She wasn't thinking clearly, and she mistook the look-alike for the real thing. It's understandable."

"And you tell me *I'm* building a case on coincidences," Frank said disgustedly.

At that moment Officer Gurney, Prewitt's partner, came out of the house and called to him! "Hey, they found him. The man she stabbed!"

Tony, Frank, and Prewitt hurried to the front door.

"HQ just phoned," Gurney said. "A couple of kids on skateboards found him about twenty-five minutes ago."

"Where?"

"Way the hell down on Sepulveda. In some supermarket parking lot. He was lying on the ground beside his van."

"Dead?"

"As a doornail."

"Did he have any ID?" Tony asked.

"Yeah," Gurney said. "It's just like the lady told us. He's Bruno Frye."

Cold.

Air conditioning thrummed in the walls. Rivers of icy air gushed from two vents near the ceiling.

Hilary was wearing a sea-green autumn dress, not of a light summery fabric, but not heavy enough to ward off a chill. She hugged herself and shivered.

Lieutenant Howard stood at her left side, still looking somewhat embarrassed. Lieutenant Clemenza was on her right.

The room didn't feel like part of a morgue. It was more like a cabin in a spaceship. She could easily imagine that the bone-freezing cold of deep space lay just beyond the gray walls. The steady humming of the air conditioning could be the distant roar of rocket engines. They were standing in front of a window that looked into another room, but she would have preferred to see endless blackness and far-away stars beyond the thick glass. She almost wished she were on a long inter-galactic voyage instead of in a morgue, waiting to identify a man she had killed.

I killed him, she thought.

Those words, ringing in her mind, seemed to make her even colder than she had been a second ago.

She glanced at her watch.

3:18.

"It'll be over in a minute," Lieutenant Clemenza said reassuringly.

Even as Clemenza spoke, a morgue attendant brought a wheeled litter into the room on the other side of the window. He positioned it squarely in front of the glass. A body lay on the cart, hidden by a sheet. The attendant pulled the shroud off the dead man's face, halfway down his chest, then stepped out of the way.

Hilary looked at the corpse and felt dizzy.

Her mouth went dry.

Frye's face was white and still, but she had the insane feeling that at any moment he would turn his head toward her and open his eyes.

"Is it him?" Lieutenant Clemenza asked.

"It's Bruno Frye," she said weakly.

"But is it the man who broke into your house and attacked you?" Lieutenant Howard asked.

"Not this stupid routine again," she said. "Please."

"No, no," Clemenza said, "Lieutenant Howard doesn't doubt your story any more, Miss Thomas. You see, we already know that man is Bruno Frye. We've established that much from the ID he was carrying. What we need to hear from you is that he was the man who attacked you, the man you stabbed."

The dead mouth was unexpressive now, neither frowning nor smiling, but she could remember the evil grin into which it had curved.

"That's him," she said. "I'm positive. I've been positive all along. I'll have nightmares for a long time."

Lieutenant Howard nodded to the morgue attendant beyond the window, and the man covered the corpse.

Another absurd but chilling thought struck her: What if it sits up on the cart and throws the sheet off?

"We'll take you home now," Clemenza said.

She walked out of the room ahead of them, miserable because she had killed a man—but thoroughly relieved and even delighted that he was dead.

They took her home in the unmarked police sedan. Frank drove, and Tony sat up front. Hilary Thomas sat in the back, shoulders drawn up a bit, arms crossed, as if she was cold on such a warm late-September day.

Tony kept finding excuses to turn around and speak to her. He didn't want to take his eyes off her. She was so lovely that she made him feel as he sometimes did in a great museum, when he stood before a particularly exquisite painting done by one of the old masters.

She responded to him, even gave him a couple of smiles, but she wasn't in the mood for light conversation. She was wrapped up in her own thoughts, mostly staring out the side window, mostly silent.

When they pulled into the circular driveway at her place and stopped in front of the door, Frank Howard turned to her and said, "Miss Thomas . . . I . . . well . . . I owe you an apology."

Tony was not startled by the admission, but he was somewhat surprised by the sincere note of contrition in Frank's voice and the supplicatory expression on his face; meekness and humility were not exactly Frank's strongest suits.

Hilary Thomas also seemed surprised. "Oh . . . well . . . I suppose you were only doing your job."

"No," Frank said. "That's the problem. I wasn't doing my job. At least I wasn't doing it well."

"It's over now," she said.

"But will you accept my apologies?"

"Well . . . of course," she said uncomfortably.

"I feel very bad about the way I treated you."

"Frye won't be bothering me any more," she said. "So I guess that's all that really matters."

Tony got out of the car and opened her door. She could not get out by herself because the rear doors of the sedan had no inside handles, a deterrent to escape-minded prisoners. Besides, he wanted to accompany her to the house.

"You may have to testify at a coroner's inquest," he said as they approached the house.

"Why? When I stabbed him, Frye was in my place, against my wishes. He was threatening my life."

"Oh, there's no doubt it's a simple case of self-defense," Tony said quickly. "If you have to appear at an inquest, it'll just be a formality. There's no chance in the world that any sort of charges will be brought or anything like that."

She unlocked the front door, opened it, turned to him, smiled radiantly. "Thank you for believing in me last night, even after what the Napa County Sheriff said."

"We'll be checking into him," Tony said. "He's got some explaining to do. If you're interested, I'll let you know what his excuse is."

"I *am* curious," she said.

"Okay. I'll let you know."

"Thank you."

"It's no bother."

She stepped into the house.

He didn't move.

She looked back at him.

He smiled stupidly.

"Is there anything else?" she asked.

"As a matter of fact, yes."

"What?"

"One more question."

"Yes?"

He had never felt so awkward with a woman before.

"Would you have dinner with me Saturday?"

"Oh," she said. "Well . . . I don't think I can."

"I see."

"I mean, I'd like to."

"You would?"

"But I really don't have much time for a social life these days," she said.

"I see."

"I've just gotten this deal with Warner Brothers, and it's going to keep me busy day and night."

"I understand," he said.

He felt like a high school boy who had just been turned down by the popular cheerleader.

"It was very nice of you to ask," she said.

"Sure. Well . . . good luck with Warner Brothers."

"Thank you."

"I'll let you know about Sheriff Laurenski."

"Thank you."

He smiled, and she smiled.

He turned away, started toward the car, and heard the door of the house close behind him. He stopped and looked back at it.

A small toad hopped out of the shrubbery, onto the stone footpath in front of Tony. It sat in the middle of the walk and peered up at him, its eyes rolled way back to achieve the necessary angle, its tiny green-brown chest rapidly expanding and contracting.

Tony looked at the toad and said, "Did I give up too easily?"

The little toad made a peeping-croaking sound.

"What have I got to lose?" Tony asked.

The toad peeped-croaked again.

"That's the way I look at it. I've got nothing to lose."

He stepped around the amphibian cupid and rang the bell. He could sense Hilary Thomas looking at him through the one-way peephole lens, and when she opened the door a second later, he spoke before she could. "Am I terribly ugly?"

"What?"

"Do I look like Quasimodo or something?"

"Really, I—"

"I don't pick my teeth in public," he said.

"Lieutenant Clemenza—"

"Is it because I'm a cop?"

"What?"

"You know what some people think?"

"What do some people think?"

"They think cops are socially unacceptable."

"Well, I'm not one of those people."

"You're not a snob?"

"No. I just—"

"Maybe you turned me down because I don't have a lot of money and don't live in Westwood."

"Lieutenant, I've spent most of my life without money, and I haven't always lived in Westwood."

"Then I wonder what's wrong with me," he said, looking down at himself in mock bewilderment.

She smiled and shook her head. "Nothing's wrong with you, Lieutenant."

"Thank God!"

"Really, I said no for just one reason. I don't have time for—"

"Miss Thomas, even the President of the United States manages to take a night off now and then. Even the head of General Motors has leisure time. Even the Pope. Even God rested the seventh day. No one can be busy all the time."

"Lieutenant—"

"Call me Tony."

"Tony, after what I've been through the last two days, I'm afraid I wouldn't be a barrel of laughs."

"If I wanted to go to dinner with a barrel of laughs, I'd take a bunch of monkeys."

She smiled again, and he wanted to take her beautiful face in his hands and kiss it all over.

She said, "I'm sorry. But I need to be alone for a few days."

"That's exactly what you don't need after the sort of experience you've had. You need to get out, be among people, get your spirits up. And I'm not the only one who thinks so." He turned and pointed to the stone footpath behind him. The toad was still there. It had turned around to look at them.

"Ask Mr. Toad," Tony said.

"Mr. Toad?"

"An acquaintance of mine. A very wise person." Tony stooped down and stared at the toad. "Doesn't she need to get out and enjoy herself, Mr. Toad?"

It blinked slow heavy lids and made its funny little sound right on cue.

"You're absolutely correct," Tony told it. "And don't you think I'm the one she should go out with?"

"*Scree-ooak,*" it said.

"And what will you do to her if she turns me down again?"

"*Scree-ooak, scree-oak.*"

"Ahhh," Tony said, nodding his head in satisfaction as he stood up.

"Well, what did he say?" Hilary asked, grinning. "What will he do to me if I won't go out with you—give me warts?"

Tony looked serious. "Worse than that. He tells me he'll get into the walls of your house, work his way up to your bedroom, and croak so loudly every night that you won't be able to sleep until you give in."

She smiled. "Okay. I give up."

"Saturday night?"

"All right."

"I'll pick you up at seven."

"What should I wear?"

"Be casual," he said.

"See you Saturday at seven."

He turned to the toad and said, "Thank you, my friend."

It hopped off the walk, into the grass, then into the shrubbery.

Tony looked at Hilary. "Gratitude embarrasses him."

She laughed and closed the door.

Tony walked back to the car and got in, whistling happily.

As Frank drove away from the house, he said, "What was that all about?"

"I got a date," Tony said.

"With her?"

"Well, not with her sister."

"Lucky stiff."

"Lucky toad."

"Huh?"

"Private joke."

When they had gone a couple of blocks, Frank said, "It's after four o'clock. By the time we get this heap back to the depot and check out for the day, it'll be five o'clock."

"You want to quit on time for once?" Tony asked.

"Not much we can do about Bobby Valdez until tomorrow anyway."

"Yeah," Tony said. "Let's be reckless."

A few blocks farther on, Frank said, "Want to have a drink after we check out?"

Tony looked at him in amazement. That was the first time in their association that Frank had suggested hanging out together after hours.

"Just a drink or two," Frank said. "Unless you have something planned—"

"No. I'm free."

"You know a bar?"

"The perfect place. It's called The Bolt Hole."

"It's not around HQ, is it? Not a place where a lot of cops go?"

"So far as I know, I'm the only officer of the law who patronizes it. It's on Santa Monica Boulevard, out near Century City. Just a couple of blocks from my apartment."

"Sounds good," Frank said. "I'll meet you there."

They rode the rest of the way to the police garage in silence—somewhat more companionable silence than that in which they had worked before, but silence nonetheless.

What does he want? Tony wondered. Why has that famous Frank Howard reserve finally broken down?

At 4:30, the Los Angeles medical examiner ordered a limited autopsy on the body of Bruno Gunther Frye. If at all possible, the corpse was to be opened only in the area of the abdominal wounds, sufficient to determine if those two punctures had been the sole cause of death.

The medical examiner would not perform the autopsy himself, for he had to catch a 5:30 flight to San Francisco in order to keep a speaking engagement. The chore was assigned to a pathologist on his staff.

The dead man waited in a cold room with other dead men, on a cold cart, motionless beneath a white shroud.

Hilary Thomas was exhausted. Every bone ached dully; every joint seemed enflamed. Every muscle felt as if it had been put through a blender at high speed and then reconstituted. Emotional strain could have precisely the same physiological effect as strenuous physical labor.

She was also jumpy, much too tense to be able to refresh with a nap. Each time the big house made a normal settling noise, she wondered if the sound was actually the squeak of a floorboard under the weight of an intruder. When the softly sighing wind brushed a palm frond or a pine branch against a window, she imagined someone was stealthily cutting the glass or prying at a window lock. But when there was a long period of perfect quiet, she sensed something sinister in the silence. Her nerves were worn thinner than the knees of a compulsive penitent's trousers.

The best cure she had ever found for nervous tension was a good book. She looked through the shelves in the study and chose James Clavell's most recent novel, a massive story set in the Orient. She poured a glass of Dry Sack on the rocks, settled down in the deep brown armchair, and began to read.

Twenty minutes later, when she was just beginning to lose herself thoroughly in Clavell's story, the telephone rang. She got up and answered it. "Hello."

There was no response.

"Hello?"

The caller listened for a few seconds, then hung up.

Hilary put down the receiver and stared at it thoughtfully for a moment. Wrong number?

Must have been.

But why didn't he say so?

Some people just don't know any better, she told herself. They're rude.

But what if it wasn't a wrong number. What if it was . . . something else.

Stop looking for goblins in every shadow! she told herself angrily. Frye's dead. It was a bad thing, but it's over and done with. You deserve a rest, a couple of days to collect your nerves and wits. But then you've got to stop looking over your shoulder and get on with your life. Otherwise, you'll end up in a padded room.

She curled up in the armchair again, but she caught a chill that brought goosebumps to her arms. She went to the closet and got a blue and green knitted afghan, returned to the chair, and draped the blanket over her legs.

She sipped the Dry Sack.

She started reading Clavell again.

In a while, she forgot about the telephone call.

After signing out for the day, Tony went home and washed his face, changed from his suit into jeans and a checkered blue shirt. He put on a thin tan jacket and walked two blocks to The Bolt Hole.

Frank was already there, sitting in a back booth, still in his suit and tie, sipping Scotch.

The Bolt Hole—or simply The Hole, as regular customers referred to it— was that rare and vanishing thing: an ordinary neighborhood bar. During the past two decades, in response to a continuously fracturing and subdividing culture, the American tavern industry, at least that part of it in cities and suburbs, had indulged in a frenzy of specialization. But The Hole had successfully bucked the trend. It wasn't a gay bar. It wasn't a singles' bar or a swingers' bar. It wasn't a bar patronized primarily by bikers or truckers or show business types or off-duty policemen or account executives; its clientele was a mixture, representative of the community. It wasn't a topless go-go bar. It wasn't a rock and roll bar or a country and western bar. And, thank God, it wasn't a sports bar with one of those six-foot television screens and Howard Cosell's voice in quadraphonic sound. The Hole had nothing more to offer than pleasantly low lighting, cleanliness, courtesy, comfortable stools and booths, a jukebox that wasn't turned too loud, hot dogs and hamburgers served from the minuscule kitchen, and good drinks at reasonable prices.

Tony slide into the booth, facing Frank.

Penny, a sandy-haired waitress with pinchable cheeks and a dimpled chin, stopped by the table. She ruffled Tony's hair and said, "What do you want, Renoir?"

"A million in cash, a Rolls-Royce, eternal life, and the acclaim of the masses," Tony said.

"What'll you settle for?"

"A bottle of Coors."

"That we can provide," she said.

"Bring me another Scotch," Frank said. When she went to the bar to get their drinks, Frank said, "Why'd she call you Renoir?"

"He was a famous French painter."

"So?"

"Well, I'm a painter, too. Neither French nor famous. It's just Penny's way of teasing me."

"You paint pictures?" Frank asked.

"Certainly not houses."

"How come you never mentioned it?"

"I made a few observations about fine art a time or two," Tony said. "But you greeted the subject with a marked lack of interest. In fact, you couldn't have shown less enthusiasm if I'd wanted to debate the fine points of Swahili grammar or discuss the process of decomposition in dead babies."

"Oil paintings?" Frank asked.

"Oils. Pen and ink. Watercolors. A little bit of everything, but mostly oils."

"How long you been at it?"

"Since I was a kid."

"Have you sold any?"

"I don't paint to sell."

"What do you do it for?"

"My own satisfaction."

"I'd like to see some of your work."

"My museum has odd hours, but I'm sure a visit can be arranged."

"Museum?"

"My apartment. There's not much furniture in it, but it's chockfull of paintings."

Penny brought their drinks.

They were silent for a while, and then they talked for a few minutes about Bobby Valdez, and then they were silent again.

There were about sixteen or eighteen people in the bar. Several of them had ordered sandwiches. The air was filled with the mouth-watering aroma of sizzling ground sirloin and chopped onions.

Finally, Frank said, "I suppose you're wondering why we're here like this."

"To have a couple of drinks."

"Besides that." Frank stirred his drink with a swizzle stick. Ice cubes rattled softly. "There are a few things I have to say to you."

"I thought you said them all this morning, in the car, after we left Vee Vee Gee."

"Forget what I said then."

"You had a right to say it."

"I was full of shit," Frank said.

"No, maybe you had a point."

"I tell you, I was full of shit."

"Okay," Tony said. "You were full of shit."

Frank smiled. "You could have argued with me a bit more."

"When you're right, you're right," Tony said.

"I was wrong about the Thomas woman."

"You already apologized to her, Frank."

"I feel like I should apologize to you."

"Not necessary."

"But you saw something there, saw she was telling the truth. I didn't even get a whiff of that. I was off on the wrong scent altogether. Hell, you even pushed my nose in it, and I couldn't pick up the right smell."

"Well, sticking strictly to nasal imagery, you might say you couldn't get the scent because your nose was so far out of joint."

Frank nodded glumly. His broad face seemed to sag into the melancholy mask of a bloodhound. "Because of Wilma. My nose is out of joint because of Wilma."

"Your ex-wife?"

"Yeah. You hit it right on the head this morning when you said I've been a woman-hater."

"Must have been bad, what she did to you."

"No matter what she did," Frank said, "that's no excuse for what I've let happen to me."

"You're right."

"I mean, you can't hide from women, Tony."

"They're everywhere," Tony agreed.

"Christ, you know how long it's been since I slept with a woman?"

"No."

"Ten months. Since she left me, since four months before the divorce came through."

Tony couldn't think of anything to say. He didn't feel he knew Frank well enough to engage in an intimate discussion of his sex life, yet it was obvious that the man badly needed someone to listen and care.

"If I don't get back in the swim pretty soon," Frank said, "I might as well go away and be a priest."

Tony nodded. "Ten months sure is a long time," he said awkwardly.

Frank didn't respond. He stared into his Scotch as he might have stared into a crystal ball, trying to see his future. Clearly, he wanted to talk about Wilma and the divorce and where he should go from here, but he didn't want to feel that he was forcing Tony to listen to his trouble. He had a lot of pride. He wanted to be coaxed, cajoled, drawn out with questions and murmured sympathy.

"Did Wilma find another man or what?" Tony asked, and knew immediately that he had gone to the heart of the matter much too quickly.

Frank was not ready to talk about that part of it, and he pretended not to hear the question. "What bothers me is the way I'm screwing up in my work. I've always been damned good at what I do. Just about perfect, if I say so myself. Until the divorce. Then I turned sour on women, and pretty soon I went sour on the job, too." He took a long pull on his Scotch. "And what the hell's going on with that damned crazy Napa County Sheriff? Why would he lie to protect Bruno Frye?"

"We'll find out sooner or later," Tony said.

"You want another drink?"

"Okay."

Tony could see that they were going to be sitting in The Bolt Hole for a long while. Frank wanted to talk about Wilma, wanted to get rid of all the poison that had been building up in him and eating at his heart for nearly a year, but he was only able to let it out a drop at a time.

It was a busy day for Death in Los Angeles. Many died of natural causes, of course, and therefore were not required by law to come under a coroner's probing scalpel. But the medical examiner's office had nine others with which to deal. There were two traffic fatalities in an accident certain to involve charges of criminal negligence. Two men were dead of gunshot wounds. One child had apparently been beaten to death by a mean-tempered drunken father.

A woman had drowned in her own swimming pool, and two young men had died of what appeared to be drug overdoses. And there was Bruno Frye.

At 7:10 Thursday evening, hoping to catch up on the backlog of work, a pathologist at the city morgue completed a limited autopsy on the body of Bruno Gunther Frye, male, Caucasian, age forty. The doctor did not find it necessary to dissect the corpse beyond the general area of the two abdominal traumata, for he was swiftly able to determine that the deceased definitely had perished from those injuries and no other. The upper wound was not critical; the knife tore muscle tissue and grazed a lung. But the lower wound was a mess; the blade ripped open the stomach, pierced the pyloric vein, and damaged the pancreas, among other things. The victim had died of massive internal bleeding.

The pathologist sewed up the incisions he had made as well as the two crusted wounds. He sponged blood and bile and specks of tissue from the repaired stomach and the huge chest.

The dead man was transferred from the autopsy table (which still bore traces of red-brown gore in the stainless-steel blood gutters) to a cart. An attendant pushed the cart to a refrigerated room where other bodies, already cut open and explored and sewn up again, now waited patiently for their ceremonies and their graves.

After the attendant left, Bruno Frye lay silent and motionless, content in the company of the dead as he had never been in the company of the living.

Frank Howard was getting drunk. He had taken off his suit jacket and his tie, had opened the first two buttons of his shirt. His hair was in disarray because he kept running his fingers through it. His eyes were bloodshot, and his broad face was doughy. He slurred some of his words, and every once in a while he repeated himself, stressing a point so often that Tony had to gently nudge him on, as if bumping a phonograph needle out of a bad groove. He was downing two glasses of Scotch to one of Tony's beers.

The more he drank, the more he talked about the women in his life. The closer he got to being completely smashed, the closer he got to the central agony of his life: the loss of two wives.

During his second year as a uniformed officer with the LAPD, Frank Howard had met his first wife, Barbara Ann. She was a salesgirl working the jewelry counter in a downtown department store, and she helped him choose a gift for his mother. She was so charming, so petite, so pretty and dark-eyed, that he couldn't resist asking for a date, even though he was certain she would turn him down. She accepted. They were married seven months later. Barbara Ann was a planner; long before the wedding, she worked out a detailed agenda for their first four years together. She would continue to work at the department store, but they would not spend one penny of her earnings. All of her money would go into a savings account that would later be used to make a down payment on a house. They would try to save as much as they could from his salary by living in a safe, clean, but inexpensive studio apartment. They would sell his Pontiac because it was a gas hog, and because they would be living close enough to the store for Barbara Ann to walk to work; her Volkswagen would be sufficient to get him to and from divisional HQ, and his equity in his car would start the house fund. She had even planned a day-to-day menu for the first six months, nourishing meals prepared within a tight budget. Frank loved this stern accountant streak in her, partly because it seemed so out of character. She was a light-hearted, cheerful woman, quick to laugh, sometimes even giddy, impulsive in matters not financial, and a wonderful bedmate, always eager to make love and damned good at it. She was not an accountant in matters of the flesh; she never planned their love-making; it was usually sudden and surprising and passionate. But she planned that they would buy a house only after they'd acquired at least forty percent of the purchase price. And she knew exactly how many rooms it should have and what size each room should be; she drew up a floor plan of the ideal place, and she kept it in a dresser drawer, taking it out now and then to stare at it and dream. She wanted children a great deal, but she planned not to have them until she was secure in her own house. Barbara Ann planned for just about every eventuality—except cancer. She contracted a virulent form of lymph cancer, which was diagnosed two years and two days after she married Frank, and three months after that, she was dead.

Tony sat in the booth at The Bolt Hole, with a beer getting warm in front of him, and he listened to Frank Howard with the growing realization that this was the first time the man had shared his grief with anyone. Barbara Ann had died in 1958, twenty-two years ago, and in all the time since, Frank had not expressed to anyone the pain he had felt while watching her waste away and die. It was a pain that had never dwindled; it burned within him now as fiercely as it had then. He drank more Scotch and searched for words to describe his agony; and Tony was amazed at the sensitivity and depth of feeling that had been so well-concealed behind the hard Teutonic face and those usually expressionless blue eyes.

Losing Barbara Ann had left Frank weak, disconnected, miserable, but he had sternly repressed the tears and the anguish because he had been afraid that if he gave in to them he would not be able to regain control. He had sensed self-destructive impulses in himself: a terrible thirst for booze that he had never experienced prior to his wife's death; a tendency to drive much too fast and recklessly, though he had previously been a cautious driver. To improve his state of mind, to save himself from himself, he had submerged his pain in the demands of his job, had given his life to LAPD, trying to forget Barbara Ann in long hours of police work and study. The loss of her left an aching hole in him that would never be filled, but in time he managed to plate over that hole with an obsessive interest in his work and with total dedication to the Department.

For nineteen years he survived, even thrived, on the monotonous regimen of a workaholic. As a uniformed officer, he could not extend his working hours, so he went to school five nights a week and Saturdays, until he earned a Bachelor of Science in Criminology. He used his degree and his superb service record to climb into the ranks of the plainclothes detectives, where he could labor well beyond his scheduled tour of duty each day without screwing up a dispatcher's roster. During his ten- and twelve- and fourteen-hour workdays, he thought of nothing else but the cases to which he had been assigned. Even when he wasn't on the job, he thought about current investigations to the exclusion of just about everything else, pondered them while standing in the shower and while trying to fall asleep at night, mulled over new evidence while eating his early breakfasts and his solitary late-night dinners. He read almost nothing but criminology textbooks and case studies of criminal types. For nineteen years he was a cop's cop, a detective's detective.

In all that time, he never got serious about a woman. He didn't have time for dating, and somehow it didn't seem right to him. It wasn't fair to Barbara Ann. He led a celibate's life for weeks, then indulged in a few nights of torrid release with a series of paid partners. In a way he could not fully understand, having sex with a hooker was not a betrayal of Barbara Ann's memory, for the exchange of cash for services made it strictly a business transaction and not a matter of the heart in even the slightest regard.

And then he met Wilma Compton.

Leaning back against the booth in The Bolt Hole, Frank seemed to choke on the woman's name. He wiped one hand across his clammy face, pushed spread fingers through his hair, and said, "I need another double Scotch." He made a great effort to articulate each syllable, but that only made him sound more thoroughly drunk than if he had slurred and mangled his words.

"Sure," Tony said. "Another Scotch. But we ought to get a bite of something, too."

"Not hungry," Frank said.

"They make excellent cheeseburgers," Tony said. "Let's get a couple of those and some French fries."

"No. Just Scotch for me."

Tony insisted, and finally Frank agreed to the burger but not the fries.

Penny took the food order, but when she heard Frank wanted another Scotch, she wasn't sure that was a good idea.

"I didn't drive here," Frank assured her, again stressing each sound in each word. "I came in a taxi 'cause I intended to get stupid drunk. I'll go home in a taxi, too. So please, you dimpled little darling, bring me another of those delicious double Scotches."

Tony nodded at her. "If he can't get a cab later, I'll take him home."

She brought new drinks for both of them. A half-finished beer stood in front of Tony, but it was warm and flat, and Penny took it away.

Wilma Compton.

Wilma was twelve years younger than Frank, thirty-one when he first met her. She was charming, petite, pretty, and dark-eyed. Slender legs. Supple body. Exciting swell of hips. A tight little ass. A pinched waist and breasts a shade too full for her size. She wasn't quite as lovely or quite as charming or quite as petite as Barbara Ann had been. She didn't have Barbara Ann's quick wit or Barbara Ann's industrious nature or Barbara Ann's compassion. But on the surface, at least, she bore enough resemblance to the long-dead woman to stir Frank's dormant interest in romance.

Wilma was a waitress at a coffee shop where policemen often ate lunch. The sixth time she waited on Frank, he asked for a date, and she said yes. On their fourth date, they went to bed. Wilma had the same hunger and energy and willingness to experiment that had made Barbara Ann a wonderful lover. If at times she seemed totally concerned with her own gratification and not at all interested in his, Frank was able to convince himself that her selfishness would pass, that it was merely the result of her not having had a satisfying relationship in a long time. Besides, he was proud that he could arouse her so easily, so completely. For the first time since he'd slept with Barbara Ann, love was a part of his love-making, and he'd thought he perceived the same emotion in Wilma's response to him. After they had been sleeping together for two months, he asked her to marry him. She said no, and thereafter she no longer wanted to date him; the only time he could see her and talk to her was when he stopped at the coffee shop.

Wilma was admirably forthright about her reasons for refusing him. She wanted to get married; she was actively looking for the right man, but the right man had to have a substantial bankroll and a damned good job. A cop, she said, would never make enough money to provide her with the lifestyle and the security she wanted. Her first marriage had failed largely because she and her husband had always been arguing about bills and budgets. She had discovered that worries about finances could burn the love out of a relationship, leaving only an ashy shell of bitterness and anger. That had been a terrible experience, and she had made up her mind never to go through it again. She didn't rule out marrying for love, but there had to be financial security as well. She was afraid she sounded hard, but she could not endure the kind of pain she had endured before. She got all shaky-voiced and teary-eyed when she spoke of it. She would not, she said, risk the unbearably sad and depressing dissolution of another love affair because of a lack of money.

Strangely, her determination to marry for money did not decrease Frank's respect for her or dampen his ardor. Because he had been lonely for so long, he was eager to continue their relationship, even if he had to wear the biggest pair of rose-colored glasses ever made in order to maintain the illusion of romance. He revealed his financial situation to her, virtually begged her to look at his savings account passbook and short-term certificates of deposit which totaled nearly thirty-two thousand dollars. He told her what his salary was and carefully explained that he would be able to retire fairly young with a fine pension, young enough to use some of their savings to start a small business and earn even more money. If security was what she wanted, he was her man.

Thirty-two thousand dollars and a police pension were not sufficient for Wilma Compton. "I mean," she said, "it's a good little piece of change, but then you don't own a house or anything, Frank." She fingered the savings account passbooks for a long moment, as if receiving sexual pleasure from them, but then she handed them back and said, "Sorry, Frank. But I want to shoot for something better than this. I'm still young, and I look five years younger than I really am. I have some time yet, a little more time to look around. And I'm afraid that even thirty-two thousand isn't a big bankroll these days. I'm afraid it might not be enough to get us through some crisis. And I won't go into something with you if there's a chance it could . . . get hateful . . . and mean . . . like it did the last time I was married."

He was crushed.

"Christ, I was acting like such a fool!" Frank wailed, pounding one fist into the table to emphasize his foolishness. "I had made up my mind that she was exactly like Barbara Ann, something special, someone rare and precious. No matter what she did, no matter how crude she was or how coarse or how unfeeling, I made excuses for her. Lovely excuses. Dandy, elaborate, creative excuses. Stupid. I was stupid, stupid, dumb as a jackass. Jesus!"

"What you did was understandable," Tony said.

"It was stupid."

"You were alone a long, long time," Tony said. "You had such a wonderful two years with Barbara Ann that you thought you'd never have anything half as good again, and you didn't want to settle for less. So you shut out the world. You convinced yourself that you didn't need anyone. But we all need someone, Frank. We all need people to care about. A hunger for love and comradeship is as natural to our species as the requirement for food and water. So the need built up inside of you all those years, and when you saw someone who resembled Barbara Ann, when you saw Wilma, you couldn't keep that need bottled up any longer. Nineteen years of wanting and needing came bubbling out of you all at once. You were bound to act kind of crazy. It would have been nice if Wilma had turned out to be a good woman who deserved what you had to offer. But you know, actually, it's surprising someone like Wilma didn't get her claws into you years ago."

"I was a sap."

"No."

"An idiot."

"No, Frank. You were human," Tony said. "That's all. Just human like the rest of us."

Penny brought the cheeseburgers.

Frank ordered another double scotch.

"You want to know what made Wilma change her mind?" Frank asked. "You want to know why she finally agreed to marry me?"

"Sure," Tony said. "But why don't you eat your burger first."

Frank ignored the sandwich. "My father died and left me everything. At first it looked like maybe thirty thousand bucks, but then I discovered the old man had collected a bunch of five- and ten-thousand dollar life insurance policies over the past thirty years. After taxes, the estate amounted to ninety thousand dollars."

"I'll be damned."

"With what I had already," Frank said, "that windfall was enough for Wilma."

"Maybe you'd have been better off if your father had died poor," Tony said.

Frank's red-rimmed eyes grew watery, and for a moment he looked as if he was about to weep. But he blinked rapidly and held back the tears. In a voice laden with despair, he said, "I'm ashamed to admit it, but when I found out how much money was in the estate, I stopped caring about my old man dying. The insurance policies turned up just one week after I buried him, and the moment I found them I thought, *Wilma.* All of a sudden I was so damned happy I couldn't stand still. As far as I was concerned, my dad might as well have been dead twenty years. It makes me sick to my stomach to think how I behaved. I mean, my dad and I weren't really close, but I owed him a lot more grieving than I gave. Jesus, I was one selfish son of a bitch, Tony."

"It's over, Frank. It's done," Tony said. "And like I said, you were a bit crazy. You weren't exactly responsible for your actions."

Frank put both hands over his face and sat that way for a minute, shaking but not crying. Finally, he looked up and said, "So when she saw I had almost a hundred and twenty-five thousand dollars, Wilma wanted to marry me. In eight months, she cleaned me out."

"This is a community property state," Tony said. "How could she get more than half of what you had?"

"Oh, she didn't take anything in the divorce."

"What?"

"Not one penny."

"Why?"

"It was all gone by then."

"Gone?"

"Poof!"

"She spent it?"

"Stole it," Frank said numbly.

Tony put down his cheeseburger, wiped his mouth with a napkin. "Stole it? How?"

Frank was still quite drunk, but suddenly he spoke with an eerie clarity and precision. It seemed important to him that this indictment of her, more than anything else in his story, should be clearly understood. She had left him nothing but his indignation, and now he wanted to share that with Tony. "As soon as we got back from our honeymoon, she announced she was taking over the bookkeeping. She was going to attend to all our banking business, watch over our investments, balance our checkbook. She signed up for a course in investment planning at a business school, and she worked out a detailed budget for us. She was very adamant about it, very businesslike, and I was really pleased because she seemed so much like Barbara Ann."

"You'd told her that Barbara Ann had done those things?"

"Yeah. Oh, Jesus, yeah. I set myself up to be picked clean. I sure did."

Suddenly, Tony wasn't hungry any more.

Frank pushed one shaky hand through his hair. "See, there wasn't any way I could have suspected her. I mean, she was so good to me. She learned to cook my favorite things. She always wanted to hear about my day when I got home, and she listened with such interest. She didn't want a lot of clothes or jewelry or anything. We went out to dinner and to the movies now and then, but she always said it was a waste of money; she said she was just as happy staying home with me and watching TV together or just talking. She wasn't in any hurry to buy a house. She was so . . . easy-going. She gave me massages when I came home stiff and sore. And in bed . . . she was fabulous. She was perfect. Except . . . except . . . all the time she was cooking and listening and massaging and fucking my brains out, she was. . . . ."

"Bleeding your joint bank accounts."

"Of every last dollar. All except ten thousand that was in a long-term certificate of deposit."

"And then just walked out?"

Frank shuddered. "I came home one day, and there was a note from her. It said, 'If you want to know where I am, call this number and ask for Mr. Freyborn.' Freyborn was a lawyer. She'd hired him to handle the divorce. I was stunned. I mean, there was never any indication. . . . Anyway, Freyborn refused to tell me where she was. He said it would be a simple case, easily settled because she didn't want alimony or anything else from me. She didn't want a penny, Freyborn said. She just wanted out. I was hit hard. Real hard. Jesus, I couldn't figure out what I'd done. For a while, I nearly went crazy trying to figure out where I went wrong. I thought maybe I could change, learn to be a better person, and win her back. And then . . . two days later, when I needed to write a check, I saw the account was down to three dollars. I went to the bank and then to the savings and loan company, and after that I knew why she didn't want a penny. She'd taken all the pennies already."

"You didn't let her get away with it," Tony said.

Frank slugged down some Scotch. He was sweating. His face was pasty and sheet-white. "At first, I was just kind of numb and . . . I don't know . . . suicidal, I guess. I mean, I didn't try to kill myself, but I didn't care if I lived either. I was in a daze, a kind of trance."

"But eventually you snapped out of that."

"Part way. I'm still a little numb. But I came part of the way out of it," Frank said. "Then I was ashamed of myself. I was ashamed of what I'd let her do to me. I was such a sap, such a dumb son of a bitch. I didn't want anyone to know, not even my attorney."

"That's the first purely stupid thing you did," Tony said. "I can understand the rest of it, but that—"

"Somehow, it seemed to me that if I let everyone know how Wilma conned me, then everyone would think that every word I'd ever said about Barbara Ann was wrong, too. I was afraid people would get the idea that Barbara Ann had been conning me just like Wilma, and it was important to me, more important than anything else in the world, that Barbara Ann's memory be kept clean. I know it sounds a little crazy now, but that's how I looked at it then."

Tony didn't know what to say.

"So the divorce went through smooth as glass," Frank said. "There weren't any long discussions about the details of the settlement. In fact, I never got to see Wilma again except for a few minutes in court, and I haven't talked to her since the morning of the day she walked out."

"Where is she now? Do you know?"

Frank finished his Scotch. When he spoke his voice was different, soft, almost a whisper, not as if he was trying to keep the rest of the story secret from other customers in The Hole, but as if he no longer had sufficient strength to speak in a normal tone of voice. "After the divorce went through, I got curious about her. I took out a small loan against that certificate of deposit she'd left behind, and I hired a private investigator to find out where she was and what she was doing. He turned up a lot of stuff. Very interesting stuff. She got married again just nine days after our divorce was final. Some guy named Chuck Pozley down in Orange County. He owns one of those electronic game parlors in a shopping center in Costa Mesa. He's worth maybe seventy or eighty thousand bucks. The way it looks, Wilma was seriously thinking about marrying him just when I inherited all the money from my dad. So what she did, she married me, milked me dry, and then went to this Chuck Pozley with my money. They used some of her capital to open two more of those game parlors, and it looks like they'll do real well."

"Oh, Jeez," Tony said.

This morning he had known almost nothing at all about Frank Howard, and now he knew almost everything. More than he really wanted to know. He was a good listener; that was both his blessing and his curse. His previous partner, Michael Savatino, often told him that he was a superior detective largely because people liked and trusted him and were willing to talk to him about almost anything. And the reason they were willing to talk to him, Michael said, was because he was a good listener. And a good listener, Michael said, was a rare and wonderful thing in a world of self-interest, self-promotion, and self-love. Tony listened willingly and attentively to all sorts of people because, as a painter fascinated by hidden patterns, he was seeking the overall pattern of human existence and meaning. Even now, as he listened to Frank, he thought of a quote from Emerson that he had read a long time ago: *The Sphinx must solve her own riddle. If the whole of history is in one man, it is all to be explained from individual experience.* All men and women and children were fascinating puzzles, great mysteries, and Tony was seldom bored by their stories.

Still speaking so softly that Tony had to lean forward to hear him, Frank said, "Pozley knew what Wilma had in mind for me. It looks like they were probably seeing each other a couple of days a week while I was at work. All the time she was playing the perfect wife, she was stealing me blind and fucking this Pozley. The more I thought about it, the madder I got, until finally I decided to tell my attorney what I should have told him in the first place."

"But it was too late?"

"That's about what it comes down to. Oh, I could have initiated some sort of court action against her. But the fact that I hadn't accused her of theft earlier, during the divorce proceedings, would have weighed pretty heavily against me. I'd have spent most of the money I had left on lawyers' fees, and I'd probably have lost the suit anyway. So I decided to put it behind me. I figured I'd lose myself in my work, like I'd done after Barbara Ann died. But I was torn up a whole lot worse than I realized. I couldn't do my job right any more. Every woman I had to deal with . . . I don't know. I guess I just . . . just saw Wilma in all women. If I had the slightest excuse, I got downright vicious with women I had to question, and then before long I was getting too rough with *every* witness, both men and women. I started losing perspective, overlooking clues a child would spot. . . . I had a hell of a falling out with my partner, and so here I am." His voice sank lower by the second, and he gave up the struggle for clarity; his words began to get mushy. "After Barbara Ann died, at least I had my work. At least I had somethin'. But Wilma took everythin'. She took my money and my self-respec', and she even took my ambition. I juss can't seem to care 'bout nothin' any more." He slid out of the booth and stood up, swaying like a toy clown that had springs for ankles. "S'cuse me. Gotta go pee." He staggered across the tavern to the men's room door, giving an exaggerated wide berth to everyone he encountered on the way.

Tony sighed and closed his eyes. He was weary, both in body and soul.

Penny stopped by the table and said, "You'd be doing him a favor if you took him home now. He's going to feel like a half-dead goat in the morning."

"What's a half-dead goat feel like?"

"A lot worse than a healthy goat, and a whole lot worse than a dead one," she said.

Tony paid the tab and waited for his partner. After five minutes, he picked up Frank's coat and tie and went looking for him.

The men's room was small: one stall, one urinal, one sink. It smelled strongly of pine-scented disinfectant and vaguely of urine.

Frank was standing at a graffiti-covered wall, his back to the door when Tony entered. He was pounding his open palms against the wall above his head, both hands at once, making loud slapping sounds that reverberated in the narrow high-ceilinged room. BAM-BAM-BAM-BAM-BAM! The noise wasn't audible in the barroom because of the dull roar of conversation and the music, but in here it hurt Tony's ears.

"Frank?"

BAM-BAM-BAM-BAM-BAM-BAM-BAM!

Tony went to him, put a hand on his shoulder, pulled him gently away from the wall, and turned him around.

Frank was weeping. His eyes were bloodshot and filled with tears. Big tears streamed down his face. His lips were puffy and loose; his mouth quivered with grief. But he was crying soundlessly, neither sobbing nor whimpering, his voice stuck far back in his throat.

"It's okay," Tony said. "Everything will be all right. You don't need Wilma. You're better off without her. You've got friends. We'll help you get over this, Frank, if you'll just let us. I'll help. I care. I really do care, Frank."

Frank closed his eyes. His mouth sagged down, and he sobbed, but still in eerie silence, making noise only when he sucked in a wheezy breath. He reached out, seeking support, and Tony put an arm around him.

"Wanna go home," Frank said mushily. "I juss wanna go home."

"All right. I'll take you home. Just hold on."

With arms around each other, like old buddies from the war, they left The Bolt Hole. They walked two and a half blocks to the apartment complex where Tony lived and climbed into Tony's Jeep station wagon.

They were halfway to Frank's apartment when Frank took a deep breath and said, "Tony . . . I'm afraid."

Tony glanced at him.

Frank was hunched down in his seat. He seemed small and weak; his clothes looked too big for him. Tears shone on his face.

"What are you afraid of?" Tony asked.

"I don't wanna be alone," Frank said, weeping thinly, shaking from the effects of too much liquor, but shaking from something else as well, some dark fear.

"You aren't alone," Tony said.

"I'm afraid of . . . dyin' alone."

"You aren't alone, and you aren't dying, Frank."

"We all get old . . . so fast. And then. . . . I want someone to be there."

"You'll find someone."

"I want someone to remember and care."

"Don't worry," Tony said lamely.

"It scares me."

"You'll find someone."

"Never."

"Yes. You will."

"Never. Never." Frank said, closing his eyes and leaning his head against the side window.

By the time they got to Frank's apartment house, he was sleeping like a child. Tony tried to wake him. But Frank would not come fully to his senses. Stumbling, mumbling, sighing heavily, he allowed himself to be half-walked, half-carried to the door of the apartment. Tony propped him against the wall beside the front door, held him up with one hand, felt through his pockets, found the key. When they finally reached the bedroom, Frank collapsed on the mattress in a loose-limbed heap and began to snore.

Tony undressed him down to his shorts. He pulled back the covers, rolled Frank onto the bottom sheet, pulled the top sheet and the blanket over him. Frank just snuffled and snored.

In the kitchen, in a junk drawer beside the sink, Tony found a pencil, a pad of writing paper, and a roll of Scotch tape. He wrote a note to Frank and taped it to the refrigerator door.

> *Dear Frank,*
> *When you wake up in the morning, you're going*
> *to remember everything you told me, and you're*
> *probably going to be a little embarrassed. Don't*
> *worry. What you told me will stay strictly*
> *between us. And tomorrow I'll tell you some*
> *outrageously embarrassing secrets of my own,*
> *so then we'll be even. After all, cleaning the*
> *soul is one thing friends are for.*
>
> *Tony.*

He locked the door on his way out.

Driving home, he thought about poor Frank being all alone, and then he realized that his own situation was not markedly better. His father was still alive, but Carlo was sick a lot these days and probably would not live more than five years, ten at the most. Tony's brothers and sisters were spread all over the country, and none of them was really close in spirit either. He had a great many friends, but it was not just friends that you wanted by you when you were old and dying. He knew what Frank had meant. When you were on your deathbed, there were only certain hands that you could hold and from which you could draw courage: the hands of your spouse, your children, or your parents. He realized that he was building the kind of life that, when complete, might well be a hollow temple of loneliness. He was thirty-five, still young, but he had never truly given much serious thought to marriage. Suddenly, he had the feeling that time was slipping through his fingers. The years went by so very fast. It seemed only last year that he had been twenty-five, but a decade was gone.

Maybe Hilary Thomas is the one, he thought as he pulled into the parking slot in front of his apartment. She's special. I can see that. Very special. Maybe she'll think I'm someone special, too. It could work out for us. Couldn't it?

For a while he sat in the Jeep, staring at the night sky, thinking about Hilary Thomas and about getting old and dying alone.

At 10:30, when Hilary was deeply involved in the James Clavell novel, just as she was finishing a snack of apples and cheese, the telephone rang.

"Hello?"

There was only silence on the other end of the line.

"Who's there?"

Nothing.

She slammed the receiver down. That's what they told you to do when you got a threatening or obscene phone call. Just hang up. Don't encourage the caller. Just hang up quickly and sharply. She had given him a real pain in the ear, but that didn't make her feel a lot better.

She was sure it wasn't a wrong number. Not twice in one night with no apology either time. Besides, there had been a menacing quality in that silence, an unspoken threat.

Even after she had been nominated for the Academy Award, she had never felt the need for an unlisted number. Writers were not celebrities in the same sense that actors and even directors were. The general public never remembered or cared who earned the screenplay credit on a hit picture. Most writers who got unlisted numbers did it because it seemed prestigious; unlisted meant the harried scribbler was so busy with so many important projects that he had no time for even the rare unwanted call. But she didn't have an ego problem like that, and leaving her name in the book was just as anonymous as taking it out.

Of course, maybe that was no longer true. Perhaps the media reports about her two encounters with Bruno Frye had made her an object of general interest where her two successful screenplays had not. The story of a woman fighting off a would-be rapist and killing him the second time—that might very well fascinate a certain kind of sick mind. It might make some animal out there eager to prove he could succeed where Bruno Frye had failed.

She decided to call the telephone company business office first thing in the morning and ask for a new, unlisted number.

At midnight, the city morgue was, as the medical examiner himself had once described it, quiet as a tomb. The dimly lighted hallway was silent. The laboratory was dark. The room full of corpses was cold and lightless and still except for the insect hum of the blowers that pumped chill air through the wall vents.

As Thursday night changed to Friday morning, only one man was on duty in the morgue. He was in a small chamber adjacent to the M.E.'s private office. He was sitting in a springbacked chair at an ugly metal and walnut-veneer desk. His name was Albert Wolwicz. He was twenty-nine years old, divorced, and the father of one child, a daughter named Rebecca. His wife had won custody of Becky. They both lived in San Diego now. Albert didn't mind working the (you should forgive the expression) graveyard shift. He did a little filing, then just sat and listened to the radio for a while, then did a bit more filing, then read a few chapters of a really good Stephen King novel about vampires on the loose in New England; and if the city remained cool all night, if the uniformed bulls and the meat wagon boys didn't start running in stretchers from gang fights or freeway accidents, it would be sweet duty all the way through to quitting time.

At ten minutes past midnight, the phone rang.

Albert picked it up. "Morgue."

Silence.

"Hello," Albert said.

The man on the other end of the line groaned in agony and began to cry.

"Who is this?"

Weeping, the caller could not respond.

The tortured sounds were almost a parody of grief, an exaggerated and hysterical sobbing that was the strangest thing Albert had ever heard. "If you'll tell me what's wrong, maybe I can help."

The caller hung up.

Albert stared at the receiver for a moment, finally shrugged and put it down.

He tried to pick up where he'd left off in the Stephen King novel, but he kept thinking he heard something shuffling through the doorway behind him. He turned around half a dozen times, but there was never anyone (or anything) there.

CHAPTER 4

FRIDAY MORNING.

Nine o'clock.

Two men from Angels' Hill Mortuary of West Los Angeles arrived at the city morgue to claim the body of Bruno Gunther Frye. They were working in association with the Forever View Funeral Home in the town of St. Helena, where the deceased had lived. One man from Angels' Hill signed the necessary release, and both men transferred the corpse from cold storage to the back of a Cadillac hearse.

Frank Howard did not appear to have a hangover. His complexion did not have that after-the-binge sallowness; he was ruddy and healthy-looking. His blue eyes were clear. Confession apparently was every bit as good for the soul as the proverb promised.

At first in the office, then in the car, Tony sensed the awkwardness he had anticipated, and he did his best to make Frank feel comfortable. In time, Frank seemed to realize that nothing had changed for the worse between them; indeed, the partnership was working far better than it had during the past three months. By mid-morning, they had established a degree of rapport that would make it possible for them to learn to function together almost as a single organism. They still did not interact with the perfect harmony that Tony had experienced with Michael Savatino, but now there did not seem to be any obstacles to the development of precisely that sort of deep relationship. They needed some time to adjust to each other, a few more months, but eventually they would share a psychic bond that would make their job immeasurably easier than it had been in the past.

Friday morning, they worked on leads in the Bobby Valdez case. There were not many trails to follow, and the first two led nowhere.

The Department of Motor Vehicles report on Juan Mazquezza was the first disappointment. Apparently, Bobby Valdez had used a phony birth certificate and other false ID to obtain a valid driver's license under the name Juan Mazquezza. But the last address the DMV could provide was the one from which Bobby had moved last July, the Las Palmeras Apartments to La Brea Avenue. There were two other Juan Mazquezzas in the DMV files. One was a nineteen-year-old boy who lived in Fresno. The other Juan was a sixty-seven-year-old man in Austin. They both owned automobiles with California registrations, but neither of them had a Jaguar. The Juan Mazquezza who had lived on La Brea Avenue had never registered a car, which meant that Bobby had bought the Jaguar using yet another phony name. Evidently, he had a source for forged documents of extremely high quality.

Dead end.

Tony and Frank returned to the Vee Vee Gee Laundry and questioned the employees who had worked with Bobby when he'd been using the Mazquezza name. They hoped that someone would have kept in touch with him after he quit his job and would know where he was living now. But everyone said Juan had been a loner; no one knew where he'd gone.

Dead end.

After they left Vee Vee Gee, they went to lunch at an omelet house that Tony liked. In addition to the main dining room, the restaurant had an open-air brick terrace where a dozen tables stood under blue- and white-striped umbrellas. Tony and Frank ate salads and cheese omelets in the warm autumn breeze.

"You doing anything tomorrow night?" Tony asked.

"Me?"

"You."

"No. Nothing."

"Good. I've arranged something."

"What?"

"A blind date."

"For me?"

"You're half of it."

"Are you serious?"

"I called her this morning."

"Forget it," Frank said.

"She's perfect for you."

"I hate match-making."

"She's a gorgeous woman."

"Not interested."

"And sweet."

"I'm not a kid."

"Who said you were?"

"I don't need you to fix me up with someone."

"Sometimes a guy does that for a friend. Doesn't he?"

"I can find my own dates."

"Only a fool would turn down this lady."

"Then I'm a fool."

Tony sighed. "Suit yourself."

"Look, what I said last night at The Bolt Hole. . . ."

"Yeah?"

"I wasn't looking for sympathy."

"Everybody needs some sympathy now and then."

"I just wanted you to understand why I've been in such a foul mood."

"And I do understand."

"I didn't mean to give you the impression that I'm a jerk, that I'm a sucker for the wrong kind of woman."

"You didn't give me that impression at all."

"I've never broken down like that before."

"I believe it."

"I've never . . . cried like that."

"I know."

"I guess I was just tired."

"Sure."

"Maybe it was all that liquor."

"Maybe."

"I drank a lot last night."

"Quite a lot."

"The liquor made me sentimental."

"Maybe."

"But now I'm all right."

"Who said you weren't?"

"I can get my own dates, Tony."

"Whatever you say."

"Okay?"

"Okay."

They concentrated on their cheese omelets.

There were several large office buildings nearby, and dozens of secretaries in bright dresses paraded past on the sidewalk, going to lunch.

Flowers ringed the restaurant terrace and perfumed the sun-coppered air.

The noise on the street was typically that of L.A. It wasn't the incessant barking of brakes and screaming of horns that you heard in New York or Chicago or most other cities. Just the hypnotic grumble of engines. And the air-cutting *whoosh* of passing cars. A lulling noise. Soothing. Like the tide on the beach. Made by machines but somehow natural, primal. Also subtly and inexpressibly erotic. Even the sounds of the traffic conformed to the city's subconscious subtropical personality.

After a couple of minutes of silence, Frank said, "What's her name?"

"Who?"

"Don't be a smartass."

"Janet Yamada."

"Japanese?"

"Does she sound Italian?"

"What's she like?"

"Intelligent, witty, good-looking."

"What's she do?"

"Works at city hall."

"How old is she?"

"Thirty-six, thirty-seven."

"Too young for me?"

"You're only forty-five, for God's sake."

"How'd you come to know her?"

"We dated for a while," Tony said.

"What went wrong?"

"Nothing. We just discovered we make better friends than lovers."

"You think I'll like her?"

"Positive."

"And she'll like me?"

"If you don't pick your nose or eat with your hands."

"Okay," Frank said. "I'll go out with her."

"If it's going to be an ordeal for you, maybe we should just forget it."

"No. I'll go. It'll be okay."

"You don't have to do it just to please me."

"Give me her phone number."

"I don't feel right about this," Tony said. "I feel like I've forced you into something."

"You haven't forced me."

"I think I should call her and cancel the arrangements," Tony said.

"No, listen, I—"

"I shouldn't try to be a matchmaker. I'm lousy at it."

"Dammit, I *want* to go out with her!" Frank said.

Tony smiled broadly. "I know."

"Have I just been manipulated?"

"You manipulated yourself."

Frank tried to scowl, but couldn't. He grinned instead. "Want to double-date Saturday night?"

"No way. You've got to stand on your own, my friend."

"And besides," Frank said knowingly, "you don't want to share Hilary Thomas with anyone else."

"Exactly."

"You really think it can work with you two?"

"You make it sound like we're planning to get married. It's just a date."

"But even for a date, won't it be . . . awkward?"

"Why should it be?" Tony asked.

"Well, she's got all that money."

"That's a male chauvinist remark if I ever heard one."

"You don't think that'll make it difficult?"

"When a *man* has some money, does he have to limit his dating to women who have an equal amount of money?"

"That's different."

"When a king decides to marry a shopgirl, we think it's too romantic for words. But when a queen wants to marry a shopboy, we think she's letting herself be played for a fool. Classic double standard."

"Well . . . good luck."

"And to you as well."

"Ready to go back to work?"

"Yeah," Tony said. "Let's find Bobby Valdez."

"Judge Crater might be easier."

"Or Amelia Earhart."

"Or Jimmy Hoffa."

Friday afternoon.

One o'clock.

The body lay on an embalming table at Angels' Hill Mortuary in West Los Angeles. A tag wired to the big toe on the right foot identified the deceased as Bruno Gunther Frye.

A death technician prepared the body for shipment to Napa County. He swabbed it down with a long-lasting disinfectant. The intestines and other soft abdominal organs were pulled out of the dead man through the only available natural body opening and discarded. Because of the stab wounds and the autopsy that had taken place the previous night, there was not much unclotted blood or other fluids remaining in the corpse, but those last few dollops were forced out nonetheless; embalming fluid took their place.

The technician whistled a Donny and Marie Osmond hit while he labored over the dead man.

The Angels' Hill Mortuary was not responsible for any cosmetic work on the corpse. That would be handled by the mortician in St. Helena. The Angels' Hill technician merely tucked the sightless eyes shut forever and sewed up the lips with a series of tight interior stitches which froze the wide mouth in a vague eternal smile. It was a neat job; none of the sutures would be visible to the mourners—if there were any mourners.

Next, the deceased was wrapped in an opaque white shroud and put into a cheap aluminum coffin that met minimum construction and seal standards set by the state for the conveyance of a dead body by any and all means of public transportation. In St. Helena, it would be transferred to a more impressive casket, one that would be chosen by the family or friends of the loved one.

At 4:00 Friday afternoon, the body was taken to the Los Angeles International Airport and put into the cargo hold of a California Airways propjet destined for Monterey, Santa Rosa, and Sacramento. It would be taken off the plane at the second stop.

At 6:30 Friday evening, in Santa Rosa, there was no one from Bruno Frye's family at the small airport. He had no relatives. He was the last of his line. His grandfather had brought only one child into the world, a lovely daughter named Katherine, and she had produced no children at all. Bruno was adopted. He never had married.

Three people waited on the Tarmac behind the small terminal, and two of them were from the Forever View Funeral Home. Mr. Avril Thomas Tannerton was the owner of Forever View, which served St. Helena and the surrounding communities in that part of the Napa Valley. He was forty-three, good-looking, slightly pudgy but not fat, with lots of reddish-blond hair, a scattering of freckles, lively eyes, and an easy warm smile that he had difficulty suppressing. He had come to Santa Rosa with his twenty-four-year-old assistant, Gary Olmstead, a slightly-built man who seldom talked more than the dead with whom he worked. Tannerton made you think of a choirboy, a veneer of genuine piety over a core of good-natured mischievousness; but Olmstead had a long, mournful, ascetic face perfectly suited to his profession.

The third man was Joshua Rhinehart, Bruno Frye's local attorney and executor of the Frye estate. He was sixty-one years old, and he had the looks that would have contributed to a successful career as a diplomat or politician. His hair was thick and white, swept back from brow and temples, not chalk-white, not yellow-white, but a lustrous silver-white. A broad forehead. A long proud nose. A strong jaw and chin. His coffee-brown eyes were quick and clear.

The body of Bruno Frye was transferred from the aircraft to the hearse, then driven back to St. Helena. Joshua Rhinehart followed in his own car.

Neither business nor personal obligations had required Joshua to make this trip to Santa Rosa with Avril Tannerton. Over the years, he had done quite a lot of work for Shade Tree Vineyards, the company that had been wholly owned by the Frye family for three generations, but he had long ago ceased to need the income from that account, and in fact it had become considerably more trouble than it was worth. He continued to handle the Frye family's affairs largely because he still remembered the time, thirty-five years ago, when he had been struggling to build a practice in rural Napa County and had been helped immeasurably by Katherine Frye's decision to give him all the family's legal business. Yesterday, when he heard that Bruno was dead, he hadn't grieved at all. Neither Katherine nor her adopted son had ever inspired affection, and they most certainly had not encouraged the special emotional ties of friendship. Joshua accompanied Avril Tannerton to the Santa Rosa airport only because he wanted to be in a position to manage the arrival of the corpse in case any reporters showed up and tried to turn the event into a circus. Although Bruno had been an unstable man, a very sick man, perhaps even a profoundly evil man, Joshua was determined that the funeral would be carried out with dignity. He felt he owed the dead man that much. Besides, for most of his life, Joshua was a stalwart supporter and promoter of the Napa Valley, championing both its quality of life and its magnificent wine, and he did not want to see the fabric of the entire community stained by the criminal acts of one man.

Fortunately, there had not been a single reporter at the airport.

They drove back to St. Helena through creeping shadows and dying light, east from Santa Rosa, across the southern end of the Sonoma Valley, into the five-mile-wide Napa Valley, then north in the purple-yellow gloaming. As he followed the hearse, Joshua admired the countryside, something he had done with ever-increasing pleasure for the last thirty-five years. The looming mountain ridges were thick with pine and fir and birch, lighted only along their crests by the westering sun, already out of sight; those ridges were ramparts, Joshua thought; great walls keeping out the corrupting influences of a less civilized world than that which lay within. Below the mountains the rolling hills were studded with black-trunked oaks and covered with long dry grass that, in the daylight, looked as blond and soft as cornsilk; but now in the gathering dusk which leeched away its color, the grass shimmered in dark waves, awash in the ebb and flow of a gentle breeze. Beyond the boundaries of the small quaint towns, endless vineyards sprang up on some of the hills and on nearly all of the rich flatland. In 1880, Robert Louis Stevenson had written of the Napa Valley; "One corner of land after another is tried with one kind of grape after another. This is a failure; that is better; a third is best. So, bit by bit, they grope about for their Clos Vougeot and Lafite . . . and the wine is bottled poetry." When Stevenson had been honeymooning in the valley and writing *Silverado Squatters*, there had been fewer than four thousand acres in vines. By the coming of the Great Plague—Prohibition—in 1920, there had been ten thousand acres producing viniferous grapes. Today, there were thirty thousand acres bringing forth grapes that were far sweeter and less acidic than those grown anywhere else in the world, as much productive land as in all of the Sonoma Valley, which was twice as large as the Napa. Tucked in among the vineyards were the great wineries and houses, some of them converted from abbeys and monasteries and Spanish-style missions, others built along clean modern lines. Thank God, Joshua thought, only a couple of the newer wineries had opted for the sterile factory look that was an insult to the eye and a blight upon the valley. Most of man's handiwork either complemented or at least did not intrude upon the truly dazzling natural beauty of this unique and idyllic place. As he followed the hearse toward Forever View, Joshua saw lights come on in the windows of the houses, soft yellow lights that brought a sense of warmth and civilization to the encroaching night. The wine *is* bottled poetry, Joshua thought, and the land from which it comes is God's greatest work of art; my land; my home; how lucky I am to be here when there are so many less charming, less pleasant places in which I might have wound up.

Like in an aluminum coffin, dead.

Forever View stood a hundred yards back from the two-lane highway, just south of St. Helena. It was a big white colonial-style house with a circular driveway, marked by a tasteful white and green hand-painted sign. As darkness fell, a single white spotlight came on automatically, softly illuminating the sign; and a low row of electric carriage lamps marked the circular driveway with a curve of amber light.

There were no reporters waiting at Forever View either. Joshua was pleased to see that the Napa County press evidently shared his strong aversion to unnecessary bad publicity.

Tannerton drove the hearse around to the rear of the huge white house. He and Olmstead slid the coffin onto a cart and wheeled it inside.

Joshua joined them in the mortician's workroom.

An effort had been made to give the chamber an airy cheerful ambience. The ceiling was covered with prettily textured acoustical tile. The walls were painted pale blue, the blue of a robin's egg, the blue of a baby's blanket, the blue of new life. Tannerton touched a wall switch, and lilting music came from stereo speakers, bright soaring music, nothing somber, nothing heavy.

To Joshua, at least, the place reeked of death in spite of everything that Avril Tannerton had done to make it cozy. The air bore traces of the pungent fumes from embalming fluid, and there was a sweet cover-up aerosol scent of carnations that only reminded him of funeral bouquets. The floor was glossy white ceramic tile, freshly scrubbed, a bit slippery for anyone not wearing rubber-soled shoes; Tannerton and Gary Olmstead were wearing them, but Joshua was not. At first, the tile gave an impression of openness and cleanliness, but then Joshua realized the floor was grimly utilitarian; it had to have a stainproof surface that would resist the corroding effects of spilled blood and bile and other even more noxious substances.

Tannerton's clients, the relatives of the deceased, would never be brought into this room, for the bitter truth of death was too obvious here. In the front of the house, where the viewing chambers were decorated with heavy wine-red velvet drapes and plush carpets and dark wood paneling and brass lamps, where the lighting was low and artfully arranged, the phrases "passed away" and "called home by God" could be taken seriously; in the front rooms, the atmosphere encouraged a belief in heaven and the ascendance of the spirit. But in the tile-floored workroom with the lingering stink of embalming fluid and the shiny array of mortician's instruments lined up on enamel trays, death seemed depressingly clinical and unquestionably final.

Olmstead opened the aluminum coffin.

Avril Tannerton folded back the plastic shroud, revealing the body from the hips up.

Joshua looked down at the waxy yellow-gray corpse and shivered. "Ghastly."

"I know this is a trying time for you," Tannerton said in practiced mournful tones.

"Not at all," Joshua said. "I won't be a hypocrite and pretend grief. I knew very little about the man, and I didn't particularly like what I did know. Ours was strictly a business relationship."

Tannerton blinked. "Oh. Well . . . then perhaps you would prefer us to handle the funeral arrangements through one of the deceased's friends."

"I don't think he had any," Joshua said.

They stared down at the body for a moment, silent.

"Ghastly," Joshua said again.

"Of course," Tannerton said, "no cosmetic work has been done. Absolutely none. If I could have gotten to him soon after death, he'd look much better."

"Can you . . . do anything with him?"

"Oh, certainly. But it won't be easy. He's been dead a day and a half, and though he's been kept refrigerated—"

"Those wounds," Joshua said thickly, staring at the hideously scarred abdomen with morbid fascination. "Dear God, she really cut him."

"Most of that was done by the coroner," Tannerton said. "This small slit is a stab wound. And this one."

"The pathologist did a good job with his mouth," Olmstead said appreciatively.

"Yes, didn't he?" Tannerton said, touching the sealed lips of the corpse. "It's unusual to find a coroner with an aesthetic sense."

"Rare," Olmstead said.

Joshua shook his head. "I still find it hard to believe."

"Five years ago," Tannerton said, "I buried his mother. That's when I met him. He seemed a little . . . strange. But I figured it was the stress and the grief. He was such an important man, such a leading figure in the community."

"Cold," Joshua said. "He was an extremely cold and self-contained man. Vicious in business. Winning a battle with a competitor wasn't always enough for him; if at all possible, he preferred to utterly destroy the other fellow. I've always thought he was capable of cruelty and physical violence. But attempted rape? Attempted murder?"

Tannerton looked at Joshua and said, "Mr. Rhinehart, I've often heard it said that you don't mince words. You've got a reputation, a much admired reputation, for saying exactly what you think and to hell with the cost. But. . . ."

"But what?"

"But when you're speaking of the dead, don't you think you ought to—"

Joshua smiled. "Son, I'm a cantankerous old bastard and not entirely admirable. Far from it! As long as truth is my weapon, I don't mind hurting the feelings of the living. Why, I've made children cry, and I've made kindly gray-haired grandmothers weep. I have little compassion for fools and sons of bitches when they're alive. So why should I show more respect than that for the dead?"

"I'm just not accustomed to—"

"Of course, you're not. Your profession requires you to speak well of the deceased, regardless of who he might have been and what heinous things he might have done. I don't hold that against you. It's your job."

Tannerton couldn't think of anything to say. He closed the lid of the coffin.

"Let's settle on the arrangements," Joshua said. "I'd like to get home and have my dinner—if I have any appetite left when I leave here." He sat down on a high stool beside a glass-fronted cabinet that contained more tools of the mortician's trade.

Tannerton paced in front of him, a freckled, mop-haired bundle of energy. "How important is it to you to have the usual viewing?"

"Usual viewing?"

"An open casket. Would you find it offensive if we avoided that?"

"I hadn't really given it a thought," Joshua said.

"To be honest with you, I don't know how . . . presentable the deceased can be made to look," Tannerton said. "The people at Angels' Hill didn't give him quite a full enough look when they embalmed him. His face appears to be somewhat drawn and shrunken. I am not pleased. I am definitely not pleased. I could attempt to pump him up a bit, but patchwork like that seldom looks good. As for cosmetology . . . well . . . again, I wonder if too much time has passed. I mean, he apparently was in the hot sun for a couple of hours after he died, before he was found. And then it was eighteen hours in cold storage before the embalming was done. I can certainly make him look a great deal better than he does now. But as for bringing the glow of life back to his face. . . . You see, after all that he's been through, after the extremes of temperature, and after this much time, the skin texture has changed substantially; it won't take makeup and powder at all well. I think perhaps—"

Beginning to get queasy, Joshua interrupted. "Make it a closed casket."

"No viewing?"

"No viewing."

"You're sure?"

"Positive."

"Good. Let me see. . . . Will you want him buried in one of his suits?"

"Is it necessary, considering the casket won't be open?"

"It would be easier for me if I just tucked him into one of our burial gowns."

"That'll be fine."

"White or a nice dark blue?"

"Do you have something in polka dots?"

"Polka dots?"

"Or orange and yellow stripes?"

Tannerton's ever-ready grin slipped from beneath his dour funeral director expression, and he struggled to force it out of sight again. Joshua suspected that, privately, Avril was a fun-loving man, the kind of hail-fellow-well-met who would make a good drinking buddy; but he seemed to feel that his public image required him to be somber and humorless at all times. He was visibly upset when he slipped up and allowed the private Avril to appear when only the public man ought to be seen. He was, Joshua thought, a likely candidate for an eventual schizophrenic breakdown.

"Make it the white gown," Joshua said.

"What about the casket? What style would—"

"I'll leave that to you."

"Very well. Price range?"

"Might as well have the best. The estate can afford it."

"The rumor is he must have been worth two or three million."

"Probably twice that," Joshua said.

"But he really didn't live like it."

"Or die like it," Joshua said.

Tannerton thought about that for a moment, then said, "Any religious services?"

"He didn't attend church."

"Then shall I assume the minister's role?"

"If you wish."

"We'll have a short graveside service," Tannerton said. "I'll read something from the Bible, or perhaps just a simple inspirational piece, something nondenominational."

They agreed on a time for burial: Sunday at two o'clock in the afternoon. Bruno would be laid to rest beside Katherine, his adoptive mother, in the Napa County Memorial Park.

As Joshua got up to leave, Tannerton said, "I certainly hope you've found my services valuable thus far, and I assure you I'll do everything in my power to make the rest of this go smoothly."

"Well," Joshua said, "you've convinced me of one thing. I'm going to draw up a new will tomorrow. When my time comes, I sure as hell intend to be cremated."

Tannerton nodded. "We can handle that for you."

"Don't rush me, son. Don't rush me."

Tannerton blushed. "Oh, I didn't mean to—"

"I know, I know. Relax."

Tannerton cleared his throat uncomfortably. "I'll . . . uh . . . show you to the door."

"No need. I can find it myself."

Outside, behind the funeral home, the night was very dark and deep. There was only one light, a hundred-watt bulb above the rear door. The glow reached only a few feet into the velveteen blackness.

In the late afternoon, a breeze had sprung up, and with the coming of the night, it had grown into a gusty wind. The air was turbulent and chilly; it hissed and moaned.

Joshua walked to his car, which lay beyond the meager semicircle of frosty light, and as he opened the door he had the peculiar feeling he was being watched. He glanced back at the house, but there were no faces at the windows.

Something moved in the gloom. Thirty feet away. Near the three-car garage. Joshua sensed rather than saw it. He squinted, but his vision was not what it had once been; he couldn't discern anything unnatural in the night.

Just the wind, he thought. Just the wind stirring through the trees and bushes or pushing along a discarded newspaper, a piece of dry brush.

But then it moved again. He saw it this time. It was crouched in front of a row of shrubs leading out from the garage. He could not see any detail. It was just a shadow, a lighter purple-black smudge on the blue-black cloth of the night, as soft and lumpy and undefined as all the other shadows—except that this one moved.

Just a dog, Joshua thought. A stray dog. Or maybe a kid up to some mischief.

"Is someone there?"

No reply.

He took a few steps away from his car.

The shadow-thing scurried back ten or twelve feet, along the line of shrubbery. It stopped in an especially deep pool of darkness, still crouching, still watchful.

Not a dog, Joshua thought. Too damned big for a dog. Some kid. Probably up to no good. Some kid with vandalism on his mind.

"Who's there?"

Silence.

"Come on now."

No answer. Just the whispering wind.

Joshua started toward the shadow among shadows, but he was suddenly arrested by the instinctive knowledge that the thing was dangerous. Horrendously dangerous. Deadly. He experienced all of the involuntary animal reactions to such a threat: a shiver up his spine; his scalp seemed to crawl and then tighten; his heart began to pound; his mouth went dry; his hands curled into claws; and his hearing seemed more acute than it had been a minute ago. Joshua hunched over and drew up his bulky shoulders, unconsciously seeking a defensive posture.

"Who's there?" he repeated.

The shadow-thing turned and crashed through the shrubs. It ran off across the vineyards that bordered Avril Tannerton's property. For a few seconds, Joshua could hear the steadily diminishing clamor of its flight, the receding *thud-thud-thud* of heavy running footsteps and the fading wheeze as it gasped for breath. Then the wind was the only sound in the night.

Looking over his shoulder a couple of times, he returned to his car. He got in, closed the door, locked it.

Already, the encounter began to seem unreal, increasingly dreamlike. Was there actually someone in the darkness, waiting, watching? Had there been something dangerous out there, or had it been his imagination? After spending half an hour in Avril Tannerton's ghoulish workshop, a man could be expected to jump at strange noises and start looking for monstrous creatures in the shadows. As Joshua's muscles relaxed, as his heart slowed, he began to think he had been a fool. The threat he had sensed so strongly seemed, in retrospect, to be a phantom, a vagary of the night and wind.

At worst, it had been a kid. A vandal.

He started the car and drove home, surprised and amused by the effect Tannerton's workroom had had upon him.

Saturday evening, promptly at seven o'clock, Anthony Clemenza arrived at Hilary's Westwood house in a blue Jeep station wagon.

Hilary went out to meet him. She was wearing a sleek emerald-green silk dress with long tight sleeves and a neckline cut low enough to be enticing but not cheap. She hadn't been on a date in more than fourteen months, and she nearly had forgotten how to dress for the ritual of courtship; she had spent two hours choosing her outfit, as indecisive as a schoolgirl. She accepted Tony's invitation because he was the most interesting man she'd met in a couple of years—and also because she was trying her best to overcome her tendency to hide from the rest of the world. She had been stung by Wally Topelis's assessment of her; he had warned her that she was using the virtue of self-reliance as an excuse to hide from people, and she had recognized the truth in what he'd said.

She avoided making friends and finding lovers, for she was afraid of the pain that only friends and lovers could inflict with their rejections and betrayals. But at the same time that she was protecting herself from the pain, she was denying herself the pleasure of good relationships with good people who would not betray her. Growing up with her drunken violent parents, she had learned that displays of affection were usually followed by sudden outbursts of rage and anger and unexpected punishment.

She was never afraid to take chances in her work and in business matters; now it was time to bring the same spirit of adventure to her personal life. As she walked briskly toward the blue Jeep, swinging her hips a little, she felt tense about taking the emotional risks that the mating dance entailed, but she also felt fresh and feminine and considerably happier than she had in a long time.

Tony hurried around to the passenger's side and opened the door. Bending low, he said, "The royal carriage awaits."

"Oh, there must be some mistake. I'm not the queen."

"You look like a queen to me."

"I'm just a lowly serving girl."

"You're a great deal prettier than the queen."

"Better not let her hear you say that. She'll have your head for sure."

"Too late."

"Oh?"

"I've already lost my head over you."

Hilary groaned.

"Too saccharine?" he asked.

"I need a bite of lemon after that one."

"But you liked it."

"Yes, I admit I did. I guess I'm a sucker for flattery," she said, getting into the Jeep in a swirl of green silk.

As they drove down toward Westwood Boulevard, Tony said, "You're not offended?"

"By what?"

"By this buggy?"

"How could I be offended by a Jeep? Does it talk? Is it liable to insult me?"

"It's not a Mercedes."

"A Mercedes isn't a Rolls. And a Rolls isn't a Toyota."

"There's something very Zen about that."

"If you think I'm a snob, why'd you ask me out?"

"I don't think you're a snob," he said. "But Frank says we'll be awkward with each other because you've got more money than I have."

"Well, based on my experience with him, I'd say Frank's judgments of other people are not to be trusted."

"He has his problems," Tony agreed as he turned left onto Wilshire Boulevard. "But he's working them out."

"I will admit this isn't a car you see many of in L.A."

"Usually, women ask me if it's my second car."

"I don't really care if it is or isn't."

"They say that in L.A. you are what you drive."

"Is that what they say? Then you're a Jeep. And I'm a Mercedes. We're cars, not people. We should be going to the garage for an oil change, not to a restaurant for dinner. Does that make sense?"

"No sense at all," Tony said. "Actually, I got a Jeep because I like to go skiing three or four weekends every winter. With this jalopy, I know I'll always be able to get through the mountain passes, no matter how bad the weather gets."

"I've always wanted to learn to ski."

"I'll teach you. You'll have to wait a few weeks. But it won't be long until there's snow at Mammoth."

"You seem pretty sure we'll still be friends a few weeks from now."

"Why wouldn't we be?" he asked.

"Maybe we'll get into a fight tonight, first thing, at the restaurant."

"Over what?"

"Politics."

"I think all politicians are power-hungry bastards too incompetent to tie their own shoelaces."

"So do I."

"I'm a Libertarian."

"So am I—sort of."

"Short argument."

"Maybe we'll fight over religion."

"I was raised a Catholic. But I'm not much of anything any more."

"Me either."

"We don't seem to be good at arguing."

"Well," she said, "maybe we're the kind of people who fight over little things, inconsequential matters."

"Such as?"

"Well, since we're going to an Italian restaurant, maybe you'll love the garlic bread, and I'll hate it."

"And we'll fight over that?"

"That or the fettucini or the manicotti."

"No. Where we're going, you'll love everything," he said. "Wait and see."

He took her to Savatino's Ristorante on Santa Monica Boulevard. It was an intimate place, seating no more than sixty and somehow appearing to seat only half that number; it was cozy, comfortable, the kind of restaurant in which you could lose track of time and spend six hours over dinner if the waiters didn't nudge you along. The lighting was soft and warm. The recorded opera— leaning heavily to the voices of Gigli and Caruso and Pavarotti—was played loud enough to be heard and appreciated, but not so loud that it intruded on conversation. There was a bit too much decor, but one part of it, a spectacular mural, was, Hilary thought, absolutely wonderful. The painting covered an entire wall and was a depiction of the most commonly perceived joys of the Italian lifestyle: grapes, wine, pasta, dark-eyed women, darkly handsome men, a loving and rotund *nonna*, a group of people dancing to the music of an accordionist, a picnic under olive trees, and much more. Hilary had never seen anything remotely like it, for it was neither entirely realistic nor stylized nor abstract nor impressionistic, but an odd stepchild of surrealism, as if it were a wildly inventive collaboration between Andrew Wyeth and Salvador Dali.

Michael Savatino, the owner, who turned out to be an ex-policeman, was irrepressibly jolly, hugging Tony, taking Hilary's hand and kissing it, punching Tony lightly in the belly and recommending pasta to fatten him up, insisting they come into the kitchen to see the new cappuccino machine. As they came out of the kitchen, Michael's wife, a striking blonde named Paula, arrived, and there was more hugging and kissing and complimenting. At last, Michael linked arms with Hilary and escorted her and Tony to a corner booth. He told the captain to bring two bottles of Biondi-Santi's Brunello di Montelcino, waited for the wine, and uncorked it himself. After glasses had been filled and toasts made, he left them, winking at Tony to show his approval, seeing Hilary notice the wink, laughing at himself, winking at her.

"He seems like such a nice man," she said when Michael had gone.

"He's some guy," Tony said.

"You like him a great deal."

"I love him. He was a perfect partner when we worked homicide together."

They fell smoothly into a discussion of policework and then screenwriting. He was so easy to talk to that Hilary felt she had known him for years. There was absolutely none of the awkwardness that usually marred a first date.

At one point, he noticed her looking at the wall mural. "Do you like the painting?" he asked.

"It's superb."

"Is it?"

"Don't you agree?"

"It's pretty good," he said.

"Better than pretty good. Who did it? Do you know?"

"Some artist down on his luck," Tony said. "He painted it in exchange for fifty free dinners."

"Only fifty? Michael got a bargain."

They talked about films and books and music and theater.

The food was nearly as good as the conversation. The appetizer was light; it consisted of two stubby crèpes, one filled with unadulterated ricotta cheese, the other with a spicy concoction of shaved beef, onions, peppers, mushrooms, and garlic. Their salads were huge and crisp, smothered in sliced raw mushrooms. Tony selected the entrée, Veal Savatino, a *specialita* of the house, incredibly tender white-white veal with a thin brown sauce, pearl onions, and grilled strips of zucchini. The cappuccino was excellent.

When she finished dinner and looked at her watch, Hilary was amazed to see that it was ten minutes past eleven.

Michael Savatino stopped by the table to bask in their praise, and then he said to Tony, "That's number twenty-one."

"Oh, no. Twenty-three."

"Not by my records."

"Your records are wrong."

"Twenty-one," Michael insisted.

"Twenty-three," Tony said. "And it ought to be numbers twenty-three and twenty-four. It was two meals, after all."

"No, no," Michael said. "We count by the visit, not by the number of meals."

Perplexed, Hilary said, "Am I losing my mind, or does this conversation make no sense at all?"

Michael shook his head, exasperated with Tony. To Hilary he said, "When he painted the mural, I wanted to pay him in cash, but he wouldn't accept it. He said he'd trade the painting for a few free dinners. I insisted on a hundred free visits. He said twenty-five. We finally settled on fifty. He undervalues his work, and that makes me angry as hell."

"Tony painted that mural?" she asked.

"He didn't tell you?"

"No."

She looked at Tony, and he grinned sheepishly.

"That's why he drives that Jeep," Michael said. "When he wants to go up in the hills to work on a nature study, the Jeep will take him anywhere."

"He said he had it because he likes to go skiing."

"That too. But mostly, it's to get him into the hills to paint. He should be proud of his work. But it's easier to pull teeth from an alligator than it is to get him to talk about his painting."

"I'm an amateur," Tony said. "Nothing's more boring than an amateur dabbler running off at the mouth about his 'art.' "

"That mural is not the work of an amateur," Michael said.

"Definitely not," Hilary agreed.

"You're my friends," Tony said, "so naturally you're too generous with your praise. And neither of you has the qualifications to be an art critic."

"He's won two prizes," Michael told Hilary.

"Prizes?" she asked Tony.

"Nothing important."

"Both times he won best of the show," Michael said.

"What shows were these?" Hilary asked.

"No big ones," Tony said.

"He dreams about making a living as a painter," Michael said, "but he never does anything about it."

"Because it's only a dream," Tony said. "I'd be a fool if I seriously thought I could make it as a painter."

"He never really tried," Michael told Hilary.

"A painter doesn't get a weekly paycheck," Tony said. "Or health benefits. Or retirement checks."

"But if you only sold two pieces a month for only half what they're worth, you'd make more than you get as a cop," Michael said.

"And if I sold nothing for a month or two months or six," Tony said, "then who would pay the rent?"

To Hilary, Michael said, "His apartment's crammed full of paintings, one stacked on the other. He's sitting on a fortune, but he won't do anything about it."

"He exaggerates," Tony told her.

"Ah, I give up!" Michael said. "Maybe you can talk some sense into him, Hilary." As he walked away from their table, he said, "Twenty-one."

"Twenty-three," Tony said.

Later, in the Jeep, as he was driving her home, Hilary said, "Why don't you at least take your work around to some galleries and see if they'll handle it?"

"They won't."

"You could at least ask."

"Hilary, I'm not really good enough."

"That mural was excellent."

"There's a big difference between restaurant murals and fine art."

"That mural was fine art."

"Again, I've got to point out that you aren't an expert."

"I buy paintings for both pleasure and investment."

"With the aid of a gallery director for the investment part?" he asked.

"That's right. Wyant Stevens in Beverly Hills."

"Then he's the expert, not you."

"Why don't you show some of your work to him?"

"I can't take rejection."

"I'll bet he won't reject you."

"Can we not talk about my painting?"

"Why?"

"I'm bored."

"You're difficult."

"And bored," he said.

"What shall we talk about?"

"Well, why don't we talk about whether or not you're going to invite me in for brandy."

"Would you like to come in for brandy?"

"Cognac?"

"That's what I have."

"What label?"

"Remy Martin."

"The best." He grinned. "But, gee, I don't know. It's getting awfully late."

"If you don't come in," she said, "I'll just have to drink alone." She was enjoying the silly game.

"Can't let you drink alone," he said.

"That's one sign of alcoholism."

"It certainly is."

"If you don't come in for a brandy with me, you'll be starting me on the road to problem drinking and complete destruction."

"I'd never forgive myself."

Fifteen minutes later, they were sitting side by side on the couch, in front of the fireplace, watching the flames and sipping Remy Martin.

Hilary felt slightly light-headed, not from the cognac but from being next to him—and from wondering if they were going to go to bed together. She had never slept with a man on the first date. She was usually wary, reluctant to commit herself to an affair until she had spent a couple of weeks—sometimes a couple of months—evaluating the man. More than once she had taken so long to make up her mind that she had lost men who might have made wonderful lovers and lasting friends. But in just one evening with Tony Clemenza, she felt at ease and perfectly safe with him. He was a damned attractive man. Tall. Dark. Rugged good looks. The inner authority and self-confidence of a cop. Yet gentle. Really surprisingly gentle. And sensitive. So much time had passed since she'd allowed herself to be touched and possessed, since she'd used and been used and shared. How could she have let so much time pass? She could easily imagine herself in his arms, naked beneath him, then atop him, and as those lovely images filled her mind, she realized that he was probably having the same sweet thoughts.

Then the telephone rang.

"Damn!" she said.

"Someone you don't want to hear from?"

She turned and looked at the phone, which was a walnut box model that stood on a corner desk. It rang, rang.

"Hilary?"

"I'll bet it's him," she said.

"Him who?"

"I've been getting these calls. . . ."

The strident ringing continued.

"What calls?" Tony asked.

"The last couple of days, someone's been calling me and then refusing to speak when I answer. It's happened six or eight times."

"He doesn't say anything at all?"

"He just listens," she said. "I think it's some nut who was turned on by the newspaper stories about Frye."

The insistent bell made her grit her teeth.

She stood up and hesitantly approached the phone.

Tony went with her. "You have a listed number?"

"I'm getting a new one next week. It'll be unlisted."

They reached the desk and stood looking at the phone. It rang again and again and again.

"It's him," she said. "Who else would let it ring that long?"

Tony snatched up the receiver. "Hello?"

The caller didn't respond.

"Thomas residence," Tony said. "Detective Clemenza speaking."

Click.

Tony put the phone down and said, "He hung up. Maybe I scared him off for good."

"I hope so."

"It's still a good idea to get an unlisted number."

"Oh, I'm not going to change my mind about that."

"I'll call the telephone company service department first thing Monday morning and tell them the LAPD would appreciate a speedy job."

"Can you do that?"

"Sure."

"Thank you, Tony." She hugged herself. She felt cold.

"Try not to worry about it," he said. "Studies show that the kind of creep who makes threatening phone calls usually gets all his kicks that way. The call itself usually satisfies him. He usually isn't the violent type."

"Usually?"

"Almost never."

She smiled thinly. "That's still not good enough."

The call had spoiled any chance that the night might end in a shared bed. She was no longer in the mood for seduction, and Tony sensed the change.

"Would you like me to stay a while longer, just to see if he calls again?"

"That's sweet of you," she said. "But I guess you're right. He's not dangerous. If he was, he'd come around instead of just calling. Anyway, you scared him off. He probably thinks the police are here just waiting for him."

"Did you get your pistol back?"

She nodded. "I went downtown yesterday and filled out the registration form like I should have done when I moved into the city. If the guy on the phone *does* come around, I can plink him legally now."

"I really don't think he'll bother you again tonight."

"I'm sure you're right."

For the first time all evening, they were awkward with each other.

"Well, I guess I'd better be going."

"It is late," she agreed.

"Thank you for the cognac."

"Thank you for a wonderful dinner."

At the door he said, "Doing anything tomorrow night?"

She was about to turn him down when she remembered how good she had felt sitting beside him on the sofa. And she thought of Wally Topelis's warning about becoming a hermit. She smiled and said, "I'm free."

"Great. What would you like to do?"

"Whatever you want."

He thought about it for a moment. "Shall we make a whole day of it?"

"Well . . . why not?"

"We'll start with lunch. I'll pick you up at noon."

"I'll be ready and waiting."

He kissed her lightly and affectionately on the lips. "Tomorrow," he said. "Tomorrow."

She watched him leave, then closed and locked the door.

All day Saturday, morning and afternoon and evening, the body of Bruno Frye lay alone in the Forever View Funeral Home, unobserved and unattended.

Friday night, after Joshua Rhinehart had left, Avril Tannerton and Gary Olmstead had transferred the corpse to another coffin, an ornate brass-plated model with a plush velvet and silk interior. They tucked the dead man into a white burial gown, put his arms straight out at his sides, and pulled a white velvet coverlet up to the middle of his chest. Because the condition of the flesh was not good, Tannerton did not want to expend any energy trying to make the corpse presentable. Gary Olmstead thought there was something cheap and disrespectful about consigning a body to the grave without benefit of makeup and powder. But Tannerton persuaded him that cosmetology offered little hope for Bruno Frye's shrunken yellow-gray countenance.

"And anyway," Tannerton had said, "you and I will be the last people in this world to lay eyes on him. When we shut this box tonight, it'll never be opened again."

At 9:45 Friday night, they had closed and latched the lid of the casket. That done, Olmstead went home to his wan little wife and his quiet and intense young son. Avril went upstairs; he lived above the rooms of the dead.

Early Saturday morning, Tannerton left for Santa Rosa in his silver-gray Lincoln. He took an overnight bag with him, for he didn't intend to return until ten o'clock Sunday morning. Bruno Frye's funeral was the only one that he was handling at the moment. Since there was to be no viewing, he hadn't any reason to stay at Forever View; he wouldn't be needed until the service on Sunday.

He had a woman in Santa Rosa. She was the latest of a long line of women; Avril thrived on variety. Her name was Helen Virtillion. She was a good-looking woman in her early thirties, very lean, taut, with big firm breasts which he found endlessly fascinating.

A lot of women were attracted to Avril Tannerton, not in spite of what he did for a living but because of it. Of course, some were turned off when they discovered he was a mortician. But a surprising number were intrigued and even excited by his unusual profession.

He understood what made him desirable to them. When a man worked with the dead, some of the mystery of death rubbed off on him. In spite of his freckles and his boyish good looks, in spite of his charming smile and his great sense of fun and his open-hearted manner, some women felt he was nonetheless mysterious, enigmatic. Unconsciously, they thought they could not die so long as they were in his arms, as if his services to the dead earned him (and those close to him) special dispensation. That atavistic fantasy was similar to the secret hope shared by many women who married doctors because they were subconsciously convinced that their spouses could protect them from all of the microbial dangers of this world.

Therefore, all day Saturday, while Avril Tannerton was in Santa Rosa making love to Helen Virtillion, the body of Bruno Frye lay alone in an empty house.

Sunday morning, two hours before sunrise, there was a sudden rush of movement in the funeral home, but Tannerton was not there to notice.

The overhead lights in the windowless workroom were switched on abruptly, but Tannerton was not there to see.

The lid of the sealed casket was unlatched and thrown back. The workroom was filled with screams of rage and pain, but Tannerton was not there to hear.

At ten o'clock Sunday morning, as Tony stood in his kitchen drinking a glass of grapefruit juice, the telephone rang. It was Janet Yamada, the woman who had been Frank Howard's blind date last night.

"How'd it go?" he asked.

"It was wonderful, a wonderful night."

"Really?"

"Sure. He's a doll."

"Frank is a doll."

"You said he might be kind of cold, difficult to get to know, but he wasn't."

"He wasn't?"

"And he's so romantic."

"Frank?"

"Who else?"

"Frank Howard is romantic?"

"These days you don't find many men who have a sense of romance," Janet said. "Sometimes it seems like romance and chivalry were thrown out the window when the sexual revolution and the women's rights movement came in. But Frank still helps you on with your coat and opens doors for you and pulls your chair out and everything. He even brought me a bouquet of roses. They're beautiful."

"I thought you might have trouble talking to him."

"Oh, no. We have a lot of the same interests."

"Like what?"

"Baseball, for one thing."

"That's right! I forgot you like baseball."

"I'm an addict."

"So you talked baseball all night."

"Oh, no," she said. "We talked about a lot of other things. Movies—"

"Movies? Are you trying to tell me Frank is a film buff?"

"He knows the old Bogart pictures almost line by line. We traded favorite bits of dialogue."

"I've been talking about film for three months, and he hasn't opened his mouth," Tony said.

"He hasn't seen a lot of recent pictures, but we're going to a show tonight."

"You're seeing him again?"

"Yeah. I wanted to call and thank you for fixing me up with him," she said.

"Am I one hell of a matchmaker, or am I one hell of a matchmaker?"

"I also wanted to let you know that even if it doesn't work out, I'll be gentle with him. He told me about Wilma. What a rotten thing! I wanted you to know that I'm aware she put a couple of cracks in him, and I won't ever hit him too hard."

Tony was amazed. "He told you about Wilma the first night he met you?"

"He said he used to be unable to talk about it, but then you showed him how to handle his hostility."

"Me?"

"He said after you helped him accept what had happened, he could talk about it without pain."

"All I did was sit and listen when he wanted to get it off his chest."

"He thinks you're a hell of a great guy."

"Frank's a damned good judge of people, isn't he?"

Later, feeling good about the excellent impression that Frank had made on Janet Yamada, optimistic about his own chances for a little romance, Tony drove to Westwood to keep his date with Hilary. She was waiting for him; she came out of the house as he pulled into the driveway. She looked crisp and lovely in black slacks, a cool ice-blue blouse, and a lightweight blue corduroy blazer. As he opened the door for her, she gave him a quick, almost shy kiss on the cheek, and he got a whiff of fresh lemony perfume.

It was going to be a good day.

Exhausted from a nearly sleepless night in Helen Virtillion's bedroom, Avril Tannerton got back from Santa Rosa shortly before ten o'clock Sunday morning.

He did not look inside the coffin.

With Gary Olmstead, Tannerton went to the cemetery and prepared the gravesite for the two o'clock ceremony. They erected the equipment that would lower the casket into the ground. Using flowers and a lot of cut greenery, they made the site as attractive as possible.

At 12:30 back at the funeral home, Tannerton used a chamois cloth to wipe the dust and smudged fingerprints from Bruno Frye's brass-plated casket. As he ran his hand over the rounded edges of the box, he thought of the magnificent contours of Helen Virtillion's breasts.

He did not look inside the coffin.

At one o'clock, Tannerton and Olmstead loaded the deceased into the hearse. Neither of them looked inside the coffin.

At one-thirty they drove to the Napa County Memorial Park. Joshua Rhinehart and a few local people followed in their own cars. Considering that it was for a wealthy and influential man, the funeral procession was embarrassingly small.

The day was clear and cool. Tall trees cast stark shadows across the road, and the hearse passed through alternating bands of sunlight and shade.

At the cemetery, the casket was placed on a sling above the grave, and fifteen people gathered around for the brief service. Gary Olmstead took up a position beside the flower-concealed control box that operated the sling and would cause it to lower the deceased into the ground. Avril stood at the front of the grave and read from a thin book of nondenominational inspirational verses. Joshua Rhinehart was at the mortician's side. The other twelve people flanked the open grave. Some of them were grape growers and their wives. They had come because they had sold their harvests to Bruno Frye's winery, and they considered their attendance at his funeral to be a business obligation. The others were Shade Tree Vineyards executives and their wives, and their reasons for being present were no more personal than those of the growers. Nobody wept.

And nobody had the opportunity or the desire to look into the coffin.

Tannerton finished reading from his small black book. He glanced at Gary Olmstead and nodded.

Olmstead pushed a button on the control box. The powerful little electric motor hummed. The casket was lowered slowly and smoothly into the gaping earth.

Hilary could not remember another day that was as much fun as that first full day with Tony Clemenza.

For lunch, they went to the Yamashiro Skyroom, high in the Hollywood Hills. The food at Yamashiro was uninspiring, very ordinary, but the ambience and the stunning view made it a fine place for an occasional light lunch or dinner. The restaurant, an authentic Japanese palace, had once been a private estate. It was surrounded by ten acres of lovely ornamental gardens. From its mountaintop perch, Yamashiro offered a breathtaking view of the entire Los Angeles basin. The day was so clear that Hilary could see all the way to Long Beach and Palos Verdes.

After lunch, they went to Griffith Park. For an hour, they walked through part of the Los Angeles Zoo, where they fed the bears, and where Tony did hilarious imitations of the animals. From the zoo they went to a special afternoon performance of the dazzling Laserium hologram show in the Griffith Park Observatory.

Later, they passed an hour on Melrose Avenue, between Doheny Drive and La Cienega Boulevard, prowling through one fascinating antique shop after another, not buying, just browsing, chatting with the proprietors.

When the cocktail hour arrived, they drove to Malibu for Mai Tais at Tonga Lei. They watched the sun set into the ocean and relaxed to the rhythmic roar of breaking waves.

Although Hilary had been an Angeleno for quite some time, her world had been composed only of her work, her house, her rose garden, her work, the film studios, her work, and the few fancy restaurants in which the motion picture and television crowd gathered to do business. She had never been to the Yamashiro Skyroom, the zoo, the laser show, the Melrose antique shops, or Tonga Lei. It was all new to her. She felt like a wide-eyed tourist—or, more accurately, like a prisoner who had just finished serving a long, long sentence, most of it in solitary confinement.

But it was not just where they went that made the day special. None of it would have been half as interesting or as much fun if she'd been with someone other than Tony. He was so charming, so quick-witted, so full of fun and energy, that he made the bright day brighter.

After slowly sipping two Mai Tais each, they were starving. They drove back to Sepulveda and went north into the San Fernando Valley to have dinner at Mel's Landing, another place with which she was not familiar. Mel's was unpretentious and moderately priced, and it offered some of the freshest and tastiest seafood she had ever eaten.

As she and Tony ate Mel's steamed clams and discussed other favorite places to eat, Hilary found that he knew ten times as many as she did. Her knowledge did not extend much beyond that handful of expensive dining spots that served the movers and shakers of the entertainment industry. The out-of-the-way eateries, the hole-in-the-wall cafés with surprising house specialties, the small mom-and-pop restaurants with plainly served but delicious food—all of that was one more aspect of the city about which she had never taken time to learn. She saw that she had become rich without ever discovering how to use and fully enjoy the freedom that her money could provide.

They ate too many of Mel's clams and then too much red snapper with too many Malaysian shrimp. They also drank too much white wine.

Considering how much they consumed, it was amazing, Hilary thought, that they had so much time between mouthfuls for conversation. But they never stopped talking. She was usually reticent on the first few dates with a new man, but not with Tony. She wanted to hear what he thought about everything, from *Mork and Mindy* to Shakespearean drama, from politics to art. People, dogs, religion, architecture, sports, Bach, fashions, food, women's liberation, Saturday morning cartoons—it seemed urgent and vital that she know what he thought about those and a million other subjects. She also wanted to tell him what she thought about all those things, and she wanted to know what he thought of what she thought, and pretty soon she was telling him what she thought of what he thought of what she thought. They chattered as if they had just learned that God was going to strike everyone in the world deaf and dumb at sunrise. Hilary was drunk, not on wine, but on the fluidity and intimacy of their conversation; she was intoxicated by communication, a potent brew for which she had built up little tolerance over the years.

By the time he took her home and agreed to come in for a nightcap, she was certain they would go to bed together. She wanted him very much; the thought of it made her warm and tingly. She knew he wanted her. She could see the desire in his eyes. They needed to let dinner settle a bit, and with that in mind, she poured white crème de menthe on the rocks for both of them.

They were just sitting down when the telephone rang.

"Oh, no," she said.

"Did he bother you after I left last night?"

"No."

"This morning?"

"No."

"Maybe that's not him."

They both went to the phone.

She hesitated, then picked it up. "Hello?"

Silence.

"Damn you!" she said, and she slammed the receiver down so hard that she wondered if she'd cracked it.

"Don't let him rattle you."

"I can't help it," she said.

"He's just a slimy little creep who doesn't know how to deal with women. I've seen others like him. If he ever got a chance to make it with a woman, if a woman offered herself to him on a silver platter, he'd run away screaming in terror."

"He still scares me."

"He's no threat. Come back to the couch. Sit down. Try to forget about him."

They returned to the sofa and sipped their crème de menthe in silence for a minute or two.

At last, she softly said, "Damn."

"You'll have an unlisted number by tomorrow afternoon. Then he won't be able to bother you any more."

"But he sure spoiled this evening. I was so mellow."

"I'm still enjoying myself."

"It's just that . . . I'd figured on more than just drinks in front of the fireplace."

He stared at her. "Had you?"

"Hadn't you?"

His smile was special because it was not merely a configuration of the mouth; it involved his whole face and his expressive dark eyes; it was the most genuine and by far the most appealing smile that she had ever seen. He said, "I've got to admit I had hopes of tasting more than the crème de menthe."

"Damn the phone."

He leaned over and kissed her. She opened her mouth to him, and for a brief sweet moment their tongues met. He pulled back and looked at her, put his hand against her face as if he was touching delicate porcelain. "I think we're still in the mood."

"If the phone rings again—"

"It won't."

He kissed her on the eyes, then on the lips, and he put one hand gently on her breast.

She leaned back, and he leaned into her. She put her hand on his arm and felt the muscles bunched beneath his shirt.

Still kissing her, he stroked her soft throat with his fingertips, then began to unbutton her blouse.

Hilary put her hand on his thigh, where the muscles were also tense beneath his slacks. Such a lean hard man. She slid her hand up to his groin and felt the huge steeliness and fierce heat of his erection. She thought of him entering her and moving hotly within her, and a thrill of anticipation made her shiver.

He sensed her excitement and paused in the unbuttoning of her blouse to lightly trace the swell of her breasts where they rose above the cups of her bra. His fingers seemed to leave cool trails on her warm skin; she could feel the lingering ghost of his touch as clearly as she could feel the touch itself.

The telephone rang.

"Ignore it," he said.

She tried to do as he said. She put her arms around him and slid down on the couch and pulled him on top of her. She kissed him hard, crushing her lips against his, licking, sucking.

The phone rang and rang.

"Damn!"

They sat up.

It rang, rang, rang.

Hilary stood.

"Don't," Tony said. "Talking to him hasn't helped. Let me handle it another way and see what happens."

He got up from the couch and went to the corner desk. He lifted the receiver, but he didn't say anything. He just listened.

Hilary could tell from his expression that the caller had not spoken.

Tony was determined to wait him out. He looked at his watch.

Thirty seconds passed. A minute. Two minutes.

The battle of nerves between the two men was strangely like a childish staring contest, yet there was nothing childish about it. It was eerie. Goosebumps popped up on her arms.

Two and a half minutes.

It seemed like an hour.

Finally, Tony put down the phone. "He hung up."

"Without saying anything?"

"Not a word. But he hung up first, and I think that's important. I figured if I gave him a dose of his own medicine he wouldn't like it. He thinks he's going to frighten you. But you're expecting the call, and you just listen like he does. At first, he thinks you're only being cute, and he's sure he can outwait you. But the longer you're silent, the more he starts to wonder if you aren't up to some trick. Is there a tap on your phone? Are you stalling so the police can trace the call? Is it even you who picked up the phone? He thinks about that, starts to get scared, and hangs up."

"*He's* scared? Well, that's a nice thought," she said.

"I doubt that he'll get up the nerve to call back. At least not until you've changed numbers tomorrow. And then he'll be too late."

"Nevertheless, I'll be on edge until the man from the phone company's done his job."

Tony held out his arms, and she moved into his embrace. They kissed again. It was still extraordinarily sweet and good and right, but the sharp edge of unrestrained passion could no longer be felt. Both of them were unhappily aware of the difference.

They returned to the couch, but only to drink their crème de menthe and talk. By twelve-thirty in the morning, when he had to go home, they had decided to spend the following weekend on a museum binge. Saturday, they'd go to the Norton Simon Museum in Pasadena to look at the German expressionist paintings and the Renaissance tapestry. Then they would spend most of Sunday at the J. Paul Getty Museum, which boasted a collection of art richer than any other in the world. Of course, in between the museums, they would eat a lot of good food, share a lot of good talk, and (they ardently hoped) pick up where they had left off on the couch.

At the front door, as he was leaving, Hilary suddenly couldn't bear to wait five days to see him again. She said, "What about Wednesday?"

"What about it?"

"Doing anything for dinner?"

"Oh, I'll probably fry up a batch of eggs that are just getting stale in the refrigerator."

"All that cholesterol's bad for you."

"And maybe I'll cut the mold off the bread, make some toast. And I should finish the fruit juice I bought two weeks ago."

"You poor dear."

"The bachelor's life."

"I can't let you eat stale eggs and moldy toast. Not when I make such a terrific tossed salad and filet of sole."

"A nice light supper," he said.

"We don't want to get bloated and sleepy."

"Never know when you might have to move fast."

She grinned. "Precisely."

"See you Wednesday."

"Seven?"

"Seven sharp."

They kissed, and he walked away from the door, and a cold night wind rushed in where he had been, and then he was gone.

Half an hour later, upstairs, in bed, Hilary's body ached with frustration. Her breasts were full and taut; she longed to feel his hands on them, his fingers gently stroking and massaging. She could close her eyes and feel his lips on her stiffening nipples. Her belly fluttered as she pictured him braced above her on his powerful arms, and then she above him, moving in slow sensuous circles. Her sex was moist and warm, ready, waiting. She tossed and turned for almost an hour before she finally got up and took a sedative.

As sleep crept over her, she held a drowsy dialogue with herself.

Am I falling in love?

—No. Of course not.

Maybe. Maybe I am.

—No. Love's dangerous.

Maybe it'll work with him

—Remember Earl and Emma.

Tony's different.

—You're horny. That's all it is. You're just horny.

That, too.

She slept, and she dreamed. Some of the dreams were golden and fuzzy about the edges. In one of them she was naked with Tony, lying in a meadow where the grass felt like feathers, high above the world, a meadow atop a towering pillar of rock, and the warm wind was cleaner than sunshine, cleaner than the electric current of a lightning bolt, cleaner than anything in the world.

But she had nightmares, too. In one of them, she was in the old Chicago apartment, and the walls were closing in, and when she looked up she saw there was no ceiling, and Earl and Emma were staring down at her, their faces as big as God's face, grinning down at her as the walls closed in, and when she opened the door to run out of the apartment, she collided with an enormous cockroach, a monstrous insect bigger than she was, and it obviously intended to eat her alive.

At three o'clock in the morning, Joshua Rhinehart woke, moaning and tussling briefly with the tangled sheets. He'd drunk a bit too much wine with dinner, which was most unusual for him. The buzz was gone, but his bladder was killing him; however, it was not merely the call of nature that had disturbed his sleep. He'd had a horrible dream about Tannerton's workroom. In that nightmare, several dead men—all of them duplicates of Bruno Frye—had risen up from their caskets and from the porcelain and stainless steel embalming tables; he had run into the night behind Forever View, but they had come after him, had searched the shadows for him, moving jerkily, calling his name in their flat dead voices.

He lay on his back in the darkness, staring at the ceiling which he could not see. The only sound was the nearly inaudible purr of the electronic digital clock on the nightstand.

Before his wife's death three years ago, Joshua had seldom dreamed. And he'd never had a nightmare. Not once in fifty-eight years. But after Cora passed away, all of that changed. He dreamed at least once or twice a week now, and more often than not the dream was a bad one. Many of them had to do with losing something terribly important but indescribable, and there always ensued a frantic but hopeless search for that which he had lost. He didn't need a fifty-dollar-an-hour psychiatrist to tell him that those dreams were about Cora and her untimely death. He still had not adjusted to life without her. Perhaps he never would. The other nightmares were filled with walking dead men who often looked like him, symbols of his own mortality; but tonight they all bore a striking resemblance to Bruno Frye.

He got out of bed, stretched, yawned. He shuffled to the bathroom without turning on a lamp.

A couple of minutes later, on his way back to bed, he stopped at the window. The panes were cold to the touch. A stiff wind pressed against the glass and made mewling sounds like an animal that wanted to be let inside. The valley was still and dark except for the lights of the wineries. He could see the Shade Tree Vineyards to the north, farther up in the hills.

Suddenly, his eye was caught by a fuzzy white dot just south of the winery, a single smudge of light in the middle of a vineyard, approximately where the Frye house stood. Lights in the Frye house? There wasn't supposed to be anyone there. Bruno had lived alone. Joshua squinted, but without his glasses, everything at a distance tended to grow hazier the harder he tried to focus on it. He couldn't tell if the light was at the Frye place or at one of the administration buildings between the house and the main winery complex. In fact, the longer he stared the less he was sure that it was a light he was watching; it was faint, lambent; it might only be a reflection of moonlight.

He went to the nightstand and, not wanting to turn on a lamp and spoil his night vision, he felt for his glasses in the dark. Before he found them, he knocked over an empty water glass.

When he got back to the window and looked up into the hills again, the mysterious light was gone. Nevertheless, he stood there for a long while, a vigilant guardian. He was executor of the Frye estate, and it was his duty to preserve it for final distribution in accordance with the will. If burglars and vandals were stripping the house, he wanted to know about it. For fifteen minutes, he waited and watched, but the light never returned.

At last, convinced that his weak eyes had deceived him, he went back to bed.

Monday morning, as Tony and Frank pursued a series of possible leads on Bobby Valdez, Frank talked animatedly about Janet Yamada. Janet was so pretty. Janet was so intelligent. Janet was so understanding. Janet was this, and Janet was that. He was a bore on the subject of Janet Yamada, but Tony allowed him to gush and ramble. It was good to see Frank talking and acting like a normal human being.

Before checking out their unmarked police sedan and getting on the road, Tony and Frank had spoken to two men on the narcotics squad, Detectives Eddie Quevedo and Carl Hammerstein. The word from those two specialists was that Bobby Valdez was most likely selling either cocaine or PCP to support himself while he pursued his unpaid vocation as a rapist. The biggest money in the L.A. drug market was currently in those two illegal but extremely popular substances. A dealer could still make a fortune in heroin or grass, but those were no longer the most lucrative commodities in the underground pharmacy. According to the narcs, if Bobby was involved in drug traffic, he had to be a pusher, selling directly to users, a man at the lower end of the production and marketing structure. He was virtually penniless when he got out of prison last April, and he needed substantial capital to become either a manufacturer or an importer of narcotics. "What you're looking for is a common street hustler," Quevedo had told Tony and Frank. "Talk to other hustlers." Hammerstein had said, "We'll give you a list of names and addresses. They're all guys who've taken falls for dealing drugs. Most of them are probably dealing again; we just haven't caught them at it yet. Put on a little pressure. Sooner or later, you'll find one of them who's run into Bobby on the street and knows where he's holed up." There were twenty-four names on the list that Quevedo and Hammerstein had given them.

Three of the first six men were not at home. The other three swore they didn't know Bobby Valdez or Juan Mazquezza or anyone else with the face in the mug shots.

The seventh name on the list was Eugene Tucker, and he was able to help them. They didn't even have to lean on him.

Most black men were actually one shade of brown or another, but Tucker was truly black. His face was broad and smooth and as black as tar. His dark brown eyes were far lighter than his skin. He had a bushy black beard that was salted with curly white hairs, and that touch of frosting was the only thing about him, other than the whites of his eyes, that was not very, very dark. He even wore black slacks and a black shirt. He was stocky, with a big chest and bigger arms, and his neck was as thick as a wharf post. He looked as if he snapped railroad ties in two for exercise—or maybe just for fun.

Tucker lived in a high-rent townhouse in the Hollywood Hills, a roomy place that was sparsely but tastefully furnished. The living room had only four pieces in it: a couch, two chairs, a coffee table. No end tables or fancy storage units. No stereo. No television set. There weren't even any lamps; at night, the only light would come from the ceiling fixture. But the four pieces that he did have were of remarkably high quality, and each item perfectly accented the others. Tucker had a taste for fine Chinese antiques. The couch and chairs, which recently had been reupholstered in jade-green velvet, were all made of hand-carved rosewood, a hundred years old, maybe twice that, immensely heavy and well-preserved, matchless examples of their period and style. The low table was also rosewood with a narrow inlaid ivory border. Tony and Frank sat on the couch, and Eugene Tucker perched on the edge of a chair opposite them.

Tony ran one hand along the rosewood arm of the couch and said, "Mr. Tucker, this is marvelous."

Tucker raised his eyebrows. "You know what it is?"

"I don't know the precise period," Tony said. "But I'm familiar enough with Chinese art to know this is definitely not a reproduction that you picked up on sale at Sears."

Tucker laughed, pleased that Tony knew the value of the furniture. "I know what you're thinking," he said good-naturedly. "You're wondering how an ex-con, just two years out of the stir, can afford all this. A twelve-hundred-dollar-a-month townhouse. Chinese antiques. You're wondering if maybe I've gotten back into the heroin trade or some allied field of endeavor."

"In fact," Tony said, "that's not what I'm asking myself at all. I *am* wondering how the devil you've done it. But I know it's not from selling junk."

Tucker smiled. "How can you be so sure?"

"If you were a drug dealer with a passion for Chinese antiques," Tony said, "you'd simply furnish the entire house at a single crack, instead of a piece or two at a time. You are clearly into something that earns a lot of bread, but not nearly as much as you'd make distributing dope like you used to do."

Tucker laughed again and applauded approvingly. He turned to Frank and said, "Your partner is perceptive."

Frank smiled. "A regular Sherlock Holmes."

To Tucker, Tony said, "Satisfy my curiosity. What do you do?"

Tucker leaned forward, suddenly frowning, raising one granite fist and shaking it, looking huge and mean and very dangerous. When he spoke he snarled: "I design dresses."

Tony blinked.

Collapsing back in his chair, Tucker laughed again. He was one of the happiest people Tony had ever seen. "I design women's clothes," he said. "I really do. My name's already beginning to be known in the California design community, and some day it'll be a household word. I promise you."

Intrigued, Frank said, "According to our information, you did four years of an eight-year sentence for wholesaling heroin and cocaine. How'd you go from that to making women's clothes?"

"I used to be one mean son of a bitch," Tucker said. "And those first few months in prison, I was even meaner than usual. I blamed society for everything that happened to me. I blamed the white power structure. I blamed the whole world, but I just wouldn't put any blame on myself. I thought I was a tough dude, but I hadn't really grown up yet. You aren't a man until you accept responsibility for your life. A lot of people never do."

"So what turned you around?" Frank asked.

"A little thing," Tucker said. "Man, sometimes it amazes me how such a little thing can change a person's life. With me, it was a TV show. On the six o'clock news, one of the L.A. stations did a five-part series about black success stories in the city."

"I saw it," Tony said. "More than five years ago, but I still remember it."

"It was fascinating stuff," Tucker said. "It was an image of the black man you never get to see. But at first, before the series began, everybody in the slammer figured it would be one big laugh. We figured the reporter would spend all his time asking the same idiot question: 'Why can't all these poor black folks work hard and become rich Las Vegas headliners like Sammy Davis, Jr.?' But they didn't talk to any entertainers or sports stars.''

Tony remembered that it had been a striking piece of journalism, especially for television, where news—and especially the human interest stories on the news—had as much depth as a teacup. The reporters had interviewed black businessmen and businesswomen who had made it to the top, people who had started out with nothing and eventually had become millionaires. Some in real estate. One in the restaurant business. One with a chain of beauty shops. About a dozen people. They all agreed that it was harder to get rich if you were black, but they also agreed that it was not as hard as they thought when they started out, and that it was easier in Los Angeles than in Alabama or Mississippi or even Boston or New York. There were more black millionaires in L.A. than in the rest of California *and* the other forty-nine states combined. In Los Angeles, almost everyone was living in the fast lane; the typical Southern Californian did not merely accommodate himself to change but actively sought it and reveled in it. This atmosphere of flux and constant experimentation drew a lot of marginally sane and even insane people into the area, but it also attracted some of the brightest and most innovative minds in the country, which was why so many new cultural and scientific and industrial developments originated in the region. Very few Southern Californians had the time or patience for outmoded attitudes, one of which was racial prejudice. Of course, there was bigotry in L.A. But whereas a landed white family in Georgia might require six or eight generations to overcome its prejudice toward blacks, that same metamorphosis of attitudes often transpired in one generation of a Southern California family. As one of the black businessmen on the TV news report had said, "The Chicanos have been the niggers of L.A. for quite some time now." But already that was changing, too. The Hispanic culture was regarded with ever-increasing respect, and the browns were creating their own success stories. Several people interviewed on that news special had offered the same explanation for the unusual fluidity of Southern California's social structures and for the eagerness with which people there accepted change: it was, they said, partly because of geology. When you were living on some of the worst fault lines in the world, when the earth could quake and move and *change* under your feet without warning, did that awareness of impermanence have a subconscious influence on a person's attitudes toward less cataclysmic kinds of change? Some of those black millionaires thought it did, and Tony tended to agree with them.

"There were about a dozen rich black people on that program," Eugene Tucker said. "A lot of guys in the slammer with me just hooted at the TV and called them all Uncle Toms. But I started thinking. If some people on that show could make it in a white world, why couldn't I? I was just as clever and smart as any of them, maybe even smarter than some. It was a completely new image of a black man to me, a whole new idea, like a light bulb going on in my head. Los Angeles was my home. If it really offered a better chance, why hadn't I taken advantage of it? Sure, maybe some of those people had to act like Uncle Toms on their way to the top. But when you've made it, when you've got that million in the bank, you're nobody's man but your own." He grinned. "So I decided to get rich."

"Just like that," Frank said, impressed.

"Just like that."

"The power of positive thinking."

"Realistic thinking," Tucker corrected.

"Why dress designing?" Frank asked.

"I took aptitude tests that said I'd do well in design work or any aspect of the art business. So I tried to decide what I'd most enjoy designing. Now, I've always liked to choose the clothes my girlfriends wear. I like to go shopping with them. And when they wear an outfit I've picked, they get more compliments than when they wear something they chose themselves. So I hooked up with a university program for inmates, and I studied design. Took a lot of business courses, too. When I was finally paroled, I worked for a while at a fast food restaurant. I lived in a cheap rooming house and kept my expenses down. I drew some designs, paid seamstresses to sew up samples, and started hawking my wares. It wasn't easy at first. Hell, it was damned hard! Every time I got an order from a shop, I walked it to the bank and borrowed money against it to complete the dresses. Man, I was clawing to hold on. But it got better and better. It's pretty good now. In a year, I'll open my own shop in a good area. And eventually you'll see a sign in Beverly Hills that says 'Eugene Tucker.' I promise you."

Tony shook his head. "You're a remarkable man."

"Not particularly," Tucker said. "I'm just living in a remarkable place and a remarkable time."

Frank was holding the manila envelope that contained the mug shots of Bobby "Angel" Valdez. He tapped it against his knee and looked at Tony and said, "I think maybe we've come to the wrong place this time."

"It sure looks that way," Tony said.

Tucker slid forward on his chair. "What was it you wanted?"

Tony told him about Bobby Valdez.

"Well," Tucker said, "I don't move in the circles I once did, but I'm not completely out of touch either. I donate fifteen or twenty hours of my time every week to Self-Pride. That's a city-wide anti-drug campaign. I feel sort of like I've got debts to pay, you know? A Self-Pride volunteer spends about half his time talking to kids, the other half working on an information-gathering program, sort of like TIP. You know about TIP?"

"Turn in Pushers," Tony said.

"Right. They have a number you can call and give anonymous tips about neighborhood drug dealers. Well, we don't wait for people to call us at Self-Pride. We canvas those neighborhoods where we know pushers work. We go door to door, talk to parents and kids, pump them for anything they know. We build up dossiers on dealers until we feel we've really got the goods, then we turn the dossiers over to the LAPD. So if this Valdez is dealing, there's a chance I'll know at least a little something about him."

Frank said, "I have to agree with Tony. You are rather remarkable."

"Hey, look, I don't deserve any pats on the back for my work at Self-Pride. I wasn't asking for congratulations. In my day I created a lot of junkies out of kids who might have done right if I hadn't been there to steer them wrong. It's going to take me a long, long time to help enough kids to balance the equation."

Frank took the photographs out of the envelope and gave them to Tucker.

The black man looked at each of the three shots. "I know the little bastard. He's one of about thirty guys we're building files on right now."

Tony's heartbeat accelerated a bit in anticipation of the chase to come.

"Only he doesn't use the name Valdez," Tucker said.

"Juan Mazquezza?"

"Not that either. I think he calls himself Ortiz."

"Do you know where we can find him?"

Tucker stood up. "Let me call the information center at Self-Pride. They might have an address on him."

"Terrific," Frank said.

Tucker started toward the kitchen to use the phone in there, stopped, looked back at them. "This might take a few minutes. If you'd like to pass the time looking at my designs, you can go into the study." He pointed to a set of double doors that opened off the living room.

"Sure," Tony said. "I'd like to see them."

He and Frank went into the study and found that it was even more sparsely furnished than the living room. There was a large expensive drawing table with its own lamp. A high stool with a padded seat and a spring back stood in front of the table, and beside the stool there was an artist's supply cabinet on wheels. Near one of the windows, a department store mannequin posed with head tilted coyly and shiny-smooth arms spread wide; bolts of bright cloth lay at its plastic feet. There were no shelves or storage cabinets; stacks of sketches and drawing tablets and draftsman's tools were lined up on the floor along one wall. Obviously, Eugene Tucker was confident that eventually he would be able to furnish the entire townhouse with pieces as exquisite as those in the living room, and in the meantime, regardless of the inconvenience, he did not intend to waste money on cheap temporary furniture.

Quintessential California optimism, Tony thought.

Pencil sketches and a few full-color renditions of Tucker's work were thumbtacked to one wall. His dresses and two-piece suits and blouses were tailored yet flowing, feminine yet not frilly. He had an excellent sense of color and a flair for the kind of detail that made a piece of clothing special. Every one of the designs was clearly the work of a superior talent.

Tony still found it somewhat difficult to believe that the big hard-bitten black man designed women's clothes for a living. But then he realized that his own dichotomous nature was not so different from Tucker's. During the day, he was a homicide detective, desensitized and hardened by all of the violence he saw, but at night, he was an artist, hunched over a canvas in his apartment-studio, painting, painting, painting. In a curious way, he and Eugene were brothers under the skin.

Just as Tony and Frank were looking at the last of the sketches, Tucker returned from the kitchen. "Well, what do you think?"

"Wonderful," Tony said. "You've got a terrific feeling for color and line."

"You're really good," Frank said.

"I know," Tucker said, and he laughed.

"Does Self-Pride have a file on Valdez?" Tony asked.

"Yes. But he calls himself Ortiz, like I thought. Jimmy Ortiz. From what we've been able to gather, he deals strictly in PCP. I know I'm not on solid ground when I start pointing the finger at other people . . . but so far as I'm concerned, a PCP dealer is the lowest kind of bastard in the drug trade. I mean, PCP is *poison*. It rots the brain cells faster than anything else. We don't have enough information in our file to turn it over to the police, but we're working on it."

"Address?" Tony asked.

Tucker handed him a slip of paper on which the address had been noted in neat handwriting. "It's a fancy apartment complex one block south of Sunset, just a couple of blocks from La Cienega."

"We'll find it," Tony said.

"Judging from what you've told me about him," Tucker said, "and from what we've learned about him at Self-Pride, I'd say this guy isn't the kind who's ever going to knuckle down and rehabilitate himself. You'd better put this one away for a long, long time."

"We're sure going to try," Frank said.

Tucker accompanied them to the front door, then outside, where the patio deck in front of the townhouse offered a wide view of Los Angeles in the basin below. "Isn't it gorgeous?" Tucker asked. "Isn't it something?"

"Quite a view," Tony said.

"Such a big, big, beautiful city," Tucker said with pride and affection, as if he had created the megalopolis himself. "You know, I just heard that the bureaucrats back in Washington made a study of mass transit possibilities for L.A. They were determined to ram some system or other down our throats, but they were stunned to find out it would cost at least one hundred billion dollars to build a rapid transit railway network that would handle only ten or twelve percent of the daily commuter crush. They still don't understand how vast the West is." He was rhapsodizing now, his broad face alight with pleasure, his strong hands tossing off one gesture after another. "They don't realize that the meaning of L.A. is space—space and mobility and freedom. This is a city with elbow room. Physical and emotional elbow room. Psychological elbow room. In L.A., you have a chance to be almost anything you want to be. Here, you can take your future out of the hands of other people and shape it yourself. It's fantastic. I love it. God, I love it!"

Tony was so impressed with the depth of Tucker's feeling for the city that he revealed his own secret dream. "I've always wanted to be an artist, to make a living with my art. I paint."

"Then why are you a cop?" Tucker asked.

"It's a steady paycheck."

"Screw steady paychecks."

"I'm a good cop. I like the work well enough."

"Are you a good artist?"

"Pretty good, I think."

"Then take the leap," Tucker said. "Man, you are living on the edge of the Western world, on the edge of possibility. Jump. Jump off. It's one hell of a thrill, and it's so damned far to the bottom that you'll never crash into anything hard or sharp. In fact, you'll probably find exactly the same thing I found. It's not like falling down at all. You'll feel like you're falling *up!*"

Tony and Frank followed the brick wall to the driveway, past a jade-plant hedge that had thick juicy leaves. The unmarked sedan was parked in the shade of a large date palm.

As Tony opened the door on the passenger's side, Tucker called to him from the patio deck, "Jump! Just jump off and fly!"

"He's some character," Frank said as he drove away from the townhouse.

"Yeah," Tony said, wondering what it felt like to fly.

As they headed for the address that Tucker had given them, Frank talked a little about the black man and then a lot about Janet Yamada. Still mulling over Eugene Tucker's advice, Tony gave his partner only half his attention. Frank didn't notice that Tony was distracted. When he was talking about Janet Yamada, he really didn't attempt to carry on a conversation; he delivered a soliloquy.

Fifteen minutes later, they found the apartment complex where Jimmy Ortiz lived. The parking garage was underground, guarded by an iron gate that opened only to an electronic signal, so they couldn't see if there was a black Jaguar on the premises.

The apartments were on two levels, in randomly set wings, with open staircases and walkways. The complex was structured around an enormous swimming pool and a lot of lush greenery. There was also a whirlpool spa. Two girls in bikinis and a hairy young man were sitting in the swirling water, drinking a martini lunch and laughing at one another's banter as tendrils of steam writhed up from the turbulent pool around them.

Frank stopped at the edge of the Jacuzzi and asked them where Jimmy Ortiz lived.

One of the girls said, "Is he that cute little guy with the mustache?"

"Baby face," Tony said.

"That's him," she said.

"Does he have a mustache now?"

"If it's the same guy," she said. "This one drives a terrific Jag."

"That's him," Frank said.

"I think he lives over there," she said, "in Building Four, on the second floor, all the way at the end."

"Is he home?" Frank asked.

No one knew.

At Building Four, Tony and Frank climbed the stairs to the second floor. An open-air balcony ran the length of the building and served the four apartments that faced onto the courtyard. Along the railing, opposite the first three doors, pots of ivy and other climbing plants had been set out to give the second level a pleasant green look like that enjoyed by ground-floor residents; but there were no plants in front of the end apartment.

The door was ajar.

Tony's eyes met Frank's. A worried look passed between them.

Why was the door ajar?

Did Bobby know they were coming?

They flanked the entrance. Waited. Listened.

The only sound came from the happy trio in the courtyard whirlpool.

Frank raised his eyebrows questioningly.

Tony pointed to the doorbell.

After a brief hesitation, Frank pressed it.

Inside, the chimes rang softly. *Bong-bing-bong.*

They waited for a response, eyes on the door.

Suddenly the air seemed perfectly still and oppressively heavy. Humid. Thick. Syrupy. Tony had trouble breathing it; he felt as if he were drawing fluid into his lungs.

No one answered the bell.

Frank rang it again.

When there was still no response, Tony reached under his jacket and slipped his revolver from its shoulder holster. He felt weak. His stomach was bubbling acidly.

Frank took out his revolver, listened closely for sounds of movement inside, then finally pushed the door all the way open.

The foyer was deserted.

Tony leaned sideways to get a better look inside. The living room, of which he could see only a small part, was shadowy and still. The drapes were shut, and there were no lights burning.

Tony shouted, "Police!"

His voice echoed under the balcony roof.

A bird chirped in an olive tree.

"Come out with your hands raised, Bobby!"

On the street, a car horn sounded.

In another apartment a phone rang, muffled but audible.

"Bobby!" Frank shouted. "You hear what he said? We're the police. It's all over now. So just come out of there. Come on! *Right now!*"

Down in the courtyard, the whirlpool bathers had grown very quiet.

Tony had the crazy notion that he could hear people in a dozen apartments as they crept stealthily to their windows.

Frank raised his voice even further. "We don't want to hurt you, Bobby!"

"Listen to him!" Tony shouted into the apartment. "Don't force us to hurt you. Come on out peacefully."

Bobby didn't respond.

"If he was in there," Frank said, "he'd at least tell us to go fuck ourselves."

"So what now?" Tony asked.

"I guess we go in."

"Jesus, I hate shit like this. Maybe we should call a backup team."

"He's probably not armed," Frank said.

"You're kidding."

"He doesn't have any prior arrests for carrying a gun. Except when he's after a woman, he's a sniveling little creep."

"He's a killer."

"Women. He's only dangerous to women."

Tony shouted again: "Bobby, this is your last chance! Now dammit, come out of there nice and slow!"

Silence.

Tony's heart was hammering furiously.

"Okay," Frank said. "Let's get this over with."

"If memory serves me right, you went in first the last time we had to do something like this."

"Yeah. The Wilkie-Pomeroy case."

"Then I guess it's my turn," Tony said.

"I know you've been looking forward to this."

"Oh, yes."

"With all your heart."

"Which is now in my throat."

"Go get him, tiger."

"Cover me."

"The foyer's too narrow for me to give you good cover. I won't be able to see past you once you go in."

"I'll stay as low as possible," Tony said.

"Make like a duck. I'll try to look over you."

"Just do the best you can."

Tony's stomach was cramping up on him. He took a couple of deep breaths and tried to calm down. That trick had no effect other than to make his heart pound harder and faster than it had been doing. At last, he crouched and launched himself through the open door, the revolver held out in front of him. He scuttled across the slippery tile floor of the foyer and stopped at the brink of the living room, searching the shadows for movement, expecting to take a bullet right between the eyes.

The living room was dimly illuminated by thin strips of sunlight that found their way around the edges of the heavy drapes. As far as Tony could tell, all of the lumpy shapes were couches and chairs and tables. The place appeared to be full of big, expensive, and utterly tasteless Americanized Mediterranean furniture. A narrow shaft of sunlight fell across a red velvet sofa that had a large and thoroughly grotesque wrought-iron fleur-de-lis bolted to its imitation oak side.

"Bobby?"

No response.

A clock ticking somewhere.

"We don't want to hurt you, Bobby."

Only silence.

Tony held his breath.

He could hear Frank breathing.

Nothing else.

Slowly, cautiously, he stood.

No one shot at him.

He felt along the wall until he located a light switch. A lamp with a garish bullfight scene on its shade came on in one corner, and he could see that both the living room and the open dining area beyond were deserted.

Frank came in behind him and motioned toward the door of the foyer closet.

Tony stepped back, out of the way.

Holding his revolver at gut-level, Frank gingerly opened the sliding door. The closet contained only a couple of light-weight jackets and several shoe boxes.

Staying away from each other in order to avoid making a single easy target of themselves, they crossed the living room. There was a liquor cabinet with ridiculously large black iron hinges; the glass in the cabinet doors was tinted yellow. A round coffee table was in the center of the room, a mammoth eight-sided thing with a useless copper-lined brazier in the middle of it. The sofa and high-backed chairs were upholstered in flame-red velvet with lots of gold fringe and black tassels. The drapes were flashy yellow and orange brocade. The carpet was a thick green shag. It was a singularly ugly place to live.

And, Tony thought, it's also an absurd place in which to die.

They walked through the dining area and looked into the small kitchen. It was a mess. The refrigerator door and a few of the cupboards were standing open. Cans and jars and boxes of food had been pulled off the shelves and dumped onto the floor. Some items appeared to have been thrown down in a rage. Several jars were broken; sharp fragments of glass sparkled in the garbage. A puddle of maraschino cherry juice lay like a pink-red amoeba on the yellow tiles; the bright red cherries gleamed in every corner. Chocolate dessert topping was splashed all over the electric stove. Cornflakes were scattered everywhere. And dill pickles. Olives. Dry spaghetti. Someone had used mustard and grape jelly to scrawl one word four times on the only blank wall in the kitchen:

Cocodrilos
Cocodrilos
Cocodrilos
Cocodrilos

They whispered:

"What is it?"

"Spanish."

"What's it mean?"

"Crocodiles."

"Why crocodiles?"

"I don't know."

"Creepy," Frank said.

Tony agreed. They had walked into a bizarre situation. Even though he could not understand what was happening. Tony knew there was great danger ahead. He wished he knew which door it would pop out of.

They looked in the den, which was as overfurnished as the other two rooms. Bobby wasn't hiding in there or in the den closet.

They moved warily back down the hall toward the two bedrooms and two baths. They didn't make a sound.

They didn't find anything out of the ordinary in the first bedroom and bathroom.

In the master bedroom, there was another mess. All of the clothes had been taken out of the closet and strewn about. They were piled on the floor, wadded into balls on the bed, draped over the dresser where they had fallen when thrown, and most if not all of them were badly damaged. Sleeves and collars had been stripped off shirts. Lapels had been torn from sports jackets and suit coats. The inseams of trousers had been ripped open. The person who had done all of that had been functioning in a blind rage, yet he had been surprisingly methodical and thorough in spite of his fury.

But who had done it?

Someone with a grudge against Bobby?

Bobby himself? Why would he mess up his own kitchen and destroy his own clothes?

What did crocodiles have to do with it?

Tony had the disturbing feeling that they were moving too fast through the apartment, that they were overlooking something important. An explanation for the strange things they'd discovered seemed to be hovering at the edge of his mind, but he could not reach out and grab it.

The door to the adjoining bath was closed. It was the only place they hadn't looked.

Frank trained his revolver on the door and watched it while he spoke to Tony. "If he didn't leave before we got here, he has to be in the bathroom."

"Who?"

Frank gave him a quick perplexed glance. "Bobby, of course. Who else?"

"You think he tore up his own place?"

"Well . . . what do you think?"

"We're missing something."

"Yeah? Like what?"

"I don't know."

Frank moved toward the bathroom door.

Tony hesitated, listening to the apartment.

The place was about as noisy as a tomb.

"*Somebody* must be in that bathroom," Frank said.

They took up positions flanking the door.

"Bobby! You hear me?" Frank shouted. "You can't stay in there forever. Come out with your hands raised!"

Nobody came out.

Tony said, "Even if you're not Bobby Valdez, no matter who you are, you've got to come out of there."

Ten seconds. Twenty. Thirty.

Frank took hold of the knob and twisted it slowly until the bolt slipped out of its slot with a soft snick. He pushed the door open and convulsively threw himself back against the wall to get out of the way of any bullets or knives or other indications that he was unwelcome.

No gunfire. No movement.

The only thing that came out of the bathroom was a really terrible stench. Urine. Excrement.

Tony gagged. "Jesus!"

Frank put one hand over his mouth and nose.

The bathroom was deserted. The floor was puddled with bright yellow urine, and feces was smeared over the commode and sink and clear glass shower door.

"What in the name of God is going on here?" Frank asked through his fingers.

One Spanish word was printed twice in feces on the bathroom wall.

Cocodrilos
Cocodrilos

Tony and Frank swiftly retreated to the center of the bedroom, stepping on torn shirts and ruined suits. But now that the bathroom door had been opened, they could not escape the odor without leaving the room altogether, so they went into the hallway.

"Whoever did this really hates Bobby," Frank said.

"So you no longer think Bobby did it to himself?"

"Why would he? It doesn't make sense. Christ, this is about as weird as they come. The hairs are up on the back of my neck."

"Spooky," Tony agreed.

His stomach muscles were still painfully cramped with tension, and his heart was thumping only slightly slower than it had been when they'd first crept into the apartment.

They were both silent for a moment, listening for the footsteps of ghosts.

Tony watched a small brown spider as it climbed the corridor wall.

Finally Frank put his gun away and took out his handkerchief and wiped his sweat-streaked face.

Tony holstered his own revolver and said, "We can't just leave it like this and put a stakeout on the place. I mean, we've gone too far for that. We've found too much that needs explaining."

"Agreed," Frank said. "We'll have to call for assistance, get a warrant, and run a thorough search."

"Drawer by drawer."

"What do you think we'll find?"

"God knows."

"I saw a phone in the kitchen," Frank said.

Frank led the way down the hall to the living room, then around the corner, into the kitchen. Before Tony could follow him across the threshold from the dining area, Frank said, "Oh, Jesus," and tried to back out of the kitchen.

"What's the matter?"

Even as Tony spoke, something cracked loudly.

Frank cried out and fell sideways and clutched at the edge of a counter, trying to stay on his feet.

Another sharp crack slammed through the apartment, echoing from wall to wall, and Tony realized it was gunfire.

But the kitchen had been deserted!

Tony reached for his revolver, and he had the peculiar feeling he was moving in slow-motion while the rest of the world rushed past in frantic double time.

The second shot took Frank in the shoulder and spun him around. He crashed down into the mess of maraschino cherry juice and dry spaghetti and cornflakes and glass.

As Frank dropped out of the way, Tony was able to see beyond him for the first time, and he spotted Bobby Valdez. He was wriggling out of the cupboard space under the sink, a spot they hadn't thought to investigate because it looked too small to conceal a man. Bobby was squirming and slithering out of there like a snake from a tight hole. Only his legs were still under the sink; he was on his side, pulling himself out with one arm, holding a .32 pistol in his other hand.

He was naked. He looked sick. His eyes were huge, wild, dilated, sunken in rings of puffy dark flesh. His face was shockingly pale, his lips bloodless. Tony took in all of those details in a fraction of a second, with senses sharpened by a flood of adrenaline.

Frank was just hitting the floor, and Tony was still reaching for his revolver when Bobby fired a third time. The bullet whacked into the edge of the archway. An explosion of plaster chips stung Tony's face.

He threw himself backward and down, twisting as he went, struck the floor too hard with his shoulder, gasped in pain, and rolled out of the dining area, out of the line of fire. He scrambled behind a chair in the living room and finally got his gun out of its holster.

Perhaps six or seven seconds had passed since Bobby had fired the first shot.

Someone was saying, "Jesus, Jesus, Jesus, Jesus," in a quivering, high-pitched voice.

Suddenly, Tony realized he was listening to himself. He bit his lip and fought off an attack of hysteria.

He now knew what had been bothering him; he knew what they had overlooked. Bobby Valdez was selling PCP, and that should have told them something when they saw the state of the apartment. They should have remembered that pushers were sometimes stupid enough to use what they sold. PCP, also called angel dust, was an animal tranquilizer that had a fairly predictable effect upon horses and bulls. But when people took the stuff, their reactions ranged from placid trances to weird hallucinations to unexpected fits of rage and violence. As Eugene Tucker said, PCP was poison; it literally ate away at brain cells, rotted the mind. Supercharged on PCP, bursting with perverse energy, Bobby had smashed up his kitchen and had done all the other damage in the apartment. Pursued by fierce but imaginary crocodiles, desperately seeking refuge from their snapping jaws, he had squirmed into the cupboard under the sink and had pulled the doors shut. Tony hadn't thought to look in the cupboard because he hadn't realized they were stalking a raving lunatic. They had searched the apartment with caution, prepared for the moves that might be expected of a mentally-disturbed rapist and incidental killer, but unprepared for the bizarre actions of a gibbering madman. The mindless destruction evident in the kitchen and master bedroom, the apparently senseless writing on the walls, the disgusting mess in the bathroom—all of those were familiar indications of PCP-induced hysteria. Tony never served on the narcotics squad, but, nevertheless, he felt he should have recognized those signs. If he had interpreted them properly, he most likely would have checked under the sink, as well as anywhere else conceivably big enough for a man to hide, even if the quarters would be brutally uncomfortable; for it was not uncommon for a person on an extremely ugly PCP trip to surrender totally to his paranoia and try to hide from a hostile world, especially in cramped, dark, womblike places. But he and Frank misinterpreted the clues, and now they were up to their necks in trouble.

Frank had been shot twice. He was badly hurt. Maybe dying. Maybe dead. *No!*

Tony tried to push that thought out of his mind as he cast about for a way to seize the initiative from Bobby.

In the kitchen Bobby began to scream in genuine terror. *"Hay muchos cocodrilos!"*

Tony translated: *There are many crocodiles!*

"Cocodrilos! Cocodrilos! Cocodrilos! Ah! Ah! Ahhhhh!" His repeated cry of alarm swiftly degenerated into a wordless wail of agony.

He sounds as if he's really being eaten alive, Tony thought, shivering.

Still screaming, Bobby rushed out of the kitchen. He fired the .32 into the floor, apparently trying to kill one of the crocodiles.

Tony crouched behind the chair. He was afraid that, if he stood up and took aim, he would be cut down before he could pull the trigger.

Doing a frantic little jig, trying to keep his bare feet out of the mouths of the crocodiles, Bobby fired into the floor once, twice.

Six shots so far, Tony thought. Three in the kitchen, three here. How many in the clip? Eight? Maybe ten.

Bobby fired again, twice, three times. One of the bullets ricocheted off something.

Nine shots had been fired. One more to go.

"*Cocodrilos!*"

The tenth shot boomed deafeningly in the enclosed space, and again the bullet ricocheted with a sharp whistle.

Tony stood up from his hiding place. Bobby was less than ten feet away. Tony held the service revolver in both hands, the muzzle lined up on the naked man's hairless chest. "Okay, Bobby. Be cool. It's all over."

Bobby seemed surprised to see him. Clearly, he was so deeply into his PCP hallucination that he didn't remember seeing Tony in the kitchen archway less than a minute ago.

"Crocodiles," Bobby said urgently, in English this time.

"There are no crocodiles," Tony said.

"Big ones."

"No. There aren't any crocodiles."

Bobby squealed and jumped and whirled and tried to shoot at the floor, but his pistol was empty.

"Bobby," Tony said.

Whimpering, Bobby turned and looked at him.

"Bobby, I want you to lay face-down on the floor."

"They'll get me," Bobby said. His eyes were bulging out of his head; the dark irises were rimmed with wide circles of white. He was trembling violently. "They'll eat me."

"Listen to me, Bobby. Listen carefully. There are no crocodiles. You're hallucinating them. It's all inside your head. You hear me?"

"They came out of the toilets," Bobby said shakily. "And out of the shower drains. And the sink drain, too. Oh, man, they're big. They're real big. And they're all trying to bite off my cock." His fear began to turn to anger; his pale face flushed, and his lips pulled back from his teeth in a wolflike snarl. "I won't let them. I won't let them bite off my cock. I'll kill all of them!"

Tony was frustrated by his inability to get through to Bobby, and his frustration was exacerbated by the knowledge that Frank might be bleeding to death, getting weaker by the second, in desperate need of immediate medical attention. Deciding to enter into Bobby's dark fantasy in order to control it, Tony spoke in a soft and reassuring voice: "Listen to me. All of those crocodiles have crawled back into the toilets and the drains. Didn't you see them going? Didn't you hear them sliding down the pipes and out of the building? They saw that we'd come to help you, and they knew they were outnumbered. Every one of them has gone away."

Bobby stared at him with glassy eyes that were less than human.

"They've all gone away," Tony said.

"Away?"

"None of them can hurt you now."

"Liar."

"No. I'm telling the truth. All of the crocodiles have gone down the—"

Bobby threw his empty pistol.

Tony ducked under it.

"You rotten cop son of a bitch."

"Hold it, Bobby."

Bobby started toward him.

Tony backstepped away from the naked man.

Bobby didn't walk around the chair. He angrily pushed it aside, knocked it over, even though it was quite heavy.

Tony remembered that a man in an angel dust rage often exhibited super-human strength. It was not uncommon for four or five burly policemen to have difficulty restraining one puny PCP junkie. There were several medical theories about the cause of this freakish increase in physical power, but no theory was of any help to an officer confronted by a raging man with the strength of five or six. Tony figured he probably wouldn't be able to subdue Bobby Valdez with anything less than the revolver, even though he was philosophically opposed to using that ultimate force.

"I'm gonna kill you," Bobby said. His hands were curled into claws. His face was bright red, and spittle formed at one corner of his mouth.

Tony put the big octagonal coffee table between them. "Stop right there, dammit!"

He didn't want to have to kill Bobby Valdez. In all his years with the LAPD, he had shot only three man in the line of duty, and on every occasion he had pulled the trigger strictly in self-defense. None of those three men had died.

Bobby started around the coffee table.

Tony circled away from him.

"Now, I'm the crocodile," Bobby said, grinning.

"Don't make me hurt you."

Bobby stopped and grabbed hold of the coffee table and tipped it up, over, out of the way, and Tony backed into a wall, and Bobby rushed him, shouting something unintelligible, and Tony pulled the trigger, and the bullet tore through Bobby's left shoulder, spinning him around, driving him to his knees, but incredibly, he got up again, his left arm all bloody and hanging uselessly at his side, and, screaming in anger rather than agony, he ran to the fireplace and picked up a small brass shovel and threw it, and Tony ducked, and then suddenly Bobby was rushing at him with an iron poker raised high, and the damned thing caught Tony across the thigh, and he yelped as pain flashed up his hip and down his leg, but the blow wasn't hard enough to break bones, and he didn't collapse, but he did drop down as Bobby swung it again, at his head this time, with more power behind it this time, and Tony fired up into the naked man's chest, at close range, and Bobby was flung backwards with one last wild cry, and he crashed into a chair, then fell to the floor, gushing blood like a macabre fountain, twitched, gurgled, clawed at the shag carpet, bit his own wounded arm, and finally was perfectly still.

Gasping, shaking, cursing, Tony holstered his revolver and stumbled to a telephone he'd spotted on one of the end tables. He dialed 0 and told the operator who he was, where he was, and what he needed. "Ambulance first, police second," he said.

"Yes, sir," she said.

He hung up and limped into the kitchen.

Frank Howard was still sprawled on the floor, in the garbage. He had managed to roll onto his back, but he hadn't gotten any farther.

Tony knelt beside him.

Frank opened his eyes. "You hurt?" he asked weakly.

"No," Tony said.

"Get him?"

"Yeah."

"Dead?"

"Yeah."

"Good."

Frank looked terrible. His face was milk-white, greasy with sweat. The whites of his eyes had an unhealthy yellowish cast that had not been there before, and the right eye was badly bloodshot. There was a hint of blue in his lips. The right shoulder and sleeve of his suit coat were soaked with blood. His left hand was clamped over his stomach wound, but a lot of blood had leaked from under his pale fingers; his shirt and the upper part of his trousers were wet and sticky.

"How's the pain?" Tony asked.

"At first, it was real bad. Couldn't stop screaming. But it's starting to get better. Just kind of a dull burning and thumping now."

Tony's attention had been focused so totally on Bobby Valdez that he hadn't heard Frank's screams.

"Would a tourniquet on your arm help at all?"

"No. The wound's too high. In the shoulder. There's no place to put a tourniquet."

"Help's on the way," Tony said. "I phoned in."

Outside, sirens wailed in the distance. It was too soon to be an ambulance or a black-and-white responding to his call. Someone must have phoned the police when the shooting started.

"That'll be a couple of uniforms," Tony said. "I'll go down and meet them. They'll have a pretty good first aid kit in the cruiser."

"Don't leave me."

"But if they've got a first aid kit—"

"I need more than first aid. Don't leave me," Frank repeated pleadingly.

"Okay."

"Please."

"Okay, Frank."

They were both shivering.

"I don't want to be alone," Frank said.

"I'll stay right here."

"I tried to sit up," Frank said.

"You just lay there."

"I couldn't sit up."

"You're going to be okay."

"Maybe I'm paralyzed."

"Your body's taken a hell of a shock, that's all. You've lost some blood. Naturally, you're weak."

The sirens moaned into silence outside of the apartment complex.

"The ambulance can't be far behind," Tony said.

Frank closed his eyes, winced, groaned.

"You'll be okay, buddy."

Frank opened his eyes. "Come to the hospital with me."

"I will."

"Ride in the ambulance with me."

"I don't know if they'll let me."

"Make them."

"All right. Sure."

"I don't want to be alone."

"Okay," Tony said. "I'll make them let me in the damned ambulance even if I have to pull a gun on them to do it."

Frank smiled thinly, but then a flash of pain burned the smile off his face. "Tony?"

"What is it, Frank?"

"Would you . . . hold my hand?"

Tony took his partner's right hand. The right shoulder was the one that had taken the bullet, and Tony thought Frank would have no use of that extremity, but the cold fingers closed around Tony's hand with surprising strength.

"You know what?" Frank asked.

"What?"

"You should do what he says."

"What who says?"

"Eugene Tucker. You should jump off. Take a chance. Do what you really want with your life."

"Don't worry about me. You've got to save your energy for getting better."

Frank grew agitated. He shook his head. "No, no, no. You've got to listen to me. This is important . . . what I'm trying to tell you. Damned important."

"Okay," Tony said quickly. "Relax. Don't strain yourself."

Frank coughed, and a few bubbles of blood appeared on his bluish lips.

Tony's heart was working like a runaway triphammer. Where was the godamned ambulance? What the hell was taking the lousy bastards so long?

Frank's voice had a hoarse note in it now, and he was forced to pause repeatedly to draw breath. "If you want to be a painter . . . then do it. You're still young enough . . . to take a chance."

"Frank, please, for God's sake, save your strength."

"*Listen to me!* Don't waste any more . . . time. Life's too goddamned short . . . to fiddle away any of it."

"Stop talking like that. I've got a lot of years ahead, and so do you."

"They go by so fast . . . so fucking fast. It's no time at all."

Frank gasped. His fingers tightened their already firm grip on Tony's hand.

"Frank? What's wrong?"

Frank didn't say anything. He shuddered. Then he began to cry.

Tony said, "Let me see about that first aid kit."

"Don't leave me. I'm afraid."

"I'll only be gone a minute."

"Don't leave me." Tears streamed down his cheeks.

"Okay. I'll wait. They'll be here in a few seconds."

"Oh, Jesus," Frank said miserably.

"But if the pain's getting worse—"

"I'm not . . . in much pain."

"Then what's wrong? Something's wrong."

"I'm just embarrassed. I don't want anyone . . . to know."

"Know what?"

"I just . . . lost control. I just . . . I . . . peed in my pants."

Tony didn't know what to say.

"I don't want to be laughed at," Frank said.

"Nobody's going to laugh at you."

"But, Jesus, I peed . . . in my pants . . . like a baby."

"With all this other mess on the floor, who's going to notice?"

Frank laughed, wincing at the pain the laughter caused, and he squeezed Tony's hand even harder.

Another siren. A few blocks away. Approaching rapidly.

"The ambulance," Tony said. "It'll be here in a minute."

Frank's voice was getting thinner and weaker by the second. "I'm scared, Tony."

"Please, Frank. Please, don't be scared. I'm here. Everything's going to be all right."

"I want . . . someone to remember me," Frank said.

"What do you mean?"

"After I'm gone . . . I want someone to remember I was here."

"You'll be around a long time yet."

"Who's going to remember me?"

"I will," Tony said thickly. "I'll remember you."

The new siren was only a block away, almost on top of them.

Frank said, "You know what? I think . . . maybe I will make it. The pain's gone all of a sudden."

"Is it?"

"That's good, isn't it?"

"Sure."

The siren cut out as the ambulance stopped with a squeal of brakes almost directly below the apartment windows.

Frank's voice was getting so weak that Tony had to lean close to hear it. "Tony . . . hold me." His grip on Tony's hand slackened. His cold fingers opened. "Hold me, please. Jesus. Hold me, Tony. Will you?"

For an instant, Tony was worried about complicating the man's wounds, but then he knew intuitively that it no longer mattered. He sat down on the floor in the garbage and blood. He put an arm under Frank and lifted him into a sitting position. Frank coughed weakly, and his left hand slid off his belly; the wound was revealed, a hideous and unrepairable hole from which intestines bulged. From the moment Bobby first pulled the trigger, Frank had begun to die; he had never had a hope of survival.

"Hold me."

Tony took Frank into his arms as best he could, held him, held him as a father would hold a frightened child, held him and rocked gently, crooned softly, reassuringly. He kept crooning even after he knew that Frank was dead, crooning and slowly rocking, gently and serenely rocking, rocking.

At four o'clock Monday afternoon, the telephone company serviceman arrived at Hilary's house. She showed him where the five extensions were located. He was just about to begin work on the kitchen phone when it rang.

She was afraid that it was the anonymous caller again. She didn't want to answer it, but the serviceman looked at her expectantly, and on the fifth ring she overcame her fear, snatched up the receiver. "Hello?"

"Hilary Thomas?"

"Yes."

"This is Michael Savatino. Savatino's Ristorante?"

"Oh, I don't need reminding. I won't forget you or your wonderful restaurant. We had a perfect dinner."

"Thank you. We try very hard. Listen, Miss Thomas—"

"Please call me Hilary."

"Hilary, then. Have you heard from Tony yet today?"

Suddenly she was aware of the tension in his voice. She *knew*, almost as a clairvoyant might know, that something awful had happened to Tony. For a moment she was breathless, and fuzzy darkness closed in briefly at the edges of her vision.

"Hilary? Are you there?"

"I haven't heard from him since last night. Why?"

"I don't want to alarm you. There was some trouble—"

"Oh, God."

"—but Tony wasn't hurt."

"Are you sure?"

"Just a few bruises."

"Is he in the hospital?"

"No, no. He's really all right."

The knot of pressure in her chest loosened a bit.

"What kind of trouble?" she asked.

In a few sentences, Michael told her about the shooting.

It could have been Tony who died. She felt weak.

"Tony's taking it hard," Michael said. "Very hard. When he and Frank first started working together, they didn't get along well. But things have improved. The past few days, they got to know each other better. In fact they'd gotten fairly close."

"Where's Tony now?"

"His apartment. The shooting was at eleven-thirty this morning. He's been at his apartment since two. I was with him until a few minutes ago. I wanted to stay, but he insisted I go to the restaurant as usual. I wanted him to come with me, but he wouldn't. He won't admit it, but he needs someone right now."

"I'll go to him," she said.

"I was hoping you'd say that."

Hilary freshened up and changed clothes. She was ready to leave fifteen minutes before the repairman had finished with the phones, and she never endured a longer quarter-hour.

In the car, on the way to Tony's place, she recalled how she had felt in that dark moment when she'd thought Tony was seriously hurt, perhaps dead. She nearly had been sick to her stomach. An intolerable sense of loss had filled her.

Last night, in bed, awaiting sleep, she had argued with herself about whether or not she loved Tony. Could she possibly love anyone after the physical and psychological torture she had suffered as a child, after what she had learned about the ugly duplicitous nature of most other human beings? And could she love a man she'd known for only a few days? The argument still wasn't settled. But now she knew that she dreaded losing Tony Clemenza in a way and to a degree that she had never feared losing anyone else in her life.

At his apartment complex, she parked beside the blue Jeep.

He lived upstairs in a two-story building. Glass wind chimes were hung from the balcony near one of the other apartments; they sounded melancholy in the late-afternoon breeze.

When he answered the door, he wasn't surprised to see her. "I guess Michael called you."

"Yes. Why didn't you?" she asked.

"He probably told you I'm a total wreck. As you can see, he exaggerates."

"He's concerned about you."

"I can handle it," he said, forcing a smile. "I'm okay."

In spite of his attempt to play down his reaction to Frank Howard's death, she saw the haunted look in his face and the bleak expression in his eyes.

She wanted to hug him and console him, but she was not very good with people in ordinary circumstances, let alone in a situation like this. Besides, she sensed that he had to be ready for consolation before she dared offer it, and he was not.

"I'm coping," he insisted.

"Can I come in anyway?"

"Oh. Sure. Sorry."

He lived in a one-bedroom bachelor apartment, but the living room, at least, was large and airy. It had a high ceiling and a row of big windows in the north wall.

"Good northern light for a painter," Hilary said.

"That's why I rented the place."

It looked more like a studio than like a living room. A dozen of his eye-catching paintings hung on the walls. Other canvases were standing on the floor, leaning against the walls, stacks of them in some places, sixty or seventy in all. Two easels held works in progress. There were also a large drawing table, stool, and artist's supply cabinet. Tall shelves were jammed full of oversized art books. The only concessions to ordinary living room decor were two short sofas, two end tables, two lamps, a coffee table—all of which were arranged to form a cozy conversation corner. Although its arrangement was peculiar, the room had great warmth and livability.

"I've decided to get drunk," Tony said as he closed the door. "Very drunk. Totally smashed. I was just pouring my first drink when you rang. Would you like something?"

"What are you drinking?" she asked.

"Bourbon on the rocks."

"Make it the same for me."

While he was in the kitchen preparing drinks, she took a closer look at his paintings. Some of them were ultra-realistic; in these the detail was so fine, so brilliantly observed, so flawlessly rendered that, in terms of realism, the paintings actually transcended mere photography. Several of the canvases were surrealistic, but in a fresh and commanding style that was not at all reminiscent of Dali, Ernst, Miro, or Tanguy. They were closer to the work of René Magritte than to anything else, especially the Magritte of *The Domain of Arnheim* and *Ready-Made Bouquet*. But Margritte had never used such meticulous detail in his paintings, and it was this realer than real quality in Tony's visions that made the surrealistic elements especially striking and unique.

He returned from the kitchen with two glasses of bourbon, and as she accepted her drink she said, "Your work is so fresh and exciting."

"Is it?"

"Michael is right. Your paintings will sell as fast as you can create them."

"It's nice to think so. Nice to dream about."

"If you'd only give them a chance—"

"As I said before, you're very kind, but you're not an expert."

He was not at all himself. His voice was drab, wooden. He was dull, washed out, depressed.

She needled him a bit, hoping to bring him to life. "You think you're so smart," she said. "But you're dumb. When it comes to your own work, you're dumb. You're blind to the possibilities."

"I'm just an amateur."

"Bullshit."

"A fairly *good* amateur."

"Sometimes you can be so damned infuriating," she said.

"I don't want to talk about art," he said.

He switched on the stereo: Beethoven interpreted by Ormandy. Then he went to one of the sofas in the far corner of the room.

She followed him, sat beside him. "What *do* you want to talk about?"

"Movies," he said.

"Do you really?"

"Maybe books."

"Really?"

"Or theater."

"What you really want to talk about is what happened to you today."

"No. That's the last thing."

"You *need* to talk about it, even if you don't want to."

"What I need to do is forget all about it, wipe it out of my mind."

"So you're playing turtle," she said. "You think you can pull your head under your shell and close up tight."

"Exactly," he said.

"Last week, when I wanted to hide from the whole world, when you wanted me to go out with you instead, you said it wasn't healthy for a person to withdraw into himself after an upsetting experience. You said it was best to share your feelings with other people."

"I was wrong," he said.

"You were right."

He closed his eyes, said nothing.

"Do you want me to leave?" she asked.

"No."

"I will if you want me to. No hard feelings."

"Please stay," he said.

"All right. What shall we talk about?"

"Beethoven and bourbon."

"I can take a hint," she said.

They sat silently side by side on the sofa, eyes closed, heads back, listening to the music, sipping the bourbon, as the sunlight turned amber and then muddy orange beyond the large windows. Slowly, the room filled up with shadows.

Early Monday evening, Avril Tannerton discovered someone had broken into Forever View. He made that discovery when he went down to the cellar, where he had a lavishly equipped woodworking shop; he saw that one of the panes in a basement window had been carefully covered with masking tape and then broken to allow the intruder to reach the latch. It was a much smaller-than-average window, hinged at the top, but even a fairly large man could wriggle through it if he was determined.

Avril was certain there was no stranger in the house at the moment. Furthermore, he knew the window hadn't been broken Friday night, for he would have noticed it when he spent an hour in his workshop, doing fine sanding on his latest project—a cabinet for his three hunting rifles and two shotguns. He didn't believe anyone would have the nerve to smash the window in broad daylight or when he, Tannerton, was at home, as he had been the previous night, Sunday; therefore, he concluded that the break-in must have occurred Saturday night, while he was at Helen Virtillion's place in Santa Rosa. Except for the body of Bruno Frye, Forever View had been deserted on Saturday. Evidently, the burglar had known the house was unguarded and had taken advantage of the opportunity.

Burglar.

Did that make sense?

A burglar?

He didn't think anything had been stolen from the public rooms on the first floor or from his private quarters on the second level. He was positive he would have noticed evidence of a theft almost immediately upon his return Sunday morning. Besides, his guns were still in the den, and so was his extensive coin collection; certainly, those things would be prime targets for a thief.

In his woodworking shop, to the right of the broken cellar window, there were a couple of thousand dollars' worth of high-quality hand and power tools. Some of them were hanging neatly from a pegboard wall, and others were nestled in custom racks he had designed and built for them. He could tell at a glance that nothing was missing.

Nothing stolen.

Nothing vandalized.

What sort of burglar broke into a house just to have a look at things?

Avril stared at the pieces of glass and masking tape on the floor, then up at the violated window, then around the cellar, pondering the situation, until suddenly he realized that, indeed, something had been taken. Three fifty-pound bags of dry mortar mix were gone. Last spring, he and Gary Olmstead had torn out the old wooden porch in front of the funeral home; they'd built up the ground with a couple truckloads of topsoil, had terraced it quite professionally, and had put down a new brick veranda. They had also torn up the cracked and canted concrete sidewalks and had replaced them with brick. At the end of the five-week-long chore, they found themselves with three extra bags of mortar mix, but they didn't return them for a refund because Avril intended to construct a large patio behind the house next summer. Now those three bags of mix were gone.

That discovery, far from answering his questions, only contributed to the mystery. Amazed and perplexed, he stared at the spot where the bags had been stacked.

Why would a burglar ignore expensive rifles, valuable coins, and other worthwhile loot in favor of three relatively inexpensive bags of dry mortar mix?

Tannerton scratched his head. "Strange," he said.

After sitting quietly beside Hilary in the gathering darkness for fifteen minutes, after listening to Beethoven, after sipping two or three ounces of bourbon, and after Hilary replenished their drinks, Tony found himself talking about Frank Howard. He didn't realize he was going to open up to her until he had already begun speaking; he seemed to hear himself suddenly in mid-sentence, and then the words poured out. For half an hour, he spoke continuously, pausing only for an occasional sip of bourbon, recalling his first impression of Frank, the initial friction between them, the tense and the humorous incidents on the job, that boozy evening at The Bolt Hole, the blind date with Janet Yamada, and the recent understanding and affection that he and Frank had found for each other. Finally, when he began to recount the events in Bobby Valdez's apartment, he spoke hesitantly, softly. When he closed his eyes he could see that garbage- and blood-spattered kitchen as vividly as he could see his own living room when his eyes were open. As he tried to tell Hilary what it had been like to hold a dying friend in his arms, he began to tremble. He was terribly cold, frigid in his flesh and bones, icy in his heart. His teeth chattered. Slouched on the sofa, deep in purple shadow, he shed his first tears for Frank Howard, and they felt scalding hot on his chilled skin.

As he wept, Hilary took his hand; then she held him in much the same way that he had held Frank. She used her small cocktail napkin to dry his face. She kissed his cheeks, his eyes.

At first, she offered only consolation, and that was all he sought; but without either of them consciously striving to alter the embrace, the quality of it began to change. He put his arms around her, and it was no longer entirely clear who was holding and comforting whom. His hands moved up and down her sleek back, up and down, and he marveled at the exquisite contours; he was excited by the firmness and strength and suppleness of her body beneath the blouse.

Her hands roamed over him, too, stroking and squeezing and admiring his hard muscles. She kissed the corners of his mouth, and he eagerly returned those kisses full on her lips. Their quick tongues met, and the kiss became hot, fiercely hot and liquid; it left them breathing harder than they had been when their lips first touched.

Simultaneously, they realized what was happening, and they froze, uncomfortably reminded of the dead friend for whom mourning had just begun. If they gave each other what they so badly needed and wanted, it might be like giggling at a funeral. For a moment, they felt that they were on the verge of committing a thoughtless and thoroughly blasphemous act.

But their desire was so strong that it overcame their doubts about the propriety of making love on this night of all nights. They kissed tentatively, then hungrily, and it was as sweet as ever. Her hands moved demandingly over him, and he responded to her touch, then she to his. He realized it was good and right for them to seek joy together. Making love now was not an act of disrespect toward the dead; it was a reaction to the unfairness of death itself. Their unquenchable desire was the result of many things, one of which was a profound animal need to prove that they were alive, fully and unquestionably and exuberantly alive.

By unspoken agreement, they got up from the couch and went to the bedroom.

Tony switched on a lamp in the living room as they walked out; that light spilled through the open doorway and was the only thing that illuminated the bed. Soft penumbral light. Warm and golden light. The light seemed to love Hilary, for it didn't merely fall dispassionately upon her as it did upon the bed and upon Tony; it caressed her, lovingly accented the milky bronze shade of her flawless skin, added luster to her raven-black hair, and sparkled in her big eyes.

They stood beside the bed, embracing, kissing, and then he began to undress her. He unbuttoned her blouse, slipped it off. He unhooked her bra; she shrugged out of it and let it fall to the floor. Her breasts were beautiful—round and full and upswept. The nipples were large and erect; he bent to them, kissed them. She took his head in her hands, lifted his face to hers, found his mouth with hers. She sighed. His hands trembled with excitement as he unbuckled her belt, unsnapped and unzipped her jeans. They slid down her long legs, and she stepped out of them, already having stepped out of her shoes.

Tony went to his knees before her, intending to pull off her panties, and he saw a four-inch-long welt of scar tissue along her left side. It began at the edge of her flat belly and curved around to her back. It was not the result of surgery: it wasn't the thin line that even a moderately neat doctor would leave. Tony had seen old, well healed bullet and knife wounds before, and even though the light was not bright, he was sure that this mark had been caused by either a gun or a blade. A long time ago, she had been hurt badly. The thought of her enduring so much pain stirred in him a desire to protect and shelter her. He had a hundred questions about the scar, but this wasn't the right time to ask them. He tenderly kissed the welt of puckered skin, and he felt her stiffen. He sensed that the scar embarrassed her. He wanted to tell her it didn't detract from her beauty or desirability, and that, in fact, this single minor flaw only emphasized her otherwise incredible physical perfection.

The way to reassure her was with actions, not words. He pulled down her panties, and she stepped out of them. Slowly, slowly, he moved his hands up her gorgeous legs, over the lovely curves of her calves, over the smooth thighs. He kissed her glossy black pubic bush, and the hairs bristled crisply against his face. As he stood, he cupped her firm buttocks in both hands, gently kneaded the taut flesh, and she moved against him, and their lips met again. The kiss lasted either a few seconds or a few minutes, and when it ended, Hilary said, "Hurry."

As she pulled back the covers and got into bed, Tony stripped off his own clothes. Nude, he stretched out beside her and took her in his arms.

They explored each other with their hands, endlessly, fascinated by textures and shapes and angles and sizes and degrees of resiliency, and his erection throbbed as she fondled it.

After a while, but long before he actually entered her, he felt strangely as if he were melting into her, as if they were becoming one creature, not physically or sexually so much as spiritually, blending together through some sort of truly miraculous psychic osmosis. Overwhelmed by the warmth of her, excited by the promise of her magnificent body, but most deeply affected by the unique murmurs and movements and actions and reactions that made her Hilary and nobody but Hilary, Tony felt as if he had taken some new and exotic drug. His perceptions seemed to extend beyond the range of his own senses, so that he felt almost as if he were seeing through Hilary's eyes as well as through his own, feeling with his hands *and* her hands, tasting her mouth with his but also tasting his mouth with hers. Two minds, meshed. Two hearts, synchronized.

Her hot kisses made him want to taste every part of her, every delicious inch, and he did, arriving at long last, at the warm juncture of her thighs. He spread her elegant legs and licked the moist center of her, opened those secret folds of flesh with his tongue, found the hidden nubble that, when softly flicked, caused her to gasp with pleasure.

She began to moan and writhe under the loving lash.

"*Tony!*"

He made love to her with his tongue and teeth and lips.

She arched her back, clutched the sheets with both hands, thrashed ecstatically.

As she raised herself, he slipped his hands under her, grabbed her rump, held her to him.

"*Oh, Tony! Yes, yes!*"

She was breathing deeply, rapidly. She tried to pull away from him when the pleasure became too intense, but then a moment later she thrust herself at him, begging for more. Eventually, she began to quiver all over, and those shallow tremors swiftly grew into wonderful wrenching shudders of pure delight. She gasped for breath and tossed her head and cried out deliriously, rode the wave within her, came and came again, lithe muscles contracting, relaxing, contracting, relaxing, until finally she was exhausted. She collapsed, and sighed.

He raised his head, kissed her fluttering belly, then moved up to tease her nipples with his tongue.

She reached down between them and gripped the iron hardness of him. Suddenly, as she anticipated this final joining, this complete union, she was filled with a new erotic tension.

He opened her with his fingers, and she released him from her hand, and he guided himself into her.

"Yes, yes, yes," she said as he filled her up. "My lovely Tony. Lovely, lovely, lovely Tony."

"You're beautiful."

It had never been sweeter for him. He braced himself above her on his fully-extended arms, looked down at her exquisite face. Their eyes locked, and after a moment it seemed that he was no longer merely staring at her, but into her, through her eyes, into the essence of Hilary Thomas, into her soul. She closed her eyes, and a moment later he closed his, and he discovered that the extraordinary bond was not destroyed when the gaze was broken.

Tony had made love to other women, but he had never been as close to any of them as he was to Hilary Thomas. Because this coupling was so special, he wanted to make it last a long time, wanted to bring her to the edge with him, wanted to take the plunge together. But this time he did not have the kind of control that usually marked his love-making. He was rushing toward the brink and could do nothing to stop himself. It was not just that she was tighter and slicker and hotter than other women he had known; it was not merely some trick of well-trained vaginal muscles; it was not that her perfect breasts drove him wild or that her silken skin was far silkier than that of any other women in his experience. All of those things were true, but it was the fact that she was special to him, extraordinarily special in a way that he had not yet even fully defined, that made being with her unbearably exciting.

She sensed his onrushing orgasm, and she put her hands on his back, pulled him down. He didn't want to burden her with his full weight, but she seemed unaware of it. Her breasts squashed against his chest as he settled onto her. She lifted her hips and ground her pelvis against him, and he thrust harder and faster. Incredibly, she started to come again just as he began to spurt uncontrollably. She held him close, held him tight, repeatedly whispering his name as he erupted and erupted within her, thickly and forcefully and endlessly within her, in the deepest and darkest reaches of her. As he emptied himself, a tremendous tide of tenderness and affection and aching need swept through him, and he knew that he would never be able to let her go.

Afterwards, they lay side by side on the bed, holding hands, heartbeats gradually easing.

Hilary was physically and emotionally wrung out by the experience. The number and startling power of her climaxes had shaken her. She'd never felt anything quite like it. Each orgasm had been a bolt of lightning, striking to the core of her, jolting through every fiber, an indescribably thrilling current. But Tony had given her a great deal more than sexual pleasure; she had felt something else, something new to her, something splendid and powerful that was beyond words.

She was aware that some people would say the word "love" perfectly described her feelings, but she wasn't ready to accept that disturbing definition. For a long, long time, since her childhood, the words "love" and "pain" had been inextricably linked in Hilary's mind. She couldn't believe that she was in love with Tony Clemenza (or he with her), dared not believe it, for if she were to do so, she would make herself vulnerable, leave herself defenseless.

On the other hand, she had difficulty believing that Tony would knowingly hurt her. He wasn't like Earl, her father. He wasn't like anyone she had ever known before. There was a tenderness about him, a quality of mercy, that made her feel that she would be perfectly safe in his hands. Perhaps she ought to take a chance with him. Maybe he was the one man who was worth the risk.

But then she realized how she would feel if their luck together went sour after she had put everything on the line for him. That would be a hard blow. She didn't know if she would bounce back from that one.

A problem.

No easy solution.

She didn't want to think about it right now. She just wanted to lay beside him, basking in the glow that they had created together.

She began to remember their lovemaking, the erotic sensations that had left her weak, some of which still lingered warmly in her flesh.

Tony rolled onto his side and faced her. He kissed her throat, her cheek. "A penny for your thoughts."

"They're worth more than that," she said.

"A dollar."

"More than that."

"A hundred dollars?"

"Maybe a hundred thousand."

"Expensive thoughts."

"Not thoughts, really. Memories."

"Hundred-thousand-dollar memories?"

"Mmmmmmm."

"Of what?"

"Of what we did a few minutes ago."

"You know," he said, "you surprised me. You seem so proper and pure—almost angelic—but you've got a wonderfully bawdy streak in you."

"I can be bawdy," she admitted.

"Very bawdy."

"You like my body?"

"It's a beautiful body."

For a while, they talked mostly nonsense, lovers' talk, murmuring dreamily. They were so mellow that everything seemed amusing to them.

Then, still speaking softly, but with a more serious note in his voice, Tony said, "You know, of course, I'm not ever going to let go of you."

She sensed that he was prepared to make a commitment if he could determine that she was ready to do likewise. But that was the problem. She wasn't ready. She didn't know if she would ever be ready. She wanted him. Oh, Jesus, how she wanted him! She couldn't think of anything more exciting or rewarding than the two of them living together, enriching each other's lives with their separate talents and interests. But she dreaded the disappointment and pain that would come if he ever stopped wanting her. She had put all of those terrible years in Chicago with Earl and Emma behind her, but she could not so easily disregard the lessons she had learned in that tenement apartment so long ago. She was afraid of commitment.

Looking for a way to avoid the implied question in his statement, hoping to keep the conversation frivolous, she said, "You're *never* going to let go of me?"

"Never."

"Won't it be awkward for you, trying to do police work with me in hand?"

He looked into her eyes, trying to determine if she understood what he had said.

Nervously, she said, "Don't hurry me, Tony, I need time. Just a little time."

"Take all the time you want."

"Right now I'm so happy that I just want to be silly. It's not the right time to be serious."

"So I'll try to be silly," he said.

"What shall we talk about?"

"I want to know all about you."

"That sounds serious, not silly."

"Tell you what. You be half-serious, and I'll be half-silly. We'll take turns at it."

"All right. First question."

"What's your favorite breakfast food?"

"Cornflakes," she said.

"Your favorite lunch?"

"Cornflakes."

"Your favorite dinner?"

"Cornflakes."

"Wait a minute," he said.

"What's wrong?"

"I figure you were serious about breakfast. But then you slipped in two silly responses in a row."

"I *love* cornflakes."

"Now you owe me two serious answers."

"Shoot."

"Where were you born?"

"Chicago."

"Raised there?"

"Yes."

"Parents?"

"I don't know who my parents are. I was hatched from an egg. A duck egg. It was a miracle. You must have read all about it. There's even a Catholic church in Chicago named after the event. Our Lady of the Duck Egg."

"Very silly indeed."

"Thank you."

"Parents?" he asked again.

"That's not fair," she said. "You can't ask the same thing twice."

"Who says?"

"I say."

"Is it that horrible?"

"What?"

"Whatever your parents did."

She tried to deflect the question. "Where'd you get the idea they did something horrible?"

"I've asked you about them before. I've asked you about your childhood, too. You've always avoided those questions. You were very smooth, very clever about changing the subject. You thought I didn't notice, but I did."

He had the most penetrating stare she'd ever encountered. It was almost frightening.

She closed her eyes so that he couldn't see into her.

"Tell me," he said.

"They were alcoholics."

"Both of them?"

"Yeah."

"Bad?"

"Oh, yeah."

"Violent?"

"Yeah."

"And?"

"And I don't want to talk about it now."

"It might be good for you."

"No. Please, Tony. I'm happy. If you make me talk about . . . them . . . then I won't be happy any more. It's been a beautiful evening so far. Don't spoil it."

"Sooner or later, I want to hear about it."

"Okay," she said. "But not tonight."

He sighed. "All right. Let's see . . . Who's your favorite television personality?"

"Kermit the Frog."

"Who's your favorite human television personality?"

"Kermit the Frog," she said.

"I said *human* this time."

"To me, he seems more human than anyone else on TV."

"Good point. What about the scar?"

"Does Kermit have a scar?"

"I mean your scar."

"Does it turn you off?" she asked, again trying to deflect the question.

"No," he said. "It just makes you more beautiful."

"Does it?"

"It does."

"Mind if I check you out on my lie detector?"

"You have a lie detector here?"

"Oh, sure," she said. She reached down and took his flaccid prick in her hand. "My lie detector works quite simply. There's no chance of getting an inaccurate reading. We just take the main plug"—she squeezed his organ—"and we insert it in socket B."

"Socket B?"

She slid down on the bed and took him into her mouth. In seconds, he swelled into pulsing, rigid readiness. In a few minutes, he was barely able to restrain himself.

She looked up and grinned. "You weren't lying."

"I'll say it again. You're a surprisingly bawdy wench."

"You want my body again?"

"I want your body again."

"What about my mind?"

"Isn't that part of the package?"

She took the top this time, settled onto him, moved back and forth, side to side, up and down. She smiled at him as he reached for her jiggling breasts, and after that she was not aware of single movements or individual strokes; everything blurred into a continuous, fluid, superheated motion that had no beginning and no end.

At midnight, they went to the kitchen and prepared a very late dinner, a cold meal of cheese and leftover chicken and fruit and chilled white wine. They brought everything back to the bedroom and ate a little, fed each other a little, then lost interest in the food before they'd eaten much of anything.

They were like a couple of teenagers, obsessed with their bodies and blessed with apparently limitless stamina. As they rocked in rhythmic ecstasy, Hilary was acutely aware that this was not merely a series of sex acts in which they were engaged; this was an important ritual, a profound ceremony that was cleansing her of long-nurtured fears. She was entrusting herself to another human being in a way she would have thought impossible only a week ago, for she was putting her pride out of the way, prostrating herself, offering herself up to him, risking rejection and humiliation and degradation, with the fragile hope that he would not misuse her. And he did not. A lot of the things they did might have been degrading with the wrong partner, but with Tony each act was exalting, uplifting, glorious. She was not yet able to tell him that she loved him, not with words, but she was saying the same thing when, in bed, she begged him to do whatever he wanted with her, leaving herself no protection, opening herself completely, until, finally, kneeling before him, she used her lips and tongue to draw one last ounce of sweetness from his loins.

Her hatred for Earl and Emma was as strong now as it had been when they were alive, for it was their influence that made her unable to express her feelings to Tony. She wondered what she would have to do to break the chains that they had put on her.

For a while, she and Tony lay in bed, holding each other, saying nothing because nothing needed to be said.

Ten minutes later, at four-thirty in the morning, she said, "I should be getting home."

"Stay."

"Are you capable of doing more?"

"God, no! I'm wiped out. I just want to hold you. Sleep here," he said.

"If I stay, we won't sleep."

"Are *you* capable of doing more?"

"Unfortunately, dear man, I'm not. But I've got things to do tomorrow, and so have you. And we're much too excited and too full of each other to get any rest so long as we're sharing a bed. We'll keep touching like this, talking like this, resisting sleep like this."

"Well," he said, "we've got to learn to spend the night together. I mean, we're going to be spending a lot of them in the same bed, don't you think?"

"Many, many," she said. "The first night's the worst. We'll adjust when the novelty wears off. I'll start wearing curlers and cold cream to bed."

"And I'll start smoking cigars and watching Johnny Carson."

"Such a shame," she said.

"Of course, it'll take a bit of time for the freshness to wear off."

"A bit," she agreed.

"Like fifty years."

"Or sixty."

They delayed her leaving for another fifteen minutes, but finally she got up and dressed. Tony pulled on a pair of jeans.

In the living room, as they walked toward the door, she stopped and stared at one of his paintings and said, "I want to take six of your best pieces to Wyant Stevens in Beverly Hills and see if he'll handle you."

"He won't."

"I want to try."

"That's one of the best galleries."

"Why start at the bottom?"

He stared at her, but he seemed to be seeing someone else. At last, he said, "Maybe I should jump."

"Jump?"

He told her about the impassioned advice he had received from Eugene Tucker, the black ex-convict who was now designing dresses.

"Tucker is right," she said. "And this isn't even a jump. It's only a little hop. You're not quitting your job with the police department or anything. You're just testing the waters."

Tony shrugged. "Wyant Stevens will turn me down cold, but I guess I don't lose anything by giving him the chance to do it."

"He won't turn you down," she said. "Pick out half a dozen paintings you feel are most representative of your work. I'll try to get us an appointment with Wyant either later today or tomorrow."

"You pick them out right now," he said. "Take them with you. When you get a chance to see Stevens, show them to him."

"But I'm sure he'll want to meet you."

"If he likes what he sees, *then* he'll want to meet me. And if he does like it, I'll be happy to go see him."

"Tony, really—"

"I just don't want to be there when he tells you it's good work but only that of a gifted amateur."

"You're impossible."

"Cautious."

"Such a pessimist."

"Realist."

She didn't have time to look at all of the sixty canvases that were stacked in the living room. She was surprised to learn that he had more than fifty others stored in closets, as well as a hundred pen and ink drawings, nearly as many watercolors, and countless preliminary pencil sketches. She wanted to see all of them, but only when she was well-rested and fully able to enjoy them. She chose six of the twelve pieces that hung on the living room walls. To protect the paintings, they carefully wrapped them in lengths of an old sheet, which Tony tore apart for that purpose.

He put on a shirt and shoes, helped her carry the bundles to her car, where they stashed them in the trunk.

She closed and locked the trunk, and they looked at each other, neither of them wanting to say goodbye.

They were standing at the edge of a pool of light cast by a twenty-foot-high sodium-vapor lamp. He kissed her chastely.

The night was chilly and silent. There were stars.

"It'll be dawn before long," he said.

"Want to sing 'Two Sleepy People' with me?"

"I'm a lousy singer," he said.

"I doubt it." She leaned against him. "Judging from my experience, you're excellent at everything you do."

"Bawdy."

"I try to be."

They kissed again, and then he opened the driver's door for her.

"You're not going to work today?" she asked.

"No. Not after . . . Frank. I have to go in and write up a report, but that'll take only an hour or so. I'm taking a few days. I've got a lot of time coming to me."

"I'll call you this afternoon."

"I'll be waiting," he said.

She drove away from there on empty early-morning streets. After she had gone a few blocks, her stomach began to growl with hunger, and she remembered that she didn't have the fixings for breakfast at home. She'd intended to do her grocery shopping after the man from the telephone company had gone, but then she'd heard from Michael Savatino and had rushed to Tony's place. She turned off at the next corner and went to an all-night market to pick up eggs and milk.

Tony figured Hilary wouldn't need any more than ten minutes to get home on the deserted streets, but he waited fifteen minutes before he called to find out if she had made the trip safely. Her phone didn't ring. All he got was a series of computer sounds—the beeps and buzzes that comprised the language of smart machines—then a few clicks and snaps and pops, then the hollow ghostly hissing of a missed connection. He hung up, dialed once more, being careful to get every digit right, but again the phone would not ring.

He was certain that the new unlisted number he had for her was correct. When she had given it to him, he had double-checked to be sure he'd gotten it right. And she read it off a carbon copy of the telephone company work order, which she had in her purse, so there wasn't any chance she was mistaken about it.

He dialed the operator and told her his problem. She tried to ring the number for him, but she couldn't get through, either.

"Is it off the hook?" he asked.

"It doesn't seem to be."

"What can you do?"

"I'll report the number out of order," she said. "Our service department will take care of it."

"When?"

"Does this number belong to either an elderly person or an invalid?"

"No," he said.

"Then it falls under normal service procedures," she said. "One of our servicemen will look into it sometime after eight o'clock this morning."

"Thank you"

He put down the receiver. He was sitting on the edge of the bed. He stared pensively at the rumpled sheets where Hilary had lain, looked at the slip of paper on which her new number was written.

Out of order?

He supposed it was possible that the serviceman had made a mistake when he'd switched Hilary's phones yesterday afternoon. Possible. But not probable. Not very likely at all.

Suddenly, he thought of the anonymous caller who had been bothering her. A man who did that sort of thing was usually weak, ineffectual, sexually stunted; almost without exception, he was incapable of having a normal relationship with a woman, and he was generally too introverted and frightened to attempt rape. Usually. Almost without exception. Generally. But was it conceivable that this crank was the one out of a thousand who *was* dangerous?

Tony put one hand on his stomach. He was beginning to feel queasy.

If bookmakers in Las Vegas had been taking bets on the likelihood of Hilary Thomas becoming the target of two unconnected homicidal maniacs in less than a week, the odds against would have been astronomical. On the other hand, during his years with the Los Angeles Police Department, Tony had seen the improbable happen again and again; and long ago he had learned to expect the unexpected.

He thought of Bobby Valdez. Naked. Crawling out of that small kitchen cabinet. Eyes wild. The pistol in his hand.

Outside the bedroom window, even though first light still had not touched the eastern sky, a bird cried. It was a shrill cry, rising and falling and rising again as the bird swooped from tree to tree in the courtyard; it sounded as if it was being pursued by something very fast and very hungry and relentless.

Sweat broke out on Tony's brow.

He got up from the bed.

Something was happening at Hilary's place. Something was wrong. Terribly wrong.

Because she stopped at the all-night market to buy milk, eggs, butter, and a few other items, Hilary didn't get home until more than half an hour after she left Tony's apartment. She was hungry and pleasantly weary. She was looking forward to a cheese omelet with a lot of finely chopped parsley—and then at least six uninterrupted hours of deep, deep sleep. She was far too tired to bother putting the Mercedes in the garage; she parked in the circular driveway.

The automatic lawn sprinklers sprayed water over the dark grass, making a cool hissing-whistling sound. A breeze rustled the palm fronds overhead.

She let herself into the house by the front entrance. The living room was pitch-black. But having anticipated a late return, she had left the foyer light burning when she'd gone out. Inside, she held the bag of groceries in one arm, closed and double-locked the door.

She switched on the living room ceiling light and took two steps out of the foyer before she realized that the place had been destroyed. Two table lamps were smashed, the shades torn to shreds. A glass display case lay in thousands of sharp pieces on the carpet; and the expensive limited-edition porcelains that had been in it were ruined; they were reduced to worthless fragments, thrown down on the stone hearth and ground underfoot. The sofa and armchairs were ripped open; chunks of foam and wads of cotton padding material were scattered all over the floor. Two wooden chairs, which apparently had been smashed repeatedly against one wall, were now only piles of kindling, and the wall was scarred. The legs were broken off the lovely little antique corner desk; all of the drawers were pulled from it and the bottoms knocked out of them. Every painting was still where she'd put it, but each hung in unrepairable ribbons. Ashes had been scooped out of the fireplace and smeared over the beautiful Edward Fields carpet. Not a single piece of furniture or decoration had been overlooked; even the fireplace screen had been kicked apart, and all of the plants had been jerked out of their pots and torn to bits.

Hilary was dazed at first, but then her shock gave way to anger at the vandals. "Son of a bitch," she said between clenched teeth.

She had passed many happy hours personally choosing every item in the room. She spent a small fortune on them, but it wasn't the cost of the wreckage that disturbed her; most of it was covered by insurance. However, there was sentimental value that could not be replaced, for these were the first really nice things that she had ever owned, and it hurt to lose them. Tears shimmered at the corners of her eyes.

Numb, disbelieving, she walked farther into the rubble before she realized that she might be in danger. She stopped, listened. The house was silent.

An icy shiver raced up her spine, and for one horrible instant she thought she felt someone's breath against the nape of her neck.

She whirled, looked behind her.

No one was there.

The foyer closet, which had been closed when she'd come into the house, was still closed. For a moment, she stared at it expectantly, afraid that it would open. But if anyone had been hiding in there, waiting for her to arrive, he would have come out by now.

This is absolutely crazy, she thought. It can't happen again. It just can't. That's preposterous. Isn't it?

There was a noise behind her.

With a soft cry of alarm, she turned and threw up her free arm to fend off the attacker.

But there was no attacker. She was still alone in the living room.

Nevertheless, she was convinced that what she had heard was not something so innocent as a naturally settling beam or floorboard. She knew she was not the only person in the house. She sensed another presence.

The noise again.

In the dining room.

A snapping. A tinkling. Like someone taking a step on broken glass or shattered china.

Then another step.

The dining room lay beyond an archway, twenty feet from Hilary. It was as black as a grave in there.

Another step: *tinkle-snap*.

She started to back up, cautiously retreating from the source of the noise, edging toward the front door, which now seemed a mile away. She wished she hadn't locked it.

A man moved out of the perfect darkness of the dining room, into the penumbral area beneath the archway, a big man, tall, and broad in the shoulders. He paused in the gloom for a second, then stepped into the brightly lit living room.

"No!" Hilary said.

Stunned, she stopped backing toward the door. Her heart leapt, and her mouth went dry, and she shook her head back and forth, back and forth: no, no, no.

He was holding a large and wickedly sharp knife. He grinned at her. It was Bruno Frye.

Tony was thankful that the streets were empty, for he couldn't have tolerated any delay. He was afraid he was already too late.

He drove hard and fast, north on Santa Monica, then west on Wilshire, putting the Jeep up to seventy miles an hour by the time he reached the first downslope just outside the Beverly Hills city limits, engine screaming, windows and loose dashboard knobs vibrating tinnily. At the bottom of the hill, the traffic light was red. He didn't brake. He pressed the horn in warning and flew through the intersection. He slammed across a shallow drainage channel in the street, a broad depression that was almost unnoticeable at thirty-five miles an hour, but at his speed it felt like a yawning ditch beneath him; for a fraction of a second he actually was airborne, thumping his head into the roof in spite of the restraining harness that he wore. The Jeep came back to the pavement with a bang, a many-voiced chorus of rattles and clanks, and a sharp bark of tortured rubber. It began to slue to the left, its rear end sliding around with a blood-chilling screech, smoke curling up from the protesting tires. For an electrifying instant, he thought he was going to lose control, but then abruptly the wheel was his again, and he was more than halfway up the next hill without realizing how he'd gotten there.

His speed was down to forty miles an hour, and he got it back up to sixty. He decided not to push it beyond that. He only had a short distance to go. If he wrapped the Jeep around a streetlamp or rolled it over and killed himself, he wouldn't be able to do Hilary any good.

He was still not obeying the rules of the road. He went much too fast and wide on what few turns there were, swinging out into the east-bound lanes, again thankful that there were no oncoming cars. The traffic signals were all against him, a perverse twist of fate, but he ignored every one of them. He wasn't worried about getting a ticket for speeding or reckless driving. If stopped, he would flash his badge and take the uniformed officers along with him to Hilary's place. But he hoped to God he wasn't given a chance to pick up those reinforcements, for it would mean stopping, identifying himself, and explaining the emergency. If they pulled him over, he would lose at least a minute.

He had a hunch that a minute might be the difference between life and death for Hilary.

As she watched Bruno Frye coming through the archway, Hilary thought she must be losing her mind. The man was dead. *Dead!* She had stabbed him twice, had seen his blood. She had seen him in the morgue, too, cold and yellow-gray and lifeless. An autopsy had been performed. A death certificate had been signed. *Dead men don't walk.* Nevertheless, he was back from the grave, walking out of the dark dining room, the ultimate uninvited guest, a large knife in one gloved hand, eager to finish what he had started last week; and it simply was not possible that he could be there.

Hilary closed her eyes and willed him to be gone. But a second later, when she forced herself to look again, he was still there.

She was unable to move. She wanted to run, but all of her joints—hips, knees, ankles—were rigid, locked, and she didn't have the strength to make them move. She felt weak, as frail as an old, old woman; she was sure that, if she somehow managed to unlock her joints and take a step, she would collapse.

She couldn't speak, but, inside, she was screaming.

Frye stopped less than fifteen feet from her, one foot in a cotton snowdrift of stuffing that had been torn from one of the ruined armchairs. He was pasty-faced, shaking violently, obviously on the edge of hysteria.

Could a dead man be hysterical?

She had to be out of her mind. *Had* to be. Stark raving mad. But she knew she wasn't.

A ghost? But she didn't believe in ghosts. And besides, wasn't a spirit supposed to be insubstantial, transparent, or at least translucent? Could an apparition be as solid as this walking dead man, as convincingly and terrifyingly *real* as he was?

"Bitch," he said. "You stinking bitch!"

His hard, low-pitched, gravelly voice was unmistakable.

But, Hilary thought crazily, his vocal cords already should have started to rot. His throat should be blocked with putrescence.

She felt high-pitched laughter building in her, and she struggled to control it. If she began to laugh, she might never stop.

"You killed me," he said menacingly, still teetering on the brink of hysteria.

"No," she said. "Oh, no. No."

"You did!" he screamed, brandishing the knife. "You killed me! Don't lie about it. I know. Don't you think I know? Oh, Jesus! I feel so strange, so alone, all alone, so empty." There was genuine spiritual agony mixed up with his rage. "So empty and scared. And it's all because of you."

He slowly crossed the few yards that separated him from her, stepping carefully through the rubble.

Hilary could see that this dead man's eyes were not blank or filmed with milky cataracts. These eyes were blue-gray and very much alive—and brimming with cold, cold anger.

"This time you'll stay dead," Frye said as he approached. "You won't come back this time."

She tried to retreat from him, took one hesitant step, and her legs almost buckled. But she didn't fall. She had more strength left than she had thought.

"This time," Frye said, "I'm taking every precaution. I'm not giving you a chance to come back. I'm going to cut your fuckin' heart out."

She took another step, but it didn't matter, she could not escape. She wouldn't have time to reach the door and throw off both locks. If she tried that, he would be on her in a second, ramming the knife down between her shoulders.

"Pound a stake through your fuckin' heart."

If she ran for the stairs and tried to get to the pistol in her bedroom, she surely wouldn't be as lucky as she had been the last time. This time he would catch her before she made it to the second floor.

"I'll cut your goddamned head off."

He loomed over her, within arm's reach.

She had nowhere to run, nowhere to hide.

"Gonna cut out your tongue. Stuff your fuckin' mouth full of garlic. Stuff it full of garlic so you can't sweet-talk your way back from hell."

She could hear her own thunderous heartbeat. She couldn't breathe because of the intensity of her fear.

"Cut your fuckin' eyes out."

She froze again, unable to move an inch.

"Gonna cut your eyes out and crush them so you can't see your way back."

Frye raised the knife high above his head. "Cut your hands off so you can't feel your way back from hell."

The knife hung up there for an eternity as terror distorted Hilary's sense of time. The wicked point of the weapon drew her gaze, nearly hypnotizing her.

"No!"

Sharp slivers of light glinted on the cutting edge of the poised blade.

"Bitch."

And then the knife started down, straight at her face, light flashing off the steel, down and down and down in a long, smooth, murderous arc.

She was holding the bag of groceries in one arm. Now, without pausing to think about what she must do, in one quick and instinctive move, she grabbed the bag with both hands and thrust it out, up, in the way of the descending knife, trying desperately to block the killing blow.

The blade rammed through the groceries, puncturing a carton of milk.

Frye roared in fury.

The dripping bag was knocked out of Hilary's grasp. It fell to the floor, spilling milk and eggs and scallions and sticks of butter.

The knife had been torn from the dead man's hand. He stopped to retrieve it.

Hilary ran toward the stairs. She knew that she had only delayed the inevitable. She had gained two or three seconds, no more than that, not nearly enough time to save herself.

The doorbell rang.

Surprised, she stopped at the foot of the stairs and looked back.

Frye stood up with the knife in hand.

Their eyes met; Hilary could see a flicker of indecision in his.

Frye moved toward her, but with less confidence than he had exhibited before. He glanced nervously toward the foyer and the front door.

The bell rang again.

Holding on to the bannister, backing up the steps, Hilary yelled for help, screamed at the top of her voice.

Outside, a man shouted: "Police!"

It was Tony.

"Police! Open this door!"

Hilary couldn't imagine why he had come. She had never been so glad to hear anyone's voice as she was to hear his, now.

Frye stopped when he heard the word "police," looked up at Hilary, then at the door, then at her again, calculating his chances.

She kept screaming.

Glass exploded with a bang that caused Frye to jump in surprise, and sharp pieces rang discordantly on a tile floor.

Although she couldn't see into the foyer from her position on the steps, Hilary knew that Tony had smashed the narrow window beside the front door.

"*Police!*"

Frye glared at her. She had never seen such hatred as that which twisted his face and gave his eyes a mad shine.

"Hilary!" Tony said.

"I'll be back," Frye told her.

The dead man turned away from her and ran across the living room, toward the dining room, apparently intending to slip out of the house by way of the kitchen.

Sobbing, Hilary dashed down the few steps she had climbed. She rushed to the front door, where Tony was calling her through the small broken window-pane.

Holstering his service revolver, Tony returned from the rear lawn, stepped into the brightly-lit kitchen.

Hilary was standing by the utility island in the center of the room. There was a knife on the counter, inches from her right hand.

As he closed the door he said, "There's no one in the rose garden."

"Lock it," she said.

"What?"

"The door. Lock it."

He locked it.

"You looked everywhere?" she asked.

"Every corner."

"Along both sides of the house?"

"Yes."

"In the shrubbery?"

"Every bush."

"Now what?" she asked.

"I'll call in to HQ, get a couple of uniforms out here to write up a report."

"It won't do any good," she said.

"You never can tell. A neighbor might have seen someone lurking here earlier. Or maybe somebody spotted him running away."

"Does a dead man have to run away? Can't a ghost just vanish when it wants to?"

"You don't believe in ghosts?"

"Maybe he wasn't a ghost," she said. "Maybe he was a walking corpse. Just your ordinary, everyday, run-of-the-mill walking corpse."

"You don't believe in zombies, either."

"Don't I?"

"You're too level-headed for that."

She closed her eyes and shook her head. "I don't know what I believe any more."

Her voice contained a tremor that disturbed him. She was on the verge of a collapse.

"Hilary . . . are you sure of what you saw?"

"It was *him*."

"But how could it be?"

"It was Frye," she insisted.

"You saw him in the morgue last Thursday."

"Was he dead then?"

"Of course he was dead."

"Who said?"

"The doctors. Pathologists."

"Doctors have been known to be wrong."

"About whether or not a person is dead?"

"You read about it in the papers every once in a while," she said. "They decide a man has kicked the bucket; they sign the death certificate; and then the deceased suddenly sits up on the undertaker's table. It happens. Not often. I admit it's not an everyday occurrence. I know it's pretty much a one in a million kind of thing."

"More like one in ten million."

"But it *does* happen."

"Not in this case."

"I *saw* him! Here. Right here. Tonight."

He went to her, kissed her on the cheek, took her hand, which was ice-cold. "Listen, Hilary, he's dead. Because of the stab wounds you inflicted, Frye lost half the blood in his body. They found him in a huge pool of it. He lost all that blood, and then he lay in the hot sun, unattended, for a few hours. He simply couldn't have lived through that."

"Maybe he could."

Tony lifted her hand to his lips, kissed her pale fingers. "No," he said quietly but firmly. "Frye would have had to die from such a blood loss."

Tony figured that she was suffering from mild shock, which was somehow responsible for a temporary short circuit of her senses, a brief confusion of memories. She just was getting this attack mixed up with the one last week. In a minute or two, when she regained control of herself, everything would clear up in her mind, and she would realize that the man who had been here tonight had not been Bruno Frye. All he had to do was stroke her a little bit, speak to her in a measured voice, and answer all her questions and wild suppositions as reasonably as possible, until she was her normal self again.

"Maybe Frye wasn't dead when they found him in that supermarket parking lot," she said. "Maybe he was just in a coma."

"The coroner would have discovered it when he did the autopsy."

"Maybe he didn't do the autopsy."

"If he didn't, another doctor on his staff did."

"Well," Hilary said, "maybe they were especially busy that day—a lot of bodies all at once or something like that—and they decided just to fill out a quick report without actually doing the work."

"Impossible," Tony said. "The medical examiner's office has the highest professional standards imaginable."

"Can't we at least check on it?" she asked.

He nodded. "Sure. We can do that. But you're forgetting that Frye must have passed through the hands of at least one mortician. Probably two. What little blood was left in him must have been drained out and replaced with embalming fluid."

"Are you sure?"

"He had to be either embalmed or cremated to be shipped to St. Helena. It's the law."

She considered that for a moment, then said, "But what if this *is* one of those bizarre cases, the one in ten million? What if he *was* mistakenly pronounced dead? What if the coroner *did* fudge on the autopsy? And what if Frye sat up on the embalmer's table, just as the mortician was starting to work on him?"

"You're grasping at straws, Hilary. Surely you can see that if anything like that happened, we'd know about it. If a mortician found himself in possession of a dead body that turned out not to be dead after all, that turned out to be a virtually bloodless man urgently in need of medical attention, then that mortician would get him to the nearest hospital in one hell of a hurry. He'd also call the coroner's office. Or the hospital would call. We'd know about it immediately."

She thought about what he had said. She stared at the kitchen floor and chewed on her lower lip. Finally, she said, "What about Sheriff Laurenski up there in Napa County?"

"We haven't been able to get a response out of him yet."

"Why not?"

"He's dodging our inquiries. He won't take our calls or return them."

"Well, doesn't that tell you that there's more to this than meets the eye?" she asked. "There's some sort of conspiracy, and the Napa sheriff is part of it."

"What sort of conspiracy did you have in mind?"

"I . . . don't know."

Still speaking softly and calmly, still certain that she would eventually respond to his gentle and reasonable arguments, Tony said, "A conspiracy between Frye and Laurenski and maybe even Satan himself? A conspiracy to cheat Death out of his due? An evil conspiracy to come back from the grave? A conspiracy to somehow live forever? None of that makes sense to me. Does it make sense to you?"

"No," she said irritably. "It doesn't make the slightest bit of sense."

"Good. I'm glad to hear that. If you said it did, I'd be worried about you."

"But, dammit, something highly unusual is happening here. Something extraordinary. And it seems to me that Sheriff Laurenski must be a part of it. After all, he protected Frye last week, actually lied for him. And now he's avoiding you because he doesn't have an acceptable explanation for his actions. Doesn't that seem like suspicious behavior to you? Doesn't he seem like a man who is up to his neck in some sort of conspiracy?"

"No," Tony said. "To me, he just seems like a very badly embarrassed policeman. For an officer of the law, he committed a damned serious error. He covered for a local big shot because he thought the man couldn't possibly be involved in rape and attempted murder. He couldn't get hold of Frye last Wednesday night, but he pretended that he had. He was totally convinced that Frye wasn't the man we wanted. But he was wrong. And now he's thoroughly ashamed of himself."

"Is that what you think?" she asked.

"That's what everyone at HQ thinks."

"Well, it's not what I think."

"Hilary—"

"I saw Bruno Frye tonight!"

Instead of gradually coming to her senses, as he had hoped she would do, she was getting worse, retreating further into this dark fantasy of walking dead men and strange conspiracies. He decided to get tough with her.

"Hilary, you didn't see Bruno Frye. He wasn't here. Not tonight. He's dead. Dead and buried. This was another man who came after you tonight. You're in mild shock. You're confused. That's perfectly understandable. However—"

She pulled her hand out of his and stepped back from him. "I am not confused. Frye was here. And he said he'd be back."

"Just a minute ago, you admitted your story doesn't make any sense at all. Didn't you?"

Reluctantly, she said, "Yes. That's what I said. It doesn't make sense. *But it happened!*"

"Believe me, I've seen how a sudden shock can affect people," Tony said. "It distorts perceptions and memories and—"

"Are you going to help me or not?" she asked.

"Of course I'm going to help you."

"How? What will we do?"

"For starters, we'll report the break-in and the assault."

"Isn't that going to be terribly awkward?" she asked sourly. "When I tell them that a dead man tried to kill me, don't you suppose they'll decide to commit me for a few days, until they can complete a psychiatric evaluation? You know me a hell of a lot better than anyone else, and even you think I'm crazy."

"I don't think you're crazy," he said, dismayed by her tone of voice. "I think you're distraught."

"Damn."

"It's understandable."

"Damn."

"Hilary, listen to me. When the responding officers get here, you won't say a word to them about Frye. You'll calm down, get a grip on yourself—"

"I've *got* a grip on myself!"

"—and you'll try to recall exactly what the assailant looked like. If you settle your nerves, if you give yourself half a chance, I'm sure you'll be surprised by what you'll remember. When you're calm, collected, more rational about this, you'll realize that he wasn't Bruno Frye."

"He was."

"He might have resembled Frye, but—"

"You're acting just like Frank Howard did the other night," she said angrily.

Tony was patient. "The other night, at least, you were accusing a man who was *alive.*"

"You're just like everyone else I've ever trusted," she said, her voice cracking.

"I want to help you."

"Bullshit."

"Hilary, don't turn away from me."

"You're the one who turned away first."

"I care about you."

"Then show it!"

"I'm here, aren't I? What more proof do you need?"

"Believe me," she said. "That's the best proof."

He saw that she was profoundly insecure, and he supposed she was that way because she had had very bad experiences with people she had loved and trusted. Indeed, she must have been brutally betrayed and hurt, for no ordinary disappointment would have made her as sensitive as she was now. Still suffering from those old emotional wounds, she now demanded fanatical trust and loyalty. The moment he showed doubts about her story, she began to withdraw from him, even though he wasn't impugning her veracity. But, dammit, he knew it wasn't healthy to play along with her delusion; the best thing he could do for her was gently coax her back to reality.

"Frye was here tonight," she insisted. "Frye and nobody else. But I won't tell the police that."

"Good," he said, relieved.

"Because I'm not going to call the police."

"What?"

Without explaining, she turned away from him and walked out of the kitchen.

As he followed her through the wrecked dining room, Tony said, "You have to report this."

"I don't have to do anything."

"Your insurance company won't pay if you haven't filed a police report."

"I'll worry about that later," she said, leaving the dining room, entering the living room.

He trailed her as she weaved through the debris in the front room, heading toward the stairs. "You're forgetting something," he said.

"What's that?"

"I'm a detective."

"So?"

"So now that I'm aware of this situation, it's my duty to report it."

"So report it."

"Part of the report will be a statement from you."

"You can't force me to cooperate. I won't."

As they reached the foot of the stairs, he grabbed her by the arm. "Wait a minute. Please wait."

She turned and faced him. Her fear had been driven out by anger. "Let go of me."

"Where are you going?"

"Upstairs."

"What are you going to do?"

"Pack a suitcase and go to a hotel."

"You can stay at my place," he said.

"You don't want a crazy woman like me staying overnight," she said sarcastically.

"Hilary, don't be this way."

"I might go berserk and kill you in your sleep."

"I don't think you're crazy."

"Oh, that's right. You think I'm just confused. Maybe a little dotty. But not dangerous."

"I'm only trying to help you."

"You've got a funny way of doing it."

"You can't live in a hotel forever."

"I'll come home once he's been caught."

"But if you don't make a formal complaint, no one's even going to be looking for him."

"I'll be looking for him."

"You?"

"Me."

Now Tony was angry. "What game are you going to play—Hilary Thomas, Girl Detective?"

"I might hire private investigators."

"Oh, really?" he asked scornfully, aware that he might alienate her further with this approach, but too frustrated to be patient any longer.

"Really," she said. "Private investigators."

"Who? Philip Marlowe? Jim Rockford? Sam Spade?"

"You can be a sarcastic son of a bitch."

"You're forcing me to be. Maybe sarcasm will snap you out of this."

"My agent happens to know a first-rate firm of private detectives."

"I tell you, this isn't their kind of work."

"They'll do anything they're paid to do."

"Not anything."

"They'll do this."

"It's a job for the LAPD."

"The police will only waste their time looking for known burglars, known rapists, known—"

"That's a very good, standard, effective investigative technique," Tony said. "But it won't work this time."

"Why? Because the assailant was an ambulatory dead man?"

"That's right."

"So you think maybe the police should spend their time looking for known *dead* rapists and burglars?"

The look she gave him was a withering mixture of anger and disgust.

"The way to break this case," she said, "is to find out how Bruno Frye could have been stone-cold dead last week—and alive tonight."

"Will you listen to yourself, for God's sake?"

He was concerned for her. This stubborn irrationality frightened him.

"I know what I said," she told him. "And I also know what I saw. And it wasn't just that I *saw* Bruno Frye in this house a little while ago. I heard him, too. He had that distinct, unmistakable, guttural voice. It was him. No one else. I saw him, and I heard him threatening to cut off my head and stuff my mouth full of garlic, as if he thought I was some sort of vampire or something."

Vampire.

That word jolted Tony because it made such a startling and incredible connection with several things that had been found last Thursday in Bruno Frye's gray Dodge van, strange items about which Hilary couldn't possibly know anything, items that Tony had forgotten until this morning. A chill swept through him.

"Garlic?" he asked. "Vampires? Hilary, what are you talking about?"

She pulled out of his grasp and hurried up the stairs.

He ran after her. "What's this about vampires?"

Climbing the steps, refusing to look at Tony or answer his questions, Hilary said, "Isn't this some swell story I've got to tell? I was assaulted by a walking dead man who thought *I* was a vampire. Oh, wow! Now you're absolutely positive that I've lost my mind. Call the little white chuckle wagon! Get this poor lady into a straitjacket before she hurts herself! Put her in a nice padded room real quick! Lock the door and throw away the key!"

In the second-floor hallway, a few feet from the top of the stairs, as Hilary was heading toward a bedroom door, Tony caught up with her. He grabbed her arm again.

"Let go, dammit!"

"Tell me what he said."

"I'm going to a hotel, and then I'm going to work this thing out on my own."

"I want to know every word he said."

"There's nothing you can do to stop me," she told him. "Now let me go."

He shouted in order to get through to her. "I have to know what he said about vampires, dammit!"

Her eyes met his. Apparently she recognized the fear and confusion in him, for she stopped trying to pull away. "What's so damned important?"

"The vampire thing."

"Why?"

"Frye apparently was obsessed with the occult."

"How do you know that?"

"We found some things in that van of his."

"What things?"

"I don't remember all of it. A deck of tarot cards, a Ouija board, more than a dozen crucifixes—"

"I didn't see anything about that in the newspapers."

"We didn't make a formal press release out of it," Tony said. "Besides, by the time we searched the van and inventoried its contents and were prepared to consider a release, all of the papers had published their first-day stories, and the reporters had filed their followups. The case just didn't have enough juice to warrant squeezing third-day coverage out of it. But let me tell you what else was in that van. Little linen bags of garlic taped above all the doors. Two wooden stakes with very sharp points. Half a dozen books about vampires and zombies and other varieties of the so-called 'living dead.' "

Hilary shuddered. "He told me he was going to cut out my heart and pound a stake through it."

"Jesus."

"He was going to cut out my eyes, too, so I wouldn't be able to find my way back from hell. That's how he put it. Those were his words. He was afraid that

I was going to return from the dead after he killed me. He was raving like a lunatic. But then again, *he* returned from the grave, didn't he?" She laughed harshly, without a note of humor, but with a trace of hysteria. "He was going to cut off my hands, so I couldn't feel my way back."

Tony felt sick when he thought of how close that man had come to fulfilling those threats.

"It *was* him," Hilary said. "You see? It was Frye."

"Could it have been make-up?"

"What?"

"Could it have been someone made up to look like Frye?"

"Why would anyone do that?"

"I don't know."

"What would he have to gain?"

"I don't know."

"You accused me of grabbing at straws. Well, this isn't even a straw you're grabbing at. It's just a mirage. It's nothing."

"But could it have been another man in make-up?" Tony persisted.

"Impossible. There isn't any make-up that convincing at close range. And the body was the same as Frye's. The same height and weight. The same bone structure. The same muscles."

"But if it was someone in make-up, imitating Frye's voice—"

"That would make it easy for you," she said coldly. "A clever impersonation, no matter how bizarre and unexplainable, is easier to accept than my story about a dead man walking. But you mentioned his voice, and that's another hole in your theory. No one could mimic that voice. Oh, an excellent impressionist might get the low pitch and the phrasing and the accent just right, but he wouldn't be able to recreate that awful rasping, crackling quality. You could only talk like that if you had an abnormal larynx or screwed-up vocal cords. Frye was born with a malformed voice box. Or he suffered a serious throat injury when he was a child. Maybe both. Anyway, that was Bruno Frye who spoke to me tonight, not a clever imitation. I'd bet every cent I have on it."

Tony could see that she was still angry, but he was no longer so sure that she was hysterical or even mildly confused. Her dark eyes were sharply focused. She spoke in clipped and precise sentences. She looked like a woman in complete control of herself.

"But Frye is dead," Tony said weakly.

"He was here."

"How could he have been?"

"As I said, that's what I intend to find out."

Tony had walked into a strange room, a room of the mind, which was constructed of impossibilities. He half-remembered something from a Sherlock Holmes story. Holmes had expressed the view to Watson that, in detection, once you had eliminated all the possibilities except one, that which was left, no matter how unlikely or absurd, must be the truth.

Was the impossible possible?

Could a dead man walk?

He thought of the inexplicable tie between the threats the assailant had made and the items found in Bruno Frye's van. He thought of Sherlock Holmes, and finally he said, "All right."

"All right what?" she asked.

"All right, maybe it was Frye."

"It was."

"Somehow . . . some way . . . God knows how . . . but maybe he did survive the stabbing. It seems utterly impossible, but I guess I've got to consider it."

"How wonderfully open-minded of you," she said. Her feathers were still ruffled. She was not going to forgive him easily.

She pulled away from him again and entered the master bedroom.

He followed her.

He felt slightly numb. Sherlock Holmes hadn't said anything about the effects of living with the disturbing thought that nothing was impossible.

She got a suitcase out of the closet, put it on the bed, and started filling it with clothes.

Tony went to the bedside phone and picked up the receiver. "Line's dead. He must have cut the wires outside. We'll have to use a neighbor's phone to report this."

"I'm not reporting it."

"Don't worry," he said. "All that's changed. I'll support your story now."

"It's too late for that," she said sharply.

"What do you mean?"

She didn't answer. She took a blouse off a hanger with such a sudden tug that the hanger clattered to the closet floor.

He said, "You're not still planning to hide out in a hotel and hire private investigators."

"Oh, yes. That's exactly what I'm planning to do," she said, folding the blouse.

"But I've said I believe you."

"And *I* said it's too late for that. Too late to make any difference."

"Why are you being so difficult?"

Hilary didn't respond. She placed the folded blouse in the suitcase and returned to the closet for other pieces of clothing.

"Listen," Tony said, "all I did was express a few quite reasonable doubts. The same doubts that anyone would have in a situation like this. In fact, the same doubts that you would have expressed if *I'd* been the one who'd said he'd seen a dead man walking. If our roles were reversed, I'd expect you to be skeptical. I wouldn't be furious with you. Why are you so damned touchy?"

She came back from the closet with two more blouses and started to fold one of them. She wouldn't look at Tony. "I trusted you . . . with everything," she said.

"I haven't violated any trust."

"You're like everyone else."

"What happened at my apartment earlier—wasn't that kind of special?"

She didn't answer him.

"Are you going to tell me that what you felt tonight—not just with your body, but with your heart, your mind—are you going to tell me that was no different from what you feel with every man?"

Hilary tried to freeze him out. She kept her eyes on her work, put the second blouse in the suitcase, began to fold the third. Her hands were trembling.

"Well, it was special for me," Tony said, determined to thaw her. "It was perfect. Better than I ever thought it could be. Not just the sex. The being together. The sharing. You got inside me like no woman ever has before. You took away a piece of me when you left my place last night, a piece of my soul, a piece of my heart, a piece of something vital. For the rest of my life, I'm not going to feel like a whole man except when I'm with you. So if you think I'm going to just let you walk away, you're in for a big surprise. I'll put up one hell of a fight to hold on to you, lady."

She had stopped folding the blouse. She was just standing with it in her hands, staring down at it.

Nothing in his entire life had seemed half so important as knowing what she was thinking at that moment.

"I love you," he said.

Still looking at the blouse, she responded to him in a tremulous voice. "Are commitments ever kept? Are promises between two people ever kept? Promises like this? When someone says, 'I love you,' does he ever really mean it? If my parents could gush about love one minute, then beat me black and blue a minute later, who the hell can I trust? You? Why should I? Isn't it going to end in disappointment and pain? Doesn't it always end that way? I'm better off alone. I can take good care of myself. I'll be all right. I just don't want to be hurt any more. I'm sick of being hurt. Sick to death of it! I'm not going to make commitments and take risks. I can't. I just can't."

Tony went to her, gripped her by the shoulders, forced her to look at him. Her lower lip quivered. Tears gathered in the corners of her beautiful eyes, but she held them back.

"You feel the same thing for me that I feel for you," he said. "I know it. I feel it. I'm sure of it. You're not turning your back on me because I had some doubts about your story. That doesn't really have anything to do with it. You're turning your back on me because you're falling in love, and you are absolutely terrified of that. Terrified because of your parents. Because of what they did to you. Because of all the beatings you took. Because of a lot of other things you haven't even told me about yet. You're running from your feelings for me because your rotten childhood left you emotionally crippled. But you love me. You do. And you know it."

She couldn't speak. She shook her head: no, no, no.

"Don't tell me it isn't true," he said. "We need each other, Hilary. I need you because all my life I've been afraid to take risks with *things*—money, my career, my art. I've always been open to people, to changing relationships but never to changing circumstances. With you, because of you, for the very first time, I'm willing to take a few tentative steps away from the security of being on the public payroll. And now, when I think seriously about painting for a living, I don't start feeling guilty and lazy, like I used to. I don't always hear Papa's lectures about money and responsibility and the cruelty of fate, like I used to. When I dream of a life as an artist, I no longer automatically start reliving all the financial crises our family endured, the times we were without enough food, the times we were almost without a roof over our heads. I'm finally able to put that behind me. I'm not yet strong enough to quit my job and take the plunge. God, no. Not yet. But because of you, I can now envision myself as a full-time painter, seriously anticipate it, which is something I couldn't do a week ago."

Tears were streaming down her face now. "You're so good," she said. "You're a wonderful, sensitive artist."

"And you need me every bit as much as I need you," he said. "Without me, you're going to build that shell a little thicker, a little harder. You're going to wind up alone and bitter. You have always been able to take risks with *things*—money, your career. But you haven't been able to take chances with people. You see? We're opposites in that respect. We complement each other. We can teach each other so much. We can help each other grow. It's like we were each only half a person—and now we've found our missing halves. I'm yours. You're mine. We've been knocking around all our lives, groping in the dark, trying to find each other."

Hilary dropped the yellow blouse that she had intended to pack in the suitcase, and she threw her arms around him.

Tony hugged her, kissed her salty lips.

For a minute or two they just held each other. Neither of them could speak. At last he said, "Look in my eyes."

She raised her head.

"You've got such dark eyes."

"Tell me," he said.

"Tell you what?"

"What I want to hear."

She kissed the corners of his mouth.

"Tell me," he said.

"I . . . love you."

"Again."

"I love you, Tony. I do. I really do."

"Was that so difficult?"

"Yeah. For me it was."

"It'll get easier the more often you say it."

"I'll make sure to practice a lot," she said.

She was smiling and weeping at the same time.

Tony was aware of a growing tightness, like a rapidly expanding bubble, in his chest, as if he quite literally were bursting with happiness. In spite of the sleepless night just passed, he was full of energy, wide awake, keenly aware of the special woman in his arms—her warmth, her sweet curves, her deceptive softness, the resiliency of her mind and flesh, the fading scent of her perfume, the pleasant animal odor of clean hair and skin.

He said, "Now that we've found each other, everything will be all right."

"Not until we know about Bruno Frye. Or whoever he is. Whatever he is. Nothing will be all right until we know he's definitely dead and buried, once and for all."

"If we stick together," Tony said, "we'll come through safe and sound. He's not going to get his hands on you so long as I'm around. I promise you that."

"And I trust you. But . . . just the same . . . I'm scared of him."

"Don't be scared."

"I can't help it," she said. "Besides, I think it's probably smart to be scared of him."

Tony thought of the destruction downstairs, thought of the sharp wooden stakes and the little bags of garlic that had been found in Frye's van, and he decided that Hilary was right. It was smart to be scared of Bruno Frye.

A walking dead man?

She shivered, and Tony caught it from her.

PART TWO

THE LIVING AND
THE LIVING DEAD

Goodness speaks in a whisper.
Evil shouts.
> —A Tibetan proverb

Goodness shouts.
Evil whispers.
> —A Balinese proverb

CHAPTER 5

TUESDAY MORNING, for the second time in eight days. Los Angeles was rocked by a middle-register earthquake. It hit as high as 4.6 on the Richter Scale as measured at Cal Tech, and it lasted twenty-three seconds.

There was no major damage, and most Angelenos spoke of the tremor only to make jokes. There was the one about the Arabs repossessing part of the country for failure to pay oil debts. And that night, on television, Johnny Carson would say that Dolly Parton had caused the seismic disturbance by getting out of bed too suddenly. To new residents, however, those twenty-three seconds hadn't been the least bit funny, and they couldn't believe that they would ever become blasé about the earth moving under their feet. A year later, of course, they would be making their own jokes about other tremors.

Until the really big one.

A never-spoken, deeply subconscious fear of the big one, the quake to end all quakes, was what made Californians joke about the smaller jolts and shocks. If you dwelt upon the possibility of cataclysm, if you thought about the treachery of the earth for too long, you would be paralyzed with fear. Life must go on regardless of the risks. After all, the big one might not come for a hundred years. Perhaps never. More people died in those snowy, sub-zero Eastern winters than in California quakes. It was as dangerous to live in Florida's hurricane country and on the tornado-stricken plains of the Midwest as it was to build a house on the San Andreas fault. And with every nation on the planet acquiring or seeking to acquire nuclear weapons, the fury of the earth seemed less frightening than the petulant anger of men. To put the quake threat in perspective, Californians made light of it, found humor in the potential disaster, and pretended that living on unstable ground had no effect on them.

But that Tuesday, as on all other days when the earth moved noticeably, more people than usual would exceed the speed limit on the freeways, hurrying to work or to play, hurrying home to families and friends, to lovers; and none of them would be consciously aware that he was living at a somewhat faster pace than he had on Monday. More men would ask their wives for divorces than on a day without a quake. More wives would leave their husbands than had done so the previous day. More people would decide to get married. A greater than usual number of gamblers would make plans to go to Las Vegas for the weekend. Prostitutes would enjoy substantial new business. And there most likely would be a marked increase in sexual activity between husbands and wives, between unwed lovers, and between inexperienced teenagers making their first clumsy experimental moves. Uncontestable proof of this erotic aspect of seismic activity did not exist. But over the years, at several zoos, many sociologists and behavioral psychologists had observed primates—gorillas, chimpanzees, and orangutans—engaging in an abnormal amount of frenzied coupling in the hours following large- and middle-sized earthquakes; and it was reasonable to assume that, at least in the matter of primal reproductive organs, man was not a great deal different from his primate cousins.

Most Californians smugly believed that they were perfectly adjusted to life in earthquake country; but in ways of which they were not aware, the psychological stress continued to shape and change them. Fear of the impending catastrophe was an everpresent whisper that propagandized the subconscious mind, a very influential whisper that molded people's attitudes and characters more than they would ever know.

Of course, it was just one whisper among many.

Hilary wasn't surprised by the police response to her story, and she tried not to let it upset her.

Less than five minutes after Tony placed the call from a neighbor's home, approximately thirty-five minutes before the morning earthquake, two uniformed officers in a black-and-white arrived at Hilary's house, lights flashing, no siren. With typical, bored, professional dispatch and courtesy, they duly recorded her version of the incident, located the point at which the house had been breached by the intruder (a study window again), made a general listing of the damage in the living room and the dining room, and gathered the other information required for the proper completion of a crime report. Because Hilary had said that the assailant had worn gloves, they decided not to bother calling for a lab man and a fingerprint search.

They were intrigued by her contention that the man who attacked her was the same man she thought she had killed last Thursday. Their interest had nothing to do with a desire to determine if she was correct in her identification of the culprit; they made up their minds about that as soon as they heard her story. So far as they were concerned, there was no chance whatsoever that the assailant could have been Bruno Frye. They asked her to repeat her account of the attack several times, and they frequently interrupted with questions; but they were only trying to determine if she was genuinely mistaken, hysterical and confused, or lying. After a while, they decided that she was slightly mixed up due to shock, and that her confusion was exacerbated by the intruder's resemblance to Bruno Frye.

"We'll work from this description you've given us," one of them said.

"But we can't put an APB on a dead man," said the other. "I'm sure you understand that."

"It was Bruno Frye," Hilary said doggedly.

"Well, there's just no way we can go with that, Miss Thomas."

Although Tony supported her story as best he could without having seen the assailant, his arguments and his position with the Los Angeles Police Department made little or no impression on the uniformed officers. They listened politely, nodded a lot, but were not swayed.

Twenty minutes after the morning earthquake, Tony and Hilary stood at the front door and watched the black-and-white police cruiser as it pulled out of the driveway.

Frustrated, she said, "Now what?"

"Now you'll finish packing that suitcase, and we'll go to my apartment. I'll call the office and have a chat with Harry Lubbock."

"Who's he?"

"My boss. Captain Lubbock. He knows me pretty damned well, and we respect each other. Harry knows I don't go out on a limb unless I've thoroughly tested it first. I'll ask him to take another look at Bruno Frye, get some deeper background on the man. And Harry can put more pressure on Sheriff Laurenski than he's done so far. Don't worry. One way or another, I'll get some action."

But forty-five minutes later, in Tony's kitchen, when he placed the call, he could not get any satisfaction from Harry Lubbock. The captain listened to everything that Tony had to say, and he didn't doubt that Hilary *thought* she had seen Bruno Frye, but he couldn't find any justification for launching an investigation of Frye in conjunction with a crime that had been committed days after the man's death. He was not prepared to consider the one-in-ten-million chance that the coroner had been wrong and that Frye miraculously had survived the massive blood loss, an autopsy, and subsequent refrigeration in the morgue. Harry was sympathetic, soft-spoken, and endlessly patient, but it was clear that he thought Hilary's observations were unreliable, her perceptions distorted by terror and hysteria.

Tony sat down beside her, on one of the three breakfast bar stools, and told her what Lubbock had said.

"Hysteria!" Hilary said. "God, I'm sick of that word! Everyone thinks I panicked. Everyone's so damned sure I was reduced to a blubbering mess. Well, of all the women I know, I'm the one least likely to lose my head in a situation like that."

"I agree with you," Tony said. "I'm just telling you how Harry sees it."

"Damn."

"Exactly."

"And your support didn't mean a thing?"

Tony grimaced. "He thinks that, because of what happened to Frank, I'm not entirely myself."

"So he's saying *you're* hysterical."

"Just upset. A little confused."

"Is that really what he said?"

"Yeah."

Remembering that Tony had used those same words to describe her when he'd first heard her story about a walking dead man, she said, "Maybe you deserved that."

"Maybe I did."

"What did Lubbock say when you told him about the threats—the stake through the heart, the mouth full of garlic, all of that stuff?"

"He agreed it was a striking coincidence."

"Just that? Just a coincidence?"

"For the time being," Tony said, "that's how he's going to look at it."

"Damn."

"He didn't say it straight out, but I'm pretty sure he thinks that, last week some time, I told you what was found in Frye's van."

"But you didn't."

"You know I didn't, and I know I didn't. But I suppose that's the way it's going to look to everyone else."

"But I thought you said that you and Lubbock were close, that there was a lot of mutual respect."

"We are, and there is," Tony replied. "But like I told you, he thinks I'm not myself right now. He figures I'll get my head on straight in a few days or a week, when the shock of my partner's death subsides. He thinks then I'll change my mind about supporting your story. I'm sure I won't because I *know* you weren't aware of the occult books and bric-a-brac in Frye's van. And I've got a hunch, too, a very strong hunch that Frye somehow *has* come back. God knows how. But I need more than a hunch to sway Harry, and I can't blame him for being skeptical."

"In the meantime?"

"In the meantime, the homicide squad has no interest in the case. It doesn't come under our jurisdiction. It'll be handled like any other break-in and attempted assault by a person or persons unknown."

Hilary frowned. "Which means not much of anything will be done."

"Unfortunately, I'm afraid that's true. There's almost nothing the police *can* do with a complaint like this one. This sort of thing is usually solved, if ever, a long way down the line, when they catch the guy in the act, breaking and entering another house or assaulting another woman, and he confesses to a lot of old, unsolved cases."

Hilary got up from the stool and began to pace in the small kitchen. "Something strange and frightening is happening here. I can't wait a week for you to convince Lubbock. Frye said he'd be back. He's going to keep trying to kill me until one of us is dead—permanently and irrevocably dead. He could pop up anytime, anywhere."

"You won't be in danger if you stay here until we can puzzle this out," Tony said, "or at least until we come up with something that'll convince Harry Lubbock. You'll be safe here. Frye—if it is Frye—won't know where to find you."

"How can you be sure of that?" she asked.

"He's not omniscient."

"Isn't he?"

Tony scowled. "Wait a minute now. You aren't going to tell me that he has supernatural powers or second sight or something like that."

"I'm not going to tell you that, and I'm not going to rule it out either," she said. "Listen, once you've accepted the fact that Frye is somehow alive, how can you rule out *anything*? I might even start believing in gnomes and goblins and Santa Claus. But what I meant was—maybe he simply followed us here."

Tony raised his eyebrows. "Followed us from your house?"

"It's a possibility."

"No. It isn't."

"Are you positive?"

"When I arrived at your place, he ran away."

She stopped pacing, stood in the middle of the kitchen, hugging herself. "Maybe he hung around the neighborhood, just watching, waiting to see what we'd do and where we'd go."

"Highly unlikely. Even if he did stay nearby after I got there, he sure as hell split when he saw the police cruiser pull up."

"You can't assume that," Hilary said. "At best, we're dealing with a madman. At worst, we're confronting the unknown, something so far beyond our understanding that the danger is incalculable. Whichever the case, you can't expect Frye to reason and behave like an ordinary man. Whatever he may be, he's most definitely *not* ordinary."

Tony stared at her for a moment, then wearily wiped one hand across his face. "You're right."

"So are you positive we weren't followed here?"

"Well . . . I didn't look for a tail," Tony said. "It never occurred to me."

"Me either. Until just now. So as far as we know, he might be outside, watching the apartment, right this very minute."

That idea disturbed Tony. He stood up. "But he'd have to be pretty damned bold to pull a stunt like that."

"He *is* bold!"

Tony nodded. "Yeah. You're right again." He stood for a moment, thinking, then walked out of the kitchen.

She followed him. "Where are you going?"

He crossed the living room toward the front door. "You stay here while I have a look around."

"Not a chance," Hilary said firmly. "I'm coming along with you."

He stopped with his hand on the door. "If Frye is out there, keeping a watch on us, you'll be a whole lot safer staying here."

"But what if I wait for you—and then it's not you who comes back?"

"It's broad daylight out there," Tony said. "Nothing's going to happen to me."

"Violence isn't restricted to darkness," Hilary said. "People get killed in broad daylight all the time. You're a policeman. You know that."

"I have my service revolver. I can take care of myself."

She shook her head. She was adamant. "I'm not going to sit here biting my nails. Let's go."

Outside, they stood by the balcony railing and looked down at the vehicles in the apartment complex parking lot. There were not many of them at that time of day. Most people had gone to work more than an hour ago. In addition to the blue Jeep that belonged to Tony, there were seven cars. Bright sunshine sparkled on the chrome and transformed some of the windshields into mirrors.

"I think I recognize all of them," Tony said. "They belong to people who live here."

"Positive?"

"Not entirely."

"See anybody in any of them?"

He squinted. "I can't tell with the sun shining on the glass."

"Let's take a closer look," she said.

Down in the parking area, they found the cars were empty. There wasn't anyone hanging around who didn't belong.

"Of course," Tony said, "even as bold as he is, it's not likely that he'd stand a watch right on our doorstep. And since there's only one driveway in and out of these apartments, he could keep an eye on us from a distance."

They walked out of the walled complex, onto the sidewalk, and looked north, then south along the tree-shaded street. It was a neighborhood of garden apartments and townhouses and condominiums, nearly all of which lacked adequate parking; therefore, even at that hour of a weekday morning, a lot of cars were lined up along both curbs.

"You want to check them out?" Hilary asked.

"It's a waste of time. If he has binoculars, he'll be able to watch this driveway from four blocks away. We'd have to walk four blocks in each direction, and even then, he could just pull out and drive away."

"But if he does, then we'll spot him. We won't be able to stop him, of course, but at least we'll know for sure that he followed us. And we'll know what he's driving."

"Not if he's two or three blocks from us when he splits," Tony said. "We wouldn't be close enough to be sure it was him. And he might just get out of his car and take a walk, then come back after we've gone."

To Hilary, the air seemed leaden; she found it somewhat taxing to draw a deep breath. The day was going to be very hot, especially for the end of September; and it would be a humid day, too, especially for Los Angeles, where the air was nearly always dry. The sky was high and clear and gas-flame blue. Already, wriggling ghost snakes of heat were rising from the pavement. High-pitched, musical laughter sailed on the light breeze; children were playing in the swimming pool at the townhouse development across the street.

On such a day as this, it was difficult to maintain a belief in the living dead.

Hilary sighed and said, "So how do we find out if he's here, watching us?"

"There's no way to be sure."

"I was afraid you'd say that."

Hilary looked down the street, which was mottled with shadow and light. Horror cloaked in sunshine. Terror hiding against a backdrop of beautiful palm trees and bright stucco walls and Spanish-tile roofs. "Paranoia Avenue," she said.

"Paranoia *City* until this is over."

They turned away from the street and walked back across the macadam parking area in front of his apartment building.

"Now what?" she asked.

"I think we both need to get some sleep."

Hilary had never been so weary. Her eyes were grainy and sore from lack of rest; the strong sunlight stung them. Her mouth felt fuzzy and tasted like cardboard; there was an unpleasant film of tartar on her teeth, and her tongue seemed to be coated with a furry mold. She ached in every bone and muscle and sinew, from her toes to the top of her head, and it didn't help to realize that at least half of the way she felt was the consequence of emotional rather than physical exhaustion.

"I *know* we need to sleep," she said. "But do you really think you can?"

"I know what you mean. I'm tired as hell, but my mind's racing. It's not going to shut off easily."

"There's a question or two I'd like to ask the coroner," she said. "Or whoever performed the autopsy. Maybe when I get some answers I'll be able to take a nap."

"Okay," Tony said. "Let's lock up the apartment and go to the morgue right now."

A few minutes later, when they drove away in Tony's blue Jeep, they watched for a tail, but they were not followed. Of course, that didn't mean Frye wasn't sitting in one of those parked cars along that tree-lined street. If he had followed them from Hilary's house earlier, he didn't need to trail after them now, for he already knew the location of their lair.

"What if he breaks in while we're gone?" Hilary asked. "What if he's hiding in there, waiting, when we come back?"

"I've got two locks on my door," Tony said. "One of them is the best deadbolt money can buy. He'd have to chop down the door. The only other way is to break one of the windows that faces on the balcony. If he's waiting in there when we come back, we'll know it long before we set foot inside."

"What if he finds another way in?"

"There isn't one," Tony said. "To get in through any of the other windows, he'd have to climb to the second floor on a sheer wall, and he'd have to do it right out in the open where he'd be sure to be seen. Don't worry. Home base is safe."

"Maybe he can pass through a door. You know," she said shakily. "Like a ghost. Or maybe he can turn into smoke and drift through a keyhole."

"You don't believe garbage like that," Tony said.

She nodded. "You're right."

"He doesn't have any supernatural powers. He had to break a windowpane to get into your house last night."

They headed downtown through heavy traffic.

Her bone-deep weariness undermined her usually strong mental defenses against the pernicious disease of self-doubt, leaving her uncharacteristically vulnerable. For the first time since seeing Frye walk out of the dining room, she began to wonder if she truly had seen what she thought she had seen.

"Am I crazy?" she asked Tony.

He glanced at her, then back at the street. "No. You're not crazy. You saw something. You didn't wreck the house all by yourself. You didn't just imagine that the intruder looked like Bruno Frye. I'll admit I thought that's what you were doing at first. But now I know you aren't confused."

"But . . . a walking dead man? Isn't that too much to accept?"

"It's just as difficult to accept the other theory—that two unassociated maniacs, both suffering from the same unique set of delusions, both obsessed with a psychotic fear of vampires, attacked you in one week. In fact, I think it's a little easier to believe that Frye is somehow alive."

"Maybe you caught it from me."

"Caught what?"

"Insanity."

He smiled. "Insanity isn't like the common cold. You can't spread it with a cough—or a kiss."

"Haven't you heard of a 'shared psychosis'?"

Braking for a traffic light, he said, "Shared psychosis? Isn't that a social welfare program for underprivileged lunatics who can't afford psychoses of their own?"

"Jokes at a time like this?"

"Especially at a time like this."

"What about mass hysteria?"

"It's not one of my favorite pastimes."

"I mean, maybe that's what's happening here."

"No. Impossible," he said. "There's only two of us. That's not enough to make a mass."

She smiled. "God, I'm glad you're here. I'd hate to be fighting this thing alone."

"You'll never be alone again."

She put one hand on his shoulder.

They reached the morgue at quarter past eleven.

At the coroner's office, Hilary and Tony learned from the secretary that the chief medical examiner had not performed the autopsy on the body of Bruno Frye. Last Thursday and Friday, he had been in San Francisco on a speaking engagement. The autopsy had been left to an assistant, another doctor on the M. E.'s staff.

That bit of news gave Hilary hope that there would be a simple solution to the mystery of Frye's return from the grave. Perhaps the assistant assigned to the job had been a slacker, a lazy man who, free of his boss's constant super- vision, had skipped the autopsy and filed a false report.

That hope was dashed when she met Ira Goldfield, the young doctor in question. He was in his early thirties, a handsome man with piercing blue eyes and a lot of tight blond curls. He was friendly, energetic, bright, and obviously too interested in his work and too dedicated to it to do less than a perfect job.

Goldfield escorted them to a small conference room that smelled of pine- scented disinfectant and cigarette smoke. They sat at a rectangular table that was covered with half a dozen medical reference books, pages of lab reports, and computer print-outs.

"Sure," Goldfield said. "I remember that one. Bruno Graham . . . no . . . Gunther. Bruno Gunther Frye. Two stab wounds, one of them just a little worse than superficial, the other very deep and fatal. Some of the best devel- oped abdominal muscles I've ever seen." He blinked at Hilary and said, "Oh yes . . . You're the woman who . . . stabbed him."

"Self-defense," Tony said.

"I don't doubt that for a second," Goldfield assured him. "In my professional opinion, it's highly unlikely that Miss Thomas could have initiated a successful assault against that man. He was huge. He'd have brushed her away as easily as one of us might turn aside a small child." Goldfield looked at Hilary again. "According to the crime report and the newspaper accounts that I read, Frye attacked you without realizing you were carrying a knife."

"That's right. He thought I was unarmed."

Goldfield nodded. "It had to be that way. Considering the disparity in body sizes, that's the only way you could have taken him without being seriously injured yourself. I mean, the biceps and triceps and forearms on that man were truly astounding. Ten or fifteen years ago, he could have entered body building competitions with considerable success. You were damned lucky, Miss Thomas. If you hadn't surprised him, he could have broken you in half. Almost literally in half. And easily, too." He shook his head, still impressed with Frye's body. "What was it you wanted to ask me about him?"

Tony looked at her, and she shrugged. "It seems rather pointless now that we're here."

Goldfield looked from one of them to the other, a vague, encouraging smile of curiosity on his handsome face.

Tony cleared his throat. "I agree with Hilary. It seems pointless . . . now that we've met you."

"You came in looking so somber and mysterious," Goldfield said pleasantly. "You pricked my interest. You can't keep me hanging like this."

"Well," Tony said, "we came here to find out if there actually had been an autopsy."

Goldfield didn't understand. "But you knew that before you asked to see me. Agnes, the M.E.'s secretary, must have told you. . . ."

"We wanted to hear it from you," Hilary said.

"I still don't get it."

"We knew that an autopsy report had been filed," Tony said. "But we didn't know for certain that the work had been done."

"But now that we've met you," Hilary said quickly, "we have no doubt about it."

Goldfield cocked his head. "You mean to say . . . you thought I filed a fake report without bothering to cut him open?" He didn't seem to be offended, just amazed.

"We thought there might be an outside chance of it," Tony admitted. "A long shot."

"Not in *this* M.E.'s jurisdiction," Goldfield said. "He's a tough old SOB. He keeps us in line. If one of us didn't do his job, the old man would crucify him." It was obvious from Goldfield's affectionate tone that he greatly admired the chief medical examiner.

Hilary said, "Then there's no doubt in your mind that Bruno Frye was . . . dead?"

Goldfield gaped at her as if she had just asked him to stand on his head and recite a poem. "Dead? Why, of course he was dead!"

"You did a complete autopsy?" Tony asked.

"Yes. I cut him—" Goldfield stopped abruptly, thought for a second or two, then said, "No. It wasn't a complete autopsy in the sense you probably mean. Not a medical school dissection of every part of the body. It was an extremely busy day here. A lot of incoming. And we were short-handed. Anyway, there wasn't any need to open Frye all the way up. The stab wound in the lower abdomen was decisive. No reason to open his chest and have a look at his heart. Nothing to be gained by weighing a lot of organs and poking around in his cranium. I did a very thorough exterior examination, and then I opened the two wounds further, to establish the extent of the damage and to be certain that at least one of them had been the cause of death. If he hadn't been stabbed in your house, while attacking you . . . if the circumstances of his death had been less clear, I might have done more with him. But it was clear there wasn't going to be any criminal charges brought in the case. Besides, I am absolutely positive that the abdominal wound killed him."

"Is it possible he was only in a very deep coma when you examined him?" Hilary asked.

"Coma? My God, no! Jesus, no!" Goldfield stood up and paced the length of the long narrow room. "Frye was checked for pulse, respiration, pupil activity, and even brainwaves. The man was indisputably dead, Miss Thomas." He returned to the table and looked down at them. "Dead as stone. When I saw him, there wasn't enough blood in his body to sustain even the barest threshold of life. There was advanced lividity, which means that the blood still in the tissues had settled to the lowest point of the body—the lowest corresponding, in this case, to the position in which he'd been when he'd died. At those places, the flesh was somewhat distended and purple. There's no mistaking that and no overlooking it."

Tony pushed his chair back and stood. "My apologies for wasting your time, Dr. Goldfield."

"And I'm sorry for suggesting you might not have done your job well enough," Hilary said as she got to her feet.

"Hold on now," Goldfield said. "You can't just leave me standing here in the dark. What's this all about?"

She looked at Tony. He seemed as reluctant as she was to discuss walking dead men with the doctor.

"Come on," Goldfield said. "Neither of you strikes me as stupid. You had your reasons for coming here."

Tony said, "Last night, another man broke into Hilary's house and attempted to kill her. He bore a striking resemblance to Bruno Frye."

"Are you serious?" Goldfield asked.

"Oh, yes," Hilary said. "Very serious."

"And you thought—"

"Yes."

"God, it must have been a shock to see him and think he'd come back!" Goldfield said. "But all I can tell you is that the resemblance must be coincidental. Because Frye is dead. I've never seen a man any deader than he was."

They thanked Goldfield for his time and patience, and he escorted them out to the reception area.

Tony stopped at the desk and asked Agnes, the secretary, for the name of the funeral home that had claimed Frye's body.

She looked through the files and said, "It was Angels' Hill Mortuary."

Hilary wrote down the address.

Goldfield said, "You don't still think—"

"No," Tony said. "But on the other hand, we've got to pursue every lead. At least, that's what they taught me at the police academy."

Eyes hooded, frowning, Goldfield watched them as they walked away.

At Angels' Hill Mortuary, Hilary waited in the Jeep while Tony went inside to talk to the mortician who had handled the body of Bruno Frye. They had agreed that he would be able to obtain the information faster if he went in alone and used his LAPD identification.

Angels' Hill was a big operation with a fleet of hearses, twelve roomy viewing chapels, and a large staff of morticians and technicians. Even in the business office, the lighting was indirect and relaxing, and the colors were somber yet rich, and the floor was covered with plush wall-to-wall carpet. The decor was meant to convey a hushed appreciation for the mystery of death; but to Tony, all it conveyed was a loud and clear statement about the profitability of the funeral business.

The receptionist was a cute blonde in a gray skirt and maroon blouse. Her voice was soft, smooth, whispery, but it did not contain even a slight hint of sexual suggestiveness or invitation. It was a voice that had been carefully trained to project consolation, heartfelt solace, respect, and low-key but genuine concern. Tony wondered if she used the same cool funeral tone when she cried encouragement to her lover in bed, and that thought chilled him.

She located the file on Bruno Frye and found the name of the technician who had worked on the body. "Sam Hardesty. I believe Sam is in one of the preparation rooms at the moment. We've had a couple of recent admissions," she said, as if she were working in a hospital rather than a mortuary. "I'll see if he can spare you a few minutes. I'm not sure how far along he is in the treatment. If he can get free, he'll meet you in the employees' lounge."

She took Tony to the lounge to wait. The room was small but pleasant. Comfortable chairs were pushed up against the walls. There were ashtrays and all kinds of magazines. A coffee machine. A soda machine. A bulletin board covered with notices about bowling leagues and garage sales and car pools.

Tony was leafing through a four-page mimeographed copy of the *Angels' Hill Employee News* when Sam Hardesty arrived from one of the preparation rooms. Hardesty looked unnervingly like an automobile mechanic. He was wearing a rumpled white jumpsuit that zipped up the front; there were several small tools (the purpose of which Tony did not want to know) clipped to Hardesty's breast pocket. He was a young man, in his late twenties, with long brown hair and sharp features.

"Detective Clemenza?"

"Yes."

Hardesty held out his hand, and Tony shook it with some reluctance, wondering what it had touched just moments ago.

"Suzy said you wanted to talk to me about one of the accounts." Hardesty had been trained by the same voice coach who had worked with Suzy, the blond receptionist.

Tony said, "I understand you were responsible for preparing Bruno Frye's body for shipment to Santa Rosa last Thursday."

"That's correct. We were cooperating with a mortuary up in St. Helena."

"Would you please tell me exactly what you did with the corpse after you picked it up at the morgue?"

Hardesty looked at him curiously. "Well, we brought the deceased here and treated him."

"You didn't stop anywhere between the morgue and here?"

"No."

"From the moment the body was consigned to you until you relinquished it at the airport, was there ever a time when it was alone?"

"Alone? Only for a minute or two. It was a rush job because we had to put the deceased aboard a Friday afternoon flight. Say, can you tell me what this is all about? What are you after?"

"I'm not sure," Tony said. "But maybe if I ask enough questions I'll find out. Did you embalm him?"

"Certainly," Hardesty said. "We had to because he was being shipped on a public conveyance. The law requires us to hook out the soft organs and embalm the deceased before putting him on a public conveyance."

"Hook out?" Tony asked.

"I'm afraid it's not very pleasant," Hardesty said. "But the intestines and stomach and certain other organs pose a real problem for us. Filled with decaying waste as they are, those parts of the body tend to deteriorate a great deal faster than other tissues. To prevent unpleasant odors and embarrassingly noisy gas accumulations at the viewing, and for ideal preservation of the deceased even after burial, it's necessary to remove as many of those organs as we can. We use a sort of telescoping instrument with a retractable hook on one end. We insert it in the anal passage and—"

Tony felt the blood drain out of his face, and he quickly raised one hand to halt Hardesty. "Thank you. I believe that's all I've got to hear. I get the picture."

"I warned you it wasn't particularly pleasant."

"Not particularly," Tony agreed. Something seemed to be stuck in his throat. He coughed into his hand. It was still down there. It would probably be down there until he got out of this place. "Well," he said to Hardesty, "I think you've told me everything I needed to know."

Frowning thoughtfully, Hardesty said, "I don't know what you're looking for, but there *was* one peculiar thing connected with the Frye assignment."

"What's that?"

"It happened two days after we shipped the deceased to Santa Rosa," Hardesty said. "It was Sunday afternoon. The day before yesterday. Some guy called up and wanted to talk to the technician who handled Bruno Frye. I was here because my days off are Wednesday and Thursday, so I took the call. He was very angry. He accused me of doing a quick and sloppy job on the deceased. That wasn't true. I did the best work I could under the circumstances. But the deceased had lain in the hot sun for a few hours, and then he'd been refrigerated. And there were those stab wounds and the coroner's incisions. Let me tell you, Mr. Clemenza, the flesh was not in very good condition when I received the deceased. I mean, you couldn't expect him to look lifelike. Besides, I wasn't responsible for cosmetic work. That was taken care of by the funeral director up there in St. Helena. I tried to tell this guy on the phone that it wasn't my fault, but he wouldn't let me get a word in edgewise."

"Did he give his name?" Tony asked.

"No. He just got angrier and angrier. He was screaming at me and crying, carrying on like a lunatic. He was in real agony. I thought he must be a relative of the deceased, someone half out of his mind with grief. That's why I was so patient with him. But then, when he got really hysterical, he told me that *he* was Bruno Frye."

"He did what?"

"Yeah. He said *he* was Bruno Frye and that some day he might just come back down here and tear me apart because of what I'd done to him."

"What else did he say?"

"That was it. As soon as he started with that kind of stuff, I knew he was a nut, so I hung up on him."

Tony felt as if he had just been given a transfusion of ice water; he was cold inside as well as out.

Sam Hardesty saw that he was shocked. "What's wrong?"

"I was just wondering if three people are enough to make it mass hysteria?"

"Huh?"

"Was there anything peculiar about this caller's voice?"

"How'd you know that?"

"A very deep voice?"

"He rumbled," Hardesty said.

"And gravelly, coarse?"

"That's right. You know him?"

"I'm afraid so."

"Who is he?"

"You wouldn't believe me if I told you."

"Try me," Hardesty said.

Tony shook his head. "Sorry. This is confidential police business."

Hardesty was disappointed; the tentative smile on his face slipped away.

"Well, Mr. Hardesty, you've been a great help. Thank you for your time and trouble."

Hardesty shrugged. "It wasn't anything."

It as something, Tony thought. Something indeed. But I sure as hell don't know what it means.

In the short hall outside the employees' lounge, they went in different directions, but after a few steps Tony turned and said, "Mr. Hardesty?"

Hardesty stopped, looked back. "Yes?"

"Answer a personal question?"

"What is it?"

"What made you decide to do . . . this kind of work?"

"My favorite uncle was a funeral director."

"I see."

"He was a lot of fun. Especially with kids. He loved kids. I wanted to be like him," Hardesty said. "You always had the feeling that Uncle Alex knew some enormous, terribly important secret. He did a lot of magic tricks for us kids, but it was more than that. I always thought that what he did for a living was very magical and mysterious, too, and that it was because of his work that he'd learned something nobody else knew."

"Have you found his secret yet?"

"Yes," Hardesty said. "I think maybe I have."

"Can you tell me?"

"Sure. What Uncle Alex knew, and what I've come to learn, is that you've got to treat the dead with every bit as much concern and respect as you do the living. You can't just put them out of mind, bury them and forget about them. The lessons they taught us when they were alive are still with us. All the things they did to us and for us are still in our minds, still shaping and changing us. And because of how they've affected us, we'll have certain influences on people who will be alive long after we're dead. So in a way, the dead never really die at all. They just go on and on. Uncle Alex's secret was just this: The dead are people, too."

Tony stared at him for a moment, not certain what he should say. But then the question came unbidden: "Are you a religious man, Mr. Hardesty?"

"I wasn't when I started doing this work," he said. "But I am now. I certainly am now."

"Yes, I suppose you are."

Outside, when Tony got behind the wheel of the Jeep and pulled the driver's door shut, Hilary said, "Well? Did he embalm Frye?"

"Worse than that."

"What's worse than that?"

"You don't want to know."

He told her about the telephone call that Hardesty had received from the man claiming to be Bruno Frye.

"Ahhh," she said softly. "Forget what I said about shared psychoses. This is proof!"

"Proof of what? That Frye's alive? He can't be alive. In addition to other things too disgusting to mention, he was embalmed. No one can sustain even a deep coma when his veins and arteries are full of embalming fluid instead of blood."

"But at least that phone call is proof that something out of the ordinary is happening."

"Not really," Tony said.

"Can you take this to your captain?"

"There's no point in doing that. To Harry Lubbock, it'll look like nothing more sinister than a crank call, a hoax."

"But the *voice!*"

"That won't be enough to convince Harry."

She sighed. "So what's next?"

"We've got to do some heavy thinking," Tony said. "We've got to examine the situation from every angle and see if there's something we've missed."

"Can we think at lunch?" she asked. "I'm starved."

"Where do you want to eat?"

"Since we're both rumpled and wrung out, I suggest some place dark and private."

"A back booth at Casey's Bar?"

"Perfect," she said.

As he drove to Westwood, Tony thought about Hardesty and about how, in one way, the dead were not really dead at all.

Bruno Frye stretched out in the back of the Dodge van and tried to get some sleep.

The van was not the one in which he had driven to Los Angeles last week. That vehicle had been impounded by the police. By now it had been claimed by a representative of Joshua Rhinehart, who was executor of the Frye estate and responsible for the proper liquidation of its assets. This van wasn't gray, like the first one, but dark blue with white accent lines. Frye had paid cash for it yesterday morning at a Dodge dealership on the outskirts of San Francisco. It was a handsome machine.

He had spent nearly all of yesterday on the road and had arrived in Los Angeles last night. He'd gone straight to Katherine's house in Westwood.

She was using the name Hilary Thomas this time, but he knew she was Katherine.

Katherine.

Back from the grave again.

The rotten bitch.

He had broken into the house, but she hadn't been there. Then she'd finally come home just before dawn, and he'd almost gotten his hands on her. He still couldn't figure out why the police had shown up.

During the past four hours, he'd driven by her house five times, but he hadn't seen anything important. He didn't know if she was there or not.

He was confused. Mixed up. And frightened. He didn't know what he should do next, didn't know how he should go about locating her. His thoughts were becoming increasingly strange, fragmented, difficult to control. He felt intoxicated, dizzy, disjointed, even though he hadn't drunk anything.

He was tired. So very tired. No sleep since Sunday night. And not much then. If he could just get caught up on his sleep, he would be able to think clearly again.

Then he could go after the bitch again.

Cut off her head.

Cut out her heart. Put a stake through it.

Kill her. Kill her once and for all.

But first, sleep.

He stretched out on the floor of the van, thankful for the sunlight that streamed through the windshield, over the front seats, and into the cargo hold. He was scared to sleep in the dark.

A crucifix lay nearby.

And a pair of sharp wooden stakes.

He had filled small linen bags with garlic and had taped one over each door. Those things might protect him from Katherine, but he knew they would not ward off the nightmare. It would come to him now as it always did when he slept, as it had all his life, and he would wake with a scream caught in the back of his throat. As always, he would not be able to recall what the dream had been about. But upon waking, he would hear the whispers, the loud but unintelligible whispers, and he would feel something moving on his body, all over his body, on his face, trying to get into his mouth and nose, some horrible *thing;* and during the minute or two that it would take for those sensations to fade away, he would ardently wish that he were dead.

He dreaded sleep, but he needed it.

He closed his eyes.

As usual, the lunchtime din in the main dining room at Casey's Bar was nearly deafening.

But in the other part of the restaurant, behind the oval bar, there were several sheltered booths, each of which was enclosed on three sides like a big confessional, and in these the distant dining room roar of conversation was tolerable; it acted as a background screen to insure even greater privacy than was afforded by the cozy booths themselves.

Halfway through lunch, Hilary looked up from her food and said, "I've got it."

Tony put down his sandwich. "Got what?"

"Frye must have a brother."

"A brother?"

"It explains everything."

"You think you killed Frye last Thursday—and then his brother came after you last night?"

"Such likeness could only be found in brothers."

"And the voice?"

"They could have inherited the same voice."

"Maybe a low-pitched voice could be inherited," Tony said. "But that special gravelly quality you described? Could that be inherited, too?"

"Why not?"

"Last night you said the only way a person could get such a voice was to suffer a serious throat injury or be born with a deformed larnyx."

"So I was wrong," she said. "Or maybe both brothers were born with the same deformity."

"A million-to-one shot."

"But not impossible."

Tony sipped his beer, then said, "Maybe brothers could share the same body type, the same facial features, the same color eyes, the same voice. But could they also share precisely the same set of psychotic delusions?"

She took a taste of her own beer while she thought about that. Then: "Severe mental illness is a product of environment."

"That's what they used to think. They're not entirely sure of that any more."

"Well, for the sake of my theory, suppose that psychotic behavior *is* a product of environment. Brothers would have been raised in the same house by the same parents—in exactly the same environment. Isn't it conceivable that they could develop identical psychoses?"

He scratched his chin. "Maybe. I remember. . . ."

"What?"

"I took a university course in abnormal psychology as part of a study program in advanced criminology," Tony said. "They were trying to teach us how to recognize and deal with various kinds of psychopaths. The idea was a good one. If a policeman can identify the specific type of mental illness when he first encounters an irrational person, and if he has at least a little understanding of how that type of psychopath thinks and reacts, then he's got a much better chance of handling him quickly and safely. We saw a lot of films of mental patients. One of them was an incredible study of a mother and daughter who were both paranoid schizophrenics. They suffered from the same delusions."

"So there!" Hilary said excitedly.

"But it was an extremely rare case."

"So is this."

"I'm not sure, but maybe it was the only one of its type they'd ever found."

"But it *is* possible."

"Worth thinking about, I guess."

"A brother. . . ."

They picked up their sandwiches and began to eat again, each of them staring thoughtfully at his food.

Suddenly, Tony said, "Damn! I just remembered something that shoots a big hole in the brother theory."

"What?"

"I assume you read the newspaper accounts last Friday and Saturday."

"Not all of them," she said. "It's sort of . . . I don't know . . . sort of embarrassing to read about yourself as victim. I got through one article; that was enough."

"And you don't remember what was in that article?"

She frowned, trying to figure out what he was talking about, and then she knew. "Oh, yeah. Frye didn't have a brother."

"Not a brother or a sister. Not anyone. He was the sole heir to the vineyards when his mother died, the last member of the Frye family, the end of his line."

Hilary didn't want to abandon the brother idea. That explanation was the only one that made sense of the recent bizarre events. But she couldn't think of a way to hold on to the theory.

They finished their food in silence.

At last Tony said, "We can't keep you hidden from him forever. And we can't just sit around and wait for him to find you."

"I don't like the idea of being bait in a trap."

"Anyway, the answer isn't here in L.A."

She nodded. "I was thinking the same thing."

"We've got to go to St. Helena."

"And talk with Sheriff Laurenski."

"Laurenski and anyone else who knew Frye."

"We might need several days," she said.

"Like I told you, I've got a lot of vacation time and sick leave built up. A few weeks of it. And for the first time in my life, I'm not particularly anxious to get back to work."

"Okay," she said. "When do we leave?"

"The sooner the better."

"Not today," she said. "We're both too damned tired. We need sleep. Besides, I want to drop your paintings off with Wyant Stevens. I've got to make arrangements for an insurance adjuster to put a price on the damage at my place, and I want to tell my house cleaning service to straighten up the wreckage while I'm gone. And if I'm not going to talk to the people at Warner Brothers about *The Hour of the Wolf* this week, then I've at least got to make excuses—or tell Wally Topelis what excuses he should make for me."

"I've got to fill out a final report on the shooting," Tony said. "I was supposed to do that this morning. And they'll want me for the inquest, of course. There's always an inquest when a policeman is killed—or when he kills someone else. But they shouldn't have scheduled the inquest any sooner than next week. If they did, I can probably get them to postpone it."

"So when do we leave for St. Helena?"

"Tomorrow," he said. "Frank's funeral is at nine o'clock. I want to go to that. So let's see if there's a flight leaving around noon."

"Sounds good to me."

"We've got a lot to do. We'd better get moving."

"One other thing," Hilary said. "I don't think we should stay at your place tonight."

He reached across the table and took her hand. "I'm sure he can't get to you there. If he tries, you've got me, and I've got my service revolver. He may be built like Mr. Universe, but a gun is a good equalizer."

She shook her head. "No. Maybe it would be all right. But I wouldn't be able to sleep there, Tony. I'd be awake all night, listening for sounds at the door and windows."

"Where do you want to stay?"

"After we've run errands this afternoon, let's pack for the trip, leave your apartment, make sure we're not followed, and check in to a room at a hotel near the airport."

He squeezed her hand. "Okay. If that'll make you feel better."

"It will."

"I guess it's best to be safe than sorry."

In St. Helena, at 4:10 Tuesday afternoon, Joshua Rhinehart put down his office phone and leaned back in his chair, pleased with himself. He had accomplished quite a lot in the past two days. Now he swiveled around to look out the window at the far mountains and the nearer vineyards.

He had spent nearly all of Monday on the telephone, dealing with Bruno Frye's bankers, stockbrokers, and financial advisers. There had been many lengthy discussions about how the assets ought to be managed until the estate was finally liquidated, and there had been more than a little debate about the most profitable ways to dispose of those assets when the time came for that. It had been a long, dull patch of work, for there had been a large number of savings accounts of various kinds, in several banks, plus bond investments, a rich portfolio of common stocks, real estate holdings, and much more.

Joshua spent Tuesday morning and the better part of the afternoon arranging, by telephone, for some of the most highly-respected art appraisers in California to journey to St. Helena for the purpose of cataloging and evaluating the varied and extensive collections that the Frye family had accumulated over six or seven decades. Leo, the patriarch, Katherine's father, now dead for forty years, had begun simply, with a fascination for elaborately hand-carved wooden spigots of the sort often used on beer and wine barrels in some European countries. Most of them were in the form of heads, the gaping or gasping or laughing or weeping or howling or snarling heads of demons, angels, clowns, wolves, elves, fairies, witches, gnomes, and other creatures. At the time of his death, Leo owned more than two thousand of those spigots. Katherine had shared her father's interest in collecting while he was alive, and after his death she had made collecting the central focus of her life. Her interest in acquiring beautiful things became a passion, and the passion eventually became a mania. (Joshua remembered how her eyes had gleamed and how she had chattered breathlessly each time that she had shown him a new purchase; he knew there had been something unhealthy about her desperate rush to fill every room and closet and drawer with lovely things, but then the rich always had been permitted their eccentricities and manias, so long as they caused no harm to anyone else.) She bought enameled boxes, turn-of-the-century landscape paintings, Lalique crystal, stained glass lamps and windows, antique cameo lockets, and many other items, not so much because they were excellent investments (which they were) but because she wanted them, needed them as a junkie always needed another fix. She stuffed her enormous house with these displays, spent countless hours just cleaning, polishing, and caring for everything. Bruno continued that tradition of almost frantic acquisition, and now both houses— the one Leo built in 1918, and the one Bruno had built five years ago—were crammed full of treasures. On Tuesday, Joshua called art galleries and prestige auction houses in San Francisco and Los Angeles, and all of them were eager to send their appraisers, for there were many fat commissions to be earned from the disposition of the Frye collections. Two men from San Francisco and two from Los Angeles were arriving Saturday morning; and, certain that they would require several days to catalogue the Frye holdings, Joshua made reservations for them at a local inn.

By 4:10 Tuesday afternoon, he was beginning to feel that he was on top of the situation; and for the first time since he was informed of Bruno's death, he was getting a fix on how long it would take him to fulfill his obligations as executor. Initially, he had worried that the estate would be so complicated that he would be tangled up in it for years, or at least for several months. But now that he had reviewed the will (which he had drawn up five years ago), and now that he had discovered where Bruno's capable financial advisers had led the man, he was confident that the entire matter could be resolved in a few weeks. His job was made easier by three factors that were seldom present in multimillion-dollar estate settlements: First, there were no living relatives to contest the will or to make other problems; second, the entire after-tax net was left to a single charity clearly named in the will; third, for a man of such wealth, Bruno Frye had kept his investments simple, presenting his executor with a reasonably neat balance sheet of easily understood debits and credits. Three weeks would see the end of it. Four at most.

Since the death of his wife, Cora, three years ago, Joshua was acutely conscious of the brevity of life, and he jealously guarded his time. He didn't want to waste one precious day, and he felt that every minute he spent bogged down in the Frye estate was definitely a minute wasted. Of course, he would receive an enormous fee for his legal services, but he already had all the money he would ever need. He owned substantial real estate in the valley, including several hundred acres of prime grape-producing land which was managed for him and which supplied grapes to two big wineries that could never get enough of them. He had thought, briefly, of asking the court to relieve him of his duties; one of Frye's banks would have taken on the job with great pleasure. He also considered turning the work over to Ken Gavins and Roy Genelli, the two sharp young attorneys who he had taken on as partners seven years ago. But his strong sense of loyalty had kept him from taking the easy out. Because Katherine Frye had given him his start in the Napa Valley thirty-five years ago, he felt he owed her the time it would take to personally preside over the orderly and dignified dissolution of the Frye family empire.

Three weeks.

Then he could spend more time on the things he enjoyed: reading good books, swimming, flying the new airplane that he'd bought, learning to cook new dishes, and indulging in an occasional weekend in Reno. Ken and Roy handled most of the law firm's business these days, and they did a damned good job of it. Joshua hadn't plunged into full retirement yet, but he sat on the edge of it a lot, dangling his legs in a big pool of leisure time that he wished he had found and used when Cora was still alive.

At 4:20, content with his progress on the Frye estate and soothed by the magnificent view of the autumn valley beyond his window, he got up from his chair and went out to the reception area. Karen Farr was pounding the hell out of an IBM Selectric II, which would have responded equally well to a feather touch. She was a slip of a girl, pale and blue-eyed and soft-voiced, but she attacked every chore with tremendous energy and strength.

"I am about to treat myself to an early whiskey," Joshua told her. "When people call and ask for me, please tell them I am in a disgraceful drunken condition and cannot come to the phone."

"And they'll all say, 'What? Again?' "

Joshua laughed. "You're a lovely and charming young woman, Miss Farr. Such a delightfully quick mind and tongue for such a mere wisp of a lass."

"And such a lot of malarkey you've got for a man who isn't even Irish. Go and have your whiskey. I'll keep the bothersome hordes away."

In his office again, he opened the corner bar, put ice in a glass, added a generous measure of Jack Daniel's Black Label. He had taken only two sips of the brew when someone knocked on his office door.

"Come in."

Karen opened the door. "There's a call—"

"I thought I was permitted to have my drink in peace."

"Don't be a grouch," she said.

"It's part of my image."

"I told him you weren't in. But then when I heard what he wanted, I thought maybe you should talk to him. It's weird."

"Who is it?"

"A Mr. Preston from the First Pacific United Bank in San Francisco. It's about the Frye estate."

"What's so weird?"

"You better hear it from him," she said.

Joshua sighed. "Very well."

"He's on line two."

Joshua went to his desk, sat down, picked up the phone, and said, "Good afternoon, Mr. Preston."

"Mr. Rhinehart?"

"Speaking. What can I do for you?"

"The business office of Shade Tree Vineyards informs me that you're the executor of the Frye estate."

"That's correct."

"Are you aware that Mr. Bruno Frye maintained accounts at our main office here in San Francisco?"

"The First Pacific United? No, I wasn't aware of that."

"A savings account, a checking account, and a safe-deposit box," Preston said.

"He had several accounts in several banks. He kept a list of them. But yours wasn't on the list. And I haven't run across any passbooks or canceled checks from your bank."

"I was afraid of that," Preston said.

Joshua frowned. "I don't understand. Are there problems with his accounts at Pacific United?"

Preston hesitated, then said, "Mr. Rhinehart, did Mr. Frye have a brother?"

"No. Why do you ask?"

"Did he ever employ a look-alike?"

"I beg your pardon?"

"Did he ever have need for a double, someone who could pass for him on fairly close inspection?"

"Are you pulling my leg, Mr. Preston?"

"I know it's a rather strange question. But Mr. Frye was a wealthy man. These days, what with terrorism on the rise and all sorts of crazies on the loose, wealthy people often have to hire bodyguards, and sometimes—not often; I admit it's rare; but in certain special cases—they even find it necessary to employ look-alikes for security reasons."

"With all due respect for your fair city," Joshua said, "let me point out that Mr. Frye lived here in the Napa Valley, not in San Francisco. We don't have that sort of crime here. We have a much different lifestyle from that which you . . . enjoy. Mr. Frye had no need for a double, and I'm certain he did not have one. Mr. Preston, what on earth is this all about?"

"We only just discovered that Mr. Frye was killed last Thursday," Preston said.

"So?"

"It is the opinion of our attorneys that the bank can in no way be held responsible."

"For what?" Joshua asked impatiently.

"As executor of the estate, it was your duty to inform us that our depositor had died. Until we received that notice—or learned of it third-hand, as we did—we had absolutely no reason to consider the account frozen."

"I'm aware of that." Slumped in his chair, staring wistfully at the glass of whiskey on his desk, afraid that Preston was about to tell him something that would disturb his rosy complacency, Joshua decided that a bit of curmudgeonly gruffness might speed the conversation along. He said, "Mr. Preston, I know that business is conducted slowly and carefully in a bank, which is fitting for an institution handling other people's hard-earned money. But I wish you could find your way clear to get to the point quickly."

"Last Thursday, half an hour before our closing time, a few hours *after* Mr. Frye was killed in Los Angeles, a man who resembled Mr. Frye entered our main branch. He had Mr. Frye's personalized checks. He wrote a check to cash, reducing that account to one hundred dollars."

Joshua sat up straight. "How much did he get?"

"Six thousand from checking."

"Ouch."

"Then he presented his passbook and withdrew all but five hundred from the savings account."

"And how much was that?"

"Another twelve thousand."

"Eighteen thousand dollars altogether?"

"Yes. Plus whatever he might have taken from the safe-deposit box."

"He hit that, too?"

"Yes. But of course, we don't know what he might have gotten out of it," Preston said. Then he added hopefully: "Perhaps nothing."

Joshua was amazed. "How could your bank release such a substantial sum in cash without requiring identification?"

"We did require it," Preston said. "And you've got to understand that he looked like Mr. Frye. For the past five years, Mr. Frye has come in two or three times every month; each time he has deposited a couple of thousand dollars in his checking. That made him noticeable. People remembered him. Last Thursday, our teller recognized him and had no reason to be suspicious, especially since he had those personalized checks and his passbook and—"

"That's not identification," Joshua said.

"The teller asked for ID, even though she recognized him. That's our policy on large withdrawals, and she handled it all according to policy. The man showed her a valid California driver's license, complete with photograph, in the name of Bruno Frye. I assure you, Mr. Rhinehart, First Pacific United has not acted irresponsibly in this matter."

"Do you intend to investigate the teller?" Joshua asked.

"An investigation has already begun."

"I'm pleased to hear that."

"But I'm quite sure it won't lead anywhere," Preston said. "She's been with us for more than sixteen years."

"Is she the same woman who let him get to the safe deposit box?" Joshua asked.

"No. That's another employee. We're investigating her as well."

"This is a damned serious matter."

"You don't have to tell me," Preston said miserably. "In all my years in banking, I've never had it happen to me. Before I phoned you, I notified the authorities, the state and federal banking officials, and First Pacific United's attorneys."

"I believe I should come down there tomorrow and have a chat with your people."

"I wish you would."

"Shall we say ten o'clock?"

"Whenever it's convenient for you," Preston said. "I'll be at your disposal all day."

"Then let's make it ten o'clock."

"I'm terribly sorry about this. But of course, the loss is covered by federal insurance."

"Except for the contents of the safe deposit box," Joshua said. "No insurance covers that loss." That was the part of it that was giving Preston a bad case of the jitters, and they both knew it. "The box might have held more of value than the savings and checking accounts combined."

"Or it might very well have been empty before he got to it," Preston said quickly.

"I'll see you in the morning, Mr. Preston."

Joshua hung up and stared at the telephone.

Finally he sipped his whiskey.

A double for Bruno Frye? A dead ringer?

Suddenly, he remembered the light he had thought he'd seen in Bruno's house at three o'clock Monday morning. He'd spotted it on his way back to bed from the bathroom, but when he'd put on his glasses, there had been no light. He'd figured that his eyes had played a trick on him. But perhaps the light had been real. Perhaps the man who had looted those Pacific United accounts had been in Bruno's house, looking for something.

Joshua had been to the house yesterday, and taken a brisk five-minute tour to be certain everything was as it should be, and he had not noticed anything awry.

Why had Bruno kept secret bank accounts in San Francisco?

Was there a dead ringer, a double?

Who? And why?

Damn!

Evidently, overseeing the complete and final settlement of the Frye estate was not going to be as short and easy a job as he had thought.

At six o'clock Tuesday evening, as Tony swung the Jeep into the street that ran past his apartment building, Hilary felt more awake than she had all day. She had entered that peculiar second-wind state of grainy-eyed alertness that came after being awake for a day and a half. Suddenly, the body and the mind seemed to decide to make the best of this forced consciousness; and, by some chemical trick, the flesh and the spirit were renewed. She stopped yawning. Her vision, which had been blurry at the edges, grew clear again. The grinding weariness receded. But she knew it would be only a short-lived reprieval from exhaustion. In an hour or two, this surprising high would end in an abrupt and inevitable crash, not unlike the sudden descent from an amphetamine energy peak, and then she would be too drained even to stay on her feet.

She and Tony had successfully dealt with all of their business that needed tending to—the insurance adjuster, the house cleaning service, the police reports, and all the rest. The only thing that hadn't gone smoothly was the stop at Wyant Stevens Gallery in Beverly Hills. Neither Wyant nor his assistant, Betty, was there, and the plump young woman in charge was reluctant to take possession of Tony's paintings. She didn't want the responsibility, but Hilary finally convinced her that she would not be sued if one of the canvases was marked or torn accidentally. Hilary had written a note to Wyant, explaining the artist's background, and then she and Tony had gone to the offices of Topelis & Associates to ask Wally to make excuses to Warner Brothers. Now the slate was clean. Tomorrow, after Frank Howard's funeral, they would catch the

11:55 PSA flight that would take them to San Francisco in time to board a connecting commuter air shuttle to Napa.

And then a rented car to St. Helena.

And then they would be on Bruno Frye's home ground.

And then—what?

Tony parked the Jeep and switched off the engine.

Hilary said, "I forgot to ask if you managed to find a hotel room."

"Wally's secretary made reservations for me while you and Wally were huddling in his office."

"At the airport."

"Yes."

"Not twin beds, I hope."

"One kingsize."

"Good," she said. "I want you to hold me while I drift off to sleep."

He leaned over and kissed her.

They took twenty minutes to pack a pair of suitcases for him and to carry their four bags down to the Jeep. During that time, Hilary was on edge, fully expecting Frye to leap out of a shadow or step around a corner, grinning.

He didn't.

They drove to the airport by a roundabout route that was full of twists and turns. Hilary watched the cars behind them.

They were not followed.

They reached the hotel at 7:30. With a touch of old-fashioned chivalry that amused Hilary, Tony signed them in as husband and wife.

Their room was on the eighth floor. It was a restful place, done in shades of green and blue.

When the bellhop left, they stood by the bed, just holding each other for a minute, silently sharing their weariness and what strength they had left.

Neither of them felt capable of going out to dinner. Tony ordered from room service, and the operator said service would take about half an hour.

Hilary and Tony showered together. They soaped and rinsed each other with pleasure, but the pleasure wasn't really sexual. They were too tired for passion. The shared bath was merely relaxing, tender, sweet.

They ate club sandwiches and french fries.

They drank half a bottle of Gamay rosé by Robert Mondavi.

They talked only a little while.

They draped a bath towel over a lamp and left the lamp on for a nightlight because, for only the second time in her life, Hilary was afraid to sleep in the dark.

They slept.

Eight hours later, at 5:30 in the morning, she woke from a bad dream in which Earl and Emma had come back to life, just like Bruno Frye. All three of them pursued her down a dark corridor that grew narrower and narrower and narrower. . . .

She couldn't get back to sleep. She lay in the vague amber glow of the makeshift nightlight and watched Tony sleep.

At 6:30 he woke, turned toward her, blinked, touched her face, her breasts, and they made love. For a short while, she forgot about Bruno Frye, but later, as they dressed for Frank's funeral, the fear came back in a rush.

"Do you really think we should go to St. Helena?"

"We have to go," Tony said.

"But what's going to happen to us there?"

"Nothing," he said. "We'll be all right."

"I'm not so sure," she said.

"We'll find out what's going on."

"That's just it," she said uneasily. "I have the feeling we'd be better off not knowing."

Katherine was gone.

The bitch was gone.

The bitch was hiding.

Bruno had awakened in the blue Dodge van at 6:30 Tuesday evening, thrown from sleep by the nightmare he could never quite remember, threatened by wordless whispers. Something was crawling all over him, on his arms, on his face, in his hair, even underneath his clothes, trying to get inside his body, trying to scuttle inside through his ears and mouth and nostrils, something unspeakably filthy and evil. He screamed and clawed frantically at himself until he finally realized where he was; then the awful whispers slowly faded, and the imaginary crawling thing crept away. For a few minutes, he curled up on his side, in a tight fetal position, and he wept with relief.

An hour later, after eating at McDonald's, he had gone to Westwood. He drove by her place half a dozen times, then parked up the street from it, in a pool of shadows between streetlamps. He watched her house all night.

She was gone.

He had the linen bags full of garlic and the sharp wooden stakes and the crucifix and the vial of holy water. He had the two very sharp knives and a small woodman's hatchet with which he could chop off her head. He had the courage and the will and the determination.

But she was gone.

When he first began to realize that she had skipped out and might not be back for days or weeks, he was furious. He cursed her, and he wept with frustration.

Then he gradually regained control of himself. He told himself that all was not lost. He would find her.

He had found her countless times before.

CHAPTER 6

WEDNESDAY MORNING, Joshua Rinehart made the short flight to San Francisco in his own Cessna Turbo Skylane RG. It was a honey of a plane with a cruising speed of 173 knots and a range of over one thousand miles.

He had begun taking flying lessons three years ago, shortly after Cora died. For most of his life, he had dreamed about being a pilot, but he had never found time to learn until he was fifty-eight years old. When Cora was taken from him so unexpectedly, he saw that he was a fool, a fool who thought that death was a misfortune that only befell other people. He had spent his life as if he possessed an infinite store of it, as if he could spend and spend, live and live, forever. He thought he would have all the time in the world to take those dreamed-about trips to Europe and the Orient, all the time in the world to relax and travel and have fun; therefore, he always put off the cruises and vacations, postponed them until the law practice was built, and then until the mortgages on their large real estate holdings were all paid, and then until the grape-growing business was firmly established, and then. . . . And then Cora suddenly ran out of time. He missed her terribly, and he still filled up with remorse when he thought of all the things that had been delayed too long. He and Cora had been happy with each other; in many ways, they had enjoyed an extremely good life together, an excellent life by most standards. They'd never wanted for anything—not food or shelter or a fair share of luxuries. There'd always been enough money. But never enough time. He could not help dwelling on what might have been. He could not bring Cora back, but at least he was determined to grab all of the joy he could get his hands on in his remaining years. Because he had never been a gregarious man, and because he felt that nine out of ten people were woefully ignorant and/or malicious, most of his pleasures were solitary pursuits; but, in spite of his preference for solitude, nearly all of those pleasures were less satisfying than they would have been if he'd been able to share them with Cora. Flying was one of the few exceptions to that rule. In his Cessna, high above the earth, he felt as if he'd been freed from all restraints, not just from the bonds of gravity, but from the chains of regret and remorse as well.

Refreshed and renewed by the flight, Joshua landed in San Francisco shortly after nine o'clock. Less than an hour later, he was at the First Pacific United Bank, shaking hands with Mr. Ronald Preston, with whom he had spoken on the phone Tuesday afternoon.

Preston was a vice-president of the bank, and his office was sumptuous. There was a lot of real leather upholstery and well-polished teak. It was a padded, plush, fat office.

Preston, on the other hand, was tall and thin; he looked brittle, breakable. He was darkly tanned and sported a neatly trimmed mustache. He talked too fast, and his hands flung off one quick gesture after another, like a short-circuiting machine casting off sparks. He was nervous.

He was also efficient. He had prepared a detailed file on Bruno Frye's accounts, with pages for each of the five years that Frye had done business with First Pacific United. The file contained a list of savings account deposits and withdrawals, another list of the dates on which Frye had visited his safe-deposit box, clear photocopies of the monthly checking account statements blown up from microfilm records, and similar copies of every check ever written on that account.

"At first glance," Preston said, "it might appear that I haven't given you copies of all the checks Mr. Frye wrote. But let me assure you that I have. There simply weren't many of them. A lot of money moved in and out of that account, but for the first three-and-a-half years, Mr. Frye wrote only two checks a month. For the last year and a half, it's been three checks every month, and always to the same payees."

Joshua didn't bother to open the folder. "I'll look at these things later. Right now, I want to question the teller who paid out on the checking and savings accounts."

A round conference table stood in one corner of the room. Six comfortably padded captain's chairs were arranged around it. That was the place Joshua chose for the interrogations.

Cynthia Willis, the teller, was a self-assured and rather attractive black woman in her late thirties. She was wearing a blue skirt and a crisp white blouse. Her hair was neatly styled, her fingernails well-shaped and brightly polished. She carried herself with pride and grace, and she sat with her back very straight when Joshua directed her into the chair opposite him.

Preston stood by his desk, silently fretting.

Joshua opened the envelope he had brought with him and took from it fifteen snapshots of people who lived or had once lived in St. Helena. He spread them out on the table and said, "Miss Willis—"

"Mrs. Willis," she corrected him.

"I'm sorry. Mrs. Willis, I want you to look at each one of those photographs, and then you tell me which is Bruno Frye. But only after you've looked at them all."

She went through the batch of photos in a minute and picked out two of them. "Both of these are him."

"Are you sure?"

"Positive," she said. "That wasn't much of a test. The other thirteen don't look like him at all."

She had done an excellent job, much better than he had expected. Many of the photographs were fuzzy, and some were taken in poor light. Joshua purposefully used bad pictures to make the identification more difficult than it otherwise might have been, but Mrs. Willis did not hesitate. And although she said the other thirteen didn't look like Frye, a few of them actually did, a little. Joshua had chosen a few people who resembled Frye, at least when the camera was slightly out of focus, but that ruse had not fooled Cynthia Willis; and neither had the trick of including two photographs of Frye, two head shots, each much different from the other.

Tapping the two snapshots with her index finger, Mrs. Willis said, "This was the man who came into the bank last Thursday afternoon."

"On Thursday morning," Joshua said, "he was killed in Los Angeles."

"I don't believe it," she said firmly. "There must have been some mistake about that."

"I saw his body," Joshua told her. "We buried him up in St. Helena last Sunday."

She shook her head. "Then you must have buried someone else. You must have buried the wrong man."

"I've known Bruno Frye since he was five years old," Joshua said. "I couldn't be mistaken."

"And I know who I saw," Mrs. Willis said politely but stubbornly.

She did not glance at Preston. She had too much pride to tailor her answers to his measurements. She knew she was a good worker, and she had no fear of the boss. Sitting up even straighter than she had been sitting, she said, "Mr. Preston is entitled to his opinion. But, after all, he didn't see the man. I did. It was Mr. Frye. He's been coming in the bank two or three times a month for the past five years. He always makes at least a two-thousand-dollar-deposit in checking, sometimes as much as three thousand, and always in cash. Cash. That's unusual. It makes him very memorable. That and the way he looks, all of those muscles and—"

"Surely he didn't always make his deposits at your window."

"Not always," she admitted. "But a lot of the time, he did. And I swear it was him who made those withdrawals last Thursday. If you know him at all, Mr. Rhinehart, you know that I wouldn't even have had to see Mr. Frye to know it was him. I would have recognized him blindfolded because of that strange voice of his."

"A voice can be imitated," Preston said, making his first contribution to the conversation.

"Not this one," Mrs. Willis said.

"It might be imitated," Joshua said, "but not easily."

"And those eyes," Mrs. Willis said. "They were almost as strange as his voice."

Intrigued by that remark, Joshua leaned toward her and said, "What about his eyes?"

"They were cold," she said. "And not just because of the blue-gray color.

Very cold, hard eyes. And most of the time he didn't seem to be able to look straight at you. His eyes kept sliding away, as if he was afraid you'd see his thoughts or something. But then, that every great once in a while when he *did* look straight at you, those eyes gave you the feeling you were looking at . . . well . . . at somebody who wasn't altogether right in the head."

Ever the diplomatic banker, Preston quickly said, "Mrs. Willis, I'm sure that Mr. Rhinehart wants you to stick to the objective facts of the case. If you interject your personal opinions, that will only cloud the issue and make his job more difficult."

Mrs. Willis shook her head. "All I know is, the man who was here last Thursday had those same eyes."

Joshua was slightly shaken by that observation, for he, too, often thought that Bruno's eyes revealed a soul in torment. There had been a frightened, haunted look in that man's eyes—but also the hard, cold, murderous iciness that Cynthia Willis had noted.

For another thirty minutes, Joshua questioned her about a number of subjects, including: the man who had withdrawn Frye's money, the usual procedures she followed when dispensing large amounts of cash, the procedures she had followed last Thursday, the nature of the ID that the imposter had presented, her home life, her husband, her children, her employment record, her current financial condition, and half a dozen other things. He was tough with her, even gruff when he felt that would help his cause. Unhappy at the prospect of spending extra weeks on the Frye estate because of this new development, anxious to find a quick solution to the mystery, he was searching for a reason to accuse her of complicity in the looting of the Frye accounts, but in the end he found nothing. Indeed, by the time he was finished quizzing her, he had come to like her a great deal and to trust her as well. He even went so far as to apologize to her for his sometimes sharp and quarrelsome manner, and such an apology was extremely rare for him.

After Mrs. Willis returned to her teller's cage, Ronald Preston brought Jane Symmons into the room. She was the woman who had accompanied the Frye look-alike into the vault, to the safe-deposit box. She was a twenty-seven-year-old redhead with green eyes, a pug nose, and a querulous disposition. Her whiny voice and peevish responses brought out the worst in Joshua; but the more curmudgeonly he became, the more querulous she grew. He did not find Jane Symmons to be as articulate as Cynthia Willis, and he did not like her as he did the black woman, and he did not apologize to her; but he was certain that she was as truthful as Mrs. Willis, at least about the matter at hand.

When Jane Symmons left the room, Preston said, "Well, what do you think?"

"It's not likely that either of them was part of any swindle," Joshua said.

Preston was relieved, but tried not to show it. "That's our assessment, too."

"But this man who's posing as Frye must bear an incredible likeness to him."

"Miss Symmons is a most astute young woman," Preston said. "If she said he looked exactly like Frye, the resemblance must, indeed, be remarkable."

"Miss Symmons is a hopeless twit," Joshua said grumpily. "If she were the only witness, I would be lost."

Preston blinked in surprise.

"However," Joshua continued, "your Mrs. Willis is keenly observant. And damned smart. And self-confident without being smug. If I were you, I'd make more of her than just a teller."

Preston cleared his throat. "Well . . . uh, what now?"

"I want to see the contents of that safe-deposit box."

"I don't suppose you have Mr. Frye's key?"

"No. He hasn't yet returned from the dead to give it to me."

"I thought perhaps it had turned up among his things since I talked to you yesterday."

"No. If the imposter used the key, I suppose he still has it."

"How did he get it in the first place?" Preston wondered. "If it was given to him by Mr. Frye, then that casts a different light on things. That would alter the bank's position. If Mr. Frye conspired with a look-alike to remove funds—"

"Mr. Frye could not have conspired. He was dead. Now shall we see what's in the box?"

"Without both keys, it'll have to be broken open."

"Please have that done," Joshua said.

Thirty-five minutes later, Joshua and Preston stood in the bank's secondary vault as the building engineer pulled the ruined lock out of the safe-deposit box and, a moment after that, slid the entire box out of the vault wall. He handed it to Ronald Preston, and Preston presented it to Joshua.

"Ordinarily," Preston said somewhat stiffly, "you would be escorted to one of our private cubicles, so that you could look through the contents without being observed. However, because there's a strong possibility you'll claim that some valuables were illegally removed, and because the bank might face a lawsuit on those charges, I must insist that you open the box in my presence."

"You haven't any legal right to insist on any such thing," Joshua said sourly. "But I have no intention of hitting your bank with a phony lawsuit, so I'll satisfy your curiosity right now."

Joshua lifted the lid of the safe-deposit box. A white envelope lay inside, nothing else, and he plucked it out. He handed the empty metal box to Preston and tore open the envelope. There was a single sheet of white paper bearing a dated, signed, typewritten note.

It was the strangest thing Joshua had ever read. It appeared to have been written by a man in a fever delirium.

> *Thursday, September 25*
> *To whom it may concern:*
> My mother, Katherine Anne Frye, died five
> years ago, but she keeps coming back to life in
> new bodies. She has found a way to return from
> the grave, and she is trying to get me. She is
> currently living in Los Angeles, under the name
> Hilary Thomas.
> This morning, she stabbed me, and I died in
> Los Angeles. I intend to go back down there and
> kill her before she kills me again. Because if she
> kills me twice, I'll stay dead. I don't have her
> magic. I can't return from the grave. Not if she
> kills me twice.
> I feel so empty, so incomplete. She killed me,
> and I'm not whole any more.
> I'm leaving this note in case she wins again.
> Until I'm dead twice, this is my own little war,
> mine and no one else's. I can't come out in the
> open and ask for police protection. If I do that,
> everyone will know what I am, who I am. Every-
> one will know what I've been hiding all my life,
> and then they'll stone me to death. But if she gets me
> again, then it won't matter if everyone finds

*out what I am, because I'll already be dead twice.
If she gets me again, then whoever finds this letter
must take the responsibility for stopping her.*

*You must cut off her head and stuff her mouth
full of garlic. Cut out her heart and pound a stake
through it. Bury her head and her heart in different
church graveyards. She's not a vampire. But I
think these things may work. If she is killed this
way, she might stay dead.*

She comes back from the grave.

Below the body of the letter, in ink, there was a fine forgery of Bruno Frye's signature. It had to be a forgery, of course. Frye was already dead when these lines were written.

The skin tingled on the back of Joshua's neck, and for some reason he thought of Friday night: walking out of Avril Tannerton's funeral home, stepping into the pitch-black night, being certain that something dangerous was nearby, sensing an evil presence in the darkness, a thing crouching and waiting.

"What is it?" Preston asked.

Joshua handed over the paper.

Preston read it and was amazed. "What in the world?"

"It must have been put in the box by the imposter who cleaned out the accounts," Joshua said.

"But why would he do such a thing?"

"Perhaps it's a hoax," Joshua said. "Whoever he is, he evidently enjoys a good ghost story. He knew we'd find out that he'd looted the checking and savings, so he decided to have some fun with us."

"But it's so . . . strange," Preston said. "I mean, you might expect a self-congratulatory note, something that would rub our faces in it. But this? It doesn't seem like the work of a practical joker. Although it's weird and doesn't always make sense, it seem so . . . *earnest.*"

"If you think it's not merely a hoax, then what do you think?" Joshua asked. "Are you telling me Bruno Frye wrote this letter and put it in the safe-deposit box *after* he died?"

"Well . . . no. Of course not."

"Then what?"

The banker looked down at the letter in his hands. "Then I would say that this imposter, this man who looks so remarkably like Mr. Frye and talks like Mr. Frye, this man who carries a driver's license in Mr. Frye's name, this man who knew that Mr. Frye had accounts in First Pacific United—this man isn't just pretending to be Mr. Frye. He actually thinks he *is* Mr. Frye." He looked up at Joshua. "I don't believe that an ordinary thief with a prankster's turn of mind would compose a letter like this. There's genuine madness in it."

Joshua nodded. "I'm afraid I have to agree with you. But where did this doppelganger come from? Who is he? How long has he been around? Was Bruno aware that this man existed? Why would the look-alike share Bruno's obsessive fear and hatred of Katherine Frye? How could both men suffer from the same delusion—the belief that she had come back from the dead? There are a thousand questions. It truly boggles the mind."

"It certainly does," Preston said. "And I don't have any answers for you. But I do have one suggestion. This Hilary Thomas should be told that she may be in grave danger."

*　　*　　*

After Frank Howard's funeral, which was conducted with full police honors, Tony and Hilary caught the 11:55 flight from Los Angeles. On the way north, Hilary worked at being bubbly and amusing, for she could see that the funeral had depressed Tony and had brought back horrible memories of the Monday morning shootout. At first, he slumped in his seat, brooding, barely responding to her. But after a while, he seemed to become aware of her determination to cheer him up, and, perhaps because he didn't want her to feel that her effort was unappreciated, he found his lost smile and began to come out of his depression. They landed on time at San Francisco International Airport, but the two o'clock shuttle flight to Napa was now rescheduled for three o'clock because of minor mechanical difficulties.

With time to kill, they ate lunch in an airport restaurant that offered a view of the busy runways. The surprisingly good coffee was the only thing to recommend the place; the sandwiches were rubbery, and the french fries were soggy.

As the time approached for their departure for Napa, Hilary began to dread going. Minute by minute, she grew more apprehensive.

Tony noticed the change in her. "What's wrong?"

"I don't know exactly. I just feel like . . . well, maybe this is wrong. Maybe we're just rushing straight into the lion's den."

"Frye is down there in Los Angeles. He doesn't have any way of knowing that you're going to St. Helena," Tony said.

"Doesn't he?"

"Are you still convinced that it's supernatural, a matter of ghosts and ghouls and whatnot?"

"I'm not ruling out anything."

"We'll find a logical explanation in the end."

"Whether we do or not, I've got this feeling . . . this premonition."

"A premonition of what?"

"Of worse things to come," she said.

After a hurried but excellent lunch in the First Pacific United Bank's private executive dining room, Joshua Rhinehart and Ronald Preston met with federal and state banking officials in Preston's office. The bureaucrats were boring and poorly prepared and obviously ineffectual; but Joshua tolerated them, answering their questions, filled out their forms, for it was his duty to use the federal insurance system to recover the stolen funds for the Frye estate.

As the bureaucrats were leaving, Warren Sackett, an FBI agent, arrived. Because the money had been stolen from a federally-chartered financial institution, the crime was within the Bureau's jurisdiction. Sackett—a tall, intense man with chiseled features—sat at the conference table with Joshua and Preston, and he elicited twice as much information as the covey of bureaucrats had done, in only half the time that those paperpushers had required. He informed Joshua that a very detailed background check on him would be part of the investigation, but Joshua already knew that and had no reason to fear it. Sackett agreed that Hilary Thomas might be in danger, and he took the responsibility for informing the Los Angeles police of the extraordinary situation that had arisen, so that both the LAPD and the Los Angeles office of the FBI would be prepared to look after her.

Although Sackett was polite, efficient, and thorough, Joshua realized that the FBI was not going to solve the case in a few days—not unless the Bruno Frye imposter walked into their office and confessed. This was not an urgent matter to them. In a country plagued by various crackpot terrorist groups, organized crime families, and corrupt politicians, the resources of the FBI could not be brought fully to bear on an eighteen-thousand-dollar case of this sort. More likely than not, Sackett would be the only agent on it full-time. He would begin slowly, with background checks on everyone involved; and then he would conduct an exhaustive survey of banks in northern California, to see if Bruno Frye had any other secret accounts. Sackett wouldn't get to St. Helena for a day or two. And if he didn't come up with any leads in the first week or ten days, he might thereafter handle the case only on a part-time basis.

When the agent finished asking questions, Joshua turned to Ronald Preston and said, "Sir, I trust that the missing eighteen thousand will be replaced in short order."

"Well. . . ." Preston nervously fingered his prim little mustache. "We'll have to wait until the FDIC approves the claim."

Joshua looked at Sackett. "Am I correct in assuming the FDIC will wait until you can assure them that neither I nor any beneficiary of the estate conspired to withdraw that eighteen thousand dollars?"

"They might," Sackett said. "After all, this is a highly unusual case."

"But quite a lot of time could pass before you're able to give them such assurances," Joshua said.

"We wouldn't make you wait beyond a reasonable length of time," Sackett said. "At most, three months."

Joshua sighed. "I had hoped to settle the estate quickly."

Sackett shrugged. "Maybe I won't need three months. It could all break fast, You never know. In a day or two, I might even turn up this guy who's a dead ringer for Frye. Then I'd be able to give the FDIC an all-clear signal."

"But you don't expect to solve it that fast."

"The situation is so bizarre that I can't commit myself to deadlines," Sackett said.

"Damnation," Joshua said wearily.

A few minutes later, as Joshua crossed the cool marble-floored lobby on his way out of the bank, Mrs. Willis called to him. She was on duty at a teller's cage. He went to her, and she said, "You know what I'd do if I were you?"

"What's that?" Joshua asked.

"Dig him up. That man you buried. Dig him up."

"Bruno Frye?"

"You didn't bury Mr. Frye." Mrs. Willis was adamant; she pressed her lips together and shook her head back and forth, looking very stern. "No. If there's a double for Mr. Frye, he's not the one who's up walking around. The double is the one who's six feet under with a slab of granite for a hat. The real Mr. Frye was here last Thursday. I'd swear to that in any court. I'd stake my life on it."

"But if it wasn't Frye who was killed down in Los Angeles, then where is the real Frye now? Why did he run away? What in the name of God is going on?"

"I don't know about that," she said. "I only know what I saw. Dig him up, Mr. Rhinehart. I believe you'll find that you've buried the wrong man."

At 3:20 Wednesday afternoon, Joshua landed at the county airport just outside the town of Napa. With a population of forty-five thousand, Napa was far from being a major city, and in fact it partook of the wine country ambiance to such an extent that it seemed smaller and cozier than it really was; but to Joshua, who was long accustomed to the rural peace of tiny St. Helena, Napa was as noisy and bothersome as San Francisco had been, and he was anxious to get out of the place.

His car was parked in the public lot by the airfield, where he had left it that morning. He didn't go home or to his office. He drove straight to Bruno Frye's house in St. Helena.

Usually, Joshua was acutely aware of the incredible natural beauty of the valley. But not today. Now he drove without seeing anything until the Frye property came into view.

Part of Shade Tree Vineyards, the Frye family business, occupied fertile black flat land, but most of it was spread over the gently rising foothills on the west side of the valley. The winery, the public tasting room, the extensive cellars, and the other company buildings—all fieldstone and redwood and oak structures that seemed to grow out of the earth—were situated on a large piece of level highland, near the westernmost end of the Frye property. All the buildings faced east, across the valley, toward vistas of seriated vines, and all of them were constructed with their backs to a one-hundred-sixty-foot cliff, which had been formed in a distant age when earth movement had sheered the side off the last foothill at the base of the more precipitously rising Mayacamas Mountains.

Above the cliff, on the isolated hilltop, stood the house that Leo Frye, Katherine's father, had built when he'd first come to the wine country in 1918. Leo had been a brooding Prussian type who had valued his privacy more than almost anything else. He looked for a building site that would provide a wide view of the scenic valley plus absolute privacy, and the clifftop property was precisely what he wanted. Although Leo was already a widower in 1918, and although he had only one small child and was not, at that time, contemplating another marriage, he nevertheless constructed a large twelve-room Victorian house on top of the cliff, a place with many bay windows and gables and a lot of architectural gingerbread. It overlooked the winery that he established, later, on the highland below, and there were only two ways to reach it. The first approach was by aerial tramway, a system comprised of cables, pulleys, electric motors, and one four-seat gondola that carried you from the lower station (a second-floor corner of the main winery building) to the upper station (somewhat to the north of the house on the clifftop). The second approach was by way of a double-switchback staircase fixed to the face of the cliff. Those three hundred and twenty steps were meant to be used only if the aerial tramway broke down—and then only if it was not possible to wait until repairs were made. The house was not merely private; it was remote.

As Joshua turned from the public road onto a very long private drive that led to the Shade Tree winery, he tried to recall everything he knew about Leo Frye. There was not much. Katherine had seldom spoken of her father, and Leo had not left a great many friends behind.

Because Joshua hadn't come to the valley until 1945, a few years after Leo's death, he'd never met the man, but he'd heard just enough tales about him to form a picture of the sort of mind that hungered for the excessive privacy embodied in that clifftop house. Leo Frye had been cold, stern, somber, self-possessed, obstinate, brilliant, a bit of an egomaniac, and an iron-handed authoritarian. He was not unlike a feudal lord from a distant age, a medieval aristocrat who preferred to live in a well-fortified castle beyond the easy reach of the unwashed rabble.

Katherine had continued to live in the house after her father died. She raised Bruno in those high-ceilinged rooms, a world far removed from that of the child's contemporaries, a Victorian world of waist-high wainscoting and flowered wallpaper and crenelated molding and footstools and mantel clocks and lace tablecloths. Indeed, mother and son lived together until he was thirty-five years old, at which time Katherine died of heart disease.

Now, as Joshua drove up the long macadam lane toward the winery, he looked above the fieldstone and wood buildings. He raised his eyes to the big house that stood like a giant cairn atop the cliff.

It was strange for a grown man to live with his mother as long as Bruno had lived with Katherine. Naturally, there had been rumors, speculations. The consensus of opinion in St. Helena was that Bruno had little or no interest in girls, that his passions and affections were directed secretly toward young men. It was assumed that he satisfied his desires during his occasional visits to San Francisco, out of sight of his wine country neighbors. Bruno's possible homosexuality was not a scandal in the valley. Local people didn't spend a great deal of time talking about it; they didn't really care. Although St. Helena was a small town, it could claim more than a little sophistication; winemaking made it so.

But now Joshua wondered if the consensus of local opinion about Bruno had been wrong. Considering the extraordinary events of the past week, it was beginning to appear as if the man's secret had been much darker and infinitely more terrible than mere homosexuality.

Immediately after Katherine's funeral, deeply shaken by her death, Bruno had moved out of the house on the cliff. He took his clothes, as well as large collections of paintings, metal sculptures, and books, which he had acquired on his own; but he left behind everything that belonged to Katherine. Her clothes were left hanging in closets and folded in drawers. Her antique furniture, paintings, porcelains, crystals, music boxes, enameled boxes—all of those things (and much more) could have been sold at auction for a substantial sum. But Bruno insisted that every item be left exactly where Katherine had put it, undisturbed, untouched. He locked the windows, drew the blinds and drapes, closed and bolt-locked the exterior shutters on both the first and second floors, locked the doors, sealed the place tight, as if it were a vault in which he could preserve forever the memory of his adoptive mother.

When Bruno had rented an apartment and had begun to make plans for the construction of a new house in the vineyards, Joshua had tried to persuade him that it was foolish to leave the contents of the cliff house unattended. Bruno insisted that the house was secure and that its remoteness made it an unlikely target of burglars—especially since burglary was an almost unheard-of crime in the valley. The two approaches to the house—the switchback stairs and the aerial tramway—were deep in Frye property, behind the winery; and the tramway operated only with a key. Besides (Bruno had argued) no one but he and Joshua knew that a great many items of value remained in the old house. Bruno was adamant; Katherine's belongings must not be touched; and finally, reluctantly, unhappily, Joshua surrendered to his client's wishes.

To the best of Joshua's knowledge, no one had been in the cliff house for five years, not since the day that Bruno had moved out. The tramway was well-maintained, even though the only person who rode it was Gilbert Ulman, a mechanic employed to keep Shade Tree Vineyards' trucks and farm equipment in good shape; Gil also had the job of regularly inspecting and repairing the aerial tramway system, which required only a couple of hours a month. Tomorrow, or Friday at the latest, Joshua would have to take the cable car to the top of the cliff and open the house, every door and window, so that it could air out before the art appraisers arrived from Los Angeles and San Francisco on Saturday morning.

At the moment, Joshua was not the least bit interested in Leo Frye's isolated Victorian redoubt; his business was at Bruno's more modern and considerably more accessible house. As he drew near the end of the road that led to the winery's public parking lot, he turned left, onto an extremely narrow driveway that struck south through the sun-splashed vineyards. Vines crowded both sides of the cracked, raggedy-edged blacktop. The pavement led him down one hill, across a shallow glen, up another slope, and ended two hundred yards south of the winery, in a clearing, where Bruno's house stood with vineyards on all sides. It was a large, single-story, ranch-style, redwood and fieldstone structure shaded by one of the nine mammoth oak trees that dotted the huge property and gave the Frye company its name.

Joshua got out of the car and walked to the front door of the house. There were only a few high white clouds against the electric-blue sky. The air flowing down from the piney heights of the Mayacamas was crisp and fresh.

He unlocked the door, stepped inside, and stood in the foyer for a moment, listening. He wasn't sure what he expected to hear.

Maybe footsteps.

Or Bruno Frye's voice.

But there was only silence.

He went from one end of the house to the other in order to get to Frye's study. The decor was proof that Bruno had acquired Katherine's obsessive compulsion to collect and hoard beautiful things. On some walls, so many fine paintings were hung so close together that their frames touched, and no single piece could claim the eye in that exquisite riot of shape and color. Display cases stood everywhere, filled with art glass and bronze sculpture and crystal paperweights and pre-Columbian statuary. Every room contained far too much furniture, but each piece was a matchless example of its period and style. In the huge study, there were five or six hundred rare books, many of them limited editions that had been bound in leather; and there were a few dozen perfect little scrimshaw figures in a display case; and there were six terribly expensive and flawless crystal balls, one as small as an orange, one as large as a basketball, the others in various sizes between.

Joshua pulled back the drapes at the window, letting in a little light, switched on a brass lamp, and sat in a modern spring-backed office chair behind an enormous 18th-century English desk. From a jacket pocket he withdrew the strange letter that he had found in the safe-deposit box at the First Pacific United Bank. It was actually just a Xerox; Warren Sackett, the FBI agent, insisted on keeping the original. Joshua unfolded the copy and propped it up where he could see it. He turned to the low typing stand that was beside the desk, pulled it over his lap, rolled a clean sheet of paper into the typewriter, and quickly tapped out the first sentence of the letter.

> *My mother, Katherine Anne Frye, died five years ago, but she keeps coming back to life in new bodies.*

He held the Xerox copy next to the sample and compared them. The type was the same. In both versions, the loop of the lower case "e" was completely filled in with ink because the keys hadn't been properly cleaned in quite a while. In both, the loop of the lower case "a" was partially occluded, and the lower case "d" printed slightly higher than any of the other characters. The letter had been typed in Bruno Frye's study, on Bruno Frye's machine.

The look-alike, the man who had impersonated Frye in that San Francisco bank last Thursday, apparently possessed a key to the house. But how had he gotten it? The most obvious answer was that Bruno had given it to him, which meant that the man was an employee, a hired double.

Joshua leaned back in the chair and stared at the Xerox of the letter, and other questions exploded like fireworks in his mind. Why had Bruno felt it necessary to hire a double? Where had he found such a remarkable look-alike? How long ago did the double start to work for him? Doing what? And how often had he, Joshua, spoken to this doppelganger, thinking the man was really Frye? Probably more than once. Perhaps more often than he'd spoken to the real Bruno. There was no way of knowing. Had the double been here, in the house, Thursday morning, when Bruno had died in Los Angeles? Most likely. After all, this was where he had typed the letter that he'd put in the safe-deposit box, so this must be where he had heard the news. But how had he learned about the death so quickly? Bruno's body had been found next to a public telephone. . . . Was it possible that Bruno's last act had been to call home and talk to his double? Yes. Possible. Even probable. The telephone company's records would have to be checked. But what had those two men said to each other as the one died? Could they conceivably share the same psychosis, the belief that Katherine had come back from the grave?

Joshua shuddered.

He folded the letter, returned it to his coat pocket.

For the first time, he realized how *gloomy* these rooms were—overstuffed with furniture and expensive ornaments, windows covered by heavy drapes, floors carpeted in dark colors. Suddenly, the place seemed far more isolated than Leo's clifftop retreat.

A noise. In another room.

Joshua froze as he was walking around the desk. He waited, listened. "Imagination," he said, trying to reassure himself.

He walked swiftly through the house to the front door, and he found that the noise had, indeed, been imaginary. He wasn't attacked. Nevertheless, when he stepped outside, closed the door, and locked it, he sighed with relief.

In the car, on his way to his office in St. Helena, he thought of more questions. Who actually had died in Los Angeles last week—Frye or his look-alike? Which of them had been at the First Pacific United Bank on Thursday—the real man or the imitation? Until he knew the answer to that, how could he settle the estate? He had countless questions but damned few answers.

When he parked behind his office a few minutes later, he realized that he would have to give serious consideration to Mrs. Willis's advice. Bruno Frye's grave might have to be opened to determine exactly who was buried in it.

Tony and Hilary landed in Napa, rented a car, and arrived at the headquarters of the Napa County Sheriff's Department by 4:20 Wednesday afternoon. The place was not somnolent like the county sheriff's offices you saw on television. A couple of young deputies and a pair of industrious clerical workers were busy with files and paperwork.

The sheriff's secretary-receptionist sat at a large metal desk, identified by a name plaque in front of her typewriter: MARSHA PELETRINO. She was a starched-looking woman with severe features, but her voice was soft, silky, and sexy. Likewise, her smile was far more pleasant and inviting than Hilary had expected.

When Marsha Peletrino opened the door between the reception area and Peter Laurenski's private office and announced that Tony and Hilary wanted to see him, Laurenski knew immediately who they were, and he didn't attempt to avoid them, as they thought he might. He came out of his office and awkwardly shook their hands. He seemed embarrassed. Clearly, he wasn't looking forward to explaining why he had provided a phony alibi for Bruno Frye last Wednesday night, but in spite of his unconcealed discomfort, he invited Tony and Hilary in for a chat.

Laurenski was somewhat of a disappointment for Hilary. He was not the sloppy, potbellied, cigar-chewing, easy to hate, small town, good old boy type that she had expected, not the sort of countrified power monger who would lie to protect a wealthy local resident like Bruno Frye. Laurenski was in his thirties, tall, blond, clean-cut, articulate, friendly, and apparently dedicated to his job, a good lawman. There was kindness in his eyes and a surprising gentleness in his voice; in some ways he reminded her of Tony. The Sheriff's Department's offices were clean and Spartan rooms where a lot of work got done, and the people who labored there with Laurenski, the deputies and civilians alike, were not patronage cronies but bright and busy public servants. After only one or two minutes with the sheriff, she knew there was not going to be any simple answer to the Frye mystery, no obvious and easily-exposed conspiracy.

In the sheriff's private office, she and Tony sat on a sturdy old railback bench that had been made comfortable with corduroy-covered foam pillows. Laurenski pulled up a chair and sat on it the wrong way, with his arms crossed on the backrest.

He disarmed Hilary and Tony by getting straight to the point and by being hard on himself.

"I'm afraid I've been less than professional about this whole thing," he said. "I've been dodging your department's phone calls."

"That's the reason we're here," Tony said.

"Is this an . . . official visit of some kind?" Laurenski asked, a bit puzzled.

"No," Tony said. "I'm here as a private citizen, not a policeman."

"We've had an extremely unusual and unsettling experience in the last couple of days," Hilary said. "Incredible things have happened, and we hope you'll have an explanation for them."

Laurenski raised his eyebrows. "Something more than Frye's attack on you?"

"We'll tell you about it," Tony said. "But first, we'd like to know why you haven't answered the LAPD."

Laurenski nodded. He was blushing. "I just didn't know what to say. I'd made a fool of myself by vouching for Frye. I guess I just hoped it would all blow away."

"And why did you vouch for him?" Hilary asked.

"It's just . . . you see . . . I really did think he was at home that night."

"You talked with him?" Hilary asked.

"No," Laurenski said. He cleared his throat. "You see, when the call came in that evening, it was taken by a night officer. Tim Larsson. He's one of my best men. Been with me seven years. A real go-getter. Well . . . when Los Angeles police called about Bruno Frye, Tim thought he'd better call me and see if I wanted to handle it, since Frye was one of the county's leading citizens. I was at home that night. It was my daughter's birthday. As far as my family was concerned, that was a pretty special occasion, and for once I was determined not to let my work intrude on my private life. I have so little time for my kids. . . ."

"I understand," Tony said. "I have a hunch you do a good job here. And I'm familiar enough with police work to know that doing a good job requires a hell of a lot more than eight hours a day."

"More like twelve hours a day, six or seven days a week," the sheriff said. "Anyway, Tim called me that night, and I told him to handle it. You see, first of all, it sounded like a ridiculous inquiry. I mean, Frye was an upstanding businessman, even a millionaire, for God's sake. Why would he throw it all away trying to rape someone? So I told Tim to look into it and get back to me as soon as he had something. As I said, he's a very competent officer. Besides, he knew Frye better than I did. Before he decided on a career in law enforcement, Tim worked for five years in the main office at Shade Tree Vineyards. During that time, he saw Frye just about every day."

"Then it was Officer Larsson who checked on Frye last Wednesday night," Tony said.

"Yes. He called me back at my daughter's birthday party. He said Frye was at home, not in Los Angeles. So I returned the call to the LAPD and proceeded to make a fool of myself."

Hilary frowned. "I don't understand. Are you saying that this Tim Larsson lied to you?"

Laurenski didn't want to have to answer that one. He got up and paced, staring at the floor, scowling. Finally he said, "I trust Tim Larsson. I always have trusted him. He's a good man. One of the best. But I just can't explain this."

"Did he have any reason to cover up for Frye?" Tony asked.

"You mean, were they buddies? No. Nothing like that. They weren't even friends. He'd only worked for Frye. And he didn't like the man."

"Did he claim to have seen Bruno Frye that night?" Hilary asked Laurenski.

"At the time," the sheriff said, "I just assumed he had seen him. But later, Tim said he figured he could identify Frye by the phone and that there wasn't any need to run all the way out there in a patrol car to have a look-see. As you must know, Bruno Frye had a very distinctive, very odd voice."

"So Larsson might have talked to someone who was covering for Frye, someone who could imitate his voice," Tony said.

Laurenski looked at him. "That's what Tim says. That's his excuse. But it doesn't fit. Who would it have been? Why would he cover for rape and murder? Where is he now? Besides, Frye's voice wasn't something that could be easily mimicked."

"So what do you think?" Hilary asked.

Laurenski shook his head. "I don't know what to think. I've been brooding about it all week. I want to believe my officer. But how can I? Something is going on here—but what? Until I can get a handle on it, I've laid Tim off without pay."

Tony glanced at Hilary, then back at the sheriff. "When you hear what we've got to tell you, I think you'll be able to believe Officer Larsson."

"However," Hilary said, "you still won't be able to make sense out of it. We're in deeper than you are, and we still don't know what's going on."

She told Laurenski about Bruno Frye being in her house Tuesday morning, five days after his death.

In his office in St. Helena, Joshua Rhinehart sat at his desk with a glass of Jack Daniel's Black Label and looked through the file that Ronald Preston had given him in San Francisco. It contained, among other things, clear photocopies of the monthly statements that had been blown up from microfilm records, plus similar copies of the front and back of every check Frye had written. Because Frye had kept the account a secret, tucked away in a city where he did no other business, Joshua was convinced that an examination of those records would yield clues to the solution of the dead ringer's identity.

During the first three-and-a-half years that the account had been active, Bruno had written two checks each month, never more than that, never fewer. And the checks were always to the same people—Rita Yancy and Latham Hawthorne—names which meant nothing to Joshua.

For reasons not specified, Mrs. Yancy had received five hundred dollars a month. The only thing Joshua could deduce from the photocopies of those checks was that Rita Yancy must live in Hollister, California, for she deposited every one of them in a Hollister bank.

No two of the checks to Latham Hawthorne were for the same amount; they ranged from a couple of hundred dollars to five or six thousand. Apparently, Hawthorne lived in San Francisco, for all of his deposits were made at the same branch of the Wells Fargo Bank in that city. Hawthorne's checks were all endorsed with a rubber stamp that read:

FOR DEPOSIT ONLY
TO THE ACCOUNT OF:
Latham Hawthorne
ANTIQUARIAN BOOKSELLER
&
OCCULTIST

Joshua stared at that last word for a while. *Occultist.* It was obviously derived from the word "occult" and was intended by Hawthorne to describe his profession, or at least half of it, rare book dealing being the other half. Joshua thought he knew what the word meant, but he was not certain.

Two walls of his office were lined with law books and reference books. He had three dictionaries, and he looked up "occultist" in all of them. The first two did not contain the word, but the third gave him a definition that was pretty much what he had expected. An occultist was someone who believed in the rituals and supernatural powers of various "occult sciences"—including, but not limited to, astrology, palmistry, black magic, white magic, demonolatry, and Satanism. According to the dictionary, an occultist could also be someone who sold the paraphernalia required to engage in any of those odd pursuits— books, costumes, cards, magical instruments, sacred relics, rare herbs, pig-tallow candles, and the like.

In the five years between Katherine's death and his own demise, Bruno Frye had paid more than one hundred and thirty thousand dollars to Latham Hawthorne. There was nothing on any of the checks to indicate what he had received in return for all that money.

Joshua refilled his glass with whiskey and returned to his desk.

The file on Frye's secret bank accounts showed that he had written two checks a month for the first three-and-a-half years, but then three checks a month for the past year and a half. One to Rita Yancy, one to Latham Hawthorne, as before. And now a third check to Dr. Nicholas W. Rudge. All of the checks to the doctor had been deposited in a San Francisco branch of the Bank of America, so Joshua assumed the physician lived in that city.

He placed a call to San Francisco Directory Assistance, then another to Directory Assistance in the 408 area code, which included the town of Hollister. In less than five minutes, he had telephone numbers for Hawthorne, Rudge, and Rita Yancy.

He called the Yancy woman first.

She answered on the second ring. "Hello?"

"Mrs. Yancy?"

"Yes."

"Rita Yancy?"

"That's right." She had a pleasant, gentle, melodic voice. "Who's this?"

"My name's Joshua Rhinehart. I'm calling from St. Helena. I'm the executor for the estate of the late Bruno Frye."

She didn't respond.

"Mrs. Yancy?"

"You mean he's dead?" she asked.

"You didn't know?"

"How would I know?"

"It was in the newspapers."

"I never read the papers," she said. Her voice had changed. It was not pleasant any more; it was hard and cold.

"He died last Thursday," Joshua said.

She was silent.

"Are you all right?" he asked.

"What do you want from me?"

"Well, as executor, one of my duties is to see that all of Mr. Frye's debts are paid before the estate is distributed to the heirs."

"So?"

"I discovered that Mr. Frye was paying you five hundred dollars a month, and I thought that might be installments on a debt of some sort."

She didn't answer him.

He could hear her breathing.

"Mrs. Yancy?"

"He doesn't owe me a penny," she said.

"Then he wasn't repaying a debt?"

"No," she said.

"Were you working for him in some capacity?"

She hesitated. Then: *click!*

"Mrs. Yancy?"

There wasn't any response. Just the hissing of the long distance line, a far-off crackle of static.

Joshua dialed her number again.

"Hello," she said.

"It's me, Mrs. Yancy. Evidently, we were cut off."

Click!

He considered calling her a third time, but he decided she would only hang up again. She wasn't handling herself well. Obviously, she had a secret, a secret she had shared with Bruno, and now she was trying to hide it from Joshua. But all she had done was feed his curiosity. He was more certain than ever that each of the people who were paid through the San Francisco bank account would have something to tell him that would help to explain the existence of a Bruno Frye look-alike. If he could only get them to talk, he might settle the estate relatively quickly after all.

As he put the receiver down, he said, "You can't get away from me that easily, Rita."

Tomorrow, he would fly the Cessna down to Hollister and confront her in person.

Now he called Dr. Nicholas Rudge, got an answering service, and left a message, including both his home and office numbers.

On his third call, he struck paydirt, although not as much of it as he had hoped to find. Latham Hawthorne was at home and willing to talk. The occultist had a nasal voice and a trace of an upper-class British accent.

"I sold him quite a number of books," Hawthorne said in answer to a question from Joshua.

"Just books?"

"That's correct."

"That's a lot of money for books."

"He was an excellent customer."

"But a hundred and thirty thousand dollars?"

"Spread out over almost five years."

"Nevertheless—"

"And most of them were extremely rare books, you understand."

"Would you be willing to buy them back from the estate?" Joshua asked, trying to determine if the man was honest.

"Buy them back? Oh, yes, I'd be happy to do that. Most definitely."

"How much?"

"Well, I can't say exactly until I see them."

"Take a stab in the dark. How much?"

"You see, if the volumes have been abused—tattered and torn and marked and whatnot—then that's quite another story."

"Let's say they're spotless. How much would you offer?"

"If they're in the condition they were when I sold them to Mr. Frye, I'm prepared to offer you quite a bit more than he originally paid for them. A great many of the titles in his collection have appreciated in value."

"How much?" Joshua asked.

"You're a persistent man."

"One of my many virtues. Come on, Mr. Hawthorne. I'm not asking you to commit yourself to a binding offer. Just an estimate."

"Well, *if* the collection still contains every book that I sold him, and *if* they're all in prime condition . . . I'd say . . . allowing for my margin of profit, of course . . . around two hundred thousand dollars."

"You'd buy back the same books for seventy thousand more than he paid you?"

"As a rough estimate, yes."

"That's quite an increase in value."

"That's because of the area of interest," Hawthorne said. "More and more people come into the field every day."

"And what is this field?" Joshua asked. "What kind of books was he collecting?"

"Haven't you seen them?"

"I believe they're on the bookshelves in his study," Joshua said. "Many of them are very old books, and a lot of them have leather bindings. I didn't realize there was anything unusual about them. I haven't taken time to look closely."

"They were occult titles," Hawthorne said. "I only sell books dealing with the occult in all its many manifestations. A high percentage of my wares are forbidden books, those that were banned by church or state in another age, those that have not been brought back into print by our modern and skeptical publishers. Limited edition items, too. I have more than two hundred steady customers. One of them is a San Jose gentleman who collects nothing but books on Hindu mysticism. A woman in Marin County has acquired an enormous library on Satanism, including a dozen obscure titles that have been published in no language but Latin. Another woman in Seattle has bought virtually every word ever printed about out-of-body experiences. I can satisfy any taste. I'm not merely polishing my ego when I say that I'm the most reputable and reliable dealer in occult literature in this country."

"But surely not all of your customers spend as much as Mr. Frye did."

"Oh, of course not. There are only two or three others like him, with his resources. But I've got a few dozen clients who budget approximately ten thousand dollars a year for their purchases."

"That's incredible," Joshua said.

"Not really," Hawthorne said. "These people feel that they are teetering on the edge of a great discovery, on the brink of learning some monumental secret, the riddle of life. Some of them are in pursuit of immortality. And some are searching for spells and rituals that will bring them tremendous wealth or unlimited power over others. Those are persuasive motivations. If they truly believe that just a little more forbidden knowledge will get them what they want, then they will pay virtually any price to obtain it."

Joshua swung around in his swivel chair and looked out the window. Low gray clouds were scudding in from the west, over the tops of the autumn-somber Mayacamas Mountains, bearing down on the valley.

"Exactly what aspect of the occult interested Mr. Frye?" Joshua asked.

"He collected two kinds of books loosely linked to the same general subject," Hawthorne said. "He was fascinated by the possibility of communicating with the dead. Séances, table knockings, spirit voices, ectoplasmic apparitions, amplification of ether recordings, automatic writing, that sort of thing. But his greatest interest, by far, lay in literature about the living dead."

"Vampires?" Joshua asked, thinking about the strange letter in the safe-deposit box.

"Yes," Hawthorne said. "Vampires, zombies, creatures of that sort. He couldn't get enough books on the subject. Of course, I don't mean that he was interested in horror novels and cheap sensationalism. He collected only serious nonfiction studies—and certain selected esoterica."

"Such as?"

"Well, for instance . . . in the esoterica category . . . he paid six thousand dollars for the hand-written journal of Christian Marsden."

"Who is Christian Marsden?" Joshua asked.

"Fourteen years ago, Marsden was arrested for the murders of nine people in and around San Francisco. The press called him the Golden Gate Vampire because he always drank his victim's blood."

"Oh, yes," Joshua said.

"And he also dismembered his victims."

"Yes."

"Cut off their arms and legs and heads."

"Unfortunately, I remember him now. A gruesome case," Joshua said.

The dirty gray clouds were still rolling across the western mountains, moving steadily toward St. Helena.

"Marsden kept a journal during his year-long killing spree," Hawthorne said. "It's a curious piece of work. He believed that a dead man named Adrian Trench was trying to take over his body and come back to life through him. Marsden genuinely felt that he was in a constant, desperate struggle for control of his own flesh."

"So that when he killed, it wasn't really him killing, but this Adrian Trench."

"That's what he wrote in his journal," Hawthorne said. "For some reason he never explained, Marsden believed that the evil spirit of Adrian Trench required other people's blood to keep control of Marsden's body."

"A sufficiently screwy story to present to a court in a sanity hearing," Joshua said cynically.

"Marsden *was* sent to an asylum," Hawthorne said. "Six years later, he died there. But he wasn't faking insanity to escape a prison sentence. He actually believed that the spirit of Adrian Trench was trying to cast him out of his own body."

"Schizophrenic."

"Probably," Hawthorne agreed. "But I don't think we should rule out the possibility that Marsden was sane and that he was merely reporting a genuine paranormal phenomenon."

"Say again?"

"I'm suggesting that Christian Marsden might really have been possessed in some way or other."

"You don't mean that," Joshua said.

"To paraphrase Shakespeare—there are a great many things in heaven and earth that we do not and cannot understand."

Beyond the large office window, as the slate-colored bank of clouds continued to press into the valley, the sun sank westward, beyond the Mayacamas, and the autumn dusk came prematurely to St. Helena.

As he watched the light bleed slowly out of the day, Joshua said, "Why did Mr. Frye want the Marsden journal so badly?"

"He believed he was living through an experience similar to Marsden's," Hawthorne said.

"You mean, Bruno thought some dead person was trying to take over his body?"

"No," Hawthorne said. "He didn't identify with Marsden, but with Marsden's victims. Mr. Frye believed that his mother—I think her name was Katherine—had come back from the dead in someone else's body and was plotting to kill him. He hoped that the Marsden journal would give him a clue about how to deal with her."

Joshua felt as if a large dose of ice-cold water had been injected into his veins. "Bruno never mentioned such a thing to me."

"Oh, he was quite secretive about it," Hawthorne said. "I'm probably the only person he ever revealed it to. He trusted me because I was sympathetic toward his interest in the occult. Even so, he only mentioned it once. He was quite passionate in his belief that she had returned from the dead, quite terrified of falling prey to her. But later, he was sorry that he had told me."

Joshua sat up straight in his chair, amazed, chilled. "Mr. Hawthorne, last week Mr. Frye attempted to kill a woman in Los Angeles."

"Yes, I know."

"He wanted to kill her because he thought that she was actually his mother hiding in a new body."

"Really? How interesting."

"Good God, sir! You knew what was going on in his mind. Why didn't you do something?"

Hawthorne remained cool and serene. "What would you have had me do?"

"You could have told the police! They could have questioned him, looked into the possibility that he needed medical attention."

"Mr. Frye hadn't committed a crime," Hawthorne said. "And beyond that, you're presuming he was crazy, and I make no such assumption."

"You're joking," Joshua said incredulously.

"Not at all. Perhaps Frye's mother did come back from the grave to get him. Maybe she even succeeded."

"For God's sake, that woman in Los Angeles was not his mother!"

"Maybe," Hawthorne said. "Maybe not."

Although Joshua was still sitting in his big office chair, and although the chair was still resting squarely on a solid floor, he felt curiously off balance. He had pictured Hawthorne as a rather cultured, mild-mannered, bookish fellow who had gotten into his unusual line of business largely because of the profits it offered. Now Joshua began to wonder if that image was altogether wrong. Maybe Latham Hawthorne was as strange as the merchandise he sold.

"Mr. Hawthorne, you're obviously a very efficient and successful businessman. You sound as if you're well-educated. You're far more articulate than most people I meet these days. Considering all of that, I find it difficult to believe that you put much credence in such things as séances and mysticism and the living dead."

"I scoff at nothing," Hawthorne said. "And in fact I think my willingness to believe is less surprising than your stubborn refusal to do so. I don't see how an intelligent man can *not* realize that there are many worlds beyond our own, realities beyond that in which we live."

"Oh, I believe the world is filled with mysteries and that we only partially perceive the nature of reality," Joshua said. "You'll get no argument from me on that. But I also think, in time, our perceptions will be sharpened and the mysteries all explained by scientists, by rational men working in their laboratories—not by superstitious cultists burning incense and chanting nonsense."

"I have no faith in scientists," Hawthorne said. "I'm a Satanist. I find my answers in that discipline."

"Devil worship?" Joshua asked. The occultist could still surprise him.

"That's a rather crude way of putting it. I believe in the Other God, the Dark Lord. His time is coming, Mr. Rhinehart." Hawthorne spoke calmly, pleasantly, as if he were discussing nothing more unusual or controversial than the weather. "I look forward to the day when He casts out Christ and all the lesser gods and takes the throne of the earth for His own. What a fine day that will be. All the devout of other religions will be enslaved or slaughtered. Their priests will be decapitated and fed to the dogs. Nuns will be ravished in the streets. Churches and mosques and synagogues and temples will be used for the celebration of black masses, and every person on the face of the earth will worship Him, and babies will be sacrificed on those altars, and Beelzebub will reign until the end of time. Soon, Mr. Rhinehart. There are signs and portents. Quite soon now. I look forward to it."

Joshua was at a loss for words. In spite of the madness that Hawthorne spouted, he sounded like a rational, reasonable man. He was not ranting or screaming. There was not even a vague trace of mania or hysteria in his voice. Joshua was more disturbed by the occultist's outward composure and surface gentleness than he would have been if Hawthorne had snarled and yelped and foamed at the mouth. It was like meeting a stranger at a cocktail party, talking with him for a while, getting to like him, and then suddenly realizing that he was wearing a latex mask, a clever false face, behind which lay the evil and grinning countenance of Death himself. A Halloween costume, but in reverse. The demon disguised as the ordinary man. Poe's nightmare come to life.

Joshua shivered.

Hawthorne said, "Could we arrange a meeting? I'm looking forward to having an opportunity to inspect the collection of books that Mr. Frye purchased from me. I can come up there almost any time. What day would be convenient for you?"

Joshua wasn't looking forward to meeting and doing business with this man. He decided to stall the occultist until the other appraisers had seen the books. Perhaps one of those men would understand the value of the collection and would make an equitable offer to the estate; then it wouldn't be necessary to traffic with Latham Hawthorne.

"I'll have to get back to you on that," Joshua said. "I've got a lot of other things to take care of first. It's a large and rather complex estate. It'll take quite a few weeks to get it all wrapped up."

"I'll be waiting for your call."

"Two more things before you hang up," Joshua said.

"Yes?"

"Did Mr. Frye say why he had such an obsessive fear of his mother?"

"I don't know what she did to him," Hawthorne said, "but he hated her with all his heart. I've never seen such raw, black hatred as when he spoke of her."

"I knew them both," Joshua said. "I never saw anything like that between them. I always thought he worshipped her."

"Then it must have been a secret hatred that he'd nurtured for a long time," Hawthorne said.

"But what could she have done to him?"

"As I said, he never told me. But there was something behind it, something so bad that he couldn't even bring himself to discuss it. You said there were two things you wanted to ask about. What's the other one?"

"Did Bruno mention a double?"

"Double?"

"A look-alike. Someone who could pass for him."

"Considering his size and his unusual voice, finding a double wouldn't be easy."

"Apparently, he managed to do it. I'm trying to find out why he thought it was necessary."

"Can't this look-alike tell you? He must know why he was hired."

"I'm having trouble locating him."

"I see," Hawthorne said. "Well, Mr. Frye never said a word about it to me. But it just occurred to me. . . ."

"Yes?"

"One reason he might need a double."

"What's that?" Joshua asked.

"To confuse his mother when she came back from the grave looking for him."

"Of course," Joshua said sarcastically. "How silly of me not to think of that."

"You misunderstand," Hawthorne said. "I know you're a skeptic. I'm not saying that she actually came back. I don't have enough information to make up my mind about that. But Mr. Frye was absolutely convinced that she *had* come back. He might have thought that hiring a double would provide him with some protection."

Joshua had to admit that Hawthorne's idea made more than a little sense. "What you're saying is that the easiest way to figure this out is to try to put myself in Frye's head, try to think like he did, like a paranoid schizophrenic."

"If he *was* a paranoid schizophrenic," Hawthorne said. "As I told you, I scoff at nothing."

"And I scoff at everything," Joshua said. "Well . . . thank you for your time and trouble, Mr. Hawthorne."

"No trouble. I'll be waiting for your call."

Don't hold your breath, Joshua thought.

After he put down the receiver, Joshua stood up, stepped to the big window, and stared out at the valley. The land was now settling into shadows under the gray clouds and the purple-blue edges of the oncoming darkness. Day seemed to be changing into night much too rapidly, and, as a sudden cold wind rattled the windowpanes, it also seemed to Joshua that autumn was giving way to winter with the same unnatural haste. The evening looked as if it belonged in gloomy, rainy January rather than early October.

In Joshua's mind, Latham Hawthorne's words spun like dark filaments of a black web on some monstrous spider's loom: *His time is coming, Mr. Rhinehart. There are signs and portents. Soon now. Quite soon.*

For the past fifteen years or so, the world had seemed to be rushing downhill with no brakes, totally out of control. A lot of strange people were out there. Like Hawthorne. And worse. Far worse. Many of them were political leaders, for that was the line of work that jackals often chose, seeking power over others; they had their hands on the controls of the planet, lunatic engineers in every nation, grinning maniacally as they pushed the machine toward derailment.

Are we living in the final days of the earth? Joshua wondered. Is Armageddon drawing near?

Bullshit, he told himself. You're just transferring your own intimations of morality to your perception of the world, old man. You've lost Cora, and you're alone, and you're suddenly aware of growing old and running out of time. Now you have the incredible, grand, egomaniacal notion that the entire world will go with you when you die. But the only doomsday drawing nigh is a very personal one, he told himself. The world will be here after you've gone. It'll be here a long, long time, he assured himself.

But he really wasn't certain of that. The air seemed to be full of ominous currents.

Someone knocked on the door. It was Karen Farr, his industrious young secretary.

"I didn't realize you were still here," Joshua said. He glanced at his watch. "Quitting time was almost an hour ago."

"I took a long lunch. I have a few things to catch up on."

"Work is an essential part of life, my dear. But don't spend all your time at it. Go home. You'll catch up tomorrow."

"I'll be finished in ten minutes," she said. "And just now two people came in. They want to see you."

"I don't have any appointments."

"They've come all the way from Los Angeles. His name's Anthony Clemenza, and the woman with him is Hilary Thomas. She's the one who was—"

"I know who she is," Joshua said, startled. "By all means, show them in."

He walked out from behind his desk and met the visitors in the middle of the room. There were awkward introductions, then Joshua saw to it that they were comfortably seated, offered drinks, poured Jack Daniels for both of them, and pulled up a chair opposite the couch where they were seated side by side.

Tony Clemenza had an air about him that appealed to Joshua. He seemed pleasantly self-assured and competent.

Hilary Thomas radiated a brisk self-confidence and quiet competence much as Clemenza did. She was also achingly lovely.

For a moment, no one seemed to know what to say. They looked at one another in silent anticipation and then tentatively sipped their whiskey.

Joshua was the first to speak. "I've never put a lot of faith in such things as clairvoyance, but, by God, I'm having a little premonition right now. You haven't come all this way just to tell me about last Wednesday and Thursday, have you? Something's happened since then."

"A lot has happened," Tony said. "But none of it makes a whole hell of a lot of sense."

"Sheriff Laurenski sent us to see you," Hilary said.

"We hope you'll have some answers for us."

"I'm looking for some answers myself," Joshua said.

Hilary tilted her head and looked curiously at Joshua. "I think maybe I'm having a premonition of my own," she said. "Something has happened here, too, hasn't it?"

Joshua took a sip of his whiskey. "If I were a superstitious man, I'd probably tell you that . . . somewhere out there . . . a dead man is walking around among the living."

Outside, the last light of day was snuffed from the sky. The coal-black night seized the valley beyond the window. A cold wind tried to find a way around the many panes of glass; it hissed and moaned. But a new warmth seemed to fill Joshua's office, for he and Tony and Hilary were drawn together by their shared knowledge of the incredible mystery of Bruno Frye's apparent resurrection.

Bruno Frye had slept in the back of the blue Dodge van, in a supermarket parking lot, until eleven o'clock that morning, when he had been awakened by a nightmare that resonated with fierce, threatening, yet meaningless whispers. For a while, he sat in the stuffy, dimly-lit cargo hold of the van, hugging himself, feeling so desperately alone and abandoned and afraid that he whimpered and wept as if he were a child.

I'm dead, he thought. Dead. The bitch killed me. Dead. The rotten, stinking bitch put a knife in my guts.

As his weeping gradually subsided, he had a peculiar and disturbing thought: But if I'm dead . . . how can I be sitting here now? How can I be alive and be dead at the same time?

He felt his abdomen with both hands. There were no tender spots, no knife wounds, no scars.

Suddenly, his thoughts cleared. A gray fog seemed to lift from his mind, and for a minute everything shone with a multifaceted, crystalline light. He began to wonder if Katherine really had come back from the grave. Was Hilary Thomas only Hilary Thomas and not Katherine Anne Frye? Was he mad to want to kill her? And all the other women he had killed over the past five years—had they actually been new bodies in which Katherine had hidden? Or had they been real people, innocent women who hadn't deserved to die?

Bruno sat on the floor of the van, stunned, overwhelmed by this new perspective.

And the whispers that invaded his sleep every night, the awful whispers that terrified him. . . .

Suddenly, he knew that, if only he concentrated hard enough, if only he searched diligently through his childhood memories, he would discover what the whispers were, what they meant. He remembered two heavy wooden doors that were set in the ground. He remembered Katherine opening those doors, pushing him into the darkness beyond. He remembered her slamming and bolting the doors behind him, remembered steps that led down, down into the earth. . . .

No!

He clamped his hands over his ears as if he could block out unwanted memories as easily as he could shut out unpleasant noise.

He was dripping sweat. Shaking, shaking.

"No," he said. "No, no, no!"

For as long as he could remember, he had wanted to find out who was whispering in his nightmares. He had longed to discover what the whispers were trying to tell him, so that, perhaps, he could then banish them from his sleep forever. But now that he was on the verge of knowing, he found the knowledge more horrifying and devastating than the mystery had been, and, panic-stricken, he turned away from the hideous revelation before it could be delivered unto him.

Now the van was full of whispers again, sibilant voices, haunting susurrations.

Bruno cried out in fear and rocked back and forth on the floor.

Strange things were crawling on him again. They were trying to climb up his arms and chest and back. Trying to get to his face. Trying to squeeze between his lips and teeth. Trying to scurry up his nostrils.

Squealing, writhing, Bruno brushed them away, slapped at them, flailing at himself.

But the illusion was fed by darkness, and there was too much light in the van for the grotesque hallucinations to hold their substance. He could see there was nothing on him, and gradually the panic drained away, leaving him limp.

For several minutes, he just sat there, his back against the wall of the van, patting his sweaty face with a handkerchief, listening to his ragged breathing grow softer and softer.

Finally, he decided it was time to start looking for the bitch again. She was out there—waiting, hiding, somewhere in the city. He had to locate her and kill her before she found a way to kill him first.

The brief moment of mental clarity, the lightning flash of lucidity was gone as if it had never existed. He had forgotten the questions, the doubts. Once again, he was absolutely certain that Katherine had come back from the dead and that she must be stopped.

Later, after a quick lunch, he drove to Westwood and parked up the street from Hilary Thomas's house. He climbed into the cargo hold again and watched her place from a small, decorative porthole on the side of the Dodge.

A commercial van was parked in the circular driveway at the Thomas house. It was painted white with blue and gold lettering on the sides:

MAIDS UNLIMITED
WEEKLY CLEANING, SPRING CLEANING
& PARTIES
WE EVEN DO WINDOWS

Three women in white uniforms were at work in the house. They made a number of trips from the house to the van and back, carrying mops and brooms and vacuum sweepers and buckets and bundles of rags, bringing out plastic bags full of trash, taking in a machine for steam-cleaning carpets, bringing out fragments of the furniture that Frye had broken during his rampage in the pre-dawn hours of yesterday morning.

Although he watched all afternoon, he didn't get even one quick glimpse of Hilary Thomas, and he was convinced that she was not in the house. In fact, he figured that she wouldn't come back until she was positive that it was safe, until she knew he was dead.

"But I'm not the one who's going to die," he said aloud as he studied the house. "Do you hear me, bitch? I'll nail you first. I'll get you before you have a chance to get me. I'll cut off your fucking head."

At last, shortly after five o'clock, the maids brought out their equipment and loaded it into the back of their van. They locked up the house and drove away.

He followed them.

They were his only lead to Hilary Thomas. The bitch had hired them. They must know where she was. If he could get one of the maids alone and force her to talk, he would find out where Katherine was hiding.

Maids Unlimited was headquartered in a single-story stucco structure on a grubby side street, half a block off Pico. The van that Frye was following pulled into a lot beside the building and parked in a row of eight other vans that bore the company name in blue and gold lettering.

Frye drove past the line of identical white vans, went to the end of the block, swung around at the deserted intersection, and headed back the way he had come. He got there in time to see the three women going into the stucco building. None of them appeared to notice him or to realize that the Dodge was the same van that had been within sight of the Thomas house all day. He parked at the curb, across the street from the housecleaning service, under the rustling fronds of a wind-stirred date palm, and he waited for one of those women to reappear.

During the next ten minutes, a lot of maids in white uniforms came out of Maids Unlimited, but none of them had been at Hilary Thomas's house that afternoon. Then he saw a woman he recognized. She came out of the building and went to a bright yellow Datsun. She was young, in her twenties, with straight brown hair that fell almost to her waist. She walked with her shoulders back, her head up, taking brisk, springy steps. The wind pasted the uniform to her hips and thighs and fluttered the hem above her pretty knees. She got in the Datsun and drove out of the lot, turned left, headed toward Pico.

Frye hesitated, trying to make up his mind if she was the best target, wondering if he should wait for one of the other two. But something felt right about this one. He started the Dodge and pulled away from the curb.

In order to camouflage himself, he tried to keep other traffic between the Dodge and the yellow Datsun. He trailed her from street to street as discreetly as possible, and she seemed utterly unaware that she was being followed.

Her home was in Culver City, just a few blocks from the MGM film studios. She lived in an old, beautifully detailed bungalow on a street of old, beautifully detailed bungalows. A few of the houses were shabby, in need of repairs, gray and sagging and mournful; but most of them were maintained with evident pride, freshly painted, with contrasting shutters, trim little verandas, an occasional stained glass window, a leaded glass door here and there, carriage lamps, and tile roofs. This wasn't a wealthy neighborhood, but it was rich in character.

The maid's house was dark when she arrived. She went inside and switched on lights in the front rooms.

Bruno parked the Dodge across the street, in shadows that were darker than the rest of the newly fallen night. He doused the headlamps, turned off the engine, and rolled down the window. The neighborhood was peaceful and nearly silent. The only sounds came from the trees, which responded to the insistent autumn wind, and from an occasional passing car, and from a distant stereo or radio that was playing swing music. It was a Benny Goodman tune from the Forties, but the title eluded Bruno; the brassy melody floated to him in fragments, at the whimsy of the wind. He sat behind the wheel of the van and waited, listened, watched.

By 6:40, Frye decided that the young woman had neither a husband nor a live-in boyfriend. If a man had shared the house with her, he most likely would have been home from work by this time.

Frye gave it another five minutes.

The Benny Goodman stopped.

That was the only change.

At 6:45, he got out of the Dodge and crossed the street to her house.

The bungalow was on a narrow lot, much too close to its neighbors to suit Bruno's purpose. But at least there were a great many trees and shrubs along the property lines; they helped screen the front porch of the maid's house from the prying eyes of those who lived on both sides of her. Even so, he would have to move fast, get into the bungalow quickly and without causing a commotion, before she had a chance to scream.

He went up two low steps, onto the veranda. The floorboards squeaked a bit. He rang the bell.

She answered the door, smiling uncertainly. "Yes?"

A safety chain was fixed to the door. It was heavier and sturdier than most chains, but it was not one-tenth as effective as she probably thought it was. A

man much smaller than Bruno Frye could have torn this one from its mount-
ings with a couple of solid blows against the door. Bruno only needed to ram his
massive shoulder into the barrier once, hard, just as she smiled and said,
"Yes?" The door exploded inward, and splinters flew into the air, and part of
the broken safety chain hit the floor with a sharp ringing sound.

He leaped inside and threw the door shut behind him. He was pretty sure
that no one had seen him breaking in.

The woman was on her back, on the floor. The door had knocked her down.
She was still wearing her white uniform. She had lovely legs.

He dropped to one knee beside her.

She was dazed. She opened her eyes and tried to look up at him, but she
needed a moment to focus.

He put the point of a knife at her throat. "If you scream," he said, "I'll cut
you wide open. Do you understand?"

Confusion vanished from her warm brown eyes, and fear replaced it. She
began to tremble. Tears formed at the corners of her eyes, shimmered but
didn't spill out.

Impatiently, he pricked her throat with the point of the blade, and a tiny
bead of blood appeared.

She winced.

"No screaming," he said. "Do you hear me?"

With an effort, she said, "Yes."

"Will you be good?"

"Please. Please, don't hurt me."

"I don't want to hurt you," Frye said. "If you're quiet, if you're nice, if you
cooperate with me, then I won't have to hurt you. But if you scream or try to
get away from me, I'll cut you to pieces. You understand?"

In a very small voice, she said, "Yes."

"Are you going to be nice?"

"Yes."

"Do you live alone here?"

"Yes."

"No husband?"

"No."

"Boyfriend?"

"He doesn't live here."

"You expecting him tonight?"

"No."

"Are you lying to me?"

"It's the truth. I swear."

She was pale under her dusky complexion.

"If you're lying to me," he said, "I'll cut your pretty face to ribbons."

He raised the blade, put the point against her cheek.

She closed her eyes and shuddered.

"Are you expecting anyone at all?"

"No."

"What's your name?"

"Sally."

"Okay, Sally, I want to ask you a few questions, but not here, not like this."

She opened her eyes. Tears on the lashes. One trickling down her face. She
swallowed hard. "What do you want?"

"I have some questions about Katherine."

She frowned. "I don't know any Katherine."

"You know her as Hilary Thomas."

Her frown deepened. "The woman in Westwood?"

"You cleaned her house today."

"But . . . I don't know her. I've never met her."

"We'll see about that."

"It's the truth. I don't know anything about her."

"Perhaps you know more than you think you do."

"No. Really."

"Come on," he said, working hard to keep a smile on his face and a friendly note in his voice. "Let's go into the bedroom where we can do this more comfortably."

Her shaking became worse, almost epileptic. "You're going to rape me, aren't you?"

"No, no."

"Yes, you are."

Frye was barely able to control his anger. He was angry that she was arguing with him. He was angry that she was so damned reluctant to move. He wished that he could ram the knife into her belly and cut the information out of her, but, of course, he couldn't do that. He wanted to know where Hilary Thomas was hiding. It seemed to him that the best way to get that information was to break this woman the way he might break a length of heavy wire: bend her repeatedly back and forth until she snapped, bend her one way with threats and another way with cajolery, alternate minor violence with friendliness and sympathy. He did not even consider the possibility that she might be willing to tell him everything she knew. To his way of thinking, she was employed by Hilary Thomas, therefore by Katherine, and was consequently part of Katherine's plot to kill him. This woman was not merely an innocent bystander. She was Katherine's handmaiden, a conspirator, perhaps even another of the living dead. He expected her to hide information from him and to give it up only grudgingly.

"I promise that I'm not going to rape you," he said softly, gently. "But while I question you, I want you to be flat on your back, so that it'll be harder for you to try to get up and run. I'll feel safer if you're on your back. So if you're going to have to lay down for a while, you might as well do it on a nice soft mattress rather than on a hard floor. I'm only thinking of your comfort, Sally."

"I'm comfortable here," she said nervously.

"Don't be silly," he said. "Besides, if someone comes up on the front porch to ring the bell . . . he might hear us and figure that something's wrong. The bedroom will be more private. Come on now. Come on. Upsy-daisy."

She got to her feet.

He held the knife on her.

They went into the bedroom.

Hilary was not much of a drinker, but she was glad that she had a glass of good whiskey as she sat on the couch in Joshua Rhinehart's office and listened to the attorney's story. He told her and Tony about the missing funds in San Francisco, about the dead ringer who had left the bizarre letter in the safe-deposit box—and about his own growing uncertainty as to the identity of the dead man in Bruno Frye's grave.

"Are you going to exhume the body?" Tony asked.

"Not yet," Joshua said. "There are a couple of things I've got to look into first. If they check out, I might get enough answers so that it's not really necessary to open the grave."

He told them about Rita Yancy in Hollister and about Dr. Nicholas Rudge in San Francisco, and he reconstructed his recent conversation with Latham Hawthorne.

In spite of the warm room and the heat of the whiskey, Hilary was chilled to the bone. "This Hawthorne sounds as if he belongs in an institution himself."

Joshua sighed. "Sometimes I think if we put all the crazies into institutions, there'd hardly be anyone left on the outside."

Tony leaned forward on the couch. "Do you believe that Hawthorne really didn't know about the look-alike?"

"Yes," Joshua said. "Curiously enough, I do believe him. He may be something of a nut about Satanism, and he may not be particularly moral in some areas, and he might even be somewhat dangerous, but he didn't strike me as a dissembler. Strange as it might seem, I think he's probably a generally truthful man in most matters, and I can't see that there's anything more to be learned from him. Perhaps Dr. Rudge or Rita Yancy will know something of more value. But enough of that. Now let me hear from the two of you. What's happened? What's brought you all the way to St. Helena?"

Hilary and Tony took turns recounting the events of the past few days.

When they finished, Joshua stared at Hilary for a moment, then shook his head and said, "You've got a hell of a lot of courage, young lady."

"Not me," she said. "I'm a coward. I'm scared to death. I've been scared to death for days."

"Being scared doesn't mean you're a coward," Joshua said. "All bravery is based on fear. Both the coward and the hero act out of terror and necessity. The only difference between them is simply that the coward succumbs to his fear while the person with courage triumphs in spite of it. If you were a coward, you would have run away for a month-long holiday in Europe or Hawaii or some such place, and you'd have counted on time to solve the Frye riddle. But you've come here, to Bruno's hometown, where you might well expect to be in even more danger than you were in Los Angeles. I don't admire much in this world, but I do admire your spunk."

Hilary was blushing. She looked at Tony, then down at her glass of whiskey. "If I was brave," she said, "I'd stay in the city and set up a trap for him, using myself as bait. I'm not really in much danger here. After all, he's busy looking for me down in L.A. And there's no way that he can find out where I've gone."

The bedroom.

From the bed Sally watched him with alert and fear-filled eyes.

He walked around the room, looking in drawers. Then he came back to her.

Her throat was slender and taut. The bead of blood had dribbled down the graceful arc of flesh to her collarbone.

She saw him looking at the blood, and she reached up with one hand, touched it, stared at her stained fingers.

"Don't worry," he said. "It's only a scratch."

Sally's bedroom, at the rear of the neat little bungalow, was decorated entirely in earth tones. Three walls were painted beige; the fourth was covered with burlap wallpaper. The carpet was chocolate brown. The bedspread and the matching drapes were a coffee and cream abstract pattern, restful swirls of natural shades that soothed the eye. The highly polished mahogany furniture gleamed where it was touched by the soft, shaded, amber glow that came from one of the two copper-plated bedside lamps that stood on the nightstands.

She lay on the bed, on her back, legs together, arms at her sides, hands fisted. She was still wearing her white uniform; it was pulled down demurely to her knees. Her long chestnut brown hair was spread out like a fan around her head. She was quite pretty.

Bruno sat on the edge of the bed beside her. "Where is Katherine?"

She blinked. Tears slid out of the corners of her eyes. She was weeping, but silently, afraid to shriek and wail and groan, afraid that the slightest sound would cause him to stab her.

He repeated the question: "Where is Katherine?"

"I told you, I don't know anyone named Katherine," she said. Her speech was halting, tremulous; each word required a separate struggle. Her sensual lower lip quivered as she spoke.

"You know who I mean," he said sharply. "Don't play games with me. She calls herself Hilary Thomas now."

"Please. Please . . . let me go."

He held the knife up to her right eye, the point directed at the widened pupil. "Where is Hilary Thomas?"

"Oh, Jesus," she said shakily. "Look, mister, there's some sort of mix-up. A mistake. You're making a big mistake."

"You want to lose your eye?"

Sweat popped out along her hairline.

"You want to be half blind?" he asked.

"I don't know where she is," Sally said miserably.

"Don't lie to me."

"I'm not lying. I swear I'm not."

He stared at her for a few seconds.

By now there was sweat on her upper lip, too, tiny dots of moisture.

He took the knife away from her eye.

She was visibly relieved.

He surprised her. He slapped her face with his other hand, hit her so hard that her teeth clacked together and her eyes rolled back in her head.

"Bitch."

There were a lot more tears now. She made soft, mewling sounds and shrank back from him.

"You must know where she is," he said. "She hired you."

"We work for her regularly. She just called in and asked for a special clean-up. She didn't say where she was."

"Was she at the house when you got there?"

"No."

"Was anyone at the house when you got there?"

"No."

"Then how did you get in?"

"Huh?"

"Who gave you the key?"

"Oh. Oh, yeah," she said, brightening a bit as she saw a way out. "Her agent. A literary agent. We had to stop at his office first to get the key."

"Where's that?"

"Beverly Hills. You should go talk to her agent if you want to know where she is. That's who you should see. He'll know where you can find her."

"What's his name?"

She hesitated. "A funny name. I saw it written down . . . but I'm not sure I remember it exactly. . . ."

He held the knife up to her eye again.

"Topelis," she said.

"Spell it for me."

She did. "I don't know where Miss Thomas is. But that Mr. Topelis will know. He'll know for sure."

He took the knife away from her eye.

She had been rigid. She sagged a bit.

He stared down at her. Something stirred in the back of his mind, a memory, then an awful realization.

"Your hair," he said. "You've got dark hair. And your eyes. They're so dark."

"What's wrong?" she asked worriedly, suddenly sensing that she was not safe yet.

"You've got the same hair and eyes, the same complexion that she had," Frye said.

"I don't understand, I don't know what's happening here. You're scaring me."

"Did you think you could trick me?" He was grinning at her, pleased with himself for not being fooled by her clever ruse.

He knew. He *knew.*

"You figured I'd go off to see this Topelis," Bruno said, "and then you would have a chance to slip away."

"Topelis knows where she is. He knows. I don't. I really don't know anything."

"*I* know where she is now," Bruno said.

"If you know, then you can just let me go."

He laughed. "You changed bodies, didn't you?"

She stared at him. "What?"

"Somehow you got out of the Thomas woman and took control of this girl, didn't you?"

She wasn't crying any more. Her fear was burning so very brightly that it seared away her tears.

The bitch.

The rotten bitch.

"Did you really think you could fool me?" he asked. He laughed again, delighted. "After everything you've done to me, how could you think I wouldn't recognize you?"

Terror reverberated in her voice. "I haven't done anything to you. You're not making sense. Oh, Jesus. Oh, my God, my God. What do you want from me?"

Bruno leaned toward her, put his face close to hers. He peered into her eyes and said, "You're in there, aren't you? You're in there, deep down in there, hiding from me, aren't you? Aren't you, Mother? I see you, Mother. I see you in there."

A few fat droplets of rain splattered on the mullioned window in Joshua Rhinehart's office.

The night wind moaned.

"I still don't understand why Frye chose me," Hilary said. "When I came up here to do research for that screenplay, he was friendly. He answered all my questions about the wine industry. We spent two or three hours together, and I never had a hint that he was anything but an ordinary businessman. Then a few weeks later, he shows up at my house with a knife. And according to that letter in the safe-deposit box, he thinks I'm his mother in a new body. Why me?"

Joshua shifted in his chair. "I've been looking at you and thinking. . . ."

"What?"

"Maybe he chose you because . . . well, you look just a bit like Katherine."

"You don't mean we've got another look-alike on our hands," Tony said.

"No," Joshua said. "The resemblance is only slight."

"Good," Tony said. "Another dead ringer would be too much for me to deal with."

Joshua got up, went to Hilary, put one hand under her chin, lifted her face, turned it left, then right. "The hair, the eyes, the dusty complexion," he said thoughtfully. "Yes, all of that's similar. And there are other things about your face that remind me vaguely of Katherine, little things, so minor that I can't really put my finger on them. It's only a passing resemblance. And she wasn't as attractive as you are."

As Joshua took his hand away from her chin, Hilary got up and walked to the attorney's desk. Mulling over what she had learned in the past hour, she stared down at the neatly arranged items on the desk: blotter, stapler, letter opener, paperweight.

"Is something wrong?" Tony asked.

The wind worked up into a brief squall. Another burst of raindrops snapped against the window.

She turned around, faced the men. "Let me summarize the situation. Let me see if I've got this straight."

"I don't think any of us has it straight," Joshua said, returning to his chair. "The whole damned tale is too twisted to be arranged in a nice straight line."

"That's what I'm leading up to," she said. "I think maybe I just found another twist."

"Go ahead," Tony said.

"So far as we can tell," Hilary said, "shortly after his mother's death, Bruno got the idea that she had come back from the grave. For nearly five years, he has been buying books about the living dead from Latham Hawthorne. For five years, he's been living in fear of Katherine. Finally, when he saw me, he decided I was the new body she was using. But why did it take him so long?"

"I'm not sure I follow," Joshua said.

"Why did he take five years to fixate on someone, five long years to select a flesh and blood target for his fears?"

Joshua shrugged. "He's a madman. We can't expect reasoning to be logical and decipherable."

But Tony was sensitive to the implications of her question. He slid forward on the couch, frowning. "I think I know what you're going to say," he told her. "My God, it gives me goose pimples."

Joshua looked from one to the other and said, "I must be getting slow-witted in my declining years. Will someone explain things to this old codger?"

"Maybe I'm not the first woman he's thought was his mother," Hilary said. "Maybe he killed the others before he came after me."

Joshua gaped at her. "Impossible!"

"Why?"

"We'd have known if he'd been running around killing women for the past five years. He'd have been caught at it!"

"Not necessarily," Tony said. "Homicidal maniacs are often very careful, very clever people. Some of them make meticulous plans—and yet have an uncanny ability to take the right risks when something unexpected throws the plans off the rails. They aren't always easy to catch."

Joshua pushed one hand through his mane of snow-white hair. "But if Bruno killed other women—where are their bodies?"

"Not in St. Helena," Hilary said. "He may have been schizophrenic, but the respectable, Dr. Jekyll-half of his personality was firmly in control when he was around people who knew him. He almost certainly would have gone out of town to kill. Out of the valley."

"San Francisco," Tony said. "He apparently went there regularly."

"Any town in the northern part of the state," Hilary said. "Any place far enough away from the Napa Valley for him to be anonymous."

"Now wait," Joshua said. "Wait a minute. Even if he went somewhere else and found women who bore a vague resemblance to Katherine, even if he killed them in other towns—he'd still have to leave the bodies behind. There would have been similarities in the way he murdered them, links that the authorities would have noticed. They'd be looking for a modern-day Jack the Ripper. We'd have heard all about it on the news."

"If the murders were spread over five years and over a lot of towns in several counties, the police probably wouldn't make any connections between them," Tony said. "This is a large state. Hundreds of thousands of square miles. There are hundreds upon hundreds of police organizations, and there's seldom as much information-sharing among them as there ought to be. In fact, there's only one sure-fire way for them to recognize connections between several random killings—and that's if at least two, and preferably three, of the murders take place in a relatively short span of time, within a single police jurisdiction, one county or one city."

Hilary walked away from the desk, returned to the couch. "So it's possible," she said, feeling as cold as the October wind sounded. "It's possible that he's been slaughtering women—two, six, ten, fifteen, maybe more—during the past five years, and I'm the first one who ever gave him any trouble."

"It's not only possible, but probable," Tony said. "I'd say we can count on it." The Xerox of the letter that had been found in the safe-deposit box was on the coffee table in front of him; he picked it up and read the first sentence aloud. " 'My mother, Katherine Anne Frye, died five years ago, but she keeps coming back to life in new bodies.' "

"Bodies," Hilary said.

"That's the key word," Tony said. "Not body, singular. Bodies, plural. From that, I think we can infer that he killed her several times and that he thought she came back from the grave more than once."

Joshua's face was ash-gray. "But if you're right . . . I've been . . . all of us in St. Helena have been living beside the most evil, vicious sort of monster. And we weren't even aware of it!"

Tony looked grim. " 'The Beast of Hell walks among us in the clothes of a common man.' "

"What's that from?" Joshua asked.

"I've got a dustbin mind," Tony said. "Very little gets thrown away, whether I want to hold on to it or not. I remember the quotation from my Catholic catechism classes a long time ago. It's from the writings of one of the saints, but I don't recall which one. 'The Beast of Hell walks among us in the clothes of a common man. If the demon should reveal its true face to you at a time when you have turned away from Christ, then you will be without protection, and it will gleefully devour your heart and rend you limb from limb and carry your immortal soul into the yawning pit.' "

"You sound like Latham Hawthorne," Joshua said.

Outside, the wind shrieked.

Frye put the knife on the nightstand, well out of Sally's reach. Then he grabbed the lapels of her uniform dress, and tore the garment open. Buttons popped.

She was paralyzed by terror. She did not resist him; she could not.

He grinned at her and said, "Now. Now, Mother. Now, I get even."

He ripped the dress all the way down the front and flung it open. She was revealed in bra and panties and pantyhose, a slim, pretty body. He clutched the cups of her bra and jerked them down. The straps bit into her skin and then broke. Fabric tore. Elastic snapped.

Her breasts were large for her size and bone structure, round and full, with very dark, pebbly nipples. He squeezed them roughly.

"Yes, yes, yes, yes, yes!" In his deep, gravelly voice, that one word acquired the eerie quality of a sinister chant, a Satanic litany.

He wrenched off her shoes, first the right, then the left, and threw them aside. One of them struck the mirror above the dresser and it shattered.

The sound of falling glass roused the woman from her shock-induced catatonic trance, and she tried to pull away from him, but fear sapped her strength; she writhed and fluttered ineffectually against him.

He held her without difficulty, slapped her twice with such force that her mouth sagged and her eyes swam. A fine thread of blood unraveled from the corner of her mouth, ran down her chin.

"You rotten bitch!" he said, furiously. "No sex, huh? I can't have any sex, you said. No sex ever, you said. Can't risk some woman finding out what I am, you said. Well, you already know what I am, Mother. You already know my secret, I don't have to hide anything from you, Mother. You know I'm different from other men. You know my prick isn't like theirs. You know who my father was. You know. You know that my prick is like his. I don't have to hide from you, Mother. I'm going to shove it into you, Mother. All the way up into you. You hear me? Do you?"

The woman was crying, tossing her head from side to side. "No, no, no! Oh, God!" But then she got control of herself, locked eyes with him, gazed intently at him (and he could see Katherine in there, beyond the brown eyes, glaring out at him), and she said, "Listen to me. Please, listen to me! You're sick. You're a very sick man. You're all mixed up. You need help."

"Shut up, shut up, shut up!"

He slapped her again, harder than he had done before, swinging his big hand in a long swift arc, into the side of her face.

Each act of violence excited him. He was aroused by the sharp sound of each blow, by her gasps of pain and her birdlike cries, by the way her tender flesh reddened and swelled. The sight of her pain-contorted face and her scared-rabbit eyes stoked his lust to an unbearable white-hot flame.

He was shaking with need, trembling, quivering, quaking. He was breathing like a bull. His eyes were wide. His mouth was watering so excessively that he had to swallow every couple of seconds to avoid drooling on her.

He mauled her lovely breasts, squeezed and stroked them, roughed them up.

She had retreated from the terror, had slipped back into that semi-trance, motionless and rigid.

On the one hand, Bruno hated her and did not care how badly he hurt her. He *wanted* to cause her pain. He wanted her to suffer for all the things she had done to him—for even bringing him into the world in the first place.

But on the other hand, he was ashamed of touching his mother's breasts and ashamed of wanting to stick his penis into her. Therefore, as he pawed her, he tried to explain himself and justify his actions: "You told me that if I ever tried to make love to a woman, she'd know right away that I'm not human. You said she'd see the difference, and she'd know. She'd call the police, and they'd take me away, and they'd burn me at the stake because they'd know who my father was. But you already know. It's no surprise to you, Mother. So I can use my prick on you. I can stick it right up in you, Mother, and no one will burn me alive."

He had never thought of putting it into her while she was alive. He'd been hopelessly cowed by her. But by the time she had come back from the dead in her first new body, Bruno had tasted freedom, and he had been full of daring and new ideas. He realized at once that he must kill her to prevent her from taking over his life again—or dragging him back to the grave with her. But he also realized that he could screw her and be safe, since she already knew his secret. She was the one who had told him the truth about himself; she'd told him ten thousand times. She knew that his father was a demon, a foul and hideous *thing,* for she had been raped by that inhuman creature, impregnated by it against her will. During her pregnancy, she had worn overlapping girdles to conceal her condition. When her time drew near, she went away to give birth under the care of a close-mouthed midwife in San Francisco. Later, she told people in St. Helena that Bruno was the illegitimate son of an old college friend who had gotten in trouble, that his real mother died shortly after his birth, and that her last wish was for Katherine to raise the boy. She brought the baby home and pretended he had been legally placed in her care and custody. She lived in constant, numbing fear that someone would discover Bruno was hers, and that his father was not human. One of the things that marked him as the progeny of a demon was his penis. He had the penis of a demon, different from that of a man. He must always hide it, she said, or he would be uncovered and burned at the stake. She had told him all about those things, had been telling him about them since he was too young to know what a penis was for. So, in a peculiar way, she had become both his blessing and his curse. She was a curse because she kept returning from the grave to regain control of him or to kill him. But she was also a blessing because, if she didn't keep coming back again and again and again, he wouldn't have anyone into whom he could empty the great, hot quantities of semen that built up like boiling lava in him. Without her, he was doomed to a life of celibacy. Therefore, while he regarded her resurrections with horror and outrage, a part of him also eagerly looked forward to each new encounter with each new body that she inhabited.

Now, as he knelt on the bed beside her, looking down at her breasts and at the dark pubic bush that was visible through her pale yellow panties, his erection grew so hard that it hurt. He was aware of the demon-half of his personality asserting itself; he felt the beast surging toward the surface of his mind.

He clawed at Sally's (Katherine's) pantyhose, shredding the nylon as he pulled it down her slim legs. He gripped her thighs in his large hands and forced them apart, and he moved around clumsily on the mattress until he was kneeling between her legs.

She snapped out of the trance again. Suddenly bucking, thrashing, kicking, she tried to rise, but he shoved her back with ease. She pummeled him with her fists, but her punches were without force. Seeing that he was unaffected by her blows, she opened her hands, made claws of them, struck at his face, raked his left cheek with her nails, then went for his eyes.

He jerked back, raised one arm to protect himself, winced as she gouged the back of his hand. Then he fell full-length upon her, crushing her with his big, strong body. He got one arm across her throat and pressed down, choking her.

Joshua Rhinehart washed the three whiskey glasses in his sink at the wet bar. To Tony and Hilary, he said, "The two of you have more at stake in this thing than I do, so why don't you come with me tomorrow when I fly down to see Rita Yancy in Hollister?"

"I was hoping you'd ask us," Hilary said.

"There's nothing we can do here right now," Tony said.

Joshua dried his hands on a dishtowel. "Good. That's settled. Now have you gotten a hotel room for the night?"

"Not yet," Tony said.

"You're welcome to stay at my place," Joshua said.

Hilary smiled prettily. "That's very kind. But we don't want to impose on you."

"You wouldn't be imposing."

"But you weren't expecting us, and we—"

"Young lady," Joshua said impatiently, "do you know how long it's been since I've had house guests? More than three years. And do you know why I haven't had any house guests in three years? Because I didn't invite anyone to stay with me, that's why. I am not a particularly gregarious man. I don't issue invitations lightly. If I felt that you and Tony would be a burden—or, worst of all, boring—I wouldn't have invited you, either. Now let's not waste a lot of time being overly polite. You need a room. I have a room. Are you going to stay at my place or not?"

Tony laughed, and Hilary grinned at Joshua. She said, "Thank you for asking us. We'd be delighted."

"Good," Joshua said.

"I like your style," she told him.

"Most people think I'm a grump."

"But a nice grump."

Joshua found a smile of his own. "Thank you. I think I'll have that engraved on my tombstone. 'Here lies Joshua Rhinehart, a nice grump.' "

As they were leaving the office, the telephone rang, and Joshua went back to his desk. Dr. Nicholas Rudge was calling from San Francisco.

Bruno Frye was still on top of the woman, pinning her to the mattress, one muscular arm across her throat.

She gagged and fought for breath. Her face was red, dark, twisted in agony. She excited him.

"Don't fight me, Mother. Don't fight me like this. You know it's useless. You know I'll win in the end."

She writhed under his superior weight and strength. She tried to arch her back and roll to one side, and when she failed to throw him off, she was shaken by violent involuntary muscle spasms as her body reacted to the growing interruption in her air supply and in the supply of blood to her brain. At last, she seemed to realize she would never be able to get free of him, that she had absolutely no hope of escape, and so she went limp in defeat.

Convinced that the woman had surrendered spiritually as well as physically, Frye lifted his arm from her bruised throat. He raised up on his knees, taking his weight off her.

She put her hands to her neck. She gagged and coughed uncontrollably.

In a frenzy now, his heart pounding, blood roaring in his ears, aching with need, Frye got up, stood beside the bed, stripped off his clothes, threw them on top of the dresser, out of the way.

He looked down at his erection. The sight of it thrilled him. The steeliness of it. The size of it. The angry color.

He climbed onto the bed again.

She was docile now. Her eyes had a vacant look.

He ripped off her pale yellow panties and positioned himself between her slim legs. Saliva drooled out of his mouth. Dripped on her breasts.

He thrust into her. He thrust his demon staff all the way into her. Growling like an animal. Stabbed her with his demonic penis. He stabbed and stabbed her, until his semen flowered within her.

He pictured the milky fluid. Pictured it flowering from him, deep inside her.

He thought of blood blossoming from a wound. Red petals spreading from a deep knife wound.

Both thoughts wildly excited him: semen and blood.

He didn't go soft.

Sweating, grunting, slobbering, he made thrust after thrust after thrust. Into her. Into. In.

Later, he would use the knife.

Joshua Rhinehart flipped a switch on his desk phone, putting the call from Dr. Nicholas Rudge on the conference speaker, so Tony and Hilary could hear the conversation.

"I tried your home number first," Rudge said. "I didn't expect you to be at the office at this hour."

"I'm a workaholic, doctor."

"You should try to do something about it," Rudge said with what sounded like genuine concern. "That's no way to live. I've treated more than a few overly-ambitious men for whom work had become the only interest in their lives. An obsessive attitude toward work can destroy you."

"Dr. Rudge, what is your medical specialty?"

"Psychiatry."

"I suspected as much."

"You're the executor?"

"That's right. I presume you heard all about his death."

"Just what the newspaper had to say."

"While handling some estate matters, I discovered that Mr. Frye had been seeing you regularly during the year and a half prior to his death."

"He came in once a month," Rudge said.

"Were you aware that he was homicidal?"

"Of course not," Rudge said.

"You treated him all that time and weren't aware that he was capable of violence?"

"I knew he was deeply disturbed," Rudge said. "But I didn't think he was a danger to anyone. However, you must understand that he didn't really give me a chance to spot the violent side of him. I mean, as I said, he only came in once a month. I wanted to see him at least once every week, and preferably twice, but he refused. On the one hand, he wanted me to help him. But at the same time, he was afraid of what he might learn about himself. After a while, I decided not to press him too hard about making weekly visits because I was afraid that he might back off altogether and even cancel his monthly appointment. I figured a little therapy was better than none, you see."

"What brought him to you?"

"Are you asking what was wrong with him, what he was complaining of?"

"That's what I'm asking, all right."

"As an attorney, Mr. Rhinehart, you ought to be aware that I can't give out that sort of information indiscriminately. I have a doctor-patient privilege to protect."

"The patient is dead, Dr. Rudge."

"That doesn't make any difference."

"It sure as hell makes a difference to the patient."

"He placed his trust in me."

"When the patient is dead, the concept of doctor-patient privilege has little or no legal validity."

"Perhaps it has no legal validity," Rudge said. "But the moral validity remains. I still have certain responsibilities. I wouldn't do anything to damage the reputation of a patient, regardless of whether he's dead or alive."

"Commendable," Joshua said. "But in this case, nothing you could tell me would damage his reputation one whit more than he damaged it himself."

"That, too, makes no difference."

"Doctor, this is an extraordinary situation. This very day, I have come into possession of information which indicates that Bruno Frye murdered a number of women over the past five years, a large number of women, and got away with it."

"You're joking."

"I don't know what sort of thing strikes you as funny, Dr. Rudge. But *I* don't make jokes about mass murder."

Rudge was silent.

Joshua said, "Furthermore, I have reason to believe that Frye didn't act alone. He may have had a partner in homicide. And that partner may still be walking around, alive and free."

"This is extraordinary."

"That's what I said."

"Have you given this information of yours to the police?"

"No," Joshua said. "For one thing, it's probably not enough to get their attention. What I've discovered convinces *me*—and two other people who are involved in this. But the police will probably say it's only circumstantial evidence. And for another thing—I'm not sure which police agency has primary jurisdiction in the case. The murders might have been committed in several counties, in a number of cities. Now it seems to me that Frye might have told you something that doesn't appear all that important by itself, but which fits in with the facts that I've uncovered. If, during those eighteen months of therapy, you acquired a bit of knowledge that complements my information, then perhaps I'll have enough to decide which police agency to approach—and enough to convince them of the seriousness of the situation."

"Well. . . ."

"Dr. Rudge, if you persist in protecting this particular patient, yet more murders may occur. Other women. Do you want their deaths on your conscience?"

"All right," Rudge said. "But this can't be done on the telephone."

"I'll come to San Francisco tomorrow, at your earliest convenience."

"My morning is free," Rudge said.

"Shall my associates and I meet you at your offices at ten o'clock?"

"That'll be fine," Rudge said. "But I warn you—before I discuss Mr. Frye's therapy, I'll want to hear this evidence of yours in more detail."

"Naturally."

"And if I'm not convinced that there's a clear and present danger, I'll keep the file sealed."

"Oh, I have no doubt that we can convince you," Joshua said. "I'm quite sure we can make the hair stand up on the back of your neck. We'll see you in the morning, doctor."

Joshua hung up. He looked at Tony and Hilary. "Tomorrow's going to be a busy day. First San Francisco and Dr. Rudge, then Hollister and the mysterious Rita Yancy."

Hilary got up from the couch where she had sat through the call. "I don't care if we have to fly halfway around the world. At least things seem to be breaking. For the first time, I feel that we're actually going to find out what's behind all of this."

"I feel the same way," Tony said. He smiled at Joshua. "You know . . . the way you handled Rudge . . . you've got a real talent for interrogation. You'd make a good detective."

"I'd add that to my tombstone," Joshua said. "Here lies Joshua Rhinehart, a nice grump who would have made a good detective." He stood up. "I'm starved. At home I've got steaks in the freezer and a lot of bottles of Robert Mondavi's Cabernet Sauvignon. What are we waiting for?"

Frye turned away from the blood-drenched bed and from the blood-spattered wall behind the bed.

He put the bloody knife on the dresser and walked out of the room.

The house was filled with an unearthly quiet.

His demonic energy was gone. He was heavy-lidded, heavy-limbed, lethargic, sated.

In the bathroom, he adjusted the water in the shower until it was as hot as he could stand it. He stepped into the stall and soaped himself, washed the blood out of his hair, washed if off his face and body. He rinsed, then lathered up again, rinsed a second time.

His mind was blank. He thought of nothing except the details of cleaning up. The sight of the blood swirling down the drain did not make him think of the dead woman in the next room; it was only dirt being sluiced away.

All he wanted to do was make himself presentable and then go sleep in the van for several hours. He was exhausted. His arms felt as if they were made of lead; his legs were rubber.

He got out of the shower and dried himself on a big towel. The cloth smelled like a woman, but it had neither pleasant nor unpleasant associations for him.

He spent a lot of time at the sink, working on his hands with a brush that he found beside the soap dish, getting every trace of blood out of his knuckle creases, taking special care with his caked fingernails.

On his way out of the bathroom, intending to fetch his clothes from the bedroom, he noticed a full-length mirror on the door, which he hadn't seen on his way to the shower. He stopped to examine himself, looking for smears of blood that he might have missed. He was as spotless and fresh and pink as a well-scrubbed baby.

He stared at the reflection of his flaccid penis and the drooping testicles beneath it, and he tried very hard to see the mark of the demon. He knew that he was not like other men; he had no doubt whatsoever about that. His mother had been terrified that someone would find out about him and that the world would learn that he was half-demon, the child of an ordinary woman and a scaly, fanged, sulphurous beast. Her fear of exposure was transmitted to Bruno at an early age, and he still dreaded being found out and subsequently burned alive. He had never been naked in front of another person. In school, he had not gone out for sports, and he had been excused from gymnasium for supposed religious objections to taking showers in the nude with the other boys. He had never even completely stripped for a physician. His mother had been positive that anyone who saw his sex organs would know at once that his manhood was the genetic legacy of a demon father; and he had been impressed and deeply affected by her fearful, unwavering certainty.

But as he looked at himself in the mirror, he couldn't see anything that made his sex organs different from those of other men. Shortly after his mother's fatal heart attack, he had gone to a pornographic movie in San Francisco, eager to learn how a normal man's penis looked. He'd been surprised and baffled to discover that the men in the film were all very much like him. He'd gone to other pictures of the same sort, but he hadn't seen even one man who was strikingly different from him. Some of them had bigger penises than his; some of them had smaller organs; some were thicker, some thinner; some were curved slightly; some of them were circumcised, and some were not. But those were all just minor variations, not the awful, shocking, fundamental differences which he had expected.

Puzzled, worried, he had gone back to St. Helena to sit with himself and discuss his discovery. His first thought was that his mother had lied to him. But that was very nearly inconceivable. She had recounted the story of his conception several times every week, for years and years, and each time that she had described the hateful demon and the violent rape, she had shuddered and wailed and wept. The experience had been real for her, not some imaginary tale that she had created to mislead him. And yet. . . . Sitting with himself that afternoon five years ago, discussing it with himself, he had been unable to think of any explanation other than that his mother was a liar; and himself agreed with him.

The following day, he had returned to San Francisco, wildly excited, fevered, having decided to risk sex with a woman for the first time in his thirty-five years. He had gone to a massage parlor, a thinly disguised brothel, where he had chosen a slim, attractive blonde as his masseuse. She called herself Tammy, and except for slightly protruding upper teeth and a neck that was just a bit too long, she was as beautiful as any woman he had ever seen; or at least that's how she seemed to him as he struggled to keep from ejaculating in his trousers. In one of the cubicles that smelled of pine disinfectant and stale semen, he agreed to Tammy's price, paid her, and watched as she took off her sweater and slacks. Her body was smooth and sleek and so desirable that he stood like a post, unable to move, awe-stricken as he considered all of the things he could do with her. She sat on the edge of the narrow bed and smiled at him and suggested he undress. He stripped down to his underpants, but when the time came for him to show her his rigid penis, he was unable to take the risk, for he could see himself in a pillar of flame, put to death because of his demonic blood. He froze. He stared at Tammy's slender legs and at her wiry pubic hair and at her round breasts, wanting her, needing her, but afraid to take her. Sensing his reluctance to reveal himself, she reached out and put one hand on his crotch, felt his penis through his shorts. She slowly rubbed him through the thin cloth and said, "Oh, I want that. It's so big. I've never had one like this before. Show me. I want to see it. *I've never had anything like it.*" And as she spoke those words he knew that somehow he *was* different, in spite of the fact that he could not see the difference. Tammy tried to pull off his shorts, and he slapped her face, knocked her backwards, flat on the bed; she bumped her head against the wall, threw her hands up to ward him off, screamed and screamed. Bruno wondered if he should kill her. Even though she had not seen his demonic prick, she might have recognized the inhuman quality of it merely by feeling it through his underwear. Before he could make up his mind what to do, the door of the cubicle flew open in answer to the girl's screams, and a man with a blackjack stepped in from the corridor. The bouncer was as big as Bruno, and the weapon gave him a substantial advantage. Bruno was certain that they were going to overpower him, revile him, curse and spit upon him, torture him, and then burn him at the stake; but to his utter amazement, they only made him put on his clothes and get out. Tammy didn't say another word about Bruno's unusual penis. Apparently, while she knew it was different, she was not aware of exactly *how* different it was; she didn't know that it was a sign of the demon that had fathered him, proof of his hellish origins. Relieved, he had dressed hurriedly and had scurried out of the massage parlor, blushing, embarrassed, but thankful that his secret had not been uncovered. He had gone back to St. Helena and had told himself about the close call he'd had, and both he and himself had agreed that Katherine had been right, and that he would have to furnish his own sex, without benefit of a woman.

Then, of course, Katherine had started coming back from the grave, and Bruno had been able to satisfy himself with her, expending copious quantities of sperm in the many lovely bodies that she had inhabited. He still had most of his sex alone, with himself, with his other self, his other half—but it was wildly exciting to thrust into the warm, tight, moist center of a woman every once in a while.

Now he stood in front of the mirror that was fixed to the door of Sally's bathroom, and he stared with fascination at the reflection of his penis, wondering what difference Tammy had sensed when she'd felt his pulsating erection in that massage parlor cubicle, five years ago.

After a while, he let his gaze travel upward from his sex organs to his flat, hard, muscular belly, then up to his huge chest, and farther up until he met the gaze of the other Bruno in the looking glass. When he stared into his own eyes, everything at the periphery of his vision faded away, and the very foundations of reality turned molten and assumed new forms; without drugs or alcohol, he was swept into an hallucinogenic experience. He reached out and touched the mirror, and the fingers of the other Bruno touched his fingers from the far side of the glass. As if in a dream, he drifted closer to the mirror, pressed his nose to the other Bruno's nose. He looked deep into the other's eyes, and those eyes peered deep into his. For a moment, he forgot that he was only confronting a reflection; the other Bruno was real. He kissed the other, and the kiss was cold. He pulled back a few inches. So did the other Bruno. He licked his lips. So did the other Bruno. Then they kissed again. He licked the other Bruno's open mouth, and gradually the kiss became warm, but it never grew as soft and pleasant as he had expected. In spite of the three powerful orgasms that Sally-Katherine had drawn from him, his penis stiffened yet again, and when it was very hard he pressed it against the other Bruno's penis and slowly rotated his hips, rubbing their erect organs together, still kissing, still gazing rapturously into the eyes that stared out of the mirror. For a minute or two, he was happier than he had been in days.

But then the hallucination abruptly dissolved, and reality came back like a hammer striking iron. He became aware that he really was not holding his other self and that he was trying to have sex with nothing more than a flat reflection. A strong electric current of emotion seemed to jump across the synapse between the eyes in the looking glass and his own eyes, and a tremendous shock blasted through his body; it was an emotional shock, but it also affected him physically, making him twitch and shake. His lethargy burned away in an instant. Suddenly he was re-energized; his mind was spinning, sparking.

He remembered that he was dead. Half of him was dead. The bitch had stabbed him last week, in Los Angeles. Now he was both dead and alive.

A profound sorrow welled up in him.

Tears came to his eyes.

He realized that he couldn't hold himself as he once had done. Not ever again.

He couldn't fondle himself or be fondled by himself as he once had done. Not ever again.

He now had only two hands, not four; only one penis, not two; only one mouth, not two.

He could never kiss himself again, never feel his two tongues caressing each other. Not ever again.

Half of him was dead. He wept.

He never again would have sex with himself as he'd had it thousands of times in the past. Now he would have no lover but his hand, the limited pleasure of masturbation.

He was alone.

Forever.

For a while, he stood in front of the mirror, crying, his broad shoulders bent under the terrible weight of abject despair. But slowly his unbearable grief and self-pity gave way to rising anger. *She* had done this to him. Katherine. The bitch. She had killed half of him, had left him feeling incomplete and wretchedly empty, hollow. The selfish, hateful, vicious bitch! As his fury mounted, he was possessed by an urge to break things. Naked, he stormed through the bungalow—living room and kitchen and bathroom—smashing furniture, ripping upholstery, breaking dishes, cursing his mother, cursing his demon father, cursing a world that he sometimes couldn't understand at all.

In Joshua Rhinehart's kitchen, Hilary scrubbed three large baking potatoes and lined them up on the counter, so that they were ready to be popped into the microwave oven as soon as the thick steaks were approaching perfection on the broiler. The menial labor was relaxing. She watched her hands as she worked, and she thought about little more than the food that had to be prepared, and her worries receded to the back of her mind.

Tony was making the salad. He stood at the sink beside her, his shirt sleeves rolled up, washing and chopping fresh vegetables.

While they prepared dinner, Joshua called the sheriff from the kitchen phone. He told Laurenski about the withdrawal of funds from Frye's accounts in San Francisco and about the look-alike who was down in Los Angeles somewhere, searching for Hilary. He also passed along the mass murder theory that he and Tony and Hilary had arrived at in his office a short while ago. There was really not much that Laurenski could do, for (so far as they knew) no crimes had been committed in his jurisdiction. But Frye was most likely guilty of local crimes of which they were, for the moment, unaware. And it was even more likely that crimes might yet be committed in the county before the mystery of the look-alike was solved. Because of that, and because Laurenski's reputation had been stained slightly when he had vouched for Frye to the Los Angeles Police Department last Wednesday night, Joshua thought (and Hilary agreed) that the sheriff was entitled to know everything that they knew. Even though Hilary could hear only one end of the telephone conversation, she could tell that Peter Laurenski was fascinated, and she knew, from Joshua's responses, that the sheriff twice suggested that they exhume the body in Frye's grave to determine whether or not it actually had been Bruno Frye. Joshua preferred to wait until Dr. Rudge and Rita Yancy had been heard from, but he assured Laurenski that an exhumation would take place if Rudge and Yancy were unable to answer all of the questions he intended to ask.

When he finished talking with the sheriff, Joshua checked on Tony's salad, debated with himself about whether the lettuce was sufficiently crisp, fretted about whether the radishes were too hot or possibly not hot enough, examined the sizzling steaks as if looking for flaws in three diamonds, told Hilary to put the potatoes in the microwave oven, and opened two bottles of California Cabernet Sauvignon, a very dry red wine from the Robert Mondavi winery just down the road. He was rather a fussbudget in the kitchen; his worrying and nitpicking amused Hilary.

She was surprised at how quickly she had developed a liking for the attorney. She seldom felt so comfortable with a person she had known only a couple of hours. But his fatherly appearance, his gruff honesty, his wit, his intelligence, and his curiously off-handed courtliness made her feel welcome and safe in his company.

They ate in the dining room, a cozy, rustic chamber with three white plaster walls, one used-brick wall, a pegged-oak floor, and an open-beam ceiling. Now and then, squalls of big raindrops burst against the charming leaded windows.

As they sat down to the meal, Joshua said, "One rule. No one talks about Bruno Frye until we've put away the last bite of our steak, the last swallow of this excellent wine, the last mouthful of coffee, and the very last sip of brandy."

"Agreed," Hilary said.

"Definitely," Tony said. "I think my mind overloaded on the subject quite some time ago. There *are* other things in the world worth talking about."

"Yes," said Joshua. "But, unfortunately, many of them are just as thoroughly depressing as Frye's story. War and terrorism and inflation and the return of the Luddites and know-nothing politicians and—"

"—art and music and movies and the latest developments in medicine and the coming technological revolution that will vastly improve our lives in spite of the new Luddites," Hilary added.

Joshua squinted across the table at her. "Is your name Hilary or Pollyanna?"

"And is yours Joshua or Cassandra?" she asked.

"Cassandra was correct when she made her prophecies of doom and destruction," Joshua said, "but time after time everyone refused to believe her."

"If no one believes you," Hilary said, "then what good is it to be right?"

"Oh, I've given up trying to convince other people that the government is the only enemy and that Big Brother will get us all. I've stopped trying to convince them of a hundred other things that seem to be obvious truths to me but which they don't get at all. Too many of them are fools who'll never understand. But it gives me enormous satisfaction just to know I'm right and to see the ever-increasing proof of it in the daily papers. *I* know. And that's enough."

"Ah," Hilary said. "In other words, you don't care if the world falls apart beneath us, just so you can have the selfish pleasure of saying, 'I told you so.'"

"Ouch," Joshua said.

Tony laughed. "Beware of her, Joshua. Remember, she makes her living being clever with words."

For three-quarters of an hour, they spoke of many things, but then, somehow, in spite of their pledge, they found themselves talking about Bruno Frye once more, long before they were finished with the wine or ready for coffee and brandy.

At one point, Hilary said, "What could Katherine have done to him to make him fear her and hate her as much as he apparently does?"

"That's the same question I asked Latham Hawthorne," Joshua said.

"What'd he say?"

"He had no idea," Joshua said. "I still find it difficult to believe that there could have been such black hatred between them without it being visible even once in all the years I knew them. Katherine always seemed to dote on him. And Bruno seemed to worship her. Of course, everyone in town thought she was something of a saint for having taken in the boy in the first place, but now it looks as if she might have been far less saint than devil."

"Wait a minute," Tony said. "She took him in? What do you mean by that?"

"Just what I said. She could have let the child go to an orphanage, but she didn't. She opened her heart and her home to him."

"But," Hilary said, "we thought he was her son."

"Adopted," Joshua said.

"That wasn't in the newspapers," Tony said.

"It was done a long, long time ago," Joshua said. "Bruno had lived all but a few months of his life as a Frye. Sometimes it seemed to me that he was more like a Frye than Katherine's own child might have been if she'd had one. His eyes were the same color as Katherine's. And he certainly had the same cold, introverted, brooding personality that Katherine had—and that people say Leo had, too."

"If he was adopted," Hilary said, "there's a chance he *does* have a brother."

"No," Joshua said. "He didn't."

"How can you be so sure? Maybe he even has a *twin!*" Hilary said, excited by the thought.

Joshua frowned. "You think Katherine adopted one of a pair of twins without being aware of it?"

"That would explain the sudden appearance of a dead ringer," Tony said.

Joshua's frown grew deeper. "But where has this mysterious twin brother been all these years?"

"He was probably raised by another family," Hilary said, eagerly fleshing out her theory. "In another town, another part of the state."

"Or maybe even another part of the country," Tony said.

"Are you trying to tell me that, somehow, Bruno and his long-lost brother eventually found each other?"

"It could happen," Hilary said.

Joshua shook his head. "Perhaps it could, but in this case it didn't. Bruno was an only child."

"You're positive?"

"There's no doubt about it," Joshua said. "The circumstances of his birth aren't secret."

"But twins. . . . It's such a lovely theory," Hilary said.

Joshua nodded. "I know. It's an easy answer, and I'd like to find an easy answer so we can wrap this thing up fast. Believe me, I hate to punch holes in your theory."

"Maybe you can't," Hilary said.

"I can."

"Try," Tony said. "Tell us where Bruno came from, who his real mother was. Maybe we'll punch holes in *your* story. Maybe it's not as open and shut as you think it is."

Eventually, after he had broken and torn and smashed nearly everything in the bungalow, Bruno got control of himself; his fiery, bestial rage cooled into a less destructive, more human anger. For a while, after his temper fell below the boiling point, he stood in the middle of the rubble he had made, breathing hard, sweat dripping off his brow and gleaming on his naked body. Then he went into the bedroom and put on his clothes.

When he was dressed, he stood at the foot of the bloody bed and stared at the brutally butchered body of the woman he had known only as Sally. Now, too late, he realized that she hadn't been Katherine. She hadn't been another reincarnation of his mother. The old bitch hadn't switched bodies from Hilary Thomas to Sally; she couldn't do that until Hilary was dead. Bruno couldn't imagine why he had ever thought otherwise; he was surprised that he could have been so confused.

However, he felt no remorse for what he had done to Sally. Even if she hadn't been Katherine, she had been one of Katherine's handmaidens, a woman sent from Hell to serve Katherine. Sally had been one of the enemy, a conspirator in the plot to kill him. He was sure of that. Maybe she had even been one of the living dead. Yes. Of course. He was positive of that, too. Yes. Sally had been exactly like Katherine, a dead woman in a new body, one of those monsters who refused to stay in the grave where she belonged. She was one of *them.* He shuddered. He was certain that she had known all along where Hilary-Katherine was hiding. But she kept that secret, and she deserved to die for her unshakable allegiance to his mother.

Besides, he hadn't actually killed her, for she would come back to life in some other body, pushing out the person whose rightful flesh it was.

Now he must forget about Sally and find Hilary-Katherine. She was still out there somewhere, waiting for him.

He must locate her and kill her before she found a way to kill him first.

At least Sally had given him one small lead. A name. This Topelis fellow. Hilary Thomas's agent. Topelis would probably know where she was hiding.

They cleared away the dinner dishes, and Joshua poured more wine for everyone before telling the story of Bruno's rise from orphan to sole heir of the Frye estate. He had gotten his facts over the years, a few at a time, from Katherine and from other people who had lived in St. Helena long before he had come to the valley to practice law.

In 1940, the year Bruno was born, Katherine was twenty-six years old and still living with her father, Leo, in the isolated clifftop house, behind and above the winery, where they had resided together since 1918, the year after Katherine's mother died. Katherine had been away from home only for part of one year that she had spent at college in San Francisco; she had dropped out of school because she hadn't wanted to be away from St. Helena just to acquire a lot of stale knowledge that she would never use. She loved the valley and the big old Victorian house on the cliff. Katherine was a handsome, shapely woman who could have had as many suitors as she wished, but she seemed to find romance of no interest whatsoever. Although she was still young, her introverted personality and her cool attitude toward all men convinced most of the people who knew her that she would be an old maid and, furthermore, that she would be perfectly happy in that role.

Then, in January of 1940, Katherine received a call from a friend, Mary Gunther, whom she'd known at college a few years earlier. Mary needed help; a man had gotten her into trouble. He had promised to marry her, and strung her along with excuse after excuse, and then had skipped out when she was six months pregnant. Mary was nearly broke, and she had no family to turn to for help, no friend half so close as Katherine. She asked Katherine to come to San Francisco a few months hence, as soon as the baby arrived; Mary didn't want to be alone at that trying time. She also asked Katherine to care for the baby until she, Mary, could find a job and build up a nest egg and provide a proper home for the child. Katherine agreed to help and began telling people in St. Helena that she would be a temporary surrogate mother. She seemed so happy, so excited by the prospect, that her neighbors said she would be a wonderful mother to her own children if she could just find a man to marry her and father them.

Six weeks after Mary Gunther's telephone call, and six weeks before Katherine was scheduled to go to San Francisco to be with her friend, Leo suffered a massive cerebral hemorrhage and dropped dead among the high stacks of oak barrels in one of the winery's huge aging cellars. Although Katherine was stunned and grief-stricken, and although she had to start learning to run the family business, she did not back out of her promise to Mary Gunther. In April, when Mary sent a message that the baby had arrived, Katherine went off to San Francisco. She was gone more than two weeks, and when she returned, she had a tiny baby, Bruno Gunther, Mary's alarmingly small and fragile child.

Katherine expected to have Bruno for a year, at which time Mary would be firmly on her feet and ready to assume complete responsibility for the tyke. But after six months, word came that Mary had more trouble, much worse this time—a virulent form of cancer. Mary was dying. She had only a few weeks to live, a month at most. Katherine took the baby to San Francisco, so that the mother could spend what little time she had left in the company of her child. During Mary's last days, she made all of the necessary legal arrangements for Katherine to be granted permanent custody of the baby. Mary's own parents were dead; she had no other close relatives with whom Bruno could live. If Katherine had not taken him in, he would have wound up in an orphanage or in the care of foster parents who might or might not have been good to him. Mary died, and Katherine paid for the funeral, then returned to St. Helena with Bruno.

She raised the boy as if he were her own, acting not just like a guardian but like a concerned and loving mother. She could have afforded nursemaids and other household help, but she didn't hire them; she refused to let anyone else tend to the child. Leo had not employed domestic help, and Katherine had her father's spirit of independence. She got along well on her own, and when Bruno was four years old, she returned to San Francisco, to the judge who had awarded her custody at Mary's request, and she formally adopted Bruno, giving him the Frye family name.

Hoping to get a clue from Joshua's story, alert for any inconsistencies or absurdities, Hilary and Tony had been leaning forward, arms on the dining room table, while they listened. Now they leaned back in their chairs and picked up their wine glasses.

Joshua said, "There are still people in St. Helena who remember Katherine Frye primarily as the saintly woman who took in a poor foundling and gave him love and more than a little wealth, too."

"So there wasn't a twin," Tony said.

"Definitely not," Joshua said.

Hilary sighed. "Which means we're back at square one."

"There are a couple of things in that story that bother me," Tony said.

Joshua raised his eyebrows. "Like what?"

"Well, even these days, with our more liberal attitudes, we still make it damned hard for a single woman to adopt a child," Tony said. "And in 1940, it must have been very nearly impossible."

"I think I can explain that," Joshua said. "If memory serves me well, Katherine once told me that she and Mary had anticipated the court's reluctance to sanction the arrangement. So they told the judge what they felt was just a little white lie. They said that Katherine was Mary's cousin and her closest living relative. In those days, if a close relative wanted to take the child in, the court almost automatically approved."

"And the judge just accepted their claim of a blood relationship without checking into it?" Tony asked.

"You have to remember that, in 1940, judges had a lot less interest in involving themselves in family matters than they seem to have now. It was a time when Americans viewed government's role as a relatively minor one. Generally, it was a saner time than ours."

To Tony, Hilary said, "You said there were a couple of things that bothered you. What's the other one?"

Tony wearily wiped his face with one hand. "The other's not something that can easily be put into words. It's just a hunch. But the story sounds . . . too smooth."

"You mean fabricated?" Joshua asked.

"I don't know," Tony said. "I don't really know what I mean. But when you've been a policeman as long as I have, you develop a nose for these things."

"And something smells?" Hilary asked.

"I think so."

"What?" Joshua asked.

"Nothing particular. Like I said, the story just sounds too smooth, too pat." Tony drank the last of his wine and then said, "Could Bruno actually be Katherine's child?"

Joshua stared at him, dumbfounded. When he could speak, he said, "Are you serious?"

"Yes."

"You're asking me if it's possible that she made up the whole thing about Mary Gunther and merely went away to San Francisco to have her own illegitimate baby?"

"That's what I'm asking," Tony said.

"No," Joshua said. "She wasn't pregnant."

"Are you sure?"

"Well," Joshua said. "I didn't personally take her urine sample and perform a rabbit test with it. I wasn't even living in the valley in 1940. I didn't get here until '45, after the war. But I've heard her story repeated, sometimes in part and sometimes in its entirety, by people who *were* here in '40. Now you'll say that they were probably just repeating what she had told them. But if she was pregnant, she couldn't have hidden the fact. Not in a town as small as St. Helena. Everyone would have known."

"There's a small percentage of women who don't swell up a great deal when they're carrying a child," Hilary said. "You could look at them and never know."

"You're forgetting that she had no interest in men," Joshua said. "She didn't date anyone. How could she possibly have gotten pregnant?"

"Perhaps she didn't date any locals," Tony said. "But at harvest time, toward the end of summer, aren't there a lot of migrant workers in the vineyards? And aren't a lot of them young, handsome, virile men?"

"Wait, wait, wait," Joshua said. "You're reaching way out in left field again. You're trying to tell me that Katherine, whose lack of interest in men was widely remarked upon, suddenly fell for a field hand."

"It's been known to happen."

"But then you're also trying to tell me that this unlikely pair of lovers carried out at least a brief affair in a virtual fish bowl without being caught or even causing gossip. And *then* you're trying to tell me that she was a unique woman, one in a thousand, a woman who didn't look pregnant when she was. No." Joshua shook his white-maned head. "It's too much for me. Too many coincidences. You think Katherine's story sounds too neat, too smooth, but next to your wild suppositions, her tale has the gritty sound of reality."

"You're right," Hilary said. "So another promising theory bites the dust." She finished her wine.

Tony scratched his chin and sighed. "Yeah. I guess I'm too damned tired to make a whole lot of sense. But I still don't think Katherine's story makes perfect sense, either. There's something more to it. Something she was hiding. Something strange."

In Sally's kitchen, standing on broken dishes, Bruno Frye opened the telephone book and looked up the number of Topelis & Associates. Their offices were in Beverly Hills. He dialed and got an answering service, which is what he had expected.

"I've got an emergency here," he told the answering service operator, "and I thought maybe you could help me."

"Emergency?" she asked.

"Yes. You see, my sister is one of Mr. Topelis's clients. There's been a death in the family, and I've got to get hold of her right away."

"Oh, I'm sorry," she said.

"The thing of it is, my sister's apparently off on a short holiday, and I don't know where she's gone."

"I see."

"It's urgent that I get in touch with her."

"Well, ordinarily, I'd pass your message right on to Mr. Topelis. But he's out tonight, and he didn't leave a number where he could be reached."

"I wouldn't want to bother him anyway," Bruno said. "I thought, with all the calls you take for him, maybe *you* might know where my sister is. I mean, maybe she called in and left word for Mr. Topelis, something that would indicate where she was."

"What's your sister's name?"

"Hilary Thomas."

"Oh, yes! I do know where she is."

"That's wonderful. Where?"

"I didn't take a message from her. But someone called in just a while ago and left a message for Mr. Topelis to pass on to her. Hold the line just a sec. Okay?"

"Sure."

"I've got it written down here somewhere."

Bruno waited patiently while she sorted through her memos.

Then she said, "Here it is. A Mr. Wyant Stevens called. He wanted Mr. Topelis to tell Miss Thomas that he, Mr. Stevens, was eager to handle the paintings. Mr. Stevens said he wanted her to know he wouldn't be able to sleep until she got back from St. Helena and gave him a chance to strike a deal. So she must be in St. Helena."

Bruno was shocked.

He couldn't speak.

"I don't know what hotel or motel," the operator said apologetically. "But there aren't really many places to stay in all of Napa Valley, so you shouldn't have any trouble finding her."

"No trouble," Bruno said shakily.

"Does she know anyone in St. Helena?"

"Huh?"

"I just thought maybe she's staying with friends," the operator suggested.

"Yes," Bruno said. "I think I know just where she is."

"I'm really sorry about the death."

"What?"

"The death in the family."

"Oh," Bruno said. He licked his lips nervously. "Yes. There have been quite a few deaths in the family the past five years. Thank you for your help."

"No trouble."

He hung up.

She was in St. Helena.

The brazen bitch had gone back.

Why? My God, what was she doing? What was she after? What was she up to?

Whatever she had in mind, it would not do him any good. That was for damned sure.

Frantic, afraid that she was planning some trick that would be the death of him, he began to call the airlines at Los Angeles International, trying to get a seat on a flight north. There were no commuter planes until morning, and all of the early flights were already booked solid. He wouldn't be able to get out of L.A. until tomorrow afternoon.

That would be too late.

He knew it. Sensed it.

He had to move fast.

He decided to drive. The night was still young. If he stayed behind the wheel all night and kept the accelerator to the floor, he could reach St. Helena by dawn.

He had a feeling his life depended on it.

He hurried out of the bungalow, stumbling through ruined furniture and other rubble, leaving the front door wide open, not bothering to be careful, not taking time to see if anyone was nearby. He sprinted across the lawn, into the dark and deserted street, toward his van.

After they enjoyed coffee with brandy in the den, Joshua showed Tony and Hilary to the guest room and connecting bath at the far end of the house from his own sleeping quarters. The chamber was large and pleasant, with deep window sills and leaded glass windows like those in the dining room. The bed was an enormous fourposter that delighted Hilary.

After they said goodnight to Joshua and closed the bedroom door, and after they drew the drapes over the windows to prevent the eyeless night from gazing blindly in at them, they took a shower together to soothe their aching muscles. They were quite exhausted, and they intended only to try to recapture the sweet, relaxing, childlike asexual pleasure of the bath that they had shared the previous night at the airport hotel in L.A. Neither of them expected passion to raise its lovely head. However, as he lathered her breasts, the gentle, rhythmic, circular movements of his hands made her skin tingle and sent wonderful shivers through her. He cupped her breasts, filled his large hands with them, and her nipples hardened and rose through the soapy foam that sheathed them. He went to his knees and washed her belly, her long slim legs, her buttocks. For Hilary, the world shrank to a small sphere, to just a few sights and sounds and exquisite sensations: the odor of lilac-scented soap, the hiss and patter of falling water, the swirling patterns of steam, his lean and supple body glistening as water cascaded over his well-defined muscles, the eager and incredible growth of his manhood as she took her turn lathering him. By the time they were finished showering, they had forgotten how tired they were; they had forgotten their aching muscles; only desire remained.

On the fourposter bed, in the soft glow of a single lamp, he held her and kissed her eyes, her nose, her lips. He kissed her chin, her neck, her turgid nipples.

"Please," she said. "Now."

"Yes," he said against the hollow of her throat.

She opened her legs to him, and he entered her.

"Hilary," he said. "My sweet, sweet Hilary."

He drove into her with great strength and yet with tenderness, filled her up.

She rocked in time with him. Her hands moved over his broad back, tracing the outlines of his muscles. She had never felt so alive, so energized. In only a minute, she began to come, and she thought she might never stop, just rise from peak to peak, on and on, forever and ever, without end.

As he moved within her, they became one body and soul in a way she had never been with any other man. And she knew Tony felt it, too, this unique and astonishingly deep bonding. They were physically, emotionally, intellectually, and psychically joined, molded into a single being that was far superior to the sum of its two halves, and in that moment of phenomenal synergism—

which neither of them had experienced with other lovers—Hilary knew that what they had was so special, so important, so rare, so powerful, that it would last as long as they lived. As she called his name and lifted up to meet his thrusts and climaxed yet again, and as he began to spurt within the deep darkness of her, she knew, as she had known the first time they'd made love, that she could trust him and rely on him as she'd never been able to trust or rely upon another human being; and, best of all, she knew that she would never be alone again.

Afterwards, as they lay together beneath the covers, he said, "Will you tell me about the scar on your side?"

"Yes. Now I will."

"It looks like a bullet wound."

"It is. I was nineteen, living in Chicago. I'd been out of high school for a year. I was working as a typist, trying to save enough money so I could get a place of my own. I was paying Earl and Emma rent for my room."

"Earl and Emma?"

"My parents."

"You called them by their first names?"

"I never thought of them as my father and mother."

"They must have hurt you a lot," he said sympathetically.

"Every chance they got."

"If you don't want to talk about it now—"

"I do," she said. "Suddenly, for the first time in my life, I *want* to talk about it. It doesn't hurt to talk about it. Because now I've got you, and that makes up for all the bad days."

"My family was poor," Tony said. "But there was love in our house."

"You were lucky."

"I'm sorry for you, Hilary."

"It's over," she said. "They've been dead a long time, and I should have exorcised them years ago."

"Tell me."

"I was paying them a few dollars rent each week, which they used to buy a little more booze, but I was socking away everything else I earned as a typist. Every penny. Not much, but it grew in the bank. I didn't even spend anything for lunch; I went without. I was determined to get an apartment of my own. I didn't even care if it was another shabby place with dark little rooms and bad plumbing and cockroaches—just so Earl and Emma didn't come with it."

Tony kissed her cheek, the corner of her mouth.

She said, "Finally, I saved up enough. I was ready to move out. One more day, one more paycheck, and I was going to be on my way."

She trembled.

Tony held her close.

"I came home from work that day," Hilary said, "and I went into the kitchen—and there was Earl holding Emma against the refrigerator. He had a gun. The barrel was jammed into her teeth."

"My God."

"He was going through a very bad siege of. . . . Do you know what delirium tremens are?"

"Sure. They're hallucinations. Spells of mindless fear. It's something that happens to really chronic alcoholics. I've dealt with people who've been having delirium tremens. They can be violent and unpredictable."

"Earl had that gun against her teeth, which she kept clenched, and he started screaming crazy stuff about giant worms that he thought were coming out of the walls. He accused Emma of letting the worms out of the walls, and he wanted her to stop them. I tried to talk to him, but he wasn't listening. And then the worms kept coming out of the walls and started slithering around his feet; he got furious with Emma, and he pulled the trigger."

"Jesus."

"I saw her face blown away."

"Hilary—"

"I need to talk about it."

"All right."

"I've never talked about it before."

"I'm listening."

"I ran out of the kitchen when he shot her," Hilary said. "I knew I couldn't make it out of the apartment and down the hall before he shot me in the back, so I ducked the other way, into my room. I closed and locked the door, but he shot the lock off. By then, he was convinced that I was the one causing the worms to come out of the walls. He shot me. It wasn't anywhere close to being a fatal wound, but it hurt like hell, like a white-hot poker in my side, and it bled a lot."

"Why didn't he shoot you again? What saved you?"

"I stabbed him," she said.

"Stabbed? Where'd you get the knife?"

"I kept one in my room. I'd had it since I was eight. I'd never used it until then. But I always thought that if one of their beatings got out of hand and it looked like they were going to finish me, I'd cut them to save myself. So I cut Earl about the same instant he pulled the trigger. I didn't hurt him any worse than he hurt me, but he was shocked, terrified at the sight of his own blood. He ran out of the room, back to the kitchen. He started shouting at Emma again, telling her to make the worms go away before they smelled his blood and came after him. Then he emptied his gun into her because she wouldn't send the worms away. I was hurting something terrible from the wound in my side, and I was scared, but I tried to count the shots. When I thought he'd used up his ammunition, I hobbled out of my room and tried to make it to the front door. But he had several boxes of bullets. He had reloaded. He saw me and shot at me from the kitchen, and I ran back to my room. I barricaded the door with a dresser and hoped help would come before I bled to death. Out in the kitchen, Earl kept screaming about the worms, and then about giant crabs at the windows, and he kept emptying the gun into Emma. He put almost a hundred and fifty rounds into her before it was all over. She was torn to pieces. The kitchen was a charnel house."

Tony cleared his throat. "What happened to him?"

"He killed himself when the SWAT team finally broke in."

"And you?"

"A week in the hospital. A scar to remind me."

They were silent for a while.

Beyond the drapes, beyond the leaded windows, the night wind coughed.

"I don't know what to say," Tony said.

"Tell me you love me."

"I do."

"Tell me."

"I love you."

"I love you, Tony."

He kissed her.

"I love you more than I ever thought I could love anyone," she said. "In just a week, you've changed me forever."

"You're damned strong," he said admiringly.

"You give me strength."

"You had plenty of that before I came along."

"Not enough. You give me more. Usually . . . just thinking about that day he shot me . . . I get upset, scared all over again, as if it just happened yesterday. But I didn't get scared this time. I told you all about it, and I was hardly affected. You know why?"

"Why?"

"Because all the terrible things that happened in Chicago, the shooting and everything that came before it, all of that is ancient history now. None of it matters any more. I have you, and you make up for all the bad times. You balance the scales. In fact, you tip the scales in my favor."

"It works both ways, you know. I need you as much as you need me."

"I know. That's what makes it so perfect."

They were silent again.

Then she said, "There's another reason that those memories of Chicago don't scare me any more. I mean, besides the fact that I've got you now."

"What's that?"

"Well, it has to do with Bruno Frye. Tonight I began to realize that he and I have a lot in common. It looks like he endured the same sort of torture from Katherine that I got from Earl and Emma. But he cracked, and I didn't. That big strong man cracked, but I held on. That means something to me. It means a lot. It tells me that I shouldn't worry so much, that I should not be afraid of opening myself to people, that I can take just about anything the world throws at me."

"That's what I told you. You're strong, tough, hard as nails," Tony said.

"I'm not hard. Feel me. Do I feel hard?"

"Not here," he said.

"What about here?"

"Firm," he said.

"Firm isn't the same as hard."

"You feel nice."

"Nice isn't the same as hard either."

"Nice and firm and warm," he said.

She squeezed him.

"*This* is hard," she said, grinning.

"But it's not hard to make it soft again. Want me to show you?"

"Yes," she said. "Yes. Show me."

They made love again.

As Tony filled her up and explored her with long silken strokes, as waves of pleasure crashed through her, she was sure that everything would be all right. The act of love reassured her, gave her tremendous confidence in the future. Bruno Frye had not come back from the grave. She wasn't being stalked by a walking corpse. There was a logical explanation. Tomorrow they would talk to Dr. Rudge and Rita Yancy, and they would learn what lay behind the mystery of the Frye look-alike. They would uncover enough information and proof to help the police, and the double would be found, arrested. The danger would pass. Then she would always be with Tony, and Tony with her, and then nothing really bad could happen. Nothing could hurt her. Neither Bruno Frye nor anyone else could hurt her. She was happy and safe at last.

Later, as she lay on the edge of sleep, a sharp crash of thunder filled the sky, rolled down the mountains, into the valley, and over the house.

A strange thought flashed through her mind: *The thunder is a warning. It's an omen. It's telling me to be careful and not to be so damned sure of myself.*

But before she could explore that thought further, she fell off the edge of sleep, all the way down into it.

* * *

Frye drove north from Los Angeles, traveling near the sea at first, then swinging inland with the freeway.

California had just come out of one of its periodic gasoline shortages. Service stations were open. Fuel was available. The freeway was a concrete artery running through the flesh of the state. The twin scalpels of his headlights laid it bare for his examination.

As he drove, he thought about Katherine. The bitch! What was she doing in St. Helena? Had she moved back into the house on the cliff? If she had done that, had she also taken control of the winery again? And would she try to force him to move in with her? Would he have to live with her and obey her as before? All of those questions were of vital importance to him, even though most of them didn't make any sense whatsoever and could not be sensibly answered.

He was aware that his mind was not clear. He wasn't able to think straight regardless of how hard he tried, and that inability frightened him.

He wondered if he should pull over at the next rest area and get some sleep. When he woke he might have control of himself again.

But then he remembered that Hilary-Katherine was already in St. Helena, and the possibility that she was setting a trap for him in his own house was far more unsettling than his temporary inability to order his thoughts.

He wondered, briefly, whether the house was actually his any longer. After all, he was dead. (Or half dead.) And they had buried him. (Or they thought they had.) Eventually, the estate would be liquidated.

As Bruno considered the extent of his losses, he got very angry with Katherine for taking so much from him, leaving him alone, without himself to touch and talk to, and now she had even moved into his house.

He pushed his foot down hard on the accelerator until the speedometer registered ninety miles an hour.

If a cop stopped him for speeding, Bruno intended to kill him. Use the knife. Cut him open. Rip him up. No one was going to stop Bruno from getting to St. Helena before sunrise.

CHAPTER 7

AFRAID THAT HE would be seen by men on the night crew at the winery, men who knew him to be dead, Bruno Frye did not drive the van onto the property. Instead, he parked almost a mile away, on the main road, and walked overland, through the vineyards, to the house that he had built five years ago.

Shining directly through ragged tears in the cloud cover, the cold white moon cast just enough light for him to make his way between the vines.

The rolling hills were silent. The air smelled vaguely of copper sulphate which had been sprayed during the summer to prevent mildew, and overlaying that was the fresh, ozone odor of the rain that had stirred up the copper sulphate. There was no rain falling now. There couldn't have been much of a storm earlier, just sprinkles, squalls. The land was only soft and damp, not muddy.

The night sky was one shade brighter than it had been half an hour ago. Dawn had not yet arrived from its bed in the east, but it would be rising soon. When he reached the clearing, Bruno hunkered down beside a line of shrubbery and studied the shadows around the house. The windows were dark and blank. Nothing moved. There was not a sound except the soft, whispery whistle of the wind.

Bruno crouched by the shrubs for a few minutes. He was afraid to move, afraid that she was waiting for him inside. But at last, heart pounding, he forced himself to forsake the cover and relative safety of the shrubbery; he got up and walked to the front door.

His left hand held a flashlight that wasn't switched on, and his right hand held a knife. He was prepared to lunge and thrust at the slightest movement, but there was no movement other than his own.

At the doorstep, he put the flashlight down, fished a key out of his jacket pocket, unlocked the door. He picked up the flash, pushed the door open with one foot, snapped on the light that he carried, and went into the house fast and low, the knife held straight out in front of him.

She wasn't waiting in the foyer.

Bruno went slowly from one gloomy, overfurnished room to another gloomy, overfurnished room. He looked in closets and behind sofas and behind large display cases.

She wasn't in the house.

Perhaps he had gotten back in time to stop whatever plot she was hatching.

He stood in the middle of the living room, the knife and the flashlight still in his hands, both of them directed at the floor. He swayed, exhausted, dizzy, confused.

It was one of those times when he desperately needed to talk to himself, to share his feelings with himself, to work out his confusion with himself and get his mind back on the track. But he would never again be able to consult himself because himself was dead.

Dead.

Bruno began to shake. He wept.

He was alone and frightened and very mixed-up.

For forty years, he had posed as an ordinary man, and he had passed for normal with considerable success. But he could not do that any more. Half of him was dead. The loss was too great for him to recover. He had no self-confidence. Without himself to turn to, without his other self to give advice and offer suggestions, he did not have the resources to maintain the charade.

But the bitch was in St. Helena. Somewhere. He couldn't sort out his thoughts, couldn't get a grip on himself, but he knew one thing: He had to find her and kill her. He had to get rid of her once and for all.

The small travel alarm was set to go off at seven o'clock Thursday morning.

Tony woke an hour before it was time to get up. He woke with a start, began to sit up in bed, realized where he was, and eased back down to the pillow. He lay on his back, in the dark, staring at the shadowy ceiling, listening to Hilary's rhythmic breathing.

He had bolted from sleep to escape a nightmare. It was a brutal, grisly dream filled with mortuaries and tombs and graves and coffins, a dream that was somber and heavy and dark with death. Knives. Bullets. Blood. Worms coming out of the walls and wriggling from the staring eyes of corpses. Walking dead men who spoke of crocodiles. In the dream, Tony's life had been threatened half a dozen times, but on each occasion, Hilary had stepped between him and the killer, and every time she had died for him.

It was a damned disturbing dream.

He was afraid of losing her. He loved her. He loved her more than he could ever tell her. He was an articulate man, and he was not the least bit reluctant to express his emotions, but he simply did not have the words to properly describe the depth and quality of his feeling for her. He didn't think such words existed; all of the ones he knew were crude, leaden, hopelessly inadequate. If she were taken from him, life would go on, of course—but not easily, not happily, not without a great deal of pain and grief.

He stared at the dark ceiling and told himself that the dream had not been anything to worry about. It had not been an omen. It had not been a prophecy. It was only a dream. Just a bad dream. Nothing more than a dream.

In the distance, a train whistle blew two long blasts. It was a cold, lonely, mournful sound that made him pull the covers up to his chin.

Bruno decided that Katherine might be waiting for him in the house that Leo had built.

He left his own house and crossed the vineyards. He took the knife and flashlight with him.

In the first pale light of dawn, while most of the sky was still blue-black, while the valley lay in the fading penumbra of the night, he went to the clifftop house. He did not go up by way of the cable car because, in order to board it, he would have to go into the winery and climb to the second floor, where the lower tramway station occupied a corner of the building. He dared not be seen in there, for he figured the place was now crawling with Katherine's spies. He wanted to sneak up on the house, and the only route by which he could do that was the stairs on the face of the cliff.

He started climbing rapidly, two steps at a time, but before he went very far, he discovered that caution was essential. The staircase was crumbling. It had not been kept in good repair, as the tramway had been. Decades of rain and wind and summer heat had leeched away much of the mortar that bound the old structure together. Small stones, pieces of virtually every one of the three hundred and twenty steps, broke off under his feet and clattered to the base of the cliff. Several times, he almost lost his balance, almost fell backwards, or almost pitched sideways into space. The safety railing was decayed, dilapidated, missing whole sections; it would not save him if he stumbled against it. But slowly, cautiously, he followed the switchback path of the staircase, and in time he reached the top of the cliff.

He crossed the lawn, which had gone to weeds. Dozens of rose bushes, once carefully tended and manicured, had sent thorny tentacles in all directions and now sprawled in tangled, flowerless heaps.

Bruno let himself into the rambling Victorian mansion and searched the musty, dust-filmed, spider-webbed rooms which stank of mildew that thrived on the drapes and carpets. The house was crammed full of antique furniture and art glass and statuary and many other things, but it did not hold anything sinister. The woman was not here, either.

He didn't know whether that was good or bad. On the one hand, she hadn't moved in, hadn't taken over in his absence. That was good. He was relieved about that. But on the other hand—where the hell was she?

His confusion was rapidly getting worse. His powers of reasoning began to fail him hours ago, but now he couldn't trust his five senses, either. Sometimes he thought he heard voices, and he pursued them through the house, only to realize it was his own mumbling that he heard. Sometimes the mildew didn't smell like mildew at all, but his mother's favorite perfume; but then a moment later it smelled like mildew again. And when he looked at familiar paintings that had hung on these walls since his childhood, he was unable to perceive what they were depicting; the shapes and colors would not resolve themselves, and his eyes were baffled by even the most simple pictures. He stood before one painting that he knew to be a landscape with trees and wildflowers, but he was not able to *see* those objects in it; he could only remember that they were there; all he saw now were smears, disjointed lines, blobs, meaningless forms.

He tried not to panic. He told himself that his bizarre confusion and disorientation were merely the results of his not having slept all night. He'd driven a long way in a short time, and he was understandably weary. His eyes were heavy, gritty, red and burning. He ached all over. His neck was stiff. All he needed was sleep. When he woke, he would be clear-headed. That was what he told himself. That was what he had to believe.

Because he had searched the house from bottom to top, he was now in the finished attic, the big room with the sloped ceiling, where he had spent so much of his life. In the chalky glow of his flashlight, he could see the bed in which he had slept during the years he'd lived in the mansion.

Himself was already on the bed. Himself was lying down, eyes closed, as if sleeping. Of course, the eyes were sewn shut. And the white nightgown was not a nightgown; it was a burial gown that Avril Tamerton had put on him. Because himself was dead. The bitch had stabbed and killed him. Himself had been stone-cold dead since last week.

Bruno was too enervated to vent his grief and rage. He went to the king-size bed and stretched out on his half of it, beside himself.

Himself stank. It was a pungent, chemical smell.

The bedclothes around himself were stained and damp with dark fluids that were slowly leaking out of the body.

Bruno didn't care about the mess. His side of the bed was dry. And although himself was dead and would never speak again or laugh again, Bruno felt good just being near himself.

Bruno reached out and touched himself. He touched the cold, hard, rigid hand and held it.

Some of the painful loneliness abated.

Bruno did not feel whole, of course. He would never feel whole again, for half of him was dead. But lying there beside his corpse, he did not feel all alone either.

Leaving the flashlight on to dispel the darkness in the shuttered attic bedroom, Bruno fell asleep.

Dr. Nicholas Rudge's office was on the twentieth floor of a skyscraper in the heart of San Francisco. Apparently, Hilary thought, the architect either had never heard of the unpleasant term "earthquake country," or he had made a very good deal with the devil. One wall of Rudge's office was glass from floor to ceiling, divided into three enormous panels by only two narrow, vertical, steel struts; beyond the window lay the terraced city, the bay, the magnificent Golden Gate Bridge, and the lingering tendrils of last night's fog. A quickening Pacific wind was tearing the gray clouds to tatters, and blue sky was becoming more dominant by the minute. The view was spectacular.

At the far end of the big room from the window-wall, six comfortable chairs were arranged around a circular teak coffee table. Obviously, group therapy sessions were held in that corner. Hilary, Tony, Joshua and the doctor sat down there.

Rudge was an affable man with the ability to make you feel as if you were the most interesting and charming individual he had encountered in ages. He was as bald as all the clichés (a billiard ball, a baby's bottom, an eagle), but he had a neatly trimmed beard and mustache. He wore a three-piece suit with a tie and display handkerchief that matched, but there was nothing of the banker or of the dandy in his appearance. He looked distinguished, reliable, yet as relaxed as if he'd been wearing tennis whites.

Joshua summed up the evidence that the doctor had said he would need to hear, and he delivered a short lecture (which seemed to entertain Rudge) about a psychiatrist's obligation to protect society from a patient who appeared to have homicidal tendencies. In a quarter of an hour, Rudge heard enough to be convinced that a claim of doctor-patient privilege was neither wise nor justified in this case. He was willing to open the Frye file to them.

"Although I must admit," Rudge said, "if only one of you had come in here with this incredible story, I'd have put very little credence in it. I'd have thought you were in need of my professional services."

"We've considered the possibility that all three of us are out of our minds," Joshua said.

"And rejected it," Tony said.

"Well, if you *are* unbalanced," Rudge said, "then you'd better make it 'the *four* of us' because you've made a believer out of me, too."

During the past eighteen months (Rudge explained), he had seen Frye eighteen times in private, fifty-minute sessions. After the first appointment, when he realized the patient was deeply disturbed about something, he encouraged Frye to come in at least once every week, for he believed that the problem was too serious to respond to once-a-month sessions. But Frye had resisted the idea of more frequent treatments.

"As I told you on the phone," Rudge said, "Mr. Frye was torn between two desires. He wanted my help. He wanted to get to the root of his problem. But at the same time, he was afraid of revealing things to me—and afraid of what he might learn about himself."

"What was his problem?" Tony asked.

"Well, of course, the problem itself—the psychological knot that was causing his anxiety and tension and stress—was hidden in his subconscious mind. That's why he needed me. Eventually, we'd have been able to uncover that knot, and we might even have untied it, if the therapy had been successful. But we never got that far. So I can't tell you what was wrong with him because I don't really know. But I think what you're actually asking me is—what brought Frye to me in the first place? What made him realize that he needed help?"

"Yes," Hilary said. "At least that's a place to start. What were his symptoms?"

"The most disturbing thing, at least from Mr. Frye's point of view, was a recurring nightmare that terrified him."

A tape recorder stood on the circular coffee table, and two piles of cassettes lay beside it, fourteen in one pile, four in the other. Rudge leaned forward in his chair and picked up one of the four.

"All of my consultations are recorded and stored in a safe," the doctor said. "These are tapes of Mr. Frye's sessions. Last night, after I spoke with Mr. Rhinehart on the phone, I listened to portions of these recordings to see if I could find a few representative selections. I had a hunch you might convince me to open the file, and I thought it might be better if you could hear Bruno Frye's complaints in his own voice."

"Excellent," Joshua said.

"This first one is from the very first session," Dr. Rudge said. "For the first forty minutes, Frye would say almost nothing at all. It was very strange. He seemed outwardly calm and self-possessed, but I saw that he was frightened and trying to conceal his true feelings. He was afraid to talk to me. He almost got up and left. But I kept working at him gently, very gently. In the last ten minutes, he told me what he'd come to see me about, but even then it was like pulling teeth to get it out of him. Here's part of it."

Rudge pushed the cassette into the recorder and snapped on the machine.

When Hilary heard the familiar, deep, gravelly voice, she felt a chill race down her spine.

Frye spoke first:

> *"I have this trouble."*
> *"What sort of trouble?"*
> *"At night."*
> *"Yes?"*
> *"Every night."*
> *"You mean you have trouble sleeping?"*
> *"That's part of it."*
> *"Can you be more specific?"*
> *"I have this dream."*
> *"What sort of dream?"*
> *"A nightmare."*
> *"The same one every night?"*
> *"Yes."*
> *"How long has this been going on?"*
> *"As long as I can remember."*
> *"A year? Two years?"*
> *"No, no. Much longer than that."*
> *"Five years? Ten?"*
> *"At least thirty. Maybe longer."*
> *"You've been having the same bad dream every night for at least thirty years?"*
> *"That's right."*
> *"Surely not every night."*
> *"Yes. There's never a reprieve."*
> *"What's this dream about?"*
> *"I don't know."*
> *"Don't hold back."*
> *"I'm not."*
> *"You want to tell me."*
> *"Yes."*
> *"That's why you're here. So tell me."*
> *"I want to. But I just don't know what the dream is."*
> *"How can you have had it every night for thirty years or more and not know what it's about?"*
> *"I wake up screaming. I always know a dream woke me. But I'm never able to remember it."*
> *"Then how do you know it's always the same dream?"*
> *"I just know."*
> *"That's not good enough."*
> *"Good enough for what?"*
> *"Good enough to convince me that it's always the same dream. If you're so sure it's just one recurring nightmare, then you must have better reasons than that for thinking so."*
> *"If I tell you . . ."*
> *"Yes?"*
> *"You'll think I'm crazy."*

"I never use the word 'crazy.' "

"You don't?"

"No."

"Well . . . every time the dream wakes me, I feel as if there's something crawling on me."

"What is it?"

"I don't know. I can never remember. But I feel as if something's trying to crawl in my nose and in my mouth. Something disgusting. It's trying to get into me. It pushes at the corners of my eyes, trying to make me open my eyes. I feel it moving under my clothes. It's in my hair. It's everywhere. Crawling, creeping . . ."

In Nicholas Rudge's office, everyone was watching the tape recorder.

Frye's voice was still gravelly, but there was raw terror in it now.

Hilary almost could see the big man's fear-twisted face—the shock-wide eyes, the pale skin, the cold sweat along his hairline.

The tape continued:

"Is it just one thing crawling on you?"

"I don't know."

"Or is it many things?"

"I don't know."

"What does it feel like?"

"Just . . . awful . . . sickening."

"Why does this thing want to get inside you?"

"I don't know."

"And you say you always feel like this after a dream."

"Yeah. For a minute or two."

"Is there anything else that you feel in addition to this crawling sensation?"

"Yeah. But it's not a feeling. It's a sound."

"What sort of sound?"

"Whispers."

"You mean that you wake up and imagine that you hear people whispering?"

"That's right. Whispering, whispering, whispering. All around me."

"Who are these people?"

"I don't know."

"What are they whispering?"

"I don't know."

"Do you have the feeling they're trying to tell you something?"

"Yes. But I can't make it out."

"Do you have a theory, a hunch? Can you make a guess?"

"I can't hear the words exactly, but I know they're saying bad things."

"Bad things? In what way?"

"They're threatening me. They hate me."

"Threatening whispers."

"Yes."

"How long do they last?"

"About as long as the . . . creeping . . . crawling."

"A minute or so?"

"Yes. Do I sound crazy?"

"Not at all."

"Come on. I sound a little crazy."

"Believe me, Mr. Frye, I've heard stories much stranger than yours."

"I keep thinking that if I knew what the whispers were saying, and if I knew what was crawling on me, I'd be able to figure out what the dream is. And once I know what it is, maybe I won't have it any more."

"That's almost exactly how we're going to approach the problem."

"Can you help me?"

"Well, to a great extent that depends on how much you want to help yourself."

"Oh, I want to beat this thing. I sure do."

"Then you probably will."

"I've been living with it so long . . . but I never get used to it. I dread going to sleep. Every night, I just dread it."

"Have you undergone therapy before?"

"No."

"Why not?"

"I was afraid."

"Of what?"

"Of what . . . you might find out."

"Why should you be afraid?"

"It might be something . . . embarrassing."

"You can't embarrass me."

"I might embarrass myself."

"Don't worry about that. I'm your doctor. I'm here to listen and help. If you—"

Dr. Rudge popped the cassette out of the tape recorder and said, "A recurring nightmare. That's not particularly unusual. But a nightmare followed by tactile and audial hallucinations—that's not a common complaint."

"And in spite of that," Joshua said, "he didn't strike you as dangerous?"

"Oh, heavens, no," Rudge said. "He was just frightened of a dream, and understandably so. And the fact that some dream sensations lingered even after he was awake meant that the nightmare probably represented some especially horrible, repressed experience buried way down in his subconscious. But nightmares are generally a healthy way to let off psychological steam. He exhibited no signs of psychosis. He didn't seem to confuse components of his dream with reality. He drew a clear line when he talked about it. In his mind, there appeared to be a sharp distinction between the nightmare and the real world."

Tony slid forward on his chair. "Could he have been less sure of reality than he let you know?"

"You mean . . . could he have fooled me?"

"Could he?"

Rudge nodded. "Psychology isn't an exact science. And by comparison, psychiatry is even less exact. Yes, he could have fooled me, especially since I only saw him once a month and didn't have a chance to observe the mood swings and personality changes that would have been more evident if we'd had weekly contact."

"In light of what Joshua told you a while ago," Hilary said, "do you feel you *were* fooled?"

Rudge smiled ruefully. "It looks as if I was, doesn't it?"

He picked up the second cassette that had been wound to a pre-selected point in another conversation between him and Frye, and he slipped it into the recorder.

> *"You've never mentioned your mother."*
> *"What about her?"*
> *"That's what I'm asking you."*
> *"You're full of questions, aren't you?"*
> *"With some patients, I hardly ever have to ask anything. They just open up and start talking."*
> *"Yeah? What do they talk about?"*
> *"Quite often they talk about their mothers."*
> *"Must get boring for you."*
> *"Very seldom. Tell me about your mother."*
> *"Her name was Katherine."*
> *"And?"*
> *"I don't have anything to say about her."*
> *"Everyone has something to say about his mother—and his father."*

For almost a minute, there was silence. The tape wound from spool to spool, producing only a hissing sound.

"I'm just waiting him out," Rudge said, interpreting the silence for them. "He'll speak in a moment."

> *"Doctor Rudge?"*
> *"Yes?"*
> *"Do you think . . . ?"*
> *"What is it?"*
> *"Do you think the dead stay dead?"*
> *"Are you asking if I'm religious?"*
> *"No. I mean . . . do you think that a person can die . . . and then come back from the grave?"*
> *"Like a ghost?"*
> *"Yes. Do you believe in ghosts?"*
> *"Do you?"*
> *"I asked you first."*
> *"No. I don't believe in them, Bruno. Do you?"*
> *"I haven't made up my mind."*
> *"Have you ever seen a ghost?"*
> *"I'm not sure."*
> *"What does this have to do with your mother?"*
> *"She told me that she would . . . come back from the grave."*
> *"When did she tell you this?"*
> *"Oh, thousands of times. She was always saying it. She said she knew how it was done. She said that she would watch over me after she died. She said that if she saw I was misbehaving and not living like she wanted me to, then she's come back and make me sorry."*
> *"Did you believe her?"*
> *" . . . "*
> *"Did you believe her?"*
> *" . . . "*
> *"Bruno?"*
> *"Let's talk about something else."*

"Jesus!" Tony said. "That's where he got the notion that Katherine had come back. The woman planted the idea in him before she died!"

To Rudge, Joshua said, "What in the name of God was the woman trying to do? What sort of relationship did those two have?"

"That was the root of the problem," Rudge said. "But we never got around to exposing it. I kept hoping I could get him to come in every week, but he kept resisting—and then he was dead."

"Did you pursue the subject of ghosts with him in later sessions?" Hilary asked.

"Yes," the doctor said. "The very next time he came in, he started off on it again. He said that the dead stayed dead and that only children and fools believed differently. He said there weren't such things as ghosts and zombies. He wanted me to know that he had never believed Katherine when she'd told him that she would come back."

"But he was lying," Hilary said. "He did believe her."

"Apparently, he did," Rudge said. He put the third tape in the machine.

"Doctor, what religion are you?"

"I was raised a Catholic."

"Do you still believe?"

"Yes."

"Do you go to church?"

"Yes. Do you?"

"No. Do you go to mass every week?"

"Nearly every week."

"Do you believe in heaven?"

"Yes. Do you?"

"Yeah. What about hell?"

"What do you think about it, Bruno?"

"Well, if there's a heaven, there must be a hell."

"Some people would argue that earth is hell."

"No. There's another place with fire and everything. And if there are angels . . ."

"Yes?"

"There must be demons. The Bible says there are."

"You can be a good Christian without taking all of the Bible literally."

"Do you know how to spot the various marks of the demons?"

"Marks?"

"Yeah. Like when a man or a woman makes a deal with the devil, he puts a mark on them. Or if he owns them for some other reason, he marks them, sort of like we brand cattle."

"Do you believe you can really make a deal with the devil?"

"Huh? Oh, no. No, that's just bunk. It's crap. But some people do believe in it. A lot of people do. And I find them interesting. Their psychology fascinates me. I read a lot about the occult, just trying to figure out the kind of people who put a lot of faith in it. I want to understand the way their minds work. You know?"

"You were talking about the marks that demons leave on people."

"Yeah. It's just something I read recently. Nothing important."

"Tell me about it."

"Well, see, there are supposed to be hundreds and hundreds of demons in hell. Maybe thousands. And each one of them is supposed to have his own mark that he puts on people whose souls he claims. Like, for instance, in the middle ages, they believed that a strawberry birthmark on the face was the mark of a demon. And another one was crossed eyes. A third breast. Some people are born with a third breast. It's really not so rare. And there are those who say it's a mark of a demon. The number

> 666. *That's the mark of the chief of all demons, Satan. His people have*
> *the number 666 burned into their skin, under their hair, where it can't*
> *be seen. I mean, that's what the True Believers think. And twins. . . .*
> *That's another sign of a demon at work."*
>
> *"Twins are the handiwork of demons?"*
>
> *"You understand, I'm not saying I believe any of this. I don't. It's*
> *junk. I'm just telling you what some nuts out there believe."*
>
> *"I understand."*
>
> *"If I'm boring you—"*
>
> *"No. I find it as fascinating as you do."*

Rudge switched off the recorder. "One comment before I let him go on. I encouraged him to talk about the occult because I thought it was just an intellectual exercise for him, a way for him to strengthen his mind to deal with his own problem. I am sorry to say that I believed him when he said he didn't take it seriously."

"But he did," Hilary said. "He took it very seriously."

"So it seems. But at the time I thought he was exercising his mind, preparing to solve his own problem. If he could find a way to explain the apparently irrational thought process of far-out people like die-hard occultists, then he would feel ready to find an explanation for the tiny piece of irrational behavior in his own personality. If he could explain occultists, it would be an easier matter to explain the dream that he could not remember. That's what I *thought* he was doing. But I was wrong. Damn! If only he'd been coming in more frequently."

Rudge started the tape recorder again.

> *"You said twins are the handiwork of demons."*
>
> *"Yeah. Not all twins, of course. Just certain special kinds of twins."*
>
> *"Such as?"*
>
> *"Siamese twins. Some people think that's the mark of a demon."*
>
> *"Yes. I can see how that superstition might develop."*
>
> *"And sometimes identical twins are born with both heads covered by*
> *cauls. That's rare. Maybe one. But not two. It's very rare for both twins*
> *to be born with cauls. When that happens, you can be pretty sure those*
> *twins were marked by a demon. At least, that's what some people think."*

Rudge took the tape out of the player. "I'm not sure how that one fits in with what's been happening to the three of you. But since there seems to be a dead ringer for Bruno Frye, the subject of twins seemed like something you'd want to hear about."

Joshua looked at Tony, then at Hilary. "But if Mary Gunther did have two children, why did Katherine bring home only one? Why would she lie and say there was just one baby? It doesn't make any sense."

"I don't know," Tony said doubtfully. "I told you that story sounded too smooth."

Hilary said, "Have you found a birth certificate for Bruno?"

"Not yet," Joshua said. "There wasn't one in any of his safe-deposit boxes."

Rudge picked up the fourth of the four cassettes that had been separated from the main pile of tapes. "This was the last session I had with Frye. Just three weeks ago. He finally agreed to let me try hypnosis to help him recall the dream. But he was wary. He made me promise to limit the range of questions. I wasn't permitted to ask him about anything except the dream. The excerpt

I've chosen for you begins after he was in the trance. I regressed him in time, not far, just to the previous night. I put him back into his dream again."

"*What do you see, Bruno?*"

"*My mother. And me.*"

"*Go on.*"

"*She's pulling me along.*"

"*Where are you?*"

"*I don't know. But I'm just little.*"

"*Little?*"

"*A little boy.*"

"*And your mother is forcing you to go somewhere?*"

"*Yeah. She's dragging me by the hand.*"

"*Where does she drag you?*"

"*To . . . the . . . the door. The door. Don't let her open it. Don't. Don't!*"

"*Easy. Easy now. Tell me about this door. Where does it go?*"

"*To hell.*"

"*How do you know that?*"

"*It's in the ground.*"

"*The door is in the ground?*"

"*For God's sake, don't let her open it! Don't let her put me down there again. No! No! I won't go down there again!*"

"*Relax. Be calm. There's no reason to be afraid. Just relax, Bruno. Relax. Are you relaxed?*"

"*Y-Yes.*"

"*All right. Now slowly and calmly and without any emotion, tell me what happens next. You and your mother are standing in front of a door in the ground. What happens now?*"

"*She . . . she . . . opens the door.*"

"*Go on.*"

"*She pushes me.*"

"*Go on.*"

"*Pushes me . . . through the door.*"

"*Go on, Bruno.*"

"*She slams it . . . locks it.*"

"*She locks you inside?*"

"*Yeah.*"

"*What's it like in there?*"

"*Dark.*"

"*What else?*"

"*Just dark. Black.*"

"*You must be able to see something.*"

"*No. Nothing.*"

"*What happens next?*"

"*I try to get out.*"

"*And?*"

"*The door's too heavy, too strong.*"

"*Bruno, is this really just a dream?*"

"*. . .*"

"*Is it really just a dream, Bruno?*"

"*It's what I dream.*"

"*But is it also a memory?*"

"*. . .*"

"Did your mother actually lock you in a dark room when you were a child?"

"Y-Yes."

"In the cellar?"

"In the ground. In that room in the ground."

"How often did she do that?"

"All the time."

"Once a week?"

"More often."

"Was it a punishment?"

"Yeah."

"For what?"

"For . . . for not acting . . . and thinking . . . like one."

"What do you mean?"

"It was punishment for not being one."

"One what?"

"One. One. Just one. That's all. Just one."

"All right. We'll come back to that later. Now we're going to go on and find out what happens next. You're locked in that room. You can't get out the door. What happens next, Bruno?"

"I'm s-s-scared."

"No. You're not scared. You feel very calm, relaxed, not scared at all. Isn't that right? Don't you feel calm?"

"I . . . guess so."

"Okay. What happens after you try to open the door?"

"I can't get it open. So I just stand on the top step and look down into the dark."

"There are steps?"

"Yes."

"Where do they lead?"

"Hell."

"Do you go down?"

"No! I just . . . stand there. And . . . listen."

"What do you hear?"

"Voices."

"What are they saying?"

"They're just . . . whispers. I can't make them out. But they're . . . coming . . . getting louder. They're coming closer. They're coming up the steps. They're so loud now!"

"What are they saying?"

"Whispers. All around me."

"What are they saying?"

"Nothing. It means nothing."

"Listen closely."

"They don't speak in words."

"Who are they? Who's whispering?"

"Oh, Jesus. Listen. Jesus."

"Who are they?"

"Not people. No. No! Not people!"

"It isn't people whispering?"

"Get them off! Get them off me!"

"Why are you brushing at yourself?"

"They're all over me!"

"There's nothing on you."

"All over me!"
"Don't get up, Bruno. Wait—"
"Oh, my God!"
"Bruno, lie down on the couch."
"Jesus, Jesus, Jesus, Jesus."
"I'm ordering you to lie down on the couch."
"Jesus, help me! Help me!"
"Listen to me, Bruno. You—"
"Gotta get 'em off, gotta get 'em off!"
"Bruno, it's all right. Relax. They're going away."
"No! There's even more of them! Ah! Ah! No!"
"They're going away. The whispers are getting softer, fainter.
They're—"
"Louder! Getting louder! A roar of whispers!"
"Be calm. Lie down and be—"
"They're getting in my nose! Oh, Jesus! My mouth!"
"Bruno!"

On the tape, there was a strange, strangled sound. It went on and on.
Hilary hugged herself. The room suddenly seemed frigid.
Rudge said, "He jumped up from the couch and ran into the corner, over there. He crouched down in the corner and put his hands over his face."
The eerie, wheezing, gagging sound continued to come from the tape.
"But you snapped him out of the trance," Tony said.
Rudge was pale, remembering. "At first, I thought he was going to stay there, in the dream. Nothing like that had ever happened to me before. I'm very good at hypnotic therapy. Very good. But I thought I'd lost him. It took a while, but finally he began to respond to me."
On the tape: rasping, gagging, wheezing.
"What you hear," Rudge said, "is Frye screaming. He's so frightened that his throat has seized up on him, so terrified that he's lost his voice. He's trying to scream, but he can't get much sound out."
Joshua stood up, bent over, switched off the recorder. His hand was shaking. "You think his mother really locked him in a dark room."
"Yes," Rudge said.
"And there was something else in there with him."
"Yes."
Joshua pushed one hand through his thick white hair. "But for God's sake, what could it have been? What was in that room?"
"I don't know," Rudge said. "I expected to find out in a later session. But that was the last time I saw him."

In Joshua's Cessna Skylane, as they flew south and slightly east toward Hollister, Tony said, "My view of this thing is going through changes."
"How?" Joshua asked.
"Well, at first, I looked at it in simple black and white. Hilary was the victim. Frye was the bad guy. But now . . . in a way . . . maybe Frye's a victim, too."
"I know what you mean," Hilary said. "Listening to those tapes . . . I felt so sorry for him."
"It's all right to feel sorry for him," Joshua said, "so long as you don't forget that he's damned dangerous."
"Isn't he dead?"
"Is he?"

* * *

Hilary had written a screenplay that contained two scenes set in Hollister, so she knew something about the place.

On the surface, Hollister resembled a hundred other small towns in California. There were some pretty streets and some ugly streets. New houses and old houses. Palm trees and oaks. Oleander bushes. Because this was one of the drier parts of the state, there was more dust than elsewhere, but that was not particularly noticeable until the wind blew really hard.

The thing that made Hollister different from other towns was what lay under it. Fault lines. Most communities in California were built on or near geological faults that now and then slipped, causing earthquakes. But Hollister was not built on just one fault; it rested on a rare confluence of faults, a dozen or more, both major and minor, including the San Andreas fault.

Hollister was a town on the move; at least one earthquake struck it every day of the year. Most of those shocks were in the middle or lower range of the Richter Scale, of course. The town had never been leveled. But the sidewalks were cracked and canted. A walk could be level on Monday, a bit hoved up on Tuesday, and almost level again on Wednesday. Some days there were chains of tremors that rattled the town gently, with only brief pauses, for an hour or two at a time; but people who lived there were seldom aware of these very minor tremors, just as those who lived in the High Sierra ski country paid scant attention to any storm that put down only an inch of snow. Over the decades, the courses of some streets in Hollister were altered by the evermoving earth; avenues that had once been straight were now a bit curved or occasionally doglegged. The grocery stores had shelves that were slanted toward the back or covered with wire screens to prevent bottles and cans from crashing to the floor every time the ground shook. Some people lived in houses that were gradually slipping down into unstable land, but the sinkage was so slow that there was no alarm, no urgency about finding another place to live; they just repaired the cracks in the walls and planed the bottoms off doors and made adjustments as they could. Once in a while, a man in Hollister would add a room to his house without realizing that the addition was on one side of a fault line and the house on the other side; and as a result, over a period of years, the new room would move with stately, turtlelike determination—north or south or east or west, depending on the fault—while the rest of the house stood still or inched in the opposite direction, a subtle but powerful process that eventually tore the addition from the main structure. The basements of a few buildings contained sinkholes, bottomless pits; these pits were spreading unstoppably under the buildings and would one day swallow them, but in the meantime, the citizens of Hollister lived and worked above. A lot of people would be terrified to live in a town where (as some residents put it) you could "go to sleep at night listening to the earth whisper to itself." But for generations the good people of Hollister had gone about their business with a positive attitude that was wondrous to behold.

Here was the ultimate California optimism.

Rita Yancy lived in a corner house on a quiet street. It was a small home with a big front porch. There were autumn-blooming white and yellow flowers in a border along the walkway.

Joshua rang the bell. Hilary and Tony stood behind him.

An elderly woman came to the door. Her gray hair was done up in a bun. Her face was wrinkled, and her blue eyes were quick, bright. She had a friendly smile. She was wearing a blue housedress and a white apron and sensible old-lady shoes. Wiping her hands on a dish towel, she said, "Yes?"

"Mrs. Yancy?" Joshua asked.

"That's me."

"My name's Joshua Rhinehart."

She nodded. "I figured you'd show up."

"I'm determined to talk to you,'" he said.

"You strike me as a man who either doesn't give up easily or never gives up at all."

"I'll camp out right here on your porch until I get what I've come for."

She sighed. "That won't be necessary. I've given the situation a great deal of thought since you called yesterday. What I decided was—you can't do anything to me. Not a thing. I'm seventy-five years old, and they don't just throw women my age into jail. So I might as well tell you what it was all about, because, if I don't, you'll just keep pestering me."

She stepped back, opened the door wide, and they went inside.

In the attic of the clifftop house, in the king-size bed, Bruno woke, screaming. The room was dark. The flashlight had gone dead while he slept.

Whispers.

All around him.

Soft, sibilant, evil whispers.

Slapping at his face and neck and chest and arms, trying to brush away the hideous things that crawled on him, Bruno fell off the bed. There seemed to be even a greater number of bustling, skittering *things* on the floor than there had been on the bed, thousands of them, all whispering, whispering. He wailed and gibbered, then clamped a hand over his nose and mouth to prevent the things from slithering inside of him.

Light.

Threads of light.

Thin lines of light like loose, luminescent threads hanging from the otherwise tenebrous fabric of the room. Not many threads, not much light, but some. It was a whole lot better than nothing.

He scrambled as fast as he could toward those faint filaments of light, flinging the *things* from him, and what he found was a window. The far side of it was covered by shutters. Light was seeping through the narrow chinks in the shutters.

Bruno stood, swaying, fumbling in the darkness for the window latch. When he found the lock, it would not turn; it was badly corroded.

Screaming, brushing frantically at himself, he stumbled back toward the bed, found it in the seamless blackness, got hold of the lamp that stood on the nightstand, carried the lamp back to the window, used it as a club, and glass shattered. He threw the lamp aside, felt for the bolt on the inside of the shutters, put his hand on it, jerked on it, skinned a knuckle as he forced the bolt out of its catch, threw open the shutters, and wept with relief as light flooded into the attic.

The whispers faded.

Rita Yancy's parlor—that was what she called it, a parlor, rather than using a more modern and less colorful word—almost was a parody of the stereotypical parlor in which sweet little old ladies like her were supposed to spend their twilight years. Chintz drapes. Handmade, embroidered wall hangings—most of them inspirational sayings framed by penny-sized flowers and cute birds—were everywhere, a relentless display of good will and humor and bad taste. Tasseled upholstery. Wingback chairs. Copies of *Reader's Digest* on a dainty occasional table. A basket filled with of balls of yarn and knitting needles. A flowered carpet that was protected by matching flowered runners. Handmade afghans were draped across the seat and the back of the sofa. A mantel clock ticked hollowly.

Hilary and Tony sat on the sofa, on the edge of it, as if afraid to lean back and risk rumpling the covering. Hilary noticed that each of the many knick-knacks and curios were dustfree and highly polished. She had the feeling that Rita Yancy would jump up and run for a dust cloth the instant anyone tried to touch and admire those prized possessions.

Joshua sat in an armchair. The back of his head and his arms rested on antimacassars.

Mrs. Yancy settled into what was obviously her favorite chair; she seemed to have acquired part of her character from it, and it from her. It was possible, Hilary thought, to picture Mrs. Yancy and the chair growing together into a single organic-inorganic creature with six legs and brushed velvet skin.

The old woman picked up a blue and green afghan that was folded on her footstool. She opened the blanket and covered her lap with it.

There was a moment of absolute silence, where even the mantel clock seemed to pause, as if time had stopped, as if they had been quick-frozen and magically transported, along with the room, to a distant planet to be put on exhibition in an extraterrestrial museum's Department of Earth Anthropology.

Then Rita Yancy spoke, and what she said totally shattered Hilary's homey image of her. "Well, there's sure as hell no point in beating around the bush. I don't want to waste my whole day on this damn silly thing. Let's get straight to it. You want to know why Bruno Frye was paying me five hundred bucks a month. It was hush money. He was paying me to keep my mouth shut. His mother paid me the same amount every month for almost thirty-five years, and when she died, Bruno started sending checks. I must admit that surprised the hell out of me. These days it's an unusual son who would pay that kind of money to protect his mother's reputation—and especially after she's already kicked the bucket. But he paid."

"Are you saying you were blackmailing Mr. Frye and his mother before him?" Tony asked, astonished.

"Call it whatever you want. Hush money or blackmail or anything you want."

"From what you've told us so far," Tony said, "I believe the law would call it blackmail and nothing else."

Rita Yancy smiled at him. "Do you think the word bothers me? Do you think I'm afraid of it? All quivery inside? Sonny, let me tell you, I've been accused of worse than that in my time. Is blackmail the word you want to use? Well, it's all right by me. Blackmail. That's what it is. We won't put a prettier face on it. But of course, if you're stupid enough to drag an old lady into court, I won't use the same word then. I'll just say that I did a great favor for Katherine Frye a long time ago, and that she insisted on repaying me with a monthly check. You don't really have any proof otherwise, do you? That's one reason I set it up on a monthly basis in the first place. I mean, blackmailers are supposed to strike and run, take it in one big bite, which is easy for the prosecutor to trace. But who's going to believe that a blackmailer would agree to a modest monthly payment on account?"

"We don't have any intention of bringing criminal charges against you," Joshua assured her. "And we haven't the slightest interest in attempting to recover the money that was paid to you. We realize that would be futile."

"Good," Mrs. Yancy said. "Because I'd make a bloody battle of it if you tried."

She straightened her afghan.

I've got to remember this one, everything about her, Hilary thought. She'd make a great little character role in a movie some day: Grandma with spice and acid and a touch of rot.

"All we want is some information," Joshua said. "There's a problem with the estate, and its holding up the disbursement of funds. I need to get answers to some questions in order to expedite the final settlement. You say you don't want to waste your whole day on this 'damn silly thing.' Well, I don't want to waste months on the Frye estate either. My only motivation in coming here is to get the information I need to wrap up this damn silly thing of *mine*."

Mrs. Yancy stared hard at him, then at Hilary and Tony. Her eyes were shrewd, appraising. Finally, she nodded with evident satisfaction, as if she had read their minds and had approved of what she'd seen in them. "I think I believe you. All right. Ask your questions."

"Obviously," Joshua said, "the first thing we want to know is what you had on Katherine Frye that made her and her son pay you nearly a quarter of a million dollars over the past forty years."

"To understand about that," Mrs. Yancy said, "you'll need a bit of background on me. You see, when I was a young woman, at the height of the Great Depression, I looked around at all the kinds of work I could do to make ends meet, and I decided that none of them offered more than mere survival and a life of drudgery. All but one. I realized that the only profession that offered me a chance at real money was the oldest profession of them all. When I was eighteen, I became a working girl. In those days, in mixed company like this, a woman like me was referred to as a 'lady of easy virtue.' Today, you don't have to tiptoe around it. You can use any damn word you want these days." A strand of gray hair had slipped out of her bun. She pushed it away from her face, tucked it behind her ear. "When it comes to sex—the old slap-and-tickle, as it was sometimes called in my day—I'm amazed at how times have changed."

"You mean you were a . . . prostitute?" Tony asked, expressing the surprise that Hilary felt.

"I was an exceptionally good-looking girl," Mrs. Yancy said proudly. "I never worked the streets or bars or hotels or anything like that. I was on the staff of one of the finest, most elegant houses in San Francisco. We catered exclusively to the carriage trade. Only the very best sort of men. There were never fewer than ten girls and often as many as fifteen, but every one of us was striking and refined. I made good money, as I had expected I would. But by the time I was twenty-four, I realized that there was a great deal more money to be made operating my own house than there was in working in someone else's establishment. So I found a house with a lot of charm and spent nearly all of my savings redecorating it. Then I lined up a stable of lovely and polished young ladies. For the next thirty-six years, I worked as a madam, and I ran a damned classy place. I retired fifteen years ago, when I was sixty, because I wanted to come here to Hollister where my daughter and her husband lived; I wanted to be close to my grandchildren, you know. Grandchildren make old age a lot more rewarding than I'd ever thought it would be."

Hilary leaned back on the couch, no longer worried about rumpling the afghans that were draped across it.

Joshua said, "This is all quite fascinating, but what does it have to do with Katherine Frye?"

"Her father regularly visited my place in San Francisco," Rita Yancy said. "Leo Frye?"

"Yes. A very strange man. I was never with him myself. I never serviced him. After I became a madam, I did very little bedwork; I was busy with the management details. But I heard all the stories that my girls told about him. He sounded like a first-class bastard. He liked his women docile, subservient.

He liked to insult them and call them dirty names while he was using them. He was a strong disciplinarian, if you know what I mean. He had some nasty things he liked to do, and he paid a high price for the right to do them with my girls. Anyway, in April of 1940, Leo's daughter, Katherine, showed up on my doorstep. I'd never met her. I didn't even know he had a child. But he'd told her about me. He'd sent her to me so that she could have her baby in total secrecy."

Joshua blinked. "Her baby?"

"She was pregnant."

"Bruno was her baby?"

"What about Mary Gunther?" Hilary asked.

"There never was such a person as Mary Gunther," the old woman said. "That was just a cover story that Katherine and Leo made up."

"I knew it!" Tony said. "Too smooth. It was just too damn smooth."

"Nobody in St. Helena knew she was pregnant," Rita Yancy said. "She was wearing several girdles. You wouldn't believe how that poor girl had bound herself up. It was horrible. From the time she missed her first period, long before she ever began to swell up, she started wearing tighter and tighter and tighter girdles, then one girdle on top of another. And she starved herself, trying to keep off all the weight she could. It's a miracle she didn't either have a miscarriage or kill herself."

"And you took her in?" Tony asked.

"I'm not going to claim I did it out of the goodness of my heart," Mrs. Yancy said. "I can't stand old women when they're smug and self-righteous, like a lot of the ones I see when I go to the bridge games at the church. Katherine didn't touch my heart or anything like that. And I didn't take her in because I felt I had an obligation to her father. I didn't owe him a thing. Because of what I'd heard about him from my girls, I didn't even like him. And he'd been dead six weeks when Katherine showed up. I took her in for one reason, and I'm not going to pretend otherwise. She had three thousand bucks with her to cover room and board and the doctor's fee. That was a good deal more money then than it is today."

Joshua shook his head. "I can't understand it. She had a reputation as a cold fish. She didn't care for men. She didn't have a lover that anyone knew about. Who was the father?"

"Leo," Mrs. Yancy said.

"Oh, my God," Hilary said softly.

"Are you sure?" Joshua asked Rita Yancy.

"Positive," the old woman said. "He'd been fooling around with his own daughter since she was four years old. He forced her to perform oral sex when she was a small child. Later, as she grew up, he did everything to her. Everything."

Bruno had hoped that a good night's sleep would clear his befuddled mind, wash away the confusion and the disorientation that had plagued him last night and early this morning. But now, as he stood in front of the broken attic window, basking in the gray October light, he was no more in command of himself than he had been six hours ago. His mind was writhing with chaotic thoughts and doubts and questions and fears; pleasant and ugly memories tangled like worms; mental images shifted and changed like puddles of quicksilver.

He knew what was wrong with him. He was alone. All alone. He was only half a man. Torn in half. That's what was wrong with him. Ever since the other half of him had been killed, he'd been increasingly nervous, increasingly unsure of himself. He no longer had the resources that he'd had when both halves of him had been alive. And now, trying to stumble along as only half a person, he was unable to cope; even the smallest problems were beginning to seem insoluble.

He turned away from the window and staggered heavily to the bed. He knelt on the floor beside the bed and put his head on the corpse, on its chest.

"Say something. Say something to me. Help me figure out what to do. Please. Please, help me."

But the dead Bruno had nothing to say to the one who was still alive.

Mrs. Yancy's parlor.

The ticking clock.

A white cat strolled in from the dining room and jumped up on the old woman's lap.

"How do you know that Leo molested Katherine?" Joshua asked. "Surely he didn't tell you about it."

"He didn't," Mrs. Yancy said. "But Katherine did. She was in a terrible state. Half out of her mind. She'd expected her father to bring her to me when her time drew near, but then he died. She was alone and terrified. Because of what she'd done to herself—the girdles and the dieting—her labor was damned difficult. I called in the doctor who gave my girls their weekly health examinations because I knew he would be discreet and willing to handle the case. He was sure the baby would be born dead. He thought there was a pretty good chance Katherine would die, too. She was in hard, agonizing labor for fourteen hours. I've never seen anyone endure the kind of pain that she went through. She was delirious a lot of the time, and when she had her wits about her, she was desperate to tell me what her father had done to her. I think she was trying to patch up her soul. She seemed to be afraid to die with the secret, and so she sort of treated me as if I was a priest listening to her confession. Her father forced her to provide oral sex shortly after her mother died. When they moved into the cliff house, which I gather is fairly isolated, he virtually set about training her to be a sex slave to him. When she was old enough for intercourse, he took precautions, but eventually, after years and years of it, they made a mistake; she got pregnant."

Hilary had the urge to lift the afghan that was draped on the couch and curl up in it to ward off the chills that swept over her. In spite of the frequent beatings, the emotional intimidation, the physical and mental torture that she suffered while living with Earl and Emma, she knew she was lucky to have escaped sexual abuse. She believed Earl had been impotent; only his inability to perform had saved her from that ultimate degradation. At least she had been spared that nightmare. But Katherine Frye had been plunged into it, and Hilary unexpectedly felt a kinship with the woman.

Tony seemed to sense what was going through her mind. He took her hand, squeezed it gently, reassuringly.

Mrs. Yancy stroked the white cat, and it made a low, rough, purring sound.

"There's something I don't understand," Joshua said. "Why didn't Leo send Katherine to you as soon as he knew she was going to have a baby? Why didn't he ask you to set up an abortion for her? Surely you had the contacts for that."

"Oh, yes," Mrs. Yancy said. "In my line of work, you had to know doctors who would handle that sort of thing. Leo could have arranged that through me. I don't know for sure why he didn't. But I suspect it was because he hoped Katherine would have a pretty baby girl."

"I'm not sure I follow," Joshua said.

"Isn't it obvious?" Mrs. Yancy asked, scratching the white cat under its fat chin. "If he had a granddaughter, then in a few years, he'd be able to start breaking her in, just like he did Katherine. Then he'd have two of them. A little harem of his own."

Unable to get a response out of his other self, Bruno got up and walked aimlessly around the huge room, stirring the dust on the floor; hundreds of whirling motes spun in the milky shaft of light from the window.

Eventually, he noticed a pair of dumbbells, each weighing about fifty pounds. They were part of the elaborate set of weights he had used six days a week, every week, between the ages of twelve and thirty-five. Most of his equipment—the barbells, heavier weights, the press bench—was down in the basement. But he had always kept a spare set of dumbbells in his room for use in those idle moments when a few extra sets of bicep curls or wrist flexes was just the thing to drive away boredom.

Now he picked up the weights and started working out with them. His enormous shoulders and powerful arms quickly got into the familiar rhythm, and he began to work up a sweat.

Twenty-eight years ago, when he'd first expressed a desire to lift weights and become a body builder, his mother had thought it was an excellent idea. Long, brutal workouts with weights helped to burn up the sexual energy that he was just then beginning to generate, caught as he was in the throes of puberty. Because he didn't dare expose his demonic penis to a girl, vigorous weight training preoccupied him, seized his imagination and his emotions as sex might otherwise have done. Katherine had approved.

Later, as he packed on muscle tissue and became a formidable specimen, she had second thoughts about the wisdom of letting him grow so strong. Afraid that he might develop his body only so he could successfully turn on her, she had tried to take his weights away from him. But when he broke into tears and begged her to reconsider, she realized that she would never have anything to fear from him.

How could she ever have thought differently? Bruno wondered as he curled the dumbbells to his shoulders and then slowly let them down again. Hadn't she realized that she would always be stronger than he was? After all, she had the key to the door in the ground. She had the power to unlock that door and make him go into that dark hole. No matter how big his biceps and triceps became, as long as she possessed that key, she would always be stronger than he was.

It was around that time, when his body began to develop, that she first told him that she knew how to come back from the dead. She'd wanted him to know that, after she died, she'd watch over him from the other side; and she'd sworn that she would come back to punish him if she saw him misbehaving or if he started getting careless about hiding his demonic heritage from other people. She had warned him a thousand times or more that, if he was bad and forced her to come back from the grave, she would throw him into the hole in the ground, lock the door, and leave him there forever.

But now, as he worked out in the dusty attic, Bruno suddenly wondered if Katherine's threat had been empty. Had she really possessed supernatural powers? Could she really come back from the dead? Or was she lying to him? Was she lying because she was afraid of him? Was she afraid he would get big and strong—and then break her neck? Was her story about coming back from the grave nothing more than feeble insurance against his getting the idea that he could kill her and then be free of her forever?

Those questions came to him, but he was not capable of holding on to them long enough to explore each one and answer it. Disconnected thoughts surged like bursts of electric current through his short-circuiting brain. Each doubt was forgotten an instant after it occurred to him.

Contrarily, each fear that rose up did *not* fade away but remained, sparking and sputtering, in the dark corners of his mind. He thought of Hilary-Katherine, the latest resurrection, and he remembered that he had to find her.

Before she found him.

He began to shake.

He dropped one dumbbell with a crash. Then the other one. The floorboards rattled.

"The bitch," he said fearfully, angrily.

The white cat licked Mrs. Yancy's hand as she said, "Leo and Katherine worked up a complex story to explain the baby. They didn't want to admit it was hers. If they did that, they had to point a finger at the man responsible, at some young suitor. But she didn't have any suitors. The old man didn't want anyone else touching her. Just him. Gives me the creeps. What kind of man would force himself on his own little girl? And the bastard started on her when she was only *four!* She wasn't even old enough to understand what was happening." Mrs. Yancy shook her gray head in shock and sorrow. "How could a grown man be aroused by a baby like that? If I made the laws, any man who did that sort of thing would be castrated—or worse: Worse, I think. I tell you, it disgusts me."

Joshua said, "Why didn't they just claim Katherine was raped by a migrant farm worker or some stranger passing through? She wouldn't have had to send an innocent man to jail to support a story like that. She could have given the police a totally phony description. And even if, by some wild chance, they'd found a guy who fit that description, some poor son of a bitch who didn't have an alibi . . . well, then she could have said he wasn't the right man. She wouldn't have been forced to railroad anyone."

"That's right," Tony said. "Most rape cases of that sort are never solved. The police would probably have been surprised if Katherine *had* made a positive identification of anybody they rounded up."

"I can understand why she wouldn't have been eager to cry rape," Hilary said. "She would have had to endure endless humiliation and embarrassment. A lot of people think every woman who's raped was just asking for it."

"I'm aware of that," Joshua said. "I'm the one who keeps saying that most of my fellow human beings are idiots, asses and buffoons. Remember? But St. Helena has always been a relatively openminded town. The people there wouldn't have blamed Katherine for being raped. At least most of them wouldn't have. She would have had to deal with a few crude characters and a measure of embarrassment, naturally, but in the long run she would have had everyone's sympathy. And it seems to me that it would have been a lot easier taking that route than trying to make everyone believe an elaborate lie about Mary Gunther—and then having to worry about maintaining that lie for the rest of her life."

The cat turned over on Mrs. Yancy's lap. She rubbed its belly.

"Leo didn't want to blame the pregnancy on a rapist because that would have brought in the cops," Mrs. Yancy said. "Leo had great respect for the cops. He was an authoritarian type. He believed the cops were better at their jobs than they really were, and he was afraid they would smell something fishy about any rape story that he and Katherine could concoct. He didn't want to draw attention to himself, not attention like that. He was scared to death the cops would sniff out the truth. He wasn't about to risk going to jail for child molestation and incest."

"Katherine told you that?" Hilary asked.

"That's right. As I said before, she'd been living with the shame of Leo's abuse all her life, and when she thought maybe she was going to die in child-birth, she wanted to tell someone, anyone, what she'd been through. Anyway, Leo was sure he'd be safe if Katherine could conceal her pregnancy, hide it completely, and fool everyone in St. Helena. Then it would be possible to pass the child off as the illegitimate baby of an unfortunate friend from Katherine's college days."

"So her father forced her to wear the girdles," Hilary said, feeling sorrier for Katherine Frye than she would have thought possible when she first walked into Mrs. Yancy's parlor. "He put her through that agony to protect himself. It was his idea."

"Yes," Mrs. Yancy said. "She'd never been able to stand up to him. She'd always done what he'd told her to do. It wasn't any different this time. She did this thing with the girdles and the dieting, even though it caused her a hell of a lot of pain. She did it because she was afraid to disobey him. Which isn't surprising when you consider that he'd spent twenty-some years breaking her spirit."

"She went away to college," Tony said. "Wasn't that an attempt to gain independence?"

"No," Mrs. Yancy said. "College was Leo's idea. In 1937, he went to Europe for seven or eight months to sell off the last of his holdings in the old country. He saw World War Two coming, and he didn't want to have any assets frozen over there. He didn't want to take Katherine on the trip with him. I suspect he intended to combine business with pleasure. He was a highly-sexed man. And I hear tell some of those European brothels offer all kinds of kinky thrills, just the sort of things to appeal to him. The dirty old goat, Katherine would have been in his way. He decided she should go to college while he was out of the country, and he arranged for her to stay with a family he knew in San Francisco. They owned a company that distributed wine, beer, and liquor in the Bay Area, and one of the things they handled was Shade Tree products."

Joshua said, "He was taking quite a chance, letting her out from under his thumb for so long."

"Apparently, he didn't think so," Mrs. Yancy said. "And he was proved right. In all those months without him around, she never began to come out of his thrall. She never told anyone about the things he'd been doing to her. She never even considered telling anyone. She was a broken spirit, I tell you. Enslaved. That's really the word for it. She was enslaved, not like a plantation worker or anything like that. Mentally and emotionally enslaved. And when he came back from Europe, he made her drop out of college. He took her back to St. Helena with him, and she didn't resist. She couldn't resist. She didn't know how."

The mantel clock chimed the hour. Two measured tones. The notes echoed softly from the parlor ceiling.

Joshua had been sitting on the edge of his chair. Now he slid back until his head touched the antimacassar again. He was pale, and dark rings circled his eyes. His white hair was no longer fluffy; it was lank, lifeless. In the short time that Hilary had known him, he appeared to her to have aged. He looked wrung-out.

She knew how he felt. The Frye family history was an unrelievedly grim tale of man's inhumanity to man. The more they poked around in that mess, the more depressed they became. The heart could not help but respond, and the spirit sagged as one awful discovery followed another.

As if talking to himself, getting it straight in his own mind, Joshua said, "So they went back to St. Helena, and they picked up their sick relationship where they'd left off, and eventually they made a mistake, and she got pregnant—and no one up there in St. Helena ever suspected a thing."

Tony said, "Incredible. Usually a simple lie is the best because it's the only kind that won't trip you up. The story about Mary Gunther was so damned involved! It was a juggling act. They had to keep a dozen balls in the air at once. Yet they brought it off without a hitch."

"Oh, hardly without a hitch," Mrs. Yancy said. "There was certainly a hitch or two."

"Such as?"

"Such as—the day she left St. Helena to come to my place to have her baby, she told people up there that this imaginary Mary Gunther had sent word that the baby had arrived. Now that was stupid. It really was. Katherine said she was going to San Francisco to pick up the child. She told them Mary's message mentioned a lovely baby, but neglected to say whether it was a boy or girl. That was Katherine's pathetic way of covering for herself, since she couldn't know what her baby's sex was until it was born. Dumb. She should have known better. That was her only mistake—saying that the child was born before she left St. Helena. Ah, I know she was a complete nervous wreck. I know she wasn't thinking straight. She couldn't have been a very well-balanced woman after all that Leo had done to her over the years. And being pregnant, having to hide it under all those girdles, then Leo's death coming at a time when she needed him most—that was bound to drive her even further over the edge. She was out of her head, and she didn't think it out well enough."

"I don't understand," Joshua said. "Why was it a mistake for her to say Mary's baby had already been born? Where's the hitch?"

Stroking the cat, Mrs. Yancy said, "What she should have told the people in St. Helena was that the Gunther baby was about to arrive, that it hadn't been born yet, but that she was going to San Francisco to be with Mary. That way she wouldn't have been committed to the story that there was *one* baby. But she didn't think of that. She didn't realize what might happen. She told everyone that it was just *one* baby, already in hand. Then she came to my place and gave birth to twins."

Hilary said, "Twins?"

"Damn," Tony said.

The surprise brought Joshua to his feet.

The white cat sensed the tension. It lifted its head out of Rita Yancy's lap and peered curiously at each person in the parlor, one after the other. Its yellow eyes appeared to shine with inner light.

The attic bedroom was large, but not nearly large enough to keep Bruno from feeling that it was gradually closing in on him. He looked for things to do because idleness made his claustrophobia worse.

He got bored with the dumbbells even before his massive arms began to ache from the exercise.

He took a book from one of the shelves and tried to read, but he wasn't able to concentrate.

His mind still hadn't settled down; it flitted from one thought to another, like a quietly desperate jeweler looking for a misplaced bag of diamonds.

He talked to his dead self.

He searched the dusty corners for spiders and squashed them.

He sang to himself.

He laughed at times without really knowing what had struck him funny.

He wept, too.

He cursed Katherine.

He made plans.

He paced, paced, paced.

He was eager to leave the house and begin searching for Hilary-Katherine, but he knew he would be a fool if he went out in daylight. He was certain that Katherine's conspirators were everywhere in St. Helena. Her friends from the grave. Other walking dead, men and women from the Other Side, hiding in new bodies. All of them would be on the lookout for him. Yes. Yes. Maybe dozens of them. He would be too conspicuous during the day. He would have to wait until sunset before he went looking for the bitch. Although night was the favorite time of the day for the undead, the time when they prowled in especially large numbers, and although he would be in terrible danger while he stalked Hilary-Katherine in the night, he would also benefit from the darkness. A night-shadow would hide him from the walking dead every bit as well as it would conceal them from him. With the scales thus balanced, the success of the hunt would depend only on who was smarter—he or Katherine—and if that was the only criterion, he might have a better than even chance of winning; for Katherine was clever and infinitely wicked and cunning, but she was not as smart as he was.

He believed that he would be safe if he stayed in the house during the day, and that was ironic, really, because he hadn't felt safe for one minute during the thirty-five years he'd lived there with Katherine. Now the house was a reliable haven because it was the last place Katherine or her conspirators would look for him. She wanted to catch him and bring him to this very place. He knew that. He knew it! She had come back from the grave for only one reason: to bring him to the top of the cliff, around the house, to the doors in the ground at the end of the rear lawn. She wanted to put him in that hole in the ground, lock him in there forever. That's what she had told him she would do if she ever had to come back to punish him. He had not forgotten. And now she would expect him to avoid the top of the cliff and the old house at all costs. She would never think to look for him in his long-abandoned attic bedroom, not in a million years.

He was so pleased with his excellent strategy that he laughed aloud.

But then he had a horrible thought. If she *did* think to look for him here, and if she came with a few of her friends, others of the living dead, enough of them to overpower him, then they wouldn't have far to drag him. The doors in the ground were right behind the house. If Katherine and her hellish friends caught him here, they would be able to carry him to those doors and throw him into that dark room, into the whispers, in little more than a minute.

Frightened, he ran back to the bed and sat down beside himself and tried to get himself to reassure him that everything would be all right.

Joshua couldn't sit still. He walked back and forth on one of the flowered runners in Mrs. Yancy's parlor.

The old woman said, "When Katherine gave birth to twins, she realized that the elaborate lie about Mary Gunther would no longer hold up. The people in St. Helena had been prepared for *one* child. No matter how she explained the second baby, she'd plant suspicion. The idea that everyone she knew would find out what she'd been doing with her own father. . . . Well, I guess it was too much for her on top of everything else that had happened in her life. She just snapped. For three days, she carried on like someone in a fever delirium, gabbling like a madwoman. The doctor gave her sedatives, but they didn't always work. She ranted and raved and babbled. I thought I'd have to call the cops and let them put her away in a little padded room. But I didn't want to do that. I sure as hell didn't."

"But she needed psychiatric help," Hilary said. "Just letting her scream and carry on for three days—that wasn't good. That wasn't good at all."

"Maybe not," Mrs. Yancy said. "But I couldn't do anything else. I mean, when you're running a fancy bordello, you don't want to see the cops except when you pass out their payoff money. They usually don't bother a classy operation like the one I had going. After all, some of my clients were influential politicians and wealthy businessmen, and the cops didn't want to embarrass any big shots in a raid. But if I sent Katherine off to a hospital, I knew damned well the newspapers would pick up on the story, and then the cops would *have* to shut me down. They couldn't just let me go on doing business after I'd gotten all that publicity. No way. Absolutely impossible. I'd have lost everything. And my doctor was worried that his career would be ruined if his regular patients found out he was secretly treating prostitutes. These days it wouldn't damage a doctor's practice even if everyone knew he gave vasectomies to alligators with the same instrument he used in his office. But in 1940, people were more . . . squeamish. So you see, I had to think about myself, and I had to protect my doctor, my girls . . ."

Joshua walked up to the old woman's chair. He looked down at her, taking in the plain dress and the apron and the dark brown support stockings and the stodgy black shoes and the silky white cat, trying to see through the grandmotherly image to the real woman underneath. "When you accepted Katherine's three thousand dollars, didn't you also take on certain responsibilities for her?"

"I didn't *ask* her to come to my place to have her baby," Mrs. Yancy said. "My business was worth a whole lot more than three thousand dollars. I wasn't going to throw it all away just for principle. Is that what you think I should have done?" She shook her gray head in disbelief. "If that's what you really think I should have done, then you're living in a dream world, my dear sir."

Joshua stared down at the woman, unable to speak for fear he would scream at her. He didn't want to be thrown out of her house until he was certain she had told him absolutely everything she knew about Katherine Anne Frye's pregnancy and about the twins. *Twins!*

Tony said, "Look, Mrs. Yancy, shortly after you took Katherine in, when you discovered that she had wrapped herself up in girdles, you knew she was likely to lose the baby. You admit the doctor told you that might happen."

"Yes."

"He told you Katherine might die, too."

"So?"

"A child's death or the death of a pregnant woman in labor—something like that would have closed up your place every bit as fast as having to call in the cops to deal with a woman who was suffering a nervous breakdown. Yet you didn't turn Katherine away when there was still time to do that. Even after you knew it was a risky proposition, you kept her three thousand dollars, and you allowed her to stay. Now surely you realized that if someone died, you'd have to report it to the police and risk getting shut down."

"No problem," Mrs. Yancy said. "If the babies had died, we'd have taken them away in a suitcase. We'd have buried them quietly in the hills up in Marin County. Or maybe we'd have weighted the suitcase and dropped it off the Golden Gate Bridge."

Joshua had an almost irresistible urge to grab the old woman by her bun of gray hair and yank her out of her chair, jerk her out of her smug complacency. Instead, he turned away and took a deep breath and began to pace along the flower-patterned runner once more, glowering at the floor.

"And what about Katherine?" Hilary asked Rita Yancy. "What would you have done if *she* had died?"

"The same as I'd done if the twins had been born dead," Mrs. Yancy said blithely. "Except, of course, we wouldn't have been able to fit Katherine into a suitcase."

Joshua stopped at the far end of the runner and looked back at the woman, aghast. She wasn't trying to be funny. She was utterly unaware of the gruesome humor in that gross remark; she was merely stating a fact.

"If anything had gone wrong, we'd have dumped the body," Mrs. Yancy said, still answering Hilary's question. "And we'd have handled it so that no one would have known that Katherine had ever come to my place. Now don't you look so shocked and disapproving, young lady. I'm no killer. We're talking about what I'd have done—what any sensible person in my position would have done—if she or the baby had died a natural death. *Natural death.* For heaven's sake, if I were a killer, I'd have done away with poor Katherine when she was out of her head, when I didn't know if she'd ever recover. She was a threat to me then. I didn't know whether or not she was going to cost me my house, my business, everything. But I didn't strangle her, you know. My goodness, such a thought never crossed my mind! I nursed the poor girl through her fits. I nursed her out of her hysteria, and then everything was all right."

Tony said, "You told us Katherine ranted and raved and babbled. That sounds as if—"

"Only for three days," Mrs. Yancy said. "We even had to tie her down to the bed to keep her from hurting herself. But she was only sick for three days. So maybe it wasn't a nervous breakdown. Just a sort of temporary collapse. Because after three days she was as good as new."

"The twins," Joshua said. "Let's get back to the twins. That's what we really want to know about."

"I think I've told you just about everything," Mrs. Yancy said.

"Were they identical twins?" Joshua asked.

"How can you tell when they're just born? They're all wrinkled and red. There's no way to tell that early if they're fraternal or identical."

"Couldn't the doctor have run a test—"

"We were a first-class bordello, Mr. Rhinehart, not a hospital." She chucked the white cat under the chin, and it playfully waved a paw at her. "The doctor didn't have the time or the facilities for what you're suggesting. Besides, why should we have cared whether the boys were identical or not?"

Hilary said, "Katherine named one of them Bruno."

"Yes," Mrs. Yancy said. "I found that out when he started sending me checks after Katherine's death."

"What did she call the other boy?"

"I haven't the foggiest. By the time she left my place, she hadn't given names to either of them yet."

"But weren't their names on their birth certificates?" Tony asked.

"There weren't any certificates," Mrs. Yancy said.

"How could that be?"

"The births weren't recorded."

"But the law—"

"Katherine insisted that the births not be recorded. She was paying good money for what she wanted, and we made sure she got it."

"And the doctor went along with this?" Tony asked.

"He got a thousand bucks for delivering the twins and for keeping his mouth shut," the old woman said. "A thousand was worth several times more in those days than it is now. He was well paid for bending a few rules."

"Were both of the babies healthy?" Joshua asked.

"They were thin," Mrs. Yancy said. "Scrawny as hell. Two pathetic little things. Probably because Katherine had been on a diet for months. And because of the girdles. But they could cry just as good and loud as any other babies. And there wasn't a thing wrong with their appetites. They seemed healthy enough, just small."

"How long did Katherine stay at your place?" Hilary asked.

"Almost two weeks. She needed that long to get her strength back after such a hard delivery. And the babies needed time to put a little flesh on their bones."

"When she left, did she take both children with her?"

"Of course. I wasn't running a nursery. I was glad to see her leave."

"Did you know that she was going to take only one of the twins to St. Helena?" Hilary asked.

"I understood that to be her intention, yes."

"Did she say what she was going to do with the other boy?" Joshua asked, taking over the questioning from Hilary.

"I believe she intended to put it up for adoption," Mrs. Yancy said.

"You *believe?*" Joshua asked exasperatedly. "Weren't you even the least bit concerned about what might happen to those two helpless babies in the hands of a woman who was obviously mentally unbalanced?"

"She had recovered."

"Baloney."

"I tell you, if you'd met her on the street, you wouldn't have thought she had any problems."

"But for God's sake, underneath that facade—"

"She was their mother," Mrs. Yancy said primly. "She wouldn't have done them any harm."

"You couldn't have been sure of that," Joshua said.

"I certainly *was* sure of it," Mrs. Yancy declared. "I've always had the highest respect for motherhood and a mother's love. A mother's love can work wonders."

Again, Joshua had to restrain himself from reaching for the bun of hair on top of her head.

Tony said, "Katherine couldn't have put the baby up for adoption. Not without a birth certificate to prove that it was hers."

"Which leaves us with a number of unpleasant possibilities to consider," Joshua said.

"Honestly, you people amaze me," Mrs. Yancy said, shaking her head and scratching her cat. "You always want to believe the worst. I've never seen three bigger pessimists. Did you ever stop to think she might have left the little boy on a doorstep? She probably abandoned him at an orphanage or maybe a church, some place where he would be found right away and given proper care. I imagine he was adopted by an upstanding young couple, raised in an excellent home, given lots of love, a good education, all sorts of advantages."

In the attic, waiting for nightfall, bored, nervous, lonely, apprehensive, sometimes stuporous, more than frenetic, Bruno Frye spent much of Thursday afternoon talking to his dead self. He hoped to soothe his roiling mind and regain a sense of purpose, but he made little or no progress along those lines. He decided that he would be calmer, happier, and less lonely if he could at least look into the other self's eyes, like in the old days, when they had often sat and stared longingly at each other for an hour or more at a time, communicating so much without benefit of words, sharing, being one, just one together. He recalled that moment in Sally's bathroom, only yesterday, when he had stopped in front of a mirror and had mistaken his reflection for his other self. Looking into eyes that he had thought were the eyes of his other self, he had felt wonderful, blissful, at peace. Now he desperately wanted to recapture that state of mind. And how much better to look into the *real* eyes of his other self, even if they were flat and sightless now. But himself lay on the bed, eyes firmly closed. Bruno touched the eyes of the other Bruno, the dead one, and they were cold orbs; the lids would not lift under his gently prodding fingertips. He explored the curves of those shuttered eyes, and he felt hidden sutures at the corners, tiny knots of thread holding the lids down. Excited by the prospect of seeing the other's eyes again, Bruno got up and hurried downstairs, looking for razor blades and delicate cuticle scissors and needles and a crocheting hook and other makeshift surgical instruments that might be of use in the reopening of the other Bruno's eyes.

If Rita Yancy had any more information about the Frye twins, neither Hilary nor Joshua would get it out of her. Tony could see that much even if Hilary and Joshua could not. Any second now, one of them was going to say something so sharp, so angry, so biting and bitter, that the old woman would take offense and order all of them out of the house.

Tony was aware that Hilary was deeply shaken by the similarities between her own childhood ordeal and Katherine's agony. She was bristling at all three of Rita Yancy's attitudes—the bursts of phony moralizing, the brief moments of equally unfelt and syrupy sentimentality, and the far more genuine and constant and stunning callousness.

Joshua was suffering from a loss of self-esteem because he had worked for Katherine for twenty-five years without spotting the quiet madness that surely must have been bubbling just below the carefully-controlled surface placidity. He was disgusted with himself; therefore, he was even more irritable than usual. And because Mrs. Yancy was, even in ordinary circumstances, the kind of person Joshua despised, the attorney's patience with her could fit into a thimble with room left over for one of Charo's stage costumes plus the collected wisdom of the last four U.S. Presidents.

Tony got up from the sofa and went to the footstool that was in front of Rita Yancy's chair. He sat down, explaining his move by pretending that he just wanted to pet the cat; but in switching seats, he was placing himself between the old woman and Hilary, and he was effectively blocking Joshua, who looked as if he might seize Mrs. Yancy and shake her. The footstool was a good position from which to continue the interrogation in a casual fashion. As Tony stroked the white cat, he kept up a constant stream of chatter with the woman, ingratiating himself with her, charming her, using the old Clemenza soft-sell which always had done well for him in his police work.

Eventually, he asked her if there had been anything unusual about the birth of the twins.

"Unusual?" Mrs. Yancy asked, perplexed. "Don't you think the whole damned thing was unusual?"

"You're right," he said. "I didn't put my question very well. What I meant to ask was whether there was anything peculiar about the birth itself, anything odd about her labor pains or her contractions, anything remarkable about the initial state of the babies when they came out of her, any abnormality, any strangeness."

He saw surprise enter her eyes as his question tripped a switch in her memory.

"In fact," she said, "there *was* something unusual."

"Let me guess," he said. "Both of the babies were born with cauls."

"That's right! How did you know?"

"Just a lucky guess."

"The hell it was." She wagged a finger at him. "You're smarter than you pretend to be."

He forced himself to smile at her. He had to force it, for there was nothing about Rita Yancy that could elicit a genuine smile from him.

"Both of them were born with cauls," she said. "Their little heads were almost entirely covered. The doctor had seen and dealt with that sort of thing before, of course. But he thought the chances of both twins having cauls was something like a million to one."

"Was Katherine aware of this?"

"Aware of the cauls? Not at the time. She was delirious with pain. And then for three days she was completely out of her mind."

"But later?"

"I'm sure she was told about it," Mrs. Yancy said. "It's not the sort of thing you forget to tell a mother. In fact . . . I remember telling her myself. Yes. Yes, I do. I recall it very clearly now. She was fascinated. You know, some people think that a child born with a caul has the gift of second sight."

"Is that what Katherine believed?"

Rita Yancy frowned. "No. She said it was a bad sign, not a good one. Leo had been interested in the supernatural, and Katherine had read a few books in his occult collection. In one of those books, it said that when twins were born with cauls, that was . . . I can't recall exactly what she said it meant, but it wasn't good. An evil omen or something."

"The mark of a demon?" Tony asked.

"Yes! That's it!"

"So she believed that her babies were marked by a demon, their souls already damned?"

"I'd almost forgotten about that," Mrs. Yancy said.

She stared beyond Tony, not seeing anything in the parlor, looking into the past, striving to remember. . . .

Hilary and Joshua stayed back, out of the way, silent; and Tony was relieved that they recognized his authority.

Eventually, Mrs. Yancy said, "After Katherine told me about it being the mark of a demon, she just clammed up. She didn't want to talk any more. For a couple of days, she was as quiet as a mouse. She stayed in bed, staring at the ceiling, hardly moving at all. She looked like she was thinking real hard about something. Then suddenly, she started acting so damned weird that I had to start wondering if I still might have to send her away to the booby hatch."

"Was she ranting and raving and violent like before?" Tony asked.

"No, no. It was all talk this time. Very wild, intense, crazy talk. She told me that the twins were the children of a demon. She said she'd been raped by a thing from hell, a green and scaly thing with huge eyes and a forked tongue and long claws. She said it had come from hell to force her to carry its children. Crazy, huh? She swore up and down that it was true. She even described this demon. A damned good description, too. Full of detail, very well done. And when she told me about how it raped her, she managed to give me the chills, even though I knew it was all a bunch of crap. The story was colorful, very imaginative. At first, I thought it was a joke, something she was doing just for laughs, except she wasn't laughing, and I couldn't see anything funny in it. I reminded her that she'd told me all about Leo, and she screamed at me. Did she scream! I thought the windows would break. She denied ever having said such things. She pretended to be insulted. She was so angry with me for suggesting incest, so self-righteous, a regular little prig, so determined to make me apologize—well, I couldn't help laughing at her. And that made her even angrier. She kept saying it hadn't been Leo, though we both knew damned well it had. She did everything she could to make me believe it was a demon that had fathered the twins. And I tell you, her act was *good!* I didn't believe it for a minute, of course. All that silly stuff about a creature from hell sticking his thing in her. What a bunch of hogwash. But I started to wonder if maybe she had convinced herself. She sure looked convinced. She was so fanatical about it. She said she was afraid that she and her babies would be burned alive if any religious people found out that she'd consorted with a demon. She begged me to help her keep the secret. She didn't want me to tell anyone about the two cauls. Then she said she knew that both twins carried the mark of the demon between their legs. She pleaded with me to keep that a secret, too."

"Between their legs?" Tony asked.

"Oh, she was carrying on like a full-fledged looney," Rita Yancy said. "She insisted that both of her babies had their father's sex organs. She said they weren't human between the legs, and she said she knew I'd noticed that, and she begged me not to tell anyone about it. Well, that was purely ridiculous. Both those little boys had perfectly ordinary pee-pees. But Katherine jabbered on and on about demons for almost two days. Sometimes she seemed truly hysterical. She wanted to know how much money I'd take to keep the secret about the demon. I told her I wouldn't take a penny for that, but I said I'd settle for five hundred a month to keep mum about Leo and all the rest of it, the rest of the *real* story. That calmed her down a little, but she still had this demon thing stuck in her head. I was just about decided that she really believed what she was saying, and I was going to call my doctor and have him examine her—and then she shut up about it. She seemed to regain her senses. Or she got tired of her joke, I guess. Anyway, she didn't say one more word about demons. She behaved herself from then on until she took her babies and left a week or so later."

Tony thought about what Mrs. Yancy had told him.

Like a witch cuddling a feline familiar, the old woman petted the white cat.

"What if," Tony said. "What if, what if, what if?"

"What if what?" Hilary asked.

"I don't know," he said. "Pieces seem to be falling into place . . . but it looks . . . so wild. Maybe I'm putting the puzzle together all wrong. I've got to think about it. I'm just not sure yet."

"Well, do you have any more questions for me?" Mrs. Yancy asked.

"No," Tony said, getting up from the footstool. "I can't think of anything else."

"I believe we've gotten what we came for," Joshua agreed.

"More than we bargained for," Hilary said.

Mrs. Yancy lifted the cat off her lap, put it on the floor, and rose from her chair. "I've wasted too much time on this silly damned thing. I should be in the kitchen. I've got work to do. I made four pie shells this morning. Now I've got to mix up the fillings and get everything in the oven. I've got grandchildren coming for dinner, and each one of them has a different kind of favorite pie. Sometimes the little dears can be a tribulation. But on the other hand, I'd sure be lost without them."

The cat leapt abruptly over the footstool, darted along the flowered runner, past Joshua, and under a corner table.

Precisely when the animal stopped moving, the house shook. Two miniature glass swans toppled off a shelf, bounced without breaking on the thick carpet. Two embroidered wall hangings fell down. Windows rattled.

"Quake," Mrs. Yancy said.

The floor rolled like the deck of a ship in mild seas.

"Nothing to worry about," Mrs. Yancy said.

The movement decreased.

The rumbling, discontented earth grew quiet.

The house was still again.

"See?" Mrs. Yancy said. "It's over now."

But Tony sensed other oncoming shockwaves—although none of them had anything to do with earthquakes.

Bruno finally opened the dead eyes of his other self, and at first he was upset by what he found. They weren't the clear, electrifying, blue-gray eyes that he had known and loved. These were the eyes of a monster. They appeared to be swollen, rotten-soft and protuberant. The whites were stained brown-red by half-dried, scummy blood from burst vessels. The irises were cloudy, muddy, less blue than they had been in life, now more the color of an ugly bruise, dark and wounded.

However, the longer Bruno stared into them the less hideous those damaged eyes became. They were, after all, still the eyes of his other self, still part of himself, still eyes that he knew better than any other eyes, still eyes that he loved and trusted, eyes that loved and trusted him. He tried not to look *at* them but *into* them, deep brown beyond the surface ruin, way down in, where (many times in the past) he had made the blazing, thrilling connection with the other half of his soul. He felt none of the old magic now, for the other Bruno's eyes were not looking back at him. Nevertheless, the very act of peering deeply into the other's dead eyes somehow revitalized his memories of what total unity with his other self had been like; he remembered the pure, sweet pleasure and fulfillment of being with himself, just he and himself against the world, with no fear of being alone.

He clung to that memory, for memory was now all that he had left.

He sat on the bed for a long time, staring down into the eyes of the corpse.

Joshua Rhinehart's Cessna Turbo Skylane RG roared north, slicing across the eastward-flowing air front, heading for Napa.

Hilary looked down at the scattered clouds below and at the sere autumn hills that lay a few thousand feet below the clouds. Overhead, there was nothing but crystal-blue sky and the distant, stratospheric vapor trail of a military jet.

Far off in the west, a dense bank of blue-gray-black clouds stretched out of sight to the north and the south. The massive thunderheads were rolling in like giant ships from the sea. By nightfall, Napa Valley—in fact, the entire northern third of the state from the Monterey Peninsula to the Oregon border— would lay under threatening skies again.

During the first ten minutes after takeoff, Hilary and Tony and Joshua were silent. Each was preoccupied with his own bleak thoughts—and fears.

Then Joshua said, "The twin has to be the dead ringer we're looking for."

"Obviously," Tony said.

"So Katherine didn't try to solve her problem by killing off the extra baby," Joshua said.

"Evidently not," Tony said.

"But which one did *I* kill?" Hilary asked. "Bruno or his brother?"

"We'll have the body exhumed and see what we can learn from it," Joshua said.

The plane hit an air pocket. It dropped more than two hundred feet in a roller coaster swoop, then soared up to its proper altitude.

When her stomach crawled back into its familiar niche, Hilary said, "All right, let's talk this thing out and see if we can come up with any answers. We're all sitting here chewing on the same question anyway. If Katherine didn't kill Bruno's twin brother in order to keep the Mary Gunther lie afloat, then what *did* she do with him? Where the devil has he been all these years?"

"Well, there's always Mrs. Rita Yancy's pet theory," Joshua said, managing to pronounce her name in such a way as to make it clear that even the need to refer to her in passing distressed him and left a bad taste in his mouth. "Perhaps Katherine did leave one of the twins bundled up on the doorstep of a church or an orphanage."

"I don't know. . . ." Hilary said doubtfully. "I don't like it, but I don't exactly know why. It's just too . . . clichéd . . . too trite . . . too romantic. Damn. None of those is the word I want. I can't think how to say it. I just sense that Katherine would not have handled it like that. It's too . . ."

"Too smooth," Tony said. "Just like the story about Mary Gunther was too smooth to please me. Abandoning one of the twins like that would have been the quickest, easiest, simplest, safest—although not the most moral—way for her to solve her problem. But people almost never do anything the quickest, easiest, simplest, and safest way. Especially not when they're under the kind of stress that Katherine was under when she left Rita Yancy's whorehouse."

"Still," Joshua said, "we can't rule it out altogether."

"I think we can," Tony said. "Because if you accept that the brother was abandoned and then adopted by strangers, you've got to explain how he and Bruno got back together again. Since the brother was an unregistered birth, there'd be no way he could trace his blood parentage. The only way he could hook up with Bruno would be by coincidence. Even if you're willing to accept that coincidence, you've still got to explain how the brother could have been raised in another home, in an altogether different environment from Bruno's, without ever knowing Katherine—and yet have such a fierce hatred for the woman, such an overwhelming fear of her."

"That's not easy," Joshua admitted.

"You've got to explain why and how the brother developed a psychopathic personality and paranoid delusions that perfectly match Bruno's in every detail," Tony said.

The Cessna droned northward.

Wind buffeted the small craft.

For a minute, the three of them sat in silence within the expensive, single-engine, overhead-wing, two-hundred-mile-per-hour, sixteen-mile-per-gallon, white and red and mustard-yellow, airborne cocoon.

Then Joshua said, "You win. I can't explain it. I can't see how the brother could have been raised entirely apart from Bruno yet wind up with the same psychosis. Genetics don't explain it, that's for sure."

"So what are you saying?" Hilary asked Tony. "That Bruno and his brother weren't separated after all?"

"She took them both home to St. Helena," Tony said.

"But where was the other twin all those years?" Joshua asked. "Locked away in a closet or something?"

"No," Tony said. "You probably met him many times."

"What? Me? No. Never. Just Bruno."

"What if. . . . What if both of them were living as Bruno? What if they . . . took turns?"

Joshua looked away from the open sky ahead, stared at Tony, blinked. "Are you trying to tell me they played some sort of childish game for forty years?" he asked skeptically.

"Not a game," Tony said. "At least it wouldn't have been a game to them. They would have thought of it as a desperate, dangerous necessity."

"You've lost me," Joshua said.

To Tony, Hilary said, "I knew you were working on an idea when you started asking Mrs. Yancy about the babies having cauls and about how Katherine reacted to that."

"Yes," Tony said. "Katherine carrying on about a demon—that bit of news gave me a big piece of the puzzle."

"For God's sake," Joshua said impatiently, gruffly, "stop being so damned mysterious. Put it together for Hilary and me in a way we can understand."

"Sorry. I was more or less still thinking aloud." Tony shifted in his seat. "Okay, look. This will take a while. I'll have to go back to the beginning. . . . To understand what I'm going to say about Bruno, you have to understand Katherine, or at least understand the way I see her. What I'm theorizing is . . . a family in which madness has been . . . sort of handed down like a legacy for at least three generations. The insanity steadily grows bigger and bigger, like a trust fund earning interest." Tony shifted in his seat again. "Let's start with Leo. An extreme authoritarian type. To be happy he needed to totally control other people. That was one of the reasons he did so well in business, but it was also the reason he didn't have many friends. He knew how to get his way every time, and he never gave an inch. A lot of aggressive men like Leo have a different approach to sex from the one they have toward everything else; they like to be relieved of all responsibility when they're in bed; they like to be ordered around and dominated for a change—but only in bed. Not Leo. Not even in bed. He insisted on being the dominant one even in his sex life. He enjoyed hurting and humiliating women, calling them names, forcing them to do unpleasant things, being a little rough, a little sadistic. We know that from Mrs. Yancy."

"It's a hell of a big step from paying prostitutes so they'll satisfy some perverse desire—to molesting your own child," Joshua said.

"But we know he did molest Katherine repeatedly, over many years," Tony said. "So it mustn't have been a big step in Leo's eyes. He probably would have said that his abuse of Mrs. Yancy's girls was all right because he was paying them and therefore owned them, at least for a while. He would have been a man with a strong sense of property rights—and with an extremely liberal definition of the word 'property.' He'd have used that argument, that same point of view, to justify what he did to Katherine. A man like that thinks of a child as just another of his possessions—'*my* child' instead of 'my *child*.' To him, Katherine was a thing, an object, wasted if not used."

"I'm glad I never met the son of a bitch," Joshua said. "If I'd ever shaken hands with him, I think I'd still feel dirty."

"My point," Tony said, "is that Katherine, as a child, was trapped in a house, in a brutalizing relationship, with a man who was capable of *anything*, and there was virtually no chance that she could maintain a firm grip on her sanity under those awful conditions. Leo was a very cold fish, a loner's loner, more than a little bit selfish, with a very strong and very twisted sex drive. It's possible, even likely, that he wasn't just emotionally disturbed. He might have been all the way gone, over the edge, psychotic, detached from reality but able to conceal his detachment. There's a kind of psychopath who has iron control over his delusions, the ability to channel a lot of his lunatic energy into socially-acceptable pursuits, the ability to pass for normal. That kind of psycho vents his madness in one narrow, generally private, area. In Leo's case, he let off a little steam with prostitutes—and a lot of it with Katherine. We've got to figure that he didn't merely abuse her physically. His desire went beyond sex. He lusted after *absolute* control. Once he'd broken her physically, he wouldn't have been satisfied until he'd broken her emotionally, spiritually, and then mentally. By the time Katherine arrived at Mrs. Yancy's place to have her father's baby, she was every bit as mad as Leo had been. But she apparently also had acquired his control, his ability to pass among normal people. She lost that control for three days when the twins arrived, but then she pulled herself together again."

"She lost control a second time," Hilary said as the plane bobbed through a patch of turbulent air.

"Yeah," Joshua said. "When she told Mrs. Yancy that she'd been raped by a demon."

"If my theory's correct," Tony said, "Katherine was going through incredible changes after the birth of the twins. She was moving from one severe psychotic state to an even *more* severe psychotic state. A new set of delusions was pushing out the old set. She had been able to maintain a surface calm in spite of her father's sexual abuse, in spite of the emotional and physical torture he put her through, in spite of becoming pregnant with his child, and even in spite of the agony of being girdled in day and night during all those months when nature was insisting she grow. Somehow she maintained an air of normalcy through all of that. But when the twins were born, when she realized her story about Mary Gunther's baby had come crashing down around her, that was too much to bear. She flipped out—until she conceived the notion that she'd been raped by a demon. We know from Mrs. Yancy that Leo was interested in the occult. Katherine had read some of Leo's books. Somewhere she had picked up the fact that some people believe twins born with cauls are marked by a demon. Because her twins were born with cauls . . . well, she began to fantasize. And the idea that she had been the innocent victim of a demonic creature that had forced itself on her—well, that was very appealing. It exonerated her of the shame and guilt of bearing her own father's babies. It was still something she had to hide from the world, but it wasn't something she had to hide from herself. It wasn't something shameful for which she had to make constant excuses for herself. No one could expect an ordinary woman to resist a demon that had supernatural strength. If she could make herself believe that she'd really been raped by a monster, then she could start thinking of herself as nothing worse than an unfortunate, innocent victim."

"But that's what she was anyway," Hilary said. "She was her father's victim. He forced himself on her, not the other way around."

"True," Tony said. "But he had probably spent a lot of time and energy brainwashing her, trying to make her think she was the one at fault, the one responsible for their twisted relationship. Transferring the guilt to the daughter—that's a fairly common way for a sick man to escape his own sense of guilt. And that sort of behavior would fit Leo's authoritarian personality."

"All right," Joshua said as they fled northward into the yielding sky. "I'll go along with what you've said so far. It may not be right, but it makes sense, and that's a welcome change in the situation. So Katherine gave birth to twins, lost herself for three days, and then got control again by resorting to a new fantasy, a new delusion. By believing that a demon had raped her, she was able to forget that her father was the one who had actually done it. She was able to forget about the incest and regain some of her self-respect. In fact, she probably hadn't ever felt better about herself in her whole life."

"Exactly," Tony said.

Hilary said, "Mrs. Yancy was the only person she'd ever told about the incest, so when she settled into the new fantasy about a demon, she was eager to let Mrs. Yancy know the 'truth.' She was worried that Mrs. Yancy thought of her as a terrible person, a wicked sinner, and she wanted Mrs. Yancy to know that she was only the victim of some irresistible supernatural *thing*. That's why she babbled on about it for so long."

"But when Mrs. Yancy didn't believe her," Tony said, "she decided to keep it to herself. She figured no one else would believe her, either. But that didn't matter to her because she was positive, in her own mind, that she knew the truth, and that truth was the demon. That was a much easier secret to keep than the other one, the one about Leo."

"And Leo had died a few weeks earlier," Hilary said, "so he wasn't around to remind her of what she had forgotten."

Joshua took his hands off the airplane controls for a moment and wiped them on his shirt. "I thought I was too damned old and too cynical to respond to a horror story anymore. But this one makes my palms sweat. There's a terrible correlation to what Hilary just said. Leo wasn't around to remind her—but she needed to keep both twins around to reinforce the new delusion. They were the living proof of it, and she couldn't put either of them up for adoption."

"That's right," Tony said. "Having them with her helped her maintain the fantasy. When she looked at those two perfectly healthy, unquestionably human babies, she really *did* see something different about their sex organs, like she told Mrs. Yancy. She saw it in her mind, imagined it, saw something that was proof, to her, that they were the children of a demon. The twins were part of her comfortable new delusion—and I say 'comfortable' only in comparison to the nightmares with which she had lived before."

Hilary's mind was racing faster than the airplane engine. She grew excited as she saw where Tony's speculations were leading. She said, "So Katherine took the twins home, to that clifftop house, but she still had to keep the Mary Gunther lie in the air, didn't she? Sure. For one thing, she wanted to protect her reputation. But there was another reason, much more important than just her good name. A psychosis is rooted in the subconscious mind, but, as I understand it, the fantasies a psychotic uses to cope with his inner turmoil are more the product of the conscious mind. So . . . while Katherine believed in the demon on a conscious level . . . at the same time, deep down, subconsciously, she knew that if she went back to St. Helena with twins and let the Mary Gunther story collapse, her neighbors would eventually realize that Leo was the father. If she had to deal with that disgrace, she wouldn't have been able to support the demon fantasy that her conscious mind had fabricated. Her new, more comfortable delusions would be replaced by the old, hard, sharp-edged ones. So to maintain the demon fantasy in her own mind, she had to present only one child to the public. So she gave the two boys just one name. She allowed only one of them to go out in public at any one time. She forced them to live one life."

"And eventually," Tony said, "the two boys actually came to think of themselves as one and the same person."

"Hold it, hold it," Joshua said. "Maybe they were able to double for each other and live under only one name, one identity, in public. Even that's asking me to believe a lot, but I'll try. But for sure, in private they still would have been two distinct individuals."

"Maybe not," Tony said. "We've come across proof that they thought of themselves as . . . sort of one person in two bodies."

"Proof? What proof?" Joshua demanded.

"The letter you found in the safe-deposit box in that San Francisco bank. In it, Bruno wrote that *he* had been killed in Los Angeles. He didn't say his brother had been killed. He said he, himself, was dead."

"You can't prove anything by that letter," Joshua said. "It was all mumbo-jumbo. It didn't make any sense."

"In a way it *does* make sense," Tony said. "It makes sense from Bruno's point of view—*if* he didn't think of his brother as another human being. If he thought of his twin as part of himself, as just an extension of himself, and not as a separate person at all, then the letter makes a lot of sense."

Joshua shook his head. "But I still don't see how two people could possibly ever be made to believe they were only one person."

"You're accustomed to hearing about split personalities," Tony said. "Dr. Jekyll and Mr. Hyde. The woman whose true story was told in *The Three Faces of Eve.* And there was a book about another woman like that. It was a best-seller several years ago. *Sybil.* Sybil had sixteen distinct, separate personalities. Well, if I'm right about what became of the Frye twins, then they developed a psychosis that's just the reverse of split personality. These two people didn't split into four or six or eight or eighty; instead, under tremendous pressure from their mother, they . . . melted together psychologically, melted into one. Two individuals with one personality, one self-awareness, one self-image, all shared. It's probably never happened before and might never happen again, but that doesn't mean it can't have happened here."

"The two would have found it virtually essential to develop identical personalities in order to take turns living in the world beyond their mother's house," Hilary said. "Even small differences between them would ruin the charade."

"But *how?*" Joshua demanded. "What did Katherine do to them? How did she make it happen to them?"

"We'll probably never know for certain," Hilary said. "But I've got a few ideas about what she might have done."

"So do I," Tony said. "But you go first."

By mid-afternoon, the amount of light coming through the east-facing attic windows grew steadily less. The quality of the light began to decrease as well; it no longer radiated out from the shaft form that the shape of the window imparted to it. Darkness slowly claimed the corners of the room.

As shadows crept across the floor, Bruno began to worry about being caught in the dark. He couldn't simply snap on a lamp because the lamps weren't in working order. There hadn't been any electric service to the house for five years, since his mother's first death. His flashlight was useless; the batteries were drained.

For a while, as he watched the room sink into purple-gray gloom, Bruno fought panic. He didn't mind being outdoors in the dark, for there was almost always some light spilling from houses, streetlamps, light from passing cars, the stars, the moon. But in a totally lightless room, the whispers and the crawling things returned, and that was a double plague he must prevent somehow.

Candles.

His mother had always kept a couple of boxes of tall candles in the pantry, off the kitchen. They were for use in the event of a power failure. He was pretty sure there would also be matches in the pantry, a hundred or more of them in a round tin with a tight-fitting lid. He hadn't touched any of those things when he had moved out; he had taken nothing but a few personal possessions and some of the collections of artwork that he had acquired himself.

He leaned over to peer into the face of the other Bruno, and he said, "I'm going downstairs for a minute."

The cloudy, blood-muddied eyes stared up at him.

"I won't be gone long," Bruno said.

Himself said nothing.

"I'm going to get some candles so I won't be caught in the dark," Bruno said. "Will I be all right alone here for a few minutes while I'm gone?"

His other self was silent.

Bruno went to the set of steps in one corner of the room. They led down into a second-floor bedroom. The stairwell was not totally dark, for some light from the attic window fell into it. But when Bruno pushed open the door at the bottom, he was shocked to find the bedroom below was black.

The shutters.

He had opened the shutters in the attic when he'd awakened in the dark this morning, but the windows were still sealed elsewhere in the house. He hadn't dared open them. It wasn't likely that Hilary-Katherine's spies would look up and notice just one pair of open attic shutters; but if he were to let light into the entire house, they would certainly spot the change and come running. Now the place was like a sepulcher, shrouded in eternal night.

He stood in the stairwell and peered into the lightless bedroom, afraid to advance, listening for whispers.

Not a sound.

No movement either.

He thought of going back to the attic. But that was no solution to his problem. In a few hours, night would have come, and he would be without a protective light. He *must* forge on to the pantry and find those candles.

Reluctantly, he moved into the second-floor bedroom, holding open the stairwell door to take advantage of the meager, smoky light that lay behind and above him. Two steps. Then he stopped.

Waited.

Listened.

No whispers.

He let go of the door and hurriedly crossed the bedroom, feeling his way between pieces of furniture.

No whispers.

He reached another door and then stepped into the second-floor hallway.

No whispers.

For a moment, enveloped in seamless velvety blackness, he could not remember whether to turn left or right to reach the stairs that led to the ground floor. Then he regained his bearings, and he went to the right, arms extended in front of him and hands opened with fingers spread in blindman fashion.

No whispers.

He almost fell down the stairs when he came to them. The floor suddenly opened under him, and he saved himself by reeling to the left and clutching the unseen bannister.

Whispers.

Clinging to the bannister, unable to see anything at all, he held his breath, cocked his head.

Whispers.

Coming after him.

He cried out and lumbered drunkenly down the steps, lost touch with the railing, then with his balance, windmilled his arms, tripped, sprawled on the landing, face down in the musty carpet, pain shooting through his left leg, just a flash of pain and then the dull echo of it in his flesh, and he lifted his head, and he heard the whispers getting closer, closer, and he got up, whimpering with fear, limped rapidly down the next flight, stumbled when he abruptly reached the ground floor, and looked back, stared up into darkness, heard the whispers rushing toward him, building to a roaring hiss, and he shouted—"*No!*

No!"—and started toward the rear of the house, along the first-floor corridor, toward the kitchen, and then the whispers were all around him, rolling over him, coming from above and below and every side, and the things were there, too, the horrible crawling things—or *thing;* one or many; he didn't know which—and as he careened toward the kitchen, bouncing from wall to wall in his terror, he brushed and slapped at himself, desperately trying to keep the crawling things off him, and then he crashed into the kitchen door, which was a swinging door, which swung open to admit him, and he felt along the perimeter of the room, felt over the stove and the refrigerator and the cupboards and the sink until he came to the pantry door, and the things slithered over him all this time, and the whispers continued, and he screamed and screamed at the top of his raspy voice, and he pulled open the pantry door, was assaulted by a nauseating stench, stepped into the pantry in spite of the overpowering odor that wafted from it, then realized he couldn't see and wouldn't be able to find the candles or the matches by touch among all the other jars and cans, whirled around, into the kitchen again, screaming, flailing at himself, wiping the wriggling *things* off his face as they tried to scurry into his mouth and nose, found the outside door that connected the kitchen to the back porch, fumbled with the stiff latches, finally freed them, and threw the door open.

Light.

Gray afternoon light, slanted down the Mayacamas Mountains from the west, rained through the open door and illuminated the kitchen.

Light.

For a while, he stood in the doorway, letting the wonderful light wash over him. He was sheathed in perspiration. His breath came hard and ragged.

When he finally calmed down, he returned to the pantry. The sickening stench came from old cans and jars of food that had swelled and exploded, spraying spoiled goods and giving rise to green-black-yellow molds and fungi. Trying to avoid the mess as best he could, he located the candles and the can of matches.

The matches were still dry and useful. He struck one to be sure. The spurting flame was a sight that lifted his heart.

To the west of the northward-streaking Cessna, a couple of thousand feet below the aircraft, at the seven- or eight-thousand-foot level, storm clouds steadily approached from the Pacific.

"How?" Joshua asked again. "How did Katherine make the twins think and act and *be* one person?"

"As I said," Hilary told him, "we'll probably never know for certain. But for one thing, it seems to me that she must have shared her delusions with the twins almost from the day she brought them home, long before they were old enough even to understand what she was saying. Hundreds and hundreds of times, perhaps thousands upon thousands of times over the years, she told them that they were the sons of a demon. She told them they'd been born with cauls, and she explained what that meant. She told them their sex organs weren't like those of other boys. She probably told them that they would be killed if other people found out what they were. By the time they were old enough to question all those things, they would have been so thoroughly brainwashed that they wouldn't have been *able* to doubt her. They'd have shared her psychosis and her delusions. They'd have been two extremely tense little boys, afraid of being found out, afraid of being killed. Fear is stress. And a lot of stress would make their psyches highly malleable. It seems to me that tremendous, unrelenting, extraordinary stress over a long period of time would provide exactly the right atmosphere for the melting together of personalities in the way that Tony has suggested. Massive, prolonged stress wouldn't, by itself, *cause* that melting together, but it would sort of set the stage for it.''

Tony said, ''From the tapes we heard in Dr. Rudge's office this morning, we know Bruno was aware that he and his brother were born with cauls. We know that he was familiar with the superstition connected with that rare phenomenon. From the way he sounded on the tape, I think we can safely assume he believed, as his mother did, that he was marked by a demon. And there's other evidence that points to the same conclusion. The letter in the safe-deposit box, for instance. Bruno wrote that he couldn't ask for police protection against his mother because the police would discover what he was and what he'd been hiding all these years. In the letter, he said that if people found out what he was, they would stone him to death. He thought he was the son of a demon. I'm sure of it. He had absorbed Katherine's psychotic delusions.''

''All right,'' Joshua said. ''Maybe both twins believed the demon bunk because they'd never had a chance *not* to believe it. But that still doesn't explain how or why Katherine shaped the two of them into one person, how she got them to . . . melt together psychologically, as you put it.''

''The *why* part of your question is the easiest to answer,'' Hilary said. ''As long as the twins thought of themselves as individuals, there would be differences between them, even if only very minor differences. And the more differences, the more likely it was that one of them would unintentionally blow the entire masquerade someday. The more she could force them to act and think and talk and move and respond alike, the safer she was.''

''As for the *how* of it,'' Tony said, ''you shouldn't forget that Katherine knew the ways and means to break and shape a mind. After all, she had been broken and shaped by a master. Leo. He had used every trick in the book to make her what he wanted her to be, and she couldn't have helped but learn something from all of that. Techniques of physical and psychological torture. She could probably have written a textbook on the subject.''

''And to make the twins think like one person,'' Hilary said, ''she'd have to treat them like one person. She'd have to set the tone, in other words. She'd have to offer them the exact same degrees of love, if any. She'd have to punish both for the actions of one, reward both for the actions of one, treat the two bodies as if they were in possession of the same mind. She had to talk to them as if they were only one person, not two.''

''And every time she caught a glimpse of individuality, she'd either have to make them both do it, or she'd have to eradicate the mannerism in the one who displayed it. And pronoun usage would be very important,'' Tony said.

''Pronoun usage?'' Joshua asked, perplexed.

''Yes,'' Tony said. ''This is going to sound pretty damned far-out. Maybe even meaningless. But more than anything else, our understanding and use of language shapes us. Language is the way we express every idea, every thought. Sloppy thinking leads to a sloppy use of language. But the opposite is also true: Imprecise language causes imprecise thinking. That's a basic tenet of semantics. So it seems logical to theorize that the selectively-twisted usage of pronouns would aid in the establishment of the kind of selectivity-twisted self-image that Katherine wanted to see the twins adopt. For example, when the twins spoke to each other, they could never be allowed to use the pronoun 'you.' Because 'you' embodies the concept of another person other than one's self. If the twins were forced to think of themselves as *one* creature, then the pronoun 'you' would have no place between them. One Bruno could never say to the other, 'Why don't you and I play a game of Monopoly?' He'd have to say, instead, something like this: 'Why don't me and I play a game of Monopoly?' He couldn't use the pronouns 'we' and 'us' when talking about himself and his brother, for those pronouns indicate at least *two* people. Instead, he'd have to say 'me and myself' when he meant 'we.' Furthermore, when one of the twins was talking to Katherine about his brother, he couldn't be permitted to use the pronouns 'he' and 'him.' Again, they embody the concept of another individual in addition to the speaker. Complicated?"

"Insane," Joshua said.

"That's the point," Tony said.

"But it's too much. It's too crazy."

"Of course, it's crazy," Tony said. "It was Katherine's scheme, and Katherine was out of her mind."

"But how could she possibly enforce all of those bizarre rules about habits and mannerisms and attitudes and pronouns and whatever the hell else?"

"The same way you'd enforce an ordinary set of rules with ordinary children," Hilary said. "If they do the right thing, you reward them. If they do the wrong thing, however, you punish them."

"But to make children behave as unnaturally as Katherine wanted the twins to behave, to make them totally surrender their individuality, the punishment would have to be something truly monstrous," Joshua said.

"And we know it *was* something monstrous," Tony said. "We all heard Dr. Rudge's tape of that last session with Bruno, when hypnosis was used. If you remember, Bruno said that she put him into some dark hole in the ground as punishment—and I quote—'for not thinking and acting like one.' I believe he meant she put both him and his brother in that dark place when they refused to think and act like a single person. She locked them in a dark place for long periods of time, and there was something alive in there, something that crawled all over them. Whatever happened to them in that room or hole . . . it was so terrible that they had bad dreams about it every night for decades. If it could leave that strong an impression so many years afterwards, I'd say it was enough of a punishment to be a good brainwashing tool. I'd say Katherine did exactly what she set out to do with the twins: melted them into one."

Joshua stared at the sky ahead.

At last, he said, "When she came back from Mrs. Yancy's whorehouse, her problem was to pass off the twins as the one child she'd talked about, thereby salvaging the Mary Gunther lie. But she could have accomplished that by locking up one of the brothers, making him a house son, while the other twin was the only one allowed to go out of the house. That would have been quicker, easier, simpler, safer."

"But we all know Clemenza's Law," Hilary said.

"Right," Joshua said. "Clemenza's Law: Damned few people ever do anything the quickest, easiest, simplest, and safest way."

"Besides," Hilary said, "maybe Katherine just didn't have the heart to keep one of the boys locked up forever while the other one was permitted to lead at least a bit of a normal life. After all the suffering she'd been through, maybe there was a limit to the amount of suffering she could force her children to endure."

"It seems to me she made them endure a whole hell of a lot!" Joshua said. "She drove them mad!"

"Inadvertently, yes," Hilary said. "She didn't intend to drive them mad. She thought she was doing what was best for them, but her own state of mind didn't make it possible for her to *know* what was best."

Joshua sighed wearily. "It's a wild theory you've got."

"Not so wild," Tony said. "It fits the known facts."

Joshua nodded. "And I guess I believe it, too. At least most of it. I just wish all of the villains in this piece were thoroughly vile and despicable. It seems wrong, somehow, to feel so much sympathy for them."

After they landed in Napa, under rapidly graying skies, they went straight to the county sheriff's office and told Peter Laurenski everything. At first, he gaped at them as if they had lost their minds, but gradually his disbelief turned into reluctant, astonished acceptance. That was a pattern of reactions, a transformation of emotions that Hilary expected they would all witness a few hundred times in the days ahead.

Laurenski telephoned the Los Angeles Police Department. He discovered that the FBI already had contacted the LAPD in regard to the San Francisco bank fraud case involving a look-alike for Bruno Frye, now believed at large in the LAPD's jurisdiction. Laurenski's news, of course, was that the suspect was not merely a look-alike, but the genuine article—even though another genuine article was dead and buried in the Napa County Memorial Park. He informed the LAPD that he had reason to believe the two Brunos had taken turns killing women and had been involved in a series of murders in the northern half of the state over the past five years, although he could not yet provide hard evidence or name specific homicides. The evidence was thus far circumstantial: a grisly but logical interpretation of the safe-deposit box letter in light of recent discoveries about Leo and Katherine and the twins; the fact that both of the twins had made attempts on Hilary's life; the fact that one of the twins had covered for the other last week when Hilary had first been attacked, which indicated complicity in at least attempted murder; and finally the conviction, shared by Hilary and Tony and Joshua, that Bruno's hatred for his mother was so powerful and maniacal that he would not hesitate to slaughter any woman who he imagined was his mother come back to life in a new body.

While Hilary and Joshua shared the railback bench that served as an office couch, and while they drank coffee provided by Laurenski's secretary, Tony took the phone at Laurenski's request and spoke with two of his own superiors in L.A. His support for Laurenski and the corroboration of facts that he provided were apparently effective, for the call concluded with a promise that L.A. authorities would take immediate action at their end. Operating under the assumption that the psychopath would be keeping a watch on Hilary's home, the LAPD agreed to establish around-the-clock surveillance on the Westwood house.

With the cooperation of the Los Angeles police assured, the sheriff quickly composed a bulletin, outlining the basic facts of the case, for distribution to all law enforcement agencies in Northern California. The bulletin doubled as an official request for information on any unsolved murders of young, attractive, brown-eyed brunettes, in jurisdictions beyond Laurenski's, during the past five years—and especially any murders involving decapitation, mutilation, or evidence of blood fetishism.

As Hilary watched the sheriff issuing orders to clerks and deputies, and as she thought about the events of the past twenty-four hours, she had the feeling that everything was moving too fast, like a whirlwind, and that this wind—filled with surprises and ugly secrets, just as a tornado is filled with swirling clods of uprooted earth and chunks of debris—was carrying her toward a precipice that she could not yet see, but over which she might be flung. She wished she could reach out with both hands and seize control of time itself, hold it back, slow it down, take a few days out to rest and to consider what she had learned, so that she would be able to follow the final few twists and turns of the Frye mystery with a clear head. She felt sure that continued haste was foolish, even deadly. But the wheels of the law, now engaged and rolling, could not be blocked. And time could not be reined in as if it were a runaway stallion.

She hoped there was no precipice ahead.

At 5:30, after Laurenski had gotten the law enforcement machinery moving, he and Joshua used the telephone to track down a judge. They found one, Judge Julian Harwey, who was fascinated by the Frye story. Harwey understood the necessity of retrieving the corpse and putting it through an extensive battery of tests for identification purposes. If the second Bruno Frye was apprehended, and if he somehow managed to pass a psychiatric examination, which was highly unlikely but not altogether impossible, then the prosecutor would need physical proof that there had been identical twins. Harwey was willing to sign an exhumation order, and by 6:30, the sheriff had that paper in hand.

"The workmen at the cemetery won't be able to open the grave in the dark," Laurenski said. "But I'll have them out there digging at the crack of dawn." He made a few more phone calls, one to the director of the Napa County Memorial Park where Frye was buried, another to the county coroner who could conduct the examination of the body as soon as it was delivered to him, and one to Avril Tannerton, the mortician, to arrange for him to transport the corpse to and from the coroner's pathology lab.

When Laurenski finally got off the telephone, Joshua said, "I imagine you'll want to search the Frye house."

"Absolutely," Laurenski said. "We want to find proof that more than one man was living there, if we can. And if Frye really has murdered other women, maybe we'll turn up some evidence. I think it would be a good idea to go through the house on the cliff, too."

"We can search the new house as soon as you like," Joshua said. "But there's no electricity in the old place. That one will have to wait until daylight."

"Okay," Laurenski said. "But I'd like to have a look at the vineyard house tonight."

"Now?" Joshua asked, getting up from the railback bench.

"None of us has had dinner," Laurenski said. Earlier, before they had told him even half of what they'd learned from Dr. Rudge and Rita Yancy, the sheriff had called his wife to tell her he wouldn't be home until very late. "Let's get a bite to eat at the coffee shop around the corner. Then we can head on out to Frye's place."

Before they left for the restaurant, Laurenski told the night receptionist where he would be and asked her to let him know immediately if word came in that the Los Angeles police had arrested the second Bruno Frye.

"It's not going to be that easy," Hilary said.

"I suspect she's right," Tony said. "Bruno has concealed an incredible secret for forty years. He may be crazy, but he's also clever. The LAPD isn't going to lay hands on him that fast. They'll have to play a lot of cat-and-mouse before they finally nail him."

When night had begun to fall, Bruno had closed the attic shutters again.

Now there were candles on each nightstand. There were two candles on the dresser. The flickering yellow flames made shadows dance on the walls and ceiling.

Bruno knew that he should already be out looking for Hilary-Katherine, but he could not find the energy to get up and go. He kept putting it off.

He was hungry. He suddenly realized he hadn't eaten since yesterday. His stomach was growling.

For a while, he sat on the bed, beside the staring corpse, and he tried to decide where he should go to get some food. A few of the cans in the pantry hadn't swelled up, hadn't burst, but he was sure that everything on those shelves was spoiled and poisonous. For almost an hour, he struggled with the problem, trying to think of where he could go to get something to eat and still be safe from Katherine's spies. They were everywhere. The bitch and her spies. Everywhere. His state of mind was still best described as confused, and even though he was hungry, he had difficulty keeping his thoughts focused on food. But at last, he remembered there was food in the vineyard house. The milk would have spoiled during the past week, and the bread would have gotten hard. But his own pantry was full of canned goods, and the refrigerator was stocked with cheese and fruit, and there was ice cream in the freezer. The thought of ice cream made him smile like a small boy.

Driven by the vision of ice cream, hoping that a good supper would give him the energy he needed to begin looking for Hilary-Katherine, he left the attic and made his way down through the house with the aid of a candle. Outside, he snuffed out the flame and tucked the candle into a jacket pocket. He descended the crumbling switchback stairs on the face of the cliff and strode off through the dark vineyards.

Ten minutes later, in his own house, he struck a match and relit the candle because he was afraid that he would attract unwanted attention if he switched on the lights. He got a spoon from a drawer by the kitchen sink, took a one-gallon, cardboard tub of chocolate ripple from the freezer, and sat at the table for more than a quarter of an hour, smiling, eating big spoonfuls of ice cream right out of the carton, until at last he was too full to swallow even one more bite.

He dropped the spoon in the half-emptied carton, put the ice cream back in the freezer, and realized that he ought to pack up canned goods to take back to the clifftop house. He might not be able to find and kill Hilary-Katherine for days, and during this time he didn't want to have to sneak back here for every meal. Sooner or later, the bitch would think to have some of her spies put a watch on this place, and then he would be caught. But she'd never look for him in the cliff house, not in a million years, so that was where he ought to have his food supply.

He went into the master bedroom and got a large suitcase from the closet, took that into the kitchen, and filled it with cans of peaches, pears, mandarin orange slices, jars of peanut butter and jars of olives, and two kinds of jelly—each jar wrapped in paper towels to cushion it and keep it from breaking—and tins of little Vienna sausages. When he finished packing, the big suitcase was extremely heavy, but he had the muscles to handle it.

He had not showered since last night, at Sally's house in Culver City, and he felt grimy. He hated being dirty, for being dirty somehow always made him think of the whispers and the awful crawling things and the dark place in the ground. He decided he could risk taking a quick shower before he carried the food back to the clifftop house even if that meant being naked and defenseless for a few minutes. But as he walked through the living room on his way to the bedroom and master bath, he heard cars approaching along the vineyard road. The engines sounded unnaturally loud in the perfect stillness of the fields.

Bruno ran to the front window and parted the drapes just an inch and looked out.

Two cars. Four headlights. Coming up the slope toward the clearing.

Katherine.

The bitch!

The bitch and her friends. Her dead friends.

Terrified, he ran to the kitchen, grabbed the suitcase, put out the candle that he was carrying, and pocketed it. He let himself out by the back door and dashed across the rear lawn, into the sheltering vineyards, as the cars stopped out front.

Crouching, lugging the suitcase, anxiously aware of every small sound he made, Bruno moved through the vines. He circled the house until he could see the cars. He put down the suitcase and sprawled beside it, hugging the moist earth and the darkest of the night shadows. He watched the people getting out of the cars, and his heart hammered faster each time that he recognized a face.

Sheriff Laurenski and a deputy. So the police were among the living dead! He had never suspected them.

Joshua Rhinehart. The old attorney was a conspirator, too! He was one of Katherine's hellish friends.

And there *she* was! The bitch. The bitch in her sleek new body. And that man from Los Angeles.

They all went into the house.

Lights came on in one room after another.

Bruno tried to remember if he'd left any signs of his visit. Maybe some drippings from the candle. But the droplets of wax would be cold and hard already. They would have no way of knowing if the drippings were fresh or weeks old. He'd left the spoon in the ice cream carton, but that might have been done a long time before, too. Thank God, he hadn't taken a shower! The water on the floor of the shower stall and the damp towel would have given him away; finding a recently used towel, they would have known instantly that he was back in St. Helena, and they would have intensified their search for him.

He got to his feet, hefted the suitcase, and hurried as fast as he could through the vineyards. He went north toward the winery, then west toward the cliff.

They would never come to the cliff house looking for him. Not in a million years. He would be safe in the cliff house because they would think he was too afraid to go there.

If he hid in the attic, he would have time to think and plan and organize. He didn't dare rush into this. He hadn't been thinking too clearly lately, not since the other half of him had died, and he didn't dare move against the bitch until he had planned for every possible contingency.

He knew how to find her now. Through Joshua Rhinehart.

He could get his hands on her whenever he wanted.

But first he needed time to formulate a foolproof plan. He could hardly wait to get back to the attic to talk it over with himself.

Laurenski, Deputy Tim Larsson, Joshua, Tony, and Hilary spread out through the house. They searched drawers and closets and cupboards and cabinets.

At first, they couldn't find anything that proved two men had been living in the house instead of one. There seemed to be quite a few more clothes than one man would need. And the house was stocked with more food than one man usually kept on hand. But that wasn't proof of anything.

Then, as Hilary was going through desk drawers in the study, she came across a stack of recently received bills that hadn't been paid yet. Two of them were from dentists—one in nearby Napa, the other in San Francisco.

"Of course!" Tony said as everyone gathered around to have a look at the bills. "The twins would have had to go to different doctors and, especially, different dentists. Bruno Number Two couldn't walk into a dentist's office to have a tooth filled when that same dentist had filled the same tooth in Bruno Number one just the week before."

"This helps," Laurenski said. "Even identical twins don't get the same cavities in the same place on the same teeth. Two sets of dental records will prove there were two Bruno Frye's."

A while later, while searching a bedroom closet, Deputy Larsson made an unsettling discovery. One of the shoe boxes did not have shoes in it. Instead, the box contained a dozen wallet-sized snapshots of a dozen young women, driver's licenses for six of them, and another eleven licenses belonging to eleven other women. In each snapshot and in each license photo, the woman looking out at the camera had things in common with all the other women in the collection: a pretty face, dark eyes, dark hair, and an indefinable something in the lines and angles of the facial structure.

"Twenty-three women who vaguely resemble Katherine," Joshua said. "My God. Twenty-three."

"A gallery of death," Hilary said, shivering.

"At least they're not all unidentified snapshots," Tony said. "With the licenses, we've got names and addresses."

"We'll get them out on the wire right away," Laurenski said, sending Larsson out to the car to radio the information to HQ. "But I think we all know what we'll find."

"Twenty-three unsolved murders spread over the past five years," Tony said.

"Or twenty-three disappearances," the sheriff said.

They spent two more hours in the house, but they didn't find anything else as important as the photographs and driver's licenses. Hilary's nerves were frayed, and her imagination was stimulated by the disturbing realization that her own driver's license had nearly wound up in that shoe box. Each time she opened a drawer or a cupboard door, she expected to find a shriveled heart with a stake through it or a dead woman's rotting head. She was relieved when the search was finally completed.

Outside, in the chilly night air, Laurenski said, "Will the three of you be coming to the coroner's office in the morning?"

"Count me out," Hilary said.

"No thanks," Tony said.

Joshua said, "There's really nothing we can do there."

"What time should we meet at the cliff house?" Laurenski asked.

Joshua said, "Hilary and Tony and I will go up first thing in the morning and open all the shutters and windows. The place has been closed up for five years. It'll need to be aired out before any of us will want to spend hours poking through it. Why don't you just come on up and join us whenever you're finished at the coroner's?"

"All right," Laurenski said. "See you tomorrow. Maybe the Los Angeles police will get the bastard during the night."

"Maybe," Hilary said hopefully.

Up in the Mayacamas Mountains, soft thunder roared.

Bruno Frye spent half the night talking to himself, carefully planning Hilary-Katherine's death.

The other half, he slept while the candles flickered. Thin streams of smoke rose from the burning wicks. The dancing flames cast jiggling, macabre shadows on the walls, and they were reflected in the staring eyes of the corpse.

Joshua Rhinehart had trouble sleeping. He tossed and turned, getting increasingly tangled in the sheets. At three o'clock in the morning, he went out to the bar and poured himself a double shot of bourbon, drank it fast. Even that didn't settle him down a whole lot.

He had never missed Cora so much as he did that night.

*   *   *

Hilary woke repeatedly from bad dreams, but the night did not go by slowly. It swept past at rocket speeds. She still had the feeling that she was hurtling toward a precipice, and she could do nothing to stop her forward rush.

Near dawn, as Tony lay awake, Hilary turned to him, came against him, and said, "Make love to me."

For half an hour, they lost themselves in each other, and although it was not better than before, it was not one degree worse either. A sweet, silken, hushed togetherness.

Afterwards, she said, "I love you."

"I love you, too."

"No matter what happens," she said, "we've had these few days together."

"Now don't get fatalistic on me."

"Well . . . you never know."

"We've got years ahead of us. Years and years and years together. Nobody's going to take them away from us."

"You're so positive, so optimistic. I wish I'd found you a long time ago."

"We're through the worst of this thing," he said. "We know the truth now."

"They haven't caught Frye yet."

"They will," Tony said reassuringly. "He thinks you're Katherine, so he's not going to stray too far from Westwood. He'll keep checking back at your house to see if you've shown up, and sooner or later the surveillance team will spot him, and it'll all be over."

"Hold me," she said.

"Sure."

"Mmmm. That's nice."

"Yeah."

"Just being held."

"Yeah."

"I feel better already."

"Everything's going to be fine."

"As long as I have you," she said.

"Forever, then."

The sky was dark and low and ominous. The peaks of the Mayacamas were shrouded in mist.

Peter Laurenski stood in the graveyard, hands in his pants pockets, shoulders hunched against the chill morning air.

Using a backhoe for most of the way, then tossing out the last eight or ten inches of dirt with shovels, workmen at Napa County Memorial Park gouged into the soft earth, tearing open Bruno Frye's grave. As they labored, they complained to the sheriff that they were not being paid extra for getting up at dawn and missing breakfast and coming in early, but they got very little sympathy from him; he just urged them to work faster.

At 7:45, Avril Tannerton and Gary Olmstead arrived in the Forever View hearse. As they walked across the green hillside toward Laurenski, Olmstead looked properly somber, but Tannerton was smiling, taking in great lungfuls of the nippy air, as if he were merely out for his morning constitutional.

"Morning, Peter."

"Morning, Avril. Gary."

"How long till they have it open?" Tannerton asked.

"They say fifteen minutes."

At 8:05, one of the workmen climbed up from the hole and said, "Ready to yank him out?"

"Let's get on with it," Laurenski said.

Chains were attached to the casket, and it was brought out of the ground by the same device that had lowered it in just last Sunday. The bronze coffin was caked with earth around the handles and in the frill work, but overall it was still shiny.

By 8:40, Tannerton and Olmstead had loaded the big box into the hearse.

"I'll follow you to the coroner's office," the sheriff said.

Tannerton grinned at him. "I assure you, Peter, we aren't going to run off with Mr. Frye's remains."

At 8:20, in Joshua Rhinehart's kitchen, while the casket was being exhumed at the cemetery a few miles away, Tony and Hilary stacked the breakfast dishes in the sink.

"I'll wash them later," Joshua said. "Let's get up to the cliff and open that house. It must smell like hell in there after all these years. I just hope the mildew and mold haven't done too much damage to Katherine's collections. I warned Bruno about that a thousand times, but he didn't seem to care if—" Joshua stopped, blinked. "Will you listen to me babble on? Of *course* he didn't care if the whole lot of it rotted away. Those were Katherine's collections, and he wouldn't have cared a damn about anything she treasured."

They went to Shade Tree Vineyards in Joshua's car. The day was dreary; the light was dirty gray. Joshua parked in the employees' lot.

Gilbert Ulman hadn't come to work yet. He was the mechanic who maintained the aerial tramway in addition to caring for all of Shade Tree Vineyards' trucks and farm equipment.

The key that operated the tramway was hanging on a pegboard in the garage, and the winery's night manager, a portly man named Iannucci, was happy to get it for Joshua.

Key in hand, Joshua led Hilary and Tony up to the second floor of the huge main winery, through an area of administrative offices, through a viniculture lab, and then onto a broad catwalk. Half the building was open from the first floor to the ceiling, and in that huge chamber there were enormous three-story fermentation tanks. Cold, cold air flowed off the tanks, and there was a yeasty odor in the place. At the end of the long catwalk, at the southwest corner of the building, they went through a heavy pine door with black iron hinges, into a small room that was open at the end opposite from where they entered. An overhanging roof extended twelve feet out from the missing wall, to keep rain from slanting into the open chamber. The four-seat cable car—a fire-engine-red number with lots of glass—was nestled under the overhang, at the brink of the room.

The pathology laboratory had a vague, unpleasant chemical odor. So did the coroner, Dr. Amos Garnet, who sucked vigorously on a breath mint.

There were five people in the room. Laurenski, Larsson, Garnet, Tannerton, and Olmstead. No one, with the possible exception of the perennially good-natured Tannerton, seemed happy to be there.

"Open it," Laurenski said. "I've got an appointment to keep with Joshua Rhinehart."

Tannerton and Olmstead threw back the latches on the bronze casket. A few remaining chunks of dirt fell to the floor, onto the plastic dropcloth that Garnet had put down. They pushed the lid back.

The body was gone.

The velvet- and silk-lined box held nothing but the three fifty-pound bags of dry mortar mix that had been stolen from Avril Tannerton's basement last weekend.

Hilary and Tony sat on one side of the cable car, and Joshua sat on the other. The attorney's knees brushed Tony's.

Hilary held Tony's hand as the red gondola moved slowly, slowly up the line toward the top of the cliff. She wasn't afraid of heights, but the tramway seemed so fragile that she could not help gritting her teeth.

Joshua saw the tension on her face and smiled. "Don't worry. The car seems small, but it's sturdy. And Gilbert does a fine job with maintenance."

As it ground gradually upward, the car swung slightly in the stiff morning wind.

The view of the valley became increasingly spectacular. Hilary tried to concentrate on that and not on the creaking and clattering of the machinery.

The gondola finally reached the top of the cable. It locked in place, and Joshua opened the door.

When they walked out of the upper station of the tramway system, a fiercely-white arc of lightning and a violent peal of thunder broke open the lowering sky. Rain began to fall. It was a thin, cold, slanting rain.

Joshua, Hilary, and Tony ran for shelter. They stomped up the front steps and across the porch to the door.

"And you say there's no heat up here?" Hilary asked.

"The furnace has been shut down for five years," Joshua said. "That's why I told both of you to wear sweaters under your coats. It's not a cold day, really. But once you've been up here awhile in this damp, the air will cut through to your bones."

Joshua unlocked the door, and they went inside, switching on the three flashlights they'd brought with them.

"It stinks in here," Hilary said.

"Mildew," Joshua said. "That's what I was afraid of."

They walked from the foyer into the hall, then into the big drawing room. The beams of their flashlights fell on what looked to be a warehouse full of antique furniture.

"My God," Tony said, "it's worse than Bruno's house. There's hardly room to walk."

"She was obsessed with collecting beautiful things," Joshua said. "Not for investment. Not just because she liked to look at them, either. A lot of things are crammed into closets, hidden away. Paintings stacked on paintings. And as you can see, even in the main rooms, there's just too damned much stuff; it's jammed too close together to please the eye."

"If every room has antiques of this quality," Hilary said, "then there's a fortune here."

"Yeah," Joshua said. "If it hasn't been eaten up by worms and termites and whatnot." He let his flashlight beam travel from one end of the room to the other. "This mania for collecting was something I never understood about her. Until this minute. Now I wonder if. . . . As I look at all of this, and as I think about what we learned from Mrs. Yancy. . . ."

Hilary said, "You think collecting beautiful things was a reaction to all the ugliness in her life before her father died?"

"Yeah," Joshua said. "Leo broke her. Shattered her soul, smashed her spirit flat and left her with a rotten self-image. She must have hated herself for all the years she let him use her—even though she'd had no choice but to let him. So maybe . . . feeling low and worthless, she thought she could make her soul beautiful by living among lots of beautiful things."

They stood in silence for a moment, looking at the over-furnished drawing room.

"It's so sad," Tony said.

Joshua shook himself from his reverie. "Let's get these shutters open and let in some light."

"I can't stand the smell," Hilary said, cupping one hand over her nose. "But if we raise the windows, the rain will get in and ruin things."

"Not much if we raise them only five or six inches," Joshua said. "And a few drops of water aren't going to hurt anything in this mold colony."

"It's a wonder there aren't mushrooms growing out of the carpet," Tony said.

They moved through the downstairs, raising windows, unbolting the inward-facing latches on the shutters, letting in the gray storm light and the fresh rain-scented air.

When most of the downstairs rooms had been opened, Joshua said, "Hilary, all that's left down here is the dining room and the kitchen. Why don't you take care of those windows while Tony and I tend to the upstairs."

"Okay," she said. "I'll be up in a minute to help out."

She followed her flashlight beam into the pitch-black dining room as the men went down the hall toward the stairs.

When he and Joshua came into the upstairs hallway, Tony said, *"Phew!* It stinks even worse up here."

A blast of thunder shook the old house. Windows rattled icily. Doors stuttered in their frames.

"You take the rooms on the right," Joshua said. "I'll take the ones on the left."

Tony went through the first door on his side and found a sewing room. An ancient treadle-powered sewing machine stood in one corner, and a more modern electric model rested on a table in another corner; both were bearded with cobwebs. There was a work table and two dressmaker's forms and one window.

He went to the window, put his flashlight on the floor, and tried to twist open the lock lever. It was rusted shut. He struggled with it as rain drummed noisily on the shutters beyond the glass.

Joshua shone his flashlight into the first room on the left and saw a bed, a dresser, a highboy. There were two windows in the far wall.

He crossed the threshold, took two more steps, sensed movement behind him, and he started to turn, felt a sudden cold thrill go through his back, and then it became a very hot thrill, a burning lance, a line of pain drawn through his flesh, and he knew he had been stabbed. He felt the knife being jerked out of him. He turned. His flashlight revealed Bruno Frye. The madman's face was wild, demoniacal. The knife came up, came down, and the cold thrill shivered through Joshua again, and this time the blade tore his right shoulder, from front to back, all the way through, and Bruno had to twist and jerk the weapon savagely, several times, to get it out. Joshua raised his left arm to protect himself. The blade punctured his forearm. His legs buckled. He went down. He fell against the bed, slid to the floor, slick with his own blood, and Bruno turned away from him and went out to the second-floor hall, out of the flashlight's glow, into the darkness. Joshua realized he hadn't even screamed, had not warned Tony, and he tried to shout, really tried, but the first wound seemed to be very serious, for when he attempted to make any sound at all, pain blossomed in his chest, and he could do no better than hiss like a goddamned goose.

Grunting, Tony put all of his strength against the stubborn window latch, and abruptly the rusted metal gave—*sweeek*—and popped open. He raised the windows, and the sound of the rain swelled. A fine spray of water misted through a few narrow chinks in the shutters and dampened his face.

The inward-facing bolt on the shutters also was corroded, but Tony finally freed it, pushed the shutters open, leaned out in the rain, and fixed them in their braces so they wouldn't bang about in the wind.

He was wet and cold. He was anxious to get on with the search of the house, hoping the activity would warm him.

As another volley of thunder cannonaded down from the Mayacamas, into the valley, over the house, Tony walked out of the sewing room and into Bruno Frye's knife.

In the kitchen, Hilary opened the shutters on the window that looked onto the back porch. She fixed them in place and paused for a moment to stare out at the rain-swept grass and the wind-whipped trees. At the end of the lawn, twenty yards away, there were doors in the ground.

She was so surprised to see those doors that, for a moment, she thought she was imagining them. She squinted through the sheeting rain, but the doors didn't dissolve miragelike, as she half expected.

At the end of the lawn, the land rose up in one of its last steps to the vertical ramparts of the mountains. The doors were set into that hillside. They were framed with timbers and mortared stones.

Hilary turned away from the window and hurried across the filthy kitchen, anxious to tell Joshua and Tony about her discovery.

Tony knew how to protect himself against a man with a knife. He was trained in self-defense, and he'd been in situations like this one on two other occasions. But this time he was caught off guard by the suddenness and total unexpectedness of the attack.

Glaring, his broad countenance split by a hideous rictus grin, Frye swung the knife at Tony's face. Tony managed to turn partly out of the blow, but the blade still tore along the side of his head, ripping scalp, drawing blood.

The pain was like an acid burn.

Tony dropped his flashlight; it rolled away, causing the shadows to leap and sway.

Frye was fast, damned fast. He struck again as Tony was just going into a defensive posture. This time the knife scored solidly if peculiarly, coming down point-first on the top of his left shoulder, driving through jacket and sweater, through muscle and gristle, between bones, instantly taking all the strength out of that arm and forcing Tony to his knees.

Somehow Tony found the energy to swing his right fist up from the floor, into Frye's testicles. The big man gasped and staggered backwards, pulling the knife out of Tony as he went.

Unaware of what was happening above her, Hilary called up from the foot of the stairs. "Tony! Joshua! Come down here and see what I've found."

Frye whirled at the sound of Hilary's voice. He headed for the steps, apparently forgetting that he was leaving a wounded but living man behind him.

Tony got up, but a napalm explosion of pain set fire to his arm, and he swayed dizzily. His stomach flopped over. He had to lean against the wall.

All he could do was warn her. "Hilary, run! Run! Frye's coming!"

*   *   *

Hilary was about to call up to them again when she heard Tony shouting to her. For an instant, she couldn't believe what he was saying, but then she heard heavy footsteps on the first flight, thumping down. He was still out of sight above the landing, but she knew he couldn't be anyone but Bruno Frye.

Then Frye's gravelly voice boomed: *"Bitch, bitch, bitch, bitch!"*

Stunned, but not frozen with shock, Hilary backed away from the foot of the stairs, and then she ran as she saw Frye reaching the landing. Too late, she realized she should have gone toward the front of the house, outside, to the cable car; but she was streaking toward the kitchen instead, and there was no turning back now.

She pushed through the swinging door, into the kitchen, as Frye jumped down the last few steps and into the hallway behind her.

She thought of searching the kitchen drawers for a knife.

Couldn't. No time.

She ran to the outside door, unlocked it, and bolted from the kitchen as Frye entered it through the swinging door.

The only weapon she had was the flashlight she had been carrying, and that was no weapon at all.

She crossed the porch, went down the steps. Rain and wind battered her. He was not far behind. He was still chanting, *"Bitch, bitch, bitch!"*

She would never be able to run around the house and all the way to the cable car before he caught her. He was much too close and gaining.

The wet grass was slick.

She was afraid of falling.

Of dying.

Tony?

She ran toward the only place that might offer protection: the doors in the ground.

Lightning flickered, and thunder followed it.

Frye wasn't screaming behind her any more. She heard a deep, animal growl of pleasure.

Very close.

Now *she* was screaming.

She reached the doors in the hillside and saw that they were latched together at both the top and bottom. She reached and threw back the top bolt, then stooped and disengaged the one on the bottom, expecting a blade to be slammed down between her shoulders. The blow never came. She pulled open the doors, and there was inky blackness beyond.

She turned.

Rain stung her face.

Frye had stopped. He was standing just six feet away.

She waited in the open doors with darkness at her back, and she wondered what was behind her other than a flight of steps.

"Bitch," Frye said.

But now there was more fear than fury in his face.

"Put the knife down," she said, not knowing if he would obey, doubting it, but having nothing to lose. "Obey your mother, Bruno. Put the knife down."

He took a step toward her.

Hilary stood her ground. Her heart was exploding.

Frye moved closer.

Shaking, she backed down the first step that lay beyond the doors.

* * *

Just as Tony reached the head of the stairs, supporting himself with one hand against the wall, he heard a noise behind him. He looked back.

Joshua had crawled out of the bedroom. He was splashed with blood, and his face was nearly as white as his hair. His eyes seemed out of focus.

"How bad?" Tony asked.

Joshua licked his pale lips. "I'll live," he said in a strange, hissing, croaking voice. "Hilary. For God's sake . . . Hilary!"

Tony pushed away from the wall and careened down the stairs. He weaved back down the hall toward the kitchen, for he could hear Frye shouting out on the rear lawn.

In the kitchen, Tony pulled open one drawer, then another, looking for a weapon.

"Come on, dammit! *Shit!*"

The third drawer held knives. He chose the largest one. It was spotted with rust but still wickedly sharp.

His left arm was killing him. He wanted to cradle it in his right arm, but he needed that hand to fight Frye.

Gritting his teeth, steeling himself against the pain of his wounds, lurching like a drunkard, he went out to the porch. He saw Frye at once. The man was standing in front of two open doors. Two doors in the ground.

Hilary was nowhere in sight.

Hilary backed off the sixth step. That was the last one.

Bruno Frye stood at the head of the stairs, looking down, afraid to come any farther. He was alternately calling her a bitch and whimpering as if he were a child. He was clearly torn between two needs: the need to kill her, and the need to get away from that hated place.

Whispers.

Suddenly she heard the whispers, and her flesh seemed to turn to ice in that instant. It was a wordless hissing, a soft sound, but growing louder by the second.

And then she felt something crawling up her leg.

She cried out and moved up one step, closer to Frye. She reached down, brushed at her leg, and knocked something away.

Shuddering, she switched on the flashlight, turned, and shone the beam into the subterranean room behind her.

Roaches. Hundreds upon hundreds of huge roaches were swarming in the room—on the floor, on the walls, on the low ceiling. They were not just ordinary roaches, but enormous things, over two inches long, an inch wide, with busy legs and especially long feelers that quivered anxiously. Their shiny green-brown carapaces appeared to be sticky and wet, like blobs of dark mucus.

The whispering was the sound of their ceaseless movement, long legs and trembling antennae brushing other long legs and antennae, constantly crawling and creeping and scurrying this way and that.

Hilary screamed. She wanted to climb the steps and get out of there, but Frye was above, waiting.

The roaches shied away from her flashlight. They were evidently subterranean insects that survived only in the dark, and she prayed her flashlight batteries would not go dead.

The whispering grew louder.

More roaches were pouring into the room. They were coming out of a crack in the floor. Coming out by tens. By scores. By hundreds. There were a couple of thousand of the disgusting things in the room already, and the chamber was no more than twenty feet on a side. They piled up two and three deep in the other half of the room, avoiding the light, but getting bolder by the moment.

She knew that an entomologist would probably not call them roaches. They were beetles, subterranean beetles that lived in the bowels of the earth. A scientist would have a crisp, clean, Latin name for them. But to her they were roaches.

Hilary looked up at Bruno.

"Bitch," he said.

Leo Frye had built a cold storage cellar, a common enough convenience in 1918. But he had mistakenly built on a flaw in the earth. She could see that he had tried many times to patch the floor, but it kept opening each time that the earth trembled. In quake country, the earth trembled often.

And the roaches came up from hell.

They were still gushing from the hole, a wriggling, kicking, squirming mass.

They mounted up on one another, five- and six- and seven-deep, covering the walls and the ceiling, moving, endlessly moving, swarming restlessly. The cold whisper of their movement was now a soft roar.

For punishment, Katherine had put Bruno in this place. In the dark. For hours at a time.

Suddenly, the roaches moved toward Hilary. The pressure of them building up in layers finally caused them to spill at her like a breaking wave, in a roiling green-brown mass. In spite of the flashlight, they surged forward, hissing.

She screamed and started up the steps, preferring Bruno's knife to the hideous insect horde behind her.

Grinning, Frye said, "See how you like it, bitch." And he slammed the door.

The rear lawn was no more than twenty yards long, but to Tony it appeared to be at least a mile from the porch to the place where Frye was standing. He slipped and fell in the wet grass, taking some of the fall on his wounded shoulder. A brilliant light played behind his eyes for a moment, and then an iridescent darkness, but he resisted the urge to just lay there. He got up.

He saw Frye close the doors and lock them. Hilary had to be on the other side, shut in.

Tony covered the last ten feet of the lawn with the awful certainty that Frye would turn and see him. But the big man continued to face the doors. He was listening to Hilary, and she was screaming. Tony slipped up on him and put the knife between his shoulder blades.

Frye cried out in pain and turned.

Tony stumbled backwards, praying that he had inflicted a mortal wound. He knew he could not win in hand-to-hand combat with Frye—especially not when he had the use of only one arm.

Frye reached frantically behind, trying to grab the knife that Tony had rammed into him. He wanted to pull it out of himself, but he could not reach it.

A thread of blood trickled from the corner of his mouth.

Tony backed up another step. Then another.

Frye staggered toward him.

Hilary stood on the top step, pounding on the locked doors. She screamed for help.

Behind her, the whispering in the dark cellar grew louder with each shattering thump of her heart.

She risked a glance backward, shining the light down the steps. Just the sight of the humming mass of insects made her gag with revulsion. The room below appeared to be waist-deep in roaches. A huge pool of them shifted and swayed and hissed in such a way that it seemed almost as if there was only one organism down there, one monstrous creature with countless legs and antennae and hungry mouths.

She realized that she was still screaming. Over and over again. Her voice was getting hoarse. She couldn't stop.

Some of the insects were venturing up the steps in spite of her light. Two of them reached her feet, and she stamped on them. Others followed.

She turned to the doors again, screaming. She pounded on the timbers with all her strength.

Then the flashlight went out. She had thoughtlessly hammered it against the door in her hysterical effort to get help. The glass cracked. The light died.

For a moment, the whispering seemed to subside—but then it rose rapidly to a greater volume than ever before.

Hilary put her back to the door.

She thought of the tape recording she had heard in Dr. Nicholas Rudge's office yesterday morning. She thought of the twins, as children, locked in here, hands clamped over their noses and mouths, trying to keep the roaches from crawling into them. All of that screaming had given both of them coarse, gravelly voices; hours and hours, days and days of screaming.

Horrified, she stared down into the darkness, waiting for the ocean of beetles to close over her.

She felt a few on her ankles, and she quickly bent down, brushed them away.

One of them ran up her left arm. She clapped a hand on it, squashed it.

The terrifying susurration of the moving insects was almost deafening now. She put her hands to her ears.

A roach dropped from the ceiling, onto her head. Screaming, she plucked it out of her hair, threw it away.

Suddenly, the doors opened behind her, and light burst into the cellar. She saw a surging tide of roaches only one step below her, and then the wave fell back from the light, and Tony pulled her out into the rain and the beautiful dirty gray light.

A few roaches clung to her clothes, and Tony knocked them from her.

"My God," he said. "My God, my God."

Hilary leaned against him.

There were no more roaches on her, but she imagined she could still feel them. Crawling. Creeping.

She shook violently, uncontrollably, and Tony put his good arm around her. He talked to her softly, calmly, bringing her down.

At last she was able to stop screaming.

"You're hurt," she said.

"I'll live. And paint."

She saw Frye. He was sprawled on the grass, face down, obviously dead. A knife protruded from his back, and his shirt was soaked with blood.

"I had no choice," Tony said. "I really didn't want to kill him. I felt sorry for him . . . knowing what Katherine had put him through. But I had no choice."

They walked away from the corpse, across the lawn.

Hilary's legs were weak.

"She put the twins in that place when she wanted to punish them," Hilary said. "How many times? A hundred? Two hundred? A thousand times?"

"Don't think about it," Tony said. "Just think about being alive, being together. Think about whether you'd like being married to a slightly battered ex-cop who's struggling to make a living as a painter."

"I think I'd like that very much."

Forty feet away, Sheriff Peter Laurenski rushed out of the kitchen, onto the back porch. "What's happened?" he called to them. "Are you all right?"

Tony didn't bother to answer him. "We've got years and years together," he told Hilary. "And from here on, it's all going to be good. For the first time in our lives, we both know who we are, what we want, and where we're going. We've overcome the past. The future will be easy."

As they walked toward Laurenski, the autumn rain hammered softly on them and whispered in the grass.

WATCHERS

This book is dedicated to
Lennart Sane
who is not only the best at what he does
but who is also a nice guy.
And to
Elisabeth Sane
who is as charming as her husband.

PART ONE

SHATTERING
THE PAST

The past is but the beginning of a beginning,
and all that is and has been
is but the twilight of the dawn.

—H.G. Wells

The meeting of two personalities is like the contact of two
chemical substances: if there is any reaction, both are
transformed.

—C.G. Jung

CHAPTER 1

1

ON HIS THIRTY-SIXTH birthday, May 18, Travis Cornell rose at five o'clock in the morning. He dressed in sturdy hiking boots, jeans, and a long-sleeved, blue-plaid cotton shirt. He drove his pickup south from his home in Santa Barbara all the way to rural Santiago Canyon on the eastern edge of Orange County, south of Los Angeles. He took only a package of Oreo cookies, a large canteen full of orange-flavored Kool-Aid, and a fully loaded Smith & Wesson .38 Chief's Special.

During the two-and-a-half-hour trip, he never switched on the radio. He never hummed, whistled, or sang to himself as men alone frequently do. For part of the drive, the Pacific lay on his right. The morning sea was broodingly dark toward the horizon, as hard and cold as slate, but nearer shore it was brightly spangled with early light the colors of pennies and rose petals. Travis did not once glance appreciatively at the sun-sequined water.

He was a lean, sinewy man with deep-set eyes the same dark brown as his hair. His face was narrow, with a patrician nose, high cheekbones, and a slightly pointed chin. It was an ascetic face that would have suited a monk in some holy order that still believed in self-flagellation, in the purification of the soul through suffering. God knows, he'd had his share of suffering. But it could

414

be a pleasant face, too, warm and open. His smile had once charmed women, though not recently. He had not smiled in a long time.

The Oreos, the canteen, and the revolver were in a small green nylon backpack with black nylon straps, which lay on the seat beside him. Occasionally, he glanced at the pack, and it seemed as if he could see straight through the fabric to the loaded Chief's Special.

From Santiago Canyon Road in Orange County, he turned onto a much narrower route, then onto a tire-eating dirt lane. At a few minutes past eight-thirty, he parked the red pickup in a lay-by, under the immense bristly boughs of a big-cone spruce.

He slipped the harness of the small backpack over his shoulders and set out into the foothills of the Santa Ana Mountains. From his boyhood, he knew every slope, vale, narrow defile, and ridge. His father had owned a stone cabin in upper Holy Jim Canyon, perhaps the most remote of all the inhabited canyons, and Travis had spent weeks exploring the wild land for miles around.

He loved these untamed canyons. When he was a boy, black bears had roamed the woods; they were gone now. Mule deer could still be found, though not in the great number he had seen two decades ago. At least the beautiful folds and thrusts of land, the profuse and varied brush, and the trees were still as they had been; for long stretches he walked beneath a canopy of California live oaks and sycamores.

Now and then he passed a lone cabin or a cluster of them. A few canyon dwellers were half-hearted survivalists who believed the end of civilization was approaching, but who did not have the heart to move to a place even more forbidding. Most were ordinary people who were fed up with the hurly-burly of modern life and thrived in spite of having no plumbing or electricity.

Though the canyons seemed remote, they would soon be overwhelmed by encroaching suburbs. Within a hundred-mile radius, nearly ten million people lived in the interconnecting communities of Orange and Los Angeles counties, and growth was not abating.

But now crystalline, revelatory light fell on the untamed land with almost as much substance as rain, and all was clean and wild.

On the treeless spine of a ridge, where the low grass that had grown during the short rainy season had already turned dry and brown, Travis sat upon a broad table of rock and took off his backpack.

A five-foot rattlesnake was sunning on another flat rock fifty feet away. It raised its mean wedge-shaped head and studied him.

As a boy, he had killed scores of rattlers in these hills. He withdrew the gun from the backpack and rose from the rock. He took a couple of steps toward the snake.

The rattler rose farther off the ground and stared intensely.

Travis took another step, another, and assumed a shooter's stance, with both hands on the gun.

The rattler began to coil. Soon it would realize that it could not strike at such a distance, and would attempt to retreat.

Although Travis was certain his shot was clear and easy, he was surprised to discover that he could not squeeze the trigger. He had come to these foothills not merely to attempt to recall a time when he had been glad to be alive, but also to kill snakes if he saw any. Lately, alternately depressed and angered by the loneliness and sheer pointlessness of his life, he had been wound as tight as a crossbow spring. He needed to release that tension through violent action, and the killing of a few snakes—no loss to anyone—seemed the perfect prescription for his distress. However, as he stared at this rattler, he realized that its existence was less pointless than his own: it filled an ecological niche, and it probably took more pleasure in life than he had in a long time. He began to shake and the gun kept straying from the target, and he could not find the will to fire. He was not a worthy executioner, so he lowered the gun and returned to the rock where he had left his backpack.

The snake was evidently in a peaceable mood, for its head lowered sinuously to the stone once more, and it lay still.

After a while, Travis tore open the package of Oreos, which had been his favorite treat when he was young. He had not eaten one in fifteen years. They were almost as good as he remembered them. He drank Kool-Aid from the canteen, but it wasn't as satisfying as the cookies. To his adult palate, the stuff was far too sweet.

The innocence, enthusiasms, joys, and voracities of youth can be recalled but perhaps never fully regained, he thought.

Leaving the rattlesnake in communion with the sun, shouldering his backpack once more, he went down the southern slope of the ridge into the shadows of the trees at the head of the canyon, where the air was freshened by the fragrant spring growth of the evergreens. On the west-sloping floor of the canyon, in deep gloom, he turned west and followed a deer trail.

A few minutes later, passing between a pair of large California sycamores that bent together to form an archway, he came to a place where sunlight poured into a break in the forest. At the far side of the clearing, the deer trail led into another section of woods in which spruces, laurels and sycamores grew closer together than elsewhere. Ahead, the land dropped steeply as the canyon sought bottom. When he stood at the edge of the sunfall with the toes of his boots in shadow, looking down that sloped path, he could see only fifteen yards before a surprisingly seamless darkness fell across the trail.

As Travis was about to step out of the sun and continue, a dog burst from the dry brush on his right and ran straight to him, panting and chuffing. It was a golden retriever, pure of breed by the look of it. A male. He figured it was little more than a year old, for though it had attained the better part of its full growth, it retained some of the sprightliness of a puppy. Its thick coat was damp, dirty, tangled, snarled, full of burrs and broken bits of weeds and leaves. It stopped in front of him, sat, cocked its head, and looked up at him with an undeniably friendly expression.

Filthy as it was, the animal was nonetheless appealing. Travis stooped, patted its head, and scratched behind its ears.

He half-expected an owner, gasping and perhaps angry at this runaway, to follow the retriever out of the brush. Nobody came. When he thought to check for a collar and license, he found none.

"Surely you're not a wild dog—are you, boy?"

The retriever chuffed.

"No, too friendly for a wild one. Not lost, are you?"

It nuzzled his hand.

He noticed that, in addition to its dirty and tangled coat, it had dried blood on its right ear. Fresher blood was visible on its front paws, as if it had been running so long and so hard over rugged terrain that the pads of its feet had begun to crack.

"Looks like you've had a difficult journey, boy."

The dog whined softly, as if agreeing with what Travis had said.

He continued to stroke its back and scratch its ears, but after a minute or two he realized he was seeking something from the dog that it could not provide: meaning, purpose, relief from despair.

"On your way now." He gave the retriever a light slap on its side, rose, and stretched.

The dog remained in front of him.

He stepped past it, heading for the narrow path that descended into darkness.

"Move along, boy."

The retriever bared its teeth and growled low in its throat.

When he tried to step past it, the retriever snarled. It snapped at his legs. Travis danced back two steps. "Hey, what's gotten into you?"

The dog stopped growling and just panted.

He advanced again, but the dog lunged at him more ferociously than before, still not barking but growling even deeper and snapping repeatedly at his legs, driving him backward across the clearing. He took eight or ten clumsy steps on a slippery carpet of dead spruce and pine needles, stumbled over his own feet, and fell on his butt.

The moment Travis was down, the dog turned away from him. It padded across the clearing to the brink of the sloping path and peered into the gloom below. Its floppy ears had pricked up as much as a retriever's ears can.

"Damn dog," Travis said.

It ignored him.

"What the hell's the matter with you, mutt?"

Standing in the forest's shadow, it continued to stare down the deer trail, into the blackness at the bottom of the wooded canyon slope. Its tail was down, almost tucked between its legs.

Travis gathered half a dozen small stones from the ground around him, got up, and threw one of the missiles at the retriever. Struck on the backside hard enough to be stung, the dog did not yelp but whipped around in surprise.

Now I've done it, Travis thought. He'll go for my throat.

But the dog only looked at him accusingly—and continued to block the entrance to the deer trail.

Something in the tattered beast's demeanor—in the wideset dark eyes or in the tilt of its big squarish head—made Travis feel guilty for having stoned it. The sorry damn dog looked disappointed in him, and he was ashamed.

"Hey, listen," he said, "*you* started it, you know."

The dog just stared at him.

Travis dropped the other stones.

The dog glanced at the relinquished missiles, then raised its eyes once more, and Travis swore he saw approval in that canine face.

Travis could have turned back. Or he could have found another way down the canyon. But he was seized by an irrational determination to forge ahead, to go where he *wanted* to go, by God. This day of all days, he was not going to be deterred or even delayed by something as trivial as an obstructive dog.

He got up, shrugged his shoulders to resettle the backpack, took a deep breath of the piny air, and walked boldly across the clearing.

The retriever began to growl again, softly but menacingly. Its lips skinned back from its teeth.

Step by step, Travis's courage faded, and when he was within a few feet of the dog, he opted for a different approach. He stopped and shook his head and gently berated the animal: "Bad dog. You're being a very bad dog. You know that? What's gotten into you? Hmmmm? You don't look as if you were born bad. You look like a good dog."

As he continued to sweet-talk the retriever, it ceased growling. Its bushy tail wagged once, twice, tentatively.

"That's a good boy," he said slyly, coaxingly. "That's better. You and I can be friends, huh?"

The dog issued a conciliatory whine, that familiar and appealing sound all dogs make to express their natural desire to be loved.

"Now, we're getting somewhere," Travis said, taking another step toward the retriever with the intention of stooping and petting it.

Immediately, the dog leaped at him, snarling, and drove him back across the clearing. It got its teeth in one leg of his jeans, shook its head furiously. He kicked at it, missed. As Travis staggered out of balance from the misplaced kick, the dog snatched the other leg of his pants and ran a circle around him, pulling him with it. He hopped desperately to keep up with his adversary but toppled and slammed to the ground again.

"Shit!" he said, feeling immeasurably foolish.

Whining again, having reverted to a friendly mood, the dog licked one of his hands.

"You're schizophrenic," Travis said.

The dog returned to the other end of the clearing. It stood with its back to him, staring down the deer trail that descended through the cool shadows of the trees. Abruptly, it lowered its head, hunched its shoulders. The muscles in its back and haunches visibly tensed as if it were preparing to move fast.

"What're you looking at?" Travis was suddenly aware that the dog was not fascinated by the trail itself but, perhaps, by something *on* the trail. "Mountain lion?" he wondered aloud as he got to his feet. In his youth, mountain lions—specifically, cougars—had prowled these woods, and he supposed some still hung on.

The retriever growled, not at Travis this time but at whatever had drawn its attention. The sound was low, barely audible, and to Travis it seemed as if the dog was both angry and afraid.

Coyotes? Plenty of them roamed the foothills. A pack of hungry coyotes might alarm even a sturdy animal like this golden retriever.

With a startled yelp, the dog executed a leaping-scrambling turn away from the shadowed deer trail. It dashed toward him, past him, to the other arm of the woods, and he thought it was going to disappear into the forest. But at the archway formed by two sycamores; through which Travis had come only minutes ago, the dog stopped and looked back expectantly. With an air of frustration and anxiety, it hurried in his direction again, swiftly circled him, grabbed at his pants leg, and wriggled backward, trying to drag him with it.

"Wait, wait, okay," he said. "Okay."

The retriever let go. It issued one woof, more a forceful exhalation than a bark.

Obviously—and astonishingly—the dog had purposefully prevented him from proceeding along the gloomy stretch of the deer trail because something was down there. Something dangerous. Now the dog wanted him to flee because that dangerous creature was drawing nearer.

Something was coming. But what?

Travis was not worried, just curious. Whatever was approaching might frighten a dog, but nothing in these woods, not even a coyote or a cougar, would attack a grown man.

Whining impatiently, the retriever tried to grab one leg of Travis's jeans again.

Its behavior was extraordinary. If it was frightened, why didn't it run off, forget him? He was not its master; it owed him nothing, neither affection nor protection. Stray dogs do not possess a sense of duty to strangers, do not have a moral perspective, a conscience. What did this animal think it was, anyway—a freelance Lassie?

"All right, all right," Travis said, shaking the retriever loose and accompanying it to the sycamore arch.

The dog dashed ahead, along the ascending trail, which led up toward the canyon rim, through thinning trees and brighter light.

Travis paused at the sycamores. Frowning, he looked across the sun-drenched clearing at the night-dark hole in the forest where the descending portion of the trail began. What was coming?

The shrill cries of the cicadas cut off simultaneously, as if a phonograph needle was lifted from a recording. The woods were preternaturally silent.

Then Travis heard something rushing up the lightless trail. A scrabbling noise. A clatter of dislodged stones. A faint rustle of dry brush. The thing sounded closer than it probably was, for sound was amplified as it echoed up through the narrow tunnel of trees. Nevertheless, the creature was coming fast. Very fast.

For the first time, Travis sensed that he was in grave peril. He knew that nothing in the woods was big or bold enough to attack him, but his intellect was overruled by instinct. His heart hammered.

Above him, on the higher path, the retriever had become aware of his hesitation. It barked agitatedly.

Decades ago, he might have thought an enraged black bear was racing up the deer trail, driven mad by disease or pain. But the cabin dwellers and weekend hikers—outriders of civilization—had pushed the few remaining bears much farther back into the Santa Anas.

From the sound of it, the unknown beast was within seconds of reaching the clearing between the lower and higher trails.

The length of Travis's spine, shivers tracked like melting bits of sleet trickling down a windowpane.

He wanted to see what the thing was, but at the same time he had gone cold with dread, a purely instinctive fear.

Farther up the canyon, the golden retriever barked urgently.

Travis turned and ran.

He was in excellent shape, not a pound overweight. With the panting retriever leading, Travis tucked his arms close to his sides and sprinted up the deer trail, ducking under the few low-hanging branches. The studded soles of his hiking boots gave good traction; he slipped on loose stones and on slithery layers of dry pine needles, but he did not fall. As he ran through a false fire of flickering sunlight and shadow, another fire began to burn in his lungs.

Travis Cornell's life had been full of danger and tragedy, but he'd never flinched from anything. In the worst of times, he calmly confronted loss, pain, and fear. But now something peculiar happened. He lost control. For the first time in his life, he panicked. Fear pried into him, touching a deep and primitive level where nothing had ever reached him before. As he ran, he broke out in gooseflesh and cold sweat, and he did not know *why* the unknown pursuer should fill him with such absolute terror.

He did not look back. Initially, he did not want to turn his eyes away from the twisting trail because he was afraid he would crash into a low branch. But as he ran, his panic swelled, and by the time he had gone a couple of hundred yards, the reason he did not look back was because he was afraid of what he might see.

He knew that his response was irrational. The prickly sensation along the back of his neck and the iciness in his gut were symptoms of a purely superstitious terror. But the civilized and educated Travis Cornell had turned over the reins to the frightened child-savage that lives in every human being—the genetic ghost of what we once were—and he could not easily regain control even though he was aware of the absurdity of his behavior. Brute instinct ruled, and instinct told him that he must run, run, stop thinking and just run.

Near the head of the canyon, the trail turned left and carved a winding course up the steep north wall toward the ridge. Travis rounded a bend, saw a log lying across the path, jumped but caught one foot on the rotting wood. He fell forward, flat on his chest. Stunned, he could not get his breath, could not move.

He expected something to pounce on him and tear out his throat.

The retriever dashed back down the trail and leaped over Travis, landing surefootedly on the path behind him. It barked fiercely at whatever was chasing them, much more threateningly than when it had challenged Travis in the clearing.

Travis rolled over and sat up, gasping. He saw nothing on the trail below. Then he realized the retriever was not concerned about anything in that direction but was standing sideways on the trail, facing the underbrush in the forest to the east of them. Spraying saliva, it barked stridently, so hard and loud that each explosive sound hurt Travis's ears. The tone of savage fury in its voice was daunting. The dog was warning the unseen enemy to stay back.

"Easy, boy," Travis said softly. "Easy."

The retriever stopped barking but did not glance at Travis. It stared intently into the brush, peeling its pebbly black lips off its teeth and growling deep in its throat.

Still breathing hard, Travis got to his feet and looked east into the woods. Evergreens, sycamores, a few larches. Shadows like swatches of dark cloth were fastened here and there by golden pins and needles of light. Brush. Briars. Climbing vines. A few well-worn toothlike formations of rock. He saw nothing out of the ordinary.

When he reached down and put a hand upon the retriever's head, the dog stopped growling, as if it understood his intention. Travis drew a breath, held it, and listened for movement in the brush.

The cicadas remained silent. No birds sang in the trees. The woods were as still as if the vast, elaborate clockwork mechanism of the universe had ceased ticking.

He was sure that he was not the cause of the abrupt silence. His passage through the canyon had not previously disturbed either birds or cicadas.

Something *was* out there. An intruder of which the ordinary forest creatures clearly did not approve.

He took a deep breath and held it again, straining to hear the slightest movement in the woods. This time he detected the rustle of brush, a snapping twig, the soft crunch of dry leaves—and the unnervingly peculiar, heavy, ragged breathing of something big. It sounded about forty feet away, but he could not pinpoint its location.

At his side, the retriever had gone rigid. Its floppy ears were slightly pricked, straining forward.

The unknown adversary's raspy breathing was so creepy—whether because of the echo effect of the forest and canyon, or because it was just creepy to begin with—that Travis quickly took off his backpack, unsnapped the flap, and withdrew the loaded .38.

The dog stared at the gun. Travis had the weird feeling that the animal knew what the revolver was—and approved of the weapon.

Wondering if the thing in the woods was a man. Travis called out: "Who's there? Come on out where I can see you."

The hoarse breathing in the brush was now underlaid with a thick menacing gnarl. The eerie guttural resonance electrified Travis. His heart beat even harder, and he went as rigid as the retriever beside him. For interminable ticking seconds, he could not understand why the noise itself had sent such a powerful current of fear through him. Then he realized that what frightened him was the noise's ambiguity: the beast's growl was definitely that of an animal . . . yet there was also an indescribable quality that bespoke intelligence, a tone and modulation almost like the sound that an enraged *man* might make. The more he listened, the more Travis decided it was neither strictly an animal nor human sound. But if neither . . . then what the hell was it?

He saw the high brush stirring. Straight ahead. Something was coming toward him.

"Stop," he said sharply. "No closer."

It kept coming.

Now just thirty feet away.

Moving slower than it had been. A bit wary perhaps. but closing in nevertheless.

The golden retriever began to growl threateningly, again warning off the creature that stalked them. But tremors were visible in its flanks, and its head shook. Though it was challenging the thing in the brush, it was profoundly frightened of a confrontation.

The dog's fear unnerved Travis. Retrievers were renowned for boldness and courage. They were bred to be the companions of hunters, and were frequently used in dangerous rescue operations. What peril or foe could provoke such dread in a strong, proud dog like this?

The thing in the brush continued toward them, hardly more than twenty feet away now.

Though he had as yet seen nothing extraordinary, he was filled with superstitious terror, a perception of indefinable but uncanny presences. He kept telling himself he had chanced upon a cougar, just a cougar, that was probably more frightened than he was. But the icy prickling that began at the base of his spine and extended up across his scalp now intensified. His hand was so slick with sweat that he was afraid the gun would slip out of his grasp.

Fifteen feet.

Travis pointed the .38 in the air and squeezed off a single warning shot. The blast crashed through the forest and echoed down the long canyon.

The retriever did not even flinch, but the thing in the brush immediately turned away from them and ran north, upslope, toward the canyon rim. Travis could not see it, but he could clearly mark its swift progress by the waist-high weeds and bushes that shook and parted under its assault.

For a second or two, he was relieved because he thought he had frightened it off. Then he saw it was not actually running away. It was heading northnorthwest on a curve that would bring it to the deer trail above them. Travis sensed that the creature was trying to cut them off and force them to go out of the canyon by the lower route, where it would have more and better opportunities to attack. He did not understand how he knew such a thing, just that he *did* know it.

His primordial survival instinct drove him into action without the need to *think* about each move he made; he automatically did what was required. He had not felt that animal surety since he had seen military action almost a decade ago.

Trying to keep his eye on the telltale tremble of the brush to his right, abandoning his backpack and keeping only the gun, Travis raced up the steep trail, and the retriever ran behind him. Fast as he was, however, he was not fast enough to overtake the unknown enemy. When he realized that it was going to reach the path well above him, he fired another warning shot, which did not startle or deflect the adversary this time. He fired twice into the brush itself, toward the indications of movement, not caring if it *was* a man out there, and that worked. He did not believe he hit the stalker, but he scared it at last, and it turned away.

He kept running. He was eager to reach the canyon rim, where the trees were thin along the ridge top, where the brush was sparse, and where a brighter fall of sunlight did not permit concealing shadows.

When he arrived at the crest a couple of minutes later, he was badly winded. The muscles of his calves and thighs were hot with pain. His heart thumped so hard in his chest that he would not have been surprised to hear the echo of it bouncing off another ridge and coming back to him across the canyon.

This was where he had paused to eat some Oreos. The rattlesnake, which earlier had been sunning on a large flat rock, was gone.

The golden retriever had followed Travis. It stood beside him, panting, peering down the slope they had just ascended.

Slightly dizzy, wanting to sit and rest but aware that he was still in danger of an unknown variety, Travis looked down the deer trail, too, and scanned what underbrush he could see. If the stalker remained in pursuit of them, it was being more circumspect, climbing the slopes without disturbing the weeds and bushes.

The retriever whined and tugged once at Travis's pants leg. It scurried across the top of the narrow ridge to a declivity by which they could make their way down into the next canyon. Clearly, the dog believed they were not out of danger and ought to keep moving.

Travis shared that conviction. His atavistic fear—and the reliance on instinct that it invoked—sent him hurrying after the dog, over the far side of the ridge, into another tree-filled canyon.

2

Vincent Nasco had been waiting in the dark garage for hours. He did not look as if he would be good at waiting. He was big—over two hundred pounds, six-three, muscular—and he always seemed to be so full of energy that he might burst at any moment. His broad face was placid, usually as expressionless as the face of a cow. But his green eyes flashed with vitality, with an edgy nervous watchfulness—and with a strange hunger that was like something you expected to see in the eyes of a wild animal, some jungle cat, but never in the eyes of a man. Like a cat, in spite of his tremendous energy, he was patient. He could crouch for hours, motionless and silent, waiting for prey.

At nine-forty Tuesday morning, much later than Nasco expected, the deadbolt lock on the door between the garage and the house was disengaged with a single hard *clack*. The door opened, and Dr. Davis Weatherby flicked on the garage lights, then reached for the button that would raise the big sectional door.

"Stop right there," Nasco said, rising and stepping from in front of the doctor's pearl-gray Cadillac.

Weatherby blinked at him, surprised. "Who the hell—"

Nasco raised a silencer-equipped Walther P-38 and shot the doctor once in the face.

Ssssnap.

Cut off in midsentence, Weatherby fell backward into the cheery yellow and white laundry room. Going down, he struck his head on the clothes dryer and knocked a wheeled metal laundry cart into the wall.

Vince Nasco was not worried about the noise because Weatherby was unmarried and lived alone. He stooped over the corpse, which had wedged the door open, and tenderly put one hand on the doctor's face.

The bullet had hit Weatherby in the forehead, less than an inch above the bridge of his nose. There was little blood because death had been instantaneous, and the slug had not been quite powerful enough to smash through the back of the man's skull. Weatherby's brown eyes were open wide. He looked startled.

With his fingers, Vince stroked Weatherby's warm cheek, the side of his neck. He closed the sightless left eye, then the right, although he knew that postmortem muscle reactions would pop them open again in a couple of minutes. With a profound gratefulness evident in his tremulous voice, Vince said, "Thank you. Thank you, Doctor." He kissed both of the dead man's closed eyes. "Thank you."

Shivering pleasantly, Vince plucked the car keys off the floor where the dead man had dropped them, went into the garage, and opened the Cadillac's trunk, being careful not to touch any surface on which he might leave a clear fingerprint. The trunk was empty. Good. He carried Weatherby's corpse out of the laundry room, put it in the trunk, closed and locked the lid.

Vince had been told that the doctor's body must not be discovered until tomorrow. He did not know why the timing was important, but he prided himself on doing flawless work. Therefore, he returned to the laundry room, put the metal cart where it belonged, and looked around for signs of violence. Satisfied, he closed the door on the yellow and white room, and locked it with Weatherby's keys.

He turned out the garage lights, crossed the darkened space, and let himself out the side door, where he had entered during the night by quietly loiding the flimsy lock with a credit card. Using the doctor's keys, he relocked the door and walked away from the house.

Davis Weatherby lived in Corona Del Mar, within sight of the Pacific Ocean. Vince had left his two-year-old Ford van three blocks from the doctor's house. The walk back to the van was very pleasant, invigorating. This was a fine neighborhood boasting a variety of architectural styles; expensive Spanish casas sat beside beautifully detailed Cape Cod homes with a harmony that had to be seen to be believed. The landscaping was lush and well tended. Palms and ficus and olive trees shaded the sidewalks. Red, coral, yellow, and orange bougainvillaeas blazed with thousands of flowers. The bottlebrush trees were in bloom. The branches of jacarandas dripped lacy purple blossoms. The air was scented with star jasmine.

Vincent Nasco felt wonderful. So strong, so powerful, so *alive*.

3

Sometimes the dog led, and sometimes Travis took the lead. They went a long way before Travis realized that he had been completely jolted out of the despair and desperate loneliness that had brought him into the foothills of the Santa Ana Mountains in the first place.

The big tattered dog stayed with him all the way to his pickup, which was parked along the dirt lane under the overhanging boughs of an enormous spruce. Stopping at the truck, the retriever looked back the way they had come.

Behind them, black birds swooped through the cloudless sky, as if engaged in reconnaissance for some mountain sorcerer. A dark wall of trees loomed like the ramparts of a sinister castle.

Though the woods were gloomy, the dirt road onto which Travis had stepped was fully exposed to the sun, baked to a pale brown, mantled in fine, soft dust that plumed around his boots with each step he took. He was surprised that such a bright day could have been abruptly filled with an overpowering, palpable sense of evil.

Studying the forest out of which they had fled, the dog barked for the first time in half an hour.

"Still coming, isn't it?" Travis said.

The dog glanced at him and mewled unhappily.

"Yeah," he said, "I feel it too. Crazy . . . yet I feel it too. But what the hell's out there, boy? Huh? What the hell is it?"

The dog shuddered violently.

Travis's own fear was amplified every time he saw the dog's terror manifested.

He put down the tailgate of the truck and said, "Come on. I'll give you a lift out of this place."

The dog sprang into the cargo hold.

Travis slammed the gate shut and went around the side of the truck. As he pulled open the driver's door, he thought he glimpsed movement in the nearby brush. Not back toward the forest but at the far side of the dirt road. Over there, a narrow field was choked with waist-high brown grass as crisp as hay, a few bristly clumps of mesquite, and some sprawling oleander bushes with roots deep enough to keep them green. When he stared directly at the field, he saw none of the movement he thought he had caught from the corner of his eye, but he suspected that he had not imagined it.

With a renewed sense of urgency, he climbed into the truck and put the revolver on the seat beside him. He drove away from there as fast as the washboard lane permitted, and with constant consideration for the four-legged passenger in the cargo bed.

Twenty minutes later, when he stopped along Santiago Canyon Road, back in the world of blacktop and civilization, he still felt weak and shaky. But the fear that lingered was different from that he'd felt in the forest. His heart was no longer drumming. The cold sweat had dried on his hands and brow. The odd prickling of nape and scalp was gone—and the memory of it seemed unreal. Now he was afraid not of some unknown creature but of his own strange behavior. Safely out of the woods, he could not quite recall the degree of terror that had gripped him; therefore, his actions seemed irrational.

He pulled on the handbrake and switched off the engine. It was eleven o'clock, and the flurry of morning traffic had gone; only an occasional car passed on the rural two-lane blacktop. He sat for a minute, trying to convince himself that he had acted on instincts that were good, right, and reliable.

He had always taken pride in his unshakable equanimity and hardheaded pragmatism—in that if nothing else. He could stay cool in the middle of a bonfire. He could make hard decisions under pressure and accept the consequences.

Except—he found it increasingly difficult to believe something strange had actually been stalking him out there. He wondered if he had misinterpreted the dog's behavior and had imagined the movement in the brush merely to give himself an excuse to turn his mind away from self-pity.

He got out of the truck and stepped back to the side of it, where he came face-to-face with the retriever, which stood in the cargo bed. It shoved its burly head toward him and licked his neck, his chin. Though it had snapped and barked earlier, it was an affectionate dog, and for the first time its bedraggled condition struck him as having a comical aspect. He tried to hold the dog back. But it strained forward, nearly clambering over the side of the cargo hold in its eagerness to lick his face. He laughed and ruffled its tangled coat.

The retriever's friskiness and the frenzied wagging of its tail had an unexpected effect on Travis. For a long time his mind had been a dark place, filled with thoughts of death, culminating in today's journey. But this animal's un-adulterated joy in being alive was like a spotlight that pierced Travis's inner gloom and reminded him that life had a brighter side from which he had long ago turned away.

"What *was* that all about back there?" he wondered aloud.

The dog stopped licking him, stopped wagging its matted tail. It regarded him solemnly, and he was suddenly transfixed by the animal's gentle, warm brown eyes. Something in them was unusual, compelling. Travis was half-mesmerized, and the dog seemed equally captivated. As a mild spring breeze rose from the south, Travis searched the dog's eyes for a clue to their special power and appeal, but he saw nothing extraordinary about them. Except . . . well, they seemed somehow more expressive than a dog's eyes usually were, more intelligent and aware. Given the short attention span of any dog, the retriever's unwavering stare *was* damned unusual. As the seconds ticked past and as neither Travis nor the dog broke the encounter, he felt increasingly peculiar. A shiver rippled through him, occasioned not by fear but by a sense that something uncanny was happening, that he was teetering on the threshold of an awesome revelation.

Then the dog shook its head and licked Travis's hand, and the spell was broken.

"Where'd you come from, boy?"

The dog cocked its head to the left.

"Who's your owner?"

The dog cocked its head to the right.

"What should I do with you?"

As if in answer, the dog jumped over the truck's tailgate, ran past Travis to the driver's door, and climbed into the pickup's cab.

When Travis peered inside, the retriever was in the passenger's seat, looking straight ahead through the windshield. It turned to him and issued a soft woof, as if impatient with the dawdling.

He got in behind the wheel, tucked the revolver under his seat. "Don't believe I can take care of you. Too much responsibility, fella. Doesn't fit in with my plans. Sorry about that."

The dog regarded him beseechingly.

"You look hungry, boy."

It woofed once, softly.

"Okay, maybe I can help you that much. I think there's a Hershey's bar in the glove compartment . . . and there's a McDonald's not far from here, where they've probably got a couple hamburgers with your name on them. But after that . . . well, I'll either have to let you loose again or take you to the pound."

Even as Travis was speaking, the dog raised one foreleg and hit the glove-compartment release button with a paw. The lid fell open.

"What the hell . . ."

The dog leaned forward, put its snout into the open box, and withdrew the candy in its teeth, holding the bar so lightly that the wrapping was not punctured.

Travis blinked in surprise.

The retriever held forth the Hershey's bar, as if requesting that Travis unwrap the treat.

Startled, he took the candy and peeled off the paper.

The retriever watched, licking its lips.

Breaking the bar into pieces, Travis paid out the chocolate in morsels. The dog took them gratefully and ate almost daintily.

Travis watched in confusion, not certain if what had happened was truly extraordinary or had a reasonable explanation. Had the dog actually understood him when he had said there was candy in the glove box? Or had it detected the scent of chocolate? Surely the latter.

To the dog, he said, "But how did you know to press the button to pop the lid open?"

It stared, licked its chops, and accepted another bit of candy.

He said, "Okay, okay, so maybe that's a trick you've been taught. Though it's not the sort of thing anyone would ordinarily train a dog to do, is it? Roll over, play dead, sing for your supper, even walk on your hind feet a little ways . . . yeah, those're things that dogs are trained to do . . . but they're not trained to open locks and latches."

The retriever gazed longingly at the last morsel of chocolate, but Travis withheld the goody for a moment.

The *timing,* for God's sake, had been uncanny. Two seconds after Travis had referred to the chocolate, the dog had gone for it.

"Did you understand what I said?" Travis asked, feeling foolish for suspecting a dog of possessing language skills. Nevertheless, he repeated the question: "Did you? Did you understand?"

Reluctantly, the retriever raised its gaze from the last of the candy. Their eyes met. Again Travis sensed that something uncanny was happening; he shivered not unpleasantly, as before.

He hesitated, cleared his throat. "Uh . . . would it be all right with you if I had the last piece of chocolate?"

The dog turned its eyes to the two small squares of the Hershey's bar still in Travis's hand. It chuffed once, as if with regret, then looked through the windshield.

"I'll be damned," Travis said.

The dog yawned.

Being careful not to move his hand, not holding the chocolate out, not calling attention to the chocolate in any manner except with words, he addressed the big tattered dog again: "Well, maybe you need it more than I do, boy. If you want it, the last bit's yours."

The retriever looked at him.

Still not moving his hand, keeping it close to his own body in a way that implied he was withholding the chocolate, he said, "If you want it, take it. Otherwise, I'll just throw it away."

The retriever shifted on the seat, leaned close to him, and gently snatched the chocolate off his palm.

"I'll be double-damned," he said.

The dog rose onto all fours, standing on the seat, which brought its head almost to the ceiling. It looked through the back window of the cab and growled softly.

Travis glanced at the rearview mirror, then at the sidemounted mirror, but he saw nothing unusual behind them. Just the two-lane blacktop, the narrow berm, the weed-covered hillside sloping down on their right side. "You think we should get moving? Is that it?"

The dog looked at him, peered out the rear window, then turned and sat with its hind legs tucked to one side, facing forward again.

Travis started the engine, put the truck in gear, pulled onto Santiago Canyon Road, and headed north. Glancing at his companion, he said, "Are you really more than you appear to be . . . or am I just cracking up? And if you are more than you appear to be . . . what the devil *are* you?"

At the rural eastern end of Chapman Avenue, he turned west toward the McDonald's of which he'd spoken.

He said, "Can't turn you loose now or take you to a pound."

And a minute later, he said, "If I didn't keep you, I'd die of curiosity, wondering about you."

They drove about two miles and swung into the McDonald's parking lot.

Travis said, "So I guess you're my dog now."

The retriever said nothing.

CHAPTER 2

1

NORA DEVON WAS AFRAID of the television repairman. Although he appeared to be about thirty (her age), he had the offensive cockiness of a know-it-all teenager. When she answered the doorbell, he boldly looked her up and down as he identified himself—"Art Streck, Wadlow's TV"—and when he met her eyes again, he winked. He was tall and lean and well-scrubbed, dressed in white uniform slacks and shirt. He was clean-shaven. His darkish-blond hair was cut short and neatly combed. He looked like any mother's son, not a rapist or psycho, yet Nora was instantly afraid of him, maybe because his boldness and cockiness seemed at odds with his appearance.

"You need service?" he asked when she hesitated in the doorway.

Although his question appeared innocent, the inflection he put on the word "service" seemed creepy and sexually suggestive to Nora. She did not think she was overreacting. But she had called Wadlow TV, after all, and she could not turn Streck away without explanation. An explanation would probably lead to an argument, and she was not a confrontational person, so she let him inside.

As she escorted him along the wide, cool hallway to the living-room arch, she had the uneasy feeling that his good grooming and big smile were elements of a carefully calculated disguise. He had a keen animal watchfulness, a coiled tension, that further disquieted her with every step they took away from the front door.

Following her much too closely, virtually looming over her from behind, Art Streck said, "You've got a nice house here, Mrs. Devon. Very nice. I really like it."

"Thank you," she said stiffly, not bothering to correct his misapprehension of her marital status."

"A man could be happy here. Yeah, a man could be very happy."

The house was of that style of architecture sometimes called Old Santa Barbara Spanish: two stories, cream-colored stucco with a red-tile roof, verandas, balconies, all softly rounded lines instead of squared-off corners. Lush red bougainvillaea climbed the north face of the structure, dripping bright blossoms. The place was beautiful.

Nora hated it.

She had lived there since she was only two years old, which now added up to twenty-eight years, and during all but one of them, she had been under the iron thumb of her Aunt Violet. Hers had not been a happy childhood or, to date, a happy life. Violet Devon had died a year ago. But, in truth, Nora was still oppressed by her aunt, for the memory of that hateful old woman was formidable, stifling.

In the living room, putting his repair kit beside the Magnavox, Streck paused to look around. He was clearly surprised by the decor.

The flowered wallpaper was dark, funereal. The Persian carpet was singularly unattractive. The color scheme—gray, maroon, royal blue—was unenlivened by a few touches of faded yellow. Heavy English furniture from the mid-nineteenth century, trimmed with deeply carved molding, stood on clawed feet: massive armchairs, footstools, cabinets suitable for Dr. Caligari, credenzas that looked as if they each weighed half a ton. Small tables were draped with weighty brocade. Some lamps were pewter with pale-gray shades, and others had maroon ceramic bases, but none threw much light. The drapes looked as heavy as lead; age-yellowed sheers hung between the side panels, permitting only a mustard-colored drizzle of sunlight to enter the room. None of it complemented the Spanish architecture; Violet had willfully imposed her ponderous bad taste upon the graceful house.

"You decorate?" Art Streck asked.

"No. My aunt," Nora said. She stood by the marble fireplace, almost as far from him as she could get without leaving the room. "This was her place. I . . . inherited it."

"If I was you," he said, "I'd heave all this stuff out of here. Could be a bright, cheery room. Pardon my saying so, but this isn't you. This might be all right for someone's maiden aunt . . . She was a *maiden* aunt, huh? Yeah, thought so. Might be all right for a dried-up maiden aunt, but definitely not for a pretty lady like yourself."

Nora wanted to criticize his impertinence, wanted to tell him to shut up and fix the television, but she had no experience at standing up for herself. Aunt Violet had preferred her meek, obedient.

Streck was smiling at her. The right corner of his mouth curled in a most unpleasant way. It was almost a sneer.

She forced herself to say, "I like it well enough."

"Not really?"

"Yes."

He shrugged. "What's the matter with the set?"

"The picture won't stop rolling. And there's static, snow."

He pulled the television away from the wall, switched it on, and studied the tumbling, static-slashed images. He plugged in a small portable lamp and hooked it to the back of the set.

The grandfather clock in the hall marked the quarter-hour with a single chime that reverberated hollowly through the house.

"You watch a lot of TV?" he asked as he unscrewed the dust shield from the set.

"Not much," Nora said.

"I like those nighttime soaps. *Dallas, Dynasty,* that stuff."

"I never watch them."

"Yeah? Oh, now, come on, I bet you do." He laughed slyly. "Everybody watches 'em even if they don't want to admit it. Just isn't anything more interesting than stories full of backstabbing, scheming, thieving, lying . . . and adultery. You know what I'm saying? People sit and watch it and cluck their tongues and say, 'Oh, how awful,' but they really get off on it. That's human nature."

"I . . . I've got things to do in the kitchen," she said nervously. "Call me when you've fixed the set." She left the room and went down the hall through the swinging door into the kitchen.

She was trembling. She despised herself for her weakness, for the ease with which she surrendered to fear, but she could not help being what she was.

A mouse.

Aunt Violet had often said, "Girl, there are two kinds of people in the world—cats and mice. Cats go where they want, do what they want, take what they want. Cats are aggressive and self-sufficient by nature. Mice, on the other hand, don't have an ounce of aggression in them. They're naturally vulnerable, gentle, and timid, and they're happiest when they keep their heads down and accept what life gives them. You're a mouse, dear. It's not bad to be a mouse. You can be perfectly happy. A mouse might not have as colorful a life as a cat, but if it stays safely in its burrow and keeps to itself, it'll live longer than the cat, and it'll have a lot less turmoil in its life."

Right now, a cat lurked in the living room, fixing the TV set, and Nora was in the kitchen, gripped by mouselike fear. She was not actually in the middle of cooking anything, as she had told Streck. For a moment she stood by the sink, one cold hand clasped in the other—her hands *always* seemed to be cold—wondering what to do until he finished his work and left. She decided to bake a cake. A yellow cake with chocolate icing. That task would keep her occupied and help turn her mind away from the memory of Streck's suggestive winking.

She got bowls, utensils, an electric mixer, plus the cake mix and other ingredients out of the cupboards, and she set to work. Soon her frayed nerves were soothed by the mundane domestic activity.

Just as she finished pouring the batter into the two baking pans, Streck stepped into the kitchen and said, "You like to cook?"

Surprised, she nearly dropped the empty metal mixing bowl and the batter-smeared spatula. Somehow, she managed to hold on to them and—with only a little clatter to betray her tension—put them into the sink to be washed. "Yes, I like to cook."

"Isn't that nice? I admire a woman who enjoys doing woman's work. Do you sew, crochet, do embroidery, anything like that?"

"Needlepoint," she said.

"That's even nicer."

"Is the TV fixed?"

"Almost."

Nora was ready to put the cake in the oven, but she did not want to carry the pan while Streck was watching her because she was afraid she would shake too much. Then he'd realize that she was intimidated by him, and he would probably get bolder. So she left the full pans on the counter and tore open the box of icing mix instead.

Streck came farther into the big kitchen, moving casually, very relaxed, looking around with an amiable smile, but coming straight toward her. "Think I could have a glass of water?"

Nora almost sighed with relief, eager to believe that a drink of cold water was all that had brought him here. "Oh, yes, of course," she said. She took a glass from the cupboard, ran the cold water.

When she turned to hand it to him, he was standing close behind her, having crept up with catlike quiet. She gave an involuntary start. Water slopped out of the glass and splattered on the floor.

She said, "You—"

"Here," he said, taking the glass from her hand.

"—startled me."

"Me?" he said, smiling, fixing her with icy blue eyes. "Oh, I certainly didn't mean to. I'm sorry. I'm harmless, Mrs. Devon. Really, I am. All I want is a drink of water. You didn't think I wanted anything else—did you?"

He was so damned bold. She couldn't *believe* how bold he was, how smart-mouthed and cool and aggressive. She wanted to slap his face, but she was afraid of what would happen after that. Slapping him—in any way acknowledging his insulting double entendres or other offenses—seemed sure to encourage rather than deter him.

He stared at her with unsettling intensity, voraciously. His smile was that of a predator.

She sensed the best way to handle Streck was to pretend innocence and monumental thickheadedness, to ignore his nasty sexual innuendos as if she had not understood them. She must, in short, deal with him as a mouse might deal with any threat from which it was unable to flee. Pretend you do not see the cat, pretend that it is not there, and perhaps the cat will be confused and disappointed by the lack of reaction and will seek more responsive prey elsewhere.

To break away from his demanding gaze, Nora tore a couple of paper towels from the dispenser beside the sink and began to mop up the water she had spilled on the floor. But the moment she stooped before Streck, she realized she'd made a mistake, because he did not move out of her way but stood over her, loomed over her, while she squatted in front of him. The situation was full of erotic symbolism. When she realized the submissiveness implied by her position at his feet, she popped up again and saw that his smile had broadened.

Flushed and flustered, Nora threw the damp towels into the wastecan under the sink.

Art Streck said, "Cooking, needlepoint . . . yeah, I think that's real nice, real nice. What other things do you like to do?"

"That's it, I'm afraid," she said. "I don't have any unusual hobbies. I'm not a very interesting person. Low-key. Dull, even."

Damning herself for being unable to order the bastard out of her house, she slipped past him and went to the oven, ostensibly to check that it was finished preheating, but she was really just trying to get out of Streck's reach.

He followed her, staying close. "When I pulled up out front, I saw lots of flowers. You tend the flowers?"

Staring at the oven dials, she said, "Yes . . . I like gardening."

"I approve of that," he said, as if she ought to care whether he approved or not. "Flowers . . . that's a good thing for a woman to have an interest in. Cooking, needlepoint, gardening—why you're just full of womanly interests and talents. I'll bet you do everything well, Mrs. Devon. I mean everything a woman should do. I'll bet you're a first-rate woman in every department."

If he touches me, I'll scream, she thought.

However, the walls of the old house were thick, and the neighbors were some distance away. No one would hear her or come to her rescue.

I'll kick him, she thought. I'll fight back.

But, in fact, she was not sure that she would fight, was not sure that she had the gumption to fight. Even if she did attempt to defend herself, he was bigger and stronger than she was.

"Yeah, I'll bet you're a first-rate woman in every department," he repeated, delivering the line more provocatively than before.

Turning from the oven, she forced a laugh. "My husband would be astonished to hear that. I'm not too bad at cakes, but I've still not learned to make a decent piecrust, and my pot roast always turns out bone-dry. My needlepoint's not half bad, but it takes me forever to get anything done." She slipped past him and returned to the counter. She was amazed to hear herself chattering on as she opened the box of icing mix. Desperation made her garrulous.

"I've got a green thumb with flowers, but I'm not much of a housekeeper, and if my husband didn't help out—why, this place would be a disaster."

She thought she sounded phony. She detected a note of hysteria in her voice that had to be evident to him. But the mention of a husband had obviously given Art Streck second thoughts about pushing further. As Nora poured the mix into a bowl and measured out the required butter, Streck drank the water she had given him. He went to the sink and put the empty glass in the dishpan with the dirty bowls and utensils. This time he did not press unnecessarily close to her.

"Well, I better get back to work," he said.

She gave him a calculatedly distracted smile, and nodded. She began to hum softly as she returned to her own task, as if untroubled.

He crossed the kitchen and pushed open the swinging door, then stopped and said, "Your aunt really liked dark places, didn't she? This kitchen would be swell, too, if you brightened it up."

Before she could respond, he went out, letting the door swing shut behind him.

In spite of his unasked-for opinion of the kitchen decor, Streck seemed to have pulled in his horns, and Nora was pleased with herself. Using a few white lies about her nonexistent husband, delivered with admirable equanimity, she had handled him after all. That was not exactly the way a cat would have dealt with an aggressor, but it was not the timid, frightened behavior of a mouse, either.

She looked around at the high-ceilinged kitchen and decided it *was* too dark. The walls were a muddy blue. The frosted globes of the overhead lights were opaque, shedding a drab, wintry glow. She considered having the kitchen repainted, the lights replaced.

Merely to contemplate making minor changes in Violet Devon's house was dizzying, exhilarating. Nora had redone her own bedroom since Violet's death, but nothing else. Now, wondering if she could follow through with extensive redecoration, she felt wildly daring and rebellious. Maybe. Maybe she could. If she could fend off Streck, maybe she could dredge up the courage to defy her dead aunt.

Her upbeat self-congratulatory mood lasted just twenty minutes, which was long enough to put the cake pans in the oven and whip up the icing and wash some of the bowls and utensils. Then Streck returned to tell her the TV set was repaired and to give her the bill. Though he had seemed subdued when he left the kitchen, he was cocky as ever when he entered the second time. He looked her up and down as if undressing her in his imagination, and when he met her eyes he gave her a challenging look.

She thought the bill was too high, but she did not question it because she wanted him out of the house quickly. As she sat at the kitchen table to write the check, he pulled the now-familiar trick of standing too close to her, trying to cow her with his masculinity and superior size. When she stood and handed him the check, he contrived to take it in such a way that his hand touched hers suggestively.

All the way along the hall, Nora was more than half-convinced that he would suddenly put down his tool kit and attack her from behind. But she got to the door, and he stepped past her onto the veranda, and her racing heart began to slow to a more normal pace.

He hesitated just outside the door. "What's your husband do?"

The question disconcerted her. It was something he might have asked earlier, in the kitchen, when she had spoken of her husband, but now his curiosity seemed inappropriate.

She should have told him it was none of his business, but she was still afraid of him. She sensed that he could be easily angered, that the pent-up violence in him could be triggered with minor effort. So she answered him with another lie, one she hoped would make him reluctant to harass her any further: "He's a . . . policeman."

Streck raised his eyebrows. "Really? Here in Santa Barbara?"

"That's right."

"Quite a house for a policeman."

"Excuse me?" she said.

"Didn't know policemen were paid so well."

"Oh, but I told you—I inherited the house from my aunt."

"Of course, I remember now. You told me. That's right."

Trying to reinforce her lie, she said. "We were living in an apartment when my aunt died, and then we moved here. You're right—we wouldn't have been able to afford it otherwise."

"Well," he said, "I'm happy for you. I sure am. A lady as pretty as you deserves a pretty house."

He tipped an imaginary hat to her, winked, and went along the walk toward the street, where his white van was parked at the curb.

She closed the door and watched him through a clear segment of the leaded, stained-glass oval window in the center of the door. He glanced back, saw her, and waved. She stepped away from the window, into the gloomy hallway, and watched him from a point at which she could not be seen.

Clearly, he hadn't believed her. He knew the husband was a lie. She shouldn't have said she was married to a cop, for God's sake; that was too obvious an attempt to dissuade him. She should have said she was married to a plumber or doctor, anything but a cop. Anyway, Art Streck was leaving. Though he knew she was lying, he was leaving.

She did not feel safe until his van was out of sight.

Actually, even then, she did not feel safe.

2

After murdering Dr. Davis Weatherby, Vince Nasco had driven his gray Ford van to a service station on Pacific Coast Highway. In the public phone booth, he deposited coins and called a Los Angeles number that he had long ago committed to memory.

A man answered by repeating the number Vince had dialed. It was one of the usual three voices that responded to calls, the soft one with a deep timbre. Often, there was another man with a hard sharp voice that grated on Vince.

Infrequently, a woman answered; she had a sexy voice, throaty and yet girlish. Vince had never seen her, but he had often tried to imagine what she looked like.

Now, when the soft-spoken man finished reciting the number, Vince said, "It's done. I really appreciate your calling me, and I'm always available if you have another job." He was confident that the guy on the other end of the line would recognize his voice, too.

"I'm delighted to hear all went well. We've the highest regard for your workmanship. Now remember this," the contact said. He recited a seven-digit telephone number.

Surprised, Vince repeated it.

The contact said, "It's one of the public phones at Fashion Island. In the open-air promenade near Robinson's Department Store. Can you be there in fifteen minutes?"

"Sure." Vince said. "Ten."

"I'll call in fifteen with the details."

Vince hung up and walked back to the van, whistling. Being sent to another public telephone to receive "the details" could mean only one thing: they had a job for him already, two in one day!

3

Later, after the cake was baked and iced, Nora retreated to her bedroom at the southwest corner of the second floor.

When Violet Devon had been alive, this had been Nora's sanctuary in spite of the lack of a lock on the door. Like all the rooms in the large house, it had been crammed with heavy furniture, as if the place served as a warehouse instead of a home. It had been dreary in all other details as well. Nevertheless, when finished with her chores, or when dismissed after one of her aunt's interminable lectures, Nora had fled to her bedroom, where she escaped into books or vivid daydreams.

Violet inevitably checked on her niece without warning, creeping soundlessly along the hall, suddenly throwing open the unlockable door, entering with the hope of catching Nora in a forbidden pasttime or practice. These unannounced inspections had been frequent during Nora's childhood and adolescence, dwindling in number thereafter, though they had continued through the final weeks of Violet Devon's life, when Nora had been a grown woman of twenty-nine. Because Violet had favored dark dresses, had worn her hair in a tight bun, and had gone without a trace of makeup on her pale, sharp-featured face, she had often looked less like a woman than like a man, a stern monk in coarse penitential robes, prowling the corridors of a black medieval retreat to police the behavior of fellow monastics.

If caught daydreaming or napping, Nora was severely reprimanded and punished with onerous chores. Her aunt did not condone laziness.

Books were permitted—if Violet had first approved of them—because, for one thing, books were educational. Besides, as Violet often said, "Plain, homely women like you and me will never lead a glamorous life, never go to exotic places. So books have a special value to us. We can experience most everything vicariously, through books. This isn't bad. Living through books is even *better* than having friends and knowing . . . men."

With the assistance of a pliable family doctor, Violet had kept Nora out of public school on the pretense of poor health. She had been educated at home, so books had been her only school as well.

In addition to having read thousands of books by the age of thirty, Nora had become a self-taught artist in oils, acrylics, watercolors, pencil. Drawing and painting were activities of which Aunt Violet approved. Art was a solitary pursuit that took Nora's mind off the world beyond the house and helped her avoid contact with people who would inevitably reject, hurt, and disappoint her.

One corner of Nora's room had been furnished with a drawing board, an easel, and a cabinet for supplies. Space for her miniature studio was created by pushing other pieces of furniture together, not by removing anything, and the effect was claustrophobic.

Many times over the years, especially at night but even in the middle of the day, Nora had been overcome by a feeling that the floor of the bedroom was going to collapse under all the furniture, that she was going to crash down into the chamber below, where she would be crushed to death beneath her own massive four-poster bed. When that fear overwhelmed her, she had fled onto the rear lawn, where she sat in the open air, hugging herself and shuddering. She'd been twenty-five before she realized that her anxiety attacks arose not only from the overfurnished rooms and dark decor of the house but from the domineering presence of her aunt.

On a Saturday morning four months ago, eight months after Violet Devon's death, Nora had abruptly been seized by an acute need for change and had frantically reordered her bedroom-studio. She carried and dragged out all the smaller pieces of furniture, distributing them evenly through the other five crowded chambers on the second floor. Some of the heavier things had to be dismantled and taken away in sections, but finally she succeeded in eliminating everything but the four-poster bed, one nightstand, a single armchair, her drawing board and stool, the supply cabinet, and the easel, which was all she needed. Then she stripped off the wallpaper.

Throughout that dizzying weekend, she'd felt as if the revolution had come, as if her life would never be the same. But by the time she had redone her bedroom, the spirit of rebellion had evaporated, and she had left the rest of the house untouched.

Now this one place, at least, was bright, even cheerful. The walls were painted the palest yellow. The drapes were gone, and in their place were Levolor blinds that matched the paint. She had rolled up the dreary carpet and had polished the beautiful oak floor.

More than ever, this was her sanctuary. Without fail, upon passing through the door and seeing what she had wrought, her spirits lifted and she found some surcease from her troubles.

After her frightening encounter with Streck, Nora was soothed, as always, by the bright room. She sat at the drawing board and began a pencil sketch, a preliminary study for an oil painting that she had been contemplating for some time. Initially, her hands shook, and she had to pause repeatedly to regain sufficient control to continue drawing, but in time her fear abated.

She was even able to think about Streck as she worked and to try to imagine just how far he might have gone if she had not managed to maneuver him out of the house. Recently, Nora had wondered if Violet Devon's pessimistic view of the outside world and of all other people was accurate; though it was the primary view that Nora, herself, had been taught, she had the nagging suspicion that it might be twisted, even sick. But now she had encountered Art Streck, and he seemed to be ample proof of Violet's contentions, proof that interacting too much with the outside world was dangerous.

But after a while, when her sketch was half finished, Nora began to think that she had misinterpreted everything Streck had said and done. Surely he could not have been making sexual advances toward her. Not toward *her.*

She was, after all, quite undesirable. Plain. Homely. Perhaps even ugly. Nora knew this was true because, regardless of Violet's faults, the old woman had some virtues, one of which was a refusal to mince words. Nora was unattractive, drab, not a woman who could expect to be held, kissed, cherished. This was a fact of life that Aunt Violet made her understand at an early age.

Although his personality was repellent, Streck was a physically attractive man, one who could have his choice of pretty women. It was ridiculous to assume he would be interested in a drudge like her.

Nora still wore the clothes that her aunt had bought for her—dark, shapeless dresses and skirts and blouses similar to those that Violet had worn. Brighter and more feminine dresses would only call attention to her bony, graceless body and to the characterless and uncomely lines of her face.

But why had Streck said that she was pretty?

Oh, well, that was easily explained. He was making fun of her, perhaps. Or, more likely, he was being polite, kind.

That thought depressed her for a while. But she redoubled her efforts on the sketch, finished it, and began another from a different perspective. As the afternoon waned she escaped into her art.

From downstairs the chimes of the ancient grandfather clock rose punctually on the hour, half-hour, and quarter-hour.

The west-falling sun turned more golden as time passed, and as the day wore on the room grew brighter. The air seemed to shimmer. Beyond the south window a king palm stirred gently in the May breeze.

By four o'clock, she was at peace, humming as she worked.

When the telephone rang, it startled her.

She put down her pencil and reached for the receiver, "Hello?"

"Funny," a man said.

"Excuse me?"

"They never heard of him."

"I'm sorry," she said, "but I think you've got the wrong number."

"This *is* you, Mrs. Devon?"

She recognized the voice now. It was him. Streck.

For a moment, she could not speak.

He said, "They never heard of him. I called the Santa Barbara police and asked to speak with Officer Devon, but they said they don't have an Officer Devon on the force. Isn't that odd, Mrs. Devon?"

"What do you want?" she asked shakily.

"I figure it's a computer error," Streck said, laughing quietly. "Yeah, sure, some sort of computer error dropped your husband from their records. I think you'd better tell him as soon as he gets home, Mrs. Devon. If he doesn't get this straightened out . . . why, hell, he might not get his paycheck at the end of the week."

He hung up, and the sound of the dial tone made her realize that she should have hung up first, should have slammed down the handset as soon as he said that he'd called the police station. She dared not encourage him even to the extent of listening to him on the phone.

She went through the house, checking all the windows and doors. They were securely locked.

4

At McDonald's on East Chapman Avenue in Orange, Travis Cornell had ordered five hamburgers for the golden retriever. Sitting on the front seat of the pickup, the dog had eaten all of the meat and two buns, and it had wanted to express its gratitude by licking his face.

"You've got the breath of a dyspeptic alligator," he protested, holding the animal back.

The return trip to Santa Barbara took three and a half hours because the highways were much busier than they had been that morning. Throughout the journey, Travis glanced at his companion and spoke to it, anticipating a display of the unnerving intelligence it had shown earlier. His expectations were unfulfilled. The retriever behaved like any dog on a long trip. Once in a while, it *did* sit very erect, looking through the windshield or side window at the scenery with what seemed an unusual degree of interest and attention. But most of the time it curled up and slept on the seat, snuffling in its dreams—or it panted and yawned and looked bored.

When the odor of the dog's filthy coat became intolerable, Travis rolled down the windows for ventilation, and the retriever stuck its head out in the wind. With its ears blown back, hair streaming, it grinned the foolish and charmingly witless grin of all dogs who had ever ridden shotgun in such a fashion.

In Santa Barbara, Travis stopped at a shopping center, where he bought several cans of Alpo, a box of Milk-Bone dog biscuits, heavy plastic dishes for pet food and water, a galvanized tin washtub, a bottle of pet shampoo with a flea- and tick-killing compound, a brush to comb out the animal's tangled coat, a collar, and a leash.

As Travis loaded those items in the back of the pickup, the dog watched him through the rear window of the cab, its damp nose pressed to the glass.

Getting behind the wheel, he said, "You're filthy, and you stink. You're not going to be a lot of trouble about taking a bath, are you?"

The dog yawned.

By the time Travis pulled into the driveway of his four-room rented bungalow on the northern edge of Santa Barbara and switched off the pickup's engine, he was beginning to wonder if the pooch's actions that morning had really been as amazing as he remembered.

"If you don't show me the right stuff again soon," he told the dog as he slipped his key into the front door of the house, "I'm going to have to assume that I stripped a gear out there in the woods, that I'm just nuts and that I imagined everything."

Standing beside him on the stoop, the dog looked up quizzically.

"Do you want to be responsible for giving me doubts about my own sanity? Hmmmmm?"

An orange and black butterfly swooped past the retriever's face, startling it. The dog barked once and raced after the fluttering prey, off the stoop, down the walkway. Dashing back and forth across the lawn, leaping high, snapping at the air, repeatedly missing its bright quarry, it nearly collided with the diamond-patterned trunk of a big Canary Island date palm, then narrowly avoided knocking itself unconscious in a head-on encounter with a concrete birdbath, and at last crashed clumsily into a bed of New Guinea impatiens over which the butterfly soared to safety. The retriever rolled once, scrambled to its feet, and lunged out of the flowers.

When it realized that it had been foiled, the dog returned to Travis. It gave him a sheepish look.

"Some wonder dog," he said. "Good grief."

He opened the door, and the retriever slipped in ahead of him. It padded off immediately to explore these new rooms.

"You better be housebroken," Travis shouted after it.

He carried the galvanized washtub and the plastic bag full of other purchases into the kitchen. He left the food and pet dishes there, and took everything else outside through the back door. He put the bag on the concrete patio and set the tub beside it, near a coiled hose that was attached to an outdoor faucet.

Inside again, he removed a bucket from beneath the kitchen sink, filled it with the hottest water he could draw, carried it outside, and emptied it into the tub. When Travis had made four trips with the hot water, the retriever appeared and began to explore the backyard. By the time Travis filled the tub more than half full, the dog had begun to urinate every few feet along the whitewashed concrete-block wall that defined the property line, marking its territory.

"When you finish killing the grass," Travis said, "you'd better be in the mood for a bath. You reek."

The retriever turned toward him and cocked his head and appeared to listen when he spoke. But it did not look like one of those smart dogs in the movies. It did not look as if it understood him. It just looked dumb. As soon as he stopped talking, it hurried a few steps farther along the wall and peed again.

Watching the dog relieve itself, Travis felt an urge of his own. He went inside to the bathroom, then changed into an older pair of jeans and a T-shirt for the sloppy job ahead.

When Travis came outside again, the retriever was standing beside the steaming washtub, the hose in its teeth. Somehow, it had managed to turn the faucet. Water gushed out of the hose, into the tub.

For a dog, successfully manipulating a water faucet would be very difficult if not impossible. Travis figured that an equivalent test of his own ingenuity and dexterity would be trying to open a child-proof safety cap on an aspirin bottle with one hand behind his back.

Astonished, he said, "Water's too hot for you?"

The retriever dropped the hose, letting water pour across the patio, and stepped almost daintily into the tub. It sat and looked at him, as if to say, *Let's get on with it, you dink.*

He went to the tub and squatted beside it. "Show me how you can turn off the water."

The dog looked at him stupidly.

"Show me,' Travis said.

The dog snorted and shifted its position in the warm water.

"If you could turn it on, you can turn it off. How did you do it? With your teeth? Had to be with your teeth. Couldn't do it with a paw, for God's sake. But that twisting motion would be tricky. You could've broken a tooth on the cast-iron handle."

The dog leaned slightly out of the tub, just far enough to bite at the neck of the bag that held the shampoo.

"You won't turn off the faucet?" Travis asked.

The dog just blinked at him, inscrutable.

He sighed and turned off the water. "All right. Okay. Be a wiseass." He took the brush and shampoo out of the bag and held them toward the retriever. "Here. You probably don't even need me. You can scrub by yourself, I'm sure."

The dog issued a long, drawn-out *woooooof* that started deep in its throat, and Travis had the feeling it was calling *him* a wiseass.

Careful now, he told himself. You're in danger of leaping off the deep end, Travis. This is a damn smart dog you've got here, but he can't really understand what you're saying, and he can't talk back.

The retriever submitted to its bath without protest, enjoying itself. After ordering the dog out of the tub and rinsing off the shampoo, Travis spent an hour brushing its damp coat. He pulled out burrs, bits of weeds that hadn't flushed away, unsnarled the tangles. The dog never grew impatient, and by six o'clock it was transformed.

Groomed, it was a handsome animal. Its coat was predominantly medium gold with feathering of a lighter shade on the backs of its legs, on its belly and buttocks, and on the underside of the tail. The undercoat was thick and soft to provide warmth and repel water. The outer coat was also soft but not as thick, and in some places these longer hairs were wavy. The tail had a slight upward curve, giving the retriever a happy, jaunty look, which was emphasized by its tendency to wag continuously.

The dried blood on the ear was from a small tear already healing. The blood on the paws resulted not from serious injury but from a lot of running over difficult ground. Travis did nothing except pour boric-acid solution, a mild antiseptic, on these minor wounds. He was confident that the dog would experience only slight discomfort—or maybe none at all, for it was not limping—and that it would be completely well in a few days.

The retriever looked splendid now, but Travis was damp, sweaty, and stank of dog shampoo. He was eager to shower and change. He had also worked up an appetite.

The only task remaining was to collar the dog. But when he attempted to buckle the new collar in place, the retriever growled softly and backstepped out of his reach.

"Whoa now. It's only a collar, boy."

The dog stared at the loop of red leather in Travis's hand and continued to growl.

"You had a bad experience with a collar, huh?"

The dog stopped growling, but it did not take a step toward him.

"Mistreated?" Travis asked. "That must be it. Maybe they choked you with a collar, twisted it and choked you, or maybe they put you on a short chain. Something like that?"

The retriever barked once, padded across the patio, and stood in the farthest corner, looking at the collar from a distance.

"Do you trust me?" Travis asked, remaining on his knees in an unthreatening posture.

The dog shifted its attention from the loop of leather to Travis, meeting his eyes.

"I will never mistreat you," he said solemnly, feeling not at all foolish for speaking so directly and sincerely to a mere dog. "You must know that I won't. I mean, you have good instincts about things like that, don't you? Rely on your instincts, boy, and trust me."

The dog returned from the far end of the patio and stopped just beyond Travis's reach. It glanced once at the collar, then fixed him with that uncannily intense gaze. As before, he felt a degree of communion with the animal that was as profound as it was eerie—and as eerie as it was indescribable.

He said, "Listen, there'll be times I'll want to take you places where you'll need a leash. Which has to be attached to a collar, doesn't it? That's the only reason I want you to wear a collar—so I can take you everywhere with me. That and to ward off fleas. But if you really don't want to submit to it, I won't force you."

For a long time they faced each other as the retriever mulled over the situation. Travis continued to hold the collar out as if it represented a gift rather than a demand, and the dog continued to stare into his new master's eyes. At last, the retriever shook itself, sneezed once, and slowly came forward.

"That's a good boy," Travis said encouragingly.

When it reached him, the dog settled on its belly, then rolled onto its back with all four legs in the air, making itself vulnerable. It gave him a look that was full of love, trust, and a little fear.

Crazily, Travis felt a lump form in his throat and was aware of hot tears scalding the corners of his eyes. He swallowed hard and blinked back the tears and told himself he was being a sentimental dope. But he knew why the dog's considered submission affected him so strongly. For the first time in three years, Travis Cornell felt needed, felt a deep connection with another living creature. For the first time in three years, he had a reason to live.

He slipped the collar in place, buckled it, gently scratched and rubbed the retriever's exposed belly.

"Got to have a name for you," he said.

The dog scrambled to its feet, faced him, and pricked its ears as if waiting to hear what it would be called.

God in heaven, Travis thought, I'm attributing human intentions to him. He's a mutt, special maybe but still only a mutt. He may look as if he's waiting to hear what he'll be called, but he sure as hell doesn't understand English.

"Can't think of a single name that's fitting," Travis said at last. "We don't have to rush this. It's got to be just the right name. You're no ordinary dog, fur face. I've got to think on it a while until I hit the right moniker."

Travis emptied the washtub, rinsed it out, and left it to dry. Together, he and the retriever went into the home they now shared.

5

Dr. Elisabeth Yarbeck and her husband Jonathan, an attorney, lived in Newport Beach in a sprawling, single-story, ranch-style home with a shake-shingle roof, cream-colored stucco walls, and a walkway of Bouquet Canyon stone. The waning sun radiated copper and ruby light that glinted and flashed in the beveled glass of the narrow leaded windows flanking the front door, giving those panes the look of enormous gemstones.

Elisabeth answered the door when Vince Nasco rang the bell. She was about fifty, trim and attractive, with shaggy silver-blond hair and blue eyes. Vince told her his name was John Parker, that he was with the FBI, and that he needed to speak with her husband in regards to a case currently under investigation.

"Case?" she said. "What case?"

"It involves a government-financed research project on which you were once involved," Vince told her, for that was the opening line that he had been told to use.

She examined his photo ID and Bureau credentials carefully.

He was not concerned. The phony papers had been prepared by the same people who had hired him for this job. The forged documents had been provided ten months ago to assist him on a hit in San Francisco, and had served him well on three other occasions.

Though he knew the ID would meet with her approval, he was not sure that he, himself, would pass inspection. He was wearing a dark blue suit, white shirt, blue tie, and highly polished black shoes—correct attire for an agent. His size and his expressionless face also served him well in the role he was playing. But the murder of Dr. Davis Weatherby and the prospect of two more murders within the next five minutes had wildly excited him, had filled him with a manic glee that was almost uncontainable. Laughter kept building within him, and the struggle to repress it grew more difficult by the minute. In the drab green Ford sedan, which he had stolen forty minutes ago expressly for this one job, he had been seized by a fit of the shakes induced not by nervousness but by intense pleasure of an almost sexual nature. He'd been forced to pull the car to the side of the road and sit for ten minutes, breathing deeply, until he had calmed down a bit.

Now, Elisabeth Yarbeck looked up from the forged ID, met Vince's eyes, and frowned.

He risked a smile, though there was a danger of slipping into uncontrollable laughter that would blow his cover. He had a boyish smile that, by its marked contrast with his size, could be disarming.

After a moment, Dr. Yarbeck also smiled. Satisfied, she returned his credentials and welcomed him into her house.

"I'll need to speak with your husband, too," Vince reminded her as she closed the front door behind them.

"He's in the living room, Mr. Parker. This way, please."

The living room was large and airy. Cream-colored walls and carpet. Pale-green sofas. Big plate-glass windows, partly shielded by green awnings, provided views of the meticulously landscaped property and of houses on the hills below.

Jonathan Yarbeck was stuffing handfuls of wood chips in among the logs that he'd piled in the brick fireplace, getting ready to light a fire. He stood up, dusting his hands together, as his wife introduced Vince . . . "John Parker of the FBI."

"FBI?" Yarbeck said, raising his eyebrows inquiringly.

"Mr. Yarbeck," Vince said, "if there are other members of the family at home, I'd also like to speak with them now, so I don't have to repeat myself."

Shaking his head, Yarbeck said, "There's just Liz and me. Kids are away at college. What's this all about?"

Vince drew the silencer-equipped pistol from inside his suit jacket and shot Jonathan Yarbeck in the chest. The attorney was flung backward against the mantel, where he hung for a moment as if nailed in place, then fell atop the brass fireplace tools.

Ssssnap.

Elisabeth Yarbeck was briefly frozen by astonishment and horror. Vince quickly moved on her. He grabbed her left arm and twisted it up behind her back, hard. When she cried out in pain, he put the pistol against the side of her head and said, "Be quiet, or I'll blow your fuckin' brains out."

He forced her to accompany him across the room to her husband's body. Jonathan Yarbeck was face-down on top of a small brass coal shovel and a brass-handled poker. He was dead. But Vince did not want to take chances. He shot Yarbeck twice in the back of the head at close range.

A strange, thin, catlike sound escaped Liz Yarbeck—then she began to sob.

Because of the distance and the smoky tint on the glass, Vince did not believe even the neighbors could see through the big windows, but he wanted to deal with the woman in a more private place. He forced her into the hall and headed deeper into the house, looking in doors as they went until he found the master bedroom. There, he gave her a hard shove, and she sprawled on the floor.

"Stay put," he said.

He switched on the bedside lamps. He went to the big sliding-glass doors that opened onto the patio and began to close the drapes.

The moment his back was turned, the woman scrambled to her feet and ran toward the hall door.

He caught her, slammed her up against the wall, drove a fist into her stomach, knocking the wind out of her, then threw her to the floor again. Lifting her head by a handful of hair, he forced her to look him in the eyes. "Listen, lady, I'm not going to shoot you. I came here to get your husband. Just your husband. But if you try to slip away from me before I'm ready to let you go, I'll have to waste you, too. Understand?"

He was lying, of course. She was the one he was being paid to hit, and the husband had to be removed simply because he was there. However, it was true that Vince was not going to shoot her. He wanted her to be cooperative until he could tie her up and deal with her at a more leisurely pace. The two shootings had been satisfying, but he wanted to draw this one out, kill her more slowly. Sometimes, death could be savored like good food, fine wine, and glorious sunsets.

Gasping for breath, sobbing, she said, "Who *are* you?"

"None of your business."

"What do you want?"

"Just shut up, cooperate, and you'll get out of this alive."

She was reduced to urgent prayer, running the words together and some-times punctuating them with small desperate wordless sounds.

Vince finished closing the drapes.

He tore the phone out of the wall and pitched it across the room.

Taking the woman by the arm again, he pulled her to her feet and dragged her into the bathroom. He searched through drawers until he found first-aid supplies; the adhesive tape was just what he needed.

In the bedroom once more, he made her lie on her back on the bed. He used the tape to bind her ankles together and to secure her wrists in front of her. From a bureau drawer, he got a pair of her flimsy panties, which he wadded up and stuffed into her mouth. He sealed her mouth shut with a final strip of tape.

She was shaking violently, blinking through tears and sweat.

He left the bedroom, went to the living room, and knelt beside Jonathan Yarbeck's corpse, with which he had unfinished business. He turned it over. One of the bullets that had entered the back of Yarbeck's head had punched out through his throat, just under his chin. His open mouth was full of blood. One eye was rolled back in his skull, so only the white showed.

Vince looked into the other eye. "Thank you," he said sincerely, reverently. "Thank you, Mr. Yarbeck."

He closed both eyelids. He kissed them.

"Thank you."

He kissed the dead man's forehead.

"Thank you for what you've given me."

Then he went into the garage, where he searched through cabinets until he found some tools. He selected a hammer with a comfortable rubberized handle and a polished steel head.

When he returned to the quiet bedroom and put the hammer on the mattress beside the bound woman, her eyes widened almost comically.

She began to twist and squirm, tried to wrench her hands loose of the looped adhesive tape, to no avail.

Vince stripped out of his clothes.

Seeing the woman's eyes fixed on him with the same terror with which she had regarded the hammer, he said, "No, please, don't worry, Dr. Yarbeck. I'm not going to molest you." He hung his suit jacket and shirt on the back of a chair. "I have no sexual interest in you." He slipped out of his shoes, socks, and trousers. "You won't have to suffer that humiliation. I'm not that sort of man. I'm just removing my clothes to avoid getting blood all over them."

Naked, he picked up the hammer and swung it at her left leg, shattering her knee. Perhaps fifty or sixty hammer strikes after he began, The Moment arrived.

Sssssnap.

Sudden energy blasted through him. He felt inhumanly alert, acutely sen-sitive of the color and texture of everything around him. And he felt stronger than ever before in his life, like a god in a man's body.

He dropped the hammer and fell to his bare knees beside the bed. He put his forehead on the bloodied bedspread and took deep breaths, shuddering with pleasure so intense it could almost not be borne.

A couple of minutes later, when he had recovered, when he had adjusted to his new and more powerful condition, he got up, turned to the dead woman, and bestowed kisses on her battered face, plus one in the palm of each of her hands.

"Thank you."

He was so deeply moved by the sacrifice she had made for him that he thought he might weep. But his joy at his own good fortune was greater than his pity for her, and the tears would not flow.

In the bathroom he took a quick shower. As the hot water sluiced the soap from him, he thought about how lucky he was to have found a way to make murder his business, to be paid for what he would have done anyway, without remuneration.

When he had dressed again, he used a towel to wipe off the few things he had touched since entering the house. He always remembered *every* move he'd made, and he never worried about missing an object in the wipe-down and leaving a stray fingerprint. His perfect memory was just another part of his Gift.

When he let himself out of the house, he discovered that night had fallen.

CHAPTER 3

1

THROUGHOUT THE EARLY part of the evening, the retriever exhibited none of the remarkable behavior that had stirred Travis's imagination. He kept a watch on the dog, sometimes directly, sometimes out of the corner of his eye, but he saw nothing that engaged his curiosity.

He made a dinner of bacon, lettuce, and tomato sandwiches for himself, and he opened a can of Alpo for the retriever. It liked the Alpo well enough, consuming the stuff in great gulps, but it clearly preferred his food. It sat on the kitchen floor beside his chair, looking at him forlornly as he ate two sandwiches at the red Formica-topped table. At last he gave it two strips of bacon.

Nothing about its doggy begging was extraordinary. It performed no startling tricks. It merely licked its chops, whined now and then, and repeatedly employed a limited repertoire of sorrowful expressions designed to elicit pity and compassion. Any mutt would have tried to cadge a treat in the same fashion.

Later, in the living room, Travis switched on the television, and the dog curled up on the couch beside him. After a while it put its head on his thigh, wanting to be petted and scratched behind the ears, and he obliged. The dog glanced occasionally at the television but had no great interest in the programs.

Travis was not interested in TV, either. He was intrigued only by the dog. He wanted to study it and encourage it to perform more tricks. Although he tried to think of ways to elicit displays of its astonishing intelligence, he could come up with no tests that would reliably gauge the animal's mental capacity.

Besides, Travis had a hunch that the dog would not cooperate in a test. Most of the time it seemed instinctively to conceal its cleverness. He recalled its witlessness and comical clumsiness in pursuit of the butterfly, then contrasted that behavior with the wit and agility required to turn on the patio water faucet: those actions appeared to be the work of two different animals. Though it was a crazy idea, Travis suspected that the retriever did not wish to draw attention to itself and that it revealed its uncanny intelligence only in times of crisis (as in the woods), or if it was very hungry (as when it had opened the glove compartment in the truck to obtain the candy bar), or if no one was watching (as when it had turned on the water faucet).

This was a preposterous idea because it suggested that the dog was not only highly intelligent for one of its species *but was aware of the extraordinary nature of its own abilities.* Dogs—all animals, in fact—simply did not possess the high degree of self-awareness required to analyze themselves in comparison to others of their kind. Comparative analysis was strictly a human quality. If a dog was especially bright and capable of many tricks, it would still not be aware it was different from most of its kind. To assume this dog was, in fact, aware of such things was to credit it not only with remarkable intelligence but with a capacity for reason and logic, and with a facility for rational judgment superior to the instinct that ruled the decisions of all other animals.

"You," Travis told the retriever, gently stroking its head, "are an enigma wrapped in a mystery. Either that, or I'm a candidate for the rubber room."

The dog looked at him in response to his voice, gazed into his eyes for a moment, yawned—and suddenly jerked its head up and stared beyond him at the bookshelves that flanked the archway between the living and dining rooms. The satisfied, dopey, doggy expression on its face had vanished, replaced by the keen interest Travis had seen before, which transcended ordinary canine alertness.

Scrambling off the sofa, the retriever dashed to the bookshelves. It ran back and forth beneath them, looking up at the colorful spines of the neatly arranged volumes.

The rental house came fully—if unimaginatively and cheaply—furnished, with upholstery chosen for durability (vinyl) or for the ability to conceal ineradicable stains (eyesearing plaids). Instead of wood, there was lots of wood-finish Formica that was resistant to chipping, scratching, abrasion, and cigarette burns. Virtually the only things in the place reflecting Travis Cornell's own tastes and interests were the books—both paperbacks and hardcovers—that filled the shelves in the living room.

The dog appeared to be intensely curious about at least some of those few hundred volumes.

Getting to his feet, Travis said, "What is it, boy? What's got your tail in an uproar?"

The retriever jumped onto its hind feet, put his forepaws on one of the shelves, and sniffed the spines of the books. It glanced at Travis, then returned to its eager examination of his library.

He went to the shelf in question, withdrew one of the volumes to which the dog had pressed its nose—*Treasure Island* by Robert Louis Stevenson—and held it out. "This? You're interested in this?"

The dog studied the painting of Long John Silver and a pirate ship that adorned the dust jacket. It looked up at Travis, then down at Long John Silver again. After a moment, it dropped back from the shelf, onto the floor, dashed to the shelves on the other side of the archway, leaped up again, and began sniffing other books.

Travis replaced *Treasure Island* and followed the retriever. It was now applying its damp nose to his collection of Charles Dickens's novels. Travis picked up a paperback of *A Tale of Two Cities.*

Again, the retriever carefully studied the cover illustration as if actually trying to determine what the book was about, then looked up expectantly at Travis.

Utterly baffled, he said, "The French Revolution. Guillotines. Beheadings. Tragedy and heroism. It's . . . uh . . . well, it's all about the importance of valuing individuals over groups, about the need to place a far greater value on one man's or woman's life than on the advancement of the masses."

The dog returned its attention to the tomes shelved in front of it, sniffing, sniffing.

"This is nuts," Travis said, putting *A Tale of Two Cities* back where he'd gotten it. "I'm giving plot synopses to a dog, for God's sake!"

Dropping its big forepaws down to the next shelf, the retriever panted and snuffled over the literature on that row. When Travis did not pull any of those books out for inspection, the dog tilted its head to get into the shelf, gently gripped a volume in its teeth, and tried to withdraw it for further examination.

"Whoa," Travis said, reaching for the book. "Keep your slobber off the fine bindings, fur face. This one's *Oliver Twist*. Another Dickens. The story of an orphan in Victorian England. He gets involved with shady characters, the criminal underworld, and the—"

The retriever dropped to the floor and padded back to the shelves on the other side of the archway, where it continued to sniff at those volumes within its reach. Travis could have sworn it even gazed up wistfully at the books that were above its head.

For perhaps five minutes, in the grip of an eerie premonition that something of tremendous importance was about to happen, Travis followed the dog, showing it the covers of a dozen novels, providing a line or two of plot description of each story. He had no idea if that was what the precocious pooch wanted him to do. Surely, it could not understand the synopses he provided. Yet it seemed to listen raptly as he spoke. He knew he must be misinterpreting essentially meaningless animal behavior, attributing complex intentions to the dog when it had none. Still, a premonitory tingle coursed along the back of his neck. As their peculiar search continued, Travis half-expected some startling revelation at any moment—and at the same time felt increasingly gullible and foolish.

His taste in fiction was eclectic. Among the volumes he took off the shelves were Bradbury's *Something Wicked This Way Comes* and Chandler's *The Long Goodbye*. Cain's *The Postman Always Rings Twice* and Hemingway's *The Sun Also Rises*. Two books by Richard Condon and one by Anne Tyler. Dorothy Sayer's *Murder Must Advertise* and Elmore Leonard's *52 Pick-Up*.

At last the dog turned away from the books and went to the middle of the room, where it padded back and forth, back and forth, clearly agitated. It stopped, confronted Travis, and barked three times.

"What's wrong, boy?"

The dog whined, looked at the laden shelves, walked in a circle, and peered up at the books again. It seemed frustrated. Thoroughly, maddeningly frustrated.

"I don't know what more to do, boy," he said. "I don't know what you're after, what you're trying to tell me."

The dog snorted and shook itself. Lowering its head in defeat, it returned resignedly to the sofa and curled up on the cushions.

"That's all?" Travis asked. "We're just giving up?"

Putting its head down on the sofa, it regarded him with moist soulful eyes.

Travis turned from the dog and let his gaze travel slowly over the books, as if they not only offered the information printed on their pages but also contained an important message that could not be as easily read, as if their colorful spines were the strange runes of a long-lost language and, once deciphered, would reveal wondrous secrets. But he could not decipher them.

Having believed that he was on the trembling edge of some great revelation, Travis felt enormously let down. His own frustration was considerably worse than what the dog had exhibited, and he could not merely curl up on the sofa, put his head down, and forget the whole thing as the retriever had done.

"What the hell was that all about?" he demanded.

The dog looked up at him, inscrutable.

"Was there any point to all of that stuff with the books?"

The dog stared.

"Is there something special about you—or have I popped the pull-tab on my brain and emptied it?"

The dog was perfectly limp and still, as if it might close its eyes at any moment and doze off.

"If you yawn at me, damn you, I'll kick your butt."

The dog yawned.

"Bastard," Travis said.

It yawned again.

"Now, *there*. What does that mean? Are you yawning on purpose because of what I said, because you're playing with me? Or are you just yawning? How am I to interpret anything you do? How am I to know whether any of it has meaning?"

The dog sighed.

With a sigh of his own, Travis went to one of the front windows and stared out at the night, where the feathery fronds of the large Canary Island date palm were backlit by the vaguely yellow glow of the sodium-vapor streetlamps. He heard the dog get off the sofa and hurry out of the room, but he refused to inquire into its activities. For the moment, he could not handle more frustration.

The retriever was making noise in the kitchen. A clink. A soft clatter. Travis figured it was drinking from its bowl.

Seconds later, he heard it returning. It came to his side and rubbed against his leg.

He glanced down and, to his surprise, saw the retriever was holding a can of beer in its teeth. Coors. He took the proffered can and discovered it was cold.

"You got this from the refrigerator!"

The dog appeared to be grinning.

2

When Nora Devon was in the kitchen making dinner, the phone rang again. She prayed it would not be *him*.

But it was. "I know what you need," Streck said. "I know what you need."

I'm not even pretty, she wanted to say. *I'm a plain, dumpy old maid, so what do you want with me? I'm safe from the likes of you because I'm not pretty. Are you blind?* But she could say nothing.

"Do *you* know what you need?" he asked.

Finding her voice at last, she said, "Go away."

"I know what you need. You might not know, but I do."

This time she hung up first, slamming the headset down so hard that it must have hurt his ear.

Later, at eight-thirty, the phone rang again. She was sitting in bed, reading *Great Expectations* and eating ice cream. She was so startled by the first ring that the spoon popped out of her hand into the dish, and she nearly spilled the dessert.

Putting the dish and the book aside, she stared anxiously at the telephone, which stood on the nightstand. She let it ring ten times. Fifteen. Twenty. The strident sound of the bell filled the room, echoing off the walls, until each ring seemed to drill into her skull.

Eventually she realized she would be making a big mistake if she did not answer. He'd know she was here and was too frightened to pick up the receiver, which would please him. More than anything, he desired domination. Perversely, her timid withdrawal would encourage him. Nora had no experience at confrontation, but she saw that she was going to have to learn to stand up for herself—and fast.

She lifted the receiver on the thirty-first ring.

Streck said, "I can't get you off my mind."

Nora did not reply.

Streck said, "You have beautiful hair. So dark. Almost black. Thick and glossy. I want to run my hands through your hair."

She had to say something to put him in his place—or hang up. But she could not bring herself to do either.

"I've never seen eyes like yours," Streck said, breathing hard. "Gray but not like other gray eyes. Deep, warm, *sexy* eyes."

Nora was speechless, paralyzed.

"You're very pretty, Nora Devon. Very pretty. And I know what you need. I do. I really do, Nora. I know what you need, and I'm going to give it to you."

Her paralysis was shattered by a fit of the shakes. She dropped the phone into its cradle. Bending forward in bed, she felt as if she were shaking herself to pieces before the tremors slowly subsided.

She did not own a gun.

She felt small, fragile, and terribly alone.

She wondered if she should call the police. But what would she tell them? That she was the object of sexual harassment? They'd get a big laugh out of that. Her? A sex object? She was an old maid, as plain as mud, not remotely the type to turn a man's head and give him erotic dreams. The police would suppose that she either was making it up or was hysterical. Or they would assume she had misinterpreted Streck's politeness as sexual interest, which is what even *she* had thought at first.

She pulled a blue robe on over the roomy men's pajamas that she wore, belted it. Barefoot, she hurried downstairs to the kitchen, where she hesitantly withdrew a butcher's knife from the rack near the stove. Light trickled like a thin stream of quicksilver along the well-honed cutting edge.

As she turned the gleaming knife in her hand, she saw her eyes reflected in the broad, flat blade. She stared at herself in the polished steel, wondering if she could possibly use such a horrible weapon against another human being even in self-defense.

She hoped she would never have to find out.

Upstairs again, she put the butcher's knife on the nightstand, within easy reach.

She took off her robe and sat on the edge of the bed, hugging herself and trying to stop shaking.

"Why me?" she said aloud. "Why does he want to pick on *me*?"

Streck said that she was pretty, but Nora knew it was not true. Her own mother had abandoned her to Aunt Violet and had returned only twice in twenty-eight years, the last time when Nora was six. Her father remained unknown to her, and no other Devon relatives were willing to take her in, a situation which Violet frankly attributed to Nora's uncomely appearance. So although Streck said she was pretty, it could not possibly be her that he wanted. No, what he wanted was the thrill of scaring and dominating and hurting her. There were such people. She read about them in books, newspapers. And Aunt Violet had warned her a thousand times that if a man ever came on to her with sweet talk and smiles, he would only want to lift her up so he could later cast her down from a greater height and hurt her all the worse.

After a while, the worst of the tremors passed. Nora got into bed again. Her remaining ice cream had melted, so she put the dish aside, on the nightstand. She picked up the novel by Dickens and tried to involve herself once more with Pip's tale. But her attention repeatedly strayed to the phone, to the butcher's knife—and to the open door and the second-floor hall beyond, where she kept imagining she saw movement.

3

Travis went into the kitchen, and the dog followed him.

He pointed to the refrigerator and said, "Show me. Do it again. Get me a beer. Show me how you did it."

The dog did not move.

Travis squatted. "Listen, fur face, who got you out of those woods, away from whatever was chasing you? I did. And who bought hamburgers for you? I did. I bathed you, fed you, gave you a home. Now you owe me. Stop being coy. If you can open that thing, *do it!*"

The dog went to the aging Frigidaire, lowered its head to the bottom corner of the enamel-coated door, gripped the edge in its jaws, and pulled backward, straining with its entire body. The rubber seal let loose with a barely audible sucking sound. The door swung open. The dog quickly insinuated itself into the gap, then jumped up and braced itself with a forepaw on each side of the storage compartment.

"I'll be damned," Travis said, moving closer.

The retriever peered into the second shelf, where Travis had stored cans of beer, Diet Pepsi, and V-8 vegetable juice. It plucked another Coors from the supply, dropped to the floor, and let the refrigerator door slip shut again as it came to Travis.

He took the beer from it. Standing with a Coors in each hand, studying the dog, he said, more to himself than to the animal, "Okay, so somebody could have taught you to open a refrigerator door. And he could even have taught you how to recognize a certain brand of beer, how to distinguish it from other cans, and how to carry it to him. But we still have some mysteries here. Is it likely that the brand you were taught to recognize would be the same one I'd have in my refrigerator? Possible, yes, but not likely. Besides, I didn't give you any command. I didn't ask you to get me a beer. You did it on your own hook, as if you figured a beer was exactly what I needed at the moment. And it *was*."

Travis put one can down on the table. He wiped the other on his shirt, popped it open, and took a few swallows. He was not concerned that the can had been in the dog's mouth. He was too excited by the animal's amazing performance to worry about germs. Besides, it had held each can by the bottom, as if concerned about hygiene.

The retriever watched him drink.

When he had finished a third of the beer, Travis said, "It was almost as if you understood that I was tense, upset—and that a beer would help relax me. Now, is that crazy or what? We're talking analytical reasoning. Okay, so pets can *sense* their masters' moods a lot of the time. But how many pets know what beer is, and how many realize what it can do to make the master more mellow? Anyway, how'd you know there was beer in the fridge? I guess you could've seen it sometime during the evening when I was fixing dinner, but still . . ."

His hands were shaking. He drank more of the beer, and the can rattled lightly against his teeth.

The dog went around the red Formica table to the twin cabinet doors below the sink. It opened one of these, stuck its head into the dark space, and pulled out the bag of Milk-Bone biscuits, which it brought straight to Travis.

He laughed and said, "Well, If I can have a beer, I guess you deserve a treat of your own, huh?" He took the bag from the dog and tore it open. "Do a few

Milk-Bones mellow you out, fur face?" He put the open bag on the floor. "Serve yourself. I trust you not to overindulge like an ordinary dog." He laughed again. "Hell, I think I might trust you to drive the car!"

The retriever finessed a biscuit out of the package, sat down with its hind legs splayed, and happily crunched up the treat.

Pulling out a chair and sitting at the table, Travis said, "You give me reason to believe in miracles. Do you know what I was doing in those woods this morning?"

Working its jaws, industriously grinding up the biscuit, the dog seemed to have lost interest in Travis for the moment.

"I went out there on a sentimental journey, hoping to recall the pleasure I got from the Santa Anas when I was a boy, in the days before . . . everything turned so dark. I wanted to kill a few snakes like I did when I was a kid, hike and explore and feel in tune with life like in the old days. Because for a long time now, I haven't cared whether I live or die."

The dog stopped chewing, swallowed hard, and focused on Travis with undivided attention.

"Lately, my depressions have been blacker than midnight on the moon. Do you understand about depression, pooch?"

Leaving the Milk-Bone biscuits behind, the retriever got up and came to him. It gazed into his eyes with that unnerving directness and intensity that it had shown before.

Meeting its stare, he said, "Wouldn't consider suicide, though. For one thing, I was raised a Catholic, and though I haven't gone to Mass in ages, I still sort of believe. And for a Catholic, suicide is a mortal sin. Murder. Besides, I'm too mean and too stubborn to give up, no matter how dark things get."

The retriever blinked but did not break eye contact.

"I was in those woods searching for the happiness I once knew. And then I ran into you."

"Woof," it said, as if it were saying, *Good*.

He took its head in both hands, lowered his face to it, and said, "Depression. A feeling that existence was pointless. How would a dog know about those things, hmmm? A dog has no worries, does it? To a dog, every day is a joy. So do you really understand what I'm talking about, boy? Honest to God, I think maybe you do. But am I crediting you with too much intelligence, too much wisdom even for a magical dog? Huh? Sure, you can do some amazing tricks, but that's not the same as *understanding* me."

The retriever pulled away from him and returned to the Milk-Bone package. It took the bag in its teeth and shook out twenty or thirty biscuits onto the linoleum.

"There you go again," Travis said. "One minute, you seem half human— and the next minute you're just a dog with a dog's interests."

However, the retriever was not seeking a snack. It began to push the biscuits around with the black tip of its snout, maneuvering them into the open center of the kitchen floor one at a time, ordering them neatly end to end.

"What the hell is this?"

The dog had five biscuits arranged in a row that gradually curved to the right. It pushed a sixth into place, emphasizing the curve.

As he watched, Travis hastily finished his first beer and opened the second. He had a feeling he was going to need it.

The dog studied the row of biscuits for a moment, as if not quite sure what it had begun to do. It padded back and forth a few times, clearly uncertain, but eventually nudged two more biscuits into line. It looked at Travis, then at the shape it was creating on the floor, then nosed a ninth biscuit into place.

Travis sipped some beer and waited tensely to see what would happen next.

With a shake of its head and a snort of frustration, the dog went to the far end of the room and stood facing into the corner, its head hung low. Travis wondered what it was doing, and then somehow he got the idea that it had gone into the corner in order to concentrate. After a while, it returned and pushed the tenth and eleventh Milk Bone into place, enlarging the pattern.

He was stricken again by the premonition that something of great importance was about to happen. Gooseflesh dimpled his arms.

This time he was not disappointed. The golden retriever used nineteen biscuits to form a crude but recognizable question mark on the kitchen floor, then raised its expressive eyes to Travis.

A question mark.

Meaning: *Why?* Why have you been so depressed? Why do you feel life is pointless, empty?

The dog apparently understood what he had told it. All right, okay, so maybe it didn't understand language exactly, didn't follow every word that he spoke, but it somehow perceived the meaning of what he was saying, or at least enough of the meaning to arouse its interest and curiosity.

And, by God, if it also understood the purpose of a question mark, then it was capable of abstract thinking! The very concept of simple symbols—like alphabets, numbers, question marks, and exclamation points—serving as short-hand for communicating complex ideas—well, that required abstract thinking. And abstract thinking was reserved for only one species on earth: humankind. This golden retriever was demonstrably *not* human, but somehow it had come into possession of intellectual skills that no other animal could claim.

Travis was stunned. But there was nothing accidental about the question mark. Crude but not accidental. Somewhere, the dog must have seen the symbol and been taught its meaning. Statistical theorists said an infinite number of monkeys, equipped with an infinite number of typewriters, would eventually be able to recreate every line of great English prose merely by random chance. He figured that this dog forming a Milk-Bone question mark in about two minutes flat, merely by purest chance, was about ten times as unlikely as all those damn monkeys recreating Shakespeare's plays.

The dog was watching him expectantly.

Getting up, he found he was a bit shaky in the legs. He went to the carefully arranged biscuits, scattered them across the floor, and returned to his chair.

The retriever studied this disarranged Milk-Bones, regarded Travis inquiringly, sniffed at the biscuits again, and seemed baffled.

Travis waited.

The house was unnaturally quiet, as if the flow of time had been suspended for every living creature, machine, and object on earth—though not for him, the retriever, or the contents of the kitchen.

At last, the dog began to push the biscuits around with its nose as it had done before. In a minute or two, it formed a question mark.

Travis chugged some Coors. His heart was hammering. His palms were sweaty. He was filled with both wonder and trepidation, with both wild joy and fear of the unknown, simultaneously awestricken and bewildered. He wanted to laugh because he had never seen anything half as delightful as this dog. He also wanted to cry because only hours ago he'd thought life was bleak, dark, and pointless. But no matter how painful it was sometimes, life was (he now realized) nonetheless precious. He actually felt as if God had sent the retriever to intrigue him, to remind him that the world was full of surprises and that despair made no sense when one had no understanding of the purpose—and strange possibilities—of existence. Travis wanted to laugh, but his laughter teetered on the brink of a sob. Yet when he surrendered to the sob, it became a laugh. When he attempted to stand, he knew that he was even shakier than before, too shaky, so he did the only thing he could do: he stayed in his chair and took another long swallow of Coors.

Cocking its head one way and then the other, looking slightly wary, the dog watched him as if it thought he had gone mad. He had. Months ago. But he was all better now.

He put down the Coors and wiped tears out of his eyes with the backs of his hands. He said, "Come here, fur face."

The retriever hesitated, then came to him.

He ruffled and stroked its coat, scratched behind its ears. "You amaze me and scare me. I can't figure where you came from or how you got to be what you are, but you couldn't have come where you're more needed. A question mark, huh? Jesus. All right. You want to know why I felt life had no purpose or joy for me? I'll tell you. I will, by God, I'll sit right here and have another beer and tell it to a dog. But first . . . I'm going to name you."

The retriever blew air out of its nostrils, as if to say, *Well, it's about time.*

Holding the dog's head, looking straight into its eyes, Travis said, "Einstein. From now on, fur face, your name is Einstein."

4

Streck called again at ten minutes past nine.

Nora snatched up the phone on the first ring, fiercely determined to tell him off and make him leave her alone. But for some reason she clenched up again and was unable to speak.

In a repulsively intimate tone of voice, he said, "You miss me, prettiness? Hmmmm? Do you wish I'd come to you, be a man for you?"

She hung up.

What's wrong with me? she wondered. Why can't I tell him to go away and stop bothering me?

Maybe her speechlessness grew from a secret desire to hear a man—any man, even a disgusting specimen like Streck—call her pretty. Although he was not the kind who would be capable of tenderness or affection, she could listen to him and imagine what it would be like to have a *good* man say sweet things to her.

"Well, you're not pretty," she told herself, "and you never ever will be, so stop mooning around. Next time he calls, tell him off."

She got out of bed and went down the hall to the bathroom, where there was a mirror. Following Violet Devon's example, Nora did not have mirrors anywhere in the house except the bathrooms. She did not like to look at herself because what she saw was saddening.

This one night, however, she wanted to take a look at herself because Streck's flattery, though cold and calculated, had stirred her curiosity. Not that she hoped to see some fine quality that she had never seen before. No. From duckling to swan overnight . . . that was a frivolous, hopeless dream. Rather, she wanted to confirm that she was undesirable. Streck's unwanted interest rattled Nora because she was *comfortable* in her homeliness and solitude, and she wanted to reassure herself that he was mocking her, that he would not act upon his threats, that her peaceful solitude would endure. Or so she told herself as she stepped into the bathroom and switched on the light.

The narrow chamber had pale-blue tile from floor to ceiling with a white-tile border. A huge claw-foot tub. White porcelain and brass fixtures. The large mirror was somewhat streaked with age.

She looked at her hair, which Streck said was beautiful, dark, glossy. But it was of one shade, without natural highlights; to her, it wasn't glossy but oily, although she had washed it that morning.

She looked quickly at her brow, cheekbones, nose, jaw line, lips, and chin. She tentatively traced her features with one hand, but she saw nothing to intrigue a man.

At last, reluctantly, she stared into her eyes, which Streck had called lovely. They were a dreary, lusterless shade of gray. She could not bear to meet her own gaze for more than a few seconds. Her eyes confirmed her low opinion of her appearance. But also . . . well, in her own eyes she saw a smoldering anger that disturbed her, that was not like her, an anger at what she had let herself become. Of course, that made no sense whatsoever because she was what nature had made her—a mouse—and she could do nothing about that.

Turning from the mottled mirror, she felt a pang of disappointment that her self-inspection had not resulted in a single surprise or reevaluation. Immediately, however, she was shocked and appalled by that disappointment. She stood in the bathroom doorway, shaking her head, amazed by her own befuddled thought processes.

Did she *want* to be appealing to Streck? Of course not. He was weird, sick, dangerous. The very last thing she wanted was to appeal to him. Maybe she wouldn't mind if another man looked on her with favor, but not Streck. She should get on her knees and thank God for creating her as she was, because if she were at all attractive, Streck would make good on his threats. He'd come here, and he'd rape her . . . maybe murder her. Who knew about a man like that? Who knew what his limits were? She wasn't being a nervous old maid when she worried about murder, not these days: the newspapers were full of it.

She realized that she was defenseless, and she hurried back to the bedroom, where she had left the butcher's knife.

5

Most people believe psychoanalysis is a cure for unhappiness. They are sure they could overcome all their problems and achieve peace of mind if only they could understand their own psychology, understand the reasons for their negative moods and self-destructive behavior. But Travis had learned this was not the case. For years, he engaged in unsparing self-analysis, and long ago he figured out why he had become a loner who was unable to make friends. However, in spite of that understanding, he had not been able to change.

Now, as midnight approached, he sat in the kitchen, drank another Coors, and told Einstein about his self-imposed emotional isolation. Einstein sat before him, unmoving, never yawning, as if intently interested in his tale.

"I was a loner as a kid, right from the start, though I wasn't entirely without friends. It was just that I always preferred my own company. I guess it's my nature. I mean, when I was a kid, I hadn't yet decided that my being friends with someone was a danger to him."

Travis's mother had died giving birth to him, and he knew all about that from an early age. In time her death would seem like an omen of what was to come, and it would take on a terrible importance, but that was later. As a kid, he wasn't yet burdened with guilt.

Not until he was ten. That was when his brother Harry died. Harry was twelve, two years older than Travis. One Monday morning in June, Harry talked Travis into walking three blocks to the beach, although their father had expressly forbidden them to go swimming without him. It was a private cove without a public lifeguard, and they were the only two swimmers in sight.

"Harry got caught in an undertow," Travis told Einstein. "We were in the water together no more than ten feet apart, and the damn undertow got him, sucked him away, but it didn't get me. I even went after him, tried to save him so I should've swum straight into the same current, but I guess it changed course just after it snatched Harry away, 'cause I came out of the water alive." He stared at the top of the kitchen table for a long moment, seeing not the red Formica but the rolling, treacherous, blue-green sea. "I loved my big brother more than anyone in the world."

Einstein whined softly, as in commiseration.

"Nobody blamed me for what happened to Harry. He was the older one. He was supposed to be the most responsible. But I felt . . . well, if the undertow took Harry, it should've taken me, too."

A night wind blew in from the west, rattled a loose windowpane.

After taking a swallow of beer, Travis said, "The summer I was fourteen, I wanted very badly to go to tennis camp. Tennis was my big enthusiasm then. So my dad enrolled me in a place down near San Diego, a full month of intense instruction. He drove me there on a Sunday, but we never made it. Just north of Oceanside, a trucker fell asleep at the wheel, his rig jumped the median, and we were wiped. Dad was killed instantly. Broken neck, broken back, skull crushed, chest caved in. I was in the front seat beside him, and I came out of it with a few cuts, bruises, and two broken fingers."

The dog was studying him intently.

"It was just like with Harry. Both of us should have died, my father and me, but I escaped. And we wouldn't have been making the damn drive if I hadn't agitated like hell about tennis camp. So this time, there was no getting around it. Maybe I couldn't be blamed for my mother dying in childbirth, and maybe I couldn't be pinned with Harry's death, but *this* one . . . Anyway, although I wasn't always at fault, it began to be clear that I was jinxed, that it wasn't safe for people to get too close to me. When I loved somebody, really loved them, they were sure as shit going to die."

Only a child could have been convinced that those tragic events meant he was a walking curse, but Travis was a child then, only fourteen, and no other explanation was so neat. He was too young to understand that the mindless violence of nature and fate often had no meaning that could be ascertained. At fourteen, he *needed* meaning in order to cope, so he told himself that he was cursed, that if he made any close friends he would be sentencing them to early death. Being somewhat of an introvert to begin with, he found it almost too easy to turn inward and make do with his own company.

By the time he graduated from college at the age of twenty-one, he was a confirmed loner, though maturity had given him a healthier perspective on the deaths of his mother, brother, and father. He no longer consciously thought of himself as jinxed, no longer blamed himself for what had happened to his family. He remained an introvert, without close friends, partly because he had lost the ability to form and nurture intimate relationships and partly because he figured he could not be shattered by grief if he had no friends to lose.

"Habit and self-defense kept me emotionally isolated," he told Einstein.

The dog rose and crossed the few feet of kitchen floor that separated them. It insinuated itself between his legs and put its head in his lap.

Petting Einstein, Travis said, "Had no idea what I wanted to do after college, and there was a military draft then, so I joined up before they could call me. Chose the army. Special Forces. Liked it. Maybe because . . . well, there was a sense of camaraderie, and I was *forced* to make friends. See, I pretended not to want close ties with anyone, but I must have because I put myself in a situation where it was inevitable. Decided to make a career out of the service.

When Delta Force—the antiterrorist group—was formed, that's where I finally landed. The guys in Delta were tight, real buddies. They called me 'The Mute' and 'Harpo' because I wasn't a talker, but in spite of myself I made friends. Then, on our eleventh operation, my squad was flown into Athens to take the U.S. embassy back from a group of Palestinian extremists who seized it. They'd killed eight staff members and were still killing one an hour, wouldn't negotiate. We hit them quick and sneaky—and it was a fiasco. They'd booby-trapped the place. Nine men in my squad died. I was the only survivor. A bullet in my thigh. Shrapnel in my ass. But a survivor."

Einstein raised his head from Travis's lap.

Travis thought he saw sympathy in the dog's eyes. Maybe because that was what he wanted to see.

"That's eight years ago, when I was twenty-eight. Left the army. Came home to California. Got a real-estate license because my dad had sold real estate, and I didn't know what else to do. Did really well, maybe 'cause I didn't care if they bought the houses I showed them, didn't push, didn't act like a salesman. Fact is, I did so well that I became a broker, opened my own office, hired salespeople."

Which was how he had met Paula. She was a tall blond beauty, bright and amusing, and she could sell real estate so well that she joked about having lived an earlier life in which she had represented the Dutch colonists when they had bought Manhattan from the Indians for beads and trinkets. She was smitten with Travis. That's what she'd told him: "Mr. Cornell, sir, I am smitten. I think it's your strong, silent act. Best Clint Eastwood imitation I've ever seen." Travis resisted her at first. He did not believe he would jinx Paula; at least, he didn't consciously believe it; he had not openly reverted to childhood superstition. But he did not want to risk the pain of loss again. Undeterred by his hesitancy, she pursued him, and in time he had to admit he was in love with her. So in love that he told her about his lifelong tag game with Death, something of which he spoke to no one else. "Listen," Paula said, "you won't have to mourn me. I'm going to outlive you because I'm not the type to bottle up my feelings. I take out my frustrations on those around me, so I'm bound to shave a decade off *your* life."

They had been married in a simple courthouse ceremony four years ago, the summer after Travis's thirty-second birthday. He had loved her. Oh God, how he had loved her.

To Einstein, he said, "We didn't know it then, but she had cancer on our wedding day. Ten months later, she was dead."

The dog put its head down in his lap again.

For a while, Travis could not continue.

He drank some beer.

He stroked the dog's head.

In time he said, "After that, I tried to go on as usual. Always prided myself in going on, facing up to anything, keeping my chin up, all that bullshit. Kept the real-estate office running another year. But none of it mattered any more. Sold it two years ago. Cashed in all my investments, too. Turned everything into cash and socked it in the bank. Rented this house. Spent the last two years . . . well, brooding. And I got squirrelly. Hardly a surprise, huh? Squirrelly as hell. Came full circle, you see, right back to what I believed when I was a kid. That I was a danger to anyone who gets close to me. But you changed me, Einstein. You turned me around in one day. I swear, it's like you were *sent* to show me that life's mysterious, strange, and full of wonders—and that only a fool withdraws from it willingly and lets it pass him by."

The dog was peering up at him again.

He lifted his beer can, but it was empty.

Einstein went to the fridge and got another Coors.

Taking the can from the dog, Travis said, "Now, after hearing the whole sorry thing, what do you think? You think it's wise for you to hang around with me? You think it's safe?"

Einstein woofed.

"Was that a yes?"

Einstein rolled onto his back and put all four legs in the air, baring his belly as he had done earlier when he had permitted Travis to collar him.

Putting his beer aside, Travis got off his chair, settled on the floor, and stroked the dog's belly. "All right," he said. "All right. But don't die on me, damn you. Don't you dare die on me."

6

Nora Devon's telephone rang again at eleven o'clock.

It was Streck. "Are you in bed now, prettiness?"

She did not reply.

"Do you wish I was there with you?"

Since the previous call, she had thought about how to handle him and had come up with several threats she hoped might work. She said, "If you don't leave me alone, I'll go to the police."

"Nora, do you sleep in the nude?"

She was sitting in bed. She sat up straighter, tense, rigid. "I'll go to the police and say you tried to . . . to force yourself on me. I will, I swear I will."

"I'd like to see you in the nude," he said, ignoring her threat.

"I'll lie. I'll say you r-raped me."

"Wouldn't you like me to put my hands on your breasts, Nora?"

Dull cramps in her stomach forced her to bend forward in bed. "I'll have the telephone company put a tap on my line, record all the calls I get, so I'll have proof."

"Kiss you all over, Nora. Wouldn't that be nice?"

The cramps were getting worse. She was shaking uncontrollably, too. Her voice cracked repeatedly as she employed her final threat: "I have a gun. I have a gun."

"Tonight you'll dream about me, Nora. I'm sure you will. You'll dream about me kissing you everywhere, all over your pretty body—"

She slammed the phone down.

Rolling onto her side on the bed, she hunched her shoulders and drew up her knees and hugged herself. The cramps had no physical cause. They were strictly an emotional reaction, generated by fear and shame and rage and enormous frustration.

Gradually, the pain passed. Fear subsided, leaving only rage.

She was so wrenchingly innocent of the world and its ways, so unaccustomed to dealing with people, that she couldn't function unless she restricted herself to the house, to a private world without human contact. She knew nothing about social interaction. She had not even been capable of holding a polite conversation with Garrison Dilworth, Aunt Violet's attorney—Nora's attorney now—during their meetings to settle the estate. She had answered his questions as succinctly as possible and had sat in his presence with her eyes downcast and her cold hands fidgeting in her lap, crushingly shy. Afraid of her own lawyer! If she couldn't deal with a kind man like Garrison Dilworth, how could she ever handle a beast like Art Streck? In the future, she wouldn't dare have a repairman in her home, no matter what broke down; she would just have to live in ever-worsening decay and ruin because the next man might be another Streck—or worse. In the tradition established by her aunt, Nora already had groceries delivered from a neighborhood market, so she did not have to go out to shop, but now she would be afraid to let the delivery boy into the house; he had never been the least aggressive, suggestive, or in any way insulting, but one day he might see the vulnerability that Streck had seen . . .

She *hated* Aunt Violet.

On the other hand, Violet had been right: Nora was a mouse. Like all mice, her destiny was to run, to hide, and to cower in the dark.

Her fury abated just as her cramps had done.

Loneliness took the place of anger, and she wept quietly.

Later, sitting with her back against the headboard, blotting her reddened eyes with Kleenex and blowing her nose, she bravely vowed not to become a recluse. Somehow she would find the strength and courage to venture out into the world more than she'd done before. She would meet people. She would get to know the neighbors that Violet had more or less shunned. She would make friends. By God, she *would*. And she wouldn't let Streck intimidate her. She would learn how to handle other problems that came along as well, and in time she would be a different woman from the one she was now. A promise to herself. A sacred vow.

She considered unplugging the telephone, thus foiling Streck, but she was afraid she might need it. What if she woke, heard someone in the house, and was unable to plug in the phone fast enough?

Before turning out the lights and pulling up the covers, she closed the lockless bedroom door and braced it shut with the armchair, which she tilted under the knob. In bed, in the dark, she felt for the butcher's knife, which she'd placed on the nightstand, and she was reassured when she put her hand directly upon it without fumbling.

Nora lay on her back, eyes open, wide awake. Pale amber light from the streetlamps found its way through the shuttered windows. The ceiling was banded with alternating strips of black and faded gold, as if a tiger of infinite length were leaping over the bed in a jump that would never end. She wondered if she would ever sleep easily again.

She also wondered if she would find anyone who could care about her—and for her—out there in the bigger world that she had vowed to enter. Was there no one who could love a mouse and treat it gently?

Far away, a train whistle played a one-note dirge in the night. It was a hollow, cold, and mournful sound.

7

Vince Nasco had never been so busy. Or so happy.

When he called the usual Los Angeles number to report success at the Yarbeck house, he was referred to another public phone. This one was between a frozen-yogurt shop and a fish restaurant on Balboa Island in Newport Harbor.

There, he was called by the contact with the sexy, throaty, yet little-girl voice. She spoke circumspectly of murder, never using incriminating words but employing exotic euphemisms that would mean nothing in a court of law. She was calling from another pay phone, one she had chosen at random, so there was virtually no chance that either of them was tapped. But it was a Big Brother world where you didn't dare take risks.

The woman had a third job for him. Three in one day.

As Vince watched the evening traffic inching past on the narrow island street, the woman—whom he had never seen and whose name he didn't know—

gave him the address of Dr. Albert Hudston in Laguna Beach. Hudston lived with his wife and a sixteen-year-old son. Both Dr. and Mrs. Hudston had to be hit; however, the boy's fate was in Vince's hands. If the kid could be kept out of it, fine. But if he saw Vince and could serve as a witness, he had to be eliminated, too.

"Your discretion," the woman said.

Vince already knew that he would erase the kid, because killing was more useful to him, more energizing, if the victim was young. It had been a long time since he'd blown away a really young one, and the prospect excited him.

"I can only emphasize," the contact said, driving Vince a little nuts with her breathy pauses, "that this option must be exercised with all due speed. We want the deal concluded tonight. By tomorrow, the competition will be aware of what we're trying to swing, and they'll get in our way."

Vince knew the "competition" must be the police. He was being paid to kill three doctors in a single day—*doctors,* when he had never killed a doctor before—so he knew there was something that linked them, something the cops would pick up on when they found Weatherby in the trunk of his car and Elisabeth Yarbeck beaten to death in her bedroom. Vince didn't know what the link was because he never knew anything about the people he was hired to kill, and he didn't really want to know anything. It was safer that way. But the cops would link Weatherby with Yarbeck and both of them with Hudston, so if Vince did not get to Hudston tonight, the police would be providing the man with protection by tomorrow.

Vince said, "I wonder . . . do you want the option exercised in the same way as the other two deals today? You want a pattern?"

He was thinking maybe he should burn the Hudston house to the ground with them in it to cover the murders.

"No, we absolutely do want a pattern," the woman said. "Same as the others. We want them to *know* we've been busy."

"I see."

"We want to tweak their noses," she said, and laughed softly. "We want to rub in the salt."

Vince hung up and walked to the Jolly Roger for dinner. He had vegetable soup, a hamburger, fries, onion rings, coleslaw, chocolate cake with ice cream, and (as an afterthought) apple pie, all of which he washed down with five cups of coffee. He was ordinarily a big eater, but his appetite increased dramatically after a job. In fact, when he finished the pie, he wasn't full. Understandable. In one busy day, he had absorbed the life energies of Davis Weatherby and the Yarbecks; he was overcharged, a racing engine. His metabolism was in high gear; he would need more fuel for a while, until his body stored the excess life energies in biological batteries for future use.

The ability to absorb the very life force of his victim was the Gift that made him different from all other men. Because of the Gift, he would always be strong, vital, alert. He would live forever.

He had never divulged the secret of his splendid Gift to the throaty-voiced woman or to any of the people for whom he worked. Few people were imaginative and open-minded enough to consider seriously such an amazing talent. Vince kept it to himself because he was afraid they'd think he was crazy.

Outside the restaurant, he stood on the sidewalk for awhile, just breathing deeply, savoring the crisp sea air. A chilly night wind blew off the harbor, sweeping scrap paper and purple jacaranda blossoms along the pavement.

Vince felt terrific. He believed he was as much of an elemental force as were the sea and wind.

From Balboa Island, he drove south to Laguna Beach. At eleven-twenty, he parked his van across the street from the Hudston house. It was in the hills, a single-story home slung on a steep slope to take advantage of ocean views. He saw lights in a couple of windows.

He climbed between the seats and sat down in the back of the van, out of sight, to wait until all of the Hudstons had gone to bed. Soon after leaving the Yarbeck house, he had changed out of his blue suit into gray slacks, a white shirt, a maroon sweater, and a dark-blue nylon jacket. Now, in the darkness, he had nothing to do except take his weapons out of a cardboard box, where they were hidden beneath two loaves of bread, a four-roll package of toilet tissue, and other items that gave the impression he had just been to the market.

The Walther P-38 was fully loaded. After finishing the job at the Yarbeck house, he had screwed a fresh silencer onto the barrel, one of the new short ones that, thanks to the high-tech revolution, was half the length of older models. He set the gun aside.

He had a six-inch switchblade knife. He put it in the right front pocket of his trousers.

When he had wound the wire garrote into a tight coil, he tucked it into the left inside pocket of his jacket.

He had a sap weighted with lead pellets. That went into his right exterior jacket pocket.

He did not expect to use anything but the gun. However, he liked to be prepared for any eventuality.

On some jobs he had used an Uzi submachine gun that had been illegally converted for automatic fire. But the current assignment did not require heavy armament.

He also had a small leather packet, half the size of a shaving kit, which contained a few simple burglary tools. He did not bother to inspect those instruments. He might not even need them because a lot of people were amazingly lax about home security, leaving doors and windows unlocked during the night, as if they believed they were living in a nineteenth-century Quaker village.

At eleven-forty he leaned between the front seats and looked through the side window at the Hudston house. All the lights were out. Good. They were in bed.

To give them time to fall asleep, he sat down in the back of the van again, ate a Mr. Goodbar, and thought about how he'd spend some of the substantial fees that he had earned just since this morning.

He'd been wanting a power ski, one of those clever machines that made it possible to water-ski without a boat. He was an ocean lover. Something about the sea drew him; he felt at home in the tides and was most fully alive when he was moving in harmony with great, surging, dark masses of water. He enjoyed scuba diving, windsailing, and surfing. His teenage years had been spent more on the beach than in school. He still rode the board now and then, when the surf was high. But he was twenty-eight, and surfing now seemed tame to him. He wasn't as easily thrilled as he had once been. He liked *speed* these days. He pictured himself skimming over a slate-dark sea on power skis, hammered by the wind, jolted by an endless series of impacts with eternally incoming breakers, riding the Pacific as a rodeo cowboy would ride a bronc . . .

At twelve-fifteen he got out of the van. He tucked the pistol under the waistband of his trousers and crossed the silent, deserted street to the Hudston house. He let himself through an unlocked wooden gate onto a side patio brightened only by moonlight filtered through the leafy branches of an enormous sheltering coral tree.

He paused to pull on a pair of supple leather gloves.

Mirrored by moonbeams, a sliding glass door connected the patio with the living room. It was locked. A penlight, extracted from the packet of burglary tools, also revealed a wooden pole laid in the interior track of the door to prevent it from being forced.

The Hudstons were more security-conscious than most people, but Vince was unconcerned. He fixed a small suction cup to the glass, used a diamond cutter to carve a circle in the pane near the door handle, and quietly removed the cutout with the cup. He reached through the hole and disengaged the lock. He cut another circle near the sill, reached inside, and removed the wooden pole from the track, pushing it under the drawn drapes, into the room beyond.

He did not have to worry about dogs. The woman with the sexy voice had told him that the Hudstons had no house pets. That was one reason why he liked working for these particular employers: their information was always extensive and accurate.

Easing the door open, he slipped through the closed drapes into the dark living room. He stood for a moment, letting his eyes adjust to the gloom, listening. The house was tomb-silent.

He found the boy's room first. It was illuminated by the green glow of the numerals on a digital clock-radio. The teenager was lying on his side, snoring softly. Sixteen. Very young. Vince liked them very young.

He moved around the bed and crouched along the side of it, face-to-face with the sleeper. With his teeth, he pulled the glove off his left hand. Holding the pistol in his right hand, he touched the muzzle to the underside of the boy's chin.

The kid woke at once.

Vince slapped his bare hand firmly against the boy's forehead and simultaneously fired the gun. The bullet smashed up through the soft underside of the kid's chin, through the roof of his mouth, into his brain, killing him instantly.

Ssssnap.

An intense charge of life energy burst out of the dying body and into Vince. It was such pure, vital energy that he whimpered with pleasure as he felt it surge into him.

For a while he crouched beside the bed, not trusting himself to move. Transported. Breathless. At last, in the dark he kissed the dead boy on the lips and said, "I accept. Thank you. I accept."

He crept cat-swift, cat-silent through the house and quickly found the master bedroom. Sufficient light was provided by another digital clock with green numerals and the soft glow of a night-light coming through the open bathroom door. Dr. and Mrs. Hudston were both asleep. Vince killed her first—

Ssssnap.

—without waking her husband. She slept in the nude, so after he received her sacrifice, he put his head to her bare breasts and listened to the stillness of her heart. He kissed her nipples and murmured, "Thank you."

When he circled the bed, turned on a nightstand lamp, and woke Dr. Hudston, the man was at first confused. Until he saw his wife's staring, sightless eyes. Then he shouted and grabbed for Vince's arm, and Vince clubbed him over the head twice with the butt of the gun.

Vince dragged the unconscious Hudston, who also slept in the nude, into the bathroom. Again he found adhesive tape, with which he was able to bind the doctor's wrists and ankles.

He filled the tub with cold water and wrestled Hudston into it. That frigid bath revived the doctor.

In spite of being naked and bound, Hudston tried to push up out of the cold water, tried to launch himself at Vince.

Vince hit him in the face with the pistol and shoved him down into the tub again.

"Who are you? What do you want?" Hudston spluttered as his face came up out of the water.

"I've killed your wife *and* your son, and I'm going to kill you."

Hudston's eyes seemed to sink back into his damp, pasty face. "Jimmy? Oh, not Jimmy, really, no."

"Your boy is dead," Vince insisted. "I blew his brains out."

At the mention of his son, Hudston broke. He did not burst into tears, did not begin to keen, nothing as dramatic as that. But his eyes went dead—*blink*—just that abruptly. Like a light going out. He stared at Vince, but there was no fear or anger in him any more.

Vince said, "What you've got here is two choices: die easy or die hard. You tell me what I want to know, and I let you die easy, quick and painless. You get stubborn on me, and I can draw it out for five or six hours."

Dr. Hudston stared. Except for bright ribbons of fresh blood that banded his face, he was very white, wet and sickly pale like some creature that swam eternally in the deepest reaches of the sea.

Vince hoped the guy wasn't catatonic. "What I want to know is what you have in common with Davis Weatherby and Elisabeth Yarbeck."

Hudston blinked, focused on Vince. His voice was hoarse and tremulous. "Davis and Liz? What are you talking about?"

"You know them?"

Hudston nodded.

"How do you know them? Go to school together? Live next door at one time?"

Shaking his head, Hudston said, "We . . . we used to work together at Banodyne."

"What's Banodyne?"

"Banodyne Laboratories."

"Where's that?"

"Here in Orange County," Hudston said. He gave an address in the city of Irvine.

"What'd you do there?"

"Research. But I left ten months ago. Weatherby and Yarbeck still work there, but I don't."

"What sort of research?" Vince asked.

Hudston hesitated.

Vince said, "Quick and painless—or hard and nasty?"

The doctor told him about the research he had been involved with at Banodyne. The Francis Project. The experiments. The dogs.

The story was incredible. Vince made Hudston run through some of the details three or four times before he was finally convinced the story was true.

When he was sure he had squeezed everything out of the man, Vince shot Hudston in the face, point-blank, the quick death he'd promised.

Ssssnap.

Back in the van, driving down the night-draped Laguna Hills, away from the Hudston house, Vince thought about the dangerous step he had taken. Usually, he knew nothing about his targets. That was safest for him and for his employers. Ordinarily he didn't *want* to know what the poor saps had done to bring so much grief on themselves, because knowing would bring *him* grief. But this was no ordinary situation. He had been paid to kill three doctors—not medical doctors, as it turned out now, but scientists—all of them upstanding citizens, plus any members of their families who happened to get in the way. Extraordinary. Tomorrow's papers weren't going to have enough room for all the news. Something very big was going on, something so important that it might provide him with a once-in-a-lifetime edge, with a shot at money so big he would need help to count it. The money might come from selling the forbidden knowledge he had pried out of Hudston . . . if he could figure out who would like to buy it. But knowledge was not only saleable; it was also dangerous. Ask Adam. Ask Eve. If his current employers, the sexy-voiced lady and the other people in L.A., learned that he had broken the most basic rule of his trade, if they knew that he had interrogated one of his victims before wasting him, they would put out a contract on Vince. The hunter would become the hunted.

Of course, he didn't worry a lot about dying. He had too much life stored up in him. Other people's lives. More lives than ten cats. He was going to live forever. He was pretty sure of that. But . . . well, he didn't know for certain how *many* lives he had to absorb in order to insure immortality. Sometimes he felt that he'd already achieved a state of invincibility, eternal life. But at other times, he felt that he was still vulnerable and that he would have to take more life energy into himself before he would reach the desired state of godhood. Until he knew, beyond doubt, that he had arrived at Olympus, it was best to exercise a little caution.

Banodyne.

The Francis Project.

If what Hudston said was true, the risk Vince was taking would be well-rewarded when he found the right buyer for the information. He was going to be a rich man.

8

Wes Dalberg had lived alone in a stone cabin in upper Holy Jim Canyon on the eastern edge of Orange County for ten years. His only light came from Coleman lanterns, and the only running water in the place was from a hand pump in the kitchen sink. His toilet was in an outhouse with a quarter-moon carved on the door (as a joke), about a hundred feet from the back of the cabin.

Wes was forty-two, but he looked older. His face was wind-scoured and sun-leathered. He wore a neatly trimmed beard with a lot of white whiskers. Although he appeared aged beyond his true years, his physical condition was that of a twenty-five-year-old. He believed his good health resulted from living close to nature.

Tuesday night, May 18, by the silvery light of a hissing Coleman lantern, he sat at the kitchen table until one in the morning, sipping homemade plum wine and reading a McGee novel by John D. MacDonald. Wes was, as he put it, "an antisocial curmudgeon born in the wrong century," who had little use for modern society. But he liked to read about McGee because McGee swam in that messy, nasty world out there and never let the murderous currents sweep him away.

When he finished the book at one o'clock, Wes went outside to get more wood for the fireplace. Wind-swayed branches of sycamores cast vague moonshadows on the ground, and the glossy surfaces of rustling leaves shone dully with pale reflections of the lunar light. Coyotes howled in the distance as they chased down a rabbit or other small creature. Nearby, insects sang in the brush, and a chill wind soughed through the higher reaches of the forest.

His supply of cordwood was stored in a lean-to that extended along the entire north side of the cabin. He pulled the latch-peg out of the hasp on the double doors. He was so familiar with the arrangement of the wood in the storage space that he worked blindly in its lightless confines, filling a sturdy tin hod with half a dozen logs. He carried the hod out in both hands, put it down, and turned to close the doors.

He realized the coyotes and the insects had all fallen silent. Only the wind still had a voice.

Frowning, he turned to look at the dark forest that encircled the small clearing in which his cabin stood.

Something growled.

Wes squinted at the night-swaddled woods, which suddenly seemed less well illuminated by the moon than they had been a moment ago.

The growling was deep and angry. Not like anything he had heard out there before in ten years of nights alone.

Wes was curious, even concerned, but not afraid. He stood very still, listening. A minute ticked by, and he heard nothing further.

He finished closing the lean-to doors, pegged the latch, and picked up the hod full of cordwood.

Growling again. Then silence. Then the sound of dry brush and leaves crackling, crunching, snapping underfoot.

Judging by the sound, it was about thirty yards away. Just a bit west of the outhouse. Back in the forest.

The thing grumbled again, louder this time. Closer, too. Not more than twenty yards away now.

He could still not see the source of the sound. The deserter moon continued to hide behind a narrow filigree band of clouds.

Listening to the thick, guttural, yet ululant growling, Wes was suddenly uneasy. For the first time in ten years as a resident of Holy Jim, he felt he was in danger. Carrying the hod, he headed quickly toward the back of the cabin and the kitchen door.

The rustling of displaced brush grew louder. The creature in the woods was moving faster than before. Hell, it was running.

Wes ran, too.

The growling escalated into hard, vicious snarls: an eerie mix of sounds that seemed one part dog, part pig, part cougar, part human, and one part something else altogether. It was almost at his heels.

As he sprinted around the corner of the cabin, Wes swung the hod and threw it toward where he judged the animal to be. He heard the cordwood flying loose and slamming to the ground, heard the metal hod clanging end over end, but the snarling only grew closer and louder, so he knew he had missed.

He hurried up the three back steps, threw open the kitchen door, stepped inside, and slammed the door behind him. He slipped the latch bolt in place, a security measure he had not used in nine years, not since he had grown accustomed to the peacefulness of the canyon.

He went through the cabin to the front door and latched it, too. He was surprised by the intensity of the fear that had overcome him. Even if a hostile animal was out there—perhaps a crazed bear that had come down from the mountains—it could not open doors and follow him into the cabin. There was no need to engage the locks, yet he felt better for having done so. He was operating on instinct, and he was a good enough outdoorsman to know that instincts ought to be trusted even when they resulted in seemingly irrational behavior.

Okay, so he was safe. No animal could open a door. Certainly, a bear couldn't, and it was most likely a bear.

But it hadn't sounded like a bear. That's what had Wes Dalberg so spooked: it had not sounded like anything that could possibly be roaming those woods.

He was familiar with his animal neighbors, knew all the howls, cries, and other noises they made.

The only light in the front room was from the fireplace, and it did not dispel the shadows in the corners. Phantoms of reflected firelight cavorted across the walls. For the first time, Wes would have welcomed electricity.

He owned a Remington 12-gauge shotgun with which he hunted small game to supplement his diet of store-bought foods. It was on a rack in the kitchen. He considered getting it down and loading it, but now that he was safely behind locked doors, he was beginning to be embarrassed about having panicked. Like a greenhorn, for God's sake. Like some lardass suburbanite shrieking at the sight of a fieldmouse. If he had just shouted and clapped his hands, he would most likely have frightened off the thing in the brush. Even if his reaction could be blamed on instinct, he had not behaved in accordance with his self-image as a hard-bitten canyon squatter. If he armed himself with the rifle now, when there was no compelling need for it, he'd lose a large measure of self-respect, which was important because the only opinion of Wes Dalberg that Wes cared about was his own. No gun.

Wes risked going to the living room's big window. This was an alteration made by someone who held the Forest Service lease on the cabin about twenty years ago; the old, narrow, multipane window had been taken out, a larger hole cut in the wall, and a big single-pane window installed to take advantage of the spectacular forest view.

A few moon-silvered clouds appeared phosphorescent against the velvety blackness of the night sky. Moonlight dappled the front yard, glistered on the grill and hood and windshield of Wes's Jeep Cherokee, and outlined the shadowy shapes of the encroaching trees. At first nothing moved except a few branches swaying gently in the mild wind.

He studied the woodland scene for a couple of minutes. Neither seeing nor hearing anything out of the ordinary, he decided the animal had wandered off. With considerable relief and with a resurgence of embarrassment, he started to turn away from the window—then glimpsed movement near the Jeep. He squinted, saw nothing, remained watchful for another minute or two. Just when he decided he had imagined the movement, he saw it again: something coming out from behind the Jeep.

He leaned closer to the window.

Something was rushing across the yard toward the cabin, coming fast and low to the ground. Instead of revealing the nature of the enemy, the moonlight made it more mysterious, shapeless. The thing was *hurtling* at the cabin. Abruptly—Jesus, God!—the creature was airborne, a strangeness flying straight at him through the darkness, and Wes cried out, and an instant later the beast exploded through the big window, and Wes screamed, but the scream was cut short.

9

Because Travis was not much of a drinker, three beers were enough to insure against insomnia. He was asleep within seconds of putting his head on the pillow. He dreamed that he was the ringmaster in a circus where all the performing animals could speak, and after each show he visited them in their cages, where each animal told him a secret that amazed him even though he forgot it as soon as he moved along to the next cage and the next secret.

At four o'clock in the morning, he woke and saw Einstein at the bedroom window. The dog was standing with its forepaws on the sill, its face limned by moonlight, staring out at the night, very alert.

"What's wrong, boy?" Travis asked.

Einstein glanced at him, then returned his attention to the moon-washed night. He whined softly, and his ears perked up slightly.

"Somebody out there?" Travis asked, getting off the bed, pulling on his jeans.

The dog dropped onto all fours and hurried out of the bedroom.

Travis found him at another window in the darkened living room, studying the night on that side of the house. Crouching beside the dog, putting a hand on the broad furry back, he said, "What's the matter? Huh?"

Einstein pressed his snout to the glass and mewled nervously.

Travis could see nothing threatening on the front lawn or on the street. Then a thought struck him, and he said, "Are you worried about whatever was chasing you in the woods this morning?"

The dog regarded him solemnly.

"What *was* it out there in the forest?" Travis wondered.

Einstein whined again and shuddered.

Remembering the retriever's—and his own—stark fear in the Santa Ana foothills, recalling the uncanny feeling that something unnatural had been stalking them, Travis shivered. He looked out at the night-draped world. The spiky black patterns of the date palm's fronds were edged in wan yellow light from the nearest streetlamp. A fitful wind harried small funnels of dust and leaves and bits of litter along the pavement, dropped them for a few seconds and left them for dead, then enlivened them again. A lone moth bumped softly against the window in front of Travis's and Einstein's faces, evidently mistaking the reflection of the moon or streetlamp for a flame.

"Are you worried that it's still after you?" he asked.

The dog woofed once, quietly.

"Well, I don't think it is," Travis said. "I don't think you understand how far north we've come. We had wheels, but it would have had to follow on foot, which it couldn't have done. Whatever it was, it's far behind us, Einstein, far down there in Orange County, with no way of knowing where we've gone. You don't have to worry about it any more. You understand?"

Einstein nuzzled and licked Travis's hand as if reassured and grateful. But he looked out the window again and issued a barely audible whimper.

Travis had to coax him back into the bedroom. There, the dog wanted to lie on the bed beside his master, and in the interest of calming the animal, Travis did not object.

Wind murmured and moaned in the bungalow's eaves.

Now and then the house creaked with ordinary middle-of-the-night settling noises.

Engine purring, tires whispering, a car went by on the street.

Exhausted from the emotional as well as the physical exertions of the day, Travis was soon asleep.

Near dawn he came half awake and realized that Einstein was at the bedroom window again, keeping watch. He murmured the retriever's name and wearily patted the mattress. But Einstein remained on guard, and Travis drifted off once more.

CHAPTER 4

1

THE DAY FOLLOWING her encounter with Art Streck, Nora Devon went for a long walk, intending to explore parts of the city that she had never seen before. She had taken short walks with Violet once a week. Since the old woman's death, Nora still went out, though less often, and she never ventured farther than six or eight blocks from home. Today, she would go much farther. This was to be the first small step in a long journey toward liberation and self-respect.

Before setting out, she considered having a light lunch later at a restaurant chosen at random along the way. But she had never been in a restaurant. The prospect of dealing with a waiter and dining in the company of strangers was daunting. Instead, she packed one apple, one orange, and two oatmeal cookies in a small paper bag. She would eat lunch alone, in a park somewhere. Even that would be revolutionary. One small step at a time.

The sky was clear. The air was warm. With vivid green spring growth, the trees looked fresh; they stirred in a breeze just strong enough to take the searing edge off the hot sunlight.

As Nora strolled past the well-kept houses, the vast majority of which were in one style of Spanish architecture or another, she looked at doors and windows with a new curiosity, wondering about the people who lived within. Were they happy? Sad? In love? What music and books did they enjoy? What food? Were they planning vacations to exotic places, evenings at the theater, visits to nightclubs?

She had never wondered about them before because she had known their lives and hers would never cross. Wondering about them would have been a waste of time and effort. But *now* . . .

When she encountered other walkers, she kept her head down and averted her face, as she had always done before, but after a while she found the courage to look at some of them. She was surprised when many smiled at her and said hello. In time, she was even more surprised when she heard herself respond.

At the county courthouse she paused to admire the yellow blossoms of the yucca plants and the rich red bougainvillaea that climbed the stucco wall and twined through the ornate wrought-iron grille over one of the tall windows.

At the Santa Barbara Mission, built in 1815, she stood at the foot of the front steps and studied the handsome façade of the old church. She explored the courtyard with its Sacred Garden and climbed the west bell tower.

Gradually, she began to understand why, in some of the many books she had read, Santa Barbara had been called one of the most beautiful places on earth. She had lived there nearly all her life, but because she had cowered in the Devon house with Violet and, on venturing out, had looked at little more than her own shoes, she was seeing the town for the first time. It both charmed and thrilled her.

At one o'clock, in Alameda Park within sight of the pond, she sat on a bench near three ancient and massive date palms. Her feet were getting sore, but she did not intend to go home early. She opened the paper bag and began lunch with the yellow apple. Never had anything tasted half as delicious. Famished, she quickly ate the orange, too, dropping the pieces of peel into the bag, and she was starting on the first of the oatmeal cookies when Art Streck sat down beside her.

"Hello, prettiness."

He was wearing only blue running shorts, running shoes, and thick white athletic socks. However, he clearly hadn't been running, for he wasn't sweating. He was muscular with a broad chest, deeply tanned, exceedingly masculine. The whole purpose of his attire was to display his physique, so Nora at once averted her eyes.

"Shy?" he asked.

She could not speak because the bite she had taken from the oatmeal cookie was stuck in her mouth. She couldn't work up any saliva. She was afraid she would choke if she tried to swallow the piece of cookie, but she couldn't very well just spit it out.

"My sweet, shy Nora," Streck said.

Looking down, she saw how badly her right hand was trembling. The cookie was being shaken to pieces in her fingers; bits of it dropped onto the paving between her feet.

She had told herself that she would go for a day long walk as a first step toward liberation, but now she had to admit there had been another reason for getting out of the house. She had been trying to avoid Streck's attentions. She was afraid to say home, afraid that he'd call and call and call. But now he had found her in the open, beyond the protection of her locked windows and bolted doors, which was worse than the telephone, infinitely worse.

"Look at me, Nora."

No.

"Look at me."

The last of the disintegrating cookie fell from her right hand.

Streck took her left hand, and she tried to resist him, but he squeezed, grinding the bones of her fingers, so she surrendered. He put her hand palm-down on his bare thigh. His flesh was firm and hot.

Her stomach twisted, and her heart thumped, and she did not know which she would do first—puke or pass out.

Moving her hand slowly up and down his bare thigh, he said, "I'm what you need, prettiness. I can take care of you."

As if it were a wad of paste, the oatmeal cookie glued her mouth shut. She kept her head down, but she raised her eyes to look out from under her brow. She hoped to see someone nearby to whom she could call for help, but there were only two young mothers with their small children, and even they were too far away to be of assistance.

Lifting her hand from his thigh, putting it on his bare chest, Streck said, "Having a nice stroll today? Did you like the mission? Hmmm? And weren't the yucca blossoms pretty at the courthouse?"

He rambled on in that cool, smug voice, asking her how she had liked other things she'd seen, and she realized he had been *following* her all morning, either in his car or on foot. She hadn't seen him, but there was no doubt he had been there because he knew every move she had made since leaving the house, which frightened and infuriated her more than anything else he had done.

She was breathing hard and fast, yet she felt as if she could not get her breath. Her ears were ringing, yet she could hear every word he said too clearly. Though she thought she might strike him and claw at his eyes, she was also paralyzed, on the verge of striking but unable to strike, simultaneously strong with rage and weak with fear. She wanted to scream, not for help but in frustration.

"Now," he said, "you've had a real nice stroll, a nice lunch in the park, and you're in a relaxed mood. So you know what would be nice now? You know what would make this a terrific day, prettiness? A really special day? What we'll

do is get in my car, go back to your place, up to your yellow room, get in that
four-poster bed—"

He'd been in her bedroom! He must have done it yesterday. When he was
supposed to have been in the living room fixing the TV, he must have sneaked
upstairs, the bastard, prowling through her most private place, invading her
sanctuary, poking through her belongings.

"—that big old bed, and I'm going to strip you down, honey, strip you down
and fuck you—"

Nora would never be able to decide whether her sudden courage arose from
the horrible realization that he'd violated her sanctuary, whether it was that he
had spoken an obscenity in her presence for the first time, or whether both, but
she snapped her head up and glared at him and spat the wad of uneaten cookie
in his face. Flecks of spittle and damp spatters of food stuck on his right cheek,
right eye, and on the side of his nose. Bits of oatmeal clung in his hair and
speckled his forehead. When she saw anger flash into Streck's eyes and contort
his face, Nora felt a surge of terror at what she'd done. But she was also elated
that she had been able to break the bonds of emotional paralysis that had
immobilized her, even if her actions brought her grief, even if Streck retaliated.

And he did retaliate swiftly, brutally. He still held her left hand, and she
was unable to wrench free. He squeezed hard, as he had done before, grinding
her bones. It hurt, Jesus, it hurt. But she did not want to give him the
satisfaction of seeing her cry, and she was determined not to whimper or beg,
so she clenched her teeth and endured. Sweat prickled her scalp, and she
thought she might pass out. But the pain was not the worst of it; the worst was
looking into Streck's disturbing ice-blue eyes. As he crushed her fingers, he
held her not merely with his hand but with his gaze, which was cold and
infinitely strange. He was trying to intimidate and cow her, and it was working—by God, it was—because she saw in him a madness with which she would
never be able to cope.

When he saw her despair, which evidently pleased him more than a cry of
pain could have done, he stopped grinding her hand, but he did not let go. He
said, "You'll pay for that, for spitting in my face. And you'll *enjoy* paying for it."

Without conviction, she said, "I'll complain to your boss, and you'll lose your
job."

Streck only smiled. Nora wondered why he did not bother to wipe the bits
of oatmeal cookie from his face, but even as she wondered about it she knew the
reason: he was going to make her do it for him. First, he said, "Lose my job?
Oh, I already quit working for Wadlow TV. Walked out yesterday afternoon.
So I'd have time for you, Nora."

She lowered her eyes. She could not conceal her fear, was shaken by it until
she thought her teeth would chatter.

"I never do stay too long in a job. Man like me, full of so much energy, gets
bored easy. I need to move around. Besides, life's too short to waste all of it
working, don't you think? So I keep a job for a while, till I've got some money
saved, then I coast as long as I can. And once in a while I run into a lady like
you, someone who has a powerful need for me, someone who's just crying for
a man like me, and so I help her along."

Kick him, bite him, go for his eyes, she told herself.

She did nothing.

Her hand ached dully. She remembered how hot and intense the pain had
been.

His voice changed, became softer, soothing, reassuring, but that frightened
her even more. "And I'm going to help you, Nora. I'll be moving in for a while.
It's going to be fun. You're a little nervous about me, sure, I understand that,

I really do. But believe me, this is what you need, girl, this is going to turn your life upside down, nothing's ever going to be the same again, and that's the best thing that could happen to you."

2

Einstein loved the park.

When Travis slipped off the leash, the retriever trotted to the nearest bed of flowers—big yellow marigolds surrounded by a border of purple polyanthuses—and walked slowly around it, obviously fascinated. He went to a blazing bed of late blooming ranunculuses, to another of impatiens, and his tail wagged faster with each discovery. They said dogs could see in only black and white, but Travis would not have bet against the proposition that Einstein possessed full-color vision. Einstein sniffed everything—flowers, shrubbery, trees, rocks, trash cans, crumpled litter, the base of the drinking fountain, and every foot of ground he covered—no doubt turning up olfactory "pictures" of people and dogs that had passed this way before, images as clear to him as photographs would have been to Travis.

Throughout the morning and early afternoon, the retriever had done nothing amazing. In fact, his I'm-just-an-ordinary-dumb-dog behavior was so convincing that Travis wondered if the animal's nearly human intelligence came only in brief flashes, sort of the beneficial equivalent of epileptic seizures. But after all that had happened yesterday, Einstein's extraordinary nature, though seldom revealed, was no longer open to debate.

As they were strolling around the pond, Einstein suddenly went rigid, lifted his head, raised his floppy ears a bit, and stared at a couple sitting on a park bench about sixty feet away. The man was in running shorts, and the woman wore a rather baggy gray dress; he was holding her hand, and they appeared to be deep in conversation.

Travis started to turn away from them, heading out toward the open green of the park to give them privacy.

But Einstein barked once and raced straight toward the couple.

"Einstein! Here! Come back here!"

The dog ignored him and, nearing the pair on the bench, began to bark furiously.

By the time Travis reached the bench, the guy in running shorts was standing. His arms were raised defensively, and his hands were fisted as he warily moved back a step from the retriever.

"Einstein!"

The retriever stopped barking, turned away from Travis before the leash could be clipped to the collar again, went to the woman on the bench, and put his head in her lap. The change from snarling dog to affectionate pet was so sudden that everyone was startled.

Travis said, "I'm sorry, He never—"

"For Christ's sake," said the guy in running shorts, "you can't let a vicious dog run loose in the park!"

"He's not vicious," Travis said, "He—"

"Bullshit," the runner said, spraying spittle. "The damn thing tried to bite me. You *enjoy* lawsuits or something?"

"I don't know what got into—"

"Get it out of here," the runner demanded.

Nodding, embarrassed, Travis turned to Einstein and saw that the woman had coaxed the retriever onto the bench. Einstein was sitting with her, facing her, his forepaws in her lap, and she was not merely petting him but hugging him. In fact, there was something a little desperate about the way she was holding on to him."

"Get it *out* of here!" the runner said furiously.

The guy was taller, broader in the shoulders, and thicker in the chest than Travis, and he took a couple of steps forward, looming over Travis, using his superior size to intimidate. By being aggressive, by looking and acting a little dangerous, he was accustomed to getting his way. Travis despised such men.

Einstein turned his head to look at the runner, bared his teeth, and growled low in his throat.

"Listen, buddy," the runner said angrily, "are you deaf, or what? I said that dog's got to be put on a leash, and I see the leash there in your hand, so what the hell are you waiting for?"

Travis began to realize something was wrong. The runner's self-righteous anger was overdone—as if he had been caught in a shameful act and was trying to conceal his guilt by going immediately and aggressively on the offensive. And the woman was behaving peculiarly. She had not spoken a word. She was pale. Her thin hands trembled. But judging by the way she petted and clung to the dog, it wasn't Einstein that frightened her. And Travis wondered why a couple would go to the park dressed so differently from each other, one in running shorts and the other in a drab housedress. He saw the woman glance surreptitiously and fearfully at the runner, and suddenly he knew that these two were not together—at least not by the woman's choice—and that the man had, indeed, been up to something about which he felt guilt.

"Miss," Travis said, "are you all right?"

"Of course she's not all right," the runner said. "Your damn dog came barking and snapping at us—"

"He doesn't seem to be terrorizing her right now," Travis said, meeting and holding the other man's gaze.

Bits of what appeared to be oatmeal batter were stuck on the guy's cheek. Travis had noticed an oatmeal cookie spilling from a bag on the bench beside the woman, and another one crumbled on the ground between her feet. What the hell had been going on here?

The runner glared at Travis and started to speak. But then he looked at the woman and Einstein, and he evidently realized that his calculated outrage would no longer be appropriate. He said sullenly, "Well . . . you should still get the damn hound under control."

"Oh, I don't think he'll bother anyone now," Travis said, coiling the leash. "It was just an aberration."

Still furious but uncertain, the runner looked at the huddled woman and said, "Nora?"

She did not respond. She just kept petting Einstein.

"I'll see you later," the runner told her. Getting no response, he refocused on Travis, narrowed his eyes, and said, "If that hound comes nipping at my heels—"

"He won't," Travis interrupted. "You can get on with your run. He won't bother you."

Several times as he jogged slowly across the park to the nearest exit, the man glanced back at them. Then he was gone.

On the bench, Einstein had settled down on his belly with his head on the woman's lap.

Travis said, "He's sure taken a liking to you."

Without looking up, smoothing Einstein's coat with one hand, she said, "He's a lovely dog."

"I just got him yesterday."

She said nothing.

He sat down on the other end of the bench, with Einstein between them. "My name's Travis."

Unresponsive, she scratched behind Einstein's ears. The dog made a contented sound.

"Travis Cornell," he said.

At last she raised her head and looked at him. "Nora Devon."

"Glad to meet you."

She smiled, but nervously.

Though she wore her hair straight and lank, though she had no makeup, she was quite attractive. Her hair was dark and glossy, her skin flawless, and her gray eyes were accented with green striations that seemed luminous in the bright May sunshine.

As if sensing his approval and frightened of it, she immediately broke eye contact, lowered her head once more.

He said, "Miss Devon . . . is something wrong?"

She said nothing.

"Was that man . . . bothering you?"

"It's all right," she said.

With her head bowed and shoulders hunched, sitting there under a tonweight of shyness, she looked so vulnerable that Travis could not just get up, walk away, and leave her with her problems. He said, "If that man was bothering you, I think we ought to find a cop—"

"No," she said softly but urgently. She slipped out from under Einstein and got up.

The dog scrambled off the bench to stand beside her, gazing at her with affection.

Rising, Travis said, "I don't mean to pry, of course—"

She hurried away, heading out of the park on a different path from the one the runner had taken.

Einstein started after her but halted and reluctantly returned when Travis called to him.

Puzzled, Travis watched her until she disappeared, an enigmatic and troubled woman in a gray dress as drab and shapeless as the garb of an Amish lady or a member of some other sect that took great pains to cloak the female figure in garments that would not lead a man into temptation.

He and Einstein continued their walk through the park. Later, they went to the beach, where the retriever seemed astounded by the endless vistas of rolling sea and by the breakers foaming on the sand. He repeatedly stopped to stare out at the ocean for a minute or two at a time, and he frolicked happily in the surf. Later still, back at the house, Travis tried to interest Einstein in the books that had caused such excitement last evening, hoping this time to be able to figure out what the dog expected to find in them. Einstein sniffed without interest at the volumes Travis brought to him—and yawned.

Throughout the afternoon, the memory of Nora Devon returned to Travis with surprising frequency and vividness. She did not require alluring clothes to capture a man's interest. That face and those green-flecked gray eyes were enough.

3

After only a few hours of deep sleep, Vincent Nasco took an early-morning flight to Acapulco, Mexico. He checked into a huge bayfront hotel, a gleaming but soulless highrise where everything was glass, concrete, and terrazzo. After he had changed into ventilated white Top-Siders, white cotton pants, and a pale-blue Ban-Lon shirt, he went looking for Dr. Lawton Haines.

Haines was vacationing in Acapulco. He was thirty-nine years old, five eleven, one hundred and sixty pounds, with unruly dark brown hair, and he was purported to look like Al Pacino, except that he had a red birthmark the size of a half-dollar on his forehead. He came to Acapulco at least twice a year, always stayed at the elegant Hotel Las Brisas on the headland at the eastern end of the bay, and frequently enjoyed long lunches at a restaurant adjacent to the Hotel Caleta, which he favored for its margaritas and its view of Playa de Caleta.

By twelve-twenty in the afternoon, Vince was seated in a rattan chair with comfortable yellow and green cushions at a table by the windows in that same restaurant. He'd spotted Haines on entering. The doctor was at another window table, three away from Vince, half-screened by a potted palm. Haines was eating shrimp and drinking margaritas with a stunning blonde. She was wearing white slacks and a gaily striped tube-top, and half the men in the place were staring at her.

As far as Vince was concerned, Haines looked more like Dustin Hoffman than like Pacino. He had those bold features of Hoffman's including the nose. Otherwise, he was exactly as he'd been described. The guy was wearing pink cotton trousers and a pale-yellow shirt and white sandals, which seemed, to Vince, to be taking tropical resort attire to an extreme.

Vince finished a lunch of albondiga soup, seafood enchiladas in salsa verde, and a nonalcoholic margarita, and paid the check by the time Haines and the blonde were ready to leave.

The blonde drove a red Porsche. Vince followed in a rental Ford, which had too many miles on it, rattled with the exuberance of percussion instruments in a mariachi band, and had fragrant moldy carpet.

At Las Brisas, the blonde dropped Haines in the parking lot, though not until they stood beside her car for at least five minutes, holding each other's asses and soul-kissing in broad daylight.

Vince was dismayed. He expected Haines to have a stronger sense of propriety. After all, the man had a *doctorate*. If educated people did not uphold traditional standards of conduct, who would? Weren't they teaching manners and deportment in the universities these days? No wonder the world got ruder and cruder every year.

The blonde departed in her Porsche, and Haines left the lot in a white Mercedes 560 SL sports coupe. It sure wasn't a rental, and Vince wondered where the doctor had gotten it.

Haines checked his car with the valet at another hotel, as did Vince. He tailed the doctor through the lobby, out to the beach, where at first they seemed embarked on an uneventful stroll along the shore. But Haines settled down beside a gorgeous Mexican girl in a string bikini. She was dark, superbly proportioned, and fifteen years younger than the doctor. She was sunbathing on a lounge, her eyes closed. Haines kissed her throat, startled her. Evidently, she knew him, for she threw her arms around him, laughing.

Vince walked down the beach and back, then sat on the sand behind Haines and the girl, with a pair of sunbathers interposed between them. He was not concerned that Haines would notice him. The doctor seemed to have eyes only for choice female anatomy. Besides, in spite of his size, Vince Nasco had a knack for fading into the background.

Out on the bay, a tourist was taking a parachute ride, hanging high in the air behind the towboat. Sun fell like an endless rain of gold doubloons on the sand and the sea.

After twenty minutes, Haines kissed the girl on the lips, and on the slopes of her breasts, then set off back the way he had come. The girl called out, "Tonight at six!" And Haines said, "I'll be there."

Then Haines and Vince went for a pleasure drive. At first Vince thought Haines had a destination in mind, but after a while it seemed they were just heading aimlessly down the coast road, taking in the scenery. They passed Revolcadero Beach and kept going, Haines in his white Mercedes, Vince following as far back as he dared in his Ford.

Eventually they came to a scenic overlook, where Haines pulled off the road and parked beside a car from which four garishly dressed tourists were emerging. Vince parked, too, and walked to the iron railing at the outer edge of the escarpment, where there was a truly magnificent view of the coastline and of waves breaking thunderously on the rocky shore more than a hundred feet below.

The tourists, in their parrot shirts and striped pants, finished exclaiming over the sights, took their last pictures, discarded their last bits of litter, and departed, leaving Vince and Haines alone on the cliff. The only traffic on the highway was an approaching black Trans Am. Vince was waiting for the car to pass. Then he was going to take Haines by surprise.

Instead of going by, the Trans Am pulled off the road and parked beside Haine's Mercedes, and a gorgeous girl, about twenty-five, got out. She hurried to Haines. She looked Mexican but with a measure of Chinese blood, very exotic. She was wearing a white halter top and white shorts, and she had the best legs Vince had ever seen. She and Haines moved farther along the railing, until they were about forty feet from Vince, where they went into a clinch that made Vince blush.

For the next few minutes, Vince edged along the railing toward them, leaning out dangerously now and then, craning his neck to gawk down at the crashing waves that threw water twenty feet into the air—saying "Whoo boy!" when a particularly big breaker hit the craggy outcroppings of stone—trying to make it look as if his movement in their direction was entirely innocent.

Though they had turned their backs to him, the breeze carried bits of their conversation. The woman seemed worried that her husband might find out that Haines was in town, and Haines was pushing her to make up her mind about tomorrow night. The guy was shameless.

The highway cleared of traffic again, and Vince decided he might not get another opportunity to nail Haines. He closed the last few feet between him and the girl, grabbed her by the nape of the neck and the belt of her shorts, plucked her off the ground, and threw her over the railing. Screaming, she plummeted toward the rocks below.

It happened so fast that Haines didn't even have time to react. The instant the woman was airborne, Vince turned on the startled doctor and punched him in the face, twice, splitting both his lips, breaking his nose, and knocking him unconscious.

As Haines crumpled to the ground, the woman hit the rocks below, and Vince received her gift even at that distance:

Ssssnap.

He would have liked to lean over the railing to take a long look at her shattered body on the rocks down there, but unfortunately he had no time to spare. The highway would not long be free of traffic.

He carried Haines back to the Ford and put him in the front seat, letting him slump against the door as if sleeping peacefully. He made sure the man's head tipped back to let the blood from his nose trickle down his throat.

From the coast highway, which was twisty and frequently in poor repair for such a major route, Vince followed a series of lesser unpaved roads, each narrower and more rugged than the one before, traveling from gravel to dirt surfaces, heading deeper into the rain forest, until he came to a lonely dead end at a green wall of immense trees and lush vegetation. Twice during the drive, Haines had begun to regain consciousness, but Vince had quieted the doctor by thumping his head against the dashboard.

Now, he dragged the unconscious man out of the Ford, through a gap in the brush, and deep under the trees, until he found a shady clearing floored with hairy moss. Cawing and trilling birds fell silent, and unknown animals with peculiar voices moved off through the underbrush. Large insects, including a beetle as big as Vince's hand, scuttled out of his way, and lizards scampered up tree trunks.

Vince returned to the Ford, where he had left some interrogation equipment in the trunk. A packet of syringes and two vials of sodium pentothal. A leather sap weighted with lead pellets. A hand-applied Taser that resembled a remote-control device for a television set. And a corkscrew with a wooden handle.

Lawton Haines was still unconscious when Vince returned to the clearing. His breath rattled in his broken nose.

Haines should have been dead twenty-four hours ago. The people who had employed Vince for three jobs yesterday had expected to use another freelancer who lived in Acapulco and operated throughout Mexico. But that guy had died yesterday morning when a long-awaited air-mail package from Fortnum & Mason in London surprisingly contained two pounds of plastic explosives instead of assorted jellies and marmalades. Out of desperate necessity, the outfit in Los Angeles had given the job to Vince, though he was getting to be dangerously overworked. It was a big break for him, for he was sure *this* doctor must also be connected with Banodyne Laboratories and could provide more details about the Francis Project.

Now, exploring the rain forest around the clearing where Haines lay, Vince found a fallen tree from which he was able to pull off a loose, curved section of thick bark that would serve as a ladle. He located an algae-mottled stream and scooped up nearly a quart of water in the bark vessel. The stuff looked foul. No telling what exotic bacteria thrived in it. But, of course, at this point the possibility of disease would not matter to Haines.

Vince threw the first ladle of water in Haines's face. A minute later he returned with a second scoopful from which he forced the doctor to drink. After a lot of sputtering, choking, gagging, and a little vomiting, Haines was at last clearheaded enough to understand what was being said to him, and to respond intelligibly.

Holding up the leather sap, the Taser, and the corkscrew, Vince explained how he'd use each of them if Haines was uncooperative. The doctor—who revealed himself to be a specialist in brain physiology and function—proved more intelligent than patriotic, and he eagerly divulged every detail of the top-secret defense work in which he was engaged at Banodyne.

When Haines swore there was no more to be told, Vince prepared the sodium pentothal. As he drew the drug into the syringe, he said, conversationally, "Doctor, what *is* it with you and women?"

Haines, lying on his back in the hairy moss with his arms at his sides, exactly as Vince had told him to lie, was not able to adjust quickly to the change of subject. He blinked in confusion.

"I been following you since lunch, and I know you got three of them on a string in Acapulco—"

"Four," Haines said, and in spite of his terror a visible pride surfaced. "That Mercedes I'm driving belongs to Giselle, the sweetest little—"

"You're using one woman's car to cheat on her with three others?"

Haines nodded and tried to smile, but he winced as the smile sent new waves of pain through his ruined nose. "I've always . . . had this way with the ladies."

"For God's sake!" Vince was appalled. "Don't you realize these aren't the sixties or seventies any more? Free love's dead. It's got a price now. Steep price. Haven't you heard about herpes, AIDS, all that stuff?" Administering the pentothal, he said, "You must be a carrier for every venereal disease known to man."

Blinking stupidly at him, Haines at first looked baffled and then was deep in a pentothal sleep. Under the drug, he confirmed all that he had already told Vince about Banodyne and the Francis Project.

When the drug wore off, Vince used the Taser on Haines, just for the fun of it, until the batteries wore out. The scientist twitched and kicked like a half-crushed water bug, back bowed, digging at the moss with his heels and head and hands.

When the Taser was of no further use, Vince beat him unconscious with the leather sap and killed him by applying the corkscrew to the space between two ribs, angling it up into the beating heart.

Ssssnap.

Throughout, a sepulchral silence hung over the rain forest, but Vince sensed a thousand eyes watching, the eyes of wild things. He believed that the hidden watchers approved of what he had done to Haines because the scientist's lifestyle made him an affront to the natural order of things, the natural order that all the creatures of the jungle obeyed.

He said, "Thank you," to Haines, but he did not kiss the man. Not on the mouth. Not even on the forehead. Haines's life energy was as invigorating and welcome as anyone's, but his body and spirit were unclean.

4

Nora went straight home from the park. The mood of adventure and the spirit of freedom that had colored the morning and the early afternoon could not be recaptured. Streck had sullied the day.

Closing the front door behind her, she engaged the regular lock, the deadbolt lock, and the brass safety chain. She went through the downstairs rooms, drawing the drapes tightly shut at all the windows to prevent Arthur Streck from seeing inside if he should come prowling around. But she could not tolerate the resultant darkness, so she turned on every lamp in every room. In the kitchen, she closed the shutters and checked the lock on the back door.

Her contact with Streck had not only terrified her but had left her feeling dirty. More than anything, she wanted a long, hot shower.

But her legs were suddenly shaky and weak, and she was seized by a spell of dizziness. She had to grab hold of the kitchen table to steady herself. She knew she would fall if she tried to climb the stairs just then, so she sat down, folded her arms on the table, put her head in her arms, and waited until she felt better.

When the worst of the dizziness passed, she remembered the bottle of brandy in the cupboard by the refrigerator, and she decided a drink might help steady her. She had bought the brandy—Remy Martin—after Violet had died because Violet had not approved of any stronger drink than partially fermented apple cider. As an act of rebellion, Nora had poured a glass of brandy for herself when she had come home from her aunt's funeral. She had not enjoyed it and had emptied most of the contents of the glass down the drain. But now it seemed that a shot of brandy would stop her shivering.

First she went to the sink and washed her hands repeatedly under the hottest water she could tolerate, using both soap and then a lot of Ivory dish-washing liquid, scrubbing away every trace of Streck. When she was done, her hands were red and looked raw.

She brought the brandy bottle and a glass to the table. She had read books in which characters had sat down with a fifth of booze and a heavy load of despair, determined to use the former to wash away the latter. Sometimes it worked for them, so maybe it would work for her. If brandy could improve her state of mind even marginally, she was prepared to drink the whole damn bottle.

But she did not have it in her to be a lush. She spent the next two hours sipping at a single glass of Remy Martin.

When she tried to turn her mind away from thoughts of Streck, she was relentlessly tormented by memories of Aunt Violet, and when she tried not to think of Violet, she was right back to Streck again, and when she forced herself to put *both* of them out of her mind, she thought of Travis Cornell, the man in the park, and dwelling on him gave her no comfort either. He had seemed nice—gentle, polite, concerned—and he had gotten rid of Streck. But he was probably just as bad as Streck. If she gave him half a chance, Cornell would probably take advantage of her the same way Streck was trying to do. Aunt Violet had been a tyrant, twisted and sick, but increasingly it seemed that she had been right about the dangers of interacting with other people.

Ah, but the *dog*. That was a different story. She had not been afraid of the dog, not even when he dashed toward the park bench, barking ferociously. Somehow, she knew that the retriever—Einstein, his master had called him—was not barking at her, that his anger was focused on Streck. Clinging to Einstein, she'd felt safe, protected, even with Streck still looming over her.

Maybe she should get a dog of her own. Violet had abhorred the very idea of house pets. But Violet was dead, forever dead, and there was nothing to prevent Nora from having a dog of her own.

Except . . .

Well, she had the peculiar notion that no other dog would give her the profound feeling of security she had gotten from Einstein. She and the retriever had enjoyed instant rapport.

Of course, because the dog rescued her from Streck, she might be attributing qualities to him that he did not possess. Naturally, she would view him as a savior, her valiant guardian. But no matter how vigorously she tried to disabuse herself of the notion that Einstein was only a dog like any other, she still felt he was special, and she was convinced no other dog would give her the degree of protection and companionship that Einstein could provide.

A single glass of Remy Martin, consumed over two hours, plus thoughts of Einstein, did in fact lift her spirits. More important, the brandy and memories of the dog also gave her the courage to go to the kitchen telephone with the determination to call Travis Cornell and offer to buy his retriever. After all, he had told her he'd owned the dog only one day, so he couldn't be deeply attached to it. For the right price, he might sell. She paged through the directory, found Cornell's number, and dialed it.

He answered on the second ring. "Hello?"

On hearing his voice, she realized that any attempt to buy the dog from him would give him a lever with which he could attempt to pry his way into her life. She had forgotten that he might be just as dangerous as Streck.

"Hello?" he repeated.

Nora hesitated.

"Hello? Is anyone there?"

She hung up without saying a word.

Before she spoke with Cornell about the dog, she needed to devise an approach that would somehow discourage him from thinking he could make a move on her if, in fact, he was like Streck.

5

When the telephone rang at a few minutes before five o'clock, Travis was emptying a can of Alpo into Einstein's bowl. The retriever was watching with interest, licking his chops but waiting until the last scraps had been scraped from the can, exhibiting restraint.

Travis went for the phone, and Einstein went for the food. When no one answered Travis's first greeting, he said hello again, and the dog glanced away from his bowl. When Travis still got no answer, he asked if anyone was on the line, which seemed to intrigue Einstein because the dog padded across the kitchen to look up at the receiver in Travis's hand.

Travis hung up and turned away, but Einstein stood there, gazing at the wall phone.

"Probably a wrong number."

Einstein glanced at him, then at the phone again.

"Or kids thinking they're being clever."

Einstein whined unhappily.

"What's eating you?"

Einstein just stood there, riveted by the phone.

With a sigh, Travis said, "Well, I've had all the bewilderment I can handle for one day. If you're going to wax mysterious, you'll have to do it without me."

He wanted to watch the early news before preparing dinner for himself, so he got a Diet Pepsi from the fridge and went into the living room, leaving the dog in peculiar communion with the telephone. He switched on the TV, sat in the big armchair, popped the tab on his Pepsi—and heard Einstein getting into some kind of trouble in the kitchen.

"What're you doing out there?"

A clank. A clatter. The sound of claws scrabbling against a hard surface. A thump, and another.

"Whatever damage you do," Travis warned, "you're going to have to pay for. And how're you going to earn the bucks? Might have to go up to Alaska and work as a sled dog."

The kitchen got quiet. But only for a moment. Then there were a couple of clunks, a rattle, a rustle, more scrabbling of claws.

Travis was intrigued in spite of himself. He used the remote-control unit to mute the TV.

Something hit the kitchen floor with a bang.

Travis was about to go see what had happened, but before he rose from the chair, Einstein appeared. The industrious dog was carrying the telephone directory in his jaws. He must have leaped repeatedly at the kitchen counter where the book lay, pawing it, until he pulled it onto the floor. He crossed the living room and deposited the book in front of the armchair.

"What do you want?" Travis asked.

The dog nudged the directory with his nose, then gazed at Travis expectantly.

"You want me to call someone?"

"Woof."

"Who?"

Einstein nosed the phone book again.

Travis said, "Now who would you want me to call? Lassie, Rin Tin Tin, Old Yeller?"

The retriever stared at him with those dark, undoglike eyes, which were more expressive than ever but insufficient to communicate what the animal wanted.

"Listen, maybe you can read my mind," Travis said, "but I can't read yours."

Whining in frustration, the retriever padded out of the room, disappearing around the corner into the short hallway that served the bath and two bedrooms.

Travis considered following, but he decided to wait and see what happened next.

In less than a minute, Einstein returned, carrying a gold-framed eight-by-ten photograph in his mouth. He dropped it beside the phone directory. It was the picture of Paula that Travis kept on the bedroom dresser. It had been taken on their wedding day, ten months before she died. She looked beautiful—and deceptively healthy.

"No good, boy. I can't call the dead."

Einstein huffed as if to say Travis was thickheaded. He went to a magazine rack in the corner, knocked it over, spilling its contents, and came back with an issue of *Time,* which he dropped beside the gold-framed photograph. With his forepaws, he scraped at the magazine, pulling it open and leafing through its pages, tearing a few in the process.

Moving to the edge of the armchair, leaning forward, Travis watched with interest.

Einstein paused a couple of times to study the open pages of the magazine, then continued to paw through it. Finally, he came to an automobile advertisement that prominently featured a striking brunette model. He looked up at Travis, down at the ad, up at Travis again, and woofed.

"I don't get you."

Pawing the pages again, Einstein found an ad in which a smiling blonde was holding a cigarette. He snorted at Travis.

"Cars and cigarettes? You want me to buy you a car and a pack of Virginia Slims?"

After another trip to the overturned magazine rack, Einstein returned with a copy of a real-estate magazine that still showed up in the mail every month even though Travis had been out of the racket for two years. The dog pawed through that one as well until he found an ad that featured a pretty brunette real-estate saleswoman in a Century 21 jacket.

Travis looked at Paula's photograph, at the blonde smoking the cigarette, at the perky Century 21 agent, and he remembered the other ad with the brunette and the automobile, and he said, "A woman? You want me to call . . . some woman?"

Einstein barked.

"Who?"

With his jaws, Einstein gently took hold of Travis's wrist and tried to pull him out of the chair.

"Okay, okay, let go. I'll follow you."

But Einstein was taking no chances. He would not let go of Travis's wrist, forcing his master to walk in a half-stoop all the way across the living room and dining room, into the kitchen, to the wall phone. There, he finally released Travis.

"Who?" Travis asked again, but suddenly he understood. There was only one woman whose acquaintance both he and the dog had made. "Not the lady we met in the park today?"

Einstein began to wag his tail.

"And you think that's who just called us?"

The tail wagged faster.

"How could you know who was on the line? She didn't say a word. And what are you up to here, anyway? Matchmaking?"

The dog woofed twice.

"Well, she was certainly pretty, but she wasn't my type, fella. A little strange, didn't you think?"

Einstein barked at him, ran to the kitchen door and jumped at it twice, turned to Travis and barked again, ran around the table, barking all the way, dashed to the door and jumped at it once more, and gradually it became apparent that he was deeply disturbed about something.

About the woman.

She had been in some kind of trouble this afternoon in the park. Travis remembered the bastard in the running shorts. He had offered to help the woman, and she had refused. But had she reconsidered and phoned him a few minutes ago, only to discover that she did not have the courage to explain her plight?

"You really think that's who called?"

The tail started wagging again.

"Well . . . even if it was her, it's not wise to get involved."

The retriever rushed at him, seized the right leg of his jeans, and shook the denim furiously, nearly tugging Travis off balance.

"All right, already! I'll do it. Get me the damn directory."

Einstein let go of him and raced out of the room, slipping on the slick linoleum. He returned with the directory in his jaws.

Only as Travis took the phone book did he realize that he had expected the dog to understand his request. The animal's extraordinary intelligence and abilities were now things that Travis took for granted.

With a jolt, he also realized that the dog would not have brought the directory to him in the living room if it had not understood the purpose of such a book.

"By God, fur face, you *have* been well named, haven't you?"

6

Although Nora usually ate dinner no earlier than seven, she was hungry. The morning walk and the glass of brandy had given her an appetite that even thoughts of Streck could not spoil. She didn't feel like cooking, so she prepared a platter of fresh fruit and some cheese, plus a croissant heated in the oven.

Nora usually ate dinner in her room, in bed with a magazine or book, because she was happiest there. Now, as she prepared a platter to take upstairs, the telephone rang.

Streck.

It must be him. Who else? She received few calls.

She froze, listening to the phone. Even after it stopped, she leaned against the kitchen counter, feeling weak, waiting for the ringing to start again.

7

When Nora Devon did not answer her telephone, Travis was ready to go back to the evening news on TV, but Einstein was still agitated. The retriever leaped up against the counter, pawed at the directory, pulled it to the floor again, took it in his jaws, and hurried out of the kitchen.

Curious about the dog's next move, Travis followed and found him waiting at the front door with the phone book still in his mouth.

"What now?"

Einstein put one paw on the door.

"You want to go out?"

The dog whined, but the sound was muffled by the directory in his mouth.

"What're you going to do with the phone book out there? Bury it like a bone? What's up?"

Although he received answers to none of his questions, Travis opened the door and let the retriever out into the golden, late-afternoon sunshine. Einstein dashed straight to the pickup parked in the driveway. He stood at the passenger door, looking back with what might have been impatience.

Travis walked to the truck and looked down at the retriever. He sighed, "I suspect you want to go somewhere, and I suspect you don't have in mind the offices of the telephone company."

Dropping the directory, Einstein jumped up, put his forepaws against the door of the truck and stood there, looking over his shoulder at Travis. He barked.

"You want me to look up Miss Devon's address in the phone book and go there. Is that it?"

One woof.

"Sorry," Travis said. "I know you liked her, but I'm not in the market for a woman. Besides, she's not my type. I already told you that. And I'm not her type, either. Fact is, I have a hunch *nobody's* her type."

The dog barked.

"No."

The dog dropped to the ground, rushed at Travis, and took hold of one leg of his jeans again.

"No," he said, reaching down and grabbing Einstein by the collar. "There's no point chewing up my wardrobe, because I'm not going."

Einstein let go, twisted out of his grasp, and sprinted to the long bed of brightly blooming impatiens, where he started to dig furiously, tossing mangled flowers onto the lawn behind him.

"What're you doing now, for God's sake?"

The dog kept digging industriously, working his way through the bed, back and forth, apparently bent on totally destroying it.

"Hey, stop that!" Travis hurried toward the retriever.

Einstein fled to the other end of the front yard and commenced digging a hole in the grass.

Travis went after him.

Einstein escaped once more to another corner of the lawn, where he began ripping out more grass, then to the birdbath, which he tried to undermine, then back to what was left of the impatiens.

Unable to catch the retriever, Travis finally halted, gasped for breath, and shouted, "Enough!"

Einstein stopped digging in the flowers and raised his head, snaky trailers of coral-red impatiens dangling from his mouth.

"We'll go," Travis said.

Einstein dropped the flowers and came out of the ruins, onto the lawn— warily.

"No tricks," Travis promised. "If it means that much to you, then we'll go see the woman. But God knows what I'm going to say to her."

8

With her dinner platter in one hand and a bottle of Evian in the other, Nora went along the downstairs hallway, comforted by the sight of lights blazing in every room. On the upstairs landing, she used her elbow to flick the switch for the second-floor hall lights. She would need to include a lot of light bulbs in her next grocery order because she intended to leave all the lights burning day and night for the foreseeable future. It was an expense she did not in the least begrudge.

Still buoyed by the brandy, she began to sing softly to herself as she headed for her room: "Moon River, wider than a mile . . ."

She stepped through the door. Streck was lying on the bed.

He grinned and said, "Hi, babe."

For an instant she thought he was a hallucination, but when he spoke she knew he was real, and she cried out, and the platter fell from her hand, scattering fruit and cheese across the floor.

"Oh my, what an awful mess you've made," he said, sitting up and swinging his legs over the edge of the bed. He was still wearing his running shorts, athletic socks, and running shoes; nothing else. "But there's no need to clean it up now. There's other business to take care of first. I been waiting a long time for you to come upstairs. Waiting and thinking about you . . . getting primed for you . . ." He stood. "And now it's time to teach you what you've never learned."

Nora could not move. Could not breathe.

He must have come to the house directly from the park, arriving before she did. He had forced entry, leaving no trace of a break-in, and he'd been waiting here on the bed all the time she'd been sipping brandy in the kitchen. There was something about his *waiting* up here that was creepier than anything else he had done, waiting and teasing himself with the promise of her, getting a kick out of listening to her putter around downstairs in ignorance of his presence.

When he was finished with her, would he kill her?

She turned and ran into the second-floor hallway.

As she put her hand on the newel post at the head of the stairs and started down, she heard Streck behind her.

She plunged down the steps, taking them two and three at a time, terrified that she was going to twist an ankle and fall, and at the landing her knee nearly buckled, and she stumbled but kept going, *leaped* down the last flight, into the first-floor hall.

Seizing her from behind, catching the baggy shoulders of her dress, Streck spun her around to face him.

9

As Travis swung to the curb in front of the Devon house, Einstein stood on the front seat, placed both forepaws on the door handle, bore down with all of his weight, and opened the door. Another neat trick. He was out of the truck and galloping up the front walkway before Travis had engaged the hand brake and switched off the engine.

Seconds later, Travis reached the foot of the veranda steps in time to see the retriever on the porch as he stood on his hind paws and hit the doorbell with one forepaw. The bell was audible from inside.

Climbing the steps, Travis said, "Now, what the devil's gotten into you?"

The dog rang the bell again.

"Give her a chance—"

As Einstein hit the button a third time, Travis heard a man shout in anger and pain. Then a woman's cry for help.

Barking as ferociously as he had done in the woods yesterday, Einstein clawed at the door as if he actually believed he could tear his way through it.

Pressing forward, Travis peered through a clear segment in the stained-glass window. The hallway was brightly lit, so he was able to see two people struggling only a few feet away.

Einstein was barking, snarling, going crazy.

Travis tried the door, found it locked. He used his elbow to smash in a couple of the stained-glass segments, reached inside, fumbled for the lock, located it and the security chain, and went inside just as the guy in running shorts pushed the woman aside and turned to face him.

Einstein didn't give Travis a chance to act. The retriever bolted along the hallway, straight toward the runner.

The guy reacted as anyone would upon seeing a charging dog the size of this one: he ran. The woman tried to trip him, and he stumbled but did not fall. At the end of the corridor, he slammed through a swinging door, out of sight.

Einstein raced past Nora Devon and reached the still-swinging door at full tilt, timing his approach perfectly, streaking through the opening as the door rocked inward. He vanished after the runner. In the room beyond the swinging door—the kitchen, Travis figured—there was much barking, snarling, and shouting. Something fell with a crash, then something else made an even louder crash, and the runner cursed, and Einstein made a vicious sound that gave Travis a chill, and the din grew worse.

He went to Nora Devon. She was leaning against the newel post at the bottom of the stairs. He said, "You okay?"

"He almost . . . almost . . ."

"But he didn't," Travis guessed.

"No."

He touched the blood on her chin. "You're hurt."

"His blood," she said, seeing it on Travis's fingertips. "I bit the bastard." She looked toward the swinging door, which had stopped moving now. "Don't let him hurt the dog."

"Not likely," Travis said.

The noise in the kitchen subsided as Travis pushed through the swinging door. Two ladder-back chairs had been knocked over. A large blue-flowered ceramic cookie jar lay in pieces on the tile floor, and oatmeal cookies were scattered across the room, some whole and some broken and some squashed. The runner was sitting in a corner, his bare legs pulled up, hands crossed defensively on his chest. One of the man's shoes was missing, and Travis suspected the dog had gotten hold of it. The runner's right hand was bleeding, which was evidently Nora Devon's work. He was also bleeding from his left calf, but that wound appeared to be a dog bite. Einstein was guarding him, staying back out of range of a kick, but ready to tear at the runner if the guy was foolish enough to attempt to leave the corner.

"Nice job," Travis told the dog. "Very nice indeed."

Einstein made a whining sound that indicated acceptance of the praise. But when the runner started to move, the happy whine turned instantly to a snarl. Einstein snapped at the man, who jerked back into the corner again.

"You're finished," Travis told the runner.

"He bit me! They *both* bit me." Petulant rage. Astonishment. Disbelief. "*Bit me.*"

Like a lot of bullies who'd had their way all their lives, this man was shocked to discover he could be hurt, beaten. Experience had taught him that people would always back down if he pressed them hard enough and if he kept a crazy-mean look in his eyes. He thought he could never lose. Now, his face was pale, and he looked as if he was in a state of shock.

Travis went to the phone and called the police.

CHAPTER 5

1

LATE THURSDAY MORNING, May 20, when Vincent Nasco returned from his one-day vacation in Acapulco, he picked up the *Times* at the Los Angeles International Airport before taking the commuter van—they called it a limousine, but it was a van—back to Orange County. He read the newspaper during the trip to his townhouse in Huntington Beach, and on page three he saw the story about the fire at Banodyne Laboratories in Irvine.

The blaze had broken out shortly after six o'clock yesterday morning, when Vince had been on his way to the airport to catch the plane to Acapulco. One of the two Banodyne buildings had been gutted before the firemen had brought the flames under control.

The people who had hired Vince to kill Davis Weatherby, Lawton Haines, the Yarbecks, and the Hudstons had almost certainly employed an arsonist to torch Banodyne. They seemed to be trying to eradicate all records of the Francis Project, both those stored in Banodyne files and those in the minds of the scientists who had participated in the research.

The newspaper said nothing about Banodyne's defense contracts, which were apparently not public knowledge. The company was referred to as "a leader in the genetic-engineering industry, with a special focus on the development of revolutionary new drugs derived from recombinant-DNA research."

A night watchman had died in the blaze. The *Times* offered no explanation as to why he had been unable to flee the fire. Vince figured the guy had been killed by intruders, then incinerated to cover the murder.

The commuter van ferried Vince to the front door of his townhouse. The rooms were cool and shadowy. On the uncarpeted floors, each footstep was hard and clearly defined, echoing hollowly through the nearly empty house.

He had owned the place for two years, but he had not fully furnished it. In fact, the dining room, den, and two of the three bedrooms contained nothing except cheap drapes for privacy.

Vince believed that the townhouse was a way station, a temporary residence from which he would one day move to a house on the beach at Rincon, where the surf and the surfers were legendary, where the vast rolling sea was the overwhelming fact of life. But his failure to furnish his current residence had nothing to do with its temporary status in his plans. He simply liked bare white walls, clean concrete floors, and empty rooms.

When he eventually purchased his dream house, Vince intended to have polished white ceramic tile installed on the floors and walls in every one of its big rooms. There would be no wood, no stone or brick, no textured surfaces to provide the visual "warmth" that other people seemed to prize. The furniture would be built to his specifications, with several coats of glossy white enamel, upholstered in white vinyl. The only deviations that he would permit from all those shiny white surfaces would be the necessary use of glass and highly polished steel. Then, there, thus encapsulated, he would at last feel at peace and at home for the first time in his life.

Now, after unpacking his suitcase, he went down to the kitchen to prepare lunch. Tuna fish. Three hard-boiled eggs. Half a dozen rye crackers. Two apples and an orange. A bottle of Gatorade.

The kitchen had a small table and one chair in the corner, but he ate upstairs in the sparsely furnished master bedroom. He sat in a chair at the window that faced west. The ocean was only a block away, on the other side of the Coast Highway and beyond a wide public beach, and from the second floor he could see the rolling water.

The sky was partially overcast, so the sea was dappled with sunshine and shadows. In some places it looked like molten chrome, but in other places it might have been a surging mass of dark blood.

The day was warm, though it looked strangely cold, wintry.

Staring at the ocean, he always felt that the ebb and flow of blood through his veins and arteries was in perfect sympathy with the rhythm of the tides.

When he finished eating, he sat for a while in communion with the sea, crooning to himself, looking through his faint reflection on the glass as if peering through the wall of an aquarium, although he felt himself to be within the ocean even now, far beneath the waves in a clean, cool, endless world of silence.

Later in the afternoon, he drove his van to Irvine and located Banodyne Laboratories. Banodyne was set against the backdrop of the Santa Ana Mountains. The company had two buildings on a multi-acre lot that was surprisingly large in an area of such expensive real estate: one L-shaped two-story structure and a larger V-shaped single story with only a few narrow windows that made it look fortresslike. Both were very modern in design, a striking mix of flat planes and sensuous curves faced in dark green and gray marble, quite attractive. Surrounded by an employee parking lot and by immense expanses of well-maintained grass, shaded by a few palms and coral trees, the buildings were actually larger than they appeared to be, for their true scale was distorted and diminished by that enormous piece of flat land.

The fire had been confined to the V-shaped building that housed the labs. The only indications of destruction were a few broken windows and soot stains on the marble above those narrow openings.

The property was not walled or fenced, so Vince could have walked onto it from the street if he had wished, although there was a simple gate and guard booth at the three-lane entrance road. Judging by the guard's sidearm and by the subtly forbidding look of the building that housed the research labs, Vince suspected the lawns were monitored electronically and that, at night, sophisticated alarm systems would alert watchmen to an intruder's presence before he had taken more than a few steps across the grass. The arsonist must have been skilled at more than setting fires; he must also have had a wide knowledge of security systems.

Vince cruised past the place, then turned and drove by from the other direction. Like spectral presences, cloud shadows moved slowly across the lawn and slid up the walls of the buildings. Something about Banodyne gave it a portentous—perhaps even slightly ominous—look. And Vince did not think that he was letting his view of the place be unduly colored by the research that he knew to have been conducted there.

He drove home to Huntington Beach.

Having gone to Banodyne in the hope that seeing the place would help him decide how to proceed, he was disappointed. He still did not know what to do next. He could not figure out to whom he could sell his information for a price worth the risk he was taking. Not to the U.S. government: it was their information to begin with. And not to the Soviets, the natural adversary, for it was the Soviets who had paid him to kill Weatherby, the Yarbecks, the Hudstons, and Haines.

Of course, he couldn't *prove* he had been working for the Soviets. They were clever when they hired a freelancer like him. But he had worked for these people as often as he had taken contracts from the mob, and based on dozens of clues over the years, he had decided they were Soviets. Once in a while he dealt with people other than the usual three contacts in L.A., and invariably they spoke with what sounded like Russian accents. Furthermore, their targets were usually political to at least some degree—or, as in the case of the Banodyne kills, military targets. And their information always proved more thorough, accurate, and sophisticated than the information he was given by the mob when he contracted for a simple gangland hit.

So who would pay for such sensitive defense information if not the U.S. or the Soviets? Some third-world dictator looking for a way to circumvent the nuclear capabilities of the most powerful countries? The Francis Project might give some pocket Hitler that edge, elevate him to a world power, and he might pay well for it. But who wanted to risk dealing with Qaddafi types? Not Vince.

Besides, he possessed information about the *existence* of the revolutionary research at Banodyne, but he did not have detailed files on how the Francis Project's miracles had been accomplished. He had less to sell than he'd first thought.

However, in the back of his mind, an idea had been growing since yesterday. Now, as he continued to puzzle over a potential buyer for his information, that idea flowered.

The dog.

At home again, he sat in his bedroom, staring out at the sea. He sat there even after nightfall, after he could no longer see the water, and he thought about the dog.

Hudston and Haines had told him so much about the retriever that he'd begun to realize his knowledge of the Francis Project, although potentially explosive and valuable, was not one-thousandth as valuable as the dog itself. The retriever could be exploited in many ways; it was a money machine with a tail. For one thing, he could probably sell it back to the government or to the Russians for a bargeload of cash. If he could find the dog, he would be able to achieve financial independence.

But how could he locate it?

All over southern California, a quiet search—almost secret yet gigantic— must be under way. The Defense Department would be putting tremendous manpower into the hunt, and if Vince crossed paths with those searchers, they would want to know who he was. He could not afford to draw attention to himself.

Furthermore, if he conducted his own search of the nearest Santa Ana foothills, into which the lab escapees had almost surely fled, he might encounter the wrong one. He might miss the golden retriever and stumble upon The Outsider, and that could be dangerous. Deadly.

Beyond the bedroom window, the cloud-armored night sky and the sea flowed together in blackness as dark as the far side of the moon.

2

On Thursday, one day after Einstein cornered Arthur Streck in Nora Devon's kitchen, Streck was arraigned on charges of breaking and entering, assault and battery, and attempted rape. Because he had previously been convicted of rape and had served two years of a three-year sentence, his bail was high; he could not meet it. And since he could not locate a bondsman who would trust him, he seemed destined to remain in jail until his case came to trial, which was a great relief to Nora.

On Friday, she went to lunch with Travis Cornell.

She was startled to hear herself accept his invitation. It was true that Travis had seemed genuinely shocked to learn of the terror and harassment she had endured at Streck's hands, and it was also true that to some extent she owed her dignity and perhaps her life to his arrival at the penultimate moment. Yet years of indoctrination in Aunt Violet's paranoia could not be washed away in a few days, and a residue of unreasonable suspicion and wariness clung to Nora. She would have been dismayed, maybe even shattered, if Travis had suddenly tried to force himself upon her, but she would not have been surprised. Having been encouraged since early childhood to expect the worst from people, she could be surprised only by kindness and compassion.

Nevertheless, she went to lunch with him.

At first, she did not know why.

However, she did not have to think long to find the answer: the dog. She wanted to be near the dog because he made her feel secure and because she'd never before been the recipient of such unrestrained affection as Einstein lavished on her. She had never previously been the object of any affection from anyone, and she liked it even if it came from an animal. Besides, in her heart Nora knew that Travis Cornell must be completely trustworthy because Einstein trusted him, and Einstein did not seem easily fooled.

They ate lunch at a café that had a few linen-draped tables outside on a brick patio, under white- and blue-striped umbrellas, where they were permitted to clip the dog's leash to the wrought-iron table leg and keep him with them. Einstein was well-behaved, lying quietly most of the time. Occasionally he raised his head to gaze at them with his soulful eyes until they relinquished scraps of food, though he was not a pest about it.

Nora did not have much experience with dogs, but she thought that Einstein was unusually alert and inquisitive. He frequently shifted his position in order to watch the other diners, with whom he seemed intrigued.

Nora was intrigued with *everything*. This was her first meal in a restaurant, and although she had read about people having lunch and dinner in thousands of restaurants in countless novels, she was still amazed and delighted by every detail. The single rose in the milk-white vase. The matchbooks with the establishment's name embossed on them. The way the butter had been molded into round pats with a flower pattern on each, then served on a bowl of crushed ice. The slice of lemon in the ice water. The chilled salad fork was an especially amazing touch.

"Look at this," she said to Travis after their entrées had been served and the waiter had departed.

He frowned at her plate and said, "Something wrong?"

"No, no. I mean . . . these vegetables."

"Baby carrots, baby squash."

"Where do they get them so tiny? And look how they've scalloped the edge of this tomato. Everything's so pretty. How do they ever find the time to make everything so pretty?"

She knew these things that astonished her were things he took for granted, knew that her amazement revealed her lack of experience and sophistication, making her seem like a child. She frequently blushed, sometimes stammered in embarrassment, but she could not restrain herself from commenting on these marvels. Travis smiled at her almost continuously, but it was not a patronizing smile, thank God; he seemed genuinely delighted by the pleasure she took in new discoveries and small luxuries.

By the time they finished coffee and desert—a kiwi tart for her, strawberries and cream for Travis, and a chocolate éclair that Einstein did not have to share with anyone—Nora had been engaged in the longest conversation of her life. They passed two and a half hours without an awkward silence, mainly discussing books because—given Nora's reclusive life—a love of books was virtually the only thing they had in common. That and loneliness. He seemed genuinely interested in her opinions of novelists, and he had some fascinating insights into books, insights which had eluded her. She laughed more in one afternoon than she had laughed in an entire year. But the experience was so exhilarating that she occasionally felt dizzy, and by the time they left the restaurant she could not precisely remember anything they had actually said; it was all a colorful blur. She was experiencing sensory overload analogous to what a primitive tribesman might feel if suddenly deposited in the middle of New York City, and she needed time to absorb and process all that had happened to her.

Having walked to the café from her house, where Travis had left his pickup truck, they now made the return trip on foot, and Nora held the dog's leash all the way. Einstein never tried to pull away from her, never tangled the leash around her legs, but padded along at her side or in front of her, docile, now and then looking up at her with a sweet expression that made her smile.

"He's a good dog," she said.

"Very good," Travis agreed.

"So well behaved."

"Usually."

"And so cute."

"Don't flatter him too much."

"Are you afraid he'll become vain?"

"He's already vain," Travis said. "If he were any more vain, he'd be impossible to live with."

The dog looked back and up at Travis, and sneezed loudly as if ridiculing his master's comment.

Nora laughed. "Sometimes it almost seems he can understand every word you're saying."

"Sometimes," Travis agreed.

When they arrived at the house, Nora wanted to invite him in. But she wasn't sure if the invitation would seem too bold, and she was afraid Travis would misinterpret it. She knew she was being a nervous old maid, knew she could—and ought to—trust him, but Aunt Violet suddenly loomed in her memory, full of dire warnings about men, and Nora could not bring herself to do what she knew was right. The day had been perfect, and she dreaded extending it further for fear something would happen to sully the entire memory, leaving her with nothing good, so she merely thanked him for lunch and did not even dare to shake his hand.

She did, however, stoop down and hug the dog. Einstein nuzzled her neck and licked her throat once, making her giggle. She had *never* heard herself giggle before. She would have clung to him and petted him for hours if her enthusiasm for the dog had not, by comparison, made her wariness of Travis even more evident.

Standing in the open door, she watched them as they got into the pickup and drove away.

Travis waved at her.

She waved, too.

Then the truck reached the corner and began to turn right, out of sight, and Nora regretted her cowardice, wished she'd asked Travis in for a while. She almost ran after them, almost shouted his name and almost rushed down the steps to the sidewalk in pursuit. But then the truck was gone, and she was alone again. Reluctantly, she went into the house and closed the door on the brighter world outside.

3

The Bell JetRanger executive helicopter flashed over the tree-filled ravines and balding ridges of the Santa Ana foothills, its shadow running ahead of it because the sun was in the west as Friday afternoon waned. Approaching the head of Holy Jim Canyon, Lemuel Johnson looked out the window in the passenger compartment and saw four of the county sheriff's squad cars lined up along the narrow dirt lane down there. A couple of other vehicles, including the coroner's wagon and a Jeep Cherokee that probably belonged to the victim, were parked at the stone cabin. The pilot had barely enough room to put the chopper down in the clearing. Even before the engine died and the sun-bronzed rotors began to slow, Lem was out of the craft, hurrying toward the cabin, with his right-hand man, Cliff Soames, close behind him.

Walt Gaines, the county sheriff, stepped out of the cabin as Lem approached. Gaines was a big man, six-four and at least two hundred pounds, with enormous shoulders and a barrel chest. His corn-yellow hair and cornflower-blue eyes would have lent him a movie-idol look if his face had not been so broad and his features blunt. He was fifty-five, looked forty, and wore his hair only slightly longer than he had during his twenty years in the Marine Corps.

Although Lem Johnson was a black man, every bit as dark as Walt was white, though he was seven inches shorter and sixty pounds lighter than Walt, though he had come from an upper-middle-class black family while Walt's folks had been poor white trash from Kentucky, though Lem was ten years younger than the sheriff, the two were friends. More than friends. Buddies. They played bridge together, went deep-sea fishing together, and found unadulterated pleasure in sitting in lawn chairs on one or the other's patio, drinking Corona beer and solving all of the world's problems. Their wives even became best friends, a serendipitous development that was, according to Walt, "a miracle, 'cause the woman's never liked anyone else I've introduced her to in thirty-two years."

To Lem, his friendship with Walt Gaines was also a miracle, for he was not a man who made friends easily. He was a workaholic and did not have the leisure to nurture an acquaintance carefully into a more enduring relationship. Of course, careful nurturing hadn't been necessary with Walt; they had clicked the first time they'd met, had recognized similar attitudes and points of view in each other. By the time they had known each other six months, it seemed they had been close since boyhood. Lem valued their friendship nearly as much as he valued his marriage to Karen. The pressure of his job would be harder to endure if he couldn't let off some steam with Walt once in a while.

Now, as the chopper's blades fell silent, Walt Gaines said, "Can't figure why the murder of a grizzled old canyon squatter would interest you feds."

"Good," Lem said. "You're not supposed to figure it, and you really don't want to know."

"Anyway, I sure didn't expect you'd come yourself. Thought you'd send some of your flunkies."

"NSA agents don't like to be called flunkies," Lem said.

Looking at Cliff Soames, Walt said, "But that's how he treats you fellas, isn't it? Like flunkies?"

"He's a tyrant," Cliff confirmed. He was thirty-one, with red hair and freckles. He looked more like an earnest young preacher than like an agent of the National Security Agency.

"Well, Cliff," Walt Gaines said, "you've got to understand where Lem comes from. His father was a downtrodden black businessman who never made more than two hundred thousand a year. Deprived, you see. So Lem, he figures he's got to make you white boys jump through hoops whenever he can, to make up for all those years of brutal oppression."

"He makes me call him 'Massah,' " Cliff said.

"I don't doubt it," Walt said.

Lem sighed and said, "You two are about as amusing as a groin injury. Where's the body?"

"This way, Massah," Walt said.

As a gust of warm afternoon wind shook the surrounding trees, as the canyon hush gave way to the whispering of leaves, the sheriff led Lem and Cliff into the first of the cabin's two rooms.

Lem understood, at once, why Walt had been so jokey. The forced humor was a reaction to the horror inside the cabin. It was somewhat like laughing aloud in a graveyard at night to chase away the willies.

Two armchairs were overturned, upholstery slashed. Cushions from the sofa had been ripped to expose the white foam padding. Paperbacks had been pulled off a corner bookcase, torn apart, and scattered all over the room. Glass shards from the big window sparkled gemlike in the ruins. The debris and the walls were spattered with blood, and a lot of dried blood darkened the light-pine floor.

Like a pair of crows searching for brightly colored threads with which to dress up their nest, two lab technicians in black suits were carefully probing through the ruins. Occasionally one of them made a soft wordless cawing sound and plucked at something with tweezers, depositing it in a plastic envelope.

Evidently, the body had been examined and photographed, for it had been transferred into an opaque plastic mortuary bag and was lying near the door, waiting to be carried out to the meat wagon.

Looking down at the half-visible corpse in the sack, which was only a vaguely human shape beneath the milky plastic, Lem said, "What was his name?"

"Wes Dalberg," Walt said. "Lived here ten years or more."

"Who found him?"

"A neighbor."

"When was he killed?"

"Near as we can tell, about three days ago. Maybe Tuesday night. Have to wait for lab tests to pinpoint it. Weather's been pretty warm lately, which makes a difference in the rate of decomposition."

Tuesday night . . . In the predawn hours of Tuesday morning, the breakout had occurred at Banodyne. By Tuesday night, The Outsider could have traveled this far.

Lem thought about that—and shivered.

"Cold?" Walt asked sarcastically.

Lem didn't respond. They were friends, yes, and they were both officers of the law, one local and one federal, but in this case they served opposing interests. Walt's job was to find the truth and bring it to the public, but Lem's job was to put a lid on the case and keep it clamped down tight.

"Sure stinks in here," Cliff Soames said.

"You should've smelled it before we got the stiff in the bag," Walt said. "Ripe."

"Not just . . . decomposition," Cliff said.

"No," Walt said, pointing here and there to stains that were not caused by blood. "Urine and feces, too."

"The victim's?"

"Don't think so," Walt said.

"Done any preliminary tests of it?" Lem asked, trying not to sound worried. "On-site microscopic exam?"

"Nope. We'll take samples back to the lab. We think it belongs to whatever came crashing through that window."

Looking up from the body bag, Lem said, "You mean the man who killed Dalberg."

"Wasn't a man," Walt said, "and I figure you know that."

"Not a man?" Lem said.

"At least not a man like you or me."

"Then what do you think it was?"

"Damned if I know," Walt said, rubbing the back of his bristly head with one big hand. "But judging from the body, the killer had sharp teeth, maybe claws, and a nasty disposition. Does that sound like what you're looking for?"

Lem could not be baited.

For a moment, no one spoke.

A fresh piny breeze came through the shattered window, blowing away some of the noxious stench.

One of the lab men said, "Ah," and plucked something from the rubble with his tweezers.

Lem sighed wearily. This situation was no good. They would not find enough to tell them what killed Dalberg, though they would gather sufficient evidence to make them curious as hell. However, this was a matter of national defense, in which no civilian would be wise to indulge his curiosity. Lem was going to have to put a stop to their investigation. He hoped he could intervene without angering Walt. It would be a real test of their friendship.

Suddenly, staring at the body bag, Lem realized something was wrong with the shape of the corpse. He said, "The head isn't here."

"You feds don't miss a trick, do you?" Walt said.

"He was decapitated?" Cliff Soames asked uneasily.

"This way," Walt said, leading them into the second room.

It was a large—if primitive—kitchen with a hand pump in the sink and an old-fashioned wood-burning stove.

Except for the head, there were no signs of violence in the kitchen. Of course, the head was bad enough. It was in the center of the table. On a plate.

"Jesus," Cliff said softly.

When they had entered the room, a police photographer had been taking shots of the head from various angles. He was not finished, but he stepped back to give them a better view.

The dead man's eyes were missing, torn out. The empty sockets seemed as deep as wells.

Cliff Soames had turned so white that, by contrast, his freckles burned on his skin as if they were flecks of fire.

Lem felt sick, not merely because of what had happened to Wes Dalberg but because of all the deaths yet to come. He was proud of both his management and investigatory skills, and he knew he could handle this case better than anyone else. But he was also a hardheaded pragmatist, incapable of underestimating the enemy or of pretending there would be a quick ending to this nightmare. He would need time and patience and luck to track down the killer, and meanwhile more bodies would pile up.

The head had not been cut off the dead man. It was not as neat as that. It appeared to have been clawed and chewed and wrenched off.

Lem's palms were suddenly damp.

Strange . . . how the empty sockets of the head transfixed him as surely as if they had contained wide, staring eyes.

In the hollow of his back, a single droplet of sweat traced the course of his spine. He was more scared than he had ever been—or had ever thought he could be—but he did not want to be taken off the job for any reason. It was vitally important to the very security of the nation and the safety of the public that this emergency be handled right, and he knew no one was likely to perform as well as he could. That was not just ego talking. Everyone said he was the best, and he knew they were right; he had a justifiable pride and no false modesty. This was his case, and he would stay with it to the end.

His folks had raised him with an almost too-keen sense of duty and responsibility. "A black man," his father used to say, "has to do a job twice as well as a white man in order to get any credit at all. That's nothing to be bitter about. Nothing worth protesting. It's just a fact of life. Might as well protest the weather turning cold in winter. Instead of protesting, the thing to do is just face facts, work twice as hard, and you'll get where you want to go. And you must succeed because you carry the flag for all your brothers." As a result of that upbringing, Lem was incapable of less than total, unhesitating commitment to every assignment. He dreaded failure, rarely encountered it, but could be thrown into a deep funk for weeks when the successful conclusion of a case eluded him.

"Talk to you outside a minute?" Walt asked, moving to the open rear door of the cabin.

Lem nodded. To Cliff, he said, "Stay here. Make sure nobody—pathologists, photographer, uniformed cops, *nobody*—leaves before I've had a chance to talk to them."

"Yes, sir," Cliff said. He headed quickly toward the front of the cabin to inform everyone that they were temporarily quarantined—and to get away from the eyeless head.

Lem followed Walt Gaines into the clearing behind the cabin. He noticed a metal hod and firewood scattered over the ground, and paused to study those objects.

"We think it started out here," Walt said. "Maybe Dalberg was getting wood for the fireplace. Maybe something came out of those trees, so he threw the hod at it and ran into the house."

They stood in the bloody-orange late-afternoon sunlight, at the perimeter of the trees, peering into the purple shadows and mysterious green depths of the forest.

Lem was uneasy. He wondered if the escapee from Weatherby's lab was nearby, watching them.

"So what's up?" Walt asked.

"Can't say."

"National security?"

"That's right."

The spruces and pines and sycamores rustled in the breeze, and he thought he heard something moving furtively through the brush.

Imagination, of course. Nevertheless, Lem was glad that both he and Walt Gaines were armed with reliable pistols in accessible shoulder holsters.

Walt said, "You can keep your lip zipped if you insist, but you can't keep me totally in the dark. I can figure out a few things for myself. I'm not stupid."

"Never thought you were."

"Tuesday morning, every damn police department in Orange and San Bernardino counties gets an urgent request from your NSA asking us to be prepared to cooperate in a manhunt, details to follow. Which puts us all on edge.

We know what you guys are responsible for—guarding defense research, keeping the vodka-pissing Russians from stealing our secrets. And since Southern California's the home of half the defense contractors in the country, there's plenty to be stolen here."

Lem kept his eyes on the woods, kept his mouth shut.

"So," Walt continued, "we figure we're going to be looking for a Russian agent with something hot in his pockets, and we're happy to have a chance to help kick some ass for Uncle Sam. But by noon, instead of getting details, we get a cancellation of the request. No manhunt after all. Everything's under control, your office tells us. Original alert was issued in error, you say."

"That's right." The agency had realized that local police could not be sufficiently controlled and, therefore, could not be fully trusted. It was a job for the military. "Issued in error."

"Like hell. By late afternoon of the same day, we learn Marine choppers from El Toro are quartering the Santa Ana foothills. And by Wednesday morning, a hundred Marines with high-tech tracking gear are flown in from Camp Pendleton to carry on the search at ground level."

"I heard about that, but it had nothing to do with my agency," Lem said.

Walt studiously avoided looking at Lem. He stared off into the trees. Clearly, he knew Lem was lying to him, knew that Lem *had* to lie to him, and he felt it would be a breach of good manners to make Lem do it while they maintained eye contact. Though he looked crude and ill-mannered, Walt Gaines was an unusually considerate man with a rare talent for friendship.

But he was also the county sheriff, and it was his duty to keep probing even though he knew Lem would reveal nothing. He said, "Marines tell us it's just a training exercise."

"That's what I heard."

"We're always notified of training exercises ten days ahead."

Lem did not reply. He thought he saw something in the forest, a flicker of shadows, a darkish presence moving through piny gloom.

"So the Marines spend all day Wednesday and half of Thursday out there in the hills. But when reporters hear about this 'exercise' and come snooping around, the leathernecks suddenly call it off, pack up, go home. It was almost as if . . . whatever they were looking for was so worrisome, so damn top-secret that they'd rather not find it at all if finding it meant letting the press know about it."

Squinting into the forest, Lem strained to see through steadily deepening shadows, trying to catch another glimpse of the movement that had drawn his attention a moment ago.

Walt said, "Then yesterday afternoon the NSA asks to be kept informed about any 'peculiar reports, unusual assaults, or exceedingly violent murders.' We ask for clarification, don't get any."

There. A ripple in the murkiness beneath the evergreen boughs. About eighty feet in from the perimeter of the woods. Something moving quickly and stealthily from one sheltering shadow to another. Lem put his right hand under his coat, on the butt of the pistol in his shoulder holster.

"But then just one day later," Walt said, "we find this poor son of a bitch Dalbert torn to pieces—and the case is peculiar as hell and about as 'exceedingly violent' as I ever hope to see. Now here *you* are, Mr. Lemuel Asa Johnson, director of the Southern California Office of the NSA, and I know you didn't come choppering in here just to ask me whether I want onion or guacamole dip at tomorrow night's bridge game."

The movement was closer than eighty feet, much closer. Lem had been confused by the layers of shadows and by the queerly distorting late-afternoon sunlight that penetrated the trees. The thing was no more than forty feet away, maybe closer, and suddenly it came straight at them, *bounded* at them through the brush, and Lem cried out, drew the pistol from his holster, and involuntarily stumbled backward a few steps before taking a shooter's stance with his legs spread wide, both hands on the gun.

"It's just a mule deer!" Walt Gaines said.

Indeed it was. Just a mule deer.

The deer stopped a dozen feet away, under the drooping boughs of a spruce, peering at them with huge brown eyes that were bright with curiosity. Its head was held high, ears pricked up.

"They're so used to people in these canyons that they're almost tame," Walt said.

Lem let out a stale breath as he holstered his pistol.

The mule deer, sensing their tension, turned from them and loped away along the trail, vanishing into the woods.

Walt was staring hard at Lem, "What's out there, buddy?"

Lem said nothing. He blotted his hands on his suit jacket.

The breeze was stiffening, getting cooler. Evening was on its way, and night was close behind it.

"Never saw you spooked before," Walt said.

"A caffeine jag. I've had too much coffee today."

"Bullshit."

Lem shrugged.

"It seems to've been an *animal* that killed Dalberg, something with lots of teeth, claws, something savage," Walt said. "Yet no damn animal would carefully place the guy's head on a plate in the center of the kitchen table. That's a sick joke. Animals don't make jokes, not sick or otherwise. Whatever killed Dalberg . . . it left the head like that to taunt us. So what in Christ's name are we dealing with?"

"You don't want to know. And you don't *need* to know 'cause I'm assuming jurisdiction in this case."

"Like hell."

"I've got the authority," Lem said. "It's now a federal matter, Walt. I'm impounding all the evidence your people have gathered, all reports they've written thus far. You and your men are to talk to no one about what you've seen here. No one. You'll have a file on the case, but the only thing in it will be a memo from me, asserting the federal prerogative under the correct statute. You're out from under. No matter what happens, no one can blame you, Walt."

"Shit."

"Let it go."

Walt scowled. "I've got to know—"

"Let it go."

"—are people in my county in danger? At least tell me that much, damn it."

"Yes."

"In danger?"

"Yes."

"And if I fought you, if I tried to hang on to jurisdiction in this case, would there be anything I could do to lessen that danger, to insure the public safety?"

"No. Nothing," Lem said truthfully.

"Then there's no point in fighting you."

"None," Lem said.

He started back toward the cabin because the daylight was fading fast, and he did not want to be near the woods as darkness crept in. Sure, it had only been a mule deer. But next time?

"Wait a minute," Walt said. "Let me tell you what I think, and you just listen. You don't have to confirm or deny what I say. All you've got to do is hear me out."

"Go on," Lem said impatiently.

The shadows of the trees crept steadily across the bristly dry grass of the clearing. The sun was balanced on the western horizon.

Walt paced out of the shadows into the waning sunlight, hands in his back pockets, looking down at the dusty ground, taking a moment to collect his thoughts. Then: "Tuesday afternoon, somebody walked into a house in Newport Beach, shot a man named Yarbeck, and beat his wife to death. That night, somebody killed the Hudston family in Laguna Beach—husband, wife, and a teenage son. Police in both communities use the same forensics lab, so it didn't take long to discover one gun was used both places. But that's about all the police in either case are going to learn because your NSA has quietly assumed jurisdiction in those crimes, too. In the interest of national security."

Lem did not respond. He was sorry he had even agreed to listen. Anyway, he was not taking direct charge of the investigation into the murders of the scientists, which were almost surely Soviet-inspired. He'd delegated that task to other men, so he'd be free to concentrate on finding the dog and The Outsider.

The sunlight was burnt orange. The cabin windows smoldered with reflections of that fading fire.

Walt said, "Okay. Then there's Dr. Davis Weatherby of Corona Del Mar. Missing since Tuesday. This morning, Weatherby's brother finds the doctor's body in the trunk of his car. Local pathologists hardly arrive at the scene before NSA agents show up."

Lem was slightly unnerved by the swiftness with which the sheriff evidently gathered, coordinated, and absorbed information from various communities that were not in the unincorporated part of the county and were not, therefore, under his authority.

Walt grinned but with little or no humor. "Didn't expect me to have made all these connections, huh? Each of these things happened in a different police jurisdiction, but as far as I'm concerned this county is one sprawling city of two million people, so I make it my business to work hand in glove with all the local departments."

"What's your point?"

"My point is that it's astonishing to have six murders of upstanding citizens in one day. This is Orange County, after all, not L.A. And it's even more astonishing that all six deaths are related to urgent matters of national security. So it arouses my curiosity. I start checking into the backgrounds of these people, looking for something that links them—"

"Walt, for Christ's sake!"

"—and I discover they all work—or did work—for something called Banodyne Laboratories."

Lem was not angry. He couldn't get angry with Walt—they were tighter than brothers—but the big man's canniness was maddening right now. Lem said, "Listen, you've no right to conduct an investigation."

"I'm sheriff, remember?"

"But none of these murders—except Dalberg here—falls into your jurisdiction to begin with," Lem said. "And even if it did . . . once the NSA steps in, you've no right to continue. In fact, you're expressly *forbidden* by law to continue."

Ignoring him, Walt said, "So I look up Banodyne, see what kind of work they do, and I discover they're into genetic engineering, recombinant DNA—"

"You're incorrigible."

"There's no indication Banodyne's at work on defense projects, but that doesn't mean anything. Could be blind contracts, projects so secret that the funding doesn't even appear on public record."

"Jesus," Lem said irritably. "Don't you understand how damn mean we can get when we've got national security laws on our side?"

"Just speculating now," Walt said.

"You'll speculate your honky ass right into a prison cell."

"Now, Lemuel, let's not have an ugly racial confrontation here."

"You're incorrigible."

"Yeah, and you're repeating yourself. Anyway, I did some heavy thinking, and I figure the murders of these people who work at Banodyne must be connected somehow to the manhunt the Marines conducted Wednesday and Thursday. And to the murder of Wesley Dalberg."

"There's no similarity between Dalberg's murder and the others."

"Of course there's not. Wasn't the same killer. I can see that. The Yarbecks, the Hudstons, and Weatherby were hit by a pro, while poor Wes Dalberg was torn to pieces. Still, there's a connection, by God, or you wouldn't be interested, and the connection must be Banodyne."

The sun was sinking. Shadows pooled and thickened.

Walt said, "Here's what I figure: they were working on some new bug at Banodyne, a genetically altered germ, and it got loose, contaminated someone, but it didn't just make him sick. What it did was severely damage his brain, turn him into a savage or something—"

"An updated Dr. Jekyll for the high-tech age?" Lem interrupted sarcastically.

"—so he slipped out of the lab before anyone knew what happened to him, fled into the foothills, came here, attacked Dalberg."

"You watch a lot of bad horror movies or what?"

"As for Yarbeck and the others, maybe they were eliminated 'cause they knew what happened and were so scared about the consequences that they intended to go public."

Off in the dusky canyon, a soft, ululant howl arose. Probably just a coyote.

Lem wanted to get out of there, away from the forest. But he felt that he had to deal with Walt Gaines, deflect the sheriff from these lines of inquiry and consideration.

"Let me get this straight, Walt. Are you saying the United States government had its own scientists *killed* to shut them up?"

Walt frowned, knowing how unlikely—if not downright impossible—his scenario was.

Lem said, "Is life really just a Ludlum novel? Killed our own people? Is it National Paranoia Month or something? Do you really believe that crap?"

"No," Walt admitted.

"And how could Dalberg's killer be a contaminated scientist with brain damage? I mean, Christ, you yourself said it was some animal that killed Dalberg, something with claws, sharp teeth."

"Okay, okay, so I don't have it figured. Not all of it, anyway. But I'm sure it's all tied in with Banodyne somehow. I'm not entirely on the wrong track—am I?"

"Yes, you are," Lem said. "Entirely."

"Really?"

"Really." Lem felt bad about lying to Walt and manipulating him, but he did it anyway. "I shouldn't even tell you that you're chasing after false spoor, but as a friend I guess I owe you something."

Additional wild voices had joined the eerie howling in the woods, confirming that the cries were only those of coyotes, yet the sound chilled Lem Johnson and made him eager to depart.

Rubbing the nape of his bull neck with one hand, Walt said, "It doesn't have anything at all to do with Banodyne?"

"Nothing. It's just a coincidence that Weatherby and Yarbeck both worked there—and that Hudston used to work there. If you insist on making the connection, you'll just be spinning your wheels—which is fine by me."

The sun set and, in passing, seemed to unlock a door through which a much cooler, brisker breeze swept into the darkening world.

Still rubbing his neck, Walt said, "Not Banodyne, huh?" He sighed. "I know you too well, buddy. You've got such a strong sense of duty that you'd lie to your own mother if that was in the best interests of the country."

Lem said nothing.

"All right," Walt said. "I'll drop it. Your case from here on. Unless more people in my jurisdiction get killed. If that happens . . . well, I might try to take control of things again. Can't promise you that I won't. I've got a sense of duty, too, you know."

"I know," Lem said, feeling guilty, feeling like a total shit.

At last, they both headed back to the cabin.

The sky—which was dark in the east, still streaked with deep orange and red and purple light in the west—seemed to be descending like the lid of a box.

Coyotes howled.

Something out in the night woods howled back at them.

Cougar, Lem thought, but he knew that now he was even lying to himself.

4

On Sunday, two days after their successful Friday lunch date, Travis and Nora drove to Solvang, a Danish-style village in the Santa Ynez Valley. It was a touristy place with hundreds of shops selling everything from exquisite Scandinavian crystal to plastic imitations of Danish beer steins. The quaint architecture (though calculated) and the tree-lined streets enhanced the simple pleasures of window-shopping.

Several times Travis felt the urge to take Nora's hand and hold it while they strolled. It seemed natural, right. Yet he sensed that she might not be ready for even such harmless contact as hand-holding.

She was wearing another drab dress, dull blue this time, nearly as shapeless as a sack. Sensible shoes. Her thick dark hair still hung limp and unstyled, as it had been when he'd first seen her.

Being with her was pure pleasure. She had a sweet temperament and was unfailingly sensitive and kind. Her innocence was refreshing. Her shyness and modesty, though excessive, endeared her to him. She viewed everything with a wide-eyed wonder that was charming, and he delighted in surprising her with simple things: a shop that sold only cuckoo clocks; another that sold only stuffed animals; a music box with a mother-of-pearl door that opened to reveal a pirouetting ballerina.

He bought her a T-shirt with a personalized message that he would not let her see until it was ready: NORA LOVES EINSTEIN. Though she professed she could never wear a T-shirt, that it wasn't her style, Travis knew she would wear it because she did, indeed, love the dog.

Perhaps Einstein could not read the words on the shirt, but he seemed to understand what was meant. When they came out of the shop and unhooked his leash from the parking meter where they'd tethered him, Einstein regarded the message on the shirt solemnly while Nora held it up for his inspection, then happily licked and nuzzled her.

The day held only one bad moment for them. As they turned a corner and approached another shop window, Nora stopped suddenly and looked around at the crowds on the sidewalks—people eating ice cream in big homemade waffle-cookie cones, people eating apple tarts wrapped in wax paper, guys in feather-decorated cowboy hats they'd bought in one of the stores, pretty young girls in short-shorts and halters, a very fat woman in a yellow muumuu, people speaking English and Spanish and Japanese and Vietnamese and all the other languages you could heat at any Southern California tourist spot—and then she looked along the busy street at a gift shop built in the form of a three-story stone-and-timber windmill, and she stiffened, looked stricken. Travis had to guide her to a bench in a small park, where she sat trembling for a few minutes before she could even tell him what was wrong.

"Overload," she said at last, her voice shaky. "So many . . . new sights . . . new sounds . . . so many different things all at once. I'm so sorry."

"It's all right," he said, touched.

"I'm used to a few rooms, familiar things. Are people staring?"

"No one's noticed anything. There's nothing to stare at."

She sat with her shoulders hunched, her head hung forward, her hands fisted in her lap—until Einstein put his head on her knees. As she petted the dog, she began gradually to relax.

"I was enjoying myself," she said to Travis, though she did not raise her head, "really enjoying myself, and I thought how far from home I was, how wonderfully far from home—"

"Not really. Less than an hour's drive," he assured her.

"A long, long way," she said.

Travis supposed that for her it was, in fact, a great distance.

She said, "And when I realized how far from home I was and how . . . *different* everything was . . . I clenched up, afraid, like a child."

"Would you like to go back to Santa Barbara now?"

"No!" she said, meeting his eyes at last. She shook her head. She dared to look around at the people moving through the small park and at the gift shop shaped like a windmill. "No. I want to stay a while. All day. I want to have dinner in a restaurant here, not at a sidewalk café but inside, like other people do, inside, and then I want to go home after dark." She blinked and repeated those two words wonderingly, "After dark."

"All right."

"Unless, of course, you hoped to get back sooner."

"No, no," he said. "I planned on making a day of it."

"This is very kind of you."

Travis raised one eyebrow. "What do you mean?"

"You know."

"I'm afraid I don't."

"Helping me step out into the world," she said. "Giving up your time to help someone . . . like me. It's very generous of you."

He was astonished. "Nora, let me assure you, it's not charity work I'm involved in here!"

"I'm sure a man like you has better things to do with a Sunday afternoon in May."

"Oh, yes," he said self-mockingly, "I could have stayed home and given all my shoes a meticulous shining with a toothbrush. Could have counted the number of pieces in a box of elbow macaroni."

She stared at him in disbelief.

"By God, you're serious," Travis said. "You think I'm here just because I've taken pity on you."

She bit her lip and said, "It's all right." She looked down at the dog again. "I don't mind."

"But I'm not here out of pity, for God's sake! I'm here because I like being with you, I really do, I like you very much."

Even with her head lowered, the blush that crept into her cheeks was visible.

For a while neither of them spoke.

Einstein looked up at her adoringly as she petted him, though once in a while he rolled his eyes at Travis as if to say, *All right, you've opened the door of a relationship, so don't just sit there like a fool, say something, move forward, win her over.*

She scratched the retriever's ears and stroked him for a couple of minutes, and then she said, "I'm okay now."

They left the little park and strolled past the shops again, and in a while it was as if her moment of panic and his clumsy proclamation of affection had not happened.

He felt as if he were courting a nun. Eventually, he realized that the situation was even worse than that. Since the death of his wife three years ago, he had been celibate. The whole subject of sexual relations seemed strange and new to him again. So it was almost as if he were a *priest* wooing a nun.

Nearly every block had a bakery, and the wares in the display windows for each shop looked more delicious than what had been for sale in the previous place. The scents of cinnamon, powdered sugar, nutmeg, almonds, apples, and chocolate eddied in the warm spring air.

Einstein stood on his hind feet at each bakery, paws on the windowsill, and stared longingly through the glass at the artfully arranged pastries. But he didn't go into any of the shops, and he never barked. When he begged for a treat, his soulful whining was discreetly low, so as not to bother the swarming tourists. Rewarded with a bit of pecan fudge and a small apple tart, he was satisfied and did not persist in begging.

Ten minutes later, Einstein revealed his exceptional intelligence to Nora. He had been a good dog around her, affectionate and bright and well-behaved, and he had shown considerable initiative in chasing and cornering Arthur Streck, but he had not previously allowed her a glimpse of his uncanny intelligence. And when she witnessed it, she did not at first realize what she was seeing.

They were passing the town pharmacy, which also sold newspapers and magazines, some of which were displayed outside in a rack near the entrance. Einstein surprised Nora with a sudden lurch toward the pharmacy, tearing his leash out of her hand. Before either Nora or Travis could regain control of him, Einstein used his teeth to pull a magazine from the rack and brought it to them, dropping it at Nora's feet. It was *Modern Bride.* As Travis grabbed for him, Einstein eluded capture and snatched up another copy of *Modern Bride,* which he deposited at Travis's feet just as Nora was picking up her copy to return it to the rack.

"You silly pooch," she said. "What's gotten into you?"

Taking up the leash, Travis stepped through the passersby and put the second copy of the magazine back where the dog had gotten it. He thought he knew exactly what Einstein had in mind, but he said nothing, afraid of embarrassing Nora, and they resumed their walk.

Einstein looked at everything, sniffing with interest at the people who passed, and he seemed immediately to have forgotten his enthusiasm for matrimonial publications.

However, they had taken fewer than twenty steps when the dog abruptly turned and ran between Travis's legs, jerking the leash out of his hands and nearly knocking him down. Einstein went directly to the pharmacy, snatched a magazine out of the rack, and returned.

Modern Bride.

Nora still did not get it. She thought it was funny, and she stooped to ruffle the retriever's coat. "Is this your favorite reading material, you silly pooch? Read it every month, do you? You know, I'll bet you do. You strike me as a complete romantic."

A couple of tourists had noticed the playful dog and were smiling, but they were even less likely than Nora to realize there was a complex intention behind the animal's game with the magazine.

When Travis bent down to pick up *Modern Bride,* intending to return it to the pharmacy, Einstein got to it first, took it in his jaws, and shook his head violently for a moment.

"Bad dog," Nora said with evident surprise that Einstein had such a devilish streak in him.

"I guess we'll have to buy it now," Travis said.

Panting, the retriever sat on the sidewalk, cocked his head, and grinned up at Travis.

Nora remained innocently unaware that the dog was trying to tell them something. Of course, she had no reason to make a sophisticated interpretation of Einstein's behavior. She was unfamiliar with the degree of his genius and did not expect him to perform miracles of communication.

Glaring at the dog, Travis said, "You stop it, fur face. No more of this. Understand me?"

Einstein yawned.

With the magazine paid for and tucked into a pharmacy bag, they resumed their tour of Solvang, but before they reached the end of the block, the dog began to elaborate on his message. He suddenly gripped Nora's hand gently but firmly in his teeth and, to her startlement, pulled her along the sidewalk to an art gallery, where a young man and woman were admiring the landscape paintings in the window. The couple had a baby in a stroller, and it was the child to whom Einstein was directing Nora's attention. He wouldn't let go of her hand until he had forced her to touch the pink-outfitted infant's chubby arm.

Embarrassed, Nora said, "He thinks your baby's exceptionally cute, I guess—which she certainly is."

The mother and father were wary of the dog at first but quickly realized he was harmless.

"How old's your little girl?" Nora asked.

"Ten months," the mother said.

"What's her name?"

"Lana."

"That's pretty."

Finally, Einstein was willing to release Nora's hand.

A few steps away from the young couple, in front of an antique shop that looked as if it had been transported brick by brick and timber by timber from seventeenth-century Denmark, Travis stopped, crouched beside the dog, lifted one of its ears, and said, "Enough. If you ever want your Alpo again, cut it out."

Nora looked baffled. "What's gotten into him?"

Einstein yawned, and Travis knew they were in trouble.

In the next ten minutes, the dog took hold of Nora's hand twice again and led her, both times, to babies.

Modern Bride and babies.

The message was painfully clear now, even to Nora: *You and Travis belong together. Get married. Have babies. Raise a family. What're you waiting for?*

She was blushing furiously and seemed unable to look directly at Travis. He was somewhat embarrassed, too.

At last Einstein seemed satisfied that he had gotten his point across, and he stopped misbehaving. Until now, if asked, Travis would have said that a dog could not look smug.

Later, at dinnertime, the day was still pleasantly warm, and Nora changed her mind about eating inside, in an ordinary restaurant. She chose a place with sidewalk tables under red umbrellas that were, in turn, sheltered by the boughs of a giant oak. Travis sensed that she was not now intimidated by the prospect of a real restaurant experience but wanted to eat in the open air so they could keep Einstein with them. Repeatedly throughout dinner, she looked at Einstein, sometimes glancing surreptitiously at him, sometimes studying him openly and intently.

Travis made no reference to what had happened and pretended to have forgotten the whole affair. But when he had the dog's attention, and when Nora was not looking, he mouthed threats at the mutt: *No more apple tarts. Choke chain. Muzzle. Straight to the dog pound.*

Einstein took every threat with great equanimity, either grinning or yawning or blowing air out his nostrils.

5

Early Sunday evening, Vince Nasco paid a visit to Johnny "The Wire" Santini. Johnny was called "The Wire" for several reasons, not least of which was that he was tall and lean and taut, and he looked as if he was constructed of knotted wires in various gauges. He also had frizzy hair the shade of copper. He had made his bones at the tender age of fifteen, when to please his uncle, Religio Fustino, don of one of New York's Five Families, Johnny had taken it upon himself to strangle a freelance shit-and-coke dealer who was operating in the Bronx without the permission of the Family. Johnny used a length of piano wire for the job. This display of initiative and dedication to the principles of the Family had filled Don Religio with pride and love, and he had wept for only the second time in his life, promising his nephew the eternal respect of the Family and a well-paid position in the business.

Now Johnny The Wire was thirty-five and lived in a million-dollar beach house in San Clemente. The ten rooms and four baths had been remade by an interior designer commissioned to create an authentic—and expensive—private Art Deco retreat from the modern world. Everything was in shades of black, silver, and deep blue, with accents of turquoise and peach. Johnny had told Vince that he liked Art Deco because it reminded him of the Roaring Twenties, and he liked the twenties because that was the romantic era of legendary gangsters.

To Johnny The Wire, crime was not just a means to make money, not simply a way to rebel against the constraints of civilized society, and not only a genetic compulsion, but it was also—and primarily—a magnificent romantic tradition. He saw himself as a brother of every eye-patched hook-handed pirate who ever sailed in search of plunder, of every highwayman who had robbed a mail coach, of every safecracker and kidnapper and embezzler and thug in all the ages of criminal endeavor. He was, he insisted, mystical kin to Jesse James,

Dillinger, Al Capone, the Dalton boys, Lucky Luciano, and legions of others, and Johnny loved them all, these legendary brothers in blood and theft.

Greeting Vince at the front door, Johnny said, "Come in, come in, big guy. Good to see you again."

They hugged. Vince didn't like hugging, but he had worked for Johnny's Uncle Religio when he'd lived back in New York, and he still did a West Coast job for the Fustino Family now and then, so he and Johnny went back a long way, long enough that a hug was required.

"You're looking good," Johnny said. "Taking care of yourself, I see. Still mean as a snake?"

"A rattlesnake," Vince said, a little embarrassed to be saying such a stupid thing, but he knew it was the kind of outlaw crap that Johnny liked to hear.

"Hadn't seen you in so long I thought maybe the cops busted your ass."

"I'll never do time," Vince said, meaning that he knew prison was not part of his destiny.

Johnny took it to mean that Vince would go down shooting rather than submit to the law, and he scowled and nodded approval. "They ever get you in a corner, blow away as many of 'em as you can before they take you out. That's the only *clean* way to go down."

Johnny The Wire was an astonishingly ugly man, which probably explained his need to feel that he was a part of a great romantic tradition. Over the years Vince had noticed that the better-looking hoods never glamorized what they did. They killed in cold blood because they liked killing or found it necessary, and they stole and embezzled and extorted because they wanted easy money, and that was the end of it: no justifications, no self-glorification, which was the way it ought to be. But those with faces that appeared to have been crudely molded from concrete, those who resembled Quasimodo on a bad day—well, many of them tried to compensate for their unfortunate looks by casting themselves as Jimmy Cagney in *Public Enemy*.

Johnny was wearing a black jumpsuit, black sneakers. He always wore black, probably because he thought it made him look sinister instead of just ugly.

From the foyer, Vince followed Johnny into the living room, where the furniture was upholstered in black fabric and the end tables were finished in glossy black lacquer. There were ormolu table lamps by Ranc, large silver-dusted Deco vases by Daum, a pair of antique chairs by Jacques Ruhlmann. Vince knew the history of these things only because, on previous visits, Johnny The Wire had stepped out of his tough-guy persona long enough to babble about his period treasures.

A good-looking blonde was reclining on a silver-and-black chaise lounge, reading a magazine. No older than twenty, she was almost embarrassingly ripe. Her silver-blond hair was cut short, in a pageboy. She was wearing Chinese-red silk lounging pajamas that clung to the contours of her full breasts, and when she glanced up and pouted at Vince, she seemed to be trying to look like Jean Harlow.

"This is Samantha," Johnny The Wire said. To Samantha, he said, "Toots, this here is a made man that nobody messes with, a legend in his own time."

Vince felt like a jackass.

"What's a 'made man'?" the blonde asked in a high-pitched voice she'd no doubt copied from the old movie star Judy Holliday.

Standing beside the lounge, cupping one of the blonde's breasts and fondling it through the silk pajamas, Johnny said, "She doesn't know the lingo, Vince. She's not one of the *fratellanza*. She's a valley girl, new to the life, unaware of our customs."

"He means I'm no greaseball guinea," Samantha said sourly.

Johnny slapped her so hard that he nearly knocked her off the chaise lounge. "You watch your mouth, bitch."

She put a hand to her face, and tears shimmered in her eyes, and in a little-girl voice, she said, "I'm sorry, Johnny."

"Stupid bitch," he muttered.

"I don't know what gets into me," she said. "You're good to me, Johnny, and I hate myself when I act like that."

To Vince, it appeared to be a rehearsed scene, but he supposed that was just because they'd been through it so many times before, both privately and publicly. From the shine in Samantha's eyes, Vince could tell she enjoyed being slapped around; she smart-mouthed Johnny just so he'd hit her. Johnny clearly liked slapping her, too.

Vince was disgusted.

Johnny The Wire called her a "bitch" again, then led Vince out of the living room and into the big study, closing the door behind them. He winked and said, "She's a little uppity, that one, but she can just about suck your brains out through your cock."

Half-sickened by Johnny Santini's sleaziness, Vince refused to be drawn into such a conversation. Instead, he withdrew an envelope from his jacket pocket. "I need information."

Johnny took the envelope, looked inside, thumbed casually through the wad of hundred-dollar bills, and said, "What you want, you got."

The study was the only room in the house untouched by Art Deco. It was strictly high-tech. Sturdy metal tables were lined up along three walls, and eight computers stood on them, different makes and models. Every computer had its own phone line and modem, and every display screen was aglow. On some screens, programs were running; data flickered across them or scrolled from top to bottom. Drapes were drawn over the windows, and the two flexible-neck work lamps were hooded to prevent glare on the monitors, so the predominant light was electronic-green, which gave Vince a peculiar feeling of being under the surface of the sea. Three laser printers were producing hard copies with only vague whispering sounds that for some reason brought to mind images of fish swimming through ocean-floor vegetation.

Johnny The Wire had killed half a dozen men, had managed bookie and numbers operations, had planned and executed bank robberies and jewelry heists. He had been involved in the Fustino Family's drug operations, extortion rackets, kidnapping, labor-union corruption, record and videotape counterfeiting, interstate truck hijacking, political bribery, and child pornography. He had done it all, seen it all, and although he had never exactly been bored by any criminal undertaking, no matter how long or often he had been involved in it, he *had* grown somewhat jaded. During the past decade, as the computer opened exciting new areas of criminal activity, Johnny had seized the opportunity to move where no mafia wiseguy had gone before, into challenging frontiers of electronic thievery and mayhem. He had a gift for it, and he soon became the mob's premier hacker.

Given time and motivation, he could break any computer security system and pry through a corporation's or a government agency's most sensitive information. If you wanted to run a major credit-card scam, charging a million bucks worth of purchases to other people's American Express accounts, Johnny The Wire could suck some suitable names and credit histories out of TRW's files and matching card numbers from American Express's data banks, and you were in business. If you were a don under indictment and about to go to trial on heavy charges, and if you were afraid of the testimony to be given by one of your cronies who had turned state's evidence, Johnny could invade the Department of Justice's most well-guarded data banks, discover the new identity that had been given the stool pigeon through the Federal Witness Relocation Program, and tell you where to send the hit men. Johnny rather grandly called himself the "Silicon Sorcerer," though everyone else still called him The Wire.

As the mob's hacker, he was more valuable than ever to all the Families nationwide, so valuable that they didn't even mind if he moved to a comparative backwater like San Clemente, where he could live the good beach life while he worked for them. In the age of the microchip, Johnny said, the world was one small town, and you could sit in San Clemente—or Oshkosh—and pick someone's pocket in New York City.

Johnny dropped into a high-backed black leather chair equipped with rubber wheels, in which he could roll swiftly from one computer to the next. He said, "So! What can the Silicon Sorcerer do for you, Vince?"

"Can you tap into police computers?"

"It's a snap."

"I need to know if, since last Tuesday, any police agency in the county has opened a file on any particularly strange murders."

"Who're the victims?"

"I don't know. I'm just looking for strange murders."

"Strange in what way?"

"I'm not exactly sure. Maybe . . . somebody with his throat torn out. Somebody ripped to pieces. Somebody all chewed up and gouged by an animal."

Johnny gave him a peculiar look. "That's strange, all right. Something like that would be in the newspapers."

"Maybe not," Vince said, thinking of the army of government security agents that would be working diligently to keep the press in the dark about the Francis Project and to conceal the dangerous developments on Tuesday at the Banodyne labs. "The murders might be in the news, but the police will probably be suppressing the gory details, making them look like ordinary homicides. So from what the papers print, I won't be able to tell which victims are the ones I'm interested in."

"All right. Can do."

"You'd also better prowl around at the County Animal Control Authority to see if they're getting any reports of unusual attacks by coyotes or cougars or other predators. And not just attacks on people, but on livestock—cows, sheep. There might even be some neighborhood, probably on the eastern edge of the county, where a lot of family pets are disappearing or being chewed up real bad by something wild. If you run across that, I want to know."

Johnny grinned and said, "You tracking down a werewolf?"

It was a joke; he did not expect or want an answer. He had not asked why this information was needed, and he would never ask, because people in their line of work did not poke into each other's business. Johnny might be curious, but Vince knew that The Wire would never indulge his curiosity.

Vince was unnerved not by the question but by the grin. The green light from the computer screens was reflected by Johnny's eyes and by the saliva on his teeth and, to a lesser extent, by his wiry copper-colored hair. As ugly as he was to begin with, the eerie luminescence made him look like a revived corpse in a Romero film.

Vince said, "Another thing. I need to know if any police agency in the county is running a quiet search for a golden retriever."

"A dog?"

"Yeah."

"Cops don't usually look for lost dogs."

"I know," Vince said.

"This dog got a name?"

"No name."

"I'll check it out. Anything else?"

"That's it. When can you put it together?"

"I'll call you in the morning. Early."

Vince nodded. "And depending on what you turn up, I might need you to keep tracking these things on a daily basis."

"Child's play," Johnny said, spinning around once in his black leather chair, then jumping to his feet with a grin. "Now, I'm gonna fuck Samantha. Hey! You want to join in? Two studs like us, going at her at the same time, we could reduce that bitch to a little pile of jelly, have her begging for mercy. How about it?"

Vince was glad for the weird green lighting because it covered the fact that he had gone ghost-pale. The idea of messing around with that infected slut, that diseased whore, that rotting and festering round-heeled pump, was enough to make him sick. He said, "Got an appointment I can't break."

"Too bad," Johnny said.

Vince forced himself to say, "Would've been fun."

"Maybe next time."

The very idea of the three of them going at it . . . well, it made Vince feel unclean. He was overcome by a desire for a steaming-hot shower.

6

Sunday night, pleasantly tired from a long day in Solvang, Travis thought he would fall asleep the moment he put his head on his pillow, but he did not. He couldn't stop thinking about Nora Devon. Her gray eyes flecked with green. Glossy black hair. The graceful, slender line of her throat. The musical sound of her laughter, the curve of her smile.

Einstein was lying on the floor in the pale-silver light that came through the window and vaguely illuminated one small section of the dark room. But after Travis tossed and turned for an hour, the dog finally joined him on the bed and put his burly head and forepaws on Travis's chest.

"She's so sweet, Einstein. One of the gentlest, sweetest people I've ever known."

The dog was silent.

"And she's very bright. She's got a sharp mind, sharper than she realizes. She sees things I don't see. She has a way of describing things that make them fresh and new. The whole *world* seems fresh and new when I see it with her."

Though still and quiet, Einstein had not fallen asleep. He was very attentive.

"When I think about all that vitality, intelligence, and love of life being suppressed for thirty years, I want to cry. Thirty years in that old dark house. Jesus. And when I think of how she endured those years without letting it make her bitter, I want to hug her and tell her what an incredible woman she is, what a strong and courageous and incredible woman."

Einstein was silent, unmoving.

A vivid memory flashed back to Travis: the clean shampoo smell of Nora's hair when he had leaned close to her in front of a gallery window in Solvang. He breathed deep and could actually smell it again, and the scent accelerated his heartbeat.

"Damn," he said. "I've only known her a few days, but damn if I don't think I'm falling in love."

Einstein lifted his head and woofed once, as if to say it was about time that Travis realized what was happening, and as if to say that he had brought them together and was pleased to take credit for their future happiness, and as if to say that it was all part of some grand design and that Travis was to stop fretting about it and just go with the flow.

For another hour, Travis talked about Nora, about the way she looked and moved, about the melodic quality of her soft voice, about her unique perspective on life and her way of thinking, and Einstein listened with the attentiveness and genuine interest that was the mark of a true, concerned friend. It was an exhilarating hour. Travis had never thought he would love anyone again. Not anyone, not at all, and certainly not this intimately. Less than a week ago, his abiding loneliness had seemed unconquerable.

Later, thoroughly exhausted both physically and emotionally, Travis slept.

Later still, in the hollow heart of night, he came half awake and was dimly aware that Einstein was at the window. The retriever's forepaws were on the windowsill, his snout against the glass. He was staring out at the darkness, alert.

Travis sensed that the dog was troubled.

But in his dream, he had been holding Nora's hand under a harvest moon, and he did not want to come fully awake for fear he would not be able to regain that pleasant fantasy.

7

On Monday morning, May 24, Lemuel Johnson and Cliff Soames were at the small zoo—mostly a petting zoo for children—in sprawling Irvine Park, on the eastern edge of Orange County. The sky was cloudless, the sun bright and hot. The immense oaks did not stir a leaf in the motionless air, but birds swooped from branch to branch, peeping and trilling.

Twelve animals were dead. They lay in bloody heaps.

During the night, someone or something had climbed the fences into the pens and had slaughtered three young goats, a white-tailed deer and her recently born fawn, two peacocks, a lop-eared rabbit, a ewe and two lambs.

A pony was dead, though it had not been savaged. Apparently, it had died of fright while throwing itself repeatedly against the fence in an attempt to escape whatever had attacked the other animals. It lay on its side, neck twisted in an improbable angle.

The wild boars had been left unharmed. They snorted and sniffed continuously at the dusty earth around the feeding trough in their separate enclosure, looking for bits of food that might have spilled yesterday and been missed until now.

Other surviving animals, unlike the boars, were skittish.

Park employees—also skittish—were gathered near an orange truck that belonged to the county, talking with two Animal Control officers and with a young, bearded biologist from the California Department of Wildlife.

Crouching beside the delicate and pathetic fawn, Lem studied the wounds in its neck until he could no longer tolerate the stench. Not all of the foul odors were caused by the dead animals. There was evidence that the killer had deposited feces and sprayed urine on its victims, just as it had done at Dalberg's place.

Pressing a handkerchief against his nose to filter the reeking air, he moved to a dead peacock. Its head had been torn off, as had one leg. Both of its clipped wings were broken, and its iridescent feathers were dulled and pasted together with blood.

"Sir," Cliff Soames called from the adjoining pen.

Lem left the peacock, found a service gate that opened into the next enclosure, and joined Cliff at the carcass of the ewe.

Flies swarmed around them, buzzing hungrily, settling upon the ewe, then darting off as the men fanned them away.

Cliff's face was bloodless, but he did not look as shocked or as nauseated as he had been last Friday, at Dalberg's cabin. Perhaps this slaughter didn't affect him as strongly because the victims were animals instead of human beings. Or perhaps he was consciously hardening himself against the extreme violence of their adversary.

"You'll have to come to this side," Cliff said from where he crouched beside the ewe.

Lem stepped around the sheep and squatted beside Cliff. Though the ewe's head was in the shadow of an oak bough overhanging the pen, Lem saw that her right eye had been torn out.

Without comment, Cliff used a stick to lever the left side of the ewe's head off the ground, revealing that the other socket was also vacant.

The cloud of flies thickened around them.

"Looks like it was our runaway, all right," Lem said.

Lowering his own handkerchief from his face, Cliff said, "There's more." He led Lem to three additional carcasses—both lambs and one of the goats— that were eyeless. "I'd say it's beyond argument. The damn thing killed Dalberg last Tuesday night, then roamed the foothills and canyons for five days, doing . . ."

"What?"

"God knows what. But it wound up here last night."

Lem used his handkerchief to mop the sweat off his dark face. "We're only a few miles north-northwest of Dalberg's cabin."

Cliff nodded.

"Which way you think it's headed?"

Cliff shrugged.

"Yeah," Lem said. "No way of knowing where it's going. Can't begin to outthink it because we haven't the slightest idea *how* it thinks. Let's just pray to God it stays out here in the unpopulated end of the county. I don't want to even consider what would happen if it decides to head into the easternmost suburbs like Orange Park Acres and Villa Park."

On the way out of the compound, Lem saw that the flies were gathered on the dead rabbit in such numbers that they looked like a piece of dark cloth draped over the carcass and rippling in a light breeze.

Eight hours later, at seven o'clock Monday evening, Lem stepped up to the lectern in a large meeting room on the grounds of the Marine Air Station at El Toro. He leaned toward the microphone, tapped it with a finger to be sure it was active, heard a loud hollow *thump,* and said, "May I have your attention, please?"

A hundred men were seated on metal folding chairs. They were all young, well-built, and healthy-looking, for they were members of elite Marine Intelligence units. Five two-squad platoons had been drawn from Pendleton and other bases in California. Most of them had been involved in the search of the Santa Ana foothills last Wednesday and Thursday, following the breakout at the Banodyne labs.

They were *still* searching, having just returned from a full day in the hills and canyons, but they were no longer conducting the operation in uniform. To deceive reporters and local authorities, they had driven in cars and pickups and

Jeep wagons to various points along the current search perimeter. They had gone into the wilds in groups of three or four, dressed as ordinary hikers: jeans or khaki pants in the rugged Banana Republic style; T-shirts or cotton safari shirts; Dodger or Budweiser or John Deere caps, or cowboy hats. They went armed with powerful handguns that could be quickly concealed in nylon backpacks or under their loose T-shirts if they encountered real hikers or state authorities. And in Styrofoam coolers, they carried compact Uzi submachine guns that could be brought into service in seconds if they found the adversary.

Every man in the room had signed a secrecy oath, which put him in jeopardy of a long prison term if he ever divulged the nature of this operation to anyone. They knew what they were hunting, though Lem was aware that some of them had trouble believing the creature really existed. Some were afraid. But others, especially those who had previously served in Lebanon or Central America, were familiar enough with death and horror to be unshaken by the nature of their current quarry. A few old timers went as far back as the final year of the Vietnam War, and they professed to believe that the mission was a piece of cake. In any event, they were all good men, and they had a wary respect for the strange enemy they were stalking, and if The Outsider could be found, they would find it.

Now, when Lem asked for their attention, they immediately fell silent.

"General Hotchkiss tells me that you've had another fruitless day out there," Lem said, "and I know you're as unhappy about that as I am. You've been working long hours in rugged terrain for six days now, and you're tired, and you're wondering how long this is going to drag on. Well, we're going to keep looking until we find what we're after, until we corner The Outsider and kill it. There is no way we can stop if it's still loose. No way."

None of the hundred even grumbled in disagreement.

"And always remember—we're also looking for the dog."

Every man in the room probably hoped that he would be the one to find the dog and that someone else would encounter The Outsider.

Lem said, "On Wednesday, we're bringing in another four Marine Intelligence squads from more distant bases, and they'll spell you on a rotating basis, giving you a couple of days off. But you'll all be out there tomorrow morning, and the search area has been redefined."

A county map was mounted on the wall behind the lectern, and Lem Johnson pointed to it with a yardstick. "We'll be shifting north-northwest, into the hills and canyons around Irvine Park."

He told them about the slaughter at the petting zoo. He gave a graphic description of the condition of the carcasses, for he did not want any of these men to get careless.

"What happened to those zoo animals," Lem said, "could happen to any of you if you let your guard down at the wrong place and time."

A hundred men regarded him with utmost seriousness, and in their eyes he saw a hundred versions of his own tightly controlled fear.

8

Tuesday night, May 25, Tracy Leigh Keeshan could not sleep. She was so excited she felt as if she might burst. She pictured herself as a dandelion gone to seed, a puffball of fragile white fuzz, and then a gust of wind would come along and all the bits of fluff would be sent spinning in every direction—poof—to the far corners of the world, and Tracy Keeshan would exist no more, destroyed by her own excitement.

She was an unusually imaginative thirteen-year-old.

Lying in bed in her dark room, she did not even have to close her eyes to see herself on horseback—on her own chestnut stallion, Goodheart, to be precise—thundering along the racetrack, the rails flashing past, the other horses in the field left far behind, the finish line less than a hundred yards ahead, and the adoring crowds cheering wildly in the grandstand . . .

In school, she routinely got good grades, not because she was a diligent student but because learning came easily to her, and she could do well without much effort. She didn't really care about school. She was slender, blond, with eyes the precise shade of a clear summer sky, very pretty, and boys were drawn to her, but she didn't spend any more time thinking about boys than she did worrying about her school work, not yet anyway, although her girlfriends were so fixated on boys, so *consumed* by the subject that they sometimes bored Tracy half to death.

What Tracy cared about—deeply, profoundly, passionately—was horses, racing thoroughbreds. She had been collecting pictures of horses since she was five and had been taking riding lessons since she was seven, though for the longest time her parents had not been able to afford to buy her a horse of her own. During the past two years, however, her father's business had prospered, and two months ago they had moved into a big new house on two acres in Orange Park Acres, which was a horsey community with plenty of riding trails. At the back end of their lot was a private stable for six horses, though only one stall was occupied. Just today—Tuesday, May 25, a day of glory, a day that would live forever in Tracy Keeshan's heart, a day that just *proved* there was a God—she had been given a horse of her own, the splendid and beautiful and incomparable Goodheart.

So she could not sleep. She went to bed at ten, and by midnight she was more awake than ever. By one o'clock Wednesday morning, she could not stand it any longer. She had to go out to the stables and look at Goodheart. Make sure he was all right. Make sure he was comfortable in his new home. Make sure he was *real*.

She threw off the sheet and thin blanket and got quietly out of bed. She was wearing panties and a Santa Anita Racetrack T-shirt, so she just pulled on a pair of jeans and slipped her bare feet into blue Nike running shoes.

She turned the knob on her door slowly, quietly, and went out into the hall, letting the door stand open.

The house was dark and quiet. Her parents and her nine-year-old brother Bobby were asleep.

Tracy went down the hall, through the living room and the dining room, not turning on lights, relying on the moonlight that penetrated the large windows.

In the kitchen, she silently pulled open the utility drawer on the corner secretary and withdrew a flashlight. She unlocked the back door and let herself out onto the rear patio, stealthily easing the door shut behind her, not yet switching on the flashlight.

The spring night was cool but not chilly. Silvered by moonlight above but with dark undersides, a few big clouds glided like white-sailed galleons across the sea of night, and Tracy stared up at them for a while, enjoying the moment. She wanted to absorb every detail of this special time, letting her anticipation build. After all, this would be her first moment *alone* with the proud and noble Goodheart, just the two of them sharing their dreams of the future.

She crossed the patio, went around the swimming pool, where the reflection of the moon rippled gently in the chlorinated water, and stepped out onto the sloping lawn. The dew-damp grass seemed to shimmer in the lambent lunar beams.

Off to the left and right, the property line was defined by white ranch fencing that appeared vaguely phosphorescent in the moonglow. Beyond the fences were other properties of at least an acre and some as large as the Keeshan place, and all across Orange Park Acres the night was still but for a few crickets and nocturnal frogs.

Tracy walked slowly toward the stables at the end of the yard, thinking about the triumphs that lay ahead for her and Goodheart. He would not race again. He had placed in the money at Santa Anita, Del Mar, Hollywood Park, and other tracks throughout California, but he had been injured and could no longer race safely. However, he could still be put to stud, and Tracy had no doubt that he'd sire winners. Within a week they hoped to add two good mares to the stable, and then they'd take the horses immediately to a breeding farm, where Goodheart would impregnate the mares. All three would be brought back here, where Tracy would care for them. Next year two healthy colts would be born, and then the young ones would be boarded with a trainer near enough so Tracy could visit constantly, and she'd help out with their training, learn all there was to learn about rearing a champion, and then—and *then*—she and the offspring of Goodheart would make racing history, oh yes, she was quite confident of making racing history—

Her fantasizing was interrupted when, about forty yards from the stables, she stepped in something mushy and slippery, and nearly fell. She didn't smell manure, but she figured it must be a pile left by Goodheart when they'd had him out in the yard last evening. Feeling stupid and clumsy, she switched on the flashlight and directed it at the ground, and instead of manure she found the remains of a brutally mutilated cat.

Tracy made a hissing sound of disgust and instantly switched off the flashlight.

The neighborhood was crawling with cats, partly because they were useful for controlling the mouse population around everyone's stables. Coyotes regularly ventured in from the hills and canyons to the east, in search of prey. Although cats were quick, coyotes were sometimes quicker, and at first Tracy thought a coyote had dug under the fence or leaped over it and had gotten hold of this unfortunate feline, which had probably been prowling for rodents.

But a coyote would have eaten the cat right on the spot, leaving little more than a bit of tail and a scrap or two of fur, for a coyote was a gourmand rather than gourmet and had a ravenous appetite. Or it would have carried the cat away for leisurely consumption elsewhere. Yet this cat had not looked even half-eaten, merely torn to pieces, as if something or someone had killed it merely for the sick pleasure of rending it apart . . .

Tracy shuddered.

And remembered the rumors about the zoo.

In Irvine Park, which was only a couple of miles away, someone apparently had killed several caged animals in the small petting zoo two nights ago. Drug-crazed vandals. Thrill killers. The story was just a hot rumor, and no one was able to confirm it, but there were indications that it was true. Some kids had bicycled out to the park yesterday after school, and they'd not seen any mangled carcasses, but they'd reported that there seemed to be fewer animals in the pens than usual. And the Shetland pony was definitely missing. Park employees had been uncommunicative when approached.

Tracy wondered if the same psychos were prowling Orange Park Acres, killing cats and other family pets, a possibility that was spooky and sickening. Suddenly, she realized that people deranged enough to slaughter cats for the sheer fun of it would also be sufficiently twisted to get a kick out of killing horses.

An almost crippling pang of fear flashed through her as she thought of

Goodheart out there in the stable all by himself. For a moment, she could not move.

Around her, the night seemed even quieter than it had been.

It *was* quieter. The crickets were no longer chirruping. The frogs had stopped croaking, too.

The galleon clouds seemed to have dropped anchor in the sky, and the night appeared to have frozen in the ice-pale glow of the moon.

Something moved in the shrubbery.

Most of the enormous lot was devoted to open expanses of lawn, but a score of trees stood in artfully placed groups—mostly Indian laurels and jacarandas, plus a couple of corals—and there were beds of azaleas, California lilac bushes, Cape honeysuckles.

Tracy distinctly heard shrubbery rustling as something pushed roughly and hurriedly through it. But when she switched on the flashlight and swept the beam around the nearest plantings, she could not see anything moving.

The night was silent again.

Hushed.

Expectant.

She considered returning to the house, where either she could wake her father to ask him to investigate, or she could go to bed and wait until morning to investigate the situation herself. But what if it *was* only a coyote in the shrubbery? In that case, she was in no danger. Though a hungry coyote would attack a very young child, it would run from anyone Tracy's size. Besides, she was too worried about her noble Goodheart to waste any more time; she had to be sure that the horse was all right.

Using the flashlight to avoid any more dead cats that might be strewn about, she headed toward the stable. She had taken only a few steps when she heard the rustling again and, worse, an eerie growling that was unlike the sound of any animal she'd ever heard before.

She began to turn, might have run for the house then, but in the stable Goodheart whinnied shrilly, as if in fear, and kicked at the board walls of his stall. She pictured a leering psycho going after Goodheart with hideous instruments of torture. Her concern for her own welfare was not half as strong as her fear that something terrible would happen to her beloved breeder of champions, so she sprinted to his rescue.

Poor Goodheart began kicking even more frantically. His hooves slammed repeatedly against the walls, drummed furiously, and the night seemed to echo with the thunder of an oncoming storm.

She was still about fifteen yards from the stable when she heard the strange guttural growling again and realized that something was coming after her, bearing down on her from behind. She skidded on the damp grass, whirled, and brought up her flashlight.

Rushing toward her was a creature that had surely escaped from Hell. It let out a shriek of madness and rage.

In spite of the flashlight, Tracy did not get a clear look at the attacker. The beam wavered, and the night grew darker as the moon slipped behind a cloud, and the hateful beast was moving fast, and she was too scared to understand what she was seeing. Nevertheless, she saw enough to know it was nothing she had ever seen before. She had an impression of a dark, misshapen head with asymmetrical depressions and bulges, enormous jaws full of sharp curved teeth, and amber eyes that blazed in the flashlight beam the way a dog's or a cat's eyes will glow in a car's headlights.

Tracy screamed.

The attacker shrieked again and leaped at her.

It hit Tracy hard enough to knock the breath clear out of her. The flash-light flew from her hand, tumbled across the lawn. She fell, and the creature came down on top of her, and they rolled over and over toward the stable. As they rolled, she flailed desperately at the thing with her small fists, and she felt its claws sinking into the flesh along her right side. Its gaping mouth was at her face, she felt its hot rank breath washing over her, smelled blood and decay and worse, and she sensed that it was going for her throat—she thought, *I'm dead, oh God, it's going to kill me, I'm dead, like the cat*—and she would have been dead in seconds, for sure, if Goodheart, less than fifteen feet away now, had not kicked out the latched half-door of his stall and bolted straight at them in panic.

The stallion screamed and reared up on its hind feet when it saw them, as if it would trample them underfoot.

Tracy's monstrous attacker shrieked again, though not in rage this time but in surprise and fear. It released her and flung itself to one side, out from under the horse.

Goodheart's hooves slammed into the earth inches from Tracy's head, and he reared up again, pawing at the air, screaming, and she knew that in his terror he might unwittingly trample her skull to mush. She threw herself out from under him, and also away from the amber-eyed beast, which had disappeared in the darkness on the other side of the stallion.

Still, Goodheart reared and screamed, and Tracy was screaming as well, and dogs were howling all over the neighborhood, and now lights appeared in the house, which gave her hope of survival. However, she sensed that the attacker wasn't ready to give up, that it was already circling the frantic stallion to make another try for her. She heard it snarling, spitting. She knew she would never reach the distant house before the thing dragged her down again, so she scram-bled toward the nearby stable, to one of the empty stalls. As she went, she heard herself chanting, "Jesus, oh Jesus, Jesus, Jesus, Jesus . . ."

The two halves of the Dutch-style stall door were bolted firmly together. Another bolt fastened the entire door to the frame. She unlatched that second bolt, pulled open the door, rushed into the straw-scented darkness, shut the door behind her, and held it with all the strength she possessed, for it could not be latched from inside.

An instant later, her assailant slammed into the other side of the door, trying to knock it open, but the frame prevented that. The door would only move outward, and Tracy hoped the amber-eyed creature was not smart enough to figure out how the door worked.

But it *was* smart enough—

(Dear Lord in Heaven, why wasn't it as dumb as it was ugly!)

—and after hitting the barrier only twice, it began to pull instead of push. The door was almost yanked out of Tracy's grasp.

She wanted to scream for help, but she needed every ounce of energy to dig in her heels and hold the stall door shut. It rattled and thumped against the frame as her demonic assailant wrestled with it. Fortunately, Goodheart was still letting loose shrill squeals and whinnies of terror, and the assailant was also shrieking—a sound that was strangely animal and human at the same time—so her father could have no doubt where the trouble was.

The door jerked open a few inches.

She yelped and pulled it shut.

Instantly the attacker yanked it partway open again and held it ajar, striving to pull the door wider even as she struggled to reclose it. She was losing. The door inched open. She saw the shadowy outline of the malformed face. The sharply pointed teeth gleamed dully. The amber eyes were faint now, barely visible. It hissed and snarled at her, and its pungent breath was stronger than the scent of straw.

Whimpering in terror and frustration, Tracy drew back on the door with all of her strength.

But it opened another inch.

And another.

Her heart was hammering loud enough to muffle the first shotgun blast. She didn't know what she'd heard until a second shot boomed through the night, and then she knew her father had grabbed his 12-gauge on the way out of the house.

The stall door slammed shut in front of her as the attacker, frightened by the gunfire, let go of it. Tracy held fast.

Then she thought that maybe, in all the confusion, Daddy might believe that Goodheart was to blame, that the poor horse had gone loco or something. From within the stall she cried out, "Don't shoot Goodheart! Don't shoot the horse!"·

No more shots rang out, and Tracy immediately felt stupid for thinking her father would blow away Goodheart. Daddy was a cautious man, especially with loaded guns, and unless he knew exactly what was happening, he wouldn't fire anything but warning shots. More likely than not, he'd just blasted some shrubbery to bits.

Goodheart was probably all right, and the amber-eyed assailant was surely hightailing it for the foothills or the canyons or back to wherever it had come from—

(What *was* that crazy damn thing?)

—and the ordeal was over, thank God.

She heard running footsteps, and her father called her name.

She pushed open the stall door and saw Daddy rushing toward her in a pair of blue pajama bottoms, barefoot, with the shotgun cradled in his arm. Mom was there too, in a short yellow nightie, hurrying behind Daddy with a flashlight.

Up near the top of the sloped yard stood Goodheart, the sire of future champions, his panic gone, unhurt.

Tears of relief sprang from Tracy at the sight of the unharmed stallion, and she stumbled out of the stall, wanting to go have a closer look at him. With her second or third step, a fiercely hot pain flamed along her entire right side, and she was suddenly dizzy. She staggered, fell, put one hand to her side, felt something wet, and realized that she was bleeding. She remembered the claws sinking into her just before Goodheart had burst from his stall, frightening off the assailant, and as if from a great distance she heard herself saying, "Good horse . . . what a good horse . . ."

Daddy dropped to his knees beside her. "Baby, what the hell happened, what's wrong?"

Her mother arrived, too.

Daddy saw the blood. "Call an ambulance!"

Her mother, not given to hesitation or hysterics in time of trouble, turned immediately and ran back toward the house.

Tracy was getting dizzier. Creeping in at the edges of her vision was a darkness that was not part of the night. She wasn't afraid of it. It seemed like a welcoming, healing darkness.

"Baby," her father said, putting a hand on her wounds.

Weakly, realizing she was slightly delirious and wondering what she was going to say, she said, "Remember when I was very little . . . just a little girl . . . and I thought some horrible thing . . . lived in my closet . . . at night?"

He frowned worriedly. "Honey, maybe you'd better be still, be quiet and still."

As she lost consciousness, Tracy heard herself say, with a seriousness that both amused and frightened her, "Well . . . I think maybe it was the boogey-man who used to live in the closet at the other house. I think maybe . . . he was real . . . and he's come back."

9

At four-twenty Wednesday morning, only hours after the attack at the Keeshan house, Lemuel Johnson reached Tracy Keeshan's hospital room at St. Joseph's in Orange. Quick as he was, however, Lem found Sheriff Walt Gaines had arrived ahead of him. Walt stood in the corridor, towering over a young doctor in surgical greens and a white lab coat; they seemed to be arguing quietly.

The NSA's Banodyne crisis team was monitoring all police agencies in the county, including the police department in the city of Orange, in whose juris-diction the Keeshan house fell. The team's night-shift leader had called Lem at home with news of this case, which fit the profile of expected Banodyne-related incidents.

"You relinquished jurisdiction," Lem pointedly reminded Walt when he joined the sheriff and doctor at the girl's closed door.

"Maybe this isn't part of the same case."

"You know it is."

"Well, that determination hasn't been made."

"It *was* made—back at the Keeshans' house when I talked with your men."

"Okay, so let's say I'm just here as an observer."

"My ass," Lem said.

"What about your ass?" Walt asked, smiling.

"It's got a pain in it, and the name of the pain is Walter."

"How interesting," Walt said. "You *name* your pains. Do you give names to toothaches and headaches as well?"

"I've got a headache right now, and its name is Walter, too."

"That's too confusing, my friend. Better call the headache Bert or Harry or something."

Lem almost laughed—he loved this guy—but he knew that, in spite of their friendship, Walt would use the laughter as a lever to pry himself back into the case. So Lem remained stone-faced, though Walt obviously knew that Lem *wanted* to laugh. The game was ridiculous, but it had to be played.

The doctor, Roger Selbok, resembled a young Rod Steiger. He frowned when they raised their voices, and he possessed some of the powerful presence of Steiger, too, because his frown was enough to chasten and quiet them.

Selbok said the girl had been put through tests, had been treated for her wounds, and had been given a painkiller. She was tired. He was just about to administer a sedative to guarantee her a restful sleep, and he did not think it was a good idea for policemen of any stripe to be asking her questions just now.

The whispering, the early-morning hush of the hospital, the scent of dis-infectants that filled the hall, and the sight of a white-robed nun gliding past was enough to make Lem uneasy. Suddenly, he was afraid that the girl was in far worse condition than he had been told, and he voiced his concern to Selbok.

"No, no. She's in pretty good shape," the doctor said. "I've sent her parents home, which I wouldn't have done if there was anything to worry about. The left side of her face is bruised, and the eye is blackened, but there's nothing serious in that. The wounds along her right side required thirty-two stitches, so we'll need to take precautions to keep the scarring to a minimum, but she's in no danger. She's had a bad scare. However, she's a bright kid, and self-reliant, so I don't think she'll suffer lasting psychological trauma. Still, I don't think it's a good idea to subject her to an interrogation tonight."

"Not an interrogation," Lem said. "Just a few questions."

"Five minutes," Walt said.

"Less," Lem said.

They kept at Selbok, and at last they wore him down. "Well . . . I guess you've got your job to do, and if you promise not to be too insistent with her—"

"I'll handle her as if she's made of soap bubbles," Lem said.

"*We'll* handle her as if she's made of soap bubbles," Walt said.

Selbok said, "Just tell me . . . what the devil happened to her?"

"She hasn't told you herself?" Lem asked.

"Well, she talks about being attacked by a coyote . . ."

Lem was surprised, and he saw Walt was startled, too. Maybe the case had nothing to do with Wes Dalberg's death and the dead animals at the Irvine Park petting zoo, after all.

"But," the physician said, "no coyote would attack a girl as big as Tracy. They're only a danger to very small children. And I don't believe her wounds are like those a coyote would inflict."

Walt said, "I understand her father drove the assailant off with a shotgun. Doesn't he know what attacked her?"

"No," Selbok said. "He couldn't see what was happening in the dark, so he only fired two warning shots. He says something dashed across the yard, leaped the fence, but he couldn't see any details. He says that Tracy first told him it was the boogeyman who used to live in her closet, but she was delirious then. She told *me* it was a coyote. So . . . do you know what's going on here? Can you tell me anything I need to know to treat the girl?"

"I can't," Walt said. "But Mr. Johnson here knows the whole situation."

"Thanks a lot," Lem said.

Walt just smiled.

To Selbok, Lem said, "I'm sorry, Doctor, but I'm not at liberty to discuss the case. Anyway, nothing I could tell you would alter the treatment you'd give Tracy Keeshan."

When Lem and Walt finally got into Tracy's hospital room, leaving Dr. Selbok in the corridor to time their visit, they found a pretty thirteen-year-old who was badly bruised and as pale as snow. She was in bed, the sheets pulled up to her shoulders. Though she had been given painkillers, she was alert, even edgy, and it was obvious why Selbok wanted to give her a sedative. She was trying not to show it, but she was scared.

"I wish you'd leave," Lem told Walt Gaines.

"If wishes were filet mignon, we'd always eat well at dinner," Walt said. "Hi, Tracy. I'm Sheriff Walt Gaines, and this is Lemuel Johnson. I'm about as nice as they come, though Lem here is a real stinker—everybody says so—but you don't have to worry because I'll keep him in line and make him be nice to you. Okay?"

Together, they coaxed Tracy into a conversation. They quickly discovered that she'd told Selbok she'd been attacked by a coyote because, though she knew it wasn't true, she didn't believe she could convince the physician—or anyone else—of the truth of what she'd seen. "I was afraid they'd think I'd been hit real hard on the head, had my brains scrambled," she said, "and then they'd keep me here a lot longer."

Sitting on the edge of the girl's bed, Lem said, "Tracy, you don't have to worry that I'll think you're scrambled. I believe I know what you saw, and all I want from you is confirmation."

She stared at him disbelievingly.

Walt stood at the foot of her bed, smiling down at her as if he were a big, affectionate teddy bear come to life. He said, "Before you passed out, you told your dad you'd been attacked by the boogeyman who used to live in your closet."

"It was sure ugly enough," the girl said quietly. "But that's not what it was, I guess."

"Tell me," Lem said.

She stared at Walt, at Lem, then sighed. "You tell me what you think I should've seen, and if you're close, I'll tell you what I can remember. But I'm not going to start it 'cause I know you'll think I'm looney tunes."

Lem regarded Walt with unconcealed frustration, realizing there was no way to avoid divulging some of the facts of the case.

Walt grinned.

To the girl, Lem said, "Yellow eyes."

She gasped and went rigid. "Yes! You do know, don't you? You know what was out there." She started to sit up, winced in pain as she pulled the stitches in her wound, and slumped back against the bed. "What was it, what *was* it?"

"Tracy," Lem said, "I can't tell you what it was. I've signed a secrecy oath. If I violated it, I could be put in jail, but more important . . . I wouldn't have much respect for myself."

She frowned, finally nodded. "I guess I can understand that."

"Good. Now tell me everything you can about your assailant."

As it turned out, she had not seen much because the night was dark and her flashlight had illuminated The Outsider for only an instant. "Pretty big for an animal . . . maybe as big as me. The yellow eyes." She shuddered. "And its face was . . . strange."

"In what way?"

"Lumpy . . . deformed," the girl said. Though she had been very pale at the start, she grew paler now, and fine beads of sweat appeared along her hairline, dampening her brow.

Walt was leaning on the footrail of the bed, straining forward, intensely interested, not wanting to miss a word.

A sudden Santa Ana wind buffeted the building, startling the girl. She looked fearfully at the rattling window, where the wind moaned, as if she was afraid something would come smashing through the glass.

Which was, Lem reminded himself, exactly how The Outsider had gotten to Wes Dalberg.

The girl swallowed hard. "Its mouth was huge . . . and the teeth . . ."

She could not stop shaking, and Lem put a reassuring hand on her shoulder. "It's okay, honey. It's over now. It's all behind you."

After a pause to regain control of herself, but still shivering, Tracy said, "I think it was kind of hairy . . . or furry . . . I'm not sure, but it was very strong."

"What kind of animal did it resemble?" Lem asked.

She shook her head. "It wasn't like anything else."

"But if you had to say it was like some other animal, would you say it was more like a cougar than anything else?"

"No. Not a cougar."

"Like a dog?"

She hesitated. "Maybe . . . a little bit like a dog."

"Maybe a little bit like a bear, too?"

"No."

"Like a panther?"

"No. Not like any cat."

"Like a monkey?"

She hesitated again, frowned, thinking, "I don't know why . . . but, yeah, maybe a little like a monkey. Except, no dog and no monkey has *teeth* like that."

The door opened from the hall, and Dr. Selbok appeared. "You're already past five minutes."

Walt started to wave the doctor out.

Lem said, "No, it's okay. We're finished. Half a minute yet."

"I'm counting the seconds," Selbok said, retreating.

To the girl Lem said, "Can I rely on you?"

She matched his gaze and said, "To keep quiet?"

Lem nodded.

She said, "Yeah. I sure don't *want* to tell anybody. My folks think I'm mature for my age. Mentally and emotionally mature, I mean. But if I start telling wild stories about . . . about monsters, they're going to think I'm not so mature after all, and maybe they'll figure I'm not responsible enough to take care of the horses, and so maybe they'll slow down the breeding plans. I won't risk that, Mr. Johnson. No, sir. So as far as I'm concerned, it was a loco coyote. But . . ."

"Yes?"

"Can you tell me . . . is there any chance it'll come back?"

"I don't think so. But it would be wise, for a while, not to go out to the stable at night. All right?"

"All right," she said. Judging by her haunted expression, she would remain indoors after dusk for weeks to come.

They left the room, thanked Dr. Selbok for his cooperation, and went down to the hospital's parking garage. Dawn had not yet arrived, and the cavernous concrete structure was empty, desolate. Their footsteps echoed hollowly off the walls.

Their cars were on the same floor, and Walt accompanied Lem to the green, unmarked NSA sedan. As Lem put the key in the door to unlock it, Walt looked around to be sure they were alone, then said, "Tell me."

"Can't."

"I'll find out."

"You're off the case."

"So take me to court. Get a bench warrant."

"I might."

"For endangering the national security."

"It would be a fair charge."

"Throw my ass in jail."

"I might," Lem said, though he knew he would not.

Curiously, though Walt's doggedness was frustrating and more than a little irritating, it was also pleasing to Lem. He had few friends, of whom Walt was the most important, and he liked to think the reason he had few friends was because he was selective, with high standards. If Walt had backed off entirely, if he had been completely cowed by federal authority, if he'd been able to turn off his curiosity as easily as turning off a light switch, he would have been slightly tarnished and diminished in Lem's eyes.

"What reminds you of a dog *and* an ape and has yellow eyes?" Walt asked. "Aside from your mama, that is."

"You leave my mama out of this, honky," Lem said. Smiling in spite of himself, he got into the car.

Walt held the door open and leaned down to look in at him. "What in the name of God escaped from Banodyne?"

"I told you this has nothing to do with Banodyne."

"And the fire they had at the labs the next day . . . did they set it themselves to destroy the evidence of what they'd been up to?"

"Don't be ridiculous," Lem said wearily, thrusting the key into the ignition. "Evidence could be destroyed in a more efficient and less drastic manner. *If* there was evidence to destroy. Which there isn't. Because Banodyne has nothing to do with this."

Lem started the car, but Walt would not give up. He held the door open and leaned in even closer to be heard above the rumble of the engine: "Genetic engineering. That's what they're involved with at Banodyne. Tinkering with bacteria and virus to make new bugs that do good deeds like manufacture insulin or eat oil slicks. And they tinker with the genes of plants as well, I guess, to produce corn that grows in acidic soil or wheat that thrives with half the usual water. We always think of gene tinkering as being done on a small scale—plants and germs. But could they screw around with an animal's genes so it produced bizarre offspring, a whole new species? Is that what they've done, and is that what's escaped from Banodyne?"

Lem shook his head exasperatedly. "Walt, I'm not an expert on recombinant DNA, but I don't think the science is nearly sophisticated enough to work with any degree of confidence on that sort of thing. And what would be the point, anyway? Okay, just supposing they could make a weird new animal by fiddling with the genetic structure of an existing species—what *use* would there be for it? I mean, aside from exhibition in a carnival freak show?"

Walt's eyes narrowed. "I don't know. You tell me."

"Listen, research money is always damn tight, and there's fierce competition for every major and minor grant, so no one's going to be able to afford to experiment with something that has no *use*. Get me? Now, because I'm involved here, you know this has to be a matter of national defense, which would mean Banodyne was squandering Pentagon money to make a carnival freak."

"The words 'squander' and 'Pentagon' have sometimes been used in the same sentence," Walt said dryly.

"Be real, Walt. It's one thing for the Pentagon to let some of its contractors waste money in the production of a needed weapons system. But it's altogether another thing for them to knowingly hand out funds for experiments with no defense potential. The system is sometimes inefficient, sometimes even corrupt, but it's never outright stupid. Anyway, I'll say it one more time: This entire conversation is pointless because *this has nothing to do with Banodyne*."

Walt stared in at him for a long moment, then sighed. "Jesus, Lem, you're good. I know you've got to be lying to me, but I half-think you're telling the truth."

"I am telling the truth."

"You're good. So tell me . . . what about Weatherby, Yarbeck, and the others? Got their killer yet?"

"No." In fact, the man Lem had put in charge of the case had reported that it appeared as if the Soviets had used a killer outside of their own agencies and perhaps outside of the political world entirely. The investigation seemed stymied. But all he said to Walt was, "No."

Walt started to straighten up and close the car door, then leaned down and in again. "One more thing. You notice it seems to have a meaningful destination?"

"What're you talking about?"

"It's been moving steadily north or north-northwest ever since it broke out of Banodyne," Walt said.

"It didn't break out of Banodyne, damn it."

"From Banodyne to Holy Jim Canyon, from there to Irvine Park, and from there to the Keeshan house tonight. Steadily north or north-northwest. I suppose you know what that might mean, where it might be headed, but of course I daren't ask you about it or you'll heave me straight into prison and let me rot there."

"I'm telling you the truth about Banodyne."

"So you say."

"You're impossible, Walt."

"So you say."

"So *everyone* says. Now will you let me go home? I'm beat."

Smiling, Walt closed the door at last.

Lem drove out of the hospital garage to Main Street, then to the freeway, heading home toward Placentia. He hoped to make it back into bed no later than dawn.

As he piloted the NSA sedan through streets as empty as midocean sealanes, he thought about The Outsider heading northward. He'd noticed the same thing himself. And he was convinced that he knew what it was seeking even if he did not know where, precisely, it was going. From the first, the dog and The Outsider had possessed a special awareness of each other, an uncanny instinctual awareness of each other's moods and activities even when they were not in the same room. Davis Weatherby had suggested, more than half seriously, that there was something telepathic about the relationship of those two creatures. Now, The Outsider was very likely still in tune with the dog and, by some sixth sense, was following it.

For the dog's sake, Lem hoped to God that was not the case.

It had been evident in the lab that the dog had always feared The Outsider, and with good reason. The two were the yin and yang of the Francis Project, the success and the failure, the good and the bad. As wonderful, right, and good as the dog was—well, The Outsider was every bit as hideous, wrong, and evil. And the researchers had seen that The Outsider did not fear the dog but *hated* it with a passion that no one had been able to understand. Now that both were free, The Outsider might single-mindedly pursue the dog, for it had never wanted anything more than to tear the retriever limb from limb.

Lem realized that, in his anxiety, he had put his foot down too hard on the accelerator. The car was rocketing along the freeway. He eased back on the pedal.

Wherever the dog was, with whomever it had found shelter, it was in jeopardy. And those who had given it shelter were also in grave danger.

CHAPTER 6

1

THROUGH THE LAST WEEK of May and the first week of June, Nora and Travis—and Einstein—were together nearly every day.

Initially, she had worried that Travis was somehow dangerous, not as dangerous as Art Streck but still to be feared; however, she'd soon gotten through that spell of paranoia. Now she laughed at herself when she remembered how wary of him she had been. He was sweet and kind, precisely the sort of man who, according to her Aunt Violet, did not exist anywhere in the world.

Once Nora's paranoia had been overcome, she'd then been convinced that the only reason Travis continued to see her was because he pitied her. Being the compassionate man he was, he would not be able to turn his back on anyone in desperate need or trouble. Most people, meeting Nora, would not think of her as desperate—perhaps strange and shy and pathetic, but not desperate. Yet she was—or had been—desperately unable to cope with the world beyond her own four walls, desperately afraid of the future, and desperately lonely. Travis, being every bit as perceptive as he was kind, saw her desperation and responded to it. Gradually, as May faded into June and the days grew hotter under the summer sun, she dared to consider the possibility that he was helping her not because he pitied her but because he really liked her.

But she couldn't understand what a man like him would see in a woman like her. She seemed to have nothing whatsoever to offer.

All right, yes, she had a self-image problem. Maybe she was not really as hopelessly drab and dull as she felt. Still, Travis clearly deserved—and could surely have—better female companionship than she could provide.

She decided not to question his interest. The thing to do was just relax and enjoy it.

Because Travis had sold his real-estate business after the death of his wife and was essentially retired, and because Nora had no job either, they were free to be together most of the day if they wanted—and they were. They went to galleries, haunted bookstores, took long walks, went on longer drives into the picturesque Santa Ynez Valley or up along the gorgeous Pacific coast.

Twice they set out early in the morning for Los Angeles and spent a long day there, and Nora was as overwhelmed by the sheer size of the city as she was by the activities they pursued: a movie-studio tour, a visit to the zoo, and a matinee performance of a hit musical.

One day Travis talked her into having her hair cut and styled. He took her to a beauty parlor that his late wife had frequented, and Nora was so nervous that she stuttered when she spoke to the beautician, a perky blonde named Melanie. Violet always cut Nora's hair at home, and after Violet's death, Nora cut it herself. Being tended by a beautician was a new experience, as unnerving as eating in a restaurant for the first time. Melanie did something she called "feathering," and cut off a lot of Nora's hair while somehow still leaving it full. They did not allow Nora to watch in the mirror, did not let her get a glimpse of herself until she was blown dry and combed out. Then they spun her around in the chair and confronted her with herself, and when she saw her reflection she was stunned.

"You look terrific," Travis said.

"It's a total transformation," Melanie said.

"Terrific," Travis said.

"You've got such a pretty face, great bone structure," Melanie said, "but all that straight, long hair made your features look elongated and pointy. *This* frames your face to its best advantage."

Even Einstein seemed to like the change in her. When they left the beauty shop, the dog was waiting for them where they had left him tethered to a parking meter. He did a canine double-take when he saw Nora, jumped up with his front paws on her, and sniffed her face and hair, whining happily and wagging his tail.

She hated the new look. When they had turned her to the mirror, she'd seen a pathetic old maid trying to pass for a pretty, vivacious young thing. The styled hair was simply not *her*. It only emphasized that she was basically a plain, drab woman. She would never be sexy, charming, with-it, or any of the other things that the new hairstyle tried to say she was. It was rather like fastening a brightly colored feather duster to the back end of a turkey and attempting to pass it off as a peacock.

Because she did not want to hurt Travis's feelings, she pretended to like what had been done to her. But that night she washed her hair and brushed it dry, pulling on it until all the so-called style had been tugged from it. Because of the feathering, it did not hang as straight and lank as it had previously, but she did the best with it that she could.

The next day, when Travis picked her up for lunch, he was clearly startled to find that she had reverted to her previous look. However, he said nothing about it, asked no questions. She was so embarrassed and afraid of having hurt his feelings that, for the first couple of hours, she was not able to meet his eyes for more than a second or two at a time.

In spite of her repeated and increasingly vigorous demurrals, Travis insisted on taking her shopping for a new dress, a bright and summery frock that she could wear to dinner at Talk of the Town, a dressy restaurant on West Gutierrez, where he said you could sometimes see some of the movie stars who lived in the area, members of a film colony second only to that in Beverly Hills—Bel Air. They went to an expensive store, where she tried on a score of dresses, modeling each for Travis's reaction, blushing and *mortified*. The saleswoman seemed genuinely approving of the way everything looked on Nora, and she kept telling Nora that her figure was perfect, but Nora couldn't shake the feeling that the woman was laughing at her.

The dress Travis liked best was from the Diane Freis collection. Nora couldn't deny that it was lovely: predominantly red and gold, though with an almost riotous background of other colors somehow more right in combination than they should have been (which apparently was a trait of Freis's designs). It was exceedingly feminine. On a beautiful woman it would have been a knockout. But it just was not *her*. Dark colors, shapeless cuts, simple fabrics, no ornamentation whatsoever—that was her style. She tried to tell him what was best for her, explained that she could never wear such a dress as this, but he said, "You look gorgeous in it, really, you look gorgeous."

She let him buy it. Dear God, she really did. She knew it was a big mistake, was wrong, and that she would never wear it. As the dress was being wrapped, Nora wondered why she had acquiesced, and she realized that, in spite of being mortified, she was flattered to have a man buying clothes for her, to have a man take an interest in her appearance. She never dreamed such a thing would happen to her, and she was overwhelmed.

She couldn't stop blushing. Her heart pounded. She felt dizzy, but it was a good dizziness.

Then, as they were leaving the store, she learned that he had paid five hundred dollars for the dress. Five hundred dollars! She had intended to hang it in the closet and look at it a lot, use it as a starting point for pleasant daydreams, which was all fine and dandy if it had cost fifty dollars, but for five hundred she would have to wear it even if it made her feel ridiculous, even if she did look like a poseur, a scrubwoman pretending to be a princess.

The following evening, during the two hours before Travis was to pick her up and escort her to Talk of the Town, she put the dress on and took it off a half dozen times. She repeatedly sorted through the contents of her closet, searching frantically for something else to wear, something more sensible, but she didn't have anything because she had never before needed clothes for a dressy restaurant.

Scowling at herself in the bathroom mirror, she said, "You look like Dustin Hoffman in *Tootsie*."

She suddenly laughed because she knew she was being too hard on herself. But she couldn't go easier on herself because that was how she felt: like a guy in drag. In this case, feelings were more important than facts, so her laughter quickly soured.

She broke down and cried twice, and considered calling him to cancel their date. But she wanted more than anything to see him, no matter how horribly humiliating the evening was going to be. She used Murine to get the red out of her eyes, and she tried the dress on again—and took it off.

When he arrived at a few minutes past seven, he looked handsome in a dark suit.

Nora was wearing a shapeless blue shift with dark-blue shoes.

He said, "I'll wait."

She said, "Huh? For what?"

"You know," he said, meaning, *Go change*.

The words came out in a nervous rush, and her excuse was limp: "Travis, I'm sorry, this is terrible, I'm so sorry, but I spilled coffee all over the dress."

"I'll wait in here," he said, walking to the living room archway.

She said, "A whole pot of coffee."

"Better hurry. Our reservation is for seven-thirty."

Steeling herself for the amused whispers if not outright laughter of everyone who saw her, telling herself that Travis's opinion was the only one that mattered, she changed into the Diane Freis dress.

She wished she had not undone the hairstyle that Melanie had given her a couple of days ago. Maybe that would help.

No, it would probably just make her look more ludicrous.

When she came downstairs again, Travis smiled at her and said, "You're lovely."

She didn't know whether the food at Talk of the Town was as good as its reputation or not. She tasted nothing. Later, she could not clearly remember the decor of the place, either, though the faces of the other customers—including the actor Gene Hackman—were burned into her memory because she was certain that, all evening, they were staring at her with amazement and disdain.

In the middle of dinner, evidently well aware of her discomfort, Travis put down his wineglass and leaned toward her and said quietly, "You really *do* look lovely, Nora, no matter what you think. And if you had the experience to be aware of such things, you'd realize that most of the men in the room are attracted to you."

But she knew the truth, and she could face it. If men really were staring at her, it was not because she was pretty. People could be expected to stare at a turkey with a feather duster trying to pass itself off as a peacock.

"Without a trace of makeup," he said, "you look better than any woman in the room."

No makeup. That was another reason they were staring at her. When a woman put on a five hundred dollar dress to be taken to an expensive restaurant, she made herself look as good as possible with lipstick, eyeliner, makeup, skin blush, and God knew what else. But Nora had never even *thought* about makeup.

The chocolate mousse dessert, though surely delicious, tasted like library paste to her and repeatedly stuck in her throat.

She and Travis had talked for long hours during the past couple of weeks, and they had found it surprisingly easy to reveal intimate feelings and thoughts to each other. She had learned why he was alone in spite of his good looks and relative wealth, and he had learned why she harbored a low opinion of herself. So when she could not choke down any more of the mousse, when she implored Travis to take her home right away, he said softly, "If there's any justice, Violet Devon is sweating in Hell tonight."

Shocked, Nora said, "Oh, no. She wasn't *that* bad."

All the way home, he was silent, brooding.

When he left her at her door, he insisted she set up a meeting with Garrison Dilworth, who had been her aunt's attorney and now took care of Nora's minor legal business. "From what you've told me," Travis said, "Dilworth knew your aunt better than anyone, so I'd bet dollars to doughnuts he can tell you things about her that will break this goddamn stranglehold she has on you even from the grave."

Nora said, "But there're no great dark secrets about Aunt Violet. She was what she appeared to be. She was a very simple woman, really. A sort of sad woman."

"Sad my ass," Travis said.

He persisted until she agreed to make the appointment with Garrison Dilworth.

Later, upstairs in her bedroom, when she tried to take off the Diane Freis, she discovered she didn't want to undress. All evening, she had been impatient to get out of that costume, for it *had* seemed like a costume on her. But now, in retrospect, the evening possessed a warm glow, and she wanted to prolong that glow. Like a sentimental high school girl, she slept in the five-hundred-dollar dress.

Garrison Dilworth's office had been carefully decorated to convey respectability, stability, and reliability. Beautifully detailed oak paneling. Heavy royal-blue drapes hung from brass rods. Shelves full of leather-bound law books. A massive oak desk.

The attorney himself was an intriguing cross between a personification of Dignity and Probity—and Santa Claus. Tall, rather portly, with thick silver hair, past seventy but still working a full week, Garrison favored three-piece suits and subdued ties. In spite of his many years as a Californian, his deep and smooth and cultured voice clearly marked him as a product of the upper-class Eastern circles in which he had been born, raised, and educated. But there was also a decidedly merry twinkle in his eyes, and his smile was quick, warm, altogether Santalike.

He did not distance himself by staying behind his desk, but sat with Nora and Travis in comfortable armchairs around a coffee table on which stood a large Waterford bowl. "I don't know what you came here expecting to learn.

There are no secrets about your aunt. No great dark revelations that will change your life—"

"I knew as much," Nora said. "I'm sorry we've bothered you."

"Wait," Travis said. "Let Mr. Dilworth finish."

The attorney said, "Violet Devon was my client, and an attorney has a responsibility to protect clients' confidences even after their death. At least that's my view, though some in the profession might not feel such a lasting obligation. Of course, as I'm speaking to Violet's closest living relative and heir, I suppose there's little I would choose not to divulge—if in fact there *were* any secrets to reveal. And I certainly see no moral constraint against my expressing an honest opinion of your aunt. Even attorneys, priests, and doctors are allowed to have opinions of people." He took a deep breath and frowned. "I never liked her. I thought she was a narrow-minded, totally self-involved woman who was at least slightly . . . well, mentally unstable. And the way she raised you was criminal, Nora. Not abusive in any legal sense that would interest the authorities, but criminal nonetheless. And cruel."

For as long as Nora could recall, a large knot had seemed to be tied tight inside of her, pinching vital organs and vessels, leaving her tense, restricting the flow of blood and making it necessary for her to live with all her senses damped down, forcing her to struggle along as if she were a machine getting insufficient power. Suddenly, Garrison Dilworth's words untied that knot, and a full, unrestricted current of life rushed through her for the first time.

She had known what Violet Devon had done to her, but knowing was not enough to help her overcome that grim upbringing. She needed to hear her aunt condemned by someone else. Travis had already denounced Violet, and Nora had felt some small release at hearing what he said. But that had not been enough to free her because Travis hadn't known Violet and, therefore, spoke without complete authority. Garrison knew Violet well, however, and his words released Nora from bondage.

She was trembling violently, and tears were trickling down her face, but she was unaware of both conditions until Travis reached out from his chair to put one hand consolingly upon her shoulder. She fumbled in her purse for a handkerchief. "I'm sorry."

"Dear lady," Garrison said, "don't apologize for breaking through that iron shell you've been in all your life. This is the first time I've seen you show a strong emotion, the first time I've seen you in any condition other than extreme shyness, and it's lovely to behold." Turning to Travis, giving Nora time to blot her eyes, he said, "What more *did* you hope to hear me say?"

"There are some things Nora doesn't know, things she ought to know and that I don't believe would violate even your strict code of client privilege if you were to divulge them."

"Such as?"

Travis said, "Violet Devon never worked yet lived reasonably well, never in want, and she left enough funds to keep Nora pretty much for the rest of her life, at least as long as Nora stays in that house and lives like a recluse. Where did her money come from?"

"Come from?" Garrison sounded surprised. "Nora knows that, surely."

"But she doesn't," Travis said.

Nora looked up and saw Garrison Dilworth staring at her in astonishment. He blinked and said, "Violet's husband was moderately well-to-do. He died quite young, and she inherited everything."

Nora gaped at him and could barely find sufficient breath to speak. "*Husband?*"

"George Olmstead," the attorney said.

"I've never heard that name."

Garrison blinked rapidly again, as if sand had blown in his face. "She never mentioned a husband?"

"Never."

"But didn't a neighbor ever mention—"

"We had nothing to do with neighbors," Nora said. "Violet didn't approve of them."

"And in fact," Garrison said, "now that I think about it, there might have been new neighbors on both sides by the time you came to live with Violet."

Nora blew her nose and put away her handkerchief. She was still trembling. Her sudden sense of release from bondage had generated powerful emotions, but now they subsided somewhat to make room for curiosity.

"All right?" Travis asked.

She nodded, then stared hard at him and said, "You knew, didn't you? About the husband, I mean. That's why you brought me here."

"I suspected," Travis said. "If she'd inherited everything from her parents, she would have mentioned it. The fact that she didn't talk about where the money came from . . . well, it seemed to me to leave only one possibility—a husband, and very likely a husband with whom she'd had troubles. Which made even more sense when you think about how down she was on people in general and on men in particular."

The attorney was so dismayed and agitated that he could not sit still. He got up and paced past an enormous antique globe that was lighted from within and seemed made of parchment. "I'm flabbergasted. So you never really understood *why* she was bitterly misanthropic, why she suspected everyone of having her worst interests at heart?"

"No," Nora said. "I didn't need to know why, I guess. It was just the way she was."

Still pacing, Garrison said, "Yes. That's true. I'm convinced she was a borderline paranoid even in her youth. And then, when she discovered that George had betrayed her with other women, the switch clicked all the way over in her. She got much worse after that."

Travis said, "Why did Violet still use her maiden name, Devon, if she'd been married to Olmstead?"

"She didn't want his name any more. Loathed the name. She sent him packing, very nearly drove him out of the house with a stick! She was about to divorce him when he died," Garrison said. "She had learned about his affairs with other women, as I've said. She was furious. Ashamed and enraged. I must say . . . I can't entirely blame poor George because I don't think he found much love and affection at home. He knew the marriage was a mistake within a month of the wedding."

Garrison paused beside the globe, one hand resting lightly on top of the world, staring far into the past. Ordinarily, he did not look his age. Now, as he gazed back across the years, the lines in his face seemed to deepen, and his blue eyes appeared faded. After a moment he shook his head and continued:

"Anyway, those were different times, when a woman betrayed by a husband was an object of pity, ridicule. But even for those days, I thought Violet's reaction was overblown. She burned all his clothes and changed the locks on the house . . . she even killed a dog, a spaniel, of which he was fond. Poisoned it. And mailed it to him in a box."

"Dear God," Travis said.

Garrison said, "Violet took back her maiden name because she didn't want his any more. The thought of carrying George Olmstead's name through life repelled her, she said, even though he was dead. She was an unforgiving woman."

"Yes," Nora agreed.

His face pinched with distaste at the memory, and Garrison said, "When George was killed, she didn't bother to conceal her pleasure."

"Killed?" Nora half-expected to hear that Violet had murdered George Olmstead yet had somehow escaped prosecution.

"It was an auto accident, forty years ago," Garrison said. "He lost control on the Coast Highway driving home from Los Angeles, went over the edge where, in those days, there wasn't a guardrail. The embankment was sixty or eighty feet high, very steep, and George's car—a large black Packard—rolled over several times on the way down to the rocks below. Violet inherited everything because, though she had initiated divorce proceedings against him, George had not gotten around to changing his will."

Travis said, "So George Olmstead not only betrayed Violet but, in dying, left her with no target for her anger. So she directed that anger at the world in general."

"And at me in particular," Nora said.

That same afternoon, Nora told Travis about her painting. She had not mentioned her artistic pursuits before, and he had not been in her bedroom to see her easel, supply cabinet, and drawing board. She was not sure why she had kept this aspect of her life a secret from him. She had mentioned an interest in art, which was why they had gone to galleries and museums, but perhaps she had never spoken of her own work because she was afraid that, on seeing her canvases, he would be unimpressed.

What if he felt that she had no real talent?

Aside from the escape provided by books, the thing that kept Nora going through many grim, lonely years was her painting. She believed that she was good, perhaps very good, though she was too shy and too vulnerable to voice that conviction to anyone. What if she was wrong? What if she had no talent and had been merely filling time? Her art was the primary medium by which she defined herself. She had little else with which to sustain even her thin and shaky self-image, so she desperately needed to believe in her talent. Travis's opinion meant more to her than she could say, and if his reaction to her painting was negative, she would be devastated.

But after leaving Garrison Dilworth's office, Nora knew that the time had come to take the risk. The truth about Violet Devon had been a key that had unlocked Nora's emotional prison. She would need a long time to move from her cell, down the long hall to the outside world, but the journey would inevitably continue. Therefore, she would have to open herself to all the experiences that her new life provided, including the awful possibility of rejection and severe disappointment. Without risk, there was no hope of gain.

Back at the house, she considered taking Travis upstairs to have a look at a half dozen of her most recent paintings. But the idea of having a man in her bedroom, even with the most innocent intentions, was too unsettling. Garrison Dilworth's revelations freed her, yes, and her world was rapidly broadening, but she was not yet *that* free. Instead, she insisted that Travis and Einstein sit on one of the big sofas in the furniture-stuffed living room, where she would bring some of her canvases for viewing. She turned on all the lights, drew the drapes away from the windows, and said, "I'll be right back."

But upstairs she dithered over the ten paintings in her bedroom, unable to decide which two she should take to him first. Finally she settled on four pieces, though it was a bit awkward carrying that many at once. Halfway down the stairs, she halted, trembling, and decided to take the paintings back and select others. But she retreated only four steps before she realized that she could spend the entire day in vacillation. Reminding herself that nothing could be gained without risk, she took a deep breath and went quickly downstairs with the four paintings that she had originally chosen.

Travis liked them. More than liked them. He raved about them. "My God, Nora, this is no hobby painting. This is the real thing. This is *art.*"

She propped the paintings on four chairs, and he was not content to study them from the sofa. He got up for a closer look, moved from one canvas to another and back again.

"You're a superb photorealist," he said. "Okay, so I'm no art critic, but by God you're as skilled as Wyeth. But this other thing . . . this eerie quality in two of these . . ."

His compliments had left her blushing furiously, and she had to swallow hard to find her voice. "A touch of surrealism."

She had brought two landscapes and two still lifes. One of each was, indeed, strictly a photorealist work. But the other two were photorealism with a strong element of surrealism. In the still life, for example, several water glasses, a pitcher, spoons, and a sliced lemon were on a table, portrayed in excruciating detail, and at first glance the scene looked very realistic; but at second glance you noticed that one of the glasses was melting into the surface on which it stood, and that one slice of lemon was penetrating the side of a glass as if the glass had been formed around it.

"They're brilliant, they really are," he said. "Do you have others?"

Did she have *others*!

She made two additional trips to her bedroom, returning with six more paintings.

With each new canvas, Travis's excitement grew. His delight and enthusiasm were genuine, too. Initially she thought that he might be humoring her, but soon she was certain he was not disguising his true reaction.

Moving from canvas to canvas and back again, he said, "Your sense of color is excellent."

Einstein accompanied Travis around the room, adding a soft woof after each of his master's statements and vigorously wagging his tail, as if expressing agreement with the assessment.

"There's such mood in these pieces," Travis said.

"Woof."

"Your control of the medium is astonishing. I've no sense that I'm looking at thousands of brush strokes. Instead, it seems as if the picture just *appeared* on the canvas magically."

"Woof."

"It's hard to believe you've had no formal schooling."

"Woof."

"Nora, these are easily good enough to sell. Any gallery would take these in a minute."

"Woof."

"You could not only make a living at this . . . I think you could build one hell of a reputation."

Because she had not dared to admit how seriously she had always taken her work, Nora had often painted one picture over another, using a canvas again and again. As a consequence, many of her pieces were gone forever. But in the attic she had stored more than eighty of her best paintings. Now, because Travis insisted, they brought down more than a score of those wrapped canvases, tore off the brown paper, and propped them on the living-room furniture. For the first time in Nora's memory, that dark chamber looked bright and welcoming.

"Any gallery would be delighted to do a show of these," Travis said. "In fact, tomorrow, let's load some of them into the truck and take them around to a few galleries, hear what they say."

"Oh no, no."

"I promise you, Nora, you won't be disappointed."

She was suddenly in the clutches of anxiety. Although thrilled by the prospect of a career in art, she was also frightened by the big step she would be taking. Like walking off the edge of a cliff.

She said, "Not yet. In a week . . . or a month . . . we'll load them in the truck and take them to a gallery. But not yet, Travis. I just can't . . . I can't handle it yet."

He grinned at her. "Sensory overload again?"

Einstein came to her and rubbed against her leg, looking up with a sweet expression that made Nora smile.

Scratching behind the dog's ears, she said, "So much has happened so fast. I can't absorb it all. I keep having to fight off attacks of dizziness. I feel a little bit as if I'm on a carousel that's whirling around faster and faster, out of control."

What she said was true, to an extent, but that was not the only reason she wished to delay going public with her art. She also wanted to move slowly in order to have time to savor every glorious development. If she rushed into things, the transformation from reclusive spinster to a full-fledged participant in life would go too fast, and later it would be just a blur. She wanted to enjoy every moment of her metamorphosis.

As if she were an invalid who had been confined since birth to a single dark room full of life-support equipment, and as if she had just been miraculously cured, Nora Devon was coming cautiously out into a new world.

Travis was not solely responsible for Nora's emergence from reclusion. Einstein had an equally large role in her transformation.

The retriever had obviously decided that Nora could be trusted with the secret of his extraordinary intelligence. After the *Modern Bride* and baby business in Solvang, the dog gave her glimpse after glimpse of his undoglike mind at work.

Taking his lead from Einstein, Travis told Nora how he had found the retriever in the woods and how something strange—and never seen—had been pursuing it. He recounted all the amazing things the dog had done since then. He also told her of Einstein's occasional bouts with anxiety in the heart of the night, when he sometimes stood at a window and stared out at the darkness as if he believed the unknown creature in the woods would find him.

They sat for hours one evening in Nora's kitchen, drinking pots of coffee and eating homemade pineapple cake and discussing explanations for the dog's uncanny intelligence. When not cadging bits of cake, Einstein listened to them with interest, as if he understood what they were saying about him, and sometimes he whined and paced impatiently, as if frustrated that his canine vocal apparatus did not permit him to speak. But they were mostly spinning their wheels because they had no explanations *worth* discussing.

"I believe he could tell us where he comes from, why he's so damn different from other dogs," Nora said.

Einstein busily swept the air with his tail.

"Oh, I'm sure of it," Travis said. "He's got a humanlike self-awareness. He *knows* he's different, and I suspect he knows why, and I think he'd like to tell us about it if he could only find a way."

The retriever barked once, ran to the far end of the kitchen, ran back, looked up at them, did a frantic little dance of purely human frustration, and finally slumped on the floor with his head on his paws, alternately chuffing and whining softly.

Nora was most intrigued by the story of the night that the dog had gotten excited over Travis's book collection. "He recognizes that books are a means of communication," she said. "And maybe he senses there's a way to use books to bridge the communications gap between him and us."

"How?" Travis asked as he lifted another forkful of pineapple cake.

Nora shrugged. "I don't know. But maybe the problem was that your books weren't the right kind. Novels, you said?"

"Yeah. Fiction."

She said, "Maybe what we need is books with pictures, images he can react to. Maybe if we gathered up a lot of picture books of all kinds, and magazines with pictures, and maybe if we spread them out on the floor and *worked* with Einstein, maybe we'd find some way to communicate with him."

The retriever leaped to his feet and padded directly to Nora. From the expression on his face and from the intent look in his eyes, Nora knew that her proposal was a good one. Tomorrow, she would collect dozens of books and magazines, and put the scheme into operation.

"It's going to take a lot of patience," Travis warned her.

"I've got oceans of patience."

"You may think you have, but sometimes dealing with Einstein gives a whole new meaning to the word."

Turning to Travis, the dog blew air out of his nostrils.

The prospects for more direct communication looked bleak during the first few sessions with the dog on Wednesday and Thursday, but the big breakthrough was not long in coming. Friday evening, June 4, they found the way, and after that their lives could never be the same.

2

"*. . . reports of screaming in an unfinished housing tract, Bordeaux Ridge—*"

Friday evening, June 4, less than an hour before nightfall, the sun cast gold and copper light on Orange County. It was the second day of blistering temperatures in the mid-nineties, and the stored heat of the long summer day radiated off the pavement and buildings. Trees seemed to droop wearily. The air was motionless. On the freeways and surface streets, the sound of traffic was muffled, as if the thick air filtered the roar of engines and blaring of horns.

"*—repeat, Bordeaux Ridge, under construction at the east end—*"

In the gently rolling foothills to the northeast, in an unincorporated area of the county adjacent to Yorba Linda, where the suburban sprawl had only recently begun to reach, there was little traffic. The occasional blast of a horn or squeal of brakes was not merely muffled but curiously mournful, melancholy in the humid stillness.

Sheriff's Deputies Teel Porter and Ken Dimes were in a patrol car—Teel driving, Ken riding shotgun—with a broken ventilation system: no air-conditioning, not even forced air coming out of the vents. The windows were open, but the sedan was an oven.

"You stink like a dead hog," Teel Porter told his partner.

"Yeah?" Ken Dimes said. "Well, you not only stink like a dead hog, you *look* like a dead hog."

"Yeah? Well, you *date* dead hogs."

Ken smiled in spite of the heat. "That so? Well, I hear from your women that you make *love* like a dead hog."

Their tired humor could not mask the fact that they were weary and uncomfortable. And they were answering a call that didn't promise much excitement: probably kids playing games; kids loved to play on construction sites. Both deputies were thirty-two, husky former high school football players. They weren't brothers—but, as partners for six years, they were *brothers*.

Teel turned off the county road onto a lightly oiled dirt lane that led into the Bordeaux Ridge development. About forty houses were in various stages of construction. Most were still being framed, but a few had already been stuccoed.

"Now there," Ken said, "is the kind of shit I just can't believe people fall for. I mean, hell, what kind of name is 'Bordeaux' for a housing tract in Southern California? Are they trying to make you believe there's going to be vineyards here one day? And they call it 'Ridge,' but the whole tract's in this stretch of flatland between the hills. Their sign promises serenity. Maybe now. But what about when they pitch up another three thousand houses out here in the next five years?"

Teel said, "Yeah, but the part that gets me is 'miniestates.' What the fuck is a *mini*estate. Nobody in his right mind would think these are estates—except maybe Russians who've spent their lives living twelve to an apartment. These are tract homes."

The concrete curbs and gutters had been poured along the streets of Bordeaux Ridge, but the pavement had not yet been put down. Teel drove slowly, trying not to raise a lot of dust, raising it anyway. He and Ken looked left and right at the skeletal forms of unfinished houses, searching for kids who were up to no good.

To the west, at the edge of the city of Yorba Linda and adjacent to Bordeaux Ridge, were finished tracts where people already lived. From those residents, the Yorba Linda Police had received calls about screaming somewhere in this embryonic development. Because the area had not yet been annexed into the city, the complaint fell into the jurisdiction of the Sheriff's Department.

At the end of the street, the deputies saw a white pickup that belonged to the company that owned Bordeaux: Tulemann Brothers. It was parked in front of three almost-completed display models.

"Looks like there's a foreman still here," Ken said.

"Or maybe it's the night watchman on duty a little early," Teel said.

They parked behind the truck, got out of the stiflingly hot patrol car, and stood for a moment, listening. Silence.

Ken shouted. "Hello! Anybody here?"

His voice echoed back and forth through the deserted tract.

Ken said, "You want to look around?"

"Shit, no," Teel said. "But let's do it."

Ken still did not believe anything was wrong at Bordeaux Ridge. The pickup could have been left behind at the end of the day. After all, other equipment remained on the tract overnight: a couple of Bob-cats on a long-bed truck, a backhoe. And it was still likely that the reported screaming had been kids playing.

They grabbed flashlights from the car because, even if electric service to the tract had been connected, there were no lamps or ceiling lights in the unfinished structures.

Resettling their gunbelts on their hips more out of habit than out of any belief that they would need weapons, Ken and Teel walked through the nearest of the partially framed houses. They were not looking for anything in particular, just going through the motions, which was half of all police work.

A mild and inconstant breeze sprang up, the first of the day, and blew sawdust ghosts through the open sides of the house. The sun was falling rapidly westward, and the wall studs cast prison-bar shadows across the floor. The last light of the day, which was changing from gold to muddy red, imparted a soft glow to the air like that around the open door of a furnace. The concrete pad was littered with nails that winked in the fiery light and clinked underfoot.

"For a hundred and eighty thousand bucks," Teel said, probing into black corners with the beam of his flashlight, "I'd expect rooms a little bigger than these."

Taking a deep breath of sawdust-scented air, Ken said, "Hell, I'd expect rooms as big as airport lounges."

They stepped out of the back of the house, into a shallow rear yard, where they switched off their flashes. The bare, dry earth was not landscaped. It was littered with the detritus of construction: scraps of lumber, chunks of broken concrete, rumpled pieces of tarpaper, tangled loops of wire, more nails, useless lengths of PVC pipe, cedar shingles discarded by roofers, Styrofoam soft-drink cups and Big Mac containers, empty Coke cans, and less identifiable debris.

No fences had yet been constructed, so they had a view of all twelve backyards along this street. Purple shadows seeped across the sandy soil, but they could see that all the yards were deserted.

"No signs of mayhem," Teel said.

"No damsels in distress," Ken said.

"Well, let's at least walk along here, look between buildings," Teel said. "We ought to give the public something for their money."

Two houses later, in the thirty-foot-wide pass-through between structures, they found the dead man.

"Damn," Teel said.

The guy was lying on his back, mostly in shadow, with only the lower half of his body revealed in the dirty-red light, and at first Ken and Teel didn't realize what a horror they'd stumbled across. But when he knelt beside the corpse, Ken was shocked to see that the man's gut had been torn open.

"Jesus Christ, his eyes," Teel said.

Ken looked up from the ravaged torso and saw empty sockets where the victim's eyes should have been.

Retreating into the littered yard, Teel drew his revolver.

Ken also backed away from the mutilated corpse and slipped his own gun out of his holster. Though he had been perspiring all day, he felt suddenly damper, slick with a different kind of sweat, the cool, sour sweat of fear.

PCP, Ken thought. Only some asshole stoned on PCP would be violent enough to do something like this.

Bordeaux Ridge was silent.

Nothing moved except the shadows, which seemed to grow longer by the second.

"Some angel-dust junkie did this," Ken said, putting his fears about PCP into words.

"I was thinking the same thing," Teel said. "You want to look any farther?"

"Not just the two of us, by God. Let's radio for assistance."

They began to retrace their steps, warily keeping a watch on all sides as they moved, and they did not go far before they heard the noises. A crash. A clatter of metal. Glass breaking.

Ken had no doubt whatsoever where the sounds came from. The racket originated inside the closest of the three houses that were nearing completion and that would serve as sales models.

With no suspect in sight and no clue as to where to begin looking for one, they would have been justified in returning to the patrol car and calling for assistance. But now that they'd heard the disturbance in the model home, their training and instinct required them to act more boldly. They moved toward the back of the house.

A plyboard skin had been nailed over the studs, so the walls were not open to the elements, and chicken wire had been fixed to the tar-papered boards, and half the place was stuccoed. In fact, the stucco looked damp, as if the job had been started only today. Most of the windows were installed; only a few cutouts were still covered with tattered sheets of opaque plastic.

Another crash, louder than the first, was followed by the sound of more glass shattering inside.

Ken Dimes tried the sliding glass door that connected the rear yard and the family room. It was not locked.

From outside, Teel studied the family room through the glass. Although some light still entered the house by way of undraped doors and windows, shadows ruled the interior. They could see that the family room was deserted, so Teel eased through the half-open door with his flashlight in one hand and his Smith & Wesson clutched firmly in the other.

"You go around front," Teel whispered, "so the bastard doesn't get out that way."

Bending down to stay below window level, Ken hurried around the corner, along the side of the house, around to the front, and every step of the way he half-expected someone to jump on him from the roof or leap out through one of the unfinished windows.

The interior had been Sheetrocked, the ceilings textured. The family room opened into a breakfast area adjoining the kitchen, all of it one large flowing space without partitions. Oak cabinets had been installed in the kitchen, but the tile floor had not yet been put down.

The air had the lime odor of drywaller's mud, with an underlying scent of wood stain.

Standing in the breakfast area, Teel listened for more sounds of destruction, movement.

Nothing.

If this was like most California tract homes, he would find the dining room to the left, beyond the kitchen, then the living room, the entrance foyer, and a den. If he went into the hallway that led out of the breakfast area, he would probably find a laundry room, the downstairs bath, a coat closet, then the foyer. He could see no advantage of one route over another, so he went into the hall and checked the laundry first.

The dark room had no windows. The door was standing half-open, and the flashlight showed only yellow cabinets and the spaces where the washer and dryer would be placed. However, Teel wanted to look at the section behind the door, where he figured there was a sink and work area. He pushed the door all the way open and went in fast, swinging the flashlight and the gun in that direction. He found the stainless-steel sink and built-in table that he expected, but no killer.

He was more on edge that he had been in years. He could not keep the image of the dead man from flickering repeatedly through his mind: those empty eye sockets.

Not just on edge, he thought. Face it, you're scared shitless.

*　　*　　*

Out front, Ken jumped across a narrow ditch and headed for the house's double entrance doors, which were still closed. He surveyed the surrounding area and saw no one trying to escape. As twilight descended, Bordeaux Ridge looked less like a tract under development than like a bombed-out neighborhood. Shadows and dust created the illusion of rubble.

In the laundry room, Teel Porter turned, intending to step into the hall, and on his right, in the group of yellow cabinets, the two-foot-wide, six-foot-high door of a broom closet flew open, and this *thing* came at him as if it were a jack-in-the-box, Jesus, for a split second he was sure it must be a kid in a rubber fright mask. He could not see clearly in the backsplash of the flashlight, which was pointed away from the attacker, but then he knew it was real because those eyes, like circles of smoky lamplight, were not just plastic or glass, no way. He fired the revolver, but it was aimed ahead, into the hall, and the slug plowed harmlessly into the wall out there, so he tried to turn, but the thing was all over him, hissing like a snake. He fired again, into the floor this time—the sound was deafening in that enclosed space—then he was driven backward against the sink, and the gun was torn out of his hand. He also lost the flashlight, which spun off into the corner. He threw a punch, but before his fist was halfway through its arc, he felt a terrible pain in his belly, as if several stilettos had been thrust into him all at once, and he knew instantly what was happening to him. He screamed, screamed, and in the gloom the misshapen face of the jack-in-the-box loomed over him, its eyes radiantly yellow, and Teel screamed again, flailed, and more stilettos sank through the soft tissue of his throat—

Ken Dimes was four steps from the front doors when he heard Teel scream. A cry of surprise, fear, pain.

"Shit."

They were double doors, stained oak. The one on the right was secured to the sill and header by sliding bolts, while the one on the left was the active door—and unlocked. Ken rushed inside, caution briefly forgotten, then halted in the gloomy foyer.

Already, the screaming had stopped.

He switched on his flashlight. Empty living room to the right. Empty den to the left. A staircase leading up to the second floor. No one anywhere in sight.

Silence. Perfect silence. As in a vacuum.

For a moment Ken hesitated to call out to Teel, for fear he would be revealing his position to the killer. Then he realized that the flashlight, without which he could not proceed, was enough to give him away; it did not matter if he made noise.

"Teel!"

The name echoed through the vacant rooms.

"Teel, where are you?"

No reply.

Teel must be dead. Jesus. He would respond if he was alive.

Or he might just be injured and unconscious, wounded and dying. In that case, perhaps it would be best to go back to the patrol car and call for an ambulance.

No. No, if his partner *was* in desperate shape, Ken had to find him fast and administer first aid. Teel might die in the time it took to call an ambulance. Delaying that long was too great a risk.

Besides, the killer had to be dealt with.

Only the vaguest smoky-red light penetrated the windows now, for the day was being swallowed by the night. Ken had to rely entirely on the flashlight, which was not ideal because, each time the beam moved, shadows leaped and swooped, creating illusory assailants. Those false attackers might distract him from real danger.

Leaving the front door wide open, he crept along the narrow hall that led to the back of the house. He stayed close to the wall. The sole of one of his shoes squeaked with nearly every step he took. He held the gun out in front of him, not aimed at the floor or ceiling, because for the moment, at least, he didn't give a damn about safe weapons procedure.

On the right, a door stood open. A closet. Empty.

The stink of his own perspiration grew greater than the lime and woodstain odors of the house.

He came to a powder room on his left. A quick sweep of the light revealed nothing out of the ordinary, though his own frightened face, reflected in the mirror, startled him.

The rear of the house—family room, breakfast area, kitchen—was directly ahead, and on his left was another door, standing open. In the beam of the flashlight, which suddenly began to quiver violently in his hand, Ken saw Teel's body on the floor of a laundry room, and so much blood that there could be no doubt he was dead.

Beneath the waves of fear that washed across the surface of his mind, there were undercurrents of grief, rage, hatred, and a fierce desire for vengeance.

Behind Ken, something thumped.

He cried out and turned to face the threat.

But the hall to the right and the breakfast area to the left were both deserted.

The sound had come from the front of the house. Even as the echo of it died away, he knew what he'd heard: the front door being closed.

Another sound broke the stillness, not as loud as the first but more unnerving: the *clack* of the door's dead bolt being engaged.

Had the killer departed and locked the door from the outside, with a key? But where would he get a key? Off the foreman that he had murdered? And why would he pause to lock up?

More likely, he had locked the door from inside, not merely to delay Ken's escape but to let him know the hunt was still under way.

Ken considered dousing the flashlight because it pinpointed him for the enemy, but by now the twilight glow at the windows was purple-gray and did not reach into the house at all. Without the flashlight, he would be blind.

How the hell was the *killer* finding his way in this steadily deepening darkness? Was it possible that a PCP junkie's night vision improved when he was high, just as his strength increased to that of ten men as a side effect of the angel dust?

The house was quiet.

He stood with his back to the hallway wall.

He could smell Teel's blood. A vaguely metallic odor.

Click, click, click.

Ken stiffened and listened intently, but he heard nothing more after those three quick noises. They had sounded like swift footsteps crossing the concrete floor, taken by someone wearing boots with hard leather heels—or shoes with cleats.

The noises had begun and ended so abruptly that he had not been able to tell where they were coming from. Then he heard them again—*click, click, click,*

click—four steps this time, and they were in the foyer, moving in this direction, toward the hall in which he stood.

He immediately pushed away from the wall, turning to face the adversary, dropping into a crouch and thrusting both the flashlight and the revolver toward where he had heard the steps. But the hallway was deserted.

Breathing through his open mouth to reduce the noise of his own rapid respiration, which he feared would mask the movements of the enemy, Ken eased along the hall, into the foyer. Nothing. The front door was closed all right, but the den and the living room and the staircase and the gallery above were deserted.

Click, click, click, click.

The noises arose from an entirely different direction now, from the back of the house, in the breakfast area. The killer had fled silently out of the foyer, across the living room and dining room, into the kitchen, into the breakfast area, circling through the house, coming around behind Ken. Now the bastard was entering the hall that Ken had just left. And though the guy had been silent while flitting through the other rooms, he was making those noises again, obviously not because he had to make them, not because his shoes clicked with every step the way Ken's shoes squeaked, but because he wanted to make the noises again, wanted to taunt Ken, wanted to say: *Hey, I'm behind you now, and here I come, ready or not, here I come.*

Click, click, click.

Ken Dimes was no coward. He was a good cop who had never walked away from trouble. He had received two citations for bravery in only seven years on the force. But this faceless, insanely violent son a bitch, scurrying through the house in total darkness, silent when he wanted to be and making taunting sounds when it suited him—he baffled and scared Ken. And although Ken was as courageous as any cop, he was no fool, and only a fool would walk boldly into a situation that he did not understand.

Instead of returning to the hall and confronting the killer, he went to the front door and reached for the lever-action brass handle, intending to get the hell out. Then he noticed the door hadn't merely been closed and dead-bolted. A length of scrap wire had been wound around the handle on the fixed door and around that on the active door, linking them, fastening them together. He would have to unwind the wire before he could get out, which might take half a minute.

Click, click, click.

He fired once toward the hallway without even looking and ran in the opposite direction, crossing the empty living room. He heard the killer behind him. Clicking. Coming fast in the darkness. Yet when Ken reached the dining room and was almost to the doorway that led into the kitchen, intending to make a break for the family room and the patio door by which Teel had entered, he heard the clicking coming from in *front* of him. He was sure the killer had pursued him into the living room, but now the guy had gone back into the lightless hallway and was coming at him from the other direction, making a crazy game of this. From the sounds the bastard was making, he seemed just about to enter the breakfast area, which would put only the width of the kitchen between him and Ken, so Ken decided to make a stand right there, decided to blow away this psycho the moment the guy appeared in the beam of light—

Then the killer shrieked.

Clicking along the hallway, still out of sight but coming toward Ken, the attacker let out a shrill inhuman cry that was the essence of primal rage and hatred, the strangest sound that Ken had ever heard, not the sound a man would make, not even a lunatic. He gave up all thought of confrontation, pitched his flashlight into the kitchen to create a diversion, turned away from the approaching enemy, and fled again, though not back into the living room, not toward any part of the house in which this game of cat and mouse could be extended, but straight across the dining room toward a window that glimmered vaguely with the last dim glow of twilight. He tucked his head down, brought his arms up against his chest, and turned sideways as he slammed into the glass. The window exploded, and he fell out into the rear yard, rolling through construction debris. Splintering scraps of two-by-fours and chunks of concrete poked painfully into his legs and ribs. He scrambled to his feet, spun toward the house, and emptied his revolver at the broken window in case the killer was in pursuit of him.

In the settling night, he saw no sign of the enemy.

Figuring he had not scored a hit, he wasted no time cursing his luck. He sprinted around the house, along the side of it, and out to the street. He had to get to the patrol car, where there was a radio—and a pump-action riot gun.

3

On Wednesday and Thursday, the second and third of June, Travis and Nora and Einstein searched diligently for a way to improve human-canine communications, and in the process man and dog had almost begun to chew up furniture in frustration. However, Nora proved to have enough patience and confidence for all of them. When the breakthrough came near sunset on Friday evening, the fourth of June, she was less surprised than either Travis or Einstein.

They had purchased forty magazines—everything from *Time* and *Life* to *McCall's* and *Redbook*—and fifty books of art and photography, and had brought them to the living room of Travis's rental house, where there was space to spread everything out on the floor. They had put pillows on the floor as well, so they could work at the dog's level and be comfortable.

Einstein had watched their preparations with interest.

Sitting on the floor with her back against the vinyl sofa, Nora took the retriever's head in both hands and, with her face close to his, their noses almost touching, she said, "Okay, now you listen to me, Einstein. We want to know all sorts of things about you: where you came from, why you're smarter than an ordinary dog, what you were afraid of in the woods that day Travis found you, why you sometimes stare out the window at night as if you're frightened of something. Lots more. But you can't talk, can you? No. And so far as we know, you can't read. And even if you can read, you can't write. So we've got to do this with pictures, I think."

From where he sat near Nora, Travis could see that the dog's eyes never wavered from hers as she spoke. Einstein was rigid. His tail hung down, motionless. He not only seemed to understand what she was telling him, but he appeared to be electrified by the experiment.

How much does the mutt really perceive, Travis wondered, and how many of his reactions am I imagining because of pure wishful thinking?

People have a natural tendency to anthropomorphize their pets, to ascribe human perceptions and intentions to the animals where none exist. In Einstein's case, where there really was exceptional intelligence at work, the temptation to see profound meaning in every meaningless doggy twitch was even greater than usual.

"We're going to study all these pictures, looking for things that interest you, for things that'll help us understand where you came from and how you got to be what you are. Every time you see something that'll help us put the puzzle together, you've got somehow to bring it to our attention. Bark at it or put a paw on it or wag your tail."

"This is nuts," Travis said.

"Do you understand me, Einstein?" Nora asked.

The retriever issued a soft woof.

"This will never work," Travis said.

"Yes, it will," Nora insisted. "He can't talk, can't write, but he can *show* us things. If he points out a dozen pictures, we might not immediately understand what meaning they have for him, how they refer to his origins, but in time we'll find a way to relate them to one another and to him, and we'll know what he's trying to tell us."

The dog, his head still trapped firmly in Nora's hands, rolled his eyes toward Travis and woofed again.

"We ready?" Nora asked Einstein.

His gaze flicked back to her, and he wagged his tail.

"All right," she said, letting go of his head. "Let's start."

Wednesday, Thursday, and Friday, for hours at a time, they leafed through scores of publications, showing Einstein pictures of all kinds of things—people, trees, flowers, dogs, other animals, machines, city streets, country lanes, cars, ships, planes, food, advertisements for a thousand products—hoping he would see something that would excite him. The problem was that he saw many things that excited him, too many. He barked at, pawed at, woofed at, put his nose to, or wagged his tail at perhaps a hundred out of the thousands of pictures, and his choices were of such variety that Travis could see no pattern to them, no way to link them and divine meaning from their association to one another.

Einstein was fascinated by an automobile ad in which the car, being compared to a powerful tiger, was shown locked in an iron cage. Whether it was the car or the tiger that seized his interest was not clear. He also responded to several computer advertisements, Alpo and Purina Dog Chow ads, an ad for a portable stereo cassette player, and pictures of books, butterflies, a parrot, a forlorn man in a prison cell, four young people playing with a striped beach ball, Mickey Mouse, a violin, a man on an exercise treadmill, and many other things. He was tantalized by a photograph of a golden retriever like himself, and was downright excited by a picture of a cocker spaniel, but curiously he showed little or no interest in other breeds of dogs.

His strongest—and most puzzling—response was to a photo in a magazine article about an upcoming movie from 20th Century-Fox. The film's story involved the supernatural—ghosts, poltergeists, demons risen from Hell—and the photo that agitated him was of a slab-jawed, wickedly fanged, lantern-eyed demonic apparition. The creature was no more hideous than others in the film, less hideous than several of them, yet Einstein was affected by only that one demon.

The retriever barked at the photograph. He scurried behind the sofa and peeked around the end of it as if he thought the creature in the picture might rise off the page and come after him. He barked again, whined, and had to be coaxed back to the magazine. Upon seeing the demon a second time, Einstein growled menacingly. Frantically, he pawed at the magazine turning its pages until, somewhat tattered, it was completely closed.

"What's so special about *that* picture?" Nora asked the dog.

Einstein just stared at her—and shivered slightly.

Patiently, Nora reopened the magazine to the same page.

Einstein closed it again.

Nora opened it.

Einstein closed it a third time, snatched it up in his jaws, and carried it out of the room.

Travis and Nora followed the retriever into the kitchen, where they watched him go straight to the trash can. The can was one of those with a foot pedal that opened a hinged lid. Einstein put a paw on the pedal, watched the lid open, dropped the magazine into the can, and released the pedal.

"What's that all about?" Nora wondered.

"I guess that's one movie he definitely doesn't want to see."

"Our own four-footed, furry critic."

That incident occurred Thursday afternoon. By early Friday evening, Travis's frustration—and that of the dog—were nearing critical mass.

Sometimes Einstein exhibited uncanny intelligence, but sometimes he behaved like an ordinary dog, and these oscillations between canine genius and dopey mutt were enervating for anyone trying to understand how he could be so bright. Travis began to think that the best way to deal with the retriever was to just accept him for what he was: be prepared for his amazing feats now and then, but don't expect him to deliver all the time. Most likely the mystery of Einstein's unusual intelligence would never be solved.

However, Nora remained patient. She frequently reminded them that Rome wasn't built in a day and that any worthwhile achievement required determination, persistence, tenacity, and time.

When she launched into these lectures about steadfastness and endurance, Travis sighed wearily—and Einstein yawned.

Nora was unperturbed. After they had examined the pictures in all of the books and magazines, she collected those to which Einstein had responded, spread them out across the floor, and encouraged him to make connections between one image and another."

"All of these are pictures of things that played important roles in his past," Nora said.

"I don't think we can be certain of that," Travis said.

"Well, that's what we've asked him to do," she said. "We've asked him to indicate pictures that might tell us something about where he's come from."

"But does he understand the game?"

"Yes," she said with conviction.

The dog woofed.

Nora lifted Einstein's paw and put it on the photograph of the violin. "Okay, pooch. You remember a violin from somewhere, and it was important to you somehow."

"Maybe he performed at Carnegie Hall," Travis said.

"Shut up." To the dog Nora said, "All right. Now is the violin related to any of these other pictures? Is there a link to another image that would help us understand what the violin means to you?"

Einstein stared at her intently for a moment, as if pondering her question. Then he crossed the room, walking carefully in the narrow aisles between the rows of photographs, sniffing, his gaze flicking left and right, until he found the ad for the Sony portable stereo cassette player. He put one paw on it and looked back at Nora.

"There's an obvious connection," Travis said. "The violin makes music, and that cassette deck reproduces music. That's an impressive feat of mental association for a dog, but does it really mean anything else, anything about his past?"

"Oh, I'm sure it does," Nora said. To Einstein she said, "Did someone in your past play the violin?"

The dog stared at her.

She said, "Did your previous master have a cassette player like that one?"

The dog stared at her.

She said, "Maybe the violinist in your past used to record his own music on a cassette system?"

The dog blinked and whined.

"All right," she said, "is there another picture here that you can associate with the violin and the tape deck?"

Einstein stared down at the Sony ad for a moment, as if thinking, then walked into another aisle between two more rows of pictures, this time stopping at a magazine open to a Blue Cross advertisement that showed a doctor in a white coat standing at the bedside of a new mother who was holding her baby. Doctor and mother were all smiles, and the baby looked as serene and innocent as the Christ child.

Crawling nearer to the dog on her hands and knees, Nora said, "Does that picture remind you of the family that owned you?"

The dog stared at her.

"Was there a mother, father, and new baby in the family you used to live with?"

The dog stared at her.

Still sitting on the floor with his back against the sofa, Travis said, "Gee, maybe we've got a real case of reincarnation on our hands. Maybe old Einstein remembers being a doctor, a mother, or a baby in a previous life."

Nora would not dignify that suggestion with a response.

"A violin-playing baby," Travis said.

Einstein mewled unhappily.

On her hands and knees in a doglike position, Nora was only two or three feet from the retriever, virtually face-to-face with him. "All right. This is getting us nowhere. We've got to do more than just have you associate one picture with another. We've got to be able to ask questions about these pictures and somehow get answers."

"Give him paper and pen," Travis said.

"This is serious," Nora said, impatient with Travis as she had never been with the dog.

"I know it's serious," he said, "but it's also ridiculous."

She hung her head for a moment, like a dog suffering in summer heat, then suddenly looked up at Einstein and said, "How smart are you really, pooch? You want to prove you're a genius? You want to have our everlasting admiration and respect? Then here's what you have to do: learn to answer my questions with a simple yes or no."

The dog watched her closely, expectantly.

"If the answer to my question is yes—wag your tail," Nora said. "But *only* if the answer is yes. While this test is under way, you've got to avoid wagging it out of habit or just because you get excited. Wagging is *only* for when you want to say yes. And when you want to say no, you bark once. Just once."

Travis said, "Two barks mean 'I'd rather be chasing cats,' and three barks mean 'Get me a Budweiser.'"

"Don't confuse him," Nora said sharply.

"Why not? He confuses me."

The dog did not even glance at Travis. His large brown eyes remained focused intently on Nora as she explained the wag-for-yes and bark-for-no system again.

"All right," she said, "let's try it. Einstein, do you understand the yes-no signs?"

The retriever wagged his tail five or six times, then stopped.

"Coincidence," Travis said. "Means nothing."

Nora hesitated a moment, framing her next question, then said, "Do you know my name?"

The tail wagged, stopped.

"Is my name . . . Ellen?"

The dog barked. *No.*

"Is my name . . . Mary?"

One bark. *No.*

"Is my name . . . Nona?"

The dog rolled his eyes, as if chastising her for trying to trick him. No wagging. One bark.

"Is my name . . . Nora?"

Einstein wagged his tail furiously.

Laughing with delight, Nora crawled forward, sat up, and hugged the retriever.

"I'll be damned," Travis said, crawling over to join them.

Nora pointed to the photo on which the retriever still had one paw. "Did you react to this picture because it reminds you of the family you used to live with?"

One bark. *No.*

Travis said, "Did you ever live with any family?"

One bark.

"But you're not a wild dog," Nora said. "You must've lived somewhere before Travis found you."

Studying the Blue Cross advertisement, Travis suddenly thought he knew all the right questions. "Did you react to this picture because of the baby?"

One bark. *No.*

"Because of the woman?"

No.

"Because of the man in the white lab coat?"

Much wagging: *Yes, yes, yes.*

"So he lived with a doctor," Nora said. "Maybe a vet."

"Or maybe a scientist," Travis said as he followed the intuitive line of thought that had stricken him.

Einstein wagged a "yes" at the mention of scientist.

"Research scientist," Travis said.

Yes.

"In a lab," Travis said.

Yes, yes, yes.

"You're a lab dog?" Nora asked.

Yes.

"A research animal," Travis said.

Yes.

"And that's why you're so bright."

Yes.

"Because of something they've done to you."

Yes.

Travis's heart raced. They actually were communicating, by God, not just in broad strokes, and not just in the comparatively crude way he and Einstein had communicated the night that the dog had formed a question mark out of Milk-Bones. This was communication with extreme specificity. Here they were, talking as if they were three people—well, almost talking—and suddenly nothing would ever be the same again. Nothing could *possibly* be the same in a world where men and animals possessed equal (if different) intellects, where faced life on equal terms, with equal rights, with similar hopes and dreams. All right, okay, so maybe he was blowing this out of proportion. Not *all* animals had suddenly been given human-level consciousness and intelligence; this was only one dog, an experimental animal, perhaps the only one of his kind. But Jesus. *Jesus*. Travis stared in awe at the retriever, and a chill swept through him, not a chill of fear but of wonder.

Nora spoke to the dog, and in her voice was a trace of the same awe that had briefly rendered Travis speechless: "They didn't just let you go, did they?"

One bark. *No.*

"You escaped?"

Yes.

"That Tuesday morning I found you in the woods?" Travis asked. "Had you just escaped then?"

Einstein neither barked nor wagged his tail.

"Days before that?" Travis asked.

The dog whined.

"He probably has a sense of time," Nora said, "because virtually all animals follow natural day-night rhythms, don't they? They have instinctive clocks, biological clocks. But he probably doesn't have any concept of *calendar* days. He doesn't really understand how we divide time up into days and weeks and months, so he has no way of answering your question."

"Then that's something we'll have to teach him," Travis said.

Einstein vigorously wagged his tail.

Thoughtfully, Nora said, "Escaped . . ."

Travis knew what she must be thinking. To Einstein, he said, "They'll be looking for you, won't they?"

The dog whined and wagged his tail—which Travis interpreted as a "yes" with a special edge of anxiety.

4

An hour after sunset, Lemuel Johnson and Cliff Soames, trailed by two additional unmarked cars carrying eight NSA agents, arrived at Bordeaux Ridge. The unpaved street through the center of the unfinished housing tract was lined with vehicles, mostly black-and-whites bearing the Sheriff's Department shield, plus cars and a van from the coroner's office.

Lem was dismayed to see that the press had already arrived. Both print journalists and television crews with minicams were being kept behind a police line, half a block from the apparent scene of the murder. By quietly suppressing details of the death of Wesley Dalberg in Holy Jim Canyon and of the associated murders of the scientists working at Banodyne, and by instituting an aggressive campaign of disinformation, the NSA had managed to keep the press ignorant of the connections among all these events. Lem hoped that the deputies manning these barriers were among Walt Gaines's most trusted men and that they would meet reporters' questions with stony silence until a convincing cover story could be developed.

Sawhorses were lifted out of the way to let the unmarked NSA cars through the police line, then were put into place again.

Lem parked at the end of the street, past the crime scene. He left Cliff Soames to brief the other agents, and he headed toward the unfinished house that appeared to be the focus of attention.

The patrol cars' radios filled the hot night air with codes and jargon—and with a hiss-pop-crackle of static, as if the whole world were being fried on a cosmic griddle.

Portable kliegs stood on tripods, flooding the front of the house with light to facilitate the investigation. Lem felt as if he were on a giant stage set. Moths swooped and fluttered around the kliegs. Their amplified shadows darted across the dusty ground.

Casting his own exaggerated shadow, he crossed the dirt yard to the house. Inside, he found more kliegs. Dazzlingly bright light bounced off white walls. Looking pale and sweaty in that harsh glare were a couple of young deputies, men from the coroner's office, and the usual intense types from the Scientific Investigation Division.

A photographer's strobe flashed once, twice, from farther back in the house. The hallway looked crowded, so Lem went around to the back by way of the living room, dining room, and kitchen.

Walt Gaines was standing in the breakfast area, in the dimness behind the last of the hooded kliegs. But even in those shadows, his anger and grief were visible. He had evidently been at home when he had gotten word about the murder of a deputy, for he was wearing tattered running shoes, wrinkled tan chinos, a brown- and red-checkered short-sleeve shirt. In spite of his great size, bull neck, muscular arms, and big hands, Walt's clothes and slump-shouldered posture gave him the look of a forlorn little boy.

From the breakfast area, Lem could not see past the lab men and into the laundry room, where the body still lay. He said, "I'm sorry, Walt. I'm so sorry."

"Name was Teel Porter. His dad Red Porter and I been friends twenty-five years. Red just retired from the department last year. How am I going to tell him? Jesus. I've got to do it myself, us being so close. Can't pass the buck this time."

Lem knew that Walt never passed the buck when one of his men was killed in the line of duty. He always personally visited the family, broke the bad news, and sat with them through the initial shock.

"Almost lost *two* men," Walt said. "Other one's badly shaken."

"How was Teel . . . ?"

"Gutted like Dalberg. Decapitated."

The Outsider, Lem thought. No doubt about it now.

Moths had gotten inside and were bashing against the lens of the klieg light behind which Lem and Walt stood.

His voice thickening with anger, Walt said, "Haven't found . . . his head. How do I tell his dad that Teel's *head* is missing?"

Lem had no answer.

Walt looked hard at him. "You can't push me all the way out of it now. Not now that one of my men is dead."

"Walt, my agency works in purposeful obscurity. Hell, even the number of agents on the payroll is classified information. But your department is subject to full press attention. And in order to know how to proceed in this case, your people would have to be told exactly what they're looking for. That would mean revealing national defense secrets to a large group of deputies—"

"*Your* men all know what's up," Walt countered.

"Yes, but my men have signed secrecy oaths, undergone extensive security checks, and are trained to keep their mouths shut."

"My men can keep a secret, too."

"I'm sure they can," Lem said carefully. "I'm sure they don't talk outside the shop about ordinary cases. But this isn't ordinary. No, this has to remain in our hands."

Walt said, "My men can sign secrecy oaths."

"We'd have to background-check everyone in your department, not just deputies but file clerks. It'd take weeks, months."

Looking across the kitchen at the open door to the dining room, Walt noticed Cliff Soames and another NSA agent talking with two deputies in the next room. "You started taking over the minute you got here, didn't you? Before you even talked to me about it?"

"Yeah. We're making sure your people understand that they must not talk of anything they've seen here tonight, not even to their own wives. We're citing the appropriate federal laws to every man, 'cause we want to be sure they understand the fines and prison terms."

"Threatening me with jail again?" Walt asked, but there was no humor in his voice, as there had been when they'd spoken days ago in the garage of St. Joseph's Hospital after seeing Tracy Keeshan.

Lem was depressed not only by the deputy's death but by the wedge that this case was driving between him and Walt. "I don't want anyone in jail. That's why I want to be sure they grasp the consequences—"

Scowling, Walt said, "Come with me."

Lem followed him outside, to a patrol car in front of the house.

They sat in the front seat, Walt behind the steering wheel, with the doors closed. "Roll up the windows, so we'll have total privacy."

Lem protested that they'd suffocate in this heat without ventilation. But even in the dim light, he saw the purity and volatility of Walt's anger, and he realized his position was that of a man standing in gasoline while holding a burning candle. He rolled up his window.

"Okay," Walt said. "We're alone. Not NSA District Director and Sheriff. Just old friends. Buddies. So tell me all about it."

"Walt, damn it, I can't."

"Tell me now, and I'll stay off the case, I won't interfere."

"You'll stay off the case anyway. You have to."

"Damned if I do," Walt said angrily. "I can walk right down the road to those jackals." The car faced out of Bordeaux Ridge, toward the sawhorses where reporters waited, and Walt pointed at them through the dusty windshield. "I can tell them that Banodyne Laboratories was working on some defense project that got out of hand, tell them that someone or something strange escaped from those labs in spite of the security, and now it's loose, killing people."

"You do that," Lem said, "you wouldn't just wind up in jail. You'd lose your job, ruin your whole career."

"I don't think so. In court I'd claim I had to choose between breaching the national security and betraying the trust of the people who elected me to office in this county. I'd claim that, in a time of crisis like this, I had to put local public safety above the concerns of the Defense bureaucrats in Washington. I'm confident just about any jury would vindicate me. I'd stay out of jail, and in the next election I'd win by even more votes than I got the last time."

"Shit," Lem said because he knew Walt was correct.

"If you tell me about it now, if you convince me that your people are better able to handle the situation than mine, then I'll step out of your way. But if you won't tell me, I'll blow it wide open."

"I'd be breaking my oath. I'd be putting my neck in the noose."

"No one'll ever know you told me."

"Yeah? Well then, Walt, for Christ's sake, why put me in such an awkward position just to satisfy your curiosity?"

Walt looked stung. "It's not as petty as that, damn you. It's not just curiosity."

"Then what is it?"

"*One of my men is dead!*"

Leaning his head back against the seat, Lem closed his eyes and sighed. Walt had to know *why* he was required to forswear vengeance for the killing of one of his own men. His sense of duty and honor would not allow him to back off without at least that much. His was not exactly an unreasonable position.

"Do I go down there, talk to reporters?" Walt asked quietly.

Lem opened his eyes, wiped a hand across his damp face. The interior of the car was uncomfortably warm, muggy. He wanted to roll down his window. But now and then men walked past on their way in or out of the house, and he really could not risk anyone overhearing what he was going to tell Walt. "You were right to focus on Banodyne. For a few years they've been doing defense-related research."

"Biological warfare?" Walt asked. "Using recombinant DNA to make nasty new viruses?"

"Maybe that, too," Lem said. "But germ warfare doesn't have anything to do with this case, and I'm only going to tell you about the research that's related to our problems here."

The windows were fogging. Walt started the car. There was no air conditioning, and the fog on the windows continued to spread, but even the vague, moist, warm breeze from the vents was welcome.

Lem said, "They were working on several research programs under the heading of the Francis Project. Named for Saint Francis of Assisi."

Blinking in surprise, Walt said, "They'd name a warfare-related project after a saint?"

"It's apt," Lem assured him. "Saint Francis could talk to birds and animals. And at Banodyne, Dr. Davis Weatherby was in charge of a project aimed at making human-animal communication possible."

"Learning the language of porpoises—that sort of thing?"

"No. The idea was to apply the very latest knowledge in genetic engineering to the creation of animals with a much higher order of intelligence, animals capable of nearly human-level thought, animals with whom we might be able to communicate."

Walt stared at him in openmouthed disbelief.

Lem said, "There've been several scientific teams working on very different experiments under the umbrella label of the Francis Project, all of which have been funded for at least five years. For one thing, there were Davis Weatherby's dogs . . ."

Dr. Weatherby had been working with the sperm and ova of golden retrievers, which he had chosen because the dogs had been bred with ever greater refinement for more than a hundred years. For one thing, this refinement meant that, in the purest of the breed, all diseases and afflictions of an inheritable nature had been pretty much excised from the animal's genetic code, which insured Weatherby of healthy and bright subjects for his experiments. Then, if the experimental pups were born with abnormalities of any kind, Weatherby could more easily distinguish those mutations of a natural type from those that were an unintended side effect of his own sly tampering with the animal's genetic heritage, and he would be able to learn from his own mistakes.

Over the years, seeking solely to increase the intelligence of the breed without causing a change in its physical appearance, David Weatherby had fertilized hundreds of genetically altered retriever ova *in vitro*, then had transferred the fertile eggs to the wombs of bitches who served as surrogate mothers. The bitches carried the test-tube pups to full term, and Weatherby studied these young dogs for indications of increased intelligence.

"There were a hell of lot of failures," Lem said. "Grotesque physical mutation that had to be destroyed. Stillborn pups. Pups that looked normal but were *less* intelligent than usual. Weatherby was doing cross-species engineering, after all, so you can figure that some pretty horrible possibilities were realized."

Walt stared at the windshield, now entirely opaqued. Then he frowned at Lem. "Cross-species? What do you mean?"

"Well, you see, he was isolating those genetic determinants of intelligence in species that were brighter than the retriever—"

"Like apes? They'd be brighter than dogs, wouldn't they?"

"Yeah. Apes . . . and human beings."

"Jesus," Walt said.

Lem adjusted a dashboard vent to direct the flow of tepid air into his face. "Weatherby was inserting that foreign genetic material into the retriever's genetic code, simultaneously editing out the dog's own genes that limited its intelligence to that of a dog."

Walt rebelled. "That's not possible! This genetic material, as you call it, surely it can't be passed from one species to another."

"It happens in nature all the time," Lem said. "Genetic material is transferred from one species to another, and the carrier is usually a virus. Let's say a virus thrives in rhesus monkeys. While in the monkey, it acquired genetic material from the monkey's cells. These acquired monkey genes become a part of the virus itself. Later, upon infecting a human host, that virus has the capability of leaving the monkey's genetic material in its human host. Consider the AIDS virus, for instance. It's believed AIDS was a disease carried by certain monkeys and by human beings for decades, though neither species was susceptible to it; I mean, we were strictly carriers—we never got sick from what we carried. But then, somehow, something happened in monkeys, a negative genetic change that made them not only carriers but *victims* of the AIDS virus. Monkeys began to die of the disease. Then, when the virus passed to humans, it brought with it this new genetic material specifying susceptibility to AIDS, so before long human beings were also capable of contracting the disease. That's how it works in nature. It's done even more efficiently in the lab."

As creeping condensation fogged the side windows, Walt said, "So Weatherby really succeeded in breeding a dog with human intelligence?"

"It was a long, slow process, but gradually he made advancements. And a little over a year ago, the miracle pup was born."

"Thinks like a human being?"

"Not *like* a human being, but maybe *as well as.*"

"Yet it looks like an ordinary dog?"

"That was what the Pentagon wanted. Which made Weatherby's job a lot harder, I guess. Apparently, brain size has at least a little bit to do with intelligence, and Weatherby might have made his breakthrough a lot sooner if he'd been able to develop a retriever with a larger brain. But a larger brain would have meant a reconfigured and much larger skull, so the dog would have looked damned unusual."

All the windows were fogged over now. Neither Walt nor Lem tried to clear the misted glass. Unable to see out of the car, confined to its humid and claustrophobic interior, they seemed to be cut off from the real world, adrift in time and space, a condition that was oddly conducive to the consideration of the wondrous and outrageous acts of creations that genetic engineering made possible.

Walt said, "The Pentagon wanted a dog that looked like a dog but could think like a man? *Why?*"

"Imagine the possibilities for espionage," Lem said. "In times of war, dogs would have no trouble getting deep into enemy territory, scouting installations and troop strength. Intelligent dogs, with whom we could somehow communicate, would then return and tell us what they had seen and what they'd overheard the enemy talking about."

"*Tell* us? Are you saying dogs could be made to talk, like canine versions of Francis the Mule or Mr. Ed? Shit, Lem, be serious!"

Lem sympathized with his friend's difficulty in absorbing these astounding possibilities. Modern science was advancing so rapidly, with so many revolutionary discoveries to be explored every year, that to laymen there was going to be increasingly less difference between the application of that science and magic. Few nonscientists had any appreciation for how different the world of the next twenty years was going to be from the world of the present, as different as the 1980s were from the 1780s. Change was occurring at an incomprehensible rate, and when you got a glimpse of what might be coming—as Walt just had—it was both inspiring and daunting, exhilarating and scary.

Lem said, "In fact, a dog probably could be genetically altered to be able to speak. Might even be easy, I don't know. But to give it the necessary vocal apparatus, the right kind of tongue and lips . . . that'd mean drastically altering its appearance, which is no good for the Pentagon's purposes. So *these* dogs wouldn't speak. Communication would no doubt have to be through an elaborate sign language."

"You're not laughing," Walt said. "This has got to be a fucking joke, so why aren't you laughing?"

"Think about it," Lem said patiently. "In peacetime . . . imagine the president of the United States presenting the Soviet premier with a one-year-old golden retriever as a gift from the American people. Imagine the dog living in the premier's home and office, privy to the most secret talks of the USSR's highest Party officials. Once in a while, every few weeks or months, the dog might manage to slip out at night, to meet with a U.S. agent in Moscow and be debriefed."

"*Debriefed?* This is insane!" Walt said, and he laughed. But his laughter had a sharp, hollow, decidedly nervous quality which, to Lem, indicated that the sheriff's skepticism was slipping away even though he wanted to hold on to it.

"I'm telling you that it's possible, that such a dog was in fact conceived by *in vitro* fertilization of a genetically altered ovum by genetically altered sperm, and carried to term by a surrogate mother. And after a year of confinement at the Banodyne labs, sometime in the early morning hours of Monday, May 17, that dog escaped by a series of incredibly clever actions that cannily circumvented the facility's security system."

"And the dog's now loose?"

"Yes."

"And that's what's been killing—"

"No," Lem said. "The dog is harmless, affectionate, a *wonderful* animal. I was in Weatherby's lab while he was working with the retriever. In a limited way, I communicated with it. Honest to God, Walt, when you see that animal in action, see what Weatherby created, it gives you enormous hope for this sorry species of ours."

Walt stared at him, uncomprehending.

Lem searched for the words to convey what he felt. As he found the language to describe what the dog had meant to him, his chest grew tight with emotion. "Well . . . I mean, if we can do these amazing things, if we can bring such a wonder into the world, then there's something of profound value in us no matter what the pessimists and doomsayers believe. If we can do this, we have the power and, potentially, the wisdom of God. We're not only makers of weapons, but makers of *life*. If we could lift members of another species up to our level, create a companion race to share the world . . . our beliefs and philosophies would be changed forever. By the very act of altering the retriever, we've altered ourselves. By pulling the dog to a new level of awareness, we are inevitably raising our own awareness as well."

"Jesus, Lem, you sound like a preacher."

"Do I? That's because I've had more time to think about this than you have. In time, you'll understand what I'm talking about. You'll begin to feel it, too, this incredible sense that humankind is on its way to godhood—and that we *deserve* to get there."

Walt Gaines stared at the steamed glass, as if reading something of great interest in the patterns of condensation. Then: "Maybe what you say is right. Maybe we're on the brink of a new world. But for now we've got to live in and deal with the old one. So if it wasn't the dog that killed my deputy—what was it?"

"Something else escaped from Banodyne the same night that the dog got out," Lem said. His euphoria was suddenly tempered by the need to admit that there had been a darker side to the Francis Project. "They called it The Outsider."

5

Nora held up the magazine ad that compared an automobile to a tiger and that showed the car in an iron cage. To Einstein, she said, "All right, let's see what else you can clarify for us. What about this one? What is it that interested you in this photograph—the car?"

Einstein barked once: *No*.

"Was it the tiger?" Travis asked.

One bark.

"The cage?" Nora asked.

Einstein wagged his tail: *Yes*.

"Did you choose this picture because they kept you in a cage?" Nora asked.

Yes.

Travis crawled across the floor until he found the photo of a forlorn man in a prison cell. Returning with it, showing it to the retriever, he said, "And did you choose this one because the cell is like a cage?"

Yes.

"And because the prisoner in the picture reminded you of how you felt when you were in a cage?"

Yes.

"The violin," Nora said. "Did someone at the laboratory play the violin for you?"

Yes.

"Why would they do that, I wonder?" Travis said.

That was one the dog could not answer with a simple yes or no.

"Did you like the violin?" Nora asked.

Yes.

"You like music in general?"

Yes.

"Do you like jazz?"

The dog neither barked nor wagged his tail.

Travis said, "He doesn't know what jazz is. I guess they never let him hear any of that."

"Do you like rock and roll?" Nora asked.

One bark, simultaneously, a wagging of the tail.

"What's that supposed to mean?" Nora asked.

"Probably means 'yes and no,' " Travis said. "He likes some rock and roll but not all of it."

Einstein wagged his tail to confirm Travis's interpretation.

"Classical?" Nora asked.

Yes.

Travis said, "So we've got a dog that's a snob, huh?"

Yes, yes, yes.

Nora laughed in delight, and so did Travis, and Einstein nuzzled and licked them happily.

Travis looked around for another picture, snatched up the one of the man on the exercise treadmill. "They wouldn't want to let you out of the lab, I guess. Yet they'd want to keep you fit. Is this how they exercised you? On a treadmill?"

Yes.

The sense of discovery was exhilarating. Travis would have been no more thrilled, no more excited, no more awestricken if he had been communicating with an extraterrestrial intelligence.

6

I'm falling down a rabbit hole, Walt Gaines thought uneasily as he listened to Lem Johnson.

This new high-tech world of space flight, computers in the home, satellite-relayed telephone calls, factory robots, and now biological engineering seemed utterly unrelated to the world in which he was born and grew up. For God's sake, he had been a child during World War II, when there had not even been jet aircraft. He hailed from a simpler world of boatlike Chryslers with tail fins, phones with dials instead of push buttons, clocks with hands instead of digital display boards. Television did not exist when he was born, and the possibility of nuclear Armageddon within his own lifetime was something no one then could have predicted. He felt as though he had stepped through an invisible barrier from his world into another reality that was on a faster track. This new kingdom of high technology could be delightful or frightening—and occasionally both at the same time.

Like now.

The idea of an intelligent dog appealed to the child in him and made him want to smile.

But something else—The Outsider—had escaped from those labs, and it scared the bejesus out of him.

"The dog had no name," Lem Johnson said. "That's not so unusual. Most scientists who work with lab animals never name them. If you've named an animal, you'll inevitably begin to attribute a personality to it, and then your relationship to it will change, and you'll no longer be as objective in your observations as you have to be. So the dog had only a number until it was clear this was the success Weatherby had been working so hard to achieve. Even then, when it was evident that the dog would not have to be destroyed as a failure, no name was given to it. Everyone simply called it 'the dog,' which was enough to differentiate it from all of Weatherby's other pups because they'd been referred to by numbers. Anyway, at the same time, Dr. Yarbeck was working on other, very different research under the Francis Project umbrella, and she, too, finally met with some success."

Yarbeck's objective was to create an animal with dramatically increased intelligence—but one also designed to accompany men into war as police dogs accompanied cops in dangerous urban neighborhoods. Yarbeck sought to engineer a beast that was smart but also deadly, a terror on the battlefield—ferocious, stealthy, cunning, and intelligent enough to be effective in both jungle and urban warfare.

Not quite as intelligent as human beings, of course, not as smart as the dog that Weatherby was developing. It would be sheer madness to create a killing machine as intelligent as the people who would have to use and control it. Everyone had read *Frankenstein* or had seen one of the old Karloff movies, and no one underestimated the dangers inherent in Yarbeck's research.

Choosing to work with monkeys and apes because of their naturally high intelligence and because they already possessed humanlike hands, Yarbeck ultimately selected baboons as the base species for her dark acts of creation. Baboons were among the smartest of primates, good raw material. They were deadly and effective fighters by nature, with impressive claws and fangs, fiercely motivated by the territorial imperative, and eager to attack those whom they perceived as enemies.

"Yarbeck's first task in the *physical* alteration of the baboon was to make it larger, big enough to threaten a grown man," Lem said. "She decided that it would have to stand at least five feet and weigh one hundred to a hundred and ten pounds."

"That's not so big," Walt protested.

"Big enough."

"I could swat down a man that size."

"A man, yes. But not this thing. It's solid muscle, no fat at all, and far quicker than a man. Stop and think of how a fifty-pound pit bull can make mincemeat of a grown man, and you'll realize what a threat Yarbeck's warrior could be at a hundred and ten."

The patrol car's steam-silvered windshield seemed like a movie screen on which Walt saw projected images of brutally murdered men: Wes Dalberg, Teel Porter . . . He closed his eyes but still saw cadavers. "Okay, yeah, I get your point. A hundred and ten pounds would be enough if we're talking about something *designed* to fight and kill."

"So Yarbeck created a breed of baboons that would grow to greater size. Then she set to work altering the sperm and ova of her giant primates in other ways, sometimes by editing the baboon's own genetic material, sometimes by introducing genes from other species."

Walt said, "The same sort of cross-species patch-and-stitch that led to the smart dog."

"I wouldn't call it patch-and-stitch . . . but yeah, essentially the same techniques. Yarbeck wanted a large, vicious jaw on her warrior, something more like that of a German shepherd, even a jackal, so there would be room for more teeth, and she wanted the teeth to be larger and sharper and perhaps slightly hooked, which meant she had to enlarge the baboon's head and totally alter its facial structure to accommodate all of this. The skull had to be greatly enlarged, anyway, to allow for a bigger brain. Dr. Yarbeck wasn't working under the constraints that required Davis Weatherby to leave his dog's appearance unchanged. In fact, Yarbeck figured that if her creation was hideous, if it was *alien*, it would be an even more effective warrior because it would serve not only to stalk and kill our enemies but terrorize them."

In spite of the warm, muggy air, Walt Gaines felt a coldness in his belly, as if he had swallowed big chunks of ice. "Didn't Yarbeck or anyone else consider the immorality of this, for Christ's sake? Didn't any of them ever read *The*

Island of Doctor Moreau? Lem, you have a goddamn moral obligation to let the public know about this, to blow it wide open. And so do I."

"No such thing," Lem said. "The idea that there's good and evil knowledge . . . well, that's strictly a religious point of view. Actions can be either moral or immoral, yes, but knowledge can't be labeled that way. To a scientist, to *any* educated man or woman, all knowledge is morally neutral."

"But, shit, *application* of the knowledge, in Yarbeck's case, wasn't morally neutral."

Sitting on one or the other's patio on weekends, drinking Corona, dealing with the weighty problems of the world, they loved to talk about this sort of thing. Backyard philosophers. Beery sages taking smug pleasure in their wisdom. And sometimes the moral dilemmas they discussed on weekends were those that later arose in the course of their police work; however, Walt could not remember any discussion that had had as urgent a bearing on their work as this one.

"Applying knowledge is part of the process of learning more," Lem said. "The scientist has to apply his discoveries to see where each application leads. Moral responsibility is on the shoulders of those who take the technology out of the lab and use it to immoral ends."

"Do you believe that bullshit?"

Lem thought a moment. "Yeah, I guess I do. I guess, if we held scientists responsible for the bad things that flowed from their work, they'd never go to work in the first place, and there'd be no progress at all. We'd still be living in caves."

Walt pulled a clean handkerchief from his pocket and blotted his face, giving himself a moment to think. It wasn't so much the heat and humidity that had gotten to him. It was the thought of Yarbeck's warrior roaming the Orange County hills that made him break out in a sweat.

He wanted to go public, warn the unwary world that something new and dangerous was loose upon the earth. But that would be playing into the hands of the new Luddites, who would use Yarbeck's warrior to generate public hysteria in an attempt to bring an end to all recombinant-DNA research. Already, such research had created strains of corn and wheat that could grow with less water and in poor soil, relieving world hunger, and years ago they had developed a man-made virus that, as a waste product, produced cheap insulin. If he took word of Yarbeck's monstrosity to the world, he might save a couple of lives in the short run, but he might be playing a role in denying the world the beneficial miracles of recombinant-DNA research, which would *cost* tens of thousands of lives in the long run.

"Shit," Walt said. "It's not a black-and-white issue, is it?"

Lem said, "That's what makes life interesting."

Walt smiled sourly. "Right now, it's a whole hell of a lot more interesting than I care for. Okay. I can see the wisdom of keeping a lid on this. Besides, if we made it public, you'd have a thousand half-assed adventurers out there looking for the thing, and they'd end up victims of it, or they'd gun down one another."

"Exactly."

"But my men could help keep the lid on by joining in the search."

Lem told him about the hundred men from Marine Intelligence units who were still combing the foothills, dressed as civilians, using high-tech tracking gear and, in some cases, bloodhounds. "I've already got more men on line than you could supply. We're already doing as much as can be done. Now will you do the right thing? Will you stay out of it?"

Frowning, Walt said, "For now. But I want to be kept informed."

Lem nodded. "All right."

"And I have more questions. For one thing, why do they call it The Outsider?"

"Well, the dog was the first breakthrough, the first of the lab subjects to display unusual intelligence. This one was next. They were the only two successes: the dog and the other. At first, they added capital letters to the way they pronounced it, The Other, but in time it became The Outsider because that seemed to fit better. It was not an improvement on one of God's creations, as was the dog; it was entirely *outside* of creation, a thing apart. An abomination—though no one actually said as much. And the thing was aware of its status as an outsider, acutely aware."

"Why not just call it the baboon?"

"Because . . . it doesn't really look much of anything like a baboon any more. Not like anything you've ever seen—except in a nightmare."

Walt did not like the expression on his friend's dark face, in his eyes. He decided not to ask for a better description of The Outsider; perhaps that was something he did not need to know.

Instead, he said, "What about the Hudston, Weatherby, and Yarbeck murders? Who was behind all that?"

"We don't know the man who pulled the trigger, but we know the Soviets hired him. They also killed another Banodyne man who was on vacation in Acapulco."

Walt felt as if he were jolting through one of those invisible barriers again, into an even more complicated world. "Soviets? Were we talking about the Soviets? How'd they get into the act?"

"We didn't think they knew about the Francis Project," Lem said. "But they did. Apparently, they even had a mole inside Banodyne who reported out to them on our progress. When the dog and, subsequently, The Outsider escaped, the mole informed the Soviets, and evidently the Soviets decided to take advantage of the chaos and do us even more damage. They killed every project leader—Yarbeck and Weatherby and Haines—plus Hudston, who had once been a project leader but no longer worked at Banodyne. We think they did this for two reasons: first, to bring the Francis Project to a halt; second, to make it harder for us to track down The Outsider."

"How would that make it harder?"

Lem slumped in his seat as if, in talking of the crisis, he was more clearly aware of the burden on his shoulders. "By eliminating Hudston, Haines, and especially Weatherby and Yarbeck, the Soviets cut us off from the people who would have the best idea how The Outsider and the dog think, the people best able to figure out where those animals might go and how they might be recaptured."

"Have you actually pinned it on the Soviets?"

Lem sighed. "Not entirely. I'm focused primarily on recovering the dog and The Outsider, so we have another entire task force trying to track down the Soviet agents behind the murders, arson, and data hijacking. Unfortunately, the Soviets seem to have used freelance hitmen outside of their own network, so we have no idea where to look for the triggermen. That side of the investigation is pretty much stalled."

"And the fire at Banodyne a day or so later?" Walt asked.

"Definitely arson. Another Soviet action. It destroyed all the paper and electronic files on the Francis Project. There were backup computer disks at another location, of course . . . but data on them has somehow been erased."

"The Soviets again?"

"We think so. The leaders of the Francis Project and all their files have been wiped out, leaving us in the dark when it comes to trying to figure how either the dog or The Outsider might think, where they might go, how they might be tricked into captivity."

Walt shook his head. "Never thought I'd be on the side of the Russians, but putting a stop to this project seems like a good idea."

"They're far from innocent. From what I hear, they've got a similar project under way at laboratories in the Ukraine. I wouldn't doubt we're working diligently to destroy their files and people the way they've destroyed ours. Anyway, the Soviets would like nothing better than for The Outsider to run wild in some nice peaceable suburb, gutting housewives and chewing the heads off little kids, because if that happens a couple of times . . . well, then the whole thing's going to blow up in our face."

Chewing the heads off little kids? Jesus.

Walt shuddered and said, "Is that likely to happen?"

"We don't believe so. The Outsider is aggressive as hell—it was designed to be aggressive, after all—and it has a special hatred for its makers, which is something Yarbeck didn't count on and something she hoped to be able to correct in future generations. The Outsider takes great pleasure in slaughtering us. But it's also smart, and it knows that every killing gives us a new fix on its whereabouts. So it's not going to indulge its hatred too often. It's going to stay away from people most of the time, moving mainly at night. Once in a while, out of curiosity, it might poke into residential areas along the edge of the developed eastern flank of the county—"

"As it did at the Keeshan place."

"Yeah. But I bet it didn't go there to kill anyone. Just plain curiosity. It doesn't want to be caught before it accomplishes its main goal."

"Which is?"

"Finding and killing the dog," Lem said.

Walt was surprised. "Why would it care about the dog?"

"We don't really know," Lem said. "But at Banodyne, it harbored a fierce hatred of the dog, worse than what it felt toward people. When Yarbeck worked with it, constructing a sign language with which to communicate complex ideas, The Outsider several times expressed a desire to kill and mutilate the dog, but it would never explain why. It was *obsessed* with the dog."

"So you think now it's tracking the retriever?"

"Yes. Because evidence seems to indicate that the dog was the first to break out of the labs that night in May, and that its escape drove The Outsider mad. The Outsider was kept in a large enclosure inside Yarbeck's lab, and everything belonging to it—bedding, many educational devices, toys—was torn and smashed to pieces. Then, apparently realizing that the dog was going to be forever out of its reach if it didn't make good its own escape, The Outsider put its mind to the problem and, by God, found its own way out."

"But if the dog got a good head start—"

"There's a link between the dog and The Outsider that no one understands. A mental link. Instinctual awareness. We don't know its extent, but we can't rule out the possibility that this link is strong enough for one of them to follow the other over considerable distances. It's apparently a sort of mild sixth sense that was somehow a bonus of the technique of intelligence enhancement used in both Weatherby's and Yarbeck's research. But we're only guessing. We don't really know for sure. There's so fucking much we don't know!"

Both men were silent for a while.

The humid closeness of the car was no longer entirely unpleasant. Given all the dangers loose in the modern world, these steamy confines seemed safe and comfortable, a haven.

Finally, not wanting to ask any more questions, afraid of the answers he might get, Walt nevertheless said, "Banodyne is a high-security building. It's designed to keep unauthorized people from getting in, but it must be hard to get *out* of the place, too. Yet both the dog and The Outsider escaped."

"Yes."

"And obviously no one ever figured they could. Which means they're both smarter than anyone realized."

"Yes."

Walt said, "In the case of the dog . . . well, if it's smarter than anyone figured, so what? The dog is friendly."

Lem, who had been staring at the opaqued windshield, finally met Walt's eyes. "That's right. But if The Outsider is smarter than we thought . . . if it's very nearly as smart as a man, then catching it's going to be even harder."

"Very nearly . . . or *as* smart as a man."

"No. Impossible."

"Or even smarter," Walt said.

"No. That couldn't be."

"Couldn't?"

"No."

"Definitely couldn't?"

Lem sighed, wearily rubbed his eyes, and said nothing. He was not going to start lying to his best friend again.

7

Nora and Travis went through the photographs one by one, learning a little more about Einstein. By barking once or vigorously wagging his tail, the dog answered questions and was able to confirm that he had chosen the advertisements for computers because they reminded him of the computers in the lab where he had been kept. The photo of four young people playing with a striped beach ball appealed to him because one of the scientists in the lab had evidently used balls of various sizes in an intelligence test that Einstein had particularly enjoyed. They were unable to determine the reason for his interest in the parrot, the butterflies, Mickey Mouse, and many other things, but that was only because they could not hit upon the pertinent yes-or-no questions that would have led to explanations.

Even when a hundred questions failed to reveal the meaning of one of the photographs, the three of them remained excited and delighted by the process of discovery, for they met with success in enough cases to make the effort worthwhile. The only time the mood changed for the worse was when they queried Einstein about the magazine picture of the demon from an upcoming horror movie. He became extremely agitated. He tucked his tail between his legs, bared his teeth, growled deep in his throat. Several times, he padded away from the photograph, going behind the sofa or into another room, where he stayed for a minute or two before returning, reluctantly, to face additional questions, and he shivered almost continuously when being quizzed about the demon.

Finally, after trying for at least ten minutes to determine the reason for the dog's dread, Travis pointed to the slabjawed, wickedly fanged, luminous-eyed movie monster and said, "Maybe you don't understand, Einstein. This isn't a picture of a real, living thing. This is a make-believe demon from a movie. Do you understand what I mean when I say make-believe?"

Einstein wagged his tail: *Yes*.

"Well, this is a make-believe monster."

One bark: *No.*

"Make-believe, phony, not real, just a man in a rubber suit," Nora said.

No.

"Yes," Travis said.

No.

Einstein tried to run off behind the sofa again, but Travis grabbed him by the collar and held him. "Are you claiming to have seen such a thing?"

The dog raised his gaze from the picture, looked into Travis's eyes, shuddered, and whimpered.

The pitiful note of profound fear in Einstein's soft whine and an indescribably disturbing quality in his dark eyes combined to affect Travis to an extent that surprised him. Holding the collar with one hand, his other hand on Einstein's back, Travis felt the shivers that quaked through the dog—and suddenly he was shivering, too. The dog's stark fear was transmitted to him, and he thought, crazily, *By God, he really has seen something like this.*

Sensing the change in Travis, Nora said, "What's wrong?"

Instead of answering her, he repeated the question that Einstein had not yet answered: "Are you claiming to have seen such a thing?"

Yes.

"Something that looks exactly like this demon?"

A bark and a wag: *Yes and no.*

"Something that looks at least a little bit like it?"

Yes.

Letting go of the collar, Travis stroked the dog's back, trying to soothe him, but Einstein continued to shiver. "Is this why you keep a watch at the window some nights?"

Yes.

Clearly puzzled and alarmed by the dog's distress, Nora began to pet him, too. "I thought you were worried that people from the lab would find you."

Einstein barked once.

"You're not afraid people from the lab will find you?"

Yes and no.

Travis said, "But you're more afraid that . . . this other thing will find you."

Yes, yes, yes.

"Is this the same thing that was in the woods that day, the thing that chased us, the thing I shot at?" Travis asked.

Yes, yes, yes.

Travis looked at Nora. She was frowning. "But it's only a movie monster. Nothing in the real world looks even a little bit like it."

Padding across the room, sniffing at the assorted photographs, Einstein paused again at the Blue Cross ad that featured the doctor, mother, and baby in a hospital room. He brought the magazine to them and dropped it on the floor. He put his nose to the doctor in the picture, then looked at Nora, at Travis, put his nose to the doctor again, and looked up expectantly.

"Before," Nora said, "you told us the doctor represented one of the scientists in that lab."

Yes.

Travis said, "So are you telling me the scientist who worked on you would know what this thing in the woods was?"

Yes.

Einstein went looking through the photographs again, and this time he returned with the ad that showed a car in a cage. He touched his nose to the cage; then, hesitantly, he touched his nose to the picture of the demon.

"Are you saying the thing in the woods belongs in a cage?" Nora asked.

Yes.

"More than that," Travis said, "I think he's telling us that it was in a cage at one time, that he saw it in a cage."

Yes.

"In the same lab where *you* were in a cage?"

Yes, yes, yes.

"Another experimental lab animal?" Nora asked.

Yes.

Travis stared hard at the photograph of the demon, at its thick brow and deeply set yellow eyes, at its deformed snoutlike nose and mouth bristling with teeth. At last he said, "Was it an experiment . . . that went wrong?"

Yes and no, Einstein said.

Now at a peak of agitation, the dog crossed the living room to the front window, jumped up and braced his forepaws on the sill, and peered out at the Santa Barbara evening.

Nora and Travis sat on the floor among the opened magazines and books, happy with the progress they had made, beginning to feel the exhaustion that their excitement had masked—and frowning at each other in puzzlement.

She spoke softly. "Do you think Einstein's capable of lying, making up wild stories like children do?"

"I don't know. Can dogs lie, or is that just a human skill?" He laughed at the absurdity of his own question. "Can dogs lie? Can a moose be elected to the presidency? Can cows sing?"

Nora laughed, too, and very prettily. "Can ducks tap-dance?"

In a fit of silliness that was a reaction to the difficulty of dealing intellectually and emotionally with the whole idea of a dog as smart as Einstein, Travis said, "I once saw a duck tap-dancing."

"Oh, yeah?"

"Yeah. In Vegas."

Laughing, she said, "What hotel was he performing at?"

"Caesar's Palace. He could sing, too."

"The duck?"

"Yeah. Ask me his name."

"What was his name?"

"Sammy Davis Duck, Jr.," Travis said, and they laughed again. "He was such a big star they didn't even have to put his entire name on the marquee for people to know who was performing there."

"They just put 'Sammy,' huh?"

"No, Just 'Jr.' "

Einstein returned from the window and stood watching them, his head cocked, trying to figure out why they were acting so peculiar.

The puzzled expression on the retriever's face struck both Travis and Nora as the most comical thing they had ever seen. They leaned on each other, held each other, and laughed like fools.

With a snort of derision, the retriever went back to the window.

As they gradually regained control of themselves and as their laughter subsided, Travis became aware that he was *holding* Nora, that her head was on his shoulder, that the physical contact between them was greater than any they had allowed themselves before. Her hair smelled clean, fresh. He could feel the body heat pouring off her. Suddenly, he wanted her desperately, and he knew he was going to kiss her when she raised her head from his shoulder. A moment later she looked up, and he did what he knew he'd do—he kissed her—and she kissed him. For a second or two, she did not seem to realize what was happening, what it meant; briefly, it was without significance, sweet and utterly innocent, not a kiss of passion but of friendship and great affection. Then the kiss changed, and her mouth softened. She began to breathe faster, and her hand tightened on his arm, and she tried to pull him closer. A low murmur of need escaped her—and the sound of her own voice brought her to her senses. Abruptly, she stiffened with complete awareness of him as a man, and her beautiful eyes were wide with wonder—and fear—at what had almost happened. Travis instantly drew back because he knew instinctively that the time was not right, not yet perfect. When at last they did make love, it must be exactly right, without hesitation or distraction, because for the rest of their lives they would always remember their first time, and the memory should be all bright and joyous, worth taking out and examining a thousand times as they grew old together. Although it was not quite time to put their future into words and confirm it with vows, Travis had no doubt that he and Nora Devon would be spending their lives with each other, and he realized that, subconsciously, he'd been aware of this inevitability for at least the past few days.

After a moment of awkwardness, as they drew apart and tried to decide whether to comment on the sudden change in their relationship, Nora finally said, "He's still at the window."

Einstein pressed his nose to the glass, staring out at the night.

"Could he be telling the truth?" Nora whispered. "Could there have been something else that escaped from the lab, something *that* bizarre?"

"If they had a dog as smart as him, I guess they might have had other things even more peculiar. And there *was* something in the woods that day."

"But there's no danger of it finding him, surely. Not after you brought him this far north."

"No danger," Travis agreed. "I don't think Einstein understands how far we came from where I found him. Whatever was in the woods couldn't track him down now. But I'll bet the people from that lab have mounted one hell of a search. It's them I'm worried about. And so is Einstein, which is why he usually plays at being a dumb dog in public and reveals his intelligence only in private to me and now you. He doesn't want to go back."

Nora said, "If they find him . . ."

"They won't."

"But if they do, what then?"

"I'll never give him up," Travis said. "Never."

8

By eleven o'clock that night, Deputy Porter's headless corpse and the mutilated body of the construction foreman had been removed from Bordeaux Ridge by the coroner's men. A cover story had been concocted and delivered to the reporters at the police barricades, and the press had seemed to buy it; they had asked their questions, had taken a couple of hundred photographs, and had filled a few thousand feet of videotape with images that would be edited down to a hundred seconds on tomorrow's TV newscast. (In this age of mass murder and terrorism, two victims rated no more than two minutes' air-time: ten seconds for lead-in, a hundred seconds for film, ten seconds for the well-coiffed anchorpersons to look respectfully grim and saddened—then on to a story about a bikini contest, a convention of Edsel owners, or a man who claimed to have seen an alien spacecraft shaped like a Twinkie.) The reporters were gone now, as were the lab men, the uniformed deputies, and all of Lemuel Johnson's agents except Cliff Soames.

Clouds hid the fragment moon. The kliegs were gone, and the only light came from the headlamps of Walt Gaine's car. He had swung his sedan around and aimed his lights at Lem's car, which was parked at the end of the unpaved street, so Lem and Cliff would not have to fumble around in the dark. In the deep gloom beyond the headlamps, half-framed houses loomed like the fossilized skeletons of prehistoric reptiles.

As he walked toward his car, Lem felt as good as he could feel under the circumstances. Walt had agreed to allow federal authorities to assume jurisdiction without a challenge. Although Lem had broken a dozen regulations and had violated his secrecy oath by telling Walt the details of the Francis Project, he was sure Walt could keep his mouth shut. The lid was still on the case, a bit looser than it had been, perhaps, but still in place.

Cliff Soames reached the car first, opened the door, and got in on the passenger's side, and as Lem opened the driver's door he heard Cliff say, "Oh, Jesus, oh God." Cliff was scrambling back out of the car even as Lem looked in from the other side and saw what the uproar was about. A head.

Teel Porter's head, no doubt.

It was on the front seat of the car, propped so it was facing Lem when he opened the door. The mouth hung open in a silent scream. The eyes were gone.

Reeling back from the car, Lem reached under his coat and pulled his revolver.

Walt Gaines was already out of his car, his own revolver in hand, running toward Lem. "What's wrong?"

Lem pointed.

Reaching the NSA sedan, Walt looked through the open door and let out a thin, anguished sound when he saw the head.

Cliff came around from the other side of the car, gripping his gun, with the muzzle pointed straight up. "The damn thing was *here* when we arrived, while we were in the house."

"Might still be here," Lem said, anxiously surveying the darkness that crowded them on all sides, beyond the beams from the patrol car's headlights.

Studying the night-swaddled housing development, Walt said, "We'll call in my men, get a search under way."

"No point to it," Lem said. "The thing will take off if it sees your men returning . . . if it's not gone already."

They were standing at the edge of Bordeaux Ridge, beyond which lay miles of open land, foothills and mountains, out of which The Outsider had come and into which it could disappear again. Those hills, ridges, and canyons were only vague forms in the meager glow of the partial moon, more sensed than seen.

From somewhere down the unlighted street came a loud clatter, as if a pile of lumber or shingles had been knocked over.

"It *is* here," Walt said.

"Maybe," Lem said. "But we're not going to go looking for it in the dark, not just the three of us. That's what it wants."

They listened.

Nothing more.

"We searched the whole tract when we first got here, before you arrived," Walt said.

Cliff said, "It must've kept one step ahead of you, making a game of dodging your men. Then it saw us arrive, and it recognized Lem."

"Recognized me from the couple of times I visited Banodyne," Lem agreed. "In fact . . . The Outsider was probably waiting here just for me. It probably understands my role in all this and knows I'm in charge of the search for it and the dog. So it wanted to leave the deputy's head for me."

"To mock you?" Walt said.

"To mock me."

They were silent, peering uneasily at the blackness within and around the unfinished houses.

The hot June air was motionless.

For a long while, the only sound was the idling engine of the sheriff's car. "Watching us," Walt said.

Another clatter of overturned construction materials. Nearer this time.

The three men froze, each looking a different direction, guarding against attack.

The subsequent silence lasted almost a minute.

When Lem was about to speak, The Outsider shrieked. The cry was alien, chilling. This time they could identify the direction from which it came: out in the open land, in the night beyond Bordeaux Ridge.

"It's leaving now," Lem said. "It's decided we can't be lured into a search, just the three of us, so it's leaving before we can bring in reinforcements."

It shrieked again, from farther away. The eerie cry was like sharp fingernails raked across Lem's soul.

"In the morning," he said, "we'll move our Marine Intelligence teams into the foothills east of here. We'll nail the damn thing. By God, we will."

Turning to Lem's sedan, evidently contemplating the unpleasant task of dealing with Teel Porter's severed head, Walt said, "Why the eyes? Why does it always tear out the eyes?"

Lem said, "Partly because the creature's just damned aggressive, bloodthirsty. That's in its genes. And partly because it really enjoys spreading terror, I think. But also . . ."

"What?"

"I wish I didn't remember this, but I do, very clearly . . ."

On one of his visits to Banodyne, Lem had witnessed a disturbing conversation (of sorts) between Dr. Yarbeck and The Outsider. Yarbeck and her assistants had taught The Outsider a sign language similar to that developed by the researchers who attempted the first experiments in communication with the higher primates, like gorillas, back in the mid-1970s. The most successful gorilla subject—a female named Koko, which had been the center of countless news stories over the past decade—was reputed to have attained a sign-language vocabulary of approximately four hundred words. When Lem had last seen it, The Outsider boasted a vocabulary considerably larger than Koko's, though still primitive. In Yarbeck's lab, Lem had watched as the man-made monstrosity in the large cage had exchanged complicated series of hand signals with the scientist, while an assistant had whispered a running translation. The Outsider had expressed a fierce hostility toward everyone and everything, frequently interrupting its dialogue with Yarbeck to dash around its cage in uncontrolled rage, banging on the iron bars, screeching furiously. To Lem, the scene was frightening and repellant, but he was also filled with a terrible sadness and pity at the plight of The Outsider: the beast would always be caged, always a freak, alone in the world as no other creature—not even Weatherby's dog—had ever been. The experience had affected him so deeply that he still remembered nearly every exchange of sign language between The Outsider and Yarbeck, and now a pertinent part of that eerie conversation came back to him:

At one point The Outsider had signed: *Tear out your eyes.*

You want to tear out my eyes? Yarbeck signed.

Tear out everyone's eyes.

Why?

So can't see me.

Why don't you want to be seen?

Ugly.

You think you're ugly?

Much ugly.

Where did you get the idea you're ugly?

From people.

What people?

Everyone who see me first time.

Like this man with us today? Yarbeck signed, indicating Lem.

Yes. All think me ugly. Hate me.

No one hates you.

Everyone.

No one's ever told you that you're ugly. How do you know that's what they think?

I know.

How do you know?

I know, I know, I know! It raced around its cage, rattling the bars, shrieking, and then it returned to face Yarbeck. *Tear out my own eyes.*

So you won't have to look at yourself?

So won't have to look at people looking at me, the creature had signed, and Lem had pitied it then, deeply, though his pity had in no way diminished his fear of it.

Now, standing in the hot June night, he told Walt Gaines about that exchange in Yarbeck's lab, and the sheriff shivered.

"Jesus," Cliff Soames said. "It hates itself, its otherness, and so it hates its maker even more."

"And now that you've told me this," Walt said, "I'm surprised none of you ever understood why it hates the dog so passionately. This poor damned twisted thing and the dog are essentially the only two children of the Francis Project. The dog is the beloved child, the favored child, and The Outsider has always known that. The dog is the child that the parents want to brag about, while The Outsider is the child they would prefer to keep locked securely in a cellar, and so it resents the dog, *stews* in resentment every minute of every day."

"Of course," Lem said, "you're right. Of course."

"It also gives new meaning to the two smashed mirrors in the upstairs bathrooms in the house where Teel Porter was killed," Walt said. "The thing couldn't bear the sight of itself."

In the distance, very far away now, something shrieked, something that was not of God's creation.

CHAPTER 7

1

DURING THE REST of June, Nora did some painting, spent a lot of time with Travis, and tried to teach Einstein to read.

Neither she nor Travis was sure that the dog, although very smart, could be taught such a thing, but it was worth a try. If he understood spoken English, as seemed to be the case, then it followed that he could be taught the printed word as well.

Of course, they could not be absolutely certain that Einstein *did* understand spoken English, even though he responded to it with apt and specific reactions. It was remotely possible that, instead, the dog did not perceive the precise meanings of the words themselves but, by some mild form of telepathy, could read the word-*pictures* in people's minds as they spoke.

"But I don't believe that's the case," Travis said one afternoon as he and Nora sat on his patio, drinking wine coolers and watching Einstein frolic in the spray of a portable lawn sprinkler. "Maybe because I don't want to believe it. The idea that he's both as smart as me *and* telepathic is just too much. If that's the case, then maybe I should be wearing the collar and he should be holding the leash!"

It was a Spanish test that appeared to indicate the retriever was not, in fact, even slightly telepathic.

In college, Travis had taken three years of Spanish. Later, upon choosing a career in the military and signing on with the elite Delta Force, he'd been encouraged to continue those language studies because his superiors believed the escalating political instability in Central and South America guaranteed that Delta would be required to conduct antiterrorist operations in Spanish-speaking countries with steadily increasing frequency. He had been out of Delta for many years, but contact with the large population of California Hispanics had kept him relatively fluent.

Now, when he gave Einstein orders or asked questions in Spanish, the dog stared at him stupidly, wagging his tail, unresponsive. When Travis persisted in Spanish, the retriever cocked his head and whuffed as if to inquire if this was a joke. Surely, if the dog was reading mental images that arose in the mind of the speaker, he would be able to read them regardless of the language that inspired those images.

"He's no mind reader," Travis said. "There are limits to his genius—thank God!"

Day after day, Nora sat on the floor of Travis's living room or on the patio, explaining the alphabet to Einstein and trying to help him understand how words were formed from those letters and how those printed words were related to the spoken words that he already understood. Now and then, Travis took charge of the lessons to give Nora a break, but most of the time he sat nearby, reading, because he claimed not to have the patience to be a teacher.

She used a ring-binder notebook to compile her own primer for the dog. On each left-hand page, she taped a picture cut from a magazine, and on each right-hand page she printed, in block letters, the name of the object that was pictured on the left, all simple words: TREE, CAR, HOUSE, MAN, WOMAN, CHAIR . . . With Einstein sitting beside her and staring intently at the primer, she would point to the picture first, then to the word, pronouncing it repeatedly.

On the last day of June, Nora spread a score or more of unlabeled pictures on the floor.

"It's test time again," she told Einstein. "Let's see if you can do better than you did on Monday."

Einstein sat very erect, his chest puffed out, his head held high, as if confident of his ability.

Travis was sitting in the armchair, watching. He said, "If you fail, fur face, we're going to trade you in on a poodle that can roll over, play dead, and beg for its supper."

Nora was pleased to see that Einstein ignored Travis. "This is not a time for frivolity," she admonished.

"I stand corrected, professor," Travis said.

Nora held up a flashcard with TREE printed on it. The retriever went unerringly to the photo of a pine tree and indicated it with a touch of his nose. When she held up a card that said CAR, he put a paw on the photo of the car, and when she held up HOUSE, he sniffed at the picture of a colonial mansion. They went through fifty words, and for the first time the dog correctly paired every printed word with the image it represented. Nora was thrilled by his progress, and Einstein could not stop wagging his tail.

Travis said, "Well, Einstein, you're still a hell of a long way from reading Proust."

Rankled by Travis's needling of her star pupil, Nora said, "He's doing fine! Terrific. You can't expect him to be reading at college level overnight. He's learning faster than a child would."

"Is that so?"

"Yes, that's so! *Much* faster than a child would."

"Well then, maybe he deserves a couple of Milk-Bones."

Einstein dashed immediately into the kitchen to get the box of dog biscuits.

2

As the summer wore on, Travis was amazed by the swift progress Nora made in teaching Einstein to read.

By the middle of July, they graduated from her homemade primer to children's picture books by Dr. Seuss, Maurice Sendak, Phil Parks, Susi Bohdal, Sue Dreamer, Mercer Mayer, and many others. Einstein appeared to enjoy all of them immensely, though his favorites were Parks and especially— for reasons neither Nora nor Travis could discern—the charming Frog and Toad books by Arnold Lobel. They brought armsful of children's books home from the city library and purchased additional stacks of them at the bookstore.

At first, Nora read them aloud, carefully moving a finger under each word as she spoke it, and Einstein's eyes followed along as he leaned in toward the book with undivided attention. Later, she did not read the book aloud but held it open for the dog and turned the pages for him when he indicated—by a whimper or some other sign—that he had finished that portion of the text and was ready to proceed to the next page.

Einstein's willingness to sit for hours, focusing on the books, seemed proof that he was actually reading them and not just looking at the cute drawings. Nevertheless, Nora decided to test him on the contents of some of the volumes by posing a number of questions about the story lines.

After Einstein had read *Frog and Toad All Year,* Nora closed the book and said, "All right. Now, answer yes or no to these questions."

They were in the kitchen, where Travis was making a cheese-and-potato casserole for dinner. Nora and Einstein were sitting on chairs at the kitchen table. Travis paused in his cooking to watch the dog take the quiz.

Nora said, "First—when Frog came to see Toad on a winter's day, Toad was in bed and did not want to come outside. Is that right?"

Einstein had to sidle around on his chair to free his tail and wag it. *Yes.*

Nora said, "But finally Frog got Toad outside, and they went ice-skating." One bark. *No.*

"They went sledding," she said.

Yes.

"Very good. Later that same year, at Christmas, Frog gave Toad a gift. Was it a sweater?"

No.

"A new sled?"

No.

"A clock for his mantel?"

Yes, yes, yes.

"Excellent!" Nora said. "Now what shall we read next? How about this one. *Fantastic Mr. Fox.*"

Einstein wagged his tail vigorously.

Travis would have enjoyed taking a more active role in the dog's education, but he could see that working intensely with Einstein was having an enormously beneficial effect on Nora, and he did not want to interfere. Indeed, he sometimes played the curmudgeon, questioning the value of teaching the pooch to read, making wisecracks about the pace of the dog's progress or its taste in reading matter. This mild naysaying was just enough to redouble Nora's determination to stick with the lessons, to spend even more time with the dog, and to prove Travis wrong. Einstein never reacted to those negative remarks, and Travis suspected the dog exhibited forbearance because he understood the little game of reverse psychology in which Travis was engaged.

Exactly why Nora's teaching chores made her blossom was not clear. Perhaps it was because she had never interacted with anyone—not even with Travis or with her Aunt Violet—as intensely as she had with the dog, and the mere process of extensive communication encouraged her to come farther out of her shell. Or perhaps giving the gift of literacy to the dog was extremely satisfying to her. She was by nature a giving person who took pleasure in sharing with others, yet she had spent all of her life as a recluse without a single previous opportunity to express that side of her personality. Now she had a chance to give of herself, and she was generous with her time and energy, and in her own generosity she found joy.

Travis also suspected that, through her relationship with the retriever, she was expressing a natural talent for mothering. Her great patience was that of a good mother dealing with a child, and she often spoke to Einstein so tenderly and affectionately that she sounded as if she were addressing her own much-loved offspring.

Whatever the reason, Nora became more relaxed and outgoing as she worked with Einstein. Gradually forsaking her shapeless dark dresses for summery white cotton slacks, colorful blouses, jeans and T-shirts, she seemed to grow ten years younger. She had her glorious dark hair redone at the beauty salon and did not brush out all the styling this time. She laughed more often and more engagingly. In conversation, she met Travis's eyes and seldom looked shyly away from him, as she had done previously. She was quicker to touch him, too, and to put an arm around his waist. She liked to be hugged, and they kissed with ease now, although their kissing remained, for the most part, that of uncertain teenagers in the early stages of courting.

On July 14, Nora received news that lifted her spirits even higher. The Santa Barbara District Attorney's Office called to tell her that it was not going to be necessary for her to appear in court to testify against Arthur Streck. In light of his previous criminal record, Streck had changed his mind about pursuing a plea of innocence and waging a defense against charges of attempted rape, assault, and breaking and entering. He had instructed his attorney to plea-bargain with the D.A. As a result, they dropped all charges except assault, and Streck accepted a prison sentence of three years, with a provision that he serve at least two years before being eligible for parole. Nora had dreaded the trial. Suddenly she was free, and in celebration she got slightly tipsy for the first time in her life.

That same day, when Travis brought home a new stack of reading material, Einstein discovered there were Mickey Mouse picture books for children and comic books, and the dog was as jubilant about that discovery as Nora was about the resolution of the charges against Arthur Streck. His fascination with Mickey and Donald Duck and the rest of the Disney gang remained a mystery, but it was undeniable. Einstein couldn't stop wagging his tail, and he slobbered all over Travis in gratitude.

Everything would have been rosy if, in the middle of the night, Einstein had stopped going through the house from window to window, looking out at the darkness with obvious fear.

3

By Thursday morning, July 15, almost six weeks after the murders at Bordeaux Ridge, two months after the dog and The Outsider had escaped from Banodyne, Lemuel Johnson sat alone in his office on an upper floor of the federal building in Santa Ana, the county seat of Orange County. He stared out the window at the pollutant-rich haze that was trapped under an inversion layer, blanketing the western half of the county and adding to the misery of hundred-degree heat. The bile-yellow day matched his sour mood.

His duties were not limited to the search for the lab escapees, but that case constantly worried him when he was doing other work. He was unable to put the Banodyne affair out of mind even to sleep, and lately he was averaging only four or five hours of rest a night. He could not tolerate failure.

No, in truth, his attitude was much stronger than that: he was *obsessed* with avoiding failure. His father, having started life dirt-poor and having built a successful business, had inculcated in Lem an almost religious belief in the need to achieve, to succeed, and to fulfill all of one's goals. No matter how much success you had, his dad often said, life could pull the rug right out from under you if you weren't diligent. "It's even worse for a black man, Lem. With a black man, success is like a tightrope over the Grand Canyon. He's up there real high, and it's sweet, but when he makes a mistake, when he fails, it's a mile-long drop into an abyss. An *abyss*. Because failure means being poor. And in a lot of people's eyes, even in this enlightened age, a poor miserable failed black man is no man at all, he's just a nigger." That was the only time his father ever used the hated word. Lem had grown up with the conviction that any success he achieved was merely a precarious toehold on the cliff of life, that he was always in danger of being blown off that cliff by the winds of adversity, and that he dared not relent in his determination to cling fast and to climb to a wider, safer ledge.

He wasn't sleeping well, and his appetite was no good. When he did eat, the meal was inevitably followed by severe acid indigestion. His bridge game had gone to hell because he could not concentrate on the cards; at their weekly get-togethers with Walt and Audrey Gaines, the Johnsons were taking a beating.

He knew why he was obsessed with closing every case successfully, but that knowledge was of no help in modifying his obsession.

We are what we are, he thought, and maybe the only time we can change what we are is when life throws us such a surprise that it's like hitting a plate-glass window with a baseball bat, shattering the grip of the past.

So he stared out at the blazing July day and brooded, worried.

Back in May, he had surmised that the retriever might have been picked up by someone and given a home. It was, after all, a handsome animal, and if it revealed even a small fraction of its intelligence to anyone, its appeal would be irresistible; it would find sanctuary. Therefore, Lem figured locating the dog would be harder than tracking down The Outsider. A week to locate The Outsider, he had thought, and perhaps a month to lay hands on the retriever.

He had issued bulletins to every animal pound and veterinarian in California, Nevada, and Arizona, urgently requesting assistance in locating the golden retriever. The flyer claimed that the animal had escaped from a medical research lab that was conducting an important cancer experiment. The loss of the dog, the bulletin claimed, would mean the loss of a million dollars of research money and countless hours of researchers' time—and might seriously impede the development of a cure for certain malignancies. The flyer included a photograph of the dog and the information that, on the inside of its left ear, it bore a lab tattoo: the number 33-9. The letter accompanying the flyer requested not only cooperation but confidentiality. The mailing had been repeated every seven days since the breakout at Banodyne, and a score of NSA agents had been doing nothing but phoning animal pounds and vets in the three states to be certain they remembered the flyer and continued to keep a lookout for a retriever with a tattoo.

Meanwhile, the urgent search for The Outsider could, with some confidence, be confined to undeveloped territories because it would be reluctant to show itself. And there was no chance that someone would think *it* was cute enough to take home. Besides, The Outsider had been leaving a trail of death that could be followed.

Subsequent to the murders at Bordeaux Ridge east of Yorba Linda, the creature had fled into the unpopulated Chino Hills. From there it had gone north, crossing into the eastern end of Los Angeles County, where its presence was next pinpointed, on June 9, on the outskirts of semirural Diamond Bar. The Los Angeles County Animal Control Authority had received numerous—and hysterical—reports from Diamond Bar residents regarding wild-animal attacks on domestic pets. Others called the police, believing the slaughter was the work of a deranged man. In two nights, more than a score of Diamond Bar's domestic animals had been torn to pieces, and the condition of the carcasses left no doubt in Lem's mind that the perpetrator was The Outsider.

Then the trail went ice-cold for more than a week, until the morning of June 18, when two young campers at the foot of Johnstone Peak, on the southern flank of the vast Angeles National Forest, reported seeing something they insisted was "from another world." They had locked themselves in their van, but the creature had tried repeatedly to get in at them, going so far as to smash a side window with a rock. Fortunately, the pair kept a .32 pistol in the van, and one of them opened fire on their assailant, driving it off. The press treated the campers as a couple of kooks, and on the evening news the happy-talk anchorpersons got a lot of mileage out of the story.

Lem believed the young couple. On a map, he traced the thinly populated corridor of land by which The Outsider could have gone from Diamond Bar to the area below Johnstone Peak: over the San Jose Hills, through Bonelli Regional Park, between San Dimas and Glendora, then into the wilds. It would have had to cross or go under three freeways that cut through the area, but if it had traveled in the deep of night, when there was little or no traffic, it could have passed unseen. He shifted the hundred men from Marine Intelligence into that portion of the forest, where they continued their search in civilian dress, in groups of three and four.

He hoped the campers had hit The Outsider with at least one shot. But no blood was found at their campsite.

He was beginning to worry that The Outsider might evade capture for a long time. Lying north of the city of Los Angeles, the Angeles National Forest was discouragingly immense.

"Nearly as large as the entire state of Delaware," Cliff Soames said after he had measured the area on the wall map pinned to the bulletin board in Lem's office and had calculated the square miles. Cliff had come from Delaware. He was relatively new to the West and still had a newcomer's amazement at the gigantic scale of everything at this end of the continent. He was also young, with the enthusiasm of youth, and he was almost dangerously optimistic. Cliff's upbringing had been radically different from Lem's, and he did not feel himself to be on a tightrope or at risk of having his life destroyed by just one error, by a single failure. Sometimes Lem envied him.

Lem stared at Cliff's scribbled calculations. "If it takes refuge in the San Gabriel Mountains, feeding on wildlife and content with solitude, venturing out only rarely to vent its rage on the people living along the periphery of the preserve . . . it might never be found."

"But remember," Cliff said, "it hates the dog more than it hates men. It *wants* the dog and has the ability to find it."

"So we think."

"And could it really tolerate a wild existence? I mean, yeah, it's part savage, but it's also smart. Maybe too smart to be content with a hardscrabble life in that rugged country."

"Maybe," Lem said.

"They'll spot it soon, or it'll do something to give us another fix on it," Cliff predicted.

That was June 18.

When they found no trace of The Outsider during the next ten days, the expense of keeping a hundred men in the field grew insupportable. On June 29, Lem finally had to relinquish the Marines that had been put at his disposal and send them back to their bases.

Day by day, Cliff was heartened by the lack of developments and was willing to believe that The Outsider had suffered a mishap, that it was dead, that they would never hear of it again.

Day by day, Lem sank deeper into gloom, certain that he had lost control of the situation and that the The Outsider would reappear in a most dramatic fashion, making its existence known to the public. Failure.

The only bright spot was that the beast was now in Los Angeles County, out of Walt Gaines's jurisdiction. If there were additional victims, Walt might not even learn of them and would not have to be persuaded, all over again, to remain out of the case.

By Thursday, July 15, exactly two months after the breakout at Banodyne, almost one month after the campers had been terrorized by a supposed extra-terrestrial or smaller cousin of Bigfoot, Lem was convinced he would soon have to consider alternate careers. No one had blamed him for the way things had gone. The heat was on him to deliver, but it was no worse than the heat he had felt on other big investigations. Actually, some of his superiors viewed the lack of developments in the same favorable light as did Cliff Soames. But in his most pessimistic moments, Lem envisioned himself employed as a uniformed security guard working the night shift in a warehouse, demoted to the status of a make-believe cop with a rinky-dink badge.

Sitting in his office chair, facing the window, staring grimly at the hazy yellow air of the blazing summer day, he said aloud, "Damn it, I've been trained to deal with *human* criminals. How the hell can I be expected to out-think a fugitive from a nightmare?"

A knock sounded at his door, and as he swiveled around in his chair, the door opened. Cliff Soames entered in a rush, looking both excited and distraught. "The Outsider," he said. "We've got a new fix on it . . . but two people are dead."

Twenty years ago in Vietnam, Lem's NSA chopper pilot had learned everything worth knowing about putting down and taking off in rugged terrain.

Now, remaining in constant radio contact with the L.A. County sheriff's deputies who were on the scene already, he had no difficulty locating the site of the murders by visual navigation, making use of natural landmarks. At a few minutes after one o'clock, he put his craft down on a wide section of a barren ridge overlooking Boulder Canyon in the Angeles National Forest, just a hundred yards from the spot where the bodies had been found.

When Lem and Cliff left the chopper and hurried along the crest of the ridge toward the gathered deputies and forest rangers, a hot wind buffeted them. It carried the scent of dry brush and pine. Only tufts of wild grass, parched and brittled by the July sun, had managed to put down roots on this high ground. Low scrub growth—including desert plants like mesquite—marked the upper reaches of the canyon walls that dropped away to the right and left of them, and down on the lower slopes and canyon floors were trees and greener undergrowth.

They were less than four air miles north of the town of Sunland; fourteen air miles north of Hollywood, and twenty miles north of the populous heart of the great city of Los Angeles, yet it seemed they were in a desolation measuring a thousand miles across, disquietingly far from civilization. The sheriff's deputies had parked their four-wheel-drive wagons on a crude dirt track three-quarters of a mile away—coming in, Lem's chopper had flown over those vehicles—and they had hiked with ranger guides to the site where the bodies had been found. Now, gathered around the corpses were four deputies, two men from the county crime lab, and three rangers, and they looked as if they, too, felt isolated in a primeval place.

When Lem and Cliff arrived, the sheriff's men had just finished tucking the remains in body bags. The zippers hadn't yet been closed, so Lem saw that one victim was male, the other female, both young and dressed for hiking. Their wounds were grievous; their eyes were gone.

The dead now numbered five innocents, and that toll conjured a specter of guilt that haunted Lem. At times like this, he wished that his father had raised him with no sense of responsibility whatsoever.

Deputy Hal Bockner, tall and tan but with a surprisingly reedy voice, apprised Lem of the identity and condition of the victims: "Based on the ID he was carrying, the male's name was Sidney Tranken, twenty-eight, of Glendale. Body has more than a score of nasty bite marks, even more claw marks, slashes. Throat, as you saw, torn open. Eyes—"

"Yes," Lem said, seeing no need to dwell on these grisly details.

The men from the crime lab pulled the zippers shut on the body bags. It was a cold sound that hung for a moment like a chain of icicles in the hot July air.

Deputy Bockner said, "At first we thought Tranken was probably knifed by some psycho. Once in a while you get a homicidal nut who prowls these forests instead of the streets, preying on hikers. So we figured . . . knifed first, then all this other damage must've been done by animals, scavengers, after the guy was dead. But now . . . we're not so sure."

"I don't see blood on the ground here," Cliff Soames said with a note of puzzlement. "There'd have been a *lot* of it."

"They weren't killed here," Deputy Bockner said, then went on with his summary at his own pace. "Female, twenty-seven, Ruth Kasavaris, also of Glendale. Also vicious bite marks, slashes. Her throat—"

Cutting him off again, Lem said, "When were they killed?"

"Best guess before lab tests is that they died late yesterday. We believe the bodies were carried up here because they'd be found quicker on the ridge top. A popular hiking trail runs along here. But it wasn't other hikers who found them. It was a routine fire-patrol plane. Pilot looked down, saw them sprawled here on the bare ridge."

This high ground above Boulder Canyon was more than thirty air miles north-northwest of Johnstone Peak, where the young campers had taken refuge from The Outsider in their van and had later fired at it with a .32 pistol on June 18, twenty-eight days ago. The Outsider would have been reckoning north-northwest by sheer instinct and no doubt would have frequently been required to backtrack out of box canyons; therefore, in this mountainous terrain it had very likely traveled between sixty and ninety miles on the ground to cover those thirty air miles. Still, that was only a pace of three miles a day, at most, and Lem wondered what the creature had been doing during the time it was not traveling or sleeping or chasing down food.

"You'll want to see where these two were killed," Bockner said. "We've found the place. And you'll want to see the den, too."

"Den?"

"The lair," one of the forest rangers said. "The damn lair."

The deputies, rangers, and crime-lab men had been giving Lem and Cliff odd looks ever since they had arrived, but Lem had not been surprised by that. Local authorities always regarded him with suspicion and curiosity because they were not accustomed to having a powerhouse federal agency like the NSA show up and claim jurisdiction; it was a rarity. But now he realized that their curiosity was of a different kind and degree than what he usually encountered, and for the first time he perceived their fear. They had found something—the lair of which they spoke—that gave them reason to believe this case was even stranger than the sudden appearance of the NSA would usually indicate.

In suits, ties, and polished street shoes, neither Lem nor Cliff was properly dressed for a hike down into the canyon, but neither of them hesitated when the rangers led the way. Two deputies, the lab men, and one of the three rangers remained behind with the bodies, which left a party of six for the descent. They followed a shallow channel carved by runoff from rainstorms, then switched to what might have been a deer trail. After descending to the very bottom of the canyon, they turned southeast and proceeded for half a mile. Soon Lem was sweaty and covered with a film of dust, and his socks and pant legs were full of prickling burrs.

"Here's where they were killed," Deputy Bockner said when he led them into a clearing surrounded by scrub pines, cottonwoods, and brush.

The pale, sandy earth and sun-bleached grass were mottled with enormous dark stains. Blood.

"And right back here," one of the rangers said, "is where we found the lair."

It was a shallow cave in the base of the canyon wall, perhaps ten feet deep, twenty feet wide, no more than a dozen steps from the small clearing where the hikers had been murdered. The mouth of the cave was about eight feet wide but low, requiring Lem to stoop a bit as he entered. Once inside, he was able to stand erect, for the ceiling was high. The place had a mildly unpleasant, musty smell. Light found its way through the entrance and through a two-foot-wide water-carved hole in the ceiling, but for the most part the chamber was shadowy and twenty degrees cooler than the canyon outside.

Only Deputy Bockner accompanied Lem and Cliff. Lem sensed that the others held back not out of any concern that the cave would be too crowded, but out of an uneasiness about the place.

Bockner had a flashlight. He switched it on and played the beam over the things he had brought them to see, dispelling some of the shadows and causing others to flit batlike across the room to roost on different perches.

In one corner, dry grass had been piled to a depth of six or eight inches to make a bed on the sandstone floor. Beside the bed was a galvanized bucket full of relatively fresh water carried from the nearest stream, evidently placed there so the sleeper could get a drink upon waking in the middle of the night.

"It was here," Cliff said softly.

"Yes," Lem agreed.

Instinctively he sensed The Outsider had made this bed; somehow, its alien presence was still in the chamber. He stared at the bucket, wondering where the creature had acquired it. Most likely, along the way from Bano-dyne, it had decided it would eventually find a burrow and hide for a while, and it had realized it would need a few things to make its life in the wild more comfortable. Perhaps breaking into a stable or barn or empty house, it had stolen the bucket and various other things that Bockner now revealed with his flashlight.

A plaid flannel blanket for when the weather turned cooler. A horse blanket, judging by the look of it. What caught Lem's attention was the neatness with which the blanket had been folded and placed on a narrow ledge in the wall beside the entrance.

A flashlight. This was on the same shelf that held the blanket. The Outsider had exceedingly good night vision. That was one of the design requirements with which Dr. Yarbeck had been working: in the dark, a good genetically engineered warrior would be able to see as well as a cat. So why would it want a flashlight? Unless . . . maybe even a creature of the night was sometimes afraid of darkness.

That thought jolted Lem, and suddenly he pitied the beast as he had pitied it that day he had watched it communicating by crude sign language with Yarbeck, the day it had said that it wanted to tear its own eyes out so it would never have to look at itself again.

Bockner moved the beam of his own flashlight and focused it on twenty candy wrappers. Apparently, The Outsider had stolen a couple family packs of candy somewhere along the way. The strange thing was that the wrappers were not crumpled but were smoothed out and laid flat on the floor along the back wall—ten from Reese's peanut butter cups and ten from Clark Bars. Perhaps The Outsider liked the bright colors of the wrappers. Or perhaps it kept them to remind itself of the pleasure that the candy had given it because, once those treats were gone, there was not much other pleasure to be had in the hard life to which it had been driven.

In the farthest corner from the bed, deep in shadows, was a pile of bones. The bones of small animals. Once the candy was eaten, The Outsider had been forced to hunt in order to feed itself. And without the means to light a fire, it had fed savagely on raw meat. Perhaps it kept the bones in the cave because it was afraid that, by disposing of them outside, it would be leaving clues to its whereabouts. By storing them in the darkest, farthest corner of its haven, it seemed to have a civilized sense of neatness and order, but to Lem it also seemed as if The Outsider had hidden the bones in the shadows because it was ashamed of its own savagery.

Most pathetically of all, a peculiar group of items was stored in a niche in the wall above the grassy bed. No, Lem decided, not just stored. The items were carefully arranged, as if for display, the way an aficionado of art glass or ceramics or Mayan pottery might display a valuable collection. There was a round stained-glass bauble of the sort that people hung from their patio covers to sparkle in the sun; it was about four inches in diameter, and it portrayed a blue flower against a pale-yellow background. Beside that bauble was a bright copper pot that had probably once contained a plant on the same—or another— patio. Next to the pot were two things that surely had been taken from inside a house, perhaps from the same place where The Outsider had stolen the candy: first, a fine porcelain study of a pair of red-feathered cardinals sitting on a branch, every detail exquisitely crafted; second, a crystal paperweight. Apparently, even within the alien breast of Yarbeck's monstrosity, there was an appreciation of beauty and a desire to live not as an animal but as a thinking being in an ambience at least lightly touched by civilization.

Lem felt sick at heart as he considered the lonely, tortured, self-hating, inhuman yet self-aware creature that Yarbeck had brought into the world.

Last of all, the niche above the grass bed held a ten-inch-high figure of Mickey Mouse that was also a coin bank.

Lem's pity swelled because he knew why the bank had appealed to The Outsider. At Banodyne, there had been experiments to determine the depth and nature of the dog's and The Outsider's intelligence, to discover how close their perceptions were to those of a human being. One of the experiments had been designed to probe their ability to differentiate between fantasy and reality. On several occasions, the dog and The Outsider had separately been shown a videotape that had been assembled from film clips of all kinds: bits of old John Wayne movies, footage from George Lucas's *Star Wars*, news films, scenes from a wide variety of documentaries—and old Mickey Mouse cartoons. The reactions of the dog and The Outsider were filmed and, later, they were quizzed to see if they understood which segments of the videotape were of real events and which were flights of the imagination. Both creatures had gradually learned to identify fantasy when they saw it; but, strangely, the one fantasy they most wanted to believe in, the fantasy they clung to the longest, was Mickey Mouse. They were enthralled by Mickey's adventures with his cartoon friends. After escaping Banodyne, The Outsider had somehow come across this coin bank and had wanted it badly because the poor damn thing was reminded of the only real pleasure it had ever known while in the lab.

In the beam of Deputy Bockner's flashlight, something on the shelf glinted. It was lying nearly flat beside the coin bank, and they almost overlooked it. Cliff stepped on the grass bed and plucked the gleaming object out of the wall niche: a three-inch-by-four-inch triangular fragment of a mirror.

The Outsider huddled here, Lem thought, trying to take heart from its meager treasures, trying to make as much of a home for itself as was possible. Once in a while it picked up this jagged shard from a mirror and stared at itself, perhaps searching hopefully for an aspect of its countenance that was *not* ugly, perhaps trying to come to terms with what it was. And failing. Surely failing.

"Dear God," Cliff Soames said quietly, for the same thoughts had apparently passed through his mind. "The poor miserable bastard."

The Outsider had possessed one additional item: a copy of *People* magazine. Robert Redford was on the cover. With a claw, sharp stone, or some other instrument, The Outsider had cut out Redford's eyes.

The magazine was rumpled and tattered, as if it had been paged through a hundred times, and now Deputy Bockner handed it to them and suggested they page through it once more. On doing so, Lem saw that the eyes of every person pictured in the issue had been either scratched, cut, or crudely torn out.

The thoroughness of this symbolic mutilation—not *one* image in the magazine had been spared—was chilling.

The Outsider was pathetic, yes, and it was to be pitied.

But it was also to be feared.

Five victims—some gutted, some decapitated.

The innocent dead must not be forgotten, not for a moment. Neither an affection for Mickey Mouse nor a love of beauty could excuse such slaughter.

But Jesus . . .

The creature had been given sufficient intelligence to grasp the importance and the benefits of civilization, to long for acceptance and a meaningful existence. Yet a fierce lust for violence, a killing instinct second to none in nature, was also engineered into it because it was meant to be a smart killer on a long invisible leash, a living machine of war. No matter how long it existed in peaceful solitude in its canyon cave, no matter how many days or weeks it resisted its own violent urges, it could not change what it was. The pressure would build within it until it could no longer contain itself, until the slaughter of small animals would not provide enough psychological relief, and then it would seek larger and more interesting prey. It might damn itself for its savagery, might long to remake itself into a creature that could exist in harmony with the rest of the world, but it was powerless to change what it was. Only hours ago, Lem had pondered how difficult it was for him to become a different man from the one his father had raised, how hard it was for *any* man to change what life had made him, but at least it was possible if one had the determination, willpower, and time. However, for The Outsider change was impossible; murder was in the beast's genes, *locked* in, and it could expect no hope of re-creation or salvation.

"What the hell is this all about?" Deputy Bockner asked, finally unable to repress his curiosity.

"Believe me," Lem said, "you don't want to know."

"What was in this cave?" Bockner asked.

Lem only shook his head. If two more people had to die, it was a stroke of good fortune that they had been murdered in a national forest. This was federal land, which meant much simpler procedures by which the NSA could assume authority in the investigation.

Cliff Soames was still turning the fragment of mirror over and over in his hand, staring at it thoughtfully.

Looking around the eerie chamber one last time, Lem Johnson made a promise to himself and to his dangerous quarry: When I find you, I won't consider trying to take you alive; no net or tranquilizer guns, as the scientists and the military types would prefer; instead, I'll shoot you quick and clean, take you down fast.

That was not only the safest plan. It would also be an act of compassion and mercy.

4

By the first of August, Nora sold all of Aunt Violet's furniture and other possessions. She had phoned a man who dealt in antiques and secondhand furniture, and he had given her one price for everything, and she had accepted it happily. Now—except for dishes, silverware, and the furniture in the bedroom that she had made her own—the rooms were empty from wall to wall. The house seemed cleansed, purified, *exorcised*. All evil spirits had been driven out, and she knew she now had the will to redecorate entirely. But she no longer wanted the place, so she telephoned a real-estate agent and put it on the market.

Her old clothes were gone, too, all of them, and she had an entirely new wardrobe with slacks and skirts and blouses and jeans and dresses like any woman might have. Occasionally, she felt too conspicuous in bright colors, but she always resisted the urge to change into something dark and drab.

She still had not found the courage to put her artistic talent on the market and see if her work was worth anything. Travis nudged her about it now and then, in ways he thought were subtle, but she was not ready to lay her fragile ego on the anvil and give just anyone a chance to swing a hammer at it. Soon, but not yet.

Sometimes, when she looked at herself in a mirror or noticed her reflection in a sun-silvered store window, she realized that, indeed, she was pretty. Not beautiful, perhaps, not gorgeous like some movie star, but moderately pretty. However, she did not seem to be able to hold on to this breakthrough perception of her appearance, at least not for long, because every few days she would be surprised anew by the comeliness of the face looking back at her from the mirror.

On the fifth of August, late in the afternoon, she and Travis were sitting at the table in his kitchen, playing Scrabble, and she was feeling pretty. A few minutes ago, in the bathroom, she'd had another of those revelations when she had looked in the mirror, and in fact she had liked her looks more than ever before. Now, back at the Scrabble board, she felt buoyant, happier than she would have once believed possible—and mischievous. She started using her tiles to spell nonsense words and then vociferously defended them when Travis questioned their legitimacy.

" 'Dofnup'?" he said, frowning at the board. "There's no such word as 'dofnup.' "

"It's a triangular cap that loggers wear," she said.

"Loggers?"

"Like Paul Bunyan."

"Loggers wear knit caps, what you call toboggan caps, or round leather caps with earflaps."

"I'm not talking about what they wear to work in the woods," she explained patiently. " 'Dofnup.' That's the name of the cap they wear to bed."

He laughed and shook his head. "Are you putting me on?"

She kept a straight face. "No. It's true."

"Loggers wear a special cap to bed?"

"Yes. The dofnup."

He was unaccustomed to the very *idea* that Nora would play a joke on him, so he fell for it. "Dofnup? Why do they call it that?"

"Beats me," she said.

Einstein was on the floor, on his belly, reading a novel. Since graduating with startling swiftness from picture books to children's literature like *The Wind in the Willows*, he had been reading eight and ten hours a day, every day. He couldn't get *enough* books. He'd become a prose junkie. Ten days ago, when the dog's obsession with reading had finally outstripped Nora's patience for holding books and turning pages, they had tried to puzzle out an arrangement that would make it possible for Einstein to keep a volume open in front of him and turn the pages himself. At a hospital-supply company, they had found a device designed for patients who had the use of neither arms nor legs. It was a metal stand onto which the boards of the book were clamped; electrically powered mechanical arms, controlled by three push buttons, turned the pages and held them in place. A quadriplegic could operate it with a stylus held in his teeth; Einstein used his nose. The dog seemed immensely pleased by the arrangement. Now, he whimpered softly about something he had just read, pushed one of the buttons, and turned another page.

Travis spelled "wicked" and picked up a lot of points by using a double-score square, so Nora used her tiles to spell "hurkey," which was worth even more points.

" 'Hurkey'?" Travis said doubtfully.

"It's a favorite Yugoslavian meal," she said.

"It is?"

"Yes. The recipe includes both ham and turkey, which is why they call it—" She couldn't finish. She broke into laughter.

He gaped at her in astonishment. "You *are* putting me on. *You* are putting me on! Nora Devon, what's become of you? When I first met you, I said to myself, 'Now, there's the grimmest-damn-most-serious young woman I've ever seen.' "

"And squirrelly."

"Well, not squirrelly."

"Yes, squirrelly," she insisted. "You thought I was squirrelly."

"All right, yeah, I thought you were so squirrelly you probably had the attic of that house packed full of walnuts."

Grinning, she said, "If Violet and I had lived in the south, we'd have been straight out of Faulkner, wouldn't we?"

"Too weird even for Faulkner. But now just look at you! Making up dumb words and dumber jokes, conning me into believing them 'cause I'd never expect Nora Devon, of all people, to do any such thing. You've sure changed in these few months."

"Thanks to you," she said.

"Maybe thanks to Einstein more than me."

"No. You most of all," she said, and abruptly she was stricken by that old shyness that had once all but paralyzed her. She looked away from him, down at her tray of Scrabble tiles, and in a low voice she said, "You most of all. I'd never have met Einstein if I hadn't met you. And you . . . cared about me . . . worried about me . . . saw something in me that I couldn't see. You remade me."

"No," he said. "You give me too much credit. You didn't have to be remade. *This* Nora was always there, inside the old one. Like a flower all cramped up and hidden inside a drab little seed. You just had to be encouraged to . . . well, to grow and bloom."

She could not look at him. She felt as if a tremendous stone had been placed on the back of her neck, forcing her to bow her head, and she was blushing. But she found the courage to say, "It's so damn hard to bloom . . . to change. Even when you want to change, want it more than anything in the world, it's hard. Desire to change isn't enough. Or desperation. Couldn't be done without . . . love." Her voice had dropped to a whisper, and she was unable to lift it. "Love is like the water and the sun that make the seed grow."

He said, "Nora, look at me."

That stone on her neck must have weighed a hundred pounds, a thousand.

"Nora?"

It weighed a *ton*.

"Nora, I love you too."

Somehow with great effort, she lifted her head. She looked at him. His brown eyes, so dark as to be almost black, were warm and kind and beautiful. She loved those eyes. She loved the high bridge and narrow line of his nose. She loved every aspect of his lean and ascetic face.

"I should have told you first," he said, "because it's easier for me to say it than it is for you. I should have said it days ago, weeks ago: Nora, by God, I love you. But I didn't say it because I was afraid. Every time I let myself love someone, I lose them, but this time I think maybe it'll be different. Maybe you'll change things for me the way I helped change them for you, and maybe this time luck's with me."

Her heart raced. She could barely get her breath, but she said, "I love you."

"Will you marry me?"

She was stunned. She did not know what she'd expected to happen, but certainly not *this*. Just hearing him say he loved her, just being able to express the same sentiments to him—that was enough to keep her happy for weeks, months. She expected to have time to walk around their love, as if it were a great and mysterious edifice that, like some newly discovered pyramid, must be studied and pondered from every angle before she dared to undertake an exploration of the interior.

"Will you marry me?" he repeated.

This was too fast, recklessly fast, and just sitting there on a kitchen chair she got as dizzy as if she had been spinning around on a carnival ride, and she was afraid, too, so she tried to tell him to slow down, tried to tell him they had plenty of time to consider the next step before taking it, but to her surprise she heard herself say, "Yes. Oh, yes."

He reached out and took both her hands.

She cried, then, but they were good tears.

Lost in his book, Einstein had nevertheless been aware of what was transpiring. He came to the table, sniffing at both of them, rubbing against their legs, and whining happily.

Travis said, "Next week?"

"Married? But it takes time to get a license and everything."

"Not in Las Vegas. I can call ahead, make arrangements with a wedding chapel in Vegas. We can go next week and be married."

Crying and laughing at the same time, she said, "All right."

"Terrific," Travis said, grinning.

Einstein wagged his tail furiously: *Yes, yes, yes, yes, yes.*

5

On Wednesday, the fourth of August, working on contract for the Tetragna Family of San Francisco, Vince Nasco hit a little cockroach named Lou Pantangela. The cockroach had turned state's evidence and was scheduled, in September, to testify in court against members of the Tetragna organization.

Johnny The Wire Santini, computer hacker for the mob, had used his high-tech expertise to invade federal computer files and locate Pantangela. The cockroach was living under the protection of two federal marshals in a safe house in, of all places, Redondo Beach, south of L.A. After testifying this autumn, he was scheduled to be given a new identity and a new life in Connecticut, but of course he was not going to live that long.

Because Vince would probably have to waste one or both of the marshals to get at Pantangela, the rubout was going to bring a lot of heat, so the Tetragnas offered him a very high price—$60,000. They had no way of knowing that the need to kill more than one man was a bonus to Vince; it made the job more—not less—attractive.

He ran surveillance on Pantangela for almost a week, using a different vehicle every day to avoid being spotted by the cockroach's bodyguards. They did not often let Pantangela outside, but they were still more confident of their hiding place than they should have been because three or four times a week they allowed him to have a late lunch in public, accompanying him to a little trattoria four blocks from the safe house.

They had changed Pantangela's appearance as much as possible. He had once had thick black hair that he had worn longish, over his collar. Now his hair was cut short and dyed light brown. He'd had a mustache, but they'd made him shave it off. He had been sixty pounds overweight, but after two months in the care of the marshals, he had lost about forty pounds. Nevertheless, Vince recognized him.

On Wednesday, August 4, they took Pantangela to the trattoria at one o'clock, as usual. At ten minutes past one, Vince strolled in to have his own lunch.

The restaurant had only eight tables in the middle and six booths along each side wall. It looked clean but had too much Italian kitsch for Vince's taste: red-and white-checkered tablecloths; garish murals of Roman ruins; empty wine bottles used as candleholders; a thousand bunches of plastic grapes, for God's sake, hanging from lattice fixed to the ceiling and meant to convey the atmosphere of an arbor. Because Californians tend to eat an early dinner, at least by Eastern standards, they also eat an early lunch, and by ten past one, the number of diners had already peaked and was declining. By two o'clock, it was likely that the only customers remaining would be Pantangela, his two bodyguards, and Vince, which was what made it such a good place for the hit.

The trattoria was too small to bother with a hostess at lunch, and a sign told guests to seat themselves. Vince walked back through the room, past the Pantangela party, to an empty booth behind them.

Vince had given a lot of thought to his clothes. He was wearing rope sandals, red cotton shorts, and a white T-shirt on which were blue waves, a yellow sun, and the words ANOTHER CALIFORNIA BODY. His aviator sunglasses were mirrored. He carried an open-topped canvas beach bag that was boldly lettered MY STUFF. If you glanced in the bag when he walked past, you'd see a tightly rolled towel, bottles of tanning lotion, a small radio, and a hairbrush, but you wouldn't see the fully automatic, silencer-equipped Uzi pistol with a forty-round magazine hidden in the bottom. With his deep tan to complement the outfit, he achieved the look he wanted: a very fit but aging surfer; a leisure-sotted, shiftless, and probably harebrained jerk who would be beaching it every day, pretending to be young, and still self-intoxicated when he was sixty.

He only glanced uninterestedly at Pantangela and the marshals, but he was aware of them giving him the once-over, then dismissing him as harmless. Perfect.

The booths had high padded backs, so from where he sat he could not see Pantangela. But he could hear the cockroach and the marshals talking now and then, mostly about baseball and women.

After a week of surveillance, Vince knew that Pantangela never left the trattoria sooner than two-thirty, usually three o'clock, evidently because he insisted on an appetizer, a salad, a main course, and dessert, the whole works. That gave Vince time for a salad and an order of linguini with clam sauce.

His waitress was about twenty, white-blond, pretty, and as deeply tanned as Vince. She had the hip look and sound of a beach girl, and she started coming on to him right away, while taking his order. He figured she was one of those sand nymphs whose brain was as sun-fried as her body. She probably spent every summer evening on the beach, doing dope of every description, spreading her legs for any stud who vaguely interested her—and most of them would interest her—which meant that, no matter how healthy she looked, she was disease-ridden. Just the idea of humping her made him want to puke, but he had to play out the role he'd chosen for himself, so he flirted with her and tried to look as if he could barely keep from drooling at the thought of her naked, writhing body pinned under him.

At five minutes past two, Vince had finished lunch, and the only other customers in the place were Pantangela and the two marshals. One of the waitresses had left for the day, and the other two were in the kitchen. It could not have been better.

The beach bag was on the booth beside him. He reached into it and withdrew the Uzi pistol.

Pantangela and the marshals were talking about the Dodgers' chances of getting in the World Series.

Vince got up, stepped around to their booth, and sprayed them with twenty to thirty rounds from the Uzi. The stubby, high-tech silencer worked beautifully, and the shots sounded like nothing more than a stuttering man having trouble pronouncing a word that began with a sibilant. It went down so fast that the marshals didn't have a chance to reach for their own weapons. They didn't even have time to be surprised.

Ssssnap.

Ssssnap.

Ssssnap.

Pantangela and his guardians were dead in three seconds.

Vince shuddered with intense pleasure, and was briefly overcome by the wealth of life energy that he had just absorbed. He could not speak. Then in a tremulous and raspy voice, he said, "Thank you."

When he turned away from the booth, he saw his waitress standing in the middle of the room, frozen in shock. Her wide blue eyes were fixated on the dead men, but now her gaze shifted slowly to Vince.

Before she could scream, he emptied the rest of the magazine into her, maybe ten shots, and she went down in a rain of blood.

Ssssnap.

"Thank you," he said, then said it again because she had been young and vital and, therefore, of more use to him.

Concerned that someone else would come out of the kitchen—or maybe someone would walk past the restaurant and look in and see the waitress on the floor—Vince stepped quickly to his booth, snatched up the beach bag, and jammed the Uzi pistol under the towel. Putting on his mirrored sunglasses, he got out of there.

He was not worried about fingerprints. He had coated the pads of his fingers with Elmer's glue. It dried nearly transparent and could not be noticed unless he turned his hands palms-up and called people's attention to it. The layer of glue was thick enough to fill the minute lines in the skin, leaving the fingertips smooth.

Outside, he walked to the end of the block, turned the corner, and got into his van, which was parked at the curb. As far as he could tell, no one gave him a second look.

He went to the ocean, looking forward to some time in the sun and an invigorating swim. Going to Redondo Beach, two blocks away, seemed too bold, so he followed the Coast Highway south to Bolsa Chica, just north of where he lived in Huntington Beach.

As he drove, he thought about the dog. He was still paying Johnny The Wire to keep tabs on animal pounds, police agencies, and anyone else who might be dragged into the search for the retriever. He knew about the National Security Agency's bulletin to veterinarians and animal-control authorities in three states, and he also knew that the NSA had so far had no luck.

Maybe the dog had been killed by a car, or by the creature that Hudston had called "The Outsider," or by a coyote pack in the hills. But Vince didn't want to believe it was dead because that would mean an end to his dream of making a huge financial killing with the dog either by ransoming it back to the authorities or selling it to a rich showbiz type who could work up an act with it, or by finding some means of using the animal's secret intelligence to pull a safe and profitable scam on unsuspecting marks.

What he preferred to believe was that someone had found the dog and had taken it home as a pet. If he could just locate the people who had the dog, he could buy it from them—or blow them away and just *take* the mutt.

But where the hell was he supposed to look? How was he supposed to find them? If they were findable, the NSA would surely reach them first.

Most likely, if the dog was not already dead, the best way to get his hands on it was to find The Outsider first and let that beast lead him to the dog, which Hudston had seemed to think it would. But that was not an easy task, either.

Johnny The Wire was also still providing him with information about particularly violent killings of people and animals throughout southern California. Vince knew about the slaughter at the Irvine Park petting zoo, the murder of Wes Dalberg, and the men at Bordeaux Ridge. Johnny had turned up the rash of reports about mutilated pets in the Diamond Bar area, and Vince had actually seen the TV news story about the young couple who had encountered what they thought was an extraterrestrial in the wilds below Johnstone Peak. Three weeks ago, two hikers had been found horribly mauled in the Angeles National Forest, and by hacking his way into the NSA's own computers, Johnny had confirmed that they had taken over jurisdiction in that case, too, which meant it had to be the work of The Outsider.

Since then, nothing.

Vince was not ready to give up. Not by a long shot. He was a patient man. Patience was part of his job. He would wait, watch, keep Johnny The Wire at work, and sooner or later he would get what he was after. He was sure of it. He had decided that the dog, like immortality, was part of his great destiny.

At Bolsa Chica State Beach, he stood for a while with the surf pounding against his thighs, staring out at the great dark masses of surging water. He felt as powerful as the sea. He was filled with scores of lives. He would not have been surprised if electricity had suddenly leaped from his fingertips the way thunderbolts flashed from the hands of the gods in mythology.

Finally, he threw himself forward, into the water, and swam against the powerful incoming waves. He went far out before turning parallel to the shore, swimming first south and then north, keeping at it until, exhausted, he at last allowed the tide to carry him back to shore.

He dozed for a while in the hot afternoon sun. He dreamed of a pregnant woman, her stomach large and round, and in the dream he strangled her to death.

He often dreamed of killing children or, even better, the unborn children of pregnant women because it was something he longed to do in real life. Child murder was, of course, much too dangerous; it was a pleasure he had to deny himself, though a child's life energy would be the richest, the purest, the most worthy of absorption. Too dangerous by far. He couldn't indulge in infanticide until he was certain he had achieved immortality, whereupon he would no longer need to fear the police or anyone else.

Although he often had such dreams, the one he woke from on Bolsa Chica Beach struck him as more meaningful than others of its type. It felt . . . different. Prophetic. He sat yawning and blinking in the westering sun, pretending not to notice the bikinied girls who were giving him the eye, and he told himself that this dream was a glimpse of pleasure to come. One day he would actually feel his hands around the throat of a pregnant woman like the one in the dream, and he would know the ultimate thrill, receive the ultimate gift, not only her life energy but the pure, untapped energy of the unborn in her womb.

Feeling like a million bucks, he returned to his van, drove home, showered, and went out to dinner at the nearest Stuart Anderson steak house, where he treated himself to filet mignon.

6

Einstein bolted past Travis, out of the kitchen, across the small dining room, disappearing into the living room. Carrying the leash, Travis went after him. Einstein was hiding behind the sofa.

Travis said "Listen, it's not going to hurt."

The dog watched him warily.

"We've got to take care of this before we go off to Vegas. The vet will give you a couple of shots, vaccinate you against distemper and rabies. It's for your own good, and it really won't hurt. Really. Then we'll get you a license, which we should've done weeks ago."

One bark. *No.*

"Yes, we will."

No.

Crouching, holding the leash by the clip with which he would attach it to the collar, Travis took a step toward Einstein.

The retriever scrambled away. He ran to the armchair, leaped up, and stood on that observation platform, watching Travis intently.

Coming slowly out from behind the sofa, Travis said, "Now, you listen up, fur face. I'm your master—"

One bark.

Frowning, Travis said, "Oh, yes, I *am* your master. You may be one damn smart dog—but you're still the dog, and I'm the man, and I'm telling you that we're going to the vet."

One bark.

Leaning against the dining-room archway, arms folded, smiling, Nora said, "I think he's trying to give you a taste of what children are like, in case we ever decide to have any."

Travis lunged toward the dog.

Einstein flew off his perch and was already out of the room when Travis, unable to halt, fell over the armchair.

Laughing, Nora said, "This is vastly entertaining."

"Where'd he go?" Travis demanded.

She pointed to the hallway that led to the two bedrooms and bath.

He found the retriever in the master bedroom, standing on the bed, facing the doorway. "You can't win," Travis said. "This is for your own good, damn it, and you're going to have those shots whether you like it or not."

Einstein lifted one hind leg and peed on the bed.

Astonished, Travis said, "What in the hell are you doing?"

Einstein stopped peeing, stepped away from the puddle that was soaking into the quilted bedspread, and stared defiantly at Travis.

Travis had heard stories of dogs and cats expressing extreme displeasure by stunts like this. When he had owned the real-estate agency, one of his saleswomen had boarded her miniature collie in a kennel for two weeks while away on vacation. When she returned and bailed out the dog, it punished her by urinating on both her favorite chair and her bed.

But Einstein was not an ordinary dog. Considering his remarkable intellect, the soiling of the bed was even more of an outrage than it would have been if he *had* been ordinary.

Getting angry now, moving toward the dog, Travis said, "This is inexcusable."

Einstein scrambled off the mattress. Realizing the dog would try to slip around him and out of the room, Travis scuttled backward and slammed the door. Cut off from the exit, Einstein swiftly changed directions and dashed to the far end of the bedroom, where he stood in front of the dresser.

"No more fooling around," Travis said sternly, brandishing the leash.

Einstein retreated into a corner.

Closing in at a crouch, spreading his arms to prevent the dog from bolting around either side of him, Travis finally made contact and clipped the leash to the collar. "Ha!"

Huddled defeatedly in the corner, Einstein hung his head and began to shudder.

Travis's sense of triumph was short-lived. He stared in dismay at the dog's bowed and trembling head, at the visible shivers that shook the animal's flanks. Einstein issued low, almost inaudible, pathetic whines of fear.

Stroking the dog, trying to calm and reassure him, Travis said, "This really is for your own good, you know. Distemper, rabies—the sort of stuff you don't want to mess with. And it will be painless, my friend. I swear it will."

The dog would not look at him and refused to take heart from his assurances.

Under Travis's hand, the dog felt as if he were shaking himself to pieces. He stared hard at the retriever, thinking, then said, "In that lab . . . did they put a lot of needles in you? Did they hurt you with needles? Is that why you're afraid of getting vaccinations?"

Einstein only whimpered.

Travis pulled the reluctant dog out of the corner, freeing his tail for a question-and-answer session. Dropping the leash, he took Einstein's head in both hands and forced his face up, so they were eye-to-eye.

"Did they hurt you with needles in the lab?"

Yes.

"Is that why you're afraid of the vet?"

Though he did not stop shuddering, the dog barked once: *No.*

"You were hurt by needles, but you're not afraid of them?"

No.

"Then *why* are you like this?"

Einstein just stared at him and made those terrible sounds of distress.

Nora opened the bedroom door a crack and peeked in. "Did you get the leash on him yet, Einstein?" Then she said, "Phew! What happened in here?"

Still holding the dog's head, staring into his eyes. Travis said, "He made a bold statement of displeasure."

"Bold," she agreed, moving to the bed and beginning to strip off the soiled spread, blanket, and sheets.

Trying to puzzle out the reason for the dog's behavior, Travis said, "Einstein, if it's not needles you're afraid of—is it the vet?"

One bark. *No.*

Frustrated, Travis brooded on his next question while Nora pulled the mattress cover from the bed.

Einstein trembled.

Suddenly, Travis had a flash of understanding that illuminated the dog's contrariness and fear. He cursed his own thickheadedness. "Hell, of course! You're not afraid of the vet—but of who the vet might report you to."

Einstein's shivering subsided a bit, and he wagged his tail briefly. *Yes.*

"If people from that lab are hunting for you—and we know they must be hunting furiously because you have to be the most important experimental animal in history—then they're going to be in touch with every vet in the state, aren't they? Every vet . . . and every dog pound . . . and every dog-licensing agency."

Another burst of vigorous tail wagging, less shivering.

Nora came around the bed and stopped down beside Travis. "But golden retrievers have to be one of the two or three most popular breeds. Vets and animal-licensing bureaucrats deal with them all the time. If our genius dog here hides his light under a bushel and plays dopey mutt—"

"Which he can do quite well."

"—then they'd have no way of knowing he was the fugitive."

Yes, Einstein insisted.

To the dog, Travis said, "What do you mean? Are you saying they would be able to identify you?"

Yes.

"How?" Nora wondered.

Travis said, "A mark of some kind?"

Yes.

"Somewhere under all that fur?" Nora asked.

One bark. *No.*

"Then where?" Travis wondered.

Pulling loose of Travis's hands, Einstein shook his head so hard that his floppy ears made a flapping noise.

"Maybe on the pads of his feet," Nora said.

"No," Travis said even as Einstein barked once. "When I found him, his feet were bleeding from a lot of hard travel, and I had to clean out the wounds with boric acid. I'd have noticed a mark on one of his paws."

Again, Einstein shook his head violently, flapping his ears.

Travis said, "Maybe on the inner lip. They tattoo racehorses on the inner lip to identify them and prevent ringers from being run. Let me peel back your lips and have a look, boy."

Einstein barked once—*No*—and shook his head violently.

At last Travis got the point. He looked in the right ear and found nothing. But in the left ear, he saw something. He urged the dog to go with him to the window, where the light was better, and he discovered that the mark consisted of two numbers, a dash, and a third number tattooed in purple ink on the pink-brown flesh: 33-9.

Looking over Travis's shoulder, Nora said, "They probably had a lot of pups they were experimenting with, from different litters, and they had to be able to identify them."

"Jesus. If I'd taken him to a vet, and if the vet had been told to look for a retriever with a tattoo . . ."

"But he has to have shots."

"Maybe he's already had them," Travis said hopefully.

"We don't dare count on that. He was a lab animal in a controlled environment where he might not have needed shots. And maybe the usual inoculations would've interfered with their experiments."

"We can't risk a vet."

"If they do find him," Nora said, "we simply won't give him up."

"They can make us," Travis said worriedly.

"Damned if they can."

"Damned if they can't. More likely than not, the government's financing the research, and *they* can crush us. We can't risk it. More than anything else, Einstein's afraid of going back to the lab."

Yes, yes, yes.

"But," Nora said, "if he contracts rabies or distemper or—"

"We'll get him the shots later," Travis said. "Later. When the situation cools down. When he's not so hot."

The retriever whined happily, nuzzling Travis's neck and face in a sloppy display of gratitude.

Frowning, Nora said, "Einstein is about the number-one miracle of the twentieth century. You really think he's ever going to cool down, that they'll ever stop looking for him?"

"They might not stop for years," Travis admitted, stroking the dog. "But gradually they'll begin to search with less enthusiasm and less hope. And the vets will start forgetting to look in the ears of every retriever that's brought to them. Until then he'll have to go without the shots, I guess. It's the best thing we can do. It's the only thing we can do."

Ruffling Einstein's coat with one hand, Nora said: "I hope you're right."

"I am."

"I hope so."

"I am."

Travis was badly shaken by how close he had come to risking Einstein's freedom, and for the next few days he brooded about the infamous Cornell Curse. Maybe it was happening all over again. His life had been turned around and made livable because of the love he felt for Nora and for this impossible damn dog. And now maybe fate, which had always dealt with him in a supremely hostile manner, would rip both Nora and the dog away from him.

He knew that fate was only a mythological concept. He did not believe there was actually a pantheon of malevolent gods looking down on him through a celestial keyhole and plotting tragedies for him to endure—yet he could not help looking warily at the sky now and then. Each time he said something even slightly optimistic about the future, he found himself knocking on wood to counter malicious fates. At dinner, when he toppled the salt shaker, he immediately picked up a pinch of the stuff to throw it over his shoulder, then felt foolish and dusted it off his fingers. But his heart began to pound, and he was filled with a ridiculous superstitious dread, and he didn't feel right again until he snatched up more salt and tossed it behind him.

Although Nora was surely aware of Travis's eccentric behavior, she had the good grace to say nothing about his jitters. Instead, she countered his mood by quietly loving him every minute of the day, by speaking with great delight about their trip to Vegas, by being in unrelievedly good humor, and by *not* knocking on wood.

She did not know about his nightmares because he did not tell her about them. It was the same bad dream, in fact, two nights in a row.

In the dream, he was wandering in the wooded canyons of the Santa Ana foothills of Orange County, the same woods in which he had first met Einstein. He had gone there with Einstein again, and with Nora, but now he had lost them. Frightened for them, he plunged down steep slopes, scrambled up hills, struggled through clinging brush, calling frantically for Nora, for the dog. Sometimes he heard Nora answering or Einstein barking, and they sounded as if they were in trouble, so he turned in the direction from which their voices came, but each time he heard them they were farther off and in a different place, and no matter how intently he listened or how fast he made his way through the forest, he was losing them, losing them—

—until he woke, breathless, heart racing, a silent scream caught in his throat.

Friday, August 6, was such a blessedly busy day that Travis had little time to worry about hostile fate. First thing in the morning, he telephoned a wedding chapel in Las Vegas and, using his American Express number, made arrangements for a ceremony on Wednesday, August 11, at eleven o'clock.

Overcome by a romantic fever, he told the chapel manager that he wanted twenty dozen red roses, twenty dozen white carnations, a good organist (no damn taped music) who could play traditional music, so many candles that the altar would be bright without harsh electric light, a bottle of Dom Perignon with which to conclude events, and a first-rate photographer to record the nuptials. When those details had been agreed upon, he telephoned the Circus Circus Hotel in Las Vegas, which was a family-oriented enterprise that boasted a recreational-vehicle campgrounds behind the hotel itself; he arranged for camp space beginning the night of Sunday, August 8. With another call to an RV campgrounds in Barstow, he also secured reservations for Saturday night, when they would pull off the road halfway to Vegas. Next, he went to a jewelry store, looked at their entire stock, and finally bought an engagement ring with a big, flawless three-carat diamond and a wedding band with twelve quarter-carat stones. With the rings hidden under the seat of the truck, Travis and Einstein went to Nora's house, picked her up, and took her to an appointment with her attorney, Garrison Dilworth.

"Getting married? That's wonderful!" Garrison said, pumping Travis's hand. He kissed Nora on the cheek. He seemed genuinely delighted. "I've asked around about you, Travis."

Surprised, Travis said, "You have?"

"For Nora's sake."

The attorney's statement made Nora blush and protest, but Travis was pleased that Garrison had been concerned about her welfare.

Fixing Travis with a measured stare, the silver-haired attorney said, "I gather you did quite well in real estate before you sold your business."

"I did all right," Travis confirmed modestly, feeling as if he were speaking with Nora's father, trying to make the right impression.

"*Very* well," Garrison said. "And I also hear you've invested the profits rather well."

"I'm not broke," Travis admitted.

Smiling, Garrison said, "I also hear you're a good, reliable man with more than your share of kindness."

It was Travis's turn to blush. He shrugged.

To Nora, Garrison said, "Dear, I'm delighted for you, happier than I can say."

"Thank you." Nora favored Travis with a loving, radiant look that made him want to knock on wood for the first time all day.

Because they intended to take a honeymoon of at least a week or ten days following the wedding, Nora did not want to have to rush back to Santa Barbara in the event her real-estate agent found a taker for Violet Devon's house. She asked Garrison Dilworth to draw up a power of attorney, giving him authority to handle all aspects of such a sale in her name during her absence. This was done in less than half an hour, signed and witnessed. After another round of congratulations and best wishes, they were on their way to buy a travel trailer.

They intended to take Einstein with them not only to the wedding in Vegas but on the honeymoon. Finding good, clean motels that would accept a dog might not always be easy where they were going, so it was prudent to take a motel-on-wheels with them. Furthermore, neither Travis nor Nora could have made love with the retriever in the same room. "It'd be like having another *person* there," Nora said, blushing as bright as a well-polished apple. Staying in motels, they would have to rent two rooms—one for them and one for Einstein—which seemed too awkward.

By four o'clock, they found what they were looking for: a middle-size, silvery, Quonset-shaped Airstream with a kitchenette, a dining nook, a living room, one bedroom, and one bath. When they retired for the night, they could leave Einstein in the front of the trailer and close the bedroom door after themselves. Because Travis's pickup was already equipped with a good trailer hitch, they were able to hook the Airstream to the rear bumper and haul it with them as soon as the sale was concluded.

Einstein, riding in the pickup between Travis and Nora, kept craning his head around to look out the back window at the gleaming, semicylindrical trailer as if amazed at the ingenuity of humankind.

They shopped for trailer curtains, plastic dishes and drinking glasses, food with which to stock the kitchenette cabinets, and a host of other items they needed before they hit the road. By the time they returned to Nora's house and cooked omelets for a late dinner, they were dragging. For once there was nothing smartass about Einstein's yawns; he was just tired.

That night, at home in his own bed, Travis slept the deep, deep sleep of ancient petrified trees and dinosaur fossils. The dreams of the previous two nights were not repeated.

Saturday morning, they set out on their journey to Vegas and to matrimony. Seeking to travel mostly on wide divided highways on which they would be comfortable with the trailer, they took Route 101 south and then east until it became Route 134, which they followed until it became Interstate 210, with the city of Los Angeles and its suburbs to the south of them and the great Angeles National Forest to the north. Later, on the vast Mojave Desert, Nora was thrilled by the barren yet hauntingly beautiful panoramas of sand, stone, tumbleweed, mesquite, joshua trees, and other cacti. The world, she said, suddenly seemed much bigger than she had ever realized, and Travis took pleasure in her bedazzlement.

Barstow, California, was a sprawling pit stop in that enormous wasteland, and they arrived at the big RV campgrounds by three that afternoon. Frank and Mae Jordan, the middle-aged couple in the next camper space, were from Salt Lake City and were traveling with their pet, a black Labrador named Jack.

To Travis's and Nora's surprise, Einstein had a terrific time playing with Jack. They chased each other around the trailers, took playful nips at each other, tangled and tumbled and sprang up and went chasing again. Frank Jordan tossed a red rubber ball for them, and they sprinted after it, vying to be the champion retriever. The dogs also made a game of trying to get the ball away from each other and then holding on to it as long as possible. Travis was exhausted just watching them.

Einstein was undoubtedly the smartest dog in the world, the smartest dog of all time, a phenomenon, a miracle, as perceptive as any man—but he was also a dog. Sometimes, Travis forgot this fact, but he was charmed every time Einstein did something to remind him.

Later, after sharing charcoal-grilled hamburgers and corn on the cob with the Jordans, and after downing a couple of beers in the clear desert night, they said goodbye to the Salt Lakers, and Einstein seemed to say goodbye to Jack. Inside the Airstream, Travis patted Einstein on the head and told him, "That was very nice of you."

The dog cocked his head, staring at Travis as if to ask what the devil he meant.

Travis said, "You know what I'm talking about, fur face."

"I know, too," Nora said. She hugged the dog. "When you were playing games with Jack, you could have made a fool of him if you'd wanted to, but you let him win his share, didn't you?"

Einstein panted and grinned happily.

After one last nightcap, Nora took the bedroom, and Travis slept on the fold-out sofa bed in the living room. Travis had thought about sleeping with her, and perhaps she had considered allowing him into her bed. After all, the wedding was less than four days away. God knew, Travis wanted her. And although she surely suffered slightly with a virgin's fear, she wanted him, too; he had no doubt of that. Each day, they were touching each other and kissing more often—and more intimately—and the air between them crackled with erotic energy. But why not do things right and proper since they were so close to the day? Why not go to their marriage bed as virgins—she as a virgin to everyone, he to her?

That night, Travis dreamed that Nora and Einstein were lost in the desolate reaches of the Mojave. In the dream, he was for some reason legless, forced to search for them at an agonizingly slow crawl, which was bad because he knew that, wherever they were, they were under attack by . . . something . . .

Sunday, Monday, and Tuesday in Las Vegas, they prepared for the wedding, watched Einstein playing enthusiastically with other campers' dogs, and took side trips to Charleston Peak and Lake Mead. In the evenings, Nora and Travis left Einstein with his books while they went to stage shows. Travis felt guilty about leaving the retriever alone, but by various means Einstein indicated that he did not want them to stay at the trailer merely because the Strip hotels were so prejudiced and shortsighted as to refuse to allow well-behaved genius dogs into the casinos and showrooms.

Wednesday morning, Travis dressed in a tuxedo, and Nora wore a simple calf-length white dress with spare lace trim at the cuffs and neckline. With Einstein between them, they drove to their wedding in the pickup, leaving the unhitched Airstream at the campgrounds.

The nondenominational, commercial chapel was the funniest place Travis had ever seen, for the design was earnestly romantic, solemn, and tacky all at the same time. Nora thought it was hilarious, too, and upon entering they had trouble suppressing their laughter. The chapel was tucked in among neon-dripping, glitzy, high-rise hotels on Las Vegas Boulevard South. It was only the size of a one-story house, pale-pink stucco with white doors. Engraved in brass above the doors was the legend YE SHALL GO TWO BY TWO . . . Instead of depicting religious images, the stained-glass windows were aglow with garishly rendered scenes from famous love stories including *Romeo and Juliet*, *Abelard and Heloise*, *Aucassin and Nicolette*, *Gone with the Wind*, *Casablanca*—and, unbelievably, *I Love Lucy* and *Ozzie & Harriet*.

Curiously, the tackiness did not deflate their buoyant mood. Nothing could diminish this day. Even the outrageous chapel was to be prized, remembered in every gaudy detail to be vividly recalled over the years, and always to be recalled fondly because it was *their* chapel on *their* day and therefore special in its own strange way.

Dogs were not ordinarily admitted. But Travis had generously tipped the entire staff in advance to insure that Einstein would not only be allowed inside but would be made to feel as welcome as anyone.

The minister, the Reverend Dan Dupree—"Please call me Reverend Dan"—was a florid-faced, potbellied fellow, a strenuous smiler and glad-hander who looked like a stereotypical used-car salesman. He was flanked by two paid witnesses—his wife and her sister—who were wearing bright summery dresses for the occasion.

Travis took his place at the front of the chapel.

The woman organist struck up "The Wedding March."

Nora had expressed a deep desire to actually walk down the aisle and meet

Travis rather than just beginning the ceremony at the altar railing. Further-more, she wanted to be "given away," as other brides were. That should have been her father's singular honor, of course, but she had no father. Nor was anyone else at hand who would be a likely candidate for the job, and at first it seemed that she would have to make the walk alone or on the arm of a stranger. But in the pickup, on their way to the ceremony, she had realized that Einstein was available, and she had decided that no one in the world was more suited to accompany her down the aisle than the dog.

Now, as the organist played, Nora entered the back of the nave with the dog at her side. Einstein was acutely aware of the great honor of escorting her, and he walked with all the pride and dignity he could muster, his head held high, his slow steps timed to hers.

No one seemed disturbed—or even surprised—that a dog was giving Nora away. This was, after all, Las Vegas.

"She's one of the loveliest brides I've ever seen," Reverend Dan's wife whispered to Travis, and he sensed that she was sincere, that she did not routinely bestow that compliment.

The photographer's flash blinked repeatedly, but Travis was too involved with the sight of Nora to be bothered by the strobe.

Vases full of roses and carnations filled the small nave with their perfume, and a hundred candles flickered softly, some in clear glass votive cups and others on brass candelabras. By the time Nora arrived at his side, Travis was oblivious of the tacky decor. His love was an architect that entirely remade the reality of the chapel, transforming it into a cathedral as grand as any in the world.

The ceremony was brief and unexpectedly dignified. Travis and Nora ex-changed vows, then rings. Tears full of reflected candlelight shimmered in her eyes, and Travis wondered for a moment why her tears should blur *his* vision, then realized that he, too, was on the verge of tears. A burst of dramatic organ music accompanied their first kiss as man and wife, and it was the sweetest kiss he had ever known.

Reverend Dan popped the Dom Perignon and, at Travis's direction, poured a glass for everyone, the organist included. A saucer was found for Einstein. Slurping noisily, the retriever joined in their toast to life, happiness, and love eternal.

Einstein spent the afternoon in the forward end of the trailer, in the living room, reading.

Travis and Nora spent the afternoon at the other end of the trailer, in bed.

After closing the bedroom door, Travis put a second bottle of Dom Perignon in an ice bucket and loaded a compact-disk player with four albums of George Winston's most mellow piano music.

Nora drew down the blind at the only window and switched on a small lamp with a gold cloth shade. The soft amber light lent the room an aura rather like that of a place in a dream.

For a while they lay on the bed, talking, laughing, touching, kissing, then talking less and kissing more.

Gradually, Travis undressed her. He'd never before seen her unclothed, and he found her even more lovely and more exquisitely proportioned than he had imagined. Her slender throat, the delicacy of her shoulders, the fullness of her breasts, the concavity of her belly, the flair of her hips, the round sauciness of her buttocks, the long smooth supple sleekness of her legs—every line and angle and curve excited him but also filled him with great tenderness.

After he undressed himself, he patiently and gently introduced her to the art of love. With a profound desire to please and with full awareness that every-thing was new to her, he showed Nora—sometimes not without delicious teasing—all the sensations that his tongue, fingers, and manhood could engen-der in her.

He was prepared to find her hesitant, embarrassed, even fearful, because her first thirty years of life had not prepared her for this degree of intimacy. But she harbored no trace of frigidity and was eager to engage in any act that might pleasure either or both of them. Her soft cries and breathless murmurs of excitement delighted him. Each time that she sighed climactically and surren-dered to a shudder of ecstasy, Travis became more aroused, until he was of a size and firmness that he had never attained before, until his need was almost painful.

When at last he let his warm seed flower within her, he buried his face in her throat and called her name and told her that he loved her, told her again and again, and the moment of release seemed so long that he half-thought time had stopped or that he had tapped an inexplicable well that could never be exhausted.

With consummation achieved, they held each other for a long time, silent, not needing to talk. They listened to music, and in a while they finally spoke of what they felt, both physically and emotionally. They drank some cham-pagne, and in time they made love again. And again.

Although the constant shadow of certain death looms over every day, the pleasures and joys of life can be so fine and deeply affecting that the heart is nearly stilled by astonishment.

From Vegas, they hauled the Airstream north on Route 95, across the immense Nevada barrens. Two days later, on Friday, August 13, they reached Lake Tahoe and connected the trailer to the electric and water lines at an RV campsite on the California side of the border.

Nora was not quite as easily overwhelmed by each new scenic vista and novel experience as she had been. However, Lake Tahoe was so stunningly beautiful that it filled her with childlike wonder again. Twenty-two miles long and twelve miles wide, with the Sierra Nevadas on its western flank and the Carson Range on the east, Tahoe was said to be the clearest body of water in the world, a shimmering jewel in a hundred amazingly iridescent shades of blue and green.

For six days, Nora and Travis and Einstein hiked in the Eldorado, Tahoe, and Toiyabe National Forests, vast primeval tracts of pine, spruce, and fir. They rented a boat and went on the lake, exploring paradisiacal coves and graceful bays. They went sunning and swimming, and Einstein took to the water with the enthusiasm indigenous to his breed.

Sometimes in the morning, sometimes in the late afternoon, more often at night, Nora and Travis made love. She was surprised by her carnal appetite. She could not get enough of him.

"I love your mind and your heart," she told him, "but God help me, I love your body almost as much! Am I depraved?"

"Good heavens, no. You're just a young, healthy woman. In fact, given the life you've led, you're emotionally healthier than you've any right to be. Really, Nora, you stagger me."

"I'd like to straddle you instead."

"Maybe you *are* depraved," he said, and laughed.

Early on the serenely blue morning of Friday the twentieth, they left Tahoe and drove across the state to the Monterey Peninsula. There, where the con-tinental shelf met the sea, the natural beauty was, if possible, even greater than that at Tahoe, and they stayed four days, leaving for home on the afternoon of Wednesday, August 25.

Throughout their trip, the joy of matrimony was so all-consuming that the miracle of Einstein's humanlike intelligence did not occupy their thoughts as much as previously. But Einstein reminded them of his unique nature when they drew near to Santa Barbara late that afternoon. Forty or fifty miles from home, he grew restless. He shifted repeatedly on the seat between Nora and Travis, sat up for a minute, then laid his head on Nora's lap, then sat up again. He began to whimper strangely. By the time they were ten miles from home, he was shivering.

"What's wrong with you, fur face?" she asked.

With his expressive brown eyes, Einstein tried hard to convey a complex and important message, but she could not understand him.

Half an hour before dusk, when they reached the city and departed the freeway for surface streets, Einstein began alternately to whine and growl low in his throat.

"What's wrong with him?" Nora asked.

Frowning, Travis said, "I don't know."

As they pulled into the driveway of Travis's rented house and parked in the shade of the date palm, the retriever began to bark. He had never barked in the truck, not once on their long journey. It was ear-splitting in that confined space, but he would not stop.

When they got out of the truck, Einstein bolted past them, positioned himself between them and the house, and continued barking.

Nora moved along the walkway toward the front door, and Einstein darted at her, snarling. He seized one leg of her jeans and tried to pull her off balance. She managed to stay on her feet and, when she retreated to the birdbath, he let go of her.

"What's gotten into him?" she asked Travis.

Staring thoughtfully at the house, Travis said, "He was like this in the woods that first day . . . when he didn't want me to follow the dark trail."

Nora tried to coax the dog closer in order to pet him.

But Einstein would not be coaxed. When Travis tested the dog by approaching the house, Einstein snarled and forced him to retreat.

"Wait here," Travis told Nora. He walked to the Airstream in the driveway and went inside.

Einstein trotted back and forth in front of the house, looking up at the door and windows, growling and whining.

As the sun rolled down the western sky and kissed the surface of the sea, the residential street was quiet, peaceful, ordinary in every respect—yet Nora felt a *wrongness* in the air. A warm wind off the Pacific elicited whispers from the palm and eucalyptus and ficus trees, sounds that might have been pleasant any other day but which now seemed sinister. In the lengthening shadows, in the last orange and purple light of the day, she also perceived an indefinable menace. Except for the dog's behavior, she had no reason to think that danger was near at hand; her uneasiness was not intellectual but instinctual.

When Travis returned from the trailer, he was carrying a large revolver. It had been in a bedroom drawer, unloaded, throughout their honeymoon trip. Now, Travis finished inserting cartridges into the chambers and snapped the cylinder shut.

"Is that necessary?" she asked worriedly.

"Something was in the woods that day," Travis said, "and though I never actually saw it . . . well, it put the hair up on the back of my neck. Yeah, I think the gun might be necessary."

Her own reaction to the whispering trees and afternoon shadows gave her a hint of what Travis must have felt in the woods, and she had to admit that the gun made her feel at least slightly better.

Einstein had stopped pacing and had taken up his guard position on the walkway again, barring their approach to the house.

To the retriever, Travis said, "Is someone inside?"

A quick wag of the tail. *Yes.*

"Men from the lab?"

One bark. *No.*

"The other experimental animal you told us about?"

Yes.

"The thing that was in the woods?"

Yes.

"All right, I'm going in there."

No.

"Yes," Travis insisted. "It's my house, and we're not going to run from this, whatever the hell it is."

Nora remembered the magazine photograph of the movie monster to which Einstein had reacted so strongly. She did not believe anything even remotely like that creature could actually exist. She believed that Einstein was exaggerating or that they had misunderstood what he had been trying to tell them about the photo. Nevertheless, she suddenly wished they had not only the revolver but a shotgun.

"This is a .357 Magnum," Travis told the dog, "and one shot, even if it hits an arm or a leg, will knock down the biggest, meanest man and keep him down. He'll feel as if he's been hit by a cannonball. I've taken firearms training from the best, and I've done regular target practice over the years to keep my edge. I really know what I'm doing, and I'll be able to handle myself in there. Besides, we can't just call the cops, can we? Because whatever they find in there is going to raise eyebrows, lead to a lot of questions, and sooner or later they'll have you back in that damn lab again."

Einstein was clearly unhappy with Travis's determination, but the dog padded up the front steps to the stoop and looked back as if to say, *All right, okay, but I'm not letting you go in there alone.*

Nora wanted to go in with them, but Travis was adamant that she remain in the front yard. She reluctantly admitted that—since she lacked both a weapon and the skill to use it—there was nothing she could do to help and that she would most likely only get in the way.

Holding the revolver at his side, Travis joined Einstein on the stoop and inserted his key in the door.

7

Travis disengaged the lock, pocketed the key, and pushed the door inward, covering the room beyond with the .357. Warily, he stepped across the threshold, and Einstein entered at his side.

The house was silent, as it should have been, but the air reeked of a bad smell that did not belong.

Einstein growled softly.

Little of the fast-fading sunlight entered the house through the windows, many of which were partly or entirely covered with drapes. But it was bright enough for Travis to see that the sofa's upholstery was slashed. Shredded foam padding spilled onto the floor. A wooden magazine rack had been hammered to pieces against the wall, gouging holes in the plasterboard. The TV screen had been smashed in with a floor lamp, which still protruded from the set. Books had been taken off the shelves, torn apart, and scattered across the living room.

In spite of the breeze blowing in through the door, the stench seemed to be getting worse.

Travis flicked the wall switch. A corner lamp came on. It did not shed much light, just enough to reveal more details of the rubble.

Looks like somebody went through here with a chainsaw and then a power mower, he thought.

The house remained silent.

Leaving the door open behind him, he took a couple of steps into the room, and the crumpled pages of the ruined books crunched crisply underfoot. He noticed dark, rusty stains on some of the paper and on the bone-white foam padding, and suddenly he stopped, realizing the stains were blood.

A moment later, he spotted the corpse. It was that of a big man, lying on his side on the floor near the sofa, half-covered by gore-smeared book pages, book boards, and dust jackets.

Einstein's growling grew louder, meaner.

Moving closer to the body, which was just a few feet from the dining-room archway, Travis saw that it was his landlord, Ted Hockney. Beside him was his Craftsman toolbox. Ted had a key to the house and Travis had no objections to his entering at any time to make repairs. Lately there had been a number of repairs required, including a leaky faucet and broken dishwasher. Evidently, Ted had walked down the block from his own house and entered with the intention of fixing something. Now Ted was broken, too, and beyond repair.

Because of the ripe stink, Travis first thought the man must have been killed at least a week ago. But on closer inspection, the corpse proved to be neither bloated with the gas of decomposition nor marked by any signs of decay, so it could not have been there for very long. Perhaps only a day, perhaps less. The hideous stench had two other sources: for one thing, the landlord had been disemboweled; furthermore, his killer had apparently defecated and urinated on and around the body.

Ted Hockney's eyes were gone.

Travis felt sick, and not only because he had liked Ted. He would have been sickened by such insane violence regardless of who the dead man had been. A death like this left the victim no dignity whatsoever and somehow diminished the entire human race.

Einstein's low growling gave way to ugly snarling punctuated with hard, sharp barks.

With a nervous twitch and a sudden hammering of his heart, Travis turned from the corpse and saw that the retriever was facing into the nearby dining room. The shadows were deep in there because the drapes were drawn shut over both windows, and only a thin gray light passed through from the kitchen beyond.

Go, get out, leave! an inner voice told him.

But he did not turn and run because he had never run away from anything in his life. Well, all right, that was not quite true: he had virtually run away from life itself these past few years when he had let despair get the best of him. His descent into isolation had been the ultimate cowardice. However, that was behind him; he was a new man, transformed by Einstein and Nora, and he was not going to run again, damned if he was.

Einstein went rigid. He arched his back, thrust his head down and forward, and barked so furiously that saliva flew from his mouth.

Travis took a step toward the dining-room arch.

The retriever stayed at Travis's side, barking more viciously.

Holding the revolver in front of him, trying to take confidence from the powerful weapon, Travis eased forward another step, treading cautiously in the treacherous rubble. He was only two or three steps from the archway. He squinted into the gloomy dining room.

Einstein's barking resounded through the house until it seemed as if a whole pack of dogs must be loose in the place.

Travis took one more step, then saw something move in the shadowy dining room.

He froze.

Nothing. Nothing moved. Had it been a phantom of the mind?

Beyond the arch, layered shadows hung like gray and black crepe.

He wasn't sure if he had seen movement or merely imagined.

Back off, get out, now! the inner voice said.

In defiance of it, Travis raised one foot, intending to step into the archway.

The thing in the dining room moved again. This time there was no doubt of its presence, because it rushed out of the deepest darkness at the far side of that chamber, vaulted onto the dining-room table, and came straight at Travis, emitting a blood-freezing shriek. He saw lantern eyes in the gloom, and a nearly man-size figure that—in spite of the poor light—gave an impression of deformity. Then the thing was coming off the table, straight at him.

Einstein charged forward to engage it, but Travis tried to step back and gain an extra second in which to squeeze off a shot. As he pulled the trigger, he slipped on the ruined books that littered the floor, and fell backward. The revolver roared, but Travis knew he had missed, had fired into the ceiling. For an instant, as Einstein scrambled toward the adversary, Travis saw the lantern-eyed thing more clearly, saw it work alligator jaws and crack open an impossibly wide mouth in a lumpish face, revealing wickedly hooked teeth.

"Einstein, no!" he shouted, for he knew the dog would be torn to pieces in any confrontation with this hellish creature, and he fired again, twice, wildly, from his position on the floor.

His cry and the shots not only brought Einstein to a halt but gave the enemy second thoughts about going up against an armed man. The thing turned—it was quick, far quicker than a cat—and crossed the unlighted dining room to the kitchen doorway. For a moment, he saw it silhouetted in the murky light from the kitchen, and he had the impression of something that had never been meant to stand erect but was standing erect anyway, something with a misshapen head twice as large as it ought to have been, a hunched back, arms too long and terminating in claws like the tines of a garden rake.

He fired again and came closer to the mark. The bullet tore out a chunk of the door frame.

With a shriek, the beast disappeared into the kitchen.

What in the name of God was it? Where had it come from? Had it really escaped from the same lab that had produced Einstein? But how had they made this monstrosity? And why? *Why?*

He was a well-read man: in fact, for the last few years, most of his time was devoted to books, so possibilities began to occur to him. Recombinant-DNA research was foremost among them.

Einstein stood in the middle of the dining room, barking, facing the doorway where the thing had vanished.

Lurching to his feet in the living room, Travis called the dog back to his side, and Einstein returned quickly, eagerly.

He shushed the dog, listened intently. He heard Nora frantically calling his name from the yard out front, but he heard nothing in the kitchen.

For Nora's benefit, he shouted, "I'm okay! I'm all right! Stay out there!"

Einstein was shivering.

Travis could hear the loud two-part thudding of his own heart, and he could *almost* hear the sweat trickling down his face, and down the small of his back, but he could hear nothing whatsoever to pinpoint that escapee from a night-mare. He did not think it had gone out the back door into the rear yard. For one thing, he figured the creature did not want to be seen by a lot of people and, therefore, only went outside at night, traveled exclusively in the dark, when it could slip even into a fair-sized town like Santa Barbara without being spotted. The day was still light enough to make the thing leery of the outdoors. Fur-thermore, Travis could sense its presence nearby, the way he might sense that someone was staring at him behind his back, the way he might sense an oncoming thunderstorm on a humid day with a lowering sky. It was out there, all right, waiting in the kitchen, ready and waiting.

Cautiously, Travis returned to the archway and stepped into the half-dark dining room.

Einstein stayed close at his side, neither whining nor growling nor barking. The dog seemed to realize that Travis needed complete silence in order to hear any sound the beast might make.

Travis took two more steps.

Ahead, through the kitchen door, he could see a corner of the table, the sink, part of a counter, half of the dishwasher. The setting sun was at the other end of the house, and the light in the kitchen was dim, gray, so their adversary would not cast a revealing shadow. It might be waiting on either side of the door, or it might have climbed onto the counters from which it could launch itself down at him when he entered the room.

Trying to trick the creature, hoping that it would react without hesitation to the first sign of movement in the doorway, Travis tucked the revolver under his belt, quietly picked up one of the dining-room chairs, eased to within six feet of the kitchen, and pitched the chair through the open door. He snatched the revolver out of his waistband and, as the chair sailed into the kitchen, assumed a shooter's stance. The chair crashed into the Formica-topped table, clattered to the floor, and banged against the dishwasher.

The lantern-eyed enemy did not go for it. Nothing moved. When the chair finished tumbling, the kitchen was again marked by a hushed expectancy.

Einstein was making a curious sound, a quiet shuddery huffing, and after a moment Travis realized the noise was a result of the dog's uncontrollable shivering.

No question about it: the intruder in the kitchen was the very thing that had pursued them through the woods more than three months ago. During the intervening weeks, it had made its way north, probably traveling mostly in the wildlands to the east of the developed part of the state, relentlessly tracking the dog by some means that Travis could not understand and for reasons he could not even guess.

In response to the chair he had thrown, a large white-enameled canister crashed to the floor just beyond the kitchen doorway, and Travis jumped back in surprise, squeezing off a wild shot before he realized he was only being taunted. The lid flew off the container when it hit the floor, and flour spilled across the tile.

Silence again.

By responding to Travis's taunt with one of its own, the intruder had displayed unnerving intelligence. Abruptly Travis realized that, coming from the same research lab as Einstein and being a product of related experiments, the creature might be as smart as the retriever. Which would explain Ein-stein's fear of it. If Travis had not already accommodated himself to the idea of a dog with humanlike intelligence, he might have been unable to credit this beast with more than mere animal cleverness; however, events of the past few months had primed him to accept—and quickly adapt to—almost anything.

Silence.

Only one round left in the gun.

Deep silence.

He had been so startled by the flour canister that he had not noticed from which side of the doorway it had been flung, and it had fallen in such a fashion that he could not deduce the position of the creature that had hurled it. He still did not know if the intruder was to the left or right of the doorway.

He was not sure he any longer cared where it was. Even with the .357 in hand, he did not think he would be wise to enter the kitchen. Not if the damn thing was as smart as a man. It would be like doing battle with an intelligent buzzsaw, for Christ's sake.

The light in the east-facing kitchen was dwindling, almost gone. In the dining room, where Travis and Einstein stood, the darkness was deepening. Even behind them, in spite of the open front door and window and the corner lamp, the living room was filling with shadows.

In the kitchen, the intruder hissed loudly, a sound like escaping gas, which was immediately followed by a *click-click-click* that might have been made by its sharply clawed feet or hands tapping against a hard surface.

Travis had caught Einstein's tremors. He felt as if he were a fly on the edge of a spider's web, about to step into a trap.

He remembered Ted Hockney's bitten, bloodied, eyeless face.

Click-click.

In antiterrorist training, he had been taught how to stalk men, and he had been good at it. But the problem here was that the yellow-eyed intruder was maybe as smart as a man but could not be counted on to *think* like a man, so Travis had no way of knowing what it might do next, how it might respond to any initiative he made. Therefore, he could never outthink it, and by its alien nature the creature had a perpetual and deadly advantage of surprise.

Click.

Travis quietly took a step back from the open kitchen door, then another step, treading with exaggerated care, not wanting the thing to discover that he was retreating because only God knew what it might do if it knew he was slipping out of its reach. Einstein padded silently into the living room, now equally eager to put distance between himself and the intruder.

When he reached Ted Hockney's corpse, Travis glanced away from the dining room, searching for the least littered route to the front door—and he saw Nora standing by the armchair. Frightened by the gunfire, she had gotten a butcher's knife from the kitchenette in the Airstream and had come to see if he needed help.

He was impressed by her courage but horrified to see her there in the glow of the corner lamp. Suddenly it seemed as if his nightmares of losing both Einstein and Nora were on the verge of coming true, the Cornell Curse again, because now they were both inside the house, both vulnerable, both possibly within striking distance of the thing in the kitchen.

She started to speak.

Travis shook his head and raised one hand to his mouth.

Silenced, she bit her lip and glanced from him to the dead man on the floor.

As Travis quietly stepped through the rubble, he was stricken by a feeling that the intruder had gone out the back of the house and was coming around the side, heading for the front door, risking being seen by neighbors in the gloom of twilight, intending to enter behind them, swift and fast. Nora was standing between Travis and the front door, so he would not have a clear shot at the creature if it came that way; hell, it would be all over Nora one second after it reached the door. Trying not to panic, trying not to think of Hockney's eyeless face, Travis moved more quickly across the living room, risking the crackle of some debris underfoot, hoping those small noises would not carry to the kitchen if the intruder was still out there. Reaching Nora, he took her by the arm and propelled her toward the front door, out onto the stoop and down the stairs, looking left and right, half-expecting to see the living nightmare rushing at them, but it was nowhere in sight.

The gunshots and Nora's shouting had drawn neighbors as far as their front doors all along the street. A few had even come outside onto porches and lawns. Somebody surely would have called the cops. Because of Einstein's status as a much-wanted fugitive, the police seemed almost as grave a danger as the yellow-eyed thing in the house.

The three of them piled into the pickup. Nora locked her door, and Travis locked his. He started the engine and backed the truck—and the Airstream— out of the driveway, into the street. He was aware of people staring.

The twilight was going to be short-lived, as it always was near the ocean. Already, the sunless sky was blackish in the east, purple overhead, and a steadily darkening blood-red in the west. Travis was grateful for the oncoming cover of nightfall, although he knew the yellow-eyed creature would be sharing it with them.

He drove past the gaping neighbors, none of whom he had ever met during his years of self-imposed solitude, and he turned at the first corner. Nora held Einstein tightly, and Travis drove as fast as he dared. The trailer rocked and swayed behind them when he took the next couple of corners at too great a speed.

"What happened in there?" she asked.

"It killed Hockney earlier today or yesterday—"

"It?"

"—and it was waiting for us to come home."

"*It?*" she repeated.

Einstein mewled.

Travis said, "I'll have to explain later." He wondered if he could explain. No description he gave of the intruder would do it justice; he did not possess the words necessary to convey the degree of its strangeness.

They had gone no more than eight blocks when they heard sirens in the neighborhood that they had just left. Travis drove another four blocks and parked in the empty lot of a high school.

"What now?" Nora asked.

"We abandon the trailer and the truck," he said. "They'll be looking for both."

He put the revolver in her purse, and she insisted on slipping the butcher's knife in there, too, rather than leave it behind.

They got out of the pickup and, in the descending night, walked past the side of the school, across an athletic field, through a gate in a chain-link fence, and onto a residential street lined with mature trees.

With nightfall, the breeze became a blustery wind, warm and parched. It blew a few dry leaves at them and harried dust ghosts along the pavement.

Travis knew they were too conspicuous even without the trailer and truck. The neighbors would be telling the police to look for a man, woman, and golden retriever—not the most common trio. They would be wanted for questioning in the death of Ted Hockney, so the search for them would not be perfunctory. They had to get out of sight quickly.

He had no friends with whom they could take refuge. After Paula died, he had withdrawn from his few friends, and he hadn't maintained relationships with any of the real-estate agents who had once worked for him. Nora had no friends, either, thanks to Violet Devon.

The houses they passed, most with warm lights in the windows, seemed to mock them with unattainable sanctuary.

8

Garrison Dilworth lived on the border between Santa Barbara and Montecito, on a lushly landscaped half acre, in a stately Tudor home that did not mesh well with the California flora but which perfectly complemented the attorney. When he answered the door, he was wearing black loafers, gray slacks, a navy-blue sports jacket, a white knit shirt, and half-lens tortoiseshell reading glasses over which he peered at them in surprise but, fortunately, not with displeasure. "Well, hello there, newlyweds!"

"Are you alone?" Travis asked as he and Nora and Einstein stepped into the large foyer floored with marble.

"Alone? Yes."

On the way over, Nora had told Travis that the attorney's wife had passed away three years ago and that he was now looked after by a housekeeper named Gladys Murphy.

"Mrs. Murphy?" Travis asked.

"She's gone home for the day," the attorney said, closing the door behind them. "You look distraught. What on earth's wrong?"

"We need help," Nora said.

"But," Travis warned, "anyone who helps us may be putting himself in jeopardy with the law."

Garrison raised his eyebrows. "What have you done? Judging by the solemn look of you—I'd say you've kidnapped the president."

"We've done nothing wrong," Nora assured him.

"Yes, we have," Travis disagreed. "And we're still doing it—we're harboring the dog."

Puzzled, Garrison frowned down at the retriever.

Einstein whined, looking suitably miserable and lovable.

"And there's a dead man in my house," Travis said.

Garrison's gaze shifted from the dog to Travis. "Dead man?"

"Travis didn't kill him," Nora said.

Garrison looked at Einstein again.

"Neither did the dog," Travis said. "But I'll be wanted as a material witness, something like that, sure as hell."

"Mmmmm," Garrison said, "why don't we go into my study and get this straightened out?"

He led them through an enormous and only half-lit living room, along a short hallway, into a den with rich teak paneling and a copper ceiling. The maroon leather armchairs and couch looked expensive and comfortable. The polished teak desk was massive, and a detailed model of a five-masted schooner, all sails rigged, stood on one corner. Nautical items—a ship's wheel, a brass sextant, a carved bullock's horn filled with tallow that held what appeared to be sailmaking needles, six types of ship lanterns, a helmsman's bell, and sea charts—were used as decoration. Travis saw photographs of a man and woman on various sailboats, and the man was Garrison.

An open book and a half-finished glass of Scotch were on a small table beside one of the armchairs. Evidently, the attorney had been relaxing here when they had rung the doorbell. Now, he offered them a drink, and they both said they would have whatever he was having.

Leaving the couch for Travis and Nora, Einstein took the second armchair. He sat in it, rather than curling up, as if prepared to participate in the discussion to come.

At a corner wet bar, Garrison poured Chivas Regal on the rocks in two glasses. Although Nora was unaccustomed to whiskey, she startled Travis by downing her drink in two long swallows and asking for another. He decided that she had the right idea, so he followed suit and took his empty glass back to the bar while Garrison was refilling Nora's.

"I'd like to tell you everything and have your help," Travis said, "but you really must understand you could be putting yourself on the wrong side of the law."

Recapping the Chivas, Garrison said, "You're talking as a layman now. As an attorney, I assure you the law isn't a line engraved in marble, immovable and unchangeable through the centuries. Rather . . . the law is like a string, fixed at both ends but with a great deal of play in it—very loose, the line of the law—so you can stretch it this way or that, rearrange the arc of it so you are nearly always—short of blatant theft or cold-blooded murder—safely on the right side. That's a daunting thing to realize but true. I've no fear that anything you tell me could land my bottom in a prison cell, Travis."

Half an hour later, Travis and Nora had told him everything about Einstein. For a man only a couple of months shy of his seventy-first birthday, the silver-haired attorney had a quick and open mind. He asked the right questions and did not scoff. When given a ten-minute demonstration of Einstein's uncanny abilities, he did not protest that it was all mere trickery and flummery; he accepted what he saw, and he readjusted his ideas of what was normal and possible in this world. He exhibited greater mental agility and flexibility than most men half his age.

Holding Einstein on his lap in the big leather armchair, gently scratching the dog's ears, Garrison said, "If you go to the media, hold a press conference, blow the whole thing wide open, then we might be able to sue in court to allow you to keep custody of the dog."

"Do you really think that would work?" Nora asked.

"At best," Garrison admitted, "it's a fifty-fifty chance."

Travis shook his head. "No. We won't risk it."

"What have you in mind to do?" Garrison asked.

"Run," Travis said. "Stay on the move."

"And what will that accomplish?"

"It'll keep Einstein free."

The dog woofed in agreement.

"Free—but for how long?" Garrison asked.

Travis got up and paced, too agitated to sit still any longer. "They won't stop looking," he admitted. "not for a few years."

"Not ever," the attorney said.

"All right, it's going to be tough, but it's the only thing we can do. Damned if we'll let them have him. He has a dread of the lab. Besides, he more or less brought me back to life—"

"And he saved me from Streck," Nora said.

"He brought us together," Travis said.

"Changed our lives."

"Radically changed us. Now he's as much a part of us as our own child would be," Travis said. He felt a lump of emotion in his throat when he met the dog's grateful gaze. "We fight for him, just as he'd fight for us. We're family. We live together . . . or we die together."

Stroking the retriever, Garrison said, "It won't only be the people from the lab looking for you. And not only the police."

"The other thing," Travis said, nodding.

Einstein shivered.

"There, there, easy now," Garrison said reassuringly, patting the dog. To Travis, he said, "What do you think the creature is? I've heard your description of it, but that doesn't help much."

"Whatever it is," Travis said, "God didn't make it. Men made it. Which means it has to be a product of recombinant-DNA research of some kind. God knows why. God knows what they thought they were doing, why they wanted to build something like that. But they did."

"And it seems to have an uncanny ability to track you."

"To track Einstein," Nora said.

"So we'll keep moving," Travis said. "And we'll go a long way."

"That'll require money, but the banks don't open for more than twelve hours," Garrison said. "If you're going to run, something tells me you've got to head out tonight."

"Here's where we could use your help," Travis told him.

Nora opened her purse and withdrew two checkbooks, Travis's and her own. "Garrison, what we'd like to do is write a check on Travis's account and one on mine, payable to you. He's only got three thousand in his checking, but he has a large savings account at the same bank, and they're authorized to transfer funds to prevent overdrawing. My account's the same way. If we give you one of Travis's checks for twenty thousand—backdated so it appears to've been written before all this trouble—and one of mine for twenty, you could deposit them into your account. As soon as they clear, you'd buy eight cashier's checks for five thousand apiece and send them to us."

Travis said, "The police will want me for questioning, but they'll know I didn't kill Ted Hockney because no *man* could've torn him apart like that. So they won't put a lock on my accounts."

"If federal agencies are behind the research that produced Einstein and this creature," Garrison said, "then they'll be hot to get their hands on you, and *they* might freeze your accounts."

"Maybe. But probably not right away. You're in the same town, so your bank should clear my check by Monday at the latest."

"What'll you do for funds in the meantime, while you're waiting for me to sent you the forty thousand?"

"We've got some cash and traveler's checks left over from the honeymoon," Nora said.

"And my credit cards," Travis added.

"They can track you by credit cards and traveler's checks."

"I know," Travis said. "So I'll use them in a town where we don't intend to stay, and we'll scoot out fast as we can."

"When I've purchased the cashier's checks for forty thousand, where do I send them?"

"We'll be in touch by phone," Travis said, returning to the couch and sitting at Nora's side. "We'll work something out."

"And the rest of your assets—and Nora's?"

"We'll worry about that later," Nora said.

Garrison frowned. "Before you leave here, Travis, you can sign a letter giving me the right to represent you in any legal matters that may arise. If anyone does try to freeze your assets, or Nora's, I can beat them off if at all possible—though I'll keep a low profile until they connect me with you."

"Nora's funds are probably safe for a while. She and I haven't told anyone but you about the marriage. The neighbors will tell the police I left in the company of a woman, but they won't know who she is. Have you told anyone about us?"

"Just my secretary, Mrs. Ashcroft. But she's not a gossip."

"All right, then," Travis said. "I don't think the authorities will find out about the marriage license, so they might take quite a while to come up with Nora's name. But when they do, they'll discover you're her attorney. If they monitor my accounts for canceled checks in the hope of learning where I've gone, they'll know about the twenty thousand I paid to you, and they'll come looking for you—"

"That doesn't give me the slightest pause," Garrison said.

"Maybe not," Travis said. "But as soon as they connect me to Nora and both of us to you, they'll be watching you closely. As soon as that happens . . . then the next time we call, you'll have to tell us at once, so we can hang up and break off all contact with you."

"I understand perfectly," the attorney said.

"Garrison," Nora said, "you don't have to involve yourself in this. We're really asking too much of you."

"Listen, my dear, I'm almost seventy-one. I still enjoy my law practice, and I still go sailing . . . but in truth I find life a bit on the dull side these days. This affair is just what I need to get my ancient blood flowing faster. Besides, I do believe you have an obligation to help keep Einstein free, not just for the reasons you mentioned but because . . . mankind has no right to employ its genius in the creation of another intelligent species, then treat it like property. If we've come so far that we can create as God creates, then we have to learn to act with the justice and mercy of God. In this case, justice and mercy require that Einstein remain free."

Einstein raised his head from the attorney's lap, gazed up admiringly, then nuzzled his cold nose under Garrison's chin.

In the three-car garage, Garrison kept a new black Mercedes 560 SEL, an older white Mercedes 500 SEL with pale-blue interior, and a green Jeep that he used primarily to drive down to the marina, where he kept his boat.

"The white one used to belong to Francine, my wife," the attorney said as he led them to the car. "I don't use it much any more, but I keep it in working order, and I drive it often enough to prevent the tires from disintegrating. I should have gotten rid of it when Franny died. It was her car, after all. But . . . she loved it so, her flashy white Mercedes, and I can remember the way she looked when she was behind the wheel . . . I'd like you to take it."

"A sixty-thousand-dollar getaway car?" Travis said, sliding one hand along the polished hood. "That's going on the run in style."

"No one will be looking for it," Garrison said. "Even if they do eventually connect me with you two, they won't know I've given you one of my cars."

"We can't accept something this expensive," Nora said.

"Call it a loan," the attorney told her. "When you're finished with it, when you've gotten another car, just park this one somewhere—a bus terminal, an airport—and give me a call to tell me where it is. I can send someone to collect it."

Einstein put his forepaws on the driver's door of the Mercedes and peered into the car through the side window. He glanced at Travis and Nora and woofed as if to say he thought they would be foolish if they turned down such an offer.

9

With Travis driving, they left Garrison Dilworth's house at ten-fifteen Wednesday night and took Route 101 north. By twelve-thirty they passed through San Luis Obispo, went by Paso Robles at one o'clock in the morning. They stopped for gasoline at a self-service station at two o'clock, an hour south of Salinas.

Nora felt useless. She was not even able to spell Travis at the wheel because she did not know how to drive. To some extent, that was Violet Devon's fault, not Nora's, just one more result of a lifetime of seclusion and oppression; nonetheless, she felt utterly useless and was displeased with herself. But she was not going to remain helpless the rest of her life. Damn it, no. She was going to learn to drive and to handle firearms. Travis could teach her both skills. Given his background, he could also instruct her in the martial arts, judo or karate. He was a good teacher. He had certainly done a splendid job of teaching her the art of lovemaking. That thought made her smile, and slowly her highly self-critical mood abated.

For the next two and a half hours, as they drove north to Salinas and then on to San Jose, Nora dozed fitfully. When not sleeping, she took comfort in the empty miles they were putting behind them. On both sides of the highway, vast stretches of farmland seemed to roll on to infinity under the frost-pale light of the moon. When the moon set, they drove long stretches in unrelieved darkness before spotting an occasional light at a farm or a cluster of roadside businesses.

The yellow-eyed thing had tracked Einstein from the Santa Ana foothills in Orange County to Santa Barbara—a distance of more than one hundred and twenty-five air miles, Travis had said, and probably close to three hundred miles on foot in the wilds—in three months. Not a fast pace. So if they went three hundred air miles north from Santa Barbara before finding a place to hole up in the San Francisco Bay area, maybe the stalker would not reach them for seven or eight months. Maybe it would never reach them. Over how great a distance could it sniff out Einstein? Surely, there were limits to its uncanny ability to track the dog. Surely.

10

At eleven o'clock Thursday morning, Lemuel Johnson stood in the master bedroom of the small house that Travis Cornell had rented in Santa Barbara. The dresser mirror had been smashed. The rest of the room had been trashed as well, as if The Outsider had been driven into a jealous rage upon seeing that the dog lived in domestic comfort while it was forced to roam the wildlands and live in comparatively primitive conditions.

In the debris that covered the floor, Lem found four silver-framed photographs that had probably stood on the dresser or nightstands. The first was of Cornell and an attractive blonde. By now Lem had learned enough about Cornell to know that the blonde at his side must be his late wife, Paula. Another photo, a black-and-white shot of a man and woman, was old enough that Lem guessed the people smiling at the camera were Cornell's parents. The third was of a young boy, about eleven or twelve, also black-and-white, also old, which might have been a shot of Travis Cornell himself but which was more likely a picture of the brother who had died young.

The last of the four photos was of ten soldiers grouped on what appeared to be the wooden steps in front of a barracks, grinning at the camera. One of the ten was Travis Cornell. And on a couple of their uniforms, Lem noticed the distinctive patch of Delta Force, the elite antiterrorist corps.

Uneasy about that last photograph, Lem put it on the dresser and headed back toward the living room, where Cliff was continuing to sift through blood-stained rubble. They were looking for something that would mean nothing to the police but might be extremely meaningful to them.

The NSA had been slow to pick up on the Santa Barbara killing, and Lem had not been alerted until almost six o'clock this morning. As a result, the press had already reported the grisly details of Ted Hockney's murder. They were enthusiastically disseminating wild speculations about what might have killed Hockney, focusing primarily on the theory that Cornell kept some kind of exotic and dangerous pet, perhaps a cheetah or panther, and that the animal had attacked the unsuspecting landlord when he had let himself into the house. The TV cameras had lingered lovingly on the shredded and blood-spattered books. It was _National Enquirer_ stuff, which did not surprise Lem because he believed the line separating sensational tabloids like the _Enquirer_ and the so-called "legitimate" press—especially electronic news media—was often thinner than most journalists cared to admit.

He had already planned and put into operation a disinformation campaign to reinforce the press's wrongheaded hysteria about jungle cats on the loose. NSA-paid informants would come forth, claiming to know Cornell, and would vouch that he did, indeed, keep a panther in the house in addition to a dog. Others who had never met Cornell would, in identifying themselves as his friends, sorrowfully report that they had urged him to have the panther de-fanged and declawed as it had reached maturity. Police would want to question Cornell—and the unidentified woman—regarding the panther and its current whereabouts.

Lem was confident the press would be nicely deflected from all inquiries that might lead them closer to the truth.

Of course, down in Orange County, Walt Gaines would hear about this murder, would make friendly inquiries with local authorities, and would swiftly conclude that The Outsider had tracked the dog this far north. Lem was relieved that he had Walt's cooperation.

Entering the living room, where Cliff Soames was at work, Lem said, "Find anything?"

The young agent rose from the debris, dusted his hands together, and said, "Yeah. I put it on the dining-room table."

Lem followed him into the dining room, where a fat ringbinder notebook was the only item on the table. When he opened it and leafed through the contents, he saw photographs that had been cut from glossy magazines and taped to the left-hand pages. Opposite each photo, on the right-hand page, was the name of the pictured object printed in large block letters: TREE, HOUSE, CAR . . .

"What do you make of it?" Cliff asked.

Scowling, saying nothing, Lem continued to leaf through the book, knowing it was important but at first unable to guess why. Then it hit him: "It's a primer. To teach reading."

"Yeah," Cliff said.

Lem saw that his assistant was smiling. "You think they must know the dog's intelligent, that it must've revealed its abilities to them? And so they . . . decided to teach it to read?"

"Looks that way," Cliff said, still smiling. "Good God, do you think it's possible? _Could_ it be taught to read?"

"Undoubtedly," Lem said. "In fact, teaching it to read was on Dr. Weatherby's schedule of experiments for this autumn."

Laughing softly, wonderingly, Cliff said, "I'll be damned."

"Before you get too much of a kick out of it," Lem said, "you better consider the situation. This guy knows the dog is amazingly smart. He might've succeeded in teaching it to read. So we have to figure he's worked out a means of communicating with it as well. He knows it's an experimental animal. He must know a lot of people are looking for it."

Cliff said, "He must know about The Outsider, too, because the dog would have found a way of telling him."

"Yes. Yet, knowing all of this, he hasn't chosen to go public. He could've sold the story to the highest bidder. But he didn't. Or if he's a crusading type, he could've called in the press and blasted the Pentagon for funding this kind of research."

"But he didn't," Cliff said, frowning.

"Which means, first and foremost, he's committed to the dog, committed to keeping it for his own and to preventing its recapture."

Nodding, Cliff said, "Which makes sense if what we've heard about him is true. I mean, this guy lost his whole damn family when he was young. Lost his wife after less than a year. Lost all those buddies in Delta Force. So he became a recluse, cut himself off from all his friends. Must've been lonely as hell. Then along comes the dog . . ."

"Exactly," Lem said. "And for a man with Delta Force training, staying undercover won't be difficult. And if we *do* find him, he'll know how to fight for the dog. Jesus, will he know how to fight!"

"We haven't confirmed the Delta Force rumor yet," Cliff said hopefully.

"I have," Lem said, and he described the photograph he had seen in the wrecked bedroom.

Cliff sighed. "We're in deep shit now."

"Up to our necks," Lem agreed.

11

They had reached San Francisco at six o'clock Thursday morning and, by six-thirty, had found a suitable motel—a sprawling facility that looked modern and clean. The place did not accept pets, but it was easy to sneak Einstein into the room.

Although a small chance existed that an arrest warrant might have been issued for Travis, he checked into the motel using his ID. He'd no choice because Nora possessed neither credit cards nor a driver's license. These days, desk clerks were willing to accept cash, but not without ID; the chain's computer demanded data on the guests.

He did not, however, give the correct make or license number of his car, for he had parked out of sight of the office for the very purpose of keeping those details from the clerk.

They paid for only one room and kept Einstein with them because they were not going to need privacy for lovemaking. Exhausted, Travis barely managed to kiss Nora before falling into a deep sleep. He dreamed of things with yellow eyes, misshapen heads, and crocodile mouths full of sharks' teeth.

He woke five hours later, at twelve-ten Thursday afternoon.

Nora had gotten up before him, showered, and dressed again in the only clothes she had. Her hair was damp and clung alluringly to the nape of her neck. "The water's hot and forceful," she told him.

"So am I," he said, embracing her, kissing her.

"Then you better cool off," she said, pulling away from him. "Little ears are listening."

"Einstein? He has big ears."

In the bathroom, he found Einstein standing on the counter, drinking out of a sinkful of cold water that Nora had drawn for him.

"You know, fur face, for most dogs, the toilet is a perfectly adequate source of drinking water."

Einstein sneezed at him, jumped down from the counter, and padded out of the bathroom.

Travis had no means of shaving, but he decided a day's growth of beard would give him the look he needed for the work he would have to do this evening in the Tenderloin district.

They left the motel and ate at the first McDonald's they could find. After lunch, they drove to a local branch of the Santa Barbara bank where Travis had his checking account. They used his computer-banking card, his Mastercard, and two of his Visa cards to make cash withdrawals totaling fourteen hundred dollars. Next they went to an American Express office, and using one of Travis's checks and his Gold Card, they acquired the maximum allowable five hundred dollars in cash and forty-five hundred in traveler's checks. Combined with the twenty-one hundred in cash and traveler's checks left over from their honeymoon, they had eighty-five hundred in liquid assets.

During the rest of the afternoon and early evening, they went shopping. With credit cards, they bought a complete set of luggage and purchased enough clothes to fill the bags. They got toiletries for both of them and an electric razor for Travis.

Travis also bought a Scrabble game, and Nora said, "You don't really feel in the mood for games, do you?"

"No," he replied cryptically, enjoying her puzzlement. "I'll explain later."

Half an hour before sunset, with their purchases packed tightly in the spacious trunk of the Mercedes, Travis drove into the heart of San Francisco's Tenderloin, which was the area of the city that lay below O'Farrell Street, wedged between Market Street and Van Ness Avenue. It was a district of sleazy bars featuring topless dancers, go-go joints where the girls wore nothing at all, rap parlors where men paid by the minute to sit with nude young women and talk about sex and where more than talk was usually accomplished.

This degeneracy was a shocking revelation to Nora, who had begun to think of herself as experienced and sophisticated. She was not prepared for the cesspool of the Tenderloin. She gaped at the gaudy neon signs that advertised peep shows, female mud wrestling, female impersonators, gay baths, and massage parlors. The meaning of some of the billboard come-ons at the worst bars baffled her, and she said, "What do they mean when the marquee says 'Get a Wink at the Pink'?"

Looking for a parking place, Travis said, "It means their girls dance entirely nude and that, during the dance, they spread their labia to show themselves more completely."

"No!"

"Yes."

"My God. I don't believe it. I mean, I *do* believe it—but I don't *believe* it. What's it mean—'Extremely Close-Up'?"

"The girls dance right at the customers' tables. The law doesn't allow touching, but the girls dance close, swinging their bare breasts in the customers' faces. You could insert one, maybe two, but not three sheets of paper between their nipples and the men's lips."

In the back seat, Einstein snorted as if with disgust.

"I agree, fella," Travis told him.

They passed a cancerous-looking place with flashing red and yellow bulbs and rippling bands of blue and purple neon, where the sign promised LIVE SEX SHOW.

Appalled, Nora said, "My God, are there other shows where they have sex with the dead?"

Travis laughed so hard he almost back-ended a carload of gawking college boys. "No, no, no. Even the Tenderloin has some limits. They mean 'live' as opposed to 'on film.' You can see plenty of sex on film, theaters that show only pornography, but that place promises live sex, on stage. I don't know if they deliver on the promise."

"And I don't care to find out!" Nora said, sounding as if she were Dorothy from Kansas and had just wandered into an unspeakable new neighborhood of Oz. "What're we doing here?"

"This is the place you come to when you're trying to find things they don't sell on Nob Hill—like young boys or really large amounts of dope. Or phony driver's licenses and other counterfeit ID."

"Oh," she said. "Oh, yes, I see. This area is controlled by the underworld, by people like the Corleones in *The Godfather*."

"I'm sure the mob owns more of these places than not," he said as he maneuvered the Mercedes into a parking space at the curb. "But don't ever make the mistake of thinking the *real* mob is a bunch of honorable cuties like the Corleones."

Einstein was agreeable to remaining with the Mercedes.

"Tell you what, fur face. If we're *real* lucky," Travis joked, "we'll get you a new identity, too. We'll make you into a poodle."

Nora was surprised to discover that, as twilight settled over the city, the breeze off the bay was chilly enough for them to need the nylon, quilt-lined jackets they had bought earlier in the day.

"Even in summer, nights can be cool here," he said. "Soon, the fog rolls in. The stored-up heat of the day pulls it off the water."

He would have worn his jacket even if the evening air had been mild, for he was carrying his loaded revolver under his belt and needed the jacket to conceal it.

"Is there really a chance you'll need the gun?" she asked as they walked away from the car.

"Not likely. I'm carrying it mainly for ID."

"Huh?"

"You'll see."

She looked back at the car, where Einstein was staring out the rear window, looking forlorn. She felt bad leaving him there. But she was quite certain that even if these establishments would admit dogs such places were not good for Einstein's moral welfare.

Travis seemed interested solely in those bars whose signs were either in both English and Spanish or in Spanish only. Some places were downright shabby and did not conceal the peeling paint and the moldy carpeting, while others used mirrors and glitzy lighting to try to hide their true roach-hole nature. A few were actually clean and expensively decorated. In each, Travis spoke in Spanish with the bartender, sometimes with musicians if there were any and if they were on a break, and a few times he distributed folded twenty-dollar bills. Since she spoke no Spanish, Nora did not know what he was asking about or why he was paying these people.

On the street, searching for another sleazy lounge, he explained that the biggest illegal migration was Mexican, Salvadoran, Nicaraguan—desperate people escaping economic chaos and political repression. Therefore, more Spanish-speaking illegals were in the market for phony papers than were Vietnamese, Chinese, or those in all other language groups put together. "So the quickest way to get a lead on a supplier of phony paper is through the Latino underworld."

"Have you got a lead?"

"Not yet. Just bits and pieces. And probably ninety-nine percent of what I've paid for is nonsense, lies. But don't worry—we'll find what we need. That's why the Tenderloin doesn't go out of business: people who come here *always* find what they need."

The people who came here surprised Nora. In the streets, in the topless bars, all kinds could be found. Asians, Latinos, whites, blacks, and even Indians mingled in an alcoholic haze, so it seemed as if racial harmony was a beneficial side effect of the pursuit of sin. Guys swaggered around in leather jackets and jeans, guys who looked like hoods, which she expected. But there were also men in business suits, clean-cut college kids, others dressed like cowboys, and wholesome surfer types who looked as if they had stepped out of an old Annette Funicello movie. Bums sat on the pavement or stood on corners, grizzled old winos in reeking clothes, and even some of the business-suit types had a weird glint in their eyes that made you want to run from them, but it seemed as if most of the people here were those who would pass for ordinary upstanding citizens in any decent neighborhood. Nora was amazed.

Not many women were on the streets or in the company of the men in the bars. No, correct that: there were women to be seen, but they looked more lascivious than the nude dancers, and only a few of them seemed not to be for sale.

At a topless bar called Hot Tips, which had signs in both Spanish and English, the recorded rock music was so loud Nora got a headache. Six beautiful girls with exquisite bodies, wearing only spike heels and sequined bikini panties, were dancing at the tables, wriggling, writhing, swinging their breasts in the sweaty faces of men who were either mesmerized or hooting and clapping. Other topless girls, equally pretty, were waitressing.

While Travis spoke in Spanish with the bartender, Nora noticed some of the customers looking at her appraisingly. They gave her the creeps. She kept one hand on Travis's arm. She couldn't have been torn away from him with a crowbar.

The stink of stale beer and whiskey, body odor, the layered scents of various cheap perfumes, and cigarette smoke made the air as heavy as that in a steambath, though less healthful.

Nora clenched her teeth and thought, I will not be sick and make a fool of myself. I simply will not.

After a couple of minutes of rapid conversation, Travis passed a pair of twenties to the bartender and was directed to the back of the lounge, where a guy as big as Arnold Schwarzenegger was sitting on a chair beside a doorway that was covered by a densely beaded curtain. He was wearing black leather pants and a white T-shirt. His arms seemed as large as tree trunks. His face looked as if it had been cast in cement, and he had gray eyes almost as transparent as glass. Travis spoke with him in Spanish and passed him two twenties.

The music faded from a thunderous din to a mere roar. A woman, speaking into a microphone, said, "All right, boys, if you like what you see, then show it—start stuffin' those pussies."

Nora twitched in shock, but as the music rose again, she saw what was meant by the crude announcement: the customers were expected to slip folded five- and ten-dollar bills into the dancers' panties.

The hulk in black leather pants got off his chair and led them through the beaded curtain, into a room ten feet wide and eighteen or twenty feet long, where six more young women in spike heels and bikini panties were getting ready to take over from the dancers already on the floor. They were checking their makeup in mirrors, applying lipstick, or just chatting with each other. They were all (she saw) as good-looking as the girls out front. Some of them had hard faces, pretty but hard, though others were as fresh-faced as schoolteachers. All were the kind of women that men probably had in mind when they talked about girls who were "stacked."

The hulk led Travis—and Travis led Nora, holding her hand—through that dressing room toward the door at the other end. As they went, one of the topless dancers—a striking blonde—put a hand on Nora's shoulder and walked beside her.

"Are you new, honey?"

"Me? No. Oh, no, I don't work here."

The blonde, who was so well-endowed that Nora felt like a boy, said, "You got the equipment, honey."

"Oh, no," was all Nora could say.

"You like my equipment?" the blonde asked.

"Oh, well, you're very pretty," Nora said.

To the blonde, Travis said, "Give it up, sister. The lady doesn't swing that way."

The blonde smiled sweetly. "If she tries it, she might like it."

They went through a door, out of the dressing room and into a narrow, shabby, poorly lit hallway before Nora realized she had been propositioned. By a woman!

She did not know whether to laugh or gag. Probably both.

The hulk took them to an office at the back of the building and left them, saying, "Mr. Van Dyne will be with you in a minute."

The office had gray walls, gray metal chairs, filing cabinets, and a gray metal desk that was battered and scarred. No pictures or calendars hung on the bare walls. No pens or notepads or reports were on the desk. The place looked as if it was seldom used.

Nora and Travis sat on the two metal chairs in front of the desk.

The music from the bar was still audible but no longer deafening. When she caught her breath, Nora said, "Where do they all come from?"

"Who?"

"All those pretty girls with their pretty boobs and tight little bottoms and long legs, and all of them willing to . . . to do *that*. Where do so many of them come from?"

"There's a breeding farm outside of Modesto," Travis said.

She gaped at him.

He laughed and said, "I'm sorry. I keep forgetting how innocent you are, Mrs. Cornell." He kissed her cheek. His stubble scratched a little, but it was nice. In spite of wearing yesterday's clothes and not having shaved, he seemed as clean as a well-scrubbed baby compared to the gauntlet they had run in order to reach this office. He said, "I should answer you straight because you don't know when I'm joking."

She blinked. "Then there *isn't* a breeding farm outside Modesto?"

"No. There's all kinds of girls who do it. Girls who hope to break into showbiz, go to L.A. to be movie stars but can't make it, so they drift into places like this in L.A. or they come north to San Francisco or they go to Vegas. Most are decent enough kids. They see this as temporary. Very good money can be made fast. It's a way to build up a stake before taking another crack at Hollywood. Then there are some, the self-haters, who do it to humiliate themselves. Others are in rebellion from their parents, from their first husbands, from the whole damn world. And some are hookers."

"The hookers meet . . . johns here?" she asked.

"Maybe, maybe not. Some probably dance to have an explicable source of income when the IRS knocks on their doors. They report their earnings as dancers, which gives them a better chance of concealing what they make from turning tricks."

"It's sad," she said.

"Yeah. In some cases . . . in a *lot* of cases, it's damn sad."

Fascinated, she said, "Will we get false IDs from this Van Dyne?"

"I believe so."

She regarded him solemnly. "You really *do* know your way around, don't you?"

"Does it bother you—that I know places like this?"

She thought a moment. Then: "No. In fact . . . if a woman's going to take a husband, I suppose he ought to be a man who knows what to do in any situation. It gives me a lot of confidence."

"In me?"

"In you, yes, and confidence that we're going to get through this all right, that we're going to save Einstein and ourselves."

"Confidence is good. But in Delta Force, one of the first things you learn is that being *overly* confident can get you killed."

The door opened, and the hulk returned with a round-faced man in a gray suit, blue shirt, and black tie.

"Van Dyne," the newcomer said, but he did not offer to shake hands. He went around the desk and sat in a spring-backed chair. He had thinning blond hair and baby-smooth cheeks. He looked like a stockbroker in a television commercial: efficient, smart, as well-meaning as he was well-groomed. "I wanted to talk to you because I want to know who's spreading these falsehoods about me."

Travis said, "We need some ID—driver's licenses, social security cards, the whole works. First-rate, with full backup, not junk."

"That's what I'm talking about," Van Dyne said. He raised his eyebrows quizzically. "Where on earth did you get the idea that I'm in that sort of business? I'm afraid you've been misinformed."

"We need first-rate paper with full backup," Travis repeated.

Van Dyne stared at him, at Nora. "Let me see your wallet. And your purse, miss."

Putting his wallet on the desk, Travis told Nora, "It's okay."

Reluctantly, she put her purse beside the wallet.

"Please stand and let Caesar search you," Van Dyne said.

Travis stood and motioned for Nora to get up as well.

Caesar, the cement-faced hulk, searched Travis with embarrassing thoroughness, found the .357 Magnum, put it on the desk. He was even more thorough with Nora, unbuttoning her blouse and boldly feeling the cups of her bra for a miniature microphone, battery, and recorder. She blushed and would not have permitted these intimacies if Travis had not explained to her what Caesar was looking for. Besides, Caesar remained expressionless throughout, as if he were a machine without the potential for erotic response.

When Caesar was finished with them, they sat down while Van Dyne went through Travis's wallet and then through Nora's purse. She was afraid he was going to take their money without giving them anything in return, but he appeared to be interested in only their ID and the butcher's knife that Nora still carried.

To Travis, Van Dyne said, "Okay. If you were a cop, you wouldn't be allowed to carry a Magnum"—he swung out the cylinder and looked at the ammunition—"loaded with magnums. The ACLU would have your ass." He smiled at Nora. "No policewoman carries a butcher's knife."

Suddenly she understood what Travis meant when he'd said he was carrying the revolver not for protection but for its value as ID.

Van Dyne and Travis haggled a bit, finally settling on sixty-five hundred as the price for two sets of ID with "full backup."

Their belongings, including the butcher's knife and revolver, were returned to them.

From the gray office, they followed Van Dyne into the narrow hall, where he dismissed Caesar, then to a set of dimly lit concrete stairs leading to a basement beneath Hot Tips, where the rock music was further filtered by the intervening concrete floor.

Nora was not sure what she expected to find in the basement: maybe men who all looked like Edward G. Robinson and wore green eye shades on elastic bands and labored over antique printing presses, producing not just false identification papers but stacks of phony currency. What she found, instead, surprised her.

The steps ended in a stone-walled storage room about forty by thirty feet. Bar supplies were stacked to shoulder height. They walked along a narrow aisle formed by cartons of whiskey, beer, and cocktail napkins, to a steel fire door in the rear wall. Van Dyne pushed a button in the door frame, and a closed-circuit security camera made a purring sound as it panned them.

The door was opened from inside, and they went through into a smaller room with subdued lighting, where two young bearded guys were working at two of seven computers lined up on work tables along one wall. The first guy was wearing soft Rockport shoes, safari pants, a web belt, and a cotton safari shirt. The other wore Reeboks, jeans, and a sweatshirt that featured the Three Stooges. They looked almost like twins, and both resembled young versions of Steven Spielberg. They were so intensely involved with their computer work that they did not look up at Nora and Travis and Van Dyne, but they were having fun, too, talking exuberantly to themselves, to their machines, and to each other in high-tech language that made no sense whatsoever to Nora.

A woman in her early twenties was also at work in the room. She had short blond hair and oddly beautiful eyes the color of pennies. While Van Dyne spoke with the two guys at the computers, the woman took Travis and Nora to the far end of the room, put them in front of a white screen, and photographed them for the phony driver's licenses.

When the blonde disappeared into a darkroom to develop the film, Travis and Nora rejoined Van Dyne at the computers, where the young men were working happily. Nora watched them accessing the supposedly secure computers of the California Department of Motor Vehicles and the Social Security Administration, as well as those of other federal, state, and local government agencies.

"When I told Mr. Van Dyne that I wanted ID with 'full backup,'" Travis explained, "I meant the driver's licenses must be able to stand up to inspection if we're ever stopped by a highway patrolman who runs a check on them. The licenses we're getting are indistinguishable from the real thing. These guys are inserting our new names into the DMV's files, actually creating computer records of these licenses in the state's data banks."

Van Dyne said, "The addresses are phony, of course. But when you settle down somewhere, under your new names, you just apply to the DMV for a change of address like the law requires, and then you'll be perfectly legit. We're setting these up to expire in about a year, at which time you'll go into a DMV office, take the usual test, and get brand-new licenses because your new names are in their files."

"What're our new names?" Nora wondered.

"You see," Van Dyne said, speaking with the quiet assurance and patience of a stockbroker explaining the market to a new investor, "we have to start with birth certificates. We keep computer files of infant deaths all over the western United States, going back at least fifty years. We've already searched those lists for the years each of you was born, trying to find babies who died with your hair and eye colors—and with your first names, too, just because it's easier for you not to have to change both first and last. We found a little girl, Nora Jean Aimes, born October twelfth of the year you were born and who died one month later, right here in San Francisco. We have a laser printer with virtually an infinite choice of type styles and sizes, with which we've already produced a facsimile of the kind of birth certificate that was in use in San Francisco at that time, and it bears Nora Jean's name, vital statistics. We'll make two Xeroxes of it, and you'll receive both. Next, we tapped into the Social Security files and appropriated a number for Nora Jean Aimes, who never was given one, and we also created a history of Social Security tax payments." He smiled. "You've already paid in enough quarters to qualify you for a pension when you retire. Likewise, the IRS now has computer records that show you've worked as a waitress in half a dozen cities and that you've faithfully paid your taxes every year."

Travis said, "With a birth certificate and legitimate Social Security number, they were then able to get a driver's license that would have real ID behind it."

"So I'm Nora Jean Aimes? But if her birth certificate's on record, so is her death certificate. If someone wanted to check—"

Van Dyne shook his head. "In those days, both birth and death certificates were strictly paper documents, no computer files. And because it squanders more money than it spends wisely, the government has never had the funds to transfer records of the precomputer era into electronic data banks. So if someone gets suspicious about you, they can't just search out the death records on computer and learn the truth in two minutes flat. They'd have to go to the courthouse, dig back through the coroner's files for that year, and find Nora Jean's death certificate. But that won't happen because part of our service involves having Nora Jean's certificate removed from public records and destroyed now that you've bought her identity."

"We're into TRW, the credit-reporting agency," one of the twin Spielberg look-alikes said with obvious delight.

Nora saw data flickering across the green screens, but none of it had any meaning for her.

"They're creating solid credit histories for our new identities," Travis told her. "By the time we settle down somewhere and put in a change of address with the DMV and TRW, our mailbox will be flooded with offers for credit cards—Visa, Mastercard, probably even American Express and Carte Blanche."

"Nora Jean Aimes," she said numbly, trying to grasp how quickly and thoroughly her new life was being built.

Because they could locate no infant who had died in the year of Travis's birth with his first name, he had to settle for being Samuel Spencer Hyatt, who had been born that January and had perished that March in Portland, Oregon.

The death would be expunged from the public record, and Travis's new identity would stand up to fairly intense scrutiny.

Strictly for fun (they said), the bearded young operators created a military record for Travis, crediting him six years in the Marines and awarding him a Purple Heart plus a couple of citations for bravery during a peace-keeping-mission-turned-violent in the Middle East. To their delight, he asked if they could also create a valid real-estate broker's license under his new name, and within twenty-five minutes they cracked into the right data banks and did the job.

"Cake and pie," one of the young men said.

"Cake and pie," the other echoed.

Nora frowned, not understanding.

"Piece of cake," one of them explained.

"Easy as pie," the other said.

"Cake and pie," Nora said, nodding.

The blonde with copper-penny eyes returned, carrying driver's licenses imprinted with Travis's and Nora's pictures.

"You're both quite photogenic," she said.

Two hours and twenty minutes after meeting Van Dyne, they left Hot Tips with two manila envelopes containing a variety of documents supporting their new identities. Out on the street, Nora felt a little dizzy and held on to Travis's arm all the way back to the car.

Fog had rolled through the city while they had been in Hot Tips. The blinking lights and flashing-rippling neon of the Tenderloin were softened yet curiously magnified by the mist, so it seemed as if every cubic centimeter of night air was awash with strange lights, with an aurora borealis brought down to ground level. Those sleazy streets had a certain mystery and cheap allure after dark, in the fog, but not if you'd seen them in daylight first and remembered what you had seen.

In the Mercedes, Einstein was waiting patiently.

"Couldn't arrange to have you turned into a poodle, after all," Nora told him as she buckled her seat belt. "But we sure did ourselves up right. Einstein, say hello to Sam Hyatt and Nora Aimes."

The retriever put his head over the front seat, looked at her, looked at Travis, and snorted once as if to say they could not fool him, that *he* knew who they were.

To Travis, Nora said, "Your antiterrorist training . . . is that where you learned about places like Hot Tips, people like Van Dyne? Is that where terrorists get new ID once they slip into the country?"

"Yeah, some go to people like Van Dyne, though not usually. The Soviets supply papers for most terrorists. Van Dyne services mostly ordinary illegal immigrants, though not the poor ones, and criminal types looking to dodge arrest warrants."

As he started the car, she said, "But if you could find Van Dyne, maybe the people looking for us can find him."

"Maybe. It'll take them a while, but maybe they can."

"Then they'll find out all about our new identities."

"No," Travis said. He turned on the defroster and the windshield wipers to clear the condensation off the outside of the glass. "Van Dyne wouldn't keep records. He doesn't want to be caught with proof of what he does. If the authorities ever tumble to him and go in there with search warrants, they won't find anything in Van Dyne's computers except the accounting and purchasing records for Hot Tips."

As they drove through the city, heading for the Golden Gate Bridge, Nora

stared in fascination at the people in the streets and in other cars, not just in
the Tenderloin but in every neighborhood through which they passed. She
wondered how many of them were living under the names and identities with
which they had been born and how many were changelings like her and Travis.

"In less than three hours, we've been totally remade," she said.

"Some world we live in, huh? More than anything else, that's what high
technology means—maximum fluidity. The whole world is becoming ever more
fluid, malleable. Most financial transactions are now handled with electronic
money that flashes from New York to L.A.—or around the world—in seconds.
Money crosses borders in a blink; it no longer has to be smuggled out past the
guards. Most records are kept in the form of electrical charges that only computers read. So everything's fluid. Identities are fluid. The past is fluid."

Nora said, "Even the genetic structure of a species is fluid these days."

Einstein woofed agreement.

Nora said, "Scary, isn't it?"

"A little," Travis said as they approached the light-bedecked southern entrance to the fog-mantled Golden Gate Bridge, which was all but invisible in
the mist. "But maximum fluidity is basically a good thing. Social and financial
fluidity guarantee freedom. I believe—and I hope—that we're heading toward
an age when the role of governments will inevitably dwindle, when there'll be
no way to regulate and control people as thoroughly as was possible in the past.
Totalitarian government won't be able to stay in power."

"How so?"

"Well, how can a dictatorship control its citizens in a high-tech society of
maximum fluidity? The only way is to refuse to allow high tech to intrude, seal
the borders, and live entirely in an earlier age. But that'd be national suicide for
any country that tried it. They couldn't compete. In a few decades, they'd be
modern aborigines, primitive by the standards of the civilized high-tech world.
Right now, for instance, the Soviets try to restrict computers to their defense
industry, which can't last. They'll have to computerize their entire economy
and teach their people to use computers—and *then* how can they keep the
screws tight when their citizens have been given the means to manipulate the
system and foil its controls on them?"

At the entrance to the bridge, no northbound toll was collected. They drove
onto the span, where the speed limit had been drastically reduced because of
the weather.

Looking up at the ghostly skeleton of the bridge, which glistened with
condensation and vanished in the fog, Nora said, "You seem to think the world
will be paradise in a decade or two."

"Not paradise," he said. "Easier, richer, safer, happier. But not a paradise.
After all, there will still be all the problems of the human heart and all the
potential sicknesses of the human mind. And the new world's bound to bring
us some new dangers as well as blessings."

"Like the thing that killed your landlord," she said.

"Yes."

In the back seat, Einstein growled.

12

That Thursday afternoon, August 26, Vince Nasco drove to Johnny The
Wire Santini's place in San Clemente to pick up the past week's report, which
was when he learned of the murder of Ted Hockney in Santa Barbara the
previous evening. The condition of the corpse, especially the missing eyes,
linked it to The Outsider. Johnny had also ascertained that the NSA had

quietly assumed jurisdiction in the case, which convinced Vince it was related to the Banodyne fugitives.

That evening, he got a newspaper and, over a dinner of seafood enchiladas and Dos Equis at a Mexican restaurant, he read about Hockney and about the man who had rented the house where the murder occurred—Travis Cornell. The press was reporting that Cornell, a former real-estate broker who had once been a member of Delta Force, kept a panther in the house and that the cat had killed Hockney, but Vince knew that the cat was bullshit, just a cover story. The cops said they wanted to talk to Cornell and to an unidentified woman seen with him, though they had not filed any charges against them.

The story also had one line about Cornell's dog: "Cornell and the woman may be traveling with a golden retriever."

If I can find Cornell, Vince thought, I'll find the dog.

This was the first break he'd had, and it confirmed his feeling that owning the retriever was a part of his great destiny.

To celebrate, he ordered more seafood enchiladas and beer.

13

Travis, Nora, and Einstein stayed Thursday night at a motel in Marin County, north of San Francisco. They got a six-pack of San Miguel at a convenience store and take-out chicken, biscuits, and coleslaw from a fast-food restaurant, and ate a late dinner in the room.

Einstein enjoyed the chicken and showed considerable interest in the beer.

Travis decided to pour half a bottle in the new yellow plastic dish they had gotten the retriever during their shopping spree earlier in the day. "But no more than half a bottle, no matter how much you like it. I want you sober for some questions and answers."

After dinner, the three of them sat on the king-size bed, and Travis unwrapped the Scrabble game. He put the board upside down on the mattress, with the playing surface concealed, and Nora helped him sort all the lettered game tiles into twenty-six piles.

Einstein watched with interest and did not seem even slightly woozy from his half-bottle of San Miguel.

"Okay," Travis said. "I need more detailed answers than we've been able to get with yes-and-no questions. It occurred to me that this might work."

"Ingenious," Nora agreed.

To the dog, Travis said, "I ask you a question, and you indicate the letters that are needed to spell out the answer, one letter at a time, word by word. You got it?"

Einstein blinked at Travis, looked at the stacks of lettered tiles, raised his eyes to Travis again, and grinned.

Travis said, "All right. Do you know the name of the laboratory from which you escaped?"

Einstein put his nose to the pile of Bs.

Nora plucked a tile off the stack and put it on the portion of the board that Travis had left clear.

In less than a minute, the dog spelled BANODYNE.

"Banodyne," Travis said thoughtfully. "Never heard of it. Is that the entire name?"

Einstein hesitated, then began to choose more letters until he had spelled out BANODYNE LABORATORIES INC.

On a pad of motel stationery, Travis made a note of the answer, then returned all the tiles to their individual stacks. "Where is Banodyne located?"

IRVINE.

"That makes sense," Travis said. "I found you in the woods north of Irvine. All right . . . I found you on Tuesday, May eighteenth. When had you escaped from Banodyne?"

Einstein stared at the tiles, whined, and made no choices.

"In all the reading you've done," Travis said, "you've learned about months, weeks, days, and hours. You have a sense of time now."

Looking at Nora, the dog whined again.

She said, "He has a sense of time now, but he didn't have one when he escaped, so it's hard to remember how long he was on the run."

Einstein immediately began to indicate letters: THATS RIGHT.

"Do you know the names of any researchers at Banodyne?"

DAVIS WEATHERBY.

Travis made a note of the name. "Any others?"

Hesitating frequently to consider possible spellings, Einstein finally produced LAWTON HANES, AL HUDSTUN, and a few more.

After noting all of them on the motel stationery, Travis said, "These will be some of the people looking for you."

YES. AND JOHNSON.

"Johnson?" Nora said. "Is he one of the scientists?"

NO. The retriever thought for a moment, studied the stacks of letters, and finally continued: SECURITY.

"He's head of security at Banodyne?" Travis asked.

NO. BIGGER.

"Probably a federal agent of some kind," Travis told Nora as she returned the letters to their stacks.

To Einstein, Nora said, "Do you know this Johnson's first name?"

Einstein gazed at the letters and mewled, and Travis was about to tell him it was all right if he didn't know Johnson's first name, but then the dog attempted to spell it: LEMOOOL.

"There is no such name," Nora said, taking the letters away.

Einstein tried again: LAMYOULL. Then again: LIMUUL.

"That's not a name either," Travis said.

A third time: LEMB YOU WILL.

Travis realized the dog was struggling to spell the name phonetically. He chose six lettered tiles of his own: LEMUEL.

"Lemuel Johnson," Nora said.

Einstein leaned forward and nuzzled her neck. He was wiggling with pleasure at having gotten the name across to them, and the springs of the motel bed creaked.

Then he stopped nuzzling Nora and spelled DARK LEMUEL.

"Dark?" Travis said. "By 'dark' you mean Johnson is . . . evil?"

NO. DARK.

Nora restacked the letters and said, "Dangerous?"

Einstein snorted at her, then at Travis, as if to say they were sometimes unbearably thickheaded. NO. DARK.

For a moment they sat in silence, thinking, and at last Travis said, "Black! You mean Lemuel Johnson is a black man."

Einstein chuffed softly, shook his head up and down, swept his tail back and forth on the bedspread. He indicated nineteen letters, his longest answer: THERES HOPE FOR YOU YET.

Nora laughed.

Travis said, "Wiseass."

But he was exhilarated, filled with a joy that he would have been hard-pressed to describe if he had been required to put it into words. They had been communicating with the retriever for many weeks, but the Scrabble tiles provided a far greater dimension to their communication than they had enjoyed previously. More than ever, Einstein seemed to be their own child. But there was also an intoxicating feeling of breaking through the barriers of normal human experience, a feeling of transcendence. Einstein was no ordinary mutt, of course, and his high intelligence was more human than canine, but he *was* a dog—more than anything else, a dog—and his intelligence was still qualitatively different from that of a man, so there was inevitably a strong sense of mystery and great wonder in this interspecies dialogue. Staring at THERES HOPE FOR YOU YET, Travis thought a broader meaning could be read into the message, that it could be directed to all humankind.

For the next half an hour, they continued questioning Einstein, and Travis recorded the dog's answers. In time they discussed the yellow-eyed beast that had killed Ted Hockney.

"What is the damned thing?" Nora asked.

THE OUTSIDER.

Travis said, " 'The Outsider'? What do you mean?"

THATS WHAT THEY CALLED IT.

"The people in the lab?" Travis asked. "Why did they call it The Outsider?"

BECAUSE IT DOES NOT BELONG.

Nora said, "I don't understand."

TWO SUCCESSES. ME AND IT. I AM DOG. IT IS NOTHING THAT CAN BE NAMED. OUTSIDER.

Travis said, "It's intelligent, too?"

YES.

"As intelligent as you?"

MAYBE.

"Jesus," Travis said, shaken.

Einstein made an unhappy sound and put his head on Nora's knee, seeking the reassurance that petting could provide him.

Travis said, "Why would they create a thing like that?"

Einstein returned to the stacks of letters: TO KILL FOR THEM.

A chill trickled down Travis's spine and seeped deep into him. "Who did they want it to kill?"

THE ENEMY.

"What enemy?" Nora asked.

IN WAR.

With understanding came revulsion bordering on nausea. Travis sagged back against the headboard. He remembered telling Nora that even a world without want and with universal freedom would fall far short of paradise because of all the problems of the human heart and all the potential sicknesses of the human mind.

To Einstein, he said, "So you're telling us that The Outsider is a prototype of a genetically engineered soldier. Sort of . . . a very intelligent, deadly police dog designed for the battlefield."

IT WAS MADE TO KILL. IT WANTS TO KILL.

Reading the words as she laid out the tiles, Nora was appalled. "But this is crazy. How could such a thing ever be controlled? How could it be counted on not to turn against its masters?"

Travis leaned forward from the headboard. To Einstein, he said, "Why is The Outsider looking for you?"

HATES ME.

"Why does it hate you?"

DONT KNOW.

As Nora replaced the letters, Travis said, "Will it continue looking for you?"

YES. FOREVER.

"But how does something like that move unseen?"

AT NIGHT.

"Nevertheless . . ."

LIKE RATS MOVE UNSEEN.

Looking puzzled, Nora said, "But how does it track you?"

FEELS ME.

"Feels you? What do you mean?" she asked.

The retriever puzzled over that one for a long time, making several false starts on an answer, and finally said, CANT EXPLAIN.

"Can you feel it, too?" Travis asked.

SOMETIMES.

"Do you feel it now?"

YES. FAR AWAY.

"Very far away," Travis agreed. "Hundreds of miles. Can it really feel you and track you from that far away?"

EVEN FARTHER.

"Is it tracking you now?

COMING.

The chill in Travis grew icier. "When will it find you?"

DON'T KNOW.

The dog looked dejected, and he was shivering again.

"Soon? Will it feel its way to you soon?"

MAYBE NOT SOON.

Travis saw that Nora was pale. He put a hand on her knee and said, "We won't run from it the rest of our lives. Damned if we will. We'll find a place to settle down and wait, a place where we'll be able to prepare a defense and where we'll have the privacy to deal with The Outsider when it arrives."

Shivering, Einstein indicated more letters with his nose, and Travis laid out the tiles: I SHOULD GO.

"What do you mean?" Travis asked, replacing the tiles.

I DANGER YOU.

Nora threw her arms around the retriever and hugged him. "Don't you even *think* such a thing. You're part of us. You're family, damn you, we're all family, we're all in this together, and we stick it out together because *that's what families do.*" She stopped hugging the dog and took his head in both hands, met him nose to nose, peered deep into his eyes. "If I woke up some morning and found you'd left us, it'd break my heart." Tears shimmered in her eyes, a tremor in her voice. "Do you understand me, fur face? It would break my heart if you went off on your own."

The dog pulled away from her and began to choose lettered tiles again: I WOULD DIE.

"You would die if you left us?" Travis asked.

The dog chose more letters, waited for them to study the words, then looked solemnly at each of them to be sure they understood what he meant: I WOULD DIE OF LONELY.

PART TWO

GUARDIAN

Love alone is capable of uniting living beings in such a way as to complete and fulfill them, for it alone takes them and joins them by what is deepest in themselves.

—Pierre Teilhard de Chardin

Greater love hath no man than this:
that he lay down his life
for his friends.
—The Gospel According to Saint John

CHAPTER 8

1

O<small>N THE</small> T<small>HURSDAY</small> that Nora drove to Dr. Weingold's office, Travis and Einstein went for a walk across the grassy hills and through the woods behind the house they had bought in the beautiful California coastal region called Big Sur.

On the treeless hills, the autumn sun warmed the stones and cast scattered cloud shadows. The breeze off the Pacific drew a whisper from the dry golden grass. In the sun, the air was mild, neither hot nor cool. Travis was comfortable in jeans and a long-sleeved shirt.

He carried a Mossberg short-barreled pistol-grip pump-action 12-gauge shotgun. He always carried it on his walks. If he ever encountered someone who asked about it, he intended to tell them he was hunting rattlesnakes.

Where the trees grew most vigorously, the bright morning seemed like late afternoon, and the air was cool enough to make Travis glad that his shirt was flannel. Massive pines, a few small groves of giant redwoods, and a variety of foothill hardwoods filtered the sun and left much of the forest floor in perpetual twilight. The undergrowth was dense in places: the vegetation included those low, impenetrable thickets of evergreen oaks sometimes called "chaparral," plus lots of ferns that flourished because of the frequent fog and the constant humidity of the seacoast air.

Einstein repeatedly sniffed out cougar spoor and insisted on showing Travis the tracks of the big cats in the damp forest soil. Fortunately, he fully understood the danger of stalking a mountain lion, and was able to repress his natural urge to prowl after them.

The dog contented himself with merely observing local fauna. Timid deer could often be seen ascending or descending their trails. Raccoons were plentiful and fun to watch, and although some were quite friendly, Einstein knew they could turn nasty if he accidentally frightened them; he chose to keep a respectful distance.

On other walks, the retriever had been dismayed to discover the squirrels, which he could approach safely, were terrified of him. They froze with fear, stared wild-eyed, small hearts pounding visibly.

WHY SQUIRRELS AFRAID? he had asked Travis one evening.

"Instinct," Travis had explained. "You're a dog, and they know instinctively that dogs will attack and kill them."

NOT ME.

"No, not you," Travis agreed, ruffling the dog's coat. "You wouldn't hurt them. But the squirrels don't know you're different, do they? To them, you look like a dog, and you smell like a dog, so you've got to be feared like a dog."

I LIKE SQUIRRELS.

"I know. Unfortunately, they're not smart enough to realize it."

Consequently, Einstein kept his distance from the squirrels and tried hard not to terrify them, often sauntering past with his head turned the other way as if unaware of them.

This special day, their interest in squirrels and deer and birds and raccoons and unusual forest flora was minimal. Even views of the Pacific did not intrigue them. Today, unlike other days, they were walking only to pass the time and to keep their minds off Nora.

Travis repeatedly looked at his watch, and he chose a circular route that would bring them back to the house at one o'clock, when Nora was expected to return.

It was the twenty-first of October, eight weeks after they had acquired new identities in San Francisco. After considerable thought, they had decided to come south, substantially reducing the distance that The Outsider would have to travel in order to put its hands on Einstein. They would not be able to get on with their new lives until the beast found them, until they killed it; therefore, they wanted to hasten rather than delay that confrontation.

On the other hand, they did not want to risk returning too far south toward Santa Barbara, for The Outsider might cover the distance between them faster than it had traveled from Orange County to Santa Barbara last summer. They could not be certain that it would continue to make only three or four miles a day. If it moved faster this time, it might come upon them before they were ready for it. The Big Sur area, because of its sparse population and because it was a hundred ninety air miles from Santa Barbara, seemed ideal. If The Outsider got a fix on Einstein and tracked him down as slowly as before, the thing would not arrive for almost five months. If it doubled its speed somehow, swiftly crossing the open farmland and the wild hills between there and here, quickly skirting populated areas, it would still not reach them until the second week of November.

That day was drawing near, but Travis was satisfied that he had made every preparation possible, and he almost welcomed The Outsider's arrival. Thus far, however, Einstein said that he did not feel his adversary was dangerously close. Evidently, they still had plenty of time to test their patience before the showdown.

By twelve-fifty, they reached the end of their circular route through the hills and canyons, returning to the yard behind their new house. It was a two-story structure with bleached-wood walls, a cedar-shingled roof, and massive stone chimneys on both the north and south sides. It boasted front and rear porches on the east and west, and either vantage point offered a view of wooded slopes.

Because no snow ever fell here, the roof was only gently pitched, making it possible to walk all over it, and that was where Travis made one of his first defensive modifications to the house. He looked up now, as he came out of the trees, and saw the herringbone pattern of two-by-fours that he had fixed across the roof. They would make it safer and easier to move quickly across those sloped surfaces. If The Outsider crept up on the house at night, it would not be able to enter by the downstairs windows because, at sundown, those were barricaded with interior locking shutters that Travis had installed himself and that would foil any would-be intruder except, perhaps, a maniacally deter-mined man with an ax. The Outsider would then most likely climb the porch posts onto the front or rear porch to have a look at the second-floor windows, which it would find also protected by interior shutters. Meanwhile, warned of the enemy's approach by an infrared alarm system that he had installed around the house three weeks ago, Travis would go onto the roof by way of an attic trap door. Up there, making use of the two-by-four handholds, he would be able to creep to the edge of the main roof, look down on the porch roof or on any portion of the surrounding yard, and open fire on The Outsider from a position where it could not reach him.

Twenty yards behind and east of the house was a small rust-red barn that backed up to the trees. Their property included no tillable land, and the original owner apparently erected the barn to house a couple of horses and some chickens. Travis and Nora used it as a garage because the dirt driveway led two hundred yards in from the highway, past the house, directly to the double doors on the barn.

Travis suspected that, when The Outsider arrived, it would scout the house from the woods and then from the cover of the barn. It might even wait in there, hoping to catch them by surprise when they came out for the Dodge pickup or the Toyota. Therefore, he had rigged the barn with a few surprises.

Their nearest neighbors—whom they had met only once—were over a quarter-mile to the north, out of sight beyond trees and chaparral. The high-way, which was closer, was not much traveled at night, when The Outsider was most likely to strike. If the confrontation involved a great deal of gunfire, the shots would echo and reecho through the woods and across the bare hills, so the few people in the area—neighbors or passing motorists—would have trouble determining where the noise originated. He ought to be able to kill the creature and bury it before someone came nosing around.

Now, more worried about Nora than about The Outsider, Travis climbed the back-porch steps, unlocked the two dead bolts on the rear door, and went into the house, with Einstein close behind him. The kitchen was large enough to serve also as the dining room, yet it was cozy; oak walls, a Mexican-tile floor, beige-tile counters, oak cabinets, a hand-textured plaster ceiling, the best appliances. The big plank table with four comfortable padded chairs and a stone fireplace helped make this the center of the house.

There were five other rooms—an enormous living room and a den at the front of the first floor; three bedrooms upstairs—plus one bath down and one up. One of the bedrooms was theirs, and one served as Nora's studio where she had done a little painting since they moved in—and the third was empty, awaiting developments.

Travis switched on the kitchen lights. Although the house seemed isolated, they were only two hundred yards from the highway, and power poles followed the line of their dirt driveway.

"I'm having a beer," Travis said. "You want anything?"

Einstein padded to his empty water dish, which was in the corner beside his food dish, and scooted it across the floor to the sink.

They had not expected to be able to afford such a house so soon after fleeing Santa Barbara—especially not when, during their first call to Garrison Dilworth, the attorney informed them that Travis's bank accounts had, indeed, been frozen. They had been lucky to get the twenty-thousand-dollar check through. Garrison had converted some of both Travis's and Nora's funds into eight cashier's checks as planned, and had sent them to Travis addressed to Mr. Samuel Spencer Hyatt (the new persona), care of the Marin County motel where they had stayed for nearly a week. But also, claiming to have sold Nora's house for a handsome six-figure price, he had sent another packet of cashier's checks two days later, to the same motel.

Speaking with him from a pay phone, Nora had said, "But even if you *did* sell it, they can't have paid the money and closed the deal so soon."

"No," Garrison had admitted. "It won't close for a month. But you need the cash now, so I'm advancing it to you."

They had opened two accounts at a bank in Carmel, thirty-odd miles north of where they now lived. They had bought the new pickup, then had taken Garrison's Mercedes north to the San Francisco airport, leaving it there for him. Heading south again, past Carmel and along the coast, they looked for a house in the Big Sur area. When they had found this one, they had been able to pay cash for it. It was wiser to buy than rent, and it was wiser to pay cash rather than finance the house, for fewer questions needed to be answered.

Travis was sure their ID would stand up, but he saw no reason to test the quality of Van Dyne's papers until necessary. Besides, after buying a house, they were more respectable; the purchase added substance to their new identities.

While Travis got a bottle of beer from the refrigerator, twisted off the cap, took a long swallow, then filled Einstein's dish with water, the retriever went to the walk-in pantry. The door was ajar, as always, and the dog opened it all the way. He put one paw on a pedal that Travis had rigged for him just inside the pantry door, and the light came on in there.

In addition to shelves of canned and bottled goods, the huge pantry contained a complex gadget that Travis and Nora had built to facilitate communication with the dog. The device stood against the rear wall: twenty-eight one-inch-square tubes made of Lucite, lined up side by side in a wooden frame; each tube was eighteen inches tall, open at the top, and fitted with a pedal-release valve at the bottom. In the first twenty-six tubes were stacked lettered tiles from six Scrabble games, so Einstein would have enough letters to be able to form long messages. On the front of each tube was a handdrawn letter that showed what it contained; A, B, C, D, and so on. The last two tubes held blank game tiles on which Travis had carved commas—or apostrophes—and question marks. (They'd decided they could figure where the periods were supposed to go.) Einstein was able to dispense letters from the tubes by stepping on the pedals, then could use his nose to form the tiles into words on the pantry floor. They had chosen to put the device in there, out of sight, so they would not be required to explain it to neighbors who might drop in unexpectedly.

As Einstein busily pumped pedals and clicked tiles against one another, Travis carried his beer and the dog's water dish out to the front porch, where they would sit and wait for Nora. By the time he came back, Einstein had finished forming a message.

COULD I HAVE SOME HAMBURGER? OR THREE WEENIES?

Travis said, "I'm going to have lunch with Nora when she gets home. Don't you want to wait and eat with us?"

The retriever licked his chops and thought for a moment. Then he studied the letters he had already used, pushed some of them aside, and reused the rest along with a K and a T and an apostrophe that he had to release from the Lucite tubes.

OK. BUT I'M STARVED.

"You'll survive," Travis told him. He gathered up the lettered tiles and sorted them into the open tops of the proper tubes.

He retrieved the pistol-grip shotgun that he'd stood by the back door and carried it out to the front porch, where he put it beside his rocking chair. He heard Einstein turn off the pantry light and follow him.

They sat in anxious silence, Travis in his chair, Einstein on the redwood floor.

Songbirds trilled in the mild October air.

Travis sipped at his beer, and Einstein lapped occasionally at his water, and they stared down the dirt driveway, into the trees, toward the highway that they could not see.

In the glove compartment of the Toyota, Nora had a .38 pistol loaded with hollow-point cartridges. During the weeks since they had left Marin County, she had learned to drive and, with Travis's help, had become proficient with the .38—also with a fully automatic Uzi pistol and a shotgun. She only had the .38 today, but she'd be safe going and coming from Carmel. Besides, even if The Outsider had crept into the area without Einstein's knowledge, it did not want Nora; it wanted the dog. So she was perfectly safe.

But where was she?

Travis wished he had gone with her. But after thirty years of dependency and fear, solo trips into Carmel were one of the means by which she asserted—and tested—her new strength, independence, and self-confidence. She would not have welcomed his company.

By one-thirty, when Nora was half an hour late, Travis began to get a sick, twisting feeling in his gut.

Einstein began to pace.

Five minutes later, the retriever was the first to hear the car turning into the foot of the driveway at the main road. He dashed down the porch steps, which were at the side of the house, and stood at the edge of the dirt lane.

Travis did not want Nora to see that he had been overly worried because somehow that would seem to indicate a lack of trust in her ability to take care of herself, an ability that she did, indeed, possess and that she prized. He remained in his rocking chair, his bottle of Corona in one hand.

When the blue Toyota appeared, he sighed with relief. As she went by the house, she tooted the horn. Travis waved as if he had not been sitting there under a leaden blanket of fear.

Einstein went to the garage to greet her, and a minute later they both reappeared. She was wearing blue jeans and a yellow- and white-checkered shirt, but Travis thought she looked good enough to waltz onto a dance floor among begowned and bejeweled princesses.

She came to him, leaned down, kissed him, Her lips were warm.

She said, "Miss me terribly?"

"With you gone, there was no sun, no trilling from the birds, no joy." He tried to say it flippantly, but it came out with an underlying note of seriousness.

Einstein rubbed against her and whined to get her attention, then peered up at her and woofed softly, as if to say, *Well?*

"He's right," Travis said. "You're not being fair. Don't keep us in suspense."

"I am," she said.

"You are?"

She grinned. "Knocked up."

"Oh my," he said.

"Preggers. With child. In a family way. A mother-to-be."

He got up and put his arms around her, held her close and kissed her, and said, "Dr. Weingold couldn't be mistaken," and she said, "No, he's a good doctor," and Travis said, "He must've told you when," and she said, "We can expect the baby the third week of June," and Travis said stupidly, "Next June?" and she laughed and said, "I don't intend to carry this baby for a whole extra year," and finally Einstein insisted on having a chance to nuzzle her and express his delight.

"I brought home a chilled bottle of bubbly to celebrate," she said, thrusting a paper bag into his hands.

In the kitchen, when he took the bottle out of the bag, he saw that it was sparkling apple cider, nonalcoholic. He said, "Isn't this a celebration worth the best champagne?"

Getting glasses from a cupboard, she said, "I'm probably being silly, a world-champion worrier . . . but I'm taking no chances, Travis. I never thought I'd have a baby, never dared dream it, and now I've got this hinkey feeling that I was never *meant* to have it and that it's going to be taken away from me if I don't take every precaution, if I don't do everything just right. So I'm not taking another drink until it's born. I'm not going to eat too much red meat, and I'm going to eat more vegetables. I never have smoked, so that's not a worry. I'm going to gain exactly as much weight as Dr. Weingold tells me I should, and I'm going to do my exercises, and I'm going to have the most perfect baby the world has ever seen."

"Of course you are," he said, filling their wine glasses with sparkling apple cider and pouring some in a dish for Einstein.

"Nothing will go wrong," she said.

"Nothing," he said.

They toasted the baby—and Einstein, who was going to make a terrific godfather, uncle, grandfather, and furry guardian angel.

Nobody mentioned The Outsider.

Later that night, in bed in the dark, after they had made love and were just holding each other, listening to their hearts beating in unison, he dared to say, "Maybe, with what might be coming our way, we shouldn't be having a baby just now."

"Hush," she said.

"But—"

"We didn't plan for this baby," she said. "In fact, we took precautions against it. But it happened anyway. There's something special about the fact that it happened in spite of all our careful precautions. Don't you think? In spite of all I said before, about maybe not being meant to have it . . . well, that's just the old Nora talking. The new Nora thinks we *were* meant to have it, that it's a great gift to us—as Einstein was."

"But considering what may be coming—"

"That doesn't matter," she said. "We'll deal with that. We'll come out of that all right. We're ready. And then we'll have the baby and really begin our life together. I love you, Travis."

"I love you," he said. "God, I love you."

He realized how much she had changed from the mousy woman he'd met in

Santa Barbara last spring. Right now, she was the strong one, the determined one, and *she* was trying to allay *his* fears.

She was doing a good job, too. He felt better. He thought about the baby, and he smiled in the dark, with his face buried in her throat. Though he now had three hostages to fortune—Nora, the unborn baby, and Einstein—he was in finer spirits than he had been in longer than he could remember. Nora had allayed his fears.

2

Vince Nasco sat in an elaborately carved Italian chair with a deep glossy finish that had acquired its remarkable transparency only after a couple of centuries of regular polishing.

To his right was a sofa and two more chairs and a low table of equal elegance, arranged before a backdrop of bookcases filled with leather-bound volumes that had never been read. He knew they had never been read because Mario Tetragna, whose private study this was, had once pointed to them with pride and said, "Expensive books. And as good as the day they were made because they've never been read. Never. Not a one."

In front of him was the immense desk at which Mario Tetragna reviewed earnings reports from his managers, issued memos about new ventures, and ordered people killed. The don was at that desk now, overflowing his leather chair, eyes closed. He looked as if he was dead of clogged arteries and a fat-impacted heart, but he was only considering Vince's request.

Mario "The Screwdriver" Tetragna—respected patriarch of his immediate blood family, much-feared don of the broader Tetragna Family that controlled drug traffic, gambling, prostitution, loan-sharking, pornography, and other organized criminal activity in San Francisco—was a five-foot-seven-inch, three-hundred-pound tub with a face as plump and greasy and smooth as an overstuffed sausage casing. It was hard to believe that this rotund specimen could have built an infamous criminal operation. True, Tetragna had been young once, but even then he would have been short, and he had the look of a man who'd been fat all his life. His pudgy, stubby-fingered hands reminded Vince of a baby's hands. But they were the hands that ruled the Family's empire.

When Vince had looked into Mario Tetragna's eyes, he instantly realized that the don's stature and his all too evident decadence were of no importance. The eyes were those of a reptile; flat, cold, hard, watchful. If you weren't careful, if you displeased him, he would hypnotize you with those eyes and take you the way a snake would take a mesmerized mouse; he would choke you down whole and digest you.

Vince admired Tetragna. He knew this was a great man, and he wished he could tell the don that he, too, was a man of destiny. But he had learned never to speak of his immortality, for in the past such talk had earned him ridicule from a man he'd thought would understand.

Now, Don Tetragna opened his reptilian eyes and said, "Let me be certain I understand. You are looking for a man. This is not Family business. It is a private grudge."

"Yes, sir," Vince said.

"You believe this man may have bought counterfeit papers and may be living under a new name. He would know how to obtain such papers, even though he is not a member of any Family, not of the *fratellanza*?"

"Yes, sir. His background is such that . . . he would know."

"And you believe he would have obtained these papers in either Los Angeles or here," Don Tetragna said, gesturing toward the window and the city of San Francisco with one soft, pink hand.

Vince said, "On August twenty-fifth he went on the run, starting from Santa Barbara by car because for various reasons he couldn't take a plane anywhere. I believe he would've wanted a new identity as quickly as he could get it. At first, I assumed he'd go south and seek out counterfeit ID in Los Angeles because that was closest. But I've spent the better part of two months talking with all the right people in L.A., Orange County, and even San Diego, all the people to whom this man could've gone for high-quality false ID, and I've had a few leads, but none panned out. So if he didn't go south from Santa Barbara, he came north, and the only place in the north where he could get the kind of quality papers he would want—"

"Is in our fair city," Don Tetragna said, gesturing again toward the window and smiling at the populous slopes below.

Vince supposed that the don was smiling fondly at his beloved San Francisco. But the smile didn't look fond. It looked avaricious.

"And," Don Tetragna said, "you would like for me to give you the names of the people who have my authorization to deal in papers such as this man needed."

"If you can see it in your heart to grant me this favor, I would be most grateful."

"They won't have kept records."

"Yes, sir, but they might remember something."

"They're in the business of *not* remembering."

"But the human mind never forgets, Don Tetragna. No matter how hard it tries, it never really forgets."

"How true. And you swear that the man you seek is not a member of any Family?"

"I swear it."

"This execution must not in any way be traced to my Family."

"I swear it."

Don Tetragna closed his eyes again, but not for as long as he had closed them before. When he opened them, he smiled broadly but, as always, it was a humorless smile. He was the least jolly fat man Vince had ever seen. "When your father married a Swedish girl rather than one of his own people, his family despaired and expected the worst. But your mother was a good wife, unquestioning and obedient. And they produced you—a most handsome son. But you're more than handsome. You're a good soldier, Vincent. You have done fine, clean work for the Families in New York and New Jersey, for those in Chicago, and also for us on this coast. Not very long ago, you did me the great service of crushing the cockroach Pantangela."

"For which you paid me most generously, Don Tetragna."

The Screwdriver waved one hand dismissively. "We're all paid for our labors. But we're not talking money here. Your years of loyalty and good service are worth more than money. Therefore, you are owed at least this one favor."

"Thank you, Don Tetragna."

"You'll be given the names of those who provide such papers in this city, and I'll see that they are all forewarned of your visit. They'll cooperate fully."

"If you say they will," Vince said, rising and bowing with only his head and shoulders, "I know that it is true."

The don motioned him to sit down. "But before you attend to this private affair, I'd like you to take another contract. There's a man in Oakland who is giving me much grief. He thinks I can't touch him because he's politically well connected and well guarded. His name is Ramon Velazquez. This will be a difficult job, Vincent."

Vince carefully concealed his frustration and displeasure. He did not want to take on a troublesome hit right now. He wanted to concentrate on tracking down Travis Cornell and the dog. But he knew Tetragna's contract was more a demand than an offer. To get the names of the people who sold false papers, he must first waste Velazquez.

He said, "I would be honored to squash any insect that has stung you. And there'll be no charge this time."

"Oh, I'd insist on paying you, Vincent."

As ingratiatingly as he knew how, Vince smiled and said, "Please, Don Tetragna, let me do this favor. It would give me great pleasure."

Tetragna appeared to consider the request, though this was what he expected—a free hit in return for helping Vince. He put both hands on his enormous belly and patted himself. "I am such a lucky man. Wherever I turn, people want to do me favors, kindnesses."

"Not lucky, Don Tetragna," Vince said, sick of their mannered conversation. "You reap what you sow, and if you reap kindness it is because of the seeds of greater kindness you've sown so broadly."

Beaming, Tetragna accepted his offer to waste Velazquez for nothing. The nostrils of his porcine nose flared as if he had smelled something good to eat, and he said, "But now tell me . . . to satisfy my curiosity, what will you do to this other man when you catch him, this man with whom you have a personal vendetta?"

Blow his brains out and snatch his dog. Vince thought.

But he knew the kind of crap The Screwdriver wanted to hear, the same hard-assed stuff most of these guys wanted to hear from him, their favorite hired killer, so he said, "Don Tetragna, I intend to cut off his balls, cut off his ears, cut out his tongue—and only then put an ice pick through his heart and stop his clock."

The fat man's eyes glittered with approval. His nostrils flared.

3

By Thanksgiving, The Outsider had not found the bleached-wood house in Big Sur.

Every night, Travis and Nora locked the shutters over the inside of the windows. They dead-bolted the doors. Retiring to the second floor, they slept with shotguns beside their bed and revolvers on their nightstands.

Sometimes, in the dead hours after midnight, they were awakened by strange noises in the yard or on the porch roof. Einstein padded from window to window, sniffing urgently, but always he indicated that they had nothing to fear. On further investigation, Travis usually found a prowling raccoon or other forest creature.

Travis enjoyed Thanksgiving more than he had thought he would, given the circumstances. He and Nora cooked an elaborate traditional meal for just the three of them; roast turkey with chestnut dressing, a clam casserole, glazed carrots, baked corn, pepper slaw, crescent rolls, and pumpkin pie.

Einstein sampled everything because he had developed a much more sophisticated palate than an ordinary dog. He was still a dog, however, and though the only thing he strongly disliked was the sour pepper slaw, he preferred turkey above all else. That afternoon he spent a lot of time gnawing contentedly on the drumsticks.

Over the weeks, Travis had noticed that, like most dogs, Einstein would go out into the yard occasionally and eat a little grass, though sometimes it seemed to gag him. He did it again on Thanksgiving Day, and when Travis asked him if he liked the taste of grass, Einstein said no. "Then why do you try to eat it sometimes?"

NEED IT.

"Why?"

I DON'T KNOW.

"If you don't know what you need it *for,* then how do you know you need it at all? Instinct?"

YES.

"Just instinct?"

DON'T KNOCK IT.

That evening, the three of them sat in piles of pillows on the living-room floor in front of the big stone fireplace, listening to music. Einstein's golden coat was glossy and thick in the firelight. As Travis sat with one arm around Nora, petting the dog with his free hand, he thought eating grass must be a good idea because Einstein looked healthy and robust. Einstein sneezed a few times and coughed now and then, but those seemed natural reactions to the Thanksgiving overindulgence and to the warm, dry air in front of the fireplace. Travis was not for a moment concerned about the dog's health.

4

On the afternoon of Friday, November 26, the balmy day after Thanksgiving, Garrison Dilworth was aboard his beloved forty-two-foot Hinckley Sou'wester, *Amazing Grace,* in his boat slip in the Santa Barbara harbor. He was polishing brightwork and, diligently bent to his task, almost didn't see the two men in business suits as they approached along the dock. He looked up as they were about to announce themselves, and he knew who they were—not their names, but who they must work for—even before they showed him their credentials.

One was named Johnson.

The other was Soames.

Pretending puzzlement and interest, he invited them aboard.

Stepping off the dock, down onto the deck, the one named Johnson said, "We'd like to ask you a few questions, Mr. Dilworth."

"What about?" Garrison inquired, wiping his hands on a white rag.

Johnson was a black man of ordinary size, even a little gaunt, haggard-looking, yet imposing.

Garrison said, "National Security Agency, you say? Surely, you don't think I'm in the hire of the KGB?"

Johnson smiled thinly. "You've done work for Nora Devon?"

He raised his eyebrows. "Nora? Are you serious? Well, I can assure you that Nora isn't the sort of person to be involved—"

"You are her attorney, then?" Johnson asked.

Garrison glanced at the freckle-faced younger man, Agent Soames, and again raised his eyebrows as if to ask if Johnson was always this chilly. Soames stared expressionlessly, taking his cue from the boss.

Oh my, we're in trouble with these two, Garrison thought.

After his frustrating and unsuccessful questioning of Dilworth, Lem sent Cliff Soames off on a series of errands: begin the procedures to obtain a court order allowing taps to be placed on the attorney's home and office telephones;

find the three pay phones nearest his office and the three nearest his house, and arrange for taps to be put on those as well; obtain telephone-company records of all long-distance calls made from Dilworth's home and office phones; bring in extra men from the Los Angeles office to staff an around-the-clock surveillance of Dilworth, starting within three hours.

While Cliff was attending to those things, Lem strolled around the boat docks in the harbor, hoping the sounds of the sea and the calming sight of rolling water would help clear his mind and focus his thoughts on his problems. God knew, he needed desperately to *get focused*. Over six months had passed since the dog and The Outsider had escaped from Banodyne, and Lem had lost almost fifteen pounds in the pursuit. He had not slept well in months, had little interest in food, and even his sex life had suffered.

There's such a thing as trying too hard, he told himself. It causes constipation of the mind.

But such admonishments did no good. He was still as blocked as a pipe full of concrete.

For three months, since they found Cornell's Airstream in the school parking lot the day after Hockney's murder, Lem had known that Cornell and the woman had been returning, on that August night, from a trip to Vegas, Tahoe, and Monterey. Nightclub table cards from Vegas, hotel stationery, matchbooks, and gasoline credit-card receipts had been found in the trailer and pickup truck, pinpointing every stop of their itinerary. He had not known the woman's identity, yet he had assumed she was a girlfriend, nothing more, but of course he should never have assumed any such thing. Only a few days ago, when one of his own agents went to Vegas to marry, Lem had finally realized that Cornell and the woman could have gone to Vegas for that same purpose. Suddenly their trip had looked like a honeymoon. Within hours, he confirmed that Cornell had, in fact, been married in Clark County, Nevada, on August 11, to Nora Devon of Santa Barbara.

Seeking the woman, he discovered that her house had been sold six weeks ago, after she'd vanished with Cornell. Looking into the sale, he found she had been represented by her attorney, Garrison Dilworth.

By freezing Cornell's assets, Lem thought he had made it harder for the man to continue a fugitive existence, but now he discovered that Dilworth had helped slip twenty thousand out of Cornell's bank and that all of the proceeds from the sale of the woman's house had been transferred to her somehow. Furthermore, through Dilworth, she had closed out her local bank accounts four weeks ago, and that money also was in her hands. She and her husband and the dog might now have sufficient resources to remain in hiding for years.

Standing on the dock, Lem stared at the sun-spangled sea, which slapped rhythmically against the pilings. The motion nauseated him.

He looked up at the soaring, cawing seagulls. Instead of being calmed by their graceful flight, he grew edgy.

Garrison Dilworth was intelligent, clever, a born fighter. Now that the link had been made between him and the Cornells, the attorney promised to take the NSA to court to unfreeze Travis's assets. "You've filed no charges against the man," Dilworth had said. "What toadying judge would grant the power to freeze his accounts? Your manipulation of the legal system to hamper an innocent citizen is unconscionable."

Lem could have filed charges against Travis and Nora Cornell for the violations of all sorts of laws designed to preserve the national security, and by doing so he'd have made it impossible for Dilworth to continue lending assistance to the fugitives. But filing charges meant attracting media attention. Then the harebrained story about Cornell's pet panther—and perhaps the

NSA's entire cover-up—would come down like a paper house in a thunderstorm.

His only hope was that Dilworth would try to get in touch with the Cornells to tell them that his association with them had been at last uncovered and that contact between them would have to be far more circumspect in the future. Then, with luck, Lem would pinpoint the Cornells through their telephone number. He did not have much hope of everything working out that easily. Dilworth was no fool.

Looking around at the Santa Barbara yacht harbor, Lem tried to relax, for he knew he needed to be calm and fresh if he was to outthink the old attorney. The hundreds of pleasure boats at the docks, sails furled or packed away, bobbed gently on the rolling tide, and other boats with unfurled sails glided serenely out toward the open sea, and people in bathing suits were sunning on the decks or having early cocktails, and the gulls darted like stitching needles across the blue and white quilt of the sky, and people were fishing from the stone breakwater, and the scene was achingly picturesque, but it was also an image of leisure, great and calculated leisure, with which Lem Johnson could not identify. To Lem, too much leisure was a dangerous distraction from the cold, hard realities of life, from the competitive world, and any leisure activity that lasted longer than a few hours made him nervous and anxious to get back to work. Here was leisure measured in days, in weeks; here, in these expensive and lovingly crafted boats, was leisure measured in month-long sailing excursions up and down the coast, so much leisure that it made Lem break into a sweat, made him want to scream.

He had The Outsider to worry about as well. There had been no sign of it since the day Travis Cornell had shot at it in his rented house, back at the end of August. Three months ago. What had the thing been doing in those three months? Where had it been hiding? Was it still after the dog? Was it dead?

Maybe, out in the wilds, it had been bitten by a rattlesnake, or maybe it had fallen off a cliff.

God, Lem thought, let it be dead, please, give me that much of a break. Let it be dead.

But he knew The Outsider was not dead because that would be too easy. Nothing in life was that easy. The damn thing was out there, stalking the dog. It had probably suppressed the urge to kill people it encountered because it knew each murder drew Lem and his men closer to it, and it did not want to be found before it had killed the dog. When the beast had torn the dog and the Cornells to bloody pieces, then it would once again begin to vent its rage on the population at large, and every death would hang heavily on Lem Johnson's conscience.

Meanwhile, the investigation into the murders of the Banodyne scientists was dead in the water. In fact, that second NSA task force had been dismantled. Obviously, the Soviets had hired outsiders for those hits, and there was no way to find out whom they had brought in.

A deeply tanned guy in white shorts and Top-Siders passed Lem and said, "Beautiful day!"

"Like hell," Lem said.

5

The day after Thanksgiving, Travis walked into the kitchen to get a glass of milk and saw Einstein having a sneezing fit, but he did not think much of it. Nora, even quicker than Travis to worry about the retriever's welfare, was also unconcerned. In California, the pollen count peaks in spring and autumn;

however, because the climate permits a twelve-month cycle of flowers, no season is pollen-free. Living in the woods, the situation was exacerbated.

That night, Travis was awakened by a sound he could not identify. Instantly alert, every trace of sleep banished, he sat up in the dark and reached for the shotgun on the floor beside the bed. Holding the Mossberg, he listened for the noise, and in a minute or so it came again; in the second-floor hallway.

He eased out of bed without waking Nora and went cautiously to the doorway. The hall, like most places in the house, was equipped with a low-wattage night-light, and in the pale glow Travis saw that the noise came from the dog. Einstein was standing near the head of the stairs, coughing and shaking his head.

Travis went to him, and the retriever looked up. "You okay?"

A quick wag of the tail. *Yes.*

He stooped and ruffled the dog's coat. "You sure?"

Yes.

For a minute, the dog pressed against him, enjoying being petted. Then he turned away from Travis, coughed a couple of times, and went downstairs.

Travis followed. In the kitchen, he found Einstein slurping water from the dish.

Having emptied the dish, the retriever went to the pantry, turned on the light, and began to paw lettered tiles out of the Lucite tubes.

THIRSTY.

"Are you sure you feel well?"

FINE. JUST THIRSTY. NIGHTMARE WOKE ME.

Surprised, Travis said, "You dream?"

DON'T YOU?

"Yeah. Too much."

He refilled the retriever's water dish, and Einstein emptied it again, and Travis filled it a second time. By then the dog had had enough. Travis expected him to want to go outside to pee, but the dog went upstairs instead and settled in the hall by the door of the bedroom in which Nora still slept.

In a whisper, Travis said, "Listen, if you want to come in and sleep beside the bed, it's all right."

That was what Einstein wanted. He curled up on the floor on Travis's side of the bed.

In the dark, Travis could reach out and easily touch both the shotgun and Einstein. He took greater reassurance from the presence of the dog than from the gun.

6

Saturday afternoon, just two days after Thanksgiving, Garrison Dilworth got in his Mercedes and drove slowly away from his house. Within two blocks he confirmed that the NSA still had a tail on him. It was a green Ford, probably the same one that had followed him last evening. They stayed well back of him, and they were discreet, but he was not blind.

He still had not called Nora and Travis. Because he was being followed, he suspected his phones were being tapped as well. He could have gone to a pay phone, but he was afraid that the NSA could eavesdrop on the conversation with a directional microphone or some other high-tech gadget. And if they managed to record the push-button tones that he produced by punching in the Cornells' number, they could easily translate those tones into digits and trace the number back to Big Sur. He would have to resort to deception to contact Travis and Nora safely.

He knew he had better act soon, before Travis and Nora phoned him. These days, with the technology available to them, the NSA could trace the call back to its origins as fast as Garrison would be able to warn Travis that the line was tapped.

So at two o'clock Saturday afternoon, chaperoned by the green Ford, he drove to Della Colby's house in Montecito to take her to his boat, the *Amazing Grace,* for a lazy afternoon in the sun. At least that was what he had told her on the phone.

Della was Judge Jack Colby's widow. She and Jack were Garrison's and Francine's best friends for twenty-five years before death broke up the four-some. Jack had died one year after Francine. Della and Garrison remained very close; they frequently went to dinner together, went dancing and walking and sailing. Initially, their relationship had been strictly platonic; they were simply old friends who had the fortune—or misfortune—to outlast everyone they most cared about, and they needed each other because they shared so many good times and memories that would be diminished when there was no longer any-one left with whom to reminisce. A year ago, when they suddenly found themselves in bed together, they had been surprised and overwhelmed with guilt. They felt as if they were cheating on their spouses, though Jack and Francine had died years ago. The guilt passed, of course, and now they were grateful for the companionship and gently burning passion that had unexpect-edly brightened their late-autumn years.

When he pulled into Della's driveway, she came out of the house, locked the front door, and hurried to his car. She was dressed in boat shoes, white slacks, a blue- and white-striped sweater, and a blue windbreaker. Although she was sixty-nine, and though her short hair was snow-white, she looked fifteen years younger.

He got out of the Mercedes, gave her a hug and a kiss, and said, "Can we go in your car?"

She blinked, "Are you having trouble with yours?"

"No," he said. "I'd just rather take yours."

"Sure."

She backed her Caddy out of the garage, and he got in on the passenger's side. As she pulled into the street, he said, "I'm afraid my car might be bugged, and I don't want them hearing what I've got to tell you."

Her expression was priceless.

Laughing, he said, "No, I've not gone senile overnight. If you'll keep an eye on the rearview mirror as you drive, you'll see we're being followed. They're very good, very subtle, but they're not invisible."

He gave her time, and after a few blocks Della said, "The green Ford, is it?"

"That's them."

"What've you gotten yourself into, dear?"

"Don't go straight to the harbor. Drive to the farmer's market, and we'll buy some fresh fruit. Then drive to a liquor store, and we'll buy some wine. By then, I'll have told you everything."

"Have you some secret life I've never suspected?" she asked, grinning at him. "Are you a geriatric James Bond?"

Yesterday, Lem Johnson had reopened a temporary headquarters in a claus-trophobic office at the Santa Barbara Courthouse. The room had one narrow window. The walls were dark, and the overhead lighting fixture was so dim it left the corners full of hanging shadows like misplaced scarecrows. The bor-rowed furniture consisted of rejects from other offices. He had worked out of here in the days following the Hockney killing, but had closed it up after a week, when there was nothing more to be done in the area. Now, with the hope that Dilworth would lead them to the Cornells, Lem reopened the cramped field HQ, plugged in the phones, and waited for developments.

He shared the office with one assisting agent—Jim Vann—who was an almost too-earnest and too-dedicated twenty-five-year-old.

At the moment, Cliff Soames was in charge of the six-man team at the harbor, overseeing not only the NSA agents spotted throughout the area, but also coordinating the coverage of Garrison Dilworth with the Harbor Patrol and the Coast Guard. The shrewd old man apparently realized he was being followed, so Lem expected him to make a break, to try to shake surveillance long enough to place a call to the Cornells in private. The most logical way for Garrison to throw off his tail was to head out to sea, go up or down the coast, put ashore on a launch, and telephone Cornell before his pursuers could relocate him. But he would be surprised to find himself accompanied out of the harbor by the local patrol; then, at sea, he would be followed by a Coast Guard cutter standing by for that purpose.

At three-forty, Cliff called to report that Dilworth and his lady friend were sitting on the deck of the *Amazing Grace,* eating fruit and sipping wine, reminiscing a lot, laughing a little. "From what we can pick up with directional microphones and from what we can see, I'd say they don't have any intention of going anywhere. Except maybe to bed. They sure do seem to be a randy old pair."

"Stay with them," Lem said. "I don't trust him."

Another call came through from the search team that had secretly entered Dilworth's house minutes after he had left. They had found nothing related to the Cornells or the dog.

Dilworth's office had been carefully searched last night, and nothing had been found there, either. Likewise, a study of his phone records did not produce a number for the Cornells; if he had called them in the past, he always did so from a pay phone. An examination of his AT&T credit card records showed no such calls, so if he *had* used a pay phone, he had not billed it to himself but had reversed the charges to the Cornells, leaving nothing to be traced. Which was not a good sign. Obviously, Dilworth had been exceedingly cautious even before he had known he was being watched.

Saturday, afraid the dog might be coming down with a cold, Travis kept an eye on Einstein. But the retriever sneezed only a couple of times and did not cough at all, and he seemed to be fit.

A freight company delivered ten large cartons containing all of Nora's finished canvases that had been left behind in Santa Barbara. A couple of weeks ago, using a friend's return address to insure that no link would exist between him and Nora "Aimes," Garrison Dilworth had shipped the paintings to their new house.

Now, unpacking and unwrapping the canvases, creating piles of paper padding in the living room, Nora was transported. Travis knew that, for many years, this work was what she had lived for, and he could see that having the paintings with her again was not only a great joy to her but would probably spur her to return to her new canvases, in the spare bedroom, with greater enthusiasm.

"You want to call Garrison and thank him?" he asked.

"Yes, absolutely!" she said. "but first, let's unpack them all and make sure none of them is damaged."

*   *   *

Posted around the harbor, posing as yacht owners and fishermen, Cliff Soames and the other NSA agents watched Dilworth and Della Colby and eavesdropped on them electronically as the day waned. Twilight descended without any indication that Dilworth intended to put to sea. Soon night fell, yet the attorney and his woman made no move.

Half an hour after dark, Cliff Soames got weary of pretending to fish off the stern of a Cheoy Lee sixty-six-foot sport yacht docked four slips away from Dilworth's. He climbed the steps, went into the pilot's cabin, and pulled the headphones off Hank Gorner, the agent who was monitoring the old couple's conversation through a directional mike. He listened for himself.

"... the time in Acapulco when Jack hired that fishing boat ..."

"... yes, the whole crew looked like pirates?"

"... we thought we'd have our throats cut, be dumped at sea ..."

"... but then it turned out they were all divinity students ..."

"... studying to be missionaries ... and Jack said ..."

Returning the headphones, Cliff said, "Still reminiscing!"

The other agent nodded. The cabin light was out, and Hank was illuminated only by a small, hooded, built-in work lamp above the chart table, so his features looked elongated and strange. "That's the way it's been all day. At least they have some great stories."

"I'm going to the john," Cliff said wearily. "Be right back."

"Take ten hours if you want. They're not going anywhere."

A few minutes later, when Cliff returned, Hank Gorner pulled off his headphones and said, "They went below decks."

"Something up?"

"Not what we'd hope. They're gonna jump each other's bones."

"Oh."

"Cliff, jeez, I don't want to listen to this."

"Listen," Cliff insisted.

Hank put one earphone to his head. "Jeez, they're undressing each other, and they're as old as my grandparents. This is embarrassing."

Cliff sighed.

"Now they're quiet," Hank said, a frown of distaste creeping over his face. "Any second they're gonna start moaning, Cliff."

"Listen," Cliff insisted. He snatched a light jacket off the table and went outside again so *he* wouldn't have to listen.

He took up his position in a chair on the stern deck, lifting the fishing pole once more.

The night was cool enough for the jacket, but otherwise it could not have been better. The air was clear and sweet, scented with just a slight tang of the sea. The moonless sky was full of stars. The water slapped lullingly against the dock pilings and against the hulls of the moored boats. Somewhere across the harbor, on another craft, someone was playing love songs from the forties. An engine turned over—*whump-whump-whump*—and there was something romantic about the sound. Cliff thought how nice it would be to own a boat and set out on a long trip through the South Pacific, toward palm-shaded islands—

Suddenly that idling engine roared, and Cliff realized it was the *Amazing Grace*. As he rose from his chair, dropping the fishing pole, he saw Dilworth's boat reversing out of its slip recklessly fast. It was a sailboat, and subconsciously Cliff had not expected it to move with sails furled, but it had auxiliary engines; they knew this, were prepared for this, but still it startled him. He hurried back to the cabin. "Hank, get Harbor Patrol. Dilworth's on the move."

"But they're in the sack."

"Like hell they are!" Cliff ran out to the bow deck and saw that Dilworth had already swung the *Amazing Grace* around and was headed toward the mouth of the harbor. No lights at the aft end of the boat, the area around the wheel, just one small light forward. Jesus, he was really making a break for it.

By the time they unpacked all one hundred canvases, hung a few, and carried the rest into the unused bedroom, they were starving.

"Garrison's probably having dinner now, too," Nora said. "I don't want to interrupt him. Let's call him after we've eaten."

In the pantry, Einstein released letters from the Lucite tubes and spelled out a message: IT'S DARK. CLOSE THE SHUTTERS FIRST.

Surprised and unsettled by his own uncharacteristic inattention to security, Travis hurried from room to room, closing the interior shutters and slipping the bolt-type latches in place. Fascinated by Nora's paintings and delighted by the pleasure she exhibited in their arrival, he had not even noticed that night had arrived.

Halfway toward the mouth of the harbor, confident that distance and the engine's roar now protected them from electronic eavesdroppers, Garrison said, "Take me close to the outer point of the north breakwater, along the channel's edge."

"Are you sure about this?" Della asked worriedly. "You're not a teenager."

He patted her bottom and said, "I'm better."

"Dreamer."

He kissed her on the cheek and edged forward along the starboard railing, where he got into position for his jump. He was wearing dark blue swim trunks. He should have had a wetsuit because the water would be chilly. But he thought he ought to be able to swim to the breakwater, around the point of it, and haul himself out on the north side, out of sight of the harbor, all in a few minutes, long before the water temperature leached too much body heat from him.

"Company!" Della called from the wheel.

He looked back and saw a Harbor Patrol boat leaving the docks to the south, coming toward them on their port side.

They won't stop us, he thought. They have no legal right.

But he had to go over the side before the Patrol swung in and took up a position astern. From behind, they would see him vault the railing. As long as they were to port, the *Amazing Grace* would conceal his departure, and the boat's phosphorescent wake would cover the first few seconds of his swim around the point of the breakwater, long enough for the Patrol's attention to have moved on with Della.

They were heading out at the highest speed with which Della felt comfortable. The Hinckley Sou'wester jolted through the slightly choppy waters with enough force to make it necessary for Garrison to hold fast to the railing. Still, they seemed to move past the stone wall of the breakwater at a frustratingly slow pace, and the Harbor Patrol drew nearer, but Garrison waited, waited, because he didn't want to go into the harbor a hundred yards short of its end. If he went in too soon, he would not be able to swim all the way out to the point and around it; instead, he would have to swim straight to the breakwater and climb its flank, within full sight of all observers. Now the patrol closed to within a hundred yards—he could see them when he rose from a crouch and looked across the Hinckley's cabin roof—and began to swing around behind them, and Garrison could not wait much longer, could not—

"The point!" Della called from the wheel.

He threw himself over the railing, into the dark water, away from the boat.

The sea was *cold*. It shocked the breath out of him. He sank, could not find the surface, was seized by panic, flailed, thrashed, but then broke through to the air, gasping.

The *Amazing Grace* was surprisingly close. He felt as if he had been thrashing in confusion beneath the surface for a minute or more, but it must have been only a second or two because his boat was not yet far away. The Harbor Patrol was close, too, and he decided that even the churning wake of the *Amazing Grace* did not give him enough cover, so he took a deep breath and went under again, staying down as long as he could. When he came up, both Della and her shadowers were well past the mouth of the harbor, turning south, and he was safe from observation.

The outgoing tide was swiftly carrying him past the point of the northern breakwater, which was a wall of loose boulders and rocks that rose more than twenty feet above the waterline, mottled gray and black ramparts in the night. He not only had to swim around the end of the barrier but had to move toward land against the resistant current. Without further delay, he began to swim, wondering why on earth he had thought this would be a snap.

You're almost seventy-one, he told himself as he stroked past the rocky point, which was illuminated by a navigation-warning light. What ever possessed you to play hero?

But he knew what possessed him: a deep-seated belief that the dog must remain free, that it must not be treated as the government's property. *If we've come so far that we can create as God creates, then we have to learn to act with the justice and mercy of God.* That was what he had told Nora and Travis—and Einstein—on the night Ted Hockney had been killed, and he had meant every word he'd said.

Salt water stung his eyes, blurred his vision. Some had gotten into his mouth, and it burned a small ulcer on his lower lip.

He fought the current, pulled past the point of the breakwater, out of sight of the harbor, then slashed toward the rocks. Reaching them at last, he hung onto the first boulder he touched, gasping, not yet quite able to pull himself out of the water.

In the intervening weeks since Nora and Travis went on the run, Garrison had plenty of time to think about Einstein, and he felt even more strongly that to imprison an intelligent creature, innocent of all crime, was an act of grave injustice, regardless of whether the prisoner was a dog. Garrison had devoted his life to the pursuit of justice that was made possible by the laws of a democracy, and to the maintenance of the freedom that grew from this justice. When a man of ideals decides he is too old to risk everything for what he believes in, then he is no longer a man of ideals. He may no longer be a man at all. That hard truth had driven him, in spite of his age, to make this night swim. Funny—that a long life of idealism should, after seven decades, be put to the ultimate test over the fate of a dog.

But *what* a dog.

And what a wondrous new world we live in, he thought.

Genetic technology might have to be rechristened "genetic art," for every work of art was an act of creation, and no act of creation was finer or more beautiful than the creation of an intelligent mind.

Getting his second wind, he heaved entirely out of the water, onto the sloped north flank of the northern breakwater. That barrier rose between him and the harbor, and he moved inland, along the rocks, while the sea surged at his left side. He'd brought a waterproof penlight, clipped to his trunks, and now he used it to proceed, barefoot, with the greatest caution, afraid of slipping on the wet stones and breaking a leg or an ankle.

He could see the city lights a few hundred yards ahead, and the vague silvery line of the beach.

He was cold but not as cold as he had been in the water. His heart was beating fast but not as fast as before.

He was going to make it.

Lem Johnson drove down from the temporary HQ in the courthouse, and Cliff met him at the empty boat slip where the *Amazing Grace* had been tied up. A wind had risen. Hundreds of craft along the docks were wallowing slightly in their berths; they creaked, and slack sail lines clicked and clinked against their masts. Dock lamps and neighboring boat lanterns cast shimmering patterns of light on the dark, oily-looking water where Dilworth's forty-two-footer had been moored.

"Harbor Patrol?" Lem asked worriedly.

"They followed him out to open sea. Seemed as if he was going to turn north, swung close by the point, but then he went south instead."

"Did Dilworth see them?"

"He had to. As you see—no fog, lots of stars, clear as a bell."

"Good. I want him to be aware. Coast Guard?"

"I've talked to the cutter," Cliff assured him. "They're on the spot, flanking the *Amazing Grace* at a hundred yards, heading south along the coast."

Shivering in the rapidly cooling air, Lem said, "They know he might try putting ashore in a rubber boat or whatever?"

"They know," Cliff said. "He can't do it under their noses."

"Is the Guard sure he sees them?"

"They're lit up like a Christmas tree."

"Good. I want him to know it's hopeless. If we can just keep him from warning the Cornells, then they'll call him sooner or later—and we'll have them. Even if they call him from a pay phone, we'll know their general location."

In addition to taps on Dilworth's home and office phones, the NSA had installed tracing equipment that would lock open a line the moment a connection was made, and keep it open even after both parties hung up, until the caller's number and street address were ascertained and verified. Even if Dilworth shouted a warning and hung up the instant he recognized one of the Cornell's voices, it would be too late. The only way he could try to foil the NSA was by not answering his phone at all. But even that would do him no good because, after the sixth ring, every incoming call was being automatically "answered" by the NSA's equipment, which opened the line and began tracing procedures.

"The only thing could screw us now," Lem said, "is if Dilworth gets to a phone we don't have monitored and warns the Cornells not to call him."

"It's not going to happen," Cliff said. "We're on him tight."

"I wish you wouldn't say that," Lem worried. As the wind got hold of it, a metal clip on a loose line clanged loudly off a spar, and the sound made Lem jump. "My dad always said the worst happens when you least expect it."

Cliff shook his head. "With all due respect, sir, the more I hear you quote your father, the more I think he must've been just about the gloomiest man who ever lived."

Looking around at the wallowing boats and wind-chopped water, feeling as if *he* was moving instead of standing still in a moving world, a little queasy, Lem said, "Yeah . . . my dad was a great guy in his way, but he was also . . . impossible."

Hank Gorner shouted, "Hey!" He was running along the dock from the Cheoy Lee where he and Cliff had been stationed all day. "I've just been on with the Guard cutter. They're playing their searchlight over the *Amazing Grace,* intimidating a little, and they tell me they don't see Dilworth. Just the woman."

Lem said, "But, Christ, he's running the boat!"

"No," Gorner said. "There's no lights in the *Amazing Grace,* but the Guard's searchlight brightens up the whole thing, and they say the woman's at the wheel."

"It's all right. He's just below deck," Cliff said.

"No," Lem said as his heart started to pound. "He wouldn't be below deck at a time like this. He'd be studying the cutter, deciding whether to keep going or turn back. He's not on the *Amazing Grace.*"

"But he has to be! He didn't get off before she pulled out of the dock."

Lem stared out across the crystalline-clear harbor, toward the light near the end of the northern breakwater. "You said the damn boat swung out close to the north point, and it looked as if he was going north, but then he suddenly swung south."

"Shit," Cliff said.

"That's where he dropped off," Lem said. "Out by the point of the northern breakwater. Without a rubber boat. Swimming, by God."

"He's too old for that crap," Cliff protested.

"Evidently not. He went around the other side, and he's headed for a phone on one of the northern public beaches. We've got to stop him, and fast."

Cliff cupped his hands to his mouth and shouted the first names of the four agents who were positioned on other boats along the docks. His voice carried, echoing flatly off the water, in spite of the wind. Men came running, and even as Cliff's shouts faded away across the harbor, Lem was sprinting for his car in the parking lot.

The worst happens when you least expect it.

As Travis was rinsing dinner dishes, Nora said, "Look at this."

He turned and saw that she was standing by Einstein's food and water dishes. The water was gone, but half his dinner remained.

She said, "When have you known him to leave a single scrap?"

"Never." Frowning, Travis wiped his hands on the kitchen towel. "The last few days . . . I've thought maybe he's coming down with a cold or something, but he says he feels fine. And today he hasn't been sneezing or coughing like he was."

They went into the living room, where the retriever was reading *Black Beauty* with the help of his page-turning machine.

They knelt beside him, and he looked up, and Nora said, "Are you sick, Einstein?"

The retriever barked once, softly: *No.*

"Are you sure?"

A quick wag of the tail: *Yes.*

"You didn't finish your dinner," Travis said.

The dog yawned elaborately.

Nora said, "Are you telling us you're a little tired?"

Yes.

"If you were feeling ill," Travis said, "you'd let us know right away, wouldn't you, fur face?"

Yes.

Nora insisted on examining Einstein's eyes, mouth, and ears for obvious signs of infection, but at last she said, "Nothing. He seems okay. I guess even Superdog has a right to be tired once in a while."

The wind had come up fast. It was chilly, and under its lash the waves rose higher than they had been all day.

A mass of gooseflesh, Garrison reached the landward end of the north flank of the harbor's northern breakwater. He was relieved to depart the hard and sometimes jagged stones of that rampart for the sandy beach. He was sure he had scraped and cut both feet; they felt hot, and his left foot stung with each step, forcing him to limp.

He stayed close to the surf, away from the tree-lined park that lay behind the beach. Over there, where park lamps lit the walkways and where spotlights dramatically highlighted the palms, he would be more easily seen from the street. He did not think anyone would be looking for him; he was sure his trick had worked. However, if anyone *was* looking for him, he did not want to call attention to himself.

The gusting wind tore foam off the incoming breakers and flung it in Garrison's face, so he felt as if he was continuously running through spiders' webs. The stuff stung his eyes, which had finally stopped tearing from his dunk in the sea, and at last he was forced to move away from the surf line, farther up the beach, where the softer sand met the lawn but where he was still out of the lights.

Young people were on the darkish beach, dressed for the chill of the night: couples on blankets, cuddling; small groups smoking dope, listening to music. Eight or ten teenage boys were gathered around two all-terrain vehicles with balloon tires, which were not allowed on the beach during the day and most likely weren't allowed at night. They were drinking beer beside a pit they'd dug in the sand to bury their bottles if they saw a cop approaching; they were talking loudly about girls, and indulging in horseplay. No one gave Garrison more than a glance as he hurried by. In California, health-food-and-exercise fanatics were as common as street muggers in New York, and if an old man wanted to take a cold swim and then run on the beach in the dark, he was no more remarkable or noteworthy than a priest in a church.

As he headed north, Garrison scanned the park to his right in search of pay phones. They would probably be in pairs, prominently illuminated, on islands of concrete beside one of the walkways or perhaps near one of the public comfort stations.

He was beginning to despair, certain that he must have passed at least one group of telephones, that his old eyes were failing him, but then he saw what he was looking for. Two pay phones with winglike sound shields. Brightly lighted. They were about a hundred feet in from the beach, midway between the sand and the street that flanked the other side of the park.

Turning his back to the churning sea, he slowed to catch his breath and walked across the grass, under the wind-shaken fronds of a cluster of three stately royal palms. He was still forty feet from the phones when he saw a car, traveling at high speed, suddenly brake and pull to the curb with a squeal of tires, parking in a direct line from the phones. Garrison didn't know who they were, but he decided not to take any chances. He sidled into the cover provided by a huge old double-boled date palm that was, fortunately, not one of those fitted with decorative spotlights. From the notch between the trunks, he had a view of the phones and of the walkway leading out to the curb where the car had parked.

Two men got out of the sedan. One sprinted north along the park perimeter, looking inward, searching for something.

The other man rushed straight into the park along the walkway. When he reached the lighted area around the phones, his identity was clear—and shocking.

Lemuel Johnson.

Behind the trunks of the Siamese date palms, Garrison drew his arms and legs closer to his body, sure that the joined bases of the trees provided him with plenty of cover but trying to make himself smaller nevertheless.

Johnson went to the first phone, lifted the handset—and tried to tear it out of the coinbox. It had one of those flexible metal cords, and he yanked on it hard, repeatedly, with little effect. Finally, cursing the instrument's toughness, he ripped the handset loose and threw it across the park. Then he destroyed the second plane.

For a moment, as Johnson turned away from the phones and walked straight toward Garrison, the attorney thought that he had been seen. But Johnson stopped after only a few steps and scanned the seaward end of the park and the beach beyond. His gaze did not appear to rest even momentarily on the date palms behind which Garrison hid.

"You damn crazy old bastard," Johnson said, then hurried back toward his car.

Crouched in shadows behind the palms, Garrison grinned because he knew whom the NSA man was talking about. Suddenly, the attorney did not mind the chill wind sweeping off the night sea behind him.

Damn crazy old bastard or geriatric James Bond—take your pick. Either way, he was still a man to be reckoned with.

In the basement switching room of the telephone company, Agents Rick Olbier and Denny Jones were tending the NSA's electronic tapping and tracing equipment, monitoring Garrison Dilworth's office and home lines. It was dull duty, and they played cards to make the time pass: two-hand pinochle and five-hundred rummy, neither of which was a good game, but the very idea of two-hand poker repelled them.

When a call came through to Dilworth's home number at fourteen minutes past eight o'clock. Olbier and Jones reacted with far more excitement than the situation warranted because they were desperate for action. Olbier dropped his cards on the floor, and Jones threw his on the table, and they reached for the two headsets as if this was World War II and they were expecting to overhear a top-secret conversation between Hitler and Göring.

Their equipment was set to open the line and lock in a tracer pulse if Dilworth did not answer by the sixth ring. Because he knew the attorney was not at home and that the phone would not be answered, Olbier overrode the program and opened the line after the second ring.

On the computer screen, green letters announced: NOW TRACING.

And on the open line, a man said, "Hello?"

"Hello," Jones said into the mike on his headset.

The caller's number and his local Santa Barbara address appeared on the screen. This system worked much like the 911 police emergency computer, providing instant identification of the caller. But now, above the address on the screen, a company's rather than an individual's name appeared: TELEPHONE SOLICITATIONS, INC.

On the line, responding to Denny Jones, the caller said, "Sir, I'm pleased to tell you that you have been selected to receive a free eight-by-ten photograph and ten free pocket prints of any—"

Jones said, "Who is this?"

The computer was now searching data banks of Santa Barbara street addresses to cross-check the ID of the caller.

The voice on the phone said, "Well, I'm calling in behalf of Olin Mills, sir, the photography studio, where the finest quality—"

"Wait a sec," Jones said.

The computer verified the identity of the telephone subscriber who placed the call: Dilworth was getting a sales pitch, nothing more.

"I don't want any!" Jones said sharply, and disconnected.

"Shit," Olbier said.

"Pinochle?" Jones said.

In addition to the six men who had been at the harbor, Lem called in four more from the temporary HQ at the courthouse.

He stationed five along the perimeter of the oceanside park, a few hundred yards apart. Their job was to watch the wide avenue that separated the park from a business district, where there were a lot of motels but also restaurants, yogurt shops, gift shops, and other retail enterprises. All of the businesses had phones, of course, and even some of the motels would have pay phones in their front offices; using any of them, the attorney could alert Travis and Nora Cornell. At this hour on a Saturday evening, some stores were closed, but some of them—and all of the restaurants—were open. Dilworth must not be permitted to cross the street.

The sea wind was stiffening and growing chillier. The men stood with their hands in their jackets, heads tucked down, shivering.

Palm fronds were rattled by sudden gusts. Tree-roosting birds shrilled in alarm, then resettled.

Lem sent another agent to the southwest corner of the park, out by the base of the breakwater that separated the public beach from the harbor on the other side. His job was to prevent Dilworth from returning to the breakwater, climbing it, and sneaking back across the harbor to phones in another part of the city.

A seventh man was dispatched to the northwest corner of the park, down by the water line, to be sure Dilworth did not proceed north onto private beaches and into residential areas where he might persuade someone to allow him to use an unmonitored phone.

Just Lem, Cliff, and Hank were left to comb through the park and adjoining beach in search of the attorney. He knew he had too few men for the job, but these ten—plus Olbier and Jones at the telephone company—were the only people he had in town. He could see no point ordering in more agents from the Los Angeles office; by the time they arrived, Dilworth would either have been found and stopped—or would have succeeded in calling the Cornells.

The roofless all-terrain vehicle was equipped with a roll bar. It had two bucket seats, behind which was a four-foot-long cargo area that could accommodate additional passengers or a considerable amount of gear.

Garrison was flat on his stomach on the floor of the cargo hold, under a blanket. Two teenage boys were in the bucket seats, and two more were in the cargo hold on top of Garrison, sprawled as if they were sitting on nothing more than a pile of blankets. They were trying to keep the worst of their weight off Garrison, but he still felt half-crushed.

The engine sounded like angry wasps: a high, hard buzzing. It deafened Garrison because his right ear was flat against the cargo bed, which transmitted and amplified every vibration.

Fortunately, the soft beach provided a relatively smooth ride.

The vehicle stopped accelerating, slowed, and the engine noise dropped dramatically.

"Shit," one of the boys whispered to Garrison, "there's a guy ahead with a flashlight, flagging us down."

They drew to a halt, and over the whispery idling of the engine, Garrison heard a man say, "Where you boys headed?"

"Up the beach."

"That's private property up there. You have any right up there?"

"It's where we live," Tommy, the driver, responded.

"Is that so?"

"Don't we look like a bunch of spoiled rich kids?" one of them asked, playing wiseass.

"What you been up to?" the man asked suspiciously.

"Beach cruisin', hangin' out. But it got too cold."

"You boys been drinking?"

You dolt, Garrison thought as he listened to the interrogator. These are *teenagers* you're talking to, poor creatures whose hormonal imbalances have thrown them into rebellion against all authority for the next couple of years. I have their sympathy because I'm in flight from the cops, and they'll take my side without even knowing what I've done. If you want their cooperation, you'll never get it by bullying them.

"Drinking? Hell no," another boy said. "Check the cooler in back if you want. Nothing in it but Dr. Pepper."

Garrison, who was pressed up against the ice chest, hoped to God the man would not come around to the back of the vehicle and have a look. If the guy got *that* close he would almost surely see there was something vaguely human about the shape under the blanket on which the boys were sitting.

"Dr. Pepper, huh? What kind of beer was in there before you drank it?"

"Hey, man," Tommy said. "Why're you hassling us? Are you a cop or what?"

"Yeah, in fact, I am."

"Where's your uniform?" one of the boys asked.

"Undercover. Listen, I'm disposed to let you kids go on, not check your breath for liquor or anything. But I have to know—did you see an old white-haired guy on the beach tonight?"

"Who cares about old guys?" one of the boys asked. "We were looking for *women*."

"You'd have noticed this old character if you'd seen him. He'd most likely have been wearing swim trunks."

"Tonight?" Tommy said. "It's almost December, man. You feel that wind?"

"Maybe he was wearing something else."

"Didn't see him," Tommy said. "No old guy with white hair. Any you guys see him?"

The other three said they had not seen any old fart fitting the description they had been given, and then they were allowed to drive on, north from the public beach, into a residential area of seaside homes and private beaches.

When they had rounded a low hill and were out of sight of the man who had stopped them, they pulled the blanket off Garrison, and he sat up with considerable relief.

Tommy dropped the other three boys off at their houses and took Garrison home with him because his parents were out for the evening. He lived in a house that looked like a ship with multiple decks, slung over a bluff, all glass and angles.

Following Tommy into the foyer, Garrison caught a glimpse of himself in a mirror. He looked nothing like the dignified silver-haired barrister known by everyone in the city's courts. His hair was wet, dirty, and matted. His face was smeared with dirt. Sand, bits of grass, and threads of seaweed were stuck to his bare skin and tangled in his gray chest hair. He grinned happily at himself.

"There's a phone in here," Tommy said from the den.

After preparing dinner, eating, cleaning up, and then worrying about Einstein's loss of appetite, Nora and Travis had forgotten about calling Garrison Dilworth and thanking him for the care with which he had packaged and shipped her paintings. They were sitting in front of the fireplace when she remembered.

In the past, when they had called Garrison, they had done so from public phones in Carmel. That had proved to be an unnecessary precaution. And now, tonight, neither of them was in the mood to get in the car and drive into town.

"We could wait and call him from Carmel tomorrow," Travis said.

"It'll be safe to phone from here," she said. "If they'd made a link between you and Garrison, he'd have called and warned us off."

"He might not know they've made a link," Travis said. "He might not know they're watching him."

"Garrison would know," she said firmly.

Travis nodded. "Yeah, I'm sure he would."

"So it's safe to call him."

She was halfway to the phone when it rang.

The operator said, "I have a collect call for anyone from a Mr. Garrison Dilworth in Santa Barbara. Will you accept the charges?"

A few minutes before ten o'clock, after conducting a thorough but fruitless search of the park and beach, Lem reluctantly admitted that Garrison Dilworth had somehow gotten past him. He sent his men back to the courthouse and harbor.

He and Cliff also drove back to the harbor to the sport yacht from which they had based their surveillance of Dilworth. When they put in a call to the Coast Guard cutter pursuing the *Amazing Grace,* they learned that the attorney's lady had turned around well short of Ventura and was heading north along the coast, back to Santa Barbara.

She entered the harbor at ten thirty-six.

At the empty slip belonging to Garrison, Lem and Cliff huddled in the crisp wind, watching her bring the Hinckley smoothly and gently into its mooring. It was a beautiful boat, beautifully handled.

She had the gall to shout at them, "Don't just stand there! Grab the lines and help tie her up!"

They obliged primarily because they were anxious to speak with her and could not do so until the *Amazing Grace* was secured.

Once their assistance had been rendered, they stepped through the railing gate. Cliff was wearing Top-Siders as part of his boater's disguise, but Lem was in street shoes and not at all sure-footed on the wet deck, especially as the boat was rocking slightly.

Before they could say a word to the woman, a voice behind them said, "Excuse me, gentlemen—"

Lem turned and saw Garrison Dilworth in the glow of a dock lamp, just boarding the boat behind them. He was wearing someone else's clothes. His pants were much too big in the waist, cinched in with a belt. They were too short in the legs, so his bare ankles were revealed. He wore a voluminous shirt.

"—please excuse me, but I've got to get into some warm clothes of my own and have a pot of coffee—"

Lem said, "God *damn* it."

"—to thaw out these old bones."

After a gasp of astonishment, Cliff Soames let out a hard bark of laughter, then glanced at Lem and said, "Sorry."

Lem's stomach cramped and burned with an incipient ulcer. He did not wince with pain, did not double over, did not even put a hand on his gut, gave no indication of discomfort because any such sign from him might increase Dilworth's satisfaction. Lem just glared at the attorney, at the woman, then left without saying a word.

"That damn dog." Cliff said as he fell into step at Lem's side of the dock, "sure inspires one hell of a lot of loyalty."

Later, bedding down in a motel because he was too tired to close the temporary field office tonight and go home to Orange County, Lem Johnson thought about what Cliff had said. Loyalty. One *hell* of a lot of loyalty.

Lem wondered if he had ever felt such a strong bond of loyalty to anyone as the Cornells and Garrison Dilworth apparently felt toward the retriever. He tossed and turned, unable to sleep, and he finally realized there was no use trying to switch off his inner lights until he satisfied himself that he was capable of the degree of loyalty and commitment that he had seen in the Cornells and their attorney.

He sat up in the darkness, leaning against the headboard.

Well, sure, he was damn loyal to his country, which he loved and honored. And he was loyal to the Agency. But to another *person*? All right, Karen. His wife. He was loyal to Karen in every way—in his heart, mind, and gonads. He loved Karen. He had loved her deeply for almost twenty years.

"Yeah," he said aloud in the empty motel room at two o'clock in the morning, "yeah, if you're so loyal to Karen, why aren't you with her now?"

But he wasn't being fair to himself. After all, he had a job to do, an important job.

"That's the trouble," he muttered, "you've always—*always*—got a job to do."

He slept away from home more than a hundred nights a year, one in three. And when he *was* home, he was distracted half the time, his mind on the latest case. Karen had once wanted children, but Lem had delayed the start of a family, claiming that he could not handle the responsibility of children until he was sure his career was secure.

"Secure?" he said. "Man, you inherited your daddy's money. You started out with more of a cushion than most people."

If he was as loyal to Karen as those people were to that mutt, then his commitment to her should mean that her desires ought to come before all others. If Karen wanted a family, then family should take precedence over career. Right? At least he should have compromised and started a family when they were in their early thirties. His twenties could have gone to the career, his thirties to child-rearing. Now he was forty-five, almost forty-six, and Karen was forty-three, and the time for starting a family had passed.

Lem was overcome with a great loneliness.

He got out of bed, went into the bathroom in his shorts, switched on the light, and stared hard at himself in the mirror. His eyes were bloodshot and sunken. He had lost so much weight on this case that his face was beginning to look downright skeletal.

Stomach cramps seized him, and he bent over, holding onto the sides of the sink, his face in the basin. He'd been afflicted only for the past month or so, but his condition seemed to be worsening with startling speed. The pain took a long time to pass.

When he confronted his reflection in the mirror again, he said, "You're not even loyal to your own self, you asshole. You're killing yourself, working yourself to death, and you can't stop. Not loyal to Karen, not loyal to yourself. Not really loyal to your country or the Agency, when it comes right down to it. Hell, the only thing you're totally and unswervingly committed to is your old man's crackpot vision of life as a tightrope walk."

Crackpot.

That word seemed to reverberate in the bathroom long after he'd spoken it. He had loved and respected his father, had never said a word against him. Yet today he had admitted to Cliff that his dad had been "impossible."And now— crackpot vision. He still loved his dad and always would. But he was beginning to wonder if a son could love a father and, at the same time, completely reject his father's teachings.

A year ago, a month ago, even a few days ago, he would have said it was impossible to hold fast to that love and still be his own man. But now, by God, it seemed not only possible but essential that he separate his love for his father from his adherence to his father's workaholic code.

What's happening to me? he wondered.

Freedom? Freedom, at last, at forty-five?

Squinting into the mirror, he said, "Almost forty-six."

CHAPTER 9

1

SUNDAY, TRAVIS NOTED that Einstein still had less of an appetite than usual, but by Monday, November 29, the retriever seemed fine. On Monday and Tuesday, Einstein finished every scrap of his meals, and he read new books. He sneezed only once and did not cough at all. He drank more water than in the past, though not an excessive amount. If he seemed to spend more time by the fireplace, if he padded through the house less energetically . . . well, winter was swiftly settling upon them, and animals' behavior changed with the seasons.

At a bookstore in Carmel, Nora bought a copy of *The Dog Owner's Home Veterinary Handbook*. She spent a few hours at the kitchen table, reading, researching the possible meanings of Einstein's symptoms. She discovered that listlessness, partial loss of appetite, sneezing, coughing, and unusual thirst could signify a hundred ailments—or mean nothing at all. "About the only thing it couldn't be is a cold," she said. "Dogs don't get colds like we do." But by the time she got the book, Einstein's symptoms had diminished to such an extent that she decided he was probably perfectly healthy.

In the pantry off the kitchen, Einstein used the Scrabble tiles to tell them: FIT AS A FIDDLE.

Stooping beside the dog, stroking him, Travis said, "I guess you ought to know better than anyone."

WHY SAY FIT AS A FIDDLE?

Replacing the tiles in their Lucite tubes, Travis said, "Well, because it means—healthy."

BUT WHY DOES IT MEAN HEALTHY?

Travis thought about the metaphor—fit as a fiddle—and realized he was not sure why it meant what it did. He asked Nora, and she came to the pantry door, but she had no explanation for the phrase, either.

Pawing out more letters, pushing them around with his nose, the retriever asked: WHY SAY SOUND AS A DOLLAR?

"Sound as a dollar—meaning healthy or reliable," Travis said.

Stooping beside them, speaking to the dog, Nora said, "That one's easier. The United States dollar was once the soundest, most stable currency in the world. Still is, I suppose. For decades, there was no terrible inflation in the dollar like in some other currencies, no reason to lose faith in it, so folks said, 'I'm as sound as a dollar.' Of course, the dollar isn't what it once was, and the phrase isn't as fitting as it used to be, but we still use it."

WHY STILL USE IT?

"Because . . . we've always used it," Nora said, shrugging.

WHY SAY HEALTHY AS A HORSE? HORSES NEVER SICK?

Gathering up the tiles and sorting them back into their tubes, Travis said, "No, in fact, horses are fairly delicate animals in spite of their size. They get sick pretty easily."

Einstein looked expectantly from Travis to Nora.

Nora said, "We probably say we're healthy as a horse because horses *look* strong and seem like they shouldn't ever get sick, even though they get sick all the time."

"Face it," Travis told the dog, "we humans say things all the time that don't make sense."

Pumping the letter-dispensing pedals with his paw, the retriever told them: YOU ARE A STRANGE PEOPLE.

Travis looked at Nora, and they both laughed.

Beneath YOU ARE A STRANGE PEOPLE, the retriever spelled: BUT I LIKE YOU ANYWAY.

Einstein's inquisitiveness and sense of humor seemed, more than anything else, to indicate that, if he had been mildly ill, he was now recovered.

That was Tuesday.

On Wednesday, December 1, while Nora painted in her second-floor studio, Travis devoted the day to inspecting his security system and to routine weapons maintenance.

In every room, a firearm was carefully concealed under furniture or behind a drape or in a closet, but always within easy reach. They owned two Mossberg pistol-grip shotguns, four Smith & Wesson Model 19 Combat Magnums loaded with .357s, two .38 pistols that they carried with them in the pickup and Toyota, an Uzi carbine, two Uzi pistols. They could have obtained their entire arsenal legally, from a local gun shop, once they purchased a house and established residence in the county, but Travis had not been willing to wait that long. He had wanted to have the weapons on the first night they settled into their new home; therefore, through Van Dyne in San Francisco, he and Nora had located an illegal arms salesman and had acquired what they needed. Of course, they could not have bought conversion kits for the Uzis from a licensed gun dealer. But they were able to purchase three such kits in San Francisco, and now the Uzi carbine and pistols were fully automatic.

Travis moved from room to room, checking that the weapons were properly positioned, that they were free of dust, that they did not need to be oiled, and that their magazines were fully loaded. He knew that everything would be in order, but he just felt more comfortable if he conducted this inspection once a week. Though he had been out of uniform for many years, the old military training and methodology were still a part of him, and under pressure they surfaced more quickly than he had expected.

Taking a Mossberg with them, he and Einstein also walked around the house, stopping at each of the small infrared sensors that were, as much as possible, placed inconspicuously against backdrops of rocks or plants, snug against the trunks of a few trees, at the corners of the house, and beside an old rotting pine stump at the edge of the driveway. He had bought the components on the open market, from an electronics dealer in San Francisco. It was dated stuff, not at all state-of-the-art security technology, but he chose it because he was familiar with it from his days in Delta Force, and it was good enough for his purposes. Lines from the sensors ran underground, to an alarm box in one of the kitchen cupboards. When the system was switched on at night, nothing larger than a raccoon could come within thirty feet of the house—or enter the barn at the back of the property—without tripping the alarm. No bells would ring, and no sirens would blare because that would alert The Outsider and might run it off. They didn't want to chase it away; they wanted to *kill* it. Therefore, when the system was tripped, it turned on clock radios in every room of the house, all of which were set at low volume so as not to frighten off an intruder but high enough to warn Travis and Nora.

Today, all the sensors were in place, as usual. All he had to do was wipe off the light film of dust that had coated the lenses.

"The palace moat is in good repair, m'lord," Travis said.

Einstein woofed approval.

In the rust-red barn, Travis and Einstein examined the equipment that, they hoped, would provide a nasty surprise for The Outsider.

In the northwest corner of the shadowy interior, to the left of the big rolling door, a pressurized steel tank was clamped in a wall rack. In the diagonally opposite southeast corner at the back of the building, beyond the pickup and car, an identical vessel was bolted to an identical rack. They resembled large propane tanks of the sort people used at summer cabins for gas cooking, but they did not hold propane. They were filled with nitrous oxide, which was sometimes inaccurately called "laughing gas." The first whiff *did* exhilarate you and make you want to laugh, but the second whiff knocked you out before the laugh could escape your lips. Dentists and surgeons frequently used nitrous oxide as an anesthetic. Travis had purchased it from a medical-supply house in San Francisco.

After switching on the barn lights, Travis checked the gauges on both tanks. Full pressure.

In addition to the large rolling door at the front of the barn, there was a smaller, man-size door at the rear. These were the only two entrances. Travis had boarded over a pair of windows in the loft. At night, when the alarm system was engaged, the smaller rear door was left unlocked in the hope that The Outsider, intending to scout the house from the cover of the barn, would let itself into the trap. When it opened the door and crept into the barn, it would trigger a mechanism that would slam and lock the door behind it. The front door, already locked from outside, would prevent an exit in that direction.

Simultaneous with the springing of the trap, the large tanks of nitrous oxide would release their entire contents in less than one minute because Travis had fitted them with high-pressure emergency-release valves tied in with the alarm system. He had caulked all of the draft-admitting cracks in the barn and had insulated the place as thoroughly as possible in order to insure that the nitrous oxide would be contained within the structure until one of the doors was unlocked from outside and opened to vent the gas.

The Outsider could not take refuge in the pickup or the Toyota, for they would be locked. No corner in the barn would be free of the gas. Within less than a minute, the creature would collapse. Travis had considered using poisonous gas of some kind, which he probably could have obtained on the underground market, but he had decided against going to that extreme because, if something went wrong, the danger to him and Nora and Einstein would be too great.

Once gas had been released and The Outsider had succumbed, Travis could simply open one of the doors, vent the barn, enter with the Uzi carbine, and kill the beast where it lay unconscious. At worst, even if the time taken airing out the building gave The Outsider a chance to regain consciousness, it would still be groggy and disoriented and easily dispatched.

When they had ascertained that everything in the barn was as it should be, Travis and Einstein returned to the yard behind the house. The December day was cool but windless. The forest surrounding the property was preternaturally still. The trees stood motionless under a low sky of slate-colored clouds.

Travis said, "Is The Outsider still coming?"

With a quick wag of the tail, Einstein said, *Yes.*

"Is it close?"

Einstein sniffed the clean, winter-crisp air. He padded across the yard to the perimeter of the northern woods and sniffed again, cocked his head, peered intently into the trees. He repeated this ritual at the southern end of the property.

Travis had the feeling that Einstein was not actually employing his eyes, ears, and nose in search of The Outsider. He had some way of monitoring The Outsider that was far different from the means by which he would track a cougar or squirrel. Travis perceived that the dog was employing an inexplicable sixth sense—call it psychic or at least quasi-psychic. The retriever's use of its ordinary senses was probably either the trigger by which it engaged that psychic ability—or mere habit.

At last, Einstein returned to him and whined curiously.

"Is it close?" Travis asked.

Einstein sniffed the air and surveyed the gloom of the encircling forest, as if he could not decide on an answer.

"Einstein? Is something wrong?"

Finally, the retriever barked once: *No.*

"Is The Outsider getting close?"

A hesitation. Then: *No.*

"Are you sure?"

Yes.

"Really sure?"

Yes.

At the house, as Travis opened the door, Einstein turned away from him, padded across the back porch, and stood at the top of the wooden steps, taking one final look around at the yard and at the peaceful, shadowed, soundless forest. Then, with a faint shiver, he followed Travis inside.

Throughout the inspection of the defenses during the afternoon, Einstein had been more affectionate than usual, rubbing against Travis's legs a great deal, nuzzling, seeking by one means or another to be petted or patted or scratched. That evening, as they watched television, then played a three-way game of Scrabble on the living-room floor, the dog continued to seek attention. He kept putting his head in Nora's lap, then in Travis's. He seemed as if he would be content to be stroked and have his ears gently scratched until next summer.

From the day of their first encounter in the Santa Ana foothills, Einstein had gone through spells of purely doggy behavior, when it was hard to believe that he was, in his own way, as intelligent as a man. Tonight, he was in one of those moods again. In spite of his cleverness at Scrabble—in which his score was second only to Nora's, and in which he took devilish pleasure forming words that made sly reference to her as yet unnoticeable pregnancy—he was nonetheless, this night, more of a dog than not.

Nora and Travis chose to finish the evening with a little light reading—detective stories—but Einstein did not want them to bother inserting a book in his page-turning machine. Instead, he lay on the floor in front of Nora's armchair and went instantly to sleep.

"He still seems a little draggy," she said to Travis.

"He ate all his dinner, though. And we did have a long day."

The dog's breathing, as it slept, was normal, and Travis was not worried. Actually, he was feeling better about their future than he had for some time. The inspection of their defenses had given him renewed confidence in their preparations, and he believed they would be able to handle The Outsider when it arrived. And thanks to Garrison Dilworth's courage and dedication to their cause, the government had been stymied, perhaps for good, in its efforts to track them down. Nora was painting again with great enthusiasm, and Travis had decided to use his real-estate license, under the name of Samuel Hyatt, to go back to work once The Outsider had been destroyed. And if Einstein was still a little draggy . . . well, he was certainly more energetic than he had been for a while and was sure to be himself by tomorrow or the day after, at the latest.

That night, Travis slept without dreaming.

In the morning, he was up before Nora. By the time he showered and dressed, she was up, too. On her way into the shower, she kissed him, nibbled on his lip, and mumbled sleepy vows of love. Her eyes were puffy, and her hair was mussed, and her breath was sour, but he would have rushed her straight back into bed if she had not said, "Try me this afternoon, Romeo. Right now, the only lust in my heart is for a couple of eggs, bacon, toast, and coffee."

He went downstairs and, starting in the living room, opened the interior shutters to let in the morning light. The sky looked as low and gray as it had been yesterday, and he would not be surprised if rain fell before twilight.

In the kitchen, he noticed that the pantry door was open, the light on. He looked in to see if Einstein was there, but the only sign of the dog was the message that he had spelled out sometime during the night.

FIDDLE BROKE. NO DOCTOR. PLEASE. DON'T WANT TO GO BACK TO LAB. AFRAID. AFRAID.

Oh shit. Oh Jesus.

Travis stepped out of the pantry and shouted, "*Einstein!*"

No bark. No sound of padding feet.

The shutters still covered the kitchen windows, and most of the room was not illuminated by the glow from the pantry. Travis snapped on the lights.

Einstein was not there.

He ran into the den. The dog was not there, either.

Heart pounding almost painfully, Travis climbed the stairs two at a time, looked in the third bedroom that would one day be a nursery and then in the room that Nora used as a studio, but Einstein was not in either place, and he was not in the master bedroom, not even under the bed where Travis was desperate enough to check, and for a moment he could not figure out where in the hell the dog had gone, and he stood listening to Nora singing in the shower—she was oblivious of what was happening—and he started into the bathroom to tell her that something was wrong, horribly wrong, which was when he thought of the downstairs bath, so he ran out of the bedroom and along the hall and descended the stairs so fast he almost lost his balance, almost fell, and in the first-floor bath, between the kitchen and the den, he found what he most feared to find.

The bathroom stank. The dog, ever considerate, had vomited in the toilet but had not possessed the strength—or perhaps the clarity of mind—to flush. Einstein was lying on the bathroom floor, on his side. Travis knelt next to him. Einstein was still but not dead, not dead, because he was breathing; he inhaled and exhaled with a rasping noise. He tried to lift his head when Travis spoke to him, but he did not have the strength to move.

His eyes. Jesus, his eyes.

Ever so gently, Travis lifted the retriever's head and saw that those wonderfully expressive brown eyes were slightly milky. A watery yellow discharge oozed from the eyes; it had crusted in the golden fur. A similar sticky discharge bubbled in Einstein's nostrils.

Putting a hand on the retriever's neck, Travis felt a laboring and irregular heartbeat.

"No," Travis said. "Oh, no, no. It's not going to be like this, boy. I'm not going to let it happen like this."

He lowered the retriever's head to the floor, got up, turned toward the door—and Einstein whimpered almost inaudibly, as if to say that he did not want to be left alone.

"I'll be right back, right back," Travis promised. "Just hold on, boy. I'll be right back."

He ran to the stairs and climbed faster than before. Now, his heart was beating with such tremendous force that he felt as if it would tear loose of him. He was breathing too fast, hyperventilating.

In the master bedroom, Nora was just stepping out of the shower, naked and dripping.

Travis's words ran together in panic: "Get dressed quick we've got to get to the vet now for god's sake hurry."

Shocked, she said, "What's happened?"

"Einstein! Hurry! I think he's dying."

He grabbed a blanket off the bed, left Nora to dress, and hurried downstairs to the bathroom. The retriever's ragged breathing seemed to have gotten worse in just the minute that Travis had been away. He folded the blanket twice, to a fourth of its size, then eased the dog onto it.

Einstein made a pained sound, as if the movement hurt him.

Travis said, "Easy, easy. You'll be all right."

At the door, Nora appeared, still buttoning her blouse, which was damp because she had not taken time to towel off before dressing. Her wet hair hung straight.

In a voice choked with emotion, she said, "Oh, fur face, no, no."

She wanted to stoop and touch the retriever, but there was no time to delay. Travis said, "Bring the pickup alongside the house."

While Nora sprinted to the barn, Travis folded the blanket around Einstein as best he could, so only the retriever's head, tail, and hind legs protruded. Trying unsuccessfully not to elicit another whimper of pain, Travis lifted the dog in his arms and carried him out of the bathroom, across the kitchen, out of the house, pulling the door shut behind him but leaving it unlocked, not giving a damn about security right now.

The air was cold. Yesterday's calm was gone. Evergreens swayed, shivered, and there was something ominous in the way their bristling, needled branches pawed at the air. Other leafless trees raised black, bony arms toward the somber sky.

In the barn, Nora started the pickup. The engine roared.

Travis cautiously descended the porch steps and went out to the driveway, walking as if he was carrying an armload of fragile antique china. The blustery wind stood Travis's hair straight up, flapped the loose ends of the blanket, and ruffled the fur on Einstein's exposed head, as if it were a wind with a malevolent consciousness, as if it wanted to tear the dog away from him.

Nora swung the pickup around, heading out, and stopped where Travis waited. She would drive.

It was true what they said: sometimes, in certain special moments of crisis, in times of great emotional tribulation, women are better than men often are. Sitting in the truck's passenger seat, cradling the blanket-wrapped dog in his arms, Travis was in no condition to drive. He was shaking badly, and he realized that he had been crying from the time he had found Einstein on the bathroom floor. He had seen difficult military service, and he had never panicked or been paralyzed with fear while on dangerous Delta Force operations, but this was different, this was Einstein, *this was his child*. If he had been required to drive, he'd probably have run straight into a tree, or off the road into a ditch. There were tears in Nora's eyes, too, but she didn't surrender to them. She bit her lip and drove as if she had been trained for stunt work in the movies. At the end of the dirt lane, they turned right, heading north on the twisty Pacific Coast Highway toward Carmel, where there was sure to be at least one veterinarian.

During the drive, Travis talked to Einstein, trying to soothe and encourage him. "Everything's going to be all right, just fine, it's not as bad as it seems, you'll be good as new."

Einstein whimpered and struggled weakly in Travis's arms for a moment, and Travis knew what the dog was thinking. He was afraid that the vet would see the tattoo in his ear, would know what it meant, and would send him back to Banodyne.

"Don't you worry about that, fur face. Nobody's going to take you away from us. By God, they aren't. They'll have to walk through me first, and they aren't going to be able to do that, no way."

"No way," Nora agreed grimly.

But in the blanket, cradled against Travis's chest, Einstein trembled violently.

Travis remembered the lettered tiles on the pantry floor: FIDDLE BROKE . . . AFRAID . . . AFRAID.

"Don't be afraid," he pleaded with the dog. "Don't be afraid. There's no reason to be afraid."

In spite of Travis's heartfelt assurances, Einstein shivered and was afraid—and Travis was afraid, too.

2

Stopping at an Arco service station on the outskirts of Carmel, Nora found the vet's address in a phone book and called him to be sure he was in. Dr. James Keene's office was on Dolores Avenue at the southern end of town. They pulled up in front of the place at a few minutes before nine.

Nora had been expecting a typically sterile-looking veterinary clinic and was surprised to find that Dr. Keene's offices were in his home, a quaint two-story Country English house of stone and plaster and exposed timbers with a roof that curved over the eaves.

As they hurried up the stone walk with Einstein, Dr. Keene opened the door before they reached it, as if he had been on the lookout for them. A sign indicated that the entrance to the surgery was around the side of the house, but the vet took them in at the front door. He was a tall, sorrowful-faced man with sallow skin and sad brown eyes, but his smile was warm, and his manner was gracious.

Closing the door, Dr. Keene said, "Bring him this way, please."

He led them swiftly along a hallway with an oak parquet floor protected by a long, narrow oriental carpet. On the left, through an archway, lay a pleasantly furnished living room that actually looked *lived*-in, with footstools in front of the chairs, reading lamps, laden bookshelves, and crocheted afghans folded neatly and conveniently over the backs of some chairs for when the evenings were chilly. A dog stood just inside the archway, a black labrador. It watched them solemnly, as if it understood the gravity of Einstein's condition, and it did not follow them.

At the rear of the large house, on the left side of the hall, the vet took them through a door into a clean white surgery. Lined along the walls were white-enameled and stainless-steel cabinets with glass fronts, which were filled with bottles of drugs, serums, tablets, capsules, and the many powdered ingredients needed to compound more exotic medicines.

Travis gently lowered Einstein onto an examination table and folded the blanket back from him.

Nora realized that she and Travis looked every bit as distraught as they would have if they'd been bringing a dying child to a doctor. Travis's eyes were red, and though he was not actively crying at the moment, he continually blew his nose. The moment she had parked the pickup in front of the house and had pulled on the hand brake, Nora had ceased to be able to repress her own tears. Now she stood on the other side of the examination table from Dr. Keene, with one arm around Travis, and she wept quietly.

The vet was apparently used to strong emotional reactions from pet owners, for he never once glanced curiously at Nora or Travis, never once indicated by any means that he found their anxiety and grief to be excessive.

Dr. Keene listened to the retriever's heart and lungs with a stethoscope, palpated his abdomen, examined his oozing eyes with an ophthalmoscope. Through those and several other procedures, Einstein remained limp, as if paralyzed. The only indications that the dog still clung to life were his faint whimpers and ragged breathing.

It's not as serious as it seems, Nora told herself as she blotted her eyes with a Kleenex.

Looking up from the dog, Dr. Keene said, "What's his name?"

"Einstein," Travis said.

"How long have you owned him?"

"Only a few months."

"Has he had his shots?"

"No," Travis said. "Damn it, no."

"Why not?"

"It's . . . complicated," Travis said. "But there're reasons that shots couldn't be gotten for him."

"No reason's good enough," Keene said disapprovingly. "He's got no license, no shots. It's very irresponsible not to see that your dog is properly licensed and vaccinated."

"I know," Travis said miserably. "I know."

"What's wrong with Einstein?" Nora said.

And she thought-hoped-prayed: It's not as serious as it seems.

Lightly stroking the retriever, Keene said, "He's got distemper."

Einstein had been moved to a corner of the surgery, where he lay on a thick, dog-size foam mattress that was protected by a zippered plastic coverlet. To prevent him from moving around—if at any time he had the strength to move—he was tethered on a short leash to a ringbolt in the wall.

Dr. Keene had given the retriever an injection. "Antibiotics," he explained. "No antibiotics are effective against distemper, but they're indicated to avoid secondary bacteriological infections."

He had also inserted a needle in one of the dog's leg veins and had hooked him to an IV drip to counteract dehydration.

When the vet tried to put a muzzle on Einstein, both Nora and Travis objected strenuously.

"It's not because I'm afraid he'll bite," Dr. Keene explained. "It's for his own protection, to prevent him from chewing at the needle. If he has the strength, he'll do what dogs always do to a wound—lick and bite at the source of the irritation."

"Not this dog," Travis said. "This dog's different." He pushed past Keene and removed the device that bound Einstein's jaws together.

The vet started to protest, then thought better of it. "All right. For now. He's too weak now, anyway."

Still trying to deny the awful truth, Nora said, "But how could it be so serious? He showed only the mildest symptoms, and even those went away over a couple of days."

"Half the dogs who get distemper never show any symptoms at all," the vet said as he returned a bottle of antibiotics to one of the glass-fronted cabinets and tossed a disposable syringe in a wastecan. "Others have only a mild illness, symptoms come and go from one day to the next. Some, like Einstein, get very ill. It can be a gradually worsening illness, or it can change suddenly from mild symptoms to . . . this. But there is a bright side here."

Travis was crouched beside Einstein, where the dog could see him without lifting his head or rolling his eyes, and could therefore feel attended, watched over, loved. When he heard Keene mention a bright side, Travis looked up eagerly. "What bright side? What do you mean?"

"The dog's condition, before it contracts distemper, frequently determines the course of the disease. The illness is most acute in animals that are ill-kept and poorly nourished. It's clear to me that Einstein was given good care."

Travis said, "We tried to feed him well, to make sure he got plenty of exercise."

"He was bathed and groomed almost *too* often," Nora added.

Smiling, nodding approval, Dr. Keene said, "Then we have an edge. We have real hope."

Nora looked at Travis, and he could meet her eyes only briefly before he had to look away, down at Einstein. It was left to her to ask the dreaded question: "Doctor, he's going to be all right, isn't he? He won't—he won't die, will he?"

Apparently, James Keene was aware that his naturally glum face and drooping eyes presented, merely in repose, an expression that did little to inspire confidence. He cultivated a warm smile, a soft yet confident tone of voice, and an almost grandfatherly manner that, although perhaps calculated, seemed genuine, and helped balance the perpetual gloom God had seen fit to visit upon his countenance.

He came to Nora, put his hands on her shoulders. "My dear, you love this dog like a baby, don't you?"

She bit her lip and nodded.

"Then have faith. Have faith in God, who watches over sparrows, so they say, and have a little faith in me, too. Believe it or not, I'm pretty good at what I do, and I deserve your faith."

"I believe you are good," she told him.

Still squatting beside Einstein, Travis said thickly, "But the chances. What're the chances? Tell us straight?"

Letting go of Nora, turning to Travis, Keene said, "Well, the discharge from his eyes and nose isn't as thick as it can get. Not nearly. No pus blisters on the abdomen. You say he's vomited, but you've seen no diarrhea?"

"No. Just vomiting," Travis said.

"His fever's high but not dangerously so. Has he been slobbering excessively?"

"No," Nora said.

"Fits of head-shaking and chewing on air, sort of as if he had a bad taste in his mouth?"

"No," Travis and Nora said simultaneously.

"Have you seen him run in circles or fall down without reason? Have you seen him lie on his side and kick violently as if he were running? Aimless wandering around a room, bumping into walls, jerking and twitching—anything like that?"

"No, no," Travis said.

And Nora said, "My God, could he *get* like that?"

"If he goes into second-stage distemper, yes," Keene said. "Then there's brain involvement. Epileptic-like seizures. Encephalitis."

Travis came to his feet in a sudden lurch. He staggered toward Keene, then stopped, swaying. His face was pale. His eyes filled with a terrible fear. "Brain involvement? If he recovered, would there be . . . brain damage?"

An oily nausea rippled in Nora. She thought of Einstein with brain damage—as intelligent as a man, intelligent enough to remember that he had once been special, and to know that something had been lost, and to know that he was now living in a dullness, a grayness, that his life was somehow less than what it had once been. Sick and dizzy with fear, she had to lean against the examination table.

Keene said, "Most dogs in second-stage distemper don't survive. But if he made it, there would, of course, be some brain damage. Nothing that would require he be put to sleep. He might have lifelong chorea, for instance, which is involuntary jerking or twitching, rather like palsy, and often limited to the head. But he could be relatively happy with that, lead a pain-free existence, and he could still be a fine pet."

Travis almost shouted at the vet: "To hell with whether he'd make a fine pet or not. I'm not concerned about *physical* effects of the brain damage. What about his *mind*?"

"Well, he'd recognize his masters," the doctor said. "He'd know you and remain affectionate toward you. No problem there. He might sleep a lot. He might have periods of listlessness. But he'd almost certainly remain housebroken. He wouldn't forget that training—"

Shaking, Travis said, "I don't give a damn if he pisses all over the house as long as he can still *think!*"

"Think?" Dr. Keene said, clearly perplexed. "Well . . . what do you mean exactly? He is a dog, after all."

The vet had accepted their anxious, grief-wracked behavior as within the parameters of normal pet-owner reactions in a case like this. But now, at last, he began to look at them strangely.

Partly to change the subject and dampen the vet's suspicion, partly because she simply had to know the answer, Nora said, "All right, but is Einstein *in* second-stage distemper?"

Keene said, "From what I've seen so far, he's still in the first stage. And now that treatment has begun, if we don't see any of the more violent symptoms during the next twenty-four hours, I think we have a good chance of keeping him in first stage and rolling it back."

"And there's no brain involvement in first stage?" Travis asked with an urgency that again caused Keene to furrow his brow.

"No. Not in first stage."

"And if he stays in first stage," Nora said, "he won't die?"

In his softest voice and most comforting manner, James Keene said, "Well, now, the chances are very high that he'd survive just first-stage distemper—and without any aftereffects. I want you to realize that his chances of recovery *are* quite high. But at the same time, I don't want to give you false hope. That'd be cruel. Even if the disease proceeds no further than first stage . . . Einstein could die. The percentages are on the side of life, but death is possible."

Nora was crying again. She thought she had gotten a grip on herself. She thought she was ready to be strong. But now she was crying. She went to Einstein, sat on the floor beside him, and put one hand on his shoulder, just to let him know that she was there.

Keene was becoming slightly impatient with—and thoroughly baffled by—their tumultuous emotional response to the bad news. A new note of sternness entered his voice as he said, "Listen, all we can do is give him top-flight care and hope for the best. He'll have to remain here, of course, because distemper treatment is complex and ought to be administered under veterinary supervision. I'll have to keep him on the intravenous fluids, antibiotics . . . and there'll be regular anticonvulsants and sedatives if he begins to have seizures."

Under Nora's hand, Einstein shivered as if he had heard and understood the grim possibilities.

"All right, okay, yes," Travis said, "obviously, he's got to stay here in your office. We'll stay with him."

"There's no need—" Keene began.

"Right, yes, no need," Travis said quickly, "but we want to stay, we'll be okay, we can sleep here on the floor tonight."

"Oh, I'm afraid that's not possible," Keene said.

"Yes, it is, oh yes, entirely possible," Travis said, babbling now in his eagerness to convince the vet. "Don't worry about us, Doctor. We'll manage just fine. Einstein needs us here, so we'll stay, the important thing is that we stay, and of course we'll pay you extra for the inconvenience."

"But I'm not running a hotel!"

"We must stay," Nora said firmly.

Keene said, "Now, really, I'm a reasonable man, but—"

With both hands, Travis seized the vet's right hand and held it tightly, startling Keene. "Listen, Dr. Keene, please, let me try to explain. I know this is an unusual request. I know we must sound like a couple of lunatics to you, but we've got our reasons, and they're good ones. This is no ordinary dog, Dr. Keene. He saved my life—"

"And he saved mine, too," Nora said. "In a separate incident."

"And he brought us together," Travis said. "Without Einstein, we would never have met, never married, and we'd both be dead."

Astonished, Keene looked from one to the other. "You mean he saved your lives—literally? And in two separate incidents?"

"Literally," Nora said.

"And then brought you together?"

"Yes," Travis said. "Changed our lives in more ways than we can count or ever explain."

Held fast in Travis's hands, the vet looked at Nora, lowered his kind eyes to the wheezing retriever, shook his head, and said, "I'm a sucker for heroic dog stories. I'll want to hear this one, for sure."

"We'll tell you all about it," Nora promised. But, she thought, it'll be a carefully edited version.

"When I was five years old," James Keene said, "I was saved from drowning by a black labrador."

Nora remembered the beautiful black lab in the living room and wondered if it was actually a descendant of the animal that had saved Keene—or just a reminder of the great debt he owed to dogs.

"All right," Keene said, "you can stay."

"Thank you," Travis's voice cracked. "Thank you."

Freeing his hand from Travis, Keene said, "but it'll be at least forty-eight hours before we can be at all confident that Einstein will survive. It'll be a long haul."

"Forty-eight hours is nothing," Travis said. "Two nights of sleeping on the floor. We can handle that."

Keene said, "I have a hunch that, for you two, forty-eight hours is going to be an eternity, under the circumstances." He looked at his wristwatch and said, "Now, my assistant will arrive in about ten minutes, and shortly after that we'll open the office for morning hours. I can't have you underfoot in here while I'm seeing other patients. And you wouldn't want to wait in the patient lounge with a bunch of other anxious owners and sick animals; that would only depress you. You can wait in the living room, and when the office is closed late this afternoon, you can return here to be with Einstein."

"Can we peek in on him during the day?" Travis asked.

Smiling, Keene said, "All right. But just a peek."

Under Nora's hand, Einstein finally stopped shivering. Some of the tension went out of him, and he relaxed, as if he had heard they would be allowed to remain close by, and was immensely comforted.

The morning passed at an agonizingly slow pace. Dr. Keene's living room had a television set, books, and magazines, but neither Nora nor Travis could get interested in TV or reading.

Every half hour or so, they slipped down the hall, one at a time, and peeked in at Einstein. He never seemed worse, but he never seemed any better, either.

Keene came in once and said, "By the way, feel free to use the bathroom. And there's cold drinks in the refrigerator. Make coffee if you want." He smiled down at the black lab at his side. "And this fella is Pooka. He'll love you to death if you give him a chance."

Pooka was, indeed, one of the friendliest dogs, Nora had ever seen. Without encouragement, he would roll over, play dead, sit up on his haunches, and then come snuffling around, tail wagging, to be rewarded with some petting and scratching.

All morning, Travis ignored the dog's pleas for affection, as if petting Pooka would in some way be a betrayal of Einstein and would insure Einstein's death of distemper.

However, Nora took comfort from the dog and gave it the attention it desired. She told herself that treating Pooka well would please the gods and that the gods would then look favorably upon Einstein. Her desperation produced in her a superstition just as fierce as—if different from—that which gripped her husband.

Travis paced. He sat on the edge of a chair, head bowed, his face in his hands. For long periods, he stood at one of the windows, staring out, not seeing the street that lay out there but some dark vision of his own. He blamed himself for what had happened, and the truth of the situation (which Nora recalled for him) did nothing to lessen his irrational sense of guilt.

Facing a window, hugging himself as if he were cold, Travis said quietly, "Do you think Keene saw the tattoo?"

"I don't know. Maybe not."

"Do you think there's really been a description of Einstein circulated to vets? Will Keene know what the tattoo means?"

"Maybe not," she said. "Maybe we're too paranoid about this."

But after hearing from Garrison and learning of the lengths to which the government had gone to prevent him from getting a warning to them, they knew that an enormous and urgent search for the dog must be still under way. So there was no such thing as being "too paranoid."

From noon until two, Dr. Keene closed the office for lunch. He invited Nora and Travis to eat with him in the big kitchen. He was a bachelor who knew how to take care of himself, and he had a freezer stocked with frozen entrées that he had prepared and packaged himself. He defrosted individually wrapped slabs of homemade lasagna and, with their help, made three salads. The food was good, but neither Nora nor Travis was able to eat much of it.

The more Nora knew of James Keene, the more she liked him. He was lighthearted in spite of his morose appearance, and his sense of humor ran toward self-deprecation. His love of animals was a light within that gave him a special glow. Dogs were his greatest love, and when he spoke of them his enthusiasm transformed his homely features and made of him a handsomer and quite appealing man.

The doctor told them of the black lab, King, that had saved him from drowning when he was a child, and he encouraged them to tell him how Einstein saved their lives. Travis recounted a colorful story about going hiking and almost walking into an injured and angry bear. He described how Einstein warned him off and then, when the half-mad bear gave chase, how Einstein challenged and repeatedly foiled the beast. Nora was able to tell a story closer to the truth: harassment by a sexual psychopath whose attack had been interrupted by Einstein and who had been held by the retriever until the police arrived.

Keene was impressed. "He really is a hero!"

Nora sensed that the stories about Einstein had so completely won the vet over that, if he *did* spot the tattoo and knew what it meant, he might conceivably put it out of his mind and might let them go in peace once Einstein was recovered. *If* Einstein recovered.

But as they were gathering up the dishes, Keene said, "Sam, I've been wondering why your wife calls you 'Travis.'"

They were prepared for this. Since assuming new identities, they had decided that it was easier and safer for Nora to continue calling him Travis, rather than trying to use Sam all the time and then, at some crucial moment, slipping up. They could claim that Travis was a nickname she'd given him, that the origin was a private joke; with winks at each other and foolish grins, they could imply there was something sexual about it, something much too embarrassing to explain further. That was how they handled Keene's question, but they were in no mood to wink and grin foolishly with any conviction, so Nora was not sure they carried it off. In fact she thought their nervous and inept performance might increase Keene's suspicions if he had any.

Just before afternoon office hours were to begin, Keene received a call from his assistant, who'd had a headache when she had gone to lunch, and who now reported that the headache had been complicated by an upset stomach. The vet was left to handle his patients alone, so Travis quickly volunteered his and Nora's services.

"We've got no veterinary training, of course. But we can handle any manual labor involved."

"Sure," Nora agreed, "and between us we've got one pretty good brain. We could do just about anything else you showed us how to do."

They spent the afternoon restraining recalcitrant cats and dogs and parrots and all sorts of other animals while Jim Keene treated them. There were bandages to be laid out, medicines to be retrieved from the cabinets, instruments to be washed and sterilized, fees to be collected and receipts written. Some pets, afflicted with vomiting and diarrhea, left messes to be cleaned up, but Travis and Nora tended to those unpleasantnesses as uncomplainingly and unhesitatingly as they performed other tasks.

They had two motives, the first of which was that, by assisting Keene, they had a chance to be in the surgery with Einstein throughout the afternoon. Between chores, they stole a few moments to pet the retriever, speak a few encouraging words to him, and reassure themselves that he was getting no worse. The downside of being around Einstein continuously was that they could see, to their dismay, that he did not seem to be getting any *better*, either.

Their other purpose was to further ingratiate themselves with the vet, to give him a reason to be beholden to them, so he would not reconsider his decision to allow them to stay the night.

The patient load was far greater than usual, Keene said, and they were not able to close the office until after six o'clock. Weariness—and the labor they shared—generated a warm feeling of camaraderie. As they made and ate dinner together, Jim Keene entertained them with a treasure of amusing animal stories culled from his experiences, and they were almost as comfortable and friendly as they would have been if they had known the vet for months instead of less than one day.

Keene prepared the guest bedroom for them, and provided a few blankets with which to make a crude bed on the floor of the surgery. Travis and Nora would sleep in the real bed in shifts, each spending half the night on the floor with Einstein.

Travis had the first shift, from ten o'clock until three in the morning. Only one light was left on in the far corner of the surgery, and Travis alternately sat and stretched out on the piled blankets in the shadows where Einstein lay.

Sometimes, Einstein slept, and the sound of his breathing was more normal, less frightening. But sometimes he was awake, and his respiration was horribly labored, and he whimpered in pain and—Travis somehow knew—in fear. When Einstein was awake, Travis talked to him, reminiscing about experiences they had shared, the many good moments and happy times over the past six months, and the retriever seemed to be at least slightly soothed by Travis's voice.

Unable to move at all, the dog was of necessity incontinent. A couple of times he peed on the plastic-covered mattress. With no distaste whatsoever, with the same tenderness and compassion a father might show in caring for a gravely ill child, Travis cleaned up. In a curious way, Travis was even pleased by the mess because, every time Einstein peed, it was proof that he still lived, still functioned in some ways, as normally as ever.

Rainsqualls came and went during the night. The sound of rain on the roof was mournful, like funeral drums.

Twice during the first shift, Jim Keene appeared in pajamas and a robe. The first time, he examined Einstein carefully and changed his IV bottle. Later, he administered an injection after the examination. On both occasions, he assured Travis that right now they did not have to see signs of improvement to be encouraged; right now, it was good enough that there were no indications of deterioration in the dog's condition.

Frequently during the night, Travis wandered to the other end of the surgery and read the words of a simply framed scroll that hung above the scrub sink:

TRIBUTE TO A DOG

The one absolutely unselfish friend that man can have in this selfish world, the one that never deserts him, the one that never proves ungrateful or treacherous, is his dog. A man's dog stands by him in prosperity and in poverty, in health and in sickness. He will sleep on the cold ground, where the wintry winds blow and the snow drives fiercely, if only he may be near his master's side. He will kiss the hand that has no food to offer; he will lick the wounds and sores that come in encounter with the roughness of the world. He guards the sleep of his pauper master as if he were a prince. When all other friends desert, he remains. When riches take wing and reputation falls to pieces, he is as constant in his love as the sun in its journey through the heavens.

—Senator George Vest, 1870

Each time he read the tribute, Travis was filled anew with wonder at Einstein's existence. What fantasy of children was more common than that their dogs were fully as perceptive and wise and clever as any adult? What gift from God would more delight a young mind than to have the family dog prove able to communicate on a human level and to share triumphs and tragedies with full understanding of their meaning and importance? What miracle could bring more joy, more respect for the mysteries of nature, more sheer exuberance over the unanticipated wonders of life? Somehow, in the very idea of a dog's personality *and* human intelligence combined in a single creature, one had a hope of a species at once as gifted as humankind but more noble and worthy. And what fantasy of adults was more common than that, one day, another intelligent species would be found to share the vast, cold universe and, by sharing it, would at last provide some relief from our race's unspeakable loneliness and sense of quiet desperation?

And what other loss could be more devastating than the loss of Einstein, this first hopeful evidence that humankind carried within it the seeds not merely of greatness but of godhood?

These thoughts, which Travis could not suppress, shook him and drew from him a thick sob of grief. Damning himself for being an emotional basket case, he went into the downstairs hall, where Einstein would not be aware of—and perhaps be frightened by—his tears.

* * *

Nora relieved him at three in the morning. She had to insist that he go upstairs, for he was reluctant to leave Keene's surgery.

Exhausted but protesting that he would not sleep, Travis tumbled into bed and slept.

He dreamed of being pursued by a yellow-eyed thing with wicked talons and foreshortened alligator jaws. He was trying to protect Einstein and Nora, pushing them in front of him, encouraging them to run, run, run. But somehow the monster got around Travis and tore Einstein to pieces, then savaged Nora—it was the Cornell Curse, which could not be avoided by a simple change of name to Samuel Hyatt—and at last Travis stopped running and fell to his knees and lowered his head because, having failed Nora and the dog, he wanted to die, and he heard the thing approaching—*click-click-click—and he was afraid but he also welcomed the death that it promised*—

Nora woke him shortly before five in the morning. "Einstein," she said urgently. "He's having convulsions."

When Nora led Travis into the white-walled surgery, Jim Keene was crouched over Einstein, ministering to him. They could do nothing but stay out of the vet's way, give him room to work.

She and Travis held each other.

After a few minutes, the vet stood up. He looked worried, and he did not make his usual effort to smile or try to lift their hopes. "I've given him additional anticonvulsants. I think . . . he'll be all right now."

"Has he gone into the second stage?" Travis asked.

"Maybe not," Keene said.

"Could he be having convulsions and still be in first stage?"

"It's possible," Keene said.

"But not likely."

"Not likely," Keene said. "But . . . not impossible."

Second-stage distemper, Nora thought miserably.

She held Travis tighter than ever.

Second stage. Brain involvement. Encephalitis. Chorea. Brain damage. *Brain damage.*

Travis would not return to bed. He remained in the surgery with Nora and Einstein the rest of the night.

They turned on another light, brightening the room somewhat but not enough to bother Einstein, and they watched him closely for signs that the distemper had progressed to the second stage: the jerking and twitching and chewing movements of which Jim Keene had spoken.

Travis was unable to extract any hope from the fact that no such symptoms were exhibited. Even if Einstein was in the first stage of the disease and remained there, he appeared to be dying.

The next day, Friday, December 3, Jim Keene's assistant was still too sick to come to work, so Nora and Travis helped out again.

By lunchtime, Einstein's fever had not fallen. His eyes and nose continued to ooze a clear though yellowish fluid. His breathing was slightly less labored, but in her despair Nora wondered if the dog's respiration only sounded easier because he was not making as great an effort to breathe and was, in fact, beginning to give up.

She could not eat even a bite of lunch. She washed and ironed both Travis's clothes and her own, while they sat around in two of Jim Keene's spare bathrobes, which were too big for them.

That afternoon, the office was busy again. Nora and Travis were kept in constant motion, and Nora was glad to be overworked.

At four-thirty, a time that she would never forget for as long as she lived, just after they finished helping Jim deal with a difficult Irish setter, Einstein yipped twice from his bed in the corner. Nora and Travis turned, both gasping, both expecting the worst, for this was the first sound other than whimpers that Einstein had made since his arrival at the surgery. But the retriever had lifted his head—the first time he'd had the strength to lift it—and was blinking at them; he looked around curiously, as if to ask where on earth he was.

Jim knelt beside the dog and, while Travis and Nora crouched expectantly behind him, he thoroughly examined Einstein. "Look at his eyes. They're slightly milky but not at all like they were, and they've stopped actively leaking." With a damp cloth, he cleaned the crusted fur beneath Einstein's eyes and wiped off his nose; the nostrils no longer bubbled with fresh excretions. With a rectal thermometer he took Einstein's temperature and, reading it, said, "Falling. Down two full degrees."

"Thank God," Travis said.

And Nora discovered that her eyes were filling with tears again.

Jim said, "He's not out of the woods yet. His heartbeat is more regular, less accelerated, though still not good. Nora, get one of those dishes over there and fill it with some water."

Nora returned from the sink a moment later and put the dish down on the floor, at the vet's side.

Jim pushed it close to Einstein. "What do you think, fella?"

Einstein raised his head off the mattress again and stared at the dish. His lolling tongue looked dry and was coated with a gummy substance. He whined and licked his chops.

"Maybe," Travis said, "if we help him—"

"No," Jim Keene said. "Let him consider it. He'll know if he feels up to it. We don't want to force water that's going to make him vomit again. He'll know by instinct if the time is right."

With some groaning and wheezing, Einstein shifted on the foam mattress, rolling off his side, half onto his belly. He put his nose to the dish, sniffed the water, put his tongue to it tentatively, liked the first taste, had another, and drank a third of it before sighing and lying down again.

Stroking the retriever, Jim Keene said, "I'd be very surprised if he doesn't recover, fully recover, in time."

In time.

That phrase bothered Travis.

How much time would Einstein require for a full recovery? When The Outsider finally arrived, they would all be better off if Einstein was healthy and if all of his senses were functioning sharply. The infrared alarms notwithstanding, Einstein was their primary early-warming system.

After the last patient left at five-thirty, Jim Keene slipped out for half an hour on a mysterious errand, and when he returned he had a bottle of champagne. "I'm not much of a drinking man, but certain occasions demand a nip or two."

Nora had pledged to drink nothing during her pregnancy, but even the most solemn pledge could be stretched under these circumstances.

They got glasses and drank in the surgery, toasting Einstein, who watched them for a few minutes but, exhausted, soon fell asleep.

"But a natural sleep," Jim noted. "Not induced with sedatives."

Travis said, "How long will he need to recover?"

"To shake off distemper—a few more days, a week. I'd like to keep him here two more days, anyway. You could go home now, if you want, but you're also welcome to stay. You've been quite a help."

"We'll stay," Nora said at once.

"But after the distemper is beaten," Travis said, "he's going to be weak, isn't he?"

"At first, very weak," Jim said. "But gradually he'll get most if not all of his old strength back. I'm sure now that he never went into second-stage distemper, in spite of the convulsions. So perhaps by the first of the year he'll be his old self, and there should be no lasting infirmities, no palsied shaking or anything like that."

The first of the year.

Travis hoped that would be soon enough.

Again, Nora and Travis split the night into two shifts. Travis took the first watch, and she relieved him in the surgery at three o'clock in the morning.

Fog had seethed into Carmel. It roiled at the windows, softly insistent.

Einstein was sleeping when Nora arrived, and she said, "Has he been awake much?"

"Yeah," Travis said. "Now and then."

"Have you . . . talked to him?"

"Yeah."

"Well?"

Travis's face was lined, haggard, and his expression was grave. "I've asked him questions that can be answered with a yes or no."

"And?"

"He doesn't answer them. He just blinks at me, or yawns, or he goes back to sleep."

"He's very tired yet," she said, desperately hoping that was the explanation for the retriever's uncommunicative behavior. "He doesn't have the strength even for questions and answers."

Pale and obviously depressed, Travis said, "Maybe. I don't know . . . but I think . . . he seems . . . confused."

"He hasn't shaken the disease yet," she said. "He's still in the grip of it, beating the damn stuff, but still in its grip. He's bound to be a little muddle-headed for a while yet."

"Confused," Travis repeated.

"It'll pass."

"Yeah," he said. "Yeah, it'll pass."

But he sounded as if he believed that Einstein would never be the same again.

Nora knew what Travis must be thinking: it was the Cornell Curse again, which he professed not to believe in but which he still feared in his heart of hearts. Everyone he loved was doomed to suffer and die young. Everyone he cared about was torn from him.

That was all nonsense, of course, and Nora did not believe in it for a moment. But she knew how hard it was to shake off the past, to face only toward the future, and she sympathized with his inability to be optimistic just now. She also knew there was nothing she could do for him to haul him out of that pit of private anguish—nothing except kiss him, hold him for a moment, then send him off to bed to get some sleep.

When Travis was gone, Nora sat on the floor beside Einstein and said, "There're some things I have to tell you, fur face. I guess you're asleep and can't hear me, and maybe even if you were awake you wouldn't understand what I'm saying. Maybe you'll never again understand, which is why I want to say these things now, while there's at least still *hope* that your mind's intact."

She paused and took a deep breath and looked around at the still surgery, where the dim lights gleamed in the stainless-steel fixtures and in the glass of the enameled cabinets. It was a lonely place at three-thirty in the morning.

Einstein's breath came and went with a soft hiss, an occasional rattle. He didn't stir. Not even his tail moved.

"I thought of you as my guardian, Einstein. That's what I called you once, when you saved me from Arthur Streck. My guardian. You not only rescued me from that awful man—you also saved me from loneliness and terrible despair. And you saved Travis from the darkness within him, brought us together, and in a hundred other ways you were as perfect as any guardian angel might hope to be. In that good, pure heart of yours, you never asked for or wanted anything in return for all you did. Some Milk-Bones once in a while, a bit of chocolate now and then. But you'd have done it all even if you'd been fed nothing but Dog Chow. You did it because you love, and being loved in return was reward enough. And by just being what you are, fur face, you taught me a great lesson, a lesson I can't easily put into words . . ."

For a while, silent and unable to speak, she sat in the shadows beside her friend, her child, her teacher, her guardian.

"But damn it," she said at last, "I've got to find words because maybe this is the last time I can even pretend you're able to understand them. It's like this . . . you taught me that I'm *your* guardian, too, that I'm Travis's guardian, and that he is my guardian and yours. We have a responsibility to stand watch over one another, we are watchers, all of us, watchers, guarding against the darkness. You've taught me that we're all needed, even those who sometimes think we're worthless, plain, and dull. If we love and allow ourselves to be loved . . . well, a person who loves is the most precious thing in the world, worth all the fortunes that ever were. That's what you've taught me, fur face, and because of you I'll never be the same."

The rest of the long night, Einstein lay motionless, lost in a deep sleep.

Saturday, Jim Keene kept hours only in the morning. At noon he locked the office entrance at the side of his big, cozy house.

During the morning, Einstein had exhibited encouraging signs of recovery. He drank more water and spent some time on his belly instead of lying limply on his side. Head raised, he looked around with interest at the activity in the vet's surgery. He even slurped up a raw-egg-and-gravy mixture that Jim put in front of him, downing half the contents of the dish, and he did not regurgitate what he had eaten. He was now entirely off intravenous fluids.

But he still dozed a lot. And his responses to Travis and Nora were only those of an ordinary dog.

After lunch, as they were sitting with Jim at the kitchen table, having a final cup of coffee, the vet sighed and said, "Well, I don't see how this can be put off any longer." From an inner pocket of his old, well-worn corduroy jacket, he withdrew a folded sheet of paper and put it on the table in front of Travis.

For a moment, Nora thought it was the bill for his services. But when Travis unfolded the paper, she saw that it was a wanted flyer put out by the people looking for Einstein.

Travis's shoulders sagged.

Feeling as if her heart had begun to sink down through her body, Nora moved closer to Travis so they could read the bulletin together. It was dated last week. In addition to a description of Einstein that included the three-number tattoo in his ear, the flyer stated the dog would most likely be found in the possession of a man named Travis Cornell and his wife, Nora, who might be living under different names. Description—and photographs—of Nora and Travis were at the bottom of the sheet.

"How long have you known?" Travis asked.

Jim Keene said, "Within an hour after I first saw him, Thursday morning. I've been getting weekly updates of that bulletin for six months—and I've had three follow-up calls from the Federal Cancer Institute to make sure I'll remember to examine any golden retriever for a lab tattoo and report it at once."

"And have you reported him?" Nora asked.

"Not yet. Didn't seem any point arguing about it until we saw whether he was going to pull through."

Travis said, "Will you report him now?"

His hound-dog face settling into an expression that was even more glum than usual, Jim Keene said, "According to the Cancer Institute, this dog was at the very center of extremely important experiments that might lead to a cancer cure. Says there that millions of dollars of research money will have been spent for nothing if the dog isn't found and returned to the lab to complete their studies."

"It's all lies," Travis said.

"Let me make one thing very clear to you," Jim said, leaning forward in his chair and folding his large hands around his coffee cup. "I'm an animal lover to the bone. I've dedicated my life to animals. And I love dogs more than anything else. But I'm afraid I don't have a lot of sympathy for people who believe that we should stop all animal experimentation, people who think medical advancements that help save human lives are not worth harming one guinea pig, one cat, one dog. People who raid labs and steal animals, ruining years of important research . . . they make me want to spit. It's good and right to love life, to dearly love it in all its most humble forms. But these people don't love life—they *revere* it, which is a pagan and ignorant and perhaps even savage attitude."

"This isn't like that," Nora said. "Einstein was never used in cancer research. That's just a cover story. The Cancer Institute isn't hunting for Einstein. It's the National Security Agency that wants him." She looked at Travis and said, "Well, what do we do now?"

Travis smiled grimly, and said, "Well, I sure can't kill Jim here to stop him—"

The vet looked startled.

"—so I guess we've got to persuade him," Travis finished.

"The truth?" Nora asked.

Travis stared at Jim Keene for a long time, and at last said, "Yeah. The truth. It's the only thing that might convince him to throw that damn wanted poster in the trash."

Taking a deep breath, Nora said, "Jim, Einstein is as smart as you or me or Travis."

"Smarter, I sometimes think," Travis said.

The vet stared at them, uncomprehending.

"Let's make another pot of coffee," Nora said. "This is going to be a long, long afternoon."

* * *

Hours later, at ten minutes past five, Saturday afternoon, Nora and Travis and Jim Keene crowded in front of the mattress on which Einstein lay.

The dog had just taken a few more ounces of water. He looked at them with interest, too.

Travis tried to decide if those large brown eyes still had the strange depth, uncanny alertness, and undoglike awareness that he had seen in them so many times before. Damn. He was not sure—and his uncertainty scared him.

Jim examined Einstein, noting aloud that his eyes were clearer, almost normal, and that his temperature was still falling. "Heart's sounding a little better, too."

Worn out by the ten-minute examination, Einstein flopped onto his side and issued a long weary sigh. In a moment, he dozed again.

The vet said, "He sure doesn't seem much like a genius dog."

"He's still sick," Nora said. "All he needs is a little more time to recover, and he'll be able to show you that everything we've said is true."

"When do you think he'll be on his feet?" Travis asked.

Jim thought about that, then said. "Maybe tomorrow. He'll be very shaky at first, but maybe tomorrow. We'll just have to see."

"When he's on his feet," Travis said, "when he's got his sense of balance back and is interested in moving around, that ought to indicate he's clearer in his head, too. So when he's up and about—that's when we'll give him a test to prove to you how smart he is."

"Fair enough," Jim said.

"And if he proves it," Nora said, "you'll not turn him in?"

"Turn him in to people who'd create this Outsider you've told me about? Turn him in to the liars who cooked up that baloney wanted flyer? Nora, what sort of man do you take me for?"

Nora said, "A good man."

Twenty-four hours later, on Sunday evening, in Jim Keene's surgery, Einstein was tottering around as if he were a little old four-legged man.

Nora scooted along the floor on her knees beside him telling him what a fine and brave fellow he was, quietly encouraging him to keep going. Every step he took thrilled her as if he were her own baby learning to walk. But what thrilled her more was the look he gave her a few times: it was a look that seemed to express chagrin at his infirmity, but there was also a sense of humor in it, as if he were saying, *Hey, Nora, am I a spectacle—or what? Isn't this just plain ridiculous?*

Saturday night he had eaten a little solid food, and all day Sunday he had nibbled at easily digestible vittles that the vet provided. He was drinking well, and the most encouraging sign of improvement was his insistence on going outside to make his toilet. He could not stay on his feet for long periods of time, and once in a while he wobbled and plopped backward on his butt; however, he did not bump into walls or walk in circles.

Yesterday, Nora had gone shopping and had returned with three Scrabble games. Now, Travis had separated the lettered tiles into twenty-six piles at one end of surgery, where there was a lot of open floor space.

"We're ready," Jim Keene said. He was sitting on the floor with Travis, his legs drawn up under him Indian-style.

Pooka was lying at his master's side, watching with baffled dark eyes.

Nora led Einstein back across the room to the Scrabble tiles. Taking his head in her hands, looking straight into his eyes, she said, "Okay, fur face.

Let's prove to Dr. Jim that you're not just some pathetic lab animal involved in cancer tests. Let's show him what you *really* are and prove to him what those nasty people really want you for."

She tried to believe that she saw the old awareness in the retriever's dark gaze.

With evident nervousness and fear, Travis said, "Who asks the first question?"

"I will," Nora said unhesitatingly. To Einstein, she said, "How's the fiddle?"

They had told Jim Keene about the message that Travis had found the morning Einstein had been so very ill—FIDDLE BROKE—so the vet understood what Nora was asking.

Einstein blinked at her, then looked at the letters, blinked at her again, sniffed the letters, and she was getting a sick feeling in her stomach when, suddenly, he began to choose tiles and push them around with his nose.

FIDDLE JUST OUT OF TUNE.

Travis shuddered as if the dread he had contained was a powerful electric charge that had leapt out of him in an instant. He said, "Thank God, thank you, God," and he laughed with delight.

"Holy shit," Jim Keene said.

Pooka raised his head very high and pricked his ears, aware that something important was happening but not sure what it was.

Her heart swelling with relief and excitement and love, Nora returned the letters to their separate piles and said, "Einstein, who is your master? Tell us his name."

The retriever looked at her, at Travis, then made a considered reply.

NO MASTER. FRIENDS.

Travis laughed. "By God, I'll settle for that! No one can be his master, but anyone should be damned proud to be his friend."

Funny—this proof of Einstein's undamaged intellect made Travis laugh with delight, the first laughter of which he had been capable in days, but it made Nora weep with relief.

Jim Keene looked on in wide-eyed wonder, grinning stupidly. He said, "I feel like a child who's sneaked downstairs on Christmas Eve and actually seen the real Santa Claus putting gifts under the tree."

"My turn," Travis said, sliding forward and putting a hand on Einstein's head, patting him. "Jim just mentioned Christmas, and it's not far away. Twenty days from now. So tell me, Einstein, what would you most like to have Santa bring you?"

Twice, Einstein started to line up the lettered tiles, but both times he had second thoughts and disarranged them. He tottered and thumped down on his butt, looked around sheepishly, saw that they were all expectant, got up again, and this time produced a three-word request for Santa.

MICKEY MOUSE VIDEOS.

They didn't get to bed until two in the morning because Jim Keene was intoxicated, not drunk from beer or wine or whiskey but from sheer joy over Einstein's intelligence. "Like a man's, yes, but still the dog, still the dog, wonderfully like, yet wonderfully different from, a man's thinking, based on what little I've seen." But Jim did not press for more than a dozen examples of the dog's wit, and he was the first to say that they must not tire their patient. Still, he was electrified, so excited he could barely contain himself. Travis would not have been too surprised if the vet had suddenly just exploded.

In the kitchen, Jim pleaded with them to retell stories about Einstein: the

Modern Bride business in Solvang; the way he had taken it upon himself to add cold water to the first hot bath that Travis had given him; and many more. Jim actually retold some of the same stories himself, almost as if Travis and Nora had never heard them, but they were happy to indulge him.

With a flourish, he snatched the wanted flyer off the table, struck a kitchen match, and burned the sheet in the sink. He washed the ashes down the drain. "To hell with the small minds who'd keep a creature like that locked up to be poked and prodded and studied. They might've had the genius to make Einstein, but they don't understand the meaning of what they themselves have done. They don't understand the greatness of it, because if they did they wouldn't want to cage him."

At last, when Jim Keene reluctantly agreed that they were all in need of sleep, Travis carried Einstein (already sleeping) up to the guest room. They made a blanket-cushioned place for him on the floor next to the bed.

In the dark, under the covers, with Einstein's soft snoring to comfort them, Travis and Nora held each other.

She said, "Everything's going to be all right now."

"There's still some trouble coming," he said. He felt as if Einstein's recovery had weakened the curse of untimely death that had followed him all of his life. But he was not ready to hope that the curse had been banished altogether. The Outsider was still out there somewhere . . . coming.

CHAPTER 10

━━━

1

ON TUESDAY AFTERNOON, December 7, when they took Einstein home, Jim Keene was reluctant to let them go. He followed them out to the pickup and stood at the driver's window, restating the treatment that must be continued for the next couple of weeks, reminding them that he wanted to see Einstein once a week for the rest of the month, and urging them to visit him not only for the dog's medical care but for drinks, dinner, conversation.

Travis knew the vet was trying to say he wanted to remain a part of Einstein's life, wanted to participate in the magic of it. "Jim, believe me, we'll be back. And before Christmas, you'll have to come out to our place, spend the day with us."

"I'd like that."

"So would we," Travis said sincerely.

On the drive home, Nora held Einstein in her lap, wrapped in a blanket once more. He still did not have his old appetite, and he was weak. His immune system had taken severe punishment, so he would be more than usually susceptible to illness for a while. He was to be kept in the house as much as possible and pampered until he had regained his previous vigor—probably after the first of the year, according to Jim Keene.

The bruised and swollen sky bulged with saturated dark clouds. The Pacific Ocean was so hard and gray that it did not appear to be water but looked more like billions of shards and slabs of slate being continuously agitated by some geological upheaval in the earth below.

The bleak weather could not dampen their high spirits.

Nora was beaming, and Travis found himself whistling. Einstein studied the scenery with great interest, clearly treasuring even the somber beauty of this nearly colorless winter day. Perhaps he had never expected to see the world outside Jim Keene's office again, in which case even a sea of jumbled stone and contusive sky were precious sights.

When they reached home, Travis left Nora in the pickup with the retriever and entered the house alone, by the back door, carrying the .38 pistol they kept in the truck. In the kitchen, where the lights had been on ever since their hasty departure last week, he immediately took an Uzi automatic pistol from its hiding place in a cabinet, and put the lighter gun aside. He proceeded cautiously from room to room, looking behind every large item of furniture and in every closet.

He saw no signs of burglary, and he expected none. This rural area was relatively crime-free. You could leave your door unlocked for days at a time without risking thieves who would take everything down to the wallpaper.

The Outsider, not a burglar, worried him.

The house was deserted.

Travis checked the barn, too, before driving the pickup inside, but it was also safe.

In the house, Nora put Einstein down and pulled the blanket off him. He tottered around the kitchen, sniffing at things. In the living room he looked at the cold fireplace and inspected his page-turning machine.

He returned to the kitchen pantry, clicked on the light with his foot pedal, and pawed letters out of the Lucite tubes.

HOME.

Stooping beside the dog, Travis said, "It's sure good to be here, isn't it?"

Einstein nuzzled Travis's throat and licked his neck. The golden coat was fluffy and smelled clean because Jim Keene had given the dog a bath, in his surgery, under carefully controlled conditions. But as fluffy and fresh as he was, Einstein still did not look himself; he seemed tired, and he was thinner, too, having lost a few pounds in less than a week.

Pawing out more letters, Einstein spelled the same word again, as if to emphasize his pleasure: HOME.

Standing at the pantry door, Nora said, "Home is where the heart is, and there's plenty of heart in this one. Hey, let's have an early dinner and eat it in the living room while we run the videotape of *Mickey's Christmas Carol*. Would you like that?"

Einstein wagged his tail vigorously.

Travis said, "Do you think you could handle your favorite food—a few weenies for dinner?"

Einstein licked his chops. He dispensed more letters, with which he expressed his enthusiastic approval of Travis's suggestion.

HOME IS WHERE THE WEENIES ARE.

When Travis woke in the middle of the night, Einstein was at the bedroom window, on his hind feet with his forepaws braced on the sill. He was barely visible in the second-hand glow of the night-light in the adjoining bathroom. The interior shutter was bolted over the window, so the dog had no view of the front yard. But perhaps, for getting a fix on The Outsider, sight was the sense on which he least depended.

"Something out there, boy?" Travis asked quietly, not wanting to wake Nora unnecessarily.

Einstein dropped from the window, padded to Travis's side of the bed, and put his head up on the mattress.

Petting the dog, Travis whispered, "Is it coming?"

Replying with only a cryptic mewl, Einstein settled down on the floor beside the bed and went to sleep again.

In a few minutes, Travis slept, too.

He woke again near dawn to find Nora sitting on the edge of the bed, petting Einstein. "Go back to sleep," she told Travis.

"What's wrong?"

"Nothing," she whispered drowsily. "I woke up and saw him at the window, but it's nothing. Go to sleep."

He did manage to fall asleep a third time, but he dreamed that The Outsider had been smart enough to learn how to use tools during its six-month-long pursuit of Einstein and now, yellow eyes gleaming, it was smashing its way though the bedroom shutters with an ax.

2

They gave Einstein his medicines on schedule, and he swallowed his pills obediently. They explained to him that he needed to eat well in order to regain his strength. He tried, but his appetite was returning only slowly. He would need a few weeks to regain the pounds he had lost and to recover his old vitality. But day by day his improvement was perceptible.

By Friday, December 10, Einstein seemed strong enough to risk a short walk outside. He still wobbled a little now and then, but he no longer tottered with every step. He'd had all of his shots at the veterinary clinic; there was no chance of picking up rabies on top of the distemper he'd just beaten.

The weather was milder than it had been in recent weeks, with temperatures in the low sixties and no wind. The scattered clouds were white, and the sun, when not hidden, laid a warm life-giving caress on the skin.

Einstein accompanied Travis on an inspection tour of the infrared sensors around the house and the nitrous-oxide tanks in the barn. They moved a bit more slowly than the last time they had walked this line together but Einstein seemed to enjoy being back on duty.

Nora was in her studio, working diligently on a new painting: a portrait of Einstein. He was not aware that he was the subject of her latest canvas. The picture was to be one of his Christmas gifts and would, once opened on the holiday, be hung above the fireplace in the living room.

When Travis and Einstein came out of the barn, into the yard, he said, "Is it getting closer?"

Upon being asked that question, Einstein went through his usual routine, though with less exertion, less sniffing of the air, and less study of the shadowy forest around them. Returning to Travis, the dog whined anxiously.

"Is it out there?" Travis asked.

Einstein gave no answer. He merely surveyed the woods again—puzzled.

"Is it still coming?" Travis asked.

The dog did not reply.

"Is it nearer than it was?"

Einstein padded a circle, sniffed the ground, sniffed the air, cocked his head one way and then the other. Finally he returned to the house and stood at the door, looking at Travis, waiting patiently.

Inside, Einstein went directly to the pantry.

MUZZY.

Travis stared at the word on the floor. "Muzzy?"

Einstein dispensed more letters and nosed them into place.

MUFFLED. FUZZY.

"Are you talking about your ability to sense The Outsider?"

A quick tail wag: *Yes.*

"You can't sense it any more?"

One bark: *No.*

"Do you think . . . it's dead?"

DON'T KNOW.

"Or maybe this sixth sense of yours doesn't work when you're sick—or debilitated like you are now."

MAYBE.

Gathering up the lettered tiles and sorting them into the tubes, Travis thought for a minute. Bad thoughts. Unnerving thoughts. They had an alarm system around the property, yes, but to some extent they were depending on Einstein for an early warning. Travis should have felt comfortable with the precautions he had taken and with his own abilities, as a former Delta Force man, to exterminate The Outsider. But he was tormented by the feeling that he had overlooked a hole in their defenses and that, come the crisis, he would need Einstein's full powers and strength to help him deal with the unexpected.

"You're going to have to get well as fast as you can," he told the retriever. "You're going to have to try to eat even when you have no real appetite. You're going to have to sleep as much as you can, give your body a chance to knit up, and don't spend half the night at the windows, worrying."

CHICKEN SOUP.

Laughing, Travis said, "Might as well try that, too."

A BOILERMAKER KILLS GERMS DEAD.

"Where'd you get that idea?"

BOOK. WHAT'S A BOILERMAKER?

Travis said, "A shot of whiskey dropped into a glass of beer.

Einstein considered that for a moment.

KILL GERMS BUT BECOME ALCOHOLIC.

Travis laughed and ruffled Einstein's coat. "You're a regular comedian, fur face."

MAYBE I SHOULD PLAY VEGAS.

"I bet you could."

ME AND PIA ZADORA.

He hugged the dog, and they sat in the pantry laughing, each in his own way.

In spite of the joking, Travis knew that Einstein was deeply troubled by the loss of his ability to sense The Outsider. The jokes were a defensive mechanism, a way to hold off fear.

That afternoon, exhausted from their short walk around the house, Einstein slept while Nora painted feverishly in her studio. Travis sat by a front window, staring out at the woods, repeatedly going over their defenses in his mind, looking for a hole.

On Sunday, December 12, Jim Keene came out to their place in the afternoon and stayed for dinner. He examined Einstein and was pleased with the dog's improvement.

"Seems slow to us," Nora said fretfully.

"I told you, it'll take time," Jim said.

He made a couple of changes in Einstein's medication and left new bottles of pills.

Einstein had fun demonstrating his page-turning machine and his letter-dispensing device in the pantry. He graciously accepted praise for his ability to hold a pencil in his teeth and use it to operate the television and the videotape recorder without bothering Nora and Travis for help.

Nora was at first surprised that the veterinarian looked less sad-eyed and sorrowful than she remembered. But she decided his face was the same; the only thing that had changed was her perception of him. Now that she knew him better, now that he was a friend of the first rank, she saw not only the glum features nature had given him but the kindness and humor beneath his somber surface.

Over dinner, Jim said, "I've been doing a little research into tattooing—to see if maybe I can remove the numbers in his ear."

Einstein had been lying on the floor nearby, listening to the conversation. He got to his feet, wobbled a moment, then hurried to the kitchen table and jumped into one of the empty chairs. He sat very erect and stared at Jim expectantly.

"Well," the vet said, putting down a forkful of curried chicken that he'd lifted halfway to his mouth, "most but not all tattoos can be eradicated. If I know what sort of ink was used and by what method it was embedded under the skin, I might be able to erase it."

"That would be terrific," Nora said. "Then even if they found us and tried to take Einstein back, they couldn't prove he's the dog they lost."

"There'd still be traces of the tattoo that would show up under close inspection," Travis said. "Under a magnifying glass."

Einstein looked from Travis to Jim Keene as if to say, *Yeah, what about that?*

"Most labs just tag research animals," Jim said. "Of those that tattoo, there're a couple of different standard inks used. I might be able to remove it and leave no trace except a natural-looking mottling of the flesh. Microscopic examination wouldn't reveal traces of the ink, not a hint of the numbers. It's a small tattoo, after all, which makes the job easier. I'm still researching techniques, but in a few weeks we might try it—if Einstein doesn't mind some discomfort."

The retriever left the table and padded into the pantry. They could hear the pumping of the letter-dispensing pedals.

Nora went to see what message Einstein was composing.

DON'T WANT TO BE BRANDED. AM NOT A COW.

His desire to be free of the tattoo went deeper than Nora had thought. He wanted the mark removed in order to escape identification by people at the lab. But evidently he also hated carrying those three numbers in his ear because they marked him as mere property, a condition that was an affront to his dignity and a violation of his rights as an intelligent creature.

FREEDOM.

"Yes," Nora said respectfully, putting a hand on his head, "I do understand. You are a . . . a *person,* and a person with"—this was the first time she had thought of this aspect of the situation—"a soul."

Was it blasphemous to think Einstein had a soul? No. She did not think blasphemy entered into it. Man had made the dog; however, if there was a God, He obviously approved of Einstein—not least of all because Einstein's ability to differentiate right from wrong, his ability to love, his courage, and his selflessness made him closer to the image of God than were many human beings who walked the earth.

"Freedom," she said. "If you've got a soul—and I know you do—then you were born with free will and the right to self-determination. The number in your ear is an insult, and we'll get rid of it."

After dinner, Einstein clearly wanted to monitor—and participate in—the conversation, but he ran out of energy and slept by the fire.

Over a short brandy and coffee, Jim Keene listened as Travis outlined their defenses against The Outsider. Encouraged to find holes in their preparations, the vet could think of nothing except the vulnerability of their power supply. "If the thing was smart enough to bring down the line that runs in from the main highway, it could plunge you into darkness in the middle of the night and render your alarm useless. And without power those tricky mechanisms in the barn wouldn't slam the door behind the beast or release the nitrous oxide."

Nora and Travis took him downstairs, into the half-basement under the rear of the house, to show him the emergency generator. It was powered by a forty-gallon tank of gasoline buried in the yard, and it would restore electricity to the house and barn alarm after only a ten-second delay following the loss of the main supply.

"As far as I can see," Jim said, "you've thought of everything."

"I think we have, too," Nora said.

But Travis scowled. "I wonder . . ."

On Wednesday, December 22, they drove into Carmel. Leaving Einstein with Jim Keene, they spent the day buying Christmas gifts, decorations for the house, ornaments for a tree, and the tree itself.

With the threat of The Outsider moving inexorably closer to them, it seemed almost frivolous to make plans for the holiday. But Travis said, "Life is short. you never know how much time you've got left, so you can't let Christmas slide by without celebrating, no matter what. Besides, my Christmases haven't been so terrific these last few years. I intend to make up for that."

"Aunt Violet didn't believe in making an event of Christmas. She didn't believe in exchanging gifts or putting up a tree."

"She didn't believe in *life*," Travis said. "and that's just one more reason to do this Christmas up right. It'll be your first good one, as well as Einstein's first."

Starting next year, Nora thought, there'll be a baby in the house to share Christmas, and won't *that* be a hoot!

Aside from suffering a little mild morning sickness and having put on a couple of pounds, she'd not yet shown any signs of pregnancy. Her belly was still flat, and Dr. Weingold said that, considering her body type, she had a chance of being one of those women whose abdomen underwent only moderate distension. She hoped she was lucky in that regard because, after the birth, getting back into shape would be a lot easier. Of course, the baby was not due for six months yet, which gave her plenty of time to get as big as a walrus.

Returning from Carmel in the pickup—the back of which was filled with packages and a perfectly formed Christmas tree—Einstein slept half on Nora's lap. He was worn out from his busy day with Jim and Pooka. They got home less than an hour before dark. Einstein led the way toward the house—

—but suddenly stopped and looked around curiously. He sniffed the chilly air, then moved across the yard, nose to the ground, as if tracking a scent.

Heading toward the back door with her arms full of packages, Nora did not at first see anything unusual in the dog's behavior, but she noticed that Travis had halted and was staring hard at Einstein. She said, "What is it?"

"Wait a second."

Einstein crossed the yard to the edge of the woods on the south side. He stood rigid, head thrust forward, then shook himself and moved on along the perimeter of the forest. He stopped repeatedly, standing motionless each time, and in a couple of minutes he came all the way around to the north.

When the retriever returned to them, Travis said, "Something?"

Einstein wagged his tail briefly and barked once: *Yes and no.*

Inside, in the pantry, the retriever laid out a message.

FELT SOMETHING.

"What?" Travis asked.

DON'T KNOW.

"The Outsider?"

MAYBE.

"Close?"

DON'T KNOW.

"Are you getting your sixth sense back?" Nora asked.

DON'T KNOW. JUST FELT.

"Felt what?" Travis asked.

The dog composed an answer only after considerable deliberation.

BIG DARKNESS.

"You felt a big darkness?"

Yes.

"What's that mean?" Nora asked uneasily.

CAN'T EXPLAIN BETTER. JUST FELT IT.

Nora looked at Travis and saw a concern in his eyes that probably mirrored the expression in her own.

A big darkness was out there somewhere, and it was coming.

3

Christmas was joyous and fine.

In the morning, sitting around the light-bedecked tree, drinking milk and eating homemade cookies, they opened presents. As a joke, the first gift that Nora gave Travis was a box of underwear. He gave her a bright orange and yellow muumuu obviously sized for a three-hundred-pound woman: "For March, when you'll be too big for anything else. Of course, by May you'll have outgrown it." They exchanged serious gifts, also—jewelry and sweaters and books.

But Nora, like Travis, felt the day belonged to Einstein more than to anyone else. She gave him the portrait on which she had been working all month, and the retriever seemed stunned and flattered and delighted that she had seen fit to immortalize him in paint. He got three new Mickey Mouse videotapes, a pair of fancy metal food and water bowls with his name engraved on them to replace the plastic dishes he had been using, his own small battery-powered clock that he could take with him to any room in the house (he was showing an increasing interest in time), and several other presents, but he was repeatedly drawn to the portrait, which they propped against the wall for his inspection. Later, when they hung it above the living-room fireplace, Einstein stood on the hearth and peered up at the picture, pleased and proud.

Like any kid, Einstein perversely took almost as much pleasure in playing with empty boxes, crumpled wrapping paper, and ribbons as he did with the gifts themselves. And one of his favorite things was a joke gift: a red Santa cap with a white pom-pom on the tip, which was held on his head by an elastic strap. Nora put it on him just for fun. When he saw himself in a mirror, he was so taken with his appearance that he objected when, a few minutes later, she tried to take the cap off him. He kept it on most of the day.

Jim Keene and Pooka arrived in the early afternoon, and Einstein herded them straight into the living room to look at his portrait above the mantel. For an hour, watched over by Jim and Travis, the two dogs played together in the back yard. That activity, having been preceded by the excitement of the morning's gift-giving, left Einstein in need of a nap, so they returned to the house, where Jim and Travis helped Nora prepare Christmas dinner.

After his nap, Einstein tried to interest Pooka in Mickey Mouse cartoons, but Nora saw that he met with only limited success. Pooka's attention span didn't even last long enough for Donald or Goofy or Pluto to get Mickey into trouble. In respect of his companion's lower IQ, and apparently not bored with such company, Einstein turned the television off and engaged in strictly doggy activities: some light wrestling in the den and a lot of lying around, nose to nose, silently communing with each other about canine concerns.

By early evening, the house was filled with the aromas of turkey, baked corn, yams, and other goodies. Christmas music played. And in spite of the interior shutters that had been bolted over the windows when the early-winter night had fallen, in spite of the guns near at hand, in spite of the demonic presence of The Outsider that always lurked in the back of her mind, Nora had never been happier.

During dinner, they talked about the baby, and Jim asked if they had given any thought to names. Einstein, eating in the corner with Pooka, was instantly intrigued by the idea of participating in the naming of their firstborn. He dashed immediately to the pantry to spell out his suggestion.

Nora left the table to see what name the dog thought suitable.

MICKEY.

"Absolutely not!" she said. "We're not naming my baby after a cartoon mouse."

DONALD.

"Nor a duck."

PLUTO.

"Pluto? Get serious, fur face."

GOOFY.

Nora firmly restrained him from pushing the letter-dispensing pedals any more, gathered up the used tiles and put them away, turned off the pantry light, and went back to the table. "You may think it's hilarious," she told Travis and Jim, who were choking with laughter, "but *he's* serious!"

After dinner, sitting around the tree in the living room, they talked about many things, including Jim's intention of getting another dog. "Pooka needs to have another of his kind," the vet said. "He's almost a year and a half old now, and I'm of the belief that human companionship isn't enough for them after they're well past the puppy stage. They get lonely like we do. And since I'm going to get him a companion, I might as well get a female purebred lab and maybe wind up with some nice puppies to sell later. So he's going to have not only a friend but a mate."

Nora had not noticed that Einstein was any more interested in that part of the conversation than in any other. However, after Jim and Pooka had gone home, Travis found a message in the pantry and called Nora over to have a look at it.

MATE. A COMPANION, PARTNER, ONE OF A PAIR.

The retriever had been waiting for them to notice the carefully arranged tiles. Now he appeared behind them and regarded them quizzically.

Nora said, "Do you think you'd like a mate?"

Einstein slipped between them, into the pantry, disarranged the tiles, and made a reply.

IT'S WORTH THINKING ABOUT.

"But listen, fur face," Travis said, "you're one of a kind. There's no other dog like you, with your IQ."

The retriever considered that point but was not dissuaded.

LIFE IS MORE THAN INTELLECT.

"True enough,'" Travis said. "But I think this needs a lot of consideration."

LIFE IS FEELINGS.

"All right," Nora said. "We'll think about it."

LIFE IS MATE. SHARING.

"We promise to think about it and then discuss it with you some more," Travis said. "Now it's getting late."

Einstein quickly made one more message.

BABY MICKEY?

"Absolutely not!" Nora said.

That night, in bed, after she and Travis made love, Nora said, "I'll bet he *is* lonely."

"Jim Keene?"

"Well, yes, I bet he's lonely, too. He's such a nice man, and he'd make someone a great husband. But women are just as choosy about looks as men are, don't you think? They don't go for husbands with hound-dog faces. They marry the good-looking ones who half the time treat them like dirt. But I didn't mean Jim. I meant Einstein. He must get lonely now and then."

"We're with him all the time."

"No, we're really not. I paint, and you do things in which poor Einstein doesn't get included. And if you do go back to real estate eventually, there'll be a lot of time when Einstein's without anyone."

"He has his books. He loves books."

"Maybe books aren't enough," she said.

They were silent for so long that she thought Travis had fallen asleep. Then he said, "If Einstein mated and produced puppies, what would they be like?"

"You mean—would they be as smart as he is?"

"I wonder . . . Seems to me there's three possibilities. First, his intelligence isn't inheritable, so his puppies would just be ordinary puppies. Second, it is inheritable, but the genes of his mate would dilute the intelligence, so the puppies would be smart but not as smart as their father; and each succeeding generation would get dimmer, duller, until eventually his great-great-grandpups would just be ordinary dogs."

"What's the third possibility?"

"Intelligence, being a survival trait, might be genetically dominant, very dominant."

"In which case his puppies would be as smart as he is."

"And their puppies after them, on and on, until in time you'd have a colony of intelligent golden retrievers, thousands of them all over the world."

They were silent again.

Finally she said, "Wow."

Travis said, "He's right."

"What?"

"It *is* something worth thinking about."

4

Vince Nasco had never anticipated, back in November, that he would need a full month to get a whack at Ramon Velazquez, the guy in Oakland who was a thorn in the side of Don Mario Tetranga. Until he wasted Velazquez, Vince would not be given the names of people in San Francisco who dealt in false ID and who might help him track down Travis Cornell, the woman, and the dog. So he had an urgent need to reduce Velazquez to a hunk of putrifying meat.

But Velazquez was a goddamn shadow. The man did not make a step without two bodyguards at his side, which should have made him more rather than less conspicuous. However, he conducted his gambling and drug enterprises—infringing on the Tetranga franchise in Oakland—with all the stealth of Howard Hughes. He slipped and slithered on his errands, using a *fleet* of different cars, never taking the same route two days in a row, never meeting in the same place, using the street as an office, never staying anywhere long enough to be made, marked, and wiped out. He was a hopeless paranoid who believed everyone was out to get him. Vince couldn't keep the man in sight long enough to match him with the photograph that the Tetrangas had supplied. Ramon Velazquez was *smoke*.

Vince didn't get him until Christmas Day, and it was a hell of a mess when it went down. Ramon was at home with a lot of relatives. Vince came at the Velazquez property from the house behind it, over the high brick wall between one big lot and the other. Coming down on the other side, he saw Velazquez and some people at a barbecue on the patio near the pool where they were roasting an enormous turkey—did people barbecue turkeys anywhere but in California?—and they all spotted him immediately though he was half an acre away. He saw the bodyguards reaching for weapons in their shoulder holsters, so he had no choice but to fire indiscriminately with his Uzi, spraying the entire patio area, taking out Velazquez, both bodyguards, a middle-aged woman who must have been somebody's wife, and an old dame who had to be somebody's grandmother.

Ssssnap.

Ssssnap.

Ssssnap.

Ssssnap.

Ssssnap.

Everyone else, inside and outside of the house, was screaming and diving for cover. Vince had to climb the wall back into the yard of the house next door—where nobody was home, thank God—and as he was hauling his ass over the top, a bunch of Latino types at the Velazquez place opened fire on him. He barely got away with his hide intact.

The day after Christmas, when he showed up at a San Francisco restaurant owned by Don Tetranga, to meet with Frank Dicenziano, a trusted Family *capo* who answered only to the don himself, Vince was worried. The *fratellanza* had a code about assassinations. Hell, they had a code about everything—probably even bowel movements—and they took their codes seriously, but the code of assassination was maybe taken a little more seriously than others. The first rule of that code was: You don't hit a man in the company of his family unless he's gone to ground and you just can't reach him any other way. Vince felt fairly safe on that score. But another rule was that you never shot a man's wife or kids or his grandmother in order to get at him. Any hit man who did such a thing would probably wind up dead himself, wasted by the very people who had hired him. Vince hoped to convince Frank Dicenziano that Velazquez was a special case—no other target had ever eluded Vince for a month—and that what had happened in Oakland on Christmas Day was regrettable but unavoidable.

Just in case Dicenziano—and by extension, the don—was too furious to listen to reason, Vince went prepared with more than a gun. He knew that, if they wanted him dead, they would crowd him and take the gun away from him before he could use it, as soon as he walked into the restaurant and before he knew the score. So he wired himself with plastic explosives and was prepared to detonate them, wiping out the entire restaurant, if they tried to fit him for a coffin.

Vince was not sure if he would survive the explosion. He had absorbed the life energies of so many people recently that he thought he must be getting close to the immortality he had been seeking—or was already there—but he could not know how strong he was until he put himself to the test. If his choice was standing at the heart of an explosion . . . or letting a couple of wiseguys pump a hundred rounds into him and encase him in concrete for a dunk in the bay . . . he decided the former was more appealing and, perhaps, offered him a marginally better chance of survival.

To his surprise, Dicenziano—who resembled a squirrel with meatballs in his cheeks—was delighted with how the Velazquez contract had been fulfilled. He said the don had the highest praise for Vince. No one searched Vince when he entered the restaurant. At a corner booth, as the first men in the room, he and Frank were served a special lunch of dishes not served on the menu. They drank three-hundred-dollar Cabernet Sauvignon, a gift from Mario Tetranga.

When Vince cautiously raised the issue of the dead wife and grandmother, Dicenziano said, "Listen, my friend, we knew this was going to be a hard hit, a demanding job, and that rules might have to be broken. Besides, these people were not *our* kind of people. They were just a bunch of wetback spics. They don't belong in this business. If they try to force their way into it, they can't expect us to play by the rules."

Relieved, Vince went to the men's room halfway through lunch and disconnected the detonator. He didn't want to set the Plastique off accidentally now that the crisis was past.

At the end of lunch, Frank gave Vince the list. Nine names. "These people—who are not all Family people, by the way—pay the don for the right to operate their ID business in his territory. Back in November, in anticipation of your success with Velazquez, I spoke to these nine, and they'll remember that the don wants them to cooperate with you in any way they can."

Vince set out the same afternoon, looking for someone who would remember Travis Cornell.

Initially, he was frustrated. Two of the first four people on the list could not be reached. They had closed up shop and gone away for the holidays. To Vince, it seemed wrong that the criminal underworld would take off for Christmas and New Year's as if they were schoolteachers.

But the fifth man, Anson Van Dyne, was at work in the basement beneath his topless club, Hot Tips, and at five-thirty, December 26, Vince found what he was after. Van Dyne looked at the photograph of Travis Cornell, which Vince had obtained from the back-issue files of the Santa Barbara newspaper. "Yeah, I remember him. He's not one you forget. Not a foreigner looking to become an instant American like half my customers. And not the usual sad-assed loser who needs to change his name and hide his face. He's not a big guy and he doesn't come on tough or anything, but you get the feeling he could mop the floor with anyone who crossed him. Very self-contained. Very watchful. I couldn't forget him."

"What you couldn't forget," said one of the two bearded boy wonders at the computers, "is that gorgeous quiff he was with."

"For her, even a dead man could get it up," the other one said.

The first said, "Yeah, even a dead man. Cake and pie."

Vince was both offended and confused by their contributions to the conversation, so he ignored them. To Van Dyne, he said, "Is there any chance you'd remember the new names you gave them?"

"Sure. We got it on file," Van Dyne said.

Vince could not believe what he had heard. "I thought people in your line of work didn't keep records? Safer for you and essential for your clients."

Van Dyne shrugged. "Fuck the clients. Maybe one day the feds or the locals hit us, put us out of business. Maybe I find myself needing a steady flow of cash for lawyer's fees. What better than to have a list of a couple of thousand bozos living under phony names, bozos who'd be willing to be squeezed a little rather than have to start all over again with new lives."

"Blackmail," Vince said.

"An ugly word," Van Dyne said. "But apt, I'm afraid. Anyway, all we care about is that *we* are safe, that there aren't any records here to incriminate *us*. We don't keep the data in this dump. Soon as we provide someone with a new ID, we transmit the record of it over a safe phone line from the computer here to a computer we keep elsewhere. The way *that* computer is programmed, the data can't be pulled out of it from here; it's a one-way road; so if we're busted, the police hackers can't reach our records from these machines. Hell, they won't even know the records exist."

This new high-tech criminal world made Vince woozy. Even the don, a man of infinite criminal cleverness, had thought these people kept no records and had not realized how computers had made it safe to do so. Vince thought about what Van Dyne had told him, getting it all sorted out in his mind. He said, "So can you take me to this other computer and look up Cornell's new ID?"

"For a friend of Don Tetranga's," Van Dyne said, "I'll do just about anything but slit my own throat. Come with me."

Van Dyne drove Vince to a busy Chinese restaurant in Chinatown. The place must have seated a hundred and fifty, and every table was occupied, mostly by Anglos rather than Asians. Although the joint was enormous and was decorated with paper lanterns, dragon murals, imitation rosewood screens, and strings of brass wind chimes in the shapes of Chinese ideograms, it reminded Vince of the kitschy Italian trattoria in which he had murdered the cockroach Pantangela and the two federal marshals last August. All ethnic art and decor—from Chinese to Italian to Polish to Irish—were, when boiled down to their essence, perfectly alike.

The owner was a Chinese man in his thirties, who was introduced to Vince simply as Yuan. With bottles of Tsingtao provided by Yuan, Van Dyne and Vince went into the owner's basement office, where two computers stood on two desks, one out in the main work area and the other shoved into a corner. The one in the corner was switched on, though nobody was working at it.

"This is my computer," Van Dyne said. "No one here ever works with it. They never even *touch* it, except to open the phone line to put the modem in operation every morning and close it every night. My computers at Hot Tips are linked to this one."

"You trust Yuan?"

"I got him the loan that started this business. He owes me his good fortune. And it's pretty much a clean loan, nothing that can be linked to me in any way, or to Don Tetranga, so Yuan remains an upstanding citizen who's of no interest to the cops. All he does for me in return is let me keep the computer here."

Sitting in front of the terminal, Van Dyne began to use the keyboard. In two minutes he had Travis Cornell's new name: Samuel Spencer Hyatt.

"And here," Van Dyne said as new data flickered up. "This is the woman who was with him. Her real name was Nora Louise Devon of Santa Barbara. Now she's Nora Jean Aimes."

"Okay," Vince said. "Now wipe them off your records."

"What do you mean?"

"Erase them. Take them out of the computer. They're not yours any more. They're mine. Nobody else's. Just *mine*."

A short while later, they were back at Hot Tips, which was a decadent place that revolted Vince.

In the basement, Van Dyne gave the names Hyatt and Aimes to the bearded boy wonders who seemed to live down there around the clock, like a couple of trolls.

First, the trolls broke into the Department of Motor Vehicle computers. They wanted to see whether, in the three months since acquiring new identities, Hyatt and Aimes had settled down somewhere and filed a change of address with the state.

"Bingo," one of them said.

An address appeared on the screen, and the bearded operator ordered a printout.

Anson Van Dyne tore the paper off the printer and handed it to Vince.

Travis Cornell and Nora Devon—now Hyatt and Aimes—were living at a rural address on Pacific Coast Highway south of the town of Carmel.

5

On Wednesday, December 29, Nora drove into Carmel alone for an appointment with Dr. Weingold.

The sky was overcast, so dark that the white seagulls, swooping against the backdrop of clouds, were by contrast almost as bright as incandescent lights. The weather had been much the same since the day after Christmas, but the promised rain never came.

Today, however, it came in torrents just as she pulled the pickup into one of the spaces in the small parking lot behind Dr. Weingold's office. She was wearing a nylon jacket with a hood, just in case, and she pulled the hood over her head before dashing from the truck into the one-story brick building.

Dr. Weingold gave her the usual thorough examination and pronounced her fit as a fiddle, which would have amused Einstein.

"I've never seen a woman at the three-month mark in better shape," the doctor said.

"I want this to be a very healthy baby, a perfect baby."

"And so it shall be."

The doctor believed that her name was Aimes and her husband's name was Hyatt, but he never once indicated disapproval of her marital status. The situation embarrassed Nora, but she supposed that the modern world, into which she had fluttered from the cocoon of the Devon house, was liberal-minded about these things.

Dr. Weingold suggested, as he had done before, that she consider a test to determine the baby's sex, and as before she declined. She wanted to be surprised. Besides, if they found out they were going to have a girl, Einstein would start campaigning for the name "Minnie."

After huddling with the doctor's receptionist to schedule the next appointment, Nora pulled the hood over her head again and went out into the driving rain. It was coming down hard, drizzling off a section of roof that had no gutters, sluicing across the sidewalk, forming deep puddles on the macadam of the parking lot. She sloshed through a miniature river on her way to the pickup, and in seconds her running shoes were saturated.

As she reached the truck, she saw a man getting out of a red Honda parked beside her. She didn't notice much about him—just that he was a big guy in a small car, and that he was not dressed for the rain. He was wearing jeans and a blue pullover, and Nora thought; the poor man is going to get soaked to the skin.

She opened the driver's door and started to get into the truck. The next thing she knew, the man in the blue sweater was coming in after her, shoving her across the seat and clambering behind the wheel. He said, "If you yell, bitch, I'll blow your guts out," and she realized that he was jamming a revolver into her side.

She almost yelled anyway, involuntarily, almost tried to keep on going across the front seat and out the door on the passenger's side. But something in his voice, brutal and dark, made her hesitate. He sounded as if he would shoot her in the back rather than let her escape.

He slammed the driver's door, and now they were alone in the truck, beyond help, virtually concealed from the world by the rain that streamed down the windows and made the glass opaque. It didn't matter; the doctor's parking lot was deserted, and it could not be seen from the street, so even out of the truck she would have had no one to whom to turn.

He was a *very* big man, and muscular, but it was not his size that was most frightening. His broad face was placid, virtually expressionless; that serenity, completely unsuited to these circumstances, scared Nora. His eyes were worse. Green eyes—and cold.

"Who are you?" she demanded, trying to conceal her fear, sure that visible terror would excite him. He seemed to be balanced on a thin line. "What do you want with me?"

"I want the dog."

She had thought: robber. She had thought: rapist. She had thought: psychopathic thrill killer. But she had not for a moment thought that he might be a government agent. Yet who else would be looking for Einstein? No one else even knew the dog existed.

"What're you talking about?" she said.

He pushed the muzzle of the revolver deeper into her side, until it hurt.

She thought of the baby growing within her. "All right, okay, obviously you know about the dog, so there's no point in playing games."

"No point." He spoke so quietly that she could hardly hear him above the roar of the rain that drummed on the roof of the cab and snapped against the windshield.

He reached over and pulled down the hood of her jacket, opened the zipper, and slid his hand down her breasts, over her belly. For a moment she was terrified that he was, after all, intent on rape.

Instead, he said, "This Weingold is a gynecologist-obstetrician. So what's your problem? You have some damn social disease or are you pregnant?" He almost spit out the words "social disease" as if merely pronouncing those syllables made him sick with disgust.

"You're no government agent." She spoke entirely from instinct.

"I asked you a question, bitch," he said in a voice barely louder than a whisper. He leaned close, digging the gun into her side again. The air in the truck was humid. The all-enveloping sound of rain combined with the stuffiness to create a claustrophobic atmosphere that was nearly intolerable. He said, "Which is it? You got herpes, syphilis, clap, or some other crotch rot? Or are you pregnant?"

Thinking that pregnancy might gain her a dispensation from the violence of which he seemed so capable, she said, "I'm going to have a baby. I'm three months pregnant."

Something happened in his eyes. A *shifting*. Like movement in a subtle kaleidoscopic pattern that was composed of bits of glass all the same shade of green.

Nora knew that admitting pregnancy was the worst thing she could have done, but she did not know *why*.

She thought about the .38 pistol in the glove compartment. She could not possibly open the glove box, grab the gun, and shoot him before he pulled the trigger of the revolver. Still, she'd have to remain constantly on the lookout for an opportunity, for a laxness on his part, that would give her a chance to go for her own weapon.

Suddenly he was climbing on top of her, and again she thought that he was going to rape her in broad daylight, in the veiling curtains of rain but still daylight. Then she realized he was just changing places with her, urging her behind the wheel while he moved into the passenger's seat, keeping the muzzle of the revolver on her the whole time.

"Drive," he said.

"Where?"

"Back to your place."

"But—"

"Keep your mouth shut and drive."

Now she was at the opposite side of the cab from the glove box. To get at it, she would have to reach in front of him. He would never be *that* lax.

Determined to keep a rein on her galloping fear, she now found that she had to rein in despair as well.

She started the truck, drove out of the parking lot, and turned right in the street.

The windshield wipers thumped nearly as loud as her heart. She wasn't sure how much of the oppressive sound was made by the impacting rain and how much of it was the roar of her own blood in her ears.

Block by block, Nora searched for a cop—although she had on idea what she should do if she saw one. She never had to figure it out because no cops were anywhere to be seen.

Until they were out of Carmel and on the Pacific Coast Highway, the blustering wind not only drove rain against the windshield but also flung bristling bits of cypress and pine needles from huge old trees that sheltered the town's streets. South along the coast, as they headed into steadily less populated areas, no trees overhung the road, but the wind off the ocean hit the pickup full force. Nora frequently felt it pulling at the wheel. And the rain, slashing straight at them from the sea, seemed to pummel the truck hard enough to leave dents in the sheet metal.

After at least five minutes of silence, which seemed like an hour, she could not longer obey his order to keep her mouth shut. "How did you find us?"

"Been watching your place for more than a day," he said in that cool, quiet voice that matched his placid face. "When you left this morning, I followed you, hoping you'd give me an opening."

"No, I mean how did you know where we lived?"

He smiled. "Van Dyne."

"That double-crossing creep."

"Special circumstances," he assured her. "The Big Man in San Francisco owed me a favor, so he put pressure on Van Dyne."

"Big Man?"

"Tetranga."

"Who's he?"

"You don't know anything, do you?" he said. "Except how to make babies, huh? You know about that, huh?"

The hard taunting note in his voice was not merely sexually suggestive: it was darker, stranger, and more terrifying than that. She was so frightened of the fierce tension that she sensed in him each time he approached the subject of sex that she did not dare reply to him.

She turned on the headlights as they encountered thin fog. She kept her attention on the rain-washed highway, squinting through the smeary windshield.

He said, "You're very pretty. If I was going to stick it into anyone, I'd stick it into you."

Nora bit her lip.

"But even as pretty as you are," he said, "you're like all the others, I'll bet. If I stuck it into you, then it'd rot and fall off because you're diseased like all the others—aren't you? Yeah. You are. Sex is death. I'm one of the few who seem to know it, even though proof is everywhere. Sex is death. But you're very pretty . . ."

As she listened to him, her throat got tight. She was having difficulty drawing a deep breath.

Suddenly his taciturnity was gone. He talked fast, still soft-voiced and unnervingly calm, considering the crazy things he was saying, but very fast: "I'm going to be bigger than Tetranga, more important. I've got scores of lives in me. I've absorbed energies from more than you'd believe, experienced The Moment, felt The Snap. It's my Gift. When Tetranga's dead and gone, I'll be here. When everyone now alive is dead, I'll be here because I'm immortal."

She didn't know what to say. He had come out of nowhere, somehow knowing about Einstein, and he was a lunatic, and there seemed to be nothing she could do. She was as angry about the unfairness of it as she was afraid. They had made careful preparations for The Outsider, and they had taken elaborate steps to elude the government—but how were they supposed to have prepared for this? It wasn't *fair*.

Silent again, he stared at her intently for a minute or more, another eternity. She could feel his icy green gaze on her as surely as she would have felt a cold, fondling hand.

"You don't know what I'm talking about, do you?" he said.

"No."

Perhaps because he found her pretty, he chose to explain. "I've only ever told one person before, and he made fun of me. His name was Danny Slowicz, and we both worked for the Carramazza Family in New York, biggest of the five Mafia Families. Little muscle work, once in a while killing people who needed killed."

Nora felt sick because he was not merely crazy and not merely a killer but a crazy *professional* killer.

Unaware of her reaction, switching his gaze from the rainswept road to her face, he continued. "See, we were having dinner in this restaurant, Danny and me, washing down clams with Valpolicella, and I explained to him that I was destined to lead a long life because of my ability to acquire the vital energies of people I wasted. I told him, 'See, Danny, people are like batteries, walking batteries, filled with this mysterious energy we call life. When I off someone, his energy becomes *my* energy, and I get stronger. I'm a bull, Danny.' I says, 'Look at me—am I a bull or what? And I got to be a bull 'cause I have this Gift of being able to take the energy from a guy.' And you know what Danny says?"

"What?" she asked numbly.

"Well, Danny was a serious eater, so he kept his attention on his plate, face in his food, until he scarfs a few more clams. Then he looks up, his lips and chin dripping clam sauce, and he says, 'Yeah, Vince, so where'd you learn this trick, huh? Where'd you learn how to absorb these life energies?' I said, 'Well, it's my Gift,' and he said 'You mean like from God?' So I had to think about that, and I said, "Who knows where from? It's my Gift like Mantle's hitting was a gift, like

Sinatra's voice was a gift.' And Danny says, 'Tell me this—suppose you waste a guy who's an electrician. After you absorb his energy, would you all of a sudden know how to rewire a house?' I didn't realize he was putting me on. I thought it was a serious question, so I explained how I absorb life energy, not personality, not all the stuff the guy knows, just his energy. And then Danny says, 'So if you blew away a carnival geek, you wouldn't all of a sudden get the urge to bite the heads off chickens.' Right then I knew Danny thought I was either drunk or nuts, so I ate clams and didn't say any more about my Gift, and that's the last time I told anyone until I'm here telling you."

He had called himself Vince, so now she knew his name. She did not see what good it would do her to know it.

He had told his story without any indication that he was aware of the insane black humor in it. He was a deadly serious man. Unless Travis could deal with him, this guy was not going to let them live.

"So," Vince said, "I couldn't risk Danny going around telling anyone what I'd told him, because he'd color it up, make it sound funny, and people would think I was nuts. The big bosses don't hire crazy hit men; they want cool, logical, balanced guys who can do the work clean. Which is what I am, cool and balanced, but Danny would have had them thinking the other way. So that night I slit his throat, took him to this deserted factory I knew, cut him into pieces, put him in a vat, and poured a lot of sulfuric acid over him. He was a favorite nephew of the don's, so I couldn't take a chance of anyone finding a body that might be traced back to me. Now I got Danny's energy in me, along with a lot of others."

The gun was in the glove box.

Some small hope could be taken from the knowledge that the gun was in the glove box.

While Nora was visiting Dr. Weingold, Travis whipped up and baked a double batch of chocolate cookies with peanut butter chips. Living alone, he had learned to cook, but he had never taken pleasure in it. During the past few months, however, Nora had improved his culinary skills to such an extent that he enjoyed cooking, especially baking.

Einstein, who usually hung around dutifully throughout a baking session, in the anticipation of receiving a sweet morsel, deserted him before he had finished mixing the batter. The dog was agitated and moved around the house from window to window, staring out at the rain.

After a while, Travis got edgy about the dog's behavior and asked if something was wrong.

In the pantry, Einstein made his reply.

I FEEL A LITTLE STRANGE.

"Sick?" Travis asked, worried about a relapse. The retriever was recovering well, but still recovering. His immune system was not in condition for a major new challenge.

NOT SICK.

"Then what? You sense . . . The Outsider?"

NO. NOT LIKE BEFORE.

"But you sense something?"

BAD DAY.

"Maybe it's the rain."

MAYBE.

Relieved but still edgy, Travis returned to his baking.

* * *

The highway was silver with rain.

The daytime fog grew slightly thicker as they drove south along the coast forcing Nora to slow to forty miles an hour, thirty in some places.

Using the fog as an excuse, could she slow the truck enough to risk throwing open her door and leaping out? No. Probably not. She would have to let their speed drop below five miles an hour in order not to hurt herself or her unborn child, and the fog simply was not dense enough to justify reducing speed that far. Besides, Vince kept the revolver pointed at her while he talked, and he would shoot her in the back as she turned to make her exit.

The pickup's headlamps and those of the few oncoming cars were refracted by the mist. Halos of light and scintillant rainbows bounded off the shifting curtains of fog, briefly seen, then gone.

She considered running the truck off the road, over the edge in one of the few places where she knew the embankment to be gentle and the drop endurable. But she was afraid she would misjudge where she was and, by mistake, drive off the brink into a two-hundred-foot emptiness, crashing with terrible force into the rocky coastline below. Even if she went over at the right point, a calculated and survivable crash might knock her unconscious or induce a miscarriage, and if possible she wanted to get out of this with her life and the life of the child within her.

Once Vince started talking to her, he could not stop. For years he had husbanded his great secrets, had hidden his dreams of power and immortality from the world, but his desire to speak of his supposed greatness evidently had never diminished after the fiasco with Danny Slowicz. It was as if he had stored up all the words he had wanted to say to people, had put them on reels of mental recording tape, and now he was playing them back at high speed, spewing out all this craziness that made Nora sick with dread.

He told her how he had learned of Einstein—the killing of the research scientists in charge of various programs under the Francis Project at Banodyne. He knew of The Outsider, too, but was not afraid of it. He was, he said, on the brink of immortality, and gaining ownership of the dog was one of the final tasks he had to complete in order to achieve his Destiny. He and the dog were destined to be together because each of them was unique in this world, one of a kind. Once Vince had achieved his Destiny, he said, nothing could stop him, not even The Outsider.

Half the time, Nora didn't understand what he was saying. She supposed that if she *did* understand it, she would be as insane as he clearly was.

But though she did not always grasp his meaning, she knew what he intended to do to her and to Travis once he had the retriever. At first, she was afraid of speaking about her fate, as if putting it into words would somehow make it irrevocable. At last, however, when they were no more than five miles from the dirt lane that turned off the highway and led up to the bleached-wood house she said, "You won't let us go when you've got the dog, will you?"

He stared at her, caressing her with his gaze. "What do you think, Nora?"

"I think you'll kill us."

"Of course."

She was surprised that his confirmation of her fears did not fill her with greater terror. His smug response only infuriated her, damping her fear while increasing her determination to spoil his neat plans.

She knew, then, that she was a radically changed woman from the Nora of last May, who would have been reduced to uncontrollable shudders by this man's bold self-assurance.

"I could run this truck right off the road, take my chances with an accident," she said.

"The moment you pulled on the wheel," he said, "I'd have to shoot you and then try to regain control."

"Maybe you couldn't. Maybe you'd die, too."

"Me? Die? Maybe. But not in anything as minor as a traffic accident. No, no. I've got too many lives in me to go that easily. And I don't believe you'll try it anyway. In your heart of hearts, you believe that man of yours will pull a sharp one, save you and the dog and himself. You're wrong, of course, but you can't stop believing in him. He won't do anything because he'll be afraid of hurting you. I'll go in there with a gun in your belly, and that will paralyze him long enough for me to blow his head off. That's why I've only got the revolver. It's all I need. His caring for you, his fear of hurting you, will get him killed."

Nora decided it was very important that she not let her fury show. She must try to look frightened, weak, utterly unsure of herself. If he underestimated her, he might slip up and give her some small advantage.

Taking her eyes off the rainy highway for a second, she glanced at him and saw that he was staring at her not with amusement or psychopathic rage, as she would have expected, and not with his usual bovine placidity either, but with something that looked very much like affection and maybe gratitude.

"I've dreamed for years of killing a pregnant woman," he said, as if that was a goal no less worthwhile and commendable than wanting to build a business empire or feed the hungry or nurse the sick. "I have never been in a situation where the risk of killing a pregnant woman was low enough to justify it. But in that isolated house of yours once I've dealt with Cornell, the conditions will be ideal."

"Please, no," she said shakily, playing the weakling, though she didn't have to fake the nervous quiver in her voice.

Still speaking calmly but with a trace more emotion than before, he said, "There'll be your life energy, still young and rich, but in the instant you die, I'll also receive the energy of the child. And that'll be perfectly pure, unused, a life that's unsoiled by the contaminants of this sick and degenerate world. You're my first pregnant woman, Nora, and I'll always remember you."

Tears shimmered at the corners of her eyes, which was not just good acting, either. Although she *did* believe Travis would find some way to handle this man, she was afraid that, in the turmoil, she or Einstein would die. And she did not know how Travis would be able to cope with his failure to save all of them.

"Don't despair, Nora," Vince said. "You and your baby will not entirely cease to exist. You'll both become a part of me, and in me you'll live forever."

Travis took the first tray of cookies out of the oven and put them on a rack to cool.

Einstein came sniffing around, and Travis said, "They're too hot yet."

The dog returned to the living room to look out the front window at the rain.

Just before Nora turned off the Coast Highway, Vince slid down on the seat, below the window level, out of sight. He kept the gun on her. "I'll blow that baby right out of your belly if you make the slightest wrong move."

She believed him.

Turning onto the dirt lane, which was muddy and slippery, Nora drove up the hill toward the house. The overhanging trees shielded the road from the worst of the rain but collected the water on their branches and sent it to the ground in fatter droplets or rivulets.

She saw Einstein at a front window, and she tried to come up with some signal that would mean "trouble," that the dog would instantly understand. She couldn't think of anything.

Looking up at her, Vince said, "Don't go all the way to the barn. Stop right beside the house."

His plan was obvious. The corner of the house where the pantry and cellar stairs were located had no windows. Travis and Einstein would not be able to see the man getting out of the truck with her. Vince could hustle her around the corner, onto the back porch, and inside before Travis realized something was wrong.

Maybe Einstein's canine senses would detect danger. Maybe. But . . . Einstein had been so ill.

Einstein padded into the kitchen, excited.

Travis said, "Was that Nora's truck?"

Yes.

The retriever went to the back door and did a dance of impatience—then stood still and cocked his head.

Nora's stroke of luck came when she least expected it.

When she parked alongside the house, engaged the hand brake, and switched off the engine, Vince grabbed her and dragged her across the seat, out of his side of the truck because that was the side against the back end of the house and most difficult to see from windows at the front corner of the structure. Climbing from the pickup, pulling her by one hand, he was looking around to be sure Travis was not nearby; distracted, he couldn't keep his revolver on Nora as closely as before. As she slid across the seat, past the glove box, she popped open the door and snatched up the .38 pistol. Vince must have heard or sensed something because he swung toward her, but he was too late. She jammed the .38 into his belly and, before he could raise his gun and blow her head off, she squeezed the trigger three times.

With a look of shock, he slammed against the house, which was only three feet behind him.

She was amazed by her own cold-bloodedness. Crazily, she thought that no one was so dangerous as a mother protecting her children, even if one child was unborn and the other was a *dog*. She fired once more, point-blank at his chest.

Vince went down hard, face-first in the wet ground. She turned from him and ran. At the corner of the house, she almost collided with Travis, who vaulted over the porch railing and landed in a crouch in front of her, holding the Uzi carbine.

"I killed him," she said, hearing hysteria in her voice, fighting to control it. "I shot him four times, I killed him, my *God*."

Travis rose from a crouch, bewildered. Nora threw her arms around him and put her head against his chest. As chilling rain beat upon them, she reveled in the living warmth of him.

"Who—" Travis began.

Behind Nora, Vince issued a shrill breathless cry and, rolling onto his back, fired at them. The bullet struck Travis high in the shoulder and knocked him backward. If it had been two inches to the right, it would have hit Nora in the head.

She was almost pulled off her feet when Travis fell because she was holding him. But she let go fast enough and went to the left, in front of the truck, out of the line of fire. She got only a quick look at Vince, who was holding his revolver in one hand and clutching his stomach with the other, trying to get off the ground.

In that glimpse, before she cowered down in front of the pickup, she had not seen any blood on the man.

What was happening here? He could not possibly have survived three rounds in the stomach and one in the chest. Not unless he actually *was* immortal.

Even as Nora scrambled for the cover of the truck, Travis had been getting off his back, sitting up in the mud. Blood was visible on *him,* spreading across his chest from his shoulder, soaking his shirt. He still had the Uzi in his right hand, which functioned in spite of the wound in that shoulder. As Vince pulled off a wild second shot, Travis opened fire with the Uzi. His position was no better than Vince's: the spray of bullets snapped into the house and ricocheted along the side of the truck, indiscriminate fire.

He stopped shooting. "Shit." He struggled onto his feet.

Nora said, "Did you get him?"

"He made it around the front of the house," Travis said, and headed that way.

Vince figured he was approaching immortality, almost there, if he had not already arrived. He was in need of—at most—only a few more lives, and his only concern was that he would be snuffed out when he was *that* close to his Destiny. As a result, he took precautions. Like the latest and most expensive model Kelvar bulletproof vest. He was wearing one under his sweater, which was what had stopped the four shots the bitch had tried to pump into him. The slugs had flattened against the vest, drawing no blood whatsoever. But, Jesus, they had hurt. The impact had knocked him against the wall of the house and had driven the breath out of him. He felt as if he had lain on a giant anvil while someone repeatedly pounded a blacksmith's hammer into his gut.

Hunched over his pain, hobbling toward the front of the house, trying to get out of the way of the damn Uzi, he was sure he was going to be shot in the back. But somehow he made it to the corner, climbed the porch steps, and got out of Cornell's line of fire.

Vince took some satisfaction in having wounded Cornell, though he knew it wasn't mortal. And having lost the element of surprise, he was in for a protracted battle. Hell, the woman looked to be almost as formidable as Cornell himself—a crazy Amazon.

He could have sworn there was something of the timid mouse in the woman, that it was her nature to submit. Obviously, he misjudged her—and that spooked him. Vince Nasco was not accustomed to making such mistakes; mistakes were for lesser men, not for the child of Destiny.

Scuttling across the front porch, certain that Cornell was coming fast behind him, Vince decided to go into the house instead of heading for the woods. They would expect him to run for the trees, take cover, and reconsider his strategy. Instead, he'd go straight into the house and find a position from which he could see both the front and rear doors. Maybe he'd take them by surprise yet.

He was passing a large window, heading for the front door, when something exploded through the glass.

Vince cried out in surprise and fired his revolver, but the shot went into the porch ceiling, and the dog—Jesus, that's what it was, the dog—hit him hard. The gun flew out of his hand. He was knocked backward. The dog clung to him, claws snagged in his clothes, teeth sunk in his shoulder. The porch railing disintegrated. They tumbled out into the front yard, into the rain.

Screaming, Vince hammered at the dog with his big fists until it squealed and let go of him. Then it went for his throat, and he just knocked it off in time to prevent it tearing open his windpipe.

His gut still throbbed, but he hitched and stumbled back to the porch, looking for his revolver—and found Cornell instead. Bleeding from the shoulder, Cornell was on the porch, looking down at Vince.

Vince felt a wild surge of confidence. He knew that he had been right all along, knew he was invincible, immortal, because he could look straight into the muzzle of the Uzi without fear, without the *slightest* fear, so he grinned up at Cornell. "Look at me, *look!* I'm your worst nightmare."

Cornell said, "Not even close," and opened fire.

In the kitchen Travis sat in a chair, with Einstein at his side, while Nora dressed his wound. As she worked, she told him what she knew about the man who had forced his way into the truck.

"He was a damn wild card," Travis said. "No way we could ever have known he was out there."

"I hope he's the *only* wild card.'

Wincing as Nora poured alcohol and iodine into the bullet hole, wincing again as she bound the wound with gauze by passing it under his armpit, he said, "Don't worry about making a great job of it. The bleeding's not bad. No artery's been hit."

The bullet had gone through, leaving a hideous exit wound, and he was in considerable pain, but for a while yet he would be able to function. He would have to seek medical attention later, maybe from Jim Keene to avoid the questions that any other doctor would surely insist on having answered. For now, he was only concerned that the wound be bound tight enough to allow him to dispose of the dead man.

Einstein was battered, too. Fortunately, he had not been cut when he smashed through the front window. He did not seem to have any broken bones, but he had taken several hard blows. Not in the best of shape to begin with, he looked bad—muddy and rain-soaked and in pain. He would need to see Jim Keene, too.

Outside, the rain was falling harder than ever, pounding on the roof, gurgling noisily through gutters and downspouts. It was slanting across the front porch and through the shattered window, but they did not have time to worry about water damage.

"Thank God for the rain," Travis said. "No one in the area will have heard the gunfire in this downpour."

Nora said, "Where will we dump the body?"

"I'm thinking." And it was hard to think clearly because the pain in his shoulder throbbed up and into his head.

She said, "We could bury him here, in the woods—"

"No. We'd always know he was there. We'd always worry about the body being dug up by wild animals, found by hikers. Better . . . there're places along the Coast Highway where we could pull over, wait until there's no traffic, drag him out of the bed of the truck, and toss him over the side. If we pick a place where the sea comes in right to the base of the slope, it'll carry him out, move him away, before anyone notices him down there."

As Nora finished the bandage, Einstein abruptly got up, whined. He sniffed the air. He went to the back door, stood staring at it for a moment, then disappeared into the living room.

"I'm afraid he's hurt worse than he appears to be," Nora said, applying a final strip of adhesive tape.

"Maybe," Travis said. "But maybe not. He's just been acting peculiar all day, ever since you left this morning. He told me it smelled like a bad day."

"He was right," she said.

Einstein returned from the living room at a run and went straight to the pantry switching on the lights and pumping the pedals that released lettered tiles.

"Maybe he has an idea about disposing of the body," Nora said.

As Nora gathered up the leftover iodine, alcohol, gauze, and tape, Travis painfully pulled on his shirt, and went to the pantry to see what Einstein had to say.

THE OUTSIDER IS HERE.

Travis slammed a new magazine into the butt of the Uzi carbine, put an extra in one pocket, and gave Nora one of the Uzi pistols that was kept in the pantry.

Judging by Einstein's sense of urgency, they had no time to go through the house closing and bolting shutters.

The clever scheme to gas The Outsider in the barn had been built upon the certainty that it would approach at night and reconnoiter. Now that it had come in daylight and had reconnoitered while they were distracted by Vince, that plan was useless.

They stood in the kitchen, listening, but nothing could be heard above the relentless roar of the rain.

Einstein was not able to give them a more precise fix on their adversary's location. His sixth sense was still not working up to par. They were just lucky that he had sensed the beast at all. His morning-long anxiety had evidently not been related to any presentiment about the man who had come home with Nora but had been, even without his knowledge, caused by the approach of The Outsider.

"Upstairs," Travis said. "Let's go."

Down here, the creature could enter by doors or windows, but on the second floor they would at least have only windows to worry about. And maybe they could get shutters closed over some of those.

Nora climbed the stairs with Einstein. Travis brought up the rear, moving backward, keeping the Uzi aimed down at the first floor. The ascent made him dizzy. He was acutely aware that the pain and weakness in his injured shoulder was slowly spreading outward though his entire body like an ink stain through a blotter.

On the second floor, at the head of the stairs, he said, "If we hear it come in, we can back off, wait until it starts to climb toward us, then step forward and catch it by surprise, blow it away."

She nodded.

They had to be silent now, give it a chance to creep into the downstairs, give it time to decide they were on the second floor, let it gain confidence, let it approach the stairs with a sense of security.

A strobe-flash of lightning—the first of the storm—pulsed at the window at the end of the hall, and thunder cracked. The sky seemed to have been shattered by the blast, and all the rain stored in the heavens collapsed upon the earth in one tremendous fall.

At the end of the hallway, one of Nora's canvases flew out of her studio and crashed against the wall.

Nora cried out in surprise, and for an instant all three of them stared stupidly at the painting lying on the hall floor, half thinking that its poltergeist-like flight had been related to the great crash of thunder and the lightning.

A second painting sailed out of her studio, hit the wall, and Travis saw the canvas was shredded.

The Outsider was already in the house.

They were at one end of the short hall. The master bedroom and future nursery were on the left, the bathroom and then Nora's studio on the right. The thing was just two doors away, in Nora's studio, demolishing her paintings.

Another canvas flew into the hallway.

Rain-soaked, muddied, battered, still somewhat weak from his battle from distemper, Einstein nevertheless barked viciously, trying to warn off The Outsider.

Holding the Uzi, Travis moved one step down the hall.

Nora grabbed his arm. "Let's not. Let's get out."

"No. We've got to face it."

"On *our* terms," she said.

"These are the best terms we're going to get."

Two more paintings flew out of the studio and clattered down on top of the growing pile of wrecked canvases.

Einstein was no longer barking but growling deep in his throat.

Together, they moved along the hall, toward the open door of Nora's studio.

Travis's experience and training told him they ought to split up, spread out, instead of grouping into a single target. But this was not Delta Force. And their enemy was not a mere terrorist. If they spread out they would lose some of the courage they needed to face the thing. Their very closeness gave them strength.

They were halfway to the studio door when The Outsider shrieked. It was an icy sound that stabbed right through Travis and quick-froze his bone marrow. He and Nora halted, but Einstein took two more steps before stopping.

The dog was shuddering violently.

Travis realized he, too, was shaking. The tremors aggravated the pain in his shoulder.

Breaking fear's hold, he rushed to the open door, treading on ruined canvases, spraying bullets into the studio. The weapon's recoil, though minimal, was like a chisel chipping into his wound.

He hit nothing, heard nothing scream, saw no sign of the enemy.

The floor in there was littered with a dozen mangled paintings and glass from the broken window by which the thing had entered after climbing onto the front porch roof.

Waiting, Travis stood with his legs spread wide. The gun in both hands. Blinking sweat out of his eyes. Trying to ignore the seething pain in his right shoulder. Waiting.

The Outsider must be to the left of the door—or behind it on the right, crouched, ready to spring. If he gave it time, maybe it would grow tired of waiting and would rush him, and he could cut it down in the doorway.

No, it's as smart as Einstein, he told himself. Would Einstein be so dumb as to rush me through a narrow doorway? No. No, it'll do something more intelligent, unexpected.

The sky exploded with thunder so powerful it vibrated the windows and shook the house. Chain lightning sizzled through the day.

Come on, you bastard, show yourself.

He glanced at Nora and Einstein, who stood a few steps away from him, with the master bedroom on one side of them and the bathroom on the other side, the stairs behind them.

He looked again through the doorway, at the window glass among the debris on the floor. Suddenly he was certain that The Outsider was no longer in the studio, that it had gone out through the window, onto the roof of the front porch, and that it was coming at them from another part of the house, through another door, perhaps out of one of the bedrooms, or from the bathroom—or maybe it would explode at them, shrieking, from the top of the steps.

He motioned Nora forward, to his side. "Cover me."

Before she could object, he went through the doorway, into the studio, moving in a crouch. He nearly fell in the rubble, but stayed on his feet and spun around, ready to open fire if the thing was looming over him.

It was gone.

The closet door was open. Nothing in there

He went to the broken window and cautiously looked out onto the roof of the rain-washed porch. Nothing.

Wind keened over the dangerously sharp shards of glass still bristling from the window frame.

He started back toward the upstairs hall. He could see Nora out there, looking at him, scared, but gamely clutching her Uzi. Behind her, the door to the future nursery opened, and it was *there,* yellow eyes aglow. Its monstrous jaws cracked wide, full of teeth far sharper than the wicked glass shards in the window frame.

She was aware of it, started to turn, but it struck at her before she had a chance to fire. It tore the Uzi out of her hands.

It had no chance to gut her with its razor-edge six-inch claws because, even as the beast was tearing the pistol out of her hands, Einstein charged it, snarling. With catlike quickness, The Outsider shifted its attention from Nora to the dog. It whipped around on him, lashed out as if its arms were constructed with more than one elbow joint. It snatched Einstein up in both horrendous hands.

Crossing the studio to the hall door, Travis had no clear shot at The Outsider because Nora was between him and that hateful thing. As Travis reached the doorway, he cried out for her to fall down, to give him a line of fire, and she did, immediately, but too late. The Outsider scooped Einstein into the nursery and slammed the door, as if it were an evil nightmare-spawned jack-in-the-box that had popped out and popped back in with its prey, all in the blink of an eye.

Einstein squealed, and Nora rushed the nursery door.

"No!" Travis shouted, pulling her aside.

He aimed the automatic carbine at the closed door and emptied the rest of the magazine into it, punching at least thirty holes in the wood, crying out through clenched teeth as pain flared through his shoulder. There was some risk of hitting Einstein, but the retriever would be in worse danger if Travis did *not* open fire. When the gun stopped spitting bullets, he ripped out the empty magazine, took a full magazine from his pocket and slammed that into the gun. Then he kicked open the ruined door and went into the nursery.

The window stood open, curtains blowing in the wind.

The Outsider was gone.

Einstein was on the floor, against one wall, motionless, covered with blood. Nora made a wrenching sound of grief when she saw the retriever.

At the window, Travis spotted splashes of blood leading across the porch roof. Rain was swiftly washing the gore away.

Movement caught his eye, and he looked toward the barn, where The Outsider disappeared through the big door.

Crouching over the dog, Nora said, "Oh my God, Travis, my God, after all he's come through and now he has to die like this."

"I'm going after the son-of-a-bitching bastard," Travis said ferociously. "It's in the barn."

She moved toward the door, too, and he said, "No! Call Jim Keene and then stay with Einstein, stay with Einstein."

"But you're the one who needs me. You can't go after it alone."

"*Einstein* needs you."

"Einstein is dead," she said through tears.

"Don't say that!" he screamed at her. He was aware that he was irrational, as if he believed Einstein would not really be dead until they *said* he was dead, but he could not control himself. "Don't say he's dead. Stay here with him, damn it. I've already hurt that fucking fugitive from a nightmare, hurt it bad I think, it's bleeding, and I can finish it off myself. Call Jim Keene, stay with Einstein."

He was also afraid that, in all of this activity, she was going to induce a miscarriage, if she had not already done so. Then they would have lost not only Einstein but the baby.

He left the room at a run.

You're in no condition to go into that barn, he told himself. You've got to cool down first. Telling Nora to call a vet for a dead dog, telling her to stay with it when, in fact, you could have used her at your side . . . No good. Letting rage and a thirst for vengeance get the best of you. No good.

But he could not stop. All his life he had lost people he loved, and except in Delta Force he'd never had anyone to strike back at because you can't take vengeance on fate. Even in Delta, the enemy was so faceless—the lumpish mass of maniacs and fanatics who were "international terrorism"—that vengeance provided little satisfaction. But here was an enemy of unparalleled evil, an enemy worthy of the name, and he would make it pay for what it had done to Einstein.

He raced down the hallway, descended the stairs two and three at a time, was hit by a wave of dizziness and nausea, and nearly fell. He grabbed at the banister to steady himself. He leaned on the wrong arm, and hot pain flared in his wounded shoulder. Letting go of the railing, he lost his balance and tumbled down the last flight, hitting the bottom hard.

He was in worse shape than he had thought.

Clutching the Uzi, he got to his feet and staggered to the back door, onto the porch, down the steps, into the yard. The cold rain cleared his fuzzy head, and he stood for a moment on the lawn, letting the storm wash some of the dizziness out of him.

An image of Einstein's broken, bloody body flashed through his mind. He thought of the amusing messages that would never be formed on the pantry floor, and he thought of Christmases to come without Einstein padding around in his Santa cap, and he thought of love that would never be given or received, and he thought of all the genius puppies who would never be born, and the weight of all that loss nearly crushed him into the ground.

He used his grief to sharpen his rage, honed his fury until it had a razored edge.

Then he went to the barn.

The place swarmed with shadows. He stood at the open door, letting the rain beat on his head and back, peering into the barn, squinting at the layered gloom, hoping to spot the yellow eyes.

Nothing.

He went through the door, bold with rage, and sidled to the light switches on the north wall. Even when the lights came on, he could not see The Outsider.

Fighting off the dizziness, clenching his teeth in pain, he moved past the empty space where the truck belonged, past the back of the Toyota, slowly along the side of the car.

The loft.

He would be moving out from under the loft in a couple of steps. If the thing was up there, it could leap down on him—

That speculation proved a dead end, for The Outsider was at the back of the barn, beyond the front end of the Toyota, crouched on the concrete floor, whimpering and hugging itself with both long, powerful arms. The floor around it was smeared with blood.

He stood beside the car for almost a minute, fifteen feet from the creature, studying it with disgust, fear, horror, and a weird fascination. He believed he could see the body structure of an ape, maybe a baboon—something in the simian family, anyway. But it was neither mostly one species nor merely a patchwork of the recognizable parts of many animals. It was, instead, a thing unto itself. With its oversized and lumpish face, its immense yellow eyes, steam-shovel jaw, and long curved teeth, with its hunched back and matted coat and too-long arms, it attained a frightful individuality.

It was staring at him, waiting.

He took two steps forward, bringing up the gun.

Lifting its head, working its jaws, it issued a raspy, cracked, slurred, but still intelligible word that he could hear even above the sounds of the storm: "*Hurt.*"

Travis was more horrified than amazed. The creature had not been designed to be capable of speech, yet it had the intelligence to learn language and to desire communication. Evidently, during the months it pursued Einstein, that desire had grown great enough to allow it to conquer, to some extent, its physical limitations. It had practiced speech, finding ways to wring a few tortured words from its fibrous voice box and malformed mouth. Travis was horrified not at the sight of a demon speaking but at the thought of how desperately the thing must have wanted to communicate with someone, anyone. He did not want to pity it, did not dare pity it, because he wanted to feel *good* about blowing it off the face of the earth.

"*Come far. Now done,*" it said, with tremendous effort, as if each word had to be torn from its throat.

Its eyes were too alien ever to inspire empathy, and every limb was unmistakably an instrument of murder.

Unwrapping one long arm from around its body, it picked up something that had been on the floor beside it but that Travis had not noticed until now: one of the Mickey Mouse tapes Einstein had gotten for Christmas. The famous mouse was pictured on the cassette holder, wearing the same outfit he always wore, smiling that familiar smile, waving.

"*Mickey,*" The Outsider said, and as wretched and strange and barely intelligible as its voice was, it somehow conveyed a sense of terrible loss and loneliness. "*Mickey.*"

Then it dropped the cassette and clutched itself and rocked back and forth in agony.

Travis took another step forward.

The Outsider's hideous face was so repulsive that there was almost something exquisite about it. In its unique ugliness, it was darkly, strangely seductive.

This time, when the thunder crashed, the barn lights flickered, and nearly went out.

Raising its head again, speaking in that same scratchy voice but with cold, insane glee, it said, "*Kill dog, kill dog, kill dog,*" and it made a sound that might have been laughter.

He almost shot it to pieces. But before he could pull the trigger, The Outsider's laughter gave way to what seemed to be sobbing. Travis watched, mesmerized.

Fixing Travis with its lantern eyes, it again said, "*Kill dog, kill dog, kill dog,*" but this time it seemed wracked with grief, as if it grasped the magnitude of the crime that it had been genetically compelled to commit.

It looked at the cartoon of Mickey Mouse on the cassette holder.

Finally, pleadingly, it said, "*Kill me.*"

Travis did not know if he was acting more out of rage or out of pity when he squeezed the trigger and emptied the Uzi's magazine into The Outsider. What man had begun, man now ended.

When he was done, he felt drained.

He dropped the carbine and walked outside. He could not find the strength to return to the house. He sat down on the lawn, huddled in the rain, and wept.

He was still weeping when Jim Keene drove up the muddy lane from the Coast Highway.

CHAPTER 11

═══════

1

ON THURSDAY AFTERNOON, January 13, Lem Johnson left Cliff Soames and three other men at the foot of the dirt lane, where it met the Pacific Coast Highway. Their instructions were to allow no one past them but to remain on station until—and if—Lem called for them.

Cliff Soames seemed to think this was a strange way to handle things, but he did not voice his objections.

Lem explained that, since Travis Cornell was an ex-Delta man with considerable combat skills, he ought to be handled with care. "If we go storming in there, he'll know who we are as soon as he sees us coming, and he might react violently. If I go in alone, I'll be able to get him to talk to me, and maybe I can persuade him to just give it up."

That was a flimsy explanation for his unorthodox procedure, and it did not wipe the frown off Cliff's face.

Lem didn't care about Cliff's frown. He went in alone, driving one of the sedans, and parked in front of the bleached-wood house.

Birds were singing in the trees. Winter had temporarily relaxed its hold on the northern California coast, and the day was warm.

Lem climbed the steps and knocked on the front door.

Travis Cornell answered the knock and stared at him through the screen door before saying, "Mr. Johnson, I suppose."

"How did you . . . oh yes, of course, Garrison Dilworth would have told you about me that night he got his call through."

To Lem's surprise, Cornell opened the screen door. "You might as well come in."

Cornell was wearing a sleeveless T-shirt, apparently because of a sizable bandage encasing most of his right shoulder. He led Lem through the front room and into a kitchen, where his wife sat at the table, peeling apples for a pie.

"Mr. Johnson," she said.

Lem smiled and said, "I'm widely known, I see."

Cornell sat at the table and lifted a cup of coffee. He offered no coffee to Lem.

Standing awkwardly for a moment, Lem eventually sat with them. He said, "Well, it was inevitable, you know. We had to catch up with you sooner or later."

She peeled apples and said nothing. Her husband stared into his coffee.

What's wrong with them? Lem wondered.

This was not remotely like any scenario he had imagined. He was prepared for panic, anger, despondency, and many other things, but not for this strange apathy. They did not seem to care that he had at last tracked them down.

He said, "Aren't you interested in how we located you?"

The woman shook her head.

Cornell said, "If you really want to tell us, go ahead and have your fun."

Frowning, puzzled, Lem said, "Well, it was simple. We knew that Mr. Dilworth had to've called you from some house or business within a few blocks of that park north of the harbor. So we tied our own computers into the telephone company's records—with their permission, of course—and put men to work examining all the long distance calls charged to all the numbers within three blocks of that park, on that one night. Nothing led us to you. But then we realized that, when charges are reversed, the call isn't billed to the number from which the call is placed; it appears on the records of the person who accepts the reversed charges—which was you. *But* it also appears in a special phone-company file so they'll be able to document the call if the person who accepted the charges later refuses to pay. We went through that special file, which is very small, and quickly found a call placed from a house along the coast, just north of the beach park, to your number here. When we went around to talk to the people there—the Essenby family—we focused on their son, a teenager named Tommy, and although it took some time, we ascertained that it had, indeed, been Dilworth who used their phone. The first part was terribly time-consuming, weeks and weeks, but after that . . . child's play."

"Do you want a medal or what?" Cornell asked.

The woman picked up another apple, quartered it, and began to strip off the peel.

They were not making this easy for him—but then his intentions were much different from what they would be expecting. They could not be criticized for being cool toward him when they did not yet know that he had come as a friend.

He said, "Listen, I've left my men at the end of the lane. Told them you might panic, do something stupid, if you saw us coming in a group. But why I really came alone was . . . to make you an offer."

They both met his eyes at last, with interest.

He said, "I'm getting out of this goddamn job by spring. Why I'm getting out . . . you don't have to know or care. Just say that I've gone through a sea change. Learned to deal with failure, and now it doesn't scare me any more." He sighed and shrugged. "Anyway, the dog doesn't belong in a cage. I don't give a good goddamn what they say, what they want—I know what's right. I know what it's like being in a cage. I've been in one most of my life, until recently. The dog shouldn't have to go back to that. What I'm going to suggest is that you get him out of here now, Mr. Cornell, take him off through the woods, let him somewhere that he'll be safe, then come back and face the music. Say that the dog ran off a couple of months ago, in some other place, and you think he must be dead by now, or in the hands of people who're taking good care of him. There'll still be the problem of The Outsider, which you must know about, but you and I can work up a way to deal with that when it comes. I'll put men on a surveillance of you, but after a few weeks I'll pull them, say it's a lost cause—"

Cornell stood up and stepped to Lem's chair. With his left hand he grabbed hold of Lem's shirt and hauled him to his feet. "You're sixteen days too late, you son of a bitch."

"What do you mean?"

"The dog is dead. The Outsider killed him, and I killed The Outsider."

The woman laid down her paring knife and a piece of apple. She put her face in her hands and sat forward in her chair, shoulders hunched, making soft, sad sounds.

"Ah, Jesus," Lem said.

Cornell let go of him. Embarrassed, depressed, Lem straightened his tie, smoothed the wrinkles out of his shirt. He looked down at his pants—brushed them off.

"Ah, Jesus," he repeated.

Cornell was willing to lead them to the place in the forest where he had buried The Outsider.

Lem's men dug it up. The monstrosity was wrapped in plastic, but they didn't have to unwrap it to know that it was Yarbeck's creation.

The weather had been cool since the thing had been killed, but it was getting rank.

Cornell would not tell them where the dog was buried.

"He never had much of a chance to live in peace," Cornell said sullenly. "But, by God, he's going to rest in peace now. No one's going to put him on an autopsy table and hack him up. No way."

"In a case where the national security is at stake, you can be forced—"

"Let them," Cornell said. "If they haul me up before a judge and try to make me tell them where I buried Einstein, I'll spill the whole story to the press. But if they leave Einstein alone, if they leave me and mine alone, I'll keep my mouth shut. I don't intend to go back to Santa Barbara, to pick up as Travis Cornell. I'm Hyatt now, and that's what I'm going to stay. My old life's gone forever. There's no reason to go back. And if the government's smart, it'll let me be Hyatt and stay out of my way."

Lem stared at him a long time. Then: "Yeah, if they're smart, I think they'll do just that."

Later that same day, as Jim Keene was cooking dinner, his phone rang. It was Garrison Dilworth, whom he had never met but had gotten to know during the past week by acting as liaison between the attorney and Travis and Nora. Garrison was calling from a pay phone in Santa Barbara.

"They show up yet?" the attorney asked.

"Early this afternoon," Jim said. "That Tommy Essenby must be a good kid."

"Not bad, really. But he didn't come to see me and warn me out of the goodness of his heart. He's in rebellion against authority. When they pressured him into admitting that I made the call from his house that night, he resented them. As inevitably as billy goats ram their heads into board fences, Tommy came straight to me."

"They took away The Outsider."

"What about the dog?"

"Travis said he wouldn't show them where the grave was. Made them believe that he'd kick a lot of ass and pull down the whole temple on everyone's heads if they pushed him."

"How's Nora?" Dilworth asked.

"She won't lose the baby."

"Thank God, That must be a great comfort."

2

Eight months later, on the big Labor Day weekend in September, the Johnson and Gaines families got together for a barbecue at the sheriff's house. They played bridge most of the afternoon. Lem and Karen won more often than they lost, which was unusual these days, because Lem no longer approached the game with the fanatical need to win that had once been his style.

He had left the NSA in June. Since then, he had been living on the income from the money he had long ago inherited from his father. By next spring, he expected to settle on a new line of work, a small business of some kind, in which he would be his own boss, able to set his own hours.

Late in the afternoon, while their wives made salads in the kitchen, Lem and Walt stood out on the patio, tending to the steaks on the barbecue.

"So you're still known at the Agency as the man who screwed up the Banodyne crisis?"

"That's how I'll be known until time immemorial."

"Still get a pension though," Walt said.

"Well, I did put in twenty-three years."

"Doesn't seem right, though, that a man could screw up the biggest case of the century and still walk away, at forty-six, with a full pension."

"Three-quarter pension."

Walt breathed deeply of the fragrant smoke rising off the charring steaks. "Still. What is our country coming to? In less liberal times, screwups like you would have been flogged and put in the stocks, at least." He took another deep whiff of the steaks and said, "Tell me again about that moment in their kitchen."

Lem had told it a hundred times, but Walt never got tired of hearing it again. "Well, the place was neat as a pin. Everything gleamed. And both Cornell and his wife are neat about themselves, too. They're well-groomed, well-scrubbed people. So they tell me the dog's been dead two weeks, dead and buried. Cornell throws this angry fit, hauls me out of my chair by my shirt, and glares at me like maybe he's going to rip my head off. When he lets go of me, I straightened my tie, smooth my shirt . . . and I look down at my pants, sort of out of habit, and I notice these golden hairs. Dog hairs. *Retriever* hairs, sure as hell. Now could it have been that these neat people, especially trying to fill their empty days and take their minds off their tragedy, didn't find the time to clean the house in more than two weeks?"

"Hairs were just all *over* your pants," Walt said.

"A hundred hairs."

"Like the dog had just been sitting there minutes before you came in."

"Like, if I'd been two minutes sooner, I'd have set right down on the dog himself."

Walt turned the steaks on the barbecue. "You're a pretty observant man, Lem, which ought to've taken you far in the line of work you were in. I just don't understand how, with all your talents, you managed to screw up the Banodyne case so thoroughly."

They both laughed, as they always did.

"Just luck, I guess," Lem said, which was what he always said, and he laughed again.

3

When James Garrison Hyatt celebrated his third birthday on June 28, his mother was pregnant with his first sibling, who eventually became his sister.

They threw a party at the bleached-wood house on the forested slopes above the Pacific. Because the Hyatts would soon be moving to a new and larger house a bit farther up the coast, they made it a party to remember, not merely a birthday bash but a goodbye to the house that had first sheltered them as a family.

Jim Keene drove from Carmel with Pooka and Sadie, his two black labs, and his young golden retriever, Leonardo, who was usually called Leo. A few close friends came in from the real-estate office where Sam—"Travis" to everyone—worked in Carmel Highlands, and from the gallery in Carmel where Nora's paintings were exhibited and sold. These friends brought their retrievers, too, all of them second-litter offsprings of Einstein and his mate, Minnie.

Only Garrison Dilworth was missing. He had died in his sleep the previous year.

They had a fine day, a grand time, not merely because they were friends and happy to be with one another, but because they shared a secret wonder and joy that would forever bind them into one enormous extended family.

All members of the first litter, which Travis and Nora could not have borne adopting out, and which lived at the bleached-wood house, were also present: Mickey, Donald, Daisy, Huey, Dewey, Louie.

The dogs had an even better time than the people, frolicking on the lawn, playing hide-and-seek in the woods, and watching videotapes on the TV in the living room.

The canine patriarch participated in some of the games, but he spent much of his time with Travis and Nora and, as usual, stayed close to Minnie. He limped—as he would for the rest of his life—because his right hind leg had been cruelly mangled by The Outsider and would not have been usable at all if his vet had not been so dedicated to the restoration of the limb's function.

Travis often wondered whether The Outsider had thrown Einstein against the nursery wall with great force and then had assumed he was dead. Or at the moment when it held the retriever's life in its hands, perhaps the thing had reached down within itself and found some drop of mercy that its makers had not designed into it but which had somehow been there anyway. Perhaps it remembered the one pleasure it and the dog had shared in the lab—the cartoons. And in remembering the sharing, perhaps it saw itself, for the first time, as having a dim potential to be like other living things. Seeing itself as like others, perhaps it then could not kill Einstein as easily as it had expected. After all, with a flick of those talons, it could have gutted him.

But though he had acquired the limp, Einstein had lost the tattoo in his ear, thanks to Jim Keene. No one could ever prove that he was the dog from Banodyne—and he could still play "dumb dog" very well when he wished.

At times during young Jimmy's third birthday extravaganza, Minnie regarded her mate and offspring with charmed befuddlement, perplexed by their attitudes and antics. Although she could never fully understand them, no mother of dogs ever received half the love that she was given by those she'd brought into the world. She watched over them, and they watched over her, guardians of each other.

At the dark end of that good day, when the guests were gone, when Jimmy was asleep in his room, when Minnie and her first litter were settling down for the night, Einstein and Travis and Nora gathered at the pantry off the kitchen.

The scrabble-tile dispenser was gone. In its place, an IBM computer stood on the floor. Einstein took a stylus in his mouth and tapped the keyboard. The message appeared on the screen:

THEY GROW UP FAST.

"Yes, they do." Nora said. "Yours faster than ours."

ONE DAY THEY WILL BE EVERYWHERE.

"One day, given time and a lot of litters," Travis said, "they'll be all over the world."

SO FAR FROM ME. IT'S A SADNESS.

"Yes, it is," Nora said. "But all young birds fly from the nest sooner or later."

AND WHEN I'M GONE?

"What do you mean?" Travis asked, stooping and ruffling the dog's thick coat.

WILL THEY REMEMBER ME?

"Oh yes, fur face," Nora said, kneeling and hugging him. "As long as there are dogs and as long as there are people fit to walk with them, they will all remember you."

ABOUT THE AUTHOR

Dean Koontz, author of the national bestsellers
Strangers, *Watchers*, and *Lightning*, won an *Atlantic
Monthly* fiction competition in 1965 at the age of twenty
and has been writing ever since. He lives in California
with his wife, Gerda—and a vivid imagination.